PRAISE FOR WILBUR SMITH

'Wilbur Smith rarely misses a trick'
Sunday Times

'The world's leading adventure writer'
Daily Express

'Action is the name of Wilbur Smith's game and
he is a master'
Washington Post

'The pace would do credit to a Porsche, and the invention
is as bright and explosive as a fireworks display'
Sunday Telegraph

'A violent saga set in Boer War South Africa, told with
vigour and enthusiasm . . . Wilbur Smith spins a fine tale'
Evening Standard

'A bonanza of excitement'
New York Times

'. . . a natural storyteller who moves confidently and
often splendidly in his period and sustains a flow of
convincing incident'
Scotsman

'Raw experience, grim realism, history and romance welded
with mystery and the bewilderment of life itself'
Library Journal

'A thundering good read'
Irish Times

GOLD MINE
and
MONSOON

WILBUR SMITH was born in Central Africa in 1933. He was educated at Michaelhouse and Rhodes University. He became a full-time writer in 1964 after the successful publication of *When the Lion Feeds,* and has since written over thirty novels, meticulously researched on his numerous expeditions worldwide. His books are now translated into twenty-six languages.

THE NOVELS OF WILBUR SMITH

THE COURTNEYS

When the Lion Feeds   The Sound of Thunder
A Sparrow Falls   Birds of Prey   Monsoon
Blue Horizon   The Triumph of the Sun

THE COURTNEYS OF AFRICA

The Burning Shore   Power of the Sword   Rage
A Time to Die   Golden Fox

THE BALLANTYNE NOVELS

A Falcon Flies   Men of Men   The Angels Weep
The Leopard Hunts in Darkness

THE EGYPTIAN NOVELS

River God   The Seventh Scroll
Warlock   The Quest

Also

The Dark of the Sun   Shout at the Devil
Gold Mine   The Diamond Hunters
The Sunbird   Eagle in the Sky
The Eye of the Tiger   Cry Wolf
Hungry as the Sea   Wild Justice
Elephant Song

WILBUR SMITH

GOLD MINE
and
MONSOON

PAN BOOKS

Gold Mine first published 1970 by William Heinemann
This edition published 1998 by Pan Books
Monsoon first published 1999 by Macmillan
This edition published 2000 by Pan Books

This omnibus first published 2008 by Pan Books
an imprint of Pan Macmillan Ltd
Pan Macmillan, 20 New Wharf Road, London N1 9RR
Basingstoke and Oxford
Associated companies throughout the world
www.panmacmillan.com

ISBN 978-0-330-50803-2

Copyright © Wilbur Smith 1970, 1999

1 3 5 7 9 8 6 4 2

A CIP catalogue record for this book is available from
the British Library.

Typeset by SetSystems Ltd, Saffron Walden, Essex
Printed in the UK by CPI Mackays, Chatham ME5 8TD

GOLD MINE

This book is for my wife and the jewel of my life

MOKHINISO

*with all my love and gratitude for the enchanted years
that I have been married to her*

– 1 –

It began in the time when the world was young, in the time before man, in the time before life itself had evolved upon this planet.

The crust of the earth was still thin and soft, distorted and riven by the enormous pressures from within.

What is now the flat, compacted shield of the African continent, stable and unchanging, was a series of alps. It was range upon range of mountains, thrown up and tumbled down by the movements of the magma at great depth. These were mountains such as man has never seen, so massive as to dwarf the Himalayas, mountains of steaming rock from whose clefts and gaping wounds the molten magma trickled.

It came up from the earth's centre along the fissures and weak places in the crust, bubbling and boiling, yet cooling steadily as it neared the surface so that the least volatile minerals were deposited deeper down, but those with a lower melting point were carried to the surface.

At one point in the measureless passage of time, another series of these fissures opened upon one of the nameless mountain ranges, but from them gushed rivers of molten gold. Some natural freak of temperature and chemical change had resulted in a crude but effective process of refinement during the journey to the earth's surface. The gold was in high concentration in the matrix, and it cooled and solidified at the surface.

If the mountains of that time were so massive as to challenge the imagination of man, then the storms of

1

wind and rain that blew around them were of equal magnitude.

It was a hellish landscape in which the gold field was conceived, cruel mountains reaching stark and sheer in the clouds. Cloud banks dark with the sulphurous gases of the belching earth, so thick that the rays of the sun never penetrated them.

The atmosphere was laden with all the moisture that was to become the seas, so heavy with it that it rained in one perpetual wind-lashed storm upon the hot rock of the cooling earth, then the moisture rose in steam to condense and fall again.

As the years passed by their millions, so the wind and the rain whittled away at the nameless mountain range with its coating of gold-rich ore, grinding it loose and carrying it down in freshets and rivers and rushes of mud and rock into the valley between this range and the next.

Now as the country rock cooled, so the waters lay longer upon the earth before evaporating, and they accumulated in this valley to form a lake the size of an inland sea.

Into this lake poured the storm waters from the golden mountains, carrying with them tiny particles of the yellow metal which settled with other sand and quartz gravel upon the lake bed, to be compacted into a solid sheet.

In time all the gold was scoured from the mountains, transported and laid down upon the lake beds.

Then, as happened every ten million years or so, the earth entered another period of intense seismic activity. The earth shuddered and heaved as earthquake after mammoth earthquake convulsed it.

One fearsome paroxysm cracked the bed of the lake from end to end draining it and fracturing the sedimentary beds, scattering fragments haphazardly so that great sheets of rock many miles across tilted and reared on end.

Again and again the earthquakes gripped and shook the

earth. The mountains tottered and collapsed, filling the valley where the lake had stood, burying some of the sheets of gold-rich rock, pulverizing others.

That cycle of seismic activity passed, and the ages wheeled on in their majesty. The floods and the great droughts came and receded. The miraculous spark of life was struck and burned up brightly, through the time of the monstrous reptiles, on through countless twists and turns of evolution until near the middle of the Pleistocene age a man-ape – Australopithecus – picked up the thigh bone of a buffalo from beside an outcrop of rock to use it as a weapon, a tool.

Australopithecus stood at the centre of a flat, sun-seared plateau that reached five hundred miles in each direction to the sea, for the mountains and the lake beds had long ago been flattened and buried.

Eight hundred thousand years later, one of the Australopithecus' distant but direct line stood at the same spot with a tool in his hand. The man's name was Harrison and the tool was more sophisticated than that of his ancestor, it was a prospector's pick of wood and metal.

Harrison stooped and chipped at the outcrop of rock that protruded from the dry brown African earth. He freed a piece of the stone and straightened with it in his hand.

He held it to catch the sun and grunted with disgust. It was a most uninteresting piece of stone, conglomerate, marbled black and grey. Without hope he held it to his mouth and licked it, wetting the surface before again holding it to the sun, an old prospectors' trick to highlight the metal in the ore.

His eyes narrowed in surprise as the tiny golden flecks in the rock sparkled back at him.

History remembers only his name, not his age nor his antecedents, not the colour of his eyes nor how he died, for within a month he had sold his claim for £10 and disappeared – in search, perhaps, of a really big strike.

He might have done better to retain his title to those claims.

In the eighty years since then an estimated five hundred million ounces of fine gold have been recovered from the fields of the Transvaal and Orange Free State. This is a fraction of that which remains, and which in time will be taken from the earth. For the men who mine the South African fields are the most patiently persistent, inventive and pig-headed of all Vulcan's brood.

This mass of precious metal is the foundation on which the prosperity of a vigorous young nation of eighteen million souls is based.

Yet the earth yields her treasure reluctantly – men must coax and wrest it from her.

– 2 –

Even with the electric fan blowing up a gale from the corner it was stinking hot in Rod Ironsides' office.

He reached for the silver Thermos of iced water at the edge of his desk, and arrested the movement as the jug began to dance before his finger tips touched it. The metal bottle skittered across the polished wooden surface; the desk itself shuddered, rustling the papers upon it. The walls of the room shook, so that the windows rattled in their frames. Four seconds the tremor lasted, and then it was still again.

'Christ!' said Rod, and snatched up one of the three telephones on his desk.

'This is the Underground Manager. Get me the rock mechanic's lab, honey, and snap it up, please.'

He drummed his fingers on the desk impatiently as he waited to be connected. The interleading door of his office opened and Dimitri put his head around the jamb.

'You feel that one, Rod? That was a bad one.'

'I felt it.' Then the telephone spoke into his ear.

'Dr Wessels here.'

'Peter, it's Rod. Did you read that one?'

'I haven't got a fix on it yet – can you hold on a minute?'

'I'll wait.' Rod curbed his impatience. He knew that Peter Wessels was the only person who could read the mass of complicated electronic equipment that filled the instrument room of the rock mechanic's laboratory. The laboratory was a joint research project by four of the major gold-mining companies; between them they had put up a quarter of a million Rand to finance an authoritative investigation of rock and seismic activity under stress. They had selected the Sonder Ditch Gold Mining Company's lease area as the site for the laboratory. Now Peter Wessels had his microphones sited thousands of feet down in the earth, and his tape recorders and stylus graphs ready to pinpoint any underground disturbance.

Another minute ticked by, and Rod swivelled his chair and stared out of the plate glass window at the monstrous head gear of No. 1 shaft, tall as a ten-storey building.

'Come on, Peter, come on, boy,' he muttered to himself. 'I've got twelve thousand of my boys down there.'

With the telephone still pressed to his ear, he glanced at his watch.

'Two-thirty,' he muttered. 'The worst possible time. They'll still be in the stopes.'

He heard the receiver picked up on the other end, and Peter Wessels' voice was almost apologetic.

'Rod?'

'Yes.'

'I'm sorry, Rod, you've had a force seven pressure burst at 9,500 feet in sector Sugar seven Charlie two.'

'Christ!' said Rod and slammed down the receiver. He was up from his desk in one movement, his face set and angry.

'Dimitri,' he snapped at his assistant still in the doorway.

'We won't wait for them to call us, it's a top sequence emergency. That was a force seven bump, with its source plumb in the middle of our eastern longwall at 95 level.'

'Sweet Mary Mother,' said Dimitri, and darted back into his own office. He bent his glossy black head of curls over the telephone and Rod heard him start his top sequence calls.

'Mine hospital . . . emergency team . . . Chief Ventilation Officer . . . General Manager's office.'

Rod turned away, as the outer door of his office opened and Jimmy Paterson, his electrical engineer, came in.

'I felt it, Rod. How's it look?'

'Bad,' said Rod, then there were the other line managers crowding into his office talking quietly, lighting cigarettes, coughing and shuffling their feet, but all of them watching the white telephone on Rod's desk. The minutes crawled by like crippled insects.

'Dimitri,' Rod called out to break the tension. 'Have you got a cage held at the shaft head?'

'They're holding the Mary Anne for us.'

'I've got five men checking the high tension cable on 95 level,' said Jimmy Paterson, and they ignored him. They were watching the white phone.

'Have you located the boss yet, Dimitri?' Rod asked again; he was pacing in front of his desk. It was only when he stood close to other men that you saw how tall he was.

'He's underground, Rod. He went down at twelve-thirty.'

'Put in an all-stations call for him to contact me here.'

'I've done that already.'

The white phone rang.

Only once, a shrill note that ripped along Rod's nerve ends. Then he had the receiver up to his ear.

'Underground Manager,' he said. There was a long silence and he could hear the man breathing on the other end.

'Speak, man, what is it?'

6

'The whole bloody thing has come down,' said the voice. It was husky, rough with fear and dust.

'Where are you speaking from?' Rod asked.

'They're still in there,' said the voice. 'They're screaming in there. Under the rock. They're screaming.'

'What is your station?' Rod made his voice cold, hard, trying to reach the man through his shock.

'The whole stope fell in on them. The whole bloody thing.'

'God damn you! You stupid bastard!' Rod bellowed into the phone. 'Give me your station!'

There was stunned silence for a moment. Then the man's voice came back, steadier now, angry from the insult.

'95 level main haulage. Section 43. Eastern longwall.'

'We're coming.' Rod hung up, picked up his yellow fibreglass hard helmet and lamp from the desk.

'43 section. The hanging wall has come down,' he said to Dimitri.

'Fatals?' the little Greek asked.

'For sure. They've got squealers under the rock.'

Rod clapped on his hat.

'Take over on surface, Dimitri.'

– 3 –

R od was still buttoning the front of his white overalls as he reached the shaft head. Automatically he read the sign above the entrance:

STAY ALERT.   STAY ALIVE.
WITH YOUR CO-OPERATION THIS MINE HAS WORKED
16 FATALITY-FREE DAYS.

'We'll have to change the number again,' Rod thought with grim humour.

The Mary Anne was waiting. Into its heavily wired confines were crowded the first aid team and emergency squad. The Mary Anne was the small cage used for lowering and hoisting personnel, there were two much larger cages that could carry one 120 men at one trip, while the Mary Anne could handle only forty. But that was sufficient for now.

'Let's go,' said Rod as he stepped into the cage, and the onsetter slammed the steel roller doors closed. The bell rang once, twice, and the floor dropped away from under him as the Mary Anne started down. Rod's belly came up to press against his ribs. They went down in one long continuous rush in the darkness. The cage jarring and racketing, the air changing in smell and taste, becoming chemical and processed, the heat building up rapidly.

Rod stood hunch-shouldered, leaning against the metal screen of the cage. The head room was a mere six foot three, and with his helmet on Rod stood taller than that. So today we get another butcher's bill, he thought angrily.

He was always angry when the earth took its payment in mangled flesh and snapping bones. All the ingenuity of man and the experience gained in sixty years of deep mining on the Witwatersrand were used in trying to keep the price in blood as low as possible. But when you go down into the ultra-deep levels below 8,000 feet and from those depths you remove a quarter of a million tons of rock each month, mining on an inclined sheet of reef that leaves a vast low-roofed chamber thousands of feet across, then you must pay, for the stress builds up in the rock as the focal points of pressure change until the moment when it reaches breaking point and she bumps. That is when men die.

Rod's knees flexed under him as the cage braked and then yoyoed to a halt at the brightly lit station on 66 level.

Here they must trans-ship to the sub-main shaft. The door rattled up and Rod left the cage, striding out down the main haulage the size of a railway tunnel; concreted and

8

whitewashed, brightly lit by the bulbs that lined the roof, it curved gently away.

The emergency team followed Rod. Not running, but walking with the suppressed nervous energy of men going into danger. Rod led them towards the sub-main shaft.

There is a limit to the depth which you can sink a shaft into the earth and then equip it to carry men suspended on a steel cable in a tiny wire cage. The limit is about 7,000 feet.

At this depth you must start again, blast out a new headgear chamber from the living rock and below it sink your new shaft, the sub-main.

The sub-main Mary Anne was waiting for them, and Rod led them into it. They stood shoulder to shoulder, and the door rattled shut and again the stomach-swooping rush down into darkness.

Down, down, down.

Rod switched on his head lamp. Now there were tiny motes in the air – air that had been sterilely clean before.

Dust! One of the deadly enemies of the miner. Dust from the burst. As yet the ventilation system had been unable to clear it.

Endlessly they fell in darkness and now it was very hot, the humidity building up so the faces about him, both black and white, were shiny with sweat in the light of his head lamp.

The dust was thicker now, someone coughed. The brightly lit stations flashed past them – 76, 77, 78 – down, down. The dust was a fine mist now. 85, 86, 87. No one had spoken since entering the cage. 93, 94, 95. The deceleration and stop.

The door rattled up. They were 9,500 feet below the surface of the earth.

'Come on,' said Rod.

There were men cluttering the lobby of 95 station, a hundred and fifty, perhaps two hundred of them. Still filthy from their work in the stopes, clothing sodden with sweat, they were laughing and chattering with the abandon of men freshly released from frightful danger.

In a clear space in the centre of the lobby lay five stretchers, on two of them the bright red blankets were pulled up to cover the faces of the men upon them. The faces of the other three men looked as though they had been dusted with flour.

'Two' – grunted Rod – 'so far.'

The station was a shambles, with men milling aimlessly; each minute more of them came back down the haulages as they were pulled out of the undamaged stopes, which were now suspect.

Quickly Rod looked about him, recognizing the face of one of his mine captains.

'McGee,' he shouted. 'Take over here. Get them sitting down in lines ready to load. We'll start hauling the shift out immediately. Get onto the hoist room, tell them I want the stretcher cases out first.'

He paused long enough to watch McGee take control. He glanced at his watch. Two fifty-six. He realized with astonishment that only twenty-six minutes had passed since he felt the pressure burst in his office.

McGee had the station under a semblance of control. He was shouting into the hoist room telephone, on Rod's authority demanding priority to clear 95 station.

'Right,' said Rod. 'Come on.' And he led into the haulage.

The dust was thick. He coughed. The hanging wall was lower here. As he trudged on once more, Rod pondered the unfortunate choice of mining terminology that had named the roof of an excavation 'the hanging wall'. It made one think of a gallows, or at the best it emphasized the fact that there were millions of tons of rock *hanging* overhead.

The haulage branched, and unerringly Rod took the right fork. In his head he carried an accurate three-dimensional map of the entire 176 miles of tunnels that comprised the Sonder Ditch's workings. The haulage came to a T-junction and the arms were lower and narrower. Right to 42 section, left to 43 section. The dust was so thick that visibility was down to ten feet. The dust hung in the air, sinking almost imperceptibly.

'Ventilations knocked out here,' he called over his shoulder. 'Van den Bergh!'

'Yes, sir.' The leader of the emergency squad came up behind him.

'I want air in this drive. Get it on. Use canvas piping if you have to.'

'Right.'

'Then I want pressure on the water hoses to lay this dust.'

'Right.'

Rod turned into the drive. Here the foot wall – the floor – was rough and the going slower. They came upon a line of steel trolleys filled with gold reef abandoned in the centre of the drive.

'Get these the hell out of the way,' ordered Rod, and went on.

Fifty paces and he stopped abruptly. He felt the hair on his forearms stand on end. He could never accustom himself to the sound, no matter how often he heard it.

In the deliberately callous slang of the miner they called them 'squealers'. It was the sound of a grown man, with his legs crushed under hundreds of tons of rock, perhaps his spine broken, dust suffocating him, his mind unhinged by

11

the mortal horror of the situation in which he was trapped, calling for help, calling to his God, calling for his wife, his children, or his mother.

Rod started forward again, with the sound of it becoming louder, a terrifying sound, hardly human, sobbing and babbling into silence, only to start again with a blood-chilling scream.

Suddenly there were men ahead of Rod in the tunnel, dark shapes looming in the dust mist, their head lamps throwing shafts of yellow light, grotesque, distorted.

'Who is that?' Rod called, and they recognized his voice.

'Thank God. Thank God you've come, Mr Ironsides.'

'Who is that?'

'Barnard.' The 43 section shift boss.

'What's the damage?'

'The whole hanging wall of the stope came down.'

'How many men in the stope?'

'Forty-two.'

'How many still in?'

'So far we've got out sixteen unhurt, twelve slightly hurt, three stretcher cases and two dead 'uns.'

The squealer started again, but his voice was much weaker.

'Him?' asked Rod.

'He's got twenty ton of rock lying across his pelvis. I've hit him with two shots of morphine, but it won't stop him.'

'Can you get into the stope?'

'Yes, there is a crawling hole.' Barnard flashed his lamp over the pile of fractured blue quartzite that jammed the drive like a collapsed garden wall. On it was an aperture big enough for a fox terrier to run through. Reflected light showed from the hole, and faintly from within came the grating sounds of movement over loose rock and the muffled voices of men.

'How many men have you got working in there, Barnard?'

'I – ' Barnard hesitated, 'I think about ten or twelve.'

And Rod grabbed a handful of his overall front and jerked him almost off his feet.

'You think!' In the head lamps Rod's face was white with fury. 'You've put men in there without recording their numbers? You've put twelve of my boys against the wall to try and save nine?' With a heave Rod lifted the shift boss off his feet and swung him against the side wall of the drive, pinning him there.

'You bastard, you know that most of those nine are chopped already. You know that stope is a bloody killing ground, and you send in *twelve* more to get the chop *and* you don't record their numbers. How the hell would we ever know who to look for if the hanging fell again?' He let the shift boss free, and stood back. 'Get them out of here, clear that stope.'

'But, Mr Ironsides, the General Manager is in there, Mr Lemmer is in there. He was doing an inspection in the stope.'

For a moment Rod was taken aback, then he snarled. 'I don't give a good damn if the State President is in there, clear the stope. We'll start again and this time we'll do it properly.'

Within minutes the rescuers had been recalled, they came squirming out of the aperture, white with dust like maggots wriggling from rotten cheese.

'Right,' said Rod, 'I'll risk four men at a time.'

Quickly he picked four of the floury figures, among them an enormous man on whose right shoulder was the brass badge of a boss boy.

'Big King – you here?' Rod spoke in Fanikalo, the lingua franca of the mines which enabled men from a dozen ethnic groups to communicate.

'I am here,' answered Big King.

'You looking for more awards?' A month before, Big King had been lowered on a rope 200 feet down a vertical

13

orepass to retrieve the body of a white miner. The bravery award by the company had been 100 rand.

'Who speaks of awards when the earth has eaten the flesh of men?' Big King rebuked Rod softly. 'But today is children's play only. Is the Nkosi coming into the stope?' It was a challenge.

Rod's place was not in the stope. He was the organizer, the co-ordinator. Yet, he could not ignore the challenge, no Bantu would believe that he had not stood back in fear and sent other men in to die.

'Yes,' said Rod, 'I'm coming into the stope.'

He led them in. The hole was only just big enough to admit the bulk of Rod's body. He found himself in a chamber the size of an average room, but the roof was only three and a half feet high. He played his lamp quickly across the hanging wall, and it was wicked. The rock was cracked and ugly, 'a bunch of grapes' was the term.

'Very pretty,' he said, and dropped the beam of his lamp.

The squealer was within an arm's length of Rod. His body from the waist up protruded from under a piece of rock the size of a Cadillac. Someone had wrapped a red blanket around his upper body. He was quiet now, lying still. But as the beam of Rod's lamp fell upon him, he lifted his head. His eyes were crazed, unseeing, his face running with the sweat of terror and insanity. His mouth snapped open, wide and pink in the shiny blackness of his face. He began to scream, but suddenly the sound was drowned by a great red-black gout of blood that came gushing up his throat, and spurted from his mouth.

As Rod watched in horror, the Bantu posed like that, his head thrown back, his mouth gaping as though he were a gargoyle, the life blood pouring from him. Then slowly the head sagged forward, and flopped face downwards. Rod crawled to him, lifted his head and pillowed it on the red blanket.

14

There was blood on his hands and he wiped it on the front of his overalls.

'Three,' he said, 'so far.' And leaving the dying man he crawled on towards the broken face of the fall.

Big King crawled up beside him with two pinch bars. He handed one to Rod.

Within an hour it had become a contest, a trial of strength between two men. Behind them the other three men were shoring up and passing back the rock that Rod and Big King loosened from the face. Rod knew he was being childish, he should have been back in the main haulage, not only directing the rescue, but also making all the other decisions and alternative arrangements that were needed now. The company paid him for his brains and his experience, not for his muscle.

'The hell with it,' he thought. 'Even if we miss the blast this evening, I'm staying here.' He glanced at Big King, and reached forward to get his hands onto a bigger piece of rock in the jam. He strained, using his arms first, then bringing the power of his whole body into it – the rock was solid. Big King placed huge black hands on the rock, and they pulled together. In a rush of smaller rock it came away, and they shoved it back between them, grinning at each other.

At seven o'clock Rod and Big King withdrew from the stope to rest and eat sandwiches, and drink Thermos coffee while Rod spoke to Dimitri over the field telephone that had been laid up to the face.

'We've pulled shift on both shafts, Rod, the workings are clear to blast. Except for your lot, there are fifty-eight men in your 43 section.' Dimitri's voice was reedy over the field telephone.

'Hold on.' Rod revolved the situation in his mind. He worked it out slower than usual, for he was tired, emotionally and physically drained. If he stopped the blast on both shafts for fear of bringing down more rock in 43 section, it would cost the Company a day's production, 10,000 tons of gold reef worth sixteen rand a ton, the formidable sum of R160,000 or £80,000 or $200,000 whichever way you looked at it.

It was highly probable that every man in the stope was already dead, and the original pressure burst had de-stressed the rock above and around the 95 level, so there was little danger of further bumps.

And yet there might be someone alive in there, someone lying pinned in the womb-warm darkness of the stope with a bunch of loose grapes hanging over his unprotected body. When they hit all the blast buttons on the Sonder Ditch Mine, they fired eighteen tons of Dynagel. The kick was considerable, it would bring down those grapes.

'Dimitri,' Rod made his decision, 'burn all longwalls on No. 2 shaft at seven-thirty exactly.' No. 2 shaft was three miles away. That would save the Company R80,000. 'Then at precisely five-minute intervals burn south, north and west longwalls here on No. 1 shaft.' Spreading the blast would reduce the disturbance, and that put another R60,000 in the shareholders' pockets. The total monetary loss inflicted by the disaster was around R20,000. Not too bad really, Rod thought sardonically, blood was cheap. You could buy it at three rand a pint from the Central Blood Transfusion Service.

'All right,' he stood up, and flexed his aching shoulders. 'I'm pulling everybody back into the safety of the shaft pillar while we blast.'

After the successive earth tremors of the blast, Rod put them back into the stope, and at nine o'clock they uncovered the bodies of two machine boys crushed against the metal of their own rock drill. Ten feet further on they found the white miner; his body was unmarked, but his head was flattened.

At eleven o'clock they found two more machine boys. Rod was in the haulage when they dragged them out through the small opening. Neither of them were recognizable as human, they looked more like lumps of raw meat that had been rubbed in dirt.

A little after midnight Rod and Big King went into the stope again to take over from the team at the face, and twenty minutes later they holed through the wall of loose rock into another chamber that had been miraculously left standing.

The air in here was steamy with heat. Rod recoiled instinctively from the filthy moist gush of it against his face. Then he forced himself to crawl forward and peer into the opening.

Ten feet away lay Frank Lemmer, the General Manager of the Sonder Ditch Mine. He lay on his back. His helmet had been knocked from his head, and a deep gash split the skin above his eye. Blood from the gash had run back into his silver hair and clotted black. He opened his eyes and blinked owlishly in the dazzle of Rod's lamp. Quickly Rod averted the beam.

'Mr Lemmer,' he said.

'What the bloody hell are you doing with the rescue team?' growled Frank Lemmer. 'It's not your job. Haven't you learned a single goddamned thing in twenty years of mining?'

'Are you all right, sir?'

'Get a doctor in here,' replied Frank Lemmer. 'You're going to have to cut me loose from this lot.'

Rod wriggled up to where he lay, and then he saw what Frank Lemmer meant. From the elbow his arm was pinned under a solid slab of rock. Rod ran his hands over the slab, feeling it. Only explosive would shift the rock. As always Frank Lemmer was right.

Rod wriggled out of the opening and called over his shoulder.

'Get the telephone up here.'

After a few minutes delay he had the receiver, and was through to the station at 95 level which had been set up as an advance aid post and rest station for the rescuers.

'This is Ironsides, get me Doctor Stander.'

'Hold on.'

Then moments later, 'Hello, Rod, it's Dan.'

'Dan, we've found the old man.'

'How is he, conscious?'

'Yes, but he's pinned – you'll have to cut.'

'Are you sure?' Dan Stander asked.

'Of course I'm bloody well sure,' snapped Rod.

'Whoa, boy!' admonished Dan.

'Sorry.'

'Okay, where's he caught?'

'Arm. You'll have to cut above the elbow.'

'Charming!' said Dan.

'I'll wait here for you.'

'Right. I'll be up in five minutes.'

'It's funny, you see them chopped time and again, but you know it will never happen to you.' Frank Lemmer's voice was steady and even. The arm must be numb, Rod thought as he lay beside him in the stope.

Frank Lemmer rolled his head towards Rod. 'Why don't you go farming, boy?'

'You know why,' said Rod.

'Yes.' Lemmer smiled a little, just a twitching of the lips. With his free hand he wiped his mouth. 'You know, I had just three months more before I went on pension. I nearly made it. You'll end like this, boy, in the dirt with your bones crunched up.'

'It's not the end,' said Rod.

'Isn't it?' asked Frank Lemmer, and this time he chuckled. 'Isn't it?'

'What's the joke?' asked Dan Stander, poking his head into the tiny chamber.

'Christ, it took you long enough to get here,' growled Frank Lemmer.

'Give me a hand, Rod.' Dan passed his bag through, then as he crawled forward he spoke to Frank Lemmer.

'Union Steel closed at 98 cents tonight. I told you to buy.'

'Over-priced, over-capitalized,' snorted Frank Lemmer. Dan lay on his side in the dirt and laid out his instruments, and they argued stocks and shares. When Dan had the syringe full of pentathol and was swabbing Frank Lemmer's stringy old arm, Lemmer rolled his head towards Rod again.

'We made a good dig here, Rodney, you and I. I wish they'd give it to you now, but they won't. You're still too young. But whoever they put in my place, you keep an eye on him, you know the ground – don't let him balls it up.'

And the needle went in.

Dan cut through the arm in four and a half minutes, and twenty-seven minutes later Frank Lemmer died of shock and exposure in the Mary Anne on his way to the surface.

– 7 –

Once he had paid Patti's alimony there was not too much of Rod's salary left for extravagances, but one of these was the big cream Maserati. Although it was a 1967 model, and had done nearly 30,000 miles when he bought it, yet the instalments still took a healthy bite out of his monthly pay cheque.

On mornings like this he reckoned the expense worthwhile. He came twisting down from the Kraalkop ridge, and when the national road flattened and straightened for the final run into Johannesburg he let the Maserati go. The car seemed to flatten against the ground like a running lion, and the exhaust note changed subtly, becoming deeper, more urgent.

Ordinarily, it was an hour's run from the Sonder Ditch Mine into the city of Johannesburg, but Rod could clip twenty minutes off that time.

It was Saturday morning, and Rod's mood was light and expectant.

Since the divorce Rod had lived a Jekyll and Hyde existence. Five days of the week he was the company man in top-line management, but on the last two days of the week he went into Johannesburg with his golf clubs in the boot of the Maserati, the keys to his luxury Hillbrow apartment in his pocket, and a chuckle on his lips.

Today the anticipation was keener than ever for, in addition to the twenty-two-year-old blonde model who was prepared to devote her evening to entertaining Rodney Ironsides, there was the mysterious summons from Dr Manfred Steyner to answer.

The summons had been delivered by a nameless female caller describing herself as 'Dr Steyner's Secretary'. It had come the day after Frank Lemmer's funeral, and was for Saturday at 11 a.m.

Rod had never met Manfred Steyner, but he had, of course, heard of him. Anyone who worked for any of the fifty or sixty companies that comprised the Central Rand Consolidated Group must have heard of Manfred Steyner, and the Sonder Ditch Gold Company was just one of the Group.

Manfred Steyner had a bachelor's degree in Economics from Berlin University, and a Doctor's degree in Business Administration from Cornell. He had joined CRC a mere twelve years previously at the age of thirty, and now he was the front runner. Hurry Hirschfeld could not live for ever, although he gave indications of doing so, and when he went down to make a takeover bid on Hades, the word was that Manfred Steyner would succeed him as Chairman of CRC.

Chairmanship of CRC was an enviable position, the incumbent automatically became one of the five most powerful men in Africa, and that included heads of state.

The betting favoured Dr Steyner for a number of good reasons. He had a brain that had earned him the nickname of 'The Computer'; no one had yet been able to detect in him the slightest evidence of a human weakness, and more than this he had taken the trouble ten years previously to catch Hurry Hirschfeld's only granddaughter as she emerged from Cape Town University and marry her.

Dr Steyner was in a strong position, and Rod was intrigued with the prospect of meeting him.

The Maserati was registering 125 miles an hour as he went under the over-pass of the Kloof Gold Mining Company property.

'Johannesburg, here I come!' Rod laughed aloud.

It was ten minutes before eleven o'clock when Rod

21

found the brass plaque reading 'Dr M. K. Steyner' in a secluded lane of the lush Johannesburg suburb of Sandown. The house was not visible from the road, and Rod let the Maserati roll gently in through the tall white gates, with their imitation Cape Dutch gables.

The gates, he decided, were a display of shocking taste but the gardens beyond them were paradise. Rod knew rock, but flowers were his weak suit. He recognized the massed banks of red and yellow against the green lawns as cannas, but after that he had no names for the blazing beauty spread about him.

'Wow!' he muttered in awe. 'Someone has done a hell of a lot of work around here.'

Around a curve in the macadamized drive lay the house. It also was Cape Dutch and Rod forgave Dr Steyner his gates.

'Wow!' he said again, and involuntarily braked the Maserati to a standstill.

Cape Dutch is one of the most difficult styles to copy effectively, where one line in a hundred out of place could spoil the effect; this particular example worked perfectly. It gave the feel of timelessness, of solidarity, and mixed it subtly with a grace and finesse of line. He guessed that the shutters and beams were genuine yellow wood and the windows hand-leaded.

Rod looked at it, and felt envy prickle and burn within him. He loved fine things, like his Maserati, but this was another concept in material possessions. He was jealous of the man that owned it, knowing that his own entire year's income would not be sufficient for a down payment on the land alone.

'So I've got my flat,' he grinned ruefully, and coasted down to park in front of the line of garages.

It was not clear which was the correct entrance to use, and he chose at random from a number of paved paths that all led in the general direction of the house.

Around a bend in this path he came on another spectacle. Though smaller it had, if anything, a more profound effect on Rod than the house had. It was a feminine posterior of equal grace and finesse of line, clad in Helanka stretch ski-pants, and protruding from a large and exotic bush.

Rod was captivated. He stood and watched as the bush shook and rustled, and the bottom wriggled and heaved.

Suddenly, in ladylike tones there issued from the bush a most unladylike oath and the bottom shot backwards and its owner straightened up with her forefinger in her mouth, sucking noisily.

'It bit me!' she mumbled around the finger. 'Damned stinkbug bit me!'

'Well, you shouldn't tease them,' said Rod.

And she spun round to face him. The first thing Rod noticed were her eyes, they were enormous, completely out of proportion to the rest of her face.

'I wasn't—' she started, and then stopped. The finger came out of her mouth. Instinctively one hand went to her hair, and the other began straightening her blouse and brushing off bits of vegetation that were clinging to her.

'Who are you?' she asked, and those huge eyes swept over him. This was fairly standard reaction for any woman between the ages of sixteen and sixty viewing Rodney Ironsides for the first time, and Rodney accepted it gracefully.

'My name is Rodney Ironsides. I've an appointment to see Dr Steyner.'

'Oh.' She was hurriedly tucking her shirt-tails into her slacks. 'My husband will be in his study.'

He had known who she was. He had seen her photographs fifty times in the Group newspaper; but in them she was usually in full-length evening dress and diamonds, not in a blouse with a tear in one sleeve nor pig-tails that were coming down. In the pictures her make-up was immaculate, now she had none at all and her face was flushed and dewed with perspiration.

'I must look a mess. I've been gardening,' said Theresa Steyner unnecessarily.

'Did you do this garden yourself?'

'Only a very little of the muscle work, but I planned it,' she answered. She decided he was big and ugly – no, not really ugly, but battered-looking.

'It's beautiful,' said Rod.

'Thank you.' No, not battered-looking, she changed her mind, tough-looking, and the chest hair curled out of the V of his open neck shirt.

'This is a protea, isn't it?' He indicated the bush from which she had recently emerged. He was guessing.

'Nutans,' she said; he must be in his late thirties, there was greying at his temples.

'Oh, I thought it was a protea.'

'It is. "Nutans" is its proper name. There are over two hundred different varieties of proteas,' she answered seriously. His voice didn't fit his appearance at all, she decided. He looked like a prize fighter but spoke like a lawyer, probably was one. It was usually lawyers or business consultants who came calling on Manfred.

'Is that so? It's very pretty.' Rod touched one of the blooms.

'Yes, isn't it? I've got over fifty varieties growing here.'

And suddenly they were smiling at each other. 'I'll take you up to the house,' said Theresa Steyner.

'**M**r Ironsides is here, Manfred.'
  'Thank you.' He sat at the stinkwood desk in a room that smelled of wax polish. He made no effort to rise from his seat.

'Would you like a cup of coffee?' Theresa asked from the doorway. 'Or tea?'

'No, thank you,' answered Manfred Steyner without consulting Rod who stood beside her.

'I'll leave you to it, then,' she said.

'Thank you, Theresa.' And she turned away. Rod went on standing where he was, he was studying this man of whom he had heard so much.

Manfred Steyner appeared younger than his forty-two years. His hair was light brown, almost blond, and brushed straight back. He wore spectacles with heavy black frames, and his face was smooth and silky-looking, soft as a girl's with no beard shadow on his chin. His hands that lay on the polished desk top were hairless, smooth, so that Rod wondered if he had used a depilatory on them.

'Come in,' he said, and Rod moved to the desk. Steyner wore a white silk shirt in which the ironing creases still showed, the cloth was snowy white and over it he wore a Royal Johannesburg Golf Club tie, with onyx cuff links. Suddenly Rod realized that neither shirt nor tie had ever been worn before; that much was true of what he had heard then. Steyner ordered his shirts hand-made by the gross and wore each once only.

'Sit down, Ironsides.' Steyner slurred his vowels slightly, just a trace of a Teutonic accent.

'Dr Steyner,' said Rod softly, 'you have a choice. You may call me Rodney or Mr Ironsides.'

There was no change in Steyner's voice nor expression.

'I would like to go over your background, please, Mr

Ironsides, as a preliminary to our discussion. You have no objection?'

'No, Dr Steyner.'

'You were born October 16th, 1931, at Butterworth in the Transkei. Your father was a native trader, your mother died January 1939. Your father was commissioned Captain in the Durban Light Infantry and died of wounds on the Po River in Italy during the winter of 1944. You were raised by your maternal uncle in East London. Matriculating from Queen's College, Grahamstown, in 1947, you were unsuccessful in obtaining a Chamber of Mines scholarship to Witwatersrand University for a B.Sc. (Mining Engineering) degree. You enrolled in the GMTS (Government Mining Training School) and obtained your blasting ticket during 1949. At which time you joined the Blyvooruitzicht Gold Mining Company Ltd as a learner miner.'

Dr Steyner stood up from his desk and crossing to the panelled wall he pressed a concealed switch and a portion of the panelling slid back to reveal a wash basin and towel rack. As he went on talking he began very meticulously to soap and wash his hands.

'In the same year you were promoted to miner and in 1952 to shift boss, 1954 to mine captain. You successfully completed the examination for the Mine Manager's ticket in 1959, and in 1962 you came to us as an Assistant Underground Manager, and in 1968 you achieved your present position as Underground Manager.'

Dr Steyner began drying his hands on a snowy white towel.

'You've memorized my company record pretty thoroughly,' Rod admitted.

Dr Steyner crumpled the towel and dropped it into a bin below the wash basin. He pressed the button and the panelling slid closed, then he came back to the desk stepping precisely over the glossy polished wooden floor, and Rod realized that he was a small man, not more than five and a half feet tall, about the same height as his wife.

'This is something of an achievement,' Steyner went on. 'The next youngest Underground Manager in the entire Group is forty-six years of age, whereas you are not yet thirty-nine.'

Rod inclined his head in acknowledgement.

'Now,' said Dr Steyner as he reseated himself and laid his freshly washed hands on the desk top. 'I would like briefly to touch on your private life – you have no objections?'

Again Rod inclined his head.

'The reason that your application for the Chamber of Mines scholarship was refused, despite your straight A matriculation, was the recommendation of your headmaster to the selection board in effect that you were of unstable and violent disposition.'

'How the hell did you know that?' ejaculated Rod.

'I have access to the board's records. It seems that once you had received your matric you immediately assaulted your former headmaster.'

'I beat the hell out of the bastard,' Rod agreed happily.

'An expensive indulgence, Mr Ironsides. It cost you a university degree.'

And Rod was silent.

'To continue: In 1959 you married Patricia Anne Harvey. Of the union was born a girl child in the same year, to be precise, seven and a half months after the wedding.'

Rod squirmed slightly in his chair, and Dr Steyner went on quietly.

'This marriage terminated in divorce in 1964. Your wife is suing you on the grounds of adultery, and receiving custody of the child, alimony and maintenance in the sum of R450.000 monthly.'

'What's all this about?' demanded Rod.

'I am attempting to establish an accurate picture of your present circumstances. It is necessary, I assure you.' Dr Steyner removed his spectacles and began polishing the lens on a clean white handkerchief. There were the marks of the frames on the bridge of his nose.

'Go on, then.' Despite himself, Rod was fascinated to learn just how much Steyner knew about him.

'In 1968 there was a paternity suit brought against you by a Miss Diane Johnson and judgement for R150.00 per month.'

Rod blinked and was silent.

'I should mention two further actions against you for assault, both unsuccessful on the grounds of justification or self-defence.'

'Is that all?' asked Rod sarcastically.

'Almost,' admitted Dr Steyner. 'It is only necessary to note further recurrent expenditure in the form of a monthly payment of R150.00 on a continental sports car, and a further R100.00 per month rental on the premises 596 Glen Alpine Heights, Corner Lane, Hillbrow.'

Rod was furious, he had believed that no one in CRC knew about the flat.

'Damn you! You've been prying into my affairs!'

'Yes,' agreed Dr Steyner levelly. 'I am guilty, but in good cause. If you bear with me, you'll see why.'

Suddenly Dr Steyner stood up from the desk, crossed the room to the concealed wash basin, and again began to wash his hands. As he dried them, he spoke again.

'Your monthly commitments are R850. Your salary, after deduction of tax, is less than one thousand Rand. You have no mining degree, and the chances of your taking the next step upwards to General Manager without it are remote. You are at your ceiling, Mr Ironsides. On your own ability you can go no further. In thirty years' time you will not be the youngest Underground Manager in the CRC Group, but the oldest.' Dr Steyner paused. 'That is, provided that your rather expensive tastes have not landed you in a debtors' prison, and that neither the quickness and heat of your temper, nor the matching speed and temperature of your genitalia have gotten you into really serious trouble.'

Steyner dropped the towel in the bin and returned to his seat. They sat in absolute silence, regarding each other for a full minute.

'You got me all the way up here to tell me this?' asked Rod, his whole body tense, his voice slightly husky. It needed only an ounce more of provocation to launch him across the desk at Steyner's throat.

'No.' Steyner shook his head. 'I got you up here to tell you that I will use all my influence, which I flatter myself is considerable, to secure your appointment – and I mean immediate appointment – to the position of General Manager of the Sonder Ditch Gold Mining Company Ltd.'

Rod recoiled in his chair as though Steyner had spat in his face. He stared at him aghast.

'Why?' he asked at last. 'What do you want in exchange?'

'Neither your friendship, nor your gratitude,' Dr Steyner told him. 'But your unquestioning obedience to my instructions. You will be my man – completely.'

Rod went on staring at him while his mind raced. Without Steyner's intervention he would wait at the very least ten years for this promotion, if it ever came. He wanted it, my God, how he wanted it. The achievement, the increase in income, the power that went with the job. His own mine! His own mine at the age of thirty-eight – and an additional 10,000 rand per annum.

Yet Rod was not gullible enough to believe that Manfred Steyner's price would be cheap. When the instruction came that he was to follow with unquestioning obedience, he knew it would stink like a ten-day corpse. But once he had the job he could refuse the instruction. Get the job first, then decide once he received the instruction whether to follow it or not.

'I accept,' he said.

Manfred Steyner stood up from the desk.

'You will hear from me,' he said. 'Now you may go.'

– 9 –

Rod crossed the wide-flagged stoep without seeing or hearing; vaguely he wandered down across the lawns towards his car. His mind was harrying the recent conversation, tearing it to pieces like a pack of wild dogs on a carcass. He almost bumped into Theresa Steyner before he saw her, and abruptly his mind dropped the subject of the General Managership.

Theresa had changed her clothing, made up her face and eyes, and the pig-tails were concealed under a lime-coloured silk scarf, all this in the half hour since their last meeting. She was hovering over a flower bed with a flower basket on one arm, as bright and pleasing as a hummingbird.

Rod was amused and flattered, vain enough to realize that the change was in his honour, and connoisseur enough to appreciate the improvement.

'Hello.' She looked up, contriving successfully to look both surprised and artless. Her eyes were really enormous, and the make-up was designed to enhance their size.

'You are a busy little bee.' Rod ran a knowledgeable appraisal over the floral slack suit she wore, and saw the colour start in her cheeks as she felt his eyes.

'Did you have a successful meeting?'

'Very.'

'Are you a lawyer?'

'No. I work for your grandfather.'

'Doing what?'

'Mining his gold.'

'Which mine?'

'Sonder Ditch.'

'What's your position?'

'Well, if your husband is as good as his word, I'm the new General Manager.'

'You're too young,' she said.

'That's what I thought.'

'Pops will have something to say on the subject.'

'Pops?' he asked.

'My grandfather.' And Rod laughed before he could stop himself.

'What's so funny?'

'The Chairman of CRC being called "Pops".'

'I'm the only one who calls him that.'

'I bet you are.' Rod laughed again. 'In fact I'd bet you'd get away with a lot of things no one else would dare.'

Suddenly the underlying sexuality of his last remark occurred to them both and they fell silent. Theresa looked down and carefully snipped the head off a flower.

'I didn't mean it that way,' apologized Rod.

'What way, Mr Ironsides?' She looked up and enquired with mischievous innocence, and they laughed together with the awkwardness gone again.

She walked beside him to the car, making it seem a completely natural thing to do, and as he slipped behind the steering-wheel she remarked:

'Manfred and I will be coming out to the Sonder Ditch next week. Manfred is to present long service and bravery awards to some of your men.' She had already refused the invitation to accompany Manfred, she must now see to it that she was re-invited. 'I shall probably see you then.'

'I look forward to it,' said Rod, and let in the clutch.

Rod glanced in the rear view mirror. She was a remarkably provocative and attractive woman. A careless man could drown in those eyes.

'Dr Manfred Steyner has got himself a big fat problem there,' he decided. 'Our Manfred is probably so busy soaping and scrubbing his equipment, that he never gets round to using it.'

– 10 –

Through the leaded windows Dr Steyner caught a glimpse of the Maserati as it disappeared around the curve in the driveway, and he listened as the throb of the engine dwindled into silence.

He lifted the receiver of the telephone and wiped it with the white handkerchief before putting it to his ear. He dialled and while it rang he inspected the nails of his free hand minutely.

'Steyner,' he said into the mouthpiece. 'Yes – yes.' He listened.

'Yes ... He has just left ... Yes, it is arranged ... No, there will be no difficulty there, I am sure.' As he spoke he was looking at the palm of his hand, he saw the tiny beads of perspiration appear on his skin and an expression of disgust tightened his lips.

'I am fully aware of the consequences. I tell you, I know.'

He closed his eyes and listened for another minute without moving as the receiver squawked and clacked, then he opened his eyes.

'It will be done in good time, I assure you. Goodbye.'

He hung up and went to wash his hands. Now, he thought, as he worked up lather, to get it past the old man.

– 11 –

He was old now, seventy-eight long hard years old. His hair and his eyebrows were creamy white. His skin was folded and creased, freckled and spotted, hanging in unexpected little pouches under his chin and eyes.

His body had dried out, so he stood gaunt and stooped like a tree that has taken a set before the prevailing winds; but there was still the underlying urgency in the way he held himself, the same urgency that had earned him the name of 'Hurry' Hirschfeld when first he bustled into the gold fields sixty years ago.

On this Monday morning he was standing before the full length windows of his penthouse office, looking down on the city of Johannesburg. Reef House stood shoulder to massive shoulder with the Schlesinger Building on the Braamfontein ridge above the city proper. From this height it seemed that Johannesburg cowered at Hurry Hirschfeld's feet, as well it should.

Long ago, even before the great depression of the 'thirties, he had ceased to measure his wealth in terms of money. He owned outright a little over a quarter of the issued share capital of Central Rand Consolidated. At the present market price of R120 per share, this was a staggering sum. In addition, through a complicated arrangement of trusts, proxy rights and interlocking directorates, he had control of a further massive block of twenty per cent of the company's voting rights.

The overhead intercom pinged softly into this room of soft fabrics and muted colours, and Hurry started slightly.

'Yes,' he said, without turning away from the window.

'Dr Steyner is here, Mr Hirschfeld,' his secretary's voice whispered, ghostly and disembodied into the luscious room.

'Send him in,' snapped Hurry. That goddamned intercom

always gave him the creeps. The whole goddamned room gave him the creeps. It was, as Hurry had said often and loudly, like a fairy brothel.

For fifty-five years he had worked in a bleak uncarpeted office with a few yellowing photographs of men and machinery on its walls. Then they had moved him in here – he glanced around the room with the distaste that five years had not lulled. What did they think he was, a bloody ladies' hairdresser?

The panelling door slid noiselessly aside and Dr Manfred Steyner stepped neatly into the room.

'Good morning, Grandfather,' he said. For ten years, even since Terry had been bird-brained enough to marry him, Manfred Steyner had called Hurry Hirschfeld that, and Hurry hated it. He remembered now that Manfred Steyner was also responsible for the design and decor of Reef House, and therefore the author of his recent irritation.

'Whatever it is you want – No!' he said, and he moved across to the air-conditioning controls. The thermostat was already set at 'high', now Hurry turned it to 'highest'. Within minutes the room would be at the correct temperature for growing orchids.

'How are you this morning, Grandfather?' Manfred seemed not to have heard, his expression was bland and neutral as he moved to the desk and laid out his papers.

'Bloody awful,' said Hurry. It was impossible to disconcert the little prig, he thought, you might as well shout insults at an efficiently functioning piece of machinery.

'I am sorry to hear that.' Manfred took out his handkerchief and touched his chin and forehead. 'I have the weekly reports.'

Hurry capitulated and went across to the desk. This was business. He sat down and read quickly. His questions were abrupt, cutting and instantly answered, but Manfred's handkerchief was busy now, swabbing and dabbing. Twice he removed his spectacles and wiped steam from the lenses.

'Can I turn the air-conditioning down a little, Grandfather?'

'You touch it and I'll kick your arse,' said Hurry without looking up.

Another five minutes and Manfred Steyner stood up suddenly.

'Excuse me, Grandfather.' And he shot across the office and disappeared into the adjoining bathroom suite. Hurry cocked his head to listen, and when he heard the taps hiss he grinned happily. The air-conditioning was the only method he had discovered of disconcerting Manfred Steyner, and for ten years he had been experimenting with various techniques.

'Don't use all the soap,' he shouted gleefully. 'You are the one always on about office expenses!'

It did not seem ludicrous to Hurry that one of the richest and most influential men in Africa should devote so much time and energy to baiting his personal assistant.

At eleven o'clock Manfred Steyner gathered his papers and began packing them carefully in his monogrammed pigskin briefcase.

'About the appointment of a new General Manager for the Sonder Ditch to replace Mr Lemmer. You will recall my memo regarding the appointment of younger men to key positions—'

'Never read the bloody thing,' lied Hurry Hirschfeld. They both knew he read everything, and remembered it.

'Well—' Manfred went on to enlarge his thesis for a minute, then ended, 'In view of this, my department, myself concurring entirely, urges the appointment of Rodney Barry Ironsides, the present Underground Manager, to the position. I hoped that you would initial the recommendation and we can put it through at Friday's meeting.'

Dexterously Manfred slid the yellow memo in front of Hurry Hirschfeld, unscrewed the cap of his pen and offered it to him. Hurry picked the memo up between thumb and forefinger as though it were someone's dirty handkerchief and dropped it into the waste-paper bin.

'Do you wish me to tell you in detail what you and your planning department can do?' he asked.

'Grandfather,' Manfred admonished him mildly, 'you cannot run the company as though you were a robber baron. You cannot ignore the team of highly trained men who are your advisers.'

'I've run it that way for fifty years. You show me who's going to change that.' Hurry leaned back in his chair with vast satisfaction and fished a powerful-looking cigar out of his inner pocket.

'Grandfather, that cigar! The doctor said—'

'And I said Fred Plummer gets the job as Manager of the Sonder Ditch.'

'He goes on pension next year,' protested Manfred Steyner.

'Yes,' Hurry nodded. 'But how does that alter the position?'

'He's an old dodderer,' Manfred tried again, there was a desperate edge to his voice. He had not anticipated one of the old man's whims cutting across his plans.

'He's twelve years younger than I am,' growled Hurry ominously. 'How's that make him an old dodderer?'

Now that the weekend was over, Rod found the apartment oppressive, and he longed to get out of it.

He shaved, standing naked before the mirror, and he caught a whiff of the reeking ashtrays and half-empty glasses in the lounge. The char would have her customary Monday-morning greeting when she came in later today. From Louis Botha Avenue the traffic noise was starting to build up and he glanced at his watch – six o'clock in the morning. A good time to examine your soul, he decided, and leaned forward to watch his own eyes in the mirror.

'You're too old for this type of living,' he told himself seriously. 'You've had four years of it now, four years since the divorce, and that's about enough. It would be nice now to go to bed with the same woman on two consecutive nights.'

He rinsed his razor, and turned on the taps in the shower cabinet.

'Might even be able to afford it, if our boy Manfred delivers the goods.' Rod had not allowed himself to believe too implicitly in Manfred Steyner's promise; but during the whole of these last two days the excitement had been there beneath the cynicism.

He stepped into the shower and soaped himself, then turned the cold tap full on. Gasping he shut it off and reached for his towel. Still drying himself, he went through and stood at the foot of the bed; as he towelled himself he examined the girl who lay among the tousled sheets.

She was tanned dark toffee brown so she appeared to be dressed in white transparent bra and panties where the skin was untouched by the sun. Her hair was a blonde-gold flurry across her face and the pillow, at odds with the jet black triangle of body hair. Her lips in sleep were fixed in a soft pink pout, and she looked disquietingly young. Rod had to make a conscious effort to remember her name, she was not the companion with whom he had begun the weekend.

'Lucille,' he said, sitting down beside her. 'Wake up. Time to roll.'

She opened her eyes.

'Good morning,' he said and kissed her gently.

'Mmm.' She blinked. 'What time is it? I don't want to get fired.'

'Six,' he told her.

'Oh, good. Plenty of time.' And she rolled over and snuggled down into the sheets.

'Like hell.' He slapped her bottom lightly. 'Move, girl, can you cook?'

'No—' She lifted her head. 'What's your name again?' she asked.

'Rod,' he told her.

'That's right – Piston Rod,' she giggled. 'What a way to die! Are you sure you aren't powered by steam?'

'How old are you?' he asked.

'Nineteen. How old are you?'

'Thirty-eight.'

'Daddy, you're vintage!' she told him vehemently.

'Yes, sometimes I feel that way.' He stood up. 'Let's go.'

'You go. I'll lock up when I leave.'

'No sale,' he said, the last one he had left in the flat had cleaned it out – groceries, liquor, glasses, towels, even the ashtrays. 'Five minutes to dress.'

Fortunately she lived on his way. She directed him to a run-down block of flats under the mine dumps at Booysens.

'I'm putting three blind sisters through school. You want to help?' she asked as he parked the Maserati.

'Sure.' He eased a five-rand note out of his wallet and handed it to her.

'Ta muchly.' And she slipped out of the red leather seat, closed the door and walked away. She did not look back before she disappeared into the block, and Rod felt an unaccountable wave of loneliness wash over him. It was so intense that he sat quiescent for a full minute before he could throw it off, then he hit the gears and screeched away from the kerb.

'My little five-rand friend,' he said. 'She really cares!'

He drove fast, so that as he topped the Kraalkop ridge the shadows were still long, and the dew lay silver on the grass. He pulled the Maserati into a layby and climbed out. Leaning against the bonnet he lit a cigarette, grimacing at the taste, and looked down at the valley.

There was no natural surface indication of the immense treasure house that lay below. It was like any of the other countless grassy plains of the Transvaal. In the centre stood the town of Kitchenerville, which for half a century had rejoiced in the fact that Lord Kitchener had camped one night here in pursuit of the wily Boer: a collection of three dozen buildings which had expanded miraculously into three thousand, around a magnificent town hall and shopping complex. Dressed in public lawns and gardens, wide streets and bright new houses, all of it paid for by the mining houses whose lease areas converged on the town.

Out of the bleak veld surrounding the town their headgears stood like colossal monuments to the gold hunger of man. Around the headgears clustered the plants and workshops. There were fourteen headgears in the valley. The field was divided into five lease areas, following the original farm titles, and was mined by five separate companies. Thornfontein Gold Mining, Blaauberg Gold Mining, West Tweefontein Mining, Deep Gold Levels, and the Sonder Ditch Gold Mining Company.

It was to this last that Rod naturally directed his attention.

'You beauty,' he whispered, for in his eyes the mountainous dumps of blue rock beside the shafts were truly beautiful. The complex but carefully thought out pattern of the works buildings, even the sulphur-yellow acres of the slimes dam, had a functional beauty.

'Get it for me, Manfred,' he spoke aloud. 'I want it. I want it badly.'

On the twenty-eight square miles of the Sonder Ditch's property lived 14,000 human beings, 12,000 of them were Bantu who had been recruited from all over Southern Africa. They lived in the multi-storied hostels near the shaft heads, and each day they went down through two small holes in the ground to depths that were scarcely credible, and came up again out of those same two holes. 12,000 men down, 12,000 up. That was not all: out of those two same holes came 10,000 tons of rock daily, and down them went timber and tools and piping and explosive, ton upon ton of material and equipment. It was an undertaking that must evoke pride in the men who accomplished it.

Rod glanced at his watch, 7.35 a.m. They were down already, all 12,000 of them. They had started going down at three-thirty that morning and now it was accomplished. The shift was in. The Sonder Ditch was breaking rock, and bringing the stuff out.

Rod grinned happily. His loneliness and depression of an hour ago were gone, swallowed up in the immensity of his involvement. He watched the massive wheels of the headgears spinning, stopping briefly, and then spinning again.

Each of those shafts had cost fifty million rand, the surface plant and works another fifty million. The Sonder Ditch represented an investment of 150 million rand, 220 million dollars. It was big, and it would be his.

Rod flicked away the butt of his cigarette. As he drove down the ridge, his eyes moved eastward down the valley. All mining activity ceased abruptly along an imaginary north-south line, drawn arbitarily across the open grassland.

There was no surface indication why this should be so, but the reason was deep down.

On that line ran a geological freak, a dyke, a wall of hard serpentine rock that had been named 'the Big Dipper'. It cut through the field like an axe stroke, and beyond it was bad ground. The gold reef existed in the bad ground, they knew this; but not one of the five companies had gone after it. They had prospected it tentatively and then shied away from it, for the boreholes that they sank were frightening in their inconsistency.

A big percentage of the Sonder Ditch lease area lay on the far side of the Dipper, and there was a diamond-drilling team working there now. They had already completed five holes.

Rod could remember accurately the results:-

Borehole SD No. 1.	Abandoned in water at 4,000 ft.	
SD No. 2.	Abandoned in dry hole at 5,250 ft.	
SD No. 3.	Intersected carbon leader reef at 6,600 ft.	
Assay valve	27,323-inch penny-weights.	
First deflection	6,212-inch penny-weights.	
Second deflection	2,114-inch penny-weights.	
SD No. 4.	Abandoned in artesian water at 3,500 ft.	
SD No. 5.	Intersected carbon leader at 8,116 ft.	
Assay valve	562-inch penny-weights.	

And they were drilling the deflections on that one now.

The problem was to build up a picture from results like that. It looked like a mess of faulted and waterlogged ground with the gold reef fragmented and fluky, showing unbelievably high values at one spot, and then more than likely pinching out fifty feet away.

They may mine it one day, thought Rod, but I hope to hell I'm on pension by the time they do.

In the distance beyond the slimes dam he could just make out the spidery triangle of the drilling rig against the grown grass.

'Go to it, boys,' he muttered. 'Whatever you find there won't make much difference to me.'

And he went in through the imposing gates at the entrance to the mine property, halting carefully at the stop sign where the railway line crossed the road and he forked two fingers at the traffic policeman lurking behind the gates.

The traffic cop grinned and waved; he had caught Rod the previous week, so he was still one up.

Rod drove down to his office.

– 13 –

That Monday morning Allen 'Popeye' Worth was preparing to drill his first deflection on the SD No. 5. borehole. Allen was a Texan – not a typical Texan. He stood five feet four inches tall, but was as tough as the steel drill with which he worked. Thirty years before he had started learning his trade on the oilfields around Odessa and he had learned it well.

Now he could start at the surface and drill a four-inch hole down 13,000 feet through the earth's crust, keeping the hole straight all the way, an almost impossible task if you took into account the whippiness and torque in a jointed rod of steel that long.

If, as happened occasionally, the steel snapped and broke off thousands of feet down, Allen could fit a fishing tool on the end of his rig, and patiently grope for the stump, find it, grapple it and pull it out of the borehole. When he hit the reef down there, he could purposely kick his drill off the line and pierce the reef again and again to sample it over an area of hundreds of feet. This was what was meant by deflecting.

Allen was one of the best. He could command his own salary and behave like a prima donna, and his bosses would still fawn on him, for the things he could do with a diamond drill were almost magical.

Now he was assessing the angle of his first deflection. The previous day he had lowered a long brass bottle to the end of his borehole and left it overnight. The bottle was half filled with concentrated sulphuric acid, and it had etched the brass of the bottle. By measuring the angle of the etching he knew just how his drill was branching off from his original hole.

In the tiny wood and iron building beside the drilling rig he finished his measurements and stood back from the work bench, grunting with satisfaction.

From his hip pocket he drew a corncob pipe and pouch. Once he had stuffed tobacco into the pipe and lit it, it became very clear as to why his nickname was 'Popeye'. He was a dead ringer for the cartoon character, aggressive jaw, button eyes, battered maritime cap and all.

He puffed contentedly, watching through the single window of the shack as his gang went about the tedious business of lowering the drilling bit down into the earth. Then he took the pipe from his mouth and spat accurately through the window, replaced the pipe and stooped to minutely check his measurements.

His foreman driller interrupted him from the doorway.

'On bottom, and ready to turn, boss.'

'Huh!' Popeye checked his watch. 'Two hours forty to get down, you don't reckon to rupture a gut do you?'

'That's not bad,' protested the foreman.

'And it sure as hell isn't good either! Okay, okay, cut the cackle and let's get her turning.' He bounced out of the shed and set off for the rig, darting quick beady little glances about him. The rig was a fifty-foot-high tower of steel girders and within it the drill rod hung down until it disappeared into the collar. The twin 200-horsepower diesel engines throbbed expectantly, waiting to provide the power, their exhausts smoking blue in the early morning sunlight. Beside the rig lay a mountainous heap of drilling rods, beyond them the 10,000-gallon puddling reservoir to provide water for the hole. Water was pumped into the hole continuously to cool and lubricate the tool as it cut into the rock.

'Stand by to turn her,' Popeye called to his gang, and they moved to their stations. Dressed in blue overalls, coloured fibreglass helmets, and leather gloves, they stood ready and tensed. This was an anxious moment for the whole team: power had to be applied with a lover's touch to the mile and a half length of rod, or it would buckle and snap.

Popeye climbed nimbly up onto the collar, and glanced about him to make sure all was in readiness. The foreman driller was at the controls, watching Popeye with complete absorption, his hands resting on the levers.

'Power up!' shouted Popeye and made the circular motion with his right hand. The diesels bellowed harshly, and Popeye reached out to lay his left hand on the drilling rod. This was how he did it, feeling the rod with his bare hand as he brought in the power, judging the tension by ear and eye and touch.

His right hand gestured and the foreman delicately let in the clutch, the rod moved under Popeye's hand, he gestured again and it revolved slowly. He could feel it was near breaking point and he cut down the power instantly, then let it in again. His right hand moved eloquently, expressively as an orchestral conductor, and the foreman followed it, the junior member of a highly skilled team.

Slowly the tension of the gang relaxed as the revolutions

of the drill built up steadily, until Popeye gave the clenched fist 'okay' and jumped down from the collar. They scattered casually to their other duties, while Popeye and the foreman strolled back to the shed, leaving the drill to grind away at a steady four hundred revolutions a minute.

'Got something for you,' said the foreman, as they entered the shed.

'What?' demanded Popeye.

'The latest *Playboy*.'

'You're kidding!' Popeye accused him delightedly, but the foreman fished the rolled magazine out of his lunch box.

'Hey, there!' Popeye snatched it from him and turned immediately to the coloured foldout.

'Isn't that something!' He whistled. 'This dolly could get a job in a stockyard beating the oxen to death with her boo-boos!'

The foreman joined the discussion of the young lady's anatomy, and so neither of them noticed the change in the sound of the drill until two minutes had passed. Then Popeye heard it through an erotic haze. He flung the magazine from him, and went through the door of the shed white-faced.

It was fifty yards from the shed to the rig, but even at that distance Popeye could see the vibration in the drilling rod. He could hear the labouring note of the diesels as they carried increased load, and he ran like a fox terrier, trying to reach the controls and shut off the engines before it happened.

He knew what it was. His drill had cut into one of the many fissures with which this badly faulted ground was criss-crossed. The puddling water from his borehole had drained away leaving the bit to run dry against dry rock. The friction head had built up, the dust from the cut was not being washed away – and in consequence the rod had jammed. It was being held tightly at one end while at the

45

other the two big diesels were straining to turn it. The whole rig was seconds away from a twist-off.

There should have been an operator at the controls to meet just such an emergency, but he was a hundred yards away, just emerging from the wood and iron latrine beyond the puddling dam. He was desperately trying to hoist his pants, clinch the buckle of his belt and run all at the same time.

'You whore's chamberpot!' roared Popeye, as he ran. 'What the hell you goofing off—'

The words choked off in his throat, for as he reached the door of the engine room there was a report like a cannon shot as the rod snapped, and immediately the diesels screamed into over-rev as they were relieved of the load. Just too late, Popeye punched the earth buttons on the magnetos, and the engines spluttered into silence.

In that silence Popeye was sobbing with exertion and frustration and anger.

'A twist-off,' he sobbed. 'A deep one. Oh no! God, no!' It might take two weeks to fish out the broken rod, pump cement into the fissure to seal it, and then start again.

He removed the cap from his head, and with all his strength hurled it on the engine room floor. He then proceeded to jump on it with both feet. This was standard procedure. Popeye jumped on his cap at least once a week, and the foreman knew that when he had finished doing that he would then assault anybody within range.

Quietly the foreman slipped behind the wheel of the Ford truck, and the rest of the gang scrambled aboard. They all bumped away down the rutted track. There was a roadhouse on the main road where they went for coffee at times like this. When the mists of rage had dispersed sufficiently from his mind for Popeye to start seeking a human sacrifice, he looked about to find the drilling area strangely still and deserted.

'Stupid bunch of yellow-bellied baboons!' he bellowed in

46

frustration after the retreating truck, and, as the next best thing, went into the shed to phone his Managing Director.

This gentleman sitting in the air-conditioned offices of 'Hart Drilling and Cementation' high above Rissik Street in Johannesburg was a little taken aback to learn from Popeye Worth that he, the Managing Director, was directly responsible for the twist-off of an expensive diamond drill at the Sonder Ditch No. 5 hole.

'If you used that sack of custard that passes for a brain, you'd fight shy of trying to sink holes into this bunch of knitting,' Popeye yelled into the mouthpiece. 'I'd prefer to stick my old man into a meat grinder than put a drill into this ground. It stinks, I tell you! It's really ugly down there. God help the poor son of a bitch who tries to mine it!'

He slammed down the phone and stuffed his pipe with trembling fingers. Ten minutes later his breathing had returned to normal and his hands were steady. He picked up the phone again and dialled the number of the road-house. The proprietor answered.

'José, tell my boys it's okay, they can come home now,' said Popeye.

– 14 –

For Rod Ironsides there was more excitement than usual in meeting and solving the dozen paper problems that lay on his desk to welcome him back to the office. As he worked he kept remembering that Manfred Steyner might be able to do it, might just be able to do it.

The Sonder Ditch might really belong to him soon. He dispatched the last problem and lay back in his swivel chair. His mind was clear of the last cobwebs of dissipation and, as always, he felt purged and cleansed.

If I get her, I'll make her the star performer in the whole field, he thought greedily, they'll talk about the Sonder

Ditch from Wall Street to the Bourse, and about the man who is running her. I know how to do it too. I'll cut the costs to the bone, I'll tighten her up solid. Frank Lemmer was a good man, he could get the stuff out of the ground, but he let it creep up on him. It cost him almost nine rand a ton to mill it.

Well, I'll get it out as well as he did *and* I'll get it out cheaper. An operation takes its temperament from the man at the head. Frank Lemmer would talk about costs every now and then, but he didn't mean it and we knew he didn't mean it. We have become a wasteful operation because we are on a rich reef, we have become big spenders. Well, I'm going to talk costs, and I'll skin the arse of anybody who thinks I'm joking.

Last year Hamilton at Western Holdings kept his working costs per ton milled down to just a touch over six rand. I could do the same here! I could jump our profits twelve million Rand in one year, if only they give me the job I'll shout the Sonder Ditch's name across the financial markets of the world.

The problem that Rod was pondering was the nightmare of the gold mining industry. Since the 1930s the price of gold had been fixed at $35 a fine ounce. Each year since then the cost of mining had crept up steadily. In those days they reckoned four penny-weights of gold in a ton of ore was payable value. Now around eight penny-weights was the marginal value.

So in the interim all those millions of tons of ore whose values fell between four and eight penny-weights had been placed beyond the reach of man until such time as they increased the price of gold.

There were many mines with vast reserves of goldbearing ore, millions in bullion, whose values lay just below the magical number eight. Those mines stood deserted and forlorn, rust reddening their headgears, and the corrugated iron roofs of the buildings collapsing wearily. Rising costs had shot the guts out of them, they were condemned by the single word 'UNPAY'.

The Sonder Ditch was running twenty to twenty-five penny-weights per ton. She was fat, but she could be fatter, Rod decided.

There was a knock at the door.

'Come in!' called Rod, and looked at his watch. It was nine o'clock already. Time for the Monday meeting of his mine captains.

They came in singly and in pairs, twelve of them. These were Rod's front-line men, his combat officers. They went down there each day, each to his own section, and directed the actual assault on the rock.

While they chatted idly, waiting for the meeting to begin, Rod looked them over surreptitiously and was reminded of a remark that Herman Koch of Anglo American had made to him once.

'Mining is a hard game, and it attracts a hard breed of men.'

These were men of the hard breed, physically and mentally tough, and Rod realized with a start that he was one of them. No, more than one of them. He was their leader, and with a fierce affection and pride he opened the meeting.

'Right, let's hear your gripes. Who is going to be first to break my heart?'

There are some men with a talent for controlling, and getting the very best results out of other men. Rod was one of them. It was more than his physical size, his compelling voice and hearty chuckle. It was a special magnetism, a personal charm and unerring sense of timing. Under his chairmanship the meeting would erupt, voices crackle and snap, then subside into chuckles and nods as Rod spoke.

They knew he was as tough as they were, and they respected that. They knew that when he spoke it made sense, so they listened. They knew that when he promised, he delivered, so they were placated. And they knew that when he made a decision or judgement, he acted upon it, so every man knew exactly where he stood.

If asked, any one of these mine captains would have admitted grudgingly that 'there was no bulldust in Ironsides'. This was the equivalent of a presidential citation.

'Very well then.' Rod terminated the meeting. 'You have spent a good two hours of the company's time beating your gums. Now, will you kindly haul arse, go down there and start sending the stuff out.'

– 15 –

As these men planned the week's operation, so their men were at work in the earth below them.

On 87 level, Kowalski moved like a great bear down the dimly-lit drive. He had switched off the lamp on his helmet, and he moved without sound, lightly for a man of such bulk. He heard their voices ahead of him in the dimly-lit tunnel, and he paused, listening intently. There was no sound of shovel crunching into loose rock, and Kowalski's Neanderthal features convulsed into a fearsome scowl.

'Bastards!' he muttered softly. 'They think I am in stopes, hey? They think it all right if they sit on fat black bum, no move da bloody rock, hey?'

He started forward again, a bear on cat's feet.

'They find plenty different from what they bloody think, soon!' he threatened.

He stepped round the angle of the drive and flashed his lamp. There were three men Kowalski had put on lashing, shovelling the loose stuff from the footwall into waiting cocopans. Two of them sat against the cocopan, smoking contentedly while the third regaled them with an account of a beer drink he had attended the previous Christmas.

Their shovels and sledge hammers leaned unemployed against the side wall of the drive.

All three of them froze into rigidity as the beam of Kowalski's lamp played over them.

'So!' The word burst explosively from Kowalski, and he snatched up a fourteen-pound hammer in one massive fist, reversed it and struck the butt of the handle against the foot wall. The steel head of the hammer fell off and Kowalski was left with a four-foot length of selected hickory in his hand.

'You, boss boy!' he bellowed, and his free hand shot out and fastened on the throat of the nearest Bantu. With one heave he jerked him off his feet onto his knees and began dragging him away up the drive. Even in his rage, Kowalski was making sure there were no witnesses. The other two men sat where they were, too horrified to move, while their companion's wails and cries receded into the darkness.

Then the first blow reverberated in the confined space of the drive, followed immediately by a shriek of pain.

The next blow, and another shriek.

The crack, thud, crack, thud, went on repeatedly, but the accompanying shrieks dwindled into moans and soft whimperings, then into complete silence.

Kowalski came back down the drive alone, he was sweating heavily in the lamp light, and the handle of the hammer in his hand was black and glistening with wet blood.

He threw it at their feet.

'Work!' he growled, and was gone, big and bearlike, into the shadows.

51

– 16 –

On 100 level, Joseph M'Kati was hosing down and sweeping the spillings from under the giant conveyor belt. Joseph had been on this job for five years, and he was a contented and happy man.

Joseph was a Shangaan approaching sixty years of age; the first frost was touching his hair. There were laughter lines around his eyes and at the corner of his mouth. He wore his helmet pushed to the back of his head, his overalls were hand-embroidered and ornamentally patched in blue and red, and he moved with a jaunty bounce and strut.

The conveyor was many hundreds of yards long. From all the levels above the shattered gold reef was scraped from the stopes and trammed back down the haulages in the cocopans. Then from the cocopans it was tipped into the mouths of the ore-passes. These were vertical shafts that dropped down to 100 level, hundreds of feet through living rock to spew the reef out onto the conveyor belt. A system of steel doors regulated the flow of rock onto the conveyor, and the moving belt carried it down to the shaft and dumped it into enormous storage bins. From there it was fed automatically into the ore cage in fifteen-ton loads and carried at four-minute intervals to the surface.

Joseph worked on happily beneath the whining conveyor. The spillings were small, but important. Gold is strange in its behaviour, it moves downwards. Carried by its own high specific gravity it works its way down through almost any other material. It would find any crack or irregularity in the floor and work its way into it. It would disappear into the solid earth itself if left long enough.

It was this behaviour of gold that accounted in some measure for Joseph M'Kati's contentment. He had worked his way to the end of the conveyor, washing and sweeping, and now he straightened, laid his bast broom aside and rubbed his kidneys with both hands, looking quickly around to make certain that there was no one else in the conveyor tunnel. Beside him was the ore storage bin into which the conveyor was emptying its load. The bin could hold many thousands of tons.

Satisfied that he was alone, Joseph dropped onto his hands and knees and crawled under the storage bin, ignoring the continuous roar of rock into the bin above him, working his way in until he reached the holes.

It had taken Joseph many months to chisel the heads off four of the rivets that held the seam in the bottom of the bin, but once he had done it, he had succeeded in constructing a simple but highly effective heavy media separator.

Free gold in the ore that was dumped into the storage bin immediately and rapidly worked its way down through the underlying rock, its journey accelerated by the vibration of the conveyor and bin as more reef was dropped. When the gold reached the floor of the bin, it sought an avenue through which to continue its downward journey, and it found Joseph's four rivet holes, beneath which he had spread a square of polythene sheet.

The gold-rich fines made four conical piles on the sheet of polythene, looking exactly like powdered black soot.

Crouched beneath the bin, Joseph carefully transferred the black powder to his tobacco pouch, replaced the polythene to catch the next filtering, stuffed the pouch into his hip pocket, and scrambled out from under the bin. Whistling a tribal planting tune Joseph picked up his broom and returned to the endless job of sweeping and hosing.

Johnny Delange was marking his shot holes. Lying on his side in the low stope of 27 section he was calculating by eye the angle and depth of a side cutter blast to straighten a slight bulge in his longwall.

In the Sonder Ditch they were on single blast. One daily, centrally fired, blast. Johnny was paid on *fathomage*, the cubic measure of rock broken and taken out of his stope. He must, therefore, position his shot holes to achieve the maximum disruption and blow-out from the face.

'So,' he grunted, and marked the position of the hole in red paint. 'And so.' With one bold stroke of the paint brush he set the angle on which his machine boy was to drill.

'Shaya, madoda!' Johnny clapped the shoulder of the black man beside him. 'Hit it, man.'

Machine boys were selected for stamina and physique; this one was a Greek sculpture in glistening ebony.

'Nkosi!' The machine boy grinned an acknowledgement, and with his assistant lugged his rock drill into position. The drill looked like a gargantuan version of a heavy-calibre machine gun.

The noise as the big Bantu opened the drill was shattering in the low-roofed, constricted space of the stope. The compressed air roared and fluttered into the drill, buffeting the eardrums. Johnny made the clenched-fist gesture of approval, and for a second they smiled at each other in the companionship of shared labour. Then Johnny crawled on up the stope to mark the next shot hole.

Johnny Delange was twenty-seven years old, and he was top rock breaker on the Sonder Ditch. His gang of forty-eight men were a tightly-knit team of specialists. Men fought each other for a place on 27 section, for that's where the money was. Johnny could pick and choose, so each month when the surveyors came in and measured up, Johnny Delange was way out ahead in fathomage.

Here was the remarkable position where the man at the lowest point of authority earned more than the man at the top. Johnny Delange earned more than the General Manager of the Sonder Ditch. Last year he had paid super-tax on an income of R22,000. Even a miner like Kowalski, who brutalized and bullied his gang until he was left with the dregs of the mine, would earn eight or nine thousand rand a year, about the same salary as an official of Rod Ironsides' rank.

Johnny reached the top of his longwall and painted in the last shot holes. Down the inclined floor of the stope below him all his drills were roaring, his machine boys lying or crouching behind them. He lay there on one elbow, removed his helmet and wiped his face, resting a moment.

Johnny was an extraordinary-looking young man. His long jet black hair was swept back and tied with a leather thong at the back of his head in a curlicue. His features were those of an American Indian, gaunt and bony. He had cut the sleeves out of his overalls to expose his arms – arms as muscular and sinuous as pythons, tattooed below the elbows, immensely powerful but supple. His body was the same, long and sinewy and powerful.

On his right hand he wore eight rings, two on each finger, and it was clear from the design of the rings that they were not merely ornamental. They were heavy gold rings with skull and cross-bones, wolves' heads and other irregularities worked into them, a mass of metal that formed a permanent knuckleduster. Of the big eyes in the one skull's head Rod Ironsides had once asked: 'Are those real rubies, Johnny?' And Johnny had replied seriously:

'If they aren't, then I've sure as hell been gypped out of three rand fifty, Mr Ironsides.'

Johnny Delange had been a really wild youngster, until

eight months ago. It was then he had met and married Hettie. Courtship and marriage occupying the space of one week. Now he was settling down very well. It was all of ten days since he had last fought anybody.

Lying in the stope he allowed himself five minutes to think about Hettie. She was almost as tall as he was, with a wondrously buxom body and chestnut red hair. Johnny adored her. He was not the best speech-maker in Kitchenerville when it came to expressing his affection, so he bought her things.

He bought her dresses and jewellery, he bought her a deep-freezer *and* a fifteen cubic foot Frigidaire, he bought her a Chrysler Monaco with leopard-skin upholstery and a Kenwood Chef. In fact, it was becoming difficult to enter the Delange household without tripping over at least one of Johnny's gifts to Hettie. The congestion was made more acute by the fact that living with them was Johnny's brother, Davy.

'Hell, man!' Happily Johnny shook his head. 'She's a bit of all-right, hey!'

There was an eye-level oven he had spotted in a furniture store in Kitchenerville the previous Saturday.

'She'll love that, man,' he muttered, 'and it's only four hundred rand. I'll get it for her on pay day.'

The decision made, he clapped his helmet onto his head and began crawling out of the stope. It was time now to go up to the station and collect the explosives for the day's blast.

His boss boy should have been waiting for him in the drive, and Johnny was furious to find no sign of him nor the piccaninny who was his assistant.

'Bastard!' he grunted, playing the beam of his lamp up and down the drive. 'He's been acting up like hell.'

The boss boy was a pock-marked Swazi, not a big man, but powerful for his size and highly intelligent. He was also a man of mean disposition; Johnny had never seen him

56

smile, and for an extrovert like Johnny it was galling to work with someone so sullen and taciturn. He tolerated the Swazi because of his drive and reliability, but he was the only man in the gang that Johnny disliked.

'Bastard!' The drive was deserted, the roar of the rock drills was muted.

'Where the hell is he?' Johnny scowled impatiently. 'I'll skin him when I find him.'

Then he remembered the latrine.

'That's where he is!' Johnny set off down the drive. The latrine was a rock chamber cut into the side of the drive. A flap of canvas served as a door; beyond was a regular four-holer over sanitary buckets.

Johnny pulled the canvas aside and stepped into the cubicle. The boss boy and his assistant were there. Johnny stared in surprise, for a moment not understanding what they were doing. They were so absorbed they were unaware of Johnny's presence.

Suddenly realization dawned, and Johnny's face tightened with revulsion and disgust.

'You filthy—' Johnny snarled, and catching the boss boy by the shoulders pulled him backwards and pinned him against the wall. He lifted his heavily metalled fist and drew it back ready to hurl it into the boss boy's face.

'Strike me and you know what happens,' said the boss boy softly, his expression flat and neutral, looking steadily into Johnny's eyes. Johnny hesitated. He knew the Company rules, he knew the Government labour officers' attitude, he knew what the police would do. If he hit him, they would crucify him.

'You are a pig!' Johnny hissed at him.

'You have a wife,' said the boss boy. 'My wife is in Swaziland. Two years I have not seen her.'

Johnny lowered his fist. Twelve thousand men, and no women. It was a fact. The actuality sickened him, but he understood why it happened.

'Get dressed.' He stepped back, releasing the boss boy. 'Get dressed both of you. Come to the station. I will meet you there.'

– 18 –

For a week now, since the fall of hanging in 43 section, Big King had been out of the stopes.

Rod had ordered it that way. The excuse was that Big King's white miner had been killed in the fall and now he must await an allocation to another section. In reality Rod wanted to rest him. He had seen the strain both physical and emotional that Big King had undergone during the rescue. When together they had unearthed the miner's corpse, the man with whom Big King had worked and laughed, Rod had seen the tears roll unashamedly down Big King's cheeks as he picked up the body and held it easily against his chest.

'Hamba gahle, madoda,' Big King had muttered. 'Go in peace, man.'

Big King was a legend on the Sonder Ditch. They boasted about him; how much Bantu beer he could drink in a sitting, how much rock he could lash single-handed in a shift, how he could dance any other man off his feet. He had been awarded a total of over a thousand rand in bravery awards. Big King set the pace, others tried to equal him.

Rod had put him in charge of a transport team. For the first few days Big King had enjoyed the opportunity of showing off his strength and socializing, for the transport team moved about the workings allowing Big King to visit most of his numerous friends during a shift. But now Big King was becoming bored. He wanted to get back into the stopes.

'This,' he told his transport team contemptuously, 'is

work for old men and young women.' And with one snatch and lift he picked up a forty-four-gallon drum of dieseline and unaided placed it on the platform of the loco.

A forty-four-gallon drum of dieseline weighs a little over 800 lbs avoirdupois.

– 19 –

All this fuss for that. Davy Delange paused in his labour of tamping the Dynagel into the shot holes. He leaned forward to inspect the reef. In the face of the stope it was a black line, drawn against the blue quartz rock.

The carbon leader reef, it was called. A thin layer of carbon never more than a few inches thick, more often half an inch. Black soot, that's what it was. Davy shook his head thoughtfully. You could not even see the gold in it.

Davy was two years older than his brother Johnny, and there was no physical or mental resemblance between the two of them. Davy's sandy hair was cropped into a conventional 'short back and sides'. He wore no personal jewellery, and his manner was quiet and reserved.

Johnny was tall and lean, Davy squat and muscular. Johnny was extravagant, Davy careful beyond the point of meanness. Their only common trait was that they were both first-class miners. If Johnny broke more rock than Davy, it was only because Davy was more careful than Johnny; he did not take the same chances, he observed all the safety procedures which Johnny frequently flouted.

Davy earned less money than Johnny, but saved every penny he could. It was for his farm. Davy was going to buy a farm one day. Already he had saved a little over R49,000 towards it. In five more years he would have enough. Then he could get himself a farm and a wife to help run it. Johnny, on the other hand, spent every penny he earned. He was usually in debt to Davy by the end of each month.

'Lend us a hundred till pay day, Davy.' Disapprovingly, Davy lent him the money. Davy disapproved of Johnny, his appearance, attire and habits.

Abandoning his microscopic inspection of the carbon leader reef, Davy resumed tamping in the explosive, working carefully and precisely on this highly dangerous procedure. The sticks of explosive were charged with detonators and ready to burn. By law, nobody but the miner-in-charge could perform this operation, but Davy did it automatically while he thought about Johnny's latest trespass. He had raised Davy's rent.

'A hundred rand a month!' Davy protested aloud. 'I've got a good mind to move out and find my own digs.'

But he knew he would do no such thing. Hettie's cooking was too good, and her presence too feminine and alluring. Davy would stay on with them.

– 20 –

'Rod.' Dan Stander's voice was serious and low. 'I've got a nasty one for you.'

'Thanks for nothing.' Rod made his own voice weary and resigned as he spoke into the telephone. 'I'm just going on my underground tour. Can't it wait?'

'No,' Dan assured him. 'Anyway, it's on your way. I'm speaking from the first-aid station at the shaft head. Come across.'

'What is it?'

'Assault. White on Bantu.'

'Christ.' Rod jerked upright in his chair. 'Bad?'

'Ugly. Worked him over with the handle of a fourteen-pound hammer. I've put in forty-seven stitches, but I am worried about a fracture of the skull.'

'Who did it?'

'Miner by the name of Kowalski.'

'Him!' Rod was breathing heavily. 'All right, Dan. Can he make a statement?'

'No. Not for a day or two.'

'I'll be there in a few minutes.'

Rod hung up the phone and crossed the office.

'Dimitri.'

'Boss?'

'Pull Kowalski out of the stopes. I want him in my office soonest. Put someone in to finish his shift.'

'Okay, Rod, what's the trouble?'

'He beat up one of his boys.'

Dimitri whistled softly, and Rod went on.

'Call personnel, get them onto the police.'

'Okay, Rod.'

'Have Kowalski here when I get back from my tour.'

Dan was waiting for him in the first-aid room.

'Take a look.' He indicated the figure on the stretcher. Rod knelt beside him, his mouth tightening into a thin pale line.

The catgut stitches lay neatly across the dark swollen gashes in the man's flesh. One ear had been torn off, and Dan had sewn it back on. There was a black gap where teeth had been behind the swollen purple lips.

'You will be all right now.' Rod spoke gently, and the Bantu's eyes swivelled towards him. 'The man who did this will be punished.'

Rod stood up. 'Let me have a written report on his injuries, Dan.'

'I'll fix it. See you for a drink at the Club after work?'

'Sure,' said Rod, but underneath he was seething with anger, and it stayed with him during the whole of his underground tour.

Rod dropped straight down to 100 level. His first duty was to get the stuff out, and he wanted to check the reserve in the ore storage bins. He came into the long brightly-lit tunnel beneath the ore passes, and paused. The loaded conveyor belt whined monotonously, speeding the broken reef towards the bins.

The tunnel was deserted, except for the lonely figure of the sweeper at the far end. It was one of the phenomena of a well-run gold mine that in a tour through the workings you encountered so few human beings. Mile after mile of haulage and drive were silent and devoid of life, and yet there were 12,000 men down here.

Rod set off towards the bins at the shaft end of the tunnel.

'Joseph,' he greeted the old sweeper with a smile.

'Nkosi.' Joseph ducked and bobbed with shy pleasure.

'All is well?' Rod asked. Joseph was one of Rod's favourites, he was always so cheerful, so uncomplaining, so patently honest and without guile. Rod always made a point of stopping to chat to him.

'It is well with me, Nkosi. Is it well with you?'

Rod's smile died suddenly, he had noticed the fine white powdering of dust on Joseph's upper lip.

'You old rogue!' he scolded him. 'How often must I tell you to hose down before you sweep? Water! You must use water!'

This was part of the ceaseless battle of the miner to keep down the dust.

'The dust will eat your lungs!'

Phthisis, the dread incurable occupational disease of the miner, caused by silica particles being drawn into the lungs and there solidifying.

Joseph grinned shamefaced, shifting from one foot to the

other. He was always embarrassed by Rod's childish obsession with dust. In Joseph's opinion this was one of the few flaws in Rod Ironsides' character. Apart from this weird delusion that dust could hurt a man, he was a good boss.

'It is much harder to sweep wet dirt than dry dirt,' Joseph explained patiently. Rod never seemed to understand this self-evident fact, Joseph had to point it out to him every time they had this particular discussion.

'Listen to me, old man, without water the dust will enter your body.' Rod was exasperated. 'The dust will kill you!'

Joseph bobbed again, grinning at Rod to placate him.

'Very well, I will use plenty water.'

To prove it he picked up the hose and began spraying the floor with enthusiasm.

'That is good!' Rod encouraged him. 'Use plenty of water.' And Rod went on down to the storage bins.

When Rod was out of sight, Joseph turned off the hose and leaned on his broom.

'The dust will kill you!' he mimicked Rod, and chuckled merrily, shaking his head in wonder at the childishness of it.

'The dust will kill you!' he repeated, and burst into delighted laughter, slapping his thigh.

He did a few shuffling dance steps, it was so funny.

The dance steps were awkward, for under his trousers, strapped to the calves of both legs, were heavy polythene bags filled with gold fines from under the bins.

– 22 –

Rod stepped out of the Mary Anne at 85 level, and paused to watch Big King loading a baulk of timber onto the loco while his transport team stood back respectfully and watched him. Turning from his task Big King saw Rod standing on the station landing and marched up to him.

'I see you,' he greeted Rod. Big King was not one to make hasty judgements, it was only after the rescue operations in 43 section that he had decided Rod was a man. He was now ready to accept him as an equal.

'I see you also, King Nkulu.' Rod returned the greeting.

'Find me work with men. I sicken of this.'

'You will be back in the stopes before the week is ended,' Rod promised.

'You are my father,' Big King thanked him and went back to the transport team.

– 23 –

Johnny Delange saw the Underground Manager coming up the haulage towards him. There was no mistaking that tall wide-shouldered silhouette, nor the man's free swinging stride.

'Whee!' Johnny whistled with relief, grateful for the premonition that had warned him to pack the fifty-pound cardboard cartons of Dynagel into the explosives locker of the railway truck, rather than, as he usually did, pile them haphazard onto the platform in defiance of safety standards.

'Stop!' Johnny commanded the boss boy and his assistant who were pushing the truck, and it trundled to a halt beside Rod.

'Morning, Johnny.'

'Hello, Mr Ironsides.'

'How's it going?'

Johnny hesitated before replying, and immediately Rod was aware of the tension between the three men. He glanced at the two Swazis, they were sullen and apprehensive.

'There's been trouble,' he thought. 'Not like Johnny, he's too clever to let tension cut down his fathomage.'

'Well—' Johnny paused again. 'Look, Mr Ironsides, get rid of this bastard for me.' He jerked his thumb at the boss boy. 'Give me someone else.'

'What's the trouble?'

'No trouble, I just can't work with him.'

Rod raised an eyebrow in disbelief, but turned to the boss boy.

'Are you happy in this section, or do you want transfer?'

'I want transfer!' growled the boss boy.

'Right.' Rod was relieved, sometimes in a case like this the Swazi would refuse transfer. 'Tomorrow you will be told your new section.'

'Nkosi!' The boss boy glanced sideways at his assistant. 'It is the wish of my friend that he transfers with me.'

So that's it, Rod thought, the ever-present spectre which we must ignore because we can find no way to lay it. Johnny had probably caught them at it.

'Your friend shall go with you,' Rod nodded, telling himself that this was not condonation, but merely practical politics. If he separated them, the boss boy would pick on someone else who might not be receptive. Then there would be more trouble, stabbings, faction fighting.

'I'll get you a replacement,' he told Johnny, and then suddenly a thought occurred to him. My God, yes! What a team they would make!

'Johnny, how would you like Big King?'

'Big King!' Johnny's gaunt bony features split into a wide smile. 'Now you're talking, boss!'

At three o'clock Rod had finished his tour and was in the cage on the way to the surface. The cage was crowded, men pressed shoulder to shoulder, the stench of sweat almost overpowering. They were hauling shift now, the day's work was over, the stopes were scraped and washed down, the shot holes drilled and charged, the fuses connected into the electrical circuit.

The men were out of the stopes now, falling back in orderly companies and battalions along the haulages to the stations. There to wait patiently for their turn to enter the cages and be whisked to the surface.

Rod was mulling over the myriad problems he had encountered during the day, and the solutions he had dreamed up. He had opened a new section in the back pages of his notebook and headed it simply 'COSTS'.

Already there were two entries there. Let them give me the job, he thought fervently, just let me have it one month and I'll move the world.

'Mr Ironsides.' The man beside him spoke. Rod glanced down at him recognizing him.

'Hello, Davy.' It was remarkable how dissimilar the two brothers were.

'Mr Ironsides, my boss boy has worked his ticket. He's going home at the end of the month. Can you see that I get a good man to replace him?'

'Your brother's boss boy has asked for transfer. Will you take him?'

'Ja!' Davy Delange nodded. 'I know him, he's a good boy.'

And that takes care of one more detail, thought Rod, as he stepped out of the cage into a bright summer's afternoon and tasted the fresh sweet air with pleasure. Now there are only the butt ends of the day's work to tidy up. Then I can go and fetch the drink that Dan promised me.

Dimitri met him in the passage outside the office.

'I've got Kowalski in my office.'

'Good,' said Rod grimly. He went into his own office and sat on the edge of his desk.

'Send him in,' he called through to Dimitri.

Kowalski came through the door and stopped. He stood very still, his long arms hanging slackly at his side, his belly bulging out over his belt.

'You call me,' he muttered thickly, his English hardly intelligible. It was a peasant's face, coarse-featured, dull-eyed. He had not shaved, dirt from the stopes clung in the thick black stubble of beard.

'You beat a man today?' Rod asked softly.

'He no work,' Kowalski nodded. 'I beat him. Maybe next time his brothers they work. No bloody nonsense!'

'You're fired,' said Rod. 'Pull your time and get the hell off this property.'

'You fire?' Kowalski blinked in surprise.

'There will be criminal charges pressed against you by the Company.' Rod went on. 'But in the meantime I want you off the property.'

'Police?' Kowalski growled. There was expression on his face now.

'Yes,' said Rod, 'police.'

The spade-sized hands at the end of Kowalski's arms balled slowly into massive fists.

'You call da bloody police!' He took a step towards the desk, big, menacing.

'Dimitri,' Rod called sharply, 'close the door.'

Dimitri had been listening intently, now he jumped up from his desk and closed the interleading door. He stood with his ear pressed to the panelling. For thirty seconds more there was the growl and mutter of voices, then suddenly a thud, a bellow, another thud and a shattering crash.

Dimitri winced theatrically.

'Dimitri!' Rod's voice, and he pushed the door open.

Rod sat on the edge of his desk, swinging one leg casually, he was sucking the knuckle of his right hand.

'Dimitri, tell them not to put so much polish on the floor. Our friend slipped and hit his jaw on the desk.'

Dimitri clucked sympathetically as he stood over the reclining hulk of the big Pole. Kowalski was snoring loudly through his mouth.

'Gave himself a nasty bump,' said Dimitri. 'Shame!'

– 25 –

D r Steyner worked on quietly for the remainder of Monday morning. He favoured the use of a tape recorder, for this cut out human contact which Manfred found vaguely repellent. He disliked having to speak his thoughts to a female who sat opposite him with skirts up around her thighs, squirming her bottom and touching her hair. However, what he really could not abide was the odour. Manfred was very sensitive to smells, even his own body smell of perspiration disgusted him. Women, he found, had a peculiar cloying odour that he could detect beneath their perfume and cosmetics. It nauseated him. This was why he had insisted on separate bedrooms for Theresa and himself. Naturally he had not told her the reason, but had insisted instead that he was such a light sleeper that he could not share a room with another person.

His office was in white and ice-blue, the air clean and cold from the air-conditioning unit, his voice was crisp and impersonal, the whirr of the recorder subdued, and with the conscious portion of his mind Manfred was happily absorbed in his conjuring tricks with figures and money, past performance and future estimates, a three-dimensional structure of variables and contingencies which only a super-normal brain could visualize. But beneath it was a sense of disquiet; he was waiting, hanging in time, and the outward sign of his agitation was the way the fingers of his right hand ran up and down his thigh as he worked, a caressing narcissistic gesture.

A few minutes before noon the unlisted direct telephone on his desk rang, and the movement of his hand stilled. Only one caller could reach him here, only one caller had that number. For a few seconds he sat unmoving, delaying the moment, then deliberately he switched off the recorder and lifted the telephone.

'Dr Manfred Steyner.' He identified himself.

'You have got our man in?' the voice enquired.

'Not yet, Andrew.'

There was silence from the other end, a dangerous crackling silence.

'But there is no cause for alarm. It is nothing. A delay merely, not a setback.'

'How long?'

'Two days – at the latest by the end of the week.'

'You will be in Paris next week?'

'Yes.' Manfred was an adviser to the Government team which was to meet the French for gold price talks.

'He will meet you there. It would be best for you that your side of the bargain were completed by then. You understand?'

'I understand, Andrew.'

The discussion was ended, but Manfred interjected to prevent the caller from hanging up.

'Andrew!'

'Yes.'

'Will you ask him if—' Manfred's tone had changed almost imperceptibly, there was an obsequious edge in it. 'Ask him if I may play tonight, please, Andrew.'

'Wait.'

The minutes drifted by, and then the voice came back on the line.

'Yes, you may play. Simon will inform you of your limits.'

'Thank you. Tell him, thank you.'

Manfred made no effort to conceal his relief as he cradled the receiver. He sat beaming at the ice-blue paper on the far wall of his office, even his spectacles seemed to sparkle.

– 26 –

There were five men in the opulently furnished room. One of the men was subservient to the others, he was younger than they, attentive to their moods and wishes. Clearly he was a servant. Of the remaining four, one was just as obviously the host. He was seated at the focus of all their attention. He was fat, but not excessively so, the fat of good living not of gluttony. He was speaking, addressing himself to his three guests.

'You have expressed doubts as to the reliability of the tool I intend using in the coming venture. I have arranged a demonstration which I hope will convince you that your concern is groundless. That is the reason for the invitation that Andrew here conveyed to you this afternoon.'

The host turned to the younger man. 'Andrew, would you be good enough to go through and wait for Dr Steyner to arrive; as soon as that happens, please let Simon seat him while you come through and inform us.' He gave his orders with dignity and courtesy, a man accustomed to command.

'Now, gentlemen, while we wait may I offer you a drink?'

The conversation that sprang up between the four of them as they sipped their drinks was knowledgeable, and extraordinarily well informed. At its root was one subject:

wealth. Mineral wealth, industrial wealth, the harvest of the land and the sea. Oil, steel, coal, fish, wheat and – gold.

There were clues to the stature of these men in the cut and quality of the cloth they wore, the sparkle of a stone on a finger, the tone of authority in a voice, the casual unaffected use of a high name.

'He is here, sir,' Andrew interrupted them from the doorway.

'Oh! Thank you, my boy.' The host stood up. 'Would you mind stepping this way, please, gentlemen.'

He crossed the room and drew aside one of the gold and maroon drapes. Behind it was a window.

The four men clustered about the window and looked through into the room beyond. It was a gaming room of an expensive gambling establishment. There were men and women sitting about a baccarat table, and none of them so much as glanced up at the window overlooking them.

'This is a one-way glass, gentlemen,' the host explained. 'So you need not worry about being seen in such a den of iniquity.'

They chuckled politely.

'What kind of profit does this place show you?' one of them asked.

'My dear Robert!' The host feigned shock. 'You don't for a moment believe that I would be in any way associated with an illegal undertaking?'

This time they chuckled with genuine amusement.

'Ha!' exclaimed the host. 'Here he is.'

Across the gaming room Dr Manfred Steyner was being ushered to a seat at the table by a tall sallow-faced young man, who in his evening dress looked like an undertaker.

'I have asked Simon to place him so that you may watch his face as he plays.'

They were intent now, leaning forward slightly, scrutinizing the man as he arranged the plaques that Simon had stacked at his elbow.

Dr Manfred Steyner began to play. His face was completely devoid of expression, but the pallor was startling. Every few seconds the pink tip of his tongue slipped out between his lips, then disappeared again. In the intervals between each coup, there was a reptilian stillness about him, the stillness of a lizard or an iguana. Only a pulse beat steadily in his throat and his spectacles glittered like a snake's eyes.

'May I direct your attention to his right hand during the play of this coup,' the host murmured, and all their eyes flicked downwards.

Manfred's right hand lay open beside the pile of his chips, but as his card was laid before him so his fingers closed.

'Carte.' Soundlessly he mouthed the word, and now his hand was a fist, the knuckles whitened, the tension was so fierce that his fist trembled. Yet, still his face was neutral.

The banker flipped his card.

'Sept!' The croupier's mouth formed the number. He faced Manfred's card, then he swept Manfred's stake away. Manfred's hand flopped open and lay soft and hairless as a dead fish on the green baize.

'Let us leave him to his pleasures,' suggested the host and drew the curtains across the window. They returned to their chairs, and they were strangely subdued.

'Jesus,' muttered one of the guests. 'That was ugly. I felt like a peeping Tom, like watching someone, you know, pulling his pudding.'

The host glanced at him quickly, surprised at his perception.

'In effect, that is exactly what you were watching,' he told him. 'You will excuse me playing the role of lecturer, but I know a little about this man. It cost me nearly four hundred rand for an analytic report on him by one of our leading psychiatrists.'

The host paused, assuring himself of their complete attention.

'The reasons are obscure, probably arising from an event or series of events during the period in which Dr Steyner was an orphan wandering through the smoking ruins of war-torn Europe.' The host coughed, deprecating his own flight of oratory. 'Be that as it may. The results are there for all to see. Dr Manfred Kurt Steyner's intelligence quotient is a genius rating of 158. He neither smokes nor drinks. He has no hobbies, plays no sport, has never made so much as an improper remark to any woman other than his wife, and there is some doubt as to just how often or to what extent she is favoured by his attentions.' The host sipped his drink conscious of their intense interest. 'Mechanically, if that is the correct term, Dr Steyner is neither impotent nor deficient in his manhood. However, he finds all bodily contact, and especially the secretions that may arise from such contact, to be utterly loathsome. For arousal he relies on the baccarat cards, for release he might endure a brief contact with a member of the opposite sex, but more likely he would – oh, what was the expression you used, Robert?'

They absorbed this in silence.

'He is, to be precise, a compulsive gambler. He is also a compulsive loser.'

They stirred with disbelief.

'You mean he tries to lose?' demanded Robert incredulously.

'No.' The host shook his head. 'Not on the conscious level. He believes he is trying to win, but he lays bets against odds that, with his magnificent brain, he must realize are suicidal. It is a deep-seated subconscious need to lose, to be humiliated. A form of masochism.'

The host opened a black leather notebook and checked its contents.

'During the period from 1958 to 1963 Dr Steyner lost

the total sum of R227,000 at this table. In 1964 he was able to arrive at an arrangement with his sole creditor to discharge the debt plus the accumulated interest.'

You could see the faces change as they rapidly searched their memories for a set of circumstances which would fit the dates and principals. Robert reached the correct deduction first. In 1964 their host had sold his majority holdings in the North Maun Copper Co. to CRC at a price that could only be considered advantageous. Just prior to this Dr Steyner had been made head of finance and planning at CRC.

'North Maun Copper,' said Robert with admiration. That is how he had done it, the cunning old fox! He had forced Steyner to buy well above market value.

The host smiled softly, deferentially, neither confirming nor denying.

'Since 1964 to the present Dr Steyner has continued to patronize this establishment. His gambling losses for this further period amount to—' He consulted his notebook again, pretending surprise at the figure, 'to a touch over R300,000.'

They sighed and moved restlessly. Even to these men it was a very large sum of money.

'I think we can rely on him.' The host closed his notebook with a snap, and smiled around at them.

– 27 –

Theresa lay in the dark. The night was warm, the stillness spoiled only by the klonking of a frog down at the fishpond. The moonlight came in through the window, playing shadow pictures through the branches of the Pride of India tree onto the wall of her bedroom.

She threw back the single sheet, and swung her legs off the bed. She could not sleep, it was too warm, her

74

nightdress kept binding under her armpits. She stood up and on a sudden reckless impulse she drew the nightdress off over her head and tossed it through the open door of her dressing-room, then, naked, she walked out onto the wide veranda. Into the moonlight, with the cool stone flags under her bare feet, and the warm night air moving like the touch of fairy hands on her skin.

She felt suddenly devilish and daring, she wanted to run down across the lawns and to have someone catch her doing it. She giggled, uncertain of this mood. It was so far removed from Manfred's conception of a good German Hausfrau's behaviour.

'He'd be furious,' she whispered with wicked delight, and then she heard the motor of the car.

She froze with horror, the headlights flicked through the trees as the car came up the driveway and she darted back into her room; in panic she dropped to her knees and searched for her nightgown, found it and ran to the bed as she dragged it on over her head.

She lay in the darkness and listened to the car door slam. There was silence until she heard him pass her door. His heels clacked on the yellow wood floor, he was almost running. Theresa knew the symptoms, the late night return, the suppressed urgency, and she lay rigid in her bed, waiting.

The minutes passed slowly, and then the interleading door from Manfred's suite swung open silently.

'Manfred, is that you?' She sat up and reached for the switch of the bedside lamp.

'Don't put the light on.' His voice was breathless, slurred as though he had been drinking but there was no trace of liquor on his breath as he stooped over her and kissed her. His lips were dry and tightly closed, as he slipped off his dressing-gown.

Two and a half minutes later he stood up from the bed, turning his back to Theresa as he quickly shrugged into the silk dressing-gown.

'Excuse me a minute, Theresa.' The breathlessness was gone from his voice. He went through the door of his own suite, and seconds later she heard the hiss of the shower and the tinkling splash of water.

She lay on her back and her fingernails cut into the palms of her hands. Her body was trembling with a mixture of revulsion and desire, it had been so fleeting a contact – enough to stir her, but so swift as to leave her with a feeling of having been used and sullied. She knew that the rest of the night would pass infinitely slowly, with restless burning tension, remorse and self-pity alternating with wild elation and half-crazed erotic fantasy.

'Damn him,' she screamed silently within her skull. 'Damn him! Damn him!'

She heard the shower stop, and then Manfred returned to her room. He smelt of 4711 Eau de Cologne, and he sat down carefully on the end of the bed.

'You may turn on the light, Theresa.'

It required a conscious effort for her to unclench her hand and reach out for the lamp switch. Manfred blinked behind his spectacles at the flood of light. His hair was damp and freshly combed, his cheeks shone like ripe apples.

'I hope you had an enjoyable day?' he asked, and listened seriously to her reply. Despite her tension, Theresa found herself falling under the almost hypnotic influence he wielded over her. His voice precise, almost monotonous. The glitter of his spectacles, the reptilian stillness of his body and features.

As she had so many times before, she thought of herself as a warm fluffy rabbit sitting tense and fascinated before the cobra.

'It is late,' he said at last and he stood up.

Looking down at her as she lay cuddled into the white silk sheets, he asked with as little emphasis as if he were requesting her to pass the sugar: 'Theresa, could you raise three hundred thousand rand without your grandfather knowing?'

'Three hundred thousand!' She sat up startled.

'Yes. Could you?'

'Good Lord, Manfred, that's a small fortune.' She truly saw nothing unusual in her choice of adjective. 'You know it's all in the Trust Fund, well, most of it. There is the farm and the – no, I couldn't find half of that without Pops knowing.'

'Pity,' murmured Manfred.

'Manfred, you aren't in – difficulties?'

'No. Good Lord, no. It was just a thought. Forget that I asked. Good night, Theresa, I hope you sleep well.'

Involuntarily she lifted her hands towards him in invitation.

'Good night, Manfred.'

He turned and left the room, she let her hands fall to her sides. For Theresa Steyner the long night had begun.

– 28 –

'Ladies and Gentlemen, it is customary for the General Manager to introduce the distinguished guest who presents our special service awards. Last week, in tragic circumstances, our General Manager, Mr Frank Lemmer, was killed in the Company's service, a loss which we all bitterly regret, and I am sure you all join me in sincere condolence to Mrs Eileen Lemmer.' Rod paused for the acknowledging murmur from his audience. There were 200 of them packed into the Mine Club hall. 'It falls upon me, therefore, as Acting General Manager, to introduce to you Dr Manfred Steyner who is a senior Director of Central Rand Consolidated, our parent company. He is also head of the Departments of Finance and Planning.'

Sitting beside her husband, Theresa Steyner had noticed

Manfred's irritation at Rod's mention of Frank Lemmer. It was company policy not to draw public attention to accidental death or injury inflicted on employees by the Company's operation. She liked Rod the better for his small tribute to Frank Lemmer.

Theresa was wearing sunglasses, for her eyes were swollen and red. In the dawning, after a sleepless night, she had succumbed suddenly to a fit of bitter weeping. The tears were without cause, or reason, and had left her feeling strangely lightheaded and with a brittle sense of well-being. However, her enormous eyes always showed up badly for hours after she had wept.

She sat with her legs demurely crossed, immaculate in a suit of cream shantung, a black silk scarf catching her hair and then letting it fall in a dark glossy brown cascade onto her shoulders. She leaned forward in polite attention to the speaker, one elbow on her knee, her chin cupped in her palm, one long tapered finger against her cheek. A lady with diamonds on her fingers and pearls at her throat, smiling an acknowledgement at Rod's reference to 'the lovely granddaughter of our Chairman'.

Except for the slight incongruity of the sunglasses, she was the perfect image of the young matron. Polished, poised, cosseted, secure in her unassailable virtue and duty.

However, the thoughts that were running through Theresa Steyner's head, and the flutterings and sensations that were prickling and tickling her, had they been known, would have broken up the assembly in disorder. All the formless fantasy and emotional disturbance of the previous night were now directed at one target – Rodney Ironsides. Suddenly, with a start of amusement and alarm, she was aware of a phenomenon that she had last experienced many years ago. She moved quickly, shifting her seat, for the cream shantung marked so easily with any moisture.

'Terry Steyner!' she thought, deliciously shocked at

herself, and found with relief that Rod had finished speaking and Manfred was standing up to reply. She joined in the applause enthusiastically to distract her errant fancy.

Manfred briefly mentioned the six gentlemen sitting in the front row of seats whose courage and devotion to duty they had come to honour, he then went on into an exploration of the prospects of an increase in the price of gold. In measured, carefully considered terms, he set out the advantages and benefits that would accrue to the industry, the nation and the world at large. It was an erudite and convincing dissertation, and there was a large contingent of newspaper men to record it. The press had been alerted by the public relations department of CRC to the text of Dr Steyner's speech and all the leading dailies, weeklies, financial gazettes and journals were represented.

At intervals a photographer would come to crouch below the platform and pop a flash bulb up at Dr Steyner. On the eve of the gold price talks with France this would make good copy, for Steyner was the boy genius in the South African team.

The six heroes sat uncomfortably, forlorn in their best suits, scrubbed like schoolboys at a prize-giving ceremony, staring up at the speaker, not understanding a single word of the foreign language, but maintaining expressions of grave dignity.

Rod caught Big King's eye and winked at him. Solemnly Big King's right eyelid drooped and rose in reply, and quickly Rod averted his gaze to prevent himself laughing out loud.

He looked straight into Theresa Steyner's face, taking her completely off her guard. Not even the dark glasses could conceal her thoughts, they were as clear as if she had spoken them aloud. Before she could drop her eyes to examine the hem of her skirt, Rod knew with a stomach swoop of excitement how it could be if he chose.

With a new awareness he examined her from the corner

of his eye, seeing her for the first time as an accessible woman, a highly desirable woman, but nevertheless still the granddaughter of Hurry Hirschfeld and the wife of Manfred Steyner. This made her as dangerous as a force ten pressure burst, he knew, but the desire and temptation were hard to deny, inflamed perhaps rather than dampened by the danger.

He saw that she was blushing now, her fingers picking nervously at the hem of her skirt. She was as agitated as a schoolgirl, she knew he was watching her. Rod Ironsides, who until five minutes before had been thinking of nothing but his speech, now found himself impelled into a completely new and exciting dimension.

After the awards had been made, tea had been drunk, biscuits consumed and the crowd had dispersed, Rod escorted the Steyners down across the vivid green lawns of Kikuyu grass to where the chauffeur was holding the Daimler.

'What a magnificent physique that Shangaan has, what was his name – King?' Terry was walking between the two men.

'King Nkulu. Big King, we call him.'

Rod found his speech unsteady, he had stuttered slightly. This thing between the two of them was suddenly overpowering, it hummed like a turbine, making the space between them crackle with tension. Unless he was deaf, Manfred Steyner must be aware of it.

'He is pretty special. There is nothing he can't do, and do it far and away better than his nearest rival. My God, you should see him dance.'

'Dance?' enquired Terry with interest.

'Tribal dancing, you know.'

'Of course.' Terry hoped the relief in her voice was not obvious; she had been racking her badly flustered brain for an excuse to visit the Sonder Ditch again or have Rod Ironsides come to Johannesburg. 'I have a friend who is absolutely mad keen on seeing the dances. She pesters me every time I see her.'

Quickly she selected a name from her list of friends, she must have one ready should Manfred ask.

'They dance every Saturday afternoon, bring her out any time.' Rod fielded the ball neatly.

'What about this Saturday?' Terry turned to her husband, 'Would that be all right, Manfred?'

'What's that?' Manfred looked at her vaguely, he had not been following the conversation. Manfred Steyner was a worried man, he was pondering his obligation to gain control of the management of the Sonder Ditch within two days.

'May we come out here on Saturday afternoon to watch the tribal dancing?' Terry repeated her question.

'Have you forgotten that I fly to Paris on Saturday morning, Theresa?'

'Oh, dear.' Terry bit her lip thoughtfully. 'It *had* slipped my mind. What a pity, I would have enjoyed it.'

Manfred frowned slightly, irritated.

'My dear Theresa, there is no reason why you shouldn't come out to the Sonder Ditch without me. I am sure you will be safe enough in Mr Ironsides' hands.'

His choice of words brought the colour to Terry's cheeks again.

– 29 –

After the award ceremony, Big King's first stop was the Recruiting Agency office at the entrance to the No.1 shaft hostel. There were men clustered about the counter, but they stood aside for Big King and he acknowledged the courtesy by slapping their backs indiscriminately and greeting them with:

'Kunjane, madoda. How is it, men?'

The clerk behind the counter hurried to serve him. Up at the Mine Club Big King might be a little out of his depth, but here he was treated like a reigning monarch.

In two neat bundles Big King placed the award money on the counter.

'Twenty-five rand you will send to my senior wife.' He instructed the clerk. 'And twenty-five rand you will put to my book.'

Big King was scrupulously fair. Half of all his earnings was remitted to the senior of his four wives, and half was added to the substantial sum already credited in his savings bank passbook.

The Agency was the procurer of labour for the insatiably man-hungry gold mines of the Witwatersrand and Orange Free State. Its representatives operated across the southern half of the continent. From the swamps and fever lagoons along the great Zambesi, from among the palm groves fringing the Indian Ocean, out of these simmering plains that the bushmen called 'the big dry', down from the mountains of Basutoland and the grass lands of Swaziland and Zululand they gathered the Bantu, the men themselves completing the first fifty or sixty miles of the journey on foot. Individuals meeting on a footpath to become pairs, arriving at a little general dealer's store in the bleak scrub desert to find three or four others already waiting, the arrival of the recruiting truck with a dozen men and their luggage aboard, the long bumping grinding progress through the bush. The stops at which more men scrambled aboard, until a full truck load of fifty or sixty disembarked at a railway siding in the wilderness.

Here the tiny trickle of humanity joined a stream, and at the first major centre they trans-shipped and became part of the great flood that washed towards 'Goldi'.

However, once they had reached Johannesburg and been allocated to one of the sixty major gold mines, the Agency's obligations towards its recruits were not yet discharged.

Between them the employing mine and the Agency must provide each man with employment, training, advice and comfort, maintain contact between him and his family, for very few of them could write, reassure him when he worried that his goats were sick or his wife unfaithful. They must provide a banking and savings service with a personal involvement unknown to any commercial banking institute. They had, in short, to make certain that a man taken from an environment that had not changed in a thousand years and deposited into the midst of a sophisticated and technological society would retain his health, happiness and sanity, so that at the end of his contract he would return to the place from which he had come and tell them all how wonderful it was at 'Goldi'. He would show them his hard helmet, and his new suitcase crammed with clothes, his transistor radio and the little blue book with its printed figures, inflaming them also with the desire to make the pilgrimage, and keep the flood washing towards 'Goldi'.

Big King completed his business transactions and went in through the gates of the hostel. He was going to take advantage of the fact that he had missed the shift and would be among the first at the ablutions and dining-hall.

He went down across the lawns to his block. Despite the size of an establishment that housed 6,000 men, the Company had tried to make it as attractive as possible. The result was an unusual design, halfway between a motel and an advanced penitentiary.

As a senior boss boy, Big King rated a room of his own. An ordinary labourer would share with five others.

Carefully Big King brushed down his suit and hung it in the built-in cupboard, wiped down his glossy shoes and racked them, then with a towel around his waist he set off for the ablution block and was irritated to find it already filled with new recruits up from the acclimatization centre.

Big King ran an appraising eye over their naked bodies and judged that this batch must be nearing the completion of their eight-day acclimatization. They were sleek and shiny, the muscle definition showing clearly through the skin.

You could not take a man straight out of his village, probably suffering from malnutrition, and put him down a gold mine to lash and bar and drill in a dry bulb heat of 91° Fahrenheit and 84% relative humidity, without running a serious risk of killing him with heat stroke or exhaustion.

Every recruit judged medically fit to work underground went into acclimatization. For eight days, eight hours a day, he and hundreds of others stood with only a loin cloth about his middle in a vast barn-like hall stepping up onto and down from a platform. The height of the platform was carefully matched to the man's height and body weight, the speed of his movements was regulated by a flashing panel of lights, the temperature and humidity were controlled at 91° and 84%, every ten minutes he was given water and his body temperature was registered by the half dozen trained medical assistants in charge of the room.

At the end of the eighth day he emerged as fit as an olympic athlete, and quite able to perform heavy physical labour in conditions of high temperature and humidity without discomfort or danger.

'Gwedeni!' growled Big King, and the nearest recruit, still white with soap suds, hurriedly vacated his shower with a respectful 'Keshle!' in deference to Big King's rank and standing. Big King removed his towel and stepped under the shower, revelling as always in the rush of hot water over his skin, flexing the great muscles of his arms and chest.

The messenger found him there.

'King Nkulu, I have word for thee.' The man used Shangaan, not the bastard Fanikalo.

'Speak,' Big King invited, soaping his belly and buttocks.

'The Induna bids you call at his house after you have eaten the evening meal.'

'Tell him I will attend his wishes,' said Big King and held his face up into the rush of steaming water.

Dressed in a white open-necked shirt and blue slacks, Big King sauntered down to the kitchens. Again the recruits were ahead of him, queueing with bowls in hand outside the serving hatches. Big King walked past them through the door marked 'No Admittance – Staff Only'.

The kitchens were cavernous, glistening with white porcelain tiles and stainless steel cookers and bins that could serve 18,000 hot meals a day.

When Big King entered a room, even one as large as this, no one was unaware of his presence. One of the assistant cooks snatched up a bowl not much smaller than a baby's bath, and hurried across to the nearest stainless steel bin. He opened the lid and looked expectantly at Big King. Big King nodded and the cook ladled about two litres of steaming sugar beans into the bowl, before passing on to the next bin where he again looked for and obtained Big King's approval. He added an equal quantity of mixed vegetables to the bowl, slammed down the lid and scampered across to where a second assistant waited with a spade beside yet another bin.

The spade was the same as those used for lashing gold reef underground, but the blade of this one had been polished to gleaming cleanliness. The second cook dug into the bin and came up with a spadeful of white maize porridge, cooked stiff as cake, the smell of it as saliva-making as the smell of new bread. This was the staple of Bantu diet. He deposited the spadeful in the bowl.

'I am hungry.' Big King spoke for the first time, and the second cook dug out another spadeful and added it to the bowl. They passed on to the end of the kitchens and at their approach another cook lifted the lid on a pressure cooker the size of a washing machine. From it arose a cloud of fragrant steam.

Apologetically the cook held out his hand and Big King produced his meat ticket. Meat was the only food that was rationed. Each man was limited to one pound of meat a day; the Company had long ago discovered to its astonishment and cost that a Bantu, offered unlimited supplies of fresh meat, was quite capable of eating his own weight of it monthly.

Having ascertained that Big King was entitled to his daily pound, the cook proceeded to ladle at least five pounds of it into the bowl.

'You are my brother,' Big King thanked him, and the little procession moved on to where yet another cook was filling a half-gallon jug of thick, gruel-like, mildly alcoholic Bantu beer from one of the multiple spiggots beneath the thousand-gallon tank.

The bowl and jug were ceremonially handed to Big King and he went out onto the covered terraces where benches and tables were set out for alfresco dining in mild weather.

While he ate, the terrace began to fill, for the shift was out of the mine now. Every man who passed his table greeted Big King, but only a few privileged persons took the liberty of seating themselves at the same table. One of them was Joseph M'Kati, the little old sweeper from 100 level.

'It has been a good week, King Nkulu.'

'You say so.' Big King was non-committal. 'I go now to a meeting with the Old One. Then we shall see.'

The Old One, the Shangaan Induna, lived in a Company house. A self-contained residence with lounge and dining-room, kitchen and bathroom. He was handsomely paid by the Company, provided with servants, food, furniture and all the other appurtenances of his rank and station.

He was the head of the Shangaan community on the Sonder Ditch. A chief of the blood, a greybeard and member of the tribal councils. In similar houses and with the same privileges and in equal style lived the Indunas of the other tribal groups that made up the labour force of the

Sonder Ditch. They were the paternal figureheads, the tribal jurists, ruling and judging within the framework of law and custom. The Company could not hope to maintain harmony and order without the assistance of these men.

'Baba!' Big King greeted his Induna from the doorway of his house, touching the forehead in respect not only for the man but also for what he represented.

'My son.' The Induna smiled his greeting. 'Come and sit by me.' He gestured for his servants to leave the room, and Big King went to squat at the feet of the old man. 'Is it true you go now to work with the mad one?' That was Johnny Delange's nickname.

They talked, the Induna questioning him on fifty matters that affected the welfare of his people. For Big King this was a comforting and nostalgic experience, for the Induna stood in the place of his father.

At last, satisfied, the Induna went on to other matters.

'There is a parcel ready tonight. Crooked Leg waits for you.'

'I shall go for it.'

'Go in peace then, my son.'

On his way through the gates of the hostel Big King stopped to chat with the guards. These men had the right to search over any person entering or leaving the hostel. Particularly they were concerned with preventing either women disguised as men or bottles of spirits entering the premises, both of which tended to have a disruptive effect on the community. As an afterthought they were also instructed to look out for stolen property entering or leaving. Big King had to ensure that none of them would ever, under any circumstances, take it into his head to search Big King.

While he stood at the gates, the last glow of the sunset faded and the lights began to come on across the valley. The clusters of red aerial warning lights atop the headgears, the massed yellow squares of the hotels, the strings of street lamps and the isolated pinpricks of the residential areas up on the ridge.

When it was truly dark, Big King left the guards and sauntered down the main road, until a bend in the road took him out of their sight. Then Big King left the road and started up the slope. He moved like a night animal, swiftly and with certainty of the path he followed.

He passed the ranch-type split-levels of the line management officials with their wide lawns and swimming-pools, pausing only once when a dog yapped nearby, then moving on again until he was into the broken rock and rank grass of the upper ridge; he crossed the skyline and started down the far side until he made out the grass-covered mound of rubble in the moonlight. He slowed and moved cautiously forward until he found the rusty barbed wire fence that guarded the entrance. He vaulted it easily and went on into the black mouth of the tunnel.

Fifty years before, a long-defunct mining company had suspected the existence of a gold reef in this area and had driven prospecting adits into the side of the ridge, exhausting its funds in the process, and finally abandoning the network of tunnels in despair.

Big King paused long enough to draw an electric torch from his pocket before going on into the tunnel, flashing the beam ahead of him. Soon the air stank of bats and their wings swished about his head. Unperturbed, Big King went on deeper and deeper into the side of the hill, taking a turning and fork in the tunnel without hesitation. At last there was a faint glow of yellow light ahead and Big King switched off his torch.

'Crooked Leg!' he called, his voice bounced and boomed along the tunnel. There was no reply.

'It is I, Big King!' he shouted again, and immediately a shadow detached itself from the sidewall and limped towards him, sheathing a wicked-looking knife as it came.

'All is ready.' The little cripple came to greet him. 'Come, I have it here.'

Crooked Leg had earned his limp and his nickname in a rockfall a dozen years ago. Now he owned and operated the concession photographic studio on the mine property, a flourishing enterprise, for dearly the Bantu love their own image on film. Not, however, as profitable as his nocturnal activities in the abandoned workings beyond the ridge.

He led Big King into a small rock chamber lit by a suspended hurricane lantern. Mingled with the bat stench was the acrid reek of sulphuric acid in high concentration.

On a wooden trestle table that occupied most of the chamber were earthenware jars, heavy glass bowls, polythene bags, and a variety of shoddy and very obviously second-hand laboratory equipment. In a clear space amongst all this clutter stood a large screw-topped bottle. The bottle was filled with a dirty yellow powder.

'Ha!' Big King exclaimed his pleasure. 'Plenty!'

'Yes. It has been a good week,' Crooked Leg agreed.

Big King picked up the bottle, marvelling once again at the unbelievable weight of it. This was not pure gold, for Crooked Leg's acid reduction methods were crude, but it was at least sixteen carats fine.

The bottle represented the week's collection of fines and concentrates by men like Joseph M'Kati from a dozen vulnerable points along the line of production; in some cases carried out from the company reduction works itself under the noses of the heavily armed guards.

All the men involved in this surreptitious milking off of the company's gold were Shangaans. There was only one man in whom was vested sufficient authority and prestige to prevent the greed and hostility which gold breeds from destroying the whole operation. That was the Shangaan Induna. There was only one man with the physical presence and necessary command of the Portuguese language to negotiate the disposal of the gold. That was Big King.

Big King placed the bottle in his pocket. The weight pulled his clothing out of shape.

'Run like a gazelle, Crooked Leg.' He turned back into the dark tunnel.

'Hunt like a leopard, King Nkulu,' chuckled the little cripple, as he disappeared into the moving shadows.

– 30 –

'A packet of Boxer tobacco,' said Big King. The eyes of José Almeida, the Portuguese owner of the mine concession store and the local roadhouse, narrowed slightly. He took down the yellow four-ounce packet from the shelves and handed it across the counter, accepted Big King's payment and counted the change into his palm.

He watched as the giant Bantu wandered down between the loaded shelves and racks of merchandise to disappear through the front door of the store into the night.

'Take charge,' he muttered in Portuguese to his plump little wife with her silky dark moustache, and she nodded in understanding, moving into José's place in front of the cash register. José went through into his storerooms and living quarters behind the store.

Big King was waiting in the shadows. When the back door opened he slipped through and José closed the door behind him. José led him through into a cubicle of an office, and from a cupboard he took down a jeweller's balance. Under Big King's watchful eye he began to weigh the gold.

José Almeida purchased the gold from the unofficial outlet of each of the five major mines on the Kitchenerville field, paying five Rands an ounce and selling again for sixteen. He justified the large profit margin he allowed

90

himself by the fact that mere possession of unregistered gold was a criminal offence in South Africa, punishable by up to five years' imprisonment.

Almeida was a man in his middle thirties with lank black hair that he continually pushed back from his forehead, bright brown inquisitive eyes and dirty fingernails. Despite his grubby and well-worn clothing and unkempt hairstyle, he was a man of substance.

He had been able to pay in cash the 40,000 rand demanded by the Company for the monopoly concession to trade on the mine property. He had, therefore, an exclusive clientele of 12,000 well-paid Bantu, and had recovered his 40,000 during his first year of trading. He did not really need to run the risk of illicit gold buying, but gold is strange material. It infects most men who touch it with a reckless greed.

'Two hundred and sixteen ounces,' said José. His scale was set to record a twenty per cent error – in José's favour.

'One thousand and eighty rand,' agreed Big King in Portuguese, and José went to the big green safe in the corner.

– 31 –

Terry Steyner entered the 'Grape and Gable' bar of the President Hotel at 1.14 p.m. precisely, and as Hurry Hirschfeld stood to greet her he reflected that fourteen minutes was hardly late at all for a beautiful woman. Terry's grandmother would have considered herself to be early if she was only that late.

'You're late,' growled Hurry. No sense in letting her get away with it unscathed.

'And you are a big, cuddly, growly, lovable old bear,' said Terry and kissed him on the tip of his nose before he could duck. Hurry sat down quickly scowling thunderously with pleasure. He decided he didn't give a good damn if Marais and Hardy, who further down the bar were listening and trying to cover their grins, repeated the incident to the entire membership of the Rand Club.

'Good day, Mrs Steyner.' The scarlet-jacketed barman smiled his greeting. 'Can I mix you a Manhattan?'

'Don't tempt me, Thomas. I'm on a diet. I'll just have a glass of soda water.'

'Diet,' snorted Hurry. 'You're skinny enough as it is. Give her a Manhattan, Thomas, and put a cherry in it. Never was a Hirschfeld woman that looked like a boy, and you'll not be the first of them.' As an afterthought, he added: 'I've ordered your lunch also, you'll not starve yourself in my company.'

'You are a shocker, Pops,' said Terry fondly.

'Now, young lady, let's hear what you've been up to since I last saw you.'

They talked together as friends, very dear and trusted friends. The affection they felt for each other went beyond the natural duty of their blood tie. There was a kinship of the spirit as well as the flesh. They sat close, heads together, watching each other's face as they talked, completely lost in the pleasure of each other's company, the murmur of their voices interrupted by a tinkling burst of laughter or a deep chuckle.

They were so absorbed that Peter, the headwaiter, came through from the Transvaal Room to find them.

'Mr Hirschfeld, the chef is in tears.'

'Good Lord.' Hurry looked at the antique clock above the bar. 'It's almost two o'clock. Why didn't someone tell me?'

The oysters had been flown up from Mossel Bay that morning, and Terry sighed with pleasure after each of them.

'I was out at the Sonder Ditch with Manfred on Wednesday.'

'Yes, I saw the photograph in the paper.' Hurry engulfed his twelfth and final oyster.

'I must say I like your new General Manager.'

Hurry laid down his fork and a little flush of anger started in his withered old cheeks.

'You mean Fred Plummer?'

'Don't be silly, Pops, I mean Rodney Ironsides.'

'Has that cold fish of yours been briefing you?' Hurry demanded.

'Manfred?' She was genuinely puzzled by the question, Hurry could see that. 'What's he got to do with it?'

'All right, forget it.' Hurry dismissed Manfred with a shake of his head. 'Why do you like Ironsides?'

'Have you heard him speak?'

'No.'

'He's very good. I'm sure he must be a first-class mining man.'

'He is.' Hurry nodded, watchful and non-commital.

Peter whisked Terry's plate away, giving her the respite she needed to gather her resources. In the previous few seconds she had realized that Rodney Ironsides was not, as she had believed, a certainty for the job. In fact, Pops had already chosen old plum-faced Plummer for the General Managership. It took another moment for her to decide that she would use even the dirtiest in-fighting to see that Rod was not overlooked.

Peter laid plates of cold rock lobster in front of them, and when he had withdrawn Terry looked up at Hurry. She had perfected the trick of enlarging her already enormous eyes. By holding them open like this she could flood them with tears. The effect was devastating.

'Do you know, Pops, he reminds me so much of the photographs of Daddy.'

Colonel Bernard Hirschfeld, Terry's father, had burned to death in his tank at Sidi Rezegh. She saw Hurry

Hirschfeld's expression crack with pain, and Terry felt a sick little flutter of guilt. Had it been necessary to use such a vicious weapon to achieve her ends?

Hurry pushed at the rock lobster with his fork, his head was bowed so she could not see his face. She reached out to touch his hand.

'Pops—' she whispered, and he looked up. There was a restrained excitement in Hurry's manner.

'You know, you're bloody well right! He does look a bit like Bernie. Did I ever tell you about the time when your father and I—'

Terry felt dizzy with relief. I didn't hurt him, she told herself, he likes the idea, he really does. With a woman's instinct she had chosen the only form of persuasion that could have moved Hurry Hirschfeld from his decision.

– 32 –

Manfred Steyner fastened his safety belt and lay back in the seat of the Boeing 707, feeling slightly nauseated with relief.

Ironsides was in, and he was safe. Hurry Hirschfeld had sent for him two hours before to wish him farewell and good luck with the talks. Manfred had stood before him, trying desperately to think of some way in which he could bring up the subject naturally. Hurry saved him the trouble.

'By the way, I'm giving Ironsides the Sonder Ditch. Reckon it's about time we had some young blood in top management.'

It was as easy as that. Manfred had difficulty in persuading himself that those threats which had kept him lying awake during the past four nights were no longer of consequence. Ironsides was in. He could go to Paris and tell them. *Ironsides is in. We are ready to go.*

The note of the jets changed, and the Boeing began to roll forward. Manfred twisted his head against the neck rest and peered through the Perspex porthole. He could not distinguish Terry's figure amongst the crowd on the observation balcony of Jan Smuts Airport. They taxied past a Pan Am Boeing which cut off his view and Manfred looked straight ahead. Instantly his nostrils flared, he looked around quickly.

The passenger in the seat beside him had stripped to his shirtsleeves. He was a big beefy individual who very obviously did not use deodorant. Almost in desperation Manfred looked about. The aircraft was full, there would be little chance of changing seats and beside him the beefy individual produced a pack of cigarettes.

'You can't smoke,' cried Manfred. 'The light's on.' The combination of body odour and cigarette smoke would be unbearable.

'I'm not smoking,' said the man, 'yet.' And placed a cigarette between his lips, his lighter ready in the other hand.

Nearly two thousand miles to Nairobi, thought Manfred, with his stomach starting to heave.

– 33 –

'Terry darling, why on earth should I go all the way out to Kitchenerville to watch a lot of savages prancing around?'

'As a favour to me, Joy,' Terry pleaded into the telephone.

'It means mucking up my whole weekend. I've got rid of the kids to their grandmother, I've got a copy of A Small Town in Germany and I was going to have a lovely time reading and—'

'Please, Joy, you're my last hope.'

'What time will we be home?' Joy was weakening. Terry sensed her advantage and pressed forward ruthlessly.

'You might meet a lovely man out at the mine, and he'll sweep you—'

'No, thanks.' Joy had been divorced a little over a year ago, some people took longer than others to recover. 'I've had lovely men in big fat chunks.'

'Oh, Joy, you can't sit around moping for ever. Come on, I'll pick you up in half an hour.'

Joy sighed with resignation. 'Damn you, Terry Steyner.'

'Half an hour,' said Terry and hung up before she could change her mind.

'I'm playing golf. It's Saturday, and I'm playing golf,' said Doctor Daniel Stander stubbornly.

'You remember when I drove all the way to Bloemfontein to—' Rod began, and Dan interrupted quickly.

'All right, all right, I remember. You don't have to bring that up again.'

'You owe me plenty, Stander,' Rod reminded him. 'All I am asking is one of your lousy Saturday afternoons. Is that so much?'

'I can't let the boys down. It's a long-standing date.' Dan wriggled to escape.

'I've already phoned Ben. It will be a pleasure for him to take your place.'

There was a long gloomy silence, then Dan asked, 'What's this bird like?'

'She's a beautiful, rich nymphomaniac, and she owns a brewery.'

'Yeah! Yeah!' said Dan sarcastically. 'All right, I'll do it. But I hereby declare all obligations and debts to you fully discharged.'

'I'll give you a written receipt,' Rod agreed.

Dan was still sulking when the Daimler came up the drive and parked in the front of the Mine Club. He and Rod were standing at the Ladies' Bar, watching for the arrival of their guests.

Dan had just ordered his third beer.

'Here they come,' said Rod.

'Is that them?' Dan's depression lifted magically as he peered through the coloured-glass windows. The chauffeur was letting the two ladies out of the Daimler. They were both in floral slack suits and dark glasses.

'That's them.'

'Jesus!' said Dan with rare approval. 'Which one is mine?'

'The blonde.'

'Ha!' Dan grinned for the first time since their meeting. 'Why the hell are we standing here?'

'Why indeed?' asked Rod, his stomach was tied up in knots that twisted tighter as he went down the front steps toward Terry.

'Mrs Steyner. I'm so glad you could come.' With a wild lift of elation he saw it was still there, he had not imagined it, it was there in her eyes and her smile.

'Thank you, Mr Ironsides.' She was like a schoolgirl again, uncertain of herself, flustered.

'I'd like you to meet Mrs Albright. Joy, this is Rodney Ironsides.'

'Hello.' He smiled at her as he clasped her hand. 'It's gin time, I think.'

Dan was waiting at the bar for them, and Rod made the introductions.

'Joy is so excited at the chance of watching the dancing,' said Terry as they sat down on the bar stools. 'She's been looking forward to it for days.' And for an instant Joy looked stunned.

'You'll love it,' agreed Dan, moving in to take up a position at Joy's elbow. 'I wouldn't miss it for anything.'

Joy was a tall slim girl with long straight golden hair that hung to her shoulders, her eyes were cool green but her mouth when she smiled was soft and warm. She smiled now full into Dan's eyes.

'Nor would I,' she said, and with relief Rod knew he could devote all his attention to Terry Steyner. Joy Albright would be more than adequately looked after. He ordered drinks, and all four of them promptly lost further interest in tribal dancing.

At one stage Rod told Terry Steyner, 'I am going up to Johannesburg this evening. There is no point in your unfortunate chauffeur sitting around all afternoon. Let him go, and I'll take you home.'

'Good,' Terry agreed immediately. 'Would you tell him, please?'

The next time Rod looked at his watch it was half past three.

'Good Lord!' he exclaimed. 'If we don't hurry, it will be all over.' Reluctantly Joy and Dan, who had their heads close together, drew apart.

The overflow from the amphitheatre pressed about them, a merry jostling throng, all inhibitions long since evaporated in the primeval excitement of the dance, much like the crowd at a bull ring.

Rod and Dan ran interference for the girls, ploughing a path through the main gateway and down to their reserved seats in the front row. All four of them were laughing and flushed by the time they were seated, the excitement about them was infectious and the liquor had heightened their sensibilities.

An expectant hum of voices.

'The Shangaans!' And the audience craned towards the entrance from which pranced a dozen drummers, their long wooden drums hung on rawhide straps about their necks, they took up stations around the circular earthen stage.

Tap, tap. Tap, tap – from one of the drummers, and silence gripped the amphitheatre.

Tap, tap. Tap, tap. Naked, except for their brief loin cloths, stooped over the drums that they clasped between their knees, they began to lay down the rhythm of the dance. It was a broken, disturbing beat, that jerked and twitched like a severed nerve. A compelling, demanding sound, the pulse of a continent and a people.

Then came the dancers, shuffling, row upon row, head-dresses dipping and rustling, the animal tail kilts swirling, war rattles at the wrists and ankles, black muscles already oiled with the sweat of excitement, coming in slowly rank upon majestic rank, moving as though the drums were pumping life into them.

A shrill blast on a duiker horn and the ranks whirled like dry leaves in a wind, they fell again into a new pattern, and through the opening in their midst came a single gigantic figure.

'Big King!' The name blew like a sigh through the audience, and immediately the drums changed their rhythm. Faster, demanding, and the dancers hissed in their throats a sound like storm surf rushing up a stony beach.

Big King flung his arms wide, braced on legs like black marble columns, his head thrown back. He sang a single word of command, shrilling it, and in instantaneous response every right knee was brought up to the level of the chest. Half a second's pause and then 200 horny bare feet stamped down simultaneously with a crash that shook the amphitheatre to its foundations. The Shangaans began to dance, and reality was gone in the moving, charging, swirling, retreating ranks.

Once Rod tore his eyes from the spectacle. Terry Steyner was sitting forward on the bench, eyes sparkling, lips slightly parted, completely lost in the erotic turmoil and barbaric splendour of it.

Joy and Dan had a firm hold on each others' hands, their shoulders and the outside of their thighs were pressed tightly together, and Rod was stabbed by a painful thrust of envy.

Afterwards, back in the Ladies' Bar of the Club, there was very little conversation but they were all of them tensed up, restless, moved by strange undercurrents and interplays of primitive desires and social restraints.

'Well,' said Rod at last, 'if I am to get you two ladies back to Johannesburg at a decent hour—'

Dan and Joy spoke together.

'Don't worry, Rod, I'll—'

'Dan says he will—' Then they stopped and grinned at each other sheepishly.

'I take it that Dan has suddenly remembered that he has to go to Johannesburg this evening also, and he has offered to give you a lift?' asked Rod dryly, and they laughed in confirmation.

'It looks as though we are on our own, Mrs Steyner.' Rod turned to Terry.

'I'll trust you,' said Terry.

'If you do that, you're crazy,' said Dan.

Outside the Maserati, darkness was falling swiftly. The horizon blending into the black sky, isolated lights winking at them out of the surrounding veld.

Rod switched on the headlights, and the instrument panel glowed softly, turning the interior into a warm secluded place, isolating them from the world. The wind whispered, and the tyres and the engine hummed a gentle intimate refrain.

Terry Steyner sat with her legs curled up under her, cuddled into the soft maroon leather of the bucket seat.

She was staring ahead down the path of the headlights, and she seemed withdrawn and yet very close. Every few minutes Rod would take his eyes from the road and study her profile briefly. He did so again, and this time she met his gaze frankly.

'You realize what is happening?' she asked.

'Yes,' he answered as frankly.

'You know how dangerous it could be for you?'

'And you.'

'No, not me. I am invulnerable. I am a Hirschfeld – but you, it could destroy you.'

Rod shrugged.

'If we counted the consequences before every action, nobody would do anything.'

'Have you thought that I might be a spoiled little rich girl amusing myself? I might do this all the time.'

'You might,' Rod agreed. They were silent for a long while, then Terry spoke again.

'Rod?' She used his given name for the first time.

'Yes?'

'I don't, you know, I really don't.'

'I guessed that.'

'Thank you.' She opened her bag. 'I need a cigarette. I feel as though I'm standing poised on the edge of a cliff and I've got this terrible compulsion to hurl myself over the edge.'

'Light me one, Terry.'

'You need one also?'

'Badly.'

They smoked in silence again, both of them staring ahead, then Terry rolled down the window and flicked the cigarette butt away.

'You've got the job, you know.' All day she had wanted to tell him, it had been bubbling inside her. Watching his face, she saw his lips stiffen, his eyes crease into slits.

'Did you hear me?' she asked at last, and he braked the

Maserati, swinging it off onto the shoulder of the road. He pulled on the hand brake and turned to face her.

'Terry, what did you say?'

'I said, you've got the job.'

'What job?' he demanded harshly.

'Pops signed the instruction this morning. You'll receive it on Monday. You're the new General Manager of the Sonder Ditch.' She wanted to go on and say – *and I got it for you. I made Pops give it to you.*

I never will, she promised, I will never spoil it for him. He must believe he won it fairly, not as my gift.

– 34 –

It was Saturday night, the big night in Dump City.

The Blaauberg Mine was the oldest producer on the Kitchenerville field. There were sections of its property which had been worked out completely, and the old waste dumps were now abandoned and overgrown. Among the scrub and head-high weed in the valleys between these man-made hills had grown up a shanty town. Dump City, the inhabitants had named it. The buildings were made of discarded galvanized iron sheets and flattened oil drums, there was no sanitation or running water.

Remote from the main roads, the residential communities of the neighbouring mines or the town of Kitchenerville, hidden among the dumps, accessible only to a man on foot, never visited by members of the South African Constabulary, it was ideally suited to the purposes for which its 300 permanent inhabitants had chosen it.

Every one of the shacks was a shebeen, a clip joint where watered liquor was sold at inflated prices, where dagga*

* Marijuana.

102

was freely obtainable and where men from the surrounding mines gathered to carouse.

They came not so much for the liquor. Each of the mine hostels had a bar where a full range of liquor was on sale at club prices. Very few of them came for the dagga. There was little addiction amongst these well-fed, hard-worked and contented men. What they came for were the women.

Five mines in the area, each employing ten or twelve thousand men. Here at Dump City were 200 women, the only available women within twenty miles. It was not necessary for the young ladies of Dump City to solicit custom, even the fat, the withered, the toothless, could behave like queens.

Big King came down the path that skirted the mine dump. With him were two dozen of his fellow tribesmen, big Shangaans wearing their regalia, carrying their fighting sticks and still tensed up from the dancing. They came at a trot, Big King leading them. They were singing, not the gentle planting or courting melodies, not the work chant nor the song of welcome.

They were singing the fighting songs, those their fore-fathers had sung when they carried the spear in search of cattle and slaves. The driving inflammatory rhythm, the fiercely patriotic words wrought so mightily on the delicate susceptibilities of the average Shangaan that the Company had found it necessary to ban the singing of these songs.

Like a Scot hearing the pipes, when a Shangaan began singing these warlike chants, he was ready for violence.

The song ended as Big King led them down to the nearest shanty, and pushed aside the sacking that acted as a door. He stooped through the opening, and his comrades crowded in behind him.

A brittle electric silence fell on the large room. The air was so thick with smoke, and the light from the suspended hurricane lamps so feeble, that it was impossible to see the far wall. The room was filled with men, forty or fifty of them, the smell of humanity and bad liquor was solid. Among this press of men were half a dozen bright spots of the girls' dresses, but with their curiosity aroused by the singing more girls were coming through from the interleading doorways at the back, some of them had men with them and were still shrugging into their clothing. When they saw Big King and his warriors in full war kit, they fell silent and watchful.

At Big King's shoulder one of his Shangaans whispered:

'Basutos! They are all Basutos!' He was right, Big King saw that they were all men of that mountainous little independent state.

Big King started forward, swaggering just enough to make his leopard tail kilt swing and swirl and the heron feathers of his head-dress rustle. He reached the primitive bar counter.

'Flying Bird,' he told the crone who owned the house, and she placed a bottle of Eagle Brandy on the counter.

Big King half filled a tumbler, conscious that every eye was on him, and drained it.

Slowly he turned and surveyed the room.

'What is it,' he asked in a voice that carried to every corner, 'that sits on top of a mountain and scratches its fleas. Is it a baboon, or a Basuto?'

A roar of delight went up from his Shangaans.

'A Basuto!' they shouted, crowding forward to the bar, while a growl and a mutter went up from the rest of the room.

'What is it,' shouted a Basuto jumping to his feet, 'that has feathers on its head and crows from a dungheap? Is it a rooster, or a Shangaan?'

Without seeming to move, Big King picked up the bottle of Eagle Brandy and hurled it. With a crack it burst against the Basuto's forehead and he went over backwards taking two of his companions with him.

The old crone snatched up her cash register and ran as the room exploded into violent movement.

There was not enough space in which to use the fighting sticks, Big King realized, so he lifted a section of the bar counter off its trestles and, holding it in front of him like the blade of a bulldozer, he charged across the room, flattening all and everything before him.

The crash of breaking furniture and the yelp and squeal of men being struck down drove Big King beyond the frontiers of sanity into the red atavistic fury of the berserker.

Basuto is also one of the fighting tribes of the N'guni group. These wiry mountaineers rushed into the conflict with the same savage joy as the Shangaans, a conflict that raged and roared out of the single room to engulf the entire population of Dump City.

One of the girls, her dress ripped from her back so she was left with only a tattered pair of bloomers, had climbed on top of the remains of the bar counter from where, with her big melon breasts swinging in the lamp light, she shrilled that peculiar ululation that Bantu women used to goad their menfolk into battle frenzy. A dozen of the other girls joined in, trilling, squealing, and the sound was too much for Big King.

With the bar top held ahead of him he charged straight through the flimsy wall of the shack, bursting it open like a paper bag. The roof sagged down wearily, and Big King raged on unchecked down the narrow dirt street, striking down any man who crossed his path, scattering chickens and yelping dogs, roaring like a bull gorilla.

He turned at the end of the encampment and came back, his frustration mounting as he found the street deserted except for a few prostrate bodies; through the gaping hole in the wall he entered the shebeen once more to find that here also the fighting had died down. A few of the participants were crawling, or moaning as they lay on the carpet of broken glass.

Big King glared about him, seeking a further outlet for his wrath.

'King Nkulu!' The girl was still on the trestle table, her eyes bright with excitement, her legs trembling with it.

Big King let out another roar, and hurled the bar top from him. It clattered against the far wall and Big King started towards her.

'You are a lion!' She shrieked encouragement at him, and she took one of her big black velvety breasts in each hand and pointed them at him, squeezing them together, shaking with excitement.

'Eat me!' she screamed, as Big King swept her off the table and, lifting her high, ran with her out into the night. Carrying her into the scrub below the mine dumps, holding her easily with one arm, ripping the leopard-tail kilt from his own waist as he ran.

– 35 –

It was Saturday night in Paris also, but there were men who were still working, for there were lights burning in the upstairs rooms of one of the big embassies in the rue Royale.

The fat man who had been the host in the gambling establishment in Johannesburg was now the guest. He sat at ease in a leather club easy chair, his corpulence and the steel-grey hair at his temples giving him dignity. His face heavy, tanned, intelligent. His eyes glittery and hard as the diamond on his finger.

He was listening intently to a man of about the same age as himself who stood before a projected image on a screen that covered one wall of the room. There was that in the man's bearing and manner that marked him as a scholar, he was speaking now, addressing himself directly to the listener in the easy chair, pointing with a marker to the screen beside him.

'You see here a plan of the working of the five producing gold mines of the Kitchenerville fields in relation to each other.' He touched the screen with the marker. 'Thornfontein, Blaauberg, Tweefontein, Deep Gold Levels and Sonder Ditch.'

The man in the chair nodded. 'I have seen and studied this diagram before.'

'Good, then you will know that the Sonder Ditch property sits in the centre of the field. It has common boundaries with the other four mines and here,' he tapped the screen again, 'it is intersected by the massive serpentine dyke which they call the Big Dipper.'

Again the fat man nodded.

'It is for these reasons we have selected the Sonder Ditch as the trigger point.' The lecturer touched a button on the wall panel and the image on the screen changed.

'Now, here is something you have not seen before.'

The man in the chair crouched forward.

'What is it?'

'It is an underground map based on the borehole results of the five companies who have been exploring the ground to the east of the Big Dipper. These results have been pooled and interpreted by some of the finest brains in the fields of geology and hydrophysics. You have here a carefully considered representation of exactly what lies on the far side of the Big Dipper fault.'

The big man moved uncomfortably in his chair.

'It's a monster!'

'Yes, a monster. Lying just beyond the fault is an underground lake, no, that is not the correct word. Let us call it an underground sea, the size of, say, Lake Eyrie. The water is held in a vast sponge of porous dolomite rock.'

'My God.' For the first time the fat man had lost his

poise. 'If this is right, why don't the mining companies arrive at the same conclusion and keep well away from it?'

'Because,' the lecturer switched off the image and the overhead lights came on, 'because of their highly competitive attitude none of them has access to the findings of the others. It is only when all the results are studied that the picture becomes clear.'

'How did your government come to be in possession of *all* the results?' demanded the fat man.

'That is not important.' The lecturer was brusque, impatient of the interruption. 'We are also in possession of the findings of a certain Dr Peter Wessels who is at present head of a research team in Rock Mechanics based on the Sonder Ditch mine property. It is Company classified information and consists of a paper that Dr Peter Wessels has written on the shatter patterns and stresses of rock. His researches are directly related to the Ventersdorp quartzites which comprise the country rock of the Sonder Ditch workings.'

The lecturer picked up a pamphlet from his desk.

'I will not weary you by asking you to wade through its highly technical findings. Instead I will give it to you in capsule form. Dr Wessels arrives at the conclusion that a column of Ventersdorp quartzite 120 feet thick would shatter under a side pressure of 4,000 pounds per square inch.'

The lecturer dropped the pamphlet back on the desk.

'As you know, by law, the gold mining companies are bound to leave a barrier of solid rock 120 feet thick along their boundaries. That is all that separates one mine's working from another, just that wall of rock. You understand?'

'Of course. It is very simple.'

'Simple? Yes, it is simple! This Dr Steyner, over whom you have control, will instruct the new General Manager of the Sonder Ditch to drive a tunnel through the Big Dipper dyke. The drive will puncture the vast underground reservoir and the water will run back and flood the entire Sonder Ditch workings. Once they are flooded, the pressure delivered by a 6,000-foot head of water at the lower levels will be in excess of 4,000 pounds per square inch. That is sufficient to burst the rock walls, and flood the Thornfontein, the Blaauberg, Deep Gold Levels and Tweefontein gold mines.'

'The entire Kitchenerville gold fields would be effectively and permanently put out of production. The consequences for the economy of the Republic of South Africa would be catastrophic.'

The fat man was visibly shaken.

'Why do you want to do it?' he asked, shaking his head in awe.

'My colleague here,' the lecturer indicated a man who was sitting quietly in one corner, 'will explain that to you presently.'

'But – people!' the fat man protested. 'There will be people down there when it bursts, thousands of them.'

The lecturer smiled, raising one eyebrow. 'If I were to tell you that six thousand men would drown, would you refuse to proceed, and forfeit the million-dollar payment my government has offered you?'

The fat man looked down, embarrassed, and muttered barely audibly, 'No.'

The lecturer chuckled. 'Good! Good! However, you may salve you aching conscience by assuring yourself that we do not expect more than forty or fifty fatalities from the flooding. Naturally, those men actually working on the face will be killed. But that tremendous volume of water under immense pressure should make it a merciful death. For the rest of them, the mine can be evacuated swiftly enough to allow them excellent chances of survival. The surrounding mines will have days to evacuate before the water pressure builds up sufficiently to burst through the boundary walls.'

There was silence then in the room for nearly a minute.

'Have you any questions?'

The fat man shook his head.

'Very well, in that case I will leave it to my colleague to complete the briefing. He will explain the necessity for this operation, will arrange the terms of payment and conditions upon which you will proceed.' The lecturer gathered up the pamphlet and other papers from the desk. 'It remains only for me to wish you good luck.' He chuckled again and left the room quickly.

The little man, who up until them had remained silent, suddenly bounced out of his chair and began pacing up and down the wall-to-wall carpeting. He spoke rapidly, shooting occasional sideways glances at his audience, his bald head shining in the fluorescent lighting, wriggling his moustache like rabbit whiskers, puffing nervously at his cigarette.

'Reasons first. I'll make it short and sweet, right? The South Africans and the Frogs have got together. They're here in Paris now cooking up mischief. We know what they're up to, they're going to launch an all-out attack on my government's currency. Gold price increase, you know. Very complicated and very nasty for us, right? They might just be able to do it, South Africa is the world's biggest gold producer. With the Frogs helping her, they might just be able to force an increase.'

He stopped in front of the fat man and thrust out an accusing finger.

'Are we going to sit back and let them have a free run? No, sir! We are going to throw down our own curve ball! In three months time the Syndicate will be ready to attack. At that precise moment we will kick the chair out from under the South Africans by cutting their gold production in half. We will flood the Kitchenerville goldfields and the attack will fizzle out like a damp squib, right?'

'As simple as that?' asked the fat man.

'As simple as that!' The bald head nodded vigorously.

'Now, my next duty is to make clear to you that the agreed million dollars is *all* the reward you receive. Neither you nor your agents may indulge in any financial transactions that might, in retrospect, show that this was a planned operation, right?'

'Right.' The fat man nodded.

'You give your assurance that you will not deal in any of the shares of the companies involved?'

'You have my solemn word.' The fat man told him earnestly, and not for the first time in his life reflected how easily and painlessly a promise could be given.

With the assistance of the three men who had watched Manfred Steyner that night at the gambling club in Johannesburg, he intended launching a bear offensive on the stock exchanges of the world.

On the day that they drilled into the Big Dipper dyke he and his partners would sell millions of the shares of the five mining companies for one of the biggest financial killings in the history of money.

'We are agreed then.' The bald head bobbed. 'Now, as for this Dr Steyner, we have had a screening and personality analysis and we believe that, despite the secure hold you have on his loyalties, he would jib at giving the order to drive on the Big Dipper if he were aware of the consequences. Therefore we have prepared a second geological report,' he produced from his brief case a thick manila folder, 'incorporating those figures which he will recognize. In other words the drilling results of the CRC exploration teams, but the other figures are fictitious. This report purports to prove the existence of a fabulously rich gold reef beyond the fault.' He crossed to the fat man and handed him the folder. 'Take it. It will help you convince Dr Steyner, and he in turn to convince the new General Manager of the Sonder Ditch gold mine.'

111

'You have been thorough,' said the fat man.

'We try to give a satisfactory service to our customers,' said the bald man.

– 36 –

The game was five-card stud poker, and there were two big winners at the table, Manfred Steyner and the Algerian.

Manfred had timed his arrival in Paris to ensure himself an uninterrupted weekend before the rest of the delegates came in on the Monday morning flight.

He had checked in at the Hotel George Cinq on Saturday afternoon, bathed and rested for three hours until eight in the evening, then he had set out for the Club Chat Noir by taxi.

He had been playing now for five hours, and a steady succession of strong cards had pushed his winnings up to a formidable sum. It lay piled in front of him, a fruit salad of garish French bank notes. Across the table sat the Algerian, a slim dark-skinned Arab with toffee eyes and a silky black moustache. His teeth were very white against the creamy brown skin. He wore a turtle-neck shirt in pink silk, and a linen jacket of baby blue. With long brown fingers he kept smoothing and stacking his own pile of bank notes.

A girl sat on the arm of his chair, an Arab girl in a skin-tight gold trouser suit. Her hair was shiny black and hung onto her shoulders, her eyes were disconcertingly level as she watched Manfred.

'Ten thousand.' Manfred's voice was explosive, like that of a teutonic drillmaster. He was betting on his fourth card which had just been dealt to him. He and the Algerian were the remaining players in the game. The others had folded their hands and were sitting back watching with the casual interest of men no longer involved.

The Algerian's eyes narrowed slightly and the girl leaned down to whisper softly in his ear. He shook his head, annoyed, and drew on his cigarette. He had a pair of queens and a six showing and he leaned forward to study Manfred's cards.

The dealer's voice prodded. 'The bet is ten thousand francs, from four, five, seven of clubs. Possible straight flush.'

'Bet or drop,' said one of the uncommitted players. 'You're wasting time.'

The Algerian flashed him a venomous glance.

'Bet,' he said, and counted out ten thousand-franc notes into the pool.

'*Carte.*' The dealer slid a card face down in front of each of them. Quickly the Algerian lifted one corner of his card with his thumb, glanced at it and then closed the face.

Manfred sat very still, the card lying inches from his right hand. His face was pale, calm, but he was seething internally. Far from a possible straight flush, Manfred was holding four, five, seven of clubs and the eight of hearts. A six was the only card that could improve his hand and one six was already showing among the Algerian's cards. His chances were remote.

His lower belly and loins were tight and hot with excitement, his chest constricted. He drew out the sensation, wanting it to last for ever.

'Pair of queens still to bet,' murmured the dealer.

'Ten thousand.' The Algerian pushed the notes forward.

He has found another queen, thought Manfred, but he is uncertain of my flush or straight.

Manfred placed his smooth white hand over his fifth card, cupping it. He lifted it.

'Table,' said Manfred calmly, and there was a gasp and rustle from the watchers. The girl's hand tightened on the Algerian's sleeve, she stared with hatred into Manfred's face.

'The gentleman has made a table bet,' intoned the croupier. 'House rules. Any player may bet the entire stake he has upon the table.' He reached across and began to count the notes in front of Manfred.

Minutes later he announced the total. 'Two hundred and twelve thousand francs.' He looked across at the Algerian. 'It is now up to you to bet against the possible straight flush.'

The girl whispered urgently into the Arab's ear, but he snapped a single word at her and she recoiled. He looked about the room, as if seeking guidance, then he lifted and examined his hole cards again.

Suddenly his face hardened, and he looked steadily across at Manfred.

'Call!' he blurted, and Manfred's clenched right hand fell open upon the table.

The Arab faced his hand. Three queens. The whole room looked expectantly at Manfred.

He flicked over his last card. Two of diamonds. His hand was worthless.

With a birdlike cry of triumph the Algerian leaped from his seat and reaching across the table began raking Manfred's stake with both arms towards him.

Manfred stood up from the table, and the Arab girl grinned maliciously at him, taunting him in Arabic. He turned quickly away and almost ran down the steps that led to the cloakrooms. Twenty minutes later, feeling weak and slightly dizzy, Manfred slipped into the back seat of a Citroën taxi cab.

'George Cinq,' he told the driver. As he entered the lobby of the hotel he saw a tall figure rise from one of the leather armchairs and follow him across to the lifts. Shoulder to shoulder they stepped into the lift and as the doors slid closed the tall man spoke.

'Welcome to Paris, Dr Steyner.'

'Thank you, Andrew. I presume you have come to give me my instructions?'

'That is correct. He wishes to see you tomorrow at ten o'clock. I will call for you.'

– 37 –

It was Saturday night in Kitchenerville and in the men's bar of the Lord Kitchener Hotel the daily-paid men from the five gold mines were bellying up to the counter three deep.

The public dance had been in progress for three hours. At tables along the veranda the women-folk sat primly sipping their port and lemonade. Although they all were admirably ignoring the absence of the men, yet a constant and merciless vigil was kept on the door to the men's bar. Most of the wives already had the automobile keys safely in their handbags.

In the dining-hall, cleared of its furniture and sprinkled liberally with French chalk, the local four-piece band who played under the unlikely name of the 'Wind Dogs' launched without preliminaries into a lively rendition of 'Die Ou Kraal Liedjie', and from the men's bar, in various stages of inebriation, answering the call to arms came the troops.

Many of them had shed their jackets, the knots of their ties had slipped, their voices were boisterous and legs were a little unsteady as they led their women onto the dance floor and immediately showed to which school of the dance they belonged.

There was the cavalry squadron which tucked partner under one arm, very much like a lance, and charged. At the other end of the scale were those who plodded grimly around the perimeter, looking neither left nor right, speaking to no one, not even their partners. Then there were the sociables who reeled about the floor, red in the face, their movements completely unrelated to the music, shouting to their friends and attempting to pinch any feminine posterior that came within range. Their unpredictable progress interfered with the revolutions of the dedicated.

The dedicated took up their positions in the centre of the floor and twisted. A half dozen years previously the twist had swept like an Asian 'flu epidemic through the world and then faded out. Gone, forgotten, except in places like Kitchenerville. Here it had been taken and firmly entrenched into the social culture of the community.

Even in this stronghold of the twist, there was one master. 'Johnny Delange? Gott man, but he can twist, hey!' they murmured with awe.

With the sinuous erotic movements of an erect cobra, Johnny was twisting with Hettie. His shiny rayon suit caught the light and the lace ruffles of his shirt fluttered at his throat. There was a fierce grin of pleasure on his hawk features, and the jewelled buckles of his pointed Italian shoes twinkled as he danced.

A big girl with copper hair and creamy skin, Hettie was light on her feet. She had a tiny waist and a swelling regal bottom under the emerald-green skirt. She laughed as she danced, a full healthy laugh to match her body.

The two of them moved with the expertise of a couple who have danced together often. Hettie anticipated each of Johnny's movements, and he grinned his approval at her.

From the veranda Davy Delange watched them. He stood in the shadows, clutching a tankard of beer, a squat, lonely figure. When another dancing couple cut off his view of Hettie's luscious revolving buttocks he would exclaim with irritation and move restlessly.

The music ended and the dancers spilled out onto the veranda, laughing and breathless, mopping streaming faces;

girls squealing and giggling as the men led them to their seats, deposited them and then headed for the bar.

'See you.' Johnny left Hettie reluctantly, he would have liked to stay with her, but he was sensitive about what the boys would say if he spent the whole evening with his wife.

He was absorbed into the masculine crowd, to join their banter and loud laughter. He was deeply involved in a discussion of the merits of the new Ford Mustang, which he was considering buying, when Davy nudged him.

'It's Constantine!' he whispered, and Johnny looked up quickly. Constantine was a Greek immigrant, a stoper on the Blaauberg Mine. He was a big strong black-haired individual with a broken nose. Johnny had broken his nose for him about ten months previously. As a bachelor Johnny would fight him on the average of once a month, nothing serious, just a semi-friendly punch-up.

However, Constantine could not understand that now-adays Johnny was forbidden by his brand new wife from indulging in casual exchanges of fisticuffs. He had developed the erroneous theory that Johnny Delange was afraid of him.

He was coming down the bar room now, holding his glass in his massive hairy right hand with the little finger extended genteely. On his hip rested his other hand and he minced along with a simpering smile on his blue-jowled granite-textured features. Stopping in front of the mirror to pat his hair into place, he winked at his cronies and then came on down to where Johnny stood. He paused and ogled Johnny heavily, fluttering his eyelids and wriggling his hips. His colleagues from the Blaauberg Mine were weak with laughter, gurgling merrily, hanging onto each other's shoulders.

Then with a bump and grind that raised another howl of laughter Constantine disappeared into the lavatories, to emerge minutes later and blow Johnny a kiss as he went back to join his friends. They plied liquor on the Greek in appreciation of his act. Johnny's smile was a little strained as he resumed the discussion on the Mustang's virtues.

Twenty minutes and half a dozen brandies later, Constantine repeated his little act again on the way to the latrine. His repertoire was limited.

'Hold it, Johnny,' whispered Davy. 'Let's go and sit on the veranda.'

'He's asking for it. I'm telling you!' Johnny's smile had disappeared.

'Come on, Johnny, man.'

'No, hell, they'll think I'm running. I can't go now.'

'You know what Hettie will say,' Davy warned him. For a moment longer Johnny hesitated.

'The hell with what Hettie says.' Johnny bunched his right fist with its array of gold rings as he moved down to Constantine and leaned beside him on the counter.

'Herby,' he called the barman, and when he had his attention he indicated the Greek. 'Please give the lady a port and lemonade.'

And the bystanders scattered for cover. Davy shot out of the door onto the veranda to report to Hettie.

'Johnny!' he gasped. 'He's fighting again.'

'Is he!' Hettie came to her feet like a red-headed Valkyrie. But her progress to the men's bar was delayed by the crowd of spectators that jammed the doorway and all the windows. The crowd was tiptoeing and climbing onto the chairs and tables for a better view, every thud or crash of breaking furniture was greeted with a roar of delight.

Hettie had her handbag clutched in her right hand, and like a jungle explorer hacking his way through the undergrowth with a machete, she opened a path for herself to the bar room door.

At the door she paused. The conflict had reached a critical stage. Among a litter of broken glass and shattered stools, Johnny and the Greek were circling each other warily, waving and feinting, all their wits concentrated upon each other. Both of them were marked. The Greek was bleeding from his lip, a thin red ribbon of blood down his chin that dripped onto his shirt. Johnny had a shiny red swelling closing one eye. The crowd was silent, waiting.

'Johnny Delange!' Hettie's voice cracked like a Mauser rifle fired from ambush. Johnny started guiltily, dropping his hands, half turning towards her as the Greek's fist crashed into the side of his head. Johnny spun from the blow, hit the wall and slid down quietly.

With a roar of triumph Constantine rushed forward to put the boot into Johnny's prostrate form, but he pitched forward to sprawl unconscious beside Johnny. Hettie had hit him with the water bottle snatched up from one of the table tops.

'Please help me get my husband to the car,' she appealed to the men around her, suddenly helpless and little-girlish.

She sat beside Davy in the front of the Monaco, fuming with anger.

Johnny lay at ease upon the back seat. He was snoring softly.

'Don't be angry, Hettie.' Davy was driving sedately.

'I've told him, not once, a hundred times.' Hettie's voice crackled like static. 'I told him I wouldn't put up with it.'

'It wasn't his fault. The Greek started it,' Davy explained softly and placed his hand on her leg.

'You stick up for him, just because he is your brother.'

'That's not true,' Davy soothed her, stroking her leg. 'You know how I feel about you, Hettie.'

'I don't believe you.' His hand was moving higher. 'You men are all the same. You all stick together.'

Her anger was fast solidifying into a burning resentment of Johnny Delange, one in which she was willing to take a calculated revenge. She knew that Davy's hand was no longer trying to comfort her and quench her anger. Before she married Johnny Delange, Hettie had had every opportunity to learn about men, and she had been an enthusiastic and receptive pupil. She placed no special importance on an act of the flesh, dispensing her favours as casually as someone might offer a cigarette-case around.

'Why not?' she thought. 'That will fix Mr Johnny Delange! Not all the way, of course, but just enough to get my own back on him.'

'No, Hettie. It's true – I tell you.' Davy's voice was husky, as he felt her knees fall apart under his hand. He touched the silky-smooth skin above her stocking top.

The Monaco slowed to almost walking pace, and it was ten minutes more before they reached the company-owned house on the outskirts of Kitchenerville.

In the back seat Johnny groaned. Immediately Davy's hand jerked back to the steering-wheel, and Hettie sat up in the seat, straightening her skirt.

'Help me get him inside,' she said, and her voice was shaky and her cheeks flushed. She was no longer angry.

– 38 –

They were both a little tipsy. They had stopped to celebrate Rod's promotion at the Sunnyside Hotel. They had sat side by side in one of the booths, drinking quickly, excitedly, laughing together, sitting close but not touching.

Terry Steyner could not remember when she had last behaved this way. It must have been all of ten years ago, her last term at Cape Town varsity, swigging draught beer in the Pig and Whistle at Randall's Hotel and talking the most inane rubbish. All the matronly dignity that Manfred insisted she maintain was gone, she felt like a freshette on a first date with the captain of the rugby team.

'Let's get out of here,' Rod said suddenly, and she stood

120

up unquestioningly. He took her arm down the stairs, and the light touch of his fingers tingled on her bare skin.

In the Maserati again she experienced the feeling of isolation from reality.

'How often do you see your daughter, Rod?' she asked as he settled into the seat beside her, and he glanced at her, surprised.

'Every Sunday.'

'Tomorrow?'

'Yes.'

'How old is she?'

'Nine next birthday.'

'What do you do with her?'

Rod pressed the starter.

'How do you mean?'

'Where do you take her, what do you do together?'

'We go rowing on Zoo Lake, or eat ice cream sundaes. If it's cold or raining we sit in the apartment and we play mah-jong.' He let in the clutch, and as they pulled away he added, 'She cheats.'

'The apartment?'

'I keep a hideaway in town.'

'Where?'

'I'll show you,' said Rod quietly.

She sat on the studio couch and looked about her with interest. She had not expected the obvious care that he had taken in furnishing the apartment. It was in wheatfield gold, chocolate brown and copper. There was a glorious glowing autumn landscape on the far wall that she recognized as a Dino Paravano.

She noticed a little ruefully how Rod stage-managed the lighting for full romantic effect, and then moved automatically to the liquor cabinet.

'Where is the bathroom?' Terry asked.

'Second left, down the passage.'

She lingered in the bathroom, opening the medicine cabinet like a thief. There were three toothbrushes hanging in the slots, and below them an aerosol can of Bidex. Quickly she shut the cabinet. Feeling disturbed, not sure if it was jealousy or guilt at her own prying.

The bedroom door was open and so she could not help seeing the double bed as she went back to the lounge. She stood in front of the painting.

'I love his work,' she said.

'Not too photographic for your taste?'

'No. I love it.'

He gave her the drink and stood beside her, studying the painting. She tinkled the ice in her glass, and he turned towards her. The feeling of unreality was still holding Terry as she felt him take the glass from her hand.

She was conscious of his hands only, they were strong and very practised. They touched her shoulders, and then moved onto her back calmly. She felt a voluptuous shudder shake her whole body, and then his mouth came down over hers and the sense of unreality was complete. It was all warm and misty, and she let him take control.

She never knew how long afterwards she jerked back to complete, chilling reality. They were on the couch. She lay in his arms. The front of her slack suit was open to the waist and her bra was unhooked. His head was bowed over her and with a handful of thick springy hair she was directing his lips in their quest. His mouth was warm and sucky on her breast.

'I must be mad!' she gasped, and struggled violently from his arms. She was trembling with fright, horrified with herself. Nothing like this had ever happened to her before.

'This is madness!' Her eyes were great dark pools in her pale face, and her fingers were frantic as she buttoned her blouse. As the last button slipped into its hole, anger replaced her fright.

'How many women have you seduced on that couch, Rodney Ironsides?'

Rod stood up, reaching out a hand to reassure her.

'Don't touch me!' She stepped back. 'I want to go home!'

'I'll take you home, Terry. Just calm down. Nothing happened.'

'That's not your fault,' she blazed.

'No, it's not,' he agreed.

'If you had your way, you'd have—' she bit it off.

'Yes, I would have.' Rod nodded. 'But only if you wanted the same thing.'

She stared at him, starting to recover her temper and her control.

'I shouldn't have come up here, I know. It was asking for trouble, but please take me home now.'

– 39 –

The telephone woke Rod. He checked his wrist watch as he tottered naked and half asleep through to the lounge. Eight o'clock.

'Ironsides!' He yawned into the mouthpiece, and then came fully awake as he recognized her voice.

'Good morning, Rodney. How's your hangover?'

He had not expected to hear from her again.

'Just bearable.'

'I called to thank you for an amusing and – instructive evening.'

'Hark at the girl!' He grinned and scratched his chest. 'She changes with the wind. Last night I expected a bullet between the eyes.'

'Last night I got one big fright,' she admitted. 'It comes

123

as a bit of a shock to discover suddenly that you are quite capable of acting the wanton. Not all the names I called you were meant.'

'I am sorry for my contribution to your distress,' Rod said.

'Don't be, you were very impressive.' Then quickly, changing the subject, 'You are picking up your daughter today?'

'Yes.'

'I'd like to meet her.'

'That could be arranged.' Rod was cautious.

'Does she like horses?'

'She's crazy about them.'

'Would you like to take her and me out to my stud farm on the Vaal river?'

Rod hesitated. 'Is it safe? I mean, being seen together?'

'It's my reputation, I'll look after it.'

'Fine!' Rod agreed. 'We'd love to visit your farm.'

'I'll meet you at your apartment. When?'

'Half past nine!'

Patti was still in her dressing-gown and she offered Rod her cheek casually to be pecked. There were curlers in her hair and from her eyes he could tell she'd had a late night.

'Hello, you're getting thin. Melly is dressing. Do you want some coffee? Your maintenance cheque was late again this month.' And she took a swipe at the spaniel pup as it squatted on the carpet. 'Damn dog pees all over the place. *Melanie*.' She raised her voice. 'Hurry up! Your Papa is here.'

'Hello, Daddy!' Melanie's voice shrieked delightedly from the interior of the apartment.

'Hello, baby.'

'You can't come in, Daddy, I haven't got any clothes on.'

'Well hurry up! I've come a million miles to see you.'

'Not a *million*!' You couldn't fool Melanie Ironsides.

'Did you say you wanted coffee? It's no trouble, it's made already.' Pattie led him through into the sitting-room.

'Thanks.'

'How are things?' she asked as she filled a cup and gave it to him.

'They've made me General Manager of the Sonder Ditch.' He could not prevent himself, it was too good. He had to boast.

Patti looked at him, startled.

'You're joking!' she accused, and then he saw her mind beginning to work like a cash register.

He almost laughed out loud. 'No. It's true.'

'God!' She sat down limply. 'It will nearly *double* your salary.'

He looked at her dispassionately, and not for the first time felt a great wash of relief as he realized he was no longer shackled to her.

'It's usual to offer congratulations,' he prompted her.

'You don't deserve it.' She was angry now. 'You are a selfish, philandering bastard, Rodney Ironsides, you don't deserve the good things that keep happening to you.' He had cheated her. She could have been the General Manager's wife, first lady of the goldfields. Now she was a divorcée, stuck with a miserable four fifty a month. It had seemed good before, but not now.

'I hope you will have enough conscience to make a suitable adjustment for Melanie and me. We are entitled to a share.'

The door burst open and Melanie Ironsides arrived at a gallop to wrap herself around Rod's neck. She had long blonde hair and green eyes.

'I got nine out of ten for spelling!'

'You're not clever, you're a genius. Also you're beautiful.'

'Will you carry me down to the car, Daddy?'

'What's wrong? Your legs in plaster?'

'Please, please, pretty please times three.'

Patti interrupted the love feast. 'Have you got your jersey, young lady?'

And Melanie flew.

'I'll have her back before seven,' said Rod.

'You haven't answered my question.' Patti was surly. 'Do we get a share?'

'Yes, of course,' said Rod. 'The same big juicy four fifty you've had all along.'

They had been in Rod's apartment ten minutes when the doorbell announced Terry's arrival. She was in jeans and a checked shirt with her hair in a plait, and she greeted Rod self-consciously. When he introduced her to Melanie, she did not look much older than his daughter.

The two girls summed each other up solemnly. Melanie was suddenly very demure and refined, and Rod was relieved to see that Terry had the good sense not to gush over the child.

They were in the Maserati and half way to the village of Parys on the Vaal River before Melanie had completed her microscopic scrutiny of Terry.

'Can I come up front and sit on your lap?' she asked at last.

'Yes, of course.' Terry was hard put to conceal her relief and pleasure. Melanie scrambled over the seat and settled on Terry's lap.

'You are pretty,' Melanie gave her considered opinion.

'Thank you. So are you.'

'Are you Daddy's girlfriend?' Melanie demanded. Terry glanced across at Rod, then burst out laughing.

'Almost,' she gurgled, and then all three of them were laughing.

They laughed often that day. It was a day of sunshine and laughter.

Terry and Rod walked together with fingers almost touching through the green paddocks along the willow-lined bank of the Vaal. Melanie ran ahead of them shrieking with glee at the antics of the foals.

They went up to the stables where Melanie fed sugar lumps to a winner of the Cape Metropolitan Handicap and then kissed his velvety muzzle.

They swam in the pool beside the elegant whitewashed homestead, laughter mingling with the splashes, and when they drove back to Johannesburg in the evening Melanie curled in exhausted slumber on Terry's lap, her head cushioned on Terry's bosom.

Terry waited in the Maserati while Rod carried the sleeping child up to her mother, and when he returned and slipped into the driver's seat, Terry murmured, 'My car is at your apartment. You'll have to take me with you.'

Neither of them spoke until they were back in Rod's sitting-room. Then he said, 'Thank you for a wonderful day.' And he took her to his chest and kissed her.

In the darkness she lay pressed to his sleeping body, clinging to him, as though he might be taken from her. She had never felt such intensity of emotion before, it was a compound of awed wonder and gratitude. She had just been admitted to a new level of human experience she had never suspected existed.

The sheets were still damp. She felt bruised internally, aching, a slow voluptuous pulse of pain that she cherished.

Lightly she touched his body, not wanting to wake him, running her fingertips through the coarse curls that covered his chest, marvelling still at the infinity that separated this from what she had known before.

She shuddered with almost unbearable pleasure as she remembered his voice describing her body to her, making her proud of it for the first time in her life. She remembered the words he had used to tell her exactly what they were doing together, and the feel of his hands, so gentle, sure, so lovingly possessive upon her.

He was so unashamed, taking such obvious joy in her, that the reserves which the barren years of her marriage had placed in her mind were swept away and she was able to go with Rodney Ironsides beyond the storm into that tranquil state where mind and body are completely at peace.

She became aware of him awakening beside her, and she touched his face, his lips and his eyes with her fingertips.

'Thank you,' she whispered, and he seemed to understand, for he took her head and drew it gently down into the hollow of his shoulder.

'Sleep now,' he told her softly, and she closed her eyes and lay very still and quiet beside him, but she did not sleep. She would not miss one moment of this experience.

– 40 –

Rod's letter of appointment lay on his desk when he arrived at his office at seven-thirty on the Monday morning.

He sat down and lit a cigarette. Then he began to read it slowly, savouring each word.

'Duly instructed by the Board of Directors,' it began, and ended, 'it remains only to tender the congratulations of the Board, and to voice their confidence in your ability.'

Dimitri came through from his office, distracted.

'Hey! Rod! Christ what a start to the week! We've got a fault in the main high voltage cable on 90 level, and—'

'Don't come squealing to me,' Rod cut him short. 'I'm not the Underground Manager.'

Dimitri gaped at him, taken by surprise.

128

'What the hell, have they fired you?'

'Next best thing,' said Rod and flipped the letter across the desk. 'Look what the bastards have done to me.'

Dimitri read and then whooped, 'My God, Rod! My God!' He shot down the passage to carry the news to the other line managers. Then they were all in his office, shaking his hand. He judged most of their reactions as favourable, though occasionally he detected a false note. A twinge of envy here, one there who had recently had his ears burned by the Ironsides tongue, and an incompetent who knew his job was now in danger. The phone rang. Rod answered it, his expression changed and he cleared his office with a peremptory wave.

'Hirschfeld here.'

'Morning, Mr Hirschfeld.'

'Well, you've got your chance, Ironsides.'

'I'm grateful for it.'

'I want to see you. I'll give you today to sort yourself out. Tomorrow morning at nine o'clock, my office at Reef Buildings.'

'I'll be there.'

'Good.'

Rod hung up, and the day dissolved into a welter of activity and reorganization, constantly interrupted by a stream of well-wishers. He was still running the Underground Manager's job in addition to the General Manager's. It would be some considerable time before a new Underground Manager was transferred in from one of the other group mines. He was trying to arrange his move to the big office in the main Administrative Block up on the ridge, when he had another visitor, Frank Lemmer's secretary, Miss Lily Jordan, looking like a wardress from Ravensbruck in a severe grey flannel suit.

'Mr Ironsides, you and I have not seen eye to eye in the past.'

129

This was the understatement of the year. 'It is unlikely that we will in the future. Therefore, I have come to tender my resignation. I have made arrangements.'

The phone rang. Dan Stander's voice, breezy and carefree.

'Rod, I'm in love.'

'Oh Christ, no!' Rod groaned. 'Not this morning.'

'I've got to thank you for introducing me to her. She's the most wonderful—'

'Yeah, yeah!' Rod cut him short. 'Look, Dan, I'm rather busy. Some other time, all right?'

'Oh yes, I forgot. You are the new General Manager they tell me. Congratulations. You can buy me a drink at the Club. Six o'clock.'

'Right. By then I'll need one.' Rod hung up, and faced the hanging-judge expression of Miss Lily Jordan.

'Miss Jordan, in the past our interests have conflicted. In the future they will not. You are the best private secretary within a hundred miles of the Sonder Ditch. I need you, the Company needs you.'

That was the magic word. Miss Jordan had twenty-five years' service with the Company. She wavered visibly.

'Please, Miss Jordan, give me a chance.' Shamelessly Rod switched on his most engaging smile. Miss Jordan's femininity was not so completely atrophied that she could resist that smile.

'Very well, then, Mr Ironsides. I'll stay on initially until the end of the month. We'll see after that.' She stood up. 'Now, I'll get your things moved up to the new office.'

'Thank you, Miss Jordan.' With relief he let her take over, and tackled the problems that were piling up on his desk. One man, two jobs. Now he was responsible for surface operation as well as underground. The phone rang, men queued up in the passage, memos kept coming through from Dimitri's office. There was no lunch hour, and by the time she rang he was exhausted.

'Hello,' she said. 'Do I see you tonight?' Her voice was as refreshing as a wet cloth on the brow of a prizefighter between rounds.

'Terry.' He simply spoke her name in reply.

'Yes or no. If it's *no*, I intend jumping off the top of Reef Building.'

'Yes,' he said. 'Pops has summoned me to a meeting at nine tomorrow morning, so I'll be staying overnight at the apartment. I'll call you as soon as I get in.'

'Goody! Goody!' said she.

At five-thirty Dimitri stuck his head around the door.

'I'm going down to No. 1 shaft to supervise the shoot, Rod.'

'My God, what time is it?' Rod checked his watch. 'So late already.'

'It gets late early around here,' Dimitri agreed. 'I'm off.'

'Wait!' Rod stopped him. 'I'll shoot her.'

'No trouble.' Dimitri demurred. Company standard procedure laid down that each day's blast must be supervised by either the Underground Manager or his assistant.

'I'll do it,' Rod repeated. Dimitri opened his mouth to protest further, then he saw that expression on Rod's face and changed his mind quickly.

'Okay then. See you tomorrow.' And he was gone.

Rod grinned at his own sentimentality. The Sonder Ditch was his now and, by God, he was going to shoot his own first blast on her.

They were waiting for him at the steel door of the blast control room at the shaft head. It was a small concrete room like a wartime pillbox, and there were only two keys to the door. Dimitri had one, Rod the other.

The duty mine captain and the foreman electrician added their congratulations to the hundreds he had received during the day, and Rod opened the door and they went into the tiny room.

'Check her out,' Rod instructed, and the mine captain began his calls to the shaft overseers at both No. 1 and No. 2 for their confirmation that the workings of the Sonder Ditch were deserted, that every human being who had gone down that morning had come out again this evening.

Meanwhile, the foreman electrician was busy at the electrical control board. He looked up at Rod.

'Ready to close the circuits, Mr Ironsides.'

'Go ahead,' Rod nodded and the man touched a switch. A green light showed up on the board.

'No. 1 north longwall closed and green.'

'Lock her in,' Rod instructed and the electrician touched another switch.

'No. 1 east longwall closed and green.'

'Lock her in.'

The green light showed that the firing circuit was intact. A red light would indicate a fault and the faulty circuit would not be locked into the blast pattern.

Circuit after circuit was readied until finally the foreman stood back from the control board.

'All green and locked in.'

Rod glanced at the mine captain.

'All levels clear, Mr Ironsides. She's ready to burn.'

'Cheesa!' said Rod, the traditional command that had come down from the days when each fuse had been individually lit by a hand-held igniter stick.

'Cheesa' was the Bantu word for 'burn'.

The mine captain crossed to the control board and opened the cage that guarded a large red button.

'Cheesa!' echoed the mine captain and hit the button with the heel of his hand.

Immediately the row of green lights on the control board was extinguished, and in its place showed a row of red lights. Every circuit had been broken by the explosions.

The ground under their feet began to tremble. Throughout the workings the shots were firing. In the stopes the head charges fired at the top of the inclines, then in succession the other shots went off behind them. Each charge taking a ten-ton bite of rock and reef out of the face.

At the end of the development drives, a more complicated pattern was shooting. First a row of *cutters* went off down the middle of the oval face. Then the *shoulder charges* at the top corners, followed by the *knee charges* at the bottom corners. A moment's respite with the dust and nitrous fumes swirling back down the drive, then a roar as the *easers* on each side shaped the hole. Another respite and then the *lifters* along the bottom picked up the heap of broken rock and threw it back from the face.

Rod could imagine it clearly. Though no human eye had ever witnessed the blast, he knew exactly what was taking place down there.

The last tremor died away.

'That's it. A full blast,' said the mine captain.

'Thank you.' Rod felt tired suddenly. He wanted that drink, even though their brief exchange that morning had warned him that Dan would probably be insufferable. He could guess the conversation would revolve around Dan's new-found love.

Then he smiled as he thought about what waited for him in Johannesburg later that night, and suddenly he wasn't all that tired.

They sat facing each other.

'Only three things worry me,' Terry told Rod.

'What are they?' Rod rubbed soap into the face flannel.

'Firstly, your legs are too long for this bath.'

Rod rearranged his limbs, and Terry shot half out of the water with a squeak.

'Rodney Ironsides, would you be good enough to take a bit more care where you put your toes!'

'Forgive me.' He leaned forward to kiss her. 'Tell me what else worries you.'

'Well, the second thing that worries me is that I'm not worried.'

'What part of Ireland did you say you were from?' Rod asked. 'County Cork?'

'I mean, it's terrible but I'm not even a little conscience-stricken. Once I believed that if it ever happened to me I would never be able to look another human being in the eyes, I'd be so ashamed.' She took the flannel from his hands and began soaping his chest and shoulders. 'But, far from being ashamed, I'd like to stand in the middle of Eloff Street at rush hour and shout "Rodney Ironsides is my lover".'

'Let's drink to that.' Rodney rinsed the soap from his hands and reached over the side of the bath to pick up the two wine glasses from the floor. He gave one to Terry and they clinked them together, the sparkling Cape burgundy glowed ruby red.

'Rodney Ironsides is my lover!' she toasted him.

'Rodney Ironsides is your lover,' he agreed and they drank.

'Now, I give *you* a toast,' he said.

'What is it?' She held her glass ready, and Rod leaned

forward and poured the red wine from the crystal glass
between her breasts. It ran like blood down her white skin
and he intoned solemnly:

'Bless this ship and all who sail in her!'

Terry gurgled with delight.

'To her captain. May he keep a firm hand on the
rudder!'

'May her bottom never hit the reef!'

'May she be torpedoed regularly!'

'Terry Steyner, you are terrible.'

'Yes, aren't I?' And they drained their glasses.

'Now,' Rod asked, 'what is your third worry?'

'Manfred will be home on Saturday.'

They stopped laughing, Rod reached down for the
burgundy bottle and refilled the glasses.

'We still have five days,' he said.

– 42 –

It had been a week of personal triumph for Manfred
Steyner. His address to the conference had been the
foundation of the entire talks, all discussion had
revolved upon it. He had been called upon to speak at the
closing banquet which General de Gaulle had attended in
person, and afterwards the General had asked Manfred to
take coffee and brandy with him in one of the ante-rooms.
The General had been gracious, had asked questions and
listened attentively to the answers. Twice he had called his
finance minister's attention to Manfred's replies.

Their farewells had been cordial, with a hint of state
recognition for Manfred, a decoration. In common with
most Germans, Manfred had a weakness for uniforms and
decorations. He imagined how a star and ribbon might look
on the snowy front of his dress shirt.

There had been a wonderful press both in France and at

home. Even a bad-tempered quarter column in *Time* magazine, with a picture, de Gaulle stooping over the diminutive Manfred solicitously, one hand on his shoulder. The caption read: 'The huntsman and the hawk. To catch a dollar?'

Now standing in the tiny cloakroom in the tail of the South African Airways Boeing, Manfred was whistling softly as he stripped his shirt and vest, crumpled them into a ball and dropped them into the waste bin.

Naked to the waist, he wiped his upper body with a wet cloth and then rubbed 4711 Eau de Cologne into his skin. From the briefcase he took an electric razor. The whistling stopped as he contorted his face for the razor.

Through his mind ran page after page of the report that Andrew had delivered that morning to his hotel room. Manfred had total recall when it came to written material. Although the report was in the briefcase beside him, in his mind's eye he could review it word for word, figure for figure.

It was a stupendous piece of work. How the authors had gained access to the drilling and exploration reports of the five Kitchenerville field companies he could not even guess, for the gold mining companies' security was as tight as that of any national intelligence agency. But the figures were genuine. He had checked those purporting to be from CRC carefully. They were correct. So therefore the other four must also be genuine.

The names of the authors of the report were legend. They were the top men in the field. Their opinions were the best in Harley Street. The conclusion that they reached was completely convincing. In effect it was this:

If a haulage was driven from 66 level of the Sonder Ditch No. 1 shaft through the Big Dipper dyke, it would pass *under* the limestone water-bearing foundations, and just beyond the fault it would intersect a reef of almost unbelievable value.

It had not needed the lecture that Manfred had received

from his corpulent creditor to show him the possibilities. The man who gave the order to drive through the Big Dipper would receive the credit. He would certainly be elected to the chairmanship of the Group when that office fell vacant.

There was another possibility. A person who purchased a big packet of Sonder Ditch shares immediately before the reef was intersected would be a very rich man when he came to sell those shares later. He would be so rich that he would no longer be dependent on his wife for the means to live the kind of life he wanted, and indulge his own special tastes.

Manfred blew the hairs from his razor and returned it to his brief case. Then as he took out a fresh shirt and vest, he began to sing the words to the tune:

> 'Heute ist der schönste Tag
> In meinem Leben.'

He would telephone Ironsides from Jan Smuts Airport as soon as he had passed through customs. Ironsides would come up to the house on Sunday morning and receive his orders.

As he knotted the silk of his tie Manfred knew that he stood at the threshold of a whole new world, the events of the next few months would lift him high above the level of ordinary men.

It was the chance for which he had worked and waited all these years.

Circumstances had changed completely since his last visit, Rod reflected, as he took the Maserati up the drive towards the Dutch gabled house.

He parked the car and switched off the ignition, sitting a while, reluctant to face the man who had sponsored his career and whom Rod in return had presented with a fine pair of horns.

'Courage, Ironsides!' he muttered and climbed out of the Maserati and went up the path across the lawns.

Terry was on the veranda in a gay print dress, with her hair loose, sprawled in a canvas chair with the Sunday papers scattered about her.

'Good morning, Mr Ironsides,' she greeted him as he came up the steps. 'My husband is in his study. You know the way, don't you?'

'Thank you, Mrs Steyner.' Rod kept his voice friendly but disinterested, then as he passed her chair he growled softly, 'I could eat you without salt.'

'Don't waste it, you gorgeous beast,' Terry murmured and ran the tip of her tongue over her lips.

Fifteen minutes later, Rod sat stony-faced and internally chilled before Manfred Steyner's desk. When at last he forced himself to speak, it felt as though the skin on his lips would tear with the effort.

'You want me to drive through the Big Dipper,' he croaked.

'More than that, Mr Ironsides. I want you to complete the drive within three months, and I want a complete security blanket on the development,' Manfred told him primly. Despite the fact that it was Sunday he was formally dressed, white shirt and dark suit. 'You will commence the drive from No. 1 shaft 66 level and make an intersect on reef at 6,600 feet with the SD No. 3 borehole 250 feet beyond the calculated extremity of the serpentine intrusion of the Big Dipper.'

'No,' Rod shook his head. 'You can't go through that. No one can take the chance. God alone knows what is on the other side, we only know that is bad ground. Stinking rotten ground.'

'How do you know that?' Manfred asked softly.

'Everybody on the Kitchenerville field knows it.'

'How?'

'Little things.' Rod found it hard to put into words. 'You get a feeling, the signs are there and when you've been in the game long enough you have a sixth sense that warns you when—'

'Nonsense,' Manfred interrupted brusquely. 'We no longer live in the days of witchcraft.'

'Not witchcraft, experience,' Rod snapped angrily. 'You've seen the drilling results from the other side of the fault?'

'Of course,' Manfred nodded. 'SD No. 3 found values of thousands of penny-weights.'

'And the other holes went dry and twisted off, or had water squirting out of them like a pissing horse!'

Manfred flushed fiercely. 'You will be good enough not to employ bar-room terminology in this house.'

Rod was taken off balance, and before he could answer Manfred went on.

'Would you put the considered opinions of,' Manfred named three men, 'before your own vague intuitions?'

'They are the best in the business,' Rod conceded reluctantly.

'Read that,' snapped Manfred. He tossed a manila folder onto the desk top, then stood up and went to wash his hands at the concealed basin.

Rod picked up the folder, opened it and was immediately engrossed. Ten minutes later, without looking up from the report, he fumbled a pack of cigarettes from his pocket.

'Please do not smoke!' Manfred stopped him sharply.

Three-quarters of an hour later, Rod closed the folder. During that time Manfred Steyner had sat with reptilian stillness behind his desk, with the glitter of his eyes the only signs of life.

'How the hell did you get hold of those figures and reports?' Rod asked with wonder.

'That does not concern you.' Manfred retrieved the folder from him, his first movement in forty-five minutes.

'So that's it!' muttered Rod. 'The water is in the limestone near the surface. We go in under it!' He stood up from the chair abruptly and began to pace up and down in front of Manfred's desk.

'Are you convinced?' Manfred asked, and Rod did not answer.

'I have promoted you above older and more experienced men,' said Manfred softly. 'If I tear you down again, and tell the world you were not man enough for the job, then, Rodney Ironsides, you are finished. No one else would take a chance on you again, ever!'

It was true. Rod knew it.

'However, if you were to follow my instructions and we intersected this highly enriched reef, then part of the glory would rub off on you.'

That was also true. Rod stopped pacing, he stood with shoulders hunched, in an agony of indecision. Could he trust that report beyond his own deep intuition? When he thought about that ground beyond the dyke, his skin tickled with gooseflesh. He almost had the stink of it in his nostrils. Yet he could be wrong, and the weight of the opposition was heavy. The eminent names on the report, the threats which he knew Manfred would not hesitate to put into effect.

'Will you give me a written instruction?' Rod demanded harshly.

'What effect would that have?' Manfred asked mildly.

'As General Manager, the decision to work certain ground or not to work it is technically yours. In the very unlikely event that you encountered trouble beyond the fault, it would be no defence to produce a written instruction from me. Just as if you murdered my wife you could not defend yourself by producing a written instruction from me to do so.'

This again was true. Rod knew he was trapped. He could refuse, and wreck his career. Or he could comply and take the consequences whatever they may be.

'No,' said Manfred, 'I will not give you a written instruction.'

'You bastard,' Rod said softly.

Manfred answered as gently. 'I warned you that you would not be able to refuse to obey me.'

And the last twinge of remorse that Rod felt for his association with Terry Steyner faded and was gone.

'You've given me three months to hit the Big Dipper. All right, Steyner. You've got it!'

Rod turned on his heel and walked out of the room.

Terry was waiting for him among the protea plants on the bottom lawn. She saw his face and dropped all pretence. She went to meet him.

'Rod, what is it?' Her hand on his arm, looking up into his eyes.

'Careful!' he warned her, and she dropped her hand and stood back.

'What is it?'

'That bloody Gestapo bastard,' Rod snarled, and then, 'I'm sorry, Terry, he's your husband.'

'What has he done?'

'I can't tell you here. When can I see you?'

'I'll find an excuse to get away later today. Wait for me at your apartment.'

141

Later she sat on the couch below the Paravano painting and listened while he told her about it. All of it, the report, the threat and the order to pierce the Big Dipper.

She listened but expressed neither approval nor disapproval of his decision.

Manfred turned away from the window and went back to his desk. Even at that distance there had been no doubt about his wife's gesture. The hand outstretched, the face turned up, the lips parted in anxious enquiry, and then the guilty start and withdrawal.

He sat down at his desk, and laid his hands neatly in front of him. For the first time he was thinking of Rodney Ironsides as a man and not a tool.

He thought how big he was, tall and as wide across the shoulders as a gallows. Any reprisal on Ironsides could not be physical, and it could not be immediate. It must be after the drive to the Big Dipper.

I can wait, he thought coldly, there is time for everything in this life.

– 44 –

Johnny and Davy Delange sat in the two chairs before Rod's desk. They were both awkward and uncomfortable up here in the big office with picture windows looking out over the Kitchenerville valley.

I don't blame them, Rod thought, even I am not accustomed to it yet. Wall-to-wall carpeting, air-conditioning, original paintings on the wood-panelled walls.

'I have sent for you because you two are the best rock breakers on the Sonder Ditch,' Rod began.

'Tin Ribs wants something,' thought Davy, with all the suspicion of the union man for management.

'We will now have a few words from our sponsor,' Johnny grinned to himself. 'Before we start the programme.'

Rod looked at their faces and knew exactly what they were thinking. He had been on daily pay himself once. Cut out the compliments, Ironsides – he advised himself – these are two tough cookies and they are not impressed.

'I am pulling you out of the stopes and putting you onto a special development end. You will take it in turns to work day and night shift. You will be directly responsible to me and there will be a security blanket on your activity.'

They watched him without reaction, their expressions guarded. Johnny broke the short silence.

'One end, one blast a day?' He was thinking of his pay. Calculated on the amount of rock broken, he would earn little more than basic salary with a blast on one small face daily.

'No.' Rod shook his head. 'Ultra-fast, multi-blast, and shaft sinkers' rates.'

And both the Delange brothers sat forward in their chairs.

'Multi-blast?' Davy asked. That meant that they could shoot just as soon as they were ready. A good team could blast three – maybe four times a shift.

'Ultra-fast?' Johnny demanded. That was language Johnny understood. It was a term employed only in emergency, as when driving in to rescue trapped men after a fall. It was tacit approval from management to waive standard safety procedure in favour of speed. Christ, Johnny exulted, I can shoot her four – maybe five times a shift.

'Shaft sinkers' rates?' they asked together. That was a 20 per cent bonus on stopers' rates. It was a fortune they were being offered.

Rod nodded affirmative to their questions, and waited for the reaction which he knew would follow. It came immediately.

The Delange brothers now began to look for the catch.

They sat stolidly turning the deal over in their minds, like two cautious housewives examining a tomato for blemishes because the price was too cheap.

'How long is this drive?' Johnny asked. If the drive was short, a few hundred feet, then it was worth nothing. They would hardly get into their stride before it was completed.

'Close on six thousand feet,' Rod assured him. They looked relieved.

'Where is it headed?' Davy discovered the rub.

'We are going to drive through the Big Dipper to intersect on reef at 6,000 feet.'

'Jesus!' said Johnny. 'The Big Dipper!' He was awed but unafraid. It excited him, the danger, the challenge. Had he been born earlier, Johnny Delange would have made a fine Spitfire pilot.

'The Big Dipper,' Davy murmured, his mind was racing. Nothing in this world or beyond would entice Davy Delange to drive through the Big Dipper. He had an almost religious fear of it. The name alone conjured up all sorts of hidden menace and unspeakable horror. Water. Gas. Friable ground, faults. Mud-rushes. All a miner's nightmare.

There was no question of him doing it, yet the money was too good to pass up. He could net ten or eleven thousand rand on those terms.

'All right, Mr Ironsides,' he said. 'I'll take the first night shifts. Johnny can start the day shifts.'

Davy Delange had made his decision. He would work until his drills hit the greenish-black serpentine rock of the dyke. He would then walk out of the drive and quit. He would go up to, but not beyond the dyke.

Afterwards, any of the other mines would snap him up, he had an impeccable record and he would force Johnny to follow him.

'Hey, Davy!' Johnny was delighted, he had expected Davy to turn the deal down flat.

Now he would be able to buy the Mustang for certain –

and perhaps an MGB GT for Hettie – and take a holiday to Durban over Christmas, and . . .

Rod was puzzled by Davy's easy agreement. He studied him a moment and decided that he had ferrety eyes. He's a sneaky little bastard, Rod decided, I'll have to watch him.

– 45 –

It took one shift only to prepare for the development. Rod selected the starting point. The main haulage curved away from the shaft on 66 level. 1,000 feet along this tunnel there was a chamber that had been cut out as a loco repair station but which was now out of use. Two large batwing ventilation doors were fitted to the opening of the chamber to provide privacy and behind them the chief underground surveyor set up his instruments and marked out the head of the tunnel that would fly arrow straight a mile and more through the living rock to strike through the Big Dipper into the unknown.

The area surrounding the head chamber was roped off band sign-posted with warnings.

DANGER
INDEPENDENT BLASTING

The mine captains were instructed to keep their men well away, and all loco traffic was rerouted through a secondary haulage.

On the doors of the chamber another notice was fixed.

FIERY MINE PROCEDURE IN FORCE
NO NAKED LIGHTS BEYOND THIS POINT

Owing to small deposits of coal and other organic substance in the upper stratas of rock, the Sonder Ditch was classed as a fiery mine and subject to the government legislation covering this subject. No matches, lighters or other spark-generating devices were allowed into a new development end, because the presence of methane gas was always suspected.

Colourless, odourless, tasteless, detectable only by test with a safety lamp, it was a real and terrifying danger. A nine per cent concentration in air was highly explosive. Stringent precautions were taken against accidental triggering of methane that may have oozed out of a fissure or cavity in the rock.

From the main compressed air-pipes running down the corners of the shaft were taken leads to air tanks in the haulage, ensuring that sixty pounds per square inch of pressure was available for the rock drills. Then drills, pinchbars, hammers, shovels, and the other tools were unloaded from the cage at 66 level and stored at the shaft head.

Lastly, explosive was placed in the red lockers at the head of the development, and on the evening of October 23rd 1968, thirty minutes after the main blast, Davy Delange and his gang disembarked from the cage and went to the disused loco shop.

Davy, with the surly little Swazi boss boy beside him, stood before the rock wall on which the surveyor had marked the outline of the tunnel. Behind him his gang had fallen unbidden to their labour, each man knowing exactly what was expected of him.

Already the machine boys and their assistants were lugging their ungainly tools forward.

'You! You! You! You!' Davy indicated to each of them the hole on which he was to begin and then stepped back.

'Shaya!' he commanded. 'Hit it!' And with a fluttering bellow that buffeted the eardrums the drive began.

The drilling ceased and Davy charged the holes. The

fuses hung like the tails of white mice from their holes. Each length carefully cut to ensure correct firing sequence.

'Clear the drive!' The boss boy's whistle shrilled, the tramp of heavy boots receded until silence hung heavy in the chemically cleaned air.

'Cheesa!' Davy and the boss boy, with the igniters burning like children's fireworks in their right hands, touched them to the hanging tails until the chamber was lit by the fierce blue light of the burning fuses. The shadows of the two men flickered gigantic and distorted upon the walls.

'All burning. Let's go!' And the two men walked quickly back to where the gang waited along the haulage.

The detonations sucked at their ears, and thrust against their lungs, so that afterwards the silence was stunning.

Davy checked his wristwatch. By law there was a mandatory thirty minutes' wait before anyone could go back to the face. There may be a hang-fire waiting to blow the eyes out of someone's head. Even if there were not, there was still the cloud of poisonous nitrous fumes that would destroy the hair follicles in a man's nostrils and render him still more vulnerable to the fine particles of rock dust that would seek to enter his lungs.

Davy waited those thirty minutes, by which time the ventilation had sucked away the fumes and dust.

Then, alone, he went up the haulage. With him he carried his safety lamp, its tiny blue flame burning behind the screen of fine brass wire mesh. That mesh was flash proof and insulated the flame from any methane in the air.

Standing before the raw circular wound in the rock wall, Davy tested for methane gas. Watching the blue flame for the tell-tale cap. There was no sign of it, and satisfied he extinguished the lamp.

'Boss boy!' he yelled, and the Swazi came up uncoiling the hose behind him.

'Water down!'

Only when the rock face and all the loose rubble below it were glistening and dripping with water was Davy satisfied that the dust was laid sufficiently to bring up his gang.

'Bar boys!' he yelled, and they came up, carrying the twelve-foot-long pinchbars, a tool like a giant crowbar.

'Bar down. Make safe!' And the bar boys attacked the bunches of loose rock that were flaking and crumbling from the hanging wall. Two of them manipulating one bar between them, with the steel point striking sparks from the rock. The dislodged fragments rained down, heavily at first and then less and less until the rock above their heads was solid and clean.

Only then did Davy scramble over the pile of rubble to reach the face and begin marking in the shot holes.

Behind him his gang were lashing the stuff into the waiting cocopans, and his machine boys were dragging the drills up to the face.

Davy's gang made three blasts that first night. As he rode up in the cage into a pink, sweet-smelling dawn, Davy was satisfied.

'Perhaps tonight we will get in four blasts,' he thought.

In the Company change house he showered, running the water steaming hot so his skin turned dull angry red, and he worked up a fat white lather of soap suds over his head and at his armpits and crotch.

He rubbed down with a rough thick towel and dressed quickly. Crossing the parking lot to his battered old Ford Anglia he felt happy and good-tired; hungry and ready for bed.

He drove into Kitchenerville at a steady forty miles an hour, and by this time the sun was just showing over the Kraalkop ridge. The dawn was misty rose, with long shadows against the earth, and he thought that this was how it would be in the early mornings on the farm.

On the outskirts of the town Johnny's Monaco roared past him going in the opposite direction. Johnny waved and blew the horn, shouting something that was lost in the howl of wind and motor.

'They'll catch him yet.' Davy shook his head in disapproval. 'The speed limit is forty-five along here.'

He parked the Anglia in the garage and let himself in through the kitchen door. The Bantu maid was busy over the stove.

'Three eggs,' he told her and went through to his bedroom. He shrugged off his jacket and threw it on the bed. Then he returned to the door and glanced quickly up and down the passage. It was deserted, and there was no sound besides the clatter of the maid in the kitchen.

Davy sidled into the passage. The door to Johnny's bedroom was ajar, and Davy moved quietly down to it. His heart was pounding in his throat, his breathing was stifled by his guilt and excitement.

He peered around the edge of the door and gasped aloud. This morning it was better than usual.

Hettie was a sound sleeper. Johnny always maintained it would take a shot of Dynagel to wake her. She never wore night clothes and she never rose before ten-thirty in the morning. She lay on her stomach, hugging a pillow to her chest, her hair a joyous tangle of flaming red against the green sheets. The morning was warm and her blankets had been kicked aside.

Davy stood in the passage. A nerve in his eyelid began to twitch, and under his shirt a drop of perspiration slid from his armpit down along his flank. On the bed Hettie mumbled unintelligibly in her sleep, drew her knees up and rolled slowly onto her back. One arm came up and flopped limply over her face, her eyes were covered by the crook of her elbow.

She sighed deeply. The twin mounds of her bosom were pulled out of shape by their own weight and the angle of her arm. The hair in her armpit and at the base of her belly was bright shiny red-gold. She was long and smooth and silky white, crowned and tipped with flame.

She moved her body languorously, voluptuously, and then settled once more into slumber.

'Breakfast ready, master,' the maid called from the kitchen. Davy started guiltily, then retreated down the passage.

He found with surprise that he was panting, as though he had run a long way.

– 46 –

Johnny Delange leaned against the sidewall of the haulage, his hard helmet tilted at a jaunty angle and a cigarette dangling from his lips.

Down at the face the shots began to fire. Johnny recognized each detonation, and when the last dull jar disrupted the air about them, he pushed himself away from the wall with his shoulder.

'That was the *lifters*,' he announced. 'Come on Big King!'

Not for Johnny Delange a thirty-minute waste of time. As he and Big King set off down the haulage together they were binding scarves over their noses and mouths. Ahead of them a bluey-white fog of dust and fumes filled the tunnel, and Big King had the hose going, using a fine mist spray to absorb the fumes and particles.

They pushed on up to the face, Johnny stooping over the safety lamp. Even he had a healthy respect for methane gas.

'Bar boys!' he bellowed, not waiting for Big King to finish watering down. They came up like ghosts in the fog. Hard behind them the machine boys hovered with their drills.

Taking calculated risks Johnny had his drills roaring

forty-five minutes sooner than Davy Delange would have in the same circumstances.

When he came back to the face from cutting fuses and priming his explosives, he found his lashing gang struggling with a massive slab of rock that had been blown intact from the face. Five of them were beating on it with fourteen-pound hammers in an attempt to crack it into manageable pieces. As Johnny reached them, Big King was berating them mercilessly.

'You look like a bunch of virgins grinding millet.'

The hammers clanged and struck sparks from the slab. Sweat oozed from every pore of the hammer boys' skin, greasing their bodies, flying from their heads in sparkling droplets with each blow.

'Shaya!' Big King goaded them on. 'Between you all you wouldn't crack the shell of an egg. Hit it, man! Hit it!'

One by one the men fell back exhausted, their chests heaving, gulping air through gaping mouths, blinded by their own sweat.

'All right,' Johnny intervened. The rock was holding up the whole blast. It warranted drastic measures to break it up.

'I'll pop her,' he said, and any government inspector or mine safety officer would have paled at those words.

'Stand far back and turn your faces away,' Big King instructed his gang. From the forehead of one of his men he took a pair of wire mesh goggles, designed to shield the eyes from flying splinters and rock fragments. He handed them to Johnny who placed them over his eyes.

From the canvas carrying bag he took out a stick of Dynagel. It looked like a candle wrapped in yellow greased paper.

'Give me your knife.' Big King opened a large clasp knife and handed it to Johnny.

Carefully Johnny cut a coin-shaped sliver of explosive from one end of the stick, a piece twice as thick as a penny.

He returned the remains of the stick to the bag and handed it to Big King.

'Get back,' he said and Big King moved away.

Johnny eyed the slab of rock thoughtfully and then placed the fragment of Dynagel in the centre of it. He adjusted the goggles over his eyes, and picked up one of the fourteen-pound hammers.

'Turn your eyes away,' he warned and took deliberate aim. Then with a smooth overhead two-handed swing he brought the hammer down on the Dynagel.

The explosion was painful in the confined space of the drive, and afterwards Johnny's ears hummed with it. A tiny drop of blood ran down his cheek from the scratch inflicted by a flying splinter. His wrists ached from the jolt of the hammer in his hands.

'Gwenyama!' grunted Big King in admiration. 'The man is a lion.'

The explosion had cracked the slab into three wedge-shaped segments. Johnny pushed the goggles onto his forehead and wiped the blood from his cheek with the back of his hand.

'Get it the hell out of here,' he grinned, then he turned to Big King.

'Come.' He jerked his head towards the end of the tunnel. 'Help me charge the holes.'

The two of them worked quickly, sliding the sticks of Dynagel into the shot holes and tamping them home with the charging sticks.

For anyone who was not in possession of a blasting licence, to charge up was an offence punishable by a fine of one hundred rand or two months' imprisonment, or both. Big King had no licence, but his assistance saved fifteen minutes on the operation.

Johnny and his gang blew the face five times that day, but as they rode up in the cage into the cool evening air he was not satisfied.

'Tomorrow we'll shoot her six times,' he told Big King.

'Maybe seven,' said Big King.

Hettie was waiting for him in the lounge when he got home. She flew to him and threw her arms about his neck.

'Did you bring me a present?' she asked with her lips against his ear, and Johnny laughed tantalizingly. It was very seldom that he did not have a gift for her.

'You did!' she exclaimed, and began to run her hands over his pockets.

'There!' She thrust her hand into the inside pocket of his jacket, and brought out the little white jeweller's box.

'Oh!' She opened it, and then her expression changed slightly.

'You don't like them?' Johnny asked anxiously.

'How much did they cost?' she enquired as she examined the porcelain and lacquer earrings, representing two vividly coloured parrots.

'Well,' Johnny looked shamefaced, 'you see, Hettie, it's the end of the month, you see, and well, like I'm a bit short till pay day, you see, so I couldn't—'

'How much?'

'Well, you see,' he took a breath, 'two rand fifty.'

'Oh,' said Hettie, 'they're nice.' And she promptly lost interest in them. She tossed the box carelessly onto the crowded mantelpiece and set off for the kitchen.

'Hey, Hettie,' Johnny called after her. 'How about we go across to Fochville? There's a dance there tonight. We go and twist, hey?'

Hettie turned back, her expression alive again.

'Gee, yes, man!' she enthused. 'Let's do that. I'll go and change, hey!' And she ran up the passage.

Davy came out of his bedroom, on his way to work.

'Hey, Davy.' Johnny stopped him. 'You got any money on you?'

'Are you broke again?'

'Just till pay day.'

'Hell, man, Johnny, you got a cheque for eleven hundred the beginning of the month. You spent it all?'

'Next month,' Johnny winked, 'I'm going to get a cheque for two or three thousand. Then watch me go! Come, Davy, lend me fifty. I'm taking Hettie dancing.'

– 47 –

For Rod the days flicked past like telegraph poles viewed from a speeding automobile. Each day he gained confidence in his own ability. He had never doubted that he could handle the underground operation and now he found that he had a firm grasp on the surface as well. He knew that his campaign to reduce working costs was having effect, but its full harvest would only be apparent when the quarterly reports were drafted.

Yet he lay awake in the big Manager's residence on the ridge in which he and his few sticks of furniture seemed lost and lonely, and he worried. There were always myriad nagging little problems, but there were others more serious.

This morning Lily Jordan had come through into his office.

'Mr Innes is coming up to see you at nine.'

'What's he want?' Herbert Innes was the Manager of the Sonder Ditch Reduction works.

'He wouldn't tell me,' Lily answered. The end of the month had come and gone and Lily was still with him. Rod presumed that he had been approved.

Herby Innes, burly and red-faced, sat down and drank the cup of tea that Lily provided, while he regaled Rod with a stroke by stroke account of his Sunday afternoon golf round. Rod interrupted him after he had hit a nine-iron short at the third and shanked his chip.

154

'Okay, Herby. What's the problem?'

'We've got a leak, Rod.'

'Bad?'

'Bad enough,' Herby grunted. To him the loss of a single ounce of gold during the process of recovery and refinement was catastrophic.

'What do you reckon?'

'Between the wash and the pour we are losing a couple hundred ounces a week.'

'Yes,' Rod agreed. 'That is bad enough.'

20,000 rand a month, 120,000 a year.

'Have you any ideas?'

'It's been going on for some time, even in Frank Lemmer's day. We have tried everything.'

Rod was a little hazy about the workings of the reduction plant, not that he would admit that, but he was. He knew that the ore was weighed and sampled when it reached the surface, from this a fairly accurate estimate of gold content was made and compared with actual recovery. Any discrepancy had to be investigated and traced.

'What is your recovery rate for the last quarter?'

'Ninety-six point seven-three.'

'That's pretty good,' Rod admitted. It was impossible to recover all the gold in the ore that was surfaced but Herby was getting most of it out. 96.73 per cent of it, to be precise. Which meant that very little of the missing 200 ounces was being lost into the dumps and the slimes dam.

'I tell you what, Herby,' Rod decided. 'I'll come down to the plant this afternoon. We'll go over it together, perhaps a fresh eye may be able to spot the trouble.'

'May do.' Herby was sceptical. 'We've tried everything else. We are pouring this afternoon. What time shall I expect you?'

'Two o'clock.'

They started at the shaft head, where the ore cage, the copie, arrived at the surface every four minutes with its cargo of rock which it dumped into a concrete shute. Each load was classified as either 'reef' or 'waste'.

The reef was dropped into the massive storage bins, while the waste was carried off on a conveyor to the wash house to be sluiced down before going to the dump. Tiny particles of gold sticking to the waste rock were gathered in this way.

Herby put his lips close to Rod's ear to make himself heard above the rumbling roar of rock rolling down the chute.

'I'm not worried about this end. It's all bulk here and very little shine.' Herby used the reduction plant slang for gold. 'The closer we get to the end, the more dangerous it is.'

Rod nodded and followed Herby down the steel ladder until they reached a door below the storage bins. They went through into a long underground tunnel very similar to the ore tunnel on 100 level.

Again there was a massive conveyor belt moving steadily along the tunnel while ore from the bins above was fed onto it. Rod and Herby walked along beside the belt until it passed under a massive electromagnet. Here they paused for a while. The magnet was extracting from the ore all those pieces of metal which had found their way into the ore passes and bins.

'How much you picking up?' Rod asked.

'Last week fourteen tons,' Herby answered, and taking Rod's arm led him through the door beside them. They were in an open yard that looked like a scrap-metal merchant's premises. A mountain of pinchbars, jumper bits, shovels, steel wire rope, snatch blocks, chains, spanners, fourteen-pound hammers, and other twisted and unrecognizable pieces of metal filled the yard. All of it was rusted, much of it unusable. It had been separated from the ore by the magnet.

Rod's mouth tightened. Here he was presented with indisputable evidence of the carelessness and it-belongs-to-the-company attitude of his men. This pile of scrap represented a waste that would total hundreds of thousands of rand annually.

'We will see about that!' he muttered.

'If one of those hammers got into my jaw mills it would smash it to pieces,' Herby told him dolefully and led him back into the conveyor tunnel.

The belt angled upwards sharply and they followed the catwalk beside it. They climbed steadily for five minutes and Herby was puffing like a steam engine. Through the holes in the honeycomb steel plate under his feet, Rod could see that they were now a few hundred feet above ground level.

The conveyor reached the head of a tall tower and dumped its load of ore into the gaping mouths of the screeners. As the rock fell down the tower to ground level again it was sorted for size, and the larger pieces diverted to the jaw crushers which chewed it into fistsize bites.

'See anything?' Herby asked, barely concealing the sarcasm.

Rod grinned at him.

They climbed down the steel ladders that seemed endless. The screeners rattling and the crushers hammering, until Rod's eardrums pleaded for mercy.

At last they reached ground level and went through into the mill room. This was a cavernous galvanized-iron shed the size of a large aircraft hangar. At least one hundred yards long and fifty feet high, it was filled with long rows of the cylindrical tube mills.

Forty of them in all, they were as thick as the boiler of a steam locomotive and about twice as long. Into one end of them was fed the ore which had been reduced in size by the jaw crushers. The tube mills revolved and the loose steel balls within them pounded the rock to powder.

If the noise before had been bad, it was hideous in the mill room. Rod and Herby made no effort to speak to each other until they had walked through into the comparative quiet of the first heavy-media separator room.

'Now,' Herby explained. 'This is where we start worrying.' He indicated the rows of pale blue six-inch piping that came through the wall from the mill room.

'In there is the powdered rock mixed with water to a smooth flowing paste. About forty per cent of the gold is free.'

'No one can get into those pipes and you've checked for any possible leak?' Rod asked. Herby nodded.

'But,' he said, 'have a look here!'

Along the far wall was a series of cages. They were made of heavy steel mesh, the perforations would not allow a man's finger through. The heavy steel doors were barred and locked. Outside each battery of cages stood a Bantu attendant in clean white overalls. They were all concentrating on the manipulation of the turncock that obviously regulated the flow of the powdered ore through the pipes.

Herby stopped at one of the cages.

'Shine!' He pointed. Beyond the heavy guard screen the grey paste of rock powder was flowing from a series of nozzles over an inclined black rubber sheet. The surface of the rubber sheet was deeply corrugated, and in each corrugation the free gold was collecting, held there by its own weight. The gold was thick as butter in a Dagwood sandwich, greasy yellow-looking in the folds of rubber.

Rod laid hold of the steel screen and shook it.

'No,' Herby laughed. 'No one will get in that way.'

'How do you clean the gold off that sheet? Does someone have access to the separator?' Rod asked.

'The separator cleans itself automatically,' Herby answered. 'Look!'

Rod noticed for the first time that the rubber sheet was moving very slowly, it was also an endless belt running round two rollers. As the belt inverted, so fine jets of water washed the gold from the corrugations into a collection tank.

'I'm the only one who has access. We change the collection tanks daily,' said Herby.

It looked foolproof, Rod had to admit.

Rod turned and glanced down the row of four Bantu attendants. They were all intent on their duties, and Rod knew that each of them had a high security rating. They had been carefully selected and screened before being allowed into the reduction works.

'Satisfied?' Herby asked.

'Okay,' Rod nodded, and the two of them went out through the door in the far wall. Locking it behind them.

Immediately they had gone the four Bantu attendants reacted. They straightened up, the scowls of concentration smoothed out to be replaced by grins of relief. One made a remark and they all laughed, and opened the waist bands of their tunics. From inside each trouser leg they drew a length of quarter-inch copper wire and began probing them through the steel screen.

It had taken Crooked Leg, the photographer, almost a year to work out a means of milking gold from the heavily screened and guarded separators. The method which he had discovered was, like all workable plans, extremely simple.

Mercury, quicksilver, absorbs gold the way blotting paper sucks up moisture. It will suck in any speck of gold that comes in contact with it. Mercury has a further property, it can be made to spread on copper like butter on bread. This layer of mercury on copper retains its powers of absorbing gold.

Crooked Leg had devised the idea of coating lengths of copper wire with mercury. The wire could be inserted through the apertures in the steel mesh and the wire laid across the corrugated rubber sheet, where it set about mopping up every speck of gold that flowed over it. The lengths of wire could be quickly slipped down the trouser leg at the approach of an official, and they could be smuggled in and out of the reduction works the same way.

Every evening Crooked Leg retrieved the gold-thickened wire, and issued his four accomplices with newly coated lengths. Every night in the abandoned workings beyond the ridge he boiled the mercury to make it release its gold.

'Now,' Herby could speak normally in the blessed quiet of the cyanide plant, 'we have skimmed off the free gold – and we are left with the sulphide gold.' He offered Rod a cigarette as they made their way between the massive steel tanks that spread over many acres. 'We pump this into the tanks and add cyanide. The cyanide dissolves the gold and takes it into solution. We tap it off and run it through zinc powder. The gold is deposited on the zinc, we burn away the zinc and we are left with the gold.'

Rod lit his cigarette. He knew all this but Herby was giving him a Cooks' tour for visiting VIPs. He flicked his lighter for Herby. 'There is no way anyone could swipe it when it's in solution.'

Herby shook his head, exhaling smoke. 'Apart from anything else, cyanide is a deadly poison.' He glanced at his watch. 'Three-twenty, they'll be pouring now. Shall we go across to the smelt house?'

The smelt house was the only brick building among all the galvanized iron. It stood a little isolated. Its windows were high up and heavily barred.

At the steel door Herby buzzed, and a peephole opened in the door. He and Rod were immediately recognized and the door swung open. They were in a cage of bars which could only be opened once the door was closed behind them.

'Afternoon, Mr Ironsides, Mr Innes.' The guard was apologetic. 'Would you sign, please?' He was a retired policeman with a paunch and a holstered revolver on his hip.

They signed and the guard signalled to his mate on the steel catwalk high above the smelt room floor. This guard tucked his pump action shotgun under one arm, and threw the switch on the walk beside him.

The cage door opened and they went through.

Along the far wall the electric furnaces were set into the brickwork. They resembled the doors of the bread ovens in a bakery.

The concrete floor of the room was uncluttered, except for the mechanical loader that carried the gold crucible in its steel arms, and the moulds before it. The half dozen personnel of the smelt house barely looked up as Rod and Herby approached.

The pour was well advanced, the arms of the loader tilted and a thin stream of molten gold issued from the spout of the crucible, and fell into the mould. The gold hissed and smoked and crackled, and tiny red and blue sparks twinkled on its surface as it cooled.

Already forty or fifty bars were laid out on the rubber-wheeled trolley beside the mould. Each bar was a little smaller than a cigar box. It had the knobby bumpy look of roughly cast metal.

Rod stopped and touched one of the bars. It was still hot and it had the slightly greasy feeling that new gold always has.

'How much?' he asked Herby, and Herby shrugged.

'About a million rand's worth, perhaps a little more.'

So that's what a million rand looks like, Rod mused, it's not very impressive.

'What's the procedure now?' Rod asked.

'We weigh it, and stamp the weight and batch number into each bar.' He pointed to a massive circular safe deposit door in the near wall. 'It's stored there overnight, and tomorrow a refinery armoured car will come out from Johannesburg and pick it up.' Herby led the way out of the smelt house. 'Anyway, that's not the trouble. Our leak is sucking off the shine before it ever reaches the smelt house.'

'Let me think about it for a few days,' Rod said. 'Then we'll get together again, try and find the solution.'

He was still thinking about it now. Lying in the darkness and smoking cigarette after cigarette.

There seemed to be only one solution. They would have to plant Bantu police in the reduction works.

It was an endless game involving all the mining companies and their reduction plant personnel. An inventive mind would devise a new system of sucking off the shine. The Company would become aware of the activity by comparison of estimated and actual recovery and they would work on the leak for a week, a month, sometimes a year. Then they would break the system. There would be prosecutions, stiff gaol sentences, and the Company would circularize its neighbours, and they would all settle back and wait for the next customer to appear.

Gold has many remarkable properties, its weight, its non-corruptibility and, not least, the greed and lust it conjures up in the hearts of men.

Rod stubbed his cigarette, rolled onto his side and pulled the bedclothes up over his shoulders. His last thought before sleep was for the major problem that, these days, was never very far from the surface of his mind.

The Delange brothers had driven almost 1,500 feet in two weeks. At this rate they would hit the Big Dipper seven weeks from now, then even the theft of gold would pale into insignificance.

– 48 –

At the time that Rod Ironsides was composing himself for sleep, Big King was taking a little wine with his business associate and tribal brother Philemon N'gabai, alias Crooked Leg.

They sat facing each other in a pair of dilapidated cane chairs with a lantern and a gallon jug of Jeripigo set between them. The bat stench of the abandoned workings did little to bring out the bouquet of the wine, which was of small concern to either man, for they were drinking not for taste but for effect.

Crooked Leg refilled the cheap glass tumbler that Big King preferred, and as the wine glug-glugged from the jar he continued his attack on the character and moral fibre of José Almeida, the Portuguese.

'For many months now I have had it in my heart to speak to you of these matters,' he told Big King, 'but I have waited until I could set a deadfall for the man. He is like a lion that preys upon our herds, we hear him roar in the night and in the dawn we see his spoor in the earth about the carcasses of our animals, but we cannot meet him face to face.'

Big King enjoyed listening to the oratory of Crooked Leg and while he listened he drank the Jeripigo as though it were water, and Crooked Leg kept refilling the tumbler for him.

'In counsel with myself I spoke thus: "Philemon N'gabai, it is not enough that thou should suspect this white man. It is necessary also that you see with your own eyes that he is eating your substance".'

'How, Crooked Leg?' Big King's voice was thickening, the level of the jug had fallen steadily and now showed less than half. 'Tell me how we shall take this man.' Big King showed a fist the size of a bunch of bananas. 'I will . . .'

163

'No, Big King.' Crooked Leg was scandalized. 'You must not hurt the man. How then would we sell our gold? We must prove he is cheating us and show him we know it. Then we will proceed as ever, but he will give us full measure in the future.'

Big King thought about that for some time, then at last he sighed regretfully. 'You are right, Crooked Leg. Still, I would have liked to . . .' He showed that fist again, and Crooked Leg went on hurriedly.

'Therefore, I have sent to my brother who drives a delivery van for SA Scale Company in Johannesburg, and he has taken from his Company a carefully measured weight of eight ounces.' Crooked Leg produced the cylindrical metal weight from his pocket and handed it to Big King who examined it with interest. 'Tonight, after the Portuguese has weighed the gold you take to him, you will say, "Now, my friend, please weigh this for me on your scale," and you will watch to see that his scale reads the correct number. Each time in the future he will weigh this on his scale before we sell our gold.'

'Hau!' Big King chuckled. 'You are a crafty one, Crooked Leg.'

Big King's eyes were smoky and blood-shot. The Jeripigo was a raw rough fortified wine, and he had drunk very nearly a gallon of it. He sat opposite the Portuguese store-keeper in the back room behind the concession store, and watched while he poured the gold dust into the pan of the jeweller's scale. It made a yellow pyramid that shone dully in the light from the single bare bulb above their heads.

'One hundred and twenty-three ounces.' Almeida looked up at Big King for confirmation, a strand of greasy black hair hung onto his forehead. His face was pale from lack of sun so that the blue stubble of beard was in heavy contrast.

'That is right,' Big King nodded. He could taste the

liquor fumes in the back of his throat, and they were as strong as his distaste for the man who sat opposite him. He belched.

Almeida removed the pan from the scale and carefully poured the dust back into the screw-top bottle.

'I will get the money.' He half rose from his chair.

'Wait!' said Big King, and the Portuguese looked at him in mild surprise.

Big King took the weight from the pocket of his jacket. He placed it on the desk.

'Weigh that on your scale,' he said in Portuguese.

Almeida's eyes flicked down to the weight, and then back to Big King's face. He sank back into his seat, and pushed the strand of hair off his forehead. He began to speak, but his voice cracked and he cleared his throat.

'Why? Is there something wrong?' Suddenly he was aware of the size of the man opposite him. He could smell the liquor on his breath.

'Weigh it!' Big King's voice was flat, without rancour. His face was expressionless, but the smoky red glare of his eyes was murderous.

Suddenly Almeida was afraid, deadly, coldly afraid. He could guess what would happen once the error in his balance was disclosed.

'Very well,' he said, and his voice was forced and off key. The pistol was in the drawer beside his right knee. It was loaded, with a cartridge under the hammer. The safety-catch was on, but that would only delay him an instant. He knew it would not be necessary to fire, once he had the weapon in his hand he would have control of the situation again.

If he did have to fire, the calibre was .45 and the heavy slug would stop even a giant like this Bantu. *Self-defence*, he was working it out feverishly. A *burglar*, I surprised him and he attacked. *Self-defence*. It would work. They'd believe it.

But how to get the pistol? Try and sneak it out of the drawer, or make a grab for it?

There was a desk between them, it would take a few seconds for the Bantu to realize what he was doing, a few more for him to get around the desk. He would have plenty of time.

He snatched the handle of the drawer, and it flew open. His fingernails scrabbled against the woodwork as he clawed for the big black U.S. Navy automatic, and with a surge of triumph his hand closed over the butt.

Big King came over the top of the desk like a black avalanche. The scale and the jar of gold dust were swept aside to clatter and shatter against the floor.

Still seated in his chair, with the pistol in his hand, Almeida was borne over backwards with Big King on top of him. Many years before, Big King had worked with a safari outfit in Portuguese East Africa, and he had seen the effect of gunshot wounds in the flesh of dead animals.

In the instant that he had recognized the weapon in Almeida's hand, he had been as afraid as the Portuguese. Fear had triggered the speed of his reaction, it was responsible for the savagery of his attack as he lay over the struggling body of the Portuguese.

He had Almeida's pistol hand held by the wrist and he was shaking it to force him to drop the firearm. With his right hand he had the Portuguese by the throat, and instinctively he was applying the full strength of his arms to both grips. He felt something break under his right hand, cracking like the kernel of a nut, and his fingers were suddenly without strength, and the gun skittered across the floor to come up against the far wall with a thump.

Only then did Big King begin to regain the sanity that fear had scattered. Suddenly he realized that the Portuguese was lying quietly under him. He released his grip and scrambled to his knees. The Portuguese was dead. His neck was twisted away from his shoulders at an impossible angle. His eyes were wide and surprised, and a smear of blood issued from one nostril over his upper lip.

Big King backed away towards the door, his gaze fixed in horror on the sprawling corpse. When he reached the door, he hesitated, fighting down the urge to run. He subdued it, and went back to kneel beside the desk. First he picked up the controversial cylindrical weight and placed it in his pocket, then he began sweeping up the scattered gold dust and the shattered fragments of the screw-topped container. He placed them into separate envelopes that he found among the papers on the desk. Ten minutes later he slipped out through the back door of the concession store, into the night.

– 49 –

At the time Big King was hurrying back towards the mine hostel, Rod Ironsides thrashed restlessly in a bed in which the sheets were already bunched and damp with sweat. He was imprisoned in his own fantasy, locked in a nightmare from which he could not break away. The nightmare was infinite and green, quivering, unearthly, translucent. He knew it was held back only by a transparent barrier of glass. He cowered before it, and he knew it was icy cold, he could see light shining through it, and he was deadly afraid.

Suddenly there was a crack in the glass wall, a hairline crack, and through it oozed a single drop. A large, pear-shaped drop, as perfect as though it had been painted by Tretchikoff. It glittered like a gemstone.

It was the most terrifying thing that Rod had ever seen in his life. He cried out in his sleep, trying to warn them, but the crack starred further, and the drop slid down the glass, to be followed by another and another. Suddenly a jagged slab of glass exploded out of the wall, and Rod screamed as the water burst through, in a frothing jet.

With a roar the entire glass wall collapsed, and a mountain high wave of green water hissed down upon him, carrying a white plume of spray at its crest.

He awoke sitting upright in his bed, a cry of horror on his lips and his body bathed in sweat. It took minutes for him to steady the wild racing of his heart. Then he went through to the bathroom. He ran a glass of water and held it up to the light. 'Water. It's there!' he muttered. 'I know it's there!' He drank from the tumbler.

Standing naked, with his sweat drying cold on his body, the tumbler held to his lips, the idea came to him. He had never heard of anyone trying it before, but then nobody he knew would be crazy enough to drive into a death trap like the Big Dipper.

'I'll drill and charge a matt of explosive into the hanging wall of the drive. I'll get the Delange boys on to it right away. Then at any time I choose I can blast the whole bloody roof in and seal off the tunnel.'

Rod was surprised at the strength of the relief that flooded over him. He knew then how it had been worrying him. He went back to the bedroom and straightened out his bedclothes. However, sleep would not come easily to him. His imagination was overheated, and a series of events and ideas kept playing through his mind, until abruptly he was presented with the image of Terry Steyner.

He had not seen her for almost two weeks, not since their meeting just after Manfred Steyner's return from Europe. He had spoken to her twice on the telephone, hasty, confused conversations that left him feeling dissatisfied. He was increasingly aware that he was missing her. His one attempt to find solace elsewhere had been a miserable failure. He had lost interest halfway through the approach manoeuvres and had returned the young lady to the bosom of her family at the unheard-of hour of eleven o'clock on a Saturday night.

Only the unremitting demands of his new job had prevented him from slipping away to Johannesburg and taking a risk.

'You know, Ironsides, you'd better start bracing up a little, don't lose your head over this woman. Remember our vow – *Never Again!*'

He punched the pillow into shape and settled into it.

Terry lay quietly, waiting for it. It was after one o'clock in the morning. It was one of those nights. He would come soon now. As never before she was filled with dread. A cold slimy feeling in the pit of her stomach. Yet she had been fortunate. He had not been near her since his return from Paris. Over two weeks, but it could not last. Tonight.

She heard the sound of the car coming up the drive and she felt physically ill. I can't do it, she decided, not any more, not ever again. It wasn't meant to be like this, I know that now. It's not dirty and furtive and horrible, it's like . . . like . . . it's the way Rod makes it.

She heard him in his bedroom, suddenly she sat up in bed. She felt desperate, hunted.

The door of her room opened softly.

'Manfred?' she asked sharply.

'It's me. Don't worry.' He came briskly towards her bed, a dark impersonal shape and he was undoing the cord of his dressing-gown.

'Manfred,' Terry blurted. 'I'm early this month, I'm sorry.'

He stopped. She saw his hands fall back to his sides, and he stood completely still.

'Oh!' he said at last, and she heard him shuffle his feet into the thick pile of the carpet. 'I just came to tell you,' he hesitated, seeking an excuse for his visit, 'that . . . that I'll be going away for five days. Leaving on Friday. I have to go to Durban and Cape Town.'

'I'll pack for you,' she said.

'What? Oh, yes – thank you.' He shuffled his feet again. 'Well, then.' He hesitated, then stooped quickly and brushed her cheek with his lips. 'Good night, Theresa.'

'Good night, Manfred.'

Five days. She lay alone in the darkness and gloated. *Five whole days alone with Rod.*

– 50 –

Detective Inspector Hannes Grobbelaar of the South African Criminal Investigation Department sat on the edge of the office chair with his hat tipped onto the back of his head and spoke into the telephone, which he held in a handkerchief-covered hand. He was a tall man with a long sad face and a mournful-looking moustache that was streaked with grey.

'Gold buying,' he said into the receiver, and then in reply to the obvious question, 'There's gold dust spilled all over the place and a jeweller's scale, and a .45 automatic with a full magazine and the safety-catch still on, dead man's prints on it.' He listened. 'Ja. Ja. All right, ja. Broken neck, looks like.' Inspector Grobbelaar swivelled his chair and looked down at the corpse that lay on the floor beside him. 'Bit of blood on his lip, but nothing else.'

One of the finger-print men came to the desk and Grobbelaar stood up to give him room to work, the receiver still held to his ear.

'Prints?' he asked in disgust. 'There are finger prints on everything, we have isolated at least forty separate sets so far.' He listened a few seconds. 'No, we will get him, all right. It must be a Bantu mine worker and we have got all

170

the finger prints of the men from outside the Republic. It's just a matter of checking them all out and then questioning. Ja, we'll have him within a month, that's for sure! I'll be back at John Vorster Square about five o'clock, just as soon as we finish up here.' He hung up the receiver, and stood looking down at the murdered man.

'Ugly bastard,' said Sergeant Hugo beside him. 'Asked for it, buying gold. It's as bad as diamonds.' He drew attention to the large envelope he carried in his hand. 'I've got a whole lot of glass fragments. Looks like the container the gold was in. The murderer tried to clean up, but he didn't make a very good job. These were under the desk.'

'Prints?'

'Only one piece big enough. It's got a smeary print on it. Might be of use.'

'Good,' Grobbelaar nodded. 'Get cracking on that, then.'

There was a feminine wail from somewhere in the interior of the building, and Hugo grimaced.

'There she starts again. Hell, I thought she'd exhausted herself. Bloody Portuguese women are the end.'

'You should hear them having a baby,' grunted Grobbelaar.

'Where did you hear one?'

'There was one in the ward next door to my old girl at the maternity home. She nearly brought the bloody roof down.'

Grobbelaar's moustache took on a more melancholy droop as he thought about the work that lay ahead. Hours, days, weeks of questioning and checking and cross-checking, with a succession of sullen and uncooperative suspects.

He sighed and jerked a thumb at the corpse. 'All right, we've finished with him. Tell the butcher boys to come and fetch him.'

It had taken Rod almost two days to design his dropblast matt. The angle and depth of the shot holes were carefully placed to achieve maximum disruption of the hanging wall. In addition he had decided to drill and charge the side walls of the drive with charges timed to explode *after* the hanging wall had collapsed. This would kick in on the rubble filling the tunnel and jam it solid.

Rod was fully aware of the power of water under pressures of 2,000 pounds per square inch and more and he had decided it was necessary to block at least 300 feet of the tunnel. His matt blast was designed to do so, and yet he knew that this would not seal off the water completely. It would, however, reduce the flow sufficiently to allow cementation crews to get in and plug the drive solid.

The Delange brothers did not share Rod's enthusiasm for the project.

'Hey man, that's going to take three or four days to drill and charge,' Johnny protested when Rod showed him his carefully drawn plan.

'Like hell it will,' Rod growled at him. 'I want it done properly. It will take at least a week.'

'You said ultra-fast. You didn't say nothing about drilling the hanging wall with more holes than a cheese!'

'Well, I'm saying it now,' Rod told him grimly. 'And I'm also saying that you will drill, but you won't charge the holes until I come down and make sure that you've gone in as deep as I want them.'

He didn't trust either Johnny or Davy to spend time drilling in twenty feet, when he could go in six feet, charge up and nobody would know the difference. Not until it was too late.

Davy Delange spoke for the first time.

'Will you credit us bonus fathomage while we fiddle around with this?' he asked.

'Four fathoms a shift.' Rod agreed to pay them for the removal of fictitious rock.

'Eight?' said Davy.

'Hell, no!' Rod exclaimed. That was robbery.

'I don't know,' Davy murmured, watching Rod with sly ferrety little eyes. 'Maybe I should talk to Brother Duivenhage, you know, ask his advice.'

Duivenhage was No. 1 shaft shop steward for the Mine Workers' Union. He had driven Frank Lemmer to the edge of a nervous breakdown and was now starting on Rodney Ironsides. Rod was pleading with Head Office to offer Duivenhage a fat job in management to get him out of the way. The last thing in the world that Rod wanted was Brother Duivenhage snooping around his drive on the Big Dipper.

'Six,' he said.

'Well . . .' Davy hesitated.

'Six is fair, Davy,' Johnny interrupted, and Davy glared at him. Johnny had snatched complete victory from his grasp.

'Good, that's agreed.' Quickly Rod closed the negotiations. 'You'll start drilling the matt right away.'

Rod's design demanded nearly 1,200 shot holes to be filled with two and a half tons of explosive. It was 1,000 feet down the drive from the main haulage on 66 level to where the matt began.

The drive now was a spacious, well lit and freshly ventilated tunnel, with the vent piping, the compressed air pipe, and the electrical cable bolted into the hanging wall, and a set of steel railway tracks laid along the floor.

All work on the face ceased while the Delange brothers set about drilling the matt. It was light work that demanded little from the men. As each hole was drilled, Davy would insert his charging rod to check the depth and then plug the entrance with a wad of paper. There was much time for drinking Thermos coffee and for thinking.

There were three subjects that endlessly occupied Davy's mind as he sat at ease, waiting for the completion of the next shot hole. Sometimes for half an hour at a time Davy would hold the image of that 50,000 rand in his mind. It was his, tax paid, painstakingly accumulated over the years and lovingly deposited with the local branch of the Johannesburg Building Society. He imagined it bundled and stacked in neat green piles in the Society's vault. Each bundle was labelled 'David Delange'.

Then his imagination would pass automatically on to the farm that the money would buy. He saw how it would be in the evenings when he sat on the wide stoep, with the setting sun striking the peaks of the Swart Berg across the valley, and the cattle coming in from the paddocks towards the homestead.

Always there was a woman sitting beside him on the stoep. The woman had red hair.

On the fifth morning Davy drove home in the dawn, he was not tired. The night's labours had been easy and unexacting.

The door of Johnny and Hettie's bedroom was closed. Davy read the newspapers with his breakfast; as always the cartoon strip adventures of Modesty Blaise and Willie Garvin intrigued him completely. This morning Modesty was depicted in a bikini and Davy studied her comparing her to the big healthy body of his brother's wife. The thought of her stayed with him as he rolled onto his bed, and he lay unsleeping, daydreaming an adventure in which

174

Modesty Blaise had become Hettie, and Willie Garvin was Davy.

An hour later he was still awake. He sat up and reached for the towel which lay across the foot of his bed. He wrapped the towel around his waist as he went down the passage to the bathroom. As he reached for the handle of the bathroom door, it opened under his hand and he was face to face with Hettie Delange.

She wore a white lace dressing-gown with ostrich-feather mules on her feet. Her face was innocent of make-up and she had brushed her hair and tied it with a ribbon.

'Oh!' she gasped with surprise. 'You gave me a fright, man.'

'I'm sorry, hey.' Davy grinned at her, holding the towel with one hand. Hettie let her eyes run quickly over his naked upper body.

Davy was muscled like a prizefighter. His chest hair was crisp and curly. On both arms the tattoos drew attention to the thickness and weight of muscle.

'Gee, you *are* built,' Hettie murmured in admiration, and Davy sucked in his belly reflexively.

'You think so?' His grin was self-conscious now.

'Yes.' Hettie leaned forward and touched his arm. 'It's hard too!'

The movement had allowed the front of her dressing-gown to gape open. Davy's face flushed as he looked down into the opening. He started to say something, but his voice had dried up on him. Hettie's fingers stroked down his arm, and she was watching the direction of his eyes. Slowly she moved closer to him.

'Do you like me, Davy?' she asked, her voice throaty and low, and with an animal cry Davy attacked her.

His hands ripping at the opening of her gown, pinning her to the wall of the bathroom with his mouth frantically hunting hers. His body pressing hard and urgent, his eyes wild, his breathing ragged.

175

Hettie was laughing, a breathless gasping laugh.

This was what she loved. When they lost their heads, when they went mad for her.

'Davy,' she said, jerking loose his towel. 'Davy.'

She kept wriggling away from his thrusting hips, knowing that it would inflame him further. His hands were tearing at her body, his eyes were maniacal.

'Yes!' she hissed into his mouth. He threw her off balance and she slid down the wall onto the floor.

'Wait,' she panted. 'Not here – the bedroom.'

But it was too late.

Davy had spent the afternoon locked in his bedroom, lying on his bed in an agony of black all-pervading remorse and guilt.

'My brother,' he kept repeating. 'Johnny is my brother.'

Once he wept, each sob tearing something in his chest. The tears squeezed out between burning eyelids, leaving him feeling exhausted and weak.

'My *own* brother,' he shook his head slowly in horrified disbelief. 'I cannot stay here,' he decided miserably. 'I'll have to go.'

He went to the washbasin and washed his eyes. Stooping over the basin, water still dripping from his face, he decided.

'I will have to tell him.' The burden of guilt was too heavy. 'I'll write to Johnny. I'll write it all, and then I'll go away.'

Frantically he searched for pen and paper, it was almost as though he could wipe away the deed by writing it down. He sat at the table by the window and wrote slowly and laboriously. When he had finished it was three o'clock. He felt better.

He sealed the four closely written pages into an envelope and slipped it into the inside pocket of his jacket. He dressed quickly, and crept out of the house, fearful of meeting Hettie, but she was nowhere about. Her big white Monaco was not in the garage, and with relief he turned out of the driveway and took the road out to the Sonder Ditch. He wanted to reach the mine before Johnny came off shift.

Davy listened to his brother's voice, as he kidded and laughed with the other off-duty miners in the company change house. He had locked himself in one of the lavatory closets to avoid meeting his brother, and he sat disconsolately on the toilet seat. The sound of Johnny's voice brought his guilt flooding back in its full strength. His letter of confession was buttoned into the top pocket of his overalls, and he took it out, broke open the flap and reread the contents.

'So long, then.' Johnny's voice sang out gaily from the change room. 'See you bastards tomorrow.'

There was an answering chorus from the other miners, then the door slammed.

Davy went on sitting alone for another twenty minutes in the stench of stale bodies and urine, dirty socks and rank disinfections from the foot baths. At last he tucked the letter away in his pocket and opened the closet door.

Davy's gang were at their waiting place at the head of the drive. They were sitting along the bench laughing and chatting. There was a holiday spirit amongst them for they knew it would be another shift of easy going.

They greeted Davy cheerfully, as he came down the haulage. Both the Delange brothers were popular with their gangs and it was unusual that Davy did not reply to the chorused greeting. He did not even smile.

The Swazi boss boy handed him the safety lamp, and Davy grunted an acknowledgement. He set off alone down the tunnel, trudging heavily, not conscious of his surroundings, his mind encased in a padding of guilt and self-pity.

A thousand feet along the drive he reached the day's work area. Johnny's shift had left the rock drills in place, still connected to the compressed air system, ready for use. Davy came to a halt in the centre of the work area, and without a conscious command from his brain his hands began the routine process of striking the wick of the safety lamp.

The little blue flame came alight behind the protective screen of wire mesh, and Davy held the lamp at eye level before him and walked slowly along the drive. His eyes were watching the flame without seeing it.

The air in the tunnel was cool and refrigerated, scrubbed and filtered, there was no odour nor taste to it. Davy walked on somnambulantly. He was wallowing in self-pity now. He saw himself in a semi-heroic role, one of the great lovers of history caught up in tragic circumstances. His brain was fully occupied with the picture. His eyes were unseeing. Blindly he performed the ritual that a thousand times before had begun the day's shift.

Slowly in its wire mesh cage the blue flame of the safety lamp changed shape. Its crest flattened, and there formed above it a ghostly pale line. Davy's eyes saw it, but his brain refused to accept the message. He walked on in a stupor of guilt and self-pity.

That line above the flame was called 'the cap', it signified that there was at least a five per cent concentration of methane gas in the air. The last shot hole that Johnny Delange's gang had drilled before going off shift had bored into a methane-filled fissure. For the previous three hours, gas had been blowing out of that hole. The ventilation system was unable to wash the air fast enough and now the gas had spread slowly down the drive. The air surrounding Davy's body was heavy with gas, he had breathed it into his lungs. It needed just one spark to ignite it.

Davy reached the end of the drive and snapped the snuffer over the wick, extinguishing the flame in the lamp.

'All safe,' he muttered, not realizing that he had spoken. He went back to his waiting men.

'All safe,' he repeated, and with the Swazi boss boy leading them the forty men of Davy Delange's gang trooped gaily into the mouth of the drive.

Moodily Davy followed them. As he walked he reached into his hip pocket and took out a pack of Lexington filter tips. He put one between his lips, returned the pack and began patting his pockets to locate his lighter.

Davy went from team to team of his machine boys, directing them in the line and spot to be drilled. Every time he spoke, the unlit cigarette waggled between his lips. He gesticulated with the hand that held his cigarette-lighter.

It took twenty minutes for him to set all his drills to work. And he stood and looked back along the tunnel. Each machine boy and his assistant formed a separate sculpture. Most of them were stripped to the waist. Their bodes appeared to be carved and polished in oiled ebony, as they braced themselves behind the massive rock drills.

Davy lifted his cupped hands, holding the cigarette-lighter near his face, and he flicked the cog wheel.

The air in the tunnel turned to flame. In a flash explosion, the flame reached the temperature of a welding torch. It seared the skin from the faces and exposed bodies of the machine boys, it burned the hair from their scalps. It turned their arms to charred stumps. It roasted their eyeballs in their sockets. It scorched their clothing, so as they fell the cloth smouldered and burned against their flesh.

In that instant, as the skin was licked from his face and hands, Davy Delange opened his mouth in a great gasp of agony. The flame shot down his throat into his gas-drenched lungs. Within the confines of his body the gas exploded and his chest popped like a paper bag, his ribs fanning outward about the massive wound like the petals of a sunflower.

Forty-one men died at the same moment. In the silence

179

after that whooshing, sucking detonation, they lay like scorched insects along the floor of the drive. One or two of them were moving still, an arched spine relaxing, a leg straightening, charred fingers unclenching, but within a minute all was absolutely still.

Half an hour later Doctor Dan Stander and Rodney Ironsides were the first men into the drive. The smell of burned flesh was overpowering. Both of them had to swallow down their nausea as they went forward.

– 52 –

D an Stander sat at his desk and looked out over the car park in front of the mine hospital. He appeared to have aged ten years since the previous evening. Dan envied his colleagues the detachment they could bring to their work. He had never been able to perfect the trick. He had just completed forty-one examinations for issue of death certificates.

For fifteen years he had been a mine doctor, so he was accustomed to dealing with death in its more hideous forms. This, however, was the worst he had ever encountered. Forty-one of them, all victims of severe burning and massive explosion trauma.

He felt washed out, exhausted with ugliness. He massaged his temples as he examined the tray of pathetic possessions that lay on the desk before him. This was the contents of the pockets of the man Delange. Extracting them from the scorched clothing had been a filthy business in itself. Cloth had burned into the flesh, the man had been wearing a cheap nylon shirt under his overalls. The fabric had melted in the heat and had become part of his blistered skin.

There was a bunch of keys on a brass ring, a Joseph Rogers pen-knife with a bone handle, a Ronson cigarette-lighter which had been clutched in the man's clawed and charred right hand, a springbok skin wallet, and a loose envelope with one corner burned away.

Dan had already passed on the effects of the Bantu victims to the agent of the Bantu Recruiting Agency, who would send them on to the men's families. Now he sighed with distaste and picked up the wallet. He opened it.

In one compartment there were half a dozen postage stamps, and five rands in notes. The other flap bulged with paper. Dan glanced through salesmen's cards, dry-cleaning receipts, newspaper cuttings offering farms for sale, a folded page from the *Farmer's Weekly* on the planning of a dairy herd, a JBS savings book.

Dan opened the savings book and whistled when he saw the total. He fanned the remaining pages.

There was a much-fingered envelope, unsealed and tucked behind the cardboard cover of the savings book. Dan opened it, and pulled a face. It contained a selection of photographs of the type which one found offered for sale in the dock area of the Mozambique port of Lourenço Marques. It was for this type of material that Dan was searching.

When the man's possessions were returned to his grieving relatives, Dan wanted to spare them this evidence of human frailty. He burned the photographs and the envelope in his ashtray and then crushed the blackened sheets to powder before spilling it into his waste-paper bin.

He went across to the window and opened it to let the smell of smoke escape. He stood at the window and searched the car park for Joy's Alfa Romeo. She had not arrived as yet and Dan returned to his desk.

The remaining envelope caught his eye and he picked it up. There was a smear of blood upon it, and the corner was burned away. Dan removed the four sheets of paper and spread them on the desk:

Dear Johnny,

When Pa died you were still little – and I always reckoned you were more like my son, you know, than my brother.

Well, Johnny, I reckon now I've got to tell you something . . .

Dan read slowly, and he did not hear Joy come into the room. She stood at the door watching him. Her expression fond, a small smile on her lips, shiny blonde hair hanging straight to her shoulders. Then she moved up quietly behind his chair and kissed his ear. Dan started and turned to face her.

'Darling,' Joy said and kissed him on the mouth. 'What is so interesting that you ignore my arrival?'

Dan hesitated a moment before telling her.

'There was a man killed last night in a ghastly accident. This was in his pocket.'

He handed her the letter and she read it slowly.

'He was going to send this to his brother?' she asked, and Dan nodded.

'The bitch,' Joy whispered, and Dan looked surprised.

'Who?'

'The girl – it's her fault, you know.' Joy opened her purse and took out a tissue to dab her eyes. 'Damn it, now I'm messing my make-up.' She sniffed, and then went on. 'It would serve her right if you gave that letter to her husband.'

'You mean I shouldn't give it to him?' Dan asked. 'We have no right to play God.'

'Haven't we?' asked Joy, and Dan watched quietly as she tore the letter to tiny shreds, screwed them into a ball, then dropped them into the waste bin.

'You are wonderful,' he said. 'Will you marry me?'

'I've already answered that question, Dr Stander.' And she kissed him again.

– 53 –

Hettie Delange was in a turmoil.

It had started with the phone call that had roused Johnny from their bed. He had said something about trouble at the shaft as he pulled on his clothes, but she had come only briefly awake and then drifted off again as Johnny hurried out into the night.

He had come in hours later and sat on the edge of the bed, his hands clasped between his knees and his head bowed.

'What's wrong, man,' she had snapped at him. 'Come to bed. Don't just sit there.'

'Davy's dead.' His voice had been listless.

There was a moment's shock that had convulsed the muscles of her belly, and brought her fully awake. Then, immediately, she had felt a swift cleansing rush of relief.

He was dead. It was as easy as that! All day she had worried. She had been stupid to let it happen. Just that moment of weakness, that self-indulgent slip and she had been dreading the consequences all that day. She had imagined Davy trailing after her with puppy eyes, trying to touch her, making it so obvious that even Johnny would see it. She had enjoyed it but just the once was enough. She wanted no repeat performance and certainly no complications to follow the original deed.

Now it was all taken care of. He was dead.

'Are you sure?' she had asked anxiously, and Johnny heard the tone as concern.

'I saw him!' Johnny had shuddered, and wiped the back of his hand across his mouth.

'Gee, that's terrible.' Hettie had remembered her role, and sat up and put her arms about Johnny. 'That's terrible for you.'

She had not slept again that night. Somehow the

thought of Davy going directly from her to his violent death was exciting. It was like in the movies, or a book, or something. Like he was an airman and he had been shot down, and she was his girl. Perhaps she was pregnant and all alone in the world, and she would have to go to Buckingham Palace and get his medal for him. And the Queen would say . . .

The fantasies had played out in her mind until the dawn, with Johnny tossing and muttering beside her.

She woke him when it was first light in the room.

'How was he?' she asked softly. 'What did he look like, Johnny?'

Johnny shuddered again, and then he started to tell her. His voice was husky, and the sentences broken and disconnected. When he stumbled into silence, Hettie found herself trembling with excitement.

'How terrible,' she kept repeating. 'Oh, how awful!' And she pressed against him. After a while Johnny made love to her, and for Hettie it was better than she had ever known it to be.

All that morning there were phone calls, and four of her friends came over to drink coffee with her. A reporter and photographer from the *Johannesburg Star* called and asked questions. Hettie was the centre of attraction, and again and again she repeated the story with all its grisly details.

After lunch Johnny came home with a little dark-haired man in a charcoal suit and black Italian shoes, with a matching black briefcase.

'Hettie, this is Mr Boart. He was Davy's lawyer. He's got something to tell you.'

'Mrs Delange. May I convey to you my sincere condolences in the tragic bereavement you and your husband have suffered.'

'Yes, it's terrible, isn't it?' Hettie was apprehensive. Had Davy told this lawyer about them? Had this man come to make trouble?

'Your brother-in-law made a will of which I am the executor. Your brother-in-law was a wealthy man. His estate is in excess of fifty thousand rand.' Boart paused portentously. 'And you and your husband are the sole beneficiaries.'

Hettie looked dubiously from Boart to Johnny.

'I don't – what's that mean? Beneficiary?'

'It means that you and your husband share the estate between you.'

'I get half of fifty thousand rand?' Hettie asked in delighted disbelief.

'That's right.'

'Gee,' exulted Hettie. 'That's fabulous!' She could hardly wait for Johnny and the lawyer to go before she phoned her friends again. All four of them returned to drink more coffee, to thrill again and to envy Hettie the glamour and excitement of it.

'Twenty-five thousand,' they kept repeating the sum with relish.

'Hell, man, he must really have liked you a lot, Hettie,' one of the girls commented with heavy emphasis, and Hettie lowered her eyes and contrived to look bereft and mysterious.

Johnny came home after six, unsteady on his feet and reeking of liquor. Reluctantly Hettie's four friends left to rejoin their waiting families, and almost immediately after that a big white sports car pulled up in the driveway and Hettie's day of triumph was complete. Not one of her friends had ever had the General Manager of the Sonder Ditch Gold Mining Company call at their home.

She had the front door open the instant the doorbell rang. Her greeting had been shamelessly plagiarized from a period movie that had recently played at the local cinema.

'Mr Ironsides, how good of you to come.'

When she led Rod through into the over-furnished lounge, Johnny looked up but did not get to his feet.

'Hello, Johnny', said Rod. 'I have come to tell you that I'm sorry about Davy, and to . . .'

'Don't give me that bull dust, Tin Ribs,' said Johnny Delange.

'Johnny,' gasped Hettie, 'you can't talk to Mr Ironsides like that.' And she turned to Rod, laying a hand on his sleeve. 'He doesn't mean it, Mr Ironsides. He has been drinking.'

'Get out of here,' said Johnny. 'Get into the bloody kitchen where you belong.'

'Johnny!'

'Get out!' roared Johnny, rising from his chair, and Hettie fled from the room.

Johnny lurched across to the chrome and glass liquor cabinet that filled one corner. He sloshed whisky into two glasses and handed one to Rod.

'God speed to my brother,' he said.

'To Davy Delange, one of the best rock hounds on the Kitchenerville field,' said Rod, and tossed the drink back in one gulp.

'The best!' Johnny corrected him, and emptied his own glass. He gasped at the sting of the whisky, then leaned forward to speak into Rod's face.

'You've come to find out if I'm game to finish your bloody drive for you, or if I'm going to quit. Davy didn't mean nothing to you and I don't mean nothing to you. Only one thing worrying you – you want to know about your bloody drive.' Johnny refilled his glass. 'Well, hear this, friend, and hear it well. Johnny Delange don't quit. That drive ate my brother but I'll beat the bastard, so you got nothing to worry about. You go home and get a good night's sleep, 'cos Johnny Delange will be on shift and breaking rock tomorrow morning first thing.'

– 54 –

A Silver Cloud Rolls-Royce was parked amongst the trees in the misty morning. Ahead was the practice track with the white-painted railings curving away towards the willow-lined river. The mist was heavier along the river and the grass was very green against it.

The uniformed chauffeur stood away from the Rolls, leaving its two occupants in privacy. They sat on the back seat with an angora wool travelling rug spread over their knees. On the folding table in front of them was a silver Thermos of coffee, shell-thin porcelain cups, and a plate of ham sandwiches.

The fat man was eating steadily, washing each mouthful down with coffee. The little bald-headed man was not eating, instead he puffed quickly and nervously at his cigarette and looked out of the window at the horses. The grooms were walking the horses in circles, nostrils streaming in the morning chill, blankets flapping. The jockeys stood looking up at the trainer. They wore hard caps and polo-necked jerseys. All of them carried whips. The trainer was speaking urgently, his hands thrust deep into the pockets of his overcoat.

'It's a very fine service,' said the little man. 'I particularly enjoyed the stop in Rio. My first visit there.'

The fat man grunted. He was annoyed. They shouldn't have sent this agent out. It was a mark of suspicion, distrust, and it would seriously hamper his market operation.

The conference between trainer and jockeys had ended. The diminutive riders scattered to their mounts, and the trainer came towards the Rolls.

'Good morning, sir.' He spoke through the open window, and the fat man grunted again.

'I'm giving him a full run,' the trainer went on. 'Emerald Isle will make pace for him to the five, Pater Noster will take over and push him to the mile, I've Tiger Shark to pace him for the run in.'

'Very well.'

'Perhaps you'd like to keep time, sir.' The trainer proffered a stop-watch, and the fat man seemed to recover his urbanity and charm.

'Thank you, Henry.' He smiled. 'He looks good, I'll say that.'

The trainer was pleased by the condescension.

'Oh! He's red-hot! By Saturday I'll have him sharpened down to razor edge.' He stood back from the window. 'I'll get them off, then.' He walked away.

'You have a message for me?' asked the fat man.

'Of course.' The other wriggled his moustache like a rabbit's whiskers. It was an annoying habit. 'I didn't fly all this way out here to watch a couple of mokes trotting around a race-track.'

'Would you like to give me the message?' The fat man hid his affront. What the agent had called a moke was some of the finest horseflesh in Africa.

'They want to know about this gas explosion.'

'Nothing.' The fat man dismissed the question with a wave of his hand. 'A flash explosion. Killed a few men. No damage to the workings. Negligence on the part of the miner in charge.'

'Will it affect our plans?'

'Not one iota.'

The two horses had jumped away from the start, shoulder to shoulder, with the wreaths of mist swirling in their wake. The glossy bay horse on the rails ran with an easy floating action while the grey plunged along beside it.

'My principals are very concerned.'

'Well, they have no need to be,' snapped the fat man. 'I tell you it makes no difference.'

'Was the explosion due to an error of judgement on the part of this man Ironsides?'

'No.' The fat man shook his head. 'It was negligence of the miner in charge. He should have detected the gas.'

'Pity.' The bald man shook his head regretfully. 'We had hoped it was a flaw in the Ironsides character.'

The grey horse was tiring, while the bay ran on smoothly, drawing away from him. From the side rail a third horse came in to replace the grey, and ran shoulder to shoulder with the bay.

'Why should the character of Ironsides concern you?'

'We have heard disturbing reports. This is no pawn to be moved at will. He is taking the job of General Manager by the throat. Already our sources indicate that he has reduced running costs on the Sonder Ditch by a scarcely believable two per cent. He seems to be tireless, inventive – a man, in short, to reckon with.'

'Well and good,' the fat man conceded. 'But I still fail to see why your – ah, principals – are alarmed. Do they expect that this man will hold back the flood waters by the sheer force of his personality?'

The second pacemaker was faltering, but still the big bay ran on alone. A far figure in the mist, passing the mile post, joined at last by the third pacemaker.

'I know nothing about horses,' said the bald man watching the two flying forms. 'But I've just seen that one,' he pointed with his cigarette at the far-off bay. 'I've just seen him run the guts out of the other two. One after the other he has broken their hearts and left them staggering along behind him. We would call him an imponderable, one who cannot be judged by normal standards.' He puffed at his cigarette before going on. 'There are men like that also, imponderable. It seems to us that Ironsides is one of them, and we don't like it. We don't like them on the opposing team. It is just possible that he could upset the entire operation, not, as you put it, by sheer force of personality, but by suddenly doing the unexpected, by behaving in a manner for which we have not allowed.'

Both men fell silent watching the galloping horses come round the last bend and hit the straight.

'Watch this.' The fat man spoke softly, and as though in response to his words the big bay lengthened his stride, reaching out, driving strongly away from the other horse. His head was going like a hammer, twin jets of steam shot from wide flaring nostrils, and thrown turf and dirt flew from his hooves. Five lengths clear of the following horse he went slashing past the finish line and the fat man clicked his stop watch.

He scrutinized the dial of the watch anxiously and then chuckled like a healthy baby.

'And he wasn't really being extended!'

He rapped on the window beside him, and immediately the uniformed chauffeur opened the driving door and slid in behind the wheel.

'To my office,' instructed the fat man, 'and close the partition.'

When the sound-proof glass panel had slid closed between driver and passengers, the fat man turned to his guest.

'And so, my friend, you consider Ironsides to be an imponderable. What do you want me to do about him?'

'Get rid of him.'

'Do you mean what I think you mean?' The fat man lifted an eyebrow.

'No. Nothing that drastic.' The bald head bobbed agitatedly. 'You have been reading too much James Bond. Simply arrange it that Ironsides is far away and well occupied when the drive holes through the Big Dipper Dyke, otherwise there is an excellent chance that he will do something to frustrate our good intentions.'

'I think we can arrange that,' said the fat man and helped himself to another ham sandwich.

As he had promised, Manfred caught the Friday evening flight for Cape Town. On the Saturday night Rod and Terry took a wild chance on not being recognized and spent the evening at the Kyalami Ranch Hotel. They danced and dined in the Africa Room, but were on their way back to the apartment before midnight.

In the dawn a playful slap with the rolled-up Sunday papers which Rod delivered to Terry's naked posterior as she slept triggered off a noisy brawl in which a picture was knocked off the wall by a flying pillow, a coffee table overturned and the shrieking and laughter reached such a pitch that it called down a storm of indignant thumping from the apartment above them.

Terry made a defiant gesture at the ceiling, but they both subsided gasping with laughter back onto the bed to indulge in activity every bit as strenuous if not nearly so noisy.

Later, much later, they collected Melanie and once again spent the Sunday at the stud farm on the Vaal. Melanie actually *rode* a horse, a traumatic experience which bade fair to alter her whole existence. After lunch they launched the speedboat from the boat house on the bank of the river and water-skied down as far as the barrage, Terry and Rod taking turns at the wheel and on the skis. It occurred to Rod that Terry Steyner looked good in a white bikini. It was dark before Rod delivered his sleeping daughter to her mother.

'Who is this *Terry* that Melanie talks about all the time?' demanded Patti; she was still sulking about Rod's promotion. Patti had a memory like a tax collector.

'Terry?' Rod feigned surprise. 'I thought you knew.' And he left Patti glaring after him as he went back down the stairs.

Terry was curled up in the leather bucket seat of the Maserati, just the tip of her nose protruding from the voluminous fur coat she wore.

'I love your daughter, Mr Ironsides,' she murmured.

'It would appear that the feeling is reciprocated.'

Rod drove slowly towards the Hillbrow ridge, and Terry's hand came out of the wide fur sleeve and lay on his knee.

'Wouldn't it be nice if we had a daughter of our own one day?'

'Wouldn't it,' Rod agreed dutifully, and then found to his intense amazement that he really meant it.

He was still investigating this remarkable phenomenon as he parked the Maserati in the basement garage of his apartment and went round to open Terry's door.

Manfred Steyner watched Terry climb out of the Maserati and lift her face towards Rodney Ironsides. Ironsides stooped over her and kissed her, then he slammed and locked the door of the Maserati, and arm in arm the two of them crossed to the elevator.

'Peterson Investigations always delivers the goods,' said the man at the wheel of the black Ford parked in the shadows of the garage. 'We will give them half an hour to get settled in comfortably, then we will go up and knock on the door of his apartment.'

Manfred Steyner sat very still and unblinking on the seat beside the private detective. He had arrived back in Johannesburg three hours previously in answer to the summons from the investigation bureau.

'You will leave me here. Drive the Ford out and park at the corner of Clarendon Circle. Wait for me there,' said Manfred.

'Hey? Aren't you going to . . . ?' The detective was taken aback.

'Do as I tell you.' Manfred's voice stung like thrown vitriol, but the detective persisted.

192

'You will need evidence for the court, you need me as a witness . . .'

'Get out,' Manfred snapped, and opening the door of the Ford he climbed out and closed the door behind him. The detective hesitated a moment longer, then started the engine and drove out of the garage leaving Manfred alone.

Manfred moved slowly towards the big shiny sports car. From his pocket he took a gold-plated pen-knife and opened the large blade.

He had recognized that the car was of special significance to the man. It was the only form of retaliation he could make at the moment. Until Rodney Ironsides completed the drive on the Big Dipper Dyke, he could not confront him nor Theresa Steyner. He could not let them know he even suspected them.

Such human emotions as love and hate and jealousy Manfred Steyner seldom experienced, except in their mildest manifestations. Theresa Hirschfeld he had never loved, as he had never loved any woman. He had married her for her wealth and station in life. The emotion that gripped him was neither hatred nor jealousy. It was affront. He was affronted that these two insignificant persons should conspire to cheat him.

He would not rush in blindly now with threats of physical violence and divorce. No, he would administer an anonymous punishment that would hurt the man deeply. This would be part payment. Later, when he had served his purpose, Manfred would crush him as coldly as though he were stepping on an ant.

As for the woman, he was aware of a mild relief. Her irresponsible behaviour had placed her completely at his mercy, both legally and morally. As soon as the strike beyond the Big Dipper had made him financially secure and independent, he could throw her aside. She would have served her purpose admirably.

The journey which he had interrupted by this hurried return to Johannesburg was connected with the purchase of Sonder Ditch shares. He was touring the major centres arranging with various firms of stock brokers that on a given date they would commence to purchase every available scrap of Sonder Ditch script.

As soon as he had completed this business he would tell the private detective to drive him out to Jan Smuts Airport where he had a reservation on the night plane to Durban where he would continue his preparations.

It had all worked out very well, he thought, as he slipped the knife blade through the rubber buffer of the triangular side window of the Maserati. With a quick twist he lifted the window catch, and pushed the window open. He reached through and turned the door handle. The door clicked open and Manfred climbed into the driver's seat.

The blade of the pen-knife was razor sharp. He started on the passenger seat and then the driver's seat, ripping the leather upholstery to shreds before moving to the back seat and repeating the process there. He slid the panel that concealed the tray of tools each in their separate foam rubber padded compartment, and selected a tyre lever.

With this he smashed all the dials on the dashboard, broken glass tinkling and falling to the carpeted floor. With the point of the tyre lever he dug into the rosewood panelling and tore out a section, splintering and cracking the woodwork into complete ruin.

He climbed out of the Maserati and struck the windshield with the tyre lever. The glass starred. He rained blows on it, unable to shatter it but reducing it to a sagging opaque sheet.

Then he dropped the tyre lever and groped for his penknife again. On his knees he slashed at the front offside tyre. The rubber was tougher than he had allowed. Annoyed, he slashed again. The knife turned in his hand, the blade folding against the blow. It sliced the ball of his thumb, a deep stinging cut. Manfred came to his feet with a cry, clutching his injured thumb. Blood spurted from the wound.

'Mein Gott! Mein Gott!' Manfred gasped, horrified by his own blood. As he staggered wildly from the basement garage, he was wrapping a handkerchief around his thumb.

He reached the waiting Ford, hauled the door open and fell into the front seat beside the detective.

'A doctor! For God's sake, get me to a doctor. I'm badly hurt. Quickly! Drive quickly!'

– 56 –

Terry's husband is due back in town today, Rod thought, as he sat down at his desk. It was not a thought that gave him strength to work through a day he knew would be filled with hectic activity.

The quarterly reports were due at Head Office tomorrow morning. In consequence the entire administration was in its usual last-minute panic. Already there was a mob in the waiting-room outside his office that Lily Jordan would soon need a stock whip to control. At three o'clock he was due at a consultants' meeting at Head Office, but before that he wanted to go underground to check the drop-blast matt that Johnny Delange had now completed and charged up.

The phone went as Lily led in his first visitor, a tall, thin, sorrowful-looking man with a droopy moustache.

'Mr Ironsides?' said the voice on the phone.

'Yes.'

'Porters Motors here. I've got an estimate on the repairs to your Maserati.'

'How much?' Rod crossed his fingers.

'Twelve hundred rand.'

'Wow!' Rod gasped.

'Do you want us to go ahead?'

'No, I'll have to contact my insurance company first. I'll call you.' He hung up. That act of unaccountable vandalism still irked him terribly. He realized that he would be reduced to the Company Volkswagen for a further indefinite period.

He turned his attention to his visitor.

'Detective Inspector Grobbelaar,' the tall man introduced himself. 'I am investigating officer in the murder of José Almeida, the concession store proprietor on this mine.'

They shook hands.

'Have you any ideas on who did it?' Rod asked.

'We have always got ideas,' said the Inspector, so sadly that for a moment Rod had the impression that his name was on the list of suspects. 'We believe that the murderer is employed by one of the mines in the district, probably the Sonder Ditch. I have called on you to ask for your co-operation in the investigation.'

'Of course.'

'I will be conducting a great number of interrogations amongst your Bantu employees. I hoped you might find a room for me to use on the premises.'

Rod lifted his phone and while he dialled he told Grobbelaar, 'I'm calling our Compound Manager.' Then he transferred his attention to the mouthpiece. 'Ironsides here. I am sending an Inspector Grobbelaar down to see you. Please see that an office is placed at his disposal and that he receives full co-operation.'

Grobbelaar stood up and extended his hand.

'I won't take up more of your time. Thank you, Mr Ironsides.'

His next visitor was Van der Bergh, his Personnel Officer, brandishing his departmental reports as though they were a winning lottery ticket.

'All finished,' he announced triumphantly. 'All we need is your signature.'

As Rod uncapped his pen, the telephone squealed again.

'My God,' he muttered with pen in one hand and telephone in the other. 'Is it worth it?'

It was well after one o'clock when Rod fled his office, leaving Lily Jordan to hold back the tide. He went directly to No. 1 shaft where he was welcomed like the prodigal son by Dimitri and his old Line Managers. They were all anxious to know who would be replacing him as Underground Manager. Rod promised to find out that afternoon when he visited Head Office, and changed into his overalls and helmet.

At the spot where Davy Delange had died, Rod found a gang fixing a screen of wire mesh over the hanging wall to protect the fuses of his drop-blast. The electric cable that carried the blasting circuit to the surface was covered with a distinctive green plastic coating and securely pegged to the roof of the drive.

In the concrete blast room at the shaft head, his electrician had already set up a separate control for this circuit. It would be in readiness at all times. He could fire it within minutes. Rod felt as though a great weight had been lifted from his shoulders as he passed through the swinging ventilation doors and tramped on up the drive to speak to Johnny Delange.

Halfway to the face he met the gigantic figure of Big King coming back towards him with a small gang of lashing boys under his command. Rod greeted him, and Big King stopped and let his gang go on out of earshot before he spoke.

'I wish to speak.'

'Speak then.' Rod noticed suddenly that Big King's face was gaunt, his eyes appeared sunken and his skin had the dusty greyish look of sickness so evident in an ailing Bantu.

'I wish to return to my wives in Portuguese Mozambique,' said Big King.

'Why?' Rod was dismayed at the prospect of losing such a valuable boss boy.

'My blood is thin.' This was as non-committal an answer as any man has ever received. In essence it meant, 'My reasons are my own, and I have no intention of disclosing them.'

'When your blood is thick again, will you return to work here?' Rod asked.

'That is with the gods.' An answer signifying no more than the one preceding it.

'I cannot stop you if you wish to go, Big King, you know that,' Rod told him. 'Report to the Compound Manager and he will mark your notice.'

'I have told the Compound Manager. He wants me to work out my ticket, thirty-three more days.'

'Of course,' Rod nodded. 'You know that it is a contract. You must work it out.'

'I wish to leave at once,' Big King replied stubbornly.

'Then you must give me your reason. I cannot let you break contract except if there is some good reason.' Rod knew better than to set a dangerous precedent like that.

'There is no reason.' Big King admitted defeat. 'I will work out the ticket.'

He left Rod and followed his gang down the drive. Since the night he killed the Portuguese, Big King had slept little and eaten less. Worry had kept his stomach in a turmoil of dysentry, he had neither danced nor sung. Nothing that Crooked Leg nor the Shangaan Induna could say comforted him. He waited for the police to come. As the days passed, so the flesh melted from his body, he knew that they could come before the thirty-three days of his contract expired.

His approach to Rod had been a last despairing effort. Now he was resigned. He knew that the police were inexorable. One day soon they would come. They would lock the silver chains on his wrists and lead him to the closed van. He had seen many men led away like that and he had heard what happened to them after that. The white man's law was the same as the tribal law of the Shangaans. The taking of life must be paid for with life.

They would break his neck with the rope. His ancestors would have crushed his skull with a war club, it was the same in the end.

Rod found Johnny Delange drinking cold tea from his canteen while his gang barred down the face.

'How's it going?' he asked.

'Now we have finished messing about, it has started moving again.' Johnny wiped cold tea from his lips and recorked the canteen. 'We have broken almost fifteen hundred feet since Davy died.'

'That's good going.' Rod ignored the reference to the methane explosion and the drop-blast matt.

'Would have been better if Davy were still alive.' Johnny disliked Campbell, the miner who had replaced Davy on the night shift. 'The night shift aren't breaking their fair ground.'

'I'll chase them up,' Rod promised.

'You do that.' Johnny turned away to shout an order at his gang.

Rod stood and stared at the end of the drive. Less than a thousand feet ahead lay the dark hard rock of the Big Dipper – and beyond it . . . ? Rod felt his skin creep as he remembered his nightmare. That cold green translucent thing waiting for them beyond the dyke.

'All right, Johnny, you are getting close now.' Rod tore his imagination away from that green horror. 'As soon as you hit the serpentine rock you are to stop work immediately and report to me. Is that understood?'

'You'd better tell that to Campbell also,' said Johnny. 'The night shift may hit the Big Dipper.'

'I'll tell him,' Rod agreed. 'But you make sure you

remember. I want to be down here when we hole through the dyke.'

Rod glanced at his watch. It was almost two o'clock. He had an hour to get to the consultant's meeting at Head Office.

'You are late, Mr Ironsides.' Dr Manfred Steyner looked up from the head of the boardroom table.

'My apologies, gentlemen.' Rod took his seat at the long oak table. 'Just one of those days.'

The men about the table murmured sympathetic acknowledgement, and Dr Steyner studied him for a moment without expression before remarking, 'I would be obliged for a few minutes of your time after this meeting, Mr Ironsides.'

'Of course, Dr Steyner.'

'Good.' Manfred nodded. 'Now that Mr Ironsides has graced the table with his presence, the meeting can come to order.' It was the closest any of them had ever heard Dr Steyner come to making a joke.

It was dark outside when the meeting ended. The participants shrugged on their coats, made their farewells and left Manfred and Rod sitting at the table with its overflowing ashtrays and littered pencils and note pads.

Manfred Steyner waited for fully three minutes after the door had closed on the last person to leave. Rod was accustomed to these long intent silences, yet he was uneasy. He sensed a new hostility in the man's attitude. He covered his awkwardness by lighting another cigarette and blowing a series of smoke rings at the portrait of Norman Hradsky, the original chairman of the Company. Flanking Hradsky's portrait were two others. One of a slim blond man, with ravaged good looks and laughing blue eyes. The caption read: 'Dufford Charleywood. Director of CRC from 1867–1872.' The other portrait in its heavy gilt frame depicted an impressively built man with mutton-chop whiskers and black Irish features. 'Sean Courtney' said the caption, and the dates were the same as Charleywood's.

These three had founded the Company, and Rod knew a little of their story. They had been as pretty a bunch of rogues as would be found in any convict settlement. Hradsky had ruined the other two in an ingenious bear raid on the stock exchange, and had virtually stolen their shares in the Company.*

We have become a lot more sophisticated since then, thought Rod. He looked instinctively towards the head of the long table and met Dr Steyner's level, unblinking stare. *Or have we?* he wondered. Just what devilment has our friend in mind?

Manfred Steyner was examining Rod with detached curiosity. So remote from any emotional rancour was Manfred, that he intended using the relationship that had developed between this man and his wife to further the instructions he had received that morning.

'How far is the end of the drive from the dyke?' he asked suddenly.

'Less than a thousand feet.'

'How much longer before you reach it?'

'Ten days. No more, possibly less.'

'As soon as the dyke is reached, all work on it must cease immediately. The timing of this is important, do you understand?'

'I have already instructed my miners not to hole through without my specific orders.'

'Good.' Manfred lapsed into silence for another full minute. Andrew had called him that morning with instructions from the man. Ironsides was to be well away from the Sonder Ditch when they pierced the dyke. It was left to Manfred to engineer his absence.

* Read *When the Lion Feeds*.

'I must inform you, Mr Ironsides, that it will be at least three weeks before I give the order to drill through. When you reach the dyke, it will be necessary for me to proceed to Europe to make certain arrangements there. I will be away for at least ten days during which time no work of any type must be allowed in the drive to the Big Dipper.'

'You will be away over Christmas?' Rod asked with surprise.

'Yes,' Manfred nodded, and could read Rod's mind.

Terry will be alone, Rod thought quickly, she will be alone over Christmas. The Sonder Ditch goes onto *essential services only* for a full seven days over Christmas. Just a skeleton crew to keep her going. I could get away for a week, a whole week away together.

Manfred waited until he knew that Rod had reached the decision to which he had been steered, then he asked: 'You understand? You will await my order to hole through. You need not expect that order until the middle of January.'

'I understand.'

'You may go.' Manfred dismissed him.

'Thanks,' Rod acknowledged drily.

There was a coffee bar in the ground-floor shopping centre of Reef Building. Rod beat a bearded hippie to the telephone booth, and dialled the Sandown number. It was safe enough, he had just left Manfred upstairs.

'Theresa Steyner,' she answered his call.

'We've got a week to ourselves,' he told her. 'One whole glorious week.'

'When?' she demanded joyously.

And he told her.

'Where shall we go?' she asked.

'We'll think of somewhere.'

A t 11.26 a.m. on December 16th, Johnny Delange blasted the face of the drive, and went forward in the fumes and dust.

In the beam of his lantern, the new rock blown from the face was completely different from the blueish Ventersdorp quartzite. It was a glassy, blackish green, veined with tiny white lines, more like marble than country rock.

'We are on the dyke.' He spoke to Big King, and stooped to pick up a lump of the serpentine rock. He weighed it in his hand.

'We've done it, we've beaten the bastard!'

Big King stood silently beside him. He did not share Johnny's elation.

'Right!' Johnny tossed the lump of rock back onto the pile. 'Bar down, and make safe. Then pull them out of the drive. We are finished here until further orders.'

'Well done, Johnny,' applauded Rod. 'Clean her up and pull out of the drive. I don't know how much longer it will be till we get the order to hole through the dyke. But take a holiday in the meantime. I'll pay you four fathoms of bonus a day while you are waiting.' He broke the connection with his finger, keeping the receiver to his ear. He dialled and spoke to the switch-board girl at Head Office. 'Get me Dr Steyner, please. This is Rodney Ironsides.' He waited a few seconds and then Manfred came on the line.

'We've hit the Big Dipper,' Rod told him.

'I will leave for Europe on tomorrow morning's Boeing,' said Manfred. 'You are to do nothing until I return.' Manfred cradled the receiver and depressed the button on his intercom.

'Cancel all my appointments,' he told his secretary. 'I am unavailable.'

'Very well, Dr Steyner.'

Manfred picked up the receiver of his unlisted, direct-line telephone. He dialled.

'Hello, Andrew. Will you tell him that I am ready to discharge my obligations. We have intersected the Big Dipper.' He listened for a few seconds, then spoke again. 'Very well, I will wait for your reply.'

Andrew replaced the telephone and went out through the sliding glass doors onto the terrace. It was a lazy summer's day, hushed with heat, and the sun sparkled on the crystal clear waters of the swimming-pool. Insects murmured languidly in the massed banks of blooms that surrounded the terrace.

The fat man stood before an artist's easel. He wore a blue beret and a white smock that hung like a maternity dress over his jutting stomach.

His model lay face down on an air mattress by the edge of the pool. She was a dainty, dark-haired girl with a pixy face and a doll-like body. Her discarded bikini lay in a damp bundle on the flags of the terrace. Drops of water caught the sun and bejewelled her creamy buttocks, giving her a paradoxical air of innocence and oriental eroticism.

'That was Steyner,' said Andrew. 'He reports that they have hit the Big Dipper.'

The fat man did not look up. He went on laying paint upon the canvas with complete concentration.

'Please lift your right shoulder, my dear, you are covering that utterly delightful bosom of yours,' he instructed, and the girl obeyed him immediately.

Finally he stepped back and regarded his own work critically.

'You may have a break now.' He wiped his brushes while the naked girl stood up, stretched like a cat and then dived into the pool. She surfaced with the water slicking her short dark hair against her head like the pelt of an otter, and swam slowly to the far end of the pool.

'Cable New York, Paris, London, Tokyo and Berlin the code word "Gothic",' he instructed Andrew. This was the word which would unleash the bear offensive on the financial markets of the world. On receipt of those cables, agents in the major cities would begin to sell the shares of the companies mining the Kitchenerville field, sell them by the millions.

'Then instruct Steyner to get Ironsides out of the way, and hole through the dyke.'

Manfred answered Andrew's return call on the unlisted line. He listened to, and acknowledged, his instructions. Afterwards he sat still as a lizard, running over his preparations. Reviewing them minutely, examining them for flaws. There were none.

It was time to begin the purchase of Sonder Ditch shares. He called his secretary on the intercom and instructed her to place calls to numbers in Cape Town, Durban and Johannesburg itself. He wanted the purchase orders to come through a number of different brokers, so that it would not be obvious that there was only one buyer in the market. There was also the question of credit; he was not covering the purchase orders with banker's guarantees. The stock brokers were buying for him simply on his name and reputation and position with CRC Manfred could not place too large a buying order with any one firm lest they ask him to provide surety. Dr Manfred Steyner had no surety to offer.

So, instead, he placed moderate orders with dozens of different firms. By three o'clock that afternoon Manfred had ordered the purchase of three quarters of a million rand's worth of shares. He had no means of paying for those shares but he knew he would never be called upon to do so. When he sold them again in a few weeks' time they would have doubled in value.

A few minutes after his final conversation with the firm of Swerling and Wright in Cape Town, his secretary came through on the intercom.

'SAA have confirmed your reservation on the Boeing to Salisbury. Flight 126 at nine a.m. tomorrow. You are booked to return to Johannesburg on the Rhodesian Airways Viking at 6 p.m. tomorrow evening.'

'Thank you.' Manfred grudged this wasted day but it was imperative that Theresa believed he had left for Europe. She must see him depart on the SAA flight. 'Please get my wife on the phone for me.'

'Theresa,' he told her, 'something important has come up. I have to fly to London tomorrow morning. I am afraid I will be away over Christmas.'

Her display of surprise and regret was unconvincing. She and Ironsides had made their own arrangements for the time he was away, Manfred was convinced of this.

It was all working out very well, he thought as he cradled the receiver, very well indeed.

– 58 –

The Daimler drew up under the portico of Jan Smuts Airport and the chauffeur opened the door for Terry and then for Manfred.

While the porter removed his luggage from the boot of the Daimler, Manfred swept the car park with a quick scrutiny. So early in the morning it was less than half filled. There was a cream Volkswagen with a Kitchenerville number plate parked near the far end. All the line and

206

senior members of the Sonder Ditch had cream Volkswagens as their official vehicles.

'The bee has come to the honeypot,' thought Manfred, and smiled bleakly. He took Terry's elbow into the main concourse of the airport.

Terry waited while Manfred went through his ticket and immigration formalities. On the outside she was a demure and dutiful wife, but she also had seen the Volkswagen and inside she was itching and bubbling with excitement. Darting surreptitious glances from behind her sunglasses, looking for that tall broad-shouldered figure among the crowds.

It seemed a lifetime until she stood alone on the observation balcony with the wind whipping her piebald calfskin coat around her legs, and blowing her hair into a snapping, dancing tangle. The long shark-like shape of the Boeing jet crouched at the far end of the runway and as it started forward Terry turned from the balcony rail and ran back into the main building.

Rod was waiting for her just inside the doors, and he swung her off her feet.

'Gottcha!'

With her feet dangling, she put her arms around his neck and kissed him.

The watchers paused and then smiled, and there was a minor traffic jam at the head of the stairs.

'Come on,' she entreated, 'let's not waste a minute of it.'

He put her on her feet, and they ran down the staircase hand in hand. Terry paused only to dismiss the chauffeur, and then they ran through the car park like children let out of school, and clambered into the Volkswagen. Their luggage was on the back seat.

'Go,' she said, 'go as fast as you can!'

Twenty minutes later Rod pulled the Volkswagen to a tyre-squealing halt in front of the hangars at the private airfield.

The twin-engined Cessna stood on the tarmac. Both engines were ticking over in readiness, and the mechanic climbed down from the cockpit when he recognized Terry.

'Hello, Terry, right on time,' he greeted her.

'Hello, Hank. You've got her warmed up already. You are a sweety!'

'Filed your flight plan also. Nothing too good for my most favourite customer.' The mechanic was a chunky grizzled little man, and he looked at Rod curiously.

'Give you a hand with the bags,' he said.

By the time they had the luggage stowed away in its compartment, Terry was in the cockpit speaking to the control tower.

Rod climbed up into the passenger seat beside her.

Terry switched off her radio and leaned over Rod's lap to speak to Hank.

'Thanks, Hank.' She paused delicately, and then went on with a rush. 'Hank, if anyone asks you, I was on my own today, okay?'

'Okay.' Hank grinned at her. 'Happy landings.' And he closed the cockpit door, and Terry taxied out onto the runway.

'Is this yours? Rod asked. It was a 100,000 rand's worth of aircraft.

'Pops gave it to me for my birthday,' Terry replied. 'Do you like it?'

'Not bad,' Rod admitted.

Terry turned upwind and applied the wheel brakes while she ran the engines up to peak revs, testing their response.

Suddenly Rod realized that he was in the hands of a woman pilot. He fell silent and his nerves began to tighten up.

'Let's go,' said Terry and kicked off the brakes. The Cessna surged forward, and Rod gripped the arm rests and froze with his gaze fixed dead ahead.

'Relax, Ironsides,' Terry advised him without taking her eyes off the runway, 'I've been flying since I was sixteen.'

At 3,000 feet she levelled out and banked gently onto an easterly heading.

'Now that didn't hurt too much did it?' She smiled sideways at him.

'You are quite a girl,' he told her. 'You can do all sorts of tricks.'

'You just wait,' she warned him. 'You ain't seen nothing yet!'

They flew in silence until the Highveld had fallen away behind them, and they were over the dense green mattress of the Bushveld.

'I'm going to divorce him.' She broke the silence, and Rod was not surprised that they were experiencing the mental telepathy of closely attuned minds. He had been thinking about her husband also.

'Good,' he said.

'You think I'd have a chance with you if I did?'

'If you played your cards right, you might get that lucky.'

'Conceited swine,' she said. 'I don't know why I love you.'

'Do you?' he asked.

'Yes.'

'And I you.'

They relapsed into a contented silence, until Terry put the Cessna in a shallow dive.

'What's wrong?' Rod asked with alarm.

'Going down to have a look for game.'

They flew low over thick olive-green bush broken by veils of golden brown grass.

'There,' said Rod, pointing ahead. A line of fat black bugs moving across one of the open places. 'Buffalo!'

'And over there.' Terry pointed left.

'Zebra and wildebeeste,' Rod identified them. 'And there

is a giraffe.' Its long stalk of a neck stuck up like a periscope. It broke into an awkward stiff-legged run as the aircraft roared overhead.

'We have arrived.' Terry indicated a pair of round granite koppies on the horizon ahead. They were as symmetrical as a young girl's breasts, and as they drew nearer Rod made out the thatched roof of a large building standing in the hollow between the koppies. Beyond it a long straight landing-strip had been cut from the trees, and the fat white sausage of a wind sock flew from its pole.

Terry throttled back and circled the homestead. On the lawns half a dozen tiny figures waved up at the Cessna, and as they watched, two of the figures climbed into a toy Land Rover and set off for the landing-strip. A ribbon of white dust blew out from behind it.

'That's Hans,' Terry explained. 'We can go down now.'

She lined the Cessna up for its approach, and then let it sink down with the motors bumbling softly. The ground came up and jarred the undercarriage, then they were taxiing to meet the racing Land Rover.

The man who piled out of the Land Rover was white-haired, and sunburned like old leather.

'Mrs Steyner!' He was making no attempt to conceal his pleasure. 'It's been much too long. Where have you been?'

'I've been busy, Hans.'

'New York? What the hell for?' said Hans surprisingly.

'This is Mr Ironsides.' Terry introduced them. 'Rod, this is Hans Kruger.'

'Van Breda?' asked Hans as they shook hands. 'You related to the van Bredas from Caledon?'

'I don't think so,' Rod muttered weakly and looked at Terry appealingly.

'He is stone deaf,' Terry explained. 'Both his ear drums blown out by a hangfire in the 1930s. He won't admit it though.'

'I'm glad to hear it,' Hans nodded, happily. 'You always

210

were a healthy girl. I remember when you were a little piccaninny.'

'He is an absolute darling though, so is his wife. They look after the shooting lodge for Pops,' Terry told Rod.

'Good idea!' Hans agreed heartily. 'Let's get your bags in the Land Rover and go up to the house. I bet Mr van Breda could use a drink also.' And he winked at Rod.

The lodge had thatch and rough-hewn timber roofing, stone-flagged floors covered with cured animal skins and Kelim rugs. There was a walk-in fireplace flanked by gun racks on which were displayed fifty fine examples of the gunsmith's art. The furniture was massive and masculine, leather-cushioned and low. The Spanish plaster walls were hung with trophies, horned heads and native weapons.

A vast wooden staircase led up to the bedrooms that opened off the gallery above the main room. The bedrooms were air-conditioned, and after they had got rid of Hans and his fat wife, Rod and Terry tested the bed to see if it was suitable.

An hour and a half later the bed had been judged eminently satisfactory, and as they went down to pass further judgement on the gargantuan lunch that fat Mrs Hans had spread for them, Terry remarked, 'Has it ever occurred to you, Mr Ironsides, that there are parts of your anatomy other than your flanks which are ferrous in character?' Then she giggled and added softly, 'And thank the Lord for that!'

Lunch was an exhausting experience and Terry pointed out that there was little sense in going out before four o'clock as the game would still be in thick cover avoiding the midday heat, so they went back upstairs.

After four o'clock Rod selected a .375 magnum Holland and Holland rifle from the rack, filled a cartridge belt with ammunition from one of the drawers, and they went out to the Land Rover.

'How big is this place?' Rod asked as he turned the Land

Rover away from the gardens and took the track out into the virgin bush.

'You can drive for twenty miles in any direction and it's all ours. Over there our boundary runs against the Kruger National Park,' Terry answered.

They drove along the banks of the river, skirting sandbanks on which grew fluffy-headed reeds. The water ran fast between glistening black rocks, then spread into slow lazy pools.

They saw a dozen varieties of big game, stopping every few hundred yards to watch some lovely animal.

'Pops obviously doesn't allow shooting here,' Rod remarked, as a kudu bull with long spiral horns and trumpet-shaped ears studied them with big wet eyes from a range of thirty feet. 'The game is as tame as domestic cattle.'

'Only family are allowed to shoot,' Terry agreed. 'You qualify as family, however.'

Rod shook his head. 'It would be murder.' Rod indicated the kudu. 'That old fellow would eat out of your hand.'

'I'm glad you feel like that,' Terry said, and they drove on slowly.

The evening was not cool enough to warrant a log fire in the cavernous fireplace of the lodge. They lit one anyway because Rod decided it would be pleasant to sit in front of a big, leaping fire, drink whisky and hold the girl you love.

– 59 –

When Inspector Grobbelaar lowered his teacup, there was a white scum of cream on the tips of his moustache. He licked it off carefully, and looked across at Sergeant Hugo.

'Who have we got next?' he asked.

Hugo consulted his notebook.

'Philemon N'gabai.' He read out the name, and Grobbelaar sighed.

'Number forty-eight, only sixteen more.' The single smeary fingerprint on the fragment of glass from the gold container had been examined by the fingerprint department. They had provided a list of sixty-four names any one of which might be the owner of that print. Each of them had to be interrogated, it was a lengthy and so far unrewarding labour.

'What do we know about friend Philemon?' Grobbelaar asked.

'He is approximately forty years old. A Shangaan from Mozambique. Height 5' 7½", weight 146 lb. Crippled right leg. Two previous convictions. 1956: 60 days for bicycle theft. 1962: 90 days for stealing a camera from a parked car,' Hugo read from the file.

'At one hundred and forty-six pounds I don't see him breaking many necks. But send him in, let's talk to him,' Grobbelaar suggested and dunked his moustache in the tea cup again. Hugo nodded to the African Sergeant and he opened the door to admit Crooked Leg and his escort of an African constable.

They advanced to the desk at which the two detectives sat in their shirt sleeves. No one spoke. The two interrogators subjected him to a calculated and silent scrutiny to set him at as great a disadvantage as possible.

Grobbelaar prided himself on being able to sniff out a guilty conscience at fifty paces, and Philemon N'gabai reeked of guilt. He could not stand still, he was sweating heavily, and his eyes darted from floor to ceiling. He was guilty as hell, but not necessarily of murder. Grobbelaar did not feel the slightest confidence as he shook his head sorrowfully and asked, 'Why did you do it, Philemon? We have found the marks of your hand on the gold bottle.'

The effect on Crooked Leg was instantaneous and

dramatic. His lips parted and began to tremble, saliva dripped onto his chin. His eyes for the first time fixed on Grobbelaar's face, wide and staring.

'Hello! Hello!' Grobbelaar thought, straightening in his chair, coming completely alert. He sensed Hugo's quickening interest beside him.

'You know what they do to people who kill, Philemon? They take them away to . . .' Grobbelaar did not have an opportunity to finish.

With a howl Crooked Leg darted for the door. His crippled gait was deceptive, he was fast as a ferret. He had the door open before the Bantu Sergeant collared him and dragged him gibbering and struggling back into the room.

'The gold, but not the man! I did not kill the Portuguese,' he babbled, and Grobbelaar and Hugo exchanged glances.

'Pay dirt!' Hugo exclaimed with deep satisfaction.

'Bull's eye!' agreed Grobbelaar, and smiled, a rare and fleeting occurrence.

– 60 –

'You see it has a little light that comes on to show you where the keyhole is,' said the salesman pointing to the ignition switch on the dashboard.

'Ooh! Johnny, see that!' Hettie gushed, but Johnny Delange had his head under the bonnet of the big glossy Ford Mustang.

'Why don't you sit in her?' the salesman suggested. He was very cute really, Hattie decided, with dreamy eyes and the most *fabulous* sideburns.

'Ooh! Yes, I'd love to.' She manoeuvred her bottom into the leather bucket seat of the sports car. Her skirt pulled up, and the salesman's dreamy eyes followed the hem all the way.

'Can you adjust the seat?' Hettie asked, innocently looking up at him.

'Here, I'll show you.' He leaned into the interior of the Mustang and reached across Hettie's lap. His hand brushed over her thigh, and Hettie pretended not to notice his touch. He smelled of Old Spice after-shave lotion.

'That's better!' Hettie murmured, and wriggled into a more comfortable position, contriving to make the movement provocative and revealing.

The salesman was encouraged, he lingered with his wrist just touching a sleek thigh.

'What's the compression ratio on this model?' Johnny Delange demanded as he emerged from the engine, and the salesman straightened up quickly and hurried to join him.

An hour later Johnny signed the purchase contract, and both he and Hettie shook the salesman's hand.

'Let me give you my card,' the salesman insisted, but Johnny had returned to his new toy, and Hettie took the cardboard business card.

'Call me if you need anything, anything at all,' said the salesman with heavy significance.

'Dennis Langley. Sales Manager,' Hettie read out aloud. 'My! You're very young to be Sales Manager.'

'Not all that young!'

'I'll bet,' Hettie murmured, and her eyes were suddenly bold. She ran the tip of a pink tongue over her lips. 'I won't lose it,' she promised, and placing the card in her handbag, walked to the Mustang, leaving him with a tantalizing promise and a memory of swaying hips and clicking heels.

They raced the new Mustang as far as Potchefstroom; Hettie encouraging Johnny to overtake slower vehicles with inches to spare for oncoming traffic. With horn blaring he tore over blind rises, forking ringed fingers at the protesting toots of other drivers. They had the speedometer registering

120 mph on the return run, and it was dark as they pulled into the driveway and Johnny hit the brakes hard to avoid running into the back of a big black Daimler that was parked outside their front door.

'Jesus,' gasped Johnny. 'That's Dr Steyner's bus!'

'Who is Dr Steyner?' Hettie demanded.

'Hell, he's one of the big shots from Head Office.'

'You're kidding!' Hettie challenged him.

'Truth!' Johnny affirmed. 'One of the real big shots.'

'Bigger than Mr Ironsides?' The General Manager of the Sonder Ditch was as high up the social ladder as Hettie had ever looked.

'Tin Ribs is chicken feed compared to this joker. Just look at his bus, it's five times better than Tin Ribs's clapped-out old Maserati.'

'Gee!' Hettie could follow the logic of this line of argument. 'What's he want with us?'

'I don't know,' Johnny admitted with a twinge of anxiety. 'Let's go and find out.'

The lounge of the Delange home was not the setting which showed Dr Manfred Steyner to best advantage.

He sat on the edge of a scarlet and gold plastic-covered armchair as stiff and awkward as the packs of china dogs that stood on every table and shelf of the show cabinet, or the porcelain wild ducks which flew in diminishing perspective along the pale pink painted wall. In contrast to the tinsel Christmas decorations that festooned the ceiling and the gay greeting cards that Hettie had pinned to strips of green ribbon, Manfred's black homburg and astrakhan-collared overcoat were unnecessarily severe.

'You will forgive my presumption,' he greeted them without rising. 'You were not at home and your maid let me in.'

'You're welcome, I'm sure,' Hettie simpered.

'Of course you are, Dr Steyner,' Johnny supported her.

'Ah! So you know who I am?' Manfred asked with satisfaction. This would make his task so much easier.

'Of course we do.' Hettie went to him and offered her hand. 'I am Hettie Delange, how do you do?'

With horror Manfred saw that her armpit was unshaven, filled with damp ginger curls. Hettie had not bathed since the previous evening. Manfred's nostrils twitched and he fought down a queasy wave of nausea.

'Delange, I want to speak to you alone.' He cowered away from Hettie's overwhelming physical presence.

'Sure.' Johnny was eager to please. 'How about you making us some coffee, honey,' he asked Hettie.

Ten minutes later Manfred sank with relief into the lush upholstery of the Daimler's rear seat. He ignored the two Delanges waving their farewells, and closed his eyes. It was done. Tomorrow morning Johnny Delange would be on shift and drilling into the glassy green rock of the Big Dipper.

By noon Manfred would own quarter of a million shares in the Sonder Ditch.

In a week he would be a rich man.

In a month he would be divorced from Theresa Steyner. He would sue with all possible notoriety on the grounds of adultery. He no longer needed her.

The chauffeur drove him back to Johannesburg.

It began on the floor of the Johannesburg Stock Exchange.

For some months nearly all the activity had been in the industrial counters, centring about the Alex Sagov group of companies and their merger negotiations.

The only spark of life in the mining and mining financials had been Anglo American Corporation and De Beers Deferred rights issues, but this was now old news and the prices had settled at their new levels. So it was that nobody was expecting fireworks when the call over of the gold mining counters began. The brokers' clerks crowding the floor were quietly spoken and behaved, when the first squib popped.

'Buy Sonder Ditch,' from one end of the hall.

'Buy Sonder Ditch,' a voice raised.

'Buy!' The throng stirred, heads turned.

'Buy.' The brokers suddenly agitated swirled in little knots, broke and reformed as transactions were completed. The price jumped fifty cents, and a broker ran from the floor to confer with his principal.

Here a broker thumped another on the back to gain his attention, and his urgency was infectious.

'Buy! Buy!'

'What the hell's happening?'

'Where is the buying coming from?'

'It's local!'

The price hit ten rand a share, and then the panic began in earnest.

'It's overseas buying.'

'Eleven rand!'

Brokers rushed to telephone warnings to favoured clients that a bull run was developing.

'Twelve fifty. It's only local buying.'

'Buy at best. Buy five thousand.'

Clerks raced back onto the floor carrying the hastily telephoned instructions, and plunged into the hysterical trading.

'Jesus Christ! Thirteen rand, sell now. Take your profit! It can't go much higher.'

'Thirteen seventy-five, it's overseas buying. Buy at best.'

In fifty brokers' offices around the country, the professionals who spent their lives hovering over the tickers regained their balance and, cursing themselves for having been taken unawares, they scrambled onto the bull wagon. Others, the more canny ones, recognized the makings of a sick run and off-loaded their holdings, selling industrial shares as well as mining shares. Prices ran amok.

At ten-fifteen there was a priority call from the offices of the Minister of Finance in Pretoria to the office of the President of the Johannesburg Stock Exchange.

'What are you going to do?'

'We haven't decided. We won't close the floor if we can possibly help it.'

'Don't let it go too far. Keep me informed.'

Sixteen rand and still spiralling when at eleven o'clock South African time, the London Stock Exchange came in. For the first fifteen wild minutes the price of Sonder Ditch gold mining rocketed in sympathy with the Johannesburg market.

Then suddenly and unexpectedly the Sonder Ditch shares ran head-on into massive selling pressure. Not only the Sonder Ditch, but all the Kitchenerville gold mining companies staggered as the pressure increased. The prices wavered, rallied a few shillings and then fell back, wavered again, and then crashed downwards, plummeting far below their opening prices.

'Sell!' was the cry. 'Sell at best!' Within minutes freshly-made paper fortunes were wiped away.

When the price of the Sonder Ditch gold mining shares

fell to five rand seventy-five cents, the committee of the Johannesburg Stock Exchange closed the door in the interests of the national welfare, preventing further trading.

But in New York, Paris and London the investing public continued to beat South African gold mining shares to death.

In the air-conditioned office of a skyscraper building, the little bald-headed man was smashing his balled fist onto the desk top of his superior officer.

'I told you not to trust him,' he was almost sobbing with anger. 'The fat greedy slug. One million dollars wasn't enough for him! No, he had to blow the whole deal!'

'Please, Colonel,' his chief intervened. 'Control yourself. Let us make a fair and objective appraisal of this financial activity.'

The bald-headed man sank back into his chair, and tried to light a cigarette with hands that trembled so violently as to extinguish the flame of his lighter.

'It sticks out a mile.' He flicked the lighter again, and puffed quickly. 'The first activity on the Johannesburg Exchange was Dr Steyner being clever. Buying up shares on the strength of our dummy report. That was quite natural and we expected it, in fact we wanted that to happen. It took suspicion away from us.' His cigarette had gone out, the tip was wet with spit. He threw it away and lit another.

'Fine! Everything was fine up to then. Dr Steyner had committed financial suicide, and we were on the pig's back.' He sucked at his new cigarette. 'Then! Then our fat friend pulls the big double-cross and starts selling the Kitchenerville shares short. He must have gone into the market for millions.'

'Can we abort the operation at this late date?' his chief asked.

'Not a chance.' The bald head shook vigorously. 'I have

sent a cable to our fat friend ordering him to freeze the work on the tunnel, but can you imagine him obeying that order? He is financially committed for millions of dollars and he will protect that investment with every means at his disposal.'

'Could we not warn the management of the Sonder Ditch company?'

'That would put the finger squarely on us, would it not?'

'Hmm!' the chief nodded. 'We could send them an anonymous warning.'

'Who would put any credence on that?'

'You're right,' the chief sighed. 'We will just have to batten down our hatches and ride out the storm. Sit tight and deny everything.'

'That is all we can do.' The cigarette had gone out again, and there were bits of tobacco in his moustache. The little man flicked his lighter.

'The bastard, the fat, greedy bastard!' he muttered.

– 62 –

Johnny and Big King rode up shoulder to shoulder in the cage. It had been a good shift. Despite the hardness of the serpentine rock that cut down the drilling rate by fifty per cent, they had been able to get in five blasts that day. Johnny reckoned they had driven more than half-way through the Big Dipper. There was no night shift working now. Campbell had gone back to the stopes, so the honour of holing through would be Johnny's. He was excited at the prospect. Tomorrow he would be through into the unknown.

'Until tomorrow, Big King,' he said as they reached the surface and stepped out of the cage.

They separated, Big King heading for the Bantu hostel, Johnny to the glistening new Mustang in the car park.

Big King went straight to the Shangaan Induna's cottage without changing from his working clothes. He stood in the doorway and the Induna looked up from the letter he was writing.

'What news, my father?' Big King asked.

'The worst,' the Induna told him softly. 'The police have taken Crooked Leg.'

'Crooked Leg would not betray me,' Big King declared, but without conviction.

'Would you expect him to die in your place?' asked the Induna. 'He must protect himself.'

'I did not mean to kill him,' Big King explained miserably. 'I did not mean to kill the Portuguese, it was the gun.'

'I know, my son.' The Induna's voice was husky with helpless pity.

Big King turned from the doorway and walked down across the lawns to the ablution block. The spring and swagger had gone from his step. He walked listlessly, slouching, dragging his feet.

– 63 –

Manfred Steyner sat at his desk. His hands lay on the blotter before him, one thumb wearing a turban of crisp white bandage. His only movement was the steady beat of a pulse in his throat and a nerve that fluttered in one eyelid. He was deathly pale, and a light sheen of perspiration gave his features the look of having been sculptured from washed marble.

The volume of the radio was turned high, so the voice of the announcer boomed and reverberated from the panelled walls.

'The climax of the drama was reached at eleven forty-five South African time when the President of the Johannesburg Stock Exchange declared the floor closed and all further trading suspended.

'Latest reports from the Tokyo Stock Exchange are that Sonder Ditch gold mining shares were being traded at the equivalent of four rand forty cents. This compares with the morning's opening price of the same share on the Johannesburg Stock Exchange of nine rand forty-five cents.

'A spokesman for the South African Government stated that although no reason for these extraordinary price fluctuations was apparent, the Minister of Mines, Doctor Carel De Wet, had ordered a full-scale commission of inquiry.'

Manfred Steyner stood up from his desk and went through into the bathroom. With his flair for figures he did not need pen and paper to compute that the shares he had purchased that morning had depreciated in value by well over one million rand at the close of business that evening.

He knelt on the tiled floor in front of the toilet bowl and vomited.

– 64 –

The sky was darkening rapidly, for the sun had long ago sunk below a blazing horizon.

Rod heard the whisper of wings, and strained his eyes upwards into the gloom. They came in fast, in V-formation, slanting down towards the pool of the river. He stood up from the blind and swung the shotgun on them, leading well ahead of the line of flight.

He squeezed off both barrels. Wham! Wham! And the duck broke formation and rocketed upwards, whirring aloft on noisy wings.

'Damn it!' said Rod.

'What's wrong, dead-eye Dick, did you miss?' asked Terry.

223

'The light's too bad.'

'Excuses! Excuses!' Terry stood up beside him, and Rod pushed a balled fist lightly against her cheek.

'That's enough from you, woman. Let's go home.'

Carrying the shotguns and bunches of dead duck, they trudged along the bank in the dusk to the waiting Land Rover.

It was completely dark as they drove back to the lodge.

'What a wonderful day it's been,' Terry murmured dreamily. 'If for nothing else, I will always be grateful to you for teaching me how to enjoy my life.'

Back at the lodge, they bathed and changed into fresh clothes. For dinner they had wild duck and pineapple, with salads from Mrs Fat Hans' vegetable garden. Afterwards, they sprawled on the leopard-skin rugs in front of the fireplace and watched the log fire without talking, relaxed and happy and tired.

'My God, it's almost nine o'clock.' Terry checked her wristwatch. 'I fancy a bit of bed myself, how about you, Mr Ironsides?'

'Let's hear the nine o'clock news first.'

'Oh, Rod! Nobody ever listens to the news here. This is fairyland!'

Rod switched on the radio and the first words froze them both. They were 'Sonder Ditch'.

In horrified silence they listened to the report. Rod's expression was granite-hard, his mouth a tight grim line. When the news report ended, Rod switched off the radio set and lit a cigarette.

'There is trouble,' he said. 'Big trouble. I'm sorry, Terry, we must go back. As soon as possible. I have to get back to the mine.'

'I know,' Terry agreed immediately. 'But Rod, I can't take off from this landing-strip in the dark. There is no flare path.'

'We'll leave at first light.'

Rod slept very little that night. Whenever she woke, Terry sensed him lying unsleeping, worrying. Twice she heard him get up and go to the bathroom.

In the very early hours of the morning she woke from her own troubled sleep and saw him silhouetted against the starlit window. He was smoking a cigarette and staring out into the darkness. It was the first night they had spent together without making love. In the dawn Rod was haggard and puffy-eyed.

They were airborne at eight o'clock and they landed in Johannesburg a little after ten.

Rod went straight to the telephone in Hank's office and Lily Jordan answered his call.

'Miss Jordan, what the hell is happening? Is everything all right?'

'Is that you, Mr Ironsides. Oh! Thank God! Thank God you've come, something terrible has happened!'

– 65 –

Johnny Delange blew the face of the drive twice before nine o'clock, cutting thirty feet further into the glassy green dyke.

He had found that by drilling his cutter blast holes an additional three feet deeper, he could achieve a shatter effect on the serpentine rock which more than compensated for the additional drilling time. This next blast he was going to flout standard regulations and experiment with double-charging his cutter holes. He would need additional explosives.

'Big King,' he shouted to make himself heard above the roar of drills. 'Take a gang back to the shaft station. Pick up six cases of Dynagel.'

He watched Big King and his gang retreat back down the drive, and then he lit a cigarette and turned his

225

attention to his machine boys. They were poised before the rock face, sweating behind their drills. The dark rock of the dyke absorbed the light from the overhead electric bulbs. It made the end of the drive a gloomy place, filled with a sense of foreboding.

Johnny began to think about Davy. He was aware suddenly of a sense of disquiet, and he moved restlessly. He felt the hair on his forearms come slowly erect, each on a separate goose pimple. *Davy is here*. He knew it suddenly, and surely. His flesh crawled and he went cold with dread. He turned quickly and looked over his shoulder. The tunnel behind him was deserted, and Johnny gave a sickly grin.

'Shaya, madoda,' he called loudly and unnecessarily to his gang. They could not hear him above the roar of the drills, but the sound of his own voice helped reassure him.

Yet the creepy sensation was still with him. He felt that Davy was still there, trying to tell him something.

Johnny fought the sensation. He walked quickly forward, standing close to his machine boys, as though to draw comfort from their physical presence. It did not help. His nerves were shrieking now, and he felt himself beginning to sweat.

Suddenly the machine boy who was drilling the cutter hole in the centre of the face staggered backwards.

'Hey!' Johnny shouted at him, then he saw that water was spurting in fine needle jets from around the drill steel. Something was squeezing the drill steel out of its hole, like toothpaste out of a tube. It was pushing the machine boy backwards.

'Hey!' Johnny started forward and at that instant the heavy metal drill was fired out of the rock with the force of a cannon ball. It decapitated the machine boy, tearing his head from his body with such savagery that his carcass was thrown far back down the drive, his blood spraying the dark rock walls.

From the drill hole shot a solid jet of water. It came out under such pressure that when it caught the machine boy's assistant in the chest it stove in his ribs as though he had been hit by a speeding automobile.

'Out!' yelled Johnny. 'Get out!' And the rock face exploded. It blew outwards with greater force than if it had been blasted with Dynagel. It killed Johnny Delange instantly. He was smashed to a bloody pulp by the flying rock. It killed every man in his gang with him, and immediately afterwards the monstrous burst of water that poured from the face picked up their mutilated remains and swept them down the drive.

Big King was at the shaft station when they heard the water coming. It sounded like an express train in a tunnel, a dull bellow of irresistible power. The water was pushing the air from the drive ahead of it, so that a hurricane of wind came roaring from the mouth of the drive, blowing out a cloud of dust and loose rubbish.

Big King and his gang stood and stared in uncomprehending terror until the head of the column of water shot from the drive, frothing solid, carrying with it a plug of debris and human remains.

Bursting into the T-junction of the main 66 level haulage, the strength of the flood was reduced, yet still it swept down towards the lift station in a waist-deep wall.

'This way!' Big King was the first to move. He leapt for the steel emergency ladder that led up to the level above. The rest of his gang were not fast enough, the water picked them up and crushed them against the steel-mesh barrier that guarded the shaft. The crest of the wave burst around Big King's legs, sucking at him, but he tore himself from its grip and climbed to safety.

Beneath him the water poured into the shaft like bath

water into a plug hole, forming a spinning whirlpool about the collar as it roared down to flood the workings below 66 level.

– 66 –

Leaving Terry at the airfield to solicit transport from Hank, the mechanic, Rod drove directly to the head of No. 1 shaft of the Sonder Ditch. He jumped from the Volkswagen into the clamouring crowd clustered above the shaft head.

Dimitri was wide-eyed and distracted, beside him Big King towered like a black colossus.

'What happened?' Rod demanded.

'Tell him,' Dimitri instructed Big King.

'I was at the shaft with my gang. A river leaped from the mouth of the drive, a great river of water running faster than the Zambesi in flood; roaring like a lion the water ate all the men with me. I alone climbed above it.'

'We've hit a big one, Rod,' Dimitri interrupted. 'It's pouring in fast. We calculate it will flood the entire workings up to 66 level in four hours from now.'

'Have you cleared the mine?' Rod demanded.

'All the men are out except Delange and his gang. They were in the drive. They've been chopped, I'm afraid,' Dimitri answered.

'Have you warned the other mines we could have a burst through into their workings?'

'Yes, they are pulling all their shifts out.'

'Right.' Rod set off for the blast control room with Dimitri trotting to keep up with him. 'Give me your keys, and find the foreman electrician.'

Within minutes the three of them were crowded into the tiny concrete control room.

'Check in the special circuit,' Rod instructed. 'I'm going to shoot the drop-blast matt and seal off the drive.'

The foreman electrician worked quickly at the control panel. He looked up at Rod.

'Ready!' he said.

'Check her in,' Rod nodded.

The foreman threw the switch. The three of them caught their breath together.

Dimitri said it for them: 'Red!'

On the control panel of the special circuit the red bulb glared balefully at them, the Cyclops eye of the god of despair.

'Christ!' swore the foreman. 'The circuit is shot. The water must have torn the wires out.'

'It may be a fault in the board.'

'No.' The foreman shook his head with certainty.

'We've had it,' whispered Dimitri. 'Goodbye the Sonder Ditch!'

Rod burst out of the control room into the expectant crowd outside.

'Johnson!' He singled out one of his mine captains. 'Go down to the Yacht Club at the dam, get me the rubber rescue dinghy. Quick as you can, man.'

The man scurried away, and Rod turned on the electrician foreman as he emerged from the control room.

'Get me a battery hand-operated blaster, a reel of wire, pliers, two coils of nylon rope. Hurry!'

The foreman went.

'Rod.' Dimitri caught his arm. 'What are you going to do?'

'I'm going down there. I'm going to find the break in the circuit and I'm going to blast her by hand.'

'Jesus!' Dimitri gasped. 'You are crazy, Rod. You'll kill yourself for sure!'

Rod completely ignored his protest.

'I want one man with me. A strong man. The strongest there is, we will have to drag the dinghy against the flood.' Rod looked about him. Big King was standing by the banksman's office. The two of them were tall enough to face each other over the heads of the men between them.

'Will you come with me, Big King?' Rod asked.

'Yes,' said Big King.

– 67 –

In less than twenty minutes they were ready. Rod and Big King were stripped down to singlets and bathing-trunks. They wore canvas tennis shoes to protect their feet, and the hard helmets on their heads were incongruous against the rest of their attire.

The rubber dinghy was ex-naval disposal. A nine-foot air-filled mattress, so light that a man could lift it with one hand. Into it was packed the equipment they would need for the task ahead. A water-proof bag contained the battery blaster, the reel of insulated wire, the pliers and a spare lantern. Lashed to the eyelets along the sides of the dinghy were two coils of light nylon rope, a small crowbar, an axe and a razor-sharp machete in a leather sheath. To the bows of the dinghy were fastened a pair of looped nylon towing lines.

'What else will you need, Rod?' Dimitri asked.

Rod shook his head thoughtfully. 'That's it, Dimitri. That should do it.'

'Right!' Dimitri beckoned and four men came forward and carried the dinghy into the waiting cage.

'Let's go,' said Dimitri and followed the dinghy into the cage. Big King went next and Rod paused a second to look up at the sky. It was very blue and bright.

Before the onsetter could close the shutter door, a Silver Cloud Rolls-Royce came gliding onto the bank. From the rear door emerged first Hurry Hirschfeld and then Terry Steyner.

'Ironsides!' roared Hurry. 'What the hell is going on?'

'We've hit water,' Rod answered him from the cage.

'Water? Where did it come from?'

'Beyond the Big Dipper.'

'You drove through the Big Dipper?'

'Yes.'

'You bastard, you've drowned the Sonder Ditch,' roared Hurry, advancing on the cage.

'Not yet, I haven't,' Rod contradicted.

'Rod.' Terry was white-faced beside her grandfather. 'You can't go down there.' She started forward.

Rod pushed the onsetter aside and pulled down the steel shutter door of the cage. Terry threw herself against the steel mesh of the guard barrier, but the cage was gone into the earth.

'Rod,' she whispered, and Hurry Hirschfeld put his arm around her shoulders and led her to the Rolls-Royce.

From the back seat of the Rolls, Hurry Hirschfeld was conducting a Kangaroo Court Trial of Rodney Ironsides. One by one he called for the line managers of the Sonder Ditch and questioned them. Even those who were loyal to Rod could say little in his defence, and there were others who took the opportunity to level old scores with Rodney Ironsides.

Sitting beside her grandfather, Terry heard such a condemnation of the man she loved as to chill her to the depths of her soul. There was no doubt that Rodney Ironsides, without Head Office sanction, had instituted a new development so risky and contrary to company policy as to be criminal in concept.

'Why did he do it?' muttered Hurry Hirschfeld. He seemed bewildered. 'What could he possibly achieve by driving through the Big Dipper? It looks like a deliberate attempt to sabotage the Sonder Ditch.' Hurry's anger began to seethe within him. 'The bastard! He has drowned the Sonder Ditch and killed dozens of men.' He punched his fist into the palm of his hand. 'I'll make him pay for this. I'll break him, so help me God, I'll smash him! I'll bring criminal charges against him. Malicious damage to property. Manslaughter. Culpable homicide! By Jesus, I'll have his guts for this!'

Listening to Hurry ranting and threatening, Terry could keep silent no longer.

'It wasn't his fault, Pops. Truly it wasn't. He was forced to do it.'

'Ha!' snorted Hurry. 'I heard you at the pithead a few minutes ago. Just what is this man to you, Missy, that you spring to his defence so nobly?'

'Pops, please believe me.' Her eyes were enormous in her pale face.

'Why should I believe you? The two of you are obviously up to mischief together. Naturally you will try and protect him.'

'Listen to me at least,' she pleaded, and Hurry checked the run of his tongue and breathing heavily he turned to face her.

'This better be good, young lady,' he warned her.

In her agitation she told it badly, and halfway through she realized that she wasn't even convincing herself. Hurry's expression became more and more bleak, until he interrupted her impatiently.

'Good God, Theresa, this isn't like you. To try and put the blame for this onto your own husband! That's despicable! To try and switch the blame for this . . .'

'It's true! As God is my witness.' Terry was almost in tears, she was tugging at Hurry's sleeve in her agitation. 'Rod was forced to do it. He had no option.'

'You have proof of this?' Hurry asked drily, and Terry fell silent, staring at him dumbly. What proof was there?

– 68 –

The cage checked and slowed as it approached 65 level. The lights were still burning, but the workings were deserted. They lugged the dinghy out onto the station.

They could hear the dull waterfall roar of the flood on the level below them. The displacement of huge volumes of water disturbed the air so that a strong cool breeze was blowing up the shaft.

'Big King and I will go down the emergency ladder. You will lower the dinghy to us afterwards,' Rod told Dimitri. 'Make sure all the equipment is tied into it.'

'Right.' Dimitri nodded.

All was in readiness. The men who had come down with them in the cage were waiting expectantly. Rod could find no reason for further delay. He felt something cold and heavy settle in his guts.

'Come on, Big King.' And he went to the steel ladder.

'Good luck, Rod.' Dimitri's voice floated down to him, but Rod saved his breath for that cold dark climb downwards.

All the lights had fused on 66 level, and in the beam of his lamp the water below him was black and agitated. It poured into the mouth of the shaft, bending the mesh barrier inwards. The mesh acted as a gigantic sieve, straining the floating rubbish from the flood. Amongst the timber and planking, the sodden sacking and unrecognizable objects, Rod made out the water-logged corpses of the dead pressed against the wire.

He climbed down and gingerly lowered himself into the water. Instantly it dragged at his lower body, shocking in its power. It was waist-deep here, but he found that by bracing his body against the steel ladder he could maintain his footing.

Big King climbed down beside him, and Rod had to raise his voice above the hissing thunder of water.

'All right?'

'Yes. Let them send down the boat.'

Rod flashed his lamp up the shaft, and within minutes the dinghy was swaying slowly down to them. They reached up and guided it right side up to the surface of the water, before untying the rope.

The dinghy was sucked firmly against the wire mesh, and Rod checked its contents quickly. All was secure.

'Right.' Rod tied a bight of the nylon rope around his waist, and climbed up the wire mesh barrier until he could reach the roof of the tunnel. Behind him Big King was paying out the nylon line.

Rod leaned out until he could get his hands on the compressed air pipes that ran along the roof of the tunnel. The pipes were as thick as a man's wrist, bolted securely into the hanging wall of the drive; they would support a man's weight with ease. Rod settled his grip firmly on the piping and then kicked his feet free from the barrier. He hung above the rushing waters, his feet just brushing the surface.

Hand over hand, swinging forward with feet dangling, he started up the tunnel. The nylon rope hung down behind him like a long white tail. It was 300 feet to where the water boiled from the drive into the main haulage, and Rod's shoulder muscles were shrieking in protest before he reached it. It seemed that his arms were being wrenched from their sockets, for the weight of the nylon rope that was dragging in the water was fast becoming intolerable.

There was a back eddy in the angle formed by the drive and the haulage. Here the flood swirled in a vortex, and

234

Rod lowered himself slowly into it. The water buffeted him, but again he was able to cower against the side wall of the haulage and hold his footing. Quickly he began tying the rope onto the rawlbolts that were driven into the sidewall to consolidate the rock. Within minutes he had established a secure base from which to operate, and when he flashed his lamp back down the haulage he saw Big King following him along the compressed air piping.

Big King dropped into the waist-deep water beside Rod, and they gripped the nylon rope and rested their burning arm muscles.

'Ready?' asked Rod at last, and Big King nodded.

They laid hold of the rope that led back to the dinghy and hauled upon it. For a moment nothing happened, the other end might just as well have been anchored to a mountain.

'Together!' grunted Rod, and they recovered a foot of rope.

'Again!' And they drew the dinghy inch by inch up the haulage against the rush of water.

Their hands were bleeding when they at last pulled the laden dinghy up to their own position and anchored it to the rawlbolts beside them. It bounced and bobbed with the water drumming against its underside.

Neither Rod nor Big King could talk. They hung exhausted on the body lines with the water ripping at their skin and gasped for breath.

At last Rod looked up at Big King, and in the lamp light he saw his own doubts reflected in Big King's eyes. The drop-blast matt was 1,000 feet up the drive. The strength and speed of the water in the drive was almost double what it was in the haulage. Could they ever fight their way against such primeval forces as these that were now unleashed about them?

'I will go next,' Big King said, and Rod nodded his agreement.

The huge Bantu drew himself up the rope until he could reach the compressed air pipe. His skin in the lamplight glistened like that of a porpoise. Hand over hand he disappeared into the gaping black maw of the drive. His lamp threw deformed and monstrous shadows upon the walls of rock.

When Big King's lamp flashed the signal to him, Rod climbed up to the pipe and followed him into the drive. Three hundred feet later he found Big King had established another base. But here they were exposed to the full force of the flood, and they were pulled so violently against the body lines that the harsh nylon smeared the skin from their bodies. Together they dragged the dinghy up to them and anchored it.

Rod was sobbing softly as he held his torn hands to his chest and wondered if he could do it again.

'Ready?' Big King asked beside him, and Rod nodded. He reached up and placed the raw flesh of his palms onto the metal piping, and felt the tears of pain flood his eyes. He blinked them back and dragged himself forward.

Vaguely he realized that should he fall, he was a dead man. The flood would sweep him away, dragging him along the jagged side walls of the drive, ripping his flesh from the bone, and finally hurling him against the mesh surrounding the shaft to crush the life from his body.

He went on until he knew he could go no farther. Then he selected a rawlbolt in the side wall and looped the rope through it. And they repeated the whole heart-breaking procedure. Twice as he strained against the dinghy rope Rod saw his vision explode into stars and pinwheels. Each time he dragged himself back from the brink of unconsciousness by sheer force of will.

The example that Big King was setting was the inspiration which kept Rod from failing. Big King worked without change of expression, but his eyes were bloodshot with exertion. Only once Rod heard him grunt like a gut-shot lion, and there was bright blood on the rope where he touched it.

Rod knew he could not give in while Big King held on.

Reality dissolved slowly into a dark roaring nightmare of pain, wherein muscles and bone were loaded beyond all endurance, and yet continued to function. It seemed that for all time Rod had hung on arms that were leadened and slow with exhaustion. He was inching his way along the compressed air pipe for yet another advance up the drive. Sweat running into his eyes was blurring his vision, so at first he did not credit what he saw ahead of him in the darkness.

He shook his head to clear his eyes, and then squinted along the beam of his lamp. A heavy timber structure was hanging drunkenly from the roof of the drive. The bolts that held it were resisting the efforts of the water to tear it loose.

Rod realized abruptly that this was what remained of the frame which had held the ventilation doors. The doors were gone, ripped away, but the frame was still in position. He knew that just beyond the ventilation doors the drop-blast matt began. They had reached it!

New strength flowed into his body and he swung forward along the pipe. The timber frame made a fine anchor point and Rod secured the rope to it, and flashed back the signal to Big King. He hung in the loop of rope and rested awhile, then he forced himself to take an interest in his surroundings. He played the beam over the distorted timber frame and saw instantly why the blasting circuit had been broken.

In the lamp light the distinctive green plastic-coated blasting cable hung in festoons from the roof of the drive; clearly it had become entangled in the ventilation doors and been severed when they were ripped away. The loose end of the cable dangled to the surface of the racing water.

Rod fastened his eyes on it, drawing comfort and strength from the knowledge that they would not have to continue their agonized journey down the drive.

When Big King came up out of the gloom, Rod indicated the dangling cable.

'There!' he gasped, and Big King narrowed his eyes in acknowledgement; he was unable to speak.

It was five minutes before they could commence the excruciating business of hauling the dinghy up and securing it to the door frame.

Again they rested. Their movements were slowing up drastically. Neither of them had much strength left to draw upon.

'Get hold of the end of the cable.' Rod instructed Big King, and he dragged himself over the side of the dinghy and lay sprawled full-length on the floor boards.

His weight forced the dinghy deeper, increasing its resistance to the racing water, and the rope strained against the wooden frame. Rod began clumsily to unpack the battery blaster. Big King stood waist-deep clinging with one arm to the wooden frame, reaching forward with the other towards the end of the green-coated cable. It danced just beyond his fingertips, and he edged forward against the current, steadying himself against the timber frame, placing a greater strain on the retaining bolts.

His fingers closed on the cable and with a grunt of satisfaction he passed it back to Rod.

Working with painstaking deliberation, Rod connected the crocodile clips from the reel of wire to the loose end of the green cable. Rod's plan was for both he and Big King to climb aboard the dinghy, and, paying out the nylon rope, let themselves be carried back down the drive. At the same time they would be letting the wire run from its reel. At a safe distance they would fire the drop-blast matt.

Rod's fingers were swollen and numbed. The minutes

passed as he completed his preparations and all that while the strain on the wooden frame was heavy and constant.

Rod looked up from his task, and crawled to his knees.

'All right, Big King,' he wheezed as he knelt in the bows of the dinghy and gripped the wooden frame to steady the dinghy. 'Come aboard. We are ready.'

Big King waded forward and at that instant the retaining bolts on one side of the heavy timber frame gave way. With a rending, tearing sound the frame slewed across the tunnel. The beams of timber crossed each other like the blades of a pair of gigantic scissors. Both Rod's arms were between the beams. The bones in his forearms snapped with the loud crackle of breaking sticks.

With a scream of pain Rod collapsed onto the floorboards of the dinghy, his arms useless, sticking out at absurd angles from their shattered bones. Three feet away Big King was still in the water. His mouth was wide open, but no sound issued from his throat. He stood still as a black statue and his eyes bulged from their sockets. Even through his own suffering Rod was horrified by the expression on Big King's contorted features.

Below the surface of the water the bottom timber beams had performed the same scissor movement, but this time they had caught Big King's lower body between them. They had closed across his pelvis and crushed it. Now they held him in a vicelike grip from which it was not possible to shake them.

The white face and the black face were but a few feet apart. The two stricken companions in disaster looked into each other's eyes and knew that there was no escape. They were doomed.

'My arms,' whispered Rod huskily. 'I cannot use them.' Big King's bulging eyes held Rod's gaze.

'Can you reach the blaster?' Rod whispered urgently. 'Take it and turn the handle. Burn it, Big King, burn it!'

Slow comprehension showed in Big King's pain-glazed eyes.

'We are finished, Big King. Let us go like men. Burn it, bring down the rock!'

Above them the rock was sown with explosive. The blaster was connected. In his agitation Rod tried to reach out for the blaster. His forearm swung loosely, the fingers hanging open like the petals of a dead flower, and the pain checked him.

'Get it, Big King,' Rod urged him, and Big King picked up the blaster and held it against his chest with one arm.

'The handle!' Rod encouraged him. 'Turn the handle!'

But instead Big King reached into the dinghy once more and drew the machete from its sheath.

'What are you doing?' Rod demanded, and in reply Big King swung the blade back over his shoulder and then brought it forward in a gleaming arc aimed at the nylon rope that held the dinghy anchored to the wooden frame. Clunk! The blade bit into the wood, severing the rope that was bound around it.

Freed by the stroke of the machete, the dinghy was whisked away by the current. Lying in the dancing rubber dinghy, Rod heard a bull voice bellow above the rush of the water.

'Go in peace, my friend.'

Then Rod was careening back along the drive, a hell ride during which the dinghy spun like a top and in the beam of his lamp the roof and walls melted into a dark racing blur as Rod lay maimed on the floor of the dinghy.

Then suddenly the air jarred against his ear drums, a long rolling concussion in the confines of the drive and he knew that Big King had fired the drop-blast matt. Rodney Ironsides slipped over the edge of consciousness into a soft warm dark place from which he hoped never to return.

Dimitri squatted on his haunches above the shaft at 65 level. He was smoking his tenth cigarette. The rest of the men waited as impatiently as he did; every few minutes Dimitri would cross to the shaft and flash his lamp down the hundred-foot hole to 66 level.

'How long have they been gone?' he asked, and they all glanced at their watches.

'An hour and ten minutes.'

'No, an hour and fourteen minutes.'

'Christ, call me a liar for four minutes!'

And they lapsed into silence once more. Suddenly the station telephone shrilled, and Dimitri jumped up and ran to it.

'No, Mr Hirschfeld, nothing yet!'

He listened a moment.

'All right, send him down then.'

He hung up the telephone, and his men looked at him enquiringly.

'They are sending down a policeman,' he explained.

'What the hell for?'

'They want Big King.'

'Why?'

'Warrant of arrest for murder.'

'Murder?'

'Ja, they reckon he murdered the Portuguese store-keeper.'

'Jeez!'

'Big King, is that so!' Delighted to have found something to pass the time, they fell into an animated debate.

The police inspector arrived in the cage at 65 level, but he was disappointing. He looked like a down-at-heel under-taker, and he replied to their eager questions with a sorrowful stare that left them stuttering.

For the fifteenth time Dimitri went to the shaft and peered down into it. The blast shook the earth around them, a long rumbling that persisted for many seconds.

'They've done it!' yelled Dimitri, and began to caper wildly. His men leapt to their feet and began beating each other on the back, shouting and laughing. The police inspector alone took no part in the celebrations.

'Wait,' yelled Dimitri at last. 'Shut up all of you! Shut up! Damn it! Listen!'

They fell silent.

'What is it?' someone asked. 'I can't hear anything.'

'That's just it!' exulted Dimitri. 'The water! It has stopped!'

Only then did they become aware that the dull roar of water to which their ears had become resigned was now ended. It was quiet; a cathedral hush lay upon the workings. They began to cheer, their voices thin in the silence, and Dimitri ran to the steel ladder and swarmed down it like a monkey.

From thirty feet up Dimitri saw the dinghy marooned amongst the filth and debris around the shaft. He recognized the crumpled figure lying in the bottom of it.

'Rod!' he was shouting before he reached the station at 66 level. 'Rod, are you all right?'

The floor of the haulage was wet, and here and there a trickle of water still snaked towards the shaft. Dimitri ran to the stranded dinghy and started to turn Rod onto his back. Then he saw his arms.

'Oh, Christ!' he gasped in horror, then he was yelling up the ladder. 'Get a stretcher down here.'

Rod regained consciousness to find himself covered with blankets and strapped securely into a mine stretcher. His arms were splinted and bandaged, and from the familiar rattle and rush of air he knew he was in the cage on the way to the surface.

He recognized Dimitri's voice raised argumentatively.

'Damn it! The man is unconscious and badly injured, can't you leave him alone?'

'I have my duty to perform,' a strange voice answered.

'What's he want, Dimitri?' Rod croaked.

'Rod, how are you?' At the sound of his voice Dimitri was kneeling beside the stretcher anxiously.

'Bloody awful,' Rod whispered. 'What does this joker want?'

'He's a police officer. He wants to arrest Big King for murder,' Dimitri explained.

'Well, he's a bit bloody late,' whispered Rod, and even through his pain this seemed to Rod to be terribly funny. He began to laugh. He sobbed with laughter, each convulsion sending bright bursts of pain along his arms. He was shaking uncontrollably with shock, sweat pouring from his face, and he was laughing wildly.

'He's a bit bloody late,' he repeated through his hysterical laughter as Dr Dan Stander pushed the hypodermic needle into his arm and shot him full of morphine.

– 70 –

Hurry Hirschfeld stood in the main haulage on 66 level. There was bustle all around him. Already the crews from the cementation company were manhandling their equipment up towards the blocked drive.

These were specialists from an independent contracting company. They were about to begin pumping thousands of tons of liquid cement into the rock jam that sealed the drive. They would pump it in at pressures in excess of 3,000 pounds per square inch, and when that concrete set it

243

would form a plug that would effectively seal off the drive for all time. It would also form a burial vault for the body of Big King, thought Hurry, a fitting monument to the man who had saved the Sonder Ditch.

He would arrange to have a commemorative plaque placed on the outer wall of the cement plug with a suitable inscription describing the man and the deed.

The man's dependants must be properly taken care of; perhaps they could be flown down for the unveiling of the plaque. Anyway he could leave that to Public Relations and Personnel.

The haulage stank of wetness and mud. It was dank and clammy cool, and it would not improve his lumbago. Hurry had seen enough; he started back towards the shaft. Faintly he was aware of the muted clangour of the mighty pumps which in a few days would free the Sonder Ditch of the water that filled her lower levels.

The laden stretchers with their grisly blanket-covered burdens stood in a row under the hastily rigged electric lights along one wall of the tunnel. Hurry's expression hardened as he passed them.

'I'll have the guts of the man responsible for this,' he vowed silently as he waited for the cage.

Terry Steyner rode in the rear of the ambulance with Rod. She wiped the mud from his face.

'How bad is it, Dan?' she asked.

'Hell, Terry, he'll be up and about in a few days. The arms of course are not very pretty, that's why I'm taking him directly to Johannesburg. I want a specialist orthopaedic surgeon to set them. Apart from that he is suffering from shock pretty badly and his hands are superficially lacerated. But he will be fine.'

Dan watched curiously as Terry fussed ineffectually with the damp hair of the drugged man.

'You want a smoke?' he asked.

'Light me one, please Dan.'

He passed her the cigarette.

'I didn't know that you and Rod were so friendly,' he ventured.

Terry looked up at him quickly.

'How very delicate you are, Dr Stander,' she mocked him.

'None of my business, of course.' Hurriedly Dan withdrew.

'Don't be silly, Dan. You're a good friend of Rod's and Joy is mine. You two are entitled to know. I am desperately, crazily in love with this big hunk. I intend divorcing Manfred just as soon as possible.'

'Is Rod going to marry you?'

'He hasn't said anything about marriage but I'll sure as hell start working on him,' Terry grinned, and Dan laughed.

'Good luck to you both, then. I'm sure Rod will be able to get another job.'

'What do you mean?' Terry demanded.

'They say your grandfather is threatening to fire him so high he'll be the first man on the moon.'

Terry relapsed into silence. Proof was what Pops had asked for, but what proof was there?

'They'll be waiting on the X-ray reports.' Joy Albright gave her opinion. Since her engagement to Dan, Joy had suddenly become something of a medical expert. She had rushed down to the Johannesburg Central Hospital at Dan's hurried telephonic request. Dan wanted her to keep Terry company while she waited for Rod to come out of emergency. They sat together in the waiting-room.

'I expect so,' Terry agreed. Something Joy had just said had jolted in her mind, something she must remember.

'It takes them twenty minutes or so to expose the plates

and develop them. Then the radiologist has to examine the plates and make his report to the surgeon.'

There, Joy had said it again. Terry sat up straight and concentrated on what Joy had said. Which word had disturbed her?

Suddenly she had it.

'The report!' she exclaimed. 'That's it. The report, that's the proof.'

She leapt out of her chair.

'Joy! Give me the keys of your car,' she demanded.

'What on earth?' Joy looked startled.

'I can't explain now. I have to get home to Sandown urgently, give me your keys. I'll explain later.'

Joy fished in her handbag and produced a leather key folder. Terry snatched it from her.

'Where are you parked?' Terry demanded.

'In the car park, near the main gate.'

'Thanks, Joy.' Terry dashed from the waiting-room, her high heels clattered down the passage.

'Crazy woman.' Joy looked after her bewildered.

Ten minutes later Dan looked into the waiting-room.

'Rod's fine now. Where's Terry?'

'She went mad—' And Joy explained her abrupt departure. Dan looked grave.

'I think we'd better follow her, Joy.'

'I think you're right, darling.'

'I'll just grab my coat,' said Dan.

There was only one place where Manfred would keep the geological report on the Big Dipper that Rod had told her about. That was in the safe deposit behind the panelling in his study. Because her jewellery was kept in the same safe, Terry had a key and the combination to the lock.

Even in Joy's Alfa Romeo, taking liberties with the traffic regulations, it was a thirty-five-minute drive out to

Sandown. It was after five in the evening when Terry coasted down the long driveway and parked before the garages.

The extensive grounds were deserted, for the gardeners finished at five, and there was no sign of life from the house. This was as it should be, for she knew Manfred was still in Europe. He was not due back for at least another four days.

Leaving the ignition keys in the Alfa, Terry ran up the pathway and onto the stoep. She fumbled in her handbag and found the keys to the front door. She let herself in, and went directly to Manfred's study. She slid the concealing panel aside and set about the lengthy business of opening the steel safe. It required both key and combination to activate the mechanism, and Terry had never developed much expertise at tumbling the combination.

Finally, however, the door swung open and she was confronted by the voluminous contents. Terry began removing the various documents and files, examining each one and then stacking them neatly on the floor beside her.

She had no idea of the shape, size nor colour of the report for which she was searching, it was ten minutes before she selected an unmarked folder and flicked open the cover. 'Confidential Report on the geological formations of the Kitchenerville gold fields, with special reference to those areas lying to the east of the Big Dipper Dyke.'

Terry felt a wonderful lift of relief as she read the titling for she had begun doubting that the report was here. Quickly she thumbed through the pages and began reading at random. There was no doubt.

'This is it!' she exclaimed aloud.

'I'll take that, thank you.' The dreaded familiar voice cut into her preoccupation, and Terry spun around and came to her feet in one movement, clutching the file protectively to her breast. She backed away from the man who stood in the doorway.

She hardly recognized her own husband. She had never

seen him like this. Manfred was coatless, and his shirt was without collar or stud. He appeared to have slept in his trousers, for they were rumpled and baggy. There was a yellow stain down the front of his white shirt.

His scanty brown hair was dishevelled, hanging forward wispily onto his forehead. He had not shaved, and the skin around his eyes was discoloured and puffy.

'Give that to me.' He came towards her with hand outstretched.

'Manfred.' She kept moving away from him. 'What are you doing here? When did you get back?'

'Give it to me, you slut.'

'Why do you call me that?' she asked, trying for time.

'Slut!' he repeated, and lunged towards her. Terry whirled away from him lightly.

She ran for the study door, with Manfred close behind her. She beat him into the passage and raced for the front door. Her heel caught in one of the Persian carpets that covered the floor of the passage, and she staggered and fell against the wall.

'Whore!' He was on her instantly trying to wrestle the report out of her hands, but she clung to it with all her strength. Face to face they were almost of a height, and she saw the madness in his eyes.

Suddenly Manfred released her. He stepped back, bunched his fist and swung it round-armed into her cheek. Her head jerked back and cracked against the wall. He drew back his fist and hit her again. She felt the quick warm burst of blood spurt from her nose, and staggered through the door beside her into the dining-room. She was dizzy from the blows and she fell against the heavy stink-wood table.

Manfred was close behind her. He charged her, sending her sprawling backwards onto the table. He was on top of her, both his hands at her throat.

'I'm going to kill you, you whore,' he wheezed. His thumbs hooked and pressed deep into the flesh of her throat. With the frenzied strength of despair, Terry clawed at his eyes with both hands. Her nails scored his face, raking long red lines into his flesh. With a cry Manfred released her, and backed away holding both hands to his injured face, leaving Terry lying gasping across the table.

He stood for a moment, then uncovered his face and inspected the blood on his hands.

'I'll kill you for that!'

But as he advanced towards her, Terry rolled over the table.

'Whore! Slut! Bitch!' he screamed at her, following her around the table. Terry kept ahead of him.

There were a matched pair of heavy Stuart crystal decanters on the sideboard, one containing port, the other sherry. Terry snatched up one of them and turned to face Manfred. She hurled the decanter with all her remaining strength at his head.

Manfred did not have time to duck. The decanter cracked against his forehead, and he fell backwards, stunned. Terry snatched up the report and ran out of the dining-room, down the passage, out of the front door and into the garden. She was running weakly, following the driveway towards the main road.

Then behind her she heard the engine of an automobile roar into life. Panting wildly, holding the report, she stopped and looked back. Manfred had followed her out of the house. He was behind the steering wheel of Joy's Alfa Romeo. As she watched he threw the car into gear and howled towards her, blue smoke burning from the rear tyres with the speed of the acceleration. His face behind the windscreen was white and streaked with the marks of her nails, his eyes were staring, insane, and she knew he was going to ride her down.

She kicked off her shoes and ran off the driveway onto the lawns.

Crouched forward in the driver's seat of the Alfa, Manfred watched the fleeing figure ahead of him.

Terry ran with the full-hipped sway of the mature woman, her long legs were tanned and her hair flew out loosely behind her.

Manfred was not concerned with the return of the geological report, its existence was no longer of significance to him. What he wanted was to completely destroy this woman. In his crazed state, she had become the symbol and the figurehead of all his woes. His humiliation and fall were all linked to her, he could exact his vengeance by destroying her, crushing that revolting warm and clinging body, bruising it, ripping it with the steel of the Alfa Romeo's chassis.

He hit second gear and spun the steering-wheel. The Alfa swerved from the driveway, and as its rear wheels left the tarmac, they skidded on the thick grass. Deftly Manfred checked the skid and lined up on Terry's running back.

Already she was among the protea bushes on the lower terrace. The Alfa buck-jumped the slope, flying bird-free before crashing down heavily on its suspension. Wheels spun and bit, and the sleek vehicle shot forward again.

Terry looked back over her shoulder, her face was white and her eyes very big and fear-filled. Manfred giggled. He was aware of a sense of power, the ability to dispense life or death. He steered for her, reckless of all consequences, intent on destroying her.

There was a six-foot-tall protea bush ahead of him, and Manfred roared through it, bursting it asunder. Scattering branches and leaves, giggling again, he saw Terry directly ahead of him. She was still looking back at him, and at that moment she stumbled and fell onto her knees.

She was helpless. Her face streaked with tears and blood,

her hair falling forward in wild disorder, kneeling as though for the headsman's stroke. Manfred felt a flood of disappointment. He did not want it to end so soon, he wanted to savour this sadistic elation, this sense of power.

At the last possible moment he yanked the wheel over and the car slewed violently. It shot past Terry with six inches to spare, and its rear wheels pelted her with clods of turf and thrown dirt.

Laughing aloud, wild-eyed, Manfred held the wheel hard over, bringing the Alfa around in a tight skidding circle, crackling sideways through another protea bush.

Terry was up and running again. He saw immediately that she was heading for the changing rooms of the swimming-pool among the trees on the bottom lawn and she was far enough ahead to elude him, perhaps.

'Bitch!' he snarled, and crash-changed into third gear, with engine revs peaking. The Alfa howled in pursuit of the running girl.

Had Terry thrown the bulky report aside, she might have reached the brick change rooms ahead of the racing sports car, but the report hampered and slowed her. She still had twenty yards to cover, she was running along the paved edge of the swimming-pool, and she sensed that the car was right on top of her.

Terry dived sideways, hitting the water flat on her side, and the Alfa roared past. Manfred trod heavily on the brakes, the Michelin metallic tyres screeched against the paving stones, and Manfred leapt out of the driver's seat the moment the Alfa stopped.

He ran back to the pool side. Terry was floundering towards the far steps. She was exhausted, weak with exertion and terror. Her sodden hair streamed down over her face, and she was gasping open-mouthed for air.

Manfred laughed again, a high-pitched, almost girlish giggle, and he dived after her, landing squarely between

Terry's shoulder blades with his full weight. She went under, sucking water agonizingly into already aching lungs, and when she surfaced she was coughing and gagging, blinded with water and her own wet hair.

Almost immediately she felt herself seized from behind and forced face down into the water. For half a minute she struggled fiercely, then her movements slowed and became weaker.

Manfred stood over her, chest deep in the clear water, gripping her around the waist and by a handful of her sodden hair, forcing her face deep below the surface. He had lost his spectacles, and he blinked owlishly. The wet silk of his shirt clung to his upper body, and the water had slicked his hair down.

As he felt the life going out of her, and her movements becoming sluggish and slow, he began to laugh again. The broken, incoherent laughter of a madman.

'Dan!' Joy pointed off through the trees. 'That's my car down there, parked by the swimming-pool!'

'What the hell is it doing there?'

'There's something wrong, Terry wouldn't drive through her beloved garden, unless there was!'

Dan braked sharply and pulled his Jaguar to the side of the driveway.

'I'm going to take a look.' He slid out of the car and started off across the lawns. Joy opened her own door and trotted after him.

Dan saw the man in the water, fully dressed, intent on what he was doing. He recognized Manfred Steyner.

'What the hell is he up to?' Dan started running. He reached the edge of the pool, and suddenly he realized what was happening.

'Christ! He's drowning her,' he shouted aloud, and he sprang into the water.

He did not waste time struggling with Manfred. He hit him a great open-handed, round-armed blow, that cracked against the side of Manfred's head like a pistol shot and sent him lurching sideways, releasing his grip on Terry.

Ignoring Manfred, Dan picked Terry from the water like a drowned kitten and waded to the steps. He carried her out and laid her face down on the paving. He knelt over her and began applying artificial respiration. He felt Terry stir under his hands, then cough and retch weakly.

Joy came up at the run and dropped on her knees beside him.

'My God, Dan, what happened?'

'That little bastard was trying to drown her.'

Dan looked up from his labours without interrupting the rhythm of his movement over Terry. She spluttered and retched again.

On the far side of the pool Manfred Steyner had dragged himself from the pool. He was sitting on the edge with his feet still dangling into the water, his head was hanging and he was fingering the side of his face where Dan had hit him. On his lap he held a wet pulpy mess that had been the geological report.

'Joy, can you take over here? Terry's not too far gone, and I want to get my hands on that little Hun.'

Joy took Dan's place over Terry's prostrate form, and Dan stood up.

'What are you going to do to him?' Joy asked.

'I'm going to beat him to a pulp.'

'Good show!' Joy encouraged him. 'Give him one for me.'

Manfred had heard the exchange and as Dan ran around the edge of the pool he scrambled to his feet, and staggered to the parked Alfa. He slammed the door and whirred the engine to life. Dan was just too late to stop him. The car shot forward across the lawns, leaving Dan running, futile, behind it.

'Look after her, Joy!' Dan shouted back.

By the time Dan had run up the terrace to his Jaguar and reversed it to point in the opposite direction, the Alfa had disappeared through the white gates with a musical flutter of its exhaust.

'Come on, girlie,' Dan spoke to his Jaguar. 'Let's go get him.'

The rear wheels spun as he pulled away.

Without his spectacles Manfred Steyner's vision was blurred and milky. The outlines of all objects on which he looked were softened and indistinct.

He instinctively checked the Alfa at the stop street at the bottom of the lane. He sat undecided, water still streaming from his clothing, squelching in his shoes. Beside him on the passenger seat lay the sodden report, its pages beginning to disintegrate from its soaking and the rough handling it had received.

He had to get rid of it. It was the shred of incriminating evidence. That was the only clear thought Manfred had. For the first time in his life the crystalline clarity of his thought processes was interrupted. He was confused, his mind jerking abruptly from one subject to another, the intense pleasure of inflicting hurt on Terry mingled with the sting and smart of his own injuries. He could not concentrate on either sensation for overlying it all was a sense of fear, of uncertainty. He felt vulnerable, hunted, hurt and shaken. His brain flickered and wavered as though a computer had developed an electrical fault. The answers it produced were nonsensical.

He looked in the rear view mirror, saw the Jaguar glide out between the white gates and turn towards him.

'Christ!' he panicked. He rammed his foot down on the accelerator and engaged the clutch. The Alfa screeched out into the main highway, swerved into the path of a heavy truck, bounded over the far kerb and swung back into the road.

Dan watched it tear away towards Kyalami.

He let the truck pass and then swung into the traffic behind it. He had to wait until the road was clear ahead before he could overtake the truck, and by that time the Alfa was a dwindling cream speck ahead of him.

Dan settled back in the leather bucket seat, and gave the Jaguar its head. He was furious, outraged by the treatment he had seen Manfred meting out to Terry. Her swollen and bruised face had shocked him and his feet were firmly set upon the path of vengeance.

His hands gripped the steering-wheel fiercely, he was muttering threats of violence as the speedometer moved up over the hundred mile per hour mark and he began relentlessly overhauling the cream sports car.

Steadily he moved up behind the Alfa until he was driving almost on its rear bumper. The Alfa was held up by a green school bus. Dan could not pass, however, for there was a steady stream of traffic coming in the opposite direction.

He fastened his attention on the back of Manfred's head, still fuming with anger.

Dan dropped down a gear, ready to pull out and overtake the Alfa when the opportunity arose. At that moment Manfred looked up into his rear view mirror. Dan saw the reflection of his white face with disordered damp hair hanging onto the forehead, saw his expression change immediately he recognized Dan and the Alfa shot out into the face of the approaching traffic.

There was a howl and blare of horns, vehicles swerved to make way for Manfred's wild rush. Dan glimpsed frightened faces flicking past, but the Alfa had squeezed around the green bus and was speeding away.

Dan dropped back, then sent the Jaguar like a thrown javelin through the gap between bus and kerb, overtaking on the wrong side and ignoring the bus driver's yell of protest.

The Jaguar had a higher top speed, and on the long straight Pretoria highway Dan crept up steadily on the cream Alfa.

He could see Manfred glancing repeatedly into his driving-mirror, and he grinned mirthlessly.

Ahead of them the highway rose and then dipped over a low rounded ridge. A double avenue of tall blue gum trees flanked each side of the road.

Travelling in the same direction as the two high per- formance sports cars was a Mini of a good vintage year. Its elderly driver was triumphantly about to overtake an over- loaded vegetable truck. Neck and neck they approached the blind rise at twenty-five miles per hour, between them they effectively blocked half the road.

The horn of the Alfa wailed a high-pitched warning, and Manfred pulled out to overtake both slower vehicles. He was level with them, well out over the white dividing line, when a cement truck popped up over the blind rise.

Dan stood on his brake pedal with all the strength of his right leg, and watched it happen.

The cement truck and the Alfa came head on towards each other at a combined speed of well over a hundred miles per hour. At the last moment the Alfa began to turn away but it was too late by many seconds.

It caught the heavy cement truck a glancing blow and was hurled across the path of the two slower vehicles, miraculously touching neither of them; it skidded sideways leaving reeking black smears of rubber on the tarmac, and hurdled the low bank. It struck one of the blue gums full on, with a force that shivered the giant tree trunk and brought down a rain of leaves.

Dan pulled the Jaguar into the side of the road, parked it, and walked back.

He knew there was no hurry. The drivers of the Mini

and the vegetable truck were there before him. They were attempting to talk each other down, both of them excited and relieved by their own escapes.

'I'm a doctor,' said Dan, and they fell back respectfully.

'He doesn't need a doctor,' said one of them. 'He needs an undertaker.'

One look was sufficient. Dr Manfred Steyner was as dead as Dan had ever seen anybody. His crushed head was thrust through the windscreen. Dan picked up the sodden bundle of paper from the seat beside the huddled body. He was aware that some particular importance was attached to it.

Dan's anger had evaporated entirely, and he felt a twinge of pity as he looked into the wreckage at the corpse. It appeared so frail and small – of such little consequence.

– 71 –

The sunlight was sparkling bright, broken into a myriad eyestinging fragments by the rippling surface of the bay.

The breeze was strong enough for the Arrow class yachts to fly their spinnakers as they came down on the wind. The sails bulged out blue and yellow and bright scarlet against the sombre green of the great whale-back bluff above Durban Bay.

Under the awning on the afterdeck of the motor yacht it was cool, but the fat man wore only a pair of white linen slacks with his feet thrust into dark blue cloth espadrilles.

Sprawled in a deck-chair, his belly bulged smooth and hard over the waistband of his slacks; he was tanned a dark mahogany colour and his body-hair grew thick and curly from chest to navel.

'Thank you, Andrew.' He extended his empty glass, and the younger man carried it to the open-air bar. The fat man watched him as he mixed another Pimms No. 1 cup.

A white-clad crew member clambered down the companion way from the bridge. He touched his cap respectfully to the fat man.

'Captain's respects, sir, and we are ready to sail when you give the order.'

'Thank you. Please tell the captain we will sail as soon as Miss du Maine comes aboard.' And the crew man ran back to the bridge.

'Ah!' The fat man sighed happily as Andrew placed the Pimms in his outstretched hand. 'I have really earned this break. The last few weeks have been nerve-racking, to say the least.'

'Yes, sir,' Andrew agreed dutifully. 'But, as usual, you snatched victory from the ashes.'

'It was close,' the fat man agreed. 'Young Ironsides gave us all a nasty fright with his drop-blast matt. I was only just able to make good my personal commitments before the price shot up again. The profit was not as high as I had anticipated, but then I have never made a habit of peering into the mouths of gift-horses.'

'It was a pity that our associates lost all that money,' Andrew ventured.

'Yes, yes. A great pity. But rather them than us, Andrew.'

'Indeed, sir.'

'In a way I am glad it worked out as it did. I am a patriotic man, at heart. I am relieved that it was not necessary to disrupt the economy of the country to make our little profit.'

He stood up suddenly, his interest quickening as a taxi cab came down onto the Yacht Club jetty. The cabby opened a rear door and from it emerged a very beautiful young lady.

'Ah, Andrew! Our guest has arrived. You may warn the captain that we will be sailing within minutes; and send a man to fetch her luggage.'

He went to the entry port to welcome the young lady.

72

In mid-summer in the Zambesi Valley the heat is a solid white shimmering thing. In the noonday nothing moves in the merciless sunlight.

At the centre of the native village grew a baobab tree. A monstrous bloated trunk with malformed branches like the limbs of a polio victim. The carrion crows sat in it, black and shiny as cockroaches. A score of grass huts ringed the tree, and beyond them lay the tilled fields. The millet stood tall and green in the sun.

Along the rude track towards the village came a Land Rover. It came slowly, lurching and jolting over the rough ground, its motor growling in low gear. Printed in black on its sides were the letters ARC, African Recruiting Corporation.

The children heard it first, and crawled from the grass huts. Naked black bodies, and shrill excited voices in the sunlight.

They ran to meet the Land Rover and danced beside it, shrieking and laughing. The Land Rover came to a halt in the meagre shade under the baobab tree. An elderly white man climbed from the cab. He wore khaki safari clothes and a wide-brimmed hat. Complete silence fell, and one of the oldest boys fetched a carved stool and placed it in the shade.

The white man sat on the stool. A girl came forward, knelt before him and offered a gourd of millet beer. The white man drank from the gourd. No one spoke, none would disturb an honoured guest until he had taken refreshment, but from the grass huts the adult members of the village came. Blinking into the sunlight, winding their loin clothes about their waists. They came and squatted in a semi-circle before the white man on his stool.

He lowered the gourd and set it aside. He looked at them.

'I see you, my friends,' he greeted them, and the response was warm.

'We see you, old one,' they chorused, but the expression of their visitor remained grave.

'Let the wives of King Nkulu come forward,' he called. 'Let them bring each their first-born son with them.'

Four women and four adolescent boys left the crowd and came shyly into the open. For a moment the white man studied them compassionately, then he stood and stepped forward. He placed a hand on the shoulder of each of the two eldest lads.

'Your father has gone to *his* fathers,' he told them. There was a stirring, an intake of breath, a startled cry, and then, as was proper, the eldest wife let out the first sobbing wail of mourning.

One by one each wife sank down onto the dry musty earth and covered her head with her shawl.

'He is dead,' the white man repeated against the background of their keening lament. 'But he died in such honour as to let his name live on forever. So great was his dying that for all their lives money will each month be paid to his wives, and for each of his sons there is already set aside a place at the University that each may grow as strong in learning as his father was in body. Of Big King there will be raised up an image in stone.

'The wives of Big King and his sons will travel in a flying machine to I'Goldi, that their eyes also may look upon the stone image of the man who was their husband and their father.' The white man paused for breath, it was a lengthy speech in the midday heat of the valley. He wiped his face and then tucked the handkerchief into his pocket.

'He was a lion!'

'Ngwenyama!' whispered the sturdy twelve-year-old boy standing beside the white man. The tears started from his eyes and greased down his cheeks. He turned away and ran alone into the millet fields.

73

Dennis Langley, the Sales Manager of Kitchenerville Motors who were the local Ford agents, stretched his arms over his head luxuriously. He sighed with deep contentment. What a lovely way to spend a working-day morning.

'Happy?' asked Hettie Delange beside him in the double bed. In reply Dennis grinned and sighed again.

Hettie sat up and let the sheet fall to her waist. Her breasts were big and white, and damp with perspiration. She looked down on his naked chest and arm muscles approvingly.

'Gee, you're built nicely.'

'So are you,' Dennis smiled up at her.

'You're different from the other chaps I've gone out with,' Hettie told him. 'You speak so nicely – like a gentleman, you know.'

Before Dennis Langley could decide on a suitable reply, the front door bell shrilled, the sound of it echoing through the house. Dennis shot into an upright position with a fearful expression on his face.

'Who's that?' he demanded.

'It's probably the butcher delivering the meat.'

'It may be my wife!' Dennis cautioned her. 'Don't answer it.'

'Of course I've got to answer it, silly.' Hettie threw back the sheet, and rose in her white and golden glory to find her dressing-gown. The sight was enough to momentarily quiet Dennis Langley's misgivings, but as she belted her gown and hid it from view he urged her again.

'Be careful! Make sure it's not her before you open the door.'

Hettie opened the front door, and immediately drew her gown more closely around her with one hand, while the other she tried to pat her hair into a semblance of order.

'Hello,' she breathed.

The tall young man in the doorway was really rather dreamy. He wore a dark business suit and carried an expensive leather briefcase.

'Mrs Delange?' he enquired. He had a nice soft dreamy voice.

'Yes, I'm Mrs Delange.' Hettie fluttered her eyelashes. 'Won't you come in?'

She led him through to the lounge, and she was pleasantly aware of his eyes on the opening of her gown.

'What can I do for you?' she asked archly.

'I am your local representative of the Sanlam Insurance Company, Mrs Delange. I have come to express my company's condolences on your recent sad bereavement. I would have called sooner, but I did not wish to intrude on your sorrow.'

'Oh!' Hettie dropped her eyes, immediately adopting the role of the widow.

'However, we hope we can bring a little light to disperse the darkness that surrounds you. You may know that your husband was a policy-holder with our Company?'

Hettie shook her head, but watched with interest while the visitor opened his briefcase.

'Yes, he was. Two months ago he took out a straight life policy with double indemnity. The policy was ceded to you.' The insurance man extracted a sheaf of papers from his case. 'I have here my company's cheque in full settlement of all claims under the policy. If you will just sign for it, please.'

'How much?' Hettie abandoned the role of the bereaved.

'With the double indemnity, the cheque is for forty-eight thousand rand.'

Hettie's eyes flew wide with delight.

'Gee!' she gasped. 'That's *fabulous*!'

– 74 –

Hurry's original intentions had expanded considerably. Instead of a plaque on the cement plug at
66 level, the monument to Big King had become
a life-sized statue in bronze. He sited it on the lawns in
front of the Adminstrative offices of the Sonder Ditch on a
base of black marble.

It was effective. The artist had captured a sense of
urgency, of vibrant power. The inscription was simple, just
the name of the man – 'King Nkulu' – and the date of his
death.

Hurry attended the unveiling in person, even though he
hated ceremonies and avoided them whenever possible. In
the front row of guests facing him his granddaughter sat
beside Doctor Stander and his very new blonde wife. She
winked at him and Hurry frowned lovingly back at her.

From the seat beside Hurry, young Ironsides stood up to
introduce the Chairman. Hurry noted the expression on his
granddaughter's face as she transferred all her attention to
the tall young man with both his arms encased in plaster of
Paris and supported by slings.

'Perhaps I should have fired him, after all,' thought
Hurry. 'He is going to cut one out of my herd.'

Hurry glanced sideways at his General Manager, and
decided with resignation, 'Too late'. Then he went on to
cheer himself. 'Anyway he looks like good breeding stock.'

His line of thought switched again. 'Better start making
arrangements to transfer him up to Head Office. He will
need a lot of grooming and polishing.'

Without thinking he fished a powerful-looking cigar
from his breast pocket. He had it halfway to his mouth

when he caught Terry's scandalized glare. Silently her lips formed the words: 'Your doctor!'

Guiltily Hurry Hirschfeld stuffed the cigar back into his pocket.

MONSOON

This book is for my wife and the jewel of my life

MOKHINISO

with all my love and gratitude for the enchanted years
that I have been married to her

T he three boys came up through the gill behind the chapel, so that they were hidden from the big house and the stables. Tom, the eldest, led them as he always did, but the youngest brother was close on his heels, and when Tom paused where the stream made its first turn above the village he renewed his argument. 'Why do I always have to be the cat? Why can I never join in the fun, Tom?'

'Because you are the littlest,' Tom told him, with lordly authority. He was surveying the tiny hamlet below them, which was now visible in the slot of the ravine. Smoke was rising from the forge in the smithy, and washing flapped in the easterly breeze behind the Widow Evans's cottage, but there was no sign of human life. At this time of day most of the men would be out in his father's fields, for the harvest was in full swing, while those women who were not toiling beside them would be at work in the big house.

Tom grinned with satisfaction and anticipation. 'No one's spotted us.' No one to carry reports back to their father.

'It's not fair.' Dorian was not so easily distracted from his argument. His coppery gold curls spilled down on to his forehead, giving him the look of an angry cherub. 'You never let me do anything.'

'Who let you fly his hawk last week? I did.' Tom rounded on him. 'Who let you fire his musket yesterday? I did. Who let you steer the cutter?'

'Yes, but—'

1

'But me no buts.' Tom glowered at him. 'Who's the captain of this crew, anyway?'

'You are, Tom.' Dorian dropped his green eyes under the force of his elder brother's stare. 'But, still—'

'You can go with Tom in my place, if you want.' Guy spoke softly for the first time. 'I'll play the cat.'

Tom turned to his younger twin, while Dorian exclaimed, 'Can I, Guy? Will you really?' It was only when he smiled that his full beauty burst out, like sunlight through parting clouds.

'No, he won't!' Tom cut in. 'Dorry's only a baby. He can't come. He'll stay on the roof to keep the cat.'

'I'm not a baby,' Dorian protested furiously. 'I'm nearly eleven.'

'If you're not a baby, show us your ball hairs,' Tom challenged him. Since he had sprouted his own, these had become Tom's yardstick of seniority.

Dorian ignored him: he had not even a pale ginger fluff to match the impressive growth of his elder brother. He went on to another tack. 'I'll just watch, that's all.'

'Yes, you'll watch from the roof.' Tom killed the argument dead in its tracks. 'Come on! We'll be late.' He struck out up the steep ravine.

The other two trailed after him with varying degrees of reluctance. 'Who could come anyway?' Dorian persisted. 'Everybody's busy. Even we should be helping.'

'Black Billy could come,' Tom replied, without looking back. That name silenced even Dorian. Black Billy was the oldest Courtney son. His mother had been an Ethiopian princess whom Sir Hal Courtney had brought back from Africa when he returned from his first voyage to that mystic continent. A royal bride and a shipload of treasure plundered from the Dutch and the pagan, a vast fortune with which their father had more than doubled the acreage of his ancient estate, and in so doing had elevated the family to among the wealthiest in all Devon, rivalling even the Grenvilles.

William Courtney, Black Billy to his younger half-brothers, was almost twenty-four, seven years older than the twins. He was clever, ruthless, handsome, in a dark wolf-like way, and his younger brothers feared and hated him with good reason. The threat of his name made Dorian shiver, and they climbed the last half-mile in silence. At last they left the stream and approached the rim, pausing under the big oak where the hen harrier had nested last spring.

Tom flopped down against the bole of the tree to catch his breath. 'If this wind holds we can go sailing in the morning,' he announced, as he removed his cap and wiped his sweaty forehead with his sleeve. There was a mallard wing feather in his cap, taken from the first bird ever killed by his own falcon.

He looked around him. From here the view encompassed almost half the Courtney estate, fifteen thousand acres of rolling hills and steep valleys, of woodland, pasture and wheatfields that stretched down to the cliffs along the shore, and reached almost to the outskirts of the port. But it was ground so familiar that Tom did not linger long on the view. 'I'll go ahead to see if the coast is clear,' he said, and scrambled to his feet. Crouching low, he moved cautiously to the stone wall that surrounded the chapel. Then he lifted his head and peered over.

The chapel had been built by his great-grandfather, Sir Charles, who had won his knighthood in the service of Good Queen Bess. As one of her sea captains he had fought with great distinction against the armada of Philip of Spain. Over a hundred years ago Sir Charles had built the chapel to the glory of God and in commemoration of the fleet action at Calais. He had earned his knighthood there, and many of the Spanish galleons had been

3

driven in flames on to the beach, the rest dispersed to the storms that Vice-Admiral Drake had called the Winds of God.

The chapel was a handsome octagonal building of grey stone, with a tall spire that, on a clear day, could be seen in Plymouth almost fifteen miles distant. Tom vaulted easily over the wall, and sneaked through the apple orchard to the iron-studded oak vestry door. He opened it a crack and listened intently. The silence was impenetrable. He crept inside and went to the door that opened into the nave. As he peeped in, the sunlight through the high stained-glass windows lit the interior like a rainbow. Those above the altar depicted the English fleet locked in battle against the Spaniards, with God the Father looking down approvingly from the clouds as the Spanish galleons burned.

The windows above the main door had been added by Tom's own father. This time the foes who were being battered into submission were the Dutch and the hordes of Islam, while above the battle stood Sir Hal, his sword raised heroically with his Ethiopian princess at his side. Both of them were armoured and on their shields was blazoned the *croix patté* of the Order of St George and the Holy Grail.

The nave was empty today. The preparations for Black Billy's wedding, which would take place next Saturday, had not yet begun. Tom had the building to himself. He ran back to the vestry door, and stuck his head out. He put two fingers in his mouth and gave a shrill whistle. Almost immediately his two brothers scrambled over the outer wall and ran to meet him.

'Up to the belfry, Dorry!' Tom ordered, and when it seemed that the redhead might still protest, he took a menacing pace towards him. Dorian scowled but disappeared up the staircase.

4

'Is she here yet?' Guy asked, with a hint of trepidation in his voice.

'Not yet. It's still early.' Tom crossed the floor and went down the dark stone staircase that led to the underground crypt. When he reached the bottom, he unbuckled the flap of the leather pouch that hung beside the sheathed dagger on his belt. He brought out the heavy iron key that he had removed from his father's study that morning, and unlocked the grille gate, then swung it open on its creaking hinges. He showed no hesitation as he entered the vault where so many of his ancestors lay in their stone sarcophagi. Guy followed him with less confidence. The presence of the dead always made him uneasy. He paused at the entrance to the crypt.

There were high windows at ground level through which glimmered an eerie light, the only illumination. Stone and marble coffins were arranged around the circular walls of the crypt. There were sixteen, all of the Courtneys and their wives since Great-grandfather Charles. Guy looked instinctively to the marble coffin that contained the earthly remains of his own mother, in the centre of the line of his father's three dead wives. There was a carved effigy of her on the lid, and she was beautiful, Guy thought, a pale lily of a girl. He had never known her, never taken suck at her bosom: the three-day labour of giving birth to twins had been too much for such a delicate creature. She had died of blood loss and exhaustion only hours after Guy had vented his birth cry. The boys had been raised by a series of nurses, and by their stepmother, who had been Dorian's mother.

He crossed to the marble coffin and knelt at the head. He read the inscription in front of him: 'Within this casket lies Margaret Courtney, beloved second wife of Sir Henry Courtney, mother of Thomas and of Guy, who departed this life on the 2nd of May 1673. Safe in the bosom of Christ.' Guy closed his eyes and began to pray.

'She can't hear you,' Tom told him, not unkindly.

'Yes, she can,' Guy replied, without raising his head or opening his eyes.

Tom lost interest and wandered down the row of coffins. To his mother's right lay Dorian's mother, his father's last wife. It was only three years ago that the cutter in which she had been sailing had overturned at the entrance to the bay, and the rip tide had swept her out to sea. Despite her husband's efforts to save her, the current had been too strong and had nearly taken Hal with her. It had cast them both up in a wind-battered cove five miles down the coast, but by then Elizabeth was drowned and Hal nearly so.

Tom felt tears welling up from deep inside of him, for he had loved her as he could not love the mother he had never known. He coughed and brushed his eyes, forcing the tears back before Guy could see his childish weakness. Although Hal had married Elizabeth mainly to provide his orphaned twins with a mother, very soon they had all come to love her, as they loved Dorian from when she had given birth to him. All of them but Black Billy, of course. William Courtney loved nobody but his father, and he was as fiercely jealous of him as a panther. Elizabeth had protected the younger boys from his vindictive attentions, until the sea took her from them and left them defenceless.

'You should never have left us,' Tom told her softly, then glanced guiltily at Guy. But Guy had not heard him, too intent on his prayers, and Tom moved across to the other coffin, which flanked his natural mother. This belonged to Judith, the Ethiopian princess, the mother of Black Billy. The marble effigy on the lid depicted a handsome woman with the fierce, almost hawk-like features that her son had inherited from her. She was in half-armour, as befitted one who had commanded armies against the pagan. There was a sword on her belt, and a shield and helmet rested on her chest, the shield blazoned with a

Coptic cross, the symbol of Christ that predated even the ministry of Rome. Her head was bared and the bush of her hair was a dense curling crown. As he looked at her Tom felt the hatred he bore her son rise in his chest. 'The horse should have thrown you before you had a chance to whelp that cub of yours.' This time he spoke aloud.

Guy stood up and came to join him. 'It's ill luck to speak so of the dead,' he cautioned his brother.

Tom shrugged. 'She can't hurt me now.'

Guy took his arm and led him to the next sarcophagus in the row. They both knew it was empty. The lid had not been sealed.

'Sir Francis Courtney born 6th January 1616 in the County of Devon. Knight of the Order of the Garter and of the Order of St George and the Holy Grail. Navigator and Sailor. Explorer and Warrior. Father of Henry and Valiant Gentleman.' Guy read the inscription aloud. 'Unjustly accused of piracy by the craven Dutch settlers of Cap de Bonne Esperance, and most cruelly executed by them on the 15th July 1668. Although his mortal remains lie on the far and savage African shore, his memory lives for ever in the heart of his son, Henry Courtney, and in the hearts of all the brave and faithful seamen who voyaged the Ocean Sea under his command.'

'How can Father set an empty coffin here?' Tom murmured.

'I think perhaps that he intends one day to fetch back Grandfather's body,' Guy answered.

Tom shot him a sharp glance. 'Did he tell you that?' He was jealous that his brother had been told something that he, the elder, had not. All the boys worshipped their father.

'No, he didn't,' admitted Guy, 'but it's what I would do for my father.'

Tom lost interest in the discussion and strode out into the centre of the open floor, which was inlaid with a weird

7

circular design in granites and marbles of many different colours. Brass cauldrons were set at the four points of the circle, which would hold the ancient elements of fire and earth, air and water, when the Temple of the Order of St George and the Holy Grail was convened at the full moon of the summer equinox. Sir Henry Courtney was a Nautonnier Knight of the order, as had been his father and his grandfather before him.

In the centre of the domed roof of the crypt there was an airhole open to the sky above. The building was so cunningly laid out that, through this opening, the rays of the full moon would strike the design on the stone floor under Tom's feet where the cryptic legend of the order was inlaid in black marble: 'In Arcadia habito.' Neither of the boys had yet learned the deeper meaning of this heraldic device.

Tom stood upon the black Gothic letters, placed his hand over his heart and began to recite the liturgy with which he, too, would one day be inducted into the order. 'These things I believe, and I will defend them with my life. I believe there is but one God in Trinity, the Father eternal, the Son eternal and the Holy Ghost eternal.'

'Amen!' cried Guy softly. They had both studied the catechism of the order assiduously and knew the hundred responses by heart.

'I believe in the communion of the Church of England, and the divine right of its representative on earth, William the Third, King of England, Scotland, France and Ireland, Defender of the Faith.'

'Amen!' Guy repeated. One day they would both be called upon to join this illustrious order, to stand in the light of the full moon and to make these vows in earnest.

'I will uphold the Church of England. I will confront the enemies of my sovereign Lord, William . . .' Tom went on, in soaring tones that had almost lost any last timbre of childhood. He broke off abruptly as a low whistle issued from the opening in the roof above his head.

'Dorry!' said Guy nervously. 'Someone's coming!' They both stood stock-still, waiting for the second sharply pitched whistle that would signal alarm and danger, but there was no further warning.

'It's her!' Tom grinned at his brother. 'I was afraid she might not come.'

Guy did not share his pleasure. He scratched his neck nervously. 'Tom, I like this not at all.'

'Bollocks to you, Guy Courtney.' His brother laughed at him. 'You'll never know how good it is unless you try it.'

They heard the rustle of cloth, the patter of light feet on the staircase, and a girl burst into the crypt. She stopped in the entrance, breathing quickly, her cheeks flushed brightly from her run up the hill.

'Did anyone see you leave the house, Mary?' Tom demanded.

She shook her head. 'Not a one of them, Master Tom. They was all too busy a-pigging thar broth.' Her voice purred with the local brogue, but its tone was light and pleasing. She was a well-set-up lass, with a full bow and stern, older than the twins so probably closer to twenty than fifteen. However, her skin was flawless and smooth as the famous Devon cream, and a tangle of dark ringlets and curls framed her pretty chubby face. Her lips were pink, soft and moist, but there was a sly slant to her bright, knowing eyes.

'Are you sure, Mary, that Master Billy didn't see you?' Tom asked insistently.

She shook her head so the ringlets danced. 'No. I looked in at the library afore I came, and he had his head in the books like always.' She placed both her small hands on her hips, and although they were rough and red from her work in the scullery, they almost encircled her tiny waist. Both twins' eyes followed the movement and settled on her body. Her full petticoats and ragged skirts reached

9

halfway down her plump calves, and although her feet were bare and grubby, her ankles were slim. She saw their eyes, their expressions, and smiled with a sense of power over them.

She lifted one hand and fiddled with the ribbon that held her bodice closed. Obediently both pairs of eyes followed her hands and she pushed out her breasts so that they strained at the retaining ribbon. 'You said I would ha' sixpence for it,' she reminded Tom, who roused himself.

'That I did, Mary.' He nodded. 'Sixpence for both of us, Guy and me.'

She tossed her head and stuck out her pink tongue at him. 'You're a sly one, Master Tom. 'Twas sixpence each, a shilling for the two, 'twas.'

'Don't be daft, Mary.' He reached into the purse on his belt and brought out a silver coin. He flipped it in the air. It glinted in the soft light as it spun and he caught it on his palm, then held it out for her to inspect. 'A whole silver sixpence, all for yourself.'

Again she shook her head, and pulled loose the bow in the ribbon. 'Shilling,' she repeated, and the front of her bodice opened an inch. Both the boys stared at the sliver of white skin that was revealed: it contrasted startlingly with the sun-browned, freckled shoulders above.

'Shilling, or naught!' She shrugged with feigned indifference. At the movement, the swell of one fat round breast popped half out, leaving just the pointed tip still hidden but with the border of the ruby aureole that encircled her nipple peeping shyly from under the frayed edge of her blouse. Both boys were speechless.

'Mice got your tongue?' she asked saucily. 'Methinks there's naught for me here.' She turned back to the staircase, flouncing her round bottom beneath the skirts.

'Wait!' Tom called, in a strangled voice. 'Shilling it is, then, Mary, my pretty.'

'Show me first, Master Tom!' She looked back over

her freckled shoulder as he scratched frantically in his purse.

'Here you are, Mary.' He held out the coin and she came to him slowly, swaying her hips in the way of the girls at the Plymouth docks. She took the coin from his fingers. 'Do you think I'm pretty, Master Tom?'

'You're the prettiest girl in all England,' Tom told her fervently, and meant every word. He reached out for the big round breast, which had now come clear of the bodice. She giggled and struck away his hand.

'What about Master Guy? I'nt he first?' She looked past Tom. 'You never done it afore, have you, Master Guy?'

Guy swallowed hard, but could not find his voice. He dropped his eyes and flushed darkly.

'It's his first time,' Tom affirmed. 'Take him first. I'll go after.'

Mary went to Guy and took his hand. 'Don't be afraid.' She smiled at him with those slanted eyes. 'I'll not hurt you, Master Guy,' she promised, and began to lead him to the far end of the crypt. Guy smelt her as she pressed against him. She had probably not bathed in a month and exuded a powerful odour of the kitchens where she worked, of bacon grease and woodsmoke, the horsy tang of her sweat, the odour of lobster boiling in the pot.

He felt his gorge rise. 'No!' he blurted out, and pulled away from her. 'I won't – I can't—' He was close to tears. 'You go first, Tom.'

'I got her for you,' Tom told him harshly. 'When you feel it, you'll go daft for it. See if you don't.'

'Please, Tom, don't make me.' Guy's voice shook, and he looked back desperately to the staircase. 'I just want to go home. Father will find out.'

'I've already given her our shilling.' Tom attempted to reason with him. 'You'll just waste it.'

Mary seized his hand again. 'Come along, now!' She tugged at his hand. 'There's a good lad. I've had you in my

11

eye, honest I have. You're a fine pretty boykin, that you are!'

'Let Tom go first!' Guy repeated, frantic now.

'Very well, then!' She flounced towards Tom. 'Let Master Tom show you the way. By now he should be able to find it blindfolded – he's been there often enough.' She grabbed Tom's arm, and dragged him to the nearest coffin, which happened to be that of Sir Charles, the hero of Calais, and leaned back against it.

'Not me only,' she giggled up into his face, 'but Mabel too, and Jill, unless they were both speaking a lie – and half the girls in the village, I've heard tell. It's a ram and a half you are, Master Tom!' She reached down and tugged at the laces of Tom's breeches. At the same time she stood on tiptoe and fastened her mouth on his. Tom shoved her back against the stone coffin. He was trying to say something to his twin, rolling his eyes in Guy's direction, but he was gagged by her soft wet lips and the long cat-like tongue she was thrusting deep into his mouth.

At last he pulled his face free and gasped for air, then grinned at Guy, his chin wet and shining with the girl's saliva. 'Now I'm going to show you the sweetest thing you ever will lay eyes on if you live a hundred year.'

Mary was still leaning back against the stone coffin. Tom stooped and, with practised fingers, loosed the drawstrings of her skirt to let the garment billow down and drape around her ankles. She wore nothing under it, and her body was very smooth and white. It looked as though it had been moulded from the finest candlewax. All three looked down at it, the twins in awe and Mary with a smirk of pride. After a long minute of silence, broken only by Tom's ragged breathing, Mary lifted her blouse over her head with both hands, and dropped it on the coffin lid behind her. She turned her head and looked into Guy's face. 'You don't want these?' she said, and took one of her own plump white breasts in each hand. 'No?' she mocked him. He was dumb and shaken. Then she ran her fingers slowly down her creamy body, past the deep pit of her navel. She kicked away her skirt and planted her feet apart, still watching Guy's face. 'You've never seen the likes of this little pussy cat, have you now, Master Guy?' she asked him. The curls rustled crisply under her fingers as she stroked herself. He made a choking sound, and she laughed triumphantly.

'Too late now, Master Guy!' she taunted him. 'You had your chance. Now you must wait your turn!'

By this time Tom had dropped his breeches to his ankles. Mary placed her hands on his shoulders and, with a little hop, pulled herself up, clinging to him with both her arms tight around his neck and her legs wrapped around his waist. She wore a necklace of cheap glass beads, which caught between them. The string snapped, the shiny beads cascaded down their bodies and scattered over the stone slabs. Neither seemed to notice.

Guy watched with a strange mixture of horror and fascination as his twin pinned the girl against the stone lid of their grandfather's sarcophagus, thrust and pounded against her, grunting, red-faced, while the girl thrust back at him. She began to make little mewing sounds, which rose higher and louder until she was yelping like a puppy.

Guy wanted to look away, but he could not. He stared in dreadful fascination as his brother threw back his head, opened his mouth wide and let out a dreadful, anguished cry.

She's killed him! Guy thought, and then, What are we going to tell Father? Tom's face was bright red and shining with sweat.

'Tom! Are you all right?' The words were out of his mouth before he could stop them.

Tom turned his head and gave him a contorted grin. 'I've never been better.' He let Mary drop to her feet, and stepped back, leaving her leaning once more against the

13

coffin. 'Now it's your turn,' he panted. 'Give her your sixpennyworth, lad!'

Mary was also breathless, but she laughed unsteadily, 'Gi' me a minute to catch my wind, then I'll take you for a gallop you'll not forget in many a year, Master Guy.'

At that moment a sharp double whistle reverberated down the airhole in the roof of the crypt, and Guy jumped back with alarm and relief. There was no mistaking the urgency of the warning.

'Cats!' he exclaimed. 'It's Dorry on the roof. Somebody's coming.'

Tom hopped on one foot, then on the other as he jerked up his breeches and hauled at the laces. 'Get you gone, Mary,' he snapped at the girl. She was scrabbling about on hands and knees, trying to gather up the fallen beads.

'Leave those!' Tom told her, but she ignored him. Her naked buttocks were marked with pink where they had caught the edge of the coffin – he could almost make out his grandfather's inscription imprinted on the white skin, and he felt a ridiculous urge to laugh. Instead he grabbed Guy by the shoulder. 'Come on! It might be Father!' That thought put wings on their feet and they flew up the stairs, jostling each other in their haste.

As they tumbled out of the vestry door, they found Dorian waiting for them, hiding in the ivy that covered the wall.

'Who is it, Dorry?' Tom gasped.

'Black Billy!' shrilled Dorian. 'He's just left the stables on Sultan and took the path straight up the hill. He'll be here in a minute.'

Tom gave vent to his most potent oath, learned from Big Daniel Fisher, his father's boatswain. 'He mustn't catch us here. Come on!' The three raced to the stone wall. Tom boosted Dorian over it, then he and Guy sprang over and pulled their younger brother down into the grass.

14

'Quiet! Both of you!' Tom was snorting with laughter and excitement.

'What happened?' Dorian piped up. 'I saw Mary go in. Did you do it with her, Guy?'

'You don't even know what it is.' Guy tried to avoid the question.

'I *do* know what it is,' Dorian told him indignantly. 'I've seen the rams at it, and the dogs and the cocks, and Hercules the bull, like this.' He rose on all fours and gave a lurid imitation, bucking and pumping his hips, sticking his tongue out of the corner of his mouth, and rolling his eyes horribly. 'Is this what you did to Mary, Guy?'

Guy flushed furiously. 'Stop that, Dorian Courtney! Do you hear me?' But Tom gave a delighted guffaw and pushed Dorian's face into the grass. 'You dirty little monkey. I bet a guinea you'd be better at it than Guy, hairs or no hairs.'

'Will you let me try next time, Tom?' Dorian pleaded, his voice muffled – his face was still buried in the turf.

'I'll let you try, when you've got a bit more to try with,' Tom said, and let him sit up, but at that moment they all heard the hoofbeats coming up the hill.

'Quiet!' Tom said, through his giggles, and they lay behind the wall in a row, trying to control their breathing and their mirth. They heard the horseman approach at a canter and rein down to a walk as he reached the gravelled area in front of the main doors of the chapel.

'Keep down!' Tom whispered to his brothers, but he pulled off the feathered cap and raised his head cautiously to peer over the top of the wall.

William Courtney sat up on Sultan. He was a superb horseman: the art had come to him naturally, perhaps some instinct from his African origins. He was slim and tall, and as usual dressed all in black. This, apart from his skin and hair pigmentation, was why his half-brothers had given him the nickname he hated so vehemently. Although

15

today he was bare-headed, he usually wore a wide-brimmed black hat decorated with a bunch of ostrich feathers. His high boots were black; his saddle and bridle were black. Sultan was a black stallion, groomed until he shone in the pale sunlight. Horse and rider were magnificent.

It was obvious that he'd come to check the arrangements for his impending marriage. The nuptials were to be held here rather than in the bride's home chapel, for other important ceremonies were to follow. These could only be held in the chapel of the Nautonnier Knights.

He stopped at the front door of the chapel and stooped low in the saddle to peer inside, then straightened and rode slowly around the side of the building to the vestry door. He looked about carefully then stared straight at Tom. Tom froze. He and the other boys were supposed to be down at the river mouth, helping Simon and his crew with the salmon nets. The itinerant labourers, whom William hired for the harvest, were fed almost entirely on salmon. It was cheap and plentiful, but they protested at this monotonous diet.

The apple-tree boughs must have concealed Tom from his brother's keen gaze for William dismounted and hitched Sultan to the iron ring beside the door. He was betrothed to the middle Grenville daughter. It was to be a splendid marriage, and their father had haggled for almost a year with John Grenville, the Earl of Exeter, to agree the dowry.

Black Billy's in a lather to get at her, Tom thought derisively, as he watched his brother pause on the chapel steps to slap the dust from his glistening black boots with the heavy lead-weighted riding-crop he always carried. Before he entered the chapel William glanced in Tom's direction once more. His skin was not black at all, but light amber in colour. He looked more Mediterranean than African, Spanish or Italian, perhaps. However, his hair was jet black, dense and shining, scraped back sleekly from his face and secured in a pigtail with a black ribbon plaited into it. He was handsome, in a formidable, dangerous fashion, with that thin, straight Ethiopian nose and the flashing dark eyes of a predator. Tom was envious of how most young women became flustered and fluttery in his presence.

William disappeared into the vestry and Tom rose to his feet. He whispered to his brothers, 'He's gone! Come on! We'll go back—' But before he could finish there was a scream from the chapel.

'Mary!' exclaimed Tom. 'I thought she had run, but the little dilly is still in there!'

'Black Billy has caught her,' gasped Guy.

'Now there'll be trouble!' said Dorian gleefully, and leaped up to get a better view of the excitement. 'What do you think he'll do.'

'I don't know,' said Tom, 'and we aren't waiting to find out.'

Before he could lead them in a precipitous retreat down the gill, Mary burst out of the vestry door. Even at that distance her terror was obvious. She ran as though pursued by a pack of wolves. A moment later William charged out into the sunlight, following the fleeing girl. 'Come back, you little slut!' His voice carried clearly to where they still crouched behind the wall. But Mary snatched up her skirts and ran all the harder. She was heading straight towards the wall where the boys were hiding.

Behind her, William freed Sultan's reins and swung up easily into the saddle. He sent the stallion after her at a full gallop. Horse and rider overhauled the running girl swiftly. 'Stop where you are, you dirty little whore. You've been up to no good.' William leaned over with the heavy riding-crop in his right hand as he caught up with her. 'You're going to tell me what you're doing here.' He slashed

17

at her, but Mary dodged away. He wheeled the stallion to follow her. 'You aren't going to escape me, bitch.' He was smiling, a cruel, cold smile.

'Please, Master William,' Mary shrieked, but he swung the crop again. It hissed in the air and she ducked under its arc with the agility of a hunted animal. Now she was running back towards the chapel, ducking through the apple trees, with William after her.

'Come on!' whispered Guy. 'Now's our chance.' He sprang up and tumbled down the steep side of the gill, Dorian behind him, but Tom still crouched by the wall. He watched in horror as his brother caught the running girl again and rose in the stirrups over her.

'I'll teach you to listen when I tell you to stop.' He lashed at her again, and this time the crop caught her between the shoulder-blades. Mary screamed at a higher pitch, a cry of agony and terror, and collapsed into the grass.

The sound of that shriek chilled Tom's spine and set his teeth on edge. 'Don't do that!' he said aloud, but William did not hear.

He stepped down out of the stirrups and stood over Mary. 'What mischief were you up to, drab?' She had fallen all in a welter of skirts and bare legs and he hit her again, aiming for her terrified white face, but Mary threw up an arm and took the lash across it. It raised a bright scarlet weal and she blubbered and writhed at the pain. 'Please don't hurt me, Master William.'

'I'm going to beat you until you bleed, and until you tell me what you were doing in the chapel when you should be in the scullery with your greasy pots and pans.' William was smiling easily, enjoying himself.

'I didn't do no harm, sir.' Mary lowered her hands to plead with him, and could not lift them again fast enough to meet the next blow that caught her full in the face. She howled and the blood rushed into her swollen cheek to colour it flaming scarlet. 'Please. Please don't hurt me any more.' She buried her injured face in her hands and rolled over in the grass trying to get away from him, but her skirt was rucked up under her.

William smiled again as he saw that she was naked beneath it and his next blow was delivered with relish across the soft white skin of her buttocks. 'What were you stealing, bitch? What were you doing in there?' He hit her again, and left a scarlet weal across the back of her thighs. Her scream struck Tom just as cruelly as the crop had sliced into her flesh.

'Leave her, damn you, Billy,' he blurted out, struck by an overpowering sense of responsibility and pity for the tortured girl. Before he had even thought about what he was doing he was over the wall and racing to Mary's rescue.

William did not hear him coming. He was absorbed in the sharp, unexpected pleasure he was experiencing from punishing this little slut. The sight of the scarlet lines on her white skin, her flailing, naked limbs, her wild shrieks, the unwashed animal smell of her all roused him keenly. 'What were you up to?' he roared. 'Are you going to tell me, or shall I beat it out of you?' He could hardly restrain his laughter as he laid a vivid scarlet stripe across her bare shoulders and watched the muscles beneath the soft skin spasm in agony.

Tom crashed into him from behind. He was a strapping lad for his age, not much shorter in height or less in weight than his older brother, and he was strengthened by his outrage and his hatred, by the injustice and cruelty of what he had watched, and by the memory of a thousand hurts and insults he and his brothers had suffered at Black Billy's hands. And he had the advantage this time of complete surprise.

He struck William in the small of the back, just as he was balanced on one leg, in the act of kicking the girl into a better position to receive the next blow from the riding-crop. He was flung forward with such force that he tripped over his victim and went sprawling, rolled over once and crashed head first into the bole of one of the apple trees. He lay there stunned.

Tom bent down and yanked the trembling, blubbering girl to her feet. 'Run!' he told her. 'As fast as you can!' He gave her a push. Mary needed no urging. She went off down the path, still weeping and howling, and Tom turned back to face the wrath of his brother.

William sat up in the grass. He was not yet certain who or what had knocked him down. He touched his scalp, pushing two fingers into the dark wavy hair, and brought them out smeared with blood from the small cut where he had hit the tree. Then he shook his head and stood up. He looked at Tom. 'You!' he said softly, almost pleasantly. 'I should have known you'd be at the bottom of this devilry.'

'She's done nothing.' Tom was still too buoyed up by his anger to regret his impulse. 'You might have wounded her sorely.'

'Yes,' William agreed. 'That was my purpose. She deserved it well enough.' He stooped and picked up the crop. 'But now she's gone, it's you I shall wound sorely, and take the deepest pleasure in doing my duty.'

He cut left and right with the weighted crop, which made a menacing hum in the air. 'Now tell me, little brother, what it was that you and that little whore were playing at? Was it something foul and dirty that our father should know about? Tell me now, before I have to whip it out of you.'

'I'll see you in hell first.' This was one of their father's favourite expressions, but despite his defiance Tom was bitterly regretting the chivalrous impulse that had propelled him into this confrontation. Now that he had lost the element of surprise he knew himself hopelessly outmatched. His elder brother's skills were not confined to his books. At Cambridge he had wrestled for King's College, and all-in wrestling was a sport without rules, except that the use of deadly weapons was frowned upon. At the fair in Exmouth last spring Tom had seen William throw and pin the local champion, a great ox of a man, after kicking and punching him half out of his mind.

He considered turning and running. But he knew that on those long legs, even wearing riding-boots, William would catch him within a hundred yards. There was nothing for it. He took his stance and raised both fists, the way Big Daniel had taught him.

William laughed in his face. 'By Peter and all the saints, the little cockerel wants to make a fight of it.' He dropped the riding-crop, but let his hands hang at his sides as he moved forward lazily. Suddenly he shot out his right fist. He had given no warning of the blow, and Tom only just managed to jump back. However, the fist grazed his lip, which swelled and immediately leaked the salty slick taste of blood into his mouth. His teeth were stained as though he had been eating raspberries.

'There we go! The first drop of claret spilt. There will be more, I warrant you, a cask of it before we're finished with this business.' William feinted with the right again, and when Tom ducked away he hooked at his head with the other hand. Tom blocked, as Big Daniel had shown him. William grinned. 'The monkey has learned a few tricks.' But his eyes narrowed: he had not expected that. He fired the same fist again, and Tom ducked under it then seized his brother's arm at the elbow in a desperate two-hand grip. Instinctively William pulled back, and Tom used the momentum to spring forward instead of resisting and, at the same time, to kick out wildly. Again he caught the other off balance, and one of his flying kicks landed squarely in his crotch. The breath went out of William in a *whoof* of pain, and he doubled over to clutch his injured parts with both hands. Tom swirled round and ran off down the path towards the house.

Although his dark features were still contorted with pain, when he saw the younger boy go, William straightened, forced himself to ignore the pain and launched himself after him. He was hampered by his injury, but even so he bore down inexorably on the fleeing Tom.

When Tom heard the racing footfalls coming up on him, he glanced over his shoulder and lost a yard. He could hear his brother grunting, and imagined he could feel his breath on the back of his neck. There was no escape, he could not run away from him. Instead he dropped to the ground and rolled himself into a ball.

William was so close, and coming on so fast, that he could not stop. The only way he could avoid Tom was to jump over him. He cleared him easily, but Tom rolled on to his back in the middle of the muddy path, and reached up to grab William's ankle while he was in mid-air. He held on with the strength of terror, and the man crashed down in the path on his face. For that instant he was helpless, and Tom scrambled to his feet, was on the point of racing away again, when his anger and hatred took over from his good sense.

He saw Black Billy sprawling in the mud. The temptation was too much for him to resist: for the very first time in his life his elder brother was at his mercy. Tom pulled back his right leg and took a full swing of the boot. He caught William in the side of the head just in front of his ear, but the result was not what he had expected. Instead of collapsing, William let out a roar of rage and clutched at Tom's leg with both hands. With a heave, he flung the boy into the bracken beside the path then hauled himself to his feet and launched himself at Tom before he could recover.

He straddled his younger brother's chest, then leaned

forward to pin his wrists to the ground above his head. Tom could not move, and could hardly breathe as William's full weight crushed his ribs. William was still gasping and wheezing, but slowly his breathing eased, and he began to smile again, a twisted, painful smile.

'You're going to pay for your fun, puppy. You're going to pay in a heavy coin, that I promise you,' he whispered. 'Just let me get my breath back and then we'll finish this business.' The sweat dripped from his chin onto Tom's upturned face.

'I hate you!' Tom hissed up at him. 'We hate you. My brothers, everybody who works here, everybody who knows you – we all hate you!'

Abruptly William released his grip on one of Tom's wrists and slashed him across the face with a vicious back-handed blow. 'For all these years I've been trying to teach you manners,' he said softly, 'and you never learn.'

Tom's eyes filled with tears of pain, but he still managed to gather a mouthful of saliva and spit it at the swarthy face above him. It splattered across William's chin, but he ignored it. 'I'll get you, Black Billy!' Tom promised, in a painful whisper. 'One day I'll get you.'

'No.' William shook his head. 'I think not.' He smiled, 'Have you not heard of the law of primogeniture, little monkey?' He landed another full-blooded, open-handed blow against the side of Tom's head. The boy's eyes glazed, and blood appeared below one nostril. 'Answer me, brother.' William swung back with the other hand, knocking Tom's head across. 'Do you know what it means?' He hit him again, right-handed. 'Answer me, my little beauty.'

The next swing was left-handed, then right-handed again, and the blows settled into a rhythm. Slam, with the right. Slam, with the left. Tom's head rolled loosely from side to side. He was swiftly losing consciousness, and the succession of blows never let up.

'Primogeniture –' Slam! ' – is the –' Slam! ' – right –' Slam! ' – of the –' Slam! ' – first-born.' Slam!

The next blow came from behind Black Billy's back. Dorian had followed them down the path and had seen what was happening to his favourite sibling. The blows raining down on Tom hurt Dorian just as painfully. He looked around desperately for a weapon. There was a thick accumulation of fallen branches along the edge of the path. He picked up a dry stick as thick as his wrist and as long as his arm and crept up behind William. He had the good sense to give no warning of what he was about to do, just quietly lifted the branch with both hands high above his head. He paused to take aim, gather all his strength, then brought down the branch on top of William's head with such force that the stick snapped in his hands.

William's hands flew to his pate and he rolled off Tom's chest. He looked up at Dorian, and let out a bellow. 'The whole stinking litter!' He came to his feet, and swayed unsteadily. 'Even the youngest cur.'

'You just leave my brother be,' Dorian threatened, white-faced with terror.

'Run, Dorry!' Tom croaked dazedly, from where he lay in the bracken, without the strength to sit up. 'He'll kill you. Run!'

But Dorian stood his ground. 'You leave him alone,' he said.

William took a step towards him. 'You know, Dorry, that your mother was a whore.' He smiled, soothingly, and took another step forward, dropping his hands from his injured head. 'That makes you the son of a whore.'

Dorian was not certain what a whore was, but he answered furiously, 'You are not to speak of my mama like that.' Despite himself he took a pace backwards, as William advanced menacingly upon him.

'Mama's baby,' William mocked him. 'Well, your whore mama is dead, baby.'

Tears flooded Dorian's eyes. 'Don't say that! I hate you, William Courtney.'

'You, too, must learn some manners, Baby Dorry.' William's hands shot out and locked around the child's neck. He lifted Dorian easily into the air, kicking, clawing.

'Manners maketh man,' William said, and pinned him against the trunk of the copper beech under which they stood. 'You must learn, Dorry.' He pressed carefully on the child's windpipe with both fingers, staring into his face, watching it swell and turn purple. Dorian's heels kicked helplessly against the tree trunk, and he scratched at William's hands, leaving red lines on his skin, but he made no sound.

'A nest of vipers,' said William. 'That's what you are, asps and vipers. I'll have to clean you out.'

Tom heaved himself out of the bracken and crawled to where his elder brother stood. He clutched at his legs. 'Please, Billy! I'm sorry. Hit me. Leave Dorry alone. Please, don't hurt him. He didn't mean anything.'

William kicked him away, still holding the child against the tree. Dorry's feet were dancing two feet above the ground.

'Respect, Dorry, you must learn respect.' He relaxed the pressure of his thumbs and allowed his victim to draw a single breath, then clamped down again. Dorian's silent struggles became frantic.

'Take me!' pleaded Tom. 'Leave Dorry alone. He's had enough.' Tom pulled himself to his feet, using the tree trunk to support himself. He tugged at William's sleeve.

'You spat in my face,' William said grimly, 'and this little viper tried to brain me. Now you may watch him choke.'

'William!' Another voice, rough with outrage, cut in from close at his side. 'What in the name of the devil do you think you're playing at?' A heavy blow fell across

25

William's outstretched arms. He let the child drop to the muddy earth and whirled to face his father.

Hal Courtney had used his scabbard to strike his eldest son's hands off the child, and now it seemed he might use it to knock William off his feet.

'Are you mad? What are you doing to Dorian?' he asked, his voice shaking with rage.

'He had to be – it was only a game, Father. We were playing.' William's own rage had miraculously evaporated, and he seemed chastened. 'He has taken no harm. It was all in good part.'

'You have half murdered the lad,' Hal snarled, then went down on one knee to pick his youngest son out of the mud. He held him tenderly against his chest. Dorian buried his face against his father's neck and sobbed, coughed and choked for air. There were livid scarlet fingermarks on the soft skin of his throat, and tears were smeared across his face. Hal Courtney glared at William. 'This is not the first time we have spoken about rough treatment of the younger ones. By God, William, we will discuss this further, after dinner, this evening in the library. Now get you out of my sight, before I lose control of myself.'

'Yes, sir,' William said humbly, and started back up the path to the chapel. As he left, though, he shot Tom a look that left no doubt in the boy's mind that the matter was far from settled.

'What happened to you, Tom?' Hal turned back to him.

'Nothing, Father,' he replied staunchly. 'It's nothing.' He wiped his bloody nose on his sleeve. It would have been a violation of his own code to carry tales, even of such a hated adversary as Black Billy.

'Then what happened to make your nose bleed and your face swell and turn red as a ripe apple?' Hal's voice was gruff but gentle: he was testing the lad.

'I fell,' Tom said.

'I know that sometimes you're a clumsy clod, Tom, but are you sure someone didn't push you?'

'If I did, then it's between him and me, sir.' Tom pulled himself up to his full height to disguise his aches and injuries.

Hal placed an arm around his shoulder. With the other he clasped Dorian to his chest. 'Come, boys, we'll go home now.' He took the pair down to where he had left his horse at the edge of the woods, and lifted Dorian up onto its neck in front of the saddle before he swung up behind him. He slipped his feet into the stirrups then reached down to take Tom by the arm and haul him up behind.

Tom placed both arms around his father's waist and pressed his swollen, bruised face into the small of his back. He loved the warmth and smell of his father's body, the hardness and strength of him. It made him feel safe from all harm. He wanted to cry but he forced back the tears. 'You're not a child,' he said to himself. 'Dorry can cry, but you can't.'

'Where is Guy?' his father asked, without looking around.

Tom almost said, 'He ran away,' but he stopped the disloyal words before they were spoken. 'He went home, I think, sir.'

Hal rode on in silence, feeling the two warm bodies pressed gratefully against him, and hurting for them as he knew they were hurt. Yet he felt a sense of angry helplessness. This was far from the first time he had been sucked into this primeval conflict of siblings, the children of his three wives. He knew it was a competition in which the odds were heavily loaded against the youngest, and from which there could be only one possible outcome.

He scowled in frustration. Hal Courtney was not yet forty-two – William had been born when he was only

27

eighteen – yet he felt old and weighed down with care when he confronted the turmoil of his four sons. The problem was that he loved William as much, if not more, than even little Dorian.

William was his first-born, the son of his Judith, that fierce, beautiful warrior-maid of Africa, whom he had loved with deep awe and passion. When she had died under the flying hoofs of her own wild steed she had left an aching void in his existence. For many years there had been nothing to fill the gap except the beautiful infant she had left behind.

Hal had reared William, had taught him to be tough and resilient, clever and resourceful. He was all those things now, and more. And in him there was something of the wildness and cruelty of that dark, mysterious continent that nothing could tame. Hal feared that and yet, in all truth, he would not have had it any other way. Hal himself was a hard, ruthless man, so how should he resent those qualities in his own first-born son?

'Father, what does primogenital mean?' Tom asked suddenly, his voice muffled by Hal's cloak.

He was so in step with Hal's own thoughts that his father started. 'Where did you learn that?' he asked.

'I heard it somewhere,' Tom mumbled. 'I forget where.' Hal could guess very well where it had been but he did not press the boy, who had been hurt enough for one day. Instead he tried to answer the question fairly, for Tom was old enough now. It was high time that he began to learn what hardships life held in store for him as a younger brother.

'You mean primogeniture, Tom. It means the right of the first-born.'

'Billy,' said Tom softly.

'Yes. Billy,' Hal agreed frankly. 'In accordance with the law of England, he follows directly in my footsteps. He takes precedence over all his younger brothers.'

'Us,' said Tom, with a touch of bitterness.

'Yes, you,' Hal agreed. 'When I am gone, everything is his.'

'When you are dead, you mean,' Dorian bored in, with indisputable logic.

'That's right, Dorry, when I am dead.'

'I don't want you to die,' Dorian wailed, his voice still hoarse from the damage to his throat. 'Promise me you won't ever die, Father.'

'I wish I could, lad, but I can't. We're all going to die one day.'

Dorian was silent for a moment. 'But not tomorrow?'

Hal chuckled softly. 'Not tomorrow. Not for many a long day, if I can help it. But one day it will happen. It always does.' He forestalled the next question.

'And when it does, Billy will be Sir William,' Tom said. 'That's what you're trying to tell us.'

'Yes. William will have the baronetcy, but that's not all. He will have everything else as well.'

'Everything? I don't understand,' said Tom, lifting his head from his father's back. 'Do you mean High Weald? The house and the land?'

'Yes. It will all belong to Billy. The estate, the land, the house, the money.'

'That not fair,' Dorian expostulated. 'Why can't Tom and Guy not have some? They're much nicer than Billy. It's not fair.'

'Perhaps it isn't fair, but that's the law of England.'

'It isn't fair,' Dorian persisted. 'Billy's cruel and horrible.'

'If you go through life expecting it to be fair, then you will have many sad disappointments, my boy,' Hal said softly, and hugged his baby. I wish I could make it different for you, he thought.

'When you're dead, Billy won't let us stay here at High Weald. He'll send us away.'

'You can't be sure of that,' Hal protested.

'Yes, I can,' Tom said, with conviction. 'He told me so, and he meant it.'

'You'll make your own way, Tom. That's why you have to be clever and tough. That's why I'm hard on you sometimes, harder than I ever was on William. You must learn to fend for yourselves after I am gone.' He paused. Could he explain this to them, when they were still so young? He had to try. He owed them that. 'The law of primogeniture has served to make England great. If every time somebody died his land was split between his surviving children, then soon the whole country would be divided into tiny, useless parcels, unable to feed a single family, and we would become a nation of peasants and paupers.'

'So what will we do?' Tom asked. 'Those of us who are driven out.'

'The army, the navy and the Church are open to you. You might go out into the world as traders or colonists and come back from its far corners, from the ends of the oceans, with treasures and wealth even greater than William will inherit when I die.'

They thought about that in silence for a long while. 'I'll be a sailor, like you, Father. I'll sail to the ends of the oceans, like you did,' said Tom, at last.

'And I will go with you, Tom,' said Dorian.

Sitting in the front pew of the family chapel, Hal Courtney had every reason to feel pleased with himself and the world around him. He watched his eldest son waiting at the altar, while organ music filled the small building with joyous sound. William was strikingly handsome and dashing in the costume he had chosen for his wedding. For once he had eschewed his sombre black

30

attire. His collar was of the finest Flemish lace, and his waistcoat of green velvet embroidered with golden stags. The pommel of his sword was encrusted with carnelians and lapis-lazuli. Most of the women in the congregation were watching him also, and the younger ones were giggling and discussing him in whispers.

'I could ask nothing more of a son,' Hal told himself. William had proved himself as an athlete and as a scholar. His tutor at Cambridge had praised his industry and capacity for learning, and he had wrestled, ridden and hawked his way to prominence. After his studies, when he had returned to High Weald, he had proved his worth yet again as an administrator and entrepreneur. Gradually Hal had given him more and more control over the running of the estate and the tin mines, until now he himself had almost withdrawn from overseeing the day-to-day running of the family estates. If there was anything that made Hal at all uneasy, it was that William was often too hard a bargainer, too ruthless in his treatment of the men who worked for him. More than once men had died at the tin face who might have been spared if a little more thought had been given to their safety, and a little more money spent on improvements to the shafts and the haulage. Yet the profits from the mines and the estate had almost doubled in the last three years. That was proof enough of his competence.

Now William was contracting this glittering marriage. Of course, Hal had pointed him in the direction of Lady Alice Grenville, but William had courted her and, in very short order, had had her so besotted with him that she had convinced her father of the suitability of the union, despite his initial reluctance. After all, William Courtney was a commoner.

Hal glanced at the Earl as he sat in the front pew across the aisle. John Grenville was older than him by ten years, a lean, man, plainly dressed as ill befitted one of the greatest landowners in England. His dark eyes were hooded in the unhealthy pallor of his face. He caught Hal's eye and nodded, his expression neither friendly nor hostile, although harsh words had been exchanged when it had come to the matter of Alice's dowry. In the end she brought with her the title to Gainesbury farms, over a thousand acres, in addition to the working tin mines of East and South Rushwold. The demand for tin seemed insatiable, these days, and Rushwold adjoined the Courtney mines that William was administering so efficiently. Run together, output would grow and lower the costs of hauling the precious ore to the surface. That was not all of Alice's dowry. The final item which he had wheedled out of the Earl pleased Hal as much as the rest: the packet of English East India Company shares, twelve thousand of the common stock with full voting rights. Hal was already a major shareholder in and governor of the Company, but these new shares would increase his voting power and make him one of the most influential men on the board after the chairman, Nicholas Childs.

Yes, he had every reason to feel smug. Then what was this strange feeling that niggled, like grit in the eye, at his contentment? Sometimes, when he rode along the cliffs and gazed out over the cold grey sea, he remembered the warm azure waters of the Ocean of the Indies. Often now when he flew a hawk and watched its rapid wing-beats against the sky, he remembered the taller, bluer sky of Africa. On some evenings he took down his charts from his library shelves and pored over them for hours, reading the notations he had made upon them two decades before, and dreaming of Africa's blue hills, its white beaches and mighty rivers.

Once, very recently, he had woken from a dream in sweat and confusion. It had all been so vivid, the reliving of those tragic events. She had been with him again, the lovely golden girl who had been his first true love. Once again she had been in his arms, dying. 'Sukeena, my love, I will die with you.' He had felt his heart break again as he said those words.

'No.' Her sweet voice began to fade. 'No, you will go on. I have travelled with you as far as I am permitted. But for you the fates have reserved a special destiny. You will live on. You will have many strong sons whose descendants will flourish in this land of Africa, and make it their own.' Hal covered his eyes and bowed his head as if in prayer – in case someone in the congregation saw the glint of a tear in his eye. After a while he opened his eyes and looked down at the sons she had foreseen all those years ago.

Tom was the closest to him in spirit and flesh, big-boned and strong for his age, with the eye and hand of a warrior. He was restless, easily bored by routine or any task that called for long, meticulous concentration. He was no scholar, but neither did he lack in brain or cunning. In looks, he was pleasant but not handsome, for his mouth and nose were too large, but he had a strong, determined face and heavy jaw. He was impulsive and sometimes rash, almost fearless, often too bold for his own good. The bruises on his face were faded now to yellow and ugly purple, but it was typical of Tom to rush in against someone so much older and of twice his strength, without a thought for the consequences.

Hal had learned the truth of the confrontation in the woods below the chapel: William had told him of Mary, the scullerymaid, and she had made to him an almost incoherent confession, sobbing bitterly the while. 'I'm a good girl, sir, God's truth I am. I didn't steal nothing like he said I did. It was just a bit of fun, nothing bad. Then Master William he came into the chapel and he said bad things to me, and he beat me.' Weeping copiously she had pulled up her skirts to show the great flaming weals across her thighs.

Hal had said hastily, 'Cover yourself, girl.' He could

33

guess just how innocent she was. He had noticed her before, although he usually took scant interest in the two dozen or so females who worked in the main house, for she had a saucy eye and a voluptuous turn of buttock and bosom that was difficult to overlook.

'Master Tom tried to stop him, else he would have killed me, Master William would. He's a good boy, is Master Tom. He didn't do nothing—' So Tom had cut his teeth on this bit of sweet meat, Hal thought. It would do the lad no harm. She had probably given him a good grounding in the old game, and when William had caught them at it, Tom had rushed to her defence. The sentiment was praiseworthy, but the action was foolhardy: the object of his knight errantry hardly worthy of such fierce loyalty. Hal had sent the girl back to the kitchens and had a quiet word with his steward. Within two days he had arranged other employment for her as a serving-wench at the Royal Oak in Plymouth, and she had disappeared quietly from High Weald. Hal didn't want her knocking at his door in nine months' time to present them with a bundle.

He sighed softly. It was not long now before he would have to find other employment for Tom too. He could not stay here much longer. He was almost a man. Aboli had recently started Tom's lessons with the sword – Hal had delayed this until the boy had the strength in his arms: he had seen youngsters who had been spoiled by a too early start with the blade. He shuddered abruptly as he thought of Tom in another fit of rage calling out his elder brother: William was a swordsman of note. He had severely wounded a fellow student at Cambridge with a thrust through the lower chest. It had been an affair of honour but it had taken all Hal's influence and a purse of gold guineas to keep it quiet. Duelling was legal, but frowned upon; had the man died, even Hal might not have been able to shield his son from the consequences. The thought of two of his sons taking up their feud with blades did not

34

bear thinking about, yet it might become more than a possibility if he did not separate them soon. He would have to find Tom a berth in one of the ships of John Company, the affectionate sobriquet for the English East India Company. Tom sensed his father's gaze upon him and turned to give him such a frank, guileless grin that Hal had to look away.

Guy sat beside his twin. Guy was another problem, Hal mused, but of a different sort from Tom. Although twins ran strongly in the Courtney line, and each generation usually threw up at least one set, Tom and Guy were not identical. To the contrary. They were different in almost every way that Hal could divine.

Guy was by far the better-looking of the two, with delicate, rather feminine features, and a graceful body that yet lacked the physical power and force of Tom's. In nature he was cautious to the point of timidity, yet he was bright and intelligent, with the ability to apply himself to even the most repetitive tasks with all his attention.

Hal did not have the gentry's usual disdain for merchants and moneylenders, and had no qualms in encouraging one of his sons to make a career in that direction. He recognized that Guy might be best suited to such a life. It was hard to imagine him as a warrior or a sailor. Hal frowned. There were numerous openings in John Company for clerks and secretaries, safe, secure jobs that could lead to swift advancement, especially for a bright, industrious young man whose father was a governor of the Company. He would speak to Childs next week when they met.

Hal intended to leave for London early the following morning, directly after he had seen William wed safely to Lady Alice, and the transfer of her dowry into the Courtney estate. The horses were standing ready and Big Daniel and Aboli could have them harnessed to the coach and on the way within an hour of Hal calling for them. Even at their best speed, though, it would take at least five days to get up to London and the quarterly meeting of the Company board was due to be held on the first day of next month.

I will have to take the boys with me, he thought suddenly, and it was a measure of his concern that he made that decision. It would be tempting providence to leave them at High Weald with William as master of the estate, and himself not there to mediate and protect. Even Dorian had best come, he decided.

He looked down fondly at his youngest son, perched beside him on the pew, and received in return a sunny, adoring smile. Dorian wriggled a little closer to him on the hard oak bench. Hal felt strangely moved by the contact of that small body. He placed a casual hand on the boy's shoulder. It's too early to tell how this one will turn out, he thought, but it seems that he might have all the good points of the others and fewer of their weaknesses. But it is still far too soon to tell.

At that moment he was distracted by the organ music as it burst dramatically into the bridal march. Then there was a rustle and hum as the congregation turned in their seats and strained for a first glimpse of the bride.

Although the sun was not yet clear of the treetops, and only a few stray rays were catching the high gables and towers of the big house, the entire household turned out to see them away to London, from William with his new bride at his side, Ben Green the estate steward, Evan the house-steward, right down to the lowest kitchen maid and groom.

In order of seniority they were marshalled down the main staircase that led up to the front doors, and the low-liest servants were gathered in orderly ranks on the front lawn. Big Daniel and Aboli were on the coachman's box, and the horses were snorting steam from their nostrils in the morning chill.

Hal embraced William briefly, while Alice, pink and glowing with happiness and love, clung adoringly to her new husband's arm. On their father's instructions the boys lined up unsmiling behind him to shake their elder brother's hand and then, whooping with excitement, raced each other down to the waiting carriage.

'Can I ride up with Aboli and Big Daniel?' Tom pleaded, and his father nodded indulgently.

'Me, too?' Dorian danced beside him.

'You ride in the coach with me and Mr Walsh.' Mr Walsh was their tutor, and Dorian faced four days of captivity with him and his books, Latin, French and arithmetic.

'Please, Father, why can't I?' Dorian demanded, then immediately answered himself. 'I know, because I'm the youngest!'

'Come on, Dorry.' Guy took his hand and pulled him into the coach. 'I'll help you with your lessons.'

The hardships and injustices of youth were immediately forgotten as Aboli cracked his whip, the carriage jerked and set off, with the gravel crunching under the iron-shod wheels. Guy and Dorian leaned from the window to wave and shout farewell to their favourites among the household staff until they turned at the crossroads and High Weald was hidden from their view.

On the box, Tom sat ecstatically between two of his favourite men. Big Daniel was a great hulk with a mane of silver hair bristling out from under his cocked hat. He possessed not a single tooth in his head so when he chewed his weathered face folded like the leather bellows of a blacksmith's forge. It was well known that, even at his age, he was the strongest man in Devonshire. Tom had seen him lift a recalcitrant horse in the air and dump it on its back with all four legs in the air and hold it there

37

effortlessly while the blacksmith shod it. He had been boatswain for Francis Courtney, and when Tom's grandfather had been killed by the Dutch, Big Daniel had served the son, had sailed the southern oceans with Hal Courtney, had fought with him against pagan and Dutchman, against pirate and renegade and a dozen other enemies. He had played nurse to William and the twins, had carried them on his back and dandled them with huge, gentle hands. He could tell the most enchanting stories that any small boy could dream of, build models of tall ships, so beautifully realistic in every detail that it seemed they might at any moment sail over the horizon to some stirring adventure, bearing Tom away with them on the quarterdeck. He had the most intriguing repertoire of oaths and sayings that Tom rehearsed only in the company of Dorian and Guy, for to recite them in the presence of William or his father, or any other grown-up, would have led to instant retribution. Tom loved Big Daniel dearly.

Outside his own immediate family there was only one other person he loved more. Aboli sat on Tom's other side, holding the reins in his huge black hands.

'You hold the blunderbuss.' Knowing what pleasure it would give him, Aboli handed the hideous weapon to Tom. Although its barrel was shorter than Tom's arm, it could hurl a devastating double handful of gooseshot from the gaping bell-shaped muzzle. 'If a highwayman tries to stop us, you give him a bellyful, Klebe.' Tom was almost overwhelmed by the honour, and sat up straight between them, silently praying for the chance to use the heavy weapon he cradled in his lap.

Aboli had used his pet name: 'Klebe' meant Hawk in the language of the forests of Africa. It was a nickname Tom delighted in. Aboli had taught him the language of the forest, 'because,' he had explained, 'that is where your destiny will take you. It has been prophesied by a wise and beautiful woman long ago. Africa awaits you. I, Aboli,

38

must prepare you for that day when you step on her soil for the first time.'

Aboli was a prince of his own tribe. The patterns of ritual scars that covered his black face in raised whorls and ridges were proof of his royal blood. He was an expert with any weapon he laid his hands on, from an African fighting stick to the finest Toledo rapier. Now that his twins were of the correct age, Hal Courtney had entrusted to Aboli the task of teaching them swordsmanship. Aboli had trained Hal at the same age, and William too. He had moulded each of them into expert swordsmen. Tom had taken to the blade with the same natural ability as his father and his half-brother but it grieved Aboli that Guy did not show the same eagerness or aptitude.

'How old do you think Aboli is?' Dorian had once asked.

Tom had replied, with all the wisdom of his superior age, 'He is even older than Father. He must be a hundred years at least!'

Aboli had not a hair on his cannonball head, not a single thread of grey to betray his true age, and though wrinkle and scar were so intertwined on his features as to be inextricable, his body was lean and muscular, his skin smooth and glossy as polished obsidian. Nobody, not even Aboli himself, knew how old he was. The stories he told were even more fascinating than Big Daniel's best. He told of giants and pygmies, of forests filled with marvellous animals, great apes who could rip a man apart as though he were a grasshopper, of creatures with necks so long they could eat the leaves off the tops of the tallest trees, of deserts where diamonds the size of apples glittered in the sun like water, and mountains made of solid gold.

'One day I'll go there!' Tom told him fervently, at the end of one of these magical stories. 'Will you come with me, Aboli?'

'Yes, Klebe. We will sail there together, one day,' Aboli promised.

Now the carriage jolted and crashed over the uneven surface, and splashed through the mud holes, and Tom perched between the two men trying to contain his excitement and impatience. When they reached the crossroads before Plymouth, a skeletal figure was hanging in chains from the gibbet, still wearing waistcoat, breeches and boots.

'He's been hanging there a month, come next Sunday.' Big Daniel lifted his cocked hat to the grinning skull of the executed highwayman, from which the crows had picked most of the flesh. 'God speed, John Warking. Put in a good word for me with Old Nick!'

Instead of continuing into Plymouth Aboli swung the horses onto the wide, well-travelled tracks that led eastward towards Southampton and London.

London, the greatest city in the world. Five days later, when they were still twenty miles off they saw its smoke on the horizon. It hung in the air and mingled with the clouds, like the great dun pall of a battlefield. The road took them along the bank of the Thames, broad and busy, bustling with an endless procession of small craft, barges, lighters and bum-boats, loaded deeply with timber and building stone, with bags of wheat and lowing cattle, with boxes, bales and kegs, the commerce of a nation. The river traffic grew denser as they approached the Pool of London, where the tall ships were anchored, and they passed the first buildings, each surrounded by open fields and gardens.

They could smell the city now, and the smoke closed over their heads, shading the sun. Each chimney stack was belching forth its dark fumes to deepen the gloom. The smell of the city grew stronger. The reek of green hides and new cloth in bales, of rotten meat and other strange, intriguing odours, of men and horses, of rats and chickens, the sulphurous stench of burning coal and raw sewage. The river waters turned dung brown, and the roadway became congested with cart and carriage, coach and dray. The open fields gave way to endless buildings of stone and brick, their roofs huddled together, and the side-streets became so narrow that two carriages could not pass each other. Now the river was almost obscured by the warehouses that stood four-square along either bank.

Aboli weaved their own carriage through the multitude, exchanging cheerful banter and insult with the other drivers. Beside him Tom could not drink it all in. His eyes darted back and around, his head twisted on his shoulders and he chattered like an excited squirrel. Hal Courtney had given in to Dorian's pleading and allowed him to scramble onto the carriage roof where he sat behind Tom and added his shouts and laughter to those of his elder brother.

At last they crossed the river on a mountainous stone bridge, so massive that the river tide built up around its piles and swirled like a brown maelstrom through the piers. There were stalls along its length where ragged hucksters shrieked their wares to the passers.

'Fresh lobsters, me darlings. Live oysters and cockles.'

'Ale! Sweet and strong. Drunk for a penny. Dead drunk for twopence.'

Tom saw one man puke copiously over the side of the bridge and a drunken drab spread her tattered skirts around her as she squatted and peed in the gutter. Officers in splendid uniforms from King William's Guards regiments, back from the wars, strutted through the throng with pretty girls in bonnets on their arms.

Warships were anchored in the river, and Tom eagerly pointed them out to Daniel.

'Aye.' Daniel spat tobacco juice over the side. 'That's the old *Dreadnought*, seventy-four guns. She was at the Medway. That one over there is the *Cambridge* . . .' Daniel reeled off the names of glory, and Tom thrilled to hear them.

41

'Look there!' he cried. 'That must be St Paul's Cathedral.' Tom recognized it from the pictures in his school books. The dome was only half complete, open to the sky and covered with a spider's web of scaffolding.

Guy had heard him and stuck his head out of the carriage window. 'New St Paul's,' he corrected his twin. 'The old cathedral was completely destroyed in the Great Fire. Master Wren is the architect, and the dome will be almost 365 feet high . . .'

But the attention of his two brothers on top of the carriage had moved on.

'What happened to those buildings there?' Dorian pointed out the smoke-blackened ruins that were interspersed with the newer edifices along the banks of the river.

'They were all burned down in the Fire,' Tom told him. 'See how the builders are at work.'

They crossed the bridge into the crowded streets of the city. Here the press of vehicles and humanity was denser still.

'I was here before the Fire,' Daniel told them, 'long before you nippers were even thought of. The streets were half as broad as they are now, and the people emptied the chamber-pots into the gutters . . .' He went on to delight the boys with other graphic details of the conditions that had prevailed in the city only twenty years previously.

In some of the open carriages they passed were grand gentlemen dressed in the height of fashion, and with them ladies in bright silk and satin, so beautiful that Tom stared at them in awe, sure that they were not mortals but heavenly angels.

Some of the other women who leaned from the windows of the houses that crowded the street did not seem so sacred. One singled out Aboli and screeched an invitation to him.

'What does she want to show Aboli?' Dorian piped wide-eyed.

Daniel ruffled his flaming red hair. 'Better for you if you never find out, Master Dorry, for once you do you'll never know peace again.'

They came at last to the Plough, and the carriage rumbled over the cobbles as Aboli wheeled it up to the entrance of the inn. The host rushed out to receive them, bowing and dry-washing his hands with delight. 'Sir Hal, welcome! We were not expecting you until the morrow.'

'The road was better than I feared. We made good time.' Hal stepped down stiffly. 'Give us a pitcher of small beer to wash the dust from our throats,' he ordered as he stamped into the inn and flung himself down into one of the chairs in the front parlour.

'I have your usual chamber ready for you, Sir Hal, and a room for your lads.'

'Good, and have your grooms take care of the horses, and find a room for my servants.'

'I have a message from Lord Childs for you, Sir Hal. He charged me most strictly to send him word the minute you arrived.'

'Have you done so?' Hal looked at him sharply. Nicholas Childs was the chairman of the governors of the English East India Company, but he ran it as though it were his personal fief. He was a man of vast wealth and influence in the city and at court. The Crown was a major shareholder in the Company, and thus Childs had the ear and favour of the sovereign himself. Not a man to treat lightly.

'I have this minute sent a message to him.' Hal quaffed from the pitcher of beer and belched politely behind his hand. 'You can show me up now.' He stood and the host led him up the stairs, backing ahead of him and bowing at every third step. Swiftly Hal approved the accommodation.

His own chamber had a salon and private dining room. The boys were in the room opposite, and Walsh, their tutor, in the room beside them. They would use this as their schoolroom, for Hal was determined that they miss not a day of their studies.

'Can we go out and see the town, please, Father?' Tom begged.

Hal glanced at Walsh. 'Have they finished the lessons you set for them on the journey?'

'Master Guy has indeed. But the others . . .' Walsh said primly.

'You complete the task that Master Walsh has given you,' Hal scowled at his sons, 'to his complete satisfaction, before you set a foot outside the front door.' As he turned away Tom made a ferocious face at Walsh's back.

The messenger from Nicholas Childs arrived before Aboli and Daniel had finished bringing up the heavy leather trunks that had been strapped on the roof of the carriage. The liveried footman bowed and handed Hal the sealed sheet of parchment. Hal gave him a coin and split the wax seal of the East India Company with his thumbnail. The letter had been penned by a secretary: 'Lord Childs requests the pleasure of your company to supper at eight of the clock this evening at Bombay House.' Below this was a note in Childs's own ornate hand: 'Oswald Hyde will be the only other guest. N.C.'

Hal whistled softly: a private supper with the old man and the Chancellor of His Majesty King William III. 'Something interesting afoot.' He smiled and felt the tingle of excitement run through his veins.

Between them Aboli and Daniel had scrubbed the mud of the road off the carriage and curried the horses until once again their coats shone like polished metal. Hal had plenty of time to bath and have his clothes sponged by the chambermaid before it was time to set out to keep his appointment with Childs.

Bombay House stood behind high walls and was set in substantial gardens within a stone's throw of the Inns of Court, an easy stroll from the headquarters of the East India Company on Leadenhall Street. There were guards at the high wrought-iron gates, but they swung open the gates as soon as Aboli announced his master. Three footmen were waiting at the double doors of the house to usher Hal in and take his cloak and hat. Then the major-domo led him on a march through a succession of grand rooms, hung with mirrors and huge oil paintings of ships, battles and exotic landscapes, and lit by forests of wax candles in crystal chandeliers and gilt oil lamps held aloft by statues of nymphs and blackamoors.

As they went further the grand public rooms gave way to meaner surroundings, and Hal realized that they had entered the private areas of the great house, closer to the kitchens and the servants' quarters. At last they paused before a door so small and insignificant that he might easily have passed it by, but the head steward knocked once with his staff.

'Enter!' boomed a familiar voice from the far side, and Hal, stooping through the opening, found himself in a small but richly decorated cabinet. The panelled walls were hung with tapestries from Arabia and the Indies, and the space was only just sufficient to accommodate the large table piled high with silver chafing dishes and gilt tureens, which emitted succulent aromas and enticing wisps of steam.

'Punctual as usual,' Lord Childs complimented him. He was sitting at the head of the table, overflowing the large padded chair. 'Forgive me for not rising to greet you properly, Courtney. Damned gout again.' He indicated his foot, swathed in bandages, resting on a stool. 'You have met Oswald, of course.'

'I have had that honour.' Hal bowed to the Chancellor. 'Good evening, my lord. We met at Mr Samuel Pepys's house last August.'

'Good evening, Sir Henry. I well recall our meeting.' Lord Hyde smiled and gave him a seated half-bow. 'You are not the kind of man one readily forgets.' It was a propitious start to the evening, Hal realized.

Childs waved him easily and informally to the chair at his side. 'Sit here, so we can talk. Take off your coat and wig, man. Let's be comfortable.' He glanced at Hal's thick dark hair, only lightly laced with silver. 'Of course, you don't wear a wig, damned sensible. We are all slaves to fashion, we unfortunates who live in the city.'

The other two had close-cropped heads, and were in their shirtsleeves, their collars loosened. Childs had a napkin tied round his neck, and they had not waited for Hal before beginning to eat. Judging by the pile of empty oyster shells, Childs had already accounted for several dozen. Hal shrugged out of his coat, passed it to a footman, then took the proffered chair.

'What do you fancy, Courtney, the hock or the Madeira?' Childs beckoned to one of the servants to fill Hal's glass. Hal selected the hock. He knew from past experience that it was to be a long evening, and that the Madeira was deceptively sweet but powerful. Once his glass was charged and a platter of huge Colchester oysters in front of him, Childs dismissed the servants with a wave so that they could talk freely. Almost immediately they were away on the vexing question of the Irish war. The deposed King James had sailed to Ireland from France to raise an

46

army among his Catholic supporters there, and was attacking the forces loyal to King William. Oswald Hyde bemoaned the cost of the campaign, but Childs rejoiced at the successful defence of Londonderry and Enniskillen by His Majesty's arms.

'You can be certain that, as soon as the King has taken care of the Irish, he will turn his full attention back to France.' Oswald Hyde sucked another oyster from its shell and looked unhappy, an expression that seemed to come to him naturally. 'I shall have to go back to Parliament for another appropriation.'

Even though he lived in the country, Hal kept himself well informed on the events of the day, for he had many good friends in London and corresponded with them regularly. He was able to follow the weighty twists and turns of the discussion and even to make his own noteworthy contributions. 'We have little choice in the matter,' he said. 'Once Louis invaded the Palatinate, we were forced to act against him in accordance with the terms of the Alliance of Vienna.' He had expressed an opinion with which the others concurred, and he sensed their approval, although Hyde continued to bewail the expense of a Continental war.

'I agree there must be war with France but, in God's name, we have not yet paid off the costs of the Dutch war and the Fire. The Black Boy and Jamie left us with debts owing to every bank in Europe.' The Black Boy was the nickname of Charles II, the Merry Monarch. Jamie was James II, who had succeeded him and ruled for three scant years before his overt Roman Catholicism forced him to flee to France. William, the Stadholder of the United Provinces of the Netherlands and fourth in line of succession, had been invited, with Mary his wife, to take the throne of England. Mary was the daughter of James, which made their claim to the throne all the more valid, and, of course, they were staunch Protestants.

Once the oysters had been dealt with, Childs called back the footmen to serve the other courses. He fell upon a Dover sole as though it were an enemy, and then they went on to the lamb and the beef, with three different flavours of soup from the silver gilt tureens to wash them down. A good red claret replaced the rather insipid hock.

Hal sipped sparingly at his glass, for the conversation was fascinating and opened insights into the interwoven structure of power and world politics which he was seldom vouchsafed. He would not let even the finest wines cloud his mind. Their talk ranged widely from the coronation of Peter as the Tsar of Russia to the incursions of the French into Canada, from the massacre of their settlers at Lachine by the Iroquois Indians, to the rebellion of the Marathas against the rule of the Mogul Emperor Aurangzeb in India.

This last item of news led the conversation directly to the true reason for this meeting, the affairs and fortunes of the English East India Company. Hal sensed the change that came over his companions in the way that they regarded him. Their eyes upon him became shrewd and appraising.

'I understand that you are a considerable shareholder in the Company?' Lord Hyde asked innocently.

'I was fortunate enough to purchase a little of the Company stock when I returned from the East, in the seventies,' Hal admitted modestly, 'and since then, from time to time, when fortune has been kind I have added to my holdings.'

Childs waved away his disclaimer. 'All the world is aware of the distinguished exploits of you and your father during the Dutch wars and thereafter, and the very considerable additions that you made to the privy purse from the prizes of war, and the fruits of your trading voyages to the spice islands and the eastern coasts of the African continent.' He turned to the Chancellor. 'Sir Henry con-

48

trols four and a half per cent of the Company stock, which does not include the dowry of Alice Grenville who so recently married his eldest son,' he concluded drily.

Hyde looked impressed as he mentally calculated the monetary value that that represented. 'A valiant and resourceful sea captain you have proved yourself,' Hyde murmured. 'And a prudent investor. You richly deserved those rewards.' He was watching Hal with a piercing gaze, and Hal knew that they were coming at last to their true purpose. 'Moreover, your personal interests are closely linked to our own,' the Chancellor went on quietly, rubbing his cropped pate so that the short, stiff hairs rasped under his fingers. 'We are all stockholders, the Crown the largest of all. Thus, the recent news from the East Indies affects us all most painfully.'

Hal felt the sudden constriction of dread in his chest. He straightened in his chair and his voice was tight as he murmured, 'Forgive me, my lord, but I arrived in London only this morning and I have heard no news.'

'You are fortunate then, for the news is not good,' Childs grunted, and lifted a lump of beef, dripping blood, to his mouth. He chewed and swallowed, then took a gulp of the claret. 'Two weeks ago the Company ship *Yeoman of York* tied up at the East India docks. She was sixty-two days out from Bombay with a cargo of cotton and cochineal, and despatches from Gerald Aungier, the governor of the colony.' Childs frowned and shook his head, reluctant to speak the next words. 'We have lost two ships. The *Minotaur* and the *Albion Spring*.'

Hal rocked back in his chair as though he had taken a punch to the head. 'Those two are the pride of the fleet,' he exclaimed.

It was almost impossible to believe. The East Indiamen, those stately, magnificent vessels, were the lords of the oceans, built not only for the carrying of cargo but for

49

the prestige of the great and prosperous company that owned them and of the English Crown under whose charter they sailed.

'Wrecked?' Hal hazarded. Even the might of the Company must be shaken by the magnitude of the loss. One such vessel sunk was a terrible blow. Two ships lost was a disaster – perhaps worth a hundred thousand pounds with the cargoes.

'Where were they wrecked?' he demanded. 'The Agulhas Bank? The coral reefs of the Mascarenes?'

'They were not wrecked,' said Childs ominously.

'What then?'

'Pirates,' said Childs. 'Corsairs.'

'Are you sure? How can we know that?' The East Indiamen were built for speed and heavily armed for just such a contingency. It would take a warship of force to capture one. When this news spread, the value of the Company stock would plunge. His own investments would be slashed by thousands, nay, tens of thousands of pounds.

'For months now, both ships have been overdue. We had no news of either,' Childs said. 'But it seems that a single seaman escaped from the *Minotaur*. He was almost forty days at sea clinging to some piece of wreckage, drinking but a few drops of rainwater and eating raw fish he was able to catch, until he was at last thrown up on the wild African coast. He walked for weeks along the shore to reach the Portuguese settlement at Lobito. There he was able to find a berth on a sloop bound for Bombay. He told his story to Governor Aungier, who sent the seaman and his despatches back to us on board the *Yeoman of York*.'

'Where is this seaman now?' Hal demanded. 'Have you spoken to him? Is he reliable?'

Childs held up one hand to halt the flood of questions. 'He is in a safe place, and well cared for, but we don't yet want him telling his story on the streets of London, or in a coffee-house.' Hal nodded: that made good sense. 'And, yes, I have spoken to him at length. He seems a sensible lad, tough and resourceful, if his account is true, which I think it is.'

'What does he say happened?'

'In essence, the *Minotaur* came upon a small dhow in distress off the island of Madagascar and took off her crew of a dozen before she sank. But that first night the survivors seized control of the deck during the middle watch. They had concealed weapons on their persons and they slit the throats of the officers of the watch. Of course, the crew of the *Minotaur* should have had small trouble regaining the ship from such a tiny band of pirates, but almost immediately a fleet of small boats swarmed out of the darkness, obviously in response to a signal, and the band of pirates already on board were able to prevent the ship's company from serving the guns or otherwise defending themselves until it was too late.'

'How did this man escape?'

'Most of the *Minotaur*'s men were massacred, but this man – Wilson is his name – convinced the pirate captain that he would enlist with his band and lead him to other plunder. Wilson then seized his first opportunity to escape and slipped overboard through a gun port with a small wooden keg as a float.' Childs opened a silver casket and brought out a long brown object that looked like a piece of dead tree bark. 'Tobacco leaves rolled into a stick,' he explained. 'Spanish, from their colonies in America. They call it a cigarro. I have come to prefer them to a pipe. Will you try one? Here, let me prepare it for you.' He made a fuss of sniffing it and cutting off a sliver of the dark tobacco from one end.

Hal accepted it and sniffed it suspiciously. The aroma was surprisingly pleasing. He followed Childs's example and lit the end of the tube from the burning taper Childs held for him. He puffed cautiously and found that, even though he was distressed by what he had just learned, the

51

taste was to his liking, better than any pipe he had ever taken.

By now both other men were puffing on their cigarros, which gave Hal a few minutes to consider the problem with which Childs had presented him. 'You said two ships were lost,' he said.

'Yes,' Childs agreed. 'The *Albion Spring* only weeks before the *Minotaur*. Taken by the same gang of cutthroats.'

'How can we be sure of that?'

'The pirate captain boasted of his exploits to this man Wilson.'

After another long silence Hal asked, 'What do you intend to do about this, my lord?' Then his pulse quickened as he saw the two men exchange glances, and he had the first inkling as to why he had been invited to this intimate meeting.

Childs wiped beef fat from his jowls with the back of his hand, then winked at Hal like a conspirator. 'We are going to send someone to deal with this pirate fellow, Jangiri. That's the rascal's name – Jangiri.'

'Who will you send?' asked Hal, already knowing the answer.

'Why, you, of course.'

'But, my lord, I am now a farmer and a county squire.'

'Of only a few years' standing,' Hyde cut in. 'Before that you were one of the most eminently successful mariners in the southern and eastern oceans.' Hal was silent. It was true, of course. These two knew everything about him. They could almost certainly detail every voyage he had made, and Hyde would have in his records every return of treasure and precious cargo he had made to the Treasury.

'My lords, I have a family, four sons to care for, and no woman to share the responsibility. That is the reason I no longer go seafaring.'

'Yes, I know why you gave up the sea, Courtney, and

you have my deepest condolences for the loss of your wife. But, on the other hand, even your youngest son must now be of the age when you yourself first went to sea. There is no reason why you cannot find berths for every one of your offspring aboard a well-found ship.' That was also true. Childs had clearly planned his strategy with great attention to detail, but Hal was determined not to make it easy for him.

'I could not leave my responsibilities at High Weald. Without careful administration of my estates I would be beggared.'

'My dear Sir Henry,' Hyde smiled, 'my own son was at King's College with your William. They are still the greatest of friends and correspond regularly. I understand that the administration of your estates has become almost solely the charge of young William, and that you spend much of your time hawking, hunting, reading and reminiscing with your old shipmates.'

Hal flushed with anger. Was that William's estimation of his worth and contribution to the running of High Weald and the mines?

'If this fellow, Jangiri, is not dealt with swiftly we will all be beggared,' Childs added. 'You are the best man for the job, and we all know it.'

'The suppression of piracy is the concern of the King's navy,' Hal retorted stubbornly.

'Indeed it is,' Hyde agreed. 'But by the end of the year we will be at war with France and the King's navy will have more pressing matters with which to attend. It may be several years before the Admiralty can turn its mind to policing the far oceans of the globe and we dare not wait that long. Jangiri already has two ships of great power under his command. Who can say that in a year or two he will not be strong enough to attack Bombay or our factories on the Carnatic coast? Your shares in the Company would be worth little if he succeeded.'

Hal moved restlessly in his chair and fiddled with the stem of his wineglass. This was what he had been waiting for secretly, during these past months of boredom and inactivity. His blood was charging, his mind raced, flitting from idea to idea like a sunbird on a flowering tree, darting from bloom to bloom to drink its nectar.

'I have no ship,' he said. He had sold the *Golden Bough* when he came back to Devon. She was tired and her hull eaten half away by ship-worm. 'I would need a ship of equal or superior force to the *Minotaur* or the *Albion Spring*.'

'I can offer you a squadron of two fine ships,' Childs countered easily. 'Your flagship would be the new *Seraph*, the finest vessel the Company has ever built. Thirty-six guns and fast as a gull. She is this very day fitting out at Deptford yard. She can be ready for sea by the month's end.'

'And the other?' Hal demanded.

'The *Yeoman of York*, the same ship that carried this lad Wilson back from Bombay. It will have completed its refit by the end of the week and be ready for sea again. Also thirty-six guns. Captain Edward Anderson, a fine seaman.'

'I know him well.' Hal nodded. 'But what authority would I sail under?' Hal was determined to resist a little longer.

'By noon tomorrow,' Hyde promised, 'I can deliver to you a commission signed by His Majesty's own hand, authority to seek out and destroy or take as prize the ships and property of the corsairs.'

'What terms of prize?' Hal turned his full attention to him.

'One third to the Crown, one third to the East India Company, and the last third to you and your crew,' Hyde suggested.

'If I were to go, and there is no guarantee that I shall, I would like to have half to myself and my men.'

'It is true, then.' Hyde looked miserable. 'You strike a hard bargain. We can discuss that when you agree to take the commission.'

'I should like to be able to trade for my own account during the voyage.'

It was one of the tenets of Company policy that its captains should not indulge in private trade, and thereby risk a conflict of interest and loyalty. Childs's face darkened and his jowls wobbled with outrage. 'Under no circumstances. I cannot agree to that. It would set a dangerous precedent.' Then he saw that Hal had prepared the trap and that he had walked straight into it.

'Very well,' Hal said quietly. 'I will forgo that right, if you grant me the half-share of the prize.' Childs gulped and spluttered at his effrontery, but Hyde smiled lugubriously.

'He has you there, Nicholas. One or the other, which is it to be? The prize money or the right to trade?'

Childs was thinking furiously. The prize money might far outstrip any trading profit that even this cunning and resourceful mariner might garner along the Asian and African coasts, but the right to trade was sacred and reserved to the Company alone.

'Very well,' he agreed at last. 'Half the prize but none of the trading profits.'

Hal scowled, but was well content. He nodded apparently reluctantly. 'I will need a week to think on it.'

'You do not have a week,' Hyde remonstrated. 'We need your answer this very night. His Majesty needs my reply at the meeting of his cabinet in the morning.'

'There is too much for me to consider before I can take up the commission.' Hal sat back and folded his arms in a gesture of finality. If he delayed there was a chance he might squeeze other concessions out of them.

'Henry Courtney, Baron Dartmouth,' Hyde murmured. 'Does not the title have a satisfying ring?' Hal unfolded his arms and leaned forward, taken so off guard that he allowed his eagerness to light his features. A peerage! He had never before allowed himself to think of it. Yet it was one of the few things in this world he lacked.

'You mock me, sir?' he murmured. 'Please make clear your meaning.'

'Take up the commission we offer immediately, and bring back the head of this Jangiri rogue in a pickle barrel, and I give you my solemn word that a barony is yours. What say you, Sir Hal?'

Hal began to grin. He was a commoner, albeit of the highest rank, but this next step up the ladder would enter him into the nobility and the House of Lords. 'You are the one who drives a hard bargain, my lord. I can no longer resist either your blandishments or my duty.' He raised his glass and the other two followed his example. 'Fair winds, and a good chase,' he suggested as the toast.

'Bright gold and glory!' Hyde made a better one and they drained their glasses.

When they lowered their glasses, Hyde dabbed his lips with his napkin and asked, 'You have not yet been presented at court, have you, Sir Hal?' When Hal shook his head he went on, 'If you are one day to become a peer of the realm, we must see to that before you leave London. Two of the clock in the afternoon on this coming Friday, at St James's Palace. The King is holding a levée before he sails for Ireland to take charge of the campaign against his father-in-law. I shall send a man to your lodgings, to guide you to the palace.'

Alfred Wilson was a surprise. With such a name Hal had expected a stalwart English tar with a Yorkshire or Somerset accent. At Hal's request Childs had released the seaman from wherever he was being held and sent him to Hal at the inn. He stood in the centre of the floor of the private salon and twisted his cap in his slim dark hands.

'You are English?' Hal demanded.

Wilson respectfully touched the hank of thick dark hair that spilled onto his forehead. 'My father was born in Bristol, Captain.'

'But your mother was not?' Hal guessed.

'She was an Indian, a Mogul, a Mussulman, sir.'

Wilson was darker even than Hal's own William, and as handsome. 'Do you speak her language, Wilson?'

'Yes, sir, and write it. My mother was of high birth, begging your pardon, sir.'

'Then you write English also?' Hal liked the look of him, and if his story of the escape from Jangiri were true he was indeed resourceful and clever to boot.

'Yes, sir.'

Hal was surprised, few seamen were literate. He considered him thoughtfully. 'Do you speak any other language?'

'Only Arabic.' Wilson shrugged self-deprecatingly.

'Better and better.' Hal smiled and switched into Arabic to test him. He had been taught it by his first wife, Judith, and had honed his knowledge of it on many voyages along the coasts of Africa and Araby. 'Where did you learn?' His tongue was a little rusty from disuse of the guttural tones of Arabia.

'I sailed many years before the mast, with a crew that was mostly Arab.' Wilson's command of the language was rapid and fluent.

'What rating did you hold on the *Minotaur*?'

'Warrant officer, sir.'

Hal was delighted. To hold the rank of a watch-keeping officer, at his age, he must be a bright one. I must have him, Hal decided. 'I want to hear from you everything you can tell me of the taking of the *Minotaur*. But more important, I want you to tell me about Jangiri.'

'Begging your pardon, Captain, but that will take a while.'

'We have all day, Wilson.' Hal pointed to the bench against the far wall. 'Sit there.' When he hesitated, Hal went on, 'You said it would take time. Sit down, man, and get on with it.'

It took almost four hours, and Walsh, the tutor, sat at the table and made notes as Hal instructed him. Wilson spoke quietly and without emotion until he had to describe the murder of his shipmates by the pirates. Then his voice choked, and when Hal looked up, he was surprised to see that Wilson's eyes were bright with tears. He sent for a pot of beer to soothe the man's throat and give him a chance to regain his composure. Wilson pushed the tankard aside. 'I don't take strong liquor, sir.'

Hal was delighted. Drink was the demon of most seamen. 'Never?' he asked.

'No, sir. My mother, you understand, sir.'

'You are a Christian?'

'Yes, sir, but I can't forget my mother's teaching.'

'Yes, I understand.' By God, I need this one, Hal thought. He's a gem among men. Then an idea occurred to him: During the voyage out I will have him teach my lads Arabic. They will need it on the coast.

By the time they had finished Hal had a vivid picture of what had happened on board the *Minotaur*, and of the man he was going out to confront. 'I want you to go over all this again in your mind, Wilson. If there is anything

58

you have forgotten, any detail that may be useful, I want you to come back and tell me.'

'Very well, Captain.' Wilson stood up to leave. 'Where will I find you, sir?'

Hal hesitated. 'I hope you can keep your tongue from wagging?' he asked, and when the man nodded, he went on, 'I know that you have been kept from telling the story of the taking of the *Minotaur*. If you can give me your word that you'll not be spouting your story into every flapping ear, then you can join my crew. I am looking for good watch-keeping officers. Will you sign up with me, lad?'

Wilson smiled almost shyly. 'I have heard of you afore, Captain,' he said. 'You see, my uncle sailed with your father aboard the *Lady Edwina*, and with you on the *Golden Bough*. He told tales of you.'

'Who was your uncle?'

'Ned Tyler, Captain, and he still is.'

'Ned Tyler!' Hal exclaimed. He had not heard that name in five years. 'Where is he?'

'On his farm near Bristol. He bought it with the prize money he won on board your ship, Captain.' Ned Tyler was one of the best men Hal had ever sailed with, and he marvelled yet again at how small and close-knit was the brotherhood of the sea.

'So what do you say, then, Wilson? Will you sign the watch-bill on the *Seraph*?'

'I would like it well to sail with you, Captain.'

Hal felt a lift of pleasure at his acceptance. 'Tell my boatswain Daniel Fisher to find lodgings for you until we can move into our quarters on the ship. Then you can exercise your penmanship by composing a letter to your uncle Ned. Tell him to stop milking cows and shovelling muck, and get on his sea boots again. I need him.'

After Wilson had clumped down the narrow wooden stairs to the parlour below, Hal moved to the small window that overlooked the cobbled stableyard. He stood there, hands clasped behind his back, and watched Aboli instruct the twins with the blade. Guy sat on a pile of hay with Dorian next to him. He must have finished his turn for he was red in the face and sweating in dark patches through his shirt. Dorian was patting his back in congratulation.

Hal watched while Aboli exercised Tom in the manual of arms, the six parries and the full repertoire of cuts and thrusts. Tom was sweating lightly when at last Aboli faced him and nodded to begin the bout. 'On guard, Klebe!'

They fought half a dozen inconclusive engagements. Hal could see that Aboli was moderating his power to match Tom, but the boy was tiring and slowing down when Aboli called to him, 'Last one, Klebe. This time I mean to hit you!'

Tom's expression hardened, and he went on guard in quarte, point high, watching Aboli's dark eyes to read his move before he launched. They touched sabres and Aboli came at him, right foot leading, graceful as a dancer, a feint into the high line and then, as Tom parried fierce and made the riposte, Aboli fluidly recoiled and made a counter-riposte in the line of engagement, fast as a striking viper. Tom attempted the correct parry low quarte, but his hand still lacked an inch of speed. There was a slither of steel over steel and Aboli's blade stopped an inch from his nipple as it showed through the white shirt.

'Faster, Klebe. Like a hawk!' Aboli admonished him, as Tom recovered smoothly, but his wrist was pronated and his blade slightly off line. It seemed he had left an opening for a cut to the right shoulder. Tom was furious

60

and scowling at the hit against him, but he spotted the opening.

Even from the high window Hal saw him make the mistake of signalling his move with a slight lift of his chin. 'No, Tom, no!' he whispered. Aboli was dangling the bait that had snared Hal himself, so often, when he was Tom's age. With consummate judgement of distance Aboli had set himself up two inches beyond the reach of Tom's cut to the shoulder: he would hit him again if Tom tried for it.

Hal crowed with delight as his son took a double step, a feint for the shoulder, but then with the agility of a monkey and extraordinary strength of wrist for his age, he changed his angle of attack and went instead for Aboli's hip. 'You almost had him!' Hal whispered, as Aboli was forced to extreme extension to protect himself with a circular parry that gathered Tom's blade and swept it back into the original line of engagement.

Aboli stepped back and broke off the engagement. He shook his head so that drops of sweat flew from his bald head, and flashed his teeth in a huge white smile. 'Good, Klebe. Never accept an enemy's invitation. Good! You came close to me there.' He placed one arm around Tom's shoulders. 'That's enough for one day. Master Walsh is waiting for you to take up the pen rather than the sabre.'

'One more hit, Aboli!' Tom pleaded. 'This time I will have you, fair and square.' But Aboli pushed the boy in the direction of the inn door.

'Aboli judges it finely,' Hal said to himself with approval. 'He will not drive them beyond their years and strength.' He touched the white scar on the lobe of his own right ear and grinned ruefully. 'But the day is not far off when he will tap a drop or two of Master Thomas's raspberry juice, as he once did mine, to moderate the boy's fine opinion of his own skills.'

Hal opened the casement and leaned out. 'Aboli, where's Big Danny?'

Aboli wiped the sweat from his forehead with his forearm. 'He was working on the carriage. Then he went off with that new lad, Wilson.'

'Find him and bring him up here. There is something I have to tell you.'

A little later, as the two big men shuffled in, Hal looked up from the document on the writing-desk in front of him. 'Sit down, both of you.' He indicated the bench and they sat side by side like two overgrown schoolboys about to be chastized. 'I had a word with Mabel.' Hal picked on Daniel first. 'She says she cannot abide another winter with you prowling around the cottage like a chained bear. She begged me to take you off somewhere, far away.'

Daniel looked stunned. Mabel was his wife, the head cook at High Weald, a plump, cheerful woman with red cheeks. 'She had no call—' Daniel began angrily, then broke off into a grin as he saw the sparkle in Hal's eyes.

Hal turned to Aboli. 'As for you, you black devil, the mayor of Plymouth tells me there has been a plague of bald brown babies born in the town and all the husbands are loading their muskets. Its time we got you away for a while also.'

Aboli rumbled and shook with laughter. 'Where are we going, Gundwane?' He used the pet name with which he had christened Hal as a boy and which meant Cane Rat in the language of the forests. He seldom used it, these days, only in moments of great affection.

'South!' Hal answered him. 'Past the Cape of Good Hope. Into that ocean you know so well.'

'And what will we do there?'

'Find a man named Jangiri.'

'And when we find him?' Aboli went on.

'We will kill him, and take his treasure for our own.'

Aboli pondered a moment. 'That sounds good to me.'

'What ship?' Big Daniel asked.

'The *Seraph*. An East Indiaman, fresh off the builder's slip. Thirty-six guns and quick as a ferret.'

'What does *Seraph* mean?'

'A seraph is one of the highest order of heavenly angels.'

'That's me to the letter Z.' Daniel showed all his pink gums in a wide smile. Of course he could not read and knew of the letter Z only by repute, which made Hal smile inwardly. 'When will we lay eyes on the *Seraph*?' he demanded.

'First thing tomorrow. Have the carriage ready at dawn. It's a long haul up to the Company's yards at Deptford.' Hal stopped them from rising. 'Before then we have much to do. To begin with we have no crew.' They both sobered immediately. Finding a crew for a new ship, even a Fifth-Rate, was always a difficult task.

He held up the document that lay on the desk in front of him. It was a poster he had drafted the day before and sent down to the printers in Cannon Street with Walsh. This was the first pull of the press.

PRIZE MONEY!
£ HUNDREDS £!

the headline bellowed in thick black type. The text below it was smaller in size but no less flamboyant and rich with hyperbole, scattered with exclamation marks and high-cast letters.

CAPTAIN SIR HAL COURTNEY, Hero of the Dutch wars, Master mariner and Famous Navigator, Captor of the Dutch Galleons *Standvastigheid* and *Heerlige Nacht*, Who in his Fabled ships *Lady Edwina* and *Golden Bough* has pursued many capital voyages to Africa and the Spice Islands of the Indies, who has fought and vanquished the foes of His Sovereign Majesty with great capture of RICH TREASURES and VAST BOOTY, has berths for Good men and True on his new ship *Seraph*, a 36-gun East Indiaman of Great Power and Speed, fitted out and victualled with attention to the Comfort and Care of officers and men. Those seamen who have had the good FORTUNE to sail under CAPTAIN COURTNEY on his previous voyages have shared PRIZE MONEY as much as £200 each man.

Sailing under LETTERS OF MARQUE issued by HIS MAJESTY WILLIAM III (GOD BLESS HIM!), CAPTAIN COURTNEY will seek out the enemies of HIS MAJESTY in the OCEAN OF THE INDIES, to their confusion and destruction and the WINNING of RICH PRIZE! Of which one half to be shared by officers AND CREW!

ALL GOOD SEAMEN seeking employment and fortune will be heartily welcome to take a pot of ale with BIG DANIEL FISHER the chief warrant officer of the *Seraph* at the PLOUGH in TAILORS LANE.

Aboli read it aloud for the benefit of Big Daniel, who always claimed that his eyes were too weak for the task but who could spot a gull on the horizon and carve the finest details on his model ships without the slightest difficulty.

When Aboli had finished his recitation, Daniel grinned. ''Tis too good a chance to pass by, and this famous captain is the man for me. Damn me, but I think I'll put my cross on his watch-bill.'

When Master Walsh returned from the printers, staggering under a heavy bundle of posters, Hal sent Dorian and the twins to help Aboli and Daniel nail them up on every street corner, and on every tavern and bawdy-house door along the river and the docks.

Aboli pulled up the carriage on the hard of the shipyard. Hal leaped down impulsively and strode to the edge of the Deptford jetty where Big Daniel and Alf Wilson were waiting for him. The river was thick with shipping of every class from bum-boats to First Rate men-o'-war. Some were merely hulks while others were in full seagoing rig with yards crossed and sails set, as they ran downriver towards Gravesend for the Channel or tacked slowly up against the wind and the stream, headed for Blackwall.

In all this multitude there was no mistaking or over-looking the *Seraph*. Hal's eye went to her immediately as she lay at anchor out of the main current, surrounded by lighters, her decks teeming with carpenters and sail-makers. As Hal watched, a huge water-barrel was swayed up out of one of the lighters and lowered into her open hatch aft.

'You beauty!' Hal whispered, as he ran his eyes over her in almost lascivious pleasure as though she were a naked woman. Although her yards were not yet crossed, her tall masts had an elegant rake and Hal could visualize the vast cloud of sail they could carry.

Her hull was a happy compromise. She had the beam and depth to accommodate a heavy cargo and her inventory of cannon, as befitted her role as an armed trader. Yet she had such a fine entry at the bows and pretty run at the stern as promised speed and handiness in any condition of wind.

'She will point high as you could wish, Captain, and sail away on a fairy's fart,' Big Daniel said gruffly behind him. It was an indication of his own enchantment that he had spoken unbidden.

The *Seraph* was dressed in splendour, as befitted the pride and prestige of the East India Company. Despite the lighters that clustered around her, and partially screened her from scrutiny, her paintwork showed through, sparkling in the pale spring sunlight. She was all gold and blue, her quarter galleries intricately carved with hosts of cherubim and seraphim, and her figurehead the winged angel, with the face of a child, for which she was named. Her gunports were picked out in gold, a pleasing chequerboard pattern that emphasized her force.

'Hail a bum-boat!' Hal ordered, and when one came in and tied up at the slimy stone steps he ran down lightly and stepped into the stern sheets.

'Run us out to the *Seraph*,' Big Daniel told the ancient who sat at the tiller, and pushed off. The skiff stank of sewage and her decks were stained with it – probably one of her duties was to remove night soil from the officers' cabins of the ships anchored in the river – but by day she carried vegetables and passengers out to the fleet.

'You be Captain Courtney, the new master of the *Seraph*?' the boatman quavered. 'Seed your poster at the tavern.'

'That he be,' Big Daniel answered, for Hal was too intent in studying his new love to hear the question.

'I have two fine strong lads as want to ship aboard with you,' the old man went on.

'Send them to see me,' Big Daniel growled. In the three days since they had hung the posters he had recruited almost a full crew. There would be no need to visit the gaol and bribe the warden to send his most likely prisoners aboard the *Seraph* in chains. On the contrary Daniel had been able to pick and choose from the mob of unemployed sailors that had besieged the inn. A berth in a Company ship was in high demand: the living conditions and the pay were infinitely better than those in the Royal Navy. Every loafer in the ports and every sailor stepping off an inward-bound ship knew full well that if war was declared against France, the naval press-gangs would be scouring every port in Britain, and hauling aboard the warships the men they caught. Every fool knew that it was wiser to grab a plum berth now and ship out to the far oceans before they began their dread work.

The master shipbuilder on the *Seraph*'s quarterdeck had recognized the tall figure standing in the bum-boat's sheets as a man of quality and guessed his identity. He was waiting at the rail to welcome him when Hal came up the ladder.

'Ephraim Greene at your service, Captain.'

'Show me the ship, Mr Greene, if you please.' Hal's eyes were already darting from the topmasts to every corner of the deck, and he strode off towards the stern with Greene scurrying to keep up with him. They went through the ship from the bilges to the main topgallant, and Hal snapped terse instructions to Big Daniel when he found the smallest thing that was not to his entire liking. Daniel grunted at Wilson, who scribbled a note in the leather-bound book he carried under his arm. Already Daniel and Wilson were shaping into a good working team.

When Aboli took Hal back to the inn, he left Daniel and Wilson to find quarters for themselves in the confusion of timber and sawdust, bundles and bags of new canvas sails and great coils of fresh hemp that cluttered the between-decks of the *Seraph*. They would hardly have time to step ashore again until the ship was ready to sail.

'I'll be back tomorrow early,' Hal promised Big Daniel. 'I'll want a list of stores that are on board already – you can get that from Master Greene – and another list of those we yet lack.'

'Aye, Captain.'

'Then we will work out a load manifest and start to get her trimmed out for her best attitude of sailing.'

'Aye, Captain.'

'Then, in your spare time, you can start to encourage Master Greene and his lads to shake out a little more

canvas and get us ready for sea before winter sets in.'
During the afternoon a nasty little wind had sprung up out
of the north-east, which smelt of ice and made the men
huddle into their cloaks as they stood on the open deck.
'It is on an evening such as this that the warm southern
winds seem to whisper my name.' Hal smiled as he took
his leave of them.

Big Daniel grinned. 'I can almost smell the hot dust of
Africa on the monsoon.'

It was well after dark when the carriage rolled into the
cobbled yard of the Plough, but all three of Hal's sons
rushed out of the warm lamp-lit front parlour to welcome him before he stepped down from the carriage, and
they trailed him up the stairs into his private salon.

Hal shouted for the landlord to bring him a pewter jug
of mulled wine, for he was chilled by the turn in the
weather, then threw off his cloak and dropped into a high-
backed chair before he faced the line of solemn boys who
stood before him. 'To what do I owe the honour of this
deputation, gentlemen?' He put on a serious mien to match
that of the young faces before him. Two heads swivelled
towards Tom, the acknowledged spokesman.

'We tried to sign up for the voyage with Big Daniel,'
Tom said, 'but he sent us to you.'

'What is your rating, and what experience do you
have?' Hal teased them.

'We have naught but a good heart and a will to learn,'
Tom admitted.

'That will serve for Tom and Guy. I will rate you
captain's servant and you will draw a guinea a month pay.'
Their faces lit like the sunrise, but Hal went on swiftly,
'But Dorian is still too young. He must stay at High Weald.'

There was an appalled silence, and the twins turned to Dorian with stricken expressions. Dorian struggled with his tears and only just held them back. 'Who will look after me when Tom and Guy have gone?'

'Your brother William will be master of High Weald while I am at sea, and Master Walsh will remain with you to see to your lessons.'

'William hates me,' said Dorian softly, with a tremor in his voice.

'You are too harsh on him. He is strict but he loves you.'

'He tried to kill me,' Dorian said, 'and if you are not there he will try again. Master Walsh will not be able to stop him.'

Hal began to shake his head, but then he had a vivid mental picture of the expression on William's face as he held the child by the throat. For the first time he faced the unpalatable reality that Dorian's extravagant claim might not be too far from the truth.

'I will have to stay and look after Dorian.' Tom broke the silence, his face pale and set.

Hal understood intuitively how much that offer had cost him: Tom's whole existence revolved around the thought of going to sea, yet he was prepared to give that up. Hal felt such devotion tug at his heart. 'If you do not wish to stay at High Weald, Dorian, you can go to your uncle John at Canterbury. He is your mother's brother and he loves you almost as much as I do.'

'If you truly love me, Father, you will not leave me behind. I would rather have brother William kill me than that.' Dorian spoke with a conviction and determination strange for one so young and Hal was taken aback: he had not been prepared for such steadfast refusal.

'Tom is right,' Guy agreed staunchly. 'We can't leave Dorian. None of us can. Tom and I will have to stay with him.' More than any other, Guy's petition swayed Hal. It was almost unheard of for Guy to take a strong stance on any issue, but when he did no threat would move him.

Hal frowned at them while his mind raced. Could he take a child of Dorian's age into a situation that would certainly mean terrible danger? Then he looked at the twins. He remembered that when his mother had died, his own father had taken him to sea and he had been . . . how old? Perhaps a year or so older than Dorian was now. For once he felt his determination waver.

Then he considered what dangers they would surely face. He imagined Dorian's perfect body torn by a storm of flying splinters as roundshot crashed through a wooden bulkhead. He thought of shipwreck and the child thrown up, drowned, on some deserted, wild African beach to be devoured by hyena and other loathsome beasts. He gazed at his son, at the red and gold head as innocent and lovely as the carved seraphic angel at the bows of his new ship. He felt the words of refusal rise again in his throat. But, at that moment, Tom placed his hand protectively on his younger brother's shoulder. It was a gesture without guile, but with a calm dignity, love and duty, and Hal felt the words to deny him dry in his throat. He took a slow breath. 'I will think on it,' he said gruffly. 'Go now, all three of you. You have given me enough trouble for one day.' They backed away, and at the door chorused, 'Goodnight, Father.'

When they reached their own chamber, Tom held Dorian by both shoulders. 'Don't cry, Dorry. You know that when he says he will think on it he means yes. But you must not cry ever again. If you are coming to sea with Guy and me, then you have to act like a man. Do you understand?' Dorian gulped and nodded vigorously, not trusting himself to reply.

There was a long line of carriages in the Mall outside the entrance to St James's Palace. The building was a fantasy toy-soldier castle with battlements and towers, built by Henry VIII and still used by the reigning sovereign. When Hal's carriage eventually pulled up, two footmen came forward to open the carriage door and the secretary whom Lord Hyde had sent to fetch him led him through the palace gates and across the courtyard.

There were pikemen, in steel helmets and half-armour, at the entrance to the stairway leading up to the Long Gallery, but when the secretary showed his credentials they let Hal pass, and a footman announced him in a stentorian voice. 'Captain Sir Henry Courtney!'

The guards saluted with a flourish of pikes and Hal filed up the staircase behind the Spanish ambassador and his entourage. When he reached the top he found that the entire length of the gallery was crowded with a splendid assembly of gentlemen, and such a collection of uniforms, medals, stars, plumed hats and periwigs that Hal felt like a country bumpkin. He looked around for the secretary who was guiding him, but the idiot had vanished in the throng and Hal was at a loss as to what he should do next.

Yet he had no call to feel out of place, for he was wearing the new burgundy-coloured velvet suit that he had had tailored for the occasion, and the buckles of his shoes were solid silver. Around his neck he wore the order of a Nautonnier Knight of the Order of St George and the Holy Grail, which had belonged to his father and grandfather before him. It was a magnificent decoration: on a massive gold chain hung the golden lion of England with ruby eyes, holding in its paws the globe of the world with diamond stars of the heavens twinkling above. It matched in splendour any of the myriad other orders and medals that glittered down the length of the gallery. At his hip hung the Blue Neptune sword, the blue sapphire, big as a pullet's egg, glowing on its pommel, the scabbard worked in gold inlay.

At that moment an avuncular grip closed on his elbow and Hyde's voice murmured in his ear, 'I am pleased you could come. We need not waste too much time here. 'Tis but a gathering of peacocks showing off their tails, but there are some it might be worth your while to meet. Let me present you to Admiral Shovel. He is to be the governor of the new naval shipyards that the King is building at Devonport, and there is Lord Ailesham, a good man to know – he gets things done.'

Oswald Hyde led Hal adroitly through the press and each knot of men opened invitingly at his approach. At Hyde's introduction they studied Hal keenly, noting him as someone of importance simply because he was the protégé of the Chancellor. Hal realized that Hyde was working his way gradually towards the panelled doors at the end of the gallery, and once there he took up a position where they would be among the first to encounter whoever came through.

Hyde leaned closer to Hal and murmured, 'His Majesty signed your commission in cabinet yesterday.' He slipped the roll of parchment out of his sleeve. It was tied with a red ribbon and secured by a wax imprint of the Great Seal of England: 'Honi soit qui mal y pense'. 'Guard it well!' He placed it in Hal's hand.

'Have no fear,' Hal assured him. That scrap of parchment might be worth a vast fortune, and a peerage.

At that moment there was a stir, and a murmur ran along the gallery as the doors were thrown open. William III, King of England and Stadholder of the Netherlands, stepped through on small neat feet in slippers encrusted with seed pearls and gold filigree. Everyone in the gallery bowed in unison.

Of course, Hal had known of his deformity, but the actuality came as a shock. The King of England stood not much taller than Dorian, and his back was hunched, so that the scarlet and blue mantle of the Order of the Garter rose in a peak behind his small bird-like head, and the massive gold chain of the order seemed almost to weigh him down. Beside him his wife, Queen Mary II, towered over him, although in truth she was only a young, slender girl in her twenties.

The King saw Hyde immediately and nodded for him to approach. Hyde bowed low before him, sweeping the ground with his hat. Two paces behind, Hal followed his example. The King looked at him over Hyde's back. 'You may present your friend,' he said, in a heavy Dutch accent. He had a deep, strong voice out of place in such a childlike form.

'Your Majesty, I present Sir Henry Courtney.'

'Ah, yes. The mariner,' said the King, and he gave Hal his hand to kiss. William had a long beaked nose, but his eyes were wide set, bright and intelligent.

Hal was amazed that he had been so readily recognized, but he said, in fluent Dutch, 'May I assure Your Majesty of my loyal devotion.'

The King looked at him sharply and replied in the same language. 'Where did you learn to speak so well?'

'I spent some years at the Cape of Good Hope, Your Majesty,' Hal replied. He wondered if the King knew of his imprisonment at the Dutch castle there. William's dark eyes sparkled with amusement, and Hal realized that he did – Hyde must have told him. Strange it was that this King of England had once been its bitter foe, and that as a soldier he had bested many of the English generals who now stood along the gallery ready to pay him deep respect and allegiance.

'I expect to have good reports of you before long,' said the little man, and the Queen nodded to Hal. He bowed again as the royal entourage moved on down the gallery. Hal's presentation was over.

'Follow me,' said Hyde, and led him surreptitiously to a side door. 'That was good. The King has a remarkable memory. He won't forget you when the time comes to claim those rewards of which we spoke.' Hyde held out his hand. 'These stairs will lead you down into the courtyard. Farewell, Sir Hal. We will not meet again before you sail, but I too expect to have good reports of your exploits in the Orient.'

The two ships went downriver in company. The *Seraph* led, with the *Yeoman of York* trailing her by two cables' length. The *Seraph* still had workers from the shipyard aboard. They had not been able to complete her final fitting out by the date they had so faithfully promised, but Hal had sailed nevertheless. 'I will send your men ashore when we reach Plymouth,' he had told Master Greene, the ship-builder, 'if they have finished their work when we reach there. If they haven't I shall drop them in the Bay of Biscay and let them swim home.'

The handling of the ship was still clumsy as the crew settled in. Hal glanced back over his stern and saw how, in sharp contrast, the *Yeoman*'s crew worked their sails with speed and expertise. Edward Anderson, the captain of the *Yeoman*, would be watching him too, and Hal flushed with mortification at the ineptitude of his men. That would change before they reached Good Hope, he vowed.

When they reached the open water of the Channel, the wind veered and strengthened into an autumn gale. The sun went behind the clouds and the sea turned sullen green and boisterous. The night came on prematurely, so that the two ships lost contact with each other in the darkness before they passed Dover.

For some days the *Seraph* slogged into a head-sea but at last they were off the Isle of Wight and Hal found the *Yeoman* only four miles distant and on the same tack as he was.

'Good!' He nodded and closed his telescope. He had reserved his judgement on Anderson. The *Yeoman*'s captain was a burly Yorkshireman, red-faced, unsmiling and taciturn, who, it seemed, resented having Hal placed in authority over him. But during those first days he had proved that, if nothing else, he was a reliable seaman.

Hal switched his attention back to the *Seraph*. Already the crew's ship-handling was improving with practice in these conditions, and the men seemed cheerful and willing, as well they should. Hal had offered good wages to secure the best, making up the difference over what the Company offered out of his own pocket.

At that moment the three boys came pelting up the companionway together, released by Master Walsh from their studies. They were excited and boisterous, showing not the least sign of sea-sickness after their time afloat in half a gale. Aboli had been able to outfit them with seagoing clothing in London, where there were numerous chandlers along the docks. They were better turned out than Hal had been when he sailed for the first time with his father. The old man had not believed in spoiling him, and he remembered the petticoats of rough canvas and the tar-daubed pea-jacket, stiff with salt crystals, that had rubbed him raw under his arms and between his thighs. He smiled ruefully at the memory of how he had slept beside Aboli on a damp straw pallet on the open deck, with the other common seamen, had eaten his meals crouched behind the shelter of one of the guns, using his fingers and dirk to spoon the stew out of his pannikin and break the hard biscuit, had used the leather bucket in the heads for his private business, and never bathed from the beginning of a voyage to the end. It did me little harm, Hal recalled, but on the other hand it did me little good. A lad does not have to be reared like a pig to make him a better seaman.

Of course, the circumstances of his first voyages with his father had been different. The old *Lady Edwina* had been less than half the size of the *Seraph*, and even his father's cabin had been a dog-kennel compared to the spacious stern cabin, which was now at Hal's disposal. Hal had ordered the workmen to partition off a small section of his own quarters, hardly larger than a cupboard, and build three narrow shelves to serve as bunks for the boys. He had signed on Master Walsh as captain's clerk, over the tutor's protestations that he was no seaman. He would continue his instruction of the boys, using his own tiny cabin as a schoolroom.

Hal watched now with approval as Daniel seized the whooping skylarking boys as soon as they appeared on deck, and sternly sent them to the duties he had devised for them. He had separated the twins, placing Tom in the starboard watch and Guy in the other. They were always a bad influence on each other. Guy's proximity encouraged Tom to show off, while Tom distracted Guy with his antics. Dorian was sent to the galley to help the cook bring up the breakfast.

Hal felt a pang of anxiety that Daniel might send the twins aloft to help handle sail, but he need not have worried: the time would come for that when their sea legs were hardened and they had learned to balance easily on the heeling, plunging deck. For the time being, Daniel kept them on the open deck, helping to handle the sheets.

Hal knew he could leave the boys under the big man's watchful eye, and turn his attention to the problems of his own seamanship. He paced up and down the quarterdeck, tuned now to the hull beneath him, the feel of how his ship responded to every alteration and trim of sail. She's down in the bows, he judged, as she took a green wave on board and the water streamed back down the deck and poured out through the scuppers. Over the last days he had been visualizing how he could reload the cargo in the hold, especially the heavy water-barrels, to achieve the trim he wanted. I can put two knots of speed on her, he estimated. Childs was sending him on a warlike expedition but, nevertheless, the main concern of the East India Company was always profit and the *Seraph*'s hold was crammed with a variety of trade goods for delivery to the Company factories at Bombay.

While part of his mind was busy with the loading and trim, the other part was on his crew. He was still short of watch-keeping officers. This was the main reason why he was putting in at Plymouth instead of hauling away directly to round Ushant on the French coast, cross the Bay of Biscay and head south for the bulge of the African continent and eventually for Good Hope. Plymouth was their home port, and Daniel and Aboli knew almost every man, woman and child in the town and surrounding countryside. 'I can fill the watch-bill with the best men in England within a day of setting foot on the Plymouth dock,' Daniel had boasted to Hal, who knew it was true.

'My uncle Ned sent word that he will be waiting for us there,' Wilson had said, to Hal's satisfaction: he had set his heart on having Ned Tyler aboard the *Seraph*.

Apart from the necessity of finding crew there were other reasons for this detour. Powder and shot were virtually unobtainable in London. The Irish war had led to the shortage of munitions and now, with a French war in the offing, the Admiralty was hoarding every barrel of powder and every round of shot. It had even embargoed the factories to take every scrap of their production.

One of the warehouses Hal owned at the Plymouth docks was piled high with powder kegs and iron shot. He had stored these here in preparation for the last voyage of the *Golden Bough*, which he had been forced to abandon when Dorian's mother had died and left him with a baby to care for. Although several years old, the new powders Hal had stored did not deteriorate as fast as the older types and should still be in good condition.

The final reason for the stop at Plymouth was that Childs had passengers for him to convey to the Company's factory at Bombay Island: they would be waiting for him in the port. Childs had not told him how many he was sending and Hal hoped they would be few. Accommodation was at a premium in any ship, even one of *Seraph*'s size, and some of his officers were bound to be evicted from their cabins to make space for them.

So engrossed was Hal with all these problems that it seemed little time had passed before they had the Isle of Wight abeam. Then they were rounding Gara Point, heading down the Sound past Drake's Island, and Plymouth Ho was opening before them. On shore, a few dozen idlers had seen the two fine ships coming down the Sound and had lined the waterfront to watch them tie up.

Daniel stopped beside Hal and murmured, 'Do you see that head of silver hair shining there like a beacon?' He pointed with his chin towards the quay. 'You cannot miss it, can you now?'

'Dear God, it's Master Ned.' Hal laughed.

'And that's Will Carter with him. Ned must have laid a line on him,' Daniel agreed. 'A good lad is our Will. With him as third and Ned as mate, looks like you've got all your watch-keepers, Captain, sir.'

As soon as they tied up alongside Ned Tyler was the first on board, and Hal had to restrain himself from embracing him. 'It's good to see you, Mr Tyler.'

'Aye,' Ned agreed. 'And she's a pretty little ship you have under you, but she's down in the bows and her sails look like a bunch of dirty shirts on washing day.'

'You'll have to see to that, then, won't you, Ned?' Hal said.

Ned nodded lugubriously. 'Aye, that I will, Captain.'

Despite the condition of the roads, Aboli had made good time down from London with the carriage and he was waiting on the dock, sitting on the box with the horses still in the traces. Hal gave orders to Daniel to begin bringing the powder down from the warehouse and to have the *Seraph*'s water-barrels off-loaded onto the quay so that they could be reloaded with better attention to her trim, before he called the boys to join him and went to where Aboli waited with the horses. Guy followed his father dutifully, even with a certain amount of relief.

On the other hand, Tom and Dorian climbed the gangplank onto dry land only after elaborate delaying tactics, including protracted farewells to all those members of the crew with whom they had made friends. They had taken to shipboard life as though born to it. Which, of course, they were, Hal thought, and grinned. 'Come on, you two. You may return tomorrow to help Big Daniel with the reloading.' As soon as they had scrambled onto the box beside Aboli, Hal said, 'Take us up to High Weald, Aboli.'

A while later, as the carriage passed through the gate in the stone wall that marked the boundary of the estate, Tom looked ahead and saw a single rider crossing the moor at a canter, aiming to intercept the carriage at the foot of the hill. There was no mistaking the tall figure dressed all in black on the back of the black stallion, coming from the direction of the tin shaft at East Rushwold. Dorian saw Black Billy at the same time, and moved a little closer to Tom as if for protection, but neither boy spoke.

William put the stallion to the hedge. Horse and rider sailed over, the black cloak billowing out behind, and landed easily, then turned up the road immediately to meet the oncoming carriage.

William ignored Aboli and his two younger brothers on the box, but wheeled his horse to canter alongside. 'Well met, Father!' he greeted Hal through the carriage window. 'Welcome back to High Weald. You were sorely missed.' Hal leaned from the window, smiling with pleasure, and the two fell at once into an animated conversation. William recounted everything that had taken place in Hal's absence, with special emphasis on the running of the mines and the reaping of the grain harvest.

They were coming up the last hill to the big house when suddenly William broke off, with an exclamation of annoyance. 'Ah! I forgot to mention that your guests have arrived from Brighton. They have been here two days awaiting your coming.'

'My guests?' Hal looked mystified.

William pointed with his riding-crop to the distant figures on the far lawns. A large, solid gentleman stood with a lady on each arm, while two girls in brightly coloured pinafores were already racing each other across the grass to meet the carriage, squealing with excitement like steam from a boiling kettle.

'Girls!' said Dorian, with disdain. 'Small girls!'

'But a big one also.' Tom's sharp eyes had picked out the slimmer of the two women on the arms of the portly gentleman. 'Damned pretty too.'

'Have a care, Klebe,' Aboli murmured. 'The last one landed you in deep water.' But Tom was like a hunting dog on point to the scent of a bird.

'Who on earth are they?' Hal asked William irritably. He was engrossed in fitting out a ship for a long voyage and it was not the time to have uninvited guests at High Weald.

'A certain Mr Beatty and his brood,' William answered. 'I was told you were expecting them, Father. Is that not the case? If so, we can send them packing.'

'Damn me!' Hal exclaimed. 'I had almost forgotten. They must be the passengers on board the *Seraph* as far as Bombay. Beatty is to be the new auditor-general for the Company factory there. But Childs never mentioned he was bringing his whole tribe with him. This is a nuisance. Four females! Where, in the devil's name, will I find berths for all of them?'

Hal concealed his annoyance when he stepped out of the carriage to greet the family. 'Mr Beatty, your servant, sir. Lord Childs has given me good reports of you. You had a pleasant enough journey down to Devon, I trust?'

The truth was that he had expected the family to find lodgings in the port rather than to arrive at High Weald, but he put a good face on it and turned to greet the wife. Mrs Beatty was full-fleshed, like her husband, for they had sat at the same dining-table for twenty years. Her face was red and round as a child's ball, but little girlish curls peeped out from under the peak of her bonnet. She gave Hal an elephantine curtsy.

'Enchanted, madam.' Hal told her gallantly.

She giggled when he kissed her hand. 'May I present my eldest daughter, Caroline?' She knew that, apart from being one of the richest men in Devon and a great landowner, Sir Henry Courtney was a widower. Caroline was almost sixteen, and lovely. There was not more than twenty-five years' difference in their ages, she estimated, the same as between Mr Beatty and herself. They would all be on a long voyage together, plenty of time for friendships to ripen, and sometimes dreams became reality.

Hal bowed to the girl, who curtsied prettily, but he made no effort to kiss her hand. His eyes moved on swiftly to the two girls, who hopped and danced around their parents like chirping sparrows. 'And who are these two fine young ladies?' he asked, with a paternal smile.

'I am Agnes!'

'And I am Sarah!'

By the time they were all moving up the staircase and through the front doors of High Weald, Hal had a child by each hand, and they were both chattering and dancing, looking up at him, vying for his attention.

'He always wished for a daughter,' Aboli said softly, watching his master fondly, 'and all he ever got was this gang of hellions.'

'They're only girls,' Dorian pointed out loftily.

Tom said nothing. He had not spoken since he had come close enough to Caroline to make out every detail of her features. Since then he had been transfixed.

Caroline and Guy were following the others up the stairs. They were walking side by side, but at the top Caroline paused and looked back. Her eyes met Tom's.

She was the most beautiful thing Tom had ever imagined. She was as tall as Guy, but her shoulders were narrow and her waist was lithe as a sapling. Her slippered feet were tiny under the flaring layers of petticoats and skirts. Her arms were bare below the puffed sleeves, the skin pale and unblemished. Her hair was a tower of shimmering curls and ribbons. Her face was exquisite, full pink lips and large violet eyes.

She looked through Tom without expression, her face calm and unsmiling: it was almost as if she had not seen him, as if for her he did not exist. Then she turned away and followed her family into the house. Tom had been holding his breath without realizing it, and now he let it out with an audible hiss.

Aboli shook his head. He had missed nothing. This may be a long voyage, he thought. And a dangerous one.

The *Seraph* lay alongside the quay for six days. Even with Ned Tyler and Big Daniel driving them relentlessly, it took that long for the workmen to finish fitting her out. No sooner was the last joint glued and pinned and the last wedge driven home than Daniel saw them all packed off on the post coach, back to the builders' yards at Deptford. By this time the cargo, provisions and armaments had been swung out of the *Seraph*'s hold and then in again and repacked, while Hal stood off in the middle of the harbour in one of the longboats to check her trim. Edward Anderson, from the *Yeoman*, proved his goodwill by sending his own crew across to help with the heavy work.

In the meantime Ned had sent all the sails to the sail-makers' yard. He had checked each seam and stitch and had those that did not please him resewn. Then he had watched each sail repacked in its canvas bag, marked and stowed away in the sail-lockers ready to hand.

Once he had dealt with the sails, Ned laid out and inspected the spare spars and yards, then sent them aboard again before the main cargo. Tom followed him around, asking questions and avidly gleaning every bit of sailing lore that he could.

Hal personally sampled a mug of water from each of the barrels before they were sent back on board, to make certain that their content was sweet and potable. He opened every third pickle barrel and had the ship's surgeon, Dr Reynolds, check that the salt pork and beef, the biscuits and flour were of the first quality. They all knew well enough that by the time they reached Good Hope the water would be green with slime, the biscuits crackling and popping with weevils, but Hal was determined that they would start off clean, and the men took notice of his concern and murmured approvingly among themselves. 'Not many captains would take those pains. Some would buy condemned pork from the Admiralty just to save a guinea or two.'

Daniel and his gunners looked at the powder to ensure that damp had not got into the kegs and caked it. After that they cleaned the muskets, one hundred and fifty of them, and made sure that the flints were firm and struck a shower of sparks when the lock was fired. The deck guns were run out and the carriages greased. On their swivel mounts the murderers and falconets were sited aloft in the crow's nests and at the break of the quarterdeck so that they could command the decks of an enemy ship as she came alongside and sweep her decks with a storm of grapeshot. The blacksmith and his mates sharpened the cutlasses and the axes, and set them back in their racks ready for when they were needed.

Hal puzzled over his quarter-bill, which assigned each man his station in a battle, then worked out the space at his disposal to accommodate his unexpected passengers. In the end he evicted the boys from their newly built cabin and gave it to the three Beatty sisters, while Will Carter, the third officer, had to give up his cabin, tiny as it was, to Mr Beatty and his wife. Those two large bodies would have to share a bunk twenty-two inches wide, and Hal grinned at the picture that called to mind.

In the stern cabin of the *Seraph*, Hal sat for hours with Edward Anderson of the *Yeoman*, working out with him a system of signals with which they could communicate at sea. Forty years previously, the three parliamentarian 'Generals at Sea' Blake, Deane and Monck had innovated a system of signalling, using flags and sails by day and lanterns and guns by night. Hal had obtained copies of their pamphlet, 'Instructions for the Better Ordering of the Fleet in Fighting', and he and Anderson used the five flags and four lanterns as the basis for their own set of signals. The meaning of the flags depended on the combinations and the position in the rigging from which they were flown. At night the lanterns would be arranged in patterns, vertical and horizontal lines, or squares and triangles, on the main mast and the main yard.

Once they had agreed the signals, they drew up a schedule of rendezvous to cover the possibility of the two ships losing contact with each other in conditions of poor visibility or during the vagaries of battle. At the end of these long discussions Hal was confident that he had come to know Anderson well, and that he could trust him to do his duty.

On the seventh day after reaching Plymouth they were ready to sail, and on their last day William laid on a splendid dinner for them in the dining room at High Weald.

Caroline was placed between William and Guy at the long dinner-table. Tom sat opposite her, but the table was too wide for easy conversation. This made little difference to him: for once he could think of nothing to say. He ate little, hardly touching the lobster and sole, his favourite foods. He could barely take his eyes off the girl's lovely tranquil face.

Guy, though, had discovered almost immediately that Caroline was a lover of music and they had formed an instant bond. Under Master Walsh's instruction, Guy had learned to play both the harpsichord and the cittern, a fashionable plucked stringed instrument. Tom had shown no aptitude for either instrument, and his singing, Master Walsh opined, was enough to make horses bolt.

During their stay in London, Master Walsh had taken Guy and Dorian to a concert. Tom had developed a severe stomach-ache, which had prevented him accompanying them – a circumstance he bitterly regretted now, as he watched Caroline listening with what seemed divine rapture to Guy describing the evening to her, the music and the glittering gathering of London society. Guy seemed able even to remember what dresses and jewellery the women had worn, and those huge violet eyes had not left his face.

Tom made an effort to drag her eyes away from Guy by embarking on an account of their visit to Bedlam at Moorfields, to see the lunatics on display in their iron cages. 'When I threw a stone at one, he picked up his own turds and threw them back at me,' he recounted with relish. 'Luckily he missed me and hit Guy instead.'

Caroline's rosebud upper lip lifted slightly as if she had smelt the missile, and her basilisk gaze passed clean through Tom leaving him stammering, before she turned back to Guy.

Dorian sat stiffly between Agnes and Sarah at the bottom of the table. The two girls were hidden from their parents by the display of flowers in the silver vases and the tall candelabra. They giggled and whispered to each other during the whole meal, or told inane, pointless jokes that they thought so rich they had to stuff their table napkins into their mouths to control their mirth.

Dorian was left squirming with embarrassment, and terror that the footmen waiting at table would recount his agony in the servants' quarters. Then even the stable-boys, who were usually his bosom pals, would despise him as a ninny.

At the top of the table Hal and William, Mr Beatty and Edward Anderson were engrossed in discussing the King. 'Lord knows, I was not entirely happy with a Dutchman on the throne, but the little gentleman in black velvet has proved himself a warrior,' Beatty said.

Hal nodded. 'He is a great opponent of Rome, and no lover of the French. For that alone he has my loyalty. But I found him also a man with a sharp eye and mind. I think he will make us a good king.'

Alice Courtney, William's new bride, sat pale and quiet beside Hal. In contrast to her initial loving, dutiful behaviour, she did not look at her new husband across the table. There was a purple bruise on the point of her jaw below the ear, which she had tried to hide with rice powder and by combing a lock of her dark hair over it. She responded in monosyllables to Mrs Beatty's chatter.

At the end of the meal William stood up and rang for

quiet on his wineglass with a silver spoon. 'As one who is duty-bound to remain behind when the rest of my beloved family voyages to far lands . . .' he began.

Tom ducked his head behind the floral decorations so that he was out of sight of William and his father, and pretended to stick his finger down his throat and throw up. Dorian found this so hilarious that he coughed and choked with laughter, and ducked his red head below the table. Caroline gave Tom a single haughty glance, then moved in her chair so that he was out of her eye-line. Oblivious to the sideshow, William was continuing, '. . . Father, I know that as you have many times before, you will return to us with your fame enhanced and the holds of your ships bearing great profit. I live for that day. But while you are away I wish you to know that the affairs of the family here in England will receive my unstinted care and attention.'

Hal leaned back in his chair, his eyes half closed, smiling encouragement as he listened to his eldest son's sonorous praises and hearty wishes for his safety and well-being. But when William included the names of his three half-brothers in his address, Hal felt a tickle of doubt: the sentiments he was expressing were too fulsome.

He opened his eyes suddenly to see William looking towards Tom at the end of the table. His cold dark eyes were so much at odds with the warmth of his words that Hal knew that little of what he had said was sincere. William sensed the depth of his father's appraisal and glanced at him, quickly masking his malevolence. At once his expression became affectionate again, tinged with sadness for the impending departure of all those he loved best.

However, what he had seen in William's eyes started a train of thought in Hal and filled him with foreboding, a sudden premonition that this was the last time he would sit around the same table with all his sons. The winds of hazard are bearing us all away, each on his own separate course. Some of us will never see High Weald again, he thought. He felt a melancholy so profound that he could not shrug it off, and had to force a smile to his lips as he rose to reply to William's toast: 'God speed and fair winds!'

At the end of the breakwater William sat on Sultan, his black stallion, and lifted his hat high in salute as the two ships put out to sea. Hal walked to the rail of the quarterdeck and returned his salute before turning away to give orders to the helm to bring the ship round for the run down the Sound to the open sea.

'What course to weather Ushant?' he asked Ned Tyler as they cleared Penlee Point, and the green hills of England began to drop away astern. Ned stood by the new-fangled steering wheel which, on such a modern ship, had replaced the ancient whipstaff. It was a marvellous invention: using the whipstaff the helmsman had been limited to five-degree turns either side of centre but with this new wheel he could lay the tiller seventy degrees across for much greater control of the ship's direction under way.

'The wind stands fair, Captain. South-west by south,' Ned answered. He knew that the question was a formality, that Hal had checked his chart carefully before leaving his cabin.

'Mark it on your traverse!' Hal told him, and Ned set a peg in a hole in the border of the circular traverse board. A peg would be added every half-hour and at the end of the watch the mean course could be found, and the ship's position calculated by dead reckoning.

Hal walked aft looking up at the sails. They were running free, with the wind coming in fresh over the port quarter. With Ned's setting, every sail was drawing beautifully, and *Seraph* was flying – she seemed to leap from wave to wave. Hal felt a wild exhilaration, the intensity of which surprised him: I thought I was too old to have this joy again from a ship and the promise of adventure, he thought. It took an effort to keep his expression calm and his gait dignified, but Big Daniel was standing by the break of the quarterdeck and they caught each other's eye. They did not smile but each understood how the other felt.

The passengers were standing amidships, lining the rail. The women's skirts whipped and fluttered in the wind, and they had to hold on to their bonnets. But as soon as *Seraph* cleared the land and felt the full thrust of the sea, the feminine squeals of excitement died away, and one after the other they left the rail and hurried below, until only Caroline was left standing beside her father.

All that day, and for several that followed, the force of the wind increased. It drove the two ships on, until one evening it was threatening a full gale, and Hal was forced to shorten sail. As darkness fell, both ships hoisted lanterns in their main tops to maintain contact, and as dawn broke Ned knocked on Hal's cabin door to tell him that the *Yeoman* was in sight two miles astern and that the light on Ushant was fine on the port bow.

Before noon they rounded Ushant and plunged headlong into the stormy waters of Biscay, which lived up to their evil reputation. For the next week the crew had good practice at handling the sails and working the ship in turbulent waters and high winds. Among the ladies only Caroline seemed unaffected, and joined Tom and Dorian for daily lessons in Master Walsh's crowded little cabin. She spoke little, and not at all to Tom, continuing to ignore even his most clever quips and witticisms. She declined when he offered to help her with the mathematical problems that Master Walsh set for them. Languages and mathematics were two of the areas in which Tom excelled. She also refused to join the lessons in Arabic that Alf Wilson gave the three boys for an hour each afternoon.

During the crossing of the Bay of Biscay, Guy was prostrated by seasickness. Hal was deeply disturbed that any son of his could succumb so to the motion of the waves. Nevertheless he had a pallet laid in the corner of the stern cabin for him, and Guy lay there, pale and groaning, as though on the point of death, unable to eat and only just able to gulp water from the mug Aboli held for him.

Mrs Beatty and her younger daughters were in no better case. None of them left their cabins, and Dr Reynolds, helped by Caroline, spent most of his days attending to them. There was much spiriting to and fro of chamberpots and dumping their contents over the side of the ship. The sour odour of vomit pervaded the stern quarters.

Hal had ordered their course laid off well to the westwards, to avoid running aground during darkness on the islands of Madeira and the Canaries and in the hope of picking up more favourable winds when they at last entered the doldrums. However, it was only when they were approaching thirty-five degrees north latitude, with Madeira a hundred leagues eastward, that the gales began at last to moderate. In these easier conditions Hal was able to set about repairs to the sails and rigging that the ship had sustained during the storms, and to exercise his crew in manoeuvres other than sail-setting and shortening. The crew were able to dry out their clothing and sodden bedding, the cook could get his fires going and serve hot fare. A different mood took over the ship.

Within days Mrs Beatty and her younger girls reappeared on deck, at first wan and listless, but soon in brighter spirits. It was not long before Agnes and Sarah had become the ship's pests. They took an especial set at Tom, for whom they had developed an overwhelming hero-worship, and it was to escape them that Tom talked Aboli into allowing him to go aloft, without his father's permission, which they knew would not be forthcoming.

Hal came on deck at the change of the forenoon watch to find Tom out on the yard thirty feet above the deck, bare feet planted firmly on the horse as he helped shake out another reef in the main topsail. Hal froze in mid-stride, his head thrown back, searching for an order that would bring Tom back to the deck without making plain his concern. He turned to the helm, saw that all the officers on deck were watching him, and casually crossed to where Aboli stood at the rail.

'I recall the first time you ever climbed to the main topmast, Gundwane,' Aboli said softly. 'It was in heavy seas off the Agulhas Bank. You did it because I had forbidden you to go higher than the main shrouds. You were two years younger than Klebe is now but, then, you always were a wild boy.' Aboli shook his head disapprovingly, and spat over the side. 'Your father, Sir Francis, wanted to take the rope end to you. I should have let him do it.'

Hal remembered the incident clearly. What had begun as boyish defiance had ended in abject terror as he had clung to the mast top while, a hundred feet below, vistas of the deck alternated with glimpses of the creaming green waves as the ship rolled and plunged, and the wake streamed away behind. Was Tom really two years older now than he had been that day? Certainly the yard from which his son was hanging was not even halfway to the topmast. 'You and I have both seen a fall from the main yard,' he growled. 'It breaks bone and kills just as surely as from the main-mast truck.'

'Klebe will not fall. He climbs like an ape.' Aboli grinned suddenly. 'It must be in his blood.'

Hal ignored the sally and returned to his cabin, ostensibly to write up his log but in truth so that he would no longer have to watch his son in the rigging. For the rest of the forenoon watch he waited to hear that terrible meaty thump on the deck above his head, or the cries of 'Man overboard!' When at last there was a knock on the door of the cabin and Tom, beaming with pride, put his head through to deliver a message from the officer of the watch, Hal almost leaped up with relief and hugged him to his chest.

When they ran into the doldrums, the ship lay becalmed, all sails drooping, without even an eddy or ripple under her counter. In the middle of the morning Hal was with Big Daniel, Ned Tyler and Wilson in his cabin, again going over Wilson's description of the capture of the *Minotaur* by Jangiri. Hal wanted all his officers to know exactly what to expect, and to have their ideas on how best to bring Jangiri to battle, or to discover the whereabouts of his sally port.

Suddenly Hal broke off from what he was saying, and cocked his head. There was some unusual activity on the deck above, footsteps, the faint sound of voices and laughter. 'Excuse me, gentlemen.' He came to his feet and hurried up the companionway. He looked about swiftly. All the off-duty hands were on deck – in fact, every loafer on board seemed to be there. All heads were craned back, looking up at the main mast. Hal followed their gaze.

Tom was sitting easily astride the main royal yard and calling encouragement to Dorian. 'Come on, Dorry. Don't look down.'

Dorian was hanging in the topmast shrouds below him. For a horrible moment Hal thought he was frozen there, eighty feet above the deck, but then the boy moved. He took one cautious step up, then he groped for a handhold on the ropework above his head and took another step.

'That's it, Dorry! Another one now!'

The strength of Hal's anger towards Tom was heightened by his fear for the child. I should have thrashed the skin off his backside when he played his first trick in the rigging, he thought, and strode to the helm and seized the hailing trumpet from its bracket. Before he could lift it to his mouth and bellow at the boys, Aboli appeared at his side.

'It will not be wise to frighten them now, Gundwane. Dorian needs both hands and all his wits for the job.'

Hal lowered the trumpet and held his breath as Dorian inched, hand over hand, up the shrouds. 'Why did you not stop them, Aboli?' he asked furiously.

'They did not ask me.'

'Even if they had, you would have let them go,' Hal said accusingly.

'I do not know, in truth.' Aboli shrugged. 'Every boy comes to manhood in his own time and in his own way.' He was still watching the small boy in the high rigging. 'Dorian is not afraid.'

'How do you know?' Hal snarled, beside himself with fear.

'Look at the way he holds his head. Watch his feet and hands as he takes his holds.'

Hal did not answer. He saw that Aboli was right. A coward clings to the ropes and closes his eyes, his hands shake and the smell of terror is strong upon him. Dorian kept moving, head up and eyes ahead. Almost every man of the crew was on deck, watching, and they were silent and tense.

Tom reached out towards his brother. 'Almost there, Dorry!' But Dorian scorned the helping hand and, with a visible effort, pulled himself up beside his big brother. He took a moment to catch his breath, then threw back his head and let out a high cry of triumph. Tom put a protective arm around his shoulders and hugged him. Their beaming faces were clear to see even at that distance from the deck. The crew burst into spontaneous cheering, and Dorian pulled his cap from his head and waved it at them. He and Tom were already the ship's favourites.

'He was ready for it,' Aboli said. 'And he has proved it.'

'My God, he's only a baby! I will forbid him to go aloft again!' Hal burst out.

'Dorian is no baby. You see with the eyes of a father,' Aboli told him. 'Soon there will be fighting, and you and I both know that in a fight the topmast is the safest place for a lad to be.' This was true, of course. When he was that age Hal's battle quarter had always been high aloft, for the enemies' fire was directed at the hull, and if the ship were boarded he would be out of harm's way.

A few days later Hal amended the quarter-bill to place both Tom and Dorian in the main-mast crow's nest when the ship went into battle. He was not certain what he should do with Guy, who had shown no indication of wishing to leave the safety of the main deck. Perhaps he could act as surgeon's mate in the sickbay, he thought. But, then, he might not take kindly to the sight of blood.

In the doldrums the wind flirted with them. For days on end it died away completely, and the sea was oily calm. The heat beat down upon the ship and they laboured for breath while sweat burst from every pore of their skins. Those on deck sought the shade of the sails as respite from the sun. Then, on the horizon, a cat's-paw would scratch the slick surface of the sea, and a breath of wind would scurry to fill the sails and bear them away for an hour or a day.

When the wind, capricious and fickle, stranded them again, and the ship lay dead in the water, Hal battle-trained his men. He worked them at the guns, watch competing against watch to be the quickest at loading, running out, firing and loading again. He gave them musketry drill, throwing a barrel overside to act as a target. Then he issued cutlasses from the arms locker and had Aboli and Daniel lead the company through the manual of arms. Tom took his place with the rest of his watch when they worked with the cutlass, and more than once Big Daniel made him stand out in front to demonstrate a finer point of style to the others.

Hal had started with hand-picked men: almost all had fought before and were old hands with pistol and cutlass, boarding pikes and axes, and at serving the cannon. After two or three weeks, he knew that this was the finest crew of fighting men he had ever commanded. One quality set them apart, which Hal found hard to define: he could think of it only as eagerness. They were hunting dogs questing for the scent of the quarry and he would be happy to lead them into any fight.

They had left the islands of Madeira and the Canaries far below the horizon to the east, but their progress slowed as they ran further and deeper into the doldrums. They lay for days at a time, sails hanging lifelessly, the surface of the ocean around them glassy smooth, as though oil had been spilled upon it, the burnished waters marred only by clumps of Sargasso weed and the dappling of flying fish as they skimmed over it. The sun was malicious and relentless.

Hal knew of the malaise that could overtake a crew in these enervating latitudes, how it could sap their vitality and resolve. He went to great lengths to keep his men from falling into this quagmire of boredom and despondency. When the battle drills were done each day, he organized relay races from the deck to the main top, and down again, setting one watch against the other. Even Tom and Dorian took part in these, to the squealing delight of the Beatty Brats, as Tom had christened Agnes and Sarah.

Then Hal ordered the carpenters and their mates on both ships to insert the thwarts into the pinnaces. They launched them, and a crew of oarsmen from the *Seraph* raced a crew from the *Yeoman* on a course set twice around the drifting ships, with a prize of a red ribbon and an extra ration of rum to the winning pinnace. The ribbon was tied to the *Seraph*'s bowsprit after the first race, and thereafter became an emblem of honour as it changed hands back and forth between the two ships.

To celebrate the winning of the red ribbon, Hal invited Edward Anderson to row across from the *Yeoman* to join him and his passengers for dinner in the stern cabin. As an afterthought he included his own sons in the invitation to help provide entertainment, for Master Walsh had suggested a musical recital after dinner. Walsh would play the flute and Guy the cittern, while Dorian, who had an extraordinary voice, would sing.

Hal served his best claret, and the dinner was noisy and convivial. With this number of guests there was barely space for all to sit, let alone move around, and when Hal called at last for silence and asked Master Walsh to play, the unmusical Tom found himself pushed into a corner, on a stool, and hidden from general view behind the carved screen that divided the day cabin from his father's sleeping quarters.

Walsh and Guy began with a rendition of several old tunes including 'Greensleeves' and 'Spanish Ladies', which delighted all except Tom, who was so thoroughly bored that, with his dirk, he was carving his initials into the wooden frame of the screen behind which he was sitting.

'And now we will have a song from Mistress Caroline Beatty and Master Dorian Courtney,' Walsh announced. Caroline stood up and, with difficulty, eased her way through the closely packed audience until she reached the end of the cabin where Tom sat. She gave him one of her cold looks, then turned half away from him and placed her hip against the carved screen to face Dorian, who stood against the opposite bulkhead.

They began with an aria by Purcell. Caroline's voice was clear and sweet, if a little stilted, while Dorian sang with a natural exuberance. The divine sounds that burst out of the angelic little boy brought tears to the eyes of those who listened.

By this time Tom was squirming with the need to escape the hot, claustrophobic cabin. He wanted to be up on deck, under the stars, hidden away behind one of the gun carriages with either Daniel or Aboli or both of them, listening to stories of the wild lands and mysterious oceans that lay ahead. But he was trapped.

Then he noticed that when Caroline reached for a high note she rose up on tiptoe: her skirt rode high enough to expose her ankles and the back of her calves. Tom's boredom evaporated. The girl's slippered feet were finely shaped. She wore dark blue stockings and her ankles blended in a lovely line into the swell of her calves above. Almost of its own volition, his hand came out of his pocket and reached towards a sculpted ankle.

'Are you mad?' he asked himself. With an effort he stopped himself touching her. 'She will make no end of a fuss, if I lay a finger on her.' He looked around guiltily. Caroline was standing directly in front of him, so close to him that she screened him from the sight of the rest of the company. He knew that every eye in the cabin was turned on Dorian. Still Tom hesitated. He started to withdraw his hand, to thrust it back safely into the depths of his pocket. Then he smelt her.

Over the other powerful odours in the cabin, of pork crackling and cabbage, of wine fumes and the smoke of his father's cigarro, he caught the warm girl smell of her body. His heart clenched like a fist and there was a pain of wanting in the pit of his stomach. He had to stifle the groan that rose to his lips.

He leaned forward on the stool and touched her ankle. It was the lightest brush of his fingertips against the sheer blue stuff of her stockings. Then he jerked away, and sat back on the stool ready to feign innocence when she rounded on him.

Caroline picked up the chorus from Dorian, without missing a beat, and Tom was perplexed at the lack of reaction from her. Again he reached out and this time laid two fingers gently on her ankle. Caroline did not move her foot and her voice continued clear and sweet. Tom stroked her foot, then slowly encircled her ankle with his fingers. It was so small, so feminine, that he felt the pressure swell in his chest. The blue stocking was glossy and silky to his touch. Very slowly, lingeringly, he ran his fingers up over the swell of her calf, savouring the warm curve, until he reached the top of her stocking and the bow of ribbon that secured it below her knee. There he hesitated and at that moment the song came to an end, in a glorious ringing together of the two young voices.

There was a moment's silence, then a burst of clapping and shouts of 'Bravo!' and 'Encore! Sing us another.'

His father's voice: 'We must not impose on Mistress Caroline. She has been too kind to us already.'

Caroline's dark curls danced on her shoulders. 'It is no imposition, Sir Henry, I assure you. We are only pleased that you enjoy it. We will sing again with the greatest of pleasure. Shall we give them "My Love She Lives In Durham Town", Dorian?'

'I suppose so,' Dorian agreed, with little enthusiasm, and Caroline opened her pretty mouth and let the song pour out. Tom had not moved his hand, and now his fingers stole over the top of her stocking to caress the soft skin at the back of her knee. She sang on, and it seemed that her voice had gained in force and feeling. Master Walsh wagged his head in delighted approbation as he blew on his flute.

Tom fondled first one knee then the other. He had lifted the hem of her skirt and he stared at the glossy skin, so soft and warm beneath his fingertips. Now that it was clear she would not scream or denounce him to the company, he was growing bolder.

He ran his fingers higher, moving up over the back of her thigh, and he felt her tremble, but her voice was still steady and she missed not a word of the song. From this angle Tom could just see his father's foot beneath the table, tapping out the rhythm with his toe. The knowledge that Hal was so close, the dangerous nature of his behaviour, enhanced Tom's excitement. His fingers were trembling as they reached the crease above which swelled Caroline's tight round buttock. She wore nothing under her petticoats and he followed the curve of her bottom until he reached the deep vertical cleft that separated one hemisphere of warm flesh from the other. He tried to slip one of his fingers high between her thighs but they were pressed tightly together – every muscle in both her legs was clenched as hard as stone. The divide was impassable and he abandoned the attempt. Instead he cupped one of her small firm buttocks in his hand and squeezed it gently.

Caroline hit a high ringing note at the end of the verse, and changed her position slightly, moving her tiny slippered feet apart and pushing out her bottom towards him. Her thighs parted, and when Tom tried again he felt the silken nest of fur between them. She made another small movement, as though to make it easier for him, then moved again, directing his touch. Mary the scullerymaid had shown Tom where to find that magical nub of hard flesh, and deftly he sought it out. Now Caroline was gently moving her whole body to the beat of the music, swaying her hips. Her eyes sparkled and her colour was high. Mrs Beatty thought that her daughter had never looked so enchantingly lovely, and she glanced around the circle of men's faces and was proud when she saw the admiration in their eyes.

The song reached its climax, and even Dorian had to extend himself to match the beauty of that last, high, ringing note, that seemed to fill the whole cabin then hang there, shimmering in the air, even after the song had

99

ended. Caroline spread out her skirts and petticoats, like the petals of a glorious tropical orchid, and sank down in such a deep curtsy that her forehead almost touched the deck.

All the men came to their feet to applaud her, even though they had to stoop beneath the heavy overhead beams. When Caroline lifted her head her lips were trembling and her cheeks were wet with tears of deep emotion. Her mother jumped up and hugged her impulsively.

'Oh, my darling, that was surpassing beautiful. You sang like an angel. But you have exhausted yourself. You may take a half-glass of wine to refresh yourself.' To expressions of congratulations and delight Caroline made her way back to her seat. The girl seemed transformed from her usual quiet, withdrawn self, and joined the conversation around her almost gaily. When Mrs Beatty deemed it time to retire and leave the men to their pipes, cigarros and port, Caroline went with her demurely. When she said goodnight and left the cabin she never so much as glanced in Tom's direction.

Tom sat back on his stool in the corner, staring at the deck above his head, trying to appear aloof and unconcerned, but both hands were thrust deeply into his pockets and he held himself hard so that no one would notice what he had grown in his breeches.

That night Tom slept hardly at all. He lay on his pallet with Dorian on one side of him, Guy on the other, and listened to the snores, the groans and muttering of the sleeping crew along the gundeck. He relived in his imagination every detail of the episode in the stern cabin, every touch and movement, the smell of her and the sound of her voice singing as he fondled her, the slippery softness of her most secret parts and the heat of them. He could barely contain himself until the following day when he would be with Caroline in Master Walsh's cabin. Even though they would all be poring over their slates and listening to Master Walsh's excruciatingly dull monologues, he longed for a glance or a touch that would confirm for him the monumental significance of what had taken place between them.

When at last she entered Master Walsh's cabin, preceded by her squealing sisters, she ignored Tom and went directly to Master Walsh. 'I find the light at my seat is too dull. It tires my eyes. May I change my place and sit beside Guy?'

'Yes, of course you may, young mistress,' Walsh acceded instantly, not at all immune to Caroline's charms. 'You should have told me earlier that you were uncomfortable beside Tom.'

Guy moved up the bench with alacrity to make a place for her, but Tom felt himself snubbed and tried to catch her attention by gazing at her fixedly across the narrow cabin. However, Caroline fastened her full attention on her slate and did not look up.

At last even Master Walsh became aware of Tom's strange behaviour. 'Are you seasick?'

Tom was appalled by and affronted at such an accusation. 'I am perfectly well, sir.'

'Then tell me what I was saying?' Walsh suggested.

Tom looked thoughtful and stroked his chin. At the same time he kicked Dorian's ankle beneath the tabletop.

Dorian came loyally to the rescue. 'You were saying that tautology is—'

'Thank you, Dorian,' Walsh stopped him. 'I was speaking to your brother, not to you.' He regarded Tom disapprovingly. It always irked him when a boy with a good brain refused to make use of its full potential. 'Now that you have been reprieved, Thomas, perhaps you will enlighten us all on the meaning of the word.'

'Tautology is the unnecessary repetition of meaning that has already been conveyed earlier in a phrase or sentence,' Tom told him.

Walsh looked disappointed. He had hoped to make him display his ignorance and suffer humiliation before his peers. 'You amaze me with your erudition,' he said stiffly. 'Will you display it further by giving us an example of tautology?'

Tom thought. 'A pedantic pedagogue?' he suggested. 'A tedious teacher?'

Dorian let out a snort of laughter, and even Guy looked up and smiled. The Beatty Brats understood not a word of it but when they saw Walsh flush scarlet and Tom fold his arms over his chest and grin triumphantly, they realized that their idol had come out on top again and tittered delightedly. Only Caroline went on writing on her slate without so much as raising her head.

Tom was baffled and hurt. It was as though nothing at all had happened between them. When his perennial fencing with Master Walsh left her unmoved, he tried in other ways to attract her attention. When Caroline was on deck, he pushed himself to the limits of his strength and experience to impress her with his new-found prowess as a topmast man. He copied the feats of his seniors, running out along the high yard, hands above his head, to his place on the rat-lines, or sliding down the mizzen stay without pause so that the rough hemp rope scorched his palms before he landed on bare feet with a thump close to where she stood. She turned away without even a second glance.

In contrast she was honeyed sweetness with Guy and Dorian, and even with Master Walsh. Tone-deaf Tom was excluded from their musical practices and Caroline seemed to take extra pleasure in Guy's company. The two would whisper together even during lessons, when Walsh made only half-hearted attempts to silence them. Tom protested,

'I'm working on a problem in trigonometry, and I cannot think when you two are chattering away all the time.'

Walsh smiled vindictively. 'I am unaware of any significant increase in your cerebral processes, Thomas, even in times of deepest silence.'

At this Caroline gave a burst of tinkling laughter and leaned on Guy's shoulder, as if to share the joke with him. The glance she threw at Tom was malicious and taunting.

Both Dorian and Tom had inherited their father's sharp eyesight so they were often sent aloft together as lookouts. Tom came to enjoy those long stints at the masthead: it was the only place in the crowded ship that they could ever be alone. Dorian had learned how to hold his tongue, and they could sit for hours in companionable silence, not intruding on each other's thoughts, each indulging his imagination and his fantasies.

Where once Tom's dreams had been of battle and glory, of the wild lands and great oceans whither they were bound, of the elephants and whales and huge apes on misty mountain peaks, which he discussed so avidly with Aboli and Big Daniel, his visions now were of Caroline. Of her warm soft body, which he had touched but never seen, of her eyes turned upon him with love and devotion, of doing with her the wondrous things he had done with Mary and the other girls from the village. Yet it seemed sacrilege, somehow, to allow those coarse creatures into the same dream as the divine Caroline.

He conjured up images of saving her when the ship was in flames and the decks swarming with pirates, leaping overboard with her in his arms and swimming to the snowy beach of a coral island where they could be alone. Alone! That was the problem that confronted him at the end of each of his dreams. How to be alone. The *Seraph* could sail on to the ends of the oceans with her on board, but they would never be alone.

He tried desperately to think of some place on board where they might spend even a few minutes away from prying eyes – even if he could entice her to follow him there. Which, he admitted, seemed highly unlikely.

There was the cargo hold, but it was battened down and had the Company seals upon it. There were the cabins in the stern quarters, but even the largest of those afforded little privacy and all were packed to overflowing with humanity. The bulkheads were so flimsy that through the partitions he had heard the three sisters arguing because there was only room in their cabin for one to stand upright at a time. Two had to crawl into their bunks so that one could dress or undress. There was certainly nowhere there for him to be alone with Caroline and to pour out his love to her, or to further his knowledge of her delights. But still his imagination would give him little rest.

On those evenings when the weather was favourable, Tom and Dorian would fetch their food bowls from the galley and take them up to the bows, where they would eat, squatting on the deck, with Aboli and sometimes Big Daniel for company. Afterwards they might lie on their backs and stare up at the night sky.

Daniel would puff on his clay pipe and point out to them how the sky changed with every day as they ran down further into the south. He showed them the great Southern Cross rising each evening higher above the horizon ahead of them, the shimmering clouds of Magellan, hovering like the aura of angels, showing at last beneath it.

Around each constellation Aboli wove the legends of the stars from his own tribe, and Big Daniel would chuckle. 'Away with you, you great black pagan. Let me tell them the Christian truth. That is Orion the mighty hunter, not some savage bushman.'

Aboli ignored him and told them, one night, the legend of the foolish hunter who fired all his arrows at the herd of zebra – here he pointed out the star cluster of Orion's belt – and thus had nothing with which to defend himself when the lion of Sirius stalked him. For his lack of forethought, the hunter ended up in the lion's belly – 'Which is a more satisfying story for the listener,' Aboli concluded complacently.

'And for the lion,' Big Daniel agreed, knocked out his pipe and stood up. 'I have work to do on this ship, unlike others it seems.' He went aft to make his rounds.

After he had gone they were silent for a while. Dorian curled up on the deck, like a puppy, and fell almost instantly asleep. Aboli sighed with contentment, then murmured, in the language of the forests, which they often used when they were alone, 'The foolish hunter might have learned many things if he had lived long enough.'

'Tell me what they are.' Tom spoke in the same language.

'Sometimes it is best not to chase after the zebra firing off your arrows wildly and from a distance.'

'What do you mean, Aboli?' Tom asked, sitting up and hugging his knees to his chest, sensing a hidden meaning to the story.

'The foolish hunter lacks guile and cunning. The harder he chases, the faster runs the game. Those who watch cry, "Behold, the stupid hunter!" and they laugh at his fruitless endeavours.'

Tom thought about this: he had come to expect hidden depths in all Aboli's stories. Suddenly the moral of the story occurred to him and he moved restlessly. 'Are you mocking me, Aboli?'

'That I would never do, Klebe, but it galls me to see lesser men laughing at you.'

'What cause have I given anyone to laugh at me?'

'You chase too hard. You let every man on board know what you are about.'

'Do you mean Caroline?' Tom's voice sank to a whisper. 'Is it so obvious, then?'

'There is no need for me to answer that. But, rather, tell me what makes you pine for her most.'

'She is beautiful—' Tom began.

'She is not ugly, at least.' Aboli smiled in the darkness. 'But what drives you mad is that she takes no notice of you.'

'I don't understand, Aboli.'

'You chase because she runs, and she runs because you chase.'

'What should I do rather?'

'Do what the wise hunter does and wait softly at the waterhole. Let the quarry come to you.'

Until that time Tom had taken any excuse to linger in Walsh's cabin after the day's lessons had ended, hoping for some small sign from Caroline that she was still interested in him. His father had stipulated that all three boys undergo three hours of formal instruction each day before attending to their duties in the ship. It must have seemed even to Hal that three hours was enough of Master Walsh's instruction, but until now Tom had braved it longer, simply to spend a few minutes longer in the presence of the object of his devotion.

After his talk with Aboli, this changed. During lessons, he forced himself to be silent and inscrutable, confining his exchanges with Walsh to bare necessities. As soon as the ship's bell sounded the change of watch, no matter if he were in the middle of some complex mathematical problem, he would pack away his books and slate and rise immediately to his feet. 'Please excuse me, Master Walsh, I must go to my duties.' Then he would stride from the cabin without even a glance at Caroline.

In the evenings when Caroline came on deck with her mother and her sisters to take their constitutional stroll in the fresh air, Tom made sure that his duties kept him as far from her as the ship's cramped conditions allowed.

For some days she gave no indication that she was aware of the change in his attitude to her. Then, one morning while they were at lessons, Tom glanced up inadvertently from his slate and caught her regarding him from the corner of her eye. She looked down instantly, but could not prevent the rise of colour to her cheek. Tom felt a flare of satisfaction. Aboli had been right. This was the first time he had ever caught her studying him.

With his resolve strengthened, it became easier each day to ignore her as she had once ignored him. This stalemate persisted for almost two weeks until he noticed a subtle change in her behaviour. During the morning lessons she became more talkative, addressing her remarks mostly to Walsh and Guy but particularly to Guy. She exchanged whispers with him, and laughed inordinately at his most fatuous remarks. Tom maintained his grim silence without raising his head, although her laughter galled him to the depths of his soul.

Once when they had been released from Walsh's cabin and were at the foot of the companionway, Caroline asked, in an irritatingly theatrical tone, 'Oh! These stairs are so steep. May I take your arm, Guy?' Then she leaned on him and looked up into his grinning face. Tom brushed past them with no display of emotion.

Somehow Guy's shipboard duties allowed him time to walk with Mrs Beatty and the girls on deck, or to spend hours in earnest conversation with Mr Beatty in his cabin. In fact, both Mr and Mrs Beatty seemed to have taken to him. He still made no attempt to leave the deck and venture aloft, even when Tom teased him about it in Caroline's hearing. Tom was surprised that he did not resent Guy's timidity. In fact, he felt relief that he did not have the responsibility of keeping an eye on his twin in the high, dangerous dimension aloft. It was enough to have Dorian in his care, even though the younger boy was already so quick and agile in the rigging that he was soon of little concern to Tom.

Although Caroline's intervention had first made it apparent, the twins had been drifting apart for some time. They spent little time in each other's company, and when they were together their talk was terse and guarded. It was a far cry from the days not so long ago when they had shared every thought and dream, and comforted each other when they encountered life's small hardships and injustices.

After dinner Hal often invited his passengers to an evening of whist in the stern cabin. He was a keen player and he had taught Tom to enjoy the game. With his bent for mathematics Tom had developed into an excellent player, and often partnered his father against Mr Beatty and Master Walsh. These games were taken seriously and contested to the knife. After each hand the play was discussed and dissected, while at the other table in the cabin, Guy, Mrs Beatty and the girls giggled and squealed over infantile games of loo and spoil five. Guy had shown neither aptitude for nor liking of the more difficult game of whist.

On one of these evenings Tom found himself placed by his father in a tenuous contract of five hearts. He knew from the outset that he had a choice of two mutually exclusive plays. He could place Mr Beatty with the queen of hearts and take the finesse through him, or he could play for a two split of trumps. He tried to calculate the odds on the hearts breaking evenly or the queen being a singleton, but the cries and feminine squeaks from the other table distracted him. He deliberated a while, then finessed for the lady. He saw his father frown as he began the play, and then, to his dismay, Master Walsh gave a snigger of triumph and made good his singleton queen.

Flustered by this miscalculation, Tom misplayed the clubs and the hand was a disaster.

His father was severe. 'You should have known from Master Walsh's bidding that he had seven clubs, and his discard to your king confirmed the unfavourable distribution.' Tom squirmed in his chair. He looked up to see that, at the other table, all play had stopped and that they were listening to his father berate him. Both Caroline and Guy were watching him, their heads close together. In Guy's expression there was a malicious glee that Tom had never witnessed before. Guy was actually glorying in his brother's humiliation.

Suddenly Tom found himself plunged into a crisis of guilt. For the first time in his life he was confronted with the realization that he did not like his twin. Guy turned his head and winked at Caroline, who placed a small white hand on his sleeve. She covered her mouth with the other and whispered something in his ear. She was looking squarely at Tom, and her eyes were mocking. With a shock Tom realized that, more than merely disliking Guy, he actually hated him and wished him harm.

For days afterwards, he wrestled with his guilt. His father had taught all his sons that loyalty within the family was sacrosanct – 'Us against the world,' he often said – and now Tom felt that once again he had fallen short of his father's expectations.

Then, unexpectedly, it seemed that he had been vindicated. At first he was only vaguely aware that something of great portent was afoot. He noticed Mr Beatty and his father in earnest conversation on the quarterdeck, and he could tell instantly that his father was deeply displeased. Over the next few days Mr Beatty spent much time closeted with Hal in the stern cabin. Then Hal despatched Dorian to summon Guy to one of these meetings.

'What were they saying?' Tom demanded of his little brother as soon as he returned.

'I don't know.'

'You should have listened at the door,' Tom muttered. He was beside himself with curiosity.

'I didn't dare,' Dorian admitted. 'If he had caught me, Father would have had me keel-hauled.' Dorian had only recently heard of this gruesome punishment, which fascinated him.

For days Guy had been dreading the summons to the stern cabin. He was busy with Ned Tyler in the powder magazine, helping him open the kegs and check the gritty black powder for damp, when Dorian came to find him.

'Father wants to see you now in his quarters.' The boy was beside himself with his importance as the bearer of such ominous tidings. Guy stood up and dusted the powder grains from his hands.

'Better go quickly,' Dorian warned him. 'Father's got his Death-to-the-Infidel face on.'

When Guy stepped into the cabin he saw at once that Dorian had not exaggerated their father's mood. Hal stood by the stern windows with his hands clasped behind his back. He wheeled around, and the thick pigtail down his back twitched like the tail of an angry lion as he regarded his son with an expression not entirely of anger. In it Guy saw a touch of concern and even dismay.

'I have been having a long talk with Mr Beatty.' He indicated him with a nod. Beatty sat at the table, stern and unsmiling. He wore his full periwig, a further indication of the seriousness of this meeting. Hal was silent for a moment, as if what he had to say next was so distasteful that he would prefer not to have to utter the words.

'I am led to believe that you have been making plans

110

for your future, without consulting me as the head of the family.'

'Forgive me, Father, but I do not want to be a sailor,' Guy blurted out miserably.

Hal stepped back involuntarily, as though his son had denied his faith in God. 'We have always been sailors. For two hundred years the Courtneys have put out to sea.'

'I hate it,' Guy said softly, his voice shaking. 'I hate the stink and cramped space aboard a ship. I feel sick and unhappy when I am out of sight of land.'

There was another long silence, then Hal went on, 'Tom and Dorian have taken to their heritage. They will surely enjoy rich adventures and profits. I had thought one day to offer you your own ship. But I see that I waste my breath.'

Guy hung his head, and reiterated miserably, 'I will never be happy out of sight of land.'

'Happy!' Hal had promised himself to keep his temper in check, but the scornful word burst from his lips before he could contain it. 'What has happiness to do with it? A man follows the path laid out for him. He does his duty to God and his king. He does what he must do, not what pleases him.' He felt the anger and outrage building in him. 'God's truth, boy, what kind of world would this be if every man did what pleased him alone? Who would plough the fields and reap the harvest, if every man had the right to say, "I don't want to do that." In this world there is a place for every man, but every man must know his place.' He paused as he saw a stubborn look come over his son's face. He turned to the stern window, looked out at the ocean and the tall blue sky streaked with gold by the setting sun. He was breathing deeply, but it took him some minutes to regain his composure. When he turned back, his features were set. 'Very well!' he said, 'Perhaps I am over-indulgent, but I will not force you to it – though,

God knows, I have thought of doing just that. You are fortunate that Mr Beatty has the good opinion of you that has been denied me by your selfish behaviour.' He sat down heavily in his sea-chair and drew towards him the document that lay on the tabletop.

'As you already know, Mr Beatty has offered you a position with the Honourable East India Company as an apprentice writer. He has been generous as regards salary and conditions of employment. If you take up this offer, then your employment in the Company will commence immediately. I will release you from your duties as a member of the crew of this ship. You will instead begin as assistant to Mr Beatty, and you will accompany him to the Company factory at Bombay. Do you understand that?'

'Yes, Father,' Guy murmured.

'Is that what you want?' Hal leaned forward and stared into his son's eyes, hoping for some denial.

'Yes, Father. That is what I want.'

Hal sighed and the anger left him. 'Well, then, I pray for your sake that you have made the right decision. Your fate is now out of my hands.' He pushed the parchment of indenture across the desk. 'Sign it. I will bear witness.'

Afterwards Hal sanded the wet ink of the signatures carefully then blew off the excess and handed the document to Mr Beatty. He turned back to Guy. 'I will explain your position to the ship's officers, and to your brothers. I have no doubt what they will think of you.'

I n the darkness the brothers discussed Guy's decision in exhaustive detail, squatting up in the bows with Aboli and Big Daniel.

'But how can Guy leave us like this? We swore that we'd always stick together, didn't we, Tom?' Dorian was distraught.

Tom avoided the direct question. 'Guy gets seasick. He could never be a real sailor,' he said. 'And he's afraid of the sea and of going aloft.' Somehow Tom could not bring himself to feel his younger brother's distress at this turn of events.

Dorian seemed to sense this and looked instead to the two older men for comfort. 'He should have stayed with us, don't you agree, Aboli?'

'There are many roads through the jungle,' Aboli rumbled. 'If we all took the same one it would become very crowded.'

'But Guy!' Dorian was almost in tears. 'He should never have deserted us.' He turned back to Tom. 'You won't ever desert me, will you, Tom?'

'Of course I won't,' Tom said gruffly.

'Promise?' A single tear ran down Dorian's cheek now, sparkling in the starlight.

'You must not cry,' Tom admonished him.

'I'm not crying. It's just that the wind makes my eyes water.' He dashed away the tear. 'Promise me, Tom.'

'I promise you.'

'No, not like that. Swear me a dreadful oath,' Dorian insisted.

With a long-suffering sigh, Tom drew the dirk from the sheath on his belt. He held up the narrow blade, which glinted in the moonlight. 'As God, Aboli and Big Daniel are my witness.' He pricked the point of the dagger into the ball of his thumb and they all watched the blood well up, black as tar, in the silvery light. He slipped the dagger back into its sheath, and with his free hand he drew Dorian's face close to his own. While he stared solemnly into the child's eyes, Tom inscribed with his thumb a bloody cross on Dorian's forehead. 'I swear you a dreadful oath that I will never leave you, Dorian,' he intoned with gravity. 'Now stop crying.'

With Guy's defection the watch-bill was altered so that Tom took over his twin's shipboard duties, adding them to his own. Now Ned Tyler and Big Daniel could concentrate the lessons in navigation, gunnery and sail-management on two students instead of three. Tom's routine had been heavy before, but now it seemed to have no limits.

Guy's duties now, though, were light and pleasant. After the daily lessons with Master Walsh, when Tom and Dorian had to hurry topsides to begin their stints, he spent a few hours writing letters and reports for Mr Beatty, or studying the Company's publications, including 'Instructions to Recruits in the Service of the Honourable English East India Company', after which he was free to read to Mrs Beatty, or to play cards with her daughters. None of this endeared him to his older brother, who sometimes, from the rigging, watched him strolling and laughing with the ladies on the quarterdeck, which was out of bounds to all but the ship's officers and the passengers.

The *Seraph* crossed the equator amid the usual jollification when all those who were making the crossing for the first time underwent initiation and paid allegiance to Neptune, god of the oceans. Aboli, in an improbable costume of oddments from the slop chest and a beard of unravelled rope, made an impressive Neptune.

Now the doldrums had swung to the northwards of the line, and as the two ships gradually shook free of their grip, they found themselves entering the belt of the southern trades. The character of the ocean changed: there was a sparkle to the ocean, which seemed alive after the sluggish, sullen waters of the doldrums. The air was fresh and invigorating, the sky dappled with mares' tails of wind-driven cirrus cloud. In sympathy, the mood of the crew became light and almost gay.

Hal shaped their course south-westerly, so that they could run on a broad reach, away from the continent of Africa, more than halfway across the Atlantic towards the coast of South America, but they traded the angle on the wind for distance run.

Every ten days Tom went down with Ned and the gunnery mates to check the contents of the magazine. It was part of his instruction in the art of gunnery to understand the character and the temperamental nature of the black powder. He had to know its composition, of sulphur, charcoal and saltpetre, how these ingredients could be safely blended and stored, how to prevent a build-up of heat and damp, which could cake the grains and cause uneven or faulty ignition in the guns. At each visit, Ned always impressed on him the danger of naked flame or spark in the magazine, which could set off an explosion and blow the ship out of the water.

Before going into battle the kegs were opened and the powder carefully weighed out into silk bags that contained the exact charge for a gun. This was rammed home down the muzzle as a cartridge and on top was placed a wad of cloth and then the shot. The bags were carried up to the gundecks by the powder monkeys or boys. Even when the ship was not expecting action, several silk bags were filled and laid out in the ready racks, in case of an emergency. Unfortunately the thin silk made the contents susceptible to damp and caking, so the bags had to be checked and repacked regularly.

When Ned and Tom worked in the magazine there was seldom any skylarking or light banter. The light from the single mesh-screened lantern was dim, and there was a cathedral hush. As the silk bags were passed up to him, Tom packed them carefully into the racks. They were firm and smooth to the touch. That would make a comfortable bunk, he thought. Suddenly he had a vision of Caroline stretched out on the silk bags – naked. He gave a low moan.

'What is it, Master Tom?' Ned looked up at him quizzically.

'Nothing. I was just thinking.'

'Leave the daydreaming to your twin. He's good at it,' Ned advised laconically. 'And you get on with the job. That's what you're good at.'

Tom went on packing in the bags, but now he was thinking furiously. The magazine was the only part of the ship that was deserted for ten days at a time, where a person could be alone, without fear of intrusion. It was just the place he had been trying so hard to find, so obvious that he had overlooked it. He glanced down at the keys that hung from Ned's belt. There were half a dozen in the bunch: those for the magazine, the arms-lockers, the galley stores and the slop chest – as well as the magazine.

When they had finished, Tom was at Ned's side when he secured the heavy oak door. He made a mental note of the key that turned the massive lock: it was quite distinctly shaped from the others on the bunch, with five tangs in the shape of a crown. He tried to think of a way to get his hands on the bunch, even for a few minutes, so that he could slip the one he wanted off the ring. But it was wasted effort: generations of seamen before him had contemplated the similar problem of how to get the key to the store where the spirits were kept.

That night he was lying on his pallet when the next idea occurred to him, so suddenly that he sat bolt upright: there must be more than one set of keys on board. If there were, he knew where they must be: in his father's cabin. In the sea-chest under his bunk, or in one of the drawers of the desk, he thought. For the rest of that night he had little sleep. Even in his privileged position of the master's eldest son aboard, he certainly could not make free with his father's quarters, and Hal's movements about the ship were unpredictable. There was never any time when his cabin was certain to be deserted. If he was not there, his steward was probably fussing with the bedclothes, or with Hal's wardrobe. He discounted the idea of making an attempt after his father had retired to his bunk. Tom knew that he was a light sleeper – he had found that out the hard way. His father was not an easy man to bamboozle.

Over the next week, Tom considered, and discarded, a few other wildly impractical plans, such as climbing down the outside of the hull and entering through the stern gallery. He knew he would have to take a calculated risk, and wait until his father ordered a major change of sail. Then both watches would be on deck, and his father would be fully engrossed above. Tom would conjure up some excuse to leave his post and hurry below.

The days went by swiftly, with the trades steady from the south-east and *Seraph* still set on the port tack. No change of sail was called for and there was no opportunity for Tom to put his plan into action.

Then the opportunity came to him in such a fortuitous manner that Tom felt an almost superstitious unease. He was squatting with the other men of his watch under the break of the forecastle, enjoying a rare few minutes of rest, when his father looked up from the compass binnacle and beckoned to him. Tom scrambled to his feet and ran to his father's side. 'Run down to my cabin, there's a good lad,' Hal told him. 'Look in the top drawer of my desk. You'll find my black notebook there. Bring it to me.'

'Aye, sir.' For a moment Tom felt quite giddy, then raced for the head of the companionway.

'Tom, not so fast.' His father's voice made him pause, his heart skipping. It had been too easy. 'If its not in the top drawer, it may be in one of the others.'

'Yes, Father.' Tom shot down the stairs.

The black notebook lay in the top drawer, exactly where his father had said it would be. Quickly Tom tried the other drawers, dreading to find them locked, but they slid open readily enough, and he searched them quickly. As he pulled open the last, he heard a heavy metal object clank and slide with the movement. Again his heart jumped.

The duplicate keys were tucked under a copy of the almanac and navigational tables. He lifted them out gingerly, and recognized the crown shape of the magazine key. He glanced up at the closed cabin door, and listened for footsteps before committing himself. Then he unscrewed the ring, slipped the key from it, thrust it into his pocket, closed the hasp of the ring, laid the depleted bunch back in the drawer and covered it with the almanac.

As he ran back on deck the key seemed as heavy in his pocket as a round shot. He had to find a hiding-place for it. The chances were that his father would not discover the theft, not unless the original was lost or mislaid. That was highly unlikely but, still, it was dangerous to carry his prize on his person.

That night he woke as usual when the ship's bell sounded the beginning of the middle watch at midnight. He waited for another hour then rose silently from his pallet. Beside him Guy sat up. 'Where are you going?' he whispered.

Tom's heart sank. 'To the head,' he whispered back. 'Go to sleep.' In future he must make some changes to their sleeping arrangements. Guy sank back on his straw pallet, and Tom slipped away in the direction of the bows, but as soon as he was out of Guy's sight he turned back quickly and slipped down the companionway to the lower deck.

In this wind and on this point of sailing the ship was never silent. Her timbers creaked and groaned, one of the seams popped regularly, loud as a pistol shot, and the waters rushed and whispered, thumped against the hull.

There was no light in the lower deck, but Tom moved with confidence, only once running into one of the bulkheads. Any noise he made was covered by the other shipboard sounds.

A single lantern was hanging from the deck at the bottom of the stern companionway. It cast a glimmering of light down the central passage. There was a sliver of light under the door to his father's cabin. He slipped past it and paused briefly outside the tiny cabin in which the three girls slept. He heard nothing, and went on.

The powder magazine was on the next deck down, right beside where the heel of the mainmast was stepped on the keelson. Tom crept down the last set of wooden stairs into the utter darkness of the lowest deck, and carefully to the door of the magazine. He knelt beside it and, by touch alone, fitted his key into the lock. The mechanism was stiff – he had to exert considerable effort before it yielded – and the door opened to his nudge. He stood in the dark opening and inhaled the sharp odour of black powder. Although he felt a sense of accomplishment, he knew there were still many obstacles before him. Quietly he pulled the door closed and locked it. He groped for and found the crack above the lintel, where he hid the key and the tinderbox he had brought with him. Then he retraced his steps through the vessel until he reached his pallet on the gundeck and crawled onto it. Beside him Guy moved restlessly. He was still awake, but neither spoke again, and soon they both drifted back to sleep.

So far all had worked in Tom's favour. So much so that the next day he had a queasy feeling that his luck must change. There had been little indication from Caroline that his plans might go any further than the point they had now reached. His courage was evaporating. He brooded on the risks he had taken, and those he must still take. More than once he determined to return the magazine key to his father's desk drawer, and abandon the whole desperate idea, but then he would sneak a glance at Caroline when she was absorbed in her lessons. The curve of her cheek, the pink lips pouting in concentration, a soft forearm below the puffed sleeves of her dress now lightly gilded by the tropical sun, and sparsely decorated with fine, peach-fluff hairs.

I have to be alone with her, even for a minute. It's worth any risk, he decided, but still he hesitated, unable to screw his courage to the act. He teetered on the brink, until she gave him the push that sent him over the edge.

At the end of the day's lessons, Caroline flounced out of the cabin ahead of Tom. But as she stepped onto the companionway, Master Walsh called out to her, 'Ah, Mistress Caroline, will you be able to attend the music practice this evening?'

Caroline turned back to answer him. Her movement was so unexpected that Tom could not avoid bumping into her. At the collision she almost lost her balance, but caught hold of his arm to steady herself, and he put the other round her waist. At that moment they were out of sight of Walsh and the two boys in the cabin behind them.

Caroline made no effort to pull away from him. Instead, she swayed towards him and pressed her lower body against his, a deliberate gyrating movement, looking up into his face with a sly, knowing expression as she did so. In that instant, the world changed for Tom. The contact was fleeting. Then she stepped round him and spoke to Master Walsh through the cabin door. 'Yes, of course. The weather is so fair we could meet on deck, don't you think?'

'What a splendid idea,' Walsh agreed, with alacrity. 'Shall we say at six o'clock, then?' Walsh still used the landlubber's calculation of time.

Ned Tyler stood beside Tom at the ship's wheel. Tom was trying to hold the *Seraph*'s heading at south-west by south, on her unswerving run across the ocean.

'Meet her!' Ned grunted, as Tom let her pay off a point. With every sail set to the royals and filled with twenty-five knots of wind, it was like trying to hold a runaway stallion.

'Look at your wake,' Ned told him sternly. Obediently Tom glanced back over the stern. 'Like a pair of snakes on honeymoon,' Ned said, which they both knew was unfair: a cable's length behind there was a barely discernible kink in the creaming wake, but Tom was allowed no leeway by his tutors. For the next ten minutes the *Seraph* cut a rapier-straight furrow through the blue waves.

'Very well, Master Thomas.' Ned nodded. 'Now, from the top of the main mast, if you please.'

'Royals, topgallants . . .' Tom called the names of the sails, without hesitation or mistake, and without allowing the ship's head to wander.

Then the trio of musicians came up from the stern quarters. Guy was carrying Caroline's songbook and his cittern. Walsh, with his flute sticking out of his back pocket, was carrying her stool in one hand and holding his wig on with the other. The group took up their usual place at the lee rail, protected from the main force of the wind.

Tom tried to keep his attention on the con of the ship, respond to Ned's inquisition and watch for the moment that Caroline opened her songbook and found the note he had placed between the pages.

'Mizen mast sails, if you please, from the top,' said Ned.

'Mizen topsail,' Tom replied, then hesitated. Caroline was ready to sing, and Walsh passed her the songbook.

'Go on,' Ned encouraged him.

'Mizen staysail,' said Tom, and paused again. Caroline opened the book, and frowned.

She was reading something between the pages. He thought he saw her pale, but then she glanced up involuntarily and looked straight at him across the full length of the open deck.

'Mizen course,' said Tom, and looked back at her. Again she gave him that sly, enigmatic look, and tossed her head so that her curls danced in the wind. From between the pages of her songbook she picked up the scrap of rice-paper, on which he had so laboriously penned his message, crumpled it into a ball between her fingers and tossed it disdainfully over the side. The wind caught it and carried it far out before dropping it into the water, where it disappeared among the pearling white caps. It was so clearly another rejection that Tom felt his world totter.

'Hold your luff!' said Ned sharply, and Tom started guiltily as he saw that he had let the *Seraph* sag down to leeward.

Even though he knew now that it was fruitless, Tom lay on his pallet through all the long first watch, awaiting the hour of midnight, and debating with himself as to whether there was any reason to take the risk and keep true to the assignation he had proposed. Her rejection had seemed categoric, and yet he knew with certainty that she had enjoyed that disturbing moment of intimacy in his father's cabin as much as he had. And that fleeting contact outside Walsh's quarters had confirmed beyond doubt that she was not averse to another adventure.

'She ain't the high and mighty lady she pretends,' Tom told himself angrily. 'Under all those fancy petticoats she loves it just like Mary or any of the other village girls. I bet a gold guinea to a pinch of dried horse droppings, she knows how to play Bury the Mannikin with the best of them.'

He had removed his pallet to a niche behind one of the cannon, so that neither Guy nor Dorian could lie beside him and keep watch on his comings and goings during the night. The hours of the watch seemed interminable. Once or twice he dozed, but then he would jerk awake, trembling with anticipation or consumed with doubts.

When seven bells in the first watch was struck on the deck above where he lay, he could contain himself no longer and crept out from under his blanket to make his way stealthily to the head of the companionway, holding his breath in case one of his younger brothers accosted him.

Once again he paused outside the tiny cabin in which the three girls slept, and placed his ear to the door. He heard nothing, and felt the temptation to tap on the panel to find out if Caroline was lying awake as he had been. Good sense prevailed, however, and he left the door to creep down onto the lower deck.

To his relief the key to the magazine was where he had left it along with the tinderbox. He unlocked the door, slipped through it, climbed onto the ready rack to reach the lantern in its gimbals then took it out into the passage and closed the door carefully so that a spark from the tinderbox would not touch off any loose grains of powder on the magazine floor.

He brought the tinderbox down from its hiding-place, and, squatting on the deck, considered the risk he was taking in striking a flint in the darkness of the ship. It was not so much the danger of explosion that worried him, but that any light might attract attention. His father's cabin was at the top of the companionway, and beside it was that of Mr Beatty and his wife. They might be sleepless, or one of them might leave the cabin to answer nature's call. The officer of the watch might move through the depths of the hull on his rounds and come to investigate any unusual illumination.

Yet Tom knew with absolute certainty that Caroline would have neither the courage nor the knowledge of the layout of the hull to find her way down to the magazine in complete darkness. At least he must give her that much encouragement.

He crouched over the tinderbox, shielding it with his body, and struck the steel to the flint. There was a blinding eruption of blue sparks and the tinder caught. His heart was beating fast as he lifted the mesh screen of the lantern, lit the wick and cupped it with his hands until it caught fairly. Then he lowered the screen, which dimmed the flame but protected it from setting off any loose grains of powder. He tucked away both key and tinderbox in their hiding-place, then carried the lantern back into the magazine and replaced it in its gimbals.

He retreated from the magazine and drew the door to behind him, adjusting the gap so that only the merest glimmer of light showed through, not enough to attract undue attention but sufficient to tempt a timid girl to try the ladder of the companionway.

Then he crouched beside the door, ready to close it at the first indication of any trouble and blot out the light. He could not hear the ship's bell down here so close to the bilges, so he lost count of time.

'She's not coming,' he told himself, after what seemed to him the passage of several hours. He half rose, but still he could not bring himself to leave. 'Just a little longer,' he decided, and settled back against the timber bulkhead. He must have dozed, for the first warning he had of her arrival was the perfume of her body, that kitten smell of a young girl, and then he heard the slither of her bare feet on the deck, very close at hand.

He sprang up, and she screamed in terror as he rose out of the darkness at her feet. He seized her desperately. 'It's me! It's me!' he whispered. 'Don't be afraid.'

She clung to him with surprising strength. 'You frightened me.' She was shaking wildly, so he held her to his chest and stroked her hair. She had let it down. It was thick and springing under his hands, reaching halfway down her back.

'It's all right. You're safe. I'm here to look after you.' In the dim light he saw that she wore a nightdress of pale cotton. It was fastened at her throat with a ribbon, and reached down to her ankles.

'I should never have come,' she whispered, her face pressed to his chest.

'Yes. Oh, yes!' he told her. 'I've waited so long. I wanted you to come so so much.' He was amazed at how small she was, and how warm her body was against his. He hugged her tighter. 'It's all right, Caroline. We're safe here.'

He ran his hands down her back. The cotton was sheer and flimsy and she wore no other garment under it. He could feel every swell and hollow of her body.

'What if my father—' Her voice was breathless and broken with fear.

'No, no.' He stopped her. 'Come with me.' He drew her swiftly into the magazine and pushed the door shut behind them. 'No one can ever find us here.'

He hugged her close and kissed the top of her head. Her hair smelt faintly aromatic. Her shaking eased, and she lifted her face and looked up at him. Her eyes were huge and luminous in the dim light of the screened lantern. 'Don't be rough with me,' she begged. 'Don't hurt me.'

The very idea appalled him. 'Oh, my darling. I could

never do that.' He found that the words of reassurance came naturally and convincingly to his lips. 'I love you – I have loved you since the first moment I laid eyes on your beautiful face.' He did not yet realize that he had the gift of eloquence that sets great lovers apart, nor did he know how well it would serve him over the years ahead. 'I loved you even when you treated me so coldly.' Her waist was so slim that he could almost encircle it with his hands. He pulled her harder against himself and her belly felt hot against his.

'I never wanted to be unkind to you,' she told him piteously, 'I wanted to be with you, but I couldn't help myself.'

'You don't have to explain,' he said, 'I know,' and he kissed her face, rained kisses on her forehead and her eyes, until at last he found her mouth. At first her lips were firmly closed to him, then slowly they opened like the fleshy petals of some exotic flower, all hot and moist and filled with a nectar that made his senses swim. He wanted to have all of it, to suck out her essence through her mouth. 'We are safe here,' he reassured her. 'No one ever comes down here.' He kept whispering reassurances, to distract her as he moved her towards the racks of silk powder bags.

'You are so lovely.' He eased her backwards. 'I have thought about you every waking moment.' She relaxed, and let herself fall backwards onto the mattress of silk and gunpowder.

Her head was thrown back, and he kissed her throat. At the same time he gently loosed the ribbon that held the top of her nightdress. His instinct warned him to proceed so slowly that she could pretend that it was not happening.

He whispered to her, 'Your hair is like silk and it smells of roses.' But his fingers were quick and light.

One of her breasts popped out of the top of her

nightgown, whereupon her whole body stiffened and she gasped, 'We mustn't do this. You must stop. Please.'

Her breast was very white, and much bigger than he had expected. He made no move to touch it, although it sagged softly against his cheek. He held her tightly and murmured assurances and flattery until slowly the tension left her body, and one of her hands groped up to the back of his head. She took a handful of his pigtail, and her grip tightened on it until his eyes watered, but he did not mind the pain.

Almost as though she was unaware of what she was doing she used the handful of his hair to direct him. The warm soft breast pressed against his face so that, for a moment, he could not breathe. Then he opened his mouth and sucked in the nipple. It was rubbery and firm in his mouth. Mary had liked him to do this – 'feeding the baby', she had called it.

Caroline made a soft humming sound in the back of her throat, and began to rock him softly as though he were an infant. Her eyes were closed and a small half-smile curved her lips as he sucked upon her rhythmically.

'Touch me,' she murmured, so faintly that he did not understand what she had said. 'Touch me,' she repeated. 'Touch me like you did before.' Her gown had rucked up almost to the top of her thighs and now she moved her knees apart. He reached down, and she sighed. 'Yes, like that.'

She began to thrust with her hips as though she was posting on a trotting pony. It did not take more than a few minutes before her back arched and he felt every muscle in her small body tense.

It's like drawing a longbow, Tom thought, when the nocked arrow is ready to loose.

Suddenly she shuddered and gave a cry that startled him, then fell back and went limp in his arms like a dead woman. He was alarmed. He looked into her face and saw

127

that it was flushed, her eyes were closed and dewy droplets of sweat sparkled on her upper lip.

She opened her eyes and stared at him blankly. Then, suddenly, she drew back and struck him a ringing open-handed blow across the cheek. 'I hate you!' she whispered fiercely. 'You should never have made me come here. You should never have touched me like that. It's all your fault,' and she burst into tears.

He recoiled in astonishment, but before he could recover she had leaped to her feet. With a rustle of cloth and small bare feet on the wooden deck she pushed open the magazine door and fled down the passageway.

It was some time before Tom had recovered sufficiently from the shock to stir himself. Still bemused, he doused the lantern then locked the magazine door behind him carefully. He would have to find an opportunity to return the key to his father's desk, but there was no urgency for that. So far there had been no indication that its absence from the drawer had been discovered. Yet it was too dangerous to keep it on his person, so he returned it to the hiding-place above the lintel.

When he crept past the door of Caroline's cabin, he found he was trembling with indignation and anger. He felt an almost irresistible urge to drag her from her bunk and vent his feelings upon her. He managed to contain himself, and to make his way back to his pallet on the gundeck.

Guy was waiting for him, a silent shadow crouching beside the gun-carriage.

'Where have you been?' he demanded, in a whisper.

'Nowhere.' Tom was taken by surprise, and the fatuous reply was out before he could stop it. 'I was in the head.'

'You've been gone since seven bells in the first watch, almost two hours,' Guy told him grimly. 'You must have filled the bucket. It's a wonder there's anything left of you.'

'I went on deck,' Tom started defensively, then broke

off. 'Anyway, I don't have to tell you. You're not my keeper.' He threw himself on the pallet, curled into a ball and pulled the blanket over his head.

Stupid little vixen, he thought bitterly. I wouldn't give a fig if she fell overboard and was eaten by the sharks.

The *Seraph* bored on into the south-west, never shortening sail during the starry nights. At noon each day Tom was on the quarterdeck with the other officers, using his own backstaff, a gift from his father, to observe the noon passage, and to calculate the ship's latitude. His father and Ned Tyler made simultaneous sunshots, then compared their results. On one unforgettable noonday Tom finished the complex calculation, and looked up from his slate. 'Well, sir?' his father asked, with an indulgent smile.

'Twenty-two degrees sixteen minutes thirty-eight seconds south latitude,' Tom answered uncertainly. 'By my reckoning, we should be only a few leagues north of the Tropic of Capricorn.'

Hal frowned dramatically and looked across at Ned. 'A gross error there, Mr Mate?'

'Indeed, Captain. He's out by at least ten seconds.'

'I make it fifteen seconds of error.' Hal's expression softened. 'No need to take the cat to him?'

'Not this time.' Ned gave one of his rare grins. The difference between the three calculations amounted to no more than a few nautical miles of the ocean's vastness. No man alive could have said which of the three was correct.

'Well done, lad.' Hal ruffled his hair. 'We might make a seaman of you yet.' The glow of pleasure those words gave Tom lasted him the rest of that day.

As they crossed the Tropic of Capricorn, the weather changed abruptly. They had entered the wet quadrant of the southern Atlantic, and the sky ahead was filled from horizon to heavens with dark, brooding thunderclouds, their immense heads flattened into the shape of the anvils of Vulcan, the blacksmith of the gods. Lightning rippled and glowed in their dark bellies. Thunderclaps beat down like the strokes of the god's hammer.

Hal passed the order to shorten sail, and made a signal to the *Yeoman* astern of them: 'Keep station on me.'

The sun went down behind the stormclouds, and stained them with its blood, then the rain fell upon the two ships in torrents. Solid sheets of water hammered the wooden decks so hard that the din drowned the men's voices and blotted out their vision. They could see nothing through the roaring curtains of water from one rail to the other. The scuppers could not clear the water from the main deck fast enough, and the helmsman stood knee-deep. The crew cavorted in this world of sweet water, holding up their faces with mouths wide open, drinking it down until their bellies bulged, stripping off their clothing and washing the salt from their bodies, laughing and splashing each other.

Hal made no effort to restrain them. The salt had galled all their bodies, in some cases forming suppurating sea-boils in the armpits and crotch. It was a relief to wash the corrosive crystals from their skins. Instead he ordered the empty water-casks filled. The men scooped up bucketfuls of the sweet, pure water and by nightfall every cask aboard was brimming.

The rain never let up all that night or the next day, and on the third day, when the sun rose over the watery wilderness of creamy whitecaps and towering cloud ranges, the *Yeoman* was nowhere in sight. Hal ordered both Tom and Dorian to the masthead, for their young eyes had already proved themselves the sharpest on the ship. Though they stayed aloft most of that day, they could make out no flash of the *Yeoman*'s canvas on the disturbed horizon.

'We won't see her again afore we drop anchor off Good Hope,' Ned Tyler opined, and secretly Hal agreed with him. There was only the remotest possibility that the two ships would find each other again in this endless expanse of wind-whipped ocean. It did not worry Hal unduly: he had planned with Anderson for just such an eventuality. Their prearranged rendezvous was in Table Bay, and from now onwards each ship would have to make its passage independently of the other.

On the fifty-second day out of Plymouth Hal ordered the *Seraph* put about on the starboard tack. By his calculation they were less than a thousand miles off the coast of South America. With the backstaff and the navigational tables he could confidently place the ship's longitude to within twenty miles. However, the determination of longitude was not an exact science but more an arcane ritual, based on a study of each day's pegs on the traverse board and a series of guesses and extrapolations of the ship's distance and course made good.

Hal knew full well that he could be several hundreds of miles adrift in his dead reckoning. To make a landfall on Good Hope, he would now have to ride the trade winds down until he struck thirty-two degrees of south latitude, then hold due east until he raised the distinctive table land that marked the tip of the African continent. This would be the slowest, most wearying leg of the voyage: with the wind almost in his face he would have to tack every few hours.

To avoid missing the Cape to the south, and running through into the Indian Ocean beyond, he must lay his course to strike the savage African shore some leagues to the north of Good Hope. There was always the danger of making that landfall in the black of night or in the dense

131

fog that so often shrouded the southern Cape – many great ships had found a watery graveyard on this treacherous shore. With this threat on his mind, Hal was thankful that, when the time came, he would have Tom's and Dorian's sharp young eyes at the masthead.

Thinking of his two sons, Hal was pleased with the progress they were making with their Arabic. Guy had dropped out of these lessons on the grounds that there was precious little Arabic spoken in Bombay, but each after-noon Tom and Dorian huddled for an hour with Alf Wilson on the forecastle and chattered away in the language like parakeets. When Hal tested them he found they could hold their own in a conversation with him. Their growing fluency in the language would stand them in good stead on the Fever Coast. It was a good strategy to speak your enemy's language, Hal thought.

Apart from the *Yeoman* they had not seen another ship since they had left Ushant, but this ocean was not an empty wasteland: there were strange and wonderful sights to intrigue and delight Tom and Dorian as they squatted shoulder to shoulder in the crow's nest high above the deck.

One day out of the great wilderness of water there came an albatross. Circling the ship on wide pinions, dipping and rising on currents of air, gliding and planing, sometimes so close to the crests of the waves that it seemed to become part of the spume, it kept station with the ship for days on end. Neither of the boys had seen a bird of that size before. At times it sailed close to where they crouched in their barrel-shaped perch, seeming to use the updraught from the *Seraph*'s mainsail to hold its position, never flapping its wings, only gently fingering the air with the black feathers at the tips. Dorian particularly delighted in the creature whose wingspan was three or four times that of his arms.

'Mollymawk!' He called it by the sailors' pet-name,

meaning 'Stupid Gull', for its trusting, confiding nature when it settled to earth. Dorian had begged scraps of food from the ship's cook and tossed them to the circling bird. Very soon the albatross had learned to trust and accept him, came winging to his whistle and cry. It sailed beside him almost close enough to touch, hanging almost motionless in the air, daintily snapping up the morsels he threw to it.

On the third day, while Tom hung on to his belt to prevent him falling, Dorian reached out as far as he could with a piece of fat salt pork in his hand. Mollymawk regarded him with a wise, ancient eye, banked in on his spreading pinions and took the offering from him with a delicate pinch of his formidable curved beak, which could easily have lopped off one of the boy's fingers.

Dorian whistled and clapped his hands in triumph while all three of the Beatty girls, who had been following his courtship of the bird from the deck below, shrieked with delight. When he came down at the end of the watch, Caroline kissed him in front of the officers of the deck and the on-duty watch.

'Girls are so soft!' Dorian told Tom, when they were alone on the gundeck, and gave a realistic imitation of puking.

Over the next few days Mollymawk grew tamer and more confiding towards Dorian. 'Do you think he loves me, Tom? I shall want to keep him for ever as my pet.' But on the eighth morning when they climbed to the masthead the bird had disappeared. Though Dorian whistled for him all that day, he was gone, and at sunset the child wept bitterly.

'What a baby you are,' Tom said, and hugged him until he stopped snuffling.

On the morning after Mollymawk disappeared, Tom took his usual seat on the bench against the bulkhead in Master Walsh's cabin. When the three girls arrived, late as usual, for the day's lessons, he resisted the temptation to look in Caroline's direction. He was still simmering with indignation at the way she had treated him. Sarah Beatty, who still hero-worshipped him, and was for ever plying him with small gifts, had today made him a paper rose as a bookmark, which she presented to him in front of everyone else in the cabin. Tom flushed with humiliation as he mumbled a churlish thanks, while behind Sarah's back Dorian held an imaginary baby in his arms and rocked it. Tom kicked his shin and reached for his books and slate, which he kept in the locker under the bench.

When he glanced at the slate, he saw that someone had rubbed out the algebra equation with which he had been struggling the previous day. He was about to accuse Dorian of the crime when he realized that the culprit had replaced his convoluted chalk scribbling with a simple line in a flowery script: 'Tonight at the same time.'

Tom stared at it. The handwriting was unmistakable. Dorian and the younger girls still had a childlike uneven scrawl, and Guy's hand was stolid and lacking in any art. Although he still hated Caroline to the depths of his soul, he would have recognized her handwriting anywhere and at any time. Suddenly he became aware that Guy was craning across, trying to read the slate over his shoulder. Tom tilted it to hide it from him and with one thumb smeared the chalk letters until they were indecipherable.

He could not stop himself glancing across to where Caroline sat. She seemed oblivious as always to his presence, absorbed in the book of poetry that Master Walsh had lent her, but she must have sensed his eyes on her because the one ear that Tom could see peeping out from under her bonnet in a tangle of curls slowly turned a deeper shade of pink. It was such a striking phenomenon that Tom forgot he hated her and stared at it in fascination.

'Thomas, have you completed the problem I set for you yesterday?'

Walsh roused him and he started guiltily. 'Yes, I mean no – I mean almost.'

For the rest of that day Tom was in a stew of emotion. At one minute he determined to scorn the tryst she had proposed and laugh in her face the next morning. He even uttered the scornful laugh aloud, and every person in the cabin stopped what he or she was doing and looked up at him expectantly.

'Is there some gem of wit or erudition that you wish to share with us, Thomas?' Walsh asked sarcastically.

'No, sir. I was just thinking.'

'Ah, I thought I heard the wheels rumbling. But let us not interrupt such a rare occurrence. Please continue, sir.'

All that day his feelings for Caroline oscillated from adoration to angry loathing. Later, when he sat high in the crow's nest, he noticed nothing except that the waters seemed as violet blue as her eyes. Dorian had to point out to him the pale feather on the horizon where a whale spouted, and even then he viewed it without interest.

When he stood beside his father and made the noonday sight through the aperture of his backstaff, he remembered the feel of a soft white bosom pressed to his face, and his thoughts drifted away.

When his father took the navigation slate from his hands and read his working, he turned to Ned Tyler. 'Congratulations, Mr Tyler. During the night you must have sailed us back into the northern hemisphere. Send a good man to the masthead. We should be making a landfall on the east coast of America at any minute now.'

Tom had no appetite for his dinner and gave his cut of salt beef to Dorian, whose appetite was legendary and who accepted it with alacrity then wolfed it down before Tom could change his mind. Then, when the gundeck lanterns were trimmed down for the night, Tom lay unsleeping in his corner behind the gun carriage and went over his preparations again and again in his mind.

The magazine key and tinderbox were still where he had left them in their niche above the door. He had been waiting for an opportunity to return the key to his father's desk, but none had presented itself. Now he was deeply grateful for that. He had decided by now that he loved Caroline beyond anything in the world and that he would not hesitate to lay down his life for her.

At seven bells in the first watch he crept from his pallet, and paused to see if anyone had seen him rise. His two brothers were smaller dark shapes beyond Aboli's bulk, stretched out on the deck in the dim light of the shuttered battle lanterns. Stepping over the huddled, snoring bodies of the rest of the crew he made his way unchallenged to the companionway.

Once again the lamp was burning in his father's cabin and Tom wondered what always kept him awake until after midnight. He moved softly past and could not prevent himself from stopping again beside the girls' cabin. He thought he heard soft breathing beyond the bulkhead and, once, the sound of one of the younger girls talking in her sleep, a few gabbled words. He passed on and took the key from its hiding-place, and went into the magazine to fetch out the lantern, light it and replace it in its gimbals.

By this time he was so overwrought that he jumped at every strange noise in the running ship, the scuffle of a rat in the bilges or the rattle and knock of a loose piece of rope or rigging. He crouched beside the magazine door and watched the foot of the ladder. This time he did not doze so he saw her bare white feet the moment they came hesitantly into view. He whistled softly to reassure her.

She stooped and looked at him. Then she came down the last few steps of the ladder with a rush. He ran to meet her, and she came into his arms and clung to him. 'I wanted to say how sorry I was that I struck you,' she whispered. 'I have hated myself for that every day since then.'

He could not trust himself to speak, and when he remained silent she lifted her face to him. It was merely a pale luminescence in the poor light but he stooped to kiss her, searching for her mouth. She moved towards him at the same moment and his first kiss was on her eyebrow, the next on the tip of her nose and then their mouths came together.

She was the first to pull back, 'Not here,' she whispered. 'Somebody may come.'

She followed him willingly as he took her hand and drew her through the door into the magazine. Without hesitation she went directly to the rack of powder bags, and drew him down beside her. Her mouth was open to his next kiss, and he felt the tip of her tongue fluttering on his lips, like a moth at the candle-flame. He sucked it in.

Still mouth to mouth she tugged at the drawstring that closed the top of his shirt and when she had it loose she thrust one small cool hand down into the opening and caressed his chest.

'You are hairy.' She sounded surprised. 'I want to see.' She lifted the front of his shirt. 'Silky. It feels so soft.' She pressed her face to his chest. Her breath was warm and tickling. It excited him in a way he had not known before. A sense of urgency came over him, as though she might be whisked away from him at any moment. He tried to loosen the ribbon that closed her nightdress but his fingers were clumsy and unskilled.

'Here.' She pushed away his hands. 'Let me do that.' He was vaguely aware that she was behaving differently from their last meeting here in the magazine: she was assertive and sure of herself. She was acting more like Mary or one of the other girls he had been with at High Weald. All at once he was convinced that his intuition had been

137

accurate. She had done this before, she knew as much as he, or perhaps more, and the knowledge goaded him on. There was no longer cause for him to hold himself back.

She knelt up, lifted the nightgown over her head in one movement and dropped it to the deck. She was mother naked now, but all he saw were her breasts, big, round and white, seeming to glow like two great pearls, hanging above him in the gloom. He reached for them, filling both his hands with their soft abundance.

'Not so hard. Don't be so rough,' she warned him. For a while she let him do what he wanted and then she whispered, 'Touch me! Touch me there, like before.'

He did as she asked, and she closed her eyes and lay quietly. Gently he moved over her, careful not to alarm her. He eased his breeches down to his knees.

Suddenly she tried to sit up, 'Why did you stop?' She looked down. 'What are you doing? No, stop that!' She tried to wriggle out from under him but he was much heavier and stronger than she was, and she could not move him.

'I won't hurt you,' he promised. She pushed ineffectually at his shoulders, but slowly she gave up. She stopped struggling and relaxed under the insistence of his touch. The rigidity went out of her body. She closed her eyes and started to make that soft humming sound in the back of her throat.

Suddenly her whole body convulsed and she gave a soft cry. 'What are you doing? Please, no! Oh, Tom, what are you doing?' She struggled again, but he held her very tightly, and after a while she lay quietly in his arms. Then both of them started to move in unison, in the natural rhythm as old as man himself.

Long afterwards they lay together with the sweat cooling on their bodies, their breathing steadying until they could speak again.

'It's late. Agnes and Sarah will be awake soon. I must go,' Caroline whispered, and reached for her nightgown.

'Will you come again?' he asked her.

'Perhaps.' She drew the gown over her head, and tied the ribbon at her throat.

'Tomorrow night?' he insisted.

'Perhaps,' she repeated, slipped off the rack and went to the magazine door. She listened there, then peeped through the crack. She pushed open the door just wide enough to slip through and was gone.

Gradually the *Seraph* sailed out of the tropical latitudes and on into the south. The days cooled and, after the stifling heat they had endured, the wind came sweet and fresh out of the south-east. This temperate ocean swarmed with life, clouded green with krill and plankton. From the masthead they could make out shadowy shoals of tuna, endless streams of huge fish effortlessly overtaking the ship, on their mysterious perambulations through the green ocean.

At last the noonday sun-shot proved that the ship had made her southing, and at thirty-two degrees south latitude Hal brought the bows around for the final run down to Good Hope.

It was a relief to him that the end of this leg of the voyage was approaching, and that they must soon be making their landfall. Only the previous day Dr Reynolds had reported to him the first cases of scurvy among the crew. This mysterious affliction was the curse of every captain undertaking a long passage. Once a ship had been at sea for six weeks, the foul miasma that bred the disease might overtake the crew and strike them down without reason or warning.

The two sick men were merely the first of many, Hal knew. They had shown the surgeon their swollen, bleeding gums and the first dark bruises on their bellies, where blood was weeping under the skin. No man could account for this pestilence, or for the miraculous manner in which it vanished, and its victims were cured, once the ship reached port.

'Let it be soon, Lord!' Hal prayed, and looked to the empty eastern horizon.

Now, as they approached the land, pods of dolphin joined them, riding the bow-wave, dodging back and forth under the hull, rising again on the far side and curving their glistening black backs through the surface, finning high with their flat tails beating, eyeing the men in the rigging with a bright eye and fixed grin.

This was the ocean of the great whales. On some days they saw their spouts blowing white on the wind wherever they looked from the masthead. The mountainous creatures wallowed and cavorted on the surface. Some were longer than the *Seraph*'s hull, and they passed so close that the boys could see the barnacles and growths of sea life that encrusted their bodies as though they were reefs of rock, not living creatures.

'There is twenty tons of oil in each fish,' Big Daniel remarked to Tom, as they leaned together on the bowsprit, and watched a leviathan rise from the depths, a cable's length ahead, and lift its massive bifurcated tail to the skies.

'That tail is as wide across as our mizen yard,' Tom marvelled.

'They do say they're the biggest creatures in creation.' Daniel nodded. 'At ten pounds the ton of his oil, we might do better at chasing whales than pirates.'

'How could you ever kill a thing that big?' Tom wondered. 'It would be like trying to kill a mountain.'

140

'Dangerous work, it is, but there's them that do it. The Dutch are great whale-hunters.'

'I should like to try,' said Tom. 'I should like to be a great hunter.'

Big Daniel pointed down the bowsprit as it rose and fell across the horizon. 'There's much to hunt where we are going, lad. It's a land swarming with wild creatures. There are elephants with ivory tusks longer than you are. You may get your wish.'

Tom's excitement was heightened with each day's run. After they had made the sun-shot, he went to the stern cabin with his father to watch him mark the ship's position: the line on the chart crept ever closer to the great landmass, shaped like the head of a horse.

His days were so filled with excitement and frantic activity that he should have been exhausted by nightfall. Most evenings he managed a few hours' sleep before midnight, but then he woke eagerly at the end of the first watch, and crept from his pallet.

He no longer had to beg and cajole: Caroline came to the magazine every night of her own accord. Tom found that he had aroused a wildcat. She was no longer hesitant or modest, but matched him in the urgency of her passion, giving vent to her emotions with voice and savage excess. Tom often carried away with him the evidence of their meetings: his back scratched by her long fingernails, his lips bitten and bruised.

However, he had become careless in his haste to keep their assignation each night and had a number of close calls. Once, when he was passing Mr Beatty's cabin, the door opened suddenly and Mrs Beatty stepped out. Tom just had time to pull his cap over his eyes as he slouched past, and disguised his voice. 'Seven bells in the first watch, and all's well,' he croaked hoarsely. He was tall as any man aboard now, and the passageway was dimly lit.

141

'Thank you, my good man.' Mrs Beatty was so flustered at being caught in her nightclothes that she ducked back into the cabin as if she were the guilty one.

On more than one night he felt he was being followed as he crept down from the gundeck. Once he was certain he had heard footsteps coming down the companionway behind him, but when he doubled back nobody was there. On another occasion he was leaving the lower deck in the small hours, at the end of the middle watch, when there came the clump of sea boots down the ladder from the quarterdeck. He only just had time to duck back when Ned Tyler came down the passage towards his father's cabin. From the shadows he watched him knock at the door, and heard his father's voice from within.

'What is it?'

'Ned Tyler, Captain. Wind's freshening. She could carry away a spar if we drive her on. Permission to take in the staysails and reef the main course.'

'I'll be on deck right away, Ned,' Tom's father replied. A minute later he burst out of his cabin shrugging on his pea-jacket, and passed a few feet from where Tom lay as he ran up the companionway to the deck.

Tom reached his pallet on the gundeck just as the boatswain's whistle shrilled and Big Daniel's voice boomed out in the darkness, 'All hands to shorten sail.' Tom had to pretend to rub the sleep out of his eyes and join the rush of men up into the blustery night.

It was in his nature not to be alarmed or cowed by these narrow escapes, and perversely he became emboldened by them. Nowadays there was a strut to his stride like that of a young rooster, which made Aboli grin and shake his head. 'This is the son of the man!'

One morning when the ship had been put about on the port tack, and her motion had eased to a long rise and thrust through the green Atlantic rollers, Tom was among the topmastmen coming down from working the canvas. Suddenly, for no reason other than high spirits and cockiness he stood up to his full height on the yard and danced a High Hornpipe.

Every person on deck froze with horror as they watched Tom's suicidal antics. Forty feet above the deck, Tom performed two full passes, three to the measure, on bare tiptoe, one hand on his hip and the other over his head, then he jumped on the shrouds and slid down to the deck below. He had had enough sense to make certain that his father was in his cabin at the time but before the day was out Hal had heard about the escapade and sent for Tom. 'Why did you do such a stupid, irresponsible thing?' he demanded.

'Because John Tudwell told me I wouldn't dare,' Tom explained, as though this was the best reason in the world.

Which perhaps it was, Hal thought, as he studied his son's face. To his astonishment, he realized that he was looking at a man, not a boy. In the few short months of the voyage Tom had toughened and matured beyond all recognition. His body was work-hardened, his shoulders had filled out from the constant exertion of climbing in the rigging and handling canvas and sheets in a heavy blow, his arms were muscled from the hours of sword drill with Aboli each day, and he balanced like a cat to the ship's pitch in the southern rollers.

But there was something else he could not quite put his finger on. He knew that Tom had always been the precocious one among all his sons, and though he had tried to control his wilder extravagances he had never wanted to fetter this bold, adventurous spirit. Secretly, Hal had admired the boy's courage and was proud of his headstrong ways. But now he was aware that something had happened that he had missed. This was a man, full-grown, who faced him with level gaze.

'Well!' Hal said at last. 'You've shown John Tudwell he was wrong, haven't you? So there's no need to do the High Hornpipe again.'

'No, Father,' Tom agreed readily. 'That is, not until somebody else tells me I lack the guts for it.' His grin was so infectious that Hal felt his own mouth pulled out of shape.

'Get away with you!' He gave Tom a shove towards the cabin door. 'There's no reasoning with a barbarian.'

Guy sat at his accustomed place on the bench beside Caroline in Master Walsh's cabin. His face was pale and he spoke little during the course of the morning, answering any question from the schoolmaster in a terse monosyllable. He kept his eyes on his book, not looking at either Tom or Caroline, even when they were reciting the texts that Walsh had asked for.

At last Caroline became aware of his strange behaviour. 'Are you out of sorts, Guy? Are you feeling seasick again?' she whispered.

Guy could not bring himself to look into her face. 'I am perfectly well,' he told her. 'You need not worry about me,' and added silently, Ever again!

Guy had conjured up a fantasy world over the past weeks since he had signed his indenture papers and his employment in the Company factory at Bombay had been secured. With his family connections, and under the patronage of Mr Beatty, he had foreseen his rapid advancement in the service of the Company. The Beatty family would have become his own, and Caroline would have been there beside him. He imagined sharing her company every day in the tropical paradise of Bombay. They would ride together through palm groves. In the evenings there would be music recitals, Guy playing and Caroline singing, and poetry readings, picnics with the family. He would walk hand in hand with her along white beaches, exchange with her pure, chaste kisses. In a few short years he would be twenty years old, high in the Company service and well able to afford to marry. Now all these dreams were shattered.

When he tried to think of the vile things he had uncovered, his mind shied away from them like a skittish horse. His hands shook and he felt the blood fuming in his brain. He could not bear another minute in the confines of the tiny cabin, with the two people he hated more than he had ever believed himself capable. He stood up abruptly. 'Master Walsh, please excuse me. I am feeling faint. I need to take a turn on deck. The fresh air—' Without waiting for permission, he stumbled to the door and fled up the ladder. He hurried to the bows and clung to a halyard, letting the wind blow in his face. His misery was bottomless and the rest of his life stretched ahead like an endless desert plain.

'I want to die!' he said aloud, and peered over the ship's side. The water was green and beautiful. It would be so peaceful down there. He stepped down onto the chains and balanced there, hanging on with one hand on the shrouds. 'It will be so easy,' he told himself. 'So quick and easy.' He began to lean outwards over the rushing, curling bow-wave.

A powerful grip closed on his free wrist, and he almost lost his balance. 'There is nothing that you have lost down there, Mbili,' Aboli's voice rumbled. 'You never were a swimmer.'

'Leave me!' Guy said bitterly. 'Why do you always interfere, Aboli? I just want to die.'

'You will have your wish, that is the only thing certain in this life,' Aboli assured him. 'But not today, Mbili.' The name he had called Guy from the day of his birth meant Number Two in the language of the forests. Gently he exerted pressure on his arm.

Guy tried vainly to resist that great strength. 'Leave me, Aboli. Please.'

'The men are looking at you,' Aboli told him softly. Guy looked round and saw that some of the watch on deck had stopped their talk and were watching this little panto-mime curiously. 'Do not shame your father and me with this stupidity.'

Guy capitulated, and hopped down clumsily onto the deck. Aboli released his wrist. 'Let us talk,' he suggested.

'I do not want to talk, to you or to anybody.'

'Then we will be silent together,' Aboli agreed, and led him to the lee rail. They squatted together there, shielded from the wind and from the eyes of the watch. Aboli was calm and silent, like a mountain, a reassuring presence. He did not look at Guy or touch him, but he was there. The long minutes drew out, then Guy blurted out wildly, 'I love her so, Aboli. It's like fangs gnawing at my belly.'

So! Aboli thought sadly. He has found out the truth. Klebe is not one to hide his tracks. He is after this filly like a young stallion that has kicked down the fence. It is a wonder that Mbili took so long to discover it. 'Yes, I know, Mbili,' he said. 'I have also loved.'

'What am I to do?' Guy demanded miserably.

'No matter how much it hurts, it will never kill you, and one day, sooner than you will believe possible, you will have forgotten the pain.'

'I will never forget it,' said Guy, with deep conviction. 'And I will never forget my love for her.'

146

Hal Courtney heard the ship's bell sound the beginning of the middle watch.

'Midnight,' he murmured. He pressed both fists into the small of his back. He had sat at his desk for many hours, he felt stiff and his eyes smarted. He stood up and trimmed the wick of the lamp, adjusting it to light the documents on his desktop, then seated himself again in the heavy oak chair and applied himself once more to his work.

The builders' drawings of *Seraph* were spread before him. He studied the plan of her gundecks for a while, then set it on one side, pulled towards him the drawing of the side elevation, and compared the two. 'We have to conceal the guns, and give her the look of an unarmed trader,' he murmured. 'It will mean stripping the lids off the gunports of the lower deck—' He broke off and frowned as he heard a soft scratching at the door of his cabin.

'Who is it?' he demanded. The weather was fair and the wind light and steady. He had not expected to be interrupted. There was no answer to his challenge, and after a moment he grunted. It must have been a rat or his imagination. He turned his attention back to the drawings.

The scratching at the door came again. This time he pushed back his chair irritably and stood up. Stooping under the beams he strode to the door and pulled it open. A slight figure stood diffidently before him. It took Hal a moment to recognize his own son. 'Guy?' He peered closely at him. 'What are you doing at this time of night? Come in, boy.' Guy stepped into the cabin, and pulled the door to behind him. He plucked his cap from his head. His face was pale and his expression nervous.

'Father, I had to tell you—' he stammered, twisting the cap in his hands.

'What is it, lad? Speak up,' Hal encouraged him.

'There is somebody in the powder magazine in the hold,' Guy blurted out. 'The door is open and there is a light.'

'What?' Hal's voice was sharp with alarm. 'In the magazine? A light?' A host of dire misgivings crowded his mind.

'Yes, sir.'

Hal whirled and crossed to his desk. He jerked open the top drawer and lifted out the wooden case of pistols. He opened it and took out one of the double-barrelled weapons, swiftly checked the flint and the priming, then thrust it into his belt. Then he checked the second of the pair and hefted it in his right hand.

'We'll see about this,' he muttered grimly, and lifted the lamp out of its gimbals. 'Come with me, Guy, but softly. We don't want to warn the rascals, whoever they are.'

He eased open the cabin door and Guy followed him out into the passageway. 'Close it quietly,' Hal warned and went to the head of the companionway. He peered down into the lower deck but saw no glimmer of light. He turned his head to Guy. 'Are you sure?'

'Yes, Father.'

Stepping lightly Hal started down the ladder, stopping on each tread to listen and look. He reached the bottom and paused again. Only then did he see the faint nimbus of light around the edges of the magazine door.

'Yes!' he whispered, and cocked both hammers of the pistol in his hand. 'Now we'll see what they're up to.' He started towards the magazine, carrying the lamp behind his back to shield the flame. Guy was close behind him.

Hal reached the door and placed his ear to the thick oak panel. Faintly, above the other noises of the ship, he heard sounds that puzzled him, soft cries and moans, a rustling and thudding he could not place.

148

He tried the lock and the handle turned readily enough in his hand. He put his shoulder against the door and gradually applied his weight. The jamb scraped softly and then the door swung open. He stood in the entrance and lifted his lantern high above his head. For a while he was deprived of the power of further movement. The scene before him was so far from his expectations that he could not make sense of what he was seeing.

The screened lamp in its gimbals on the bulkhead above the ready racks added its light to the rays of his own lantern. Clothing was jumbled on the deck at Hal's feet, and human bodies sprawled over the silk powder bags before him. It took a moment for him to realize they were naked. Pale skin gleamed bright in the lamplight, and he stared in disbelief. A woman's curls, tangled limbs, red mouth open wide, small feet that kicked spasmodically towards the deck beams above, slim hands that clutched and twisted in a man's hair, the man's head buried between her pearly thighs, her back and buttocks thumping against the mattress of powder bags as she writhed in transport.

The pair seemed oblivious to anything but each other. Even the lantern turned full upon them had not alarmed them for the girl's eyes were tightly closed and her features so contorted with passion that she seemed a stranger to Hal.

He stood there transfixed and only roused himself when Guy tried to push his way into the magazine. He moved to block his entrance and screen the scene from him.

'Get back, Guy,' he said, and his voice penetrated the curtains of passion that shrouded the pair on the rack. The woman's eyes flew open, then slowly expanded like the petals of a violet bloom as she stared at Hal in horror and disbelief. Her mouth twisted into a silent scream of despair, and she struggled up on one elbow, her breasts swinging round and white in the lamplight. With both hands she tore at the dark hair of the head lodged between her thighs, but could not budge it.

'Tom!' Hal found his voice at last. He saw the muscles in the boy's broad white back convulse with shock, as though a dagger had been plunged into them. Then Tom lifted his face and stared at his father. It seemed an eternity that all three were frozen like that.

Tom's face was suffused with blood, as though he had run a race, or wrestled a heavy bout. His gaze was as unfocused and vague as that of a drunkard.

'In the name of God, girl, cover yourself!' Hal grated. His own shame flared up as he found it took a huge effort on his part to tear his eyes from her spreadeagled body.

At his words she kicked Tom away with both feet and tumbled from the rack onto the deck. She snatched up her discarded nightdress and held it to her chest with both hands, trying to cover her nudity, crouching there on her knees like a wild animal in a trap. Hal turned his back on her and found Guy pressing close behind him, craning to see what was happening in the magazine. Hal shoved him roughly out into the passageway. 'Get you back to your bed!' he snarled. 'This is not your business.' Guy backed away at the venom in his father's voice. 'Tell no one of what you have seen here tonight, for if you do I will flay the skin from your back.' Guy backed slowly and reluctantly up the ladder, and Hal turned into the magazine.

Caroline had pulled the gown over her head and now it covered her to her ankles. She stood before him, hanging her head. The thick curls and ringlets fell forward and covered her face. She looked like a little girl, young and innocent. Which she has, as the devil is witness, proven she is not, Hal thought grimly, and looked at his son, who was hopping on one leg trying to get his other into his breeches. There was no longer any trace of his usual cockiness or braggadocio. He hauled his breeches up to his waist and buckled his belt, then stood abjectly beside the girl, neither of them able to meet Hal's stern gaze.

'Mistress Caroline,' Hal ordered, 'you will go this very instant to your cabin.'

'Yes, Captain,' she whispered.

'I can only say that I am disgusted by your behaviour. I never expected anything of the like from a lady of your breeding.' He felt vaguely ridiculous as he said it. As though the lower classes are the only ones who should make the beast with two backs, he mocked himself silently, and searched for some pronouncement less fatuous. 'What will your father make of it when I tell him?' he demanded. She looked up at him with real terror dissolving her prettiness.

'You won't tell him!' Suddenly, embarrassingly, she fell at his feet, and hugged his knees. 'Please don't tell him, Captain. I will do anything, only please don't tell him.'

'Get up, girl.' Hal lifted her to her feet, his anger fading. It took an effort to fan the flames. 'Go to your cabin, and stay there until I send for you.'

'You won't tell my father?' she pleaded. Tears were streaming down her face now.

'I make you no promise on that,' he said. 'You richly deserve the horse-whip that I know he will take to you.' He led her out, and pushed her towards her cabin. She fled up the ladder and he heard her door open and close softly.

Hal turned back to Tom and tried to glare at him, but felt the flames of indignation subside. Despite himself he journeyed back over the years, to another boy and girl in a dark ship's cabin in these southern seas. He had been Tom's age, and the Dutch girl five years his senior when she had carried him over the threshold into manhood. She had possessed golden hair and the face of an innocent angel, but the body of a wanton and the nature of a she-devil. He blinked as he brought his mind back from

151

twenty-five years ago, and found Tom still standing contritely before him. 'Miss Beatty is a passenger on this ship, and therefore in my care,' he said. 'You have shamed yourself and me.'

'I am sorry, Father.'

'I don't think you are.' Hal studied his face, and saw him struggling with the truth.

'I mean, I'm sorry I shamed you.' Tom qualified himself. 'But as nobody but us knows of it, then your shame need never be made public, sir.'

Hal had to stop himself gasping at his son's effrontery, but then he followed the quick-witted logic.

'You are a barbarian, sir,' he said gravely, and thought, As I was – as every red-blooded young buck is at your age.

'I shall try to improve myself,' Tom promised.

Hal stared at him. He would never have dared address his own father in that fashion. He had been terrified of his father. This boy was not terrified of him – respected and admired him, perhaps, loved him, certainly, but felt no terror when they stood face to face like this. Have I failed in my duty? Should I have made him fear me? he wondered. No, I am glad of it. I have made him a man.

'Father, I will readily accept whatever punishment you see fit to lay on me. But if you tell Caroline's family of this, you will bring disgrace upon her and ruin her life.' Tom spoke up with barely a tremor in his voice. 'She does not deserve that from us.'

'I agree with you,' Hal admitted reluctantly. 'Do I have your undertaking never to try to be alone with the girl again while she is on this ship?'

'I promise you that.' Tom raised his right hand. 'I swear it to you.'

'Then we shall not speak of it again, and I will say nothing to Mr Beatty.'

'Thank you, sir.'

Hal felt rewarded when he saw the expression in his

son's eyes, then had to cough to clear the constriction in his throat. He cast around swiftly for some way to avoid having to pursue the subject. 'How did you get into the magazine?'

'I borrowed the key from your desk,' Tom answered straight.

'Borrowed?' Hal demanded.

'Yes, sir. I would have returned it when I was finished with it.'

'You have no further need of it now, that I assure you,' Hal told him grimly. Tom went obediently to the doorway, reached up to the niche and brought down the key.

'Lock the door,' Hal ordered, and when Tom had done so, 'Give it to me.' Tom placed it in his hand.

'I think that is more than enough for one night,' Hal said. 'Go to your mattress now.'

'Goodnight, Father, and I truly am sorry that I have caused you distress.'

Hal watched him disappear up the ladder, then grinned ruefully. Perhaps I could have conducted that little skirmish with more aplomb, he thought, but the devil tell me how.

Guy waited expectantly for the uproar that must follow his disclosure of the sinful pair. He expected Caroline to be castigated by her father, perhaps beaten like a scullerymaid caught stealing, reviled by her mother and sisters, become such an outcast that she would have only him to turn to for comfort.

In his imaginings, she came to him and begged his forgiveness for having betrayed the pure, honest love he held for her. She threw herself on his mercy, and promised that if he forgave her she would try for the rest of her life to make amends to him. The thought of it warmed him and made up for the terrible suffering he had endured since the night when he had first followed Tom down to the lower deck and discovered the filth in which he was engaged.

Then he hoped that his father might haul Tom before the ship's company and order him placed on the triangle and publicly flogged, though in his heart he knew that this was too much to hope for. But at least he might force Tom to apologize to Mr and Mrs Beatty and forbid him ever again to speak to Caroline or any other member of the family. Tom would become the ship's pariah. Perhaps his father might have him removed from the *Seraph* when they reached Good Hope, even sent back to England in disgrace to suffer the tyranny of Black Billy at High Weald.

He waited eagerly for some or all of these things to happen. His chagrin deepened as each day passed as though nothing earth-shattering had occurred, as if his emotional turmoil and suffering were of no consequence.

It was true that for several days thereafter Caroline was quiet and withdrawn, starting whenever she heard footsteps outside the cabin where they laboured together over their books, looking terrified when she heard her father's voice booming out from the deck above, never glancing in Tom's direction but keeping her eyes on her books. Guy noticed, with some small satisfaction, that if Tom came on deck when she was there with her mother and sisters, she immediately made some excuse and went down to her own little cabin, staying there alone for hours.

This lasted less than a week, then she rapidly recovered her old poise and appealing manners. The roses bloomed once more in her cheeks, she laughed and joked with Master Walsh, and sang as prettily in the duets with Dorian during the musical recitals. For some time Guy refused to take part in these evenings, pleading ill-health, and he lay miserably on his pallet on the gundeck listening to the faint sounds of music and laughter from the deck below. In the end he allowed Master Walsh to persuade him to return with his cittern, although his expression and mien while he played were heroically tragic.

As for Tom, he showed precious little remorse for his treachery and deceit. True, for a while he made no effort to talk to Caroline or even catch her attention, but this was nothing new. It was one of his perfidious ways. Then, during one of their lessons, Guy intercepted an exchange between the pair.

Caroline dropped her chalk to the deck and before Guy could retrieve it for her she had stooped and groped for it under the table. The ship rolled and the chalk skittered across the deck towards Tom, who scooped it up and, with a mock-gallant bow, handed it to her, at the same time taking the opportunity to peer down her décolletage. Caroline, with dancing eyes, turned so that Master Walsh could not see her face and stuck out her tongue at Tom. It was not a childlike gesture, but suggestive and inviting, fraught with sexual undertones. Tom acknowledged it with a leer and a wink that made Caroline blush prettily, and struck Guy like a blow in the face from a clenched fist.

He brooded on it for the rest on that day, but could think of only one way in which to try to show Caroline how much she had hurt him, how she had destroyed his trust in her and shattered his life. He moved his seat in the classroom. The following day, without permission or explanation, he left the bench beside Caroline and went to the low, uncomfortable stool in the corner furthest from her.

This tactic had unforeseen and undesirable results. Master Walsh took in the rearrangement of his classroom at a glance, then looked across at Guy. 'Why have you moved?'

'I am more comfortable here,' Guy replied sullenly, without looking at him or Caroline.

155

'In that case,' Walsh looked across at Tom, 'I think it would be better if Tom moved over beside Mistress Caroline. There I can better keep him under my eye.'

Tom needed no second invitation, and for the rest of the morning Guy was forced to witness the play between the two. While frowning at his slate, Tom surreptitiously moved one of his great clodhoppers under the table to touch her elegant satin slipper. Caroline smiled secretly to herself, as though at something she had just read, but made no move to withdraw her foot.

Then, a little later, Tom wrote something on his slate and, when Walsh was busy marking Dorian's arithmetic, held it so that she could read it. Caroline glanced at what he had written then flushed and tossed her curls as if in annoyance, but her eyes danced. Then she scribbled on her own slate and let Tom read it. He grinned like the lout Guy knew he was.

Guy was consumed with jealous rage, but he was helpless. He was forced to watch them flirting, teasing each other, and his hatred boiled up until he felt he could no longer contain it. He was haunted by the images of the terrible things he had witnessed in the magazine. His father's bulk had screened from him most of the horror of that night, and the light had been poor, but the gleam of her white skin and the tantalizing roundness and soft shapes of her body flashed before him again, until he hated her but at the same time ached with longing for her. Then he saw again his brother, and the unspeakable act he was committing, degrading that perfect pure and lovely form. He was like a pig, like a filthy boar guzzling and snorting at the trough. He tried to find the most extreme words in his lexicon to portray the depth of his revulsion, but they fell short of his true feelings. I hate him, he thought fiercely, and then, I will kill him. He felt a stab of guilt at the thought, but almost immediately that evaporated to be replaced by a savage joy.

Yes. I will kill him. It was the only way now open to him.

G uy watched for his opportunity. At noon the next day he was strolling with Mr Beatty up and down the forecastle while the officers of the watch, including his father and Tom, made the sun-shot with their backstaffs.

Mr Beatty was explaining to him in detail how the affairs of the Company were administered in the Orient. 'We have two factories on the Carnatic coast, do you know where that is, Courtney?'

'Yes, sir.' Guy had studied the huge pile of books and documents that Mr Beatty had given him to read. 'The Carnatic is that stretch of country in south-east India, between Eastern Ghats and the Coromandel Coast. It is one of the richest trading areas in the Orient,' he recited dutifully.

Mr Beatty nodded. 'I see you are taking your duties seriously,' he said.

Guy tried to keep his mind on the conversation, but his attention kept wandering to the group on the quarter-deck. He saw them confer over the traverse board at the helm, then Tom scribbled on his slate and showed the result to his father. 'Well done, lad. I'll mark it so on the chart.' His father's voice carried even against the wind. The commendation irked Guy and increased his determination to carry through his plan.

His father took a last turn up and down the deck, darting sharp glances at the set of the sails, and the course in the binnacle. He was an imposing figure, tall and broad-shouldered, with handsome well-formed features and thick dark hair knotted at the back of his head. Guy felt daunted at the prospect of having to confront him. At last Hal handed over the deck to the officer of the watch and disappeared down the companionway to his own quarters.

'Sir.' Guy turned to Mr Beatty. 'Will you please excuse me? There is something of the utmost importance I must discuss with my father.'

'Of course.' Mr Beatty waved him away. 'I shall be here when you return. We shall continue our conversation then. I find it most diverting.'

Guy knocked at the door of the stern cabin, and opened it when his father's voice called from within, 'Enter!' He looked up from the ship's log, in which he was recording the noon position, with the plume of his pen poised over the page. 'Yes, lad, what is it?'

Guy took a deep breath. 'I want to challenge Tom to a duel.'

Carefully Hal replaced the goose quill in the inkwell, and rubbed his chin reflectively, before he looked up again. 'What is this about?'

'You know, Father, you were there. It is so disgusting that I cannot bring myself to discuss it, but Tom has given deep offence to Mistress Caroline.'

'Ah!' Hal sighed. 'So that's it.' As he studied Guy's taut features silently, he thought, If what the little trollop was doing on her back in the powder magazine was taking offence, then she has a remarkable way of demonstrating it. At last he said, 'And what is she to you?'

'I love her, Father,' said Guy, with a simple, touching dignity that took Hal unawares.

He stopped the smile that was already rising to his lips. 'And is the lady aware of your feelings?'

'I know not,' Guy admitted.

'You have not declared them to her? You are not betrothed? You have not spoken to Mr Beatty for his daughter's hand?'

Guy faltered, 'No, Father, not yet. I am but seventeen and . . .'

'Then I fear that you might have left it a trifle late.' Hal spoke not unkindly – he remembered the agony of young love full well. 'Which, in the circumstances, is probably fortunate.'

'I do not follow your meaning, sir.' Guy drew himself up stiffly.

Now I have to qualify myself to the little prig, Hal thought, with secret amusement, 'Simply put, now that you are painfully aware of the . . . predilections, shall we say? of Mistress Beatty, you may wish to review your affection for her. Is she worthy of such noble love as that which you bear her? Has your brother not done you a service by bringing her true nature, even as forcefully as he did, to your attention?' He was going to add, 'It seems clear that Mistress Caroline is a little strumpet,' but he bit back the words, thinking, I do not want to be challenged to a duel by my own son.

'Tom forced her to it,' Guy answered, with grim determination. 'That is why I must challenge him.'

'Did he drag her down to the magazine against her will?'

'Perhaps not, but he enticed her. He seduced her.'

'If you call Tom out, will not the entire ship's company become aware of what has transpired between Tom and her? Do you want her father to learn of her little indiscretion? Do you want her to suffer the full force of parental disapproval?'

Guy looked flustered, and Hal pressed his advantage. 'The sole reason I have not been more severe in my condemnation of your brother's part in this is to spare the young lady's reputation and prospects. Do you wish to expose her now?'

'I will not have to tell anyone else why I am doing this, but I want to fight him.'

'Well, then.' Hal gave up. 'If you are determined, and there is nothing more that I can say to persuade you, then fight him you shall. I will arrange a wrestling bout between the two of you—'

'No, Father,' Guy interrupted, 'you do not understand. I wish to challenge him to a duel with pistols.'

Hal's expression hardened instantly. 'What nonsense is this, Guy? Tom is your brother.'

'I hate him,' said Guy, and his voice quivered with passion.

'Have you considered that, if you call him out, Tom will have the choice of weapons? He will certainly choose sabres. Would you wish to face Tom with a sabre in his hand? I don't think I would. Aboli has turned him into a swordsman who can hold his own in any company. You would not last a minute against him. He would humiliate you, or he would kill you,' Hal told him bluntly and cruelly.

'I don't care, I want to fight him.'

Hal lost his temper. He slammed the palm of his hand on the desk with such violence that the ink sprayed from its well onto the pages of the ship's log. 'That's enough! I have tried to reason with you. Now I forbid this notion of yours. There will be no duelling on this ship, and certainly none between my own sons. If there is one more word from you on the subject, I will have you chained in the forward hold and as soon as we reach Good Hope I will have you transferred to another ship and sent back to England. Do you hear me, boy?'

Guy recoiled at the strength of his father's anger. He had seldom witnessed such fury from him. However, he tried to stand his ground. 'But, Father—'

'Enough!' Hal snapped. 'I have had my say and the subject is closed for all time. Now get about your duties with Mr Beatty. I will hear no more of this nonsense.'

160

The sea changed in colour and mood as the *Seraph* tacked back and forth, battling her way steadily eastward. The confused and disordered wave formations of the ocean changed their character and became great serried ranks, an army of giants marching in battle array towards the land still hidden beneath the horizon.

'The Cape rollers,' Ned Tyler told Tom and Dorian, and pointed ahead towards the misted horizon. 'Cold waters meeting the warm African airs, some call it the Cape of Good Hope, but others call it the Sea of Fogs and others still the Cape of Storms.'

Each day a sense of excitement grew stronger in the ship, which had been so long out of sight of land. The birds came out to meet them from the distant continent, gannets winging in long formations with slashes of black down their yellow throats, gulls with snowy breasts and sable mantles following with raucous cries and tiny petrels splattering the surface of the water with webbed feet.

Then they saw the first dark clumps of drifting kelp, torn from the rocks by the stormy seas and washed out by the current, waving their long stems and bunched fronds like the tentacles of deformed octopods. Vast shoals of small sardine-like fish seethed upon the surface of the cold green waters, and legions of slippery, glistening seals frolicked and fed upon this abundance. As the ship ploughed on they lifted their heads to regard the men on the deck with huge swimming eyes and stiff, cat-like whiskers.

Now each evening Hal shortened sail, so that the ship was barely holding her own against the swirling green current. At first light he sent Tom and Dorian to the masthead to make sure that no reef or rock lay ahead to claw out the ship's guts. As soon as he was certain that the way ahead was clear, he shook out the reefs and clapped on all canvas.

In the middle of the seventy-third morning since leaving Plymouth Ho, Dorian pointed out to his elder brother the cloud that stood stationary dead ahead above the horizon, while the other heavenly cohorts tumbled and streamed away upon the wind. Both boys studied it for a while, until suddenly it swirled, opened, and they saw a hard blue line beneath it, straight as a sabre cut.

'Land!' whispered Tom.

'Can it be?' Dorian asked, wonderingly.

'Yes! Yes!' Tom's voice rose sharply. 'It's the land!' He leaped to his feet in the swaying perch and pointed ahead with a finger that shook. 'Land!' he shrieked. 'Land ho!'

Below him the deck erupted into life, the watch below came streaming up and joined the scramble into the rigging. Soon every shroud and yard was clustered with men, hanging like bunches of ripe fruit, shouting and roaring with laughter and excitement.

Hal Courtney came rushing up from the stern cabin in his shirtsleeves, clutching the brass barrel of his telescope under his arm, and climbed up to where his sons perched at the masthead. He climbed fast and strongly, never stopping until he reached the crow's nest. Tom noticed with pride that, despite the long climb, his breathing was light and even.

He lifted the telescope to his eye and studied the blue silhouette through the glass, picking out the shadowy seams and folds of rugged rock. 'Well, Master Thomas, you've made your first landfall.' He handed the glass to Tom. 'What do you make of it?' Crouched between the two boys he placed an arm around each of them.

'It's a mountain!' Tom cried. 'A great mountain, with a flat top.'

'Table Mountain!' Hal agreed. Tom did not yet realize

what a feat of navigation this was. More than seventy days without sight of land, and his father had brought them in precisely on the thirty-fourth degree of south latitude. 'Look well upon this land ahead of you,' Hal told them. He felt a strange sense of prescience as though the curtains that veiled the future had opened for an instant before his eyes. 'For this is where your destiny lies.'

'Mine also, Father?' Dorian piped.

'Both of you. This is where Fate has led you.' Both boys were silent, rendered speechless for once by their father's vehemence.

The three sat together at the masthead while the sun reached its zenith. 'No need of sun-shot today.' Hal chuckled. 'We can leave that to Ned Tyler and Alf Wilson. We know where we are, don't we?' The sun started down the sky, and the *Seraph* plugged on gamely, beating her way slowly into the rushing south-east wind, gaining slowly so that the table-topped mountain rose with solemn majesty out of the sea, until it seemed to fill the sky ahead of them, and they could even make out the white specks of human habitation at the foot of the sheer rock cliffs.

'We helped build that fort.' Hal pointed it out to them. 'Aboli and Daniel and Ned Tyler and me.'

'Tell us the story!' Dorian pleaded.

'You've heard it a hundred times,' Hal protested.

Tom added his entreaties. 'It doesn't matter, Father. We want to hear it again.'

So, as they sat together in the rigging, Hal related to them the events of the war twenty-five years ago, how the entire crew of their grandfather's ship had been captured by the Dutch, and brought in chains to Good Hope. Sir Francis Courtney had been tortured to reveal the whereabouts of the treasure he had taken from the Dutch galleons he had captured. When he had stood fast against his tormentors, steadfastly enduring the most vile and inhuman suffering inflicted on him, the Dutch had taken him out onto the parade ground and publicly executed him.

Hal and the rest of the crew had been condemned to hard labour on the walls of the Dutch fort, and they had toiled and suffered there for three long years before they had made good their escape.

'So is that the mountain where Grandfather Francis is buried?' Tom asked. 'Do you know where his grave is, Father?'

'Aboli knows, for it was he who took the body down from the scaffold in the night. Under a staring moon he carried it up the mountain to a secret place.'

Tom was silent for a while, thinking about the empty sarcophagus in the chapel on the hill behind High Weald with his grandfather's name graven upon it. He guessed what his father was planning, but this was not the time to thrust himself forward. He would bide his time.

The *Seraph* came level with the small rocky island that guarded the entrance to the bay below the mountain. Forests of waving black kelp clogged the waters around it and hordes of glistening seals thronged the rocky shore of Robben Island, so called because *robben* was the Dutch name for seal.

'Now I must go down to see the ship safely into the anchorage,' Hal told them.

'Race you to the deck!' Dorian cried, as he sprang into the rigging. Tom gave him a lead, then flew after him. Their feet danced over the rat-lines, and they dropped as though falling free, but Tom was soon narrowing the gap between them until, when he was almost level, he slowed to let Dorian reach the deck a foot ahead of him.

'I won! I won!' Dorian exulted.

Tom ruffled his shining coppery curls. 'Don't gloat,' he said, and pushed him away. Then he looked at the small group in the *Seraph*'s bows. Mr and Mrs Beatty stood there with all their daughters, Guy with them. They were animated and excited, pointing out to each other the landmarks of this famous headland, next to Cape Agulhas, the most southerly point of the African landmass.

'They call the white cloud sitting on top of the mountain the tablecloth.' Guy was lecturing the group. 'And that little hill there to the south of the settlement is called Lion's Head. You can see the shape of it.' As always he had studied the navigation books and knew all the details.

'Guy, why don't you go to the masthead?' Tom called to him, not unkindly. 'You'll get a much better view from there.'

Guy glanced coldly at him, 'Thank you, but I'm quite happy where I am.' He stepped a little closer to Caroline, and began to turn away.

'No need to be afraid,' Tom assured him. 'It's quite safe.'

Guy rounded on him. 'Are you calling me a coward?' His face was suffused with blood and his voice cracked with indignation.

'That's not what I said.' Tom laughed, and turned on his heel to go to the helm. 'But take it any way you wish,' he flung over his shoulder.

Guy glared at him, and mortification flooded over him. Tom had disparaged his courage, then dismissed him casually in front of the Beatty family and Caroline. Something snapped in his mind, and before he truly realized what he was about, he launched himself down the deck at a full run.

'Tom, look out!' Dorian yelled, but he was too late. Tom was turning to protect himself but Guy crashed into him with all his weight and momentum while he was balanced on only one foot. It sent him reeling against the gunwale, with such force that the wind was driven from his lungs.

Guy leaped onto his back and threw a full arm-lock around his neck. All the boys had taken regular wrestling instruction from Big Daniel, and though Guy was slow and maladroit at the sport, he knew all the holds and throws, and now that he had this killer grip he was making the most of it. He braced himself with one knee in Tom's back, and used the counter-thrust of one arm against the crook of the other, to block off Tom's windpipe and put the strain on his spine so that at any moment the vertebrae must snap. Tom reeled about the deck tearing at Guy's arms with desperate fingers, gradually weakening, his mouth wide open as he gasped for air.

The crew came running to watch the show, hooting with excitement, stamping and shouting encouragement to their favourites. Then, above the clamour, a bull voice roared, 'Back throw, Klebe,' and Tom reacted instantly. Instead of resisting the hold that was dragging him backwards, he changed direction, throwing all his weight and strength into a back somersault. Guy found himself hurled backwards with such force that he had no choice but to release his grip and fling back both arms to break his fall, otherwise his ribs would have been stove in.

Tom turned in the air like a cat, and was on top of his twin before he hit the deck. As they crashed together onto the planks he drove down with both elbows and knees into Guy's chest and belly.

Guy screamed like a girl and tried to double up to clutch his injured stomach, but Tom was sitting astride him, pinning him to the deck. He bunched his fist and took a full back swing to drive it into Guy's face.

'Tom, no!'

It was his father's voice, and Tom froze. The wild anger faded slowly from his eyes. He lowered his fist and stood up. He looked down contemptuously at Guy. 'Next time,' he warned, 'you won't get off so lightly.' He turned away. Behind him, Guy came to his feet, still clutching his stomach and braced himself against one of the cannon. The watchers drifted away, disappointed that the show had ended so tamely.

'Tom!' Guy called, and Tom looked back. 'I'm sorry,' Guy said. 'Let's shake hands. Let's be friends.' He staggered towards his brother, looking contrite and abject, his right hand outstretched.

Immediately Tom grinned and strode back. He seized the proffered hand. 'I don't know why we ever fought,' he said.

'I do,' Guy told him, and the pathetic expression on his face changed in an instant to one of blackest hatred. Quick as a viper he drew the dagger from the sheath on his belt. The blade was six inches of bright steel with a needle point. He held it at the level of Tom's navel and thrust hard, at the same time using his grip on his right hand to jerk Tom towards him with all his strength, trying to pull him on to the dagger.

'I hate you!' he screamed at Tom, spittle spraying from his lips in the sunlight. 'I'll kill you for what you've done.'

Tom's eyes flew wide with fright and he twisted violently aside. The point of the dagger scored his flank, slit open his shirt and ploughed a shallow furrow in the flesh beneath. Instantly the blood burst out, soaking the cotton and flooding down his leg.

Caroline screamed in a high ringing voice, 'You've killed him!' and a roar went up from the crew as they raced back to watch the sport.

Guy knew that he had bungled the stroke, and he thrust and slashed desperately at Tom's face and chest. But Tom danced and dodged each thrust until, suddenly and unexpectedly, he leaped forward and slammed the heel of his left hand up under Guy's chin. His twin's head snapped back and he let go his death grip on Tom's right hand.

Guy staggered back against the gunwale, blood oozing from the corner of his mouth where he had bitten through his tongue. He still held the dagger and pointed it at Tom's face, snarling, 'I'll kill you!' His teeth were stained with his own blood. 'I'm going to kill you, you filthy swine.'

With one hand Tom massaged his injured throat, but with the other he drew his own dagger from its sheath. 'You make a fine speech, brother,' he said grimly. 'Now let's see you do the killing you boast of.' He went after Guy, right foot leading, moving on his toes, the dagger weaving in his hand like an erect cobra, his eyes fastened on his brother's face. Guy retreated before him.

Hal moved forward quickly, opened his mouth to shout at them to stop, but before he could utter a sound Aboli was beside him and gripped his upper arm. 'No, Gundwane!' His voice was low but urgent, lost to all but Hal in the screams of the women and the howls of the men. 'Never try to separate fighting dogs. You will only give one the advantage.'

'In God's name, Aboli, these are my sons.'

'They are no longer children, Gundwane. They are men. Treat them like men.'

Tom jumped forward, the point of his dagger held low, and feinted for Guy's belly. Guy ran backwards, almost tripping over his own feet. Tom circled out to his right, and Guy backed away towards the bows. The men there scattered to give them space in which to fight, and Hal saw what Tom was doing: he was driving Guy as a sheep-dog moves the flock, shepherding him into the bows.

Tom's expression was cold and set, with no sign of emotion, but his eyes glowed as he watched his twin's face. Hal had fought many men, and he knew that only the most dangerous swordsmen had that cold menace in their gaze when they closed in for the kill. He knew that Tom was no longer seeing a brother but an enemy to be destroyed. He had become a killer, and Hal was afraid as he had seldom been for himself. He was afraid for Guy, but he knew that Aboli was right. There was nothing he could do to stop this now. He could not call off Tom – it would be like trying to call off a hunting leopard.

Tom was still bleeding from the cut across his flank. The slash in his shirt flapped open to show the white skin beneath and the wound like a smiling mouth, from which the red tide oozed. It dripped onto the deck, and into his shoes so that they squelched with each step he took. But he was unconscious of the injury: all he saw was the man who had inflicted it.

Guy came up against the rail. With his left hand he groped behind him, testing the oak timbers. The realization that he was trapped dawned on him, and the wild anger faded from his eyes, replaced at once by fear. He glanced quickly about him, seeking an avenue of escape. Then his fingers touched the shaft of one of the pikes in the rack below the gunwale, and the fear dissolved like sea mist at the coming of the sun. A fierce joy lit his features as he dropped the dagger, and snatched the pike from the rack. In the face of the heavy spear with its barbed steel head, Tom dropped back a pace. Guy grinned at him, his mouth a bloody gash. 'Now we shall see,' he gloated, lowered the pike head and charged. Tom sprang back and Guy wheeled after him, thrusting with the long shaft, well out of the reach of the dagger in Tom's right hand. He gathered himself and charged again. Tom dropped the dagger, hurled himself aside to escape the gleaming steel point, then leaped back before Guy could round on him and seized the oak shaft.

They wrestled back and forth along the deck, with the shaft between them, thrusting and pushing, grunting and bleeding, mouthing garbled oaths and insults at each other. Eventually Tom pushed Guy against the side of the ship until they were locked together, face to face and chest to chest, with the pike shaft between them.

Slowly Tom forced the shaft up until it was in line with his brother's throat, then put all his weight and strength behind it. Guy's back arched as he bent over the rail, the thick oak shaft under his chin. Fear was in his eyes again: he could hear the water gurgling along the ship's side beneath him and his toes left the deck. He was going over, and he was no swimmer – water terrified him.

Tom's feet were firmly planted, but in a puddle of his own blood, slippery as oil. His feet shot out from under him, and he went down heavily on the deck. Guy was free, and he staggered to the shrouds on the foremast, gasping for breath, sweat soaking his shirt. He caught at the shrouds for support, and looked back over his shoulder.

Tom rolled to his feet, and stooped to pick up his dagger, then went after Guy like a charging leopard.

'Stop him!' Guy screamed in terror. 'Make him stop!' But the clamour of the watchers was deafening, rising higher still with wild excitement as Tom ran in with the dagger in his hand and madness in his eyes.

Guy turned and, with the strength of panic, leaped into the shrouds and began to climb hand over hand. Below him Tom paused only long enough to clamp the dagger between his teeth, then followed him up.

The audience on deck stood with heads thrown back. None had ever seen Guy in the rigging before, and even Hal was amazed at how fast he moved. Tom could gain on him only gradually.

Guy reached the yard and scrambled onto it. He looked down and experienced a moment of giddy vertigo. Then he saw Tom's face below him, coming closer as he raced up the rat-lines. He saw the merciless set of his mouth and the blood that splattered his face and soaked his shirt. Desperately he looked up the mast, but his spirit quailed at the height to the topmast and he knew that with every foot he climbed the advantage passed more firmly into Tom's hands. There was only one way for him to go, and he crawled painfully out along the high yard. He could hear Tom coming after him, and the sound drove him on. He could not look down at the rushing green water so far below him. He was sobbing with terror, but still he crawled on until he had reached the end of the yard. He looked back over his shoulder.

Tom was a pace behind him. Guy was trapped and helpless. Tom checked and sat upright on the swinging yard. He took the blade from between his teeth – he was a ghastly sight, all splashed with blood, his face white and set with rage, and the shining weapon was in his hand.

'Please, Tom,' Guy wailed. 'I didn't mean to hurt you.' He threw up both hands to shield his face, and lost his precarious balance on the yard. He teetered wildly, windmilling his arms, then leaned further and further outwards until, with a wild shriek, he went over, twisting and turning in the air, dropping free until he hit the water in an untidy tangle of limbs and went deep under.

Tom sat rigid as the fog of killing rage cleared from his brain, and looked down in horror at what he had caused. Guy was gone, there was no sign of him below the green surface, no head bobbing in the ship's long creaming wake.

He can't swim! The dreadful reality struck Tom so hard that he reeled on his perch. *I've done it. I've killed my own brother.* The biblical horror of the deed flashed through him. He leaped to his feet, stood tall on the high yard, and peered back along the wake. Then he saw Guy come to the surface, his arms waving and his cries faint and plaintive as those of a wounded gull.

He heard his father's orders to the helm bellowed from the deck below. 'Heave her to! Launch a boat! Man overboard!'

Before the ship could even respond to her helm and turn her bows up into the wind, Tom gathered himself and sprang far out from the yard. Head first, arms stretched far out above his head, he arced over, his legs straight out behind him. He struck the surface of the ocean cleanly, and went so deep that the dark waters closed around him and crushed his chest. Then he turned and struck up for the surface. He burst out waist-high, the breath whistling in his throat. The ship was past him, already swinging her bows round and into the wind.

He looked back along the path of the wake and saw nothing, but still he struck out overarm, swimming with all his strength, churning the waters behind him, hardly feeling the sting of salt in the long shallow wound down his flank. He judged roughly how far back he had last seen Guy's head, paused, and trod water, panting for breath, looking about him. There was no sign of his brother.

Oh, God, if he drowns I will never— He did not finish the thought but sucked in a mighty breath, doubled over until his head was pointed at the bottom of the sea, kicked his feet high in the air and slid smoothly below the surface. With eyes wide open he saw only the green, shot through with bars of sunlight, and swam downwards until his lungs craved air. He must turn back to breathe.

Then he saw something below him, a blur of white and blue, Guy's shirt and jacket, turning end over end, lifeless as a piece of flotsam. With aching lungs Tom swam on down until he touched his brother's shoulder. He seized the collar of his jacket and turned for the surface. Although he kicked out strongly, the drag of the limp body hampered him. The seconds stretched out into an infinity of pain. His chest burned and the need to breathe consumed him. He felt the strength going out of his legs. His hold on Guy's collar slackened and he felt him slip away. The greenness filled his head and his vision faded, stars of light exploding silently in the darkness.

Be strong! he screamed soundlessly at himself, then forced his fingers to close tighter on Guy's jacket, and willed his legs to keep kicking.

The light grew stronger, the green faded and suddenly his head burst out into the air and the sunlight. He drew a breath that filled his chest to the point of bursting, then another – honey-sweet, he felt it pervade his body and the strength flood back. He reached down, and grabbed a handful of Guy's thick, sodden locks and pulled his head out into the air.

Guy was drowned. There was no life in him. His eyes were open, blind and staring. His face was waxen.

'Breathe! For the love of God, breathe!' Tom shouted, into his white, still face and he seized him with both arms around the chest and squeezed. Aboli had shown him this trick, and it worked. The dead, stale air gushed out of Guy, mingled with gouts of sea-water and vomit. It spewed into Tom's face and he released his grip. Guy's chest expanded reflexively, sucking in air through his gaping mouth. Twice more Tom squeezed the water out of him, fighting to hold his face clear of the surface.

With the third breath, Guy coughed and choked and he struggled to breathe of his own accord. His eyes blinked, still unseeing, then slowly focusing. He was breathing but with great difficulty, racked every few seconds with paroxysms of coughing, but slowly expression returned to his eyes.

'I hate you,' he whispered into Tom's face. 'I still hate you. I will always hate you.'

'Why, Guy, why?'

'You should have let me drown, for one day I will kill you.'

'Why?' Tom repeated.

'You know,' Guy gasped. 'You know why!'

Neither twin had heard the boat approaching, but Hal Courtney shouted to them now, from close at hand, 'Hold hard, lads! I'm here.'

The crew of the longboat were pulling with a will and, at the tiller, Hal steered them in close. At his order they shipped their oars and strong hands reached down to seize both boys and drag them from the water.

Dr Reynolds was waiting at the rail as Guy was lifted

aboard the *Seraph*. Tom stood next to his father on the deck, and watched, strangely forlorn, as the surgeon's mates carried his brother below.

'He hates me, Father,' he whispered.

'Let's see to that cut, lad,' Hal said gruffly.

Tom glanced down without interest at his wound. The sea-water had reduced the bleeding to a slow weep. 'It's nothing,' he said. 'A scratch.' Then he looked up again at Hal. 'He hates me. It was the first thing he said when I pulled him to the surface. What am I to do?'

'Guy will get over it.' Hal ripped open Tom's shirt to get at the dagger cut. 'He will forget and forgive.'

'No, he will not.' Tom shook his head. 'He said he will always hate me. He is my brother. Help me, Father. What can I do?'

Hal could give him no answer. He knew all too well the younger twin's obstinacy and tenacity: they were at once his strength and his weakness. He knew that Tom was right. Guy would never forgive him.

It was the most beautiful landfall in all the oceans Hal had ever sailed. The mountain was a towering wall against the sky, and the wind sweeping over the top frothed like boiling milk into a soft pulsating cloud, touched with shades of oyster shell and pink pearl, colours borrowed from the lowering sun. The slopes of the mountain below the rocky ramparts were green with forests, and the beaches were white, rimed with a frosting of surf.

Such beauty should have delighted Hal, yet every memory that crowded back upon him was touched with pain and horror. The walls of the castle were clear to see from this range, and on the crenellated battlements the cannon glared out at them, their muzzles dark, empty eye-sockets. In the dungeons beneath those walls he had lived out three cruel Cape winters, and he shivered now at the memory of the cold in his bones. It was on those walls that Hal had laboured until the skin and flesh were torn from his palms, and he reeled with fatigue. It was on the builders' scaffolding that he had seen so many good men die, and there that he had made the difficult transition from boy to man.

He lifted the telescope to his eye to survey the other ships at anchor in the bay. He was amazed at their numbers. He counted twenty-three sail, all big trading vessels, Dutchmen for the most part. He spotted one Englishman among them, another East Indiaman from the look of her, but he saw with disappointment that she was not the *Yeoman of York*. There was no sign of his companion in the anchorage.

Without lowering the telescope, he swept the waters of the bay towards the land. His eye stopped on the open parade below the castle's walls, and the memories of his father's execution flooded back to him in all their stark, terrible detail. He had to force them from his mind to be able to concentrate on bringing the *Seraph* into the anchorage.

'We will anchor out of range of the guns in the fort, Mr Tyler.' He gave the order, and there was no need to qualify it. Ned knew his mind, and his expression was also sombre. Perhaps he too was reliving those days of horror as he put up the helm, and gave the order to take in the canvas.

The anchor went down with a splash that wet the forecastle, and the cable smoked out through the hawsehole. *Seraph* snubbed up hard, and then pirouetted gracefully with her head to the wind and became quiescent, transformed from a vital, living, straining sea creature to something lovely and tranquil as a drifting swan.

The crew lined the *Seraph*'s bare yards and hung in the shrouds, staring at the land, shouting comment, speculation and question as they watched the bum-boats rowing out to meet them. Seamen called this fair cape the Tavern of the Seas. It had been colonized over fifty years before to serve as a victualling station for the fleet of the Dutch East India Company, and the bum-boats were laden with all the things that a crew craved after three months at sea.

Hal called his officers to him. 'Watch that no strong drink is smuggled into the ship,' he warned Alf Wilson. 'The rum-sellers will try to slip it in through the gunports. We will have half the men puking drunk by nightfall if you let them hoodwink you.'

'Aye, Captain.' The fourth officer touched his cap. As a man of abstinence, he was a good choice for the duty.

'Aboli, place men armed with cutlass and pistol at the rail. We don't want those thieving rogues coming aboard to strip the ship bare, nor whores plying their trade on the gundeck. Otherwise the daggers will be out—' He had almost said, 'again', but stopped himself. He did not want to remind them of the conflict between his sons.

'Mr Fisher, you will do the bargaining with the bum-boats, you're good at that.' He could rely on Big Daniel to get his shilling's worth, and to check every piece of fruit and vegetable that came aboard. 'Mr Walsh will assist you and pay the boatmen.' Walsh had many duties, from schoolmaster to writer and purser.

The officers scattered to the tasks he had set them, and Hal strode to the rail. He looked down into the bum-boats as they came alongside. They were laden to the gunwales with fresh produce: potatoes with the earth still on them, green cabbages and apples, figs and pumpkins, sides of fresh red mutton and plucked chickens. The crew would gorge themselves this evening. Saliva squirted from under Hal's tongue as he looked down upon this cornucopia. This hunger for fresh food was a consuming lust that overcame every seaman at the end of a long voyage. Some of his men were already leaning out over the side and bargaining for the wares. Those with money paid as much as a ha'penny for a single fresh potato: a ludicrous price. They were frantic with greed, wiping the clinging earth off the fat white tubers against the skirts of their petticoats as though they were apples, then wolfing them down raw, crunching the astringent white flesh with every evidence of enjoyment.

Dr Reynolds came to Hal's side. 'Well, sir, it's a relief to be in port again. Twenty-six cases of scurvy on board already, but we will see those cured before we sail again. It's a miracle and a mystery, but the air from the land heals even the worst cases, men who have lost their teeth and are too weak to stand.' He handed Hal a ripe apple. 'I stole a couple of these from Master Walsh's stock.'

Hal bit into it and had to close his eyes in ecstasy. 'The food of the gods,' he said, as the juices flooded his mouth and slid, like sweet oil, down his throat. 'My father used to say it was lack of fresh food that caused the scurvy,' he told the surgeon.

Dr Reynolds smiled pityingly, and took a huge bite of his own apple. 'Well, Captain, sir, no reflection on your sainted father, for all the world knows he was a great and good man, but ship's biscuit and salt beef is food enough for any seaman.' Reynolds wagged his head wisely. 'You do hear some marvellous theories from men not trained in the physic arts, but it's the sea air that causes scurvy, and nothing else.'

'How are my two sons, Doctor?' Hal asked, changing the subject adroitly.

'Thomas is a healthy young animal and, fortunately, the wound was not deep and did little damage. I have closed it with cat-gut stitches, and it will be healed in next to no time – that is if it does not mortify.'

'What of Guy?'

'I have sent him to the bunk in your cabin. His lungs

177

were flooded with salt water, and that sometimes breeds morbid humours. But in a few days he, too, should be none the worse for his ducking.'

'I am thankful to you, Doctor.'

At that moment there was a commotion amidships. Aboli had picked out one of the Hottentot lads, who had carried a crate of fruit up the ladder from the bum-boat alongside, and grabbed his shoulder. 'Hey there, pretty boy,' he challenged. 'Or are you a boy?' His victim had a heart-shaped face, flawless golden skin and slanted Asiatic eyes. He reacted to Aboli's challenge with a flood of high-pitched abuse, in a strange, tongue-clicking language, and struggled in Aboli's great hands. Laughing, Aboli jerked the hat from his head, and a thick black mane fell onto the fellow's shoulders. Then Aboli lifted him high with one hand, and with the other jerked his breeches down around his knees.

The crew let out a howl of delight as a plump yellow bottom was revealed and shapely thighs, between which nestled the dark, furry, triangular badge of womanhood. High in the air, the girl rained blows with both hands on Aboli's bald head, and when this had no effect on him, she clawed at his eyes with long, sharp fingernails, and kicked wildly at him with both feet.

Aboli walked to the ship's rail and tossed her over the side as effortlessly as if she had been a stray kitten. Her companions hoisted her back into the bum-boat, streaming water, hoisting her breeches, and still shrieking abuse at the seamen who jeered at her from the rail.

Hal turned away to hide his smile, and walked across to where Mr Beatty stood with his family around him at the foot of the main mast, all of them gazing across at the shore and animatedly discussing this new land. Hal lifted his hat to the ladies, and Mrs Beatty beamed with pleasure. In contrast, Caroline avoided his eyes. She had been shame-faced in his company ever since the night in the magazine.

178

Hal turned back to Mr Beatty. 'We will be anchored here for many days, possibly weeks. I must await the arrival of the *Yeoman*, and there is much else I must see to. I'm sure that you will want to take your family ashore, to give the ladies an opportunity to escape from the confines of their cabins and to stretch their legs. I know that there are comfortable lodgings to be had in the town.'

'What a capital idea, sir!' Beatty responded enthusiastically. 'I'm sure it is no hardship to you, Sir Hal, but for us land-dwellers the confined spaces on board become irksome.'

Hal nodded agreement. 'I shall send young Guy ashore with you. I'm sure you will want your secretary at hand.' He was pleased to have achieved his most urgent purposes: first to separate Tom from Guy, and second to separate Tom from Caroline. Both situations could blow up like a powder-keg at any moment. 'I will have you conveyed ashore as soon as the boats are launched, although it is perhaps too late this evening.' He glanced at the setting sun. 'You might wish to pack your chests now and wait until tomorrow to go ashore.'

'You are very kind, Captain.' Beatty bowed.

'When you have an opportunity you might be good enough to make a courtesy call upon the Dutch governor – van der Stel is his name, Simon van der Stel. I will be much occupied with the ship's management, and you will be doing me a great service by undertaking this duty on my and the Company's behalf.'

Beatty bowed again. 'With the greatest of pleasure, Sir Hal.'

It was over twenty years since Hal had escaped with his crew from imprisonment in the castle dungeons, and it was unlikely that anyone in the settlement would recognize him, but he was a convicted felon, with a life sentence hanging over his head. During the escape from the castle he and his men had been forced to kill many of their gaolers and pursuers in self-defence, but the Dutch might see it in a different light. If he were recognized he might find himself before a Dutch tribunal charged with those crimes and facing the prospect of serving out his life sentence or even paying for his crimes on the gallows, as his father had. A formal call on the governor of the colony would not be a wise move. Much better to send Beatty.

Then again, he must gather all the news available in the settlement. Every ship returning from the Orient, no matter its nationality, called here at the Cape. He could not hope for better intelligence than was readily available in the taverns and bawdy-houses of the waterfront. He excused himself from the Beatty family and called Big Daniel and Aboli to him. 'As soon as it's dark, we're going ashore. Have one of the boats made ready.'

The moon was four days from full. The mountain loomed dark and monstrous over them, its gullies and bluffs touched with silver, as they followed the shimmering path of moonlight to the beach. Hal sat between Aboli and Big Daniel in the stern sheets. All three were muffled with cloaks and hats, and they carried pistols and swords under their cloaks. The rowers were also armed, twelve good men under Alf Wilson.

They came into the beach on one of the Atlantic swells, hissing over the sands on the foaming crest. As soon as the wave began to retreat, the rowers jumped out and dragged the longboat high and dry.

'Keep the men under your eye, Alf. Don't let them sneak away to look for drink and women,' Hal warned Wilson. 'We may be in a hurry when we return.'

They trudged together through the soft beach sand, and as soon as they found the path they set out for the huddle of buildings below the fort. Some of the windows showed the glimmer of lanterns, and as they drew nearer they could hear music, singing and drunken shouts.

'It has changed little since our last visit,' Aboli grunted.

'Trade is still good,' Big Daniel agreed, and stooped into the door of the first tavern on the edge of the settlement.

The light was so dim and the fog of tobacco smoke so dense that it took a few seconds for their vision to adjust. The room was full of dark figures, and the reek of sweating bodies, rank pipe smoke and bad liquor. The noise was deafening, and as they paused in the entrance, a seaman reeled past them. He staggered to the edge of the sand dunes, dropped to his knees and threw up loudly and copiously. Then he toppled forward and fell face down in the puddle of his own vomit.

The three men stepped together into the room and pushed their way through the throng towards the far corner, where there was a trestle table and a bench on which another comatose drunk sprawled. Big Daniel lifted him as though he were a sleeping child and laid him gently on the cow-dung floor. Aboli swept the clutter of empty tankards and platters of half-eaten food from the table, while Hal took a seat on the bench with his back to the wall to survey the dim room and the men who crowded it.

They were mostly sailors, though there were a few troopers, in their blue jackets and white cross-belts, from the castle garrison. Hal listened to their talk, but it was a drunken babble of wild boasting, cursing and mindless laughter.

'Dutchmen,' Aboli murmured, as he took his seat on the bench beside Hal. They listened for a while. As a matter of survival all three had learned to speak the language during their captivity.

A group of five tough-looking sailors sat at the table beside them. They seemed less drunk than the others, but they were speaking loudly to make themselves heard above the din. Hal listened for a while but heard nothing of interest. A Hottentot serving-wench brought them foaming pots of beer.

Daniel tasted his and made a face. 'Piss! Still warm from the pig,' he said, but took another swig.

Hal did not touch his, because he had just heard the Dutchman at the next table say, 'We will be lucky if the devil-damned convoy ever leaves this pestilent port.'

The mention of a convoy intrigued Hal. Traders usually sailed alone. Only in times of war or other emergency did they form convoys and place themselves under the protective guns of men-o'-war. He leaned forward to hear the rest.

'Ja. I for one will not weep if I never drop anchor again in this nest of black whores and thieving Hottentots. I have spent nearly the last guilder in my purse, and all I have to show for it is a sore head and a raw pizzle.'

'I say the skipper should take his chances and sail alone. The hell with this bastard Jangiri and his heathen crew! *Die Luipard* is a match for any son of the prophet. We don't need to sit around here until van Rutyers is ready to nursemaid us.'

Hal's pulse spurted at the name Jangiri. It was the first time he had heard it outside Nicholas Childs's cabinet.

'Who is van Rutyers?' Big Daniel asked quietly, and took another pull at his poisonous beer. He, too, had been eavesdropping on the Dutch sailors.

'The Dutch admiral of the Ocean of the Indies,' Hal told him. 'He is based in the Dutch factory at Batavia.' He slid a silver shilling over the dirty tabletop. 'Buy them a pot of beer, Big Danny, and listen to what they have to tell you,' he ordered, but as Daniel stood up from the bench he found himself confronted by a woman.

She stood, arms akimbo, and looked up at him with a

seductive grin that lacked only a few teeth. 'Come to the back room with me, you big bull,' she told him, 'and I will give you something you've never had before.'

'What have you got, my darling?' Big Daniel showed her his bare gums in a wide grin. 'Leprosy?'

Hal surveyed the drab swiftly, and realized that she could be a better source of information than any drunken Dutchman. 'Shame on you, Master Daniel,' he said, 'that you don't recognize a lady of quality when you see one.' The woman ogled Hal, taking in the cut and quality of his coat, the silver buttons on his waistcoat.

'Sit you down, your ladyship,' Hal invited her. She giggled and preened like a girl, pushing straggling grey strands back from her face with grimy fingers whose nails were broken and black-rimmed. 'Take a little something, for your throat's sake. Daniel, get the lady a glass of gin. No, no, let us not be mean. Get a full bottle.'

The woman fluffed out her grubby petticoats, and dropped onto the bench opposite Hal. 'You're a real prince, you are.' She peered into his face. 'And handsome as the devil, too.'

'What is your name, my beauty?' Hal asked.

'Mevrouw Maakenberg,' she answered. 'But you may call me Hannah.' Daniel returned with a square bottle of gin and a tumbler. He poured it to the brim. Hannah lifted it with her little finger raised and took a ladylike sip. She did not wince at the ferocity of the pale spirit.

'So, Hannah,' Hal smiled at her, and she wriggled like a puppy under his gaze, 'there is nothing that goes on here at Good Hope that you don't know about, is there, now?'

'That's God own truth, if I say it myself.' She showed the gaps in her teeth again. 'Anything you want to know, sir, you ask old Hannah.'

She was as good as her word. For the next hour Hal sat opposite her and listened to what she had to tell him.

He found that behind the raddled face and bleary gin-sodden eyes lurked the remnants of a once bright intelligence.

It seemed that she knew the sexual mores and leanings of every male and female in the settlement, from Governor van der Stel to the dock-workers and transport drivers. She could tell them the price of all the produce in the market, from potatoes to *mampoer*, the fiery peach brandy made by the burghers. She knew which slaves were for sale, the prices their owners were asking and what they would accept. She knew the sailing dates of every ship in the bay, her captain's name, her cargo and every port of call on her route. She could give them an account of each ship's latest voyage, the hazards and hardships she had encountered.

'Tell me, Hannah, why there are so many VOC ships lying in the bay?' He was referring to the Verenigde Oostindische Compagnie, the Dutch East India Company.

'Those are all outward bound for Batavia. Governor van der Stel has ordered that all ships sailing eastward must sail in convoy under the protection of warships.'

'Why, Hannah, would he want to do that?'

'Because of Jangiri. You have heard of Jangiri, have you not?'

Hal shook his head. 'No. Who is he – or it?'

'The Sword of the Prophet – that's what he calls himself. But he's nothing more than a bloody pirate, worse than Franky Courtney hisself, that's what he is.'

Hal exchanged a glance with Aboli. Both men were taken aback to have his father's name thrown at them so carelessly, and to know that Sir Francis and his exploits were still so well remembered hereabouts.

Hannah had not noticed their reaction. She took a gulp of her gin, and laughed raucously. 'In the last six months three VOC ships have disappeared from the Ocean of the Indies. Everybody knows it's Jangiri's doing. They do say he's cost the Company a million guilders already.'

Her eyes lit up with wonder. 'A million guilders! I did not know there was that much money in the world.' She leaned across the table to stare into Hal's face. Her breath smelt like a dung-heap, but Hal did not recoil. He did not want to risk giving her offence.

'You look like somebody I know.' She puzzled over it for a moment. 'Were you ever here at Good Hope before? I never forget a face.'

Hal shook his head and Big Daniel chuckled. 'Perhaps, missus, if he showed you his pink end you would recognize it for certain, better than his face, that is.'

Hal frowned at him but by this time the gin bottle was half empty and Hannah cackled. 'I'd pay a million guilders for sight of that!' She leered at Hal. 'Do you want to come in the back with Hannah? There'll be no charge for it, such a lovely man you are.'

'Next time,' Hal promised her.

'I do know you,' she insisted. 'When you smile like that, I know you. It'll come back to me. I never forget a face.'

'Tell me more about Jangiri,' he suggested to divert her, but she was losing her wits now.

She refilled her tumbler and held up the empty bottle. 'Everyone I love goes off and leaves me,' she said, tears flooding her eyes. 'Even the bottle don't stay with me long.'

'Jangiri,' Hal insisted. 'Tell me about Jangiri.'

'He's a bloody Mussulman pirate. He burns Christian sailors just to hear them scream.'

'Where does he come from? How many ships does he command? What strength are they?'

'One of my friends was on a ship that Jangiri chased but didn't catch,' she slurred. 'He's a lovely boy. He wants to marry me and take me home to Amsterdam.'

'Jangiri?' Big Daniel asked.

'No, you stupid clod of earth.' Hannah bristled. 'My

boyfriend. I forget his name, but he wants to marry me. He saw Jangiri. He was lucky to escape that bloodthirsty heathen.'

'Where did this happen, Hannah? When did your friend run across Jangiri?'

'Not two months past – off the Fever Coast it was, near the isle of Madagascar.'

'What force did Jangiri have?' Hal pressed.

'Many great ships,' Hannah said uncertainly. 'A fleet of warships. My friend's ship fled.'

Hal realized that she was floundering. There was little more she could tell him of importance. But he asked a last question. 'Do you know which route the VOC convoy takes on its way to Batavia?'

'South,' she said. 'They say far south. I've heard that they keep well clear of Madagascar and the islands, for that's where Jangiri skulks, the filthy heathen.'

'When will the convoy in the bay sail?' Hal asked.

But she was gone into the fogs of alcohol. 'Jangiri is the devil,' she whispered. 'He is the Antichrist, and all true Christians should dread him.' Slowly her head sagged forward, then flopped face down into the puddle of gin on the tabletop.

Daniel took a hank of her greasy grey hair and lifted her head to look into her eyes. 'The lady has left us,' he said, and let it drop again to hit the wood with a crack. She rolled off the bench and lay on the floor, snoring loudly. Hal took a silver ten-guilder coin from the purse on his sword-belt and pushed it down Hannah's bodice.

'That's more than she'll earn on her back in a month of Sundays,' Big Daniel grunted.

'But well worth it.' Hal stood up. 'That's better intelligence than we could get from Admiral van Ruyters himself.'

On the beach Alf Wilson was waiting for them with the longboat. As they rowed back across the bay to the

Seraph Hal sat quietly, digesting all the news Hannah had given him, and weaving it into his plans. By the time he had climbed the rope-ladder to the main deck he knew what he had to do.

'Some things seem clear from what Daniel's ladyfriend told us last night.' Hal looked around at the intent faces of his officers, who were crowded into the stern cabin. 'The first is that Jangiri has his nest somewhere along here.' Hal leaned over the chart spread on his desk and placed his finger on the outline of Madagascar. 'From here he can harry the trade routes to the south and east with the greatest ease.'

Aboli grunted, 'Finding his sally-port will be the trick. He does not have to use one of the big islands as his base. There are hundreds of other smaller ones, scattered over two thousand leagues from the Oman coast in the Arabian Sea to the Mascarene islands in the south.'

'You are right.' Hal nodded. 'Added to those, there are almost certainly dozens of other islands we do not know, that are neither named nor shown on any chart. We might sail a hundred years and not discover or explore them all.' He looked around their faces. 'If we cannot go to him, then what should we do?'

'Bring him to us,' said Ned Tyler.

Again Hal nodded. 'Bring him out of his lair. Give him a bait to tease him. The place to do that is off the Fever Coast. We will have to cruise off the islands of Madagascar and Zanzibar, trail our cloak along the African shore.' They muttered in agreement.

'You can be certain he has agents in every port in the Indian Ocean. They send him word of every prize that calls,' Daniel told them. 'At least, that's what I would do, if I were a heathen pirate.'

'Yes.' Hal turned to him. 'We'll call in at every port, let them know how rich we are, and how poorly armed.'

'Two fighting ships of thirty-six guns apiece?' Ned Tyler chuckled. 'That's enough force to daunt any pirate.'

'One ship,' Hal said, and smiled when they looked askance. 'I will send the *Yeoman* on alone to Bombay as soon as she arrives here. She can carry our passengers and all the urgent cargo of which we can rid ourselves and cram into her hold. We will sail the Fever Coast on our own.'

'The *Seraph* is still a ship of force,' Alf Wilson pointed out. 'Enough to frighten off most pirates.'

'She will not look like one by the time we are ready to sail.' Hal unrolled the drawings of the ship's hull, on which he had been working since they had crossed the equator. 'A Trojan horse, gentlemen. That is what we shall prepare for Mr Jangiri.'

They crowded round the desk, voicing approval, making eager comment and suggestion as they began to see what Hal had in mind.

'What we want to make her into is a rich, fat, unarmed trader. The gunports first . . .'

The next morning, Hal had himself rowed round the ship as she lay at anchor. Ned Tyler and the two ship's carpenters were with him, and he pointed out to them the changes he wanted made to the *Seraph*'s appearance. 'We can leave all the carving and gold work as they are.' He pointed to the beautiful decorative features on the stern and bows. 'They give her a nice decadent air, like the Lord Mayor's barge.'

'More like a French whorehouse.' Big Daniel sniffed.

'Besides which Lord Childs will be greatly put out if we damage his little masterpiece.' He pointed to the *Seraph*'s sides. 'It's the gunports that must be our prime concern.' The sills of the gunports were picked out in gold leaf, which gave a pleasing chequered effect to the hull but emphasized the *Seraph*'s warlike capability. 'You will begin work on them first,' Hal ordered the carpenters. 'I want the joints of the lids to the gunports concealed. Caulk them with tar and repaint them so they blend into the timber-work of the hull.' For an hour longer they studied the ship from the longboat and decided on other small touches to the *Seraph*'s outline that would make her appear more innocuous.

As they rowed back to the ship, Hal remarked to Big Daniel, 'One of the reasons I anchored so far off-shore, apart from out-ranging the guns on the fort, was to keep out of sight of prying eyes on the beach.' He nodded at the bum-boats and other small craft still clustered around the ship. 'As soon as the work begins, I want you to warn off those boats. We must believe that Jangiri has agents in the settlement, and act on that belief. I don't want beady eyes watching everything we do, and busy tongues passing on the news.'

Once back in his cabin, Hal penned a letter to Mr Beatty addressed to his lodgings in the town, explaining that he and his family would complete the voyage to Bombay in the *Yeoman of York*, when she arrived, and that Guy would accompany him. Hal was glad to arrange this by note, rather than having to persuade Mr Beatty to make the change by discussion and argument.

'Well, now!' he said aloud as he sanded the ink on the paper. 'That arrangement will also take care of Master Tom's pugilistic and amorous proclivities.' Once he had placed his wax seal on it, he sent for Big Daniel to carry the letter ashore. 'No sign of the *Yeoman* yet?' he demanded, as soon as Big Daniel stuck his head in at the door.

'Nothing yet, Captain.'

'Tell the officer of the watch to call me the minute she puts her topmasts above the horizon.' He had given the same order more than once before, and Big Daniel rolled his eyes and sucked his gums to illustrate his forbearance. Hal concealed a smile. Big Daniel was allowed such familiarity.

He stood on the scaffold in the bright morning sunlight. He was still only a lad, perhaps eighteen years of age, certainly no older. He was very good-looking – Hannah Maakenberg loved it when they were. He was tall and straight-limbed, with long waving hair, raven's-wing black, falling to his shoulder. He was terrified, which excited her as it excited the large crowd around her. Every man, woman and child in the settlement was there, every burgher and housewife, slave and Hottentot. They were in high spirits, boisterous and playful. Even the very young children were among them, infected by the spontaneous gaiety of the occasion, they chased each other, squealing, between the legs of the adults.

Beside Hannah stood one of the free burgher's wives, a plump, kindly looking woman in an apron dusted with flour. She had obviously come directly from baking bread in her kitchen. Her tiny daughter clutched at her apron. She was an angelic child, who sucked her thumb and stared solemnly at the man on the scaffold with huge blue eyes.

'It's her first execution,' the mother explained to Hannah. 'She feels a little strange and afraid of all the people.'

The prisoner's hands were manacled behind his back. He wore ragged seaman's petticoats and his feet were bare. The magistrate stepped to the front of the scaffold to read the charge and the sentence, and the crowd swayed and jostled with anticipation.

'Now hear the verdict of the court of the colony of Good Hope, by the grace of God and the power vested in me by Charter of the States General of the Republic of Holland.'

'Get on with it!' howled one of the burghers at the back of the crowd. 'Let's see him do his little dance for us.'

'It is hereby decreed that, Hendrik Martinus Ockers, having been found guilty of the crime of murder . . .'

'I was there,' Hannah told the housewife beside her proudly. 'I saw it all. I even gave evidence at the court, yes, I did!'

The woman looked suitably impressed. 'Why did he do it?' she asked.

'Why do any of them do it?' Hannah shrugged. 'They was both pissing, puking drunk.' She remembered the two figures circling each other with the long knives gleaming in the eerie lantern light, throwing distorted shadows on the tavern walls, and the shouts and the stamping of the watchers.

'How did he do it?'

'A knife, dearie. He was quick, for all the liquor in his belly. Like a panther, he was.' She made a slashing gesture. 'Like that, right across his belly. Opened him up like a fish on the block. His guts fell clean out of him, tangled in his feet, so he tripped and fell on his face.'

'Ooh!' The housewife shuddered with horrified fascination. 'Like animals, these sailors.'

'All of them, dearie, not just the sailors.' Hannah nodded primly. 'All men are the same.'

'And that's God's truth!' The woman agreed, picked up the child and placed her on her shoulder.

'There you are, *lieveling*. You will get a better view from up there,' she told her.

The magistrate reached the end of the proclamation of sentence: 'The aforesaid Hendrik Martinus Ockers is hereby condemned to death by hanging. Sentence to be carried out in public on the parade ground of the castle on the morning of the third day of September at ten of the

191

clock in the forenoon.' He moved heavily down the ladder from the scaffold and one of the guards helped him down the last few steps. The executioner, who had been standing behind the condemned man, stepped forward and placed a black cotton bag over his head.

'I hate it when they do that,' Hannah grumbled. 'I like to see his face when he's on the end of the rope, all purple and screwed up.'

'Slow John never covered their faces,' the woman beside her agreed.

'Ah! Do you remember Slow John? He was an artist.'

'I'll never forget when he executed Sir Franky, the English pirate. That was a show.'

'Remember it like yesterday,' Hannah agreed. 'Worked on him for nearly half an hour, before he chopped him—' She broke off as something else nudged her memory. Something to do with the pirates, and the pretty lad on the scaffold. She shook her head with irritation – the gin had fuddled her mind.

The executioner placed the noose over the prisoner's head and pulled it snug under his left ear. The lad was trembling now. Hannah wished again that she could see his face. The whole scene reminded her of someone.

The executioner stood back, and picked up his heavy wooden mallet. He took a full swing at the wedge that held the trap-door. The condemned man gave a pitiful cry: 'In God's name, have mercy!'

The watchers hooted with laughter. The executioner swung the mallet again and the wedge was knocked out. With a crash the trap flew open, and the man dropped through. He came up short on the rope's end, his neck stretched and his head jerked to the side. Hannah heard the vertebrae snap like a dry twig, and was disappointed again. Slow John would have judged it better, and had him kicking and jerking at the rope's end for many tantalizing minutes with the life being slowly choked out of him. This executioner was ham-fisted, lacking subtlety. For Hannah it was all over too swiftly. A few shuddering tremors ran through the condemned man's body and then he hung quietly, revolving slowly on the noose, his neck twisted at an impossible angle.

Hannah turned away, disgruntled. Then she stopped. The memory that had eluded her so long came back with a rush. 'The pirate's boy!' she said. 'Sir Franky, the pirate's boy. I never forget a face. I said I knew him.'

'Who are you talking about?' the woman with the child on her shoulder asked. 'Franky's boy? Who's Franky's boy?'

Hannah did not bother to reply but she hurried away, hugging her secret to herself, trembling with excitement. The memory of the events of twenty years ago crowded back. The trial of the English pirates; Hannah had been young and pretty in those days, and she had given one of the guards a little something for free to let her into the courtroom. She had followed the entire trial from her seat in the back row. It had been better entertainment than any play or fair.

She saw again the lad, Franky's son, chained to the pirate, standing side by side with him, as old Governor van der Velde sentenced the one to death and the other to a life sentence at hard labour on the castle walls. What was the lad's name? When she closed her eyes she could see his face so clearly in her mind's eye.

'Henry!' she exclaimed. 'Henry Courtney!'

Then three years later the pirates, led by this same Henry Courtney, had broken out of their dungeon in the castle. Hannah would never forget the sounds of shouting and fighting and of musket fire, then the earth-shaking explosion and the vast towering cloud of smoke and dust that rose high in the air as the English ruffians blew up the powder magazine in the castle. With her own eyes she had watched them gallop out of the castle gates in the carriage they had stolen, and take the road that led out into the wilderness. Although the troops from the garrison had pursued them as far as the savage mountains to the north, they had got clean away. After that, she remembered seeing the reward posters in the market, and in every tavern along the waterfront.

'Ten thousand guilders!' she whispered to herself. 'It was ten thousand guilders.' She tried to imagine such a vast sum of money. 'With that money, I could go back to Amsterdam. I could live like a grand lady for the rest of my life.' Then her spirits plunged. Will they still pay the reward after all these years? Her whole body sagged with despair as the great fortune receded from her grasp. I will send Annetjie to find out from her sport at the castle. Annetjie was one of the younger, prettier whores who worked the taverns along the waterfront. Among her regular clients was the Governor's clerk, her steamer, in the vernacular of the trade. Hannah lifted her skirts and set off at a run for the waterfront. She knew that Annetjie had a room in Die Malmok, one of the most popular of the sailors' taverns, named after the wandering albatross.

She was in luck: Annetjie was still stretched out on her stained mattress in the tiny room beneath the eaves. The room stank of men's sweat and lust. Annetjie sat up with her dense black curls in a tangle and her eyes dulled with sleep. 'What are you waking me for at this hour? Are you mad?' she whined angrily. Hannah flopped down beside her and blurted out her story.

The girl sat up and wiped the cheesy granules of sleep from the inner corners of her eyes. Her expression changed as she listened. 'How much?' she asked in disbelief, and crawled off the mattress to gather up her clothing, which was scattered across the floor. 'What ship is this *kerel* on?' she demanded, as she pulled her shift over her head and down over her wobbling white bosom. Hannah baulked at

194

the question. There were over twenty ships in the bay, and she had no idea which one her prey was on. Then her expression cleared. Henry Courtney was an English pirate, and there were only two English ships in the flotilla lying out there at anchor. He must be on one of them. 'You let me worry about that, *lieveling*,' she told the girl. 'All you have to do is find out if there is still a reward, and how we can collect it.'

The *Seraph* had been lying at anchor for fifteen days before the *Yeoman of York* finally beat into Table Bay against the south-easter and dropped anchor a cable's length astern of her. Edward Anderson had himself rowed across directly, and as he came up the ladder to the *Seraph*'s deck he greeted Hal. 'I hardly recognized you, Sir Henry. The *Seraph* looks like a different ship.'

'Then I have succeeded in my purpose.' Hal took him by the arm and led him to the companionway. 'What kept you so long?'

'Foul winds ever since we parted company. I was carried down within sight of the coast of Brazil,' Anderson grumbled. 'But I am pleased we are together again.'

'Not for long,' Hal assured him, as he waved him to a chair, and poured a glass of Canary wine for him. 'As soon as you have revictualled and refurbished the *Yeoman*, I am sending you on to Bombay alone, while I am going up the coast to seek out this Mussulman rover.'

'That was not what I expected,' Anderson spluttered into his wine, as he saw the chance of prize money snatched from him. 'I have a good fighting ship and a crew—'

'Perhaps too good,' Hal stopped him. 'From news that I have had since arriving here, it seems that our best chance of coming at Jangiri is to offer him a bait. Two fighting ships are likely to drive him off rather than suck him in.'

'Ah! So that's why you've changed your appearance?' Anderson asked.

Hal nodded, and went on, 'Besides which, there are passengers, urgent mail and cargo for Bombay. Mr Beatty is in lodgings in the town, waiting for you to convey him and his family to Bombay. The trade winds will not stand fair much longer before the season changes and the winds turn foul for a crossing of the Ocean of the Indies.'

Anderson sighed. 'I understand your reasoning, sir, though it is of scant comfort. I am loath indeed to part company with you again.'

'By the time you reach Bombay the monsoon wind will have changed. You will be able to discharge your cargo, and catch that wind to hasten your passage back across the Ocean of the Indies to the Fever Coast, where I will be waiting to rendezvous with you.'

'That will take several months, the round trip,' Anderson pointed out gloomily.

Hal was pleased that he showed this eager spirit. Other Company captains would have been delighted to avoid danger, and were well content with the peaceable life of a trader. He tried to mollify him. 'By the time we meet up again, I will have much better intelligence of Jangiri. By then I may have smelt out his lair. You can be certain that it will need both our forces to smoke him out, and that I will not attempt such an enterprise without the assistance of you and your crew, sir.'

Anderson brightened a little. 'Then I must make all haste to prepare myself for the next leg of the voyage to Bombay.' He drained his glass and stood up. 'I shall go ashore immediately to speak to Mr Beatty and have him prepare himself and his family to continue the voyage.'

'I shall send Daniel Fisher, my officer, ashore with you

to guide you to Mr Beatty's lodgings. I would go with you myself, but for various reasons that is not prudent.' He escorted Anderson up the companionway to the deck, and at the rail he told him, 'I shall have all the cargo and mail for Governor Aungier loaded into my pinnaces and sent across to you tomorrow. I intend to hoist anchor three days from now, and set out to begin the hunt for Jangiri.'

'My men will be standing by to receive your cargo. By the grace of God, I should be ready to sail myself within ten days, or less.'

'If you would give me the pleasure of being my guest at dinner tomorrow, we can use the opportunity to agree the details of our future plans.'

They shook hands, and Anderson seemed a great deal happier as he went down into the longboat, Big Daniel following him.

Hannah sat on the top of one of the tall sand dunes above the beach, from where she could look out to the flotilla anchored in the bay. Two others were with her: Annetjie and Jan Oliphant.

Jan Oliphant was Hannah's bastard son. His father was Xia Nka, a powerful Hottentot chief. Thirty years previously, while she still had her looks and golden hair, Hannah had accepted from him the gift of a beautiful *kaross*, made from the pelts of the red jackal, in exchange for a night of her favours. Liaisons between white women and coloured men were strictly forbidden by the VOC but Hannah had never paid heed to the silly laws made by seventeen old men in Amsterdam.

Although Jan Oliphant favoured his father in looks and skin colour, he was proud of his European ancestry. He spoke Dutch fluently, carried a sword and musket, and dressed like a burgher. He had earned the name Oliphant from his vocation. He was a famous elephant hunter, and a hard, dangerous man. By decree of the VOC none of the Dutch burghers was allowed to venture beyond the boundaries of the colony. By virtue of his Hottentot lineage, Jan Oliphant was not subject to these restrictions. He could come and go at will, free to range out into the trackless wilderness beyond the mountains, and return to sell the precious ivory tusks in the markets of the settlement.

His swarthy visage was horrifically mutilated, his nose twisted and his mouth riven through by the shining white scars that started in the thick woolly mat of his hair and ran down to his chin. His shattered jawbone had set askew, giving him a perpetual gaping grin. On one of his first ventures into the interior, while lying by his camp-fire, a hyena had crept up on his sleeping form, and seized a mouthful of his face in its massively powerful jaws.

Only a man of Jan Oliphant's formidable physique and strength could have survived such an attack. The beast had dragged him away into the darkness, dangling him beneath its chest, like a cat with a mouse. It had ignored the shouts and stones hurled by Jan's companions. Its long yellow fangs were sunk so deeply into his face that the bone of his jaw was crushed, and his mouth and nose were tightly sealed, so that he was unable to draw breath.

Jan had reached for the knife on his belt, and with the other hand groped under the beast's chest until he found the gap in its ribs through which he could feel the beating of its heart. He had placed the point of the knife carefully and then made a single, powerful upward stroke to kill the brute.

He crouched now on the dune between the two women, and his voice was distorted by the damaged nostrils and twisted jawbone. 'Mother, are you certain this is the same man?'

'My son, I never forget a face,' Hannah told him doggedly.

'Ten thousand guilders?' Jan Oliphant snorted with laughter. 'No man living or dead is worth that much.'

'It is true,' Annetjie cut in vehemently. 'The reward still stands. I have spoken to my sport at the castle. He says that the VOC will still pay the full amount.' She grinned avariciously. 'They will pay dead or alive, as long as we can prove that he is Henry Courtney.'

'Why don't they send the soldiers out to his ship and fetch him off?' Jan Oliphant wanted to know.

'If they arrest him, do you think they will give the reward to us?' Annetjie asked contemptuously. 'We have to catch him ourselves.'

'He may have sailed already,' Jan pointed out.

'No!' Hannah shook her head with certainty. 'No, my *lieveling*. No English ship has set sail from the anchorage in the last three days. Another has arrived, but none has sailed. Look!' She pointed out across the bay. 'There they are.'

The waters were flecked with white, curling waves, and the ships of the fleet danced a graceful minuet to the music of the wind, bowing and prancing at their moorings, with their banners and colours unfurling and waving in a shifting rainbow. Hannah knew the name of every one of them. She reeled them off, until she came to the two Englishmen that lay so far out in the bay that it was impossible to distinguish their colours.

'That's the *Seraph*, and the one further back, towards Robben Island, is the *Yeoman of York*.' She mutilated the names with her heavy accent, then shaded her eyes. 'There is a boat leaving the *Seraph*. Perhaps we are in luck, and our pirate is in it.'

'It will take nearly half an hour to reach the beach. We have plenty of time.' Jan Oliphant lay back in the sun, rubbed his bulging crotch expansively. 'I have a great itch here. Come, Annetjie, scratch it for me.'

She bridled coyly. 'You know it's against the Company

law for us white ladies to milk a pint from any of you black bastards.'

Jan Oliphant chortled. 'I won't report you to Governor van der Stel, though I hear he likes a slice of dark meat himself.' Jan Oliphant wiped the trickle of saliva that ran down his chin from between his twisted lips. 'My mother can stand guard for us.'

'I don't trust you, Jan Oliphant. You bilked me last time. Let me see your coin first,' Annetjie protested.

'I thought we were sweethearts, Annetjie.' He leaned over and squeezed one of her fat round tits. 'When we have the ten thousand guilders from the reward, I might even marry you.'

'Marry me?' She screeched with laughter. 'I wouldn't even walk in the street with you, you ugly monkey.'

He grinned at her. 'It's not walking in the street we are discussing.' He grabbed her around the waist and kissed her on the mouth. 'Come, my little pudding, we have plenty of time before the longboat reaches the beach.'

'Two guilders,' she insisted. 'That's my special price for all my best sweethearts.'

'Here's half a florin.' He pushed the coin into her cleavage.

She reached out and massaged his crotch, feeling it grow in her hand. 'One florin, or you can dip it in the ocean to cool it off.'

He snorted through his deformed nostrils and wiped the saliva from his chin as he scratched another coin from his purse. Annetjie took it from him, then tossed her head, throwing the wind-tangled mane of hair out of her face, and stood up. He picked her up in his arms and carried her down into the hollow between the dunes.

Hannah watched them with disinterest from her seat on the top of the dune. She was worrying about her share of the reward money. Jan Oliphant was her son, but she had no illusions that he would not cheat her if he had the

200

slightest opportunity. She would have to make certain that the reward money was placed in her own hands but, then, neither Annetjie nor Jan would trust her either. She puzzled over the dilemma as she watched Jan butting away at Annetjie, his belly slapping loudly against hers. He was snorting and exhorting himself to greater effort with loud cries. 'Yah! Yah! Like a hurricane! Like Leviathan spouting! Like the father of all elephants tearing down the forest! Yah! Here comes Jan Oliphant.' He let out a final bellow, slid off her and collapsed in a heap on the sand beside her.

Annetjie stood up, rearranged her skirts and looked down at him disdainfully. 'More like a goldfish blowing bubbles than a whale spouting,' she said, and scrambled back up the dune to sit beside Hannah again. The longboat from the *Seraph* was close in to the beach now, its oars flashing and dipping, riding the crest of one of the swells.

'Can you see the men in the stern?' Hannah asked eagerly.

Annetjie shaded her eyes with one hand. '*Ja*, two of them.'

'That one.' Hannah pointed out the figure in the stern sheets. 'He was with Henry Courtney that night. They are shipmates, I could tell that.'

A big man stood up and called an order to the rowers. In unison they shipped their long oars, and held them straight in the air, like the lances of a cavalry troop. The boat slid in over the sands, and came to rest high and dry.

'He *is* a big bastard,' Annetjie remarked.

'That's him for sure.'

They watched Big Daniel and Captain Anderson step out of the longboat, and strike out along the beach towards the settlement.

'I'll go down and talk to the boatmen,' Annetjie volunteered. 'I'll find out which ship our man is on and if he is truly the son of Franky the pirate.'

Hannah and Jan Oliphant watched her saunter along the water's edge towards the boat. The crew saw her coming and laughed and nudged each other, grinning expectantly.

'Annetjie will have to be the one who collects the reward money for us,' Hannah told her son.

'Ja! I was thinking the same thing. It's her boyfriend will be paying out.'

They watched the girl laughing and bantering with the sailors. Then she nodded and led one of them into a small grove of dark green milkwood trees above the beach.

'How much have you promised her as her share?' Jan Oliphant asked.

'Half.'

'Half?' He was shocked by such profligacy. 'That's too much.'

The first seaman emerged from among the trees, retying the length of rope that held up his breeches. His mates gave him an ironic cheer, and a second man jumped out of the boat and hurried into the grove, followed by a chorus of whistles and clapping.

'Ja, it's too much,' Hannah agreed. 'She's a greedy bitch. You watch, she will serve every last one of those English pigs.'

'Ja, she charged me two guilders. She is a greedy bitch. We will have to get rid of her.' Jan shrugged philosophically.

'You're right, my son. She deserves it. But only after she has picked up the reward money for us.'

They waited patiently in the warm sunlight, chatting idly, making plans to spend the great fortune that would soon be theirs, watching the procession of English seamen disappearing among the milkwood trees, and returning minutes later, sheepishly acknowledging the friendly jeers and hoots of their companions.

'I told you she would fix every last one of them,'

Hannah said, with prim disapproval, as the last sailor returned to the longboat. A few minutes later Annetjie emerged from among the trees, brushing grains of sand out of her hair and clothing. She struggled up to where Hannah and Jan Oliphant sat, with a smug expression on her chubby pink face. She flopped down beside Hannah.

'Well?' Hannah demanded.

'The captain of the English East Indiaman *Seraph* is Sir Henry Courtney,' Annetjie announced grandly.

'And you have the separate testimony of eight of his sailors to prove it,' said Hannah sarcastically.

Annetjie was unflustered, and went on, 'It seems that Henry Courtney is a rich English Milord. He owns great property in England.'

Jan Oliphant grinned. 'As a hostage he may be worth even more than ten thousand. Me and my bullies will be waiting here on the beach to meet him when he comes ashore.'

Hannah looked worried. 'Don't take chances by trying to hold him for ransom. He looks a slippery fish to me. Grab him, chop off his head and hand it over to the VOC. Take the reward and forget about the ransom.'

'Dead or alive?' Jan Oliphant asked Annetjie.

'*Ja*, that's what I said.'

'My mother is right. A dead fish will not slip through our fingers. A fish with its throat cut,' Jan mused.

'I will wait with you until he comes ashore. I will point him out to you and then it's up to you and your boys,' Hannah told her son.

'If he comes ashore a second time,' Annetjie reminded her spitefully, and Hannah began to worry again.

The cargo for Bombay had been taken out of the *Seraph* and ferried across to the *Yeoman*. The water-barrels had been scoured and refilled from the stream that meandered down from the slopes of Table Mountain. Stores of lamp-oil, salt, flour, biscuit and other dry goods, which had been depleted during the long voyage south, were replenished. Hal had retrimmed the ship to her best attitude for sailing. The crew were in good health and spirits, fat and happy on this diet of fresh fruit, vegetables and meat, and the twenty-six scurvy cases had recovered since Hal had sent them ashore to lodgings in the settlement. Now they came back aboard, cheerful and eager to continue the voyage.

'I will sail with the dawn tomorrow,' Hal told Captain Anderson of the *Yeoman*. 'Do you also make all speed to get to sea again?'

'Have no fear of that,' Anderson assured him. 'I will be waiting at the rendezvous on the first day of December.'

'And I will have good employment for you then,' Hal promised him. 'There is one last matter in which I must ask your assistance.'

'You have only to name it.'

'I am going ashore tonight to attend to some business of importance to me.'

'Pardon my impertinence, Sir Henry, but is that wise? As you have confided in me, and as I have myself ascertained by discreet enquiry to the Dutch authorities in the colony, they have unfinished business with you. If you fall into their hands, that will certainly redound to your disadvantage.'

'I am grateful for your concern, sir, but my business ashore cannot be neglected. When it is done, I shall have a small chest for you to convey to Bombay on my behalf.

From there I will be in your debt if you can consign it by the very next vessel leaving that port to my eldest son in Devon.'

'You may have complete confidence that I shall do so, Sir Henry.'

Tom and Dorian had watched the preparations for the shore expedition with mounting fascination. They had discussed it between themselves for several days. When Hal picked out the men who were to accompany him, and issued equipment and weapons to them, their curiosity overflowed.

Gathering their courage, the two crept down to their father's cabin when they knew he was safely closeted there with his officers. While Dorian played the cat on the companionway ladder, Tom sneaked to the door and listened at the panel. He could hear his father's voice.

'You, Mr Tyler, will have charge of the ship while I am ashore. We may be hard pressed by the Dutch, and in some haste when we return, so the boat crew waiting for us on the beach must be alert and well armed, ready to take us off at any instant. You must be ready to come to our assistance, Mr Tyler, and as soon as we are back on board to weigh anchor and set sail, even in the dark of night.'

Tom led Dorian back on deck. The two climbed into the rigging and sat side by side on the main yard. This was the place where they went when they wanted not to be overheard.

'It's tonight. I heard Father giving his orders. He's taking an armed raiding party ashore tonight,' Tom told his little brother. 'So now we know what the chest is for, don't we?'

'Do we?' Dorian asked doubtfully. They had watched a

working party under Big Daniel bring the mysterious chest up from the hold. It was the size of a small sea-chest, made of polished teak, beautifully dovetailed and joined, with a screw-down lid.

'Of course we know,' Tom said importantly. 'Father is going to fetch Grandfather's body from the place where Aboli hid it.'

Immediately Dorian was intrigued. 'Will he let us go with him?'

Tom lifted his cap and scratched his head dubiously.

Dorian persisted, 'You aren't afraid to ask him, are you, Tom?' He knew that challenge was the best way to get Tom to do what he wanted.

'Of course not,' Tom denied indignantly. Nevertheless, he had to screw his courage to the sticking point before he could bring himself to venture again to the stern cabin.

'You let me do the talking,' he whispered to Dorian, as he knocked at the door.

'Enter!' his father called brusquely, and then, as he saw who it was, 'Oh, it's you two, is it? However important your business, lads, I have no time to attend to it now. You will have to come back later. We will talk tomorrow.'

Caps in hand, but with dogged expressions, the pair stood their ground. Tom pointed at the polished teak chest that now reposed in the centre of the cabin deck. 'Dorian and I know that you are going to fetch Grandfather Francis tonight. That's the coffin you have brought from home for him.'

Hal was drawing the loads from the pair of pistols that lay on the desk in front of him, inserting the corkscrew down the barrels and pulling out the old ball, wad and powder charge to replace them. He looked up from the task, and studied their serious expressions. At last, he sighed. 'You have found me out,' he grunted. 'No point in denying it.'

'We want to come with you,' Tom said.

Hal looked up at him, startled, then dropped his eyes back to the pistol and went on with the loading. Deliberately he measured a charge of powder from the flask, poured it into the muzzle and rodded it home firmly. Then he took a cloth patch from the brass patch box and wrapped the half-ounce lead ball with it. This would make a perfect fit in the barrel. The pistol was a lovely weapon, built by George Truelock of London. The grip was of curlicue-grained walnut. 'Your wound is not yet healed, Tom,' he said, still without looking up.

'It's healed clean,' Tom protested, and touched his flank. 'It was naught but a scratch, even at its worst.'

Hal made a pretence of admiring the locks of the double-barrelled pistol. They were chased with a gold inlay, and the octagonal barrels were rifled. This would impart spin to the ball in flight and stabilize it to an accuracy that was unheard-of in smooth-bored weapons. If he trusted himself to hold true, Hal knew he could hit a target the size of his own thumbnail with every shot at twenty paces. He tapped the wrapped ball home with a small wooden mallet, then primed the pan. 'Even so, I don't think that yours is a very good idea,' he said.

'He was our grandfather. We are his family,' Tom insisted. 'It's our duty to be there with you.' He had chosen his words with care and rehearsed them. Family and duty were two concepts his father never took lightly. Now he reacted to them as Tom had hoped he would. He laid aside the loaded pistol, stood up and went to the stern window. For a while he remained there, hands clasped behind his back, staring out at the land. At last he spoke. 'Perhaps you're right, Tom. You are old enough, and you know how to take care of yourself in a fight.' He turned back to the pair.

Tom was exultant, his expression shining. 'Thank you, Father.'

Dorian was tense with expectation, watching his father's lips for his next utterance.

'But not you, Dorian. You're still too young.' Hal tried to soften the blow with a kindly smile. 'We don't want to lose you yet.'

Dorian seemed to crumble beneath the rejection. His expression was stricken, and his eyes welled. Tom nudged him sharply, and whispered out of the side of his mouth, 'Don't cry. Don't be a baby.'

Dorian gathered himself, and with huge effort fought back the tears. 'I'm not a baby.' He stood brave and tragic.

He's a beautiful boy, Hal thought, as he studied his son's face. Dorian's skin was gilded by the tropical sun, and his curls caught a ray of sunlight through the stern window and shimmered like spun copper. Hal was struck again by the child's resemblance to his mother. He felt his resolve waver.

'I'm not a baby. Give me a chance to prove it, please, Father.'

'Very well.' Hal could not resist him, though he knew it was unwise. 'You may come with us.'

Dorian's face was incandescent with joy, and Hal hastened to qualify his agreement. 'But only as far as the beach. You will wait for us there with Alf Wilson and the boat crew.' He held up one hand to forestall the protests he saw coming. 'That's enough. No argument. Tom, go to Big Daniel and tell him to issue you with pistol and cutlass.'

They went down into the longboat an hour before sunset. There were only four of them in the shore party: Hal, Aboli, Daniel Fisher and Tom. They each carried a tinderbox and a bull's-eye lantern. Under their dark boat cloaks they were armed with a cutlass and a brace of pistols apiece. Aboli had a large leather sack folded and tied around his waist.

As soon as they were settled on the thwarts, Alf

Wilson gave the order to cast off. The boat crew pulled on the long sweeps and they crept in towards the beach. In both bows and stern long-barrelled falconets were mounted, murderous small hand-cannon loaded with grapeshot. There were pikes and cutlasses laid on the deck, between the rowers' feet, ready to hand.

No one spoke, and the oars dipped and swung without a sound except the drip of sea-water from the blades. Alf Wilson had muffled the rowlocks. In the silence, Tom and Dorian exchanged excited grins; this was one of the adventures they had dreamed about and discussed with fevered anticipation so often during their long duties in the crow's nest. It had begun.

Hannah Maakenberg was lying in the grove of milkwoods above the beach. She had been there every daylight hour for the last three days, keeping watch on the distant silhouette of the *Seraph* as she rode at anchor. Three times she had seen boats coming from the English ship, and had watched them eagerly through the lens of the long brass telescope that Jan Oliphant had lent her. Each time she had been disappointed when Hal Courtney was not on board.

At last she was becoming discouraged. Perhaps Annetjie was right, perhaps he would not come ashore again. Her own son was rapidly losing interest in the hunt also. For the first two days he had been at her side, watching with her, but in the end he had given up hope and gone off to join his men in the drinking hells along the waterfront.

Now she watched the shape of the longboat coming from the *Seraph*, barely visible against the darkening waves. She could not contain her excitement. *He comes in the darkness, like he did last time, so that no one will recognize him.* She held the longboat in the round field of the lens. She watched its prow touch the beach and her heart leaped with excitement, then raced. There was merely a glimmering of light remaining in the western sky as the tall figure stepped from the longboat on to the white sand, and looked around the dunes and scattered bush with an alert turn of his head. For an instant he stared directly at Hannah's hiding-place and a fluke of the light struck his face, picking out his features unmistakably. Then the light faded and died away so that even through the glass the boat and its crew were just a dark blob at the edge of the white beach.

'It's him!' Hannah breathed. 'I knew he would come.' She strained her eyes as a small party of men detached itself from the dark shape of the boat. They picked their way through the heaps of white driftwood that were piled at the highwater mark, then came towards where she lay. She closed the telescope and shrank back against the bole of the nearest milkwood.

The men came on without speaking, until they were so close she thought she must be discovered. Then, without check, their boots crunching in the loose sand, they passed her by, so close she might have reached out and touched their legs. Looking up she saw Hal Courtney's face lit by the last of the sunset. Then the men passed on to disappear into the thick scrub, heading inland.

She gave them several minutes to get well clear then lurched to her feet and ran down the path leading to the town. Her heart was singing and she exulted aloud: 'I've got him now. I'm going to be rich. All that money! I'm going to be rich.'

I n single file, Aboli leading, they skirted the settlement, giving it a wide berth. They encountered no human being even when they crossed the road that ran along the base of the mountain towards Salt River and the scattered farms of Constantia. Once a dog must have scented them, for it burst into hysterical barking as they passed, but no one challenged them.

The slope of the mountain reared beneath their feet and they leaned forward against it. The bush became thicker, but Aboli seemed by instinct to find the narrow game paths, and led them upwards. The dense forest closed out the stars above them, and both Hal and Big Daniel stumbled occasionally. As Tom's eyes were young, his night vision was still sharp: he picked his way sure-footedly through the shadows. Aboli was a creature of the forests and moved silently as a panther ahead of them. Suddenly they came out on a bluff of bare rock high above the settlement.

'We will rest here,' Hal ordered. As he found a seat on one of the lichen-covered stones, Tom was amazed at how high they had climbed. The stars seemed very close, vast whorls of silvery light, bewildering in their infinite multitudes. Below them, the pinpricks of yellow candlelight in the windows of the buildings were insignificant against that splendid display.

Tom drank from the leather bottle Aboli handed him, but no one spoke. Yet the night was no longer silent. Small creatures scurried in the forest around them, and the night birds hooted and screeched. From down the slope came the hideous giggling chorus of a pack of hyenas scavenging the rubbish heaps and dung-hills of the Dutch settlement. It was a sound that made the hackles rise on the back of Tom's neck, and he had to resist the impulse to draw closer to Aboli's dark, protective bulk.

Suddenly a warm puff of wind struck him in the face, and he looked up at the night sky to see the stars blotted out swiftly as a heavy bank of cloud swept in from the sea.

'Storm coming,' Aboli grunted, and as he said it another gust swept over them on the exposed bluff. In contrast to the first it was icy cold, and Tom shivered and pulled his cloak tighter around his shoulders.

'We must hurry on,' Hal said, 'before the storm hits us.' Without another word they rose and went on into the night, which was dark with stormclouds and clamorous with wind. The trees thrashed and clattered their branches overhead.

As he stumbled along behind Aboli's tall figure, Tom began to doubt that anyone, even Aboli, could find his way through this dark night and darker forest to a secret place he had last visited twenty years ago.

At last, when it seemed that half the night had wasted away, Aboli stopped below a sheer cliff of splintered rock, whose summit was lost against the dark sky above them. Both Hal and Big Daniel were panting audibly from the long climb. Aboli was the oldest of them all, but he and Tom were the only ones still breathing easily.

Aboli knelt and placed his lantern on a flat rock in front of him. He opened the shutter and worked with the tinderbox. A shower of bright sparks flew from the flint and steel and he held the flaming tinder to the lamp wick. Holding the lantern high he moved along the foot of the cliff, shining the pale beam onto the lichen-painted rock.

A narrow cleft opened abruptly in the cliff face, and Aboli grunted with satisfaction. He moved into it – it was only just wide enough to accommodate his broad shoulders. A short distance in, the crack was choked with trailing lianas and dangling shrubs. Aboli hacked them away with his cutlass, then dropped to his knees when he reached the end of the cleft.

'Hold the lantern, Klebe.' He handed it to Tom. In its beam Tom saw that the end of the cleft was sealed with rocks and boulders. With his bare hands Aboli prised one free from the wall, and handed it back to Daniel. They worked in silence, gradually clearing the opening to a low, natural tunnel in the cliff. When it was open Aboli turned back to Hal. 'It is fitting that only you and Klebe should enter your father's resting place,' he said softly. 'Daniel and I will wait here.'

He unwound the leather sack from around his waist, and handed it to Hal, then stooped to light the wicks of the other lanterns. When he had finished he nodded to Daniel and both men moved away along the foot of the cliff, leaving Hal and Tom alone to complete their sacred duty. They stood in silence for a while, with the storm wind buffeting them and flapping their cloaks like vultures' wings. The light of the lanterns cast weird shadows on the rocky walls of the cliff.

'Come, lad.' Hal led Tom into the rock cleft, then went down on hands and knees to enter the dark mouth of the tunnel. Tom passed him the lantern and followed. The sounds of the storm faded behind them, and suddenly the tunnel opened into a cavern. Hal rose to his feet, the rock roof hanging only inches above his head.

Tom stood up beside him and blinked in the yellow light of the lantern. He found himself in a tomb that smelt of the dusts of antiquity, and he was struck with a religious awe that stifled his breathing and made his hand tremble.

At the far end of the cavern there was a natural stone platform. A gaunt human figure squatted upon it, staring directly at him with huge empty eye-sockets. Tom recoiled from it instinctively, and choked back the sob that rose in his throat.

'Steady, lad.' Hal reached out and took his hand. He led him step by step towards the seated figure. The wavering lantern light disclosed the details as they drew nearer. The head was a skull.

Tom knew that the Dutch had beheaded his grandfather, but Aboli must have replaced his head upon his shoulders. Fragments of dried skin still hung on the bone like the dead bark of a fever-tree trunk. Long dark hair hung down the back of the bony head, lovingly dressed and combed.

Tom quailed, for his grandfather's empty eyes seemed to be looking deep into his soul. He drew back once more, but his father held his hand firmly, and chided him gently. 'He was a good man. A brave man with a great heart. There is no reason for you to fear him.'

The body was bound in the skin of a beast, a pelt of black hair, which the bacon beetles had gnawed off in patches, giving it a leprous look. Hal knew that the executioner had quartered his grandfather's body, crudely hacking it into pieces on the scaffold with a cleaver. Aboli had tenderly assembled those parts and bound them up in the hide of a freshly killed buffalo. On the floor below the stone platform were the remains of a small ritual fire, a circle of ash and black charcoal sticks.

'We will pray together,' Hal said softly, and drew Tom down beside him on the stone floor of the cavern.

'Our Father, which art in heaven . . .' Hal began, and Tom clasped his hands before his eyes and joined in the recital, his voice growing more confident as the familiar words rolled off his tongue. '. . . Thy will be done, on earth, as it is in heaven.'

While Tom prayed he scrutinized, from between his fingers, the array of strange objects that had been laid out on the rock platform, grave offerings that he realized Aboli must have placed there all those years ago when he had laid Grandfather's body to rest.

There was a wooden crucifix, set with abalone shell, and bone and water-worn pebbles that shone softly in the lantern light. There was a crudely fashioned model of a three-masted ship, with the name *Lady Edwina* carved into her transom, then a wooden bow and a knife. Tom realized that these were symbols of the forces that had dominated his grandfather's life. The one true God, a tall ship, and the weapons of a warrior. Aboli had chosen his last gifts with love and perception.

When they had finished the prayer they were silent for a while, then Hal opened his eyes and lifted his head. He spoke quietly to the skeletal skin-bound figure on the platform above them. 'Father, I have come to take you home to High Weald.'

He laid out the sack on the platform. 'Hold its mouth open,' he ordered Tom, then knelt over the body of his father and lifted it in his arms. It was surprisingly light. The dry skin crackled and small tufts of hair and flakes of skin fell away. After all this time, there was no odour of putrefaction, just the scent of fungus and dust.

He slid the hunched body into the sack, feet first, until only the ancient, ravaged head remained exposed. He paused to stroke the long black tresses of hair, shot through with strands of silver. Watching that gesture Tom was struck with the love and respect it demonstrated.

'You loved him,' he said.

Hal looked up. 'If you had known him, you would have loved him also.'

'I know how much I love you,' Tom replied, 'so I can guess.'

Hal slipped one arm around his son's shoulders and hugged him briefly but hard. 'Pray God you never have to perform such an onerous duty for me,' he said, then pulled the sack over Francis Courtney's head and secured the leather laces tightly. He stood up. 'We must go now, Tom, before the storm reaches its height.' He lifted the sack carefully and swung it over his shoulder, then stooped to the entrance tunnel of the cave.

Aboli was waiting for them outside the cavern, and he made as if to relieve Hal of his burden, but Hal shook his head. 'I will carry him, Aboli. Do you lead us down this mountain.'

The descent was more hazardous than the climb had been. In the darkness and the roaring wind, it would have been easy to miss the path, and step out over a precipice, or stumble on one of the treacherous scree slopes and break a leg, but Aboli led them unerringly through the night, until Tom felt the gradient ease, and the rock and rolling pebbles under his feet give way to firm soil then to crunching beach sand.

A bolt of vivid blue lightning tore open the clouds and, for an instant, turned the night to brilliant noonday. In that moment they saw the sweep of the bay before them, its surface churned to confusion by the gale, boiling and foaming, leaping and spouting white. Then the blackness closed over them again and the thunder crashed down in an avalanche of sound that numbed their eardrums.

'The longboat is still there.' Hal shouted his relief above the wind. The stark, fleeting image of the boat was imprinted upon his vision. 'Hail them, Aboli!'

'*Seraph*!' Aboli bellowed into the night, and heard the reply faint upon the storm.

'Ahoy!' It was Alf Wilson's voice, and they started down the dunes towards it. Hal's burden, which had weighed so lightly at the beginning of the descent, now bowed him over, but he refused to relinquish it. They reached the foot of the dunes in a close group. Aboli opened the shutter of the lantern and shone the feeble yellow beam ahead.

'On guard!' he shouted a desperate warning, as he saw in the light that they were surrounded by the dark figures of men or beasts, he could not be certain which. 'Defend yourselves!' he cried, and they threw open their cloaks and drew their blades, instinctively forming a ring, back to back, facing outwards, the points of their levelled weapons forming a circle of steel.

Then lightning broke over them again, a blinding bolt that split the low clouds, lit the beach and the gale-beaten waters. In its light they saw a phalanx of menacing shapes charging down upon them. The lightning flashed on the naked blades they wielded, on the clubs and spears they brandished, and for a moment it revealed their faces. They were all Hottentots, not a Dutch face among them.

Tom felt a rush of superstitious dread as he saw the man coming at him. He was as hideous as a thing from a nightmare. Long tresses of black hair writhed in the wind, like serpents, about the terrible face, a livid scar slashed through the bloated nose and purple lips, the mouth was twisted and deformed, drooling saliva, and the eyes flashed fiercely as the creature rushed at him.

Then the darkness closed over them all again, but Tom had seen the man's sword raised over his head, and he anticipated the stroke, twisting aside his shoulders and ducking under it. He heard the blade hiss past his ear, and the explosive grunt of the effort his attacker put into the blow.

All Aboli's training came to the fore. Tom went smoothly on the riposte, lunging for the sound of the man's breathing, and felt his blade sink into living flesh, a sensation he had never experienced before, which startled him. His victim shouted with pain, and Tom felt a surge of savage joy. He recoiled and shifted his feet, quick as a cat, and lunged blindly again. Once more he felt the hit, the soggy slide of steel into flesh, then the clash as the point struck bone. The man squealed, and for the first time in his life Tom rode the wild exhilaration of battle lust.

The lightning flamed across the heavens, and Tom saw his victim reel away, his sword dropped into the sand.

217

He was clutching at his deformed face. His cheek was laid open to the bone, and the blood was black as tar in the blue light, pouring in a sheet down his chin and splashing over his chest.

Tom saw in the same flash of lightning that both his father and Aboli had killed: their victims were down, one kicking and convulsing in the sand, the other curled into a ball clutching his wound with both hands, his mouth open in a silent cry of agony.

Big Daniel was engaged, blade to blade with a tall, sinewy figure naked to the waist, body black and shiny as an eel-skin. But the rest of the attackers were backing away, repulsed by the vigour of the little knot of defenders.

Darkness shut down over them like the slamming of a door, and Tom felt Aboli's fingers close on his upper arm, his voice close to his ear: 'Back to the boat, Klebe. Keep together.' They ran blindly through the soft sand, bumping into each other.

'Is Tom with us?' His father's voice was harsh with concern for him.

'Here, Father!' he shouted.

'Thank God! Danny?'

'Here!' Big Daniel must have killed his man, for his voice was close and clear.

'*Seraph!*' Hal bellowed. 'On me!'

'*Seraph!*' Alf's voice acknowledged the order, and the lightning flared again to reveal it all. The four of them were still a hundred paces from where the longboat lay at the edge of the roaring sea. Led by Alf, the eight men waiting with it were running to join the fight, brandishing their pikes, cutlasses and boarding axes. But the pack of Hottentots had rallied and like hunting dogs were baying at their heels.

Tom glanced over his shoulder and saw the man that he had wounded had recovered and was charging along at

218

the head of them. Though his face was a mask of blood he was slashing the air with his sword, and screeching a war-cry in a strange language. He had singled out Tom, and was rushing directly at him.

Tom tried to estimate how many there were. Perhaps nine or ten, he guessed, but the darkness closed down again before he could be sure. His father and Alf Wilson were shouting to keep contact with each other, and now the two groups came together. Immediately Hal called, 'Meet them! Skirmish line!'

Even in darkness they smoothly executed the man-oeuvre they had practised so often on the *Seraph*'s deck. Shoulder to shoulder they stood to meet the attack, which burst into them like a wave out of the night. There was the clatter and clash of metal on metal and the shouts and curses of men struggling together. Then the lightning flared again.

Hannah staggered to the edge of the milkwood grove with fifteen men. The night had been too long for them, the fury of the storm debilitating, and the boredom of the ambush had overcome them. They had crept away into the grove to find a spot out of the wind in which to curl up and sleep. Then the shouting and the sounds of battle had roused them. They had seized their weapons and now poured out from among the trees.

The lightning revealed the struggling, evenly matched men, close to the water's edge where the empty longboat lay. In the same flash, Hannah saw Henry Courtney clearly. He was in the first rank of the fight, his face turned towards her, his cutlass lifted high in his right hand then slashing down at the head of one of the Hottentots.

'*Dis hom!*' Hannah screeched. 'It's him! Ten thousand guilders for the picking. *Kom kerels!* Come, lads!' She waved the pitchfork with which she was armed, and charged down the dune. The men, who had hesitated at the edge of the grove, were galvanized by her example. Now they raced down behind her, a howling, shrieking mob.

Dorian was alone in the longboat. He had been curled up asleep on the floorboards when the fighting started, but now he crawled to the bows and knelt behind the falconet. He was wide-eyed with sleep, but in the lightning he had seen Tom and his father beset by the enemy, and the new threat rushing down upon them from out of the dunes.

During battle practice on the *Seraph*, Aboli had shown Tom how to swing and aim the falconet in its swivel seating, and how to fire it. Dorian had watched avidly and begged for a chance to try it. As always, he had been met with the infuriating answer, 'You are too small. When you are older.'

Now was the chance he had been denied, and Tom and his father needed him. He reached for the length of burning match in the tub of sand below the gun. Alf Wilson had lit it and placed it at hand for just such an emergency. He took it in one hand, seized the long monkey-tail of the falconet with the other and swivelled it in the direction of the screams and shouts of the mob charging down the dunes. He looked over the barrel but could not see the sights of the gun, nor any glimpse of his target in the darkness.

Then the thunder crashed directly overhead, and the beach was lit brilliantly by the lightning. Directly under his barrel Dorian saw them coming, led by a witch from mythology, a terrible female creature waving a pitchfork, long grey hair streaming out behind her, her white dugs swinging and flopping out of the bodice of her gown, a face ravaged by age and debauchery, screaming. Dorian pressed the burning match to the touchhole of the falconet.

Twenty feet of flame shot from its muzzle, and a bucketful of grapeshot, each ball the size of a man's eye, was hurled down the beach. The range was just sufficient for the blast to reach its optimum spread. Hannah caught the full brunt of it: a dozen lead balls shattered her chest, and one struck her in the centre of the forehead, taking the top off her skull like the shell off an egg. She was flung backwards into the white sand with another six of her troop down around her. The rest staggered with the shock and disruption of the air around them. Three of those still on their feet howled with terror and fled back towards the protection of the grove. The others were stunned, and milled in confusion, stumbling over their dead companions, some bleeding from their wounds, uncertain which way to turn.

The burning wad from the falconet was blown into the long windrow of dry driftwood at the top of the beach. The flames took hold swiftly and, fanned by the wind, burned brightly, showering blue sparks from the salt crystals, which lit the beach with a wavering, flickering light.

The fight swung back and around. Although they had reduced the odds against them with pike and blade, Hal's men were still heavily outnumbered. Hal had three men against him, circling him like a pack of hyena harassing a black-maned lion. He was fighting for his life and could not even glance in the direction of his son.

Jan Oliphant was intent on his revenge for the gaping slash across his cheek, and he went after Tom, swearing and shouting his rage, using only the edge of his sabre with wild cuts and overhead slashes. Tom gave ground before him, outmatched in height, reach and strength by the burly Hottentot. For these fatal seconds Tom was on his own: he could count on no help from Aboli or Daniel, or even his

221

father. His manhood would have its full flowering this night, or he would die on these blood-soaked sands. He was afraid, but not unmanned by his fear. Rather, it gave power to his wrist and sword arm. He found something within him that he had not known was there until this moment.

He fell naturally into the rhythmic fighting grace that Aboli had instilled into him through all these years of training. Now that the flames from the burning driftwood were lighting the beach, he found his confidence growing. He felt the steel in his arm, as he realized that the brute he faced was a brawler and not a swordsman, although the power in his swinging blade was enormous – it was as irresistible as a landslide. Tom did not make the mistake of trying to match it. Instead, he anticipated each wild, hacking stroke before it was launched. There was no subtlety in the way Jan Oliphant signalled his intention with his glaring eyes and contorted blood-smeared face, or in how he moved his feet and opened his shoulders to make the stroke.

As it came whistling down at Tom's head, he reached out and touched it with his own blade, never attempting to stop it in the air, lightly deflecting it, so that it flew harmlessly an inch past his head. Each time Tom did this Jan Oliphant's rage swelled until it overwhelmed him. He held his sword high above his head with both hands and rushed straight at Tom, roaring like a bull seal in the rut. He made no attempt to cover himself from any counter-stroke, and his body was wide open.

Hal winged one of his antagonists, hitting him high in the right shoulder with his riposte. The man screamed and reeled back, dropping his sword, clutching at his wound. The other two Hottentots fighting on each side of him lost heart and dropped back. Hal had an instant of respite to glance around in the flickering light of the flames.

His heart froze in his chest as he saw Tom stand full in the path of the towering Hottentot captain. They were too far for Hal to intervene before Jan Oliphant charged home. A shout of warning and despair rose in his throat, but he choked it back. It would have served only to distract Tom.

Tom was as pale as the sand beneath his feet, but his face was set and hard with determination, his eyes bright and intent, no glimmer of fear in them as he sighted over the weaving point of his sabre. Hal expected him to drop back before the charge of the huge beast of a man bearing down on him. The set of his shoulders and the balance of his slim body signalled just that intention. But suddenly his left foot swung forward and he launched himself en flèche, like an arrow from a bow, straight at Jan Oliphant's throat. The big man had no time to bring down his guard or turn aside from the thrust. Tom's point caught him precisely in the hollow at the base of his neck, an inch above where his collarbones met. It flew deep, a handspan through Jan Oliphant's throat, found the juncture of two vertebrae in his spine and severed them cleanly. The steel drove on until, smeared pink with blood in the firelight, it sprang out a foot from the nape.

The raised sword fell from Jan Oliphant's nerveless fingers, and his limbs flew wide, for a moment forming a dark crucifix against the flames. Then he fell backwards, hitting the sand with all his slack, lifeless weight. Tom's blade jerked free, plucked from the dead man's throat by his own weight and momentum, and the air from Jan Oliphant's lungs was driven out through his punctured windpipe in an explosive sigh by the force of his fall. It burst from the wound in his throat in a tall pink feather of froth.

There was a long moment when every man on the beach froze, and stared at the grotesque corpse. Then one of the Hottentots facing Hal wailed with despair, turned and fled up the dunes. In an instant the others were racing after him in panic, leaving their dead and wounded where they had fallen.

Tom was still staring down at the man he had killed. His face crumpled and he started to shake with shock and the release of fear and rage. Hal went to him immediately and placed an arm around his shoulders. 'Well fought, lad,' he said, and hugged him.

'I killed him!' Tom whispered, in tones of disbelief.

'Before he killed you,' Hal told him. He looked around at his men scattered along the beach.

'Which of you fired the falconet?' he shouted against the wind. 'That saved us all.'

'Not me.'

'Nor me.'

All heads turned towards the longboat, and they stared at the small figure in the bows.

'Not you, Dorian?' Hal asked, in wonder.

'Yes, Father.' Dorian held up the smoking slow-match in his hand.

'Two cubs of the old lion,' said Aboli softly. 'But now we should go, before the garrison from the castle comes to that cannon and the fire.' He gestured at the piles of burning driftwood.

'Did we lose anyone?' Hal shouted.

'I saw Dick Foster go down,' Alf Wilson shouted back,

and went to kneel beside the body. There was a fearsome wound in the chest. Alf felt for the carotid artery in the man's throat beside his windpipe. 'He's gone.'

'Any others?' Hal asked.

'No, only the one,' Alf replied.

Hal felt a lift of relief. It could have been much worse – he could have lost a son, or a dear friend. 'Right, then. Get Dick into the boat. We'll give him a Christian burial when we get to sea.' He picked up the leather sack that held his father's remains.

'What shall we do with this trash?' Big Daniel kicked one of wounded Hottentots, and the man groaned. 'We should slit their throats.'

'Leave them. Don't waste time.' Hal looked around and saw that half of his crew had shallow cuts and sword nicks, but none had bothered to remark on it. This was the first time he had seen them fight. They're a good hard crew indeed, he thought, with satisfaction. They will give good account against Jangiri, or any other foe.

'Back to the boat!' he ordered, and four men picked up Dick Foster's body, handling it with respect, and laid it on the floorboards. Hal placed the leather bag beside it, then jumped over the stern to take his place at the tiller. The men seized hold of the boat and ran it down over the sands as easily as if it were a coracle. The bows were thrown high by the first wave and they leaped aboard and seized the oars.

'Heave away!' Hal shouted, and the next storm-driven wave crashed over the bows, tumbling aboard so that they were flooded knee-deep.

'Heave!' Hal exhorted them, and they shot forward, climbing at an impossible angle up the steep slope of the next wave. They reached the crest and hovered a moment on the very brink of capsizing end over end, then dropped forward and hit the trough with a crash.

'Heave!' Hal roared, and they shot out into the clear

where the waves were tall but not steep enough to up-end them. Half the men set aside their oars and began to bail her out, while the others rowed hard for the distant *Seraph*.

'Dorian!' Hal called the boy to him. 'Sit by me.' He spread the wing of his cloak over his son and under its cover hugged him close. 'How did you learn to fire the falconet?'

'Tom showed me,' Dorian said uncertainly. 'Did I do wrong?'

'You did well.' Hal hugged him harder. 'God knows, you could not have done better.'

Hal carried the leather sack into the stern cabin. The two boys followed him, sea-water pouring from their clothing onto the deck. The *Seraph* plunged and rolled at her anchor cables as the storm lashed her mercilessly.

Hal laid the sack and its precious burden on the deck beside the coffin. The screws that held down the lid were already loosened and it took only a few turns to free them. Hal lifted the lid and laid it aside. Carefully he placed the leather sack in the chest. He had to turn and angle it to get it to fit, then he packed raw oakum around his father's corpse, to prevent the fragile bones being shaken and broken during the long voyage ahead. Tom helped him replace the lid. He took the turn-screw from his father's hands. 'Let me have the honour, Father.'

'You have earned it,' Hal agreed. 'Both of you. Let Dorian help you.'

He handed the younger boy another turn-screw from the tool chest, and watched them secure the coffin lid.

'We will give your grandfather a ¯Christian service when we lay him in the stone sarcophagus in the crypt at High Weald that I prepared for him twenty years ago,' he told them, and wondered if all his sons would be together on that day. He put the gloomy doubt from his mind, as he watched them finish the task. 'Thank you,' he said simply, when they had finished. 'Go and change into dry clothes. Then see if, in this foul weather, the cook still has a fire burning in his galley and can give you something hot to eat and drink.'

At the door he stopped Dorian. 'We can never call you a baby again,' he said. 'You proved tonight that you are a man in everything but size. You saved all our lives.' Dorian's smile was so radiant, and even with his sea-wet locks dangling in his face he looked so beautiful, that it twisted Hal's heart.

Soon he heard the two brothers chattering away in the tiny cabin beside his, which had been vacated by the Beatty daughters, then their running footsteps in the passageway as they went off to importune the cook.

Hal lit two candles and placed them on the lid of his father's coffin. Then he knelt on the deck in front of it and began the long vigil. Sometimes he prayed aloud, for the peace of his father's soul and the forgiveness of his sins. Once or twice he spoke quietly to him, remembering incidents from their life together, reliving the frightful agony of Sir Francis's death. Though the night was long, and he was exhausted and cold, his vigil ended only when the dawn light, grey with the storm, crept through the stern windows. Then he roused himself and went on deck.

'Good morrow, Mr Tyler. Call both watches to get the ship under way,' he bellowed above the wind. The watch came tumbling up on the heaving deck. The forecastlemen manned the capstan and the pawls clanked as they recovered her anchor cable. In the meantime the topmen poured into the rigging and manned the yards.

Hal ordered the foresail spread for a moment to give the ship way to break out the anchor flukes from the sandy bottom, then furled the sail again as she came up hard. He listened to the capstan pawls: clank, then clank again, silence for a long moment, then clank and clank, coming faster until it became a rattling chorus as the anchor broke out and the cable slithered in through the hawsehole.

'Head sails!' Hal roared, and as they broke out the storm snatched them drum-tight. The *Seraph* quivered eagerly, and as Hal ordered the helm put over she spun on her heel and frolicked away. The men in the rigging let out a spontaneous cheer. A moment later Tom's voice hailed from the masthead, 'On deck there! A boat!'

'Where away?' Hal shouted back.

'Putting out from the beach. Now there are two of them – no, three!'

Hal crossed to the lee rail, and raised his telescope. The sea was dreary grey, flecked with whitecaps. Low cloud scudded across the sky and obscured the mountain-top. He picked out the three longboats battling the wind and the tide, throwing bursts of spray over their bows, heading towards the *Seraph*.

'Visitors, Captain,' said Ned at his elbow.

Hal grunted and focused his telescope. He could pick out the Dutch uniforms and the glint of bayonets. 'I do not think they have anything to tell us that we want to hear, Mr Tyler.' He shut it with a snap. Clearly, they were troops from the castle. Last night's fracas on the beach had stirred them up. He turned his back on the distant flotilla and smiled as he gave the next order. 'Lay the ship on a course to pass the *Yeoman of York* close to leeward, if you please, Mr Tyler.'

Half a cable's length from the *Yeoman*, the *Seraph* hove to, and launched the longboat. The teak chest was lowered into her as she danced alongside, then Hal dropped down the ladder and took the tiller before he gave the order to pull across to the anchored *Yeoman*. Anderson was at the rail, and Hal stood in the stern sheets and hailed him. 'I have the cargo for you.'

'I'm ready to receive it,' Anderson shouted back, and his crew lowered a tackle from the main yard. The longboat crept in under it and, working swiftly and deftly, they secured the teak chest to it.

'Hoist away!' Hal called, and his father's coffin was raised and swung in onto the *Yeoman*'s deck.

'I am greatly obliged to you, sir,' Hal cried to the deck high above.

'My great pleasure, sir,' Anderson answered. 'I wish you a fair wind.' He touched the brim of his cocked hat in salute.

'Until we meet again,' Hal said.

Then Guy's head appeared at the rail. He looked pale, as if the first throes of seasickness had already overtaken him. Nevertheless, he smiled bravely and waved his cap over his head. 'Farewell, Father, until we meet in Bombay.'

'Farewell and farewell,' Hal replied, and felt a sharp pang of sorrow at this parting. Would that our fates had treated us all more kindly, he thought, but he smiled encouragingly at Guy, trying to convey a message of love and hope to him, until he was forced to give his whole attention to bringing the longboat back alongside the *Seraph*.

Although the whipping pendulum action of the *Seraph*'s foremast in this wind and sea had made the climb both hazardous and frightening, Tom and Dorian were at last secure in the crow's nest. They could look down from there onto the *Yeoman*'s deck as they passed the anchored ship so closely that they could clearly make out the expressions of the passengers and crew looking up at them.

'There's Guy!' Dorian whipped off his cap to wave at his brother. 'Guy! Ahoy there, Guy!'

Guy raised his head and looked up at them. But his hands remained clasped behind his back, and no smile relieved the severity of his expression.

'Why does he not answer me?' Dorian asked plaintively. 'I have not given him offence.'

'Don't trouble yourself, Dorry. It's not you he hates, it's me,' Tom said quietly, and returned his twin's cold glare.

Behind Guy, the Beatty family stood in a small group together. With him, they had come on board the *Yeoman* days before from their lodgings in the settlement, ready for the sailing of the ship to Bombay. Caroline stood a few paces separated from the rest of her family, and Tom picked her out. She made a pretty picture in these surroundings, her skirts and petticoats rippling and flirting in the wind, holding her bonnet on with one hand, her curls dancing on cheeks pink from the wind's touch, eyes sparkling as she looked across at the other tall ship.

'Caroline!' Tom yelled. 'Up here! Ahoy!' The devil was in him, and he called her more to infuriate his twin than for any other reason. Caroline raised her eyes and saw him high in the crow's nest. She did a little impromptu dance of excitement, and waved with her free hand.

'Tom!' The wind whipped her voice away, but Tom's sharp eyes could read her lips. 'God speed!'

Guy spun round when he heard her voice, then strode across the deck and stood close by her side. He did not touch her, but his posture was possessive and belligerent as he stared across at his brother.

The *Seraph* broke out more sail, and she heeled sharply and flew away on the wind. The figures on the *Yeoman*'s deck dwindled in size and then were lost to sight. From the crow's nest they stared back at the other ship until she was a distant shape on the horizon, almost lost beneath the dark mountain and the towering ranges of sullen, bruised cloud.

'Now it's just you and me,' Dorian said sadly.

Tom did not answer. He could think of nothing to say.

'You won't ever forget the oath you swore to me?' Dorian insisted. 'You won't ever leave me?'

'I won't forget it,' Tom said.

'It was a dreadful oath,' Dorian reminded him. 'The very strongest kind.'

'I know,' said Tom, and repeated, 'I won't forget it.' He rubbed the tiny white scar at the end of his thumb.

After leaving Table Bay the *Seraph* was twenty-three days without glimpse of land or the sun. They ran into torrential downpours of rain, so copious that it seemed the very ocean had been upended and was crashing down on the deck. The rains lasted days and nights without cessation. In such conditions, even Hal's navigation was sketchy and without substance, relying entirely on the traverse board and dead reckoning of each day's run.

'This is usually a placid, sunny ocean,' Aboli remarked, looking up at the tumbling clouds low overhead. 'The sea devils have turned it on its head.'

'There is some great disturbance out there in the east,' Ned Tyler agreed. 'The wind turns over us like a wheel, always altering the direction of its thrust.'

'We have met these winds before,' Big Daniel reminded them. 'They spin around like a child's top. I have heard that they are not uncommon in these latitudes at this season of the year. But we are not at the centre—' He broke off as a mountainous swell even taller than all the others marched down upon the ship with ponderous dignity. It was so high as to dwarf the *Seraph* and its crest reached above her foretop yard. The yawning trough between this one and the swell that had preceded it was over a league wide.

Hal left his position by the lee rail and crossed quickly to the helm. 'Bring her up two points,' he ordered quietly. 'Meet her!' he said. As the wave crashed down, they wallowed in the trough for a long moment. The men around the wheel held their breath, then released it together as the *Seraph* kicked up her head.

'Mr Fisher is right.' Hal nodded at him. 'These storms spread out from their centre for hundreds of sea miles. They will sweep the entire ocean from end to end. But give thanks to God that we are not at the centre of this one. The strength of the wind there could probably rip out the main mast, though we flew not a scrap of canvas upon her.'

Big Daniel spoke again. 'In the Mascarene Islands I have seen one of these devil winds tear out the largest palm tree by its roots and carry it a mile out to sea, flying as though it were a kite.'

'Pray for a sight of the sun,' Ned Tyler looked up at the looming overcast sky, 'that we might at last be able to fix our latitude.'

'I have given us a wide berth of the land.' Hal glanced at the binnacle, then looked into the west. 'We should be at least two hundred miles clear of the African mainland.'

'But Madagascar is one of the largest islands in the world, almost ten times the size of Ireland, and it lies right across our path,' Ned pointed out quietly, so that the helmsman could not hear him. There was nothing to be gained in alarming the crew by discussing the hazards of navigation in their hearing.

At that moment there came a hail from the masthead. 'Deck! Flotsam! Fine on the port bow!'

The group of officers peered ahead, and Hal shouted, through the hailing trumpet, 'Masthead! What do you make of it?'

'Looks like the spar of a ship, or the—' The lookout broke off, then went on excitedly, 'No! It's a small boat, but almost swamped. There are men in her.'

Hal hurried up to the bows, and jumped onto the bowsprit. 'Yes, by God,' he said. 'Castaways, by the look of them. Alive too – I can see one of them moving. Stand by to launch a boat and pick them up.'

Bringing the *Seraph* down on the small boat was difficult, dangerous work in these conditions of sea and wind, but at last Hal could lower a boat and send Big Daniel and a crew to the rescue. There were only two men in the battered craft, which Big Daniel abandoned, for it was not worth the labour of salvaging it. They brought the two survivors up in a boatswain's chair, for they were far too weak to climb the ladder.

Dr Reynolds was there to meet them, and he examined them as they lay on the deck. They were both only semi-conscious. The salt had flayed the skin off their faces. Their eyes were swollen almost shut, and their tongues were blue and bloated from thirst so that they filled their mouths and protruded between their lips. 'Water is their first need,' he grunted. 'Then I will bleed them both.'

Their tongues were so swollen that they could not drink, so Reynolds introduced a brass syringe into the back of their throats and squeezed sweet water into them. Then he smeared mutton grease thickly over their salt-scalded lips, faces and arms. The effect on the younger of the two was miraculous: within two hours he had recovered sufficiently to be able to speak lucidly. However, the older man was still unconscious and seemed to be sinking fast. At Dr Reynolds's summons, Hal went down to the corner of the gundeck where they were lying on straw pallets. He squatted beside them and watched the surgeon bleed the younger patient. 'I should take another pint,' he told Hal as he finished, 'but this one is rallying strongly, and I have always been a conservative physician. One pint will do for now.' He closed the wound with a dab of tar and bound it up with a clean cloth. 'The older man is not faring as well. I shall take two pints from him.' He began work on the still figure on the other pallet.

Hal observed that the younger man indeed seemed brighter after this treatment, and leaned over him to ask, 'Do you speak English?'

'Aye, Captain. That I do,' the sailor whispered. The Welsh lilt was unmistakable.

'What is your name, lad, and what ship?'

'Taffy Evans, begging your pardon, Captain. From off the Company's ship *Nile*, God have mercy on her.'

Slowly and gently Hal drew his story out of him. As a precaution against piracy, the *Nile* had been sailing in a convoy with two other ships, outward-bound from Bombay to England, with a cargo of cloth and spices, when they had run full into this terrible cyclonic storm a hundred leagues north of the Mascarene Islands. Battered by the ferocious winds and gigantic seas, the *Nile* had become separated from the other ships of the convoy and taken on water. On the fifth day, during the second dog-watch, she had been hit by a monstrous swell. Heavy with the water in her bilges she had capsized and gone under. So swift had been her end that only a handful of men had got away in a boat, but they had neither water nor food with them and most had perished swiftly. After twelve days only the two remained alive.

While he was talking, Dr Reynolds had bled two pints from the other patient. He had just sent away his assistant to empty the blood-filled bowl overside, when he exclaimed, with chagrin, 'Devil take it, the poor wretch is dead. I had hoped to save him.' He turned his full attention back to Taffy Evans. 'I think we will get this one through, though.'

'When you are fully recovered there will be a berth for

you on full pay, and with a share of the prize money.' Hal stooped under the low deck. 'Will you sign the watch-bill?'

Taffy touched his forehead with a weak grin. 'Right gladly, Captain. I owe you a life.'

'Welcome aboard, sailor.' Hal ran up the ladder to the deck, and paced easily against the heavy roll and pitch of the ship. Finding these castaways had been fortuitous, as was the storm that was now gradually dissipating its power. They gave him the excuse for which he had been seeking. When he had the details of his plan firmly in mind, he called his officers down to his cabin. They gathered around the chart spread on his writing-desk.

'All of you know that for two hundred years the centre of all trade and commerce on the Fever Coast has been here,' he said, and touched the tiny cluster of islands marked on the chart. 'Zanzibar. Logically that is where our search for Jangiri must begin.'

They nodded in agreement. Every one of them had sailed this ocean before and they knew well how the three small islands of the Zanzibar group were situated ideally for India, the Red Sea and the Persian Gulf, and only a few leagues off the African mainland. The islands lay full in the track of the monsoon winds, which reversed themselves with the change of the seasons. The south-easterly monsoon carried shipping from India to Africa, and when the season changed, the north-westerly monsoon facilitated the return voyage. Added to this, Zanzibar had a secure harbour on the main island of Unguja, and even in the worst season of the rains, it was relatively free of the dreaded malarial fevers that turned the African mainland into a death-trap. Since as far back as the rise of Islam it had always been the entrepôt to Africa and the Ocean of the Indies, and the market where the produce of Africa – slaves, gold, ivory, gum arabic, the precious frankincense – was traded.

Alf Wilson spoke up diffidently. 'While I was their captive, I heard the pirates speak often of Zanzibar. I formed the impression that they visited it regularly to trade part of their booty, to sell their captives in the slave market and to refit and revictual their fleet.'

'Did it seem to you that Jangiri used Zanzibar as his main base?' Hal asked him.

'No, Captain, it did not. I believe that he would not place himself in the power of the Omani sultan by doing so. I believe that Jangiri has another secret hideaway, but that he uses Zanzibar as his trading port.'

'It has been my intention ever since our quest began to call at Zanzibar. However, what has troubled me is to explain what business an English ship of force is doing in these waters, so far from the regular trade route between India and Good Hope.' Hal looked around the circle of their intent faces and saw both Big Daniel and Ned Tyler nod. 'Indeed, if we sail into Zanzibar the word will spread down the coast within a week that a squadron of pirate hunters has arrived, and Jangiri will take fright. We will never bring him to battle unless we can give good, innocent reasons for being in these waters.

'The storm has given us that reason,' Hal told them, 'and the castaways we found have suggested the excuse we lacked.' They looked at him curiously.

'What story will you tell the consul in Zanzibar?' Ned Tyler asked.

'I shall tell him that we were part of the convoy from Bombay that included the luckless *Nile*. My story will be that we are laden with rich cargo. I will dream up the details of a treasure so fabulous that it will have Jangiri salivating in his beard when he hears of it.' They all laughed delightedly at the thought. 'We ran into the heart of the great storm and were battered by it just as the *Nile* was.' Hal looked across the desk at Ned Tyler. 'We have already concealed the greater part of our armament, but now I want you to send down some of our yards and spars to give the appearance of storm-damage to rigging and hull that will convince a watcher from the shore of the truth of our story. Can you do that, Mr Tyler?'

'Indeed I can, Captain,' Ned said, with relish.

'Such damage will give us the excuse to linger in Zanzibar roads, while the news of our plight is carried by every spy and trading dhow up and down the coast.' Hal enlarged on his plan. 'By the time we leave port again, every corsair and rover from the coast to Jiddah will be drawn to us like wasps to a pot of honey.'

Despite the heavy seas, the work of transforming the *Seraph* was begun at once. Ned seemed inspired by the task that Hal had set him, and his carpenters used paint of mixed colours to patch and dapple the hull. He had an old suite of sails from the Atlantic voyage brought on deck then deliberately sullied and tattered it. He selected certain parts of the rigging, including some of the upper yards and spars, for removal so that the ship's sailing qualities would not be too adversely affected. These would be sent down as soon as land was in sight. The *Seraph* would present a truly sad, bedraggled appearance when she limped into Zanzibar harbour.

Three days later, the skies began to clear and, although the seas were still high and unruly, the tropical sun burned down on them once again. The effect on the spirits of the crew was gratifying to Hal as he watched them set about their duties with new heart and vigour. At noon he was able to make his first sun-shot in all those weeks of sailing. He found that the ship's position was on the twelfth parallel of south latitude, two hundred and fifty miles further north than his dead reckoning had suggested. 'Depending on our eastings, we should raise Madagascar island within the week,' he commented, as he marked the new position in the ship's log, and ordered a change of course up into the west, towards the island and the African mainland.

As always, the birds gave warning of the proximity of land. These were of species that neither Tom nor Dorian had ever seen before. They saw fairy terns, with plumage white as frost on a December morning at High Weald, and long-tailed tropicbirds hovered over the shoals of small fish that darkened the surface in their multitudes. Closer to the island, they came across villainous-looking frigate birds, black as hell with scarlet throats, hanging on the high currents of the monsoon wind. They were lying in ambush for the flocks of terns as they returned from their fishing forays. Tom and Dorian watched them dive on their quarry with wings shaped like the blade of a half-folded clasp knife, forcing their victims to disgorge the hard-won fruits of their labours, then swooping to gobble the partly digested fish from their crops.

The sea changed colour, taking on a yellowish hue. When the boys asked why, Aboli explained, 'The rains of the great storm have engorged the rivers of the mainland, and they have discharged their muddy flood-waters into the sea. We are very close to land now.'

The next morning as the dawn exploded silently in the eastern sky behind them, and turned the horizon the colour of fire opals and rose petals, from the masthead they saw a blue wavy line scored across the horizon ahead of the ship's bows. 'Land!' The joyous cries rang through the ship.

Hal knew these islands well, and as the day wore on he climbed into the rigging and was able to identify the blue mountains of the north tip of Madagascar as they rose higher and higher from the sea.

All that day both watches laboured at the heavy work of slinging down the spars from the topmasts to make the ship appear storm-crippled. Without her top canvas the

Seraph became baulky and recalcitrant, and when close-hauled she refused to sail more than eight points to the wind. However, the trade winds were behind her and Hal was able to free her sails and lay her on a direct course towards the land. It was as well that they completed this work before the ship sailed closer in and met any of the small fishing dhows that would report their arrival in these waters and describe the *Seraph*'s condition.

The following noon Cap d'Ambre, at the northern tip of Madagascar, lay ten leagues off their port beam. With this fix on his position Hal was able to shape a course directly across the Mozambique Channel for Zanzibar. This inner sea was bejewelled with lovely little islands. The *Seraph* wove her way between them, sometimes so close that they could see the dark, half-naked islanders waving from the white beaches. The sailors climbed into the rigging and waved back lustily, speculating on the gender of the tiny figures on the sand.

These waters were dotted with the sail of small trading vessels and fishing dhows. As the *Seraph* passed, their crews called questions in Arabic and other unintelligible languages. To the delight of the *Seraph*'s men, there were women in some of the dhows.

'By God, I can see that one's titties from here. Brown as a pair of Easter buns hot from the oven.'

'Then I'll lick the sugar coating off them, so help me, I will.'

'Say you'll marry me, you little heathen beauty, and I'll jump overboard this moment,' one of the topmastmen shouted.

'They don't understand the word marry. Just tell them jig-jig. They'll understand that well enough!' his mate suggested. The faint tinkle of delighted feminine laughter from the dhow drifted back to confirm the wisdom of this counsel.

Through his telescope Hal could make out damage to

the palm trees and the other vegetation on the islands they passed, while the debris and floating rubbish that speckled the surface of the ocean confirmed the storm's passage, and that their excuse for being in these waters would be strengthened when they reached Zanzibar. 'If we do not run into Jangiri first,' Ned Tyler pointed out drily. 'We have already made such a ripple in these waters that news of our arrival must be speeding ahead of us.'

Hal was aware of the danger of Jangiri springing the trap prematurely, for they were now in his home waters. He redoubled his vigilance. The lookouts were warned of the danger, and the crew kept in a state of alert. Because of the work on the gunports Hal could not exercise the gun-crews, but he kept them busy with sword practice and musketry. These precautions proved superfluous, though, for they saw no large ships, and within ten days they had raised the African mainland.

Since leaving Good Hope this was Tom and Dorian's first sight of Africa, and whenever they could escape from their labours in Master Walsh's classroom, from the Arabic lessons with Alf Wilson or their other duties, the boys climbed to a masthead and sat for hours discussing the mysterious land out there, the wonders and adventures it promised them. The *Seraph* bore northwards along the coast, sometimes close in to the capes and coral reefs of the mainland, and the boys longed for glimpses of weird beasts and savage black tribes, but Africa seemed vast, enigmatic and deserted.

Finally Unguja appeared ahead. There were two other smaller islands in the group: Pemba and Latham. But when sailors spoke of Zanzibar, this was the island to which they usually referred. It was crowned by the massive fort, built of sparkling white coral blocks that glistened like an iceberg in the sunlight. Its ramparts bristled with heavy cannon. Hal tacked into the entrance of the ancient harbour.

A mass of fore-and-aft-rigged craft was anchored in wild disorder, congesting the harbour. Some of the ocean-going dhows were almost as large as the *Seraph*. These were the traders from India, Muscat and the Red Sea. However, there was no way of telling if any were corsairs. *Probably all of them are, given a chance.* Hal smiled to himself, then gave his full attention to bringing the *Seraph* safely to rest. He dipped his colours to the fort in courtesy to the Sultan's representative, and dropped anchor at the limit of random shot from the batteries. He had learned long ago to mistrust even the most warm, open welcome of any African potentate.

A swarm of small boats came out to greet them as soon as they were at anchor, offering wares to cater for every need or vice, from green coconuts to bundles of narcotic *bhang* leaves and flowers, from the carnal services of small brown slave boys and girls to porcupine quills filled with gold dust.

'Make certain that none of this rabble are allowed on board,' Hal warned Big Daniel. 'And keep a weather eye on our own lovely lads that they do not try to sneak ashore for a bottle and a bit of fun. I'm going to visit the British consul, although I do not expect him to be the same man I saw twenty years ago, when last we visited this place. What was the fellow's name?'

'Grey, as I recall, Captain.'

'That's right, Daniel. William Grey, and as likely a rogue as remains unhanged.'

Hal took a small party ashore with him, including Aboli and five armed seamen. The longboat deposited them on the stone quay below the thick white walls of the fort. Aboli cleared a way through the throng of merchants and idlers and they entered the warren of small alleys and lanes that were barely wide enough for three men to walk abreast.

The stench from the open sewers that ran down to the

harbour was strong enough to catch in their throats, and made Hal's gorge rise. The heat where no breeze entered was stifling and their sweat had soaked through the back of their shirts before they had gone a hundred paces. Some of the buildings were three storeys high, and none of the walls was true – they leaned and bulged out, almost meeting overhead. The upper balconies were screened with intricate latticework, and faceless female creatures in black veils peered at them through the zenana screens.

This was the season of the monsoon, which brought the slavers from all the far reaches of the eastern shores. Aboli led them through the main slave market. It was a large souk, open to the sky but shaded by a grove of banyan trees, with weird serpentine trunks and thick, dark green foliage.

The ranks of slaves for sale squatted in the shade of the spreading boughs. Hal knew they had worn their chains from the day of their capture deep in the African interior, during the long heartbreaking journey down to the coast and in the slave decks of the dhows that had brought them across the channel. Some of the men were branded on the forehead, the scars still pink and freshly healed. These markings denoted that they had been castrated in the barracoons on the beaches of the mainland. They were destined for the China trade: the emperor had decreed that no black slaves could be imported who were capable of bastardizing the pure bloodline of his people. The price of these gelded creatures was almost doubled as losses, due to the crude surgery and cauterization, were high.

The buyers from the ships in the harbour were inspecting the offerings, and haggling with the slave-masters in their ankle-length robes and headcloths. Hal shouldered his way past them and entered the maze of lanes on the far side of the souk.

Although two decades had elapsed since his last visit, Aboli led them unerringly to the heavy door of African mahogany that opened on to the noisome street. It was studded with iron nails and intricately carved with Islamic designs and texts from the Koran, in which no figure of man or animal, which might be construed as idolatry, was depicted. A slave, in long black robes and turban, answered the jangling bell.

'*Salaam aliekum.*' He touched breast and lips and bowed in welcome. 'My master knows of your coming, and waits eagerly to welcome you.' He looked at the small party that followed Hal. 'There is refreshment for your men.' He clapped his hand for another slave to lead them away, and Hal followed him into the courtyard where a fountain played and banks of flowering hibiscus sweetened the stench from the street.

For a moment he did not recognize the monstrous figure that lay on a pile of cushions in the shade beside the fountain. He hesitated, and stared at him until behind the bloated features he could make out the vestiges of the man he had once known.

'*Salaam aliekum.*' William Grey, His Majesty's consul to the Sultanate of Zanzibar, greeted him.

Hal almost replied in the same language, but stopped himself. He did not want to let Grey know that he was fluent in Arabic. Instead he said, 'I'm afraid I have not a word of that heathen tongue, sir. I was led to understand that you were English. Do you not speak a Christian language?'

'Pardon me, sir. It is a matter of habit.' Grey smiled ingratiatingly. 'I am William Grey, His Majesty's consular representative to the Omani sultanate. Forgive me not rising to greet you.' Grey made a deprecatory gesture that took in his ruined body and swollen elephantine legs, which were covered in running ulcers. Hal recognized the ravages of dropsy. 'Please be seated, sir. I have been expecting your visit since I received reports of your arrival in the harbour.'

'Good day to you, sir. Captain John Black, at your service.' Hal remembered that Grey was a Christian apostate, who had embraced Islam. He suspected that the man's change of faith had been more for financial and economic considerations than from religious conviction.

Obviously Grey neither recognized nor remembered Hal, and it had been a safe bet that he would not. Hal had banked on this when he had given Grey a false name: it was essential that the pirates did not become aware of his true identity. Twenty years before, Hal had earned the Arabic name of El Tazar, the Barracuda, for his fighting exploits when he had spread terror throughout the fleets of Islam during the Ethiopian war in the Horn of Africa. If he were to lure Jangiri to attack him, his enemies must not be given any inkling of the true identity of the man against whom they were pitted.

Hal seated himself on the cushions that had been placed for him. A female slave carried in a tray, on which were set out two silver coffee thimbles, and a second woman carried a tall silver pot, on its own charcoal brazier. The slave girls were both young, slim and supple-waisted. Grey would have paid at least two hundred rupees for each. Hal remembered that Grey had made a vast fortune from trafficking in the slave trade, and the sale of licences and commissions from the Sultan. At their last meeting, he had tried to interest Hal in both these propositions. Hal guessed that this was not the limit of his nefarious activities, and he had no illusions as to the man's integrity or morals. That he was in league with Jangiri and his ilk was not beyond the bounds of probability.

One of the girls knelt before Grey and filled the thimbles with the bitter black beverage, viscous as honey. Idly Grey caressed her arm, as he would a pet cat, with a hand on which the gold rings and jewels had sunk into the putty-soft flesh of his swollen white fingers. 'You have had a good voyage, Captain?'

'A voyage not without incident, sir,' Hal answered. Grey must already know every detail of the condition of the *Seraph*, and was merely seeking confirmation. 'After leaving Bombay, in convoy with two other ships of the Honourable East India Company, we were beset by a fearful gale off the coast of Madagascar. One of the other vessels went down with all hands lost, and we escaped only with great damage to our hull and rigging. This is the main reason why we have called at this port, which was not my original intention.'

'I am sorry to hear of your misfortune,' Grey shook his head in sympathy, 'but grateful that you have graced us with your presence, and that of your fine ship. I pray only that I may be of service to you, and provide you with whatever stores you need.'

Hal gave him a seated bow, and thought, No doubt at inflated prices, and for a goodly commission. He marvelled at the changes that age and the disease had wrought in Grey. He had been young and vigorous when last they had met but now his pate was bald and his beard silver white. His eyes were weak and rheumy and the smell of death was upon him.

'Thank you, sir. I am grateful for your good offices, particularly since I am conveying a cargo of peculiar value and political importance to His Majesty King William.'

Grey stirred his vast body, and a sparkle of interest shone in his watery eyes. 'As I am His Majesty's direct representative in these parts,' he murmured, 'might I be permitted to know the nature of this cargo?'

Hal drew in his breath sharply at the suggestion, then lowered his gaze to study the ornamental fish that drifted in the waters of the fountain. He rubbed his temples thoughtfully and made a show of pondering the wisdom of acceding to this request. At last he sighed. 'As His Majesty's representative,' he said, 'you of all persons should be informed.' He hesitated again, then seemed to make up his mind. He lowered his voice to a conspiratorial level. 'I am entrusted with the conveyance of the gift that Aurangzeb, the Mogul Emperor of India, is sending to His Majesty to celebrate his coronation.'

Grey raised his bulk on one elbow and gaped at Hal. Then, slowly, avarice bloomed in his eyes. He tried to mask his greed, but the idea of a royal tribute, the gift of one sovereign to another, filled him with almost religious awe.

The Mogul dynasty had been founded by Babur, and he in turn was the direct descendant of Timur and Genghis Khan. His father, Shah Jehan, had built the fabulous Taj Mahal as a mausoleum for a favourite wife. The Mogul empire was the most powerful and the richest ever to emerge from the Orient. What might be the value of the gift of such a mighty emperor?

Hal lowered his voice further to a whisper. 'I have been informed by the Governor of Bombay, to whom the gift was delivered, that it comprises a suite of emeralds, twenty stones perfect in fire, and each the size of a green pomegranate.'

Grey gasped softly, then struggled for breath.

Hal went on, 'Governor Aungier confided in me that the value of these stones is five lakhs of rupees.'

Grey tried to sit up, but the effort was too much for him. He fell back on the cushions and stared wordlessly at Hal. One lakh was a hundred thousand rupees. Half a million rupees was worth almost a hundred thousand pounds. This was a fortune almost too large for the mind to encompass.

'Indeed, Captain Black, such a vital cargo must be given all priority,' Grey managed. 'You may be certain that I will do all in my power to assist with the repairs to your ship, and to expedite your departure.'

'Thank you, sir.'

'How long do you estimate that these repairs will

occupy you?' Grey asked anxiously. 'When do you expect to be able to resume your voyage, Captain?'

'With your help I should be ready to sail again within the month.'

Grey was silent for a moment, evidently making rapid calculations. Then he looked relieved. With each of these tiny indications Hal was becoming more strongly convinced that Grey was in league with the corsairs.

Grey gave him a pasty, oleaginous smile. 'The damage must be greater than it appears from a casual examination,' he said, which confirmed what Hal had suspected: that he had been on the rooftop overlooking the harbour to scrutinize the *Seraph* through his telescope.

'Of course, I will try to leave sooner than that, but we are taking water heavily and I believe there may be underwater damage to the hull. We will be here for two or three weeks at least.'

'Good!' Grey declared. 'I mean, I am sure your ship will be in all respects ready for sea by that time.'

Hal smiled pleasantly and thought, And, unless I am very much mistaken, your business partner Jangiri will by that time be ready to greet us and give us a rousing welcome as soon as we enter the Mozambique Channel again.

Grey gestured to the slave-girls to refill the coffee thimbles. 'Apart from ship's stores, I am able to offer you other items for your personal profit – goods that will be worth three and four times the purchase price once you reach England again. Would that interest you, Captain?'

'Despite the decrees of John Company against private trade, I believe every man is entitled to the fruits of his own labour and ingenuity,' Hal replied.

Grey nodded enthusiastically. 'My view entirely. I have a dozen slaves in my own barracoon of such quality as is seldom seen in the souk.' He leaned forward and winked at Hal in such a suggestive, obscene fashion that

Hal had to force himself not to show his disgust by either gesture or expression. 'In fact, I might bring myself to part with one or both of my special treasures.' He stroked the head of the girl who knelt in front of him, then smiled at her lovingly and said in Arabic, 'Smile at the infidel pig!' The girl looked up sideways at Hal and showed small white teeth in a shy smile. 'Is she not a beauty?' Grey asked. 'And well worth a hundred and fifty pounds at Good Hope. I can let you have her, as a favour, you understand, for seventy.' He caressed the girl again. 'Show the infidel your tits,' he ordered in Arabic. The girl hesitated. 'Show him, or I will have the skin whipped off your back.' She was hardly more than a child, not above sixteen years, but she raised the hem of her blouse and displayed one half-ripe brown breast, tipped with a nipple like a black pearl, at the same time hanging her head modestly. 'Her more intimate parts are of equal perfection, should you wish to examine them,' Grey assured him.

'She is beautiful. But, alas, I have no accommodation for her aboard,' Hal said firmly, and the girl covered her bosom.

Grey was not deterred by this refusal. 'I have a quantity of frankincense, of the very finest quality,' he said. 'I assure you it is very much in demand. You cannot but make a handsome profit upon it.'

Hal knew that if he were to remain on civil terms with Grey, it would be politic to avail himself of at least one of the man's offerings. He haggled for ten baskets of frankincense, a total weight of one hundred and fifty pounds.

Grey's slaves carried in the baskets and set them in a row down the centre of the courtyard while Hal examined the contents. He knew that this aromatic gum came from trees in the African mountains. The trunks were deeply incised, and the sap that oozed from the wounds hardened when it was exposed to the air. After four months the gum formed into large gemlike globules, which could then be scraped off. This first milking of the sap produced a gum of a semi-opaque greenish hue, which bespoke its superior quality. Hal checked the offerings for these characteristics and affirmed his acceptance.

Grey seemed impressed with his knowledge. 'I can see you're a gentleman of taste and discernment, Captain. A pair of ivory elephant tusks arrived in the Zanzibar market recently, such as I have never seen in all my years on the island. I would hesitate to offer them to any but a gentleman of your quality, sir.' He clapped his hands, and five hefty male slaves, who must have been waiting for the order, staggered in under the weight of one of the great tusks.

'Ten feet in length!' Grey told Hal proudly. 'Two hundred and five pounds in weight!' It was an incredible shaft of curved ivory. The butt, which had been buried in the beast's skull, was creamy white, while the rest was stained yellow brown by the sap of the great trees that it had shattered and stripped of their bark. When the slaves laid the twin beside it, it was almost impossible to tell the two tusks apart, so perfectly were they matched.

Hal had been fascinated by the monstrous pachyderms since he had first laid eyes on a herd of them on the wild African shores. Then he had been a lad of around Tom's age. He stroked one of the tusks. He seemed to be touching the very soul of that immense, savage continent. He knew that he had to have this pair at any price. Grey recognized the longing in his eyes and drove a hard bargain. Hal paid more for them than he would have for a dozen slave-girls.

Later, when the tusks were swung up onto the *Seraph*'s deck to lie there gleaming like ancient amber in the sunlight, Hal knew that he had made the best of the bargain. In his old age, in the depths of an English winter, when the final chill crept into his bones, he would need only to stretch out his hand to touch his Africa and be transported back to an age and place where he was young again, with all the wonder and fire of that land still in his breast.

He stood, almost reverently, looking down at the magnificent pair. His sons came to stand on either side of him. Even Dorian was silent and awed, the same spell held them all. When Tom spoke at last his voice was almost inaudible. 'They're so big,' he whispered. 'One day I would like to hunt a creature such as this must have been.'

Hal made a lengthy show of repairing the *Seraph*. He wanted to give the news of his presence in Zanzibar an opportunity to filter down the islands and to seep along the Fever Coast until it reached the ear of Jangiri, wherever he might be. Then it would take time for the corsair to rally his forces and deploy them in ambush in the channel. Hal was certain that even Jangiri would never attempt to cut out the *Seraph* while she lay at moorings in the harbour. He was, after all, the guest of the Sultan and under his protection.

Hal understood the teachings of the Prophet well, and he knew that in the world of Islam there was a duty on the host, a burden of honour, that the Sultan would not allow any of his subjects to flout. Once the *Seraph* was on the open sea, though, she would become fair game once more, and the Sultan would probably accept his share of the booty without the least qualm.

Another consideration that Hal had to take into account was the progress of the *Yeoman of York* under Captain Edward Anderson, and when his arrival at the rendezvous might reasonably be expected. Hal was more than willing to face Jangiri in a single-ship action upon the open sea but he was certain that once he had sniffed out the corsair's land base, he would find it heavily fortified and garrisoned: he knew he would need every man and ship available to storm and seize it.

If Edward Anderson had left Good Hope a week after the *Seraph*, then he would probably have missed the worst of the great storm, and the high winds that were its aftermath would have hastened him on the voyage to Bombay. They stood now at the change of the seasons. Soon the monsoon would swing about and aid Anderson on his return voyage to the African coast. Nevertheless, it would be many more weeks before Hal could expect him to reach the rendezvous. No, indeed, there was no great hurry.

In a leisurely fashion the crew of the *Seraph* began the long business of swinging the upper yards and spars aloft and reseating them at the masthead, while the carpenters went through the motions of repairing and repainting the hull.

A week after his visit to the British consul, Hal sent Aboli ashore to make some purchases in the souk. That evening he called Tom and Dorian to his cabin. Both boys had pestered him to be allowed to go ashore whenever a boat put off for the quay. Their high spirits, too long contained, had led them lately into some dangerous pranks and it would be as well for them to have a run off the ship to rid themselves of this pent-up mischief. 'Aboli and I are going ashore this evening to listen to the gossip in the streets and marketplaces of the town,' he said. 'I am in need of a pair of slave-boys to attend me.' He spoke in Arabic, and smiled when Tom entered into the spirit of the occasion and replied in the same language.

'Revered Father, you would do me great honour if we were to be allowed to accompany you.'

Hal corrected his mistakes, but he was gratified by the progress the lad had made. Of course, he could not yet pass as a native of Arabia but he would be able to make himself understood in most company. He glanced at Dorian. 'What does my youngest son have to say on the matter?'

Dorian made a respectful obeisance. 'Beloved Father, for such kindness my gratitude would spring forth like sweet water from a desert fountain.'

'I have sired a veritable poet!' Hal laughed. Dorian's Arabic was far superior to that of his elder brother. His vocabulary was impressive, and of exactly the type a true Arab would use in similar circumstances. 'Aboli has purchased clothing for both of you. Be ready to come with me after you have eaten your dinner.'

Hal wore the long ankle-length robe and sandals Aboli had bought for him. His wide belt was of gold filigree with a curved dagger in its sheath over his stomach. The handle of the weapon was of rhinoceros horn, polished like opaque yellow agate. His waistcoat was embroidered with gold and silver thread, and his turban was black. With his thick black moustache, his beaked nose and his skin tanned the colour of oiled teak, he looked like a prosperous dhow captain, perhaps a slaver or a Red Sea rover. He took the precaution of slipping the brace of double-barrelled pistols into the gold belt, under the tail of his waistcoat.

The skin of both boys was also so sun-darkened that they needed no stain, and their headcloths covered their hair. Dorian's eyes were of such a startling green that they stood out against his coppery gold skin, but many of the Pathan tribes from the north of India had fair skins and pale eyes.

After dark they went down into the longboat and, rather than disembarking at the stone quay of the harbour, Hal steered around the breakwater to land on a quiet beach a mile from the town. He left the boat in the charge of Big Daniel, and they followed the well-used track into the town.

The town was without walls and the narrow streets unlit, except for an occasional lamp beam from an upstairs window, so they had no difficulty in entering unremarked. When they reached the main souk they found most of the stalls and small shops still open for business. Hal chose the shop of a rug-seller he had noticed on his last visit to Consul Grey. Some of the carpets in it were of beautiful design and texture. The proprietor, whose name was Salim bin-Talf, welcomed him effusively, seated him on a carpet of lustrous silk and offered him thick sweet coffee, flavoured with cardamom. Aboli and the two slave-boys sat well back in the shadows and, following Hal's instructions, maintained a respectful silence throughout the evening.

'So what is the news, *effendi*?' Bin-Talf asked the ritual question of Hal.

'The news is good,' Hal told him. He would have given the customary reply if he had just been robbed of all his worldly possessions, if all his wives had been raped, and if his eldest son had died of a snake-bite. 'What of your news?'

'My news is also good.' They sipped coffee and, as they chatted, three or four of bin-Talf's family and friends, drawn by the presence of a stranger in their midst, came to join the circle. Slowly, and with due regard to manners and protocol, the questions were asked and the true state of affairs discussed.

'Your speech is not of the north, *effendi*?' They had picked out his accent.

'I am from Morbi in Gujarat, in the empire of the Great Mogul. My ship lies in the harbour.' He had studied a number of the sea-going dhows anchored close to the *Seraph* so that he could give a description to satisfy his listeners. 'I have come to buy slaves and trade goods in the souks of Zanzibar and Lamu.'

'And how is it in your land?'

'The tribes of Marathas and the Sikhs are in revolt against the Emperor, but with God's help he will defeat them.'

'By God's grace!'

'In this sailing season his eldest son, Asaf Khan, will make the pilgrimage to Mecca, with a fleet of a hundred ships.'

'Praise be to God!'

'There is but one God.'

All this was news that Hal had gathered while in Good Hope, but its authenticity confirmed his identity to bin-Talf and his party. They became more friendly and relaxed, the conversation flowed freely. Hal haggled genteelly for a magnificent silk carpet from Persia, and when he paid with gold mohurs, coins of fifteen rupees' value, the warmth of the vendors was unreserved.

'Have you seen the English ship in the harbour?' a cousin of bin-Talf asked. 'The one with the black hull anchored at the far end of the breakwater?'

'My own ship is anchored close by the Englishman. She seems to have been damaged, for her crew work upon her masts.'

'They say it happened in the great storm last month.'

'I also encountered the same storm but, by God's grace, we survived its fury.'

'Thanks be to God!'

'They say that the English ship is outward-bound from your country, from Bombay in the kingdom of the Great Mogul.' Bin-Talf glanced around to make certain there were no spies to overhear him. 'She carries a vast treasure to a king of Franks from the Mogul.'

'I too have heard of this treasure.' It took an effort for Hal to repress his smile. 'There was much talk of it when I left Allahabad.' He also lowered his voice. 'They say it is a treasure of diamonds worth twenty lakhs.'

'Nay!' whispered the cousin excitedly, 'I heard it was

emeralds and that it was worth fifty lakhs. They say the Great Mogul has emptied his treasury.'

'Truly it must be one of the greatest treasures the world has ever seen,' Hal breathed in awe. 'And now it lies here among us. I should like to lay my eyes upon such a treasure.'

They were all silent as they considered the possibilities that Hal's words presented. Their eyes sparkled with greed as they thought about it.

'I should like to hold such a treasure in my hand,' said bin-Talf at last. 'Just to be able to boast to my grand-children that I had done so.' His cousin laughed spitefully. 'Al-Auf would take it from your hand, cousin.'

They all laughed then, and another said, 'Al-Auf would take your hand also.'

'By God, that is the truth.'

'True! True!' They laughed without restraint.

'Who is this Bad One?' Hal asked innocently, for that was the meaning of al-Auf.

'You are a seafarer and you have not heard of him?' bin-Talf marvelled. 'I thought every sailor must tremble at that name.'

'I am an ignorant one from a far country,' Hal admitted.

'Musallim bin-Jangiri, the scourge of the infidel and the Sword of Islam. That is al-Auf, the Bad One.'

Hal felt his pulse throb at the name, but he kept his expression neutral and stroked his chin thoughtfully.

'Al-Auf is then a corsair?' he asked.

'He is the father and mother of all corsairs.' Bin-Talf smiled.

'He sounds like one who should be avoided. But where would a man find al-Auf, if he were stupid enough to seek him out?'

Bin-Talf chuckled, and took a long pull on his hookah pipe. The water bubbled in the bowl and the musky *bhang* smoke streamed from his lips. 'You are right, *effendi*. Only a madman would wish to seek out al-Auf. But if you can fathom the track of the tiger shark across the ocean, then you will know where to look for his ship. If you know where the sea mist rises, then you may discern the shadow of his black sails.'

'He sounds like a djinn, a spirit of the sea, and not a man of flesh and blood,' Hal said.

'He is a man indeed. For I have seen him with my own eyes,' boasted the cousin.

'Where did you see him? What is he like?'

'I saw him at Lamu. He was in the harbour there in his ship. I saw him on the deck. He has the proud mien and the bold eye of a hero of old, a mighty man and terrible to look upon.'

'How was his ship?' Hal knew that any description of Jangiri would be coloured brightly with blind terror and unlikely to bear much resemblance to the man. He had better prospects of an accurate description of his ship.

'Strange to tell, it is not a dhow, as you might expect. It is a Frankish ship, with many sails,' said the cousin. 'But the sails are black.'

'A ship like the English ship in the harbour?' Hal asked.

'Yes! Yes! Like that but much bigger and with many more guns.'

This must surely be the captured *Minotaur* they had seen, Hal thought. 'How many guns?' he enquired.

'Many! Perhaps a hundred,' the cousin hazarded. Clearly he was no seaman and the question had no significance to him. 'If the English ship ever meets al-Auf, then her infidel crew must look to Allah for mercy, for they will receive none from al-Auf.'

Soon afterwards, Hal made his farewells, and left with Aboli and the boys.

When they rowed back to the *Seraph*, he sat alone in the stern and listened with half an ear to Tom and Dorian chatting excitedly to Big Daniel and Alf, relating in detail all they had seen and heard in the port. He was satisfied with the results of the visit. He had told nobody but Consul Grey of the putative Mogul treasure, and yet it was common talk in the souk. By now the news must have reached the ears of the corsair.

The *Seraph* lingered another three weeks at her moorings in the harbour, then Hal paid a final call on the consul. After all the flowery compliments and greetings had been exchanged, Hal told him, 'I have at last completed the repairs to my ship, and I am once again ready for sea.'

'When do you plan to sail?' Grey hauled his great bulk into a sitting position, and peered at Hal with interest.

'In three days' time, with the morning ebb.'

'Although I have been honoured by your presence in my house, I understand your eagerness to recommence your interrupted voyage. Especially in view of the fact that you carry such precious cargo. I can only wish you fair winds and God speed.' He showed not the least interest in delaying Hal's departure – rather, he seemed anxious to see him on his way. To Hal, this meant only one thing: Jangiri – al-Auf – had been summoned and must even now be lying in ambush in the Mozambique Channel.

The last three days in Zanzibar harbour were spent in the final preparations for battle. Big Daniel supervised the loading of the cannon with fresh charges, and the silk ready bags in the magazine were filled and placed at the gun stations. Aboli saw that all the muskets and pistols were fitted with new flints, and fully loaded. The whetstones whirred and sparks flew as the cutlass blades were

257

sharpened to a razor edge, and the points of the pikes were whetted by hand. Yet all this warlike activity was hidden carefully from any spy on the quay or on the battlements of the fort.

Hal watched for any unusual movement of the other shipping in the anchorage. Since he had last spoken to Grey, it seemed that there had been an increase in the number of small dhows entering and leaving the harbour. Many steered close to the *Seraph* and the crews hung over the gunwale to gape at the tall ship. This might have been due only to natural curiosity, but Hal was certain that the news of their imminent departure was being conveyed to interested ears out there in the blue.

During their last night in Zanzibar harbour there was a heavy thunderstorm, and while the thunder rolled great boulders across the roof of the sky and the lightning turned night to day, the rain cascaded on to the *Seraph*'s decks. The men on the gundecks had to shout to make themselves heard.

After midnight the clouds cleared, and myriad stars flared and flickered across the sky, reflecting in the surface of the harbour. It was so still that Hal, lying sleepless in his bunk, heard an Arab watchman in one of the dhows anchored nearby singing softly,

> God is Great.
> Man is as spume in the track of the monsoon.
> Hold the Pleiades overhead,
> And the Morning Star in your eye.
> Only God knows all the ways of the ocean.
> Only God endures for ever.

As the first promise of the dawn lightened the eastern sky and snuffed out the stars Hal roused himself and went on deck. The land breeze came in warm puffs from the island, and the *Seraph* stirred on her moorings, eager to be on her way. Hal nodded to Ned Tyler, who called both watches to get the ship under way.

The crew poured up into the rigging, and the sails billowed out, flapped and shook until the breeze filled them tightly and *Seraph* heeled, then swung her bows towards the harbour entrance. Hal walked back to the stern rail and saw that four dhows had slipped their moorings, hoisted their single lateen sails and were following them.

'They could have chosen the beginning of the ebb to get under way,' Ned murmured, at his elbow, as they stood looking back.

'Anything is possible, Mr Tyler – even that Consul Grey is an honest man,' Hal agreed.

'I think that may be reaching for the moon, Captain,' Ned said seriously.

Hal lifted his eyes to the high walls of the fort, glowing in the early light with a pearly luminosity, and grunted with sudden interest. There was a spark of fire on the eastern tower-top. As he watched it, a thin column of white smoke rose into the air, then drifted away on the monsoon wind. 'Do you think they're warming themselves up there?' Hal asked quietly.

'That smoke will be clear to see on the mainland across the channel,' was Ned's opinion.

'Or twenty leagues out at sea.'

The channel was so narrow that, as the sun pushed its glowing rim above the horizon, they saw the African mainland etched in stark detail before them, its distant mountains ablaze with the sun's fire.

Hal looked back over the stern. The small flotilla of dhows from the harbour was still following in their wake. He had not yet set all sail, and there were still three reefs in the main, so the *Seraph* was loafing along easily. Two of the larger following vessels were faster than the others. They were keeping pace with the *Seraph*, while the others dropped back gradually.

'Deck! There's more smoke from the mainland.' Tom's voice floated down from the masthead, and Hal crossed to the lee rail. A thin column rose from the green back of one of the headlands, which guarded a curving beach of white coral sand. The smoke was an unnatural silvery white, and rose straight upwards until suddenly the wind caught it and smeared it in a long trail across the tops of the green hills.

They sailed on southwards all that day. Keeping pace with their progress, more fires were lit upon the shore, always when the *Seraph* was level with some headland or bluff, and each billowed with the same silver smoke, which must have been visible for many miles around.

The straggling fleet of small dhows scattered down-channel continued to dog them, the two larger vessels keeping station two or three miles back in their wake. But as the sun dipped down towards the horizon, and turned the tumbled cumulus clouds red and gold, the two dhows shook out the reefs in their sails and almost imperceptibly closed the gap, until even in the fading light they were in clear view from the *Seraph*'s main deck. Through the lens, Hal made out the mass of men crowded into them. 'I think we can expect something to happen very soon,' he told Ned Tyler. 'I want the crew to be given their dinner while it's still daylight. They may be required to fight a night action.'

Ned looked grave: even a powerful fighting ship was at a disadvantage in a night action against an inferior but numerous enemy. Under cover of darkness a fleet of small dhows might be able to creep up on the larger ship, and put a mass of armed men onto her decks before the gunners could see to drive them off.

At that moment there was a hail from the lookout. 'Deck! There's a small boat dead ahead! She seems to be in difficulties!'

Hal strode to the rail and raised his telescope. Over

the bows he could make out the hull of a fishing dhow wallowing low down in the water, with only her bottom planking exposed. There was a cluster of human heads in the water around her. As the *Seraph* bore down upon them they waved and their shouts came thin on the wind.

'For the love of God!'

'Mercy! God has sent you to save us.'

When they were close enough to make out the features of the men struggling around the wreckage, Hal gave the order to heave to. The *Seraph* swung round, head to the wind, and drifted closer to the swamped dhow.

'Send a boat to pick them up!' Hal ordered, and while the longboat was launched and pulled across to them, he counted the heads. 'Twenty-two. A large crew for such a small boat, Mr Tyler.'

'Indeed, Captain, an uncommonly large crew.'

Hal strolled across to the rail, where Big Daniel and Alf Wilson waited with a gang of armed men.

'Are we ready to give them a fitting welcome, Mr Fisher?'

'As loving a welcome as they will ever get this side of Paradise,' said Big Daniel grimly. The longboat was now crowded with the sodden, bedraggled survivors from the dhow. It began to pull back towards the *Seraph*, low in the water.

Suddenly Alf Wilson whistled softly, and his dark, handsome features lit with a devilish pleasure. 'That big one in the bows, with the beard.' He pointed to one of the survivors. 'I know him. By God, it will be a pleasure to greet him again. He was the leader of the gang of cut-throats who boarded the *Minotaur* under exactly the same ruse as this.'

'Stand back, please, Mr Wilson,' Hal warned him softly, 'lest he recognize you also. Let us get him on board before he sees you.'

The longboat hooked on to the *Seraph*'s chains, and

the first of the rescued men came up the ladder and fell upon his hands and knees. He pressed his forehead to the deck, and the sea-water streamed from his long sodden robe to form a puddle around him.

'The blessings of Allah and all his saints be upon this ship. Your kindness and mercy shall be written in the golden book—'

'Enough of that, my lad.' Big Daniel lifted him to his feet with a kindly hand, and his men hustled the startled Arab to the far rail and surrounded him closely. The next man up the ladder and over the rail was the tall bearded one. He spread his arms, and his long wet robes clung to his lanky frame. 'This is a most auspicious day. My children and my grandchildren—' he began, in sonorous tones.

'*Salaam aliekum*, Rachid,' Alf Wilson greeted him. 'My eyes have hungered many long days for the sight of your beauteous countenance.'

Rachid stared at him in alarm. Then Alf stepped closer and smiled at him. The Arab recognized him and looked about with wild dismay, seeking an avenue of escape, then leaped for the ship's side. Alf Wilson seized him while he was in the air and bore him to the deck. He placed his knee in the small of his back and the point of his dirk against the soft skin under his ear. 'I beg of you, Beloved of the Prophet, give me reason to slit your throat.' He pricked the man so that he squealed and writhed on the deck. Alf ran his free hand over Rachid's body, then groped under his wet robe and brought out a murderously curved dagger. He tested the edge against Rachid's ear and shaved away the lobe cleanly. A trickle of blood ran down into the man's beard.

'Ah! Sharp enough,' Alf said happily. 'This must be the same blade with which you cut the nose off my old shipmate Ben Brown, and murdered Johnnie Waite.'

Rachid sobbed, howled and pleaded for mercy. 'God is

my witness, I am innocent. You have mistaken me for another. I am a poor honest fisherman.'

The others were hustled onto the deck to stand in a bewildered group, surrounded by a ring of drawn cutlasses. Alf jerked the whining, cringing Rachid to his feet and shoved him across the deck to join his men. 'If any one of you attempts to escape, or to draw one of the weapons you have concealed under your robes, my men have orders to lop off his head,' Hal warned them. Then he turned to Ned Tyler. 'Please get the ship under way again.'

When the *Seraph* was on the wind and sailing down channel once more, Hal snapped at the prisoners, 'Disrobe, all of you! Down to your unwashed skins.'

There were cries of protest. '*Effendi*, it is not fitting. Our own nudity must shame us in the sight of God.'

Hal pulled one of the pistols from his belt and drew back the hammers. He placed the muzzle against Rachid's head. 'All your clothes! Amaze us with the girth and length of your circumcised pricks, as you will delight the houris in the gardens of Paradise when I send you to them.'

Reluctantly Rachid stripped off his wet robe, and stood in his loincloth.

'All of it!' Hal insisted, and one after the other the Arabs shed their clothing. They laid it down with exaggerated care so that whatever was hidden in the folds did not clink or bump weightily against the deck timbers. At last they stood in a miserable huddle trying to cover their private parts with cupped hands, wailing and protesting their innocence. Their discarded clothing lay in a heap on the deck.

'Search these!' Hal ordered, and Aboli and Big Daniel ran each item through their hands, pulling out the selection of daggers concealed in the wet folds. By the time they had finished there was a heap of weapons on the deck.

'Rachid!' Hal singled out the leader, who fell on his

knees with tears streaming down to mingle with the blood from his injured ear. 'What is the plan of al-Auf? What signal were you to make to show him that you had seized control of my ship?'

'I do not understand you, *effendi*. I know of no man named al-Auf. Have mercy on a poor fisherman! Without me to provide for them my children will starve.'

'Allah, the All Merciful, will provide for your wretched orphans,' Hal assured him, and ran his eye over the terrified prisoners. 'That one!' He selected a villainous-looking rogue, with a scarred face and one empty eye-socket. Aboli dragged him out of the huddle. He wound a short length of heavy chain around his neck and secured it with a shackle. 'I will ask you once more.' Hal grinned at Rachid. 'What is the signal?'

'In God's name, *effendi*, I do not know this person, al-Auf. I know of no signal.'

Hal jerked his head at Aboli, who picked up the chained Arab as if he were a child and carried him to the rail. He lifted him high over his head and threw him over the side. The man hit the water and disappeared instantly, snatched beneath the surface by the weight of the chain. A horrified silence fell over every man on deck, even the English sailors. They had never guessed that their captain could be so ruthless. Then the group of naked prisoners let out a soft wail and, as one man, dropped to their knees, hands clasped before their eyes as they pleaded for their lives.

'The signal?' Hal asked quietly, looking straight at Rachid.

'As God is my witness, I know of no signal.'

'Take him,' Hal said to Aboli. He seized Rachid by his wounded ear and dragged him, squealing and bleeding, to the ship's side. He threw him flat on the deck, placed one huge bare foot between his shoulder-blades to pin him down and wound another length of chain around his neck.

Then he lifted him easily over his head. 'Throw him to the sharks,' ordered Hal, 'though even they will sicken on such offal.'

'I will tell you,' Rachid howled, kicking in the air. 'Only tell this black *shaitan* to put me down and I will tell you.'

'Hold him over the side,' Hal ordered.

Aboli changed his grip and held Rachid by the ankles far out above the *Seraph*'s rushing bow-wave. 'Speak,' he rumbled softly, 'for my arms grow tired. They will not support your weight much longer.'

'Two lights,' shrieked Rachid. 'Two red lanterns at the masthead. That is the signal to al-Auf that we have taken the ship.'

Aboli pulled him back on board and dropped him to grovel on the deck.

'What course did he order you to steer? Where were you to meet him?' asked Hal.

'He told me to steer south and stay close to the land, heading for Ras Ibn Khum.' Hal knew that that was a prominent headland that jutted out into the channel.

'Chain all of them and lock them in the forecastle with a guard to watch them at all times. Shoot the first one who tries to escape,' Hal ordered Aboli, in Arabic for benefit of the prisoners.

As the sun sank smouldering into the sea, Hal shortened sail and stood further off-shore, as any prudent captain would with a lee shore looming so close at hand. They sailed on slowly southwards, and once or twice during the early part of the night the lookouts made out a dim lantern light on one or other of the dhows shadowing them.

On board the *Minotaur*, wherever she was lurking, al-

Auf would expect his men to seize the *Seraph* only after most of her crew were asleep. Therefore, Hal waited until four bells in the middle watch – two o'clock in the morning – before he ordered the two red signal lanterns lit and placed at bows and masthead. They glared out into the night like dragon's eyes.

Then he ordered Aboli and twenty other chosen men to don the still-damp discarded robes of the captured Arabs. While they were winding on their headcloths, Hal went down to his cabin and dressed quickly in the clothing he had worn on the night of the visit to the souk in Zanzibar. When he came on deck again the *Seraph* was sailing quietly on through the dark waters. When the moon set, the dark shape of the land, with its pearly necklace of phosphorescent surf, was lost in the darkness.

Hal went down the deck and spoke to each group of men squatting beneath the gunwales. 'This is the dangerous time,' he told them softly. 'Be alert. They can be upon us before we see them.'

Two hours before dawn, in that darkest time of the night, Hal sent for the two boys. When they came to him, Tom was alert and snapping with excitement, but Dorian must have been curled on his pallet for he was still half-asleep, yawning and rubbing his eyes.

'I want both of you to go now to your battle quarters at the masthead,' he said sternly. 'If the ship becomes engaged you are to stay there, no matter what is happening on the decks below you. Do you understand me?'

'Yes, Father.' Tom's face was intent in the dim light from the binnacle.

'I place you in charge of your brother, Tom,' Hal said, as he had so many times before. 'Dorian, you are to obey Tom, whatever he tells you to do.'

'Yes, Father.'

'I shall be much occupied. I will not be able to keep

an eye on you. I want to know you are both safe and high above the fighting.'

He walked with them to the foremast shrouds and, under cover of the darkness, placed a hand on their shoulders and squeezed. 'God love you, lads, as I do. Don't try to be heroes. Just stay well out of harm's way.' He watched them clamber up the shrouds then disappear into the darkness above. He went back to his place on the quarterdeck.

With the dawn it rained again, so the night was prolonged. Then, simultaneously with the sunrise, the rainclouds parted, and the day burst upon them with dramatic suddenness. During the night, with the vagaries of the current in the narrow channel, the *Seraph* had been carried in close to the land.

Two miles to starboard the African mainland was rimmed with white beaches, and the fangs of coral reefs snarled in the shallow green inshore lagoons. Dead ahead was the whale-backed headland of Ras Ibn Khum, which thrust out into the channel. Hal quietly ordered a change of course to carry them clear of it.

During the night the fleet of following dhows, guided by the signal lanterns at *Seraph*'s masthead, had closed the gap between them. The leading vessel, a ship of some hundred tons and packed with men, was less than a cable's length astern of the ship. As soon as they saw the *Seraph* appear, with magical suddenness, out of the darkness ahead of them, they burst out cheering and fired their jezails into the air. Clearly they believed from the signal lamps that the ship was already in al-Auf's hands. Feathers of gun-smoke spurted into the air, while their voices and the popping of their weapons carried thinly across the dark, choppy waters as they danced and waved them.

'Greet them, lads,' Hal told his men in Arab gear. They capered and waved back at the dhow, their robes flapping and billowing in the morning breeze off the land. Hal made no move to slow the ship so the gap between them was not reduced.

He looked ahead, judging his safe distance off the green headland that jutted out ahead, then felt his chest tighten and his breathing come short as, not two miles ahead, another square-rigged ship with black sails came charging around the point.

At once Hal realized that she had been lying at anchor in the bay beyond, waiting in ambush while the signal fires along the coast warned her of the *Seraph*'s approach. Now she rushed out to meet them, with a bow-wave curling white under her forefoot. She was followed by a horde of small craft, a dozen or more small dhows.

Alf Wilson ran back to Hal, his dark eyes dancing with excitement. 'That's the old *Minotaur*,' he shouted. 'I'd know her anywhere, Captain.'

'Thank you, Mr Wilson, I suspected as much.' Hal kept his expression neutral, then turned to glance at Ned Tyler. 'Hold her on this course.'

As the two tall ships came together swiftly, Hal examined the *Minotaur* through his telescope. It was less than two years since she had been captured by al-Auf, but Hal saw at once that her sails and rigging had been allowed to deteriorate into a sorry state. No English captain would ever neglect his ship like that. Added to which, she was being handled sloppily. Perhaps her captain was accustomed to the lateen rig, and lacked expertise in the complicated setting of the high tiers of square sails. Now, her topsails were luffing and her mains were not properly trimmed around so the wind was spilling, the black canvas shaking and trembling as if with palsy. Hal could tell by the leeway she was making that her bottom must be foul and thick with weeds.

A disorderly swarm of men lined her sides and crowded into the rigging, prancing and waving their weapons, wild with glee. Hal estimated that there were several hundred, and he felt a chill of apprehension as he imagined that wild horde pouring aboard the *Seraph*. But he took no avoiding action that might alert the corsair. Meanwhile, the disguised English seamen on the *Seraph* were going through a delirious pantomime of welcome to the corsair.

The *Minotaur* carried twenty-five guns a side and the weight of her broadside was almost double that of the *Seraph*'s. If she were deftly handled, the *Seraph* would be no match for her. Let us hope that her fighting skills match her sailing qualities, Hal thought, as the two ships raced together head-on, until they seemed on the point of collision. The *Minotaur*'s attendant dhows straggled along behind her like ducklings.

They were so close now that Hal could make out the figurehead at her bows, the horned beast of mythology, half man and half bull. Swiftly the two ships closed until Hal could make out her name, *Minotaur*, even though the gold-leaf lettering was chipped, faded and coated with salt crystals.

Hal lifted his telescope and swept her deck. Almost at once he picked out a tall figure in black robes who stood out from the rabble of Arab seamen. There was no doubt in his mind that this was al-Auf, the Bad One. How had the cousin of bin-Talf described him? 'He has the proud mien and the bold eye of a hero of old, a mighty man and terrible to look upon.' Not too great an exaggeration, Hal thought grimly.

Al-Auf's green turban was coiled high and the gem that secured its folds glittered above his forehead in the slanting rays of the early sun. The promise of hard muscle showed in his wide shoulders, and beneath the drapes of his robes his body was graceful and poised, as that of one of the great predatory cats. His beard was oiled and barbered into twin forks that blew back over his shoulders. The two ships plunged closer towards each other, until Hal could discern al-Auf's features: dark eyes framed with beetling black brows, an eagle beak of a nose above a thin sword-cut of a mouth. A face as hard and cruel as the merciless Arabian desert that had fashioned it.

Hal saw that all the *Minotaur*'s gunports were open and all her heavy guns run out. A fine haze of blue smoke swirling back from her decks in the wind warned him that all her slow-match was lit, that her gunners waited behind their cannon. Al-Auf was cunning and wary enough not to accept the evidence of the red lanterns at the *Seraph*'s masthead as conclusive.

Hal's eyes narrowed as the gap between them shortened to a cable's length, and al-Auf showed no sign of giving way. Some of the crew in the bows of the *Minotaur* ceased their capering and looked around uneasily.

'Run out the guns!' Hal had left it to the last possible moment and his order was repeated in a yell down the companionways to the decks below. Immediately the sound of heavy blows reverberated through the ship. The wedges were being driven out with mallets. There followed a series of crashes as the lids of the gunports flew open, then the rumble of the gun carriages. From the gaping ports poked out the black muzzles of her cannon. Hal imagined the consternation on board the *Minotaur* as they saw what they had believed was a helpless, unarmed victim transformed before their eyes into a dangerous, warlike adversary.

As Hal watched, al-Auf reacted immediately. He whirled to his helm, but the order he shouted was lost in the wind and the cheers of his own crew. The *Minotaur* put up her helm and swung her bows into the wind. It was an ill-judged manoeuvre, intended to avoid collision and the sudden unexpected menace of the *Seraph*'s gaping broadside of cannon.

'Not a wise decision,' Hal murmured, with satisfaction. 'You would have done better to trade shot for shot,' and he held his course.

'Mr Fisher!' Hal called. 'I'm going to cross her bows. Fire as you bear!' Big Daniel strode to the leading starboard gun-team. Swiftly he checked the laying of the heavy weapons and pulled out the gunner's wedge to depress the aim. The range would be point-blank. Aiming down into her would send the roundshot plunging through the *Minotaur*'s vitals.

Al-Auf's ill-considered turn into the wind had taken the *Minotaur* aback. She was in irons, stalled, with the wind pressing into the front of her sails so that she could not pay off again on either tack.

'Come up a point to windward,' Hal ordered the helmsman. The *Seraph* turned in slightly towards the *Minotaur*, and began to cross her bows so closely that she almost ran into the jutting bowsprit. Not one of the other ship's guns could bear, while every single gun in succession on the *Seraph*'s starboard side would be aimed directly into the gilded bows. Big Daniel pressed the lighted match into the touch-hole of the leading gun, which fired with a tremendous roar and leaped back against its restraining tackle. The long plume of gunsmoke touched the *Minotaur*'s bows, and her planking burst open to the shot in a humming cloud of splinters.

The single shot raked the *Minotaur*, tearing through her lower decks where her gunners waited by their cannon. On board the *Seraph* they could clearly hear the screams and the cries to God as the ball tore along the gundeck. Big Daniel strode back to the second gun, and checked its aim. Sedately the *Seraph* glided on past the wallowing *Minotaur* until the cannon was pointing straight into her. Daniel touched it off in another bellowing blast of fire and gunsmoke. The heavy iron ball smashed through her bows, and the shrieks of wounded and dying men carried clearly on the wind.

One after the other, the *Seraph*'s guns crashed out, and the *Minotaur* shivered and reeled, unable to respond, under the heavy blows. Hal could see the green turban of al-Auf standing out in the panic-stricken mob of his crew as he tried to rally them, to get the sails trimmed around so that his ship would come on the wind and turn away from the terrible blows that were raking her from stem to stern.

In the *Seraph*'s rigging men were firing muskets down onto the *Minotaur*'s deck. Even with their inaccurate smooth-bored guns nearly every shot was telling among the densely packed throng of robed figures milling about in wild confusion. The deafening boom of the cannon was punctuated by the sharper crack of the falconets that swept the *Minotaur*'s deck with grapeshot. Hal glanced up at the foremast to make certain the two boys were safe, and saw Tom busy reloading the falconet. Dorian's head was close beside his brother's, bobbing with excitement, and Hal thought he could hear his high, excited voice even above the din of battle.

Every one of the *Seraph*'s starboard batteries had been discharged into the helpless *Minotaur*, and the slaughter was terrible. Hal could see blood running out of her open gunports and scuppers in bright rivulets that dribbled down her sides.

'I will lay us alongside,' Hal warned Ned. He waited until the last gun had fired and the *Seraph* had swept past her victim, then shouted the order in the lull. 'One broadside into her as we come alongside, and we will board her in the smoke.' The crew cheered and brandished their boarding weapons, pikes, cutlasses and axes. Once they were on the *Minotaur*'s deck they would still be outnum-bered, but Hal trusted in their training, their fighting spirit and the confusion of the Arabs to carry the ship with the first rush.

He gave the order and the *Seraph* pivoted neatly, coming around so that the two ships presented their broadsides to each other. But the *Seraph*'s way had carried her wide and they were still a full musket shot apart. Hal ordered all the mainsails taken in so that she was down to fighting sail, then he backed the foretopsail to take some of the way off her and bring her in more rapidly towards the *Minotaur*. One of the small dhows that had been following the enemy ship found itself directly under the *Seraph*'s bows, unable to avoid collision. Her crew looked up in terror as the high ship reared over them. Some threw themselves overboard, others were frozen with terror as the *Seraph* trod the dhow down. Her planking shattered and snapped as she rolled clean under, and the screams of her crew were drowned abruptly.

As the *Seraph* gybed through the wind she gathered speed and rushed down on the *Minotaur*, but the enemy ship was at last paying off and swinging on to the opposite tack.

They were at half musket shot, a hundred yards apart, and Hal could see al-Auf driving his men back to their battle quarters with angry shouts and blows. One or two of the *Minotaur*'s heavy cannon roared out. Some of the shot flew wide, missing the *Seraph* by fifty yards, skipping across the surface of the water like a child's game of ducks and drakes. A few balls howled through the *Seraph*'s rigging high above the deck, and one of her stays parted with a crack like a pistol shot. Still she bore down remorselessly on the other ship. The *Minotaur* was gathering speed only slowly, and most of her sails were still shaking and flapping. The yards were so close now that they were almost touching.

'Stand by to grapple her!' Hal cried, and glanced at the men in the chains. They were already swinging the heavy iron hooks in looping circles above their heads, working up the momentum to launch them across the narrow gap and grip the enemy.

Hal saw al-Auf abandon his futile efforts to rally his men to face the *Seraph*. Instead he ran to one of the unfired cannon, which had been deserted by its crew. Hal saw no sign of fear on his bearded face as he snatched up a burning match from the tub beside the gun and glared across at the *Seraph*. Then he stared straight at Hal and his thin lips curled into an angry sneer. In that instant Hal sensed that neither of them would ever forget the other. Then al-Auf thrust the smoking, spluttering match into the touch-hole of the cannon. He had no time to train it around. It was a despairing gesture of defiance, a wild throw of the dice in the hazard of battle.

With a long blast of flame and smoke, the heavy iron ball smashed through the *Seraph*'s gunwale, blew two English seamen to bloody shreds then smashed into the base of the *Seraph*'s foremast. It shivered, swayed, then began to topple, swinging slowly outwards, stays and shrouds popping and whipping, the timber tearing and cracking, gathering speed and momentum as it fell.

Hal watched his ship transforming before his eyes from a sleek fighting machine to a crippled hulk. Then, from the crow's nest at the top of the falling mast, he saw two human figures hurled like pebbles from a slingshot. For a moment they were outlined against the grey rainclouds, then they dropped towards the surface of the sea.

'Tom!' Hal cried, in agony. 'Oh, my God, Dorian!'

From the crow's nest, Tom looked down onto the *Minotaur*'s decks, onto the horde of turbaned Arabs in their multicoloured robes. He was swinging the falconet on its swivel mounting, training it almost straight downwards so that he had to hang out over the side of the crow's nest to bring it to bear.

'Shoot!' Dorian shouted beside him. 'Shoot, Tom!'

Tom could see clearly the terrible damage that the *Seraph*'s guns had inflicted on the enemy ship. Her gunwales were shattered, raw white timbers exposed, her bow-sprit had been shot away with a tangle of foresails and ropes hanging into the water. One of her deck cannon had taken a direct hit and been hurled from its carriage. The bodies of two Arab gunners were pinned under its massive black barrel.

Dead and wounded men littered the deck, and the terrified crew slithered and fell on the red-washed decks, tripping over the corpses of their fellows as they crowded to the side of the ship furthest from the *Seraph*'s menacing banks of cannon.

'Shoot!' Dorian was pounding his brother's shoulder with a clenched fist. 'Why don't you shoot?'

Tom was waiting for the right moment. He knew it might take five minutes to reload the long-barrelled fal-conet in his awkward perch in the crow's nest and in that time his best chance might pass while his gun was empty.

'Always wait for your moment,' Big Daniel had drummed into him. 'Don't blaze away at long range. Get in close and make every shot count to the full.'

The far rail of the *Minotaur* was densely crowded. Some of her crew had scrambled onto the ship's rail, prepared to throw themselves into the sea and try to swim to one of the small dhows, rather than face the *Seraph*'s broadside and the wave of infidel devils who would come swarming aboard. They were pushing and fighting to reach safety, packed six and seven deep. Tom saw clearly their brown, terror-stricken faces looking back over their shoulders as the *Seraph* loomed high over them.

He aimed carefully into the thick of them, then touched off the falconet. Smoke and fragments of burning wad flew out in a dense cloud and were blown back into his face by the wind so that, for several seconds, he was blinded. Then the smoke was whipped away and he saw the hole that the blast of grapeshot had blown in the frenzied ranks on the deck below. At least a dozen robed figures were down, struggling and kicking convulsively in their own blood.

'Oh, good shot! Good shot!' Dorian screeched.

'Help me reload,' Tom said and swung the falconet's stubby barrel upwards until it was pointed at the sky.

Dorian reached up, swabbed out the barrel, and poured a charge of black powder from the leather bucket into the gaping muzzle, and Tom thrust in the oakum wad to ram it home.

It was at that moment that the mast lurched and shuddered under them, and the shivering impact of the iron cannonball fired by al-Auf was carried through the timbers. Tom dropped the ramrod and snatched a hand-hold on the side of the crow's nest. He flung his other arm around Dorian's body and hugged him close.

'Tom, what's happening?' Dorian cried, in wild alarm, and clung to his brother.

'Hold hard, Dorry!' Tom tried to quell his own terror as the mast swayed, teetered, then leaned out until they saw the tossing waves directly beneath them. 'We're going over, Dorry. Hold on to me.'

Unhurriedly the foremast swung outwards, and the boys were overwhelmed by the squeal of tortured timbers, the snap and whip of parting ropes and sundering tackle. Faster and still faster the toppling mast sent them plummeting downwards so their breath was trapped in their lungs.

'I can't hold on—' Tom cried in despair. Still clinging to each other they were thrown clear of the canvas bucket and dropped through the thicket of twisting ropes and tumbling spars, a long, swooping, breath-stopping fall, until they struck the surface of the sea and were driven deep beneath the green water.

Dorian was torn from Tom's hands by the force with which they hit the water. Even while he was deep below the surface, Tom opened his eyes and tried to look for him, groping wildly as he kicked upwards. When he burst out again and gasped for air, his only thought was for his little brother. Through eyes that streamed and stung with salt water he looked around him. 'Dorry!' He choked. 'Where are you?'

The *Seraph*'s shattered mast lay over the side, its canvas in dreadful disarray, hanging in the water like a huge drogue anchor, dragging the bows around, so that the *Minotaur* was pulling away from her rapidly. Tom found himself enmeshed in a tangle of rope and canvas, and struggled to free himself. He kicked off a length of trailing rope that wound itself around his legs, and grabbed at a shattered spar to lift himself high enough to look about him.

'Dorry!' His voice was high with terror and panic. At that moment Dorian's head popped above the surface thirty feet from where Tom floundered. He was half drowned, choking and coughing up gouts of water. The way that the ship was swinging through the water was drawing them swiftly apart.

'Dorry, hold on!' Tom shouted. 'I'm coming.' He let go of the spar and struck out overarm towards his brother. Immediately the rope wrapped itself around his legs again.

'Tom!' Dorian saw him, and reached out a hand towards him. 'Save me, Tom. Please, please, Tom!' He was out in the open water, drifting swiftly away.

'I'm coming, Dorry.' Tom kicked and struggled with the rope that held him, but it was like trying to throw off the tenacious grip of an octopus. A wave broke over Dorian's head, driving him under again. When he surfaced he was twenty feet further away, flapping his arms uselessly, trying to keep his head clear of the surface.

'Swim, Dorry!' Tom yelled at him. 'Like I taught you.' Dorian heard him, and controlled his frenzied struggles a little.

'Kick, Dorry!' Tom called again. 'Use your hands.' Dorian trod water more determinedly, but the current had him in its grip, and Tom was being pulled away swiftly by the rope that bound him to the broken spar. He ducked below the surface, groped for the rope end and unwound it from around his legs. But the drag of the sea was tightening the loops of line and, although he tore at the rough hemp with bleeding fingers, it would not yield. He had to breathe and he dragged himself back to the surface.

He sucked in air, and once his eyes were clear looked about for Dorian. He saw him a hundred yards away, his expression unreadable with distance but his voice a despairing wail. 'Tom, help me!'

At that moment the spar rolled end over end in the water, and Tom was plucked under again, but this time so deep that his eardrums squeaked and the pain shot through his skull like a gimlet. As he tore at the rope that held him he felt the skin on his fingertips smear and his nails tear out at the roots. The pain in his chest, the need to breathe, was insufferable, but he fought on even as the strength went out of him. His vision faded into blackness, and he was left with nothing but the will to go on. I'm not going to give in. It was the only thought left to him. Dorry needs me. I cannot let myself drown.

Then he felt powerful hands seize him. When he opened his eyes again and forced back the darkness, he saw Aboli's face only inches from his, his eyes wide open and the weird patterns of his tattoos giving him the aspect of some terrible monster of the deep. He held a knife between his filed teeth and silver bubbles streamed from the corners of his lips.

Aboli had seen the two boys fall with the shattered mast and, without any hesitation, had deserted his battle station. In the time it had taken him to cross the deck and reach the weather rail, Dorian had drifted fifty yards out from the *Seraph*'s side. In desperate haste Aboli had ripped

278

off his Islamic robes and headdress and, wearing only his breeches, he had sprung to the rail and balanced there an instant while he decided which of the boys was in deepest peril.

Dorian seemed to be treading water easily, but he was drifting down to where the fleet of Arab dhows hovered. Tom, though, was trapped in the welter of billowing canvas and tangled ropes. Aboli hesitated, torn between his love for and duty to the boys. He found it impossible to decide between them.

Then, with a loud snap, one of the foremast spars cracked through and rolled over in the water. Tom was entangled in the ropes and had been plucked beneath the surface. Aboli threw one last desperate glance at Dorian's drifting head, tiny in the distance, drew the knife from the sheath on his belt, clamped the blade between his teeth and dived over the side. He came up almost over the spot where Tom had gone down, snatched another quick breath and dived again. He used the trailing ropes to pull himself down, and peered through the water, which was curtained with whirlpools of turbulence and clouds of bright bubbles.

As he went deeper he saw Tom's form appear out of the green haze beneath him. He was moving only feebly, near the point of drowning, and the yellow rope was wound around his legs like a python. Aboli reached down and seized his shoulders, then peered into the boy's face. He saw Tom's eyes open and squeezed his shoulders hard to brace him and give him hope. Then he snatched the blade from between his teeth and reached down to the rope that bound Tom's legs. He did not hack wildly at it, for the blade was razor sharp and might inflict a serious wound in the boy's bare legs. Instead, he worked carefully to sort out the tangle, sawing one loop at a time until the last strand dropped away and Tom was free. Then Aboli seized him under the armpits and shot upwards towards the surface. They broke out together, and even while Aboli hunted for air, his great chest filling and purging like a blacksmith's bellows, he was holding Tom's face well clear of the water and peering into his eyes for signs of life. Suddenly Tom coughed violently, vomited a gush of sea-water and fought for breath. Aboli dragged him onto the fallen mast and draped him over it, slamming his back with the flat of his hand so that the water Tom had swallowed erupted out of his gaping mouth and the air whistled in his throat.

Meanwhile Aboli was looking about desperately for sight of Dorian. The surface of the sea was misted with gunsmoke, which drifted in a heavy bank towards the land. The guns were still crashing out a discordant chorus, but gradually sinking into silence as the two ships pulled further and further apart.

At a glance Aboli saw that the *Minotaur* was already half a mile or more away, all her sails set and drawing, bearing up into the north. She was making no attempt to take advantage of the *Seraph*'s crippled state by attacking her while she was unable to manoeuvre. Instead she was fleeing to safety. Aboli wasted no more time on her but searched again for Dorian.

He saw three of the small dhows circling the *Seraph* at a wary distance, like jackals around a wounded lion. If the *Seraph* showed she was capable of giving chase to them, Aboli knew they would immediately head into the shallow water of the lagoon and the shelter of the coral reefs where the big ship could not follow them. Hampered by the tangle of wreckage hanging over her side, the *Seraph* was unable to come on the wind. She was drifting down with it and the current towards the fatal coral.

Aboli saw that Big Daniel already had a gang of men with swinging axes clearing away the wreckage. He tried to shout to the men on the deck for help, but they were too intent on their work and his voice did not reach them above the thump of the axe-heads into the timbers and the shouted orders. Then, suddenly, he saw the hull of one of the longboats swing out over the *Seraph*'s side and drop swiftly to the surface. Immediately the men at the oars pulled furiously towards where Aboli and Tom clung to the shattered foremast. Aboli saw with amazement that Hal was at the tiller. He must have left the ship in Ned Tyler's charge to come to the rescue of his sons. Now he was on his feet, yelling to Aboli as he approached, 'Where is Dorian? In God's name, have you seen him?' Aboli could not spare the air from his tortured lungs to reply but the longboat reached them within a minute and three men leaned over to haul them aboard. They dropped Tom onto the deck timbers between the thwarts before they jumped back to take their places at the oars. Aboli saw with relief that Tom was struggling to sit up, and reached down to help him as Hal repeated his question. 'For God's sake, Aboli, where is Dorian?'

As yet unable to use his voice Aboli pointed out into the banks of drifting gunsmoke. Hal leaped onto the thwart and balanced there easily, shading his eyes against the reflected glare of the low morning sun.

'There he is!' he yelled, with wild relief, and then to the oarsmen, 'Pull, lads! Pull for all you're worth!' The longboat built up speed under the thrust of the long oars, pulling for where the tiny speck of Dorian's head bobbed a quarter of a mile away.

This sudden precipitous dash out into the open sea, away from the *Seraph*'s safety, must have caught the attention of the men aboard one of the dhows that were stalking the ship. The Arab crew pointed to Dorian's drifting head and their excited shouts carried faintly to the men in the longboat. The man in the stern of the dhow hauled the long steering sweep hard across and she altered course. Her crew scrambled to trim her single lateen sail around, and she bore down swiftly towards the child, racing the long-boat to be first to reach him.

'Pull!' Hal roared, as he realized the danger.

Aboli dropped Tom back onto the deck, and leaped to a place on the thwart. He pushed the man already there to one side and threw all his massive weight onto the oar. His muscles bulged and bunched with the effort. 'All together, pull!' He set the stroke and the longboat leaped forward, the waves bursting over her bows and splattering over the straining backs of her crew as they raced towards Dorian.

Just then a taller wave lifted the boy high and he saw the longboat coming towards him. Dorian lifted one hand and waved. They were still not close enough to see the expression on his face but it was clear that he had not noticed the dhow skimming in towards him from the opposite direction.

'Swim, lad!' Hal shouted. 'Swim towards us!' But Dorian could not hear him. He waved again weakly, and it was clear that his strength was waning. The morning breeze was light and fitful, and the longboat was making better speed than the dhow, but they were further away from Dorian.

'We're gaining, lads!' Hal told them. 'We'll reach him before they do.'

He felt the wind puff on his cheek, die away for a moment, then come again stronger and with more determination. He watched it darken the surface of the sea, pass over Dorian's head, then swell the dhow's sail tight as a wineskin. The dhow heeled then sped ahead, her bow-wave curling white in the early sun.

Dorian must have heard the cries of the Arabs as they bore down on him for his head swivelled round and then he began to swim, his arms flopping and splashing with exhaustion as he tried to drag himself away from the racing dhow towards the longboat. He made little headway through the choppy, disturbed water.

With dismay Hal tried to estimate the relative distance and speed of the two vessels, and saw that they could not outrun the dhow. 'Pull!' he cried in despair. 'A hundred golden guineas if you reach him first! Pull! For God's sake, pull!'

There were at least twenty men in the dhow. It was an ugly little craft, the sail tattered, patched and stained with filth, the paintwork peeling from the hull, the planking zebra-striped where her crew had defecated over her gunwale. One of them lifted a long-barrelled jezail, and aimed over the narrowing gap at the longboat. White smoke spurted from the ancient weapon, and Hal heard the ball snap past his head but he did not even flinch.

Aboli heaved on the long oar with such force and effort that his eyes bulged from their sockets, suffused with blood, and his tattooed face locked in a horrible, snarling rictus. The oar bent like a green branch in his great hands, and the water hissed softly under the bows to spread in an arrow-straight shining wake behind.

The dhow was swifter still, though, and she had less distance to travel. Hal felt the ice of dread encase his chest as he realized, at last, that they could not win: they were still a hundred yards from Dorian as the dhow captain came level with him and rounded up into the wind, heaving to just long enough for five of his men to lean out over the side and reach down to seize the child.

They lifted him, struggling and kicking, from the sea with the water streaming from his clothing, his terrified shrieks ringing in Hal's head. Hal drew the pistol from under his waistcoat and pointed it in despair, but he knew it was futile even before Aboli growled, 'No, Gundwane! You might hit the boy.'

Hal lowered it and watched as Dorian was dragged over the filthy gunwale and the dhow captain put over the sweep and swung the craft back on to the wind. Her sail filled with a clap and she bore away, coming round with surprising speed and handiness on to her best point of sailing. She sped away towards the land. The Arab crew screamed abuse and mockery at them. A few fired their jezails and the bullets splashed into the sea around the longboat.

Hal's crew collapsed gasping and streaming with sweat on their oars and watched her go. No one spoke, just stared after the speeding dhow, devastated at the loss of the winsome lad who was everyone's favourite.

Then two of the Arabs lifted Dorian's small struggling body high in the air, so that the men in the longboat could see his pale face clearly. One drew the curved dagger from its sheath at his belt and lifted it high over his own head so that the silver blade caught the sunlight and glinted. Then he lifted Dorian's chin and pulled back his head like a pig for the slaughter. Deliberately he placed the blade against his throat and held it there, grinning back at the other men in the dhow.

Hal felt part of himself shrivel and die deep inside, and a whisper forced itself unbidden from his lips: 'Lord, I pray you, spare my boy. Anything you ask of me, I will do, but spare me this.'

Dorian was still struggling in the Arab's grip, and suddenly the cap fell from his head. His red-gold locks tumbled down onto his shoulders and shone in the sunlight. In obvious consternation, the man jerked the blade away from his throat. There was a sudden commotion in the dhow and the rest of the crew crowded around Dorian, gesticulating and shouting. Then he was bundled away out of their sight. On its wide triangular sail the dhow sped away.

It was two miles distant before Hal could bring himself to give the order to row back to the drifting *Seraph*, but all the way he was looking back over his shoulder. He saw the dhow following the tiny shape of the *Minotaur* up the channel into the north.

'That is where I will look for them,' he whispered. 'And I will never cease until I find them.'

On board the *Seraph* there was desperate work to be done to save the ship. This helped Hal to survive the first dreadful hours of his loss. The ship could not steer up into the wind with the foremast, sails and rigging dragging through the water like an enormous sea anchor. Hal set all sail on the standing masts to try to hold her off the lee shore, but this merely delayed the moment when she would be carried aground.

Led by Aboli and Big Daniel, ten axemen clambered out on to the foremast and hacked away the twisted mass of ropes and canvas. It was dangerous work: as every rope parted under the axe-blades, the strain was transferred unevenly and the mast rolled and kicked, threatening to throw the men into the water.

Closer they drifted to the coral reefs while the *Seraph* fought the immense drag of her shattered tackle, and Hal hurried from one side of her to the other, watching the closing land and directing the axemen in their efforts, pointing out to them the vital strands of rope that still held the fallen mast.

Always the green, humped back of Ras Ibn Khum loomed closer and higher above the ship as she battled for her life. The swells reared up under the hull as the bottom shelved towards the reef and the fangs of black coral grinned at the *Seraph*, waiting to tear the bowels out of her.

But at last the broken mast was held only by the single ten-inch manila rope of the forestay. It was stretched as tight and hard as a bar of iron, so that under the immense strain the sea-water jetted from the twisted strands. Big Daniel sent all the other axemen back on deck while he balanced easily on top of the heaving mast. He braced himself and judged his stroke, then swung the axe-head high and brought it down again on the stretched cable. He had judged it so finely that the thick cable-laid rope was not severed through all at once and only five of the strands parted.

As the remaining strands unravelled and gave under the strain, with a series of loud snaps and whipcracks and the mast rolled ponderously under his feet, Big Daniel had just time enough to race back up its slanting length and leap onto the deck. Then the butt-end of the broken mast rasped and grated over the side and at last dropped away and floated clear of the ship's side.

Immediately the *Seraph* responded gratefully to the release from her bonds. The heavily canted deck levelled itself, and she answered her helm almost joyously. Her bows came round, aiming at last to clear the headland of Ras Ibn Khum that had threatened to entrap her.

Hal crossed quickly to the lee rail and watched the jettisoned foremast drift away towards the reef, carefully marking the spot where it must be thrown ashore. Then he turned all his attention to bringing his ship into a safe anchorage.

By altering and adjusting the sail setting on the two standing masts, and making small changes in the helm, he managed to slip the grievously wounded *Seraph* past the point of the headland and into the bay beyond. Then he saw at once why al-Auf had chosen it as the place in which to lay his ambush.

It was an enclosed bay, of water so deep that it glowed blue as lapis-lazuli in the sunlight. It was protected from the monsoon wind by the tall headland, and when he looked down over the side he could see the smooth, sandy bottom ten fathoms down.

'Stand by to drop anchor, Mr Tyler,' he said, and as it splashed over the bows and the cable roared out through the hawsehole, the flood of grief that had threatened for these last dreadful hours to overwhelm him came down upon him with a black weight that threatened to crush the very life out of him. He could think of nothing but Dorian. The picture of the small body in the hands of the Arab corsairs, the knife held at his throat, was engraved in his mind and he knew it would never be expunged. He was unmanned by sorrow. It seemed to have sucked the strength from his limbs, the very breath from his lungs. He wanted to seek oblivion. Then he longed to go to his cabin and throw himself on his bunk and give himself over to his grief.

He stood alone on the quarterdeck, for his officers and all the crew kept clear of him, and none even looked in his direction. With the innate tact of hard, rough-hewn men, they were leaving him to his agony. Hal stared at the empty horizon to the north. The blue waters of the channel sparkled prettily in the sunlight, but they were void of any sail or promise of succour. Dorian was gone. He could not even rouse himself to consider his next action, to form his next order to the men who waited without looking at him.

Then Aboli went to him and touched his arm. 'Gund-wane, there will be a time for this later. If you wish to save your son, you must have the ship ready to follow him.' He glanced down the deck at the stump of the foremast, the raw timber shattered by the heavy iron ball. 'While you weep, the day steals away from you. Give the order.'

Hal looked at him with the blank eyes of a *bhang* smoker. 'He is so young, Aboli, so small.'

'Give the order, Gundwane.'

'I am so tired,' said Hal, 'so very tired.'

'No matter how it aches within you, you cannot rest,' Aboli said softly. 'Now, give the order.'

Hal shuddered with the effort, then lifted his chin. 'Mr Tyler! I want both pinnaces and the boats launched.' The words came tentatively to his lips, as though he spoke a foreign language.

'Aye, Captain.' Ned hurried to him, relief apparent on his face.

Hal felt the strength flow back into his body, and his resolve hardened. His voice firmed as he went on, 'The boat crews will recover the jettisoned mast. In the meantime the carpenters are to trim the stump of the foremast ready to fish her back in place. Sail-makers to break out the spare sails and the ropes and cables to rig the new mast.' As he reeled off the string of orders to begin the repairs to the ship, he glanced at the sun. It was already past its zenith. 'Let the crew eat by watches. There'll be precious little time to rest or eat again until we have the ship under way once more.'

Hal was at the tiller of the leading pinnace as the little flotilla of small boats rounded the point of Ras Ibn Khum. The two pinnaces had been reassembled. They were open boats, twenty-five feet in length, but weatherly, capable of long voyages in the open sea or of the type of heavy work Hal had in mind.

No sooner had they rounded the point of the headland than Hal spotted the foremast. Even from two miles away, it was easy to pick out, wrapped in its own gleaming white canvas against the black coral reef that held it. As they approached Hal saw that it would take hard work to free the long shaft of pine, for the canvas and the trailing ropes were tangled in the jagged coral and the humped swells coming in from the channel were bursting upon the reef and swirling over the mast in whirlpools of foam and white water.

Alf Wilson took one of the longboats through a pass in the coral reef into the quieter waters of the lagoon: from there it was safer and easier to land a crew on the reef armed with knives and axes. As the water burst and foamed around them they clung to the stranded mast.

In the meantime five of the strongest swimmers, led by Aboli and Big Daniel, had swum from the pinnaces and

288

the longboats to the reef, trailing light lines secured around their waists. They passed the ends to the men already clinging to the foremast, then swam back unhindered to the boats.

The light lines were used to pass heavier, stronger lines to the men on the mast. Once they had secured the ends to its butt, the small boats fanned out and began the attempt to haul the sixty-foot length of heavy pine off the reef.

All the boats held double crews, so that as one team tired the next could take over. They took up the slack in the lines, and when they came taut heaved together. The axemen on the mast hacked at the trailing lines and bundled canvas that were now woven into the jagged spines and needles of coral, trying to free it from this tenacious embrace. The oar blades thrashed the water, churning it white as the boats hauled at the stubborn load. The mast shifted, slid a few yards, and the crews shouted with triumph, but immediately it came up short again, stuck just as firmly as before. The backbreaking work had to begin all over again. A reluctant foot at a time the coral grudgingly yielded its grip, but Hal had to change the teams on the rowing benches three times before the mast rolled off the reef and they could tow it out into deeper water.

Alf Wilson rescued his men, who were still clinging to the mast. When they were dragged from the water, their arms and legs were lacerated and torn from contact with the merciless coral. Hal knew that many of those wounds would fester, for the coral was as poisonous as a serpent's venom.

By this time the sun was setting. Hal changed the teams again, and the little boats set out on the long row around the point into the lagoon beyond. With the heavy load they were dragging it seemed that they were standing still in the water, straining to no avail on the long sweeps, their arms and backs burned red as raw beef by the tropical sun, their sweat puddling on the decks under the thwarts. Dwarfed by their load the boats inched painfully along the seaward side of the reef, but when they tried to tow the mast around the point of Ras Ibn Khum, the current that swirled along the headland took them in its jaws, and held them fast.

While they battled against it the sun sank into the sea. Though they were near exhaustion, every muscle in their bodies racked and aching, their eyes glazed with the agony of their efforts, they could not pause to rest: if they had, the current would have thrown them back immediately onto the reef. As an example to his men, Hal stripped off his jacket and shirt and took his turn at the oars. Neither his back muscles nor his hands were hardened to this heavy work as were those of his men, and after the first hour he was in a trance of pain, the loom of the oar stained and sticky with blood from his raw palms. But the agony that gripped his body and the hypnotic swing and heave of rowing served to distract him from the deeper pain of the loss of his son.

A little before midnight the tide changed and the ebb around the point began to work in their favour. They moved slowly around it and into the sheltered lagoon. At last, in the moonlight, they saw the *Seraph* lying peacefully at her anchor on the tranquil waters speckled by the reflection of the stars. When they secured the floating mast alongside the ship, few had strength left to climb the ladder to the deck and most slumped in the bottom of the small boats, dead asleep before their heads hit the deck.

Hal forced himself wearily up the ladder to Ned Tyler, who was waiting for him at the rail. In the lantern light there was respect in his eyes as he evaluated Hal's state of exhaustion and saw his bloody hands. 'I will have the surgeon see to you right away.'

He stepped forward to help Hal off the ladder, but Hal

shook him off. 'Where is Tom?' he asked huskily. 'Where is my son?'

Ned looked upwards and, following his gaze, Hal saw a small, lonely figure high in the rigging of the main mast.

'He's been up there ever since we dropped anchor,' Ned said.

'Give the men a tot of rum with their breakfast, Mr Tyler,' Hal ordered, 'but get them up again at first light. God knows, they've earned a rest, but I cannot give it to them, not until the *Seraph* is ready for sea again.'

Although every muscle in his own body screamed for rest and he reeled on his feet with fatigue, he crossed to the main-mast shrouds and began the long climb to the yard.

When Hal reached the main yard, Tom made room for him and they sat together wordlessly. Hal's grief, which he had kept at bay all day and night, came rushing back upon him, sweeping away his exhaustion so that it was sharp and painful, burning coal in his chest. He put his arm around Tom's shoulders, partly to comfort him and partly to seek comfort for himself.

Tom leaned against him, but still they were silent. The stars moved in their majestic orbit above, and the Pleiades sank below the headland before Tom began to sob silently, his hard young body racked with unbearable pain. Hal held him tightly, but Tom's voice was broken and desolate as he whispered, 'It is my fault, Father.'

'It is nobody's fault, Tom.'

'I should have saved him. I gave him my promise. I made him a dreadful oath that I would never leave him.'

'No, Tom, it is not your fault. There was nothing any of us could do.' But he thought grimly, If there is any fault, it is mine. I should have left Dorian safe at High Weald. He was too young for this. All the remaining days of my life I will regret that I did not do so.

'We have to find him, Father. We have to rescue Dorian.' Tom's voice was firmer. 'He is out there somewhere. Aboli says they will never kill him. They will sell him as a slave. We have to find him.'

'Yes, Tom. We will find him.'

'We must swear another oath together,' Tom said, and looked up into his father's face. It was gaunt in the starlight, the eyes dark pits and mouth hard as if carved in marble. Tom groped for his father's hand. It was sticky with half-dried blood.

'You make the oath for both of us,' Hal told him, and Tom lifted their intertwined hands to the starry sky, 'Hear our oath, O God,' he said. 'We swear that we shall neither rest nor cease until we find Dorian again, wherever he may be in all the world.'

'Amen!' whispered Hal. 'And amen!' The stars were blurred by the tears that flooded his eyes.

The carpenters chamfered the stub of the broken foremast, sawing and chiselling away at the torn, splintered butt to form a step on to which the end of the mast could be rabbeted. Meanwhile the mast itself was floated ashore and another team shaped the end to make the joint. The work went on through the day and continued after dark by lantern light. Hal was demon-driven and spared none, especially not himself.

Hal and Ned Tyler observed the set of the tides in the bay and surveyed the beach. The sandy bottom was ideal for their purpose and the tide rise was above two and a half fathoms. When the mast had been prepared for fitting to its butt, they warped the *Seraph* onto the beach at high tide, and secured her there with heavy cables attached to palm trees at the water's edge.

When the tide ebbed out from under her, the *Seraph* was left high and dry on the white sands. Using the cables they hove her over at an angle of thirty degrees. They had to work swiftly then, for in six hours the tide would float her once more. Using a system of blocks and tackles, the old mast was restepped into its rabbeted butt, and pinned with long iron spikes dipped in boiling tar.

Hal used this opportunity to inspect the ship's bottom for evidence of the presence of the teredo worm, which in these warm waters could eat away the bottom timbers of a ship. At times these creatures grew as long as a man's arm and as thick as his thumb. During heavy infestations they drilled their holes so close to each other that only a thin layer of wood was left between them. A ship so afflicted could have the bottom drop out of her in heavy seas. Hal was relieved to find that the layer of tar and canvas that covered the hull had deterred not only the ship-worm but also the growth of weed that would slow the *Seraph*'s passage through the water. She was as clean as he could hope for, but he could not afford the time to scrape away the light growth of weed and barnacles.

As soon as the tide lifted her off the sand they towed the *Seraph* back to her anchorage in the deep water of the bay. The joint in the foremast was not strong enough to withstand the pressure of sails in a high wind, and the carpenters worked to reinforce it. First they fashioned hardwood fishes to act as splints over the joint. When these were in place they clapped on seizings of soaked hemp rope and tightened these with the capstan. When the rope dried, it was iron hard.

When Hal inspected the finished work, the master carpenter boasted, 'That joint is stronger than the mast itself. Once the stays and shrouds are rigged, no matter what you do to her, no matter how much canvas you pile on her in any gale, she'll never break at the same place again.'

'Good fellow!' Hal commended him. 'Now stand by to swing aloft her new yards and spars.'

When the work was done, and *Seraph* rode at anchor under her new foremast with all her canvas furled under the gaskets, ready to be cast loose, Ned Tyler came to Hal on the quarterdeck, with all the other ship's officers behind him, and made the formal report. 'Shipshape, and in all respects ready for sea, Captain.'

'Very good, Mr Tyler.'

Ned hesitated, then took his courage in both hands. 'If you please, sir, whither are we bound? Do you have a course for me to steer?'

'I hope to have a course for you in very short order,' Hal promised grimly. No one had seen him smile since they had lost Dorian. 'Have the prisoners paraded on deck.'

The Arab captives were brought out of the forecastle, dressed only in their loin cloths and wearing leg shackles. The links of the chains clinked as they hobbled in a bedraggled file to the foredeck and stood there, blinking in the strong sunlight.

Hal ignored them and crossed instead to the ship's rail. He stared down into the water. It was so clear that he could see the sea cucumbers crawling along the sandy bottom, and the shoals of small fish that hovered around the *Seraph*'s hull. Then, abruptly, a dark shape glided from under the ship. It was as long as one of the longboats, and as broad. Its back was banded with darker wavy lines and the monstrous tail beat to a lazy rhythm.

The *Seraph* had been long enough at this mooring for the galley slops and sewage she had dumped into the bay to attract the tiger sharks from the deep water beyond the reef. Hal felt his skin prickle as he watched the monster turn with a flick of its tail and disappear under the ship.

The tiger shark was the creature that haunted the nightmares of every mariner in these tropical waters.

Hal left the rail and walked slowly down the line of prisoners. At last his grief had a target on which to focus. It took all his will-power to keep his anger under control and his expression neutral as he peered into the faces of the corsairs. Rachid was at the far end of the line. A filthy bloodstained rag of a bandage covered his injured ear. Hal stopped in front of him.

'What is the penalty for piracy?' he asked Rachid quietly, still holding his rage in check. 'What does the Koran say of the murderer and the rapist? Speak to me of the law of Shari'ah. Expound to me the law of Islam.'

Rachid could not meet his eyes, but he trembled like a man in fever and the sweat ran down his cheeks to drip from his chin. He had learned how ruthless was this Frankish sea-devil who confronted him now.

'Does not the Prophet tell us what must be the fate of the murderer? Does he not give the killer into the hands of the father of the victim?' Hal asked. 'Does he not exhort us, have no mercy upon him who has the blood of the innocent upon his hands?'

Rachid fell to his knees on the deck and tried to kiss Hal's feet. 'Mercy, great lord! I place my worthless soul in your hands.' Hal kicked him away as though he were a cur, and walked back down the line.

'The Prophet tells us that the penalty for murder is death. You are all murderers taken bloody-handed in the act of piracy. I am a servant of the English king, charged and empowered by His Majesty with the duty of ridding these seas of such offal as you.'

Hal turned to Ned Tyler. 'Mr Tyler, have a rope reeved at the yard-arm for each of the prisoners.' He stood with his hands clasped behind his back, head thrown back to watch the ropes carried aloft and run through the sheaves.

'Ready to proceed with punishment,' Ned reported at last, when the nooses were set and a party of sailors stood ready at the tail of each rope.

'Leave that rogue for last.' Hal gestured at Rachid, who still cringed upon his knees. 'Hang the others.'

Still in their chains, squealing and struggling, crying to Allah for mercy, the nooses were dropped over their heads and tightened around their necks. Then the men on the rope tails walked away with them, stamping their bare feet on the deck in unison and chanting as though they were setting the mainsail. Three and four at a time, the Arabs were hoisted kicking and gasping to the high yard. Gradually their struggles quieted and they hung there like bunches of grotesque fruit, their necks twisted awkwardly, their tongues protruding, purple and swollen, from their gaping mouths.

At last Rachid was alone on the deck. Hal went back to stand over him. 'I gave them an easy death,' he said. 'But you have deprived me of my youngest son. You will not be so fortunate, unless you can tell me what I need to know.'

'Anything in my power, *effendi*,' Rachid blubbered. 'You need only ask it of me.'

'I need to know where I can find al-Auf and my son.'

'I do not know that, *effendi*.' Rachid shook his head so violently that his tears sprayed like water from a spaniel's back. Hal reached down and lifted him to his feet, twisted one arm up between his shoulder-blades and marched him to the ship's rail.

'Look down there!' he whispered in the man's mutilated ear. 'See what waits you.' Rachid let out a piercing wail, as the tiger shark slid silently through the bright waters below, rolling slightly so that they could see every detail of the grotesque foreshortened head. It looked up at them with a single pig-like eye.

'Where can I find al-Auf? Where is his sally-port? Tell

it to me and you will die swiftly and go to your God in one piece, not through the maw of that unclean creature down there.'

'I know not.' Rachid sobbed. 'Very few men know where al-Auf has his citadel. I am only a poor fisherman.'

'Aboli!' Hal called, and the tall black man strode to his side with the tail of the last hanging rope in his hand. 'Head first!' Hal ordered.

Aboli knelt swiftly and looped the rope through the chains that fettered the Arab's ankles. 'Heave away!' he told the sailors who held the rope's other end and Rachid was hoisted feet first into the air, swinging out like a pendulum over the ship's side.

'Where is al-Auf?' Hal called to him. 'Where can I find my son?'

'I know not. I call on God to witness,' Rachid screamed.

'Lower away!' Hal told the men on the rope end, and Rachid dropped jerkily towards the surface of the water. 'Avast!' He stopped them when Rachid's face was only a foot above the water. The man tried to turn his head to look back at Hal, who was leaning far out over the rail.

'I know not. I swear by all things holy,' he screamed. 'I know not where al-Auf has your son.'

Hal nodded to Aboli. 'Feed the beast!' Aboli lifted one of a row of leather buckets filled with slops from the galley that he had ready beside the rail. He poured the contents over the side and the mess of fish-heads, guts and peelings splattered into the sea. The shoals of small fish darted upwards to the feast and churned the surface in their frantic greed. Aboli threw another bucketful overboard.

Within a minute there was a dark, menacing movement below the tiny milling shoals. Then a broad, striped back pushed up from the depths with awful majesty. The shoals of smaller fish scattered and the behemoth rose to the surface and opened its jaws, which could have engulfed a man's torso. It's multiple rows of teeth rose erect as it snapped at the scraps, stirring the waters even though it was still deep beneath where Rachid hung suspended. 'You can never pass through the gates of Paradise if your body has been devoured by such an obscene, unclean fish,' Hal called down to him.

His prisoner wriggled helplessly on the end of the line. His voice was shrill and incoherent. 'No! I know not. Mercy, great lord.'

'Down!' Hal gestured to the men on the rope, and they let Rachid drop until his head and shoulders were submerged. 'Hold him there.' Hal watched him kick and struggle. The great shark sensed the disturbance and circled under him, rising slowly and cautiously out of the depths. Rachid's movements were becoming weak and spasmodic as he drowned.

'Heave away!' Hal signalled, and they lifted Rachid clear of the surface. He dangled there upside down. He had lost the bloody bandage from around his head, and his long sodden locks dangled in the water. He was fighting for breath, twisting and writhing at the end of the rope.

'Speak to me!' Hal bellowed. 'Speak to me of my youngest son.' He felt cold, devoid of any pity or compassion. The shark smelt the blood on the drifting bandage and rose to it. Again, the huge jaws opened and it sucked in the scrap of cloth. As it dived, arching its back, its tail fin broke through the surface and struck the hanging man a heavy blow. Rachid squealed with terror and swung back and forth on the rope.

'Speak!' Hal encouraged him. 'I wait to hear about my son.'

'I cannot tell what I do not know,' Rachid howled back, and Hal waved to the men on the rope. They dropped him back into the water, as far as his waist. Deep down the shark swirled with an agility and speed that seemed impossible in such a huge creature and rushed up towards the surface, growing even larger as it approached.

'Heave!' Hal called sharply, and they lifted Rachid clear just as the great jaws snapped closed, plucking him out of their reach with only inches to spare.

'It is still not too late,' Hal said, just loudly enough to reach Rachid through his terror and failing strength. 'Tell me and end it swiftly.'

'I do not know where you can find al-Auf, but I know a man who does,' Rachid answered, his voice broken and rough with terror.

'Give me his name.'

'His name is Grey *effendi* in Zanzibar. He was the one who told us of the great treasure you carry in your ship.'

'Down!' Hal gave the signal, and as they lowered Rachid, the tiger shark rushed up to meet him. This time Hal did not attempt to pluck him away – he was of no further value. He sent Rachid to his punishment without a qualm, and watched dispassionately as the shark's jaws closed over the man's head, engulfing him to the shoulders.

The shark hung from the rope, flexing and whipping its tail from side to side, jack-knifing its massive body, working its fangs in a shearing action, cutting through flesh and bone. Its great weight and the violence of its movements jerked the men on the other end of the rope off their feet, and sent them skidding across the deck.

Then the fangs met and sheared away Rachid's head cleanly. The shark dropped back, leaving his corpse dangling and twitching over the surface, blood spraying from the severed neck and clouding the waters.

Hal drew his sword from the sheath on his belt and with a single back-handed slash cut the rope. The headless body dropped into the sea and sank slowly, turning end over end in dark curtains of its own blood. The shark came back and, like a dog accepting a titbit, took the body almost gently in its half-moon mouth and swam away with it into the deeper water. Hal moved away from the ship's side.

'The tide will turn in an hour, Mr Tyler.' He looked up at the dead men hanging at the yard-arm. 'Rid the ship of those. Throw them overboard. We will sail for Zanzibar on the ebb tide.'

They rounded the point of Ras Ibn Khum with every sail set to the royals and came on to the wind in a broad reach.

'Your new course is north-east by north, Mr Tyler,' Hal said. 'With this wind, we should be off Zanzibar again before sunset tomorrow evening.'

Hal did not wish to give forewarning of his arrival so during the night he hove to in the channel, and took the *Seraph* into Zanzibar harbour in the dawn. He dipped his colours in courtesy to the fort, and the moment the anchor grabbed a hold on the bottom he ordered the longboat away. Then he hurried down to his cabin and took the brace of double-barrelled rifled pistols from his desk and thrust them into his sword-belt.

As he stepped out of his cabin, Tom was waiting for him. He had his cap on his head, a sword on his belt and boots on his usually bare feet.

'I wish to come with you, sir,' Tom said. Hal hesitated – there might be fighting ashore – but Tom went on quickly, 'I shared the oath with you, Father.'

'Come on, then.' Hal ran onto the deck. 'Be ready to sail again at a moment's notice,' he told Ned Tyler, and went down into the longboat with Tom and a dozen men. At the quay he left Alf Wilson and four seamen to take care of the boat. 'Stand off from the quay, but be ready to come in and pick us up in a hurry,' he told Alf, then said to Aboli, 'Take us back to the consul's house. Go swiftly. Stay together.'

They went through the narrow streets at a trot, in double file, shoulder to shoulder, their weapons at the ready. When they reached the front door of Grey's house Hal nodded at Aboli, who beat on the carved panels with the butt of the pike he carried. The blows reverberated through the quiet house. After an interval they heard shuffling footsteps approaching from the other side of the door, and the latch was lifted. An ancient female slave stared out at the party of armed men. Her wrinkled features crumpled in consternation, and she tried to slam the door shut again. Aboli blocked it with his shoulder.

'You have nothing to fear, old mother,' Hal told her gently. 'Where is your master?'

'I dare not say,' the woman whispered, but her eyes flicked to the broad stone staircase that led from the courtyard to the upper storeys of the house.

'Bolt the door again,' Hal ordered Aboli, 'and leave two men to guard it.' Then he went up the staircase two steps at a time, and came out at the second level. He paused there and glanced around the salon in which he stood. It was richly furnished with ornamental rugs and heavy dark furniture inlaid with ivory and mother-of-pearl. Hal knew the usual layout of this type of mansion: the zenana, the women's quarters, would be on the top floor; where he stood were the main living rooms, with the master's suite beyond the elaborately carved ebony and ivory screens at the far end. Hal slipped quietly between the screens into a smaller salon. The floor was strewn with silk-covered cushions and in the centre a hookah pipe stood on a low table, which was cluttered with used food bowls. The room reeked with the smell of stale *bhang* smoke, the heavy aroma of food spices and the peculiar musky odour of Grey's disease.

Hal crossed to another set of screens and stepped through into the room beyond. A low bed filled half the floor space. He stopped in the doorway, taken by surprise. On the bed was a tangle of bodies, white limbs and brown entwined. It took a long moment for Hal to realize what he was seeing. Consul Grey lay upon his back, his swollen limbs spread, his huge belly distended as though he were in the last stages of child-bearing, his chest covered with an animal skin of coarse, curling black hair. His grossly deformed legs were studded with open red ulcers, the stigmata of his disease. The room reeked so strongly of the yellow discharge from these uncovered sores, that Hal felt his gorge rise.

Two slave-girls were kneeling over him, one above his face, the other straddling his body. One raised her head. Hal and she stared at each other, until she screamed. Both girls sprang up and fled from the room, disappearing beyond another screen like a pair of startled gazelles, leaving Grey wallowing upon the bed.

Grey heaved himself on to his side and lifted himself on one elbow. 'You!' He gaped at Hal. 'I did not expect—' He broke off, and his mouth opened and closed without uttering another sound.

'I know full well what you expected, sir,' Hal told him. 'And I apologize for disappointing you.'

'You have no right to trespass in my house.' Grey wiped the girl's juices from his face with the back of his hand. Then surprise gave way to anger and he snarled, 'I have armed guards. I shall summon them.' He opened his mouth to shout, but Hal placed the point of his sword against the man's throat. Grey subsided like a punctured bladder and tried to wriggle away from the steel.

'Cover yourself.' Hal picked up a silk robe from the floor beside the bed and threw it at him. 'The sight of your carcass sickens me.'

Awkwardly, Grey drew on the robe and seemed to

recover a little of his poise and confidence. 'I did not mean to threaten you,' he smiled ingratiatingly, 'but you startled me. Your arrival was at an embarrassing moment.' He winked lewdly. 'And I expected you to be halfway to Good Hope by this time.'

'Again I must apologize,' Hal said. 'I have not been altogether honest with you. I am not a trader, nor am I a servant of the East India Company. My true name is Henry Courtney. I am a servant of His Majesty King William.'

'We are all servants of the King.' Grey's tone was reverent and his expression sanctimonious. He wriggled to the edge of the bed and, with a great effort, hoisted himself to his feet.

Hal placed the point of his sword on Grey's distended belly and gently pushed him down again. 'Pray, do not discommode yourself,' he said politely. 'When I say that I am the King's servant, I mean that I carry the King's commission. Included among the powers conferred upon me by this commission is the power of summary trial and execution of any person taken in the act of piracy, or in aiding and abetting any person in the crime of piracy upon the high seas.' Hal drew the rolled parchment from under his cloak. 'Do you wish to peruse it?'

'I am sure it is as you say.' Grey spoke lightly and with assumed confidence, but his colour had faded to a sickly sepia. 'However, I am at a loss to see how this affects me.'

'I beg you to allow me to explain.' Hal slipped the parchment back into the lining of his cloak. 'There is no cargo of treasure aboard my ship. You were the only person who believed that. I told you as a test of your honesty. I was baiting a trap for the pirate known as al-Auf.'

Grey stared at him, and sweat broke out in a rash of droplets across his chin and forehead.

'I also told you the date on which I would sail from Zanzibar, and the route I would take. Al-Auf could not have waylaid my ship without that information. He had been given the precise intelligence that could only have come from one person.' Hal touched his chest lightly with the sword-point. 'From you, sir.'

'That is not true!' Grey gobbled frantically. 'I am a loyal servant of the King, a man of honour.'

'If further evidence were needed, one of al-Auf's men has given me your name. You are in league with the corsair. You are guilty of aiding and abetting the enemies of the King. We need not debate this further. I condemn you to death by hanging.' He raised his voice. 'Aboli!'

Aboli appeared at his shoulder, his tattooed face so forbidding that Grey rolled to the far side of the bed and quaked like a beached jelly-fish.

'Rig the rope for an execution.'

Aboli had the coiled rope over his shoulder. He strode to the window, which reached from floor to ceiling, and kicked open the carved shutters. He looked down into the courtyard where the fountain splashed and gurgled, shook out the noose and let it drop and dangle halfway down the wall. Then he tied the end to the central upright frame of the window with a bowline knot. 'The drop is too long for such a barrel of lard. It will pull off his head like a chicken,' Aboli grunted, and shook his head. 'It will be messy.'

'We cannot be overly neat and tidy about this,' Hal said. 'Put him into the noose.'

Grey screamed and floundered on the bed. 'For God's sake, Courtney, you cannot do this to me.'

'I think I can. Let us put my theory to the test.'

'I am an Englishman! I demand a fair trial by an English judge!'

'You have just had one,' Hal pointed out. 'Mr Fisher, please help to prepare the prisoner for punishment!'

'Aye, Captain.' Big Daniel led his men into the room and they surrounded the man on the bed.

'I am a sick man!' Grey blubbered.

'We have the perfect cure for whatever ails you,' said

Big Daniel calmly. He rolled Grey onto his belly and, with a light line, pinioned his hands behind his back. His men hoisted the heavy body off the bed and dragged the consul to the window. Aboli had the noose ready and slipped it over his head. They turned Grey to face Hal again. They had to support him for his grossly swollen legs could not carry his weight.

'You will be gratified to hear that your ally, Musallim bin-Jangiri, also known as al-Auf, slipped out of the trap I laid for him.' Hal sat down on the end of the bed. 'He has disappeared out into the ocean. We must presume that he has slunk back to his lair to lick the wounds I was able to inflict upon him.'

'I know nothing of this.' Grey hung in the arms of his captors, shaking wildly with terror. 'You must believe me, Sir Henry.'

Hal went on as if he had not spoken. 'My problem is exacerbated by al-Auf's capture of my youngest son. I am sure you will appreciate that I will do anything to rescue my boy and I think you know where I can find him.' He reached out and placed the point of his sword at Grey's throat. 'Let him stand on his own two feet,' he said to the men who held him, and they stepped aside.

'I beg of you, Sir Henry!' Grey swayed in the open window. 'I am an old man.'

'And an evil one,' Hal agreed, and pressed the sword a little harder against his throat. A bright drop of blood welled up from the pricked skin and stained the tip of the engraved Toledo blade. 'Where can I find al-Auf? And my son?'

A bubbling, spluttering sound came from under Grey's robe and his liquid faeces, brown as tobacco juice, streamed down his bloated legs to puddle on the floor between his feet. The stench was sharp and nauseating in the small hot room, but Hal's expression did not change. 'Where can I find my son?' he repeated.

'The Flower of the Sea!' Grey screamed. 'Flor de la Mar, the old Portuguese fort on the island. That is al-Auf's sally-port.'

'I have to point out to you, sir, that your ability to provide this information confirms your guilt beyond any shadow of doubt.'

Slowly he increased the pressure of the steel at Grey's throat. Grey tried to resist it, arching his back, while his feet slid in his own dung until his heels were over the sill of the open window. He teetered there a moment and then, with a despairing wail, fell out backwards. The rope hissed after him, then came up with a thump as Grey's full weight stretched it hard over the sill.

Hal led his band down the staircase into the courtyard. There he paused to glance at the bloated body, which dangled quiescent at the rope's end. Grey was suspended over the fish pool. From the lining of his cloak Hal drew the parchment he had prepared the night before, and handed it to Aboli. 'Hang that around his neck.'

Aboli jumped onto the parapet of the fountain and reached up to slip the loop of twine over Grey's head. The parchment hung down onto his chest. Hal's proclamation was written in both English and Arabic.

Having been tried and found guilty of complicity with the corsair known as al-Auf in acts of piracy on the high seas, the prisoner, William Grey, was sentenced to death by hanging. Sentence was duly carried out by me, Henry Courtney, under power vested in me by commission of His Majesty King William III.

Tom stood beside his father and read aloud the Arabic text of the proclamation. When he came to the end he said, 'It is signed "El Tazar". That means the Barracuda. Why?'

'It's the name I was given by the Mussulmen when

first I voyaged in these waters.' Hal looked down at his son. Once again, he felt a pang of concern that one as young as Tom should have been witness to such grisly proceedings. Then he remembered that Tom was seventeen, and that with sword and cannon he had already killed more than one man himself. He was no child, and he had been prepared by vocation and training for such grim work. 'Our work here is completed,' Hal said quietly. 'Back to the ship.' He turned to the tall carved doors, and Big Daniel gave the order to the men who stood guard there. They swung them open.

The old crone who had met them on their arrival and given them access to the house now stood on the threshold. The street behind her was crowded with guards. There were at least a dozen, armed with jezails and curved scimitars, a fearsome band of ruffians who surged forward as the doors opened.

'See what the infidels have done to our lord,' the old woman wailed, as she saw Grey's body hanging from the rope. 'Murder!' She opened her toothless mouth and gave forth the high, keening cry that Arab women use to goad their men into a murderous rage.

'*Allah akbar!*' screamed the leader of the guards. 'God is great!' He flung up the long jezail to his shoulder and fired it into the band of English seamen. The ball struck one of Hal's sailors full in the face, blowing out most of his teeth, shattering his jaw and driving on deep into his skull. He dropped without a cry, and Hal stepped forward with one of the rifled pistols levelled in his left hand.

His first shot hit the guards' leader in the right eye. His eyeball burst, leaving a gaping hole in the socket, and the jelly trickled down his cheek. As he dropped, Hal fired the second barrel at the man who appeared in the gap behind him, and hit him cleanly in the centre of his forehead. The dead man fell back into the pack of his companions, knocking one off his feet.

'Have at them, lads!' Hal shouted, and his seamen charged through the doorway in a solid phalanx.

'*Seraph!*' They yelled the war-cry, as they carried the mob of robed figures before their charge. None of their foes was able to lift his long musket in the close ruck of bodies, and all were driven back by the bright hedge of cutlasses. Three more went down, then Hal's party was in the street where they had more room for sword-play.

Hal had the second, unfired pistol in his left hand, but he reserved the shots, and instead used his blade to cut down another Arab who blocked his way. He glanced round for Tom and found him a pace behind him. In that brief glimpse he noticed that Tom's blade was held high, its point already dulled with blood. He too had scored a hit. 'Good lad,' Hal grunted. 'Stay close.' He ran at the remaining Arabs. They had seen the fate of their comrades at the front of the line. Now they were confronted by the ferocious white faces bearing down on them in a pack. They broke away and fled back down the alley.

'Let them go!' Hal restrained Tom sharply. 'Back to the boat.'

'What about old Bobby?' Big Daniel asked, and indicated the dead seaman behind them. He was surrounded by the corpses of the Arabs they had cut down.

'Bring him,' Hal ordered. It was bad for the men to see one of their mates left on a battlefield. They must know that, dead or wounded, he would never desert them. 'As soon as we are at sea again, we will give him a decent burial.'

Daniel stooped and Aboli helped him haul the body over his shoulder. Then, bared cutlass in hand, the two big men led the rest at a run back through the narrow streets towards the quay. So early in the morning, there were few townsfolk abroad, and those who saw them coming disappeared swiftly into the alleys and doorways. They reached the harbour unchallenged and Alf Wilson brought in the longboat to pick them up.

As they pulled back to where the *Seraph* lay, a few bolder souls came out of hiding to fire their muskets and shout insults or bold challenges across the waters of the harbour, but the range was already long and none of the musket-balls came near the longboat. Ned Tyler had the anchor cable firmed up and a dozen men standing by the capstan. As soon as they had swarmed up the ladder and the longboat was lifted out of the water, he gave the order to hoist the anchor and set the sails.

As the *Seraph* came round, and lined up for the harbour entrance, the long green banner of the Sultan rose to the top of the flagpole on the west tower of the fort, and the battery of cannon on the ramparts opened up on them.

Even from the deck, they could clearly see the white-robed gunners frantically serving their pieces. Through the telescope Hal could make out the panic and confusion among them. As each of the massive cannon was reloaded and run out again, no attempt was made to correct their aim. As he watched, one of the over-enthusiastic gunners touched off his gigantic weapon while his team were still behind it, heaving on the tackles to run out the carriage. The recoil drove it back over them, crushing bones and amputating limbs. Hal could hear the agonized screams of the mutilated gunners even across the distance of two full cables' lengths that separated them.

Hal saw the huge stone ball in flight: it soared upwards from the battlements and seemed to pause, like a tiny black speck, at the zenith of its trajectory, then arced down towards them. For a moment Hal thought it might strike the ship, but instead it plunged into the sea alongside and threw up such a towering fountain of spray and water that it fell across the quarterdeck and splashed Hal's boots to the knees.

'We must acknowledge such a rousing farewell.' Hal looked at Ned Tyler, without a smile. 'Kindly dip our colours in courtesy to the Sultan, Mr Tyler. Then bring the ship on to a southerly heading.'

'It is not marked,' Hal muttered, as he pored over the chart spread on his desktop, 'yet I swear I have heard the name before. Flor de la Mar, the Flower of the Sea. With that name, and as Grey said, it must indeed be one of the old Portuguese possessions, of course.' He had already questioned his officers, and sent them to ask the men, but none knew of it.

Piled beside the chart were eight heavy books bound in black calf leather. These volumes were among Hal's dearest possessions. He selected one from the pile, opened the stiff crackling pages and gazed briefly at the beautiful flowing script and the ink drawings that closely covered every page on both sides. The writing was so familiar it seemed part of his very existence. It was that of his father, Sir Francis Courtney. These log books were part of the legacy Hal had received from him. The eight volumes covered thirty years of his father's voyages and wanderings on the oceans of the globe, a lifetime's accumulation of knowledge and experience, of such intrinsic and sentimental value that, for Hal, they were beyond any price in gold.

Almost reverentially, he thumbed through the pages, searching for the name he had read somewhere in them so many years before. His search was spasmodic, as every so often he was diverted by some gem of observation or a captivating drawing of a foreign harbour, an exotic landfall, a portrait of a man, a bird or a fish that had caught his father's keen eye and been faithfully recorded by his skilful pen.

Unsuccessful in his initial search, he laid the first volume aside and chose another, whose cover was marked, 'Ocean of the Indies, Anni Domini 1632 to 1641.' Hal's search lasted so long that he had to refill the oil in the lamp. Then, suddenly, the name leaped out of the page into his red, aching eyes. He gave a heartfelt sigh of relief. 'Isla Flor de la Mar': it was the notation beneath the ink line-drawing of a landfall seen from the ocean, which depicted what was clearly an island. The compass rose and a scale of distances were marked in underneath. These showed an overall size for the landmass from south to north of five sea miles. Below the name was written the position, '11 degrees 25 minutes south lat. 47 degrees 32 minutes east long.', and in smaller letters, 'Known to the Mussulmen as Daar Al Shaitan or the Harbour of the Devil.'

Quickly Hal referred back to his chart. With ruler and compass he picked out the co-ordinates his father had given. Although he treated even Sir Francis's estimate of longitude with reserve, he found that these measurements gave him a position about a hundred and fifty sea miles north of the Glorietta islands. However, on Hal's chart nothing was marked at this location except the open sea. He referred back to his father's log. Sir Francis had written a full page of description. Hal started to read and was immediately entranced. 'This island was first reported by Affonse d'Albuquerque in 1508 when he was preparing to capture the Arab cities along the Fever Coast of the eastern African continent. From this sally-port he launched his attacks on Zanzibar and Dar Es Salaam.' Hal nodded. He knew that Albuquerque had been known as the Great by his peers, and as al-Shaitan, the Devil, by the Arabs for the success of his naval forays into the Ocean of the Indies. He, more than even Tristão da Cunha, had been responsible for securing the pre-eminence of Portuguese power and influence on the Fever Coast and in the Persian Gulf.

His ships had been the first of any European power to penetrate the Arab stronghold of the Red Sea. Hal turned back to his father's writing.

Albuquerque constructed a considerable fort on the north point of the island, hewing coral stone blocks for the construction, and employing Mussulmen prisoners for the heavy work. He armed the fort with cannon captured during his conquest of Ormuz and Aden. He named the island after his own flagship, *Flor de la Mar*. Some years later, in 1508, this same ship was wrecked on the coral reefs off the coast of Goa, and Albuquerque lost the vast personal treasure he had accumulated during his campaigns in these Oceans. After the success of his attacks on the African mainland Albuquerque abandoned his base on the island and transferred his flag to Zanzibar. The fort on Flor de la Mar was allowed to fall into disrepair.

I called here on the 2nd of November 1637. The island is five and a quarter sea miles in length and half a sea mile wide at its broadest point. The east side is exposed to the scend of the ocean and the prevailing winds, and offers no secure anchorage. The bay on the north-west extremity is well protected and guarded by a coral reef. The bottom is sand and shell and affords excellent holding. There is a passage through the reef which runs directly under the walls of the fort. Thus when the battlements were manned by the Portuguese any vessel entering the bay could have been brought under heavy fire by the batteries of the garrison.

In the middle of the page Hal's father had made a detailed map of the bay and the fort, showing the passage through the reef and the various bearings and soundings. 'Thank you, Father,' Hal murmured, with feeling, and went on with his study of the text.

I went ashore and found that the walls of the fort had well stood the passage of almost a century and a half. They were sturdily built and would be impervious to all but modern siege engines. The brass cannon were still sited in their embrasures but the metal of the barrels was much corroded by the salt sea airs. The catchments and cisterns for the gathering of rainwater remained in working order, and we were able to refill our casks from them. There was a vast colony of sea birds nesting on the south point of the island. During the hours of daylight the multitudes of these birds formed a dark canopy over the island that could be discerned from many miles out at sea. The chorus of their combined voices was of such volume as to give offence to the ear and astound the senses. The flesh of these fowl was oily and strongly flavoured with fish but when salted and smoked became palatable. I despatched a shore party to gather in their eggs. They returned with ten large baskets, and all hands feasted upon them. There was besides much fish and oysters to be taken in the bay, and we lingered ten days and employed all hands in the catching and smoking of these bounties to replenish the ship's stores. We sailed again on the 12th of November, bound for the Bab al Mandeb at the foot of the Red Sea.

Hal closed the log book with the same reverence as if it had been the family Bible – which, in a manner of speaking, it was – and turned his attention to the chart. Carefully he marked in the position of the island his father had given, then ruled in the course and bearing from their present position at the southern extremity of the Zanzibar Channel.

When he went on deck the sun was lying only a finger above the horizon, so shrouded in purple sea fret that he could look directly at its fuming red orb with his naked eye. With the coming of dusk, the monsoon wind had eased but still had sufficient force to fill every sail tight and pearly as the breasts of a wet-nurse.

'Mr Tyler, bring her up to the wind as close as she can sail on this tack,' he ordered grimly. 'Full and by.'

'Full and by, it is, Captain.' Ned touched his cap.

Hal left him and strode forward, glancing up to the yards of the foremast as he passed beneath them. Tom was still up there, as he had been ever since they had cleared the harbour at Zanzibar. Hal empathized with him, but he would not go up to join his vigil. He too wanted to be alone.

When he reached the stem he stepped up onto the base of the bowsprit and clung to the forestay, peering ahead into the darkening sea, which was turning the colour of overripe plums. At intervals the *Seraph* tore the crest off a larger wave, and tossed it back over the bows, dashing a spattering of drops into his face. He made no effort to wipe them away, but let them drip down from his chin onto his chest.

Far behind them, Africa had disappeared into the distance and the hazy dusk. There was no sight of land ahead. The dark ocean was boundless and wide. What hope to find one small boy in all its limitless expanses? he wondered. 'And yet I will, should it take me the rest of my natural life,' he whispered. 'And no mercy on any who stand in my way.'

The dhow was a slaver, employed in carrying its cargo of misery from the mainland across the channel to the markets of Zanzibar. It stank of the waste of the human body, and of the agony of the human spirit. It was a foul miasma that hung over the little vessel, and permeated the hair and clothing of all aboard her. It

314

entered Dorian's lungs with every breath he drew, and seemed to corrode his very soul.

He was chained in the lower deck. The iron staples were driven through the heavy timber main frame and the heads were riveted. His leg-irons were hand forged and the chain was passed through the eye of his fetters. There was space for a hundred captives in the long low hold, but Dorian was alone. He squatted on one of the dhow's main frames, trying to keep his feet out of the noisome bilges, which slopped back and forth with each pitch and roll of the narrow hull, filled with fish scales and pieces of sodden copra – the dhow's alternative cargoes.

Every hour or so, the hatch above his head was thrown open and one of the Arab crew peered down at him anxiously. His gaoler would pass down a bowl of rice and fish stew or a green coconut from which the top had been hacked away. The coconut juice was sweet and faintly effervescent, and Dorian drank it eagerly although he spurned the stew made from half-rotten sun-dried fish.

Apart from his fetters and the foul confines of the cabin, his Arab captors had treated him with the utmost consideration. More than that, they were evidently concerned for his welfare, and made certain that he went neither hungry nor thirsty.

Four times in the last two days the captain of the dhow had come down into the slave deck and stood over him, staring at him attentively, with an expression that was difficult to fathom. He was a tall man with very dark pockmarked skin and a beaked nose. It was he who had pulled Dorian from the sea and held the dagger to his throat. On his first visit he had attempted to question the boy.

'Who are you? Where are you from? Are you a true believer? What where you doing on an infidel ship?' The captain's accent was strange and his pronunciation of some words much different from the manner in which Dorian had been taught by Alf Wilson but he understood the man without difficulty, and could have replied fluently. Instead he had hung his head and refused to look up at him. He wanted desperately to vent his fear and his anger on the Arab. He wanted to warn him that he was the son of a powerful, wealthy man, but he sensed that this would be the utmost folly. He wanted to blurt out, 'My father will come for me soon, and when he does he will have no mercy upon you, or any man of yours.' Instead he had bitten down painfully on his tongue to prevent himself from responding to these questions.

In the end, the captain had given up the attempt to make him speak, had squatted down beside him and taken a handful of his thick curls. Then he had fondled them almost lovingly. To Dorian's astonishment he had whispered a prayer. 'God is great. There is no God but God, and Muhammad is his Prophet.'

On his subsequent visits to the slave deck, he had made no further efforts to question Dorian. However, each time he had gone through the same ritual of stroking and caressing Dorian's head and muttering the prayer.

On his last visit he had suddenly pulled the dagger from the sheath on his belt. Dorian had been lulled by his previous behaviour, so now he was shocked as the bright razor-sharp blade was flashed in his face. He prevented himself from crying out, but shrank away fearfully.

The Arab bared his twisted, discoloured teeth in a horrible grin, which was meant to be placatory, and instead of injuring Dorian had merely cut off a long lock of his red-gold hair before he slipped the dagger back into its sheath.

Dorian was puzzled and confused by this behaviour, and he had much time to ponder it in the dark, stinking slave hold. He realized that it was the colour and texture of his hair that fascinated his captors, and had some special significance for them. When first he had been hauled from the sea, it had seemed certain that the Arabs would vent their anger and spite upon him. He could vividly remember the sting of the dagger held to his throat and even now, when he ran his fingertips over it, he could feel the scabs on the scratch that the blade had left on his skin.

It was only when the captain had pulled the Monmouth cap from his head and Dorian's long hair had streamed out in the wind that he had lifted the blade from the boy's throat. In the terror of those moments, Dorian had taken no heed of the jabbering and loud arguments of his captors as they hustled him below deck and chained him in the slave hold, but he remembered that every man in the dhow had taken a chance to touch or stroke his head. Now he recalled snatches of their excited talk.

Many had mentioned a 'prophecy' and some had called out a name, which was obviously revered by them all for the others had chorused, 'May Allah show him mercy,' after anyone mentioned it. To Dorian the name had sounded like 'Taimtaim'. Afraid, and so alone, he crouched on the rough stool in the dark, stinking hold and thought of Tom and his father, pined for them with a longing that threatened to crush his heart in his chest. Sometimes he dozed for a few minutes, but each time he was jerked awake by the plunging hull as the dhow was struck by a larger wave, and he slipped off his precarious perch. He was able to keep a check on the procession of day and night when the hatch above his head was opened and food and drink was passed down to him, or when the captain came down to gloat over him, and it was on the twelfth day after his capture that the iron fetters were knocked off his ankles. He was dragged out through the hatch onto the deck were the sunlight was so strong after the gloom below that he had to shield his eyes against it. It took him many minutes to adjust to its brilliance, and then, still blinking painfully, he looked about him. He found that half the crew were gathered around him in a fascinated circle. This time he took note of what they were saying.

'This is verily part of the prophecy, God be praised.'

'It cannot be so, for al-Amhara does not speak the tongue of the Prophet.' Dorian understood that by al-Amhara, which translated as the Red One, they meant him.

'Beware that you speak no blasphemy, O Ishmael. It is not for you to judge whether he be the child of the prophecy or not.'

'God's ways are marvellous and cannot be fathomed,' said another, and they all chorused, 'Praise be to God!'

Dorian looked beyond the circle of dark, bearded faces and out over the bows. The waves ahead were wind-driven and curled silver-headed in the sunlight, but on the horizon lay a dark, unnatural cloud. He stared at it so hard that his eyes watered in the wind. It seemed to be smoke that swirled and eddied, but then, with his sharp young eyes, he picked out the tiny shapes of palm trees beneath it, and realized that he was seeing a great flock of birds.

Even as he watched, smaller flocks of ten or twenty sea birds flew past the dhow, hurrying to join that vast agglomeration. He wanted to see more of what lay ahead, and at the same time to test the mood of his captors, to see how much latitude they would allow him. He walked forward, and the circle of Arabs gave way before him: they stepped respectfully out of his path as if afraid or reluctant to check him. One touched his head as he passed but Dorian ignored him.

'Watch him well,' the captain of the dhow shouted from the tiller. 'He must not escape.'

'Ah! So, Yusuf,' one answered him, 'is al-Amhara then so blessed that he can fly like the angel Gibrael?' They all laughed but none made any effort to restrain Dorian. He went forward and leaned against the single stubby mast.

Gradually the fringe of palm trees below the cloud of sea birds hardened, and then he could make out the shape of a promontory to the north end of what was clearly a small island. Closer still, and the walls of a square building, made of white blocks, glinted in the sunlight. Then he saw cannon on the walls and a flotilla of ships moored in the bay beneath the fort.

'The *Minotaur*!' he exclaimed suddenly, as he recognized the tall masts and shape of the ship that the *Seraph* had fought only days previously. With her superior speed she must have arrived well ahead of the tiny dhow. She was anchored in the middle of the bay under bare yards, and as they sailed closer Dorian could make out clearly the damage that the *Seraph*'s guns had inflicted upon her. Closer still he could just read the new name that had been painted in Arabic script on the transom, replacing her English name: *Breath of Allah*.

She was not the only square-rigged ship in the bay: there were four others, one larger and three smaller than the *Minotaur*. Dorian reasoned that these must also have been captured by the corsair from the convoys of the European fleets trading in the Orient. Five great ships loaded with precious cargo was an enormous booty. No wonder the name of al-Auf was so feared across the length and breadth of this ocean.

His thoughts were interrupted by a cry of 'Ready about!' from Yusuf, the captain at the tiller, and the rush of bare feet along the deck as the crew leaped to tack the dhow. The long yard was run back then forward on to the opposite side of the mast. The single sail filled on the starboard tack and the captain steered into the narrow passage through the reef that guarded the entrance to the bay.

'Take al-Amhara into the forward cabin. Hide him from the eyes of the watchers on the walls of the fort,' Yusuf shouted, and two of the men took Dorian's arms, led him gently to the small cabin on the foredeck and pushed him into it. Though the door was barred, there were port-holes on both sides of the cabin. Dorian peered out: he had a good view of the bay as the dhow ran in.

The channel took a dog-leg turn through the coral, then passed close under the walls of the fort. Dorian looked up at the cannon that poked through the embrasures and saw the brown faces of the gunners behind them. The faint blue smoke from their slow-match drifted along the top of the stone wall, and the faint welcoming cries of the garrison were answered eagerly by the crew of the dhow. The captain dropped anchor close to the stern of the *Breath of Allah* and called across the calm, clear waters to one of the skiffs drawn up on the beach below the fort. Three men paddled it out and tied up alongside the dhow. There was a long, heated argument among the crew, which Dorian could follow through the thin wooden partition of the cabin, as to who would accompany the captain and al-Amhara ashore. Finally Yusuf settled it by picking out three men and ordering them down into the skiff to act as an escort. Then he came into the cabin, and displayed his yellow teeth in that dreadful false smile. 'We are going ashore to meet al-Auf.'

Dorian stared at him dumbly, still giving no indication of having understood, so Yusuf signed and gestured his intention. 'We must cover your beautiful hair. I wish it to astound al-Auf.' He took down a grubby grey robe from a wooden peg beside the door, and signed for Dorian to don it. Though it stank of stale sweat and rotten fish, Dorian obeyed. Yusuf arranged the hood of the robe to cover his head and shield his face, then took Dorian's arm and hustled him down into the waiting skiff.

They were rowed to the beach, where they climbed out onto crunching white coral sand. The three Arabs closed in around Dorian, and Yusuf led them up into the palm grove and along the path towards the walls of the fort. They passed through a small cemetery in the midst of the grove. Some of the tombs it contained were ancient, the coral plaster cracked and peeling from their walls in chunks. The Christian crosses at the head were broken and fallen. At the far end there were newer graves, without headstones, the mounds of freshly turned soil marked only by white flags on short poles, covered with prayers and quotations in Arabic script. The grave flags fluttered in the streaming winds of the monsoon.

They left the cemetery and the path was winding through the grove towards the fort when abruptly they stepped into another clearing. Dorian stopped in his tracks with shock and fear: naked human bodies were hanging on tripods of rough timber along both sides of the track. This was clearly an execution ground.

Some of the victims on the tripods were still alive, They were breathing, making small painful movements. One stiffened his whole body and groaned loudly before slumping back against his bonds. Many of the others were dead, and some had been so for several days, their features frozen in the rictus of their last agony, their bellies bloated with gas, and their skins scorched pink and raw by the sun. All of them, both living and dead, had been cruelly tortured. Dorian stared in horror at one who had charred and blackened stumps instead of hands or feet. Others had empty sockets in their faces where their eyes had been put out with heated irons. Tongues had been hacked from mouths and flies swarmed in a blue cloud down gaping throats. Some of those still living called hoarsely for water, and still others called for God. One watched Dorian with huge dark eyes as he passed, repeating, in a monotonous whisper, 'God is great, God is great.' His tongue was so blackened and swollen with thirst that the words were barely audible.

One of Dorian's guards laughed and stepped off the path. He looked up at the dying man, and told him, 'On your lips the name of Allah is blasphemy!' He drew his curved dagger and, with the other hand, reached out and grasped the shrivelled bunch of the dying man's genitals. With a single stroke of the blade he severed them, and thrust them into the victim's open mouth. 'That will keep you quiet!' He chuckled. The tormented man showed no sign of pain, his anguish was already past bearing.

'You were always the buffoon, Ishmael,' Yusuf reprimanded him prissily. 'Come, now, you are wasting time with your clowning.'

Dorian's guards dragged him on until they reached the doorway in the rear wall of the fort. It stood wide open and a few robed guards squatted in the shade of the arch, their jezails stacked against the wall.

Tom had always impressed upon Dorian the need to notice and remember every detail of any new surroundings. His hood hid Dorian's face but did not cover his eyes, and he saw that the main doors of the fort were ancient and rotted, the hinges almost eaten away by rust, but that the walls were very thick. They would be proof even against the heaviest bombardment.

The guards were well acquainted with the dhow captain: they did not bother to rise to their feet but exchanged the customary florid greetings with him, then waved the party through. They entered the courtyard of the fort, and again Dorian looked around him keenly. He saw that the original buildings must be very old. The coral stone blocks were weathered and, in some places, had tumbled down. However, recent repairs had been made and even now a gang of masons was working on the staircase that led up to the battlements. The old roofs had been replaced with a thatch of palm leaves that were still only half dried. He estimated that close to two hundred men were loitering in the shade along the base of the walls. Some had spread their prayer-mats and were stretched out upon them. Others were gathered in small groups, playing dice or sharing tall hookahs, chatting together as they cleaned their muskets or whetted the edges of their scimitars. Some called the traditional greeting: '*Salaam aliekum!*' which Dorian's captors returned, '*Aliekum ya salaam.*'

Under a thatched lean-to with open sides, which stood in the centre of the expansive courtyard, was a line of cooking-fires. Veiled women were working over them, baking bread on the iron griddles or stirring the contents of the black, three-legged pots that stood over the coals. They looked up as Dorian and his guards passed but their eyes were inscrutable behind their veils and they offered no greeting.

There were rooms built into the outer walls of the fort, their doors opening out into the courtyard. Some were being used as storerooms or powder magazines, for there were guards at each. Yusuf spoke to his men: 'Wait for me here. Perhaps you can beg food from the women to fill your ever empty bellies.' He took Dorian firmly by the arm and dragged him towards the doorway in the centre of the fortifications.

Two guards barred their way. 'What is your business, Yusuf?' one demanded. 'What brings you uninvited to the door of Musallim bin-Jangiri?'

They argued for a while, Yusuf protesting his right of access, and the guard exerting his power to deny it to him. Then, at last, the guard shrugged. 'You have chosen an inappropriate hour. The master has already ordered two men to their deaths this very day. Now he confers with the traders from the mainland. But you have ever been a reckless man, Yusuf, one who likes to swim with the tiger shark. Enter at your peril.' He lowered his sword and stood aside with a smirk.

Yusuf took a firmer grip on Dorian's arm, but his fingers trembled. He drew the boy through the door into the room beyond and hissed in his ear, 'Down! Down on your belly!'

Dorian feigned ignorance of his meaning, and resisted the man's efforts to pull him to the floor. They struggled for a while at the threshold, then Yusuf released him and allowed him to remain standing while he crawled across the room towards the group of four men seated at the far end.

Still on his feet, Dorian tried to quell his uneasiness and gazed about him. At a glance he saw that although the walls of the room were of raw, unplastered coral stone blocks they had been covered with rugs of bright colours and pleasing designs. The other furnishings were sparse: the rough floor was well swept but bare, except for a single low table and an array of cushions on which the four men sat. They watched with apparent disdain as Yusuf crept towards them, chanting a litany of praises and apologies. 'Great lord! Beloved of Allah! Sword of Islam! Slayer of the infidel! Peace be upon you!'

Dorian recognized the man who sat facing him. He had last seen him upon the quarterdeck of the Minotaur. He knew that he would never forget that face.

Under a green turban, it seemed carved from teak or some other hard, unyielding material. The skin was drawn tightly over the skull so that the man's cheekbones seemed too close to the surface. His brow was high and smooth, his nose narrow and bony. The beard that hung to his waist was groomed into a forked shape, and dyed with henna to a bright ginger hue, but streaks of grey showed through the dye. Under the drooping moustache his mouth was a thin, tight line.

This lipless reptilian mouth opened now, and the voice that issued from it was soft and melodious, its gentleness given the lie by the cruel tar-black eyes above. 'You must have good reason to disturb our deliberations,' said al-Auf.

'Mighty lord, I am a piece of camel dung drying in the

sunshine of your countenance.' Three times Yusuf touched the stone floor with his forehead.

'That at least is true,' al-Auf agreed.

'I have brought you a great treasure, Beloved of the Prophet.' Yusuf raised his head long enough to indicate Dorian.

'A slave?' al-Auf asked. 'I have filled the markets of the world with slaves. You bring me one more?'

'A lad,' Yusuf confirmed.

'I am no pederast,' said al-Auf. 'I prefer the honeypot to the dung-heap.'

'A lad,' jabbered Yusuf nervously. 'But no ordinary lad, this.' He pressed his forehead once more to the stones. 'A golden boy, but more precious than gold.'

'You speak in riddles and circles, thou son of a diseased forest hog.'

'May I have your permission to display this treasure to your benevolent gaze, O mighty one? Then you will see the truth of what I tell you.'

Al-Auf nodded and stroked his dyed beard. 'Swiftly, then. Already I grow weary of your inanities.'

Yusuf rose to his feet, but with his back bent almost double and his head bowed with deep respect. He took Dorian's hand and pulled him forward. He was sweating with terror. 'Do as I tell you now,' he whispered ferociously, trying to cover his own fear, 'or I will have you gelded and give you to my crew as their whore.' He dragged Dorian to the centre of the room, and stood behind him. 'Great lord, Musallim bin-Jangiri, I will show you something you have never seen before!' He paused to let the anticipation build up and then, with a flourish, he drew back the hood that covered Dorian's head. 'Behold! The Crown of the Prophet, foretold in the prophecy!'

The four seated men stared at Dorian in silence. By this time Dorian had become accustomed to this reaction from any Arab who looked upon him for the first time.

'You have dyed his head with henna,' al-Auf said at last, 'as I have dyed my beard.' But his voice was uncertain and his expression awed.

'Not so, lord.' Yusuf was gaining confidence. He had contradicted al-Auf without a qualm, a trespass for which many men had died. 'It is God alone who has dyed his hair, just as he dyed the hair of Muhammad, his one true Prophet.'

'Praise be to God,' the others murmured automatically.

'Bring him here!' ordered al-Auf. Yusuf seized Dorian by the shoulder and almost yanked him off his feet in his eagerness to obey.

'Gently!' al-Auf cautioned him. 'Treat him with care!' Yusuf rejoiced in this reprimand for it showed that al-Auf had not rejected outright the validity of his claims for the slave-boy. He pulled Dorian forward more carefully and forced him to his knees in front of the corsair.

'I am an Englishman.' Unfortunately his childish voice quavered, robbing it of its force. 'Keep your dirty blood-stained hands off me.'

'The heart of a black-maned lion in an unweaned cub.' Al-Auf nodded with approval. 'But what did he say?' No one could answer him, and al-Auf looked back at Dorian. 'Do you speak Arabic, little one?'

An angry retort in the same language rose to Dorian's lips, but he fought it back and spoke in English. 'You can go straight to hell, and give the devil my compliments when you get there.' This was one of his father's expressions and he felt his courage return. He tried to rise from his knees but Yusuf held him down.

'He does not speak Arabic,' said al-Auf, and there was a drop of disappointment in his tone. 'That was part of the prophecy of the holy St Taimtaim, may his name be blessed for ever.'

'He can be taught,' Yusuf suggested, with a hint of desperation. 'If you leave him with me I will have him quoting the whole of the Koran within a month.'

'It is not the same.' Al-Auf shook his head. 'The prophecy is that the child would come from the sea wearing the red mantle of the Prophet on his head, and that he would speak the language of the Prophet.' He stared at Dorian in silence. The unlikely proposition was dawning slowly upon Dorian that none of the Arabs had ever seen red hair in their lives. He was beginning to understand that they looked upon it as some sacred religious stigmata: they spoke of their Prophet Muhammad having the same colouring. He had a vague recollection of Alf Wilson also mentioning this during one of his long lectures on the beliefs of Islam. Obviously al-Auf had dyed his own beard in imitation of the Prophet.

'Perhaps his hair is only cunningly dyed after all,' al-Auf said gloomily. 'If that is so,' he scowled suddenly at Yusuf, 'I will send both you and the child to the execution ground.'

Dorian felt fresh terror choke his breathing at the thought. The memory of the tormented wretches on the tripods in the palm grove was sickeningly fresh in his mind.

Yusuf was down on his knees once more, blabbering his innocence, and trying to kiss al-Auf's feet. The corsair kicked him away and raised his voice. 'Send for Ben Abram, the physician.'

Within minutes a venerable Arab came hurrying to make his obeisance before al-Auf. He had a silver-white beard and brows. His skin was eggshell pale and his eyes bright and intelligent. Even al-Auf spoke to him in a kindly tone. 'Examine this Frankish lad, old uncle. Is his hair a natural colour or has it been stained? Tell me if he is healthy and well formed.'

The doctor's hands on Dorian's head were gentle but firm, and Dorian submitted to his touch with bad grace, holding his whole body stiff and uncompromising. Ben Abram rubbed the silky red locks between his fingers, making sharp little sucking sounds between his teeth. Then he parted the hair and examined Dorian's scalp closely, turning his head to catch the light from the high, barred windows. He sniffed at his head, trying to detect any odour of chemicals or herbs. 'I have never seen any like it in fifty years of medicine, not on man or woman, though I have heard of peoples in the north of Parthia who are crowned thus,' Ben Abram said at last.

'It is not dyed, then.' Al-Auf sat forward on his cushions, his interest reawakening.

'It is his natural colour,' Ben Abram confirmed.

'What of the rest of his body?'

'We shall see. Tell him to disrobe.'

'He does not speak the language of the Prophet. You must undress him yourself.'

Even with Yusuf holding him down, they could not carry out the order. Dorian fought them like a cat being forced head first into a bucket of cold water. He clawed and kicked and bit, and in the end they had to call two guards from the door to restrain him. At last he stood naked before them, a guard holding each wrist to prevent Dorian cupping his hands over himself.

'See the colour and texture of his skin,' Ben Abram marvelled. 'It is as beautiful as the finest white silk, the same as the hide of the Sultan's stallion. It is without blemish. It complements the red of his hair exactly, and proves beyond the last doubt that what I say is correct. His colouring is natural.'

Al-Auf nodded. 'What of the rest of his body?'

'Hold him!' Ben Abram told the guards. The bite on his wrist was still bleeding. He reached out warily and began to palpate Dorian's small white genitals. 'His eggs have not yet descended into their pouch, but they are intact.' He took the childish white penis between his fingers. 'As you can see, he is not yet circumcised, but—' He drew back Dorian's foreskin and the pink cherry-top popped out.

Dorian writhed in the grip of the guards and all his resolutions of silence were swept away by his shame and humiliation. 'You heathen pig!' he screamed in Arabic. 'Take your filthy hands off my prick, or I swear to God I will kill you.'

Al-Auf recoiled on his cushions, shock and religious awe suffusing his gaunt features. 'He speaks! It is the prophecy!'

'Allah is merciful! Praise His Glorious Name!' the men on either side of him chorused. 'It is the prophecy of St Taimtaim.'

'Deck!' Tom screamed from his perch high on the foremast, cupping both hands around his mouth against the wind. 'Sail-oh!'

'Where away?' Ned Tyler hailed back.

'Fine on the port bow. Two leagues distant.'

Hal heard the shouts in his cabin, and jumped to his feet so vigorously that drops from the ink-pot splattered his chart. He wiped them away quickly and ran to the door. He came on deck in his shirtsleeves.

'Masthead! What do you make of her?' he called up.

'A small craft, lateen-rigged.' Tom's reply floated down. 'Ah! She has seen us. She's going about.'

'Only a guilty man runs.' Big Daniel had come on deck and stood by the helm.

'Or a prudent one!' said Ned Tyler.

'I bet a guinea to a pinch of dung that she's coming from al-Auf's island,' said Big Daniel.

Hal looked back at them. 'We'll bespeak her, Mr Tyler. Clap on all your canvas, and lay the ship on a course to intercept her, whoever she is.'

Trying to claw her way back to windward through the wind-chopped seas, the small dhow was no match for the *Seraph*. Within half an hour she was hull up, and the big square-rigged ship was bearing down on her remorselessly.

'Give her a gun, Mr Fisher,' Hal ordered, and Big Daniel hurried forward to the bow-chasers. Minutes later a single cannon shot thudded out. Hal watched through his telescope, and a few seconds after the shot he saw a brief fountain of white spray erupt from the surface half a cable's length to one side of the fleeing dhow.

'I think even the infidel will understand that language,' he muttered, and was proved correct immediately as the dhow surrendered to the inevitable. She dropped her single sail and rounded up into the wind.

'Have an armed boarding-party ready to send into her,' Hal ordered Big Daniel, as they raced down on the tiny vessel.

Big Daniel took his party across in the longboat. He jumped up onto the dhow's deck and disappeared into her hold. In the meantime his men secured the vessel, and herded her small crew forward under the threat of their cutlasses. Within ten minutes Big Daniel was back on deck, and hailed the *Seraph*. 'Captain, she has a full cargo of silk, all of the bales stamped with the seal of John Company.'

'Pirate booty, by God.' Hal smiled for the first time in days, then called back, 'Leave Mr Wilson and five men to sail her. Bring the captain and all his crew back to this ship under guard.'

Big Daniel brought the confused, frightened Arabs on board, while Alf Wilson put the dhow under sail and followed in the *Seraph*'s wake as she resumed her previous course close-hauled on the wind.

The Arab captain needed little persuasion to talk. 'I am Abdulla Wazari of Lamu. I am an honest trader,' he protested, part defiant and part servile.

'Where did you trade for your present cargo, Wazari?' Hal asked.

'I paid for it in honest coin and in good faith, as Allah is my witness,' said the captain, becoming evasive.

'No doubt it escaped your notice that the bales in your hold bear the chop of the English East India Company.'

'I am no thief. I did not steal them. I purchased them in fair trade.'

'Who sold them to you, then, O Wazari the Honest Trader? And where?'

'A man named Musallim bin-Jangiri sold them to me. I had no way of knowing that they were the property of this English company.'

'Nothing except the evidence of your own eyes,' said Hal drily in English. Then he went on, in Arabic, 'And where did you meet Jangiri?'

'On the island of Daar Al Shaitan.'

'Where is this island? When did you sail from there?'

'It is fifty leagues distant, perhaps.' Wazari shrugged. 'We sailed with the dawn wind yesterday.'

This estimate of the island's position agreed with the co-ordinates from his father's log book. Hal turned away and paced back and forth slowly while he pondered this fresh intelligence. It seemed apparent that al-Auf was conducting an open market on the island of Flor de la Mar, selling off his booty. Probably Arab traders from all the western seas were flocking to him to fill their holds with stolen goods at bargain prices. He came back to Wazari. 'You saw Jangiri himself, not one of his lieutenants?'

'I saw him. He was freshly returned from a terrible battle with an infidel ship. His own vessel lies in the bay, and it is pitifully damaged—' Wazari broke off as the possibility dawned upon him that he stood on the deck of the very same infidel ship he was describing. His expression became shifty.

'Did Jangiri tell you he had taken any infidel prisoners in this battle?' Hal asked. Wazari shook his head. 'He did not boast to you and you heard no talk that he had taken a Frankish child as slave? A boy of eleven or twelve summers?' Hal tried to make it seem a casual question, but saw a sudden flash of interest in Wazari's expression, which the man masked quickly as a good trader should.

'I am an old man and my memory fails me,' said Wazari. 'Perhaps some act of hospitality or kindness might restore my memory.'

'What kindness?' Hal asked.

'That you, my lord, allow me and my ship to go on our way without further let. That would be a kindness that would be written against your name in the golden book.'

'One kindness deserves another,' Hal said. 'Be kind to me, Wazari, then perhaps I shall be kind to you. Did you hear of a Frankish child when you were with Jangiri, who is also known as al-Auf?'

The Arab tugged at his beard indecisively, then sighed. 'Ah, now, I do recall something of that nature.'

'What do you recall?' Hal demanded, and instinctively touched the hilt of the dagger on his belt.

It was a gesture not wasted on the Arab. 'I recall that two days ago Jangiri offered to sell me a slave, a Frankish child, but one who spoke the language of the Prophet.'

'Why did you not buy from him?' Hal leaned so close to him that he could smell Wazari's last meal of sun-dried fish on his breath.

Wazari laughed. 'His price was a lakh of rupees.' He repeated, in wonder, 'A lakh of rupees for one slave-boy!'

'That is a ransom for a prince, not a slave,' Hal agreed. 'Did you see the boy?'

'At one lakh?' Wazari looked incredulous. 'He said I

must show him the gold before I may see the boy. I am a poor man, and I told Jangiri that. Where would I find a lakh?'

'How could he dare to ask such a price?' Hal insisted.

'He said that it was the child of the prophecy of Taimtaim,' Wazari said.

'I do not know of this prophecy.'

'The saint prophesied that a child with strange-coloured hair would come from the sea.'

'What colour?'

'Red!' said Wazari. 'The Red Crown of the Prophet. Jangiri says that this child of his has hair the colour of the sunset.'

Hal felt his heart leap as though to be free of his chest, and his spirit soared. He turned away so that Wazari should not see it on his face and went to the weather rail. He stood there for a long while and let the wind tangle his dark hair around his face. Then he smoothed it back with both hands and returned to face Wazari. 'You have been kind indeed,' he said, and when he turned to Ned Tyler he was smiling. 'Take this man and all his crew back to the dhow. Let them go on their way.'

Ned was startled, 'Let them go? Begging your pardon, Captain, but what about the stolen silk?'

'Let him keep it!' Hal laughed aloud, and every man within earshot gaped at him. They had not heard his laughter in many days. 'It is small reward for what he has given me.'

'What has he given you, Captain?' Ned asked. 'Though it's none of my business.'

'Hope!' said Hal. 'He has given me hope.'

The pinnace crept in around the south point of Flor de la Mar during the night. The moon would not rise for another hour, and it was very dark. Hal could judge his approach only by the phosphorescence of the breaking surf on the beach. He had lowered the sail, for even though the canvas was stained black he had to minimize the chances of being spotted from the shore.

Hal had kept the *Seraph* below the horizon during the hours of daylight so as not to alert al-Auf. She had come in to drop the pinnace only after the sun had set and was waiting for them now two miles off-shore. Hal had arranged a series of rocket signals with Ned Tyler. If they should run into trouble, the *Seraph* would stand in to take them off. So far they had encountered no difficulty, and the south end of the island seemed deserted, although they had seen the wavering lights from lanterns and cooking-fires at the north end as they sailed past.

If his father's drawings were accurate, Hal expected to find a sheltered cove tucked away behind the southern tail of the island, and he steered for it now. There were twenty men in the pinnace, but he intended to take only the smallest party ashore with him. He did not plan an attack on the fort or the shipping anchored in the bay: this was a scouting foray, to assess the strength of the Mussulman corsairs and to try to find where Dorian was being held. He hoped to slip ashore and get away again without alarming the garrison, or giving them an inkling of his presence.

He heard the splash of the lead, then moments later the whisper from the bows, 'By the mark four.' Big Daniel was taking the soundings himself, trusting no other with this vital task. The bottom was shelving sharply. A big swell passed under the boat, lifting them high, and Hal wished he had more light to guide them in. The breaking surf was close ahead.

'Ready for it now, lads,' Hal told the rowers softly, and then, as he felt the stern start to lift on the next swell, 'Heave away!' The pinnace caught the wave and sped forward. Delicately Hal coaxed her to stay on the wave with small adjustments of the tiller. The crest burst all around them, but on she raced in the creaming waters until suddenly she ran onto the sand.

The three leaped out waist-deep and, holding their pistols, waded ashore. Behind them, Big Daniel took the pinnace out into the deeper water beyond the surf-line to await their return.

They halted above the high-water mark. 'Aboli, leave the rockets here,' Hal said, and Aboli set down the heavy canvas-wrapped packet. 'We must hope we never need them,' he grunted. 'Now look to your priming.'

There were metallic clicks and snaps as Tom and Aboli reprimed their pistols. The long row into the beach and wading through the surf would have given the sea-water ample opportunity to degrade the priming. They had not armed themselves with the long-barrelled muskets, which were heavy and awkward to carry, and of little advantage in the night.

'Are you all right, Tom?' Hal dropped his voice even lower. He had agonized over the decision to bring the lad ashore with him.

'All right,' Tom whispered back. Hal wished he had not taken that oath in Tom's company. His son used it against him whenever he tried to shield him from danger. He had not been able to deny Tom a place in this shore party, but Hal consoled himself now with the fact that Tom's night vision far surpassed his or even Aboli's. They might be thankful for those sharp young eyes before this night was done.

'Take the lead,' he ordered Tom now, and they moved forward in Indian file, with himself in second place and Aboli bringing up the rear. The ground was open, devoid of any shrub or sea grass, but they had to follow carefully in Tom's footsteps. The nests of the sea birds were set so close together on the coral sand that there was scarcely space to step between them, and the birds' backs were sooty black, which made them almost invisible. They cackled and squawked irritably as the men stepped over them, but this noise was absorbed by the low susurration of the vast colony. Occasionally one pecked painfully at a bare ankle, drawing blood, but there was no general outcry and at last they reached the palm grove at the far end of the colony.

Tom led them on at a faster pace, keeping in the cover of the grove but just above the white coral sands of the beach. Within half an hour he had stopped them again and when Hal went to his side he pointed ahead. 'There is the horn of the bay,' he whispered. 'I can just make out the ships lying in the anchorage, though I cannot be certain which is the *Minotaur*.' To Hal's eyes, the darkness ahead was unrelieved. However, Wazari had assured him that the *Minotaur* had been in the bay four days ago and, with the damage that the *Seraph* had inflicted upon her, it seemed unlikely that she would have sailed since then.

'The moon will be up very soon,' Hal murmured. 'We will be able to make certain of her then. But, in the meantime, take us closer.'

They crept forward through the dense jungle beneath the trees. The ground was littered with fallen palm fronds, dry and noisy underfoot. They had to rely on Tom to steer them through this hazard. Hal wrinkled his nose as he smelt the smoke from the cooking-fires and the other less pleasing odours of the corsair's encampment, of rotting fish-heads and offal, of refuse and uncovered dung-heaps.

Then he stopped again as he smelt the unmistakable stench of decomposing human corpses. He had been on too many battlefields not to recognize it. Immediately he thought of Dorian, and made an effort to put the thought of his son's vulnerability out of his mind, and instead to concentrate on the task in hand. They went on slowly.

There was the sparkle of lights through the trees, and when they paused again they could hear the faint murmur of voices. Someone began to chant an Islamic prayer, and someone else was chopping firewood. Mingled with these sounds was the tapping and soft clatter of shrouds and spars, the clank of an anchor chain from the ships lying in the bay. They reached the edge of the grove and could make out the dark curve of the bay before them.

'That's the *Minotaur*,' Tom said softly. 'No mistaking her.' To Hal she was merely a darker blob in the darkness.

'The moon rises very soon,' he said, and they settled down to wait.

Eventually it came softly in its silver radiance, and the shapes of the craft in the bay materialized before them until they could make out the *Minotaur*'s bare yards against the stars. Hal saw that there were three other square-rigged vessels in the anchorage, which was as Wazari had described it to him. All these vessels had been captured by al-Auf.

'Tom, you stay here,' Hal whispered.

'Father—' he protested.

'No arguments!' Hal said firmly. 'You have done your job well, but you will stay here out of harm's way until we return.'

'But, Father—' Tom was outraged.

Hal ignored him. 'If anything happens – if we become separated, you must head back to the beach where we landed and call in the pinnace.'

'What are you going to do?' Tom demanded.

'Aboli and I are going to get a closer look at the shipping in the bay. There is nothing more you can do to help.'

'I want—' Tom began again, but Hal cut him off.

'Enough! We will meet you back here! Come, Aboli.'

The two rose quietly and, within seconds, had disappeared, leaving Tom alone at the edge of the forest. Tom was not afraid – he was too angry for that. He had been cheated, treated like a child when he had proved many times over that he was not.

'I am oath-bound,' he fumed. 'I cannot sit here while there is the least chance that I can help Dorry.' Still, it needed all his courage to defy his father, deliberately to flout his direct orders. He rose hesitantly to his feet. 'It's my duty.' He steeled himself. He did not follow directly behind his father and Aboli. Instead, he circled away from the beach. His father had shown him the chart of the island and the drawings of the old fort that his grandfather had made fifty years before, so he had a good idea of the ground ahead and where he was going.

The moon was above the trees by now so he moved swiftly. He saw its light reflected from the pale battlements of the fort ahead, and when he started towards it he struck a path leading in the same direction. As he went forward the odour of decaying human flesh became stronger, until at last he stepped out into an opening in the forest and stopped in alarm.

A field of dead bodies lay before him. Naked human corpses hung suspended from a series of crude gallows, weird and chilling in the moonlight. He felt a chill of superstitious dread and could not bring himself to walk out among the dead men. Instead he skirted the opening, keeping among the trees. It was as well he did, for before he was halfway round a file of robed figures came along the path through the forest from the direction of the fort. Had he remained on the path he would have run straight into them.

After they had passed, he kept to the cover of the palm grove, and within minutes he was crouching below the thick moon-silver walls of the fort. By now his anger had subsided and he felt very much alone and unprotected. He knew that what he should do now was admit his stupidity and sneak back to the rendezvous, before his father found out that he was missing. It won't take long. He rationalized his disobedience. Cautiously he started to circle the fort, until he came almost opposite the main gates, which stood open, but guards were huddling under the arch. It looked as though they were asleep but he could not take the chance of approaching any closer. He crouched in the shadows a few minutes longer. A torch was burning in a bracket to one side of the opening of the gateway. By its light he could make out the massive, sturdy timbers of the door.

He turned back and started to retrace his steps around the perimeter of the walls. On the eastern side the moonlight played full upon the pale coral blocks, and Tom could see that in places the walls were in ruins: some of their outer cladding had collapsed and the jungle growth was taking over. The ficus trees had probed their roots deep into the joints between the blocks, and the stems of wild lianas crawled up the walls, looking like monstrous black pythons in the moonlight.

A preposterous idea struck him: he would climb up into the fort, using a liana as a ladder, to search for Dorry. He was considering this when suddenly he heard a soft cough. He shrank back into the trees, looking for where the sound had come from. Then he saw the shape of a man's turbaned head in a corner of the battlement. He realized that guards were posted at intervals along the top of the walls and his heart tripped when he realized how close he had come to climbing up into disaster. He moved on stealthily around the outside of the fort and turned the corner at the north-western extremity.

He noticed that along this section there were loop-holes in the outside of the walls, set high up, too narrow for any but a child to squeeze through. Most of these slits were dark, but behind one or two the soft yellow light of an oil lamp or lantern showed. There were cells or rooms behind those windows.

Crouching close under the walls, he stared up at them wistfully. Behind any of those windows Dorian might be lying in his slave cell. He imagined his little brother's terror and loneliness, and shared those emotions to the full extent of his love.

Suddenly, almost without conscious volition Tom pursed his lips and whistled the opening bars of 'Spanish Ladies':

> Farewell and adieu to you, fair Spanish ladies,
> Farewell and adieu to you, ladies of Spain.
> For we've received orders to sail for old England . . .

Then he lay quietly and waited for some response. There was none. After a short while he stood up and moved quietly a little further along the wall. Again he whistled the tune, and waited.

Then movement caught his eye. Behind one of the high narrow windows someone had moved the lamp. He saw the angle of the shadows change. Tom's heart thumped against his ribs and he crept closer. He was about to whistle the tune again when the dark shape of a head appeared between the lamp and the window. Some-one was peering out through the loophole, but he could not see the face. Then a sweet unbroken voice whispered in the night,

We'll rant and we'll roar, all o'er the wild ocean,
We'll rant and we'll roar, all o'er the wild seas . . .

'Dorry!' Tom wanted to scream it out loud, but he stopped himself before it reached his lips. He crept closer to the foot of the wall, leaving the dense cover of the forest. He saw that a twisted liana rope climbed up the coral blocks to pass an arm's length from the lighted loophole where the shadow of Dorian's head still showed. He reached up and tried his weight on it. His hands were shaking with excitement and trepidation, but the liana was firm and solidly rooted. He slipped off his sword-belt and laid it, with his pistol, at the foot of the creeper.

Then he swung himself up on the liana. His body and every muscle in it had been forged and hardened in the ship's rigging and he climbed with the agility of a monkey. He came level with the loophole and leaned out towards the opening. 'Dorry?' he whispered.

The reply was instant. 'Tom! Oh, I knew you would come. I knew you would keep your promise.'

'Shh, Dorry! Not so loud. Can you climb out through the window?'

'No, I'm chained to the wall.'

'Don't cry, Dorry. They'll hear you.'

'I'm not crying.' Dorian's sobs were pitiful, even though he covered his mouth with both hands to muffle them.

'Do you think I can climb through your window?' Tom demanded. 'I'll come across and get you free.'

'I don't know, Tom. It's so small, and you're so big.'

'There's nothing else for it. I'm going to try.' Tom moved out hand over hand, onto the branch of the liana that passed closest to the loophole. He felt it bend in his grip, but he kept moving carefully until he reached the end. He was still at least three feet from the sill of the

341

window, and twenty feet above the ground. He let go with one hand and reached across.

'Tom, be careful!'

Tom found a crack in the stonework that gave him a solid hold and took his other hand from the vine. He swung across the gap, hanging on his right hand, searching frantically with his left for another support. His toes clawed at the smooth coral beneath the sill but found no step.

'Here!' Dorian reached both hands through the loop-hole. 'Give me your hand.'

Gratefully Tom locked hands with him in the sailors' overlapping monkey-grip. His weight jerked the smaller boy forward and jammed his shoulders in the opening. Tom saw instantly that if it was too narrow for Dorian's small frame, then his own broad shoulders, heavily muscled now from his exertions as a topmastman, could never pass through the opening. He was trapped. There was no entrance for him through the window, and the liana vine was three feet away, a long reach with his left hand.

'It's no good, Dorry.' Their faces were only a foot apart. 'We'll have to come back for you.'

'Please don't leave me here, Tom.' Dorian's voice rose hysterically.

'The *Seraph* is waiting just off-shore. Father, Big Danny, Aboli and me, we're all here. We'll be back for you soon.'

'Tom!'

'Dorry, don't make so much noise. I swear to you we'll come back for you.'

Tom was reaching back for his hold on the vine, but Dorian clung to his other wrist like a drowning man.

'Tom! Don't leave me alone, Tom!'

'Let go, Dorry! You'll make me fall!'

There was a shout from the battlements above them. A voice cried out in Arabic, 'Who is it? Who is down there?'

'The guards, Dorry! Let me go!' Tom looked up and saw two heads outlined against the starry sky, peering down at him from the battlements. He was stretched out along the wall, one hand with a precarious grip on the liana, the other clutched by his brother. He saw one of the men above him swing a long-barrelled jezail over the top of the wall and aim it directly into his face. 'Let go of me, Dorry.' Tom braced both feet against the coral blocks and flung himself backwards just as the jezail roared and a bright tongue of flame and powder sparks shot from the muzzle.

Tom heard the ball whip past his head, but he was falling free, plummeting down the wall, dropping twenty feet with his guts swooping up against his ribs, until he slammed into the ground with stunning force. The wind was driven out of his body and he lay for a while, trying to fill his empty lungs.

Another shot from the top of the wall galvanized him. He did not hear the ball this time, but he scrambled to his feet, still wheezing and whistling for air. He tried to run back into the grove, but when he put weight on his left foot pain shot up from his ankle into his groin like the stab of a giant hornet's sting.

He forced himself forward, running through the pain. He found his cutlass and pistol and snatched them up. Hopping and skipping to keep the weight off his injured ankle, he ran for the edge of the trees. Behind him he could hear Dorian's faint heartbreaking cries, shrill and desolate, only Tom's name uttered coherently. They were more agonizing to him than his injured ankle. Before he had covered a hundred yards the shots and the shouting had roused the entire corsair garrison.

Tom paused, and leaned against a tree-trunk. While he strapped on his sword-belt he tried to reorientate himself and decide what to do. He knew he could not make it back unaided to the south point where the boat waited for them. He had to hope that his father and Aboli would be alerted by the uproar and come back to find him. In the darkness that seemed a forlorn hope.

He did not have much time to reach a decision, for suddenly the grove seemed alive with men. They were shouting to each other, and every few minutes there was a rapid flurry of gunfire as they shot at the shadows.

'Who is it? What is happening?' More were coming up from the beach, cutting off Tom from his rendezvous.

'It is a Frank, an infidel. I saw his face.'

'Where is he now?'

'He went towards the bay.'

'Where did he come from? There is no infidel ship.'

The voices were coming closer and Tom could hear men running and crashing through the undergrowth. He pushed himself off the tree trunk, taking his weight on the ankle again, and hobbled forward. He had not gone fifty yards when there was a shout close behind him. 'There he is! Don't let him get away!' Another shot boomed out and Tom heard the ball crack into the trunk of one of the palms beside him. He placed his crippled foot full on the ground and forced himself to a run.

He was streaming with the sweat of agony. It poured down his face and into his eyes, half blinding him. Each pace was a torment that made his vision star into bright lights, but he ran on. His pursuers were gaining on him – he looked back over his shoulder and saw their white robes flitting through the forest behind him.

He skirted a clump of bush too thick to plunge through and, as he came round the other side, suddenly, shockingly, he was seized from behind and borne to the ground. He struck out wildly at his captor, but the grip upon his wrist was like an iron shackle. The weight of the man on his back crushed him into the soft sandy earth.

'Tom!' his father's voice was in his ear. 'Don't struggle. Don't make a sound.' He felt a great rush of relief. 'Are you hurt?' Hal demanded urgently. 'Why are you limping?'

'My ankle,' Tom blurted out. 'I fell. I think it's broken.'

The sounds of pursuit were close now.

'Have you seen him?' an Arab called. 'Which way did he go?'

'I saw him go that way,' someone answered. They were closing in. Then Aboli's voice rumbled, 'The lad cannot outrun them. I will lead them away to give you a chance to get back to the boat.' He rose to his feet from where he had been lying beside Hal, and darted away into the night. When he was twenty yards from where they lay he bellowed in Arabic, 'There he goes! He is doubling back towards the far side of the island. Head him off!' He fired his pistol and loped away through the forest.

Immediately there was a hubbub of shouts and shots. 'There he goes.'

'This way! Head him off!

Hal pushed Tom's face down into the dried leaves. 'Lie still! Don't move!'

Footsteps pounded close to Tom's head, but he did not try to look up. He heard the pursuit swing away and crash through the scrub towards the east side of the island, and Aboli's shouts growing fainter.

Gradually silence returned and Hal released his grip on the back of Tom's neck. 'Which leg is it?' he snapped unsympathetically.

Tom sat up, still panting wildly. 'This one.'

Hal ran his fingers over the ankle. 'You left your post,' he accused Tom as he worked. 'You could have got us all killed. Your pig-headed stupidity has put Aboli in dire danger.'

'I'm sorry, but I just had to do it,' Tom panted, and then, with a rush, he said, 'I found Dorry.'

Hal's hands froze and he looked up at Tom, his face pale in the moonlight filtered through the trees. 'You found him? Where?'

'In the fort. I spoke to him through the window.'

'My God!' Hal whispered, his anger subsiding. 'How is he?'

'Very frightened, but they have not hurt him. They've chained him up in one of the cells on the north-west side.'

Hal considered this. Then, 'There's nothing we can do for him now. We have to get back to the ship.' He squeezed Tom's shoulder hard. 'You did well, Tom, but never disobey me again. Your ankle is swelling very rapidly and we must get back to the beach.' He stood up and hauled Tom to his feet, 'Lean on me. Come.'

It took them most of what was left of the night to struggle back through the forest to the south point of the island. Even through the agony in his ankle, Tom fretted aloud about Aboli. They stopped every half-hour or so to listen for him, or for sounds of chase behind them, but they heard nothing more.

The moon was slanting down towards the African mainland when at last they staggered together out into the open ground of the sea-bird colony. By this time Tom's ankle was blown up like a pig's bladder, and Hal was half carrying and half dragging him along.

The eggs crunched and popped under their feet, and the birds rose in a black cloud around them, shrieking and circling their heads in the moonlight. They swooped down to peck at their heads, but both Hal and Tom were wearing caps.

'Cover your eyes,' Hal muttered, as they tried to beat away the creatures with their hands. 'Their beaks are like spears.'

'Al-Auf's men will hear this din from miles off.'

At last, even through the cacophony of the birds, they heard the surf breaking on the beach of the cove, and staggered the last few yards. Hal saw the dark blob against the sand where he had left the packet of rockets.

'Thank the Lord,' he gasped, for they were both almost

at the end of their strength. Then he cried with alarm, 'Look out! It's an ambush.'

A huge dark form rose out of the darkness before them. Hal dropped Tom to the sand and drew his sword.

'What took you so long, Gundwane? It will be light in an hour.' Aboli spoke from the darkness.

'Aboli! God love you!'

'The longboat is waiting just beyond the surf-line,' Aboli told him, and lifted Tom in his arms as though he were a baby. 'Do not send up a rocket. It will alert the enemy. Come, it is time we left this place.'

He whistled once, high and sharp, and was answered from out on the dark sea. Then Tom heard the sound of oars creaking in rowlocks as Big Daniel brought in the pinnace to pick them up.

The *Seraph* stood in towards the land in the dark of the moon. It was two nights after Hal and Tom's landing and fortuitous escape from the island.

Silently the *Seraph* glided the last mile and then, at Hal's quiet order to the helm, she turned into the light breeze and hove to. Hal crossed to the weather rail and listened intently. The booming of the surf on the outer beaches of Flor de la Mar was faint, but unmistakable.

'We're about a mile off-shore.' Ned Tyler confirmed Hal's own estimate.

'Launch the boats,' Hal ordered. 'I leave you in charge of the ship, Mr Tyler. Hold your station here, and await our signal.'

'Aye, Captain. And good luck, sir.'

The boats were lined up on the open deck. One after the other they were swung out and dropped to the surface of the water alongside. Then the armed men went down into them quickly and quietly, and took their places on the rowing benches.

As Hal went to the rail and the ladder, Tom was waiting for him. He was hunched over the crutch that one of the carpenters had made for him. 'Would that I were coming with you, Father,' he burst out. 'I would gladly cut off this leg of mine to do so.' He stamped the crutch on the deck in frustration. Dr Reynolds had determined that although the bone was not broken Tom would not be able to walk on it for many weeks.

'We could have found use for your strong right arm, Tom,' Hal told him. He had forgiven his son's disobedience, which had placed them all in such danger.

'Will you try to find Dorry?'

'You know that we're only attacking the shipping in the bay. After the other night al-Auf must know we're in the offing, and his men will be on the alert. Without the advantage of surprise, we could never hope to carry the fort with so few men.'

'I am mad with worrying about what those swines are doing to poor Dorry.'

'So are we all, but once we have seized or burned al-Auf's ships we will have him trapped on the island. He won't be able to escape with Dorian. Then, when Captain Anderson returns with the *Yeoman*, we will have sufficient strength to storm the fort. We must contain ourselves until then.'

'I pray to God that the *Yeoman* returns swiftly.'

'Yes, lad. Pray! That never hurt anyone. But, in the meantime, we will reinforce your prayers with a little powder and steel,' said Hal grimly, and went down into the waiting pinnace.

They pushed off from the *Seraph*'s side, Hal leading the flotilla in the first pinnace. Big Daniel had command of the second, and Alf Wilson was in charge of the two longboats. Behind them, the *Seraph* came on the wind under shortened sails, prepared to wait out the long hours until the men returned.

The oars of the small boats were muffled and the crews enjoined to strict silence as they crept in towards the island. Hal navigated by the compass, stopping every once in a while to listen for the sound of the surf. Each time it was louder, and then the man in the bows pointed ahead. Hal jumped up on the stern sheets and picked out the bright speckling of fires, which marked the encampment below the walls of the fort. He realized at once that the current had pushed them down towards the south, and altered course to head for the pass through the coral reef into the bay.

Hal could almost smell the nervous tension in the crew of the pinnace. For all fighting seamen there was a peculiar allure in the cutting out of an enemy ship from a protected anchorage. This bearding of the lion was an English speciality, an innovation of men like Drake, Frobisher and Hawkins.

Hal had enough men to take out only two of the ships he had seen in the bay. He and Aboli had studied them all carefully from the beach, and though it had been dark, the moon had given him light enough to make his selection. First, of course, had been the *Minotaur*. Though she had been badly neglected in the hands of the corsairs, and severely damaged in her short encounter with the *Seraph*, she was still a well-found vessel of great value. Hal estimated she would be worth ten thousand pounds when he tied her up in London. He had no way of knowing how much of her cargo remained on board, but it might be considerable.

The other ship he had selected was a Dutchman that, clearly, had been pirated from the VOC. She was a big-bottomed vessel built in the Rotterdam style that would fetch as much as the *Minotaur*. If he could bring both ships out, it would mean twenty thousand pounds for the night's work.

He leaned forward in his seat at the tiller and whispered to the men nearest him, 'There's twenty pounds a man lying there in the bay for the picking. Pass that along.' They chuckled fiercely, and turned on the thwarts to send the message down the length of the pinnace.

There's nothing like the smell of gold to raise a bloodthirst in an English seamen, Hal thought, and smiled to himself in the dark. It was a great shame that he could not bring out the other craft. Two more tall ships and a dozen dhows of varying shapes and sizes would add nicely to the bag, but he would have to settle for the smell of the smoke of their funeral pyres.

As they approached the pass through the reef the other boats moved into a single column behind him to follow him through. This was where the entire expedition could end before it had begun in bloody disaster. He had only his father's chart and his own instinctive seamanship to carry them through.

He stood as high as he could on the thwart and stared ahead. He was watching the snore of the surf curling white on the murderously jagged spikes of the reef, picking out the dark spot towards the north end where the deeper water remained unbroken.

'Start the lead,' he whispered, and heard the plop as it was thrown out ahead of the bows.

Seconds later came the soft call of the leadsman. 'No bottom with this line.'

They were still beyond the drop-off. Suddenly there was a startled cry from the bows and Hal looked ahead. He saw a large dhow coming down the channel directly towards them, her triangular sail catching the moonlight, and her wake leaving a long glossy slick through the passage. She was on a collision course with the pinnace.

Hal had a moment's temptation. She was a large vessel, and she was almost certainly stuffed with treasure she had traded from al-Auf. She was unsuspecting and vulnerable. It would take only minutes to board her and subdue her crew. Five of his men could sail her out to where the *Seraph* waited.

Hal hesitated. If they could take her cleanly it would be gold in the purse of every man-jack on the *Seraph*, but if they ran into resistance, and there was a fight on her deck, the sounds of the struggle would carry to the corsairs on the beach.

'Take her or let her go!' Hal had only seconds in which to decide. He glanced beyond the oncoming dhow, into the heart of the bay, and saw the bare masts of the *Minotaur* stand tall and proud against the stars. Then he looked back at the oncoming dhow. Let her go. He made the fateful decision, and aloud he whispered to his crew, ''Vast heaving.'

The rowers held their beat and the tips of the long oars dragged over the surface, taking the way off her, until she lay quiet and low in the dark waters. Behind her the other boats conformed to her example.

The big dhow made the final turn out through the passage. Unchecked and unmolested, she swept past where the pinnace lay. A lookout on her deck spotted them and hailed them in Arabic.

'What boat are you?'

'Fishing boats with the night's catch.' Hal pitched his voice so that it would not carry to the shore. 'What boat are you?'

'The ship of the Prince Abd Muhammad al-Malik.'

'Go with Allah!' Hal called after her as she bore away into the west and disappeared on the dark plains of the ocean. 'Haul away!' he ordered, and watched the long oars sweep forward and dip, swing and rise in unison, dripping liquid fire from their tips. He aimed the bows for the exact spot where the big dhow had come through.

'By the mark ten.' The lead had found bottom. Sir Francis's chart was proved accurate once again, confirmed for Hal by the passage of the dhow. They rowed on into the gap. Suddenly water was breaking on either side of them.

'By the mark five.' They were entering the throat.

'Drop the number-one buoy!' Hal ordered. The leadsman in the bows let it go over the side, and the line attached to the small white-painted keg peeled out. Hal looked round and saw the keg bobbing in their wake. It would give him his marks when he brought out the captured *Minotaur*. He turned back and squinted at the walls of the fort, which showed pale in the moonlight, lining them up with the tip of the reef. 'Now!' he muttered, and made the first turn of the dog-leg. The other boats followed him round.

'By the mark four, and a half four.'

'Too close to the outer reef.' Hal altered course slightly to keep down the centre of the channel.

Suddenly there was suppressed urgency in the voice of the man on the lead. 'By the mark two!'

With that warning Hal picked up the shape of the coral, dark and menacing as some monster, dead ahead. He put the tiller hard over, bringing her round only just in time for they had almost overrun the channel.

'By the mark seven!' There was relief in the leadsman's tone. They had passed through the coral jaws and were into the open harbour where the unsuspecting enemy ships lay.

'Drop the number-two buoy!' Hal whispered, and they left it standing in the middle of the pass to mark their way out. He glanced back over his shoulder. The other boats were fanning out.

He had given each of them their targets. Hal would take the *Minotaur*. In the second pinnace Big Daniel would take the Dutchman, and the longboats would attack and burn all the other craft in the anchorage. Hal steered for the big East Indiaman, where she lay in the deepest water directly opposite the fort. Let us find out how bright-eyed is her anchor watch, he thought, as he waited for the first alarm to be given. But the *Minotaur* stood tall, dark and silent as they came up under her quarter and hooked on to her chains.

Aboli went first, swinging up over the side. With the double-headed axe in one hand he landed on the deck, his bare feet making almost no sound, and ran forward lightly while a rush of men followed him up from the pinnace. Halfway down the deck a watchman struggled to his feet from where he had been lying asleep under the gunwale. He was unsteady on his feet and obviously only half awake. 'Who are you?' His voice was sharp with alarm. 'I know you not!' He grabbed for the musket that leaned against the gunwale beside him.

'Go with God!' said Aboli, and swung the axe in a wide, flashing arc. It took the man full in the side of his neck, severing it cleanly. His head toppled forward and rolled down his chest, while his trunk stood erect before it slumped to the deck. The air escaped from his lungs in a whistling blast of frothy blood from the open windpipe.

Aboli jumped over the corpse and, with a dozen long strides, reached the anchor cable stretched tautly through its hawsehole. He looked back over his shoulder and saw that Hal was already at the helm. The rest of the *Minotaur*'s skeleton crew had been subdued without any outcry, and their robed bodies were scattered along the open deck. Looking upwards he saw that most of the *Seraph*'s seamen were swarming up the rigging and swinging out along the yards. The *Minotaur* had been built in the same yard as the *Seraph*, and the rigging of her masts was almost identical. There was no hesitation in the way the topmastmen did their work.

As the main course spread, like the wings of a butterfly emerging from the chrysalis sheath, Aboli swung the axe high above his head and, with both hands, brought the blade flashing down again. The axe buried itself with a thump in the deck timber and the anchor cable parted with a twang.

The *Minotaur* paid away before the night breeze, until the rudder and push of the spreading sails checked her. Hal spun the wheel full to starboard and, lightly as a lover, the *Minotaur* came on the wind.

Only then could Hal spare a glance for the other boats of the flotilla. There was fighting on the deck of the Dutchman, and he heard the tinny clank of cutlass blade on scimitar, then the faint death-cry of a man hit through the heart. The sails spread on the yards and the big ship turned for the bay entrance.

At that moment there was a flicker of light, which grew swiftly in strength until it lit the deck of the *Minotaur*. Hal could make out Aboli's features clearly as he strode down the deck towards him. He swung round and saw that the square-rigged ship closest to him was on fire. The men from the longboat commanded by Alf Wilson had climbed aboard her, killed her crew and tossed tar-soaked torches into her holds and rigging.

The flames caught in her hull and jumped up into the rigging. The fire raced up as though it were gun match, tracing fiery strings against the dark sky. It reached the furled canvas on her yards, and exploded in a tall writhing tower of light higher than the palm trees on the beach.

Alf's men tumbled back into the longboat and rowed lustily across to the next ship in the anchorage, whose crew saw them coming and did not linger to greet them. They fired a few wild shots at them, then threw aside their weapons and jumped over the ship's side, hitting the water in a series of white splashes and swimming frantically for the beach.

One after the other the anchored ships burst into flame, and lit the anchorage as though it were noon. The shadows and light played vividly over the walls of the fort, and the first cannon shot banged out from the battlements. Hal did not see where the ball struck for he was bringing the *Minotaur* around and lining her up for the entrance. The keg they had left floating to mark the passage stood out clearly in the firelight, and the flames were so bright that he could even make out the loom of the reef beneath the surface. 'Ready about!' Hal bellowed, and began the delicate manoeuvre of tacking ship with so few men in the confines of the bay. There was no latitude for error here. One false turn would put them up on the beach, or send the *Minotaur* crunching into the coral. He was towing the pinnace behind the ship and its weight and drag affected the *Minotaur*'s handling. He would have to allow for this when he made his turn.

The *Minotaur* was heading directly towards the fort, and in the dancing light of the flames Hal could see the gunners scurrying to their weapons. Before he had reached the keg that marked the entrance a cannon fired, then another. He saw a clean round hole appear miraculously in the mainsail as a ball flew through it, and realized that the gunners had made no effort to depress their aim: all their shots were flying high. He glanced back over the stern and saw that Big Daniel, in the Dutchman, was following only a cable's length behind. He was towing his pinnace too: they would leave no consolation prize for the enemy.

Deeper in the bay the longboats had completed their work of destruction and every enemy ship was on fire. The anchor cable of one of the big square-rigged vessels burned through and she began to drift towards the beach, a moving bonfire. Suddenly the fire reached her powder magazine and she blew up with a thunderous roar. Her main mast was hurled aloft like a javelin, and as it fell back it skewered one of the small dhows, smashing clean through her decks so that the bottom was torn out of her and she sank stern first. The shockwave of the explosion capsized two of the dhows nearest her, and raised a tidal wave that swept through the anchorage.

Hal searched for sight of the longboats, worried that they had been overwhelmed by the force of the explosion, but then he saw them, bobbing and rolling in the disturbed waters, but making good speed to catch up with the *Minotaur* as their crews heaved frantically on the oars. Hal turned all his attention to taking the ship out through the channel.

He passed the marker keg by an oar's length on the port side, and they entered the mouth of the pass at speed, passing close under the guns on the battlements of the fort. Hal had a few seconds before the next turn came upon them, and he looked up at the batteries above.

Some of the gunners seemed to have realized their error and were training their pieces down. Hal saw the angle of the protruding barrels depressing as they strained at the training tackles.

'Stand by the main course,' Hal told his tiny crew. Each man was forced to do the work of three, but when he put up the helm, and shouted, 'Lee ho!' they jumped to it with a shout and a will, the *Minotaur* came round handily and glided down the passage between the menacing arms of coral, disaster lurking close on either hand. Hal looked back and saw Big Daniel make the same turn in the slick path of the *Minotaur*'s wake. 'Stout fellow!' Hal applauded him, under his breath.

The battery on the walls behind him was firing furiously: the gunsmoke was a thick rolling bank through which the flashes of the bombardment cut long bright shafts. The gunners had managed to lower their barrage now, and a ball raised a gleaming fountain of spray close under the *Minotaur*'s counter.

Hal smiled wolfishly. The turn was taking the ship almost directly away from the fort and now the cannon shots were flying too low. It would take the gunners some time to realize this, and by then Hal hoped to be clear of the pass and bearing out into the open sea.

'Ready about!' he yelled, as he saw the number-one marker buoy dancing in the firelight directly ahead. One of his seamen ran to take his place at the main sheet. As he passed within arm's length of where Hal stood, a chance shot from the battery hit them. There was a blast of disrupted air that almost threw Hal off his feet. He had to clutch with both hands at the spokes of the wheel for support. The stone ball, reeking of the powder fumes that had sent it on its way, struck the running seaman high in his back. It mangled his body and popped his skull so that half of his brains were flung into Hal's face like a mugful of warm custard. Hal gagged and recoiled at the horror of it, so distracted as almost to misjudge the final turn. At the last moment he gathered himself, wiped the running yellow mess from his face, and shouted, with the sickening taste on his lips, 'Let go your courses!' and put the wheel hard over.

The *Minotaur* came round, skimming the edge of the coral, and lifted her bows to the first swell of the open sea. As the reef fell away behind him, Hal turned anxiously to watch Big Daniel negotiate the last turn. He made a neater job of it than Hal had. The Dutchman switched her fat bottom round, heeled slightly to the change in the angle of the wind and then, with all the aplomb and dignity of a dowager following her more agile and skittish daughter, came trundling after the *Minotaur* into the deep, open waters.

'We're through,' Hal said softly, then raised his voice in a triumphant shout. 'We've made it, lads! Give yourselves a cheer.'

They hooted and howled like mad dogs, and from the ship that followed Big Daniel's men cheered as wildly. In the longboats they jumped on the thwarts, and danced and capered until they were in danger of capsizing. The guns of the battery banged away in frustration, a futile, fading accompaniment, and the flames of the burning fleet began to subside as they sailed out to meet the waiting *Seraph*.

As dawn broke next morning the squadron of Hal's ships lay hove to ten miles south-west of Flor de la Mar. Hal came on deck, having changed only his shirt, and gobbled down an early breakfast, just as the sun pushed its upper rim above the horizon.

When Hal looked across at her from the quarterdeck of the *Seraph*, the *Minotaur*'s blemishes were apparent in the brilliant early sunlight. She was shot-ridden and neglected, her sails ragged and discoloured, her hull stained and battered. She rode high and light in the water. A cursory examination the previous night had disclosed that her hold was empty of all cargo, but her magazine was almost full of munitions, and the powder-kegs seemed in good condition. These stores would stand Hal in good stead when the time came to make his final assault on al-Auf's beleaguered stronghold.

Yet despite her appearance the *Minotaur* needed only small attention and work upon her to restore her to first-class condition. Hal had no reason to revise his opinion of her value. She was worth at least ten thousand pounds of prize money, of which his personal share would be close to three thousand. He smiled with satisfaction and turned the lens of his telescope on the other prize they had taken the previous night.

There was no doubt at all that she was a VOC ship, just as Hal had surmised. Through the glass he read her name in gold letters on her transom: *Die Lam*, which translated as the *Lamb*. Hal thought it described her well: she looked plump and docile, yet her lines were solid and workmanlike, appealing to his sailor's eye. She was newly built and had not been long enough in the hands of the corsairs to suffer degradation. The hatches were still on her cargo hold but from her depth in the water it was clear that she was still fully laden: her cargo had not been taken ashore by al-Auf.

'Call away the longboat, Mr Tyler.' Hal snapped shut his telescope. 'I am going across to visit Mr Fisher on the *Lamb* to see just what we have captured.'

Big Daniel met him at the entryport of the Dutch ship with a wide, toothless grin. 'Congratulations, Captain. She's a beauty.'

'Well done yourself, Mr Fisher. I could have asked for no more from you and your rascals.' He smiled around at the grinning seamen who pressed close behind Big Daniel. 'All of you will have bulging purses when you step ashore on Plymouth Ho.' They cheered him raucously.

'How many of your brave lads were killed?' Hal lowered his voice as he touched on such a morbid subject.

Daniel answered loudly, 'Not a single one, praise God. Though young Peter here lost a finger, shot away. Show the captain, lad.' The young sailor held up the stump of his forefinger, swathed in a grubby rag.

'I will add an extra gold guinea to your prize money,' Hal promised him, 'to help soothe the pain.'

'At that price you can have the other four fingers as well, Captain.' The seaman grinned hugely, and his mates hooted with laughter as they went back to their stations.

Big Daniel led Hal forward. 'We found these still chained in her forecastle.' He indicated the band of strangers in rags who huddled by the foremast. 'They are the survivors of the Dutch crew. Twenty-three lovely little cheeseheads, all consigned by al-Auf to the slave markets.' Hal looked them over quickly. They were thin but not emaciated, and though the galls left by their chains were obvious on ankles and wrists and there were weals on their backs and limbs, which had been laid upon them with the Arab *kiboko*, they seemed in reasonable health. Like the *Lamb* they had not been long enough in captivity to have suffered too severely.

'It is your lucky day, *Jongens*,' Hal greeted them in Dutch. 'You are free men again.' At that their faces brightened. Hal was delighted to have them. With two extra prize ships to handle, he would need every man he could find. 'Will you sign up with me for the rest of the voyage, for a guinea a month and a share of the prize?' he asked. Their smiles expanded, and their acceptance was wholehearted.

'Are any of you officers?' Hal asked.

'No, *mijn heer*,' their spokesman replied. 'Our Captain van Orde and all his officers were murdered by that heathen scum. I was captain's coxswain.'

'You will retain your rank,' Hal told him. 'All these men are under your command.' If he kept all the Dutchmen together the language problem would be solved. Then again Big Daniel had learned to speak Dutch well while they were in captivity at Good Hope . . .

'They are your little lambs, Mr Fisher,' Hal said. 'Let them put their marks on the quarter-bill, and give them fresh clothing from the slop chest. And now let's see what we have caught ourselves here.' He led the way down to the captain's quarters in the stern.

The main cabin had been looted by the corsairs. The captain's desk and lockers had been broken open and ransacked. Every item of value had been stolen. The ship's books and papers were littered over the deck, trampled and torn, although many were still legible. Hal retrieved the log and the cargo manifest from among the mess. One glance at the manifest made him whistle with surprise and delight. 'By God, if all this is still in her holds, then the *Lamb* is a treasure indeed.' He was about to show Big Daniel the stiff sheet of parchment but remembered that he could not read, was sensitive about this, and instead said, 'Tea from China, Mr Fisher. She's crammed with it – enough to swamp every coffee-house in London.' He laughed and repeated the slogan he had seen above the front door of Garway's coffee-house in Fleet Street: '"That Excellent and by all Physitians approved China Drink, Tea."'

'Is it worth anything, Captain?' Big Daniel asked lugubriously.

'Worth anything?' Hal laughed at him. 'Probably more than its own weight in silver bars, Danny.' He flipped through the ledger to the final tally of the manifest. 'To be precise, it was worth one hundred and twenty-three thousand six hundred and ninety-two guilders on the quay at Jakarta, twice as much in London. Say thirty thousand guineas as a rough estimate. More than the *Lamb*, herself.'

At noon that same day Hal called all his officers on board the *Seraph* to receive their orders.

'We are going to be stretched to the limit for men to work all three ships,' he told them, as they assembled in the stern cabin. 'I'm sending the *Minotaur* and the *Lamb* with skeleton crews south to the Glorietta Islands to make the rendezvous with Captain Anderson in the *Yeoman*. Mr Fisher will have the *Lamb* and overall command.' He glanced at Big Daniel, and thought, By God, I shall miss him. 'Mr Wilson will have command of the *Minotaur*.' Alf Wilson bowed his gypsy-dark head in acknowledgement.

'Grand Glorietta is two hundred and thirty sea miles

from here. Not too far. There is a safe anchorage at the south end of the island, and fresh water in the creek there. I will give you four of the carpenters to undertake the repairs to the *Minotaur* and to get her back into fighting trim. That will be your first concern.'

'Aye, Captain.' Big Daniel nodded.

'By my calculations, the *Yeoman* should arrive at the rendezvous within the next three weeks. As soon as she does, you are to leave the *Lamb* anchored at Grand Glorietta with a skeleton crew aboard, and if the *Minotaur* is repaired by then you will bring her and Captain Anderson back here to take part in the assault on Flor de la Mar.'

'I understand, Captain,' Big Daniel answered. 'When do you want me to leave, sir?'

'As soon as you possibly can, Mr Fisher. Captain Anderson may already be waiting at the rendezvous. With Dorian a prisoner on Flor de la Mar, every day is precious. I shall remain here to keep al-Auf blockaded.'

Standing alone on the quarterdeck of the *Seraph*, while the sunset incarnadined the western sky, Hal watched the *Minotaur* and the *Lamb* detach and head off into the south. As the shapes of the two ships dwindled with distance and were at last engulfed by the gathering shades of dusk, Hal gave the order to take the *Seraph* back to her station off Flor de la Mar.

In the first rays of the next day's sunrise Hal sailed his ship boldly across the entrance to the bay, just out of range of the guns on the walls of the fort. His purpose was to warn al-Auf that he was under blockade, and at the same time to survey the island thoroughly. Through the lens of the telescope, the consternation in the Arab camp was clear to see. A throng of corsairs abandoned the huts and lean-to shelters among the palms and swarmed up to the shelter of the fort. The great teak doors swung shut before all had passed through and those left outside clamoured and beat at the door with fists and muskets. Hal was pleased to see how undisciplined they were; their lack of training and control had been just as apparent in their wild gunnery.

Hal could make out the turbaned heads of the gunners above the top of the wall as they rushed to man the cannon. The first shot boomed out, and the ball struck the surface of the sea halfway between the shore and the *Seraph*. It skipped along the surface, slowing with each bounce until it was quite clear to the eye. Half a cable's length from the *Seraph* it plunged below the surface and disappeared.

Then the rest of the battery opened up. Soon the walls of the fort were hazed with a fog of gunsmoke, and plumes of sea-water rose like a forest between the shore and the ship. The *Seraph* was still well out of range – Hal had overestimated the range of the Arab ordnance.

He switched his attention to the anchorage. No ships were left lying in the bay, not even the smallest fishing dhow. Their attack had swept it clean. Charred wreckage littered the surface and lay thickly along the high-water mark of the beach. The burned-out hull of the three-masted ship lay high and dry, canted over to expose her bottom, the masts burned out of her.

'She'll never go to sea again,' Ned Tyler remarked with satisfaction. 'You've got the rat bottled up in his hole, Captain.'

'Our next trick is to winkle him out,' Hal declared. 'Send Master Tom to me.' Tom came sliding down the backstay of the foremast and hobbled across on his injured foot. It seemed to be healing more speedily than Dr Reynolds had predicted. Hal watched him come down the deck with a critical eye. Tom was taller now than most of the other men on board, with the wide shoulders and brawny arms of a swordsman. His hair had not felt the scissors since they had sailed from England and it hung down his back, thick and curling, dark like a horse's tail.

Recently Hal had given him a straight razor, so his cheeks were clean but darkly tanned. He had the Courtney nose and piercing green eyes. A likely lad, Hal thought. It seemed that since he had lost Dorian, his paternal feelings had become sharper, more intense, and he had to dam back the flood of sentiment that threatened to overwhelm him. He handed the telescope to Tom, and said gruffly, 'Point out to me the exact spot where you climbed the walls of the fort, and the opening of Dorian's cell.'

They gazed across the water at the island. The barrage of cannon-fire still raged, and the thick bank of drifting gunsmoke resisted the efforts of the monsoon wind to sweep it aside.

'The north-western corner.' Tom pointed. 'Do you see the clump of three taller palms? Directly above them there is a notch in the wall with the green bushes growing out of it, and it's the first loophole to the left of that. I think that's the one, though I cannot be absolutely certain.'

Hal took back the telescope and gazed through it at the fortifications. With the early sunlight slanting across the walls, the slits formed by the loopholes were in shadowy contrast to the coral white blocks. He gazed at the one Tom had indicated, and felt that his loss was almost too painful to be endured.

'If you put me back on the island again, with Aboli and a small party of good men—' Tom began earnestly.

Hal cut him off with a curt shake of the head. 'No, Tom.' He had lost one son, he would not chance losing another.

'I know exactly where to find Dorry,' Tom pleaded. 'There are any number of places where we would be able to climb the walls.'

'They would be expecting you.'

'We can't just do nothing.' Tom's voice rose passionately. 'God alone knows what will become of Dorry if we don't get him out of their clutches.'

'We will go in as soon as we are certain of success. In the meantime, al-Auf will not hurt Dorian. It seems some religious legend is protecting him, a prophecy by an Islamic saint.'

'I don't understand. A prophecy and Dorry? How do you know that, Father.'

'From Wazari, the Arab captain we intercepted. It's Dorian's red hair. Legend has it that the Prophet Muhammad had red hair. It's rare among the peoples of the East, and they hold it in superstitious esteem.'

'We can't rely on the colour of Dorry's hair!'

'That's enough now, Tom. Go back to your battle station.' Hal's expression was not unkind, and it took all his good sense and determination to resist the lad's entreaties.

The *Seraph* drew away from the fort and gradually the guns fell silent, while smoke drifted away on the wind. Hal put her on the other tack, and they rounded the north point, slowly beginning a circuit of the island. He scrutinized every feature of the shore, coming in as close as was prudent to the edge of the reef.

Hal had made a fair copy of Sir Francis's old chart and it was now spread out beside the binnacle. On it he made notes of his own observations beside those noted by his father fifty years previously. He put a leadsman in the chains to take the soundings, and once he launched the longboat and sent Aboli inshore to investigate a lead through the coral. Aboli almost reached the beach on the far side of the lagoon before a party of a hundred or more Arabs appeared out of the palm forest and from close range opened a heavy musket fusillade on the longboat. One of the rowers was wounded in the shoulder before Aboli could bring them out through the passage again.

By the time he had completed the circuit of the island, Hal had picked out a dozen places where he could put a landing-party ashore, and he marked them carefully on the chart. When they came opposite the bay once more, he hove to, and made a detailed examination of all he could see of the fortifications, and the outworks that the Arabs had thrown up around the foot of the walls.

He tried to make some estimate of the number of men that al-Auf had under his command. Finally he decided that it was at least a thousand, but knew that the true figure might be twice that.

Every few minutes the telescope in his hands seemed to take on a life of its own and swivel back to the loophole in the thick white walls Tom had pointed out to him. 'It's going to be a long, weary wait until Edward Anderson gets here,' he predicted gloomily, and every man on the *Seraph* settled down into the monotonous routine of blockade.

Hal tried to keep the men alert by constant drilling, with musket and cutlass and cannon, but still the days dragged by. Four times, during the weeks that followed, the monotony was broken when they spotted vessels approaching Flor de la Mar from the west. Each time the *Seraph* piled on all sail and, the monsoon behind her, raced down to intercept them.

Three proved easy prey, and were overhauled and boarded without any loss. However, the fourth vessel was a beautiful 130-foot dhow, not much smaller than the *Seraph* herself. She led the *Seraph* on a glorious chase, showing a startling turn of speed, and was handled adroitly by her terrified crew. The *Seraph* almost lost her when darkness fell. However, Hal outguessed the dhow's captain, and in darkness doubled back towards the island. At daybreak the dhow was discovered trying to sneak into the bay at Flor de la Mar. The *Seraph* pounced and cut her off only half a mile short of her goal. Her crew put up a stout fight, and one of Hal's men was shot dead while three others were wounded before they carried her decks. It turned out that she was owned by Prince Abd Muhammad al-Malik.

The Prince was not on board but his personal cabin

was furnished like the throne room of an Oriental potentate. Hal had the carpets and furniture stripped from the
bulkheads and taken to his own cabin in the *Seraph*.

The Prince's name was familiar to Hal. He recalled
clearly the other ship they had hailed on the night they
had cut out the *Minotaur* and the *Lamb* from the bay of
Flor de la Mar, and that he had deliberately let go. She
had belonged to the same man, and now that Hal was
presented with such evidence of great riches he doubted
the wisdom of that decision. He ordered a rope reeved at
the masthead and the noose placed over the head of the
dhow's captain. Standing at the condemned man's side Hal
questioned him at length.

'Yes, *effendi*,' the man was terrified for his life, and
answered freely, 'al-Malik is a rich and powerful man. He
is the younger brother of the Caliph in Muscat. He has
more than one hundred trading vessels in his fleet. They
ply to every port in Africa and India and the lands of the
Prophet. We call regularly at Daar Al Shaitan to trade
with Jangiri.'

'You know full well that al-Auf is a corsair, that all
the goods you buy from him have been stolen from Christian ships, that many innocent seamen have been slaugh-
tered by the corsair to win them, and those who survive
are sold into slavery?'

'I know only that my master has sent me to trade with
Jangiri because the prices for his goods are favourable. As
to how he obtained them, this is not my concern or that
of my master.'

'I shall now make it your concern,' Hal told him
harshly. 'By trading with the corsair in stolen goods, you
have put yourself in equal guilt.' He turned to Aboli.
'Search the ship carefully.' The three dhows they had
captured earlier had all been intent on trading with al-Auf,
just as was this captain. It seemed that the news of the
magnificent bargains to be had on Daar Al Shaitan had

spread from the Persian Gulf to the Coromandel Coast. The three other ships had been carrying coin and specie to pay for the wares they expected to obtain. 'Let's see if this ruffian can make a further contribution to the expense of maintaining the blockade of the island.'

Hal paced the deck while his men ransacked the dhow. Within half an hour they had uncovered the hiding-place of the captain's money chests. The captain tore at his beard and ripped his robe with anguish when the four chests were dragged onto the deck of the dhow. They were too heavy to carry.

'Have mercy, *effendi*,' the captain wailed. 'That does not belong to me. It belongs to my master.' The man fell to his knees. 'If you take it from me then you condemn me to my death.'

'Which you deserve well enough,' Hal told him drily, then turned back to Aboli. 'Is there anything else of value in her holds?'

'She is empty, Gundwane.'

'Very well, take the booty across to the *Seraph*.' Hal faced the wailing dhow captain. 'These chests are the price of your freedom and that of your ship. Warn your master that this is but a small part of the price I will extract from him if ever again he is foolish enough to traffic with corsairs. Now, go with God, and thank him for your deliverance.'

From the deck of the *Seraph* he watched the dhow scudding away, back towards the African mainland. Then he went down to his cabin where Aboli had stacked the captured chests against the bulkhead.

'Open them,' Hal demanded, and with a crow-bar Aboli ripped away the locks.

The three vessels Hal had captured earlier had yielded rich pickings, but those were insignificant in comparison to what was revealed when the lids of the four chests were thrown back.

The coin they contained was packed into small canvas bags. Hal slit one open with his dagger and a stream of glittering gold poured out onto his desktop. He saw at once that most of the coins were mohurs, each punch-stamped with the three mountains and the elephant of the Mogul empire. But other coinage was mixed in with them: gold dinars of the Islamic sultans covered with religious script, a few ancient tetradrachms of the Persian satraps, whose rarity value far surpassed the intrinsic value of the metal.

'It would take ten men a week to count this hoard,' Hal said. 'We'll weigh it instead. Have Mr Walsh bring down the ship's scales and give him two men to help him.'

Walsh laboured the rest of that day and half the night before he could bring Hal the final tally. 'It is difficult to obtain a true measure in a moving ship,' Walsh told him primly, 'the arms of the balance can never come to rest.'

'I shall not hold you accountable for an ounce or two each way,' Hal assured him. 'Give me your honest tally, and I will be content with that until we weigh it at the court of assizes in England.'

'The weight is six hundred and five pounds to be precise – or, rather, to be imprecise.' Walsh chuckled at his own joke, while Hal stared at him in astonishment. He had not expected so much. By God, that was very close to a lakh of rupees. A vast fortune in any coinage. To that must be added the gold and silver coin he had taken from the three other dhows he had captured. It's total value far outstripped the value of the two tall ships he had taken as prizes.

'A lakh of rupees,' Hal mused aloud, and his eyes went back to the four chests with their broken seals standing along the bulkhead. There was something about that particular amount that jogged his memory. 'A lakh of rupees! That's the price that Wazari said al-Auf had placed on the red head of the child of the prophecy. Dorian's slave price.'

The more he pondered it, the more it seemed feasible. The gold was the purchase money for Dorian. The pleasure this thought gave him far outweighed the gold itself. If al-Malik was sending gold to al-Auf to buy Dorian, that proved that his son was still on the island and still contained within his blockade.

'Thank you, Mr Walsh. You have done good work.'

'I never thought to find the sight of so much gold distasteful.' Walsh contemplated the labour of counting it, and Hal went back on deck to resume the endless vigil.

'Please, God, let Anderson come soon,' he whispered, as he looked across sparkling blue waters at the emerald green island rimmed with white coral sands. 'Or at least give me the strength to contain myself.'

Another week dragged by. Then, one dazzling morning when the sea lay oily and quiescent under the stinging assault of the sun, heaving to a slow rhythm as though it were making love to itself in the breathless heat, there was a joyous cry from Tom at the masthead. 'Sail ho!'

Too impatient to wait for the reports from the lookout, Hal clambered up the rigging and squeezed into the crow's nest beside Tom.

'There!' Tom pointed to the south. For many minutes Hal thought he must have been mistaken for the horizon was deserted, then he picked out an ephemeral speck that disappeared again immediately. He trained the glass on the spot and suddenly it was there again, a tiny snowy pinnacle.

'You're right,' he rejoiced. 'A square-rigged ship.'

'Two!' Tom corrected him. 'Two ships. They can only be the *Yeoman* and the *Minotaur*.'

'We'll go down to meet them, and bid them welcome.'

Swiftly the approaching ships resolved into the *Yeoman* and the *Minotaur*. Hal examined them eagerly through the telescope and hardly recognized the *Minotaur*. Big Daniel had worked wonders in the short time he had given to refit her. She was resplendent under a new coat of paint, and even when she drew closer there was no sign of the shot damage to her hull or her rigging. On the other hand, the old *Yeoman* was sea-weary and showing all the telltale signs of her long voyage.

Hal exchanged flag signals of greeting with her, and when they were alongside each other both ships hove to and the *Yeoman* launched a boat. Edward Anderson's bright red face glowed in the stern like a port lamp as he was rowed across, and he scrambled up the ladder with surprising agility for such a big man. He grasped Hal's outstretched hand. 'I hear from your Mr Fisher that you've been hard at work in my absence, Sir Henry, and that you have taken great prize.' His chagrin was apparent in his tone and expression: only those captains who were in sight of the prize when she was captured were entitled to a share.

'I have urgent employment for your ship, sir, and the promise of even greater treasure in the offing,' Hal assured him – he thought it would be excessively cruel at this stage to mention the booty taken from the Arab dhows. 'Come to my cabin.'

As soon as they were seated, Hal's servant poured a glass of Madeira wine for each of them, then left them alone.

'I bear letters for you from Mr Beatty and from your son Guy,' Captain Anderson told him, and produced the canvas-wrapped package from the folds of his cloak.

Hal laid it aside to be opened and perused later. 'How is Guy?' The question was casual for he was anxious to get on with more urgent matters, but still Anderson's reply startled him.

'He was in good health when last I saw him, but I understand that he is to be married very shortly.'

'Good Lord, man! He is only seventeen years of age.' Hal scowled at him. 'I was not consulted in the matter. You must be mistaken, sir.'

'I assure you there is no mistake, Sir Henry.' Anderson

was even redder in the face than usual, and he moved uncomfortably in the chair.

'Who is the woman?' Hal demanded. 'Surely there must be a dearth of young ladies in Bombay.' He jumped to his feet in his agitation and began to pace the deck, frustrated at the lack of leg room in the tiny cabin, now made even smaller by the lavish furnishings purloined from al-Malik's dhow.

'I am informed that it is Mistress Caroline Beatty.' Edward Anderson pulled a luridly coloured handkerchief from his tunic and mopped his face of the sweat of embarrassment, before he could continue. 'I am led to believe that there is some urgency in the marriage. In fact, it was set to take place only a day or two after I sailed from Bombay. So your son is almost certainly a married man by this time.'

Hal came up short as the unsavoury truth started to break in upon him. 'Tom!' he said aloud.

'No, Sir Henry, you misunderstand me. Guy, not Tom.'

'Forgive me, I was thinking aloud,' Hal apologized. The shock had distracted him from the more urgent business, but Anderson brought him back to it with his next remark.

'Mr Fisher has told me the truly horrifying news that your youngest son has fallen into the hands of the enemy. You have my deepest sympathy, Sir Henry.'

'Thank you, Captain Anderson. I shall rely heavily on your help to rescue my boy.'

'My ship and crew are entirely at your disposal. That goes without saying.'

'Then let us see to our dispositions.'

Hal had had weeks to make his plans for the assault on Flor de la Mar, and now he laid them out in detail for Anderson. They spent the rest of that day closeted in the stern cabin of the *Seraph*, going over every detail of the

372

campaign, from the system of flag signals they would use ship to ship, and ship to shore, to the disposition of seamen to be used in the assault, and the delegation of the lesser commands to the various officers. Then they pored for another hour over the charts Hal had prepared. The sun was setting before Anderson was ready to go back to the *Yeoman*.

'Bear in mind, Captain Anderson, what I have told you. Al-Auf has been ensconced in the fort for some years. All that time the Arab traders from every corner of the ocean have been drawn to the island, like flies to the dung-heap. They have brought with them vast quantities of bullion to trade for slaves and stolen goods. The prizes I have captured before your arrival will fade into insignificance in comparison. I believe that on Flor de la Mar we will find a treasure to outweigh anything that Drake or Hawkins ever brought home from their adventures.'

Edward Anderson's blue eyes twinkled at the thought, and Hal went on to inspire him further. 'You will merit a knighthood for your part in this venture, and I will use all my influence with the Honourable Company to see that you obtain it. With your share of the prize you will be able to afford a fine country estate. After this you need never put to sea again.'

They shook hands briefly. 'Until the morrow!' Anderson's ruddy features split in a wide grin, and the grip of his huge fist was hearty.

'Warn your men that my son is in the fortress.' Hal struck a harsher note. 'In the heat of the fighting, let there be no mistakes.'

Hal gave the orders to put the *Seraph* on course to resume her blockade of the island and returned at once to his cabin. He slit the stitching on the canvas package of letters that Anderson had brought from Bombay. He recognized Guy's spidery handwriting on one of the folded sheets and set it aside to read later. He unfolded the letter from Beatty, and frowned as he read it.

The Residence
Bombay
6th Day November

Sir Henry,

The pleasure I experience in addressing you is somewhat mitigated by the circumstances that make it necessary. Not to put too fine a point on it, my daughter Caroline Beatty has been discovered to be with child. Dr Goodwin, the surgeon at the factory here in Bombay, puts the duration of her pregnancy at three months. This would set a date of conception to the time when my family was lodging ashore at Good Hope. You will recall that your son, Guy Courtney, was with us at the guest-house.

I am pleased to be able to inform you that your son, Guy Courtney, has behaved in a most gentlemanly fashion in this matter. He has admitted paternity of the child, and has asked if he might be allowed to marry my daughter. As he is now above the age of seventeen years he is quite within his legal rights to contract a marriage. My daughter Caroline turns eighteen years of age on Friday next so there is no difficulty as to the ages of the two young people.

My wife and I have thought it politic to give our

permission to the marriage, and the date has been set down for next Friday, the same date as my daughter's eighteenth birthday. Thus it is likely that the matter will have been accomplished by the time this epistle comes to your hand.

I have been able to provide my daughter with a dowry of £500. The Company will set a house in the cantonment at the disposal of the young married couple. Thus their immediate needs will be taken account of. No doubt you will see fit to provide your son with a suitable allowance to eke out his salary, and you will use your considerable influence on the board of governors of the Honourable Company to advance his career.

In this respect I am able to inform you that Guy has settled well into his new employment, and has received favourable comment on his efforts from Governor Aungier.

My wife joins me in assuring you, sir, of our highest esteem and duty,

your servant,

Thurston Beatty

Hal crumpled it in his fist, and glared at the letter from Guy, which lay unopened on the desktop. 'The idiot! He has laid claim to the bird brought down by Tom's arrow. What in the world could have possessed him?'

He tore Beatty's letter into shreds and threw it out of the cabin window, watching the scraps floating away on the ship's wake. Then, with a sigh, he turned his attention to the letter from Guy.

It added nothing to what Beatty had already written, except to express Guy's ecstatic joy at his good fortune in having won the hand of the lovely Caroline. 'Brother Tom did all the digging to unearth that diamond for you,' Hal muttered, with disgust, and considered sending for Tom, informing him as to the fruits of his endeavours and venting his displeasure upon the elder twin. Then he sighed again. 'To what possible advantage?' he asked himself. 'The deed is done, and all parties seem well enough pleased with the outcome, although nobody seems to have solicited the bride's views on the subject.' He balled Guy's letter, tossed it through the stern window and watched it bob away until at last it sank waterlogged below the surface.

At that moment there was a discreet knock on the cabin door, and a seaman called through the panel, 'Begging your pardon, Captain, Mr Tyler sends his compliments and Flor de la Mar is in sight dead ahead.'

Hal's domestic problems were in the instant submerged as deeply as Guy's sodden missive. He girded on his swordbelt and hurried on deck.

The Seraph led the Minotaur in line astern across the entrance of the bay. Ned Tyler had command of the Seraph, for Hal was not on board. As the two great ships drew within range they opened a steady bombardment on the Arab positions among the palm trees and on the walls of the fort. The months of practice that the gun-crews had endured now showed to good advantage, and even though their numbers were sorely depleted, their fire was rapid and accurate. Relying on the ineptitude demonstrated by the Arab gunners, Ned brought the Seraph close enough to skirt the outer edge of the reef. He was well within range of the heavy cannon on the walls of the fort, but the Seraph's fire knocked chunks of coral off the battlements and threw the defenders into further disarray. Their return fire was spasmodic and erratic. The attacking ships were well under their guns, and although a few of the huge stone balls they fired fell close enough to throw spray onto the *Seraph*'s decks, most flew well out to sea.

The Arab encampment among the groves was within long musket shot of the two ships, and half their fire was directed into the thatched huts and lean-to shelters. The guns were loaded with grapeshot, and the lead balls swept through the throng of men and women who were scurrying for the sheltering walls of the fort. They left swathes of brown bodies lying along the pathway, like corn behind the reapers.

After the first pass the ships tacked in succession then came back again, as close as the reef would allow, their fire unrelenting. By now the Arab gunners had recovered from much of their initial confusion. Their stone balls fell close around the *Seraph*, and one crashed in through the frail wooden bulwark. It chopped off both legs of one of the powder boys as he came scampering up the companionway from the magazine, laden with the silk bags of black powder.

Ned glanced at the boy's legless torso as it writhed in a spreading pool of blood close to where he stood at the helm. The dying boy was calling pitifully for his mother, but both branches of his femoral artery were spurting like open taps, and no man could be called from his duties to render him assistance. The thought of withdrawing beyond the range of the guns in the fort to prevent further losses did not occur to Ned. Hal had asked him to keep the ship close in-shore, the shore batteries engaged and the Arabs bottled up in the fort for as long as he was able. Ned would not flinch from his task, even though he mourned the loss of a single one of his brave lads.

On the far side of the island Hal heard the regular controlled gunfire of the two ships, and wiped the sweat from his face with the back of his arm. 'Stout fellow!' he applauded Ned's determination, then turned all his attention to landing the rest of the men from the *Yeoman of York*. The boats were coming in through the pass he had marked in the reef so many weeks before. The four pinnaces were packed with men, riding so deeply in the water that they had barely a hand's breadth of free board.

As the keel of each boat touched the sand the men jumped out knee-deep in the clear, warm lagoon water and waded ashore. Big Daniel and Alf Wilson marshalled them into columns and led them off the beach into the shelter of the palm grove.

Even with all the men that Anderson could spare from the *Yeoman*, Hal had less than four hundred in his landing-force to match al-Auf's horde. The enemy might well be more than the thousand, or two, Hal had estimated, but so far they had not opposed his landing. It seemed that the bombardment by the *Seraph* and the *Minotaur* had produced the desired effect of sending all the defenders into the shelter of the fort.

The last boatload of seamen came trotting up the beach, heavily laden with weapons, powder-flasks and water-bottles, for fighting in this heat would be a thirsty business. Hal watched the empty boats rowing back towards the *Yeoman*, which was hovering off-shore, not more than half a mile outside the reef, then followed the tail of the marching column up into the forest.

The order of march had been carefully planned. Big Daniel had command of the vanguard with scouts thrown out ahead to prevent them running into an ambush. There were musket men sent out as flankers on both sides of the column. Hal kept the command of the main body of men under his own hand.

It was less than three miles from the cove in which they had landed to the fort on the north end and Hal pushed them hard, keeping up a trot through the soft, sandy footing. They had not covered a mile before there was a volley of musket fire in the forest ahead, and wild cries and screams. Hal hurried forward, fearful that Big Daniel had run into a set ambush, and dreading what he would find. Nine dead Arabs were scattered on both sides of the wide path trampled by the advancing seamen, and the sounds of the fighting were dwindling among the trees as the remaining Arabs fled back towards the fort with Daniel's seamen in furious pursuit. A single sailor sat with his back to the trunk of a palm tree, wrapping a strip of cloth around the musket-ball wound in his thigh. Hal detailed a man to help him back to the beach to be taken off by the *Yeoman*, then hurried on after Big Daniel. The guns still boomed and thundered from the far side of the island, and now they were close enough to the fort to see the clouds of gunsmoke billowing over the tops of the trees not far ahead.

'Ned Tyler is keeping the sons of the Prophet from their prayers,' Hal muttered, sweat pouring down his face into his beard and soaking his shirt as though he had stood under a waterfall.

For many minutes he had been aware of a foul stench, which was becoming insufferably strong in the humid heat of the forest. When they burst out into open ground, Hal stopped so suddenly that the men who followed him ran into his back. Even in his haste and urgency he was taken aback by the horrors of al-Auf's execution ground. The sun-blackened corpses hanging on the tripods were grotesquely bloated with their own stomach gases and a few had burst open like overripe fruit. They were covered by a moving iridescent mat of blue flies.

Hal could not stop himself from searching the ranks of dead bodies for a smaller one with bright red hair, and felt a swoop of relief in the pit of his stomach when he did not find what he was looking for. He forced himself to go on between the hanging figures and to ignore the clouds of buzzing insects that rose thickly around him and brushed against his face.

Aboli and Tom were waiting for him in the trees on the far side of the clearing. 'Can we go now?' Tom shouted, from a distance of thirty paces. He, Aboli and the three men with them were all dressed in Arab robes and head-cloths. Hal saw that his son's face was set with determination and impatience, and that his sabre was bared in his right hand. He felt another stab of regret that he had given in to Tom's entreaties and had allowed him to go with Aboli. The one consideration that had influenced him was that Tom was the only man among the attackers who had been on the walls and knew where they could be scaled by a small party of determined men. Tom also knew the cell in which they were holding Dorian. Dressed as corsairs, they would try to reach Dorian and protect him from the fighting and slaughter that would follow the storming of the fort.

Hal grabbed Aboli's arm and hissed, 'Keep Tom under your eye. Don't let him do anything stupid. Cover his back at every moment.'

Aboli looked back at Hal with smoky dark eyes and did not deign to answer. Hal went on, 'Don't let him begin the climb until we draw every man on top of the wall away to the east side.'

Aboli whispered back fiercely, 'Do your work, Gund-wane, and I will do mine.'

'Go to it, then.' Hal pushed him away lightly, and watched the small party, Tom and Aboli running shoulder to shoulder at its head, jog away, circling out through the forest to reach the far side of the fortress.

As they disappeared Hal looked up at the tops of the walls just showing above the trees ahead, and cocked his head to listen for sounds of the bombardment. Although this end of the island was wreathed in thick eddies of gunsmoke and the taste of burnt powder was rank in the back of his throat, the thunder of the guns was fading away. Ned was taking the *Seraph* and the *Minotaur* out to safer waters.

Hal looked back over his shoulder and saw that, even after the long, hard run through forest, the column of seamen was closing up behind him, with few stragglers. He led them on and found Big Daniel waiting at the edge of the trees.

Across a hundred and fifty paces of open ground the white walls of the fort stood fifty feet high. The arched gates were closed, heavy beams of mahogany reinforced by iron studs. There were no defenders in sight on the battlements. They must all be on the west wall facing the sea. As the last shots of the bombardment died away, Hal heard their thin, distant cheers as they saw off the squadron of attacking ships.

'We have them at a disadvantage,' Hal told Big Daniel, 'but we must work quickly if we are to keep the element of surprise.'

Behind him the men of the column were still coming up, bowed under their loads. Sweating and panting they flopped down and raised their water-bottles, gulping down long draughts greedily. Hal strode among them, rallying them and sending them to take up their positions along the edge of the treeline.

'Keep your heads down. Keep out of sight. See to your priming, but do not fire until I give the order!'

The teams carrying the five heavy powder-kegs had fallen back to the rear of the column, but at last they came staggering up with each of the fifty-pound kegs slung on a pole between two men. They stacked them under the palm trees and Hal and Daniel set to work to prepare the fuses.

Hal had cut slow-match as short as he dared, and this was always a delicate business, for no two pieces of match would burn at the same rate. They tapped each length of fuse with the handle of a knife to try to spread the fulminate evenly, then they threaded a fuse through the bung-hole of each cask. Every second was precious now and they could not spare time to make certain that each fuse was perfect. If one failed there were four others to set off the explosives.

'Ready?' Hal looked up from his task.

Big Daniel plugged the final fuse in place with a handful of soft pitch. 'Ready as we'll ever be.'

'Light the slow-match!' Hal ordered, and Daniel struck the flint with the steel. The tinder caught. One after the other they touched a short length of slow-match to the flame, and watched it smoulder and smoke.

'Shoulder the kegs!' Hal ordered, and five fresh men, each chosen for his brawn, rose from where they had been squatting and came forward. Another rank was waiting behind them, ready to run forward and take up a keg if one of the porters was shot down by enemy musket fire from the walls of the fort.

Hal drew his sword, and strode to the edge of the forest. He peered from the cover across the open ground. There was still no sign of any defenders on the walls. He drew a deep breath and steeled himself. 'Quietly, lads! Follow me!'

Without a shout or cheer they ran forward in a group. The bare feet of the heavily burdened seamen sank deep into the sandy soil with each pace, but they covered the ground fast and were almost to the gates when there was a yell and a shot from the battlement above the gates. Hal saw a turbaned head in the stone opening and the muzzle of a smoking jezail aimed down at them. The range was short and the ball took one of the running seamen squarely in his naked chest. The wounded man sprawled full length in the sand, and the keg rolled from his shoulder.

Big Daniel was running only a pace behind him, and scooped up the keg as lightly as though it were a ninepin. With it tucked under his arm he jumped over the dying man and was the first to reach the gates. He dropped the keg against the hinges, and beckoned to the men coming up behind him. 'Here! Bring them here!'

As the first man came up, snorting and panting with the effort, Big Daniel snatched his burden from him. 'Get back to the trees!' he barked and laid the keg beside the other. 'Well done, lad.' He grabbed the next keg and stacked it in a pyramid upon the first two.

By now a crowd of shrieking Arabs was on the battlements above them, and a ragged fusillade of musket shots rang out as Daniel's men tried to reach the cover of the treeline. Another was shot down and lay groaning in the open ground, with spurts of dust kicking up around him as the musketeers on the wall tried to finish him off. From the trees the seamen hidden there opened answering fire. Their musket-balls cracked against the stone blocks, and rained chips of coral down on the men crouched at the foot of the massive gates.

Hal knelt beside Big Daniel as he placed the fifth powder-keg on top of the stack. He blew on the smouldering end of the slow-match in his hand, and it flared up redly. 'Get you gone, Danny,' he told the big man. 'I'll see to the rest of it.'

But Daniel had his own slow-match smoking in his hand. 'Beg your pardon, Captain, but I'll give you a hand to kiss the devil's daughter.' He knelt beside Hal and touched the match to the fuse of one of the powder-kegs. Hal did not waste words in argument and bent to the same task. Working without haste, they lit each of the five fuses and waited to make certain that they were burning evenly.

By this time half the garrison of the fort was swarming along the wall above them, firing as fast as they could reload into the edge of the forest. Four hundred British sailors were yelling and cheering and sending in a withering fusillade over the battlements.

Hal and Daniel were protected from the fire of the

men above them by the slight overhang below the battle-ments, but as soon as they left its shelter they would be fully exposed during their return across the open ground. Hal took a last look at the furiously burning fuses – only an inch or so protruded from the bung-hole of each keg – and rose to his feet. 'I think the time has come to leave.'

'I can see no reason to linger, Captain.' Big Daniel grinned at him with his bald gums, and the two launched themselves side by side into the open.

Immediately the shouts from the battlements behind them redoubled, and every Arab on the walls turned his fire upon the running pair. The heavy lead balls whirred about their heads and ploughed into the soft sand at their flying feet. From the trees the seamen yelled encourage-ment and fired as wildly as the Arabs on the walls.

'*Seraph*!' they screamed. 'Come on, Danny! Run for it, Captain!'

Time seemed to slow down for Hal. It was as though he was under water, each stride seeming to last many minutes. The line of the forest seemed to come no nearer, and the musket-balls flew around them as thick as hail.

Then Big Daniel was struck, not once but almost simultaneously by two balls. One hit him in the back of the knee, broke the bone, and his leg folded under him like a carpenter's rule. The second ball struck him in the hip and shattered the neck of the femur. He went down in the sand with both legs twisted and useless under him.

Hal ran on four paces before he realized he was alone. Then he paused and looked back.

'Go on!' Big Daniel yelled at him. 'You can't help me. Both my legs are gone.' His face had dived into the sand, and his eyes and mouth were filled with it. Hal whirled and ran back to him through the storm of musket fire.

'No! No!' Big Daniel bellowed, sand and spittle flying from his mouth in a cloud. 'Go back, you fool. Go back.'

Hal reached him and stooped to seize his shoulders.

He tried to lift him, and was appalled by the weight of the great body. With both his legs shot away, Daniel could not help him take the strain. Hal took another deep breath and readjusted his grip, then heaved up again. This time he lifted the top half of Daniel's torso clear of the ground and tried to get his shoulder under the other man's armpit.

'It's no use,' Big Daniel gasped in his ear, swamped in agony as the shattered bones in his hip grated against each other. 'Go on, save yourself!'

Hal had no breath to reply, so he gathered the last ounce of his strength and lifted, straining with every sinew and fibre of his body. At the effort his vision darkened and starred into whirling comets of light, but slowly Big Daniel's huge frame lifted clear of the sandy earth and he threw his right arm around Hal's shoulders. They stood there for a long moment, locked together, unable to move another step.

'You're mad,' Big Daniel whispered, his lips an inch from Hal's ear. 'The powder's going to blow—'

On the high battlements behind them an Arab musketeer poured a handful of coarse black powder into the muzzle of his jezail, and rammed down a wad on top of it. He was holding the ball between his teeth. It was an irregular lump of soft pig-iron that he had hand-forged to a rough fit in the barrel. He spat the ball into the muzzle and used the long wooden ramrod to drive it home. Then he reversed the weapon and laid the forestock across the stone sill of the embrasure. With shaking fingers, he poured a fine stream of powder into the pan of the lock, snapped the frizzen closed and drew back the hammer to full cock.

When he lifted the stock to his shoulder and peered down the long brass-bound barrel, he saw that out in the open ground the two infidels were still struggling helplessly, clinging to each other like lovers.

He aimed carefully at their heads, which were close together, then pulled hard on the stiff trigger. The hammer dropped and the flint struck a starburst of sparks from the steel of the frizzen. The powder in the pan ignited in a puff of white smoke, and for a moment it seemed that the jezail would misfire but then, with a deafening bellow, it leaped in his hands, kicking the barrel head high.

The beaten slug of pig-iron started to tumble end over end as soon as it left the muzzle. It whirred through the air to where Hal and Big Daniel were dragging themselves away. It had been aimed at Hal's head, but it dropped so sharply in flight that it almost missed him completely. In the end it struck him with a loud thump on the side of his ankle, tore away his heel and shattered the fragile bones of his left foot.

As his foot was knocked out from under him Hal dropped under Big Daniel's weight and the two lay side by side, flat upon the ground.

'Run! In the name of God!' Big Daniel shouted into Hal's face. 'The kegs are going to go up at any moment!'

'I can't!' Hal blurted through the pain. 'I'm hit! I can't stand!'

Big Daniel heaved himself up on one elbow and looked down at Hal's foot. He saw at once that the wound was crippling, then glanced back at the pyramid of powder-kegs under the arch of the gate, only thirty yards from where they lay. One of the burning fuses reached the bung-hole and flared brightly in the plug of soft pitch. It was on the point of exploding.

Big Daniel seized Hal in a smothering bear-hug and rolled on top of him, forcing his face into the soft earth, covering him with his own great body.

'Get off me, damn you!' Hal struggled beneath him, but at that instant the bottom keg blew up, and set off an instantaneous sympathetic explosion in every one of the four others piled on top of it.

Two hundred and fifty pounds weight of black powder was consumed in a single flash and the blast was cataclysmic. It ripped the heavy doors from their hinges and blew their splintered beams across the courtyard beyond. It collapsed the stonework of the arch and brought the battlements tumbling down in an avalanche of coral blocks, mortar and dust. A score or more of the Arabs on the wall were brought down with it, crushed and buried in the rubble.

The smoke and dust shot two hundred feet straight up into the air, then boiled into the anvil head of a thundercloud. The shockwave blew out across the open ground in front of the walls and struck the edge of the forest, bringing heavy branches crashing down, bowing the palm trees and thrashing through their fronds like the winds of a hurricane.

Big Daniel and Hal lay full in the path of the blast. It swept over them in a rolling wave of dust and debris. It sucked the air from their lungs and hammered them into the earth like the hoofs of a herd of stampeding buffalo. Hal felt his eardrums balloon, and the shock clubbed his brain. His senses were driven from him, and he seemed to hurtle through black space with the stars bursting in his head.

He came back slowly from that far away dark place, and his damaged eardrums roared and sang with the memory of that terrible blast, but through it he heard the thin, disembodied cheers of his seamen as they charged forward from the forest. In a pack they raced past where he lay and reached the destroyed gateway. They scrambled and shoved each other over the piles of rubble that blocked it, then they fought their way through the dust and the smoke, and swarmed into the courtyard of the fort. With their cutlasses in their hands, giving tongue like a pack of deerhounds when the stag stands at bay, they fell upon the dazed defenders in a savage orgy of battle lust.

Blinded with dust, Hal tried to sit up but there was an immense weight on his chest that suffocated him and pinned him to the ground. He coughed, choked, and tried to blink the grit out of his streaming eyes. Though he clawed feebly at the huge slack body above him he did not have the strength to free himself.

Gradually Hal's vision cleared and the roaring in his ears faded to the buzz of a hive of bees trapped in his skull. He saw Big Daniel's face above him: his eyes were wide and staring and his head rolled from side to side as Hal tried to push him off. His toothless mouth gaped open, and his tongue lolled. A mixture of his blood and spittle dribbled warm over Hal's cheek.

The horror of it goaded Hal, and he made a supreme effort and wriggled out from under the great slack body. Groggily he raised himself into a sitting position and looked down at the other man. By shielding him, Big Daniel had taken the full force of the blast. It had stripped away his clothing so that he was naked except for his boots and sword-belt. The driven sand had blasted away the skin from his back and buttocks, so that he looked like a freshly flayed deer. Chunks of stone and flying debris had ripped through his back and flanks, exposing the white bone shards of his ribs and broken spine.

'Danny?' Hal called. 'Danny? Can you hear me?' The question was futile, borne of his own stunned senses. He tried to move closer to him, but found his own legs would not obey his will. He glanced down at them. They were the only part of his body that had not been protected by Daniel's. Both his legs had been stripped of the cloth of his breeches and Hal saw that his flesh had been mangled as though caught in the iron teeth of a revolving capstan. Splinters of white bone protruded from the bloody mess. There was no pain, so his mind discounted the evidence of his eyes. He could not believe that he had lost both his legs. He did not want to gaze upon that destruction any longer.

Hal used his elbows now to drag himself closer to Big

Daniel, digging them into the soft soil and his shattered legs slithered along behind him. He lay beside the great body and gathered it in his arms. He rocked it gently as once he had soothed his infant son to sleep. 'It will be all right. We'll come through this together, like we always do,' he whispered. 'It's going to be all right, Danny.'

He did not realize that he was weeping until he saw his own tears falling into Daniel's upturned face, like warm drops of tropical rain washing away the white grains of sand that coated the staring eyeballs.

Dr Reynolds, coming up through the grove with his two surgeon's mates, found them lying there.

'Take care of Danny first,' Hal pleaded.

'God has already taken him into his care,' Dr Reynolds answered gently, and between them they lifted Hal onto the stretcher with his legs dangling.

Tom looked back over the bay. From where they lay at the top of a low white dune he could see the two square-rigged ships a mile out beyond the reef, the graceful *Seraph* leading and the *Minotaur*, with her black sails, looking menacing and potent. As he watched they tacked in succession and turned back into the south, taking up their blockade station across the mouth of the bay.

Tom rose on one knee and stared over the top of the dune at the walls of the fort, two hundred paces away. The heavy mist of gunsmoke was dissipating, blowing away on the monsoon wind, streaming out to sea. The top of the wall was lined with hundreds of heads, dark bearded faces below their *keffiya* headcloths and turbans. The defenders were brandishing their muskets and dancing on the ramparts in triumph. Tom could hear the excited jabber of their voices, and even understood some of their shouted insults aimed at the two English ships:

'May God blacken the face of the infidel.'

'God is great! He has given us the victory.'

Tom started to rise to his feet. 'Something has gone wrong. They should have blown the gates by now.'

Aboli reached up and seized his wrist. He drew him down to his side. 'Steady, Klebe! Sometimes the cruellest part of the battle is the waiting.'

Then they heard musket fire from the far side of the fortress, and all the Arab heads along the breastworks turned in that direction. Their shouts and taunts died away.

'The infidel is attacking the gates!' a voice screamed in Arabic, and there was an immediate stampede. Even the gunners deserted their cannon and raced away along the catwalk to counter this new threat. In seconds the parapets were deserted, and Tom scrambled to his feet again.

'Now is our chance! Follow me!'

Aboli pulled him down again. 'Patience, Klebe!'

Tom struggled to break his grip. 'We can't wait any longer. We have to get to Dorry!'

Aboli shook his head. 'Even you cannot fight a thousand men on your own.'

Tom stared across at the loophole in the top of the wall where he knew Dorian was incarcerated. 'He should have the sense to signal, to show us where he is. He should wave his shirt, or something.' Then swiftly he made allowance for his brother. 'But he's only a baby. He doesn't always know what to do.'

From the far side of the fort the scattered sound of musket shots crescendoed into a furious fusillade.

'Listen, Klebe.' Aboli restrained him. 'Danny and your father are laying the charges under the gates. It will not be long now.'

Then the blast stung their eardrums, and the thunder of the explosion stunned them. A tower of dust and smoke shot into the sky and boiled over at the crest, spreading out into a bulging thunderhead. The dustcloud was thick with hurtling debris, with lumps of rock and burning fragments that spun smoke-trails against the blue. Tom watched a brass cannon thrown a hundred feet into the air. Human bodies and dismembered limbs were hurled even higher, along with heavy baulks of timber and other wreckage.

Before Tom could recover his wits, Aboli was on his feet and loping away across the open ground towards the fort. Tom leaped up and charged after him, but the skirts of his robe hampered him and he could not catch Aboli before he reached the foot of the wall.

Aboli knelt and made a stirrup with his intertwined fingers. Without pausing Tom placed one booted foot into it and Aboli boosted him high into the branches of a strangler fig tree, whose roots were woven into the joints between the stone blocks. Tom climbed upwards like a monkey: neither the sword scabbard banging against his legs nor the brace of pistols thrust into his belt could slow him. Aboli and the three other men followed him up, but Tom reached the top of the parapet ahead of them. He scrambled into the gap where the wall had begun to collapse and threw his legs over the top.

A startled brown face confronted him. One Arab had not been drawn away from his post by the tumult of the assault on the gates. With a shout of astonishment, he recoiled before Tom's sudden appearance, and tried to level the musket in his hands, but the curved hammers hooked in a fold of his robe and while he struggled to free them the sabre flew from Tom's scabbard as though it was a bird. His thrust caught the man in the throat and severed his vocal cords so that his next shout was stillborn. He tottered backwards and dropped, arms flailing, fifty feet into the courtyard behind him.

While Aboli and the three seamen scrambled over the battlements, Tom cast a quick look around the walls and the courtyard of the fort. Through the thick billows of dust and smoke he saw the indistinct shapes of the Arabs stumbling away from the ruins of the gateway. Along the catwalks at the top of the parapet a wailing mob was fighting to get away from the smoking shambles that had been the gate to the fort.

Then, through the shattered gateway poured a yelling mob of English seamen. They struggled over the rubble and raced up the ramps to fall upon the Arabs on the walks of the ramparts. There were a few scattered musket shots and Tom saw one seaman fall backwards down the ramp. Then the two sides met and became a confused mass of howling, hacking, fighting men.

Tom looked for his father in the mob. Usually Hal's height and his black beard distinguished him even in the worst mêlée, but Tom could not find him. However, he could not spare the time to search longer. 'This way!' he called, and led his party along the catwalk to the ramp furthest from the gate. Their robes disguised them, and the Arabs around them let them pass without a second glance. Tom went down the ramp at a run, and reached the halfway landing unchecked. From there an arched doorway opened into the interior.

Two guards were at the entrance. One gawked at Tom's pale eyes and European features, then swung his scimitar above his head. '*Ferenghi!*' he screamed, and swung a full-blooded cut at Tom's head with the curved blade.

Tom ducked under it and riposted with a clean thrust high in the line of engagement, which went deep into the Arab's chest. As he withdrew his blade, the breath from the guard's punctured lungs whistled out of the wound, and he dropped to his knees. Aboli killed the other guard as swiftly. Then they jumped over the corpses and ran into the dark narrow passage beyond.

'Dorry!' Tom screamed. 'Where are you?' He flung the

robes back from his face and tore the turban from his head. He no longer needed the disguise and he wanted Dorian to recognize him. 'Dorian!' he cried again. His voice echoed weirdly along the passage and was answered by wild shouts in a babble of different languages.

Along both sides of the passage were the entrances to a dozen or more cells. The original doors must have rotted away a half-century ago, for they had been replaced by others of raw timber and crudely barred construction. Tom saw gaunt, bearded white faces peering through the openings and clawed hands reaching out towards him in supplication. He knew at once that these were the prisoners from the ships captured by al-Auf. Dorian must be among them, and his spirits soared.

'Dorian!'

An English voice answered, 'Jesus love you, sir, we have prayed for your coming.'

Aboli lifted the heavy locking bar from its brackets, the door burst open and the prisoners forced their way out of the tiny stone cell into the passageway. Tom was almost trapped in the flood of ragged, stinking humanity, and fought himself clear, hurrying on to peer into other cells.

'Dorian!' he bawled above the hubbub. He was trying to work out in which of the cells he had last seen his brother, but he was uncertain of his bearings.

He grabbed one of the released prisoners and shouted at him as he shook his shoulders. 'Is there a young white boy here, with red hair?'

The man stared at him as though he was mad, then pulled himself free and ran to join the flood of released men streaming down into the courtyard. Tom reached the end of the passage and the last cell. The door was ajar and he stepped into the tiny stone-walled room. It was empty. There was a mattress of dried palm fronds against the wall but no other furnishing. The sunlight slanted in through the loophole set in the far wall, and Tom crossed to it quickly. He looked out at the sweep of the bay and the two ships lying off-shore.

'This is the one,' he muttered. He jumped onto the step below the loophole and stuck his head through the opening. The liana grew up the outside of the wall, almost close enough to touch. 'This is the cell they had Dorry in. But where is he now?'

He jumped down from the step and looked around the empty cell. Iron rings were cemented into the stone blocks, to which men had been chained. The walls were covered with graffiti, scratched into the soft coral. He read Portuguese names and dates a hundred years old, worn and overgrown with moss and fungi. There were more recent additions in Arabic script, and he picked out a religious exhortation, a line from Sura 17 of the Koran that he recognized because Alf Wilson had made him learn it by heart: 'The seven heavens and the earth, and all things therein, declare His glory.' Below that there were was another scratching, made with a belt buckle or some other metal implement. It was fresh and raw, in lopsided childish letters: 'DORIAN COURTNEY – 3RD FEBRUARY 1691.'

'He was here!' Tom shouted aloud. 'Aboli, Dorry was here!'

Aboli appeared in the doorway, blocking it with his massive dark body. 'Where is he now, Klebe?'

'We will find him.'

Tom paused only to rip off the constricting robe that hampered his movements, and hurled it against the wall. Then they ran together back down the passage and out into the sunlight. The fighting was still surging through the courtyard below them and over the ramparts of the fortress, but at a glance it was obvious that the defenders were in rout. Hundreds had escaped through the shattered gateway. They had thrown away their weapons and were streaming into the forest. Others were trapped within the walls. Many were on their knees pleading for quarter, but Tom saw others leap from the ramparts rather than face the English cutlasses. With their white robes ballooning around their bodies, they shrieked as they plunged to earth.

However, a few were still fighting. One isolated group of a dozen men was holding the east bastion and screaming their defiance, 'Allah akbar! God is great,' but as Hal watched, the Englishmen swarmed over them, cut them down and threw their bodies over the battlements.

Tom looked desperately for a small figure and a fiery patch of hair in the confusion, but there was no glimpse of his brother. A woman raced up the ramp towards Tom. Her black veil had blown away and her head was uncovered. Tom saw that she was little more than a child. Her long black hair streamed back from her terrified face, and her kohl-darkened eyes were those of a fawn pursued by the hounds. Shouting with excited laughter, four seamen followed her, their shirts soaked with the blood of the men they had killed, their faces speckled with bloody droplets, swollen and inflamed with lust.

They caught the girl at the edge of the ramp and threw her down. Three pinned her to the stone flags and, though she struggled, they pulled up the skirts of her robe and exposed her slim brown limbs and her smooth naked belly. The fourth sailor ripped open his own breeches and fell on top of her.

'Grease the pink lane for us!' his mates encouraged him. Tom had never imagined anything so horrific. As a novice of the Order of St George and the Holy Grail, he had been taught that war was noble and all true warriors were gallant. He ran forward to intervene, but Aboli seized his arm and held it in a grip of iron. 'Leave them, Klebe. It is the right of the victors. Our duty is now to Bomvu.' He used his pet name for Dorian, which meant 'Red' in the language of the forests.

'We can't let them!' Tom blurted.

'We can't stop them.' Aboli cut him short. 'They will kill you if you try. Let us find Bomvu instead.' The girl was sobbing pitifully but Aboli dragged Tom down the ramp to the ground level.

At this end of the courtyard they found a maze of old walls and doorways. Some of the doors stood open, but most were heavily barred and the windows shuttered. Dorian could be behind any of those. Tom knew his little brother would be lost and terrified. They had to find him before he was hurt in the fighting and the looting.

'Take the far end,' he shouted at Aboli, pointing down the covered terrace. 'I will start here.'

He did not look back to see if Aboli had obeyed him, but ran to the nearest door. It was locked. He tried to barge it open with his shoulder, then stood back and tried to kick out the massive iron lock. It stood solidly, resisting his attempts. Tom looked about him and recognized one of the topmastmen from the *Seraph*, who was running down the terrace, carrying a long-handled axe in one hand and a pistol in the other. His arms were bloody to the elbows and his expression was rapturous with the joy of battle.

'Charley!' Tom yelled at him, and even through the mists of fighting madness the man heard him. 'Break this door in,' Tom ordered.

Charley grinned at the invitation to further destruction. 'Stand back, Tommy me lad,' he cried, and rushed at the door. With two mighty swings of the axe he had dashed in the panels and sent the door sagging back on its hinges. Tom kicked it open the rest of the way and jumped through. He found himself in a labyrinth of small rooms and passageways. He ran forward, glancing into each room as he passed. Clearly they had all been hastily deserted: bedding and clothing were thrown about in disarray.

Suddenly he heard a loud thudding over his head, and looked up a rickety staircase at the end of the passage. It sounded as though someone was trying to escape from a

locked room. Perhaps it's Dorry! His heart pounded. Without another thought Tom raced up the stairs, taking them
two at a time. He reached the top and found a heavy door
standing open, the huge iron key still in the lock. He ran
through into a long narrow room. The windows were
shuttered, and it was in semi-darkness.

'Dorry!' he shouted, as he looked about him quickly.
He saw at once that this was no prison. Along the wall
opposite the shuttered windows was packed an assortment
of small wooden chests. They were very similar to the
chests they had captured from the dhow of al-Malik, the
chests that had contained the ransom money for Dorian.
He realized that this must be one of al-Auf's storerooms,
probably the one where he kept his most valuable booty.

Four of the chests stood open, the lids thrown back.
Even in his concern for his brother, Tom was fascinated by
the contents that were revealed. He recognized the typical
Arab coin bags that filled them. He took up one and hefted
it in his hand. The weight and the shape of the coins
through the cloth dispelled any doubts he might have had.
'Gold,' he whispered. Then he noticed that someone had
left a leather saddle-bag on the stone floor beside the chest.
It was half filled with the bullion sacks. He must have
interrupted someone in the act of filling it before making
his escape from the beleaguered fortress. The banging
noises Tom had heard were of the chests being broken
open.

Whoever it was must still be here. As the realization
dawned upon Tom, he heard the slither of a stealthy
footstep on the stone flags behind him. The sound galvanized him, and he whirled towards the doorway.

Al-Auf had hidden behind the open door when he
heard Tom's running footsteps coming up the stairs and
now Tom recognized him instantly. He had seen him on
the deck of the *Minotaur* as the *Seraph* engaged the corsair.
He was taller than Tom had thought, and his predatory

eyes in their deep sockets were dark and fierce as those of a vulture. His head was bare – he wore no turban. His thick black tresses, laced with silver, fell to his shoulders, and merged with the curls of his beard. His lips were drawn back in a savage grimace as he lifted the pistol in his left hand and aimed at Tom's head.

For a fleeting moment Tom looked deep into the gaping muzzle of the barrel, then into al-Auf's bright eye, aiming at him over the sights of the pistol. With a metallic click that sounded deafening in the confines of the small room, the hammer fell and the pan flashed in a puff of white smoke. Tom winced as he waited for the ball to smash into his face, but it never came. The pistol had misfired.

For an instant al-Auf was blinded by the smoke and the flash in the pan, and in that brief time Tom had covered the space between them. He had seen that the pistol was double-barrelled, and that al-Auf's forefinger was hooking around the second trigger. He knew that luck could not favour him twice, and that the second barrel would kill him.

He swung the sabre at the outstretched pistol hand, and the blade slashed across the inside of al-Auf's wrist. Like a razor, it opened the cluster of veins and arteries beneath the brown skin, and the pistol dropped from the nerveless fingers. Hilt first, it struck the stone floor and with a vicious roar the second barrel fired. The ball splintered the wood of one of the bullion chests, and al-Auf reeled back, groping for the scimitar on the gem-encrusted belt around his waist. He cleared his blade just in time to counter the thrust that Tom sped at the centre of his sternum.

Tom had not expected him to be so quick. The silver streaks in al-Auf's hair and beard had misled him. The corsair was leopard fast, and the power in the blade was that of a man half his age. As Tom recovered from his thrust, al-Auf dropped on one knee and slashed back-handed for his ankles, a stroke that might have maimed him. Tom did not have time to recoil. Instead he bounded into the air and the curved blade flickered under the soles of his boots. Still airborne, Tom cut at the Arab's dark head, but al-Auf slipped away from him like a serpent sliding under a rock. He had left a puddle of blood on the stones, and his wrist was still spurting. Tom blocked the riposte and made a feint high in the tierce, but al-Auf countered, and lunged under his blade, aiming for his stomach. Tom jumped back and the thrust came up short. They circled, holding each other's eyes, trying to divine the other's thoughts. Their blades rasped and thrummed together as each probed for a weakness.

Tom's foot slipped in the blood, and the moment he was off-balance al-Auf released himself like a bolt from a cross-bow, going low again, trying for the hip. Tom deflected, and forced him to scramble away. Tom was reading his man now. He was fast and elusive, and age had not eroded the strength in his wrist. If they continued fencing then in the end al-Auf's experience would tell. Tom knew that he must turn it into trial of strength.

He swayed across the Arab's strong side, flirting with him, offering a fleeting opening, but as al-Auf accepted and thrust low again, Tom blocked his blade with a dead hit, and trapped it with his own. Now they were almost chest to chest, their blades crossed at eye-level. Tom put all the weight of his broad young shoulders into it, and al-Auf gave a step. Tom could feel the strength going out of him, dribbling from the open veins in his left wrist. Tom heaved again, but al-Auf was not as weak as he had pretended. He gave way so rapidly that Tom stumbled forward against no resistance, and again al-Auf went low. Tom should have read it, for he knew his man well enough by now to guard against the low thrust. It was only by a miracle of speed and catlike balance that he swayed his lower body aside and the thrust grazed his thigh. It split the stuff of his breeches and opened a shallow cut in the rubbery muscle of his leg.

It was not a damaging wound, and at the end of his thrust al-Auf was at full extension. As he tried desperately to recover Tom gathered up his blade, and forced him into a rolling engagement. The two swords swirled together, the sound of steel on steel screeching so shrilly as to set their nerves on edge, the hilts vibrating in their hands.

Tom had succeeded at last in making it a straight trial of strength, for al-Auf dared not try to disengage. To do so he must open his guard, and he knew the riposte would come like a lightning bolt. This was the classic prolonged engagement, which Tom had learned from Aboli. 'With this coup, your father killed Schreuder,' Aboli had told him, 'and that Dutchman was the greatest swordsman I have ever seen wield a blade – after your father, that is.'

Tom leaned all his weight into his wrist and al-Auf gave a pace. Round and round the two blades swirled, and sweat broke out across the brown forehead, which by now was deeply creased with effort, and streamed down into the eyes and beard. Triumphantly Tom felt the other man weakening. The blood still fell in heavy drops from his wound, and al-Auf's lips twisted into a horrid rictus of despair. Dismay and death bloomed in his eyes.

Suddenly Tom changed the angle of his wrist, the point of his sword flashed an inch from al-Auf's eyes, and he broke. Against the Arab's will, his long brown fingers opened and the hilt of his scimitar slipped from them. Tom used his own blade to pluck it away and, with a flick of his wrist, hurled it against the far wall where it fell and clattered on the stone floor.

Al-Auf tried to duck and dart to the doorway, but Tom had the point of his sword in his beard, probing gently up under his chin, and he forced him back against the wall. Tom was panting deeply, and it took him a while to recover his breath sufficiently to speak. 'There is only one thing that you can do now to save your own life,' he said, between ragged breaths. Al-Auf's eyes narrowed as he heard the infidel speak his own language so fluently. 'You can give me the Frankish boy you are holding here.'

Al-Auf stared at him. He held his injured arm against his chest, trying to staunch the bleeding by squeezing his wrist with his other hand.

'Answer me,' Tom said, and pressed the sword-point deeper into his throat. 'Speak to me, you offspring of a diseased sow. Give me the boy and I will let you live.'

The Arab winced at the prick of the steel. 'I do not know this child of whom you speak.'

'You know him well. The one with red hair,' Tom interrupted his protests.

Al-Auf twisted his lips into a mocking smile. 'Why do you want al-Amhara, the Red One?' He said, and there was a terrible hatred in his eyes. 'Was he your bum-boy?'

Tom's sword hand trembled with anger at the insult. 'Al-Amhara is my brother.'

'Then you are too late,' al-Auf gloated. 'He has gone where you will never find him.'

Tom felt as though an iron hoop was tightening around his chest. His breathing came short. Dorian was gone. 'You are lying.' In his distress the Arabic words tripped his tongue. 'I know he is here. I saw him with my own eyes. I will find him.'

'He is not on this island, search where you will.' Al-Auf laughed now, a painful, twisted sound.

Tom cut it short with the pressure of the steel point. He stared into the Arab's dark eyes, and a confused jumble of thoughts raced through his brain. 'No!' Tom did not want to believe it. 'You're hiding my brother here. You are lying.' But there was something in al-Auf's manner that warned Tom he was telling the truth. He knew they had lost little Dorry and, slowly, black despair filled the empty place that Dorry had left in his heart.

He lowered the sword blade from al-Auf's throat, and turned away. He started towards the door, desperate to search every corner of the island, if merely to set his heart at rest.

Al-Auf was so surprised that for a moment he stood rigid. Then he dropped his uninjured right hand to the hilt of the curved dagger in the gold filigree scabbard on his belt. The burnished blade made a small slippery sound as it slid from its sheath.

Tom was not too far gone in misery to ignore that fatal whisper, and as he spun around to face him, al-Auf launched himself across the gap between them with the dagger raised above his head, to plunge it into Tom's back.

At that treachery, Tom's despair turned to a consuming rage. He jumped forward to meet the attack and drove his sword-point into the centre of the Arab's chest. He felt the steel glance off a rib, then slide through heart and lung and thrill in his grip as the point hit the spine.

Al-Auf froze and the dagger dropped from his hand. It clattered loudly on the floor, and the hatred in his black eyes faded. Tom placed one booted foot against the man's chest, and pushed him backwards as he pulled the red blade free.

Al-Auf slumped to his knees and his head drooped forward, but Tom's rage was not yet assuaged. He lifted the sabre high and swung it down again, using the full power of his shoulders, his arm and the snap of his wrist so that the blade hissed in the air as it descended. It fell across the back of al-Auf's neck. The head toppled from the spouting stump, struck the floor with a meaty thump and rolled to Tom's feet.

Tom stared down into al-Auf's face. The dark eyes were wide open and fierce. His lips opened and it seemed he tried to speak, but then his lids fluttered, the light went out of his eyes, which turned dull and opaque, and his jaw went slack.

'It is done, and well done!' said Aboli from the doorway. He stepped into the room and slipped off the Arabic gown he wore. He knelt and spread the garment on the floor, then lifted the severed head by a handful of its lank black hair.

Tom watched him as he wrapped al-Auf's head in the cloak. He felt little emotion and no remorse as the blood soaked through the folds of the cloth. Aboli stood up and slung the gruesome bundle over his shoulder. 'We will take it to your father. Al-Auf's head is worth a barony to him when he presents it to the governors of the Honourable Company in London.'

With the naked sword in his hand, Tom followed Aboli like a sleep-walker down the passage and out into the sunlight. He felt no elation, only the crushing weight of the knowledge that he had lost Dorian for ever.

Tom pushed his way through the excited seamen who rampaged through the passages and inner rooms of the fort. They were guffawing and shouting loud banter at each other as they ransacked the building. Every so often there was a shout and a scream as they found another Arab hiding in one of the cells and dragged him out into the courtyard.

The prisoners were stripped naked. The seamen had learned how readily they could conceal a dagger under their voluminous robes. Even the women were treated in this way. The captured weapons were thrown in a pile in the centre of the courtyard, while the valuables, the purses of the men and the gold jewellery of the women, were thrown on a spread canvas sail.

Then the prisoners were dragged away to join the ranks of naked brown bodies that already knelt along the north wall of the courtyard, guarded by grinning sailors with pistols cocked and cutlasses drawn.

Tom strode across to the ranks of squatting Arabs and picked out one. Despite his nudity the man had noble features and an intelligent, dignified gaze.

'What is your name, old father?' Tom asked, making an effort to keep his address respectful.

The old man looked startled to be spoken to in Arabic, but he responded to Tom's gentle tone. 'My name is Ben Abram.'

'You have the look of a scholar or a holy man,' Tom flattered him.

Again the old man responded. 'I am a physician.'

'There was a boy here on the island. He would now be twelve, with red hair. He was captured by al-Auf. Do you know him?'

'I know him.' Ben Abram nodded, and Tom's spirits soared.

'He is my brother. Where is he now? Is he here on the island?' he demanded eagerly, but Ben Abram shook his head.

'He is gone. Al-Auf sold him into slavery.'

At last Tom had to accept this corroboration of al-Auf's boast. For a minute he thought that he would not be able to bear the pain of it. 'Where did they send him? What is the name of the man who bought my brother as a slave?'

Ben Abram shook his head again, but his eyes slid away from Tom's face and his expression was guarded. 'I do not know,' he whispered.

Tom knew he was lying and his hand went to the hilt of his sword. He would force it out of the old man, but then he saw the strong, determined set of Ben Abram's

404

features and his intuition warned him that he would get nothing from him by force.

To give himself time to think, he looked around the inner walls of the fort. Dead Arabs were scattered along the ramparts, with many wounded among them who groaned and writhed in the dirt. He called across to the coxswain who was in command of the guard. 'This man is a surgeon. Give him back his clothes and let him tend to the enemy wounded.'

'Aye, Mr Courtney.' The man knuckled his forehead.

Tom turned back to Ben Abram. 'Many of your men need your care. You may go to them.'

'May Allah reward your compassion.' Ben Abram rose to his feet and pulled on the robe that the coxswain tossed to him. Tom watched the old man hurry away and kneel beside one of the badly wounded Arabs at the foot of the ramp.

Now he must find his father and tell him the dread news he had learned of Dorian. Tom looked about him again, then started towards the gate. As he went he stopped every crewman from the *Seraph* he recognized. 'Have you seen the captain? Where is he?'

When none could answer, Tom felt concern well up in him. Then he saw Captain Anderson near the devastated gateway. Anderson was bright red in the face and roaring like a wounded bull, trying to get his rampaging troops organized into gangs to start retrieving the contents of the storerooms in which the pirate booty was stored. Already some sailors were staggering out of the fort under the weight of bales and barrels, to stack them beside the gate, ready to be carried down to the beach and loaded aboard the waiting ships.

Tom pushed his way to Anderson's side. Anderson swivelled to face him, and his expression softened in a way that puzzled Tom. 'I have killed al-Auf.' Tom raised his voice to make himself heard above the uproar. 'Aboli has his head.' Tom indicated the tall black man and the bloodstained bundle he carried slung over his shoulder.

'Mother Mary!' Anderson looked mightily impressed. 'That's good work. I was wondering where that rascal had vanished to. His head will be worth a lakh in London.'

'There's a room full of bullion chests at the head of the stairs behind that doorway at the end of the ramparts. The good Lord only knows how much gold al-Auf has squirrelled away there. Captain Anderson, I believe it best that you send a reliable officer to guard it before our lads begin helping themselves.'

Anderson shouted for his coxswain, and gave the orders. With five hastily recruited men, the officer hurried away, and Tom could ask the question that had been burning his tongue. 'Have you seen my father, Captain? I've been searching for him. He should be here to help you take command.'

Anderson looked down at him and his eager expression melted with pity. 'He is down, lad. I saw him struck by the blast of the powder explosion at the gates.'

As his premonition of disaster was realized, Tom felt his heart clutched by the icy hand of dread. 'Where is he, sir?'

'The last I saw of him, he was in front of the gates.' Anderson's voice was gruff with sympathy. 'I'm sorry, lad, but from what I saw he is almost certainly killed.'

Tom fled from him, even Dorian forgotten at that moment. He scrambled over the piles of rubble that blocked the gateway and saw one shattered body lying out in the open ground. He ran and dropped to his knees beside it. It was so badly mangled, stripped of its clothing, the skin flayed away from the raw flesh, that Tom could not be sure whom he was looking at. Gently he turned the shattered head. 'Danny,' he said softly, and felt the tears start in his eyes. He had not known how much he had loved the big man until now. He blinked back the tears. Close up, death was uglier than his worst nightmares. Big Daniel's eyes were open and staring, clustered with blue flies. Tom brushed them away and stroked the lids closed with the palm of his hand. He stood up again uncertainly, and found Aboli beside him. 'Where is my father? Captain Anderson said he was here.'

Tom could see no other body that might have been his father's. There were thirty or forty dead Arabs lying along the edge of the forest, killed as they tried to escape. A few seamen were picking over the corpses, making certain they were not feigning death, a favourite Arab trick, and searching them for anything of value.

'Your father is not here,' Aboli said. 'They must have taken him away.'

Tom ran to the nearest seaman who was squatting beside a body. Tom did not recognize him – he must have been off the *Yeoman of York*. 'Have you seen Sir Henry, the captain of the *Seraph*?'

The man looked up at him. 'Aye, lad. The old man was sore wounded. I saw the sawbones take him off down to the bay.' He gestured with his cupped hands full of gold jewellery.

Over the tops of the trees the masts of the squadron showed. As soon as the flags had been hoisted on the ramparts to announce the capture of the fort, all three ships had come into the bay. Tom took the pathway through the trees and ran down through the soft white coral sand. He came out on the beach, with Aboli only a pace behind him, and looked across at the tall ships lying at anchor in the clear, tranquil waters of the lagoon.

The small boats were already busy ferrying between the vessels and the beach, bringing ashore those men who had been freed from their shipboard duties. Tom saw a longboat coming from the *Seraph*, and hailed it as soon as its keel hit the sand.

407

'Where is the captain?'

'He is on board already, Master Tom,' the boatswain shouted back.

'I must go to him. Take me out to the ship.'

'Right you are, Master Tom. Jump aboard.'

When the longboat bumped against the *Seraph*'s hull, Tom was the first man up the ladder, with Aboli still close behind him. There was only a handful of the ship's depleted crew on deck, and they were lining the rail, wistfully watching the commotion ashore, eager to join the fighting and looting.

'Where is the captain?' Tom demanded.

'They took him to his quarters.'

Tom flew down the deck and when he reached the door to the stern cabin he came up short as a terrible groan echoed along the quiet deck. He paused with his right hand outstretched, unable to summon the courage to open the door and discover what horrors awaited him on the far side. Aboli reached past him and quietly pushed it open. Tom stared into his father's cabin.

They had rigged a wooden grating under the stern windows where the light was strongest. His father was laid on his back upon the grating. Dr Reynolds stood over him. He wore his black frock coat, his formal operating attire. The thick serge cloth was greenish with age and stiff with old dried blood. Reynolds was already perspiring freely in the hot little cabin. He looked up at Tom and nodded. 'Good! Come in, lad. Don't just stand there gawking! I need another pair of strong hands,' he said grimly, and began to roll his sleeves above the elbows.

Tom advanced on leaden feet until he stood beside the grating and looked down at his father's torn body. The fiery stench of raw spirit filled the heated cabin. One of the two surgeon's mates was forcing the neck of a three-quarters empty bottle of rum into Hal Courtney's mouth. The spirit was running down his cheeks and into his hair.

Hal was gagging and even in his semi-conscious condition trying to turn away his head.

Tom snatched the bottle from the man's hand. 'Slowly, curse you for a clumsy oaf! You will drown him.'

'He needs the rum to get him through the pain,' the surgeon's mate protested.

Tom ignored him, and lifted his father's head as gently as if he were an infant. He gave him the bottle with care, allowing only a sip at a time to trickle between his lips, then waiting for him to swallow.

He looked down at the injured legs. Reynolds had buckled leather straps around each one, halfway up the thighs, and twisted these tourniquets to stem the bleeding, but the wounds were still weeping. They had placed a bucket beneath the grating to catch the blood, and the steady drip-drip sounded to Tom like a water clock counting out the seconds of his father's life.

Reynolds finished his preparations, and selected an ivory-handled scalpel from the canvas surgeon's roll that lay on the grating beside the maimed legs. He began to cut away the ragged blood-soaked legs of Hal's breeches. Tom blanched and felt his senses swim as the carnage beneath the cloth was revealed.

The blast had jellified the flesh, bruised it to the colour of minced liver. Sand and coral chips had been driven into it as though fired from a musket, and splinters of bone stood out of the bloody meat like flint arrowheads.

Reynolds palpated the legs. They were soft and boneless in his hands. He pursed his lips and shook his head. 'They have to come off. Both of them. I cannot save them.'

'No!' Tom gasped. 'You cannot take his legs! He will never again ride a horse or command a ship. You must not do it!'

'Then he will die. His legs will rot, and he will be dead of the gangrene in a week, or less if he is lucky.' He nodded at his two mates. 'Hold him!'

409

Aboli stepped forward, and Reynolds said, 'Yes, you too. We need strong arms here.' He selected a scalpel, which looked to Tom more like a butcher's knife than a surgical instrument, and tested the edge on his own thumb. Tom saw the specks of rust on the blade where old blood had not been properly scrubbed away. 'Master Tom, you will hold his head.' Reynolds handed him a wooden wedge. 'Keep that between his teeth. He must have something to bite on when the pain hits him, or his teeth will crack.'

He dipped a sponge into the bowl of hot water that his mate held, and swabbed away some of the blood and dirt from Hal's left leg so that he could see where to make the first cut. Then he gave another twist to the strap of the tourniquet and ran the edge of the blade across the tightly drawn skin. The flesh parted and Tom, who was holding the wooden wedge between his father's jaws, felt his body convulse and his back arch, every muscle and sinew drawn tight as though by a capstan.

A terrible cry issued from Hal's throat, and then he clamped down on the wedge, locking his jaws so that the wood was crushed between his teeth. Tom tried to hold his head as it thrashed from side to side, but his father had the strength of a madman.

'Hold him!' Reynolds grunted, as he cut down, and Aboli and the men holding Hal were thrown about by the strength of his convulsions. Tom heard the steel of the blade strike the femur deep in his father's thigh. Quickly Reynolds laid the knife aside and took up the hank of black catgut. He tied off the open ends of the blood vessels, which were running freely despite the tourniquet. The blood cascaded into the bucket beneath the grating. Tom could not believe that there was so much of it.

Reynolds picked a saw out of the canvas roll, and inspected the fine teeth. Then he seized the shattered leg in his left hand and, like a carpenter dividing a plank, he placed the blade in the deep scalpel wound and made the first stroke.

The steel teeth grated shrilly against the bone, and despite the weight of four men trying to hold him down Hal doubled in the middle and came up into a sitting position. His head was thrown back and ropes of muscle and ligaments stood proud in his throat and shoulders. Another tortured scream tore out of his gaping mouth and rang through the ship. Then his body went slack and he fell back limply on the grating. 'Thank the Lord for that,' Reynolds whispered. 'We must work swiftly now, before he comes around again.'

With three more long strokes, the bone parted. The leg sagged and the surgeon laid aside the saw, and picked up the knife again. 'I will leave him a good thick pad on the stump, so that the end of the bone is well covered.' He shaped the flesh with a few rapid slices, and Tom gagged as the shattered leg came free and flopped on the grating. One of the surgeon's mates picked it up and dropped it on the deck. It lay there like a fresh-caught cod thrown on the floorboards of a fishing skiff, twitching softly as the nerve ends died.

Reynolds threaded a length of catgut through the eye of a sail-maker's needle, then folded the flap of flesh over the exposed bone that protruded from the stump. He hummed in his throat as he probed the point of the needle through the tough skin and began to lay his neat little stitches along the seam. The loose ends of the sutures with which he had tied off the blood vessels dangled out of the closed wound.

Within minutes Reynolds stood back and held his head to one side, like a seamstress judging a piece of embroidery. 'Nice,' he said. 'Very nice, even if I say it myself.' He made a little clucking sound of self-approval. To Tom the stump looked like the head of a new-born baby, round and bald and bloody.

411

'Now, let's have a look at his other pin.' Reynolds nodded at his mate. The man seized Hal's remaining ankle in his big hairy hands and pulled the mangled leg straight. The agony roused Hal from the dark fogs of unconsciousness. He uttered another shuddering groan, and struggled weakly, but they held him down.

Reynolds examined the leg, starting high on the thigh, just below the tourniquet, then working down over the knee, probing his powerful stubby fingers deep into the flesh to feel for broken bone.

'Good!' he encouraged himself. 'Excellent! I think I can risk cutting much lower here. I will save the knee. That's important. We will be able to articulate a wooden leg. He may even learn to walk again.'

The thought that his father, who had been the vigorous centre of his existence for as long as he could remember, might never be able to walk again was suddenly thrust upon Tom's dazed mind. It was almost as unbearable as the horrors he was forced to witness now as Reynolds picked up the bloody scalpel and laid the first incision on the remaining leg. Hal bucked and screamed in his sweat-slippery hands, and chewed the wooden wedge to splinters.

Tom was panting and grunting with the effort of holding the squirming body, and fighting back the waves of nausea that threatened to overwhelm him as the second leg fell away and dropped to the blood-slick deck under their feet. This time Hal had not been granted the release of coma. He had endured every exquisite agony of the knife and the hacksaw. Tom was filled with awe and a strange sense of pride as he watched the way his father fought back against the agony and only succumbed when it soared to another pinnacle. Even then he tried to choke back his cries.

At last Tom could bend over him and place his lips an inch from Hal's ear and whisper, 'It's over, Father. It's all over.'

Unbelievably his father heard him and understood. He tried to smile, and that smile was a terrible thing to see. 'Thank you.' Hal's lips formed the words, but no sound issued from his tortured throat. Tom's vision swam as tears threatened to overwhelm him, but he forced them back, and then he kissed his father on the lips, something he could not remember doing in all his life. Hal made no effort to roll his head aside to avoid the embrace.

Ned Tyler hurried to meet Tom as he stepped out onto the deck. 'How is he?' he asked.

'He is alive,' Tom replied, and then, when he saw how real was Ned's concern, he took pity on him. 'As well as we can expect. We will not know for some days yet. Dr Reynolds says that he must rest.'

'Thank God for that at least.' Ned said, then looked at Tom expectantly.

For a moment Tom did not know what he was waiting for. Suddenly he realized: Ned needed orders. He shied away from it. He felt too tired and uncertain of himself to take on the responsibility that was being thrust upon him. Then, with an effort, he rallied his resources. 'Our first concern now is to get all our wounded back on board where Dr Reynolds can attend them properly.'

'Aye, Mr Courtney.' Ned looked relieved and turned away to pass on the orders. Tom was astonished at how easily it had happened. He was no longer Master Tom, but Mr Courtney. As Hal's son, the mantle of command had passed naturally to him. He was only seventeen and he bore no official rank, but this was not a naval vessel, and Tom had proved time and again that he had a level head on his shoulders, that he could hold his own in any fight. The officers and men liked him. It did not have to be debated. If Ned Tyler accepted his right to command, then so would every man aboard the *Seraph*.

He tried to think what his father would want him to do even though his instinct was to hurry back to Hal's bedside, and stay there until he was strong enough to care for himself. But he knew that Dr Reynolds and his mates were better equipped for the business of nursing him back to health.

Thinking quickly, he told Ned to secure the ship and see to the routine details of management, then he went on, 'I leave the ship in your hands, Mr Tyler.' The words he had heard his father utter so often came easily to his lips. 'I'm going ashore to take command there.'

'Aye, sir,' Ned replied.

With Aboli close behind him, Tom strode back to the fort. Some sort of order had been restored, but he found Anderson and every one of the men still engrossed in ransacking the storerooms of the fortress. A mountain of plunder was piled in the centre of the courtyard, and a wild confusion of men milled about it, adding more bales and boxes to the pile.

'Captain Anderson,' Tom hailed him, 'there are three or four hundred of the enemy escaped into the forest. Many of them are still armed. I want the ramparts manned against a counter-attack.'

Anderson stared at him incredulously, but Tom went on resolutely, 'Please put your best officer in command, and have the enemy cannon reloaded with grape and trained round to cover the edge of the forest.'

Anderson's face started to swell and turn a brighter crimson. Every sailor within earshot had stopped whatever he was doing and now stood idle and gaping, following the exchange avidly.

'Then please have the open gateway barricaded to repel an attack,' Tom went on. He was as tall as Anderson, and he held his eye without blinking.

For a long minute Anderson looked at him, and it seemed that he was on the point of challenging the order, but then he wavered, and looked away at the open gateway, at the unprepared rabble of his men. The sense of what Tom had ordered was irrefutable. 'Mr McNaughton,' he roared, unnecessarily loudly, for his mate was only five paces from where he stood, 'fifty men to barricade the gates, and a hundred to man the captured guns. Load with grape and cover the approaches to the fort.' He turned back to Tom.

'There is only an hour or two of daylight left to us,' Tom went on. 'We will clear the fugitives out of the forest at first light tomorrow.' He looked across at the ranks of naked prisoners, who still knelt in the dust. 'As a matter of common humanity I want those people clothed and given water, then they can be confined in the cells of the fort. How many of our men are wounded?'

'I'm not certain.' Anderson looked guilty, and the red faded slowly from his complexion.

'Have your writer draw up the butcher's bill,' Tom ordered. 'The casualties must be sent on board the ships where they can be attended by the surgeons.'

Tom looked around quickly and saw that Ben Abram, the Arab surgeon, was still at work attending to the enemy wounded. Someone had had the sense to give him four of the prisoners to assist him. 'We will bury the dead tomorrow before they start to poison the air. The Mussulmen have certain strict rituals for the disposal of their dead. Pirates that they are, we must honour their traditions.'

Tom worked with Anderson until long after the sun had set. By the light of burning torches they restored order, had the fort secured and the booty placed under strict guard. By then Tom was weaving on his feet with fatigue. The shallow sword wound across his thigh, which al-Auf had inflicted, burned and every muscle in his body ached brutally.

'It is safe now, Klebe. All is taken care of until tomorrow. You must rest.' Aboli was suddenly at his shoulder.

'There is still one thing that cannot wait until tomorrow.' Tom led the way out through the gates to where Big Daniel still lay. Between them they wrapped the great body in a sheet of canvas and one of the stretcher parties carried it down to the beach.

It was after midnight when Tom staggered down the passage to the *Seraph*'s stern cabin. A surgeon's mate sat beside the bunk on which Hal lay. Tom told him, 'I will take over,' sent him away and threw himself down on the hard deck. Twice during the night his father's groans woke him. Once he gave him the water he pleaded for, and later he held the pewter bowl for him to urinate. It troubled him deeply to see Hal brought so low, to the level of an infant, but the pleasure of being able to serve him outweighed his exhaustion and his pity.

Tom woke again before dawn, and thought for a dreadful moment that his father had died during the night, but when he touched Hal's cheek the flesh was warm. He held the steel shaving mirror to his mouth and, with relief, watched the shining surface cloud. Hal's breath was still tainted with the odour of stale rum, but he was alive.

Tom wanted to stay with him, but he knew that that would not be what his father expected of him. He left him in the care of the surgeon's mate, and before the sun rose went ashore with Aboli.

There was still so much to be done. He placed Master Walsh and the writer from the *Yeoman of York* in charge of tallying the booty they had captured. Anderson took command of packing the treasure and sealing the chests, which were carried down to the beach and placed in the charge of a trusted officer and an armed guard.

Then Tom sent for Ben Abram. The old man looked exhausted, and Tom wondered if he had slept. 'I know it is your custom to bury your dead before sunset on the second day.'

Ben Abram nodded. 'You know our customs as well as our language.'

'How many are there?'

Ben Abram looked grave. 'Three hundred and forty-three, that I have been able to count.'

'If you give me your parole for their good behaviour, I will release fifty of your men from the stockade to dig the graves.'

Ben Abram selected a burial site at the far end of the ancient Islamic cemetery and put his men to work. It went quickly in the soft sandy soil. Before noon they had carried the bodies, each wrapped in a sheet of clean white trade cotton, down from the fort. Al-Auf's headless corpse was in the centre of the long row laid along the bottom of the shallow pit and covered with earth. Ben Abram recited the Islamic prayers for the dead, and afterwards came to find Tom on the beach. 'I call down the blessings of Allah upon you for your compassion. Without your mercy none of the dead could have entered the garden of Paradise. One day, may the man who kills you extend to you the same consideration.'

'Thank you, old father,' said Tom grimly. 'But my mercy will end with the dead. The living must face the consequences of their crimes.'

He left the old man and went to where Alf Wilson and Aboli were waiting at the head of three hundred fully armed men, who included the prisoners of al-Auf whom he had released.

'Very well,' Tom said. 'Let's round up those who escaped from the fort.'

Tom used the steady wind of the monsoon and sent small groups of men to put fire into the eastern fringe of the forest. It caught readily and flames roared through the undergrowth in towering clouds of thick black smoke. Those Arabs still hiding in the forest were driven before the fire.

When they came running out from among the trees few had any fight left in them. They threw down their weapons, pleaded for mercy and were marched away to join their comrades. By nightfall on the second day almost every fugitive had been rounded up and penned in the stockades of the fort.

'The only sweet water on the island is in the rainwater cisterns of the fort,' Tom told Anderson, when they met on the beach at sunset. 'If we missed any, they will have to give themselves up before noon tomorrow or die of thirst.'

Anderson studied the boy, who had so swiftly become a man. Tom's face was blackened by the soot of the fires, and there were bloodstains on his shirt, for some of the Arabs had chosen to fight rather than accept the dubious mercy of the *ferenghi*. Yet despite the fatigue of battle, there was a commanding set to Tom's shoulders and a new authority in his voice. Anderson noticed that the men responded without hesitation to the orders he gave. By God, he thought, the pup has become a fighting dog overnight. He has the manner and look of his sire. I would not like to get on the wrong side of either of them. Without questioning his own subservience, he reported, quite naturally, 'The writers have finished the tally of the prize. I warrant it will surprise you, for it did me. The weight of the gold alone is almost three lakhs at a conservative estimate.'

'Please see that it is divided into four equal portions,' Tom said, 'one portion to be sent aboard each of the ships of the squadron, including the *Lamb*.'

Anderson looked puzzled. 'Surely Sir Henry will want it all under his own eye?' he demurred.

'Captain Anderson, we have the long voyage back to England ahead of us, with countless hazards of sea and weather to face. If we are unfortunate enough to lose a ship, it may be the wrong one and we lose all the gold. If we spread the risk, then we stand to lose only a quarter and not the whole.'

Why the hell did I not consider that? Anderson thought, but said reluctantly, 'They screwed your head on the right way—' He had almost called Tom 'lad' but that no longer fitted. 'I will give the orders, Mr Courtney.'

'We have twenty-six of our own men wounded, five of them seriously. I want a gang to build comfortable airy shelters above the beach to house them, and the carpenters to make beds for them. Now, as to our dead,' Tom glanced across at the eight canvas-wrapped corpses lying in the shade of the grove, 'I want them taken aboard the *Minotaur*. We will give them a proper burial at sea. The *Minotaur* will sail out into the deep water at first light tomorrow. Will you be good enough to conduct the service, Captain Anderson?'

'I will be honoured to do so.'

'Now, I will have Mr Walsh issue a keg of brandy from the *Seraph*'s stores to Aboli in which to pickle al-Auf's head.'

When Tom entered the stern cabin, Hal stirred on the bunk and whispered, 'Is that you, Tom?' Swiftly Tom went to kneel beside him. 'Father, it is so good to have you back. You have been unconscious these last three days.'

'Three days? So long? Tell me what has happened since.'

419

'We prevailed, Father. Thanks to the sacrifice you made, we carried the fort. Al-Auf is dead. Aboli has his head pickled in a brandy keg, and we have taken a vast treasure from the fort.'

'Dorian?' Hal asked.

At that question, Tom felt the joy go out of him. He looked down at his father's face. It was so pale that it seemed to have been dusted with white flour, and there were deep purple half-moons under his eyes. 'Dorian is not here.' Tom's whisper was as soft as his father's. Hal closed his eyes, and Tom thought he had passed out again. They were silent for a long while. When Tom started to rise to his feet, Hal opened his eyes again and rolled his head. 'Where is he? Where is Dorian?'

'Al-Auf sold him into slavery, but I do not know where they took him except that it must be somewhere on the mainland.'

Hal struggled to sit up, but he did not have the strength to lift his shoulders from the mattress. 'Help me, Tom. Help me to my feet, I must go on deck. I must ready the ship to go after him. We have to find Dorian.'

Tom reached out to restrain him, thinking, He does not know. He felt a sorrow so deep it threatened to drown him. *How do I tell him?*

'Come, lad. Help me up. I am weak as a new-born foal.'

'Father, you cannot stand. They have taken your legs.'

'Don't talk nonsense, Tom. You test my patience.' His father was becoming so agitated that Tom feared that he might injure himself. Dr Reynolds had warned that any violent movement might rupture the sutures and start the bleeding again. *I have to convince him, for his own good.*

Tom stooped over Hal and drew back the light cotton coverlet from his lower body. 'Forgive me, Father. I have to show you.' Very gently he placed an arm under Hal's shoulders and lifted him until he could look down at his own body.

The grotesquely foreshortened limbs lay on the mattress, each swathed in a turban of bandages on which the blood had dried in dirty brown stains. Hal stared at them for a long while, then fell back on his pillows. For a minute Tom thought he had fainted again. But then he saw tears squeezing from between the tightly closed eyelids. That was too much for him to bear. He could not watch his father weep. He had to leave him now to make his own terms with his destiny. He drew the sheet over him to hide those terrible injuries and tiptoed from the cabin, closing the door silently behind him.

When he came on deck, the longboat was ready to take him across to the waiting *Minotaur*. Captain Anderson was on the quarterdeck, speaking quietly to Alf Wilson.

Tom glanced at the eight canvas-wrapped bodies. Each one was lying on its own grating, and a large round shot had been sewn into the foot of each shroud. He could recognize Daniel Fisher by his bulk: he dwarfed the others who lay beside him.

'Mr Wilson, kindly get us under way and put the ship on a course to clear the passage.'

The *Minotaur*'s black sails were appropriate to this sombre voyage. She left the island and bore out towards the west while the colour of the water beneath her keel changed from the turquoise green of the shallows to the royal purple of the ocean depths.

'Heave the ship to, please, Mr Wilson.'

The *Minotaur* rounded head to the wind, and Anderson began to intone the sonorous words of the burial service. 'Out of the deep have I called unto thee . . .' The wind mourned in the rigging, while Tom stood bareheaded by the main mast and thought of how much he had lost in these last days: a father, a brother and a dear friend.

'We therefore commit their bodies to the deep . . .' A sailor was standing by the head of each grating, and at the words they lifted them in unison so that the shrouded bodies slid out over the ship's side and plunged feet first into the sea, drawn swiftly under by the iron shot.

Alf Wilson nodded to the gunners standing by their cannon and the first shot of the salute crashed out in a long spurt of silver gunsmoke.

'Goodbye, Big Danny. Goodbye, old friend,' Tom whispered.

Later that evening Tom sat beside his father's bunk and, in a low voice, reported the day's events to him. He was not certain that Hal could yet understand everything he told him, for he made no comments and seemed to drift in and out of consciousness. However, talking to him made Tom feel closer to him in spirit, and helped to assuage the loneliness of command, the onerous burden of which he was coming to know for the first time.

When Tom at last fell silent and was about to go to his pallet on the deck, Hal fumbled for his hand and squeezed it weakly. 'You're a good lad, Tom,' he whispered, 'probably the best of all of them. I only wish—' He broke off and let Tom's hand slide from his grip. His head rolled to the side and he snored softly. Tom would never know what it was he had wished.

Over the next few days Tom noticed a slight improvement in his father's strength. He was able to concentrate for more than just a few minutes on what Tom had to report to him before he slumped into unconsciousness.

Within a week Tom was able to ask him for advice, and receive a reasoned reply. However, when he consulted Dr Reynolds as to when his father would be strong enough to begin the return voyage to England, the doctor shook his head. 'I will be able to remove the sutures from his legs in three days' time – that is fourteen days from the amputation. If you sail in a month from now, you will still be subjecting him to severe risk, especially if we run into heavy weather. To be safe, we should wait at least two months. He needs time to build up his strength.'

Tom went to find Anderson, and found him supervising the final loading of the heavy cargo they had captured. This was mostly spices and cloth, including magnificent silks from China.

'Captain Anderson, I have discussed with my father the question of the Arab prisoners.'

'I hope he does not think of releasing them. They are pirates, plain and simple. They have murdered hundreds of honest seamen.'

'We could never countenance releasing them,' Tom agreed. 'Apart from any other consideration, it would set a dangerous precedent. We cannot let loose such a pack of tiger sharks to prey upon the sea lanes.'

'I am pleased to hear that,' Anderson grunted. 'The rope's end should be their final destination.'

'By the last count we have five hundred and thirty-five of them. That's a great deal of rope, Captain Anderson, and I doubt we have enough yard-arms on which to hang all of them out to dry.'

Anderson sucked his pipe as he thought about the logistical problems of executing so many men.

'On the other hand, they would be worth at least thirty pounds a head on the slave block, perhaps more,' Tom pointed out.

Anderson stared at him, his blue eyes popping. He had not thought of that. 'God's blood, they deserve it. But you cannot sell them in Zanzibar,' he said at last. 'The Sultan would never let you put Mussulmen up for sale in his markets. We would have another war on our hands.'

'The Dutch have no such qualms,' Tom said. 'They are always on the lookout for slaves to work their cinnamon plantations in Ceylon.'

'You are right.' Anderson chuckled with delight. 'It's a round voyage of five thousand miles to Ceylon and back again, but the winds are fair and at thirty pounds a head it will be well worth the detour.' He did a quick mental calculation. 'Sweet heavens, that's within spitting distance of sixteen thousand pounds.' He was silent again as he worked out his own share of that amount, then grinned. 'Al-Auf had sufficient slave chains stored in the fort to accommodate all his own men quite handsomely. That has a fine touch of justice to it.'

'According to Dr Reynolds, my father will not be well enough to sail for at least two months. I propose that you should load the captives on board the *Yeoman* and convey them to Colombo. When you have sold them to the VOC governor there, you will rejoin us here. In the meantime I will send the captured dhow south to summon the *Lamb* from where she is lying in the Gloriettas. We will make the return voyage to England in convoy. With fair winds and God's grace, we can drop anchor in Plymouth Ho before Christmas.'

The following day they loaded the Arabs on board the *Yeoman*. The blacksmiths from all the ships were needed for the work of riveting the leg irons on to the ankles of the long ranks of men. They were chained in batches of ten, then led down to the beach.

Tom was with Reynolds in the thatched hospital they had set up under the palm trees. He was visiting the wounded sailors lying there, hoping to give them a little cheer and encouragement. Two had already died when their wounds mortified and turned into the dreaded gas gangrene, but four had recovered sufficiently to return to their duties on board ship, and Reynolds was optimistic that the others would soon follow them.

Tom left the hospital and paused to watch the batches of prisoners shuffling past on their way to the waiting longboats. He felt a certain squeamishness at the thought that he was sending these men into a life of captivity. The Dutch were not famous as the gentlest of gaolers: he remembered the tales his father, Big Daniel and Aboli had told of their own experiences in the fort at Good Hope under their Dutch captors. Then he consoled himself that the decision had not been his alone: his father had concurred and signed the warrant for their transportation, under the powers granted him by the royal commission, while Captain Anderson had been positively delighted with the prospect of turning a fat profit on their sale. They were blood-smeared pirates, after all. When he thought of little Dorian, condemned to the same fate, any pity he had felt for the prisoners withered.

Anyway, he had argued with his elders and convinced both his father and Anderson to exempt the women and children of the garrison from the sentence of transportation into slavery. There were fifty-seven of these unfortunates, some of them infants only months old. Many of the women were heavily and obviously pregnant. Touchingly, five had elected to follow their husbands into captivity rather than suffer separation. The others would be kept here on Flor de la Mar until suitable transport to Zanzibar could be arranged for them.

He was about to turn away when the familiar face and silver beard of Ben Abram among the prisoners caught his eye. 'Bring that man to me,' he called to the guards, who pulled him out of the ranks and dragged him to where Tom stood.

'A pox on you,' Tom reprimanded them. 'He is an old man. Treat him gently.' Then he spoke to Ben Abram. 'How is it that a man like you was with al-Auf?'

Ben Abram shrugged. 'There are sick to be tended everywhere, even among the outlaws. I never ask of a man's good deeds or of his crimes when he comes to me to be healed.'

'So, you treated the *ferenghi* prisoners of al-Auf as well as the true believers?' Tom asked.

'Of course. That is the will of Allah, the Compassionate.'

'You cared for my brother? You gave him comfort?'

'He is a winsome boy, your brother. I did what I could for him,' Ben Abram said. 'But Allah knows, it was not as much as I would have wished.'

Tom hesitated slightly before he countermanded his father's orders, but then he reached a decision. 'You have earned your freedom for that. I will send you back to Zanzibar with the women and children.' He turned to the guards. 'Have this man's chains struck off, then bring him back to me. He is not to be transported to Ceylon with the rest of these blackguards.' When Ben Abram returned, free of his chains, Tom sent him to help the surgeon's mates in the makeshift thatched-roof hospital.

Laden with her human cargo, the *Yeoman* sailed with the following dawn, and Tom watched her from the beach until she disappeared below the eastern horizon. He knew that Anderson was optimistic in thinking he could make the long voyage across the Indian Ocean to Ceylon and return to Flor de la Mar within two months. 'The longer he takes, the more time for Father to grow strong again,' Tom whispered, as he closed the telescope and called for the longboat.

As soon as Tom entered the stern cabin he realized that his father was worse than when he had left him only hours before.

There was the sour smell of sickness in the cabin and Hal was flushed, restless. Once again he had relapsed into delirium. 'There are rats crawling on my body. Black rats, hairy—' He broke off and screamed, and struck out at things Tom could not see. In a panic Tom sent the longboat back to the island to fetch Dr Reynolds.

Tom bent over Hal and touched his face. The skin was so hot that he jerked away his hand in surprise. Aboli brought a bowl of cool water and they stripped back the sheets from Hal's emaciated body, from which the fever had burned the flesh. As they exposed the stumps of his legs the stench of corruption rose in a thick cloud, strong enough to make Tom gag. 'Tell the doctor to hurry!' he bellowed and heard his order relayed to the approaching longboat. Aboli and Tom bathed the fever-hot body and laid wet cloths over Hal's trunk to try to reduce his temperature. Tom was relieved when at last Reynolds came down the passage and hurried to Hal's side. He unwound the bandages. Immediately the stink in the small hot cabin was stronger.

Tom stood behind him and peered in horror at the stumps of his father's legs. They were swollen purple red, and the stitches of black cat-gut were almost hidden in the puffy flesh.

'Ah!' Reynolds murmured, and leaned forward to sniff the wounds like a connoisseur nosing a fine claret. 'They have ripened very prettily. At last I can pluck the sutures.'

He rolled up his sleeves, and called for the pewter bowl. 'Hold it like that under the stump,' he told Tom.

'Hold him down!' he ordered Aboli, who leaned over Hal and took his shoulders gently in his huge hands.

Reynolds took a firm hold of the end of one of the strings of cat-gut that hung out between the pursed crimson lips of the wound, and tugged at it. Hal stiffened and screamed, and the sweat burst out across his forehead in a white rash. The black string came free and slithered out of the wound, followed by a gush of greenish yellow pus, which dripped thick as cream into the pewter bowl. Hal dropped back on the pillows in a dead faint.

Reynolds took the bowl from Tom and sniffed the vile effluent again. 'Lovely! It's benign, not a taint of gas gangrene to it.'

While Tom knelt at his side, he plucked out the other sutures one at a time from the inflamed, swollen flesh. Each had a tiny piece of yellow detritus, the remains of the decayed blood vessel, caught in the knot at the end. He dropped them into the bowl. When he had finished he rebandaged the stumps with fresh white cotton strips.

'Should we not wash the legs first?' Tom asked diffidently.

Reynolds shook his head firmly. 'We will let them heal in the pus. It is safer to let nature take its own course without interference,' he said, sternly. 'Your father's chances of survival are now very much improved, and within another few days I will be able to remove the main stitches that are holding the flaps of the stumps.'

That night his father rested much easier, and by the morning the heat and inflammation of his wounds had abated considerably.

Three days later Reynolds removed the remaining stitches. He snipped the black threads with a pair of scissors and used ivory tweezers to pull the last remaining pieces of cat-gut from the tormented flesh.

Within days thereafter Hal was able to sit up with

pillows propped behind his back, and to take a keen, intelligent interest in the reports Tom gave him of events.

'I have sent the captured dhow south to the Gloriettas to fetch the *Lamb*. She should rejoin the squadron within two weeks at the latest,' Tom told him.

'I shall be relieved when we have her and that fat cargo of tea once more under our guns,' Hal said. 'She's very vulnerable lying down there unprotected.'

Tom's estimate was accurate, and it was exactly fourteen days later that the two vessels, the small dhow and the matronly *Lamb*, sailed through the pass in the reef and dropped anchor once more in the lagoon of Flor de la Mar.

Tom had Mustapha, the captain of the dhow, and his terrified crew brought down from the cells in the fort where they had been imprisoned since their capture by the *Minotaur*. When they were paraded before him, they fell on their knees before him in the white beach sand, fully believing that the hour of their execution had come at last.

'I do not believe you are guilty of piracy,' Tom said, to calm their fears.

'As Allah is my witness, what you say is the truth, exalted one,' Mustapha agreed fervently, and touched the sand with his forehead. When he looked up again his forehead was dusted with the white grains like a sugared bun.

'I am setting you free,' Tom reassured him, 'but I make only one condition. You must take certain passengers back with you to the port of Zanzibar. The chief of these is, like you, an honest man and a son of the Prophet. There are also the women and children who were with al-Auf when we captured the island.'

'The blessings of Allah upon you, wise and compassionate one!' Mustapha genuflected again and tears of joy streamed down into his beard.

'However,' Tom cut short this show of gratitude, 'there is no doubt in my mind that you came here to trade with al-Auf, and that you knew full well that the goods he offered were the plunder of a pirate and that they were besmirched with the blood of innocent men.'

'I call on God to witness that I did not know,' Mustapha cried passionately.

Tom cocked his head on one side and looked heavenwards for a minute. Then he said drily, 'God does not seem to answer your call. Therefore, I will fine you the amount of sixty-five thousand gold dinars, which is, by a remarkable coincidence, exactly the sum we found in your chest when we searched your ship.'

Mustapha wailed with horror at such terrible injustice, but Tom turned away and told the guards, 'Release them. Give them back the dhow and let them go. They will take all the women and children. The Arab physician, Ben Abram, will go with them too, but send him to me before he goes aboard the dhow.'

When Ben Abram came, Tom led him away to the end of the long white beach so that they could make their farewells in privacy. 'Mustapha, the owner of the dhow, has agreed to take you to Zanzibar when he sails.' Tom gestured across the water of the lagoon to where the small ship lay at anchor. 'He is taking the women and children from the garrison on board now.'

They watched the refugees being ferried aboard, clutching their infants and pathetic bundles of their possessions.

Ben Abram nodded gravely. 'I offer you my thanks, but Allah will write your true reward against your name. You are young, but you will grow up to be a man of power.

430

I have seen you fight. Any man who can overcome al-Auf in single combat is a warrior indeed.' He nodded again as he considered that feat of arms. 'The manner in which you have treated those weaker than yourself, the widows and orphans, shows that you temper your strength with compassion, and that will make you great.'

'You are also a man of great heart,' Tom told him. 'I have watched you work with the sick and wounded, even those who do not follow the teachings of your Prophet.'

'God is great,' Ben Abram intoned. 'In his sight we are all worthy of mercy.'

'Even the young children.'

'Especially the young children,' Ben Abram agreed.

'That is why, old father, you are going to tell me those things concerning my brother that so far you have kept from me.'

Ben Abram came up short and stared at Tom, but Tom returned his gaze steadily and Ben Abram dropped his eyes.

'You know the name of the man who bought my brother from al-Auf,' Tom insisted. 'You know his name.'

Ben Abram stroked his beard and looked out to sea. Then, at last, he sighed. 'Yes,' he said quietly. 'I know his name, but he is a mighty man, of royal blood. I cannot betray him. That is why I have concealed his name from you, even though I have sympathy for your loss.'

Tom was silent, allowing the old man to wrestle with his conscience and his sense of duty. Then Ben Abram said, 'You already know the man's name.' Tom stared at him, puzzled. 'You captured one of his dhows,' Ben Abram prompted him.

Tom's expression cleared. 'Al-Malik!' he exclaimed. 'Prince Abd Muhammad al-Malik?'

'I did not say the name,' said Ben Abram. 'I did not betray my prince.'

'So the lakh of rupees that was on board the dhow of al-Malik was indeed the payment for my brother, as we suspected?' Tom asked.

'I cannot say if that is true.' Ben Abram ruffled his silver beard. 'But neither can I say that it is false.'

'Both my father and I believed that was so, but I could not understand how Dorry could be gone from Flor de la Mar before the payment arrived on the island. I cannot believe that al-Auf would trust anyone with such a valuable slave as Dorry without receiving full payment first.'

The old man replied, 'The Prince is the most powerful man in Araby, save only for his elder brother, the Caliph himself. Al-Malik cannot count his ships and his gold, his warriors and his camels, his slaves and his wives. His fame spreads from the mighty River Nile and the deserts of the north, east to the kingdom of the Great Mogul, west to the forbidden forests of Africa, and south to the land of the Monamatapa.'

'You are saying that al-Auf trusted him with the debt of a lakh of rupees?' Tom demanded.

'I am saying that al-Auf trusted no living man, but Prince Abd Muhammad al-Malik.'

'When you leave here, Ben Abram, will you return to Lamu, where al-Malik is the governor?'

'I will return to Lamu,' the old man agreed.

'Perchance you will see my brother again?'

'That is in the hands of God.'

'If God is kind, will you give a message to my brother?'

'Your brother is a boy of great beauty and courage.' Ben Abram smiled at the memory. 'I called him my little red lion cub. Because of the kindness you have shown me, and because of the affection I have for the child, I will carry your message to him.'

'Tell my brother that I will be true to the dreadful oath I swore to him. I will never forget that oath, not even on the day of my death.'

Dorian sat on a mattress on the stone floor. The only air in his cell came through the narrow loophole opposite him. It was a faint eddy of the monsoon that reached him, and kept the heat bearable. When he listened he could hear the sounds of prisoners in the other cells along the passage, their muttering broken at intervals by outbursts of abusive shouting at their Arab guards and bitter argument among themselves. They were like dogs confined in cages too small for their numbers, and in the oppressive heat these naturally aggressive, violent sailors became murderous. Only yesterday he had heard the sounds of a terrible conflict, and of a man being strangled to death in the next cell while his mates cheered on the murder. Dorian shuddered now, and reapplied himself to the task he had chosen to while away the monotony of his captivity. He was using a link of his leg-irons to scratch his name into the wall. Many others who had been confined in this cell had left their marks carved into the soft coral blocks. 'Perhaps one day Tom will find my name here and know what happened to me,' he told himself, as he rubbed away at the stone.

His captors had put the chains on him only the previous morning. At first they had left him unfettered, then yesterday they had caught him trying to wriggle out through the narrow loophole in the far wall. Dorian had not been daunted by the thirty-foot drop below the opening, and he had succeeded in forcing the top half of his small body through it before there had been cries of alarm behind him, his gaolers had seized his ankles and dragged him back into the cell.

They held him while he struggled like a fish on a hook. 'Al-Auf will have no mercy on us if the infidel puppy injures himself. Bring the slave chains.' A blacksmith had altered the fetters to fit his small ankle. 'Make certain that the iron does not gall him. Al-Auf will kill the man who marks his white skin or harms one red hair on his head.'

Apart from the leg-irons, they treated him with consideration and respect. Every morning, despite his struggles, two veiled women took him down to the courtyard. They stripped him and oiled his body, then bathed him at the rainwater cistern. On board ship Dorian had gone for months at a time without bathing – there was no fresh water for such extravagance, added to which all seamen knew that too much washing reduced the natural oils of the skin and was bad for the health. The Mussulmen were strangely addicted to these excesses of personal cleanliness – Dorian had watched them wash five times a day, before they went through the ritual of their prayers – so even though it threatened his health, he had to resign himself to this daily ordeal by water. He even grew to welcome the break in the dreary routine of his captivity, and had more trouble each time in rousing his temper to register his protests.

Occasionally he made a rather half-hearted attempt to bite one of the women, especially when they handled the more intimate parts of his anatomy. Soon, though, they were ready for this, and avoided his attacks while shrieking with laughter. They exclaimed endlessly over Dorian's hair as they fondled, combed, brushed and coiled it into thick shiny ropes. They had replaced his noisome, tattered rags with a clean white robe.

In every other way, too, they took good care of him. They had placed a soft, beautifully tanned sheepskin over the palm fronds of his mattress. They had given him a silk pillow for his head, and an oil lamp to light the long hours of the night. There was always a water-jar within his reach and the evaporation through the porous clay kept the contents cool. The women fed him three times a day, and although at first he had vowed to starve himself to death simply to spite them, the aroma of the food they offered him was too tempting for his young appetite to resist.

Although his solitary existence was hard to bear, he knew that he should be grateful that he had not been placed in the crowded cells further along the passageway. He had been warned by both his father and Tom about what could happen to a pretty little boy if he were placed at the mercy of vile, depraved older men.

His chain was just long enough for him to reach the step below the loophole, and though he could climb up and look out through the tiny window he could not repeat his previous escape attempt. When he was not busy carving his name into the wall he spent hours gazing out over the lagoon where al-Auf's fleet was anchored. He longed for even a glimpse of the white topsails of the *Seraph* over that distant blue horizon. 'Tom will come,' he promised himself each dawn, as he searched the lightening ocean.

Each dusk he watched until the horizon receded into the wine-purple shades of night, and he bolstered himself with the same words: 'Tom promised, and he always keeps his promises. He will come tomorrow. I know he will.'

Every few days his gaolers came to take him down to Ben Abram. The Mussulman doctor had named Dorian Lion Cub, which had stuck. His gaolers were as wary of his temper as the women, and handed him over to Ben Abram with relief. The doctor examined him carefully from the top of his shining head to his bare feet for any sign of neglect or abuse. He was especially concerned that the leg-irons had not marked his white skin, and that he had been properly fed and attended to. 'Are they treating you well, little red Lion Cub?'

'No, they beat me every day,' Dorian replied defiantly. 'And they burn me with red-hot irons.'

'Are they feeding you well?' Ben Abram smiled kindly at this patent lie.

'They give me worms to eat and rat's piss to drink.'

'You are thriving on that diet,' Ben Abram remarked. 'I should try it myself.'

'My hair is falling out,' Dorian contradicted him. 'Soon I will be bald and then al-Auf will send you to the execution ground.' Dorian was aware of the peculiar value that the Mussulmen placed on his hair, but the old man had fallen for his threat of baldness only once.

Now he smiled again and ruffled the luxuriant tresses. 'Come with me, my bald Lion Cub.' He took Dorian's hand, and for once the boy did not try to pull away. In his aching loneliness, which he tried so hard to conceal, Dorian was drawn irresistibly to the kindly old man. He went along with him to the audience chamber where al-Auf was waiting.

There was a ritual to these gatherings in which Dorian was displayed to the latest prospective buyer. While they argued and haggled, inspected his hair and his naked body, Dorian stood rigid, staring at them with a scowl of theatrical fury and hatred, silently composing the most foul insult his increasing command of Arabic afforded him.

Always there came the moment during the negotiations when the buyer asked, 'But does he speak the language of the Prophet?'

Then al-Auf would turn back to Dorian and order, 'Say something, child.'

Dorian would draw himself up and let fly with his latest composition. 'May Allah blacken thy face, and rot the teeth in thy cursed jaws.' Or 'May he fill thy bowels with worms, and dry the milk in the udders of all the goats whom thou hast ever taken to wife.' There was always consternation among the prospective buyers at these sallies. Afterwards when Ben Abram walked him back to his cell he would reprimand Dorian primly. 'Where did such a beautiful child learn such evil words?' But his eyes would twinkle merrily in their webs of wrinkles.

But on the final occasion when he entered the audience chamber, Dorian was aware of a different atmosphere. The man to whom he was being shown was not some rough dhow captain or fat oleaginous merchant: he was a prince.

He sat in the centre of the floor on a pile of silk cushions and rugs, yet his back was straight and his mien was regal. Although a dozen attendants sat behind him in attitudes of fawning subservience, there was no arrogance in the man. His dignity was imperious and his presence monumental. In the family Bible at High Weald there was a picture of St Peter, the Rock. The resemblance of this man to him was so striking that Dorian thought that they must be the same person. He was overcome with religious awe.

'Greet the mighty Prince al-Malik,' al-Auf insisted, when Dorian stood speechless before this reincarnation of Christ's apostle. Evidently al-Auf was nervous of Dorian's reaction to this command for he tugged anxiously at his beard. 'Show the Prince respect or I will have you thrashed,' he urged.

Dorian knew that the threat was baseless: al-Auf would never mark him and spoil his value. He continued to stare at the man before him in awe.

'Make your *salaams* to the Prince!' al-Auf urged him.

Dorian felt his rebellious instincts shrivel in the presence of this man. Without conscious thought he made an obeisance of deep respect.

Al-Auf looked startled, and decided to press this unexpected advantage. He hoped that the boy would eschew any reference to female goats or rotting teeth. 'Speak to the exalted Prince! Greet him in the language of the Prophet,' he commanded.

Without having to think about it, Dorian recalled an exercise Alf Wilson had set them during a long afternoon on the after-deck when the *Seraph* had lain becalmed in the doldrums. He had been trying to explain the similarities between Islamic and Christian beliefs. Now, in his sweet, unbroken voice, Dorian recited from the Koran: 'I am but a man like yourselves, but the inspiration has come to me that your God is one God. Whoever expects to meet his Lord, let him work righteousness.'

There was a sharp intake of breath from every man in the chamber. Even the Prince leaned forward quickly, and stared raptly into Dorian's clear green eyes.

Dorian was delighted with the sensation he had created. He had always enjoyed the theatrical performances Master Walsh had arranged at High Weald and on board ship, when Dorian had usually been cast as a woman. However, this was undoubtedly his most acclaimed performance.

In the long silence the Prince straightened slowly and turned to the man who sat immediately behind him. Dorian saw by his dress that he was a mullah, a religious leader, the Islamic equivalent of a priest. 'Expound on the child's words,' the Prince ordered.

'It is verse one hundred and ten of Sura eighteen,' the mullah admitted reluctantly. His face was round and glossy with good living, and a pot belly bulged on to his lap. His straggly goatee beard had been dyed a faded orange with henna. 'The child has quoted it accurately, but even a parrot can be trained to mouth words he does not understand.'

The Prince turned back to Dorian. 'What do you understand by righteousness, child?'

Alf Wilson had prepared him for that, and Dorian did not hesitate. 'It is the true respect for God, which shuns the worship of idols, or deified men, or the forces of nature, or especially of one's own self.'

Al-Malik turned back to his mullah. 'Are those the words of a parrot?' he asked.

The holy man looked discomfited. 'They are not, lord. They are wise words indeed.'

438

'How old are you, child.' Al-Malik fixed Dorian with his dark, piercing gaze.

'I am eleven, almost twelve,' Dorian told him proudly.

'Are you of Islam?'

'I would rather my nose were eaten away with leprosy,' Dorian replied. 'I am a Christian.'

Neither the Prince nor the mullah showed shock or anger at such a vehement denial. They, too, would have rejected any suggestion of apostasy as strongly.

'Come here, boy,' al-Malik ordered, not unkindly, and Dorian stepped closer to him. He reached out and took a handful of Dorian's freshly washed, glistening hair. Dorian submitted patiently as he ran it through his fingers. 'Thus must have been the very hair of the Prophet,' he said softly.

Every man in the room echoed, 'Praise be to God.'

'You may send him away now,' al-Malik told al-Auf. 'I have seen enough and we must talk.'

Ben Abram took Dorian's hand and they went to the door.

'Guard him well,' al-Malik called after them, 'but treat him gently.' Ben Abram made the gesture of respect and obedience, touching his lips and his heart, and led Dorian back to his cell.

Al-Auf's servants brought fresh pots of coffee. While one recharged the Prince's tiny cup of pure gold with the tarry thick brew, another relit his hookah.

The bargaining for such a momentous purchase could not be hurried. Gradually with long, pregnant pauses and elaborate exchanges, expressed in poetic, flowery phrases, the two men moved closer to an agreement. Al-Auf had doubled his asking price to two lakhs in order to give himself latitude within which to manoeuvre, and gradually allowed himself to be beaten down.

It was long after dark when, by the light of the oil-lamps and in the fragrant smoke of the pipe, they reached agreement on the slave price for the child.

'I do not travel with so much gold in my ship,' al-Malik said. 'I will take the child with me when I sail on the morrow, and I will send a fast dhow back to you as soon as I reach Lamu. You will have your lakh before the rise of the new moon. My sacred oath on it.'

Al-Auf barely hesitated. 'As the great Prince decrees.'

'Leave me now, for the hour grows late and I wish to pray.'

Al-Auf rose immediately. He had relinquished his own quarters to al-Malik for he was honoured to play host to such an exalted guest, and as he backed towards the door he made a series of deep genuflections. 'May the houris of paradise attend your dreams, great Prince.

'May your awakening be perfumed with the scent of violets, mighty one.

'May your prayers fly like gold-tipped arrows straight to the ears of Allah, O Beloved of the Prophet.'

Dorian could not sleep. The sense of elation he had experienced after his meeting with the Prince had long since evaporated and left him frightened and lonely once more. He knew that, yet again, his circumstances had changed and that he was about to be thrown on dark, uncertain waters. Much as he hated his present dreary captivity, it was something to which he had grown accustomed. And there were small consolations in his present position: he had grown to like and depend upon the old Arab doctor. Ben Abram was a friendly face and Dorian sensed he had his interests at heart. Also, while he was on this island there was always a chance that his father and Tom would be able to follow the trail that led to him. If he were to be taken off to some other place by this fearsome prince, what chance then that they would still be able to track him down?

He was too afraid to blow out the flame of the oil-lamp, although it attracted the mosquitoes to his tiny cell, and preferred to scratch rather than lie awake in the dark. Below the walls of the fort, the palm fronds clattered softly in the unrelenting winds of the monsoon. He hugged himself and listened to the mournful sound of the wind, fighting back the temptation to give in to his tears.

Then he heard a different sound on the wind, so light that at first it did not quite penetrate the dark mists of his misery. It died away, then came back stronger and more clearly. He sat up and reached for the lamp. His fingers were trembling so that he almost dropped it.

He stumbled across the cell to the step below the loophole, and came up at the full stretch of his chain. He placed the lamp on the sill and listened again. There was no mistake: somebody was whistling softly down there at the edge of the forest, and as he recognized the tune his heart leaped and soared.

It's Tom. He wanted to scream it aloud, and he strained against his chain to reach the opening. He tried to sing the next line of the song, but his voice broke and his lips were numb with excitement. He gathered himself and tried again, pitching his voice so softly that it would not carry to the guards at the end of the passage or to the watchmen on the ramparts of the fort above him:

> *We'll rant and we'll roar, all o'er the wild ocean,*
> *We'll rant and we'll roar, all o'er the wild seas.*

The whistling out there in the night broke off abruptly. He strained his ears but heard no more. He wanted to call out but knew it might alert someone so held his tongue, though it burned in his mouth like a live coal.

Suddenly there was a scrabbling sound close outside the loophole, and Tom's voice. 'Dorry!'

'Tom! Oh, I knew you would come. I knew you would keep your promise.'

'Shh, Dorry! Not so loud. Can you climb out through the window?'

'No, Tom. I'm chained to the wall.'

'Don't cry, Dorry. They'll hear you.'

'I'm not crying.' Dorian stuffed his fingers into his mouth to muffle the sounds of his weeping.

Tom's head appeared in the opening of the window.

'Here!' Dorian gulped back the last sob and reached with both hands through the loophole. 'Give me your hand.' Tom struggled to force his way through the tiny opening but at last fell back. 'Its no good, Dorry.' Their faces were only a foot apart. 'We'll have to come back for you.'

'Please don't leave me here, Tom,' Dorian begged.

'The *Seraph* is waiting just off-shore. Father, Aboli and I, we are all here. We will be back for you soon.'

'Tom!'

'No, Dorry. Don't make so much noise. I swear to you we'll come back for you.'

'Tom, don't leave me alone! Tom!' His brother was going, he could not bear it. Dorian pulled desperately at his arm, trying to force him to stay.

'Let go, Dorry! You'll make me fall.'

Then there was a shout from the battlements above them, and a voice cried out in Arabic: 'Who is it? Who is down there?'

'The guards, Dorry. Let me go.'

Suddenly Dorian felt his brother's arm torn from his grip and at the same time there came the roar of a musket shot from close above their heads. He knew his brother had been hit, and he heard his body slide down the wall, then, with a terrible thump, hit the ground far below.

'Oh, no! Please, God, no!' Dorian cried. He tried to put his head through the loophole far enough to see if his brother was truly killed, but the chain held him back.

There was a chorus of shouts and a wild fusillade of musket fire from the top of the walls. Quickly, confusion spread through the garrison. Within minutes he heard Arab voices at the foot of the wall below his window.

'There is nobody here,' someone shouted up at the guards on the ramparts above Dorian's head.

'I know I hit him!' the guard shouted down. 'He *must* be there.'

'No, there is no one here – but I see the marks where he fell.'

'He must have escaped into the forest.'

'Who was it?'

'A Frank. His face was very white in the moonlight.'

Their voices receded into the forest. Then Dorian heard more shouting and musket fire, and the sound of men blundering about among the trees. Gradually the noises receded into the distance.

Dorian stood by the loophole for the rest of that night, waiting and listening. But slowly the last sparks of hope flickered out, and when the grey dawn at last lit the bay and the ocean beyond, there was no sight of the *Seraph*. Only then did he creep back to his sheepskin, and bury his face in the silk pillow to stifle his sobs and to soak up his tears.

They came to fetch him at noon. The two women who had taken care of him were weeping and wailing at the prospect of losing their charge, and when the gaoler unlocked his leg-iron he said gruffly, 'Go with God, little monkey. There will be nobody to make us laugh when you are gone.'

Ben Abram took him down to where al-Auf waited for him, hands clasped angrily on his hips, beard bristling with rage. 'What Frankish dogs were those that came sniffing around your kennel last night, puppy?' he demanded.

'I know nothing of this.' Although he still felt bereft and tearful, Dorian put on a show of defiance. 'I was sleeping and I heard nothing in the night. Perhaps the devil sent you evil dreams.' He would never betray Tom to them.

'I do not have to accept your impudence any longer.' Al-Auf stepped closer. 'Answer me, you seed of Satan! Who was at the window of your cell? The guards heard you talking to the intruder.'

Dorian stared up at him silently, but he was gathering a ball of spit under his tongue.

'I am waiting!' al-Auf told him menacingly, and lowered his face until their eyes were only inches apart.

'Wait no longer,' Dorian said, and spat his mouthful into al-Auf's face. The pirate recoiled in astonishment, then a terrible rage distorted his features and he whipped the curved dagger from his belt.

'You will never do that again,' he swore. 'I'll have your infidel heart for it!'

As he started his stroke, Ben Abram leaped forward. For a man of such age he was quick and agile. He locked both hands on al-Auf's knife wrist. Although he did not have the strength to stop the stroke, he deflected it from

444

Dorian's chest. The glittering point of the dagger snagged in the sleeve of his white robe and left a clean rent in the material.

Al-Auf staggered back, thrown off-balance by the unexpected attack. Then, almost contemptuously, he threw the old man to the ground. 'You will pay for that, you ancient fool.' He stepped over him.

'Lord, do not harm the child. Think of the prophecy and of the gold,' Ben Abram pleaded, and seized the hem of al-Auf's robe. The corsair hesitated. The warning had touched him. 'A lakh of rupees to lose,' Ben Abram insisted. 'And the curse of St Taimtaim upon your head if you kill him.'

Al-Auf stood uncertainly, but his lips twitched and his knife hand trembled. He stared at Dorian with such hatred that at last the boy's courage failed and he shrank back against the wall.

'The spittle of an infidel! It is worse than the blood of a swine! He has defiled me!' Al-Auf was whipping up his faltering anger. He started forward again, then froze as a peremptory voice boomed across the chamber.

'Stop! Put down that knife! What madness is this?' Prince al-Malik towered in the entrance to the chamber. Summoned by the shouting and the uproar, he had come through from the sleeping quarters at the back. Al-Auf dropped the dagger and prostrated himself on the stone flags. 'Forgive me, noble Prince,' he blubbered. 'For a moment Shaitan stole my wits.'

'I should send you to visit your own execution field,' al-Malik said coldly.

'I am dust in your sight,' al-Auf whimpered.

'The child is no longer your property. He belongs to me.'

'I will atone for my stupidity in any way you wish, only do not turn the face of wrath upon me, great Prince.'

Al-Malik did not deign to reply, but looked at Ben

Abram. 'Take the child down to the lagoon at once and have him placed on board my dhow. The captain is expecting his arrival. I will follow presently. We will sail with the high tide this very night.'

Two of the Prince's men escorted Dorian down to the lagoon, and Ben Abram walked with him, holding his hand. Dorian's face was pale, his jaws clenched hard in the effort to maintain a brave face. They did not speak until they reached the beach and the skiff from the royal dhow was waiting to take Dorian out to where she lay at anchor.

Then Dorian begged Ben Abram, 'Please come with me.'

'I cannot do that.' The old man shook his head.

'Just as far as the dhow, then. Please. You are the only friend I have left in the whole world.'

'Very well, but only as far as the dhow.' Ben Abram climbed into the boat beside him, and Dorian moved up close beside him.

'What will happen to me now?' he asked in a whisper.

Ben Abram replied gently, 'Whatever is the will of God, my Lion Cub.'

'Will they hurt me? Will they sell me to some other person?'

'The Prince will keep you beside him always,' Ben Abram reassured him.

'How can you be so certain?' Dorian laid his head on Ben Abram's arm.

'Because of the prophecy of St Taimtaim. He will never let you go. You are too valuable to him.'

'What is this prophecy?' Dorian sat up again and looked into his face. 'Everyone speaks of the prophecy, but nobody tells me what it says.'

'It is not the time for you to know.' Ben Abram drew the child's head down again. 'One day it will all be made clear to you.'

'Can't you tell me now?'

'It might be dangerous for you to know. You must be patient, little one.'

The skiff bumped against the side of the dhow, men were waiting to receive Dorian. 'I don't want to go.' He clung to Ben Abram.

'It is the will of God.' Gently the old man disentangled Dorian's fingers. The sailors reached down and lifted him onto the deck.

'Please stay with me a little longer,' Dorian said imploringly, looking down into the small boat.

Ben Abram could not refuse the appeal. 'I will stay with you until you sail,' he agreed, and followed Dorian down to the small cabin that had been set aside for him. He sat beside him on the mattress and reached into the pouch on his belt.

'Drink this.' He brought out a small green glass vial, and proffered it.

'What is it?'

'It will soften the pain of our parting, and make you sleep.'

Dorian drank the contents of the vial and pulled a face. 'It tastes awful.'

'Like rat's piss?' Ben Abram smiled, and Dorian burst out in laughter that was close to a sob, and hugged him.

'Now lie down.' The old man pushed Dorian back on the mattress, and for a while they talked together quietly. Then Dorian's eyelids began to droop. He had not slept at all the night before and his weariness and the drug soon overpowered him.

Ben Abram stroked his head for the last time. 'Go with God, my child,' he said softly, rose from the mattress and went on deck.

The clumping of feet above his head and the movement of the hull through the water as the dhow got under way woke Dorian. He looked around for Ben Abram, but found him gone. Instead a strange woman was squatting on the deck beside his mattress. In her black robe and veil, she looked like a roosting vulture.

Dorian stood up groggily and staggered to the small porthole in the cabin. Outside it was dark, and the stars were dancing on the waters of the lagoon. The sweet night air blowing into his face revived him, and cleared his mind a little. He wanted to go up on deck but when he turned to the doorway the woman stood up and barred his way. 'You must not leave here until the Prince calls for you.'

Dorian argued with her for a while but then gave up the futile effort and returned to the porthole. He watched the walls of the fort glide by, glistening white in the moonlight, as the dhow left the lagoon and threaded its way through the channel. Then he felt the deck surge under his feet at the first strong scend of the ocean. As the ship turned towards the west his view of the moonlit island was cut out. He jumped down from the porthole and threw himself on the mattress.

The black-veiled woman went to the porthole and closed the heavy wooden shutter over it. At that moment the lookout on the deck just above Dorian's head shouted, so suddenly that Dorian jumped, 'What boat are you?'

'Fishing boats with the night's catch,' came the answer. The reply was faint, almost inaudible with distance and the closed shutter over the porthole, but Dorian's heart leaped against his ribs, then raced away with excitement.

'Father!' he gasped. Although the voice had spoken in Arabic, he had recognized it instantly. He flung himself across the cabin, and tried to reach the window, but the woman seized him.

'Father!' he screamed, as he wrestled with her, but she was heavily built, with big breasts and a full soft belly. And although she was fat, she was powerful. She caught him round the chest and threw him back onto the mattress.

'Let me go!' he screamed at her in English. 'That's my father. Let me go to him.'

The woman lay on top of him with her full weight, pinning him down. 'You cannot leave the cabin,' she grunted. 'It is the command of the Prince.'

Dorian wrestled with her, but then froze as from out there in the night his father hailed the dhow again. 'What boat are you?' His voice was growing fainter. The dhow must be pulling away fast.

'The ship of the Prince Abd Muhammad al-Malik,' the lookout called back, his voice strong and clear.

'Go with Allah!' Hal's voice was so faint and far away that it came as a whisper to Dorian's ears.

'Father!' he yelled, with all his strength, but the woman's weight was pressing on his chest, smothering him. 'Don't go! It's me! It's Dorry!' he cried, in despair because he knew that his muffled cry could never carry from the closed cabin across the water to his father's ear.

With a sudden twist and heave he threw off the big woman and slipped out from under her. Before she could hoist her bulk to her feet he had darted to the cabin door. As he struggled with the lock, she lumbered at him. He just managed to throw open the door as her fingers hooked into the collar of his robe. He threw himself forward with such force that the cotton ripped and he wriggled free.

Dorian shot up the companionway with the woman hard after him, screeching at the top of her voice, 'Stop him! Catch the infidel!'

An Arab seaman was waiting for Dorian at the top of the stairs and blocked his way with outstretched arms, but

Dorian dropped to the deck and, quick as a ferret, wriggled between his legs. He raced down the deck towards the stern.

He could see the dark shape of the longboat from the *Seraph* moving across the slick waters of the dhow's wake, pulling away swiftly towards the island, the oars swinging and dripping phosphorescence from their blades. A figure stood tall in the stern. Dorian knew it was his father. 'Don't leave me!' His voice was small in the night.

He reached the stern rail and jumped onto it, gathering himself to dive overboard into the dark waters, but a strong hand closed on his ankle and dragged him down. Within seconds he was covered by the weight of half a dozen Arab crewmen. They carried him back down the companionway, kicking, biting and scratching, and pushed him into the cabin.

'If you had jumped into the sea, they would have thrown me after you to be eaten by the fish,' the fat old woman complained bitterly. 'How can you be so cruel to me?' She huffed and fussed, and sent to ask the captain to post two men outside the cabin door, then she made certain the shutter over the porthole and the cabin door were both securely barred to prevent another escape attempt. Dorian was so distraught and exhausted that when he fell asleep at last it was as though he were still drugged.

It was almost midday when she woke him. 'The Prince has sent for you,' she told him, 'and he will be angry with old Tahi if you are dirty and smelly as a kid goat.' Once again he submitted to being bathed and having his hair combed and dressed with perfumed oil. Then he was led to the pavilion on the foredeck of the dhow.

A roof of canvas shaded the area from the scorching tropical sun almost directly overhead, but the sides of the tentlike structure were raised to let the cool winds of the monsoon blow through. The deck had been covered with silk rugs and the Prince reclined on a slightly raised dais, on a bed of cushions, while the mullah and four others of his personal retinue sat cross-legged below him. They were in deep discussion when Dorian was brought to them, but al-Malik gestured them to silence as Tahi brought the child to stand before him.

She prostrated herself on the deck, and when Dorian refused to follow her example, she tugged at his ankle. 'Show respect for the Prince!' she hissed at him. 'Or else he will have you beaten.'

Dorian was determined to resist her order. He set his jaw and raised his eyes to stare into the Prince's face. After only a few seconds he felt his determination waver and he dropped his eyes. Somehow he found it impossible to defy this regal person. He made the gesture of respect. '*Salaam aliekum*, lord!' he whispered, and prostrated himself.

Al-Malik's expression remained stern, but little laughter lines crinkled around his eyes. 'And peace unto you also, al-Ahmara.' He beckoned Dorian to come closer, then indicated a cushion below his dais, close to his right hand. 'Sit here, where I can stop you jumping over the ship's side when next the *cafard*, the madness, overtakes you.'

Dorian obeyed without protest, whereupon the men ignored him and continued with their discussions. For a while Dorian attempted to follow their conversation, but they spoke swiftly and in a formal manner that tested his understanding to the limits. Their talk was full of the names of men and places of which he was ignorant. One place name he recognized, though, was Lamu. He tried to orientate himself, and conjured up in his mind's eye the charts of the Fever Coast that he had been made to study so often during his navigation lessons with Ned Tyler.

Lamu was several hundred leagues north of Zanzibar. It was a smaller island and, from what he remembered of the sailing orders in his father's log book, it was another major trading port and centre of government of the Omani empire.

He could tell by the wind direction and the angle of the afternoon sun that the dhow was on an approximately north-westerly heading, which would indicate that Lamu was probably where they were heading. He wondered what fate awaited him there, then craned his neck to look back over the stern.

There was no sign of Flor de la Mar on the horizon behind them. During the night they must have run the island under and severed all contact with the *Seraph*, his father and Tom. At the thought he felt again that enervating mood of despair, but determined not to let himself capitulate to it. He made another effort to follow the discussions of the Prince and his retainers. 'Father will expect me to remember everything they say. It could be very valuable to him in making his plans,' he told himself, but just then the mullah stood up and went to the bows. From there he began the call to prayer, in a high, quavering voice. The Prince and his men broke off their discussions and made preparations for the midday worship. Slaves brought ewers of fresh water for the Prince and his retinue to wash.

In the stern, the helmsman pointed up into the north, indicating the direction of the holy city of Mecca, and every man aboard who could be spared from the running of the dhow faced that way.

In unison, following the plaintive cries of the holy man, they performed the ritual of standing, kneeling and prostrating themselves on the deck, submitting themselves to the will of Allah and offering him their devotions.

This was the first time Dorian had been caught up in such an efflorescence of devotion. Although he sat apart from it, he felt himself strangely moved by its force. He had never felt the same way during the weekly services in the chapel at High Weald, and he followed the chanting and the exaltations with a keener interest than their local clergyman had ever evoked in him.

He looked up towards the heavens, into the vast blue bowl of the African sky, filled with the cloud ranges marching ahead of the monsoon winds. In religious awe, he imagined he could see in the eddies of silver cloud the beard of God and his terrible features adumbrated in the shapes and outlines of the thunderheads.

Prince Abd Muhammad al-Malik rose from his position of prostration and stood erect on the low dais, still facing towards the holy city, crossing his hands over his breast in the final expression of his devotion. Dorian looked up at his bearded face, and thought that perhaps God looked like that, so noble, so terrifying, and yet so benign.

The dhow was running before the monsoon, her huge lateen sail filled tight and hard as a water-skin. The single boom was carved from joined lengths of some dark, heavy tropical timber, almost as thick as a man's waist, and longer in all than the dhow herself. Its full weight was held aloft on the stubby mast by the main halyard. As the dhow rolled to the swells, the shadow of the boom swung back and forth across the deck, alternately shading the Prince's regal figure, then allowing the full brilliance of the tropical sunlight to pour down upon him. He stood to his full height under the swinging boom. The Arab helmsman's attention was diverted, and he allowed the bows of the ship to come up too far into the eye of the wind. The sail jarred and creaked ominously.

Dorian had been taught by Ned Tyler that the lateen sail was notoriously fickle and unstable in any real blow of wind, and he could sense the ship's distress at the rough handling to which she was being subjected.

From the corner of his eye he noticed a sudden change in the sail shadow cast across the deck below the dais. His eyes flickered up into the rigging, and he saw the main halyard begin to unravel just below the heavy wooden sheave block. The rope untwisted like a nest of mating serpents as, one after the other, the strands gave way. Dorian stared in horror, for precious seconds too appalled to move or cry out. He had watched the boom being lowered and trained around when the dhow was tacked, so he knew what a vital role the main halyard played in the lateen rigging.

He started to rise to his feet, still staring up at the single mast, but as he did so the last strand of the halyard parted with a crack like a pistol shot. With a rush and roar of canvas the boom hurtled down from on high, half a ton of heavy timber, swinging towards the deck like the stroke of an executioner's blade. The Prince was oblivious to everything but his religious devotions, and stood directly under the falling boom.

Dorian threw himself forward, shoulder first into the back of al-Malik's knees. The Prince was taken completely unprepared, balancing himself in the contrary direction to meet the ship's movement. He was thrown off the raised dais face downward onto the deck. The piles of rugs and cushions strewn across the timbers broke his fall, and Dorian's small body landed on top of him.

Behind them the hardwood boom crashed through the roof of the low deck-house, shattering it into a heap of broken planking and raw splinters. The great baulk of timber snapped at the splice and the fore-end whipped down, gaining velocity as it struck the foredeck. It crushed the low wooden dais on which, moments before, the Prince had been standing, smashed through the bulwarks of the bows and stove in most of the deck planking.

The single lateen sail ballooned down behind it and covered the foredeck, smothering the men lying there under its stiff canvas shroud. The dhow's motion altered drastically as she was relieved of all the pressure of her canvas. Her bows fell off into the wind and she began to roll viciously and wallow in the swells of the monsoon.

For long seconds there was silence on board except for the banging and clattering of loose tackle and sundered rope ends. Then there came a chorus of startled shouts and the screams of injured men. Two sailors on the after-deck had been crushed and killed instantly, and three others were terribly mutilated, limbs shattered and bones crushed. Their cries were pitifully thin in the wind.

Under the shouted orders of the dhow captain, the unhurt sailors rushed forward to hack away the tangle of ropes and canvas that covered the men on the foredeck.

'Find the Prince!' the captain shrieked, fearful for his own life if his master were hurt or, Allah forbid, killed under the massive weight of the boom.

Within minutes they had ripped away the folds of the sail and, with exclamations of relief and expressions of thanks to God, lifted him out from under the wreckage.

The Prince stood aloof in the pandemonium, ignoring the rapturous cries of thanks for his deliverance, and surveyed the remains of his dias. The boom had even sheared through the thick silk folds of the precious prayer rug on which he had been standing. The mullah rushed down the deck to his side. 'You are uninjured, thanks be to Allah. He spread his wings over you, for you are the Beloved of the Prophet.'

Al-Malik fended off his hands and asked, 'Where is the child?' The question triggered another frantic search under the mountains of canvas. At last they dragged Dorian out and stood him in front of the Prince.

'Are you hurt, little one?'

Dorian was grinning with delight at the devastation that surrounded them. He had not enjoyed himself so much since he had last been with Tom. 'I am fine, sir.' In the excitement of the moment he had lapsed into English. 'But your ship is fairly buggered.'

Tom knew that the men must be kept busy during the days and weeks that they had to wait for the return of Anderson from Ceylon. Idle seamen soon find mischief with which to occupy themselves; they become a threat to themselves and to each other.

He also realized that, for his own well-being and peace of mind, he must find solace in work. Otherwise he would spend the long, tropical days brooding on Dorian's fate and his father's terrible injuries and slowly deteriorating state of health. He found himself torn between these two conflicting loyalties. He knew that, as soon as Hal was fit to travel, he must try to get his father home to the peace and security of High Weald, where he could be nursed back to health by English surgeons and cared for by a staff of loyal servants.

On the other hand, this would mean leaving Dorian to his fate as a slave in an alien world. He felt the irresistible force of his oath to his brother summoning him towards that awful coast that was Africa.

He went to Aboli to help him resolve this dilemma. 'If my father would let me take command of the *Minotaur*, and gave me a small crew of good men, then you and I could go after Dorian. I know where to start to search for him. Lamu!'

'Then what of your father, Klebe? Are you ready to desert him, now that he needs you most? What will you feel when the news reaches you when you are somewhere out there,' Aboli pointed to the west where the mysterious continent lay beneath the horizon, 'that your father is dead, and that perhaps you could have been there to save him?'

'Do not even speak of it, Aboli,' Tom flared at him, then subsided with a sigh of uncertainty. 'Perhaps by the time Captain Anderson and the *Yeoman* return, my father will be strong enough to make the voyage home without us. I will wait until then before I decide, but in the meantime we must get the *Minotaur* ready for any call we make upon her.'

Despite the work already done on her, she still showed the effects of her sojourn at the hands of al-Auf, and they both knew that her hull was probably heavily infested with ship-worm, the curse of tropical waters. That very day Tom ordered her to be careened. He had never had to do this before and knew he must rely heavily on the expertise of Ned Tyler and Alf Wilson. The ship was unloaded of all her cargo and heavy gear, including her cannon and water-barrels. All this was ferried to the beach and stored under thatched lean-to shelters in the palm grove and the guns arranged to protect the camp. Then the lightened hull was warped in parallel to the beach on the high spring tide.

Lines were run through heavy sheave blocks from the top of all three masts to the shore, and secured to the largest, strongest palms above the beach. Then, with three fathoms of water under her hull, the *Minotaur* was hove over. Twenty men on each of the capstans and the rest of the men on the shore-lines strained and chanted and heaved. Gradually the ship took on a heavy list to star-board, and her planking on the opposite side was exposed until she was in danger of rolling clean under. But by this time the tide was in full ebb and the *Minotaur* settled on the sandy bottom with her entire port side exposed. Before the tide was fully out, Tom and Ned Tyler waded out to inspect her planking.

The *Minotaur* had been in these waters for almost four years and her bottom was foul with weed and barnacles. Although these would affect her speed and sailing charac-teristics, they would not threaten her existence. However, when they scraped away the weed they found what they had most feared: everywhere ship-worm had bored their holes into the timbers of the hull below the waterline. Tom was able to thrust his forefinger full length into one of these burrows, and feel the worm squirm as his fingertip touched it. In some places the holes were so close together that the wood resembled a Swiss cheese.

The carpenters had iron vats of pitch boiling over fires on the beach. Ned poured a ladleful, bubbling, into one of the worm-holes. The loathsome creature came writhing and twisting, in its death throes, out into the open. It was as thick as his finger, and when Tom seized its head and held it up as far as he could reach, the red serpentine body hung down as far as his knees.

'The old lady would never have made it back home with this filthy crew aboard,' Ned told him. 'Her hull would have broken up in the first real gale she ran into.' With an expression of disgust, Tom flung the parboiled worm far out into the lagoon, where a shoal of small silver fish churned the water white as they devoured it.

The carpenters and their mates came wading out to join them in the work of ridding the hull of these vermin, and kept at it until the tide turned and the rising water drove them back to the beach. They worked through five successive low tides to scrape off the weed and shellfish, then cooked out the worms and plugged their holes with pitch and oakum. Those planks that were riddled and rotten past saving were cut out and replaced with bright new timbers. The scoured bottom was painted with a thick coat of pitch, covered with a mixture of pitch and tallow, then another two coats of pitch before Ned and Tom were satisfied.

With the next high tide the *Minotaur* was floated off, and in deeper water turned round. Then she was brought back to the same spot on the beach and the whole process repeated, but this time with her starboard side rolled uppermost.

When, finally, she was brought back to her moorings

in the deeper waters of the lagoon, the topmastmen went aloft to send down her yards. These were carefully examined and any weak spot was repaired before being sent aloft again. Next, all the lines and sheets of her rigging were minutely inspected and the greater part replaced with fresh manila of the finest quality from the *Seraph*'s stores. The old black sails were in rags and tatters – most had been roughly patched and cobbled by al-Auf's men. 'We will replace them all,' Tom decided, and sent Ned to rifle the lockers of the *Seraph*. The sail-makers squatted in rows on the open deck, making up new canvas and altering the sails from the *Seraph*'s lockers to suit the *Minotaur*'s masts and yards.

The lower decks were in the same state of degradation as the *Minotaur*'s rigging. She was lousy with vermin and rats, and stank like a dung-heap. Ned concocted a fearsome brew of gunpowder, brimstone and vitriol, and they placed pots of this in the lower decks and set them alight. As the noxious smoke and fumes billowed from the pots, they hurried out onto the deck and into the fresh air. Then they battened down all her ports and hatches, and let the smoke seep into every corner and cranny of the hull.

Within minutes the rats began to desert the ship, wriggling out through the hawsehole and every crack in the gunports. Some were as big as rabbits. As they swam frantically for the beach, the crew had great sport shooting at them with pistol or musket and wagering on the bag.

When the hull and the rigging had been taken care of, Tom turned his attention to the paintwork. This was faded and peeling. They rigged cradles over her sides and teams of men sanded her down, then gave her three coats of gleaming white down to the waterline. In a transport of artistic zeal, Tom had them pick out her gunports in a gay sky blue, and regild the horned figurehead and the carvings of the stern gallery. After six weeks of unrelenting work the *Minotaur* looked like a ship just off the builders' slip.

Her lovely lines and her sweet sheer were displayed to full advantage.

Looking across at her from the stern windows over his sick bed, Hal Courtney smiled wanly with approval. 'By Jesus, she's as pretty as a bride on her wedding day. Well done, my boy. You have added five thousand pounds to her value.'

His father's words gave Tom the courage to make a request. Hal listened quietly as he asked for the *Minotaur* and an independent command. Then he shook his head. 'I have lost one son,' he said softly. 'I am not yet prepared to lose another, Tom.'

'But, Father, I gave Dorry my sacred oath.'

Shadows of terrible pain, worse than those he had undergone on the grating when they took his legs, passed behind Hal's eyes. 'I know, Tom, I know,' he whispered. 'But the *Minotaur* is not mine to give you – it belongs to John Company. Even that would not stop me if I thought we could help your brother. But I cannot give you the ship and let you go off into terrible danger without a full crew to help you.'

Tom opened his mouth to argue further, but Hal reached up from the rumpled sick-bed on which he lay and placed his hand on his son's arm. 'Listen to me, lad.' His voice was husky and the pale bony hand on Tom's arm was light as the wing of a bird. 'I cannot let you go alone. This al-Malik is a man of power. He commands armies and hundreds of ships. On your own, you will not prevail against one such as him.'

'Father—' Tom broke in again, but his father stopped him.

'Hear me out, Tom. We must see through this voyage together. I have a duty to my King and to the men who placed their trust in me. When we have discharged that duty, I will have you inducted into the Order. You will become a Knight Templar of the Order of St George and the Holy Grail, with all the power that gives you. You will be able to call on the assistance of your brother knights, men like Lord Childs and Lord Hyde.'

'That will take a year,' Tom cried, in physical pain at the prospect. 'No, it may take two or three years.'

'We will achieve nothing by rushing in unprepared against a powerful nobleman in a far country, a country that is alien and where we have no allies or influence.'

'Years!' Tom repeated. 'What will happen to Dorry in the meantime?'

'By then I will be recovered from these wounds.' Hal looked down at his pitifully truncated legs. 'We will sail together to find Dorian, you and I, in a fleet of fine, powerful ships, manned with good, fighting men. Believe me, Tom, this is Dorian's best chance, and ours.'

Tom stared at his father aghast. Since his injury Hal Courtney had turned into a frail old man, with silvering beard and crippled body. Did he truly believe that he would ever again command another squadron or fight another battle? It was a forlorn dream. Tom felt the tears rising behind his eyes, but forced them back.

'Trust me, Tom,' Hal murmured. 'I give you my word. Will you give me yours?'

'Very well, Father.' Tom had to summon all his courage to make the oath, but he could not deny his own father. 'I give you my word.'

'Thank you, Tom.' The hand dropped from Tom's arm and Hal's chin drooped onto his chest. His eyes closed and his breathing was so soft that it was inaudible. With a flare of dismay Tom thought he had lost him. Then he saw the gentle rise and fall of Hal's wasted chest.

Tom rose from the bedside and moved towards the door, walking softly so that he did not disturb his father's sleep.

The monsoon died away, and they lay for months in the torpid grip of the great calm between the seasons. Then the palm trees stirred their fronds and the clouds turned back upon their tracks across the heavens and marched away in the opposite direction.

'These two mighty winds are the great wonder of all the oceans of the Indies,' Alf Wilson told Tom, as they sat on the foredeck. He spoke in Arabic, for Hal still insisted that Tom practise this language every day, and Tom knew that it would stand him in good stead in his quest to find his brother. 'From November to April they blow out of the north-east, and the Arabs call them the *kaskazi*,' Alf went on. 'From April to November they turn back upon themselves and blow out of the south-east. Then the Arabs call them the *kusi*.'

It was the *kusi* that had brought Captain Edward Anderson back to Flor de la Mar in the bright dawn of another windswept day. While the crews of the other ships of the squadron manned the yards and lined the rails to cheer her in, Anderson brought the *Yeoman of York* through the passage in the coral and dropped anchor alongside the *Seraph*. Hardly had the ship snubbed up to her cable than Tom sent the longboat across to fetch Anderson to see his father.

Edward Anderson came up the ladder looking mighty pleased with himself and his accomplishments, but his first words were to enquire after Hal Courtney's health.

'My father makes a strong recovery from his wounds,' Tom gave him the white lie, 'and I am most grateful for your concern, Captain Anderson.'

He led Anderson to the stern cabin. Tom had seen to it that the linen on the bunk was freshly washed and ironed, and that Hal's hair had been trimmed and combed by the surgeon's mate. He was propped up on bolsters and looked healthier than he really was.

'I give thanks to God to see you in such fine fettle, Sir Henry,' Anderson greeted him, and took the chair beside the bunk to which Hal pointed.

Tom served them each a glass of Madeira. 'Do you wish me to leave you alone with Captain Anderson, Father?' he asked, as he handed the twist-stemmed glass to Hal.

'Of course not,' Hal told him quickly, then said to Anderson, 'My son has taken command in my stead, while I am indisposed.'

Tom stared at him. This was the first time his promotion had been mentioned.

However, Anderson showed no surprise. 'He does you credit, Sir Henry.'

'Enough of our doings here on the island.' Hal tried to sit higher, but pain stabbed him. He winced and lay back on the pillows. 'I'm eager to have a report of your exploits since we parted.'

'All my news is good.' Anderson was neither shy nor reticent. 'The outward voyage to Ceylon was accomplished without mishap, and the loss of only a dozen of the captives. Van Groote, the Dutch governor in Colombo, was courteous in his reception, and most amenable in his desire to trade. It seems that our timing was most propitious, as a recent epidemic of smallpox in his barracoons had reduced his population of slaves most drastically. Fortunately I had been apprised of this prior to opening negotiations with him, so I was able to agree with him a very satisfactory price.'

'How much?'

'Thirty-seven pounds a head.' Anderson looked smug.

'My felicitations, Captain Anderson.' Hal reached out to shake his hand. 'That is considerably more than we expected.'

'The good news does not end there.' Anderson chuckled. 'The smallpox plague and the predations of al-Auf in these oceans meant that van Groote had been unable to ship much of the last two years' cinnamon crop. His warehouses were filled to overflowing.' Anderson winked. 'Instead of taking a note on the VOC bankers in Amsterdam for the sale price of the slaves, I loaded my ship with bales of cinnamon at these bargain prices. I have no doubt that we will double our investment when we reach the Pool of London again.'

'Again I must commend your good sense and acumen.' Anderson's news had visibly cheered Hal. Tom had not seen his father look so keen and vigorous since his injury. 'The wind stands fair for Good Hope. We should sail as soon as you are ready to take your *Yeoman* back to sea, Captain Anderson. When will that be?'

'I have a few cases of scurvy among my crew, but I expect them to recover quickly now that we are in harbour. I need only replenish my water-barrels and take on a load of coconuts. I will be ready to sail within the week.'

Four days later the squadron weighed anchor, and tacked out through the passage in line astern. As soon as they reached the open sea they set all plain sail and headed down into the south, to pass through the Mozambique Channel and forge on to the south cape of the African continent.

For the first few weeks the weather remained fair and the wind favourable. Hal's health responded favourably to being at sea again in the fresh air and to the kindly motion of the *Seraph*. He spent time each day rehearsing Tom in the rites of the Order of St George and the Holy Grail, preparing him for his entry into the knighthood, and expressed pleasure at his son's progress.

After the first week, Tom ordered a day-bed set up on the deck, on the weather side of the quarterdeck, and had his father carried up and laid where he could once again feel the wind and sun on his face. Although Tom took full responsibility for the running of the ship, he made time each day to be with his father. During these days Tom felt himself growing closer to Hal than he had ever been before. Often their talk turned to Dorian and their plans to find and rescue him. They discussed Guy and his marriage to Caroline Beatty only once. To Tom's astonishment his father spoke to him as to a man full grown. 'You do realize, Tom, that the child might well be yours and not Guy's?'

'That had occurred to me.' Tom hid his embarrassment as well as he was able, and answered as forthrightly as his father had broached the subject.

'I fear you have made an enemy of your twin brother. Be wary of Guy. He does not forgive an injury, and he has an endless capacity for hatred.'

'I doubt we shall ever meet again. He is in India, and I – well, I shall be at the ends of the oceans.'

'Fate plays us shabby tricks, Tom, and the oceans may not be as broad as you think.'

The squadron made its southings and at forty-three degrees south latitude swung up on to a westerly heading to make the landfall on the tip of Good Hope. Soon they saw the surf beating white on the southern cliffs of Africa. That same day Hal summoned Tom to the stern cabin and showed him the record of his promotion entered in the ship's log.

'Apart from a demonstration of the trust I have in you, Tom, this also means that you will be entitled to an officer's share of the prize,' his father told him. 'That might be as much as a thousand pounds.'

'Thank you, Father.'

'There is much that I would do for you that is beyond my powers. William is my first-born, and you know the significance of that. Everything goes to him.'

'You need not worry about me. I can make my own way in the world.'

'Of that I am sure.' Hal smiled, and gripped his arm. He was stronger now than when they had left Flor de la Mar – Tom could feel the power in his fingers, and the sun had put new colour in his cheeks. 'It must be because we have doubled the Cape and are northward-bound that my thoughts turn once again to High Weald. Do not hate your elder brother, Tom.'

'It is not I who hate him, Father. It's Black Billy who hates me.'

'That contemptuous name betrays your true feelings for him, but when I am gone he will be the head of our family and he has a right to your respect and loyalty.'

'It was you who taught me, Father, that respect and loyalty have to be earned and not demanded.'

They anchored well off the beach of the little Dutch settlement at the Cape of Good Hope. They watered and revictualled with fresh vegetables and meat, and had neither truck nor bother with the Dutch administration ashore. Within the week they were on their way northwards once more. As suddenly as the squadron entered the Atlantic Ocean, the character of the waters changed, and Hal Courtney's health with it.

The Cape rollers came marching down upon them, great grey ridges of water with deep valleys between, to batter the squadron day and night. The seas creamed over the ships' bows and tore away any weak plank or fitting from the decks. The howl of the wind was the voice of this wolf-pack, and the onslaught was merciless and unrelenting. Each day Hal grew weaker again, and when Tom entered his cabin one gale-driven morning he found his father flushed and sweating. His nostrils flared as he detected the familiar stench of corruption in the air, and when he drew back the bedclothes he found telltale stains of yellow pus on the white linen.

He shouted to the watch above to call Dr Reynolds, who came immediately. He unwrapped the bandages from Hal's left leg, and his kindly features crumpled with dismay. The stump was horribly swollen, and the lips of the freshly healed wound were hot purple and splitting open with pus oozing from the edges. 'I'm afraid there is a deep corruption in the wound, Sir Henry.' Dr Reynolds sniffed at the pus, and pulled a face. 'I do not like these humours. There is the taint of gangrene in them. I must lance the wound at once.'

While Tom held his father's shoulders, the surgeon pressed the point of a long scalpel deeply into the wound as Hal writhed and whimpered with the pain. When Reynolds withdrew the blade, it was followed by a copious gush of yellow and purple pus, stained with fresh blood, that covered the bottom of the bowl the surgeon's mate held under the stump. 'I think we have drained the source of the evil.' Reynolds looked pleased with the quantity and colour of the discharge. 'Now I will bleed you to reduce the fever.' He nodded to his mate. They rolled back the sleeve of Hal's nightshirt and wound a leather thong around his upper arm. When they twisted it tight the veins on the inside of Hal's elbow stood proud, like blue ropes beneath the pale skin. Reynolds cleaned the pus and blood from the blade of the scalpel by wiping it on his sleeve, then tested the point on the ball of his thumb before pricking the swollen vein and watching the dark red blood dribble into the pewter bowl to mingle with the yellow pus.

'A single pint should be sufficient,' he muttered. 'I think now we have drained off the morbid humours. Though I do say it myself, that's as good a job as you'll see this side of Land's End.'

Over the following weeks of the voyage, Hal's strength fluctuated widely. For days he lay wan and inert in his bunk, seeming on the point of death. Then he would rally strongly. When they crossed the equator, Tom was able to have him taken on deck again to enjoy the hot sunshine, and Hal talked eagerly of home, longing for the green fields and wild moorland of High Weald. He spoke of the books and papers in his library. 'All the log books of your grandfather's early voyages are there. These I can leave to you, Tom, for you are the sailor in the family and they will be of little interest to William.'

Thinking of Sir Francis made his mood swing again, and he was saddened. 'Your grandfather's body will be waiting for us at High Weald, for Anderson sent him back from Bombay. We will lay him in his sarcophagus in the crypt of the chapel. He will be glad to be home again, as glad as I will.' His expression was tragic as he thought about it. 'Tom, will you see to it that I have a place in the crypt? I would like to lie with my father and the three women I have loved. Your mother—' He broke off, unable to continue.

'That day is still far off, Father,' Tom assured him with a desperate edge to his voice. 'We still have a quest to undertake. We exchanged oaths. We have to go after Dorian. You must get well and strong again.'

With an effort, Hal shrugged off the black mood of despair. 'Of course, you are right. This moping and complaining will profit us not at all.'

'I have had the carpenters begin to fashion new legs for you, of strong English oak,' Tom told him brightly. 'We will have you up before you see High Weald again.'

Tom sent for the head carpenter. The little gnarled Welshman brought the two peg-legs, still only crudely carved, to show Hal. Then he and Tom made a show of measuring and fitting them to Hal's stumps.

Hal seemed to take a lively interest, and laughed with them, making fatuous suggestions. 'Can we not fit them with a compass and weather cock to aid my navigation?' But when the carpenter had gone below, he lapsed back into his dark mood. 'I will never be too handy with those timber yards on my legs. I fear that you might have to go after Dorian on your own, Tom.' He held up a hand to still Tom's quick protest. 'But I will stand by my word. You shall have all the help I can give you.'

Two weeks later, while the ship lay becalmed on the edge of the sluggish Sargasso Sea at thirty degrees north latitude and sixty degrees west Tom went down to his father's cabin in the humid calm and found him shrunken in his bunk. His skin was stretched over the bone of his skull, tight and parchment yellow, like the face of the Egyptian mummy that one of Tom's ancestors had brought back from a voyage to Alexandria, and which stood in its open coffin against one of the back walls of the library at High Weald. Tom called for Dr Reynolds and left his father in his care. Then, unable to bear the atmosphere in the stern cabin any longer, he hurried on deck, and took long draughts of the warm air. 'Will this voyage never end?' he lamented. 'If we do not get him home soon, he will never see High Weald again. Oh, for a wind to hasten us on.'

He ran to the main-mast shrouds and climbed aloft, never stopping until he reached the truck. He hung there, peering at the horizon to the north, vague and smoky with sea fret. Then he drew the dagger from the sheath on his belt and slammed it into the wood of the mast. He left it there, for Aboli had taught him that this was the way to call up the wind. He started to whistle 'Spanish Ladies', but that made him think of Dorian, so he changed to 'Greensleeves'.

All that morning he whistled for the wind, and before the sun had reached noon, he looked back over the stern. The surface of the sea was a polished mirror, broken only by the floating clumps of yellow Sargasso weed. Then he saw the dark blue line of the wind racing swiftly towards them over the shining surface. 'Deck!' he yelled down.

'Squall line! Dead astern.' And he saw the tiny figures of the watch on deck scramble to the sheets to trim the sails to the coming wind. It picked up all four ships of the squadron and bore them away. The *Seraph* was still in the van, and the *Yeoman*, the *Minotaur* and the matronly *Lamb* trailed after her. From then onwards it blew steadily out of the west, never faltering, not even during the night. Tom left his dagger pegged into the top of the main mast.

They made their landfall off the Isles of Scilly, and hailed the first sail they had seen in two months. It was a small open fishing-boat with a crew of three.

'What news?' Tom hailed them. 'We have had no news for eighteen months.'

'War!' the reply was shouted back. 'War with the French.'

Tom called Edward Anderson and the other captains on board the *Seraph* for a hasty council of war. It would be tragic to complete such a perilous voyage and then, almost in sight of home, to fall victim to French privateers. Hal was enjoying one of his stronger periods, and lucid enough to take part in the discussions, so Tom gathered them in the stern cabin. 'We have a choice,' he told them. 'We can dock in Plymouth, or we can run up-Channel for the mouth of the Thames.'

Anderson was for Plymouth, but Ned Tyler and Alf Wilson wanted to head for London. When each had given his opinion, Tom spoke out: 'Once we are at Blackwall we can offload our cargoes directly into the Company warehouses, and our prize can be on the Company auction floors within days.' He looked to his father for encouragement. When Hal nodded, Tom went on, 'If we go into Plymouth, we may be bottled up there for the good Lord only knows how long. I say we run the gauntlet of the French privateers and set a course to weather North Foreland.'

'Tom's right. The sooner we can deliver our cargo, the happier I will be,' said Hal.

They stood the crews to and, with loaded cannon and double lookouts at the mastheads, they ran up-Channel. Twice during the days that followed they saw strange sails that flew no colours but had the look of Frenchies about them. Tom gave the flag signal to close up their formation and the strangers veered off, heading back into the east where the French coast lay just below the horizon.

They raised the light on North Foreland two hours before dawn, and were past Sheerness by noon. In the gloaming of that winter's day all four ships tied up at the Company docks in the river. Before the gangplank was down, Tom had shouted across to the Company agent, who waited on the wharf to greet them, 'Send a message to Lord Childs that we have taken great prize. He must come at once.'

Two hours before midnight Childs's carriage, with the two outriders at full gallop clearing the way, and the side-lights glaring, came clattering through the gates of the yard. The driver reined in the team at the edge of the dock, and Childs almost tumbled from the carriage door before the wheels had stopped turning. He came stumping up the Seraph's gangplank, his face flushed, his wig awry and his mouth working with excitement.

'Who are you?' he blared at Tom. 'Where is Sir Henry?'

'My lord, I am Sir Henry's son, Thomas Courtney.'

'Where is your father, lad?'

'He waits for you below, my lord.'

Childs swivelled around and pointed at the Minotaur. 'What ship is that? She has the look of an Indiaman, but I know her not.'

'That's the old Minotaur, my lord, under a fresh coat of paint.'

471

'The *Minotaur*! You retook her from the corsair?' Childs did not wait for his reply. 'That other ship beyond her.' He pointed at the *Lamb*. 'What ship is that?'

'Another prize, my lord. A Dutchman with a full cargo of China tea.'

'Jesus love you, lad. You are a herald of great good tidings. Lead me to your father.'

Hal was sitting up in the captain's chair, with a velvet cloak draped across his lap to hide his injuries. He wore a dark blue velvet coat. On his chest glittered the gold and jewelled emblem of the Order of St George and the Holy Grail. Although his face was deadly pale and his eyes sunk into dark cavities, he held himself straight and proud. 'Welcome aboard, my lord,' he greeted Childs. 'Please excuse me for not rising, but I am a little indisposed.'

Childs seized his hand. 'You are welcome indeed, Sir Henry. I am eager to hear the extent of your successes. I have seen the two prizes tied up alongside the wharf, and your son has given me some idea of the cargo you carry.'

'Please be seated.' Hal indicated the chair at his side. 'My report will take some little time. I have written it all out, but I should like to tell you of our expedition man to man, and face to face. But, first, a glass of wine.' He gestured to Tom to fill the glasses that stood ready on a silver tray.

Childs sat forward in his chair and listened intently as Hal began his tale. Occasionally he asked a question, but mostly he listened in rapt silence, as Hal read aloud the cargo manifests of the four ships of the squadron. When at last he fell silent, drained by the effort of the long recital, Childs leaned over and took the parchments from his hand. He scrutinized them carefully, his eyes shining with cupidity. At last he looked up again. 'Since the outbreak of war with the French, the price of commodities has almost doubled. With the two captured ships, the value of

472

the prize you have won for us might be as much as five hundred thousand pounds. The directors of the Company will be more than grateful, and I think I can speak for His Majesty when I say that the Crown will honour its solemn undertaking to you. You will be Henry Courtney, Baron Dartmouth, before the week is out.'

Childs saluted him with a raised glass. 'I knew that I had chosen the right man when I sent you. May I drink to your health and fortune, Sir Henry?'

'Thank you, my lord. I am happy that you are pleased.'

'Pleased?' Childs laughed. 'There are no words to express the extent of my pleasure, my admiration, my amazement at your resourcefulness, your courage.' He leaned across to place his hand on Hal's knee. A comical expression of astonishment came over his face. He looked down and groped for Hal's missing limb.

'Sir Henry, I am overcome.' He looked down at Hal's lower body. 'Good God, man! Your legs! You have lost your legs!'

Hal smiled wanly. 'Yes, my lord, there was a certain price to pay. We seamen call it the butcher's bill.'

'We must get you out of this ship. You will be my guest at Bombay House while you recuperate. My carriage is on the wharf. I will call my physicians, the best in London. You will lack for nothing. I promise you that.'

One of the first things Hal did after he arrived at Bombay House was write to William, giving him the momentous tidings of the prize he had taken, and of his imminent elevation to the peerage. It took the letter over a week to reach his son in Devon.

With the letter still in his hand, William shouted for his horse and within the hour was riding furiously out through the gates of High Weald and galloping up the main road to London as fast as the relays of fresh horses from the post-houses could carry him.

Five days after leaving High Weald, he rode into the grounds of Bombay House in the middle of the afternoon in a downpour of rain. He left his hired horse in the stableyard; then, soaked and muddy to the waist, he strode through the main doors, brushing aside the steward and footmen who tried to bar his entrance. 'I am the eldest son of Sir Henry Courtney. I wish to be taken to my father immediately.'

As soon as he heard the name, one of the secretaries came hurrying forward. In the last few days the name of Courtney had taken the city by storm. Every news-sheet had carried pages of print concerning the exploits of Sir Henry Courtney in the Ocean of the Indies. Some were wildly fanciful, yet as an item of gossip he had supplanted the news of the latest English victory in France, and his name was bandied about every tavern and fashionable gathering in London. To add to the excitement, broadsheets handed out in the street advertised the forthcoming auction sale of the cargo and the prizes at the premises of John Company in Leadenhall Street, describing them as 'The Greatest Treasures ever taken from an Enemy on the High Seas!'

Within days of the squadron's arrival, shares in 'The United Company of Merchants of England Trading to the East Indies', which was the full and ringing title of John Company, increased in value by over 15 per cent. Over the past five years the Company had paid an annual dividend of 25 per cent, but anticipation of the distribution of this vast treasure drove the shares to unheard-of heights.

'Thank God you have arrived, sir,' the secretary greeted William. 'Your father has been asking for you every day. Please allow me to lead you to him.'

He took William up the broad curving marble staircase. When they reached the first landing, William halted abruptly under the massive Holbein portrait of Lord Childs's great-great-grandfather, and looked up at the two men descending the stairs towards him. His severe features knitted, and his dark eyes glittered as he took in the younger of the pair.

'Well met, brother dear. It seems my prayers are unanswered and you have returned to plague me. You, and that great black savage.' He glanced at Aboli.

Tom stopped on the landing facing William. He was an inch taller now than his elder brother. He looked him up and down, starting at his muddy boots and ending at his arrogant, saturnine head, and smiled coldly. 'I'm touched deeply by your expression of affection. Please be assured that it is returned in full measure.'

Although he did not show it, William was taken aback by the transformation that the years had wrought in Tom. He had become tough and tall, full of self-confidence. A man to reckon with.

'No doubt we shall have the opportunity to continue this pleasant discourse at a later date.' William inclined his head in dismissal. 'But now I have my duty as the first-born to attend our father.'

Tom did not acknowledge the barbed reference to William's seniority of birth, although it stung. He stood aside and bowed slightly. 'Your servant, brother.'

William swept past him and, without looking back, reached the long portrait gallery of the house. The secretary led him to the end of the passage, and rapped with his cane on the double doors. They were opened immediately and William went through into the elaborate bed-chamber beyond. Four black-clad surgeons were clustered about the huge four-poster bed on its raised dais. William could tell their profession by the old bloodstains on their clothing. They opened their ranks as he approached.

When he saw the figure lying on the pillows William

came to a halt. He remembered the robust and vigorous man he had seen sail away from Plymouth harbour. This frail old fellow with silver beard, shaven head and pain-fretted features could not be the same man.

'I have prayed God for your arrival,' Hal whispered. 'Come, kiss me, William.'

William started forward again and hurried to the bedside. He knelt and pressed his lips to his father's pale cheek. 'I give thanks to God that he has spared you, and that you are so well recovered from your wounds,' William told him, with a sincere and joyous mien, which disguised his true feelings. He is dying, William thought, with a mixture of elation and alarm. The estate is almost mine, and this famous treasure which he has brought back from his marauding. 'I hope you are as well as you appear?' he asked, and gripped the thin, cold hand that lay on top of the brocaded bedclothes. By Jesus, he thought, if the old pirate dies before the investiture, the barony will be lost. Without the belt of nobility around my waist, the taste of even this great fortune he has raided from the heathen will be soured.

'You are a fine and loving son, William, but don't weep for me yet. Even these coffin fillers,' he gestured at the four eminent surgeons who surrounded his bed, 'even they will be hard put to bury me.' He attempted a feckless laugh, which rang hollow in the vast echoing chamber. None of the doctors smiled.

'My love for you is enhanced by the pride I feel for the glory you have achieved. When will you take your seat in the Lords, Father?'

'Within the next few days,' Hal answered. 'And, as the eldest son, you will be with me to see me honoured.'

'Sir Henry,' one of the physicians interjected, 'we do not feel that it is wise for you to visit the House of Lords in your present state of health. We are seriously concerned—'

476

William sprang to his feet and rounded on the doctor before he could finish expressing his misgivings. 'Nonsense, fellow. It is plain for any fool to see that my father is strong enough to honour the summons of his sovereign lord. I shall be with him at every minute. With my own hands I shall see to his every want.'

Five days later the servants carried Hal down the staircase on a litter. with William hovering anxiously at his side. Lord Childs's carriage stood ready in front of the main doors, and Tom and Aboli stood separated from the troop of horsemen who would escort the carriage.

The footmen set down the litter down next to the carriage and there was a moment of confusion when nobody seemed certain what to do next. Tom stepped forward quickly, elbowing his elder brother aside, and before the doctors could intervene, he lifted his father easily and stepped into the carriage with the wasted body in his arms. 'Father, this is not wise. You are taxing your strength with this journey,' he whispered, as he settled Hal in the carriage and spread the fur rug over him.

'The King may return to the Continent soon to pursue the war, and who knows when next he will return to England?'

'Then Aboli and I should go with you,' Tom pleaded, 'but William has forbidden it.'

'William will take good care of me.' Hal pulled the lustrous furs around his shoulders. 'You must stay here with Walsh to take care of our interest at the auction house. I place great trust in you, Tom.'

Tom knew that the true reason for his refusal was that his father did not want to throw him together with his half-brother. 'As you wish, Father,' he acquiesced.

'As soon as this business at the Lords is done with, and the sale completed, we can go back to High Weald and make our plans for the rescue of Dorian.'

'I will be waiting here when you return,' Tom promised

him, and climbed down to stand at the rear wheel. William stepped into the carriage, settled himself in the seat beside their father, the driver whipped up the horses and the carriage rolled out through the gates.

Tom turned to Aboli. 'It is bad enough that Black Billy will drag him around in that bone-shaker. I will not let him do the same on the return to High Weald. The long journey down to Devon over those rough roads will kill him. We must take him by ship to Plymouth. The sea will be gentler on him, and you and I can take better care of him.'

'You do not have a ship, Klebe,' Aboli reminded him. 'The *Seraph* and the *Minotaur* belong to John Company.'

'Then we must find another to charter.'

'There are French privateers in the Channel.'

'We need something small and handy – small enough not to attract their interest and fast enough to give them the slip if they decide to chase us.'

'I think I know the master of such a craft,' Aboli said thoughtfully. 'Unless things have changed in the time we have been away.'

The auction sale at the Company's magnificent premises at Leadenhall Street took four days to accomplish. Tom sat beside Master Walsh throughout to note the prices bid on the booty.

The main saleroom was shaped like a cockpit, with tiers of benches rising up from the circular floor where the auctioneer had his dais. The benches were so crowded with merchants, their secretaries and book-keepers that there were not enough seats for all. Many found standing room only against the back walls, but they joined in boisterously, roaring their bids and waving their catalogues to attract the attention of the auctioneer.

As Tom listened to the prices being driven up with mad abandon, he thought of the chests of coin stored in the vaults beneath the auction rooms. They had brought them up from the Company wharf the night that the squadron had docked, driving the coaches through the dark, cobbled streets while a guard of fifty armed seamen marched in an escort around them.

It was clear that the prices Lord Childs had predicted would be far surpassed in the hysteria that surrounded the sale. Each day it continued Tom saw his share increase in value.

'Dear Lord!' he marvelled on the last day, as he scribbled his calculations on his slate. 'With good fortune, I will take away more than a thousand pounds.' That was as much as one of the miners or farm labourers at High Weald might earn in his entire working life. He was bewildered by such dreams of wealth, until he thought of what his father's share would be worth. 'Almost a hundred thousand!' he exclaimed. 'Together with the ermine cloak and jewelled sword-belt of a baron.' Then his mouth hardened with anger. 'And all of it will drop neatly into Black Billy's clutching paws. Black Billy, who pukes his guts out every time he has a ship under him.'

While he was still brooding on the injustice of it the auctioneer announced, in a loud, braying voice, the next item for sale. 'My lords, ladies and gentlemen, we are pleased and privileged to offer for your delectation a rare and wonderful trophy that will delight and intrigue even the most sophisticated and world-weary among you.' With a flourish, he lifted the covering cloth from a large jar of thick, transparent glass, which stood on the table in front of him. 'None other than the pickled head of the notorious and bloodthirsty brigand and corsair Jangiri, or al-Auf, the Bad One.'

A buzz and stir swept over the tiers of merchants and they craned forward to peer ghoulishly at the disembodied head swimming in its bath of spirits. Tom felt a physical shock as he looked once again into al-Auf's face. His dark hair floated like seaweed around his head. One of his eyes was open: it seemed to single out Tom and stare up at him with mild astonishment. There was a pained expression on his lips, as if he could still feel the stinging kiss of the blade that had parted head from trunk.

'Come, gentlemen!' the auctioneer wheedled. 'This is an item of value. Many persons across the land would be pleased to pay their sixpence for a peek at it. Do I hear five pounds bid?'

Slowly, a sense of outrage overcame Tom. He had taken the head as proof to the directors of John Company of the success of their expedition, not to become a bizarre sideshow in a travelling circus. His instincts and his training had instilled in him the concept of compassion and respect for a vanquished foe. That al-Auf had captured and sold Dorian into slavery did not enter into it.

Without thinking, he shouted angrily, 'Ten pounds!' He did not have that sum at his disposal, but his share of the prize was owing to him. All around the hall heads turned and faces peered at him curiously. He heard their whispers.

'It's Hal Courtney's lad, the one who cropped the head.'

'That's him. He lopped al-Auf.'

'What's his name?'

'Tom Courtney. He's Sir Hal's boy.'

The auctioneer bowed theatrically to him. 'The bold swordsman and executioner himself has bid ten pounds. Is there any advance on ten pounds?'

Someone in the front row of benches began to clap, and it was taken up by those around him. Slowly the applause became a roar until they were all clapping and stamping their feet.

Tom wanted to shout to them to stop. He wanted to

tell them that he had not killed the man for their approbation. But there were no words to describe what he had
felt as he took al-Auf's head, and what he felt now as he
watched it floating in a bottle, offered for the sport of
gawking peasants.

'Going for the first time! Going for the second time!
Sold to Mr Tom Courtney for the sum of ten pounds!'

'Pay them out of my share,' Tom snapped at Walsh,
and jumped to his feet. He wanted to get out into the fresh
air, away from the stares and the grins of this host of
strangers. He shouldered his way out of the chamber and
ran down the great staircase.

When he strode out into Leadenhall Street it was
raining. He swung his cloak over his shoulders, crammed
the wide-brimmed hat with its cavalier's feather onto his
head and adjusted his sword-belt before he stepped out
from under the portico. There was a touch on his shoulder,
and he swung round. In his preoccupation he had not seen
Aboli among the crowd of loafers at the entrance to the
salerooms.

'I have found our man, Klebe.' Aboli led forward a tall
lean fellow swathed in a sea cloak, whose features were
hidden by the Monmouth cap pulled low over his eyes. For
a moment Tom was not certain of Aboli's meaning. 'The
man to take your father back to Plymouth by sea, instead
of over the roads,' Aboli prompted him.

'Then let's all take a pot of ale while we discuss it,'
Tom suggested and they ran through the rain to the ale-
house at the corner of Cornhill.

In the stuffy front room, crowded with lawyers and
clerks, and redolent of the smoke of tobacco pipes, the
yeasty odours of the beer-kegs, they threw off their cloaks
and hats, and Tom turned to study the face of the man
Aboli had brought him. 'This is Captain Luke Jervis,'
Aboli told him. 'He sailed with your father and me in the
old *Pegasus*.'

Tom liked him immediately. He had a sharp, intelligent eye, and the look of a tough seaman. His skin was tanned and creased by the sun and salt.

'Luke has a fast cutter, and he knows every inch of the Channel, especially the French ports, like the back of his hand.' Aboli smiled significantly. 'He can give the slip to any Excise man or Froggie.' Tom did not catch his meaning immediately, but then Aboli went on, 'If it's a shipment of good Limousin cognac you're looking for, then Luke is your man.'

Tom grinned when he realized that Luke was a smuggler. If that was the case, he was the perfect choice for taking them on a quick voyage down the Channel. His vessel would be quick as a ferret, and he would be able to navigate the dangerous waters on a moonless night in a gale. Tom shook his hand. 'Aboli has told you what we want. What would be the price of your hire, Captain?'

'I owe Sir Henry my life and more,' said Luke Jervis, and touched the long white scar that ran down his left cheek. 'I will not charge him a brass farthing. It would make me proud to be of service to him.'

Tom did not ask about the scar, but thanked him. Then he said, 'Aboli will bring you word when my father is ready to leave London.'

When Lord Courtney returned from his first visit to the House of Lords, Tom could see at a glance how the journey and the ceremony had taxed him. He carried him tenderly up the staircase to the bedroom in Bombay House and Hal fell asleep almost immediately. Tom sat by his bed until evening when a footman brought up a dinner tray.

'Where is William?' Hal asked weakly, as Tom fed him spoonfuls of soup.

'He is with Master Samuels at the bank. Lord Childs handed over the Company note to him for the share of the prize, and he has gone to deposit it,' Tom told him. He did not remark on how swiftly William's concern for his father's health had abated once his barony was established, and its succession to William's person assured. William's main interest now was to see the gold safely lodged with the bankers in the Strand where it would be under his control.

'You must rest now, Father. You must regain your strength for the journey home. Our business here in London is almost done. The sooner we can get you back to High Weald, the sooner you will be restored to full health.'

'Yes, Tom.' Hal showed sudden animation. 'I want to go home now. Did you know that William and Alice have given me a grandson? They have named him Francis, after your grandfather.'

'Yes, Father,' Tom answered. 'William told me.' William had made the point quite clear that, now he had fathered an heir, the inheritance of the title and estate had passed out of Tom's reach for ever. 'I have engaged a vessel to take us back to Plymouth. The captain is Luke Jervis. Do you remember him? He says that you saved his life.'

Hal smiled. 'Luke? He was a likely lad, a good fellow. I'm happy to hear he has his own ship now.'

'It's only a small cutter, but a fast one.'

'I would like to sail at once, Tom.' Hal gripped his arm. There was an eagerness in his expression.

'We should wait for the doctors to give the word.'

It was another week before the four surgeons agreed, reluctantly, to allow Hal to be taken aboard the *Raven*, Luke Jervis's ship. They sailed from the Company wharf in the late afternoon to make the most dangerous part of the voyage at night.

William was not with them. Now that the prize money from the auction was safely deposited with Samuels Bank in the Strand, he had been anxious to get back to take care of the running of the estate. 'Every hour that I am away costs us money. I mistrust those rogues and imbeciles I had to leave in charge during my absence. I will post down to Plymouth at once. I will meet your ship when you arrive, Father.'

The *Raven* proved as swift as her reputation had promised. As they ran south in the night, Tom stood beside Luke Jervis at the tiller. Luke wanted to hear every detail of their voyage to the Indies, and he questioned Tom avidly. 'Sweet Jesus! If only I had known, I would have signed on with Captain Hal, quick as you can say Jack Flash.'

'What about your wife and babes?' Aboli grinned, showing white teeth in the darkness.

'If I never hear another brat squeal or a goodwife scold it will not break my heart.' Luke pulled at his pipe and the glow lit his rugged face. Then he took the stem out of his mouth and pointed with it into the east. 'See those lights over there. That's Calais. I was in there three nights ago to take on a cargo of brandy and baccy. The roads are thick with shipping, like fleas on a mangy dog.' He smiled wolfishly in the starlight. 'If a man had a letter of marque, he wouldn't have to sail all the way to the Orient to find a prize.'

'Doesn't it trouble your conscience to trade with the French when we're at war with them?' Tom asked, puzzled.

'Somebody has to do it,' Luke said. 'Otherwise there would be no brandy and baccy to comfort our fighting lads. I'm a patriot, I am.' He said it seriously and Tom did not pursue it, but he mused on what Luke had said about the French shipping crowding the Channel ports.

When the *Raven* tied up at the quay in Plymouth, William proved as good as his word. He had a big, well-sprung coach on the dock, and servants standing ready to carry Hal into it. They set out at a sedate pace on the road for High Weald, and all along the way they passed small groups of men and women, the labourers, miners and tenant farmers of the estate, gathered to cheer his lordship home. Hal insisted on sitting up so that they could see him, and when he recognized a face among them he made the driver halt so that he could shake the fellow's hand through the coach window.

When they wheeled through the gates and crunched up the drive to the big house, all the servants were drawn up on the front steps. Some of the women wept to see Hal's state as the footmen carried him in, and the men muttered gruff greetings.

'Jesus love you, me lord. It does our hearts good to have you safe home.'

Alice Courtney, William's wife, waited at the top of the stairs. She had the baby in her arms, a tiny creature, Tom saw, with a bright red, wrinkled face. He squalled petulantly when Alice placed him for a moment in Hal's arms, but Hal smiled proudly and kissed the top of his head, which was covered with a thick black cap of hair.

It looks like a monkey, Tom thought. Then he looked more closely at Alice's face. Although there had never been the opportunity to get to know her when she married William, he had liked her instinctively. She had been pretty and gay, but now he hardly recognized her. There was an air of melancholy about her. Her eyes were sad, and though her skin was still peach soft and unblemished she seemed careworn. When Hal was carried inside the main doors she lingered on the top step to greet Tom. 'Welcome home, brother.' She kissed his cheek, and dropped a curtsy.

'You have a beautiful baby.' Tom touched the little

face awkwardly and jerked away his fingers when the child squealed again. 'As beautiful as his mother,' he finished lamely.

'Thank you, Tom,' she said and smiled, then she dropped her voice so that none of the servants could hear her. 'I must talk to you – not here, but at the first opportunity.' She turned away quickly and handed the baby to a nurse, while Tom followed his father up the stairs.

As soon as he was free to do so, Tom went down the passage towards the back stairs, but he had to pass Dorian's room. He opened the door, stood on the threshold, and felt a nostalgic pang as he looked about the small chamber. It was as his little brother had left it. There were the companies of lead soldiers in pretty painted uniforms arrayed along the window-ledge, and the kite Tom had made for him hanging above the bed. The memories were too painful. He closed the door quietly and went down the back stairs.

He slipped through the kitchen and stableyards and ran lightly up the hill towards the chapel. It was dark and cool in the vault, just a thin beam of sunlight burning down from the opening in the centre of the domed roof. He saw with relief that the chest containing his grandfather's body stood against the far wall, beside the stone sarcophagus that had been prepared so long ago to receive it. It had made the long voyage up from Bombay and the Cape of Good Hope safely. He went to the coffin, laid his hand on the lid and whispered, 'Welcome home, Grandfather. You will be more comfortable here than in that cave in a far and savage land.'

Then he passed down the line of stone tombs until he reached the one in the centre. He stopped before it and read the inscription aloud: 'Elizabeth Courtney, wife of Henry and mother of Dorian. Taken by the sea before her full flowering. Rest in peace.'

486

'Dorian is not here today. But he will be soon,' he said aloud. 'I swear it.'

He went on to the tomb of his own mother, stooped over it to kiss the cold marble lips of her effigy. Then he knelt before it. 'I am safe home, Mother, and Guy is well. He is in India now, working for John Company. He is married. You would like Caroline, his wife. She is a pretty girl, with a lovely voice.' He spoke to her as though she were alive and listening, and he stayed beside her sarcophagus until the sunbeam on the stone walls had made its full circuit and at last winked out, leaving the vault in semi-darkness. Then he groped his way up the stairs and out into the dusk.

He stood and gazed down upon the darkling landscape he remembered so well, but which now seemed so alien to him. Beyond the rolling hills he saw the distant sea. It seemed to beckon to him from beyond the twinkle of lights that marked the harbour. He felt as though he had been away for a lifetime, but far from being content, he felt restless, consumed with the need to move on. Africa was out there, and that was where his heart longed to be.

'I wonder,' he whispered, as he started down the hill, 'if I will ever be happy in one place again.'

As he reached the bottom of the hill the pile of the house was only a dark shadow looming in the evening mists that drifted across the lawns. Tom stopped abruptly below the ha-ha wall as he glimpsed a ghostly figure beneath the outspread branches of one of the old oak trees that stood dark and massive upon the lawns. It was a female figure, dressed all in white, and Tom felt a stir of superstitious awe, for it appeared ethereal and wraith-like. There were many legends of the ghosts that haunted High Weald. When he and Guy were boys their nurse had frightened them with those tales. 'I'll not be bettered by any ghost,' Tom resolved, gathered his courage and strode towards the white girl. She seemed oblivious of his approach until he was almost upon her. Then she looked up, her face frightened, and he saw it was his sister-in-law, Alice. The moment she recognized him she gathered up her skirts and fled towards the house.

'Alice!' he called and ran after her. She did not look back but increased her pace. He caught up with her on the gravel drive below the façade of the house, and grabbed her wrist. 'Alice, it's me, Tom,' he said. 'Don't be alarmed.'

'Let me go,' she said, in a terrified tone, and looked up at the windows of the house, which were already glowing cheerfully with yellow candlelight.

'You wanted to speak to me,' he reminded her. 'What is it you want to tell me?'

'Not here, Tom. He will see us together.'

'Billy?' Tom was puzzled. 'What can he do?'

'You don't understand. You must let me go.'

'I'm not afraid of Black Billy,' he told her, with youthful arrogance.

'Then you should be,' she said, pulled her hand free and ran lightly up the steps into the house. Standing in the middle of the carriageway with both hands on his hips, Tom watched her go. He was about to turn away when something made him look up.

His elder brother stood at one of the tall bedroom windows on the second floor. The light was behind him so he was merely a slim, elegant silhouette. Neither of them moved for a long moment, then Tom made an impatient dismissive gesture and followed Alice into the house.

Tom was in his bedchamber when he heard a faint sound that was out of place even in the old house with its creaking timbers and windswept roof. He stood still, with his stock half tied, and cocked his head to listen. After a few seconds the sound came again, like a rabbit in a snare, the wail of distress high and plaintive. He went to the window and opened the latch. When he threw wide the shutters the night breeze off the sea rushed in, and the cries were stronger. He recognized them as human. It was a woman's weeping, punctuated by deeper male tones.

Tom leaned out of the window. Now he could hear that the sounds came from the floor below, where the main bedchambers were situated. Abruptly the voices fell silent, and he was about to close his window again when he heard the sound of a blow. It must have been a heavy one to carry so clearly, and Tom's heart tripped as the woman cried out again. This time it was a scream of pain so high and clear that he could not mistake who had uttered it.

'The swine!' he blurted out, and whirled to the door. In his shirtsleeves, his stock loosening, its ends dangling down his chest, he raced along the passage to the staircase, and bounded down, three steps at a time.

As he reached the door to his father's apartment he hesitated. The double doors stood wide open and the curtains of the four-poster bed across the room were drawn aside, so he could see Hal's figure lying under the embroidered bedclothes. He was propped up on the pillows, and he called urgently to Tom as he passed the open doors. 'No, Tom. Come here!'

Tom ignored his summons and ran on to the doors of William's apartment further down the passage. He tried the handle but it was locked, so he hammered on it with his clenched fists. 'Open up, damn you, Billy!' he bellowed. There was a long silence beyond, and he filled his lungs to shout again, when the door opened quietly and William stood in the opening, blocking it with his body so that Tom could not see past him. 'What is it you want?' William asked. 'How dare you come yelling at the door to my private rooms.' He was also in shirtsleeves, but his face was darkly flushed, with anger or exertion, and his eyes burned with fury. 'Get away with you, you impertinent puppy.'

'I want to speak to Alice.' Tom stood his ground stubbornly.

'You have already spoken to her once this evening. Alice is busy. You cannot see her now.'

'I heard someone cry out.'

'It was not here. Perhaps you heard a gull, or the wind in the eaves.'

'There is blood on your shirt.' Tom pointed at the tiny scarlet specks on his brother's white sleeve. William looked down and smiled coldly through his anger. Then he brought out his right hand from behind his back and sucked the cut on his swollen knuckle. 'I caught my hand in the cupboard doors.'

'I must see Alice.'

Tom made to push past him, but at that Alice's voice called urgently, 'Tom, please go away. I cannot see you now.' Her voice was gusty with tears and pain. 'Please Tom, listen to my husband. You cannot come in here.'

'Now do you believe me?' William asked scornfully. 'Alice will not talk to you.' He stepped back and closed the door.

Tom stood indecisively in front of it. He lifted his hand to knock again, but his father's voice stopped him. Hal was calling again. 'Tom, come here. I want you.'

Tom turned away from the door and went to stand beside the four-poster bed. 'Father, I heard—'

'You heard nothing, Tom. Nothing.'

'But I did.' Tom's voice was tight with outrage.

'Close the doors, Tom. There is something I must say to you.' Tom did as he was told, then came back to the bed.

'There is one thing you must remember for the rest of your life, Tom. You must never interfere between a husband and wife. Alice is William's chattel, he can do with her as he wishes, and if you try to step between them he is within his rights to kill you. You heard nothing, Tom.'

When he went down to supper Tom was still seething

with anger. Three places were set at the long polished table, and William was already seated at its head.

'You are late, Thomas,' he said, and he was smiling, relaxed and handsome, with a heavy gold chain around his neck and a bright ruby brooch hanging on his chest. 'We sit down to supper at eight o'clock at High Weald. Please try to abide by the custom of the house while you are a guest here.'

'High Weald is my home,' Tom protested coldly. 'I am not a guest.'

'That is a matter for debate, but I hold the contrary view.'

'Where is Alice?' Tom looked pointedly at the empty place on William's left-hand side.

'My wife is indisposed,' William answered smoothly. 'She will not be joining us this evening. Please take your seat.'

'It is passing strange, but I find myself without appetite. There is something hereabouts that has put me off my food. I will not be dining with you this evening, brother William.'

'As you wish.' William shrugged, and turned his attention to the stemmed glass the butler was filling with red wine.

In his present mood Tom could not trust himself to spend the night in the same house as his brother. He threw on a cloak and stormed down to the stables. He shouted for the grooms, who came tumbling down the ladder from their quarters in the loft above and saddled one of the horses for him. Tom galloped the first mile, standing in the stirrups and driving his mount on through the night. The night air cooled his rage a little, so he took pity on the horse and reined him in to a trot along the Plymouth road.

He found Aboli with Luke Jervis in the taproom of the Royal Oak near the harbour. They welcomed him with unfeigned pleasure, and Tom drank the first pot of ale without taking it from his lips or drawing breath.

At one stage of the evening he climbed the back stairs to a small room, overlooking the harbour, with a pretty, laughing lass who helped him when he lost his balance and steadied him when he almost fell back down the stairs.

Her naked body was very white in the lamplight, and her embrace was warm and engulfing. She laughed in his ear as she clung to him, and he spent his anger on top of her. Later, she giggled and waved away the coin he offered her.

'I should be the one who pays you, Master Tom.' Nearly everyone in the town had known Tom since childhood. 'What a darling boy you've grown into. It's been many a month since my porridge pot was so well stirred.'

Much later Aboli prevented him from accepting a challenge to arms from another over-refreshed seaman, and dragged him out of the tavern, helped him up onto his horse, and led him swaying in the saddle, singing lustily, to High Weald.

Early the next morning Tom rode up onto the moors with one of his saddle-bags bulging. Aboli was waiting for him at the crossroads, a dark, exotic figure in the thick mist. He wheeled his horse in beside Tom's. 'I think the good burghers of Plymouth would have preferred an attack by the French rather than your last visit.' He looked sideways at Tom. 'Do you not suffer still from last night's alarms and excursions, Klebe?'

'I slept like the innocent child I am, Aboli. Why should I suffer?' Tom tried to smile but his eyes were bloodshot.

'The joy and folly of youth.' Aboli shook his head in mock wonder. Tom grinned, put the spurs to his mount and sent him soaring over the hedge. Aboli followed him and they galloped over the brow of the hill to where a grove of dark trees nestled in the fold of ground beyond. Tom pulled up, jumped down, tied his horse to one of the branches, then strode into the field of ancient stones that stood in the grove. They were mossy with age, and legend said that they marked the graves of the old people who had been buried here back in the infancy of time.

He chose a propitious spot among them, allowing his feet, not his head, to guide him. At last he stamped his heel into the damp turf. 'Here!' he said, and Aboli stepped forward with the spade in his hand. He drove the blade deep into the soft earth and began to dig. When he paused for breath, Tom took his turn and stopped when the hole was waist-deep. He climbed out of it and went back to where he had tethered his horse. He unbuckled the flap of his saddle-bag and carefully lifted out a cloth-wrapped burden. He carried it back and set it down on the lip of the hole they had dug. He unwrapped the cloth from the jar. Through the glass, al-Auf glared back at him with one sardonic eye.

'Will you say the prayer for the dead, Aboli? Your Arabic is better than mine.'

Aboli recited it in a deep, strong voice that echoed weirdly in the dark grove. When he fell silent Tom rewrapped the jar, hiding its grisly contents, and laid it in the bottom of the grave they had prepared for it. 'You were a brave man, al-Auf. May your God, Allah, pardon your sins, for they were many and grievous.' He closed the grave and stamped down the loose soil. Then he packed the green sods over it to hide the disturbed earth.

They went to the horses and mounted. From the saddle, Aboli looked back into the grove for the last time. 'You killed your man in single combat,' he said softly, 'and you have treated his corpse with honour. You have become a warrior indeed, Klebe.'

They turned the horses' heads and rode together down the moor towards the sea.

I t was as though Hal Courtney had realized that the hour-glass of his life was dribbling out the last grains of sand. His thoughts dwelt much on death and its trappings. From his bed he sent for the master stone-mason from the town, and showed him the design he had drawn for his tomb.

'I know full well what you want of me, my lord.' The mason was grey and grizzled, with the stone dust etched into his pores.

'Of course you do, John,' Hal said. The man was an artist with chisel and mallet. He had carved the sarcophagus for Hal's father and for all his wives. It was fitting that he should do the same for the master of High Weald.

Then Hal ordered the funeral of his father to be conducted by the Bishop. His body would be laid to rest at last in the sarcophagus that John, the master mason, had prepared for it almost two decades before.

The chapel was filled with the family and all those who had known Sir Francis Courtney. The servants and labourers from the estate, dressed in their best clothes, filled the back pews and overflowed into the churchyard.

Hal sat in the centre of the aisle, in a special chair that the estate carpenters had adapted for him, with high sides to steady him and handles at each corner so that he could be carried about by four sturdy footmen.

The rest of the Courtney family sat in the front pew. There were a dozen cousins, uncles and aunts as well as the closer relatives. William was in the seat nearest his father and Alice sat beside him. This was the first time she had appeared in public since the night Tom had tried to force his way into their private apartments. She was dressed in mourning black, with a dark veil covering her face. But when she raised the corner of it to dab at her eyes, Tom leaned forward and saw that the side of her face was swollen, a deep cut in her lip was covered with a black scab and an ugly old bruise on her cheek had faded purple and green. She sensed Tom's eyes on her and hurriedly dropped the veil.

In the pew on the other side of the aisle sat the guests of honour: four knights of the Order of St George and the Holy Grail. Nicholas Childs and Oswald Hyde had come down from London together. Alice's father, John Grenville, Earl of Exeter, had ridden across from his own vast estates, which bordered High Weald, with his younger brother Arthur.

After the ceremony, the party returned to the big house for the funeral banquet. The family and the guests of honour ate in the great dining room, while trestle tables groaning with food and drink were set up in the stableyard for the peasantry.

Hal's hospitality was so bountiful, the offerings from the cellars of High Weald so copious, that before the afternoon was out two peers of the realm were forced to retire to their rooms to rest. The Bishop was so overcome by the exigencies of his office and the fine claret that he had to be assisted up the main staircase by two footmen, pausing on the landing to dispense blessings on the mourners gathered below to watch his progress.

The revellers in the stableyard, after freely availing themselves of the pots of foaming cider, took advantage of the hedgerows and haystacks for similar purposes, and others less sedate. Mingled with the snores of the imbibers were the lusty rustle of hay, the giggles and happy cries of young couples otherwise occupied.

At dusk the four knights of the Order came down from their rooms in various stages of recovery from the mourning banquet, and climbed into the waiting carriages. The small cavalcade left the house, and followed Hal and Tom in the leading carriage back up the hill to the chapel.

In the vault, the ceremonials of the Order had been set out in the crypt. The mosaic design on the floor was in the shape of the five-pointed star and in the centre were three bronze cauldrons containing the ancient elements of fire, earth and water. The flames from the brazier danced on the stone walls and cast weird shadow shapes in the corners beyond the lines of stone tombs.

Hal's chair stood ready to receive him at the door of the chapel. Once he was seated in it, his brother knights carried him down the steps into the vault and set down the chair in the centre of the pentacle, with the three cauldrons surrounding him.

Tom, wearing the simple white robes of an acolyte, waited alone in the nave of the chapel above, praying before the altar in the light of the torches in their brackets set high on the walls. He could hear the voices of the knights murmuring and echoing softly from the vault below, as they opened the Lodge in the first degree. Then there was a heavy footstep on the stone stairs as the Earl of Exeter, Tom's sponsor, came up to summon him.

Tom followed him down the stairs, to where the other knights were waiting for him within the sacred circle. Their swords were drawn and they wore the gold rings and chains of their offices as Nautonnier knights, the navigators of the first degree of the Order. Tom knelt at the border of the pentacle and begged for entrance. 'In the name of the Father, the Son and the Holy Ghost!'

'Who would enter the Lodge of the Temple of the Order of St George and the Holy Grail?' his father challenged him, in a gusty voice, like a man saved from drowning.

'A novice who presents himself for initiation to the mysteries of the Temple.'

'Enter on peril of your eternal life,' his father invited

him, and Hal's gentle tone made the warning more poignant. Tom rose to his feet and stepped over the mosaic marble pattern that marked the boundaries of the mystic circle. He had not expected to feel anything, but suddenly he shivered as though an enemy had marked his grave with the thrust of a sword into the earth.

'Who sponsors this novice?' Hal asked, in the same reedy voice. The Earl spoke up boldly. 'I do.'

Hal looked back at his son, and his mind wandered away to the hilltop in the savage, untamed land far below the equator where he had made his own vows so long ago. He looked out of the circle to the stone sarcophagus, which at last held his own father's body. He smiled almost dreamily as he considered the continuity, the enchanted chain of the knighthood that linked one generation to the next. He felt his own mortality creeping towards him like a man-eating beast stalking him from the darkness. It will be easier to meet the dark one when I have placed the future firmly in the hands of my sons, he thought, and it seemed then that he could see that future merging with the past and evolving before his eyes. He saw shadowy figures he recognized: the enemies he had fought, the men and women he had loved and who were long dead, mingling with others whom he knew had not yet passed into the mist of days to come.

The Earl reached out gently and placed a hand on Hal's bowed shoulder to call him back to the present. Hal roused himself and looked at Tom again. 'Who are you?' He began the long catechism.

'Thomas Courtney, son of Henry and of Margaret.'

Hal felt the tears rise in his eyes at the mention of the woman he had loved so dearly. The melancholy was deep in his soul. He felt an exhaustion of the spirit, and he wanted to rest, but he knew he could not until he had completed the tasks appointed to him. He roused himself once more and offered Tom the blade of the blue Neptune sword, which he had inherited from his own father. The light of the torches danced on the gold inlay of the blade and glowed in the depths of the sapphire on the pommel. 'I call on you to confirm the tenets of your faith upon this blade.'

Tom touched the blade and began the recital: 'These things I believe. That there is but one God in Trinity, the Father eternal, the Son eternal and the Holy Ghost eternal.'

'Amen!' said the Nautonnier knights together.

The question and answer continued, while the torches guttered. Each question adumbrated the code of the Order, taken almost entirely from that of the Knights Templar.

The catechism outlined the history of the Templars. It recalled how in the year 1312 the Poor Knights of Christ and the Temple of Solomon had been attacked and destroyed by the King of France, Philippe Le Bel, in connivance with his puppet Pope Clement V of Bordeaux. The Templars' vast fortune in bullion and land was confiscated by the Crown, and their master was tortured and burned at the stake. However, warned by their allies, the Templar mariners slipped their moorings in the French Channel harbours and stood out to sea. They steered for England, and sought the protection of King Edward. Since then they had opened their Lodges in Scotland and England under new names, but with the basic tenets of the Order intact.

At last all the questions had been asked and answered. Tom knelt, and the knights formed a circle around him. They laid one of their hands on his bowed head, the other on the hilt of the Neptune sword. 'Thomas Courtney, we welcome you into the Grail Company, and we accept you as a brother knight of the Temple of the Order of St George and the Holy Grail.'

They lifted him to his feet and one after the other embraced him. This was all part of the ancient ritual, but as Tom stooped to kiss his father, Hal departed from the time-honoured form. He placed the hilt of the Neptune sword in Tom's hand and closed his fingers over it. 'It is yours now, my son. Wield it with courage and honour.'

Tom knew that the beautiful blade was one of his father's most prized possessions. He could find no words then to express his gratitude but he stared deep into Hal's eyes. He saw that his father indeed understood the silent message of love and duty he was trying to send him.

After the funeral guests and the four knights of the Order had left, High Weald seemed silent and deserted. Alice spent most of her days in her private apartment. Tom saw her once, riding alone on the moors, and though he watched her from a distance he remembered the consequences of their last brief encounter and did not approach her.

William was engrossed in the management of the estate, and passed his days at the offices of the tin mine, conferring with his steward, or riding around the estate making unannounced appearances, with the object of catching malingerers and wrong-doers among his servants. Misdemeanours were punished with the whip and instant expulsion from the estate. He returned to the house in the evenings to spend an hour with his father before the punctual eight o'clock supper. He ate alone, for Alice did not join him and Tom found excuse to eat in his room or at one of the local taverns where, with Aboli and Luke Jervis, Ned Tyler and Alf Wilson, he could find more convivial company.

As the months passed Tom grew increasingly restless and impatient. While William was out of the house he spent the greater part of each day with his father. He carried Hal down to the library and sat him on his chair at the head of the long oak table, then brought down from the crowded shelves the books and maps for which Hal asked. They spread them on the table and pored over them earnestly, discussing the details of the voyage that Tom knew his father would never make.

Master Walsh, with a pair of newly purchased spectacles perched on his nose, sat at the far end of the table and took down the notes Hal dictated to him. They drew up detailed inventories of the stores and equipment they would need, and watch-bills for the men who would crew the ships of the expedition back to the Indian Ocean.

'Two ships,' Hal decided. 'Not as large as the *Seraph* or the *Minotaur*. Fast, handy vessels, but well armed, for we will certainly have to fight the pagan again. Not too deep a draught, as we will probably have to take them up the estuaries and rivers of the Fever Coast.'

'I will send Ned Tyler and Alf Wilson to look for ships that will suit us,' Tom cut in eagerly. 'They can ride along the coast and call in at every harbour between Plymouth and Margate. But with war raging on the Continent, the right ships will not be easy to find.'

'If you have gold to pay for them, you will be amazed at how easy they will be to find,' Hal demurred. 'If I have to spend every farthing of the prize we took from al-Auf to win back Dorian from the Arabs, it will be money well spent.'

'We could put a notice in a broadsheet,' suggested Master Walsh.

'A good suggestion!' Hal said.

'We could also ask Lord Childs for a Company ship.' Tom looked up from the chart.

'No!' Hal shook his head. 'If Childs knows we are taking a squadron back into the domain of John Company, he will do his best to prevent us. The Company is strongly opposed to what they call interlopers trading, or even sailing, into their territory.'

Day after day they continued with the planning and discussions. Then, fifteen days after Tom had despatched them along the coast, Ned Tyler and Alf Wilson returned with news that they had found a ship. It was ideal for the task, but the owners were asking the criminally exorbitant sum of seven thousand pounds for her. They had with them a letter of acceptance for Hal to sign, and a request from the owners that they be paid by a banker's draft.

Hal questioned the pair keenly on the condition and standing of the ship, then closed his eyes and sat in silence for so long that Tom became alarmed. 'Father!' He jumped up from his chair, and went to Hal's side. He touched his cheek and found that it was burning with fever. 'His lordship is not well. Give me a hand, lads. We must take him up to his bed.' Even Master Walsh grabbed a handle of the chair, and between them they rushed Hal up the stairs.

Once he was safely laid in the big bed, Tom sent Aboli down to Plymouth to summon Dr Reynolds from his lodgings in the town. Then he dismissed Ned Tyler and the others, and sent them to wait below. When they were gone he locked the doors to the bedchamber to be alone with his father. He turned back the bedclothes and, with trepidation, began to unwrap the bandages from the stumps of his legs.

By this time Hal was flushed with the sudden fever in his blood, and muttering incoherently in delirium. When Tom lifted off the last cloth he saw that the scar had burst open again, and that the discharge was pouring yellow from the open wound. The familiar cloying odour filled the chamber, and Tom knew that, once again, the deep corruption had flared up, but this time more virulently than ever before. The entire stump was riven with scarlet lines as though it had been lashed with a whip. Dr Reynolds had warned him of this symptom, and now he groped with trembling fingers in his father's groin, afraid of what he might find. The glands were swollen hard and lumpy as walnut shells, and Hal moaned in agony when Tom touched them.

'It is the gas gangrene,' Dr Reynolds confirmed when he arrived. 'This time I cannot save him.'

'Can you not cut it away?' Tom shouted at him. 'Can you not drain the corruption like you did before?'

'It has gone too high.' Reynolds traced, with his fingertips, the furious red lines that were appearing over Hal's lower belly even as they stared at it.

'You must be able to do something,' Tom pleaded.

'It burns through all his body like a fire in dry grass. Your father will be dead by morning,' Reynolds told him simply. 'You should send for your elder brother to pay his last respects.'

Tom sent Aboli to find William, but he was down the main shaft of the tin mine at East Rushwold. Aboli waited until evening when Hal's eldest son returned to the surface. When he heard of his father's sudden turn for the worse, William galloped back to the house. He burst into Hal's bedchamber with such a show of concern that Tom thought it might readily be mistaken for eagerness.

'How is he?' William demanded from Dr Reynolds.

'It grieves me to tell you, but his lordship is sinking fast.'

William ignored Tom, and went to kneel at the far side of the bed. 'Father, it's William. Can you hear me?' Hal stirred at the sound of his voice but did not open his eyes.

'Speak to me,' William insisted, but Hal's breathing was shallow and light.

'He is going,' William said.

Tom looked up at him sharply. He thought he had detected a note of satisfaction in his tone. 'Not long to wait now, Billy,' he agreed, his tone expressionless. 'By morning you should be Lord Courtney.'

'You are a despicable little toad,' William snarled. 'I will make you pay for that gibe in heavy coin.'

Neither spoke again for an hour, then suddenly William rose from his knees. 'It's eight of the clock, and I am famished. I have not eaten all day. Will you come down to supper?'

'I will stay here.' Tom did not look at him. 'He may wake and need us.'

'Reynolds will call us. It will take only a minute to come up from the dining room.'

'You go, Billy. I will call you,' Tom promised, and William went stiffly to the door.

He was back within half an hour wiping his lips with the napkin he carried. 'How is he now?' he asked, with a touch of diffidence in his voice.

'He has not missed you,' Tom answered. 'Do not worry, Billy. He cannot disinherit you for taking a good supper.'

They settled down for the long vigil, one on each side of the bed and Reynolds stretched out fully dressed on the bed in the dressing room, snoring softly.

The big house seemed to be holding its breath, and outside the night was so still and quiet that Tom could hear the clock in the steeple of the chapel on the hill chiming the passage of the hours. When it struck one in the morning he looked across at William on the opposite side of the four-poster. His head had slumped forward onto the bedcover, and he was breathing heavily.

Tom laid a hand on his father's brow. It's a little cooler, he thought. Perhaps the fever is receding again as it has so often before. For the first time that night he felt a small lift of hope.

His father stirred at his touch and opened his eyes. 'Are you there, Tom?'

'Here I am, Father,' Tom replied, trying to make his tone joyous. 'You are going to be well. We will sail together again as we planned.'

'I will not be coming with you, lad.' Hal had admitted at last what Tom had known all along. 'This is a voyage you will have to make on your own.'

'I wish—' Tom began, but his father groped for his hand.

'Don't waste time denying it,' he whispered. 'There is little time left. Give me your word you will find Dorian for me.'

'I give you my word, as I gave my solemn oath to Dorry.'

Hal sighed and closed his eyes again. With a flare of alarm Tom thought the worst, but then he opened them again. 'William? Where is William?'

The sound of his own name roused William, who lifted his head. 'I am here, Father.'

'Give me your right hand, William,' Hal demanded. 'And you, Tom, give me yours.' They gave them to him, and he went on, 'William, you know what terrible fate has befallen your youngest brother?'

'Yes, Father.'

'I have charged Tom with the duty of finding him, and rescuing him. Tom has accepted that duty. Now I charge you also. Are you listening, William?'

'Yes, Father.'

'I lay on you the solemn duty that you will do all in your power to help Tom with his quest to rescue Dorian. You will provide him with the ships he needs. You will pay for the crews, the stores and all else. You will not stint him, but you will make good the manifest that Tom and I have drawn up together.'

William nodded. 'I understand what it is you wish, Father.'

'Then swear it to me,' Hal insisted, his voice rising. 'There is little time left.'

'I swear it,' William said, quietly and sincerely.

'Thank God for that,' Hal murmured. He lay for a

while as if gathering his strength for one last effort. But he clung to their hands with surprising strength. Then he spoke again. 'You are brothers. Brothers should never be enemies. I want you to forget the old disputes that have torn you apart and, for my sake, become brothers in the full sense.'

William and Tom were silent, neither looking at Hal nor at each other.

'It is my dying wish. Please grant it to me,' Hal begged.

Tom spoke first. 'I am ready to forget what is past. In the future I will give William the respect and affection he deserves.'

'I can ask for no more,' Hal gasped. 'Now it is your turn, William. Swear it to me.'

'If Tom keeps to that promise, I will return the same respect and affection,' William said, without looking across at Tom.

'Thank you. Thank you, both,' Hal whispered. 'Now stay with me this little time that we have left together.'

The night was long. More than once Tom thought Hal was dead, but when he listened at his father's lips he heard the soft sigh and hiss of his breathing. Then he must have dozed for the next he heard was the crowing of the cocks in the stableyard. He started guiltily and looked across at William and saw that he was slumped half across the bed, snoring softly. The lamp had burned out, but the first pale glimmer of dawn showed beyond the curtains.

Tom touched his father's face and, with a terrible stab of grief, felt that the skin was cold. He moved his fingers to search his throat for the pulse of the carotid. There was nothing, no flicker of life.

I should have stayed awake. I failed him at the last. Tom leaned over and kissed his father's lips. Tears coursed down his cheeks, and dripped on to Hal's face. He used a corner of the sheet to wipe them away, and kissed him again.

He waited for almost half an hour, until the light in the bedchamber was stronger. Then he examined his own face in the mirror on the far wall, to make certain that he had full control of his grief. He did not want Black Billy to see him so unmanned. He reached across and shook his elder brother. 'Wake up, Billy. Father is gone.'

William lifted his head and stared at him, dazed. In the dim light of dawn his eyes were bleary and unfocused. Then he looked down at Hal's pale face. 'So it's over at last,' he said. He stood up stiffly and stretched. 'Sweet Jesus, but the old rogue took his time. I thought he would never move over for me.'

'Father is dead!' Tom thought he had not understood. Not even Black Billy could be so callous.

'We'd best call Reynolds to make certain of that, and then seal him up in his fancy new tomb before he changes his mind.' William smiled at his own grim humour, then bellowed for the surgeon, who came stumbling through from the dressing room, still half asleep. Swiftly he examined Hal, listened at his mouth for breathing, then ran his hand inside his nightshirt to feel for his heart. At last he shook his head and looked up at William. 'Your father is indeed gone, my lord.' Tom was stunned by how swift and simple it was. Billy was now Baron Dartmouth. 'Do you wish me to order the laying out and other preparations for interment, my lord?'

'Of course,' William said. 'I will be engaged. There is much that I have to see to. I will have to go up to London as soon as possible.' He was talking to himself now, rather than to the others. 'I must take my seat in the House of Lords, then meet Master Samuels at the bank—' He broke off, and looked at Tom. 'I want you to make the arrangements for the funeral. It's time you started to earn your keep.'

'I would be honoured.' Tom tried to shame him, but William went on without check.

'A quiet funeral, just the immediate family. We will get it over as soon as possible. The Bishop can do the honours, if we can keep him sober long enough. A week from today,' he decided abruptly. 'I leave the details to you.' He stretched again. 'By God, but I'm hungry. I will be at breakfast if you need me.'

There was no time for all of Hal's brother knights to assemble for his funeral. The Earl of Exeter and his brother were the only ones close enough to attend. However, the officers and men who had sailed with Hal straggled in from every corner of the county and every seaport along the coast. Some walked fifty miles to be there. Ned Tyler, Alf Wilson and Luke Jervis found pews near the front of the chapel, and the common sailors and labourers from the estate crowded the nave and overflowed outside.

'I will not spend my hard-earned guineas on food and drink for every loafer and tippler in the land,' William decided, and paid only for the hospitality offered to his invited guests. From his own prize money, Tom purchased funeral meat and drink for the men who had come to honour his father.

Two days after Hal's body had been sealed in the new stone tomb in the vault of the family chapel, William took the coach up to London, and was gone for almost three weeks. Before he left, he sent Alice and the baby to her father. Tom was certain that this was to prevent him speaking to her. He found the empty house so oppressive that he took rooms at the Royal Oak and spent his days there with Ned Tyler, Alf Wilson and Master Walsh, planning the final details of the expedition to find Dorian.

Working from the watch-bills and manifests that he and Hal had drawn up, he prepared a budget to present to

William on his return to High Weald. Time was running against Tom, for autumn was once again coming on apace. He had little more than three months to equip and man the ships, cross the Bay of Biscay and reach the more clement southern waters before the gales of winter blocked his passage. 'It will cost us another year of waiting if winter catches us,' Tom fretted. He spoke for the stores they needed from the chandlers, and pledged his word against the return of William. The credit of the new Lord Courtney was good as any banker's. He hired a large warehouse at the docks to store the goods, then sent Ned and Aboli to call up the men they needed. After the triumph of their last expedition, there was little trouble in finding the best crew, all of whom who had sailed on the *Seraph*. Most had already spent their prize money, and were eager to take a berth with Tom.

Ned Tyler and Alf found the second ship they needed, and haggled the best price for her. However, the owners refused to hand over either ship until they had been paid in full. Tom had to curb his impatience.

At the end of September William returned from London to High Weald. He came in triumph: he had taken his seat in the House of Lords and had been presented at court. He had been the guest of Lord Childs at Bombay House for his entire stay in the city. Childs had sponsored his entry to fashionable London society, had introduced him to the halls of power, and had prevailed upon him to take a seat on the board of governors of John Company. Using the prize money he had inherited, William had increased his investment in the Company to 7 per cent of the issued share capital, to make himself one of the five major shareholders after the Crown.

The gossip in the town was that Alice had come back with him from her father's house, and it was said too that she was expecting another infant.

As soon as he heard of William's return, Tom rode up

from the town to High Weald, excited and eager to discuss his plans for the expedition with his brother. He carried two metal despatch cases in his saddle-bags. In them were all the papers he had assembled over the past weeks of waiting: the deeds of purchase of the two ships, the bills from the chandlers and suppliers of ships' stores and trade goods.

He arrived at the big house in the middle of the morning, to find that William was already closeted in the library, in consultation with his bailiff. Tom was astonished to find a throng waiting their turn to see Lord Courtney. They crowded the entrance lobby and, at a rough count, Tom made it sixteen in all. Most of them he knew. There was the family lawyer, John Anstey the high sheriff of the county, overseers and engineers from the mine, and the mayor and senior aldermen from the town. The others Tom did not recognize, but he greeted them all politely and chatted with Anstey while he waited for his brother to see him.

When noon struck, he decided that William did not know he was waiting with the others so he sent a note through with Evan, the steward, who returned almost immediately, looking uncomfortable. 'His lordship says he will call you when he is ready to see you. In the meantime you are to wait.'

The afternoon passed slowly. At intervals Evan came to summon the others through to the library. By the evening Tom was the last one left.

'His lordship will see you now, Master Thomas,' Evan said apologetically.

Carrying a despatch box under each arm, and trying to conceal his irritation at the way in which he had been treated, Tom went through to the library. He found William standing at the fireplace, his hands clasped behind his back, lifting the tail of his coat to present his backside to the warmth of the flames.

509

'Good afternoon, William. I hope that you have had a successful visit to London. I heard of your presentation at court. I offer you my congratulations.' He placed the despatch boxes on the library table.

'How kind of you, brother.' William's tone was distant. At that moment Evan returned with two goblets on a silver tray, and offered one first to William. Then he came to Tom, and as Tom took the other goblet, Evan asked him, 'Will you be staying to supper this evening, sir?'

Before Tom could reply, William cut in, 'I think not, Evan. Master Thomas will not be staying long. I am sure he has plans to dine with his rough friends in the town.'

Both Tom and Evan stared at him in astonishment, but he went on smoothly, 'That will be all, thank you, Evan. Supper at eight o'clock as usual. I do not want to be disturbed before then.'

He sipped the cognac and raised an eyebrow as he glanced at the black-painted tin despatch boxes. 'I am sure that you did not come merely to congratulate me.'

'I have for your approval the manifest for the expedition. Also the bills for the expenses I have already incurred.'

'What expedition?' William pretended puzzlement. 'I do not remember asking you to run up any bills on my behalf. Perhaps I misheard you.'

'Your undertaking to our father.' Tom tried not to show that he was put out by the denial. 'I have almost completed the preparations.' He opened the boxes and laid out the documents in neat piles down the length of the table. 'These are the watch-bills. I have found one hundred and fifty good seamen. That's all the crew I will need. Every man jack of them sailed with our father, and I know them well. I can answer for every one.'

William stayed at the fireplace. There was a small enigmatic smile on his lips, but his eyes were cold.

'These are the bills of sale for the two ships. I have

510

inspected both. They are ideal for our purposes, and I have managed to beat down the owners' asking price by almost four thousand pounds.' He looked up at William, but his brother remained silent. Tom waited a while for him to speak, and when he did not he went on doggedly. 'This is a complete manifest of the stores and equipment we will need. I have already purchased most of it, and I have it stored in Patchley's warehouse at the docks. I am afraid I was forced to pay high prices. The Admiralty is buying up all available stores to equip the navy. Powder and shot, rope and sails are in desperately short supply. Prices have more than doubled since the beginning of the war.'

He waited for William to reply, then said lamely, 'I have given my word on the payment. I will need the money for these bills, and notes for the owners of the ships at once. The rest can wait a while.'

William sighed, crossed to one of the leather chairs and threw himself into it. Tom started to speak again, but William cut him off by bellowing for one of the parlourmaids.

'Susan!'

She must have been waiting outside the door, anticipating his call, for she came at once. Tom knew her. She had been a child when he sailed with his father, but in his absence she had grown into a pretty girl, with dark ringlets peeping out from under her cap and sparkling blue eyes with naughty lights in them. She dropped Tom a quick curtsy, then ran to answer William's call.

William lifted one of his legs. She took it between her own legs with her bottom pointed towards him, and seized his boot at toe and heel. She used the grip of her knees to prise it off his foot. When the boot slid off William wriggled his stockinged toes and gave her the other foot. She repeated the process, but as the boot came free William thrust his foot up under her petticoats. She squealed playfully and blushed scarlet. 'My lord!' she cried, but instead of pulling away she bent a little further over to let him explore with his toes as he wished.

After a minute, William laughed. 'Go on with you, you saucy little baggage.' He pulled his foot out from under her skirts, placed it firmly on her rump and gave her a playful shove towards the door. She scampered away, looking back archly over her shoulder as she closed the door.

'When you are done with exercising your rights as master of High Weald, may we return to the business of the expedition?' Tom asked.

'Please go on, Thomas,' William invited, with a wave of his hand.

'Will you consider the list of costs?'

'Damn me, Thomas. Don't tire me with your lists. Come straight out and tell me how much you are begging for?'

'I am begging only for that my father promised to me.' Tom was having difficulty controlling his temper. 'The two ships are the main expense—'

'Speak out!' William snapped. 'Chase the fox into the open. How much is it?'

'In all it amounts to a little over nineteen thousand pounds,' Tom said, 'but that includes trade goods. I will trade along the coast for ivory, gold, copper and gum arabic. I expect to turn a handsome profit—' He broke off as William began to laugh. It started as a chuckle, then escalated to a full belly laugh. Tom stood and watched him, wrestling with his temper. William was choking on his mirth, and had to gasp for breath before he could go on.

At last Tom could conceal his irritation no longer. 'Perhaps I am slow, but I am not certain what it is that amuses you so, brother.'

'Yes, Thomas, you are slow. It has not yet penetrated to the depths of your thick skull that I am now the master of High Weald and that you are beholden to me for every penny, not to our father's shadow.'

'What I need is not for myself. It's for Dorian. It's for the oath you swore to our father,' Tom said grimly. 'You gave him your word. You are oath-bound.'

'I think not, Thomas.' William stopped laughing abruptly. 'At the end Father was in delirium. He was wandering in his mind. If I said anything, it was merely to placate him. I had no serious intent. It would be folly to squander my inheritance on the whim of a dying man. Nineteen thousand pounds! You must have lost your senses if you think for one minute that I will hand that sum of money over to you so that you can go chasing off to the end of the world. No, dear brother. Put it out of your head.'

Tom stared at him speechlessly. 'You are going back on your solemn word? Billy, I am not chasing off for my own pleasure. We are talking about the rescue of your own brother from the hands of the infidel.'

'Don't call me Billy, not ever again.' William lifted his goblet and swigged the last drops of the cognac.

'No, I agree that there are better names for you than that. Cheat? Twister? What else would you call the man who denies his own younger brother and goes back on an oath to his father?'

'Don't address me in that disrespectful tone!' William hurled his goblet into the fireplace. It shattered. He got to his feet and advanced on Tom menacingly. 'You will have to learn your place, or I will beat it into you.' His face was dark with rage.

Tom stood his ground. 'As you beat it into Alice?' he asked bitterly. 'You are a fierce, hard man when it comes to bullying servants and women, brother. You are a prince of liars when it comes to breaking your word and cheating on your sworn obligations, too.'

'You little turd.' William's face had turned dark red

513

and seemed now to swell. He was no longer handsome and debonair. 'You will not speak like that of my wife.'

Tom had found the weakness, the way to reach and wound him. 'Have a care, Billy. Alice might hit back. You would be no match for her in a fair fight. You might be reduced to beating her baby. That should give you real pleasure. Turning little Francis's face purple and blue with your whip.' He was watching his man, poised on his toes, his fists clenched at his sides, watching William's eyes to read his intention, ready to meet him when he attacked.

'Tom, please, Tom.' To Tom's astonishment, William's face crumpled. The anger flowed out of him and he looked distraught. 'Don't say that. Please!' His shoulders sagged, and he held out his hands towards his brother in appeal. 'You are right, I owe a duty to our father's memory. We promised to set aside our differences.' He came towards Tom with his right hand outstretched. 'Here's my hand on it, Tom. Come, take it.'

Tom was thrown off-balance by this sudden change in William. He hesitated, but his anger and outrage were subsiding and William was smiling at him warmly. And what he had said was true: they *had* promised their father. He forced himself to relax and, awkwardly, he put out his own hand to take William's. His brother gripped it firmly, and smiled into Tom's eyes. Then suddenly, with all his strength, he heaved Tom towards him. At the same time he lowered his chin and butted the top of his head into Tom's face, catching him across the bridge of the nose.

Tom's vision exploded in a burst of flashing light, and he felt the cartilage in his nose crack. A wash of blood shot from both his nostrils, and he reeled backwards. But William still had a grip on his right hand, and again he pulled him forward. William was left-handed and this was his strong side. Tom's vision was starred with fireballs of light and he was dazed. He did not see the fist coming. It cracked into the side of his head and sent him flying backwards over the library table. The sheafs of paper on the tabletop scattered like leaves in a high wind, and Tom smashed into the floor on his shoulder-blades. Though he was half stunned, he was already scrabbling at the floor-boards in an effort to get back on his feet and into the fight.

But William jerked the dagger from the sheath on his hip, and launched himself over the table as Tom came up on his knees. Through his fractured vision Tom saw the glint of the blade, and hooked up under it with his forearm, deflecting it from the centre of his chest where it was aimed. The point scraped over the top of his shoulder, slicing through his waistcoat. Tom barely felt the sting of the steel, before William's weight hit him squarely and they went over together, chest to chest. Tom grappled for his wrist as William tried to stab the dagger into his eye, and they rolled across the polished floorboards, first one on top then the other.

'I'll cut your liver out,' William grunted, and changed the angle of his thrusts. Tom had to rally all his scattered wits and strength to hold him off. The point of the dagger was inches from his face. Even though William had led the sedate life of a gentleman these last three years, his wrestling skill and muscle seemed unimpaired.

They crashed into the bookcase at the end of the room. At that moment Tom was on top, and he used the brief instant of respite to slam his brother's dagger hand into the sharp edge of one of the oak shelves. William yelped, and his grip on the hilt slackened. Tom used all his strength to repeat the blow. He saw blood spring up across William's knuckles where they hit the wood, but he did not loose the dagger. Again Tom pounded his fist against the edge of the shelf and this time William gasped with the agony, his fingers opened and the weapon slipped from them.

Neither of them could reach for it without loosing his

515

grip on the other. For a moment, they matched strength, then Tom curled up his legs under him and started to rise. William came up with him. They were standing now, chest to chest, gripping each other's wrists. William tried to swing Tom off his feet, but he stood solid. He tried again and Tom went with the swing, using the impetus to fling William into the bookshelves. Loaded with heavy books, they reached almost to the high ceiling of the room and William crashed into them with such force that an entire section came free of the wall and swung down on top of them. An avalanche of leatherbound volumes cascaded down on the pair, and the falling shelves gathered momentum. Anyone trapped under them would be crushed under their weight. They realized this simultaneously and sprang apart. As they scrambled aside the shelves thundered down in a chaos of splintering wood and glass.

Panting, they confronted each other over the wreckage. Blood bubbled from Tom's broken nose and dribbled down his shirt-front. But his vision and strength came back to him, and with them his rage. 'You were ever the cheat, Billy. You king-hit me.'

He started forward, but William whirled and ran to the display of military arms hanging upon the far wall. There were steel shields, surrounded by hundreds of edged weapons arranged in decorative patterns, collected by the Courtney ancestors from every battlefield on which they had fought. William snatched down a heavy sword that had been used by a Cavalier officer in King Charles's cavalry. 'Now we will finish this once and for all,' he said grimly, as he turned on Tom. He cut and thrust at the air with the long blade, to test its balance and feel.

Tom retreated slowly before him. He could not reach the far wall and select a weapon of his own, neither could he escape through the double doors. To do so he would give William his chance. He thought of the dagger his brother had dropped, but that was buried under the books.

With his sleeve, he wiped the blood from his face and backed away.

'Ha! Ha!' William shouted, and came on faster, driving at him with a rapid series of lunges. Tom was forced to jump away, twisting and dodging. William was working him towards the corner furthest from the door.

Tom saw the trap, but when he tried to break out, his brother blocked him, cutting right and left at his head, forcing him back once more. Tom was evaluating his style and expertise. He saw that he had not improved since the days when he had watched him practising with Aboli. William was still a better wrestler than a bladesman. His eyes gave away his intention, and although he was as swift as a striking adder on the thrust and the left-handed cut, he was weak on the reverse cut and tardy on the recovery from a thrust.

Now he charged in suddenly, underestimating his unarmed adversary. Tom gave with a series of quick-running steps backwards, watching his eyes. His back came up hard against a section of bookshelf that was still standing, and he saw the triumph in William's dark eyes. 'Now, sir!' He thrust high in the natural line, and Tom let him commit to the stroke before he rolled his body away from it. The thrust went under his armpit, and the blade sank into the spine of a book on the shelf behind him. Briefly the blade was trapped, but Tom did not make the mistake of trying to wrestle it from his grip and lacerating his hands on the razor steel. While William struggled to free it, Tom stooped quickly and gathered up one of the heavy books from the floor at his feet. He hurled it into William's face. It struck him on the forehead, but as he staggered back the blade came free.

As Tom bounded past him William struck out at him, but he was slow on his weak side and still off-balance. The point touched Tom's flank and drew more blood, but it was a flesh wound, and Tom was past. He started for the wall display of weapons, but he heard the soft slither of William's stockinged feet close behind him. Instinctively he knew that William would catch him before he could get another sword down off the wall, and that he would receive a killing thrust into his unprotected back. He changed direction and heard William swear as he slipped on the polished floor – his stockings gave him no purchase.

Tom reached the table and snatched up the massive silver candlestick from the centrepiece. Holding it in front of him, he whirled to face William's next charge. His brother raised the sword high and hacked at Tom's head. It was a poor stroke, one that would have been fatal folly if Tom had had a sword in his hand. Tom raised the candlestick and the blade clattered against the soft metal. He knew that the shock had jarred his brother's hand. William winced and gasped, but raised the sword to repeat the wild overarm stroke.

Quicker on the recovery, Tom swung the silver candlestick like a battleaxe into William's ribs under the raised sword. He heard a bone break, like a green stick, and William shouted with the pain, but though his aim was thrown askew he could not stop the blow he had already launched. It hissed past Tom's head and buried itself in the tabletop, shattering the magnificently grained walnut.

Tom hit him again with the candlestick, but William ducked, avoiding the full force of the blow. Still it sent him staggering back to trip on the pile of books. He almost went down but, with a wild windmill of his right arm, recovered his balance. Tom had darted away towards the door and William went after him again, cutting left and right at his back, the blows falling just short.

Tom raced for the door out into the hall, and through it saw his sword-belt hanging in the alcove where Matthew had hung it for him when he entered the house. The great sapphire in the pommel flashed at him like a harbour beacon welcoming a gale-blasted ship.

As he ran through the open doors he reached out and slammed one shut in William's face. William blocked the swing of the door with his shoulder and threw it back, but the check had given Tom just enough leeway to cross the hall and tear down his sword-belt from the rack. He whirled and used the engraved and lacquered scabbard to block William's next wild thrust. He leaped back and, before William could follow up, he had drawn the steel of the blue Neptune sword out of its scabbard.

The blade came clear with a soft snick and quivered in his right hand like a beam of solid sunlight. The reflections danced on the walls and the ceiling above where he stood four-square to face William on equal terms at last. William came up short as the inlaid steel weaved like a standing cobra in his face and winked gold sparks into his eyes.

'Yes, brother. Now we will finish this, once and for all.' Tom threw William's threat back into his teeth, and came forward, staring deep into his brother's dark eyes, right foot leading, taking light, rapid steps. William gave ground before his advance and Tom saw fear bloom in his eyes. He realized what he had known all along: William was a coward.

Why should I be surprised? he thought grimly. Bullies are usually cowards. To test him, he attacked en flèche, the attack of the arrow, driving in a storm of rapid thrusts. William almost fell over backwards in his haste to avoid the flashing blade.

'You are quick as a frightened rabbit, brother.' Tom laughed in his face, but he was holding himself in check, never relaxing his vigilance. The frightened leopard is the most dangerous. There was also danger in facing a left-handed bladesman. All the coups were reversed and he might lay himself open to the left-handed cut from William's strong side. Fortunately, Aboli had emphasized this during so many practice sessions. Aboli was ambidextrous

519

and he had often changed his sword into his left hand in the middle of a bout, shifting the symmetry of the engagement, trying to throw Tom off his stroke. In the beginning he had succeeded, but Tom had been an apt student.

William stumbled and slipped, dropped to one knee. It looked natural, but Tom had seen his eyes and the way his blade had drifted back into position for the left-handed cut in the low line – a stroke that would sever Tom's Achilles tendon and cripple him. Instead of stepping into the snare, Tom jumped back and circled swiftly into his weak quarter.

'You waste your talents, brother.' Tom smiled through the blood of his broken nose. 'You might have an illustrious career at the Globe.'

William was forced to scramble to his feet as Tom came in again from the right, and drove him back to the foot of the grand staircase with a fierce series of cuts and thrusts, changing his angle and line with each blow. William was hard put to block each successive stroke: his breathing turned ragged and his eyes filled slowly with terror. The sweat popped out in little transparent blisters across his forehead.

'Don't be afraid, Billy.' Tom smiled at him over the darting steel. 'It's like a razor. You'll hardly feel it go in.' His next thrust split open the front of William's shirt without cutting the ivory-smooth skin beneath. 'Just like that,' Tom said. 'No pain at all.'

William reached the staircase and whirled. He went up it with long elastic bounds, three treads at a time, but Tom was after him, gaining with every stride. William heard him and was forced to turn to defend himself on the first landing. He reached instinctively for the dagger on his belt, but the sheath was empty.

'It's gone, Billy,' his brother reminded him. 'No more dirty little tricks. You'll have to fight with what you have.'

To begin with William had the advantage of height as

Tom came up from below him. He went for the overhead slash, but it was not the stroke to attempt on a bladesman of Tom's calibre. He blocked it with a dead hit, and trapped the blade as he came up onto the landing to face him. They strained together, their weapons locked before their eyes.

'When you're gone, Billy, the title will pass to little Francis.' Tom tried not to let the strain distort his voice, but William was powerful in the shoulders and their blades trembled and shook with the pressure each was applying.

'Alice will be his guardian. She would never let Dorian down,' he said, and threw William away from him with a heave of his shoulders. At the same time he stepped back and dropped the point to the level of his brother's throat. 'You see, I have to kill you, Billy, if only for Dorian's sake.' And he lunged for William's throat. It was a mortal stroke, but to avoid it William hurled himself backwards wildly. He crashed into the banisters behind him, which gave way with a splintering crackle of timbers.

William fell in a tangle of limbs into the entrance hall ten feet below. He hit the boards with a shuddering crash, and the sword flew from his grip. For a moment, the wind was driven from his lungs and he lay on his back, dazed and helpless.

Tom jumped over the shattered banisters, and dropped feet first, bracing himself in mid-air with cat-like grace to land lightly, breaking the force of his fall with a flexing of his legs and going down on one knee before springing up again. He kicked away William's sword, sending it skidding across the floor to the far wall. Then he stood tall over William's sprawling body.

He placed the point of his blade at the base of his brother's throat, in the V of his white shirt-front, where the crisp black hairs of his chest curled out of the opening.

'As you said, Billy, once and for all. It's over between us,' Tom told him grimly, and began the death thrust. Yet it was as though a steel manacle was holding back his sword hand. He pricked the skin at William's throat, but could not go deeper. He tried again, exerting all his strength, but a force outside himself held back the blade.

He stood over William, a terrible blood-splattered figure, the sword trembling in his hands and his face distorted into an ugly mask by his rage and frustration. *Do it!* The voice of his resolve rang in his ears, and again he tried to stab downwards, but his right arm would not obey. *Do it! Kill him now. For Dorry's sake, if not your own.*

Then the echo of his father's voice overrode the murderous command. 'You are brothers. Brothers should never be enemies. I want you to forget the old disputes that have torn you apart and, for my sake, become brothers in the full sense.'

He wanted to shout back, 'I have to do this.'

William lay on his back pinned under the blade, and tears of terror filled his eyes. He opened his mouth to plead for his life, but no words came, only a dreadful croak like the cry of a raven.

Tom felt the muscles and sinews of his right hand bunching with the effort he had to make to force them to obey his will, and the point moved down an inch and pierced the soft skin. Bright blood welled up from the shallow scratch and William squirmed. 'Please, I will give you the money, Tom,' he whispered. 'I swear it. This time I will give you the money.'

'I can never trust you again. You have broken one sacred oath. You are beyond the call of honour,' Tom said, and his revulsion for his brother's cowardice and perfidy gave him the strength to carry through the dreadful deed. This time his right arm would obey.

'Tom!'

A dreadful cry rang through the silent house. For a moment Tom thought it was his mother's voice, from beyond the grave. He looked up. A wraith-like figure stood at the head of the stairs, and Tom was seized by a superstitious dread. Then he saw that it was Alice with her infant in her arms. 'No, Tom. You must not kill him.'

Tom wavered. 'You don't understand. He is evil. You yourself know he is the very devil.'

'He is my husband, and Francis's father. Don't do it, Tom. For my sake.'

'Both you and the baby will be better off with his death.' Tom turned his attention back to the creature who lay, craven and whimpering, at his feet.

'It's murder, Tom. They will hunt you down, wherever you run, and they will find you and drag you to the scaffold.'

'I don't care,' Tom said, and meant it.

'Without you, there will be nobody to go to Dorian. For his sake, if not for mine, you must not do this evil thing.'

The truth of what she said struck Tom like a blow in the face, and he flinched at the sting of it. Then he stepped back.

'Go!' he ordered, and William scrambled to his feet. Tom saw there was no fight left in him. 'Get out of my sight.' His voice was thick with disgust. 'And remember next time you raise your hand to your wife that she saved your life this day.'

William backed away to the stairs and then, when he was at a safe distance, he turned, ran up them, and disappeared down the long gallery.

'Thank you, Tom.' Alice looked down at him with tragic eyes.

'You and I will live to regret this,' Tom told her.

'That is in God's hands.'

'I have to go away,' Tom said. 'I cannot stay here to protect you.'

'I know that.' Her voice was a resigned whisper.

'I shall never return to High Weald,' he went on doggedly.

'I know that also,' she agreed. 'Go with God, Tom. You are a good man, as your father was.' She turned and vanished around the corner of the gallery.

Tom stood for a while, considering the enormity of what he had just said. He would never return to High Weald. When he was dead, he would not lie in the vault of the chapel on the hill with his ancestors. His grave would be in a far and wild land. He shivered at the knowledge. Then he stooped to gather up his sword-belt and scabbard where he had dropped them. He strapped the Neptune sword around his waist.

He looked through the doors into the library. His papers were scattered over the floor. He went into the old room, and was about to gather them up, when he stopped himself. There will be no call for those now, he thought darkly. Slowly he looked around the room. It was filled with wonderful memories of his father. Another tie with his childhood would part here. Then his eye fell on the row of his father's journals on the shelf beside the door, the faithful record of all Hal's voyages. Each page, written in his hand, contained sailing directions and information more valuable then any other item in the house Tom was leaving for ever. That much I will take with me, he thought. He swept them off the shelves and went out into the hall.

Evan, the house-steward, and two of the footmen were waiting there. Evan had a cocked pistol in each hand. 'His lordship has sent for the sheriff's men. He has ordered me to detain you until he arrives, Master Tom.'

'So, what are you going to do, Evan?' Tom laid his hand on the hilt of his sword.

'Your horse is waiting outside, Master Tom.' Evan

lowered the pistols. 'I hope you find Master Dorian. All of us at High Weald will miss you. Come back to us one day.'

'Goodbye, Evan.' Tom's voice was gruff. 'Thank you.'

He went down the steps, put the journals into his saddle-bags and sprang up into the saddle. He turned the horse's head towards the sea, and rode down the long gravel drive. At the gates he resisted the urge to look back. 'It's over,' he told himself, 'it's all over,' and he spurred on, down the dark road.

Tom decided not to wait for the sheriff's men to come for him with the charges he knew William would trump up. He found his men in the taproom of the Royal Oak. They stared in astonishment at his bloodstained clothing and broken nose. 'We will sail immediately,' he told Aboli, Ned Tyler and Alf Wilson. Then he looked across at Luke Jervis on the far side of the fireplace. Luke owned the tiny *Raven* and was his own man, but he nodded his acceptance of the order without demur.

When they were about to slip the lines from the dock, a lone horseman came pounding down Plymouth Ho at a gallop. He almost fell over the horse's neck as he reined in. 'Wait for me, sir!' Tom smiled as he recognized Master Walsh's voice. 'You cannot leave me behind.'

A small group of the old stalwarts gathered on the open deck as the *Raven* slipped out into the night sea. 'What course, sir?' Luke asked as they cleared the headland.

Tom looked longingly towards the south. Down there lay Good Hope and the gateway to the Orient. Oh, for a ship, a real ship and not this cockle-shell, he thought, then turned firmly from that direction. 'London,' he said. His voice was blurred for his nose was swollen and blocked. 'I will pay you for this voyage,' he added. He still had most of his prize money in Samuels Bank in London.

'We will settle that later,' Luke grunted, then shouted the order to his three-man crew to tack the little cutter on to an easterly heading.

The *Raven* slipped quietly up the Thames and into the Pool of London, drawing no attention in the busy throng of small craft. Luke set them ashore with their meagre baggage on the stone wharf below the Tower of London. Aboli found cheap lodgings in the mean streets alongside the river.

'If fortune favours, we will need these rooms for only a few days.' Tom looked around the dingy wooden shack.

'We will need good fortune to survive the rats and cockroaches,' Alf Wilson remarked, while Tom changed into the best clothes he had brought with him. The dark blue coat and breeches, not too fancy, gave him a sober, businesslike appearance.

'I will go with you, Klebe,' Aboli volunteered. 'You will probably lose your way without me.'

The day was cold and rainy, a forerunner of autumn. It was a long walk through the maze of narrow streets, but Aboli threaded his way through them as unerringly as if they had been his native forests. They came out at the Cornhill end of Leadenhall Street, and crossed to the imposing façade of the Company headquarters. 'I will wait for you at the tavern on the corner,' Aboli told Tom as they parted.

When he entered the foyer of the building one of the secretaries recognized Tom, and greeted him respectfully. 'I will see if his lordship will receive you,' he said. 'In the meantime will you wait in the parlour, Mr Courtney.'

A uniformed footman took Tom's boat cloak, and brought him a glass of Madeira. While he sat in an easy chair before the crackling fire, Tom rehearsed the appeal he intended to put to Nicholas Childs. He could be reasonably certain that Childs had not yet heard from brother William. Unless he had become clairvoyant, William would not expect him to call here, so he was unlikely to have sent an urgent message to Childs to warn him not to offer Tom assistance.

On the other hand, Tom had realized the futility of asking Childs for command of a Company ship. There were many captains of vast experience and long service who would take precedence over him. Tom had never had his own full command, and Childs would never give him one of the magnificent Indiamen. The best he could expect was a berth as a junior officer on a ship bound for India, and Dorian was in Africa.

As he turned the problem over Tom frowned into the fire and sipped his wine. Lord Childs knew all about Dorian's capture – in fact, Tom had heard him discussing it with Hal when they were guests at Bombay House. If Tom asked for a ship he would realize his intention of going after his captured brother, instead of trading for profit. Furthermore, if Tom procured any other vessel, Childs would do his best to prevent him even rounding the Cape. Hal had said that the Company was bitterly opposed to interlopers in their chartered territories. No, best to feign disinterest in that part of the world. I'll take the skin off this cat from the tail end, he decided grimly.

Lord Childs kept him waiting less than an hour, which Tom took as a mark of high favour. The chairman of the board of the East India Company was probably one of the busiest men in London, and Tom had arrived without invitation or warning.

On the other hand I am a brother knight of the Order, and my family owns 7 per cent of the shares in the Company. He cannot guess that, only days ago, I came close to slitting Billy's throat.

The secretary led him up the main staircase, and

through the antechamber to Childs's office. The furnishings bespoke the Company's vast wealth and circumstance. The carpets underfoot were of lustrous silk and the paintings that hung upon the panelled walls were imposing seascapes depicting the ships of the Company in full sail off the exotic shores of the Carnatic and Coromandel coasts. When Tom passed under a chandelier that looked like an inverted ice mountain and entered the inner chamber through carved and gilt doors, Lord Childs rose from his desk and came to meet him. This was enough to allay any misgivings that Tom still might have about his reception. 'My dear young Thomas.' Childs clasped his hand and, with thumb and forefinger, gave him the recognition grip of brother knights of the Order. 'This is a pleasant surprise.'

Tom gave him the counter-sign. 'My lord, it is gracious of you to receive me at such short notice.'

Childs made a deprecatory gesture. 'Not at all. I am only sorry that I was forced to make you wait. The Dutch ambassador . . .' He shrugged. 'I'm sure you understand.' Childs wore a full wig and the star of the Garter on his gold-embroidered lapels. 'How is your dear brother, William?'

'In the best of health, my lord. He asked me to convey his deepest respects.'

'I was most sad not to be able to attend your father's funeral, but Plymouth is so far from London.' Childs led Tom to a chair below the tall windows that looked out over the rooftops to a distant view of the river and its shipping. 'A remarkable man, your father. He will be greatly missed by all of us who knew him well.'

For a few minutes more they exchanged pleasantries, then Childs leaned back and reached down over his ample midriff to haul the gold watch from his fob pocket. 'Bless my soul, 'tis past ten, and I am expected at St James's.' He stuffed it back into his pocket. 'I am sure you did not come here merely to pass the time of day.'

'My lord, if I may come to the point, I am in need of employment.'

'You have come to the right quarter.' Childs nodded so vehemently that his jowls wobbled like a turkey cock. 'The *Seraph* sails in ten days for the Carnatic. Edward Anderson is her master. You know both him and his ship, of course. He has a berth for a third officer, which is yours for the asking.'

'I had in mind something more – more warlike?'

'Ah, Mr Pepys is a personal friend of mine, and he knew your father. I have not the least doubt that we can find a berth for you on one of the men-o'-war. I think a fighting frigate might suit a young man of your temperament.'

'Again, sir, may I be blunt?' Tom interrupted apologetically. 'I have at my disposal a small cutter. She is very fast and handy, an ideal craft to raid French commercial shipping in the Channel.' Childs stared at him in astonishment, and Tom hurried on before he could refuse. 'I also have a crew of fighting seamen to serve her, some of the same men who served under my father on the *Seraph*. All I lack is a letter of marque to attack the French.'

Childs chuckled so heartily that his belly bounced on his lap like a rubber ball. 'The apple does not fall too far from the tree, does it? Like your father, you want to lead rather than follow. Of course, your warlike exploits are common knowledge. You should have al-Auf's severed head incorporated into the escutcheon of your coat-of-arms when you receive your own knighthood one of these fine days.'

Abruptly he stopped laughing, and Tom had a glimpse of the shrewd, calculating mind behind the benign blue eyes. Childs stood up and went to the window. He stood there, staring out at the river, until Tom began to fidget in his chair. Then it dawned upon him that the pause was deliberate. He said, 'My lord, I would want you to have a share of any prize I am able to take under this commission. I thought five per cent might be an appropriate expression of my gratitude.'

'Ten per cent might be even more appropriate,' Childs observed.

'Ten per cent indeed,' Tom agreed. 'And, of course, the sooner I can sail, the sooner I will be able to make good those ten points to you.'

Childs turned to him, rubbing his hands together briskly, his expression affable. 'I will be talking to certain personages at St James's this very morning, gentlemen who have commissions in their gift. Call upon me again in three days' time, that is Thursday, at ten of the clock. I may have news for you then.'

Those three days of waiting passed like a funeral procession, every minute filled with fears and misgivings. If William had taken the precaution of contacting all the powerful men he knew in London, all doors would close to Tom. Just enough time had elapsed since he had left High Weald for a messenger to dash all his plans.

Even if Childs could deliver a commission he had no ship and no crew, for he could not broach the subject with any of the men before he had the King's letter in his pocket. Luke Jervis had already sailed on another of his nefarious trips to meet a French counterpart somewhere in mid-Channel. This time he might run foul of the King's Excise men, and he might never return. The doubts gathered like circling vultures to plague not only Tom's waking hours but his dreams. When Luke did return, would he be willing to risk his little *Raven* in such a hazardous enterprise? He must already be a rich man, and Aboli had said that he had a wife and a brood of infants.

During those three days, his men looked at him expectantly, but Tom could offer them nothing. He dared not even tell them what Childs had promised, lest he raise their hopes too high. On the Thursday morning he slipped out of his lodgings like a thief, without even telling Aboli where he was going.

The clock in the steeple of the little church in Leadenhall Street had barely struck ten when Lord Childs's secretary came down to the visitors' parlour to summon him.

One glance at Childs's genial expression was enough to set at rest all the nightmares that had beset Tom. As soon as they had greeted each other and were seated face to face, Childs picked up the heavy parchment document from the desktop in front of him. Tom recognized the great red seal of the Chancellor of England at the foot of the single page. It was identical to the commission under which his father had sailed when the *Seraph* put out to sea. Childs read out the first line in a pedantic tone. 'Be it known by these presents that our trusty and well-beloved subject, Thomas Courtney . . .' He read no further, but looked up and smiled at Tom.

'By heaven's grace, you have it!' Tom interjected excitedly.

'I doubt that any other captain has received his commission with such despatch,' Childs remarked. 'This augurs well for our enterprise.' He emphasized the possessive plural as he set aside the commission, and picked up another document. 'This is a separate contract that embodies our agreement. I have left the name of the ship blank, but we should fill that in now.' He picked up a quill and sharpened the tip before he dipped it in the inkwell and looked up at Tom expectantly. Tom took a deep breath before he committed himself. 'The *Raven*,' he said.

'The *Raven*!' Childs wrote, in a stylish hand, and then looked up at Tom. 'Now I will need your signature.'

Tom barely glanced at the deed of joint venture before he scrawled his acceptance. Childs counter-signed, then sanded the page. Still smiling affably, he crossed to a side table on which stood a platoon of crystal decanters and poured two glasses to the rim. He handed one to Tom and saluted him with the other.

'Perdition to Louis the Fourteenth and a black pox on the French!'

Aboli haggled for a ferryman to row them upriver to where Luke Jervis had his moorings on a small island with the unlikely name of Eel Pie. From a cable's length they saw that the *Raven* had returned from her most recent jaunt and was tied up at the wooden jetty. As they closed the distance Luke came out of the cottage set among a stand of willow trees and sauntered out onto the jetty to meet them, leaving a thin stream of blue pipe smoke in the air behind him. Tom sprang ashore while Aboli paid the ferryman his sixpence. 'A profitable voyage, Master Luke?' he asked.

'The Excise men gave us a run off Sheerness. I had to toss three hogsheads of brandy overboard before we could give them the slip. All my profits for the last six months gone down to Davy Jones.' He rubbed the scar on his cheek and looked mournful. 'I think I'm getting too old for the game, Mr Courtney.'

'Perhaps I can interest you in something less taxing on your nerves,' Tom suggested.

Luke perked up noticeably. 'I thought you had something in mind. You remind me of your father. He was ever the man with an eye to the main chance.'

At that moment a woman appeared in the doorway of the cottage. Her apron was grimy from the cooking-fire and she carried a naked infant with a dirty bottom on her hip. The child clung with both hands to the soft white breast that dangled, limp as a spaniel's ear, from the opening of her blouse. 'Luke Jervis, don't you dare go off carousing with your riff-raff friends and leave me here with no food in the house and six hungry babes to feed!' she screeched, her hair dangling lankly down her face.

Luke winked at Tom. 'My little angel. Marriage is a fine and noble state. Too good for the likes of me, I oftimes think.'

The woman shrieked, 'It's time you looked for honest work, instead of sneaking away in the night and coming home with some cock-and-bull story about losing your coin, when I know full well you've been lying at anchor with some poxy slut in Pussy Bay.'

'Do you have honest work for me, Mr Courtney? Any work that takes me well out of earshot of my good wife?'

'That is what I came to talk to you about.' Tom grinned with relief.

Three nights later, the *Raven* crept inshore of the French coast with a leadsman in the bows. 'By the mark five!' He called the depth softly, then opened the shutter of the lantern a crack to examine the tallow on the end of the lead to see what it had picked up from the sea bottom. 'Sand and shell!' he reported, little louder than a whisper.

'Huitre Bank.' Luke nodded in the dark, his position confirmed. 'That's Calais over to starboard, Honfleur beyond the headland.' His pronunciation of the difficult names was fluent. Tom knew from Aboli that he spoke the language like a native. 'The beach shoals in very gently here, and with this breath of wind from the east we'll be able to wade ashore without difficulty,' he told Tom. 'Be ready to drop over when I give the word.'

Tom had decided that only he and Luke would go ashore to scout the anchorage of Calais. Luke knew the ground and might be able to talk them out of any trouble they met. He had been tempted to take Aboli with them, but the smallest party was prudent, and Aboli's black face would be hard to pass off if they were challenged by a French patrol.

'By the mark two!' came the soft call from the bows.

'Ready now,' Luke murmured, and handed the wheel to his mate. He and Tom picked up their leather sacks and moved up to the bows. Both men were dressed in rough fishermen's clothes with clogs on their feet and leather jerkins over wool petticoats. Their heads were covered with wool caps. At that moment they felt the *Raven* take the bottom, a soft bump on the sandy beach.

''Vast heaving!' Luke whispered, to the men on the long sweeps, and they rested on the oars. He went over the side first and the water came to his armpits. Tom handed down the two sacks to him, then followed him over. The water was cold enough to take his breath away.

'Heave away!' the mate called quietly to the oarsmen, and the *Raven* backed slowly off the sand. Luke had chosen the incoming tide to make certain they would not be stranded. Within a dozen strokes the little boat had disappeared into the night, and Tom shivered again, not only from the cold. It was an eerie feeling to be alone on an enemy shore, not knowing what waited for them on the beach.

The water shallowed quickly and they came out on the hard wet sand and crouched there, listening. There was only the flop and hiss of the low surf, so they jumped up and hurried into the dunes. They rested there for a few minutes to listen again and catch their breath, then moved quickly through the dunes and low scrub towards the headland. Half a mile further along, they almost ran into the wreckage of an ancient shipwreck stranded above the high-water mark.

'It's the old *Bonheur*, a Breton coaster,' Luke told Tom. 'A good landmark for our return.' He dropped on his knees and scratched a hole in the sand under the bone-white ribs of the hull. Then he dropped one of the leather sacks into it and covered it with the loose sand. 'We'll find it here when we need it.'

They went on faster now, and climbed the headland. On the crest they moved slower, using the low salt scrub as cover, trying to keep out of sight as they searched for a hiding-place. They found one in the ruins of a stone-built structure that Luke said had been a French army block-house during the Dutch wars. It had been sited to give an unrestricted view over the approaches and the main anchorage. They scouted the area around the fort to make certain that it was deserted and that there were no signs of recent occupation before they settled in. From his sack Luke brought out a pair of pistols for each of them. They loaded them with fresh powder, checked the priming and laid them ready to hand. Then they waited for the dawn. Eventually, the eastern horizon turned lemon and rosebud pink and cast a lovely warm glow over the scene below them.

Even at this hour there was a swarm of activity around the fleet of French men-o'-war that lay at anchor in the harbour. Through the lens of his telescope Tom counted fifteen three-deckers, with eighty guns apiece, and a huge gathering of lesser ships. Many did not have their yards crossed and workmen swarmed over their decks.

The activity on shore was also brisk, and as soon as the sun rose out of the morning haze, they saw companies of troops marching into the town along the road from Paris. The sunlight glittered on the bayonets of their sloped muskets, and the feathers and ribbons in their tricorn hats bobbed and fluttered with each pace. A train of wagons was following, rumbling over the rutted roadway.

A little later a squadron of cavalry in gold-frogged jackets and blue capes with polished black high boots trotted out from the town. For a heartstopping moment Tom thought they were heading straight up the slope towards their hiding-place. He let out his breath in a sigh of relief as they turned away at the crossroads outside the town and rode southwards along the road, flanked on both sides with lines of poplar trees. Their dustcloud disappeared in the direction of Honfleur.

As the sun climbed higher, burning off the low cloud, and the light strengthened, Tom could concentrate his telescope on a search of the harbour. There were dozens of smaller craft among the warships. Some were lighters and barges taking out stores and men to the larger vessels. A barge flying warning flags rowed slowly to one of the three-deckers, riding low in the water under the high-piled kegs of black powder.

Other craft were tied up at the wharf or anchored higgledy-piggledy about the bay. Many were rigged fore and aft, with single mast and bowsprit. In smaller vessels this new arrangement of sails had some advantages over the more traditional square-rigged ships, and was becoming increasingly popular in all modern navies. They could be handled by fewer men and were faster on the wind. They were often employed as scouts and auxiliaries to the main battle fleet. An intermittent stream of these vessels and other small ships was coming and going in and out of the bay, all keeping well in-shore to avoid the attentions of the Royal Navy. The English fleet was blockading the main Channel ports, waiting for the French to sally forth in any strength. Out in mid-Channel Tom had caught an occasional glimpse of the distant sails of the English fleet. The *Raven* was also out there somewhere, waiting for nightfall before coming into the beach again and picking them up out of the shallows.

Tom turned his attention from the shipping out in the Channel and avidly studied the smaller French vessels in the anchorage. Most were much larger than the little *Raven*, and many were armed with small cannon. He picked out a dozen that might serve his purpose well, but then was forced to discard one after the other as he discovered their defects. Some were in a poor state of repair or too lightly armed, others were coasters and not suited to long voyages and heavy seas, still others did not have the burden to carry the cargo and men he required.

In the middle of the day Tom and Luke lay on their bellies in the warm sand and ate a meal of bread, ham and hard-boiled eggs that Luke produced from his sack, and they passed between them the flask of beer. Tom tried not to become despondent, but there seemed little here for them.

As the sun dipped towards the horizon he was left with a choice of two out of the dozens of vessels he had scrutinized. Then one of these hoisted her mainsail and tacked out to sea, by default leaving him with no option but a nondescript old drab of a cutter, which had seen better days and fairer times.

'She will have to do,' he decided unhappily, and they gathered up their pistols and equipment ready to retreat down to the beach as soon as it was dark. Suddenly Tom seized Luke's arm and pointed back towards the north. 'There she is!' he exulted. 'That's her!'

Greyhound lean and swift, a sloop came flying round the headland, then tacked neatly into the fairway and shot into the harbour. 'Look at her! She's heavily laden, you can see that from her waterline, but still she could turn fifteen knots on a virgin's fart,' Luke whispered, in awe of her beauty. She was flush-decked, no poop or forecastle. Her single mast was elegantly raked and proportioned to the length of her hull. Tom estimated that she was fifty foot overall.

'Ten guns!' Tom counted through his lens. 'Enough to frighten off any Arab dhow.'

She flew a gaff mainsail with a boom, from her square

yard a large topsail, and from her bowsprit two jibs. In the fading light she had a ghostly, ethereal appearance, a thing of wind and wave spume and sea fret.

'I love her already, and I don't even know her name.'

'We will choose a new name for her,' Tom promised him.

The sloop rounded up to the hard. Down came her canvas, and was whisked away like a wizard's trick. They strained their eyes to watch her tie up. Tom counted her crew, and made it nine, but he guessed she could accommodate thirty fighting seamen on a long voyage, although they might have to alter her lower deck to take so many.

'Mark her well, Luke,' Tom said, without taking the telescope from his eye. 'You must find her again in the dark.'

'She is burned into my eye,' Luke assured him.

In the last of the light they saw six men leave the ship and make their way down the wharf to where the lanterns in the windows of the taverns were being lit. 'You can smell their thirst from here. They'll not be back before dawn,' Tom whispered. 'That leaves only three men aboard.'

As the last of the light faded, they hurried back down the dunes to the beach. Luke dug out the other sack from under the wreck, and lit the lantern it contained with flint and steel. He pointed it out towards the sea and lifted the shutter, flashing three times. He waited a while then flashed again. On the fourth attempt his signal was answered with three short flashes out on the dark sea.

They waded out until the low surf was breaking into their faces, and when they heard the creak of oars out in the night Luke whistled sharply. Minutes later the *Raven* loomed over them. They reached up and pulled themselves on board.

Still dripping sea-water, Luke took the helm and they backed off from the shelving beach. As soon as he had sufficient water under her he set the mainsail and jib. Tom stripped naked and dried his body on the rough cloth Aboli handed him, then pulled on dry clothes. A league off-shore Luke hove the *Raven* to, and they squatted in a circle around a shaded lantern on the open deck.

'We have found a ship,' Tom told his men. Their faces were wolfish in the lantern light. 'But it's not going to be light winds and fair weather to take her out under the noses of the French.' He did not want them to become over-confident. 'We will wait until the middle watch, when they are tucked into their hammocks. Master Luke will take us into the harbour and lay us alongside the sloop. If we're challenged, Luke will answer for us, the rest of you hold your tongues.' He frowned at them to impress on them the need for silence.

'As we come alongside, I will give the word and lead the boarding-party. Aboli and Alf Wilson will help me clear the deck of the enemy. Most are ashore and look to be there all night. We should have no more than three men to deal with. No pistols, only clubs and fists. Use your blades only as a last resort. Silence is our main concern and a man with steel in his belly will squeal like a sow giving birth. Fred will throw off the head lines and Reggie the stern. Cut and run, lads, so have your jack-knives handy.'

Then Tom spoke to each man in turn, making him repeat his orders so that there would be no confusion in the dark. With Luke and his crew of three, there were fifteen of them; the rest were old salts from the *Seraph* whom Alf and Aboli had been able to gather at such short notice. More than enough to do the job.

'The wind is easterly, and Luke reckons it will strengthen before midnight. I didn't see them put gaskets on the main, so it should come free at a pull on the halyard.' Tom looked at Ned Tyler, his gnarled features highlighted by the yellow glow of the lantern. 'Mr Tyler, you will go to the helm, don't get into the fighting. Luke will lead us out in the *Raven*, he will show a shaded light over his stern.' When every man knew what Tom wanted of him, Tom checked their weapons and made sure every one had a club and knife. Tom would be the only man to carry a long blade. He strapped the Neptune sword around his waist.

He had made certain before they sailed that each of them was dressed in dark-coloured clothing, and now he passed the lantern round the circle, and they smeared the soot from the chimney on their faces and hands. There were the usual jokes about Aboli not needing this addition to his natural pigmentation, and then they settled down below the gunwales wrapped in their sea cloaks to eat some bread and cold meat, before trying to snatch a few hours' sleep.

At the end of the first watch Luke started to ease the *Raven* closer in-shore. With the off-shore breeze they could hear the sounds from the land quite clearly, and a church clock in the town struck twelve so loudly that they could count each stroke. Tom passed the word and they shook the sleepers awake – there were few of them: most were already tense and nervous.

They had to beat into the harbour against the breeze, but this was a price Tom was pleased to pay in exchange for a straight run out. Soon they were among the French fleet, passing so close to one tall three-decker that they could hear the anchor watch on her main deck talking drowsily. No one challenged them and Luke threaded the *Raven* quietly towards the stone wharf where they had last seen the sloop. Tom crouched in the bows, peering ahead for the first glimpse of the French vessel. There was always a chance that she had sailed or moved away from the wharf, but Tom prayed that most of her crew were still swilling ale in the taverns and that her captain intended waiting until morning to offload her cargo.

Slowly the *Raven* closed with the dark wharf, weaving her way between two anchored ships. Tom strained his eyes, cupping his hands to cut out reflected light from the lamps of the houses along the waterfront. Now he could hear laughter and singing from the alehouses, but the rest of the fleet was silent, showing only their riding lamps at the mastheads.

'She is gone!' Tom's spirits plummeted as they drew within half a pistol shot of where he had last seen the sloop, and there was still no sight of her. He cursed himself for not having taken the precaution of picking out a secondary target for just such an eventuality. He was about to call to Luke at the helm for him to sheer off, when his heart leaped and thudded against his ribcage. He had seen her bare main mast outlined against the dull glow of lamplight from the town, and he realized that with the low tide the sloop's hull had dropped below the level of the wharf so that it did not show up against the stonework.

'Still there, waiting for us!' He glanced back to make sure his men were ready. They were crouched, like him, below the gunwales. With blackened faces, they looked like untidily stacked cargo along the deck. Only Luke stood tall at the wheel. Now he spun it to full lock, and his mate at the halyard, without waiting for an order, let the mainsail come down with a soft rush. The *Raven* slowed and drifted in until she touched the side of the moored French vessel. The deck of the sloop was six feet higher than the *Raven*'s and Tom steadied himself to leap up onto her.

At the jolt of the two hulls coming together a sleepy French voice exclaimed, '*Nom de Dieu!*'

'I have a message for Marcel,' Luke answered, in the same language.

'There is no Marcel here,' the Frenchman protested irritably. 'You're spoiling my paintwork with your dung-boat.'

541

'I have the fifty francs that Jacques owes him,' Luke insisted. 'I will send one of my crew to bring it to you.'

The mention of such a large sum stilled any further protest, and the Frenchman's tone became cunning and ingratiating. '*Très bien*. Give it to me. I will see that Marcel gets it.'

Tom sprang over the *Raven*'s side and hauled himself lithely up onto the sloop's deck. The Frenchman was leaning over the rail, a woollen cap on his head and a clay pipe clenched between his teeth. He straightened and removed the pipe from his mouth. 'Give it to me.'

As he came across the deck, with hand outstretched, Tom saw he had a magnificent pair of twirling moustaches. 'Certainly,' he said and tapped the man above the left ear with a controlled swing of the club. Without a sound he went down in a heap. In the next second Aboli came over the side and landed like a panther on silent bare feet. Tom saw that one of the hatches in the bows was open, and that faint lamplight was reflected from below. He dropped down the companionway with Aboli close behind him. A lantern swung from gimbals in the deck overhead, and by its light Tom saw that three hammocks were slung across the far end of the cabin. He realized that he had miscounted the numbers of the French crew. As he crossed the cabin, a man sat bolt upright suddenly in the nearest hammock. '*Qui est là?*' he asked.

By way of reply Tom hit him with a full swing. The man fell back, but another shouted with alarm in the next hammock. Aboli swung it upside down and dumped him on the deck. Before he could shout again Tom swung his club and he collapsed. A third Frenchman leaped from the last hammock and tried to run for the companionway, but Tom seized his bare ankle and hauled him back. Aboli bunched one huge fist, slammed it into the side of the man's head, and he went down.

'Any more?' Tom looked around swiftly.

'That's the last.' Aboli raced up the ladder and Tom followed him up onto the deck. Fred and Reggie had cut the mooring ropes and the sloop was already drifting away from the wharf. The Frenchman's shout in the cabin must have been muffled and had not raised the alarm. The harbour seemed as quiet and somnolent as before.

'Ned?' Tom whispered, and the reply came instantly from the stern.

'Aye, Captain.' Even in the heat of that moment it gave Tom a thrill to hear the term of address. He had a ship and he was a captain once more.

'Well done. Where is the *Raven?*'

'Dead ahead. She's already under sail.'

There was some delay among the men at the halyards of the sloop's main mast. In the dark and on a strange, foreign ship, they were having difficulty sorting out the lines: the French used a different system of rigging. Tom ran to them and they set about the unravelling.

But the sloop was gathering stern way and drifting down rapidly on one of the anchored ships. Tom saw that they would crash into it with sufficient force to do damage. A Frenchman aboard the other ship shouted.

'Have a care, you stupid oafs. You're going to ram us.'

'Stand by to fend off!' one of Tom's crew said, in English.

There was an immediate shout from the other vessel. *'Merde! Ils sont Anglais!'*

Tom snatched the main halyard out of the tangle of lines. 'Smartly now! Heave!'

The mainsail soared up the mast, the sloop checked her sideways drift and picked up the breeze. She began to sail, but she still had weigh on her, and struck the anchored ship, dragged lightly along her side.

By now other voices were shouting, 'English! The English are attacking.'

A sentry on the wharf, rudely wakened from sleep,

fired his musket and immediately there was uproar through the entire anchorage. But Ned had the sloop sailing, picking up speed sweetly. When Tom looked ahead he saw the *Raven*, her stern lantern glimmering, heading down the fairway towards the open sea.

'Jib sheets!' Tom snapped, and led a rush of bare feet down the deck towards the bows. They were getting the hang of her sails now, and the jibs went up with only scant delay. Immediately the sloop heeled and leaped forward, the water rustled under her forefoot, and they began to overhaul the *Raven*. But the French fleet was coming awake, there were shouts from ship to ship, and on some battle lanterns were lit and running up the masts.

Inspired by the mounting turmoil, Tom ran to one of the sloop's guns. It was a toy compared to the huge armaments of the ships-of-the-line anchored all around them. He could only hope that it was loaded.

'Help me!' he called to Aboli, and between them they swung open the lid of the gunport and ran out the cannon. Tom looked up and saw that they were passing half a pistol shot from one of the ships-of-the-line, a mountainous seventy-four, that blotted out half the night sky above them. He did not even have to aim the little cannon, but merely fired as she lay. The lock sparked but there was a long moment as the weapon hung fire. Then, abruptly, it bellowed and leaped back against its tackle.

Tom heard the ball strike into the heavy planking of the warship with a crash. Wild yells of anger pursued them, but the sloop was running on. She was so low against the water that she was swiftly lost in the dark.

Somewhere further down the line another gun fired and Tom saw from the long flash of flame that it was aimed nowhere near them. He never knew where the shot struck. There were more shouts and then a stuttering of cannon-fire built up into a deafening fusillade as the big ships fired at the imaginary English fleet attacking them. Powder smoke drifted in a dense fog over the two smaller ships. They were almost obscured from each other, and Tom had to stare hard into the smoke to pick out the faint light of the *Raven*'s guiding lantern.

Swiftly the shouting and gunfire fell behind them and they sailed out of the smoke into a sweet clear night. He heard faint voices on the breeze, English voices, and he realized that the tiny crew of the *Raven* were cheering them. His own crew paused at their work with the sheets and cheered back. It was unwise to give any French pursuit a lead, but Tom did not try to stop them. He saw Aboli's teeth gleaming white in the darkness and he grinned back. 'Where are the Frenchmen?' he demanded, and the three bedraggled figures were dragged up from the cabin to join their captain in the stern.

'There's a skiff in the bows,' Tom said. 'We'll heave to, and put them into it. Send them home, with our best compliments.'

They bundled the four men into the little boat and cast them off. When he realized what was happening the French captain stood in the bows of the tiny craft, his moustaches bristling with fury, shaking both fists at them, and saw them off with a string of vituperation.

'Your mother was a cow, and she slipped you from the wrong hole, you lumps of wet turd. I piss in your mother's milk. I stamp on your father's testicles.'

'Speak English!' Luke shouted back. 'The beauty of your poetry is wasted on the night air.' And the captain's outrage faded swiftly into the darkness behind them.

Aboli helped Tom trim the mainsail and when it was drawing tight and hard, he said, 'She is yours now, Klebe. What will you call her?'

'What did the French christen her?' Alf Wilson leaned far out over the stern and craned down to read the name on her transom in the light of the stern lamp.

'*Hirondelle*. What does that mean?'

'The *Swallow*,' Luke translated.

'It's a good name,' they all agreed at once. 'God knows, she flies like a bird.'

'But not in that God-forsaken language,' Tom demurred. 'In sweet Mother English. The *Swallow*! We will drink her health when we tie up in the river.' And they gave her a cheer.

When the sun came up they were off Sheerness, and although she had all sail set the *Raven* was far astern, unable to keep up with the *Swallow*. The sloop was on a broad reach, ripping white bursts of spray off the tops of the pewter-grey waves as she tore through them.

'She loves to run free,' Ned rejoiced, his face creased into a hundred wrinkles of delight. 'You would have to hang a drogue over her stern to hold her back.'

In the sparkling morning light she was as pretty as a maiden in her wedding dress, her canvas so new and bright that it gleamed like mother-of-pearl. Her paintwork was so fresh Tom could whiff the turpentine, and her decks had been holystoned until they were white as a snowfield.

Tom turned his thoughts to the cargo they were carrying in the *Swallow*'s hold. He beckoned to Aboli and sent him to investigate. They lifted the hatches and Aboli and Alf Wilson went down with lighted lanterns into the dark holds. Half an hour later they emerged again, looking delighted with their discovery.

'She's stuffed to the gills with canvas cloth. The finest quality. Enough to clothe a squadron of ships-of-the-line.'

Tom's face lit as happily. He knew what prices that commodity would fetch in the Company's auction rooms. 'The sinews of war,' he declared. 'Good as gold!'

They offloaded the cargo of canvas at the Company's wharf, then Tom sent a note to Lord Childs and took the *Swallow* upriver to Luke's mooring at Eel Pie Island. He stayed long enough with his men to get them started on the work of altering the sloop's 'tween decks to accommodate a larger crew, and installing tiny cabins for the master and the three officers. These would be not much larger than cubbyholes, comprising a bunk, a sea-chest, the lid of which could be used as a writing-desk or chart table, and not much else. The headroom under the deck beams would force the occupant to bend almost double when entering and leaving.

Tom made plans to lay out the forecastle so that it would accommodate twenty men. He moderated his original estimate of the number of men he would need to sail and fight the ship in an emergency, and still carry a sufficient cargo of stores for a three-year cruise and trade goods to ensure a profit at the end of that time.

As it was, the conditions in the crew's quarters would be crowded even in fine weather when most of the men would sleep on the open deck, but in foul weather, when they were all forced below, it would become too cramped even for hardened old sea salts like the men Alf and Aboli had recruited.

Once the new interior had been planned and the carpenters put to work, Tom and Aboli hired a ferryboat to take them downriver. When they called at Leadenhall Street, the secretary told them that Lord Childs was at the House of Lords, and would be there all day. However, he had received Tom's note and was expecting Tom to call. His secretary handed Tom a note he had left.

My dear Thomas,

I was not expecting to receive word of your successes at such an early date. The cargo from your prize has already been sold to the Admiralty, and we have received a goodly price for the entire amount. I need to discuss this with you. Please attend me at the Lords, where a steward will bring a message to me in the House.

Your servant,

N.C.

Tom and Aboli made their way down the embankment to where the enormous edifice of government, the Palace of Westminster, stood on the bank of the Thames. The steward accepted the letter that Tom proffered at the visitors' door of the House of Lords, and he waited for a remarkably short time before Lord Childs, looking flustered and distraught, came puffing down the stairs and seized Tom's arm. Without any preamble he blurted out, 'Your brother, William, is in the House. I left him not ten minutes hence. You should have given me warning of the state of affairs that exists between you.' He shouted for his carriage. 'I think you should be warned that he is intent on retribution for the injuries you have done him.'

''Tis Billy who was to blame,' Tom started angrily, but Childs bundled him in through the door of the carriage as it drew up at the entrance. 'Bombay House!' he ordered the driver. 'As fast as you like.' Then he tumbled onto the seat beside Tom. 'Your boatswain can ride up with the footman,' he said, and Tom shouted to Aboli to climb on the footplate.

The carriage started off with a jerk, and Childs lifted his wig to mop his pate. 'Your brother is a major shareholder in the Company. Not a man to trifle with. He must not see us together. For the sake of good order, I have told him that I have had no dealings with you.'

'He cannot do anything to me,' Tom said, with more certainty than he felt. He had to cling to the side strap of the lurching carriage and raise his voice above the clatter of hoofs and the thunder of the steel-shod wheels over the cobbles.

'I think you underestimate the strength of your brother's animosity, Courtney,' said Childs, and he stuffed the wig back on his shaven head. 'No matter what the right and wrong of the situation, if a person in my position – dare I say a man of certain influence? – does not wish to fall foul of him, then how much more should you, a disinherited younger son, keep out of the path of his vengeance?' Childs was silent a little while, then said reflectively, 'I have seldom heard such malice, such pure venom, from any other human being.'

They were silent for the rest of the drive to Bombay House. However, when they drove in through the gates Childs leaned out of the window and called to the driver, 'Take us to the stables, not the main door.'

In the stableyard he led Tom to a small rear door into the mansion. 'I know your brother has spies out looking for you. It is best that he does not learn of our meeting today.'

Tom hurried after Childs along what seemed an endless series of passages and stairways, until he found himself in a small cabinet with tapestry-hung walls and a large ormolu and gilt escritoire in the centre of the floor. Childs waved him to a chair beside his own, then scrabbled through the documents that covered the top of the desk and picked out one. 'Here is the bill of sale of the cargo of canvas from the French sloop *Hirondelle* to the Admiralty.' He passed it to Tom. 'You will see that I have deducted the usual handling fee from the total.'

'Twenty per cent!' Tom burst out in amazement.

'It is customary,' Childs said briskly. 'If you care to reread our agreement, you will see it is covered in clause fifteen.'

Tom made a gesture of resignation. 'What about the *Hirondelle*, herself? Will you take your twenty per cent on her value also?'

They began to bargain, and Tom soon discovered why Nicholas Childs had risen so high in the world of trade and commerce. He had the sinking feeling that he was matched against a swordsman far out of his class. At one point Childs excused himself and left Tom alone for so long that he began to fidget and finally jumped up from the chair to pace the room impatiently.

Meanwhile, in the room next door Childs dashed off a long message on a sheet of parchment. While he sanded and folded it, he told his secretary quietly, 'Send Barnes to me.'

When the coachman stood before him, Childs said, 'Barnes, this message is for Lord Courtney at the House of Lords. You must see it safely into his hands. 'Tis a matter of life and death.'

'Very good, my lord.'

'When you return, I shall want you to take my guest and his servant to the river landing at the Tower of London. However, you are not to proceed there immediately. This is what you are to do . . .' Childs gave the driver detailed instructions, and when he had finished asked, 'Do you understand, Barnes?'

'Perfectly, my lord.'

Childs bustled back into the cabinet where Tom waited and made his apologies. 'Forgive me, but there were demanding matters to which I had to attend with despatch.' He patted Tom's arm genially. 'Now, back to business.'

By the middle of that afternoon Tom found that he

had the deeds of ownership to the *Hirondelle*, but that he would receive no monies from the sale of the cargo. In addition, Nicholas Childs had wanted to retain a 25 per cent interest in any future profits that Tom accrued under the commission Childs had procured for him. Tom knew that he was a chicken to Childs's fox, but he held out stubbornly.

The one thing Tom had in his favour was that Childs had not seen the *Swallow*, and the description he had been given did not do the sloop justice, so did not excite his avarice. Childs had no employment for such a tiny craft and Tom sensed that he was willing to let her go. He stood his ground and, in the end, Childs dropped his exorbitant demands, and agreed to deliver the deeds of the sloop to Tom clear of any impediment to the title. In exchange Childs retained the proceeds of the cargo.

Childs looked well pleased with his bargain, as well he should, Tom thought grimly. He wondered how he was going to be able to explain to the men who had fought to seize the *Hirondelle* in Calais Roads that they would not be seeing any monetary rewards for their efforts.

'You would be a wise man, Courtney, to leave England as soon as you can hoist a sail, and to stay at the ends of the ocean as long as your brother's memory lasts.' Childs smiled magnanimously. 'I am offering the means for you to escape from a dangerous situation with your hide intact.'

At that juncture there was a soft tap on the door of the cabinet, and the secretary stepped in at Childs's command. 'The matter has been attended to, my lord. Barnes has returned and is waiting to convey your guests.'

'Very good.' Childs nodded. 'Excellent, indeed.' He rose at once to his feet and smiled at Tom. 'I think that concludes our business, Courtney. I understand you wish to take a ferry-boat from the Tower?'

In friendly fashion he saw Tom to the front door of the mansion, where Barnes waited with the carriage. As they shook hands, Childs asked guilelessly, 'Where will you take your new ship? And when will you sail?'

Tom knew that the question was barbed and he sidestepped the thrust. 'I have only this minute become her new owner.' He laughed. 'I have not yet had time to consider that question.' Childs was staring into his eyes, watching for any attempt to prevaricate, and Tom was forced to go on. 'I think the ports of southern France on the Mediterranean would be my best area of endeavour. Or perhaps the French territory of Louisiana on the Gulf of Mexico. I might take the *Swallow*, for that is her new name, across the Atlantic.'

Childs grunted, not entirely convinced. 'I do most sincerely hope, Courtney, that you do not harbour any thought of rounding the Cape of Good Hope and searching for your lost brother in the Ocean of the Indies?'

'Sweet Jesus, no, sir!' Tom laughed again. 'I am not fool enough to try the Cape of Storms in a paper hat like the *Swallow*.'

'All the territories beyond the Cape have been granted by royal charter to the Honourable Company. Any interloper will be dealt with in the harshest manner the law allows.' It was clear from the steely gleam in his blue eyes that he would not be bound by the law in his retribution. There was an old maritime saying that 'There is no law beyond the line', which meant that civilized law did not always apply at the ends of the ocean.

Childs gripped his arm hard to make the point unmistakable. 'In fact, I think you would be wise to fear me more than your brother, if you were rash enough to sail across my bows.'

'I assure you, my lord, that I look upon you as my good friend and that I would do nothing to change that,' Tom told him earnestly.

'Then we understand each other.' Childs masked his hard expression with a smile as earnest as Tom's, and they shook hands. It matters not a jot, Childs told himself smugly. I think this lad's final destination is in the hands of his elder brother now. Aloud he said, 'Go with God,' and added silently, Or the devil! and waved a pudgy white hand.

Tom leaped lightly into the carriage and beckoned Aboli to take the seat beside him. Childs stepped back and nodded at the coachman, who returned a significant look then touched the brim of his hat with the whip. He shook up the reins, and the carriage rolled away.

Tom and Aboli were so deep in conversation that neither noticed the route the driver followed. The narrow streets were so homogeneous that there were no landmarks for them to orientate themselves. As the carriage lurched along, Tom related to Aboli all the details of the meeting with Childs.

At the end Aboli said, 'It is not as bad a bargain as you think, Klebe. You have the *Swallow*, and a crew to sail her.'

'I have to pay Luke Jervis and the men who came with us to Calais out of my own purse,' Tom demurred. 'They are expecting a share of the cargo.'

'Offer them a share and a berth in this next voyage. It will make them more eager to serve.'

'I have but six hundred pounds left of my prize money from the *Seraph* to fit out the *Swallow* and provision her.'

'No,' said Aboli. 'You have twelve hundred pounds.'

'What nonsense is this, Aboli?' Tom turned in the seat to stare at him.

'I have the prize money I earned with your father during all the years we sailed together. I will add it to yours.' Aboli shrugged. 'I have no other use for it.'

'You will be my full partner. I will sign a deed.' Tom made no effort to hide his delight.

'If I cannot trust you by now,' Aboli almost smiled, 'what good will a piece of paper do me? It is only money, Klebe.'

'With twelve hundred pounds we can refit and provision the *Swallow*, and fill her holds with trade goods. You will not regret this, my old friend, I swear it to you.'

'I regret few things in my life,' Aboli said impassively. 'And when we find Dorian I will have no regrets at all. Now, if you have done chattering, I will sleep a little.'

He leaned back in the seat and closed his eyes. Tom studied his face surreptitiously, musing on the simple philosophy and inner strength that made Aboli a man content and complete in himself. He is without vice, Tom thought, not driven by the need to command or to amass wealth, possessed of a strong sense of loyalty and honour, a stoic and a man of deep natural wisdom, a man at peace with himself, able to enjoy all the gifts he has been given by his strange forest gods, and to endure without complaint all the ills and hardships the world can hurl against him.

He studied the polished black cranium on which grew not a single hair, neither black nor silver, to betray his age. Then he looked closer at the face. The elaborate patterns of the tattoo that covered it hid any ravages that time might have left upon it. I wonder how old he truly is? He seemed as ageless as a cliff of black obsidian, although he must have been a great deal older than Tom's father, none of his faculties or strength had been impaired by the passing of the years. He is all I have left now, Tom thought, and found himself in awe at the depth of his respect and affection for the big man. He is my father and my counsellor. More than that, he is my friend.

Without opening his eyes, Aboli spoke suddenly, startling Tom from his reverie. 'This is not the way to the river.'

'How do you know that?' Tom glanced out of the window, and saw only dark buildings that seemed derelict in the eerie fading light. The narrow streets were deserted, except for a few stray heavily cloaked figures hurrying he knew not where, or standing, sinister and still, in dark doorways, their faces hidden so he could not tell if they were man or woman. 'How do you know?' he repeated.

'We have been travelling away from the river,' Aboli said. 'Long ago we should have reached the landing at the Tower, if that is where he is taking us.'

Tom did not doubt Aboli's sense of time and direction: it was infallible. He leaned out of the window and hailed the driver on the box. 'Where are you taking us, fellow?'

'Where his lordship ordered. To Spitalfields Market.'

'No, you idiot,' Tom shouted, 'we want to go to the Tower of London.'

'I must have heard wrong. I'm sure his lordship ordered—'

'A pox on what his lordship said! Take us where I tell you. We need a ferry-boat to take us upriver.'

Grumbling loudly, the driver turned the carriage, backing and filling in the narrow lane, with the footman tugging at the bridle of the lead horse to force him to obey. 'We will not get there till after six of the clock,' the driver warned Tom. 'You will find no ferry-boat at that hour.'

'We will take our chance on that,' Tom snarled back at him. 'Do as you are told, man.'

Sullenly, the driver whipped up the horses into a trot, and they lurched and swayed through the ruts and puddles back the way they had come. Gradually they were enveloped in a soft, creeping fog that heralded the approach of evening. The buildings they passed now were wreathed in smoking grey tendrils and even the sounds of the carriage wheels and the horses' hoofs were deadened by the thick white blanket. It was colder suddenly. Tom shivered and drew his cloak closer around his shoulders.

'Is your sword loose in its scabbard, Klebe?' Aboli asked.

Tom looked at him in alarm. 'Why do you ask?' But

he laid his hand upon the blue sapphire in the hilt and held the scabbard tight between his knees.

'You may have need of it,' Aboli grunted. 'I smell treachery. The fat old man sent us out of our way for good reason.'

'It was a mistake by the driver,' Tom said, but Aboli laughed softly.

'It was no mistake, Klebe.' His eyes were open now, and he eased his own sword in its scabbard, drawing the blade an inch then reseating it with a soft, scraping sound. After another long silence he spoke again. 'We are near the river now.' Tom opened his mouth to ask how he knew, but Aboli forestalled him. 'I can feel the damp and smell the water.'

Hardly had he spoken when they came out of the narrow lane, and the coachman reined in his team on the edge of a stone wharf. Tom looked out. The surface of the river was steaming with mist so dense that he could not see the far bank. The light was going fast now, and with the darkness came a sense of icy foreboding.

'This is not the landing,' Tom challenged the driver.

'Follow the path down that way.' The man pointed with his whip. ''Tis no more than two hundred paces from here.'

'Drive us there, if it's so close.' Tom's suspicions were fully aroused.

'The coach is too wide for the path, and it is a long way round by the road. It will take you but a minute on foot.'

Aboli touched Tom's arm, and said softly, 'Do as he says. If this is a trap, we are better able to defend ourselves in the open.'

They clambered down onto the muddy verge, and the coachman smirked at them. 'A proper gentleman would have a sixpence for my trouble.'

'I am no gentleman, and you have taken no trouble,'

Tom replied. 'Next time listen to your orders and bring us on the right road.'

The driver cracked his whip angrily, and the carriage rumbled away. They watched the sidelights disappear back up the lane, and Tom took a deep breath. The river stench was strong, damp and clammy cold, thick with the raw sewage that drained directly into its waters. The mist opened and closed like a curtain, playing tricks on the eye. But the towpath along the bank lay in front of them. On their left there was a drop of two fathoms or more from the edge to the water below, and a blank brick wall hedged it in on the right.

'Take the right side,' Aboli murmured. 'I will be on the river verge.'

Tom saw that he had shifted his scabbard on to his right hip: he had arranged it so that if he fought left-handed, which, of course, he could, they would not hamper each other's sword arms. 'Stay to the centre of the path.'

They stepped onto the towpath shoulder to shoulder, their cloaks drawn up to the chin but ready to throw open in an instant and clear their sword arms. The silence and the gathering darkness pressed in upon them. There was a faint glimmer of light through the mist ahead, just sufficient to illuminate the edge of the stone wharf. As they moved towards it, Tom saw that it was a single unmasked lantern.

Closer still, and from the light of the lantern, he recognized through the darkening mists the open stone steps of the river landing.

'This is the right place,' he said softly so that only Aboli would hear. 'Look, there is a ferry-boat waiting, and the boatman.'

The boatman was a tall dark figure at the head of the landing. A wide-brimmed hat hid his eyes, and the collar of the cloak covered his mouth. His boat was moored from one of the iron rings set into the wharf. He had placed his lantern on the top step, and it cast his long shadow upon the stonework of the bridge behind him. Tom hesitated. 'I like it not. This has the feel of a set stage, with an actor waiting to speak his lines.' He spoke in Arabic so that no hidden listener could follow what he said. 'Why is the boatman waiting, unless he knew we were coming?'

'Softly, Klebe,' Aboli warned him. 'Don't let the boatman hold your eye. He is not the danger. There will be others.'

They walked on steadily towards the solitary figure, but their eyes flitted through the shadows that crowded in upon them. Suddenly another figure detached itself from the darkness and stepped into their path just beyond reach of a sword blade. The figure lifted the cowl from its head and let it drop back over her shoulders, revealing a head of thick golden curls that sparkled in the dim light.

'Good night and good cheer, lovely gentlemen.' The woman's voice was husky and enticing, but Tom saw the repellent patches of rouge on her cheeks and the thick paint on her broad mouth, which was blue as a corpse's lips in the poor light. 'For a shilling I will give you both a sight of heaven's gate.'

She had forced them to halt in a narrow part of the towpath, where they were cramped, and now she swung her hips and leered at Tom in a dreadful parody of lust.

'Behind!' Aboli breathed in Arabic, and Tom heard the soft slither of a footfall on the cobbles. 'I will take him, but you watch the whore,' Aboli warned, before Tom could turn, 'for by the sound of her she has a fine set of balls under her skirt.'

'Sixpence for the two of us, darling,' Tom said, and stepped towards her, bringing her into sword reach. At that moment he heard Aboli whirl, but did not take his eyes from the whore. Aboli lunged smoothly at the first of the two men who were closing in on them out of the darkness from behind. It was so swift that his victim did not even raise his blade to meet the thrust. The point went in under his ribs, and came out of his back at the level of his kidneys. He screamed.

Aboli used the buried blade and the strength of his left arm to swing him like a gaffed fish and hurl him into the man behind him. His sword blade slipped out of the man's belly, and the assailants staggered back, clutching at each other, the wounded man still screaming, a wild, eerie sound in the night, but he was blocking his comrade's sword arm. Aboli sent his next thrust over his shoulder, full into the face of the man behind him.

Struck full in the mouth, the man dropped his weapon and covered his face with both hands. The blood squirted out between his fingers, black and thick. He staggered away, and fell backwards over the edge of the wharf. There was a single splash as he hit the dark waters below and sank immediately under the surface.

The other man dropped to his knees holding his stomach, and toppled forward on to his face. Aboli whirled to help Tom, but he was too late.

The whore had drawn a sword from under the cloak and as she sprang at Tom the wig dropped off and revealed her cropped head and coarse, masculine features. Tom was ready for him and jumped forward to meet his charge. The assassin was taken by surprise: he had not expected such a swift response and he had not given himself the time to take his guard.

Tom went high in the natural line, the quick kill to the base of the throat where there is no bone to turn the stroke. His blade went through the windpipe and the great arteries of the neck to grate on the spine. He recovered and thrust again, an inch lower. This time the steel found the joint of the vertebrae and went clear through.

'You are learning, Klebe,' Aboli hissed as the whore

dropped and lay without a twitch, his skirts pulled up over thin hairy white legs. 'But we are not finished yet. There will be others.'

They came out of the dark doorways and the shadows like pariah dogs smelling offal. Tom did not bother to count them, but they were many.

'Back to back,' Aboli ordered, and changed his sword to the stronger side. Now the narrow neck of the pathway, which had seemed to be a trap, became their stronghold. The river guarded their one flank, and the blank window-less wall of a triple-storeyed house the other.

Tom guessed that many more assailants were crowding in upon them from both ends of the path. But they could only attack one at a time. The next man to come at Tom was armed with an iron-tipped stave, and as he swung at Tom's head it was instantly apparent that he was an expert with this ugly weapon. Tom was thankful for all the hours that Aboli had forced him to use one in the practice yard at High Weald. He ducked under the long, heavy staff, not risking the delicate blade of the Neptune sword against such a brutal blow, but he was ready for the reverse, which he knew would be a thrust to his head. He could not give ground for Aboli's broad back was pressed to his. The six-foot length of the staff had kept the attacker out of reach of the blue blade until he thrust with the iron tip. The sharp iron tip came at Tom's head like an arrow from a longbow, but Tom rolled his head at the last moment and let it fly past his cheek. Then, with his left hand he grasped the oaken shaft, and let the man pull him forward within sword range. He reached forward, the blue blade sighed in the air and flickered, like summer sheet lightning.

Clean as a straight razor it opened the man's throat under his jaw-line, and the air rushed from his open windpipe with a squeal like a piglet denied the teat.

The man behind him stared at the dreadful sight, as the dying man staggered in a circle. He was so entranced that he was slow to meet Tom's next lunge. Tom went high again, for the base of the throat, but at the last moment his victim jerked aside and the point went in through his shoulder. The weapon he carried fell from his hand and clattered on the cobbles. He clutched his wound and shouted, 'In the name of God, I am killed,' turned and blundered into the men coming up behind him. They formed a dark, struggling bunch of humanity, so closely packed that it was difficult for Tom to pick out a clear target. He stabbed three times fast and hard into the pack, and with each stroke there was another agonized screech. One staggered backwards and toppled over the edge of the path, arms swinging wildly as he fell from sight and hit the water in a flash of spray. The others scrambled back, holding their injuries, their faces dirty grey in the dull light.

Tom heard sounds behind him, somebody moaning hollowly and another sobbing with agony. A third person was flopping and kicking on the ground like a horse down with a broken leg. Tom dared not take his eyes off the men who still confronted him, but he must know that Aboli still covered his back.

'Aboli, are you hit?' he asked quietly.

At once there was a deep voice close behind him filled with scorn. 'These are apes, not warriors. They defile my blade with their blood.'

'Be not so fastidious, I beg you, old friend. How many more are there?'

'Many, but methinks they have lost stomach for the fare we are serving.'

A knot of men was hovering in front of Aboli, just out of sword-play. He saw their first backward paces, and suddenly he threw back his head and let forth such a cry that even Tom was startled. Despite himself he turned his head to look back.

Aboli's mouth was a great red cavern, and the tattooed

features were convulsed in a mask of animal ferocity. The cry he gave was the bellow of a great bull ape, a sound that shocked the ears and stunned the senses. The men before him were racing away into the darkness while the echoes rang across the dark river. The same panic seized those facing Tom: they whirled away and ran. Two were limping and weaving with their wounds, but they straggled away up a side-street and the sounds of their running feet dwindled into the silence of the encroaching mist.

'I think you will have summoned the watch.' Tom stooped and wiped his blade on the skirts of the dead whore. 'They will be on us in a minute.'

'Then let us go,' Aboli agreed, in a voice that seemed mild and soothing after the terrible cry that had preceded it.

They stepped over the crumpled bodies, and ran towards the head of the steps. Aboli raced down to where the ferry-boat was moored, but Tom turned aside and went to the boatman. 'A gold guinea for your hire!' Tom promised, as he ran to meet him. He was less than ten paces from him when the boatman threw open the folds of his cloak and raised the pistol he had concealed beneath it. Tom saw that it had twin barrels arranged side by side, and that the muzzles were like a pair of black eyeless sockets.

As he stared into those blank eyes of death, the passage of the seconds seem to freeze. Everything took on an unreal, dreamlike quality. Although his eyesight seemed sharpened, and every sense was heightened, yet his movements were slowed as though he were wading through clinging mud.

He saw that both hammers of the pistol were at full cock. From under the brim of the wide hat a single dark eye glittered over the barrels at Tom, and a pale forefinger was hooked through the trigger guard, tightening inexorably.

Tom watched the hammer on the left barrel drop, the puff and flash of the priming as the flint struck the steel. He tried to hurl himself aside but his limbs obeyed only lazily. The boatman's pistol hand was thrown head high and the weapon fired with a shattering blast. A cloud of blue gunsmoke filled the air between them. At the same instant Tom was struck a heavy blow in the body that threw him backwards. He went down heavily and lay on his back on the stones. I am hit, he thought, with surprise, as he sprawled on the top step. He felt the numb heaviness in his chest. He knew what that presaged. Perhaps I am killed, was his next thought and it made him angry. He glared up at the man who had shot him.

He still had the Neptune sword in his right hand, as he saw the pistol coming down, like a fatal basilisk, levelling its terrible blank gaze upon him. If I am killed then I can no longer move my sword arm. The thought fumed in his brain, forcing him to pour every ounce of his strength and determination into his right arm.

To his astonishment the arm had lost none of its force. It whipped forward and the sword flew from his fingers, thrown like a javelin. He watched its flight, point first, unwavering and true, the lantern-light sending golden sparks from the precious inlaid metal as it flew.

Standing over him, the boatman's cloak had opened to expose his chest. He wore only a black silk shirt beneath it, laced at the throat. Before the second barrel of the pistol fired, the steel pierced the soft material under the raised pistol arm, and Tom watched its full glistening length disappear magically into the man's torso.

The boatman stood rigid, locked in a mortal spasm, his heart cloven by the blade. Then he swayed backwards and his long legs, booted in polished black leather, gave way under him. He fell backwards, lay and writhed against the agony of the blade. Then swiftly his movements stilled.

Tom lifted himself on one elbow, and saw Aboli come bounding up the steps. 'Klebe! Where are you struck?'

'I know not. I feel nothing.'

Aboli pulled aside the folds of his cloak, then ripped open the cloth of his shirt. He groped the hard young flesh beneath, and Tom exclaimed, 'By God, gently! If I am not dead already you will soon see to it.'

Aboli seized the lantern, which still burned on the top step, and opened the shutter fully. He shone the beam on to Tom's naked chest. There was blood, much blood. 'Low in the right side,' he muttered, 'not the heart but perhaps the lungs.' He shone the light into Tom's eyes, and watched the pupils contract. 'Good! Now cough for me.'

Tom did what he ordered, and wiped his mouth with the back of his hand. 'No blood!' he said, as he studied his unsullied palm.

'Thank all your gods and mine, Klebe,' Aboli grunted, as he pushed Tom back. 'This will hurt,' he promised. 'Shout if you will, but I must gauge the track of the ball.'

He found the opening of the wound, and before Tom could brace himself slipped one long thick finger full length into it. Tom arched his back and screamed like a virgin being rudely deflowered.

'It has struck a rib, and glanced aside.' Aboli pulled his bloody finger out. 'It has not entered the cavity of your chest.' He ran his hand, slippery with warm blood, around the side of Tom's chest under his arm, and felt the lump of the ball near his shoulder-blade. 'It has run between the bone and the skin. We will cut for it later.'

Then he lifted his great tattooed head as a shout echoed from the mouth of the dark lane that led down to the landing. It had the tone of harsh authority. 'Stand and yield, villains, in the name of the King!'

'The watch!' Aboli said. 'They must not take us here, surrounded by dead men.' He hauled Tom to his feet. 'Come, I will help you to the boat.'

'Unhand me!' Tom snapped at him, shrugging himself free. 'I have lost my sword.'

Doubled over to favour his wounded side, Tom hobbled to where the boatman lay on his back. He placed his boot on the dead man's chest and pulled free the long, shining blade. He was about to turn away and go down the steps but, on an impulse, he used the point of the blade to flick the wide-brimmed hat off the corpse's head.

He stared at the dark, handsome face, surrounded by the garland of Nubian black hair that shone in the lamplight. The mouth was slack, no longer cruel, and the eyes stared into the night sky, blank and unseeing.

'Billy!' Tom whispered. He stared in horror at the face of his dead brother, and for the first time his legs went weak under him. 'Billy! I have murdered you.'

'There was no murder.' Aboli's great arm closed around his shoulders. 'But if the watch take us here, there might well be.'

He swept Tom half off his feet, and down the steps. Then he tumbled him into the ferry-boat and leaped in beside him. With a slash of his sword he severed the painter that secured them to the iron mooring ring in the stone wharf and seized the oars. The boat leaped forward with the strength of his stroke.

'Stop! Surrender yourselves,' a hoarse voice shouted from the shore. In the mist there was the sound of running footsteps and the voices of more men. 'Stop, or I will fire upon you! This is the King's watchman!'

Aboli pulled with both oars, grunting with the effort, and the mist banks closed around them. The dark stones of the wharf disappeared in the swirling silver clouds. Then there was the heavy detonation of a blunderbuss, and the hum as a swarm of lead shot cut through the mist. It fell like hail on the surface of the river around them and a few pellets struck the woodwork of the boat. Tom crouched on the floorboards, hugging his injured side. Aboli heaved on the oars, sending them further out on the broad waters. The shouts of the watch faded swiftly behind them and Aboli stopped rowing.

'Please do not piss on me. Keep that black python locked in your breeches,' Tom pleaded, in mock terror of Aboli's infamous treatment for all wounds.

Aboli grinned as he tore a strip of cloth from his undershirt. 'You do not deserve such pleasures. What stupidity to walk up to an enemy offering him money!' Aboli altered his tone to mimic Tom. '"A gold guinea for your hire!"' He chuckled. 'He surely gave you your guinea's worth.'

Aboli folded the piece of cloth into a pad and placed it over the bullet wound. 'Hold that there,' he told Tom. 'Press hard to staunch the bleeding!' Then he seized the oars again. 'The tide is with us. We will be at Eel Pie before midnight.'

They were silent for an hour, rowing on quietly in the mist banks. Aboli found his way along the dark, hidden river as though it were broad day. Tom spoke at last. 'He was my brother, Aboli.'

'He was also your enemy to the death.'

'I swore to my father on his deathbed.'

'You spared him once. All oaths to your father were discharged.'

'I will have to answer for his death at Judgement Day.'

'That is long hence.' Aboli spoke in rhythm with the swinging oars. 'Let it wait until then, and I will bear witness for you, if your God will listen to the testimony of a heathen. How is your wound?'

'The bleeding is staunched, but it hurts.'

'That is good. When a wound does not hurt, you are dead.'

They were silent again, until Tom heard the chimes of a church clock on the riverbank strike eight. He roused himself, and winced at the pain of the wound. 'Nicholas

566

Childs must have sent word to Billy where to find us,' he said softly. 'In the middle of our discussion, he suddenly left the room. He was gone for a long time, time enough to send word to him.'

'Of course. He sent us out of our way in the carriage to afford your brother time to welcome us with his friends at the landing,' Aboli agreed.

'Childs will point to us as the murderers. The magistrates will send their bailiffs to take us. Childs will have many witnesses against us. The watchmen on the landing probably saw our faces. We will end up on the gallows tree, if they lay their hands upon us.'

This was so obviously the truth that Aboli made no comment.

'Childs wanted the *Swallow*. That is why he warned Billy where to find us. I thought the swine had resigned himself to our bargain, but he wanted it all from me – the cargo and the ship.'

'He is fat and greedy,' Aboli agreed.

'Childs knows where to send them. I told him the *Swallow* was moored at Eel Pie.'

'You are not to blame. You could not see the harm in it.'

Tom moved restlessly, trying to ease the pain of the stiffening wound. 'Billy was a peer of the realm, an important man with powerful friends. They will be like bulldogs. They will not let us go.' Aboli grunted, but never interrupted the rhythm of the oars.

'We must sail tonight,' Tom said firmly. 'We dare not wait until morning.'

'At last you have seen what was clear all along,' Aboli applauded wryly. Tom settled back against the thwart. Now that the decision was made he could rest easier. He dozed intermittently, but the pain kept waking him.

An hour before midnight he was roused by the change in the stroke of the oars, and he looked up to see the outline of the *Swallow*'s sleek and lovely hull appearing out of the mist just ahead. There was a riding light at her masthead, and the dark figure of the anchor watch rose from behind her gunwale and challenged them sharply. 'Who goes there?'

'*Swallow*!' Tom shouted the traditional reply when the ship's captain was returning, and there was an immediate stir and bustle aboard the sloop. As soon as they came alongside many hands were ready to lift Tom on board.

'We must send for a surgeon,' Ned Tyler said, as soon as he saw the blood, and learned the cause and extent of Tom's injury.

'No! The watch is after us,' Tom stopped him. 'We must sail within the hour. The tide has turned already. We must run downriver on the ebb.'

'The work below decks is not complete,' Ned warned him.

'I know that,' Tom answered. 'We will find a safe port on the south coast to finish it. We cannot use Plymouth – it is too close to home. That is the first place they will look for us. Dr Reynolds lives at Cowes on the Isle of Wight. It is off the mainland. The bailiffs will not immediately look for us there. We can send word to the men we need to join us, and finish fitting out before we sail for Good Hope.'

He struggled to his feet. 'Where is Luke Jervis?'

'Ashore with his wife and brats,' Ned replied.

'Send for him.'

Luke came, still muzzy with sleep. Swiftly Tom explained what had happened, how he had lost the cargo to Childs, and the desperate need to fly downriver at once. 'I know that I owe you the share of the *Swallow* and her cargo, as I promised, but I cannot pay you now. I will give you my note on the debt. I may never be able to return to England, but I will send the monies to you when I have them.'

'No!' Luke had woken up fully during Tom's rapid recounting of the facts. 'I will not trust you for such a large sum.' His voice was harsh. Tom stared at him, at a loss for words, but Luke's face split suddenly into a wolfish grin. 'I must come along with you to protect my debt.'

'You don't understand,' Tom said roughly. 'I am going to Africa.'

'I have always wanted to taste one of them cokey-nuts,' Luke said. 'It will take me a minute to fetch my ditty-bag, Captain. Don't slip your moorings before I return.'

Tom refused to go below to the half-finished cabin so Aboli placed a mattress on the open deck for him, with a tarpaulin rigged over it to keep off the mist. Within ten minutes Ned had come to him. 'All shipshape and ready for sea, Captain,' he reported.

'Where is Luke Jervis?' Tom demanded.

'He should be back at any minute—' Ned started, but broke off as a scream tore through the night, the cry of a woman in terrible distress. They started in alarm and reached for their weapons, just as two dark figures came running down the wooden jetty towards the *Swallow*.

''Tis only Luke,' Alf Wilson said, with relief, 'and his missus after him. We best get under way. She could make us all suffer.'

'Cast off!' Luke yelled, when he was only halfway down the jetty. 'The she-devil is after me.'

They threw off the lines and ran to the halyards. The *Swallow* drew away from the jetty. Luke raced the last few yards with his wife gaining on him, screeching with rage and swinging at him with a long staff. Luke leaped across the space between dock and ship.

'Luke Jervis, come back! You will not leave me here with the brood of bastards you got out of my belly, and no food or coin to feed or clothe us. You will not go running off to Afriky to rut on them black savage whores.'

'Farewell, my bonny dove.' Jervis scrambled to his feet, bold now that twenty feet of water separated them. He blew her a kiss. 'I will see you again in three years, or maybe four, or perhaps more.'

'What will become of me and my innocent babes?' she whined, as her mood changed. 'Have you not a morsel of pity?' She burst out into pitiful wails.

'Sell the *Raven*,' Luke shouted back. 'She'll fetch enough to keep you and your litter for twenty years.'

'I'll not wait for you to come back, Luke Jervis.' Her tone changed again. 'There's many a good man will be pleased to take your place in my bed.'

'Brave men all of them.' Luke waved his cap over his head. 'They deserve you more than I do, my little geranium.'

They lay up in the River Medina half a mile upwater from Cowes. Tom had ordered Ned to have the sloop's French name painted over, but they did not replace it with her new name. She did not stand out among the other small craft in the anchorage. All the crew were enjoined to silence and warned not to speak to anyone ashore about her origins, her business or final destination.

Dr Reynolds came out to the ship immediately he received Tom's message. He cut for the ball with Tom lying on a grating in his tiny new cabin. Aboli held his arms and Alf Wilson his legs. Reynolds found the soft lead ball on the first incision, and popped it out of the swollen, inflamed flesh like the stone of a prune. There was a bright smear on the metal where it had struck Tom's rib.

Then while Tom writhed and sweated on the grating he probed the channel the ball had cut along his ribcage. 'There they are! All the wadding and the piece of your shirt it carried in with it.' Proudly the surgeon displayed these reeking trophies, holding them up in the forceps to show Tom, who lay in a sweat of agony champing on the wooden wedge between his teeth.

'I think it will heal cleanly now.' Reynolds sniffed the pus and detritus from the wound. 'Sweet as a good Devon cider. The corruption has not yet taken a strong hold in your blood. However, I will leave a quill in the wound to help it drain thoroughly. I will return in three days to remove it.'

When Reynolds removed the quill, he proclaimed the operation to have been a masterpiece of the surgeon's art. Then he drank a quart jug of the rough cider Tom offered him. Under its subtle influence he agreed, without protest or demur, to accept the post of ship's surgeon that Tom pressed upon him. 'This last year I have near died of boredom. Never a decent musket-ball wound nor sword cut to lighten my days. Nothing but running noses and trickling bums,' he confided over the second jug of cider, as they sat on the open deck beside the main mast. 'I have thought often of those balmy days on the Fever Coast.'

There was a burst of heavy hammering from below, and minutes later the master carpenter stuck his head out of the hatch. 'The work's all done, Captain. You're ready to sail whenever you've a mind.'

Tom had hired a gang of three local carpenters to help complete the refitting of the *Swallow*. They had worked in shifts, all day and by lantern-light late into the night to meet Tom's demands. He paid them off for the excellent work they had done, and bade them farewell.

In the meantime he had sent Alf Wilson and Ned Tyler by ferry across the Solent to find the best of the men they had already contracted to the voyage. They were scattered down the coast in the ports and fishing villages between Plymouth and Portsmouth, waiting for Tom to summon them.

Tom and Master Walsh went with them as far as Southampton. They visited the chandlers and merchants to purchase the stores and trade goods they needed to complete fitting out the *Swallow* and provision her for an extended trading voyage. From the last voyage with his father, Tom knew what goods were most in demand among the black African tribes.

He ordered and paid for almost two tons of Merikani cotton cloth, two thousand axe-heads, five tons of copper wire, five hundred hand mirrors, a ton of Venetian glass beads, twenty pounds of needles, a hundred cheap muskets with powder flasks and shot bags, and a ton of assorted trinkets and gewgaws. Most of these goods were safely delivered across the Solent and stored on board within the week.

Tom left Master Walsh in Southampton to see to the purchase of the last of the trade goods, and went back to the ship. He fretted throughout the last few days as his crew began to come in across the Solent in singles and small groups, carrying their bags slung over their shoulders. He greeted each by name as they came aboard and had them place their marks on the watch-bill. They were the best of all those who had sailed on the *Seraph* and the other ships of the squadron. Tom was delighted and relieved to have them on board. He paid each his silver shilling of joining money and sent them below to claim the pegs on which to hang their hammocks.

Master Walsh arrived back from their buying expedition aboard the barge he had hired to bring the last consignment of trade goods and ship's stores down Southampton Water and across the Solent to where the *Swallow* was anchored in the Medina. When these goods were loaded, the *Swallow*'s holds were filled and she lay low in the water. However, Ned Tyler and Alf Wilson had not yet returned, and they were forced to wait for them. There was not an hour that passed when Tom did not look to the shore and worry about the threat of the bailiffs that hung over him.

He was certain that the officers of the law were already scouring all the ports along the south coast. He guessed they had started at Plymouth and were spreading out from there, searching for the sloop. It was only a matter of time before they reached the Isle of Wight and began to make the enquiries that would lead them to where the *Swallow* lay.

There was another worry. The autumn was far advanced and soon winter would cast her stormy net across the seaways to the south, and lock them in. However, these days of grace gave his wound time to heal. By now he was vigorous and strong again, eager to be on his way.

At night in his tiny cabin he was haunted by the murder of his brother, and he brooded on his guilt. In his Bible, with its worn leather cover, he read and reread the story of Cain and Abel, and found little there to comfort him. Then, at the end of two weeks, Alf Wilson and Ned Tyler returned. The two were surprised by the warmth and enthusiasm of his welcome. 'Jeremy Compton has changed his mind, and we could not find Will Barnes or John Birdham.' Ned was apologetic.

'No harm done, Ned,' Tom assured him expansively, and they went over the watch-bill together, assigning each man to his station. Ned was the first mate. Alf, Luke and Aboli the other officers, with a crew of twenty-seven tried and tested old salts to make up the full complement.

'There is only one more load of trade goods to arrive, two hundredweight of red and green Venetian glass beads,' Tom told his officers. 'With luck they will come in tomorrow. We'll sail with the next tide after they are stowed.'

They settled in for what was to be their last night before sailing. As the sun set behind a thick mattress of grey cloud, a deputation led by Luke Jervis came to Tom where he sat brooding in the bows, staring across the water at the lamplights in the village, taking his leave of England for ever, saddened by the looming exile into which he was condemned for the rest of his life, and yet elated at the prospect of being able at last to begin the search for Dorian and his return to that mysterious, beckoning land so far to the south.

'There is some of the lads that would take a last pot of ale in the tavern and kiss a pretty Christian girl once more before we sail on the morrow. Will you give them permission to go ashore for an hour, Captain?' Luke asked respectfully.

Tom thought about it for a minute. It was not wise to allow men ashore, for when they had liquor in them even the best seamen were wild and untrustworthy.

'They will not taste a good English ale these next three years.' Luke prodded him delicately.

He was right, Tom thought, it would be hard on them if he refused. He could see the lighted windows of the tavern across the water. They would be almost within hail. There could be little harm in it. 'Will you go with them, Mr Jervis, and see to it that it is an hour and no more?'

'Why do you not come across with us your good self, Captain? They will mind their manners and come away prompt and sober if they are under your eye.'

'It will be better than sitting here worrying about things that might never happen, Klebe,' Aboli said softly, from where he sat beside the mast. 'The lads will take it well, to have you buy them a jug and drink with them to the success of our voyage.'

Tom left Ned in command of the sloop, and with him a few who would rather be in their hammock than in their cups. The rest rowed ashore in one of the longboats.

The taproom of the tavern was noisy and crowded with lobstermen and fishermen, and the crews off the Royal Navy's men-o'-war. The air was thick and blue with tobacco smoke. Tom ordered jugs of ale for his lads, and he and Aboli retired to a corner where they could watch the room and the door. Jim Smiley and one or two of the others started a boisterous conversation with a trio of women in the far corner, and within minutes they slipped away in couples. Although it had started raining lightly, they disappeared into the night.

'They will not be far off,' Aboli quieted Tom's misgivings. 'I told them to stay within call.'

Tom had not lowered the contents of his jug an inch from the rim when two strange men came in through the front door and stood on the threshold, beating the raindrops off their cocked hats and the shoulders of their cloaks.

'I do not like the looks of these,' said Tom uneasily, and set aside his jug. They were both big, brawny fellows, with grim, stolid faces. 'They have not come here to revel and carouse.'

'Stay here,' Aboli said, and rose to his feet. 'I will find out more about their business.'

He made his way casually through the crowd of drinkers, and followed the pair as they pushed through the crowd to where the goodwife and two wenches were filling ale jugs from the spigot of a twenty-gallon keg. 'Good morrow, mistress,' the elder of the strange pair greeted the wife. 'I would like a word.'

'Words are cheap.' She looked up and brushed the hair from her eyes. 'Let's see your ha'pence for a pot and you can talk as much as you like.' The man slapped a coin on the table, and Aboli drifted closer so that he could listen to every word, while remaining unobtrusive.

'I am looking for a ship,' said the big man.

'Then you have come to the right place. There are ships aplenty hereabouts. Yonder is Spithead and the whole bloody navy. Take your pick.'

'The ship I seek is a little sloop.' The man grinned at

her ingratiatingly, but his eyes were cold and hard. 'A pretty little ship with the name of the *Hirondelle*.' His pronunciation of the French name was murderous. 'Or perhaps the *Swallow*.'

Aboli did not wait for the goodwife's reply but turned away and strode towards where most of the crew of the sloop were standing in a group, laughing and swigging from their pots.

Tom was watching him across the smoky room and Aboli jerked his head in an unmistakable summons. Tom came to his feet and went among the crowd, but not so obviously as to draw attention, singling out his men, tapping each on the shoulder, and giving them a quiet word. Aboli was doing the same, and shepherding the seamen out into the drizzling rain.

'What is it?' Luke demanded.

'Bailiffs are drawing our covert,' Aboli told him. 'Where are John Smiley and his mates?'

'Unloading their cargo into some pretty little pink port, like as not,' Luke said.

'Whistle them up,' Tom ordered. 'We will not wait on the tide.'

Luke lifted the whalebone whistle that hung from a lanyard around his neck and blew two sharp blasts. Almost immediately John Smiley came running out of the shadows at the rear of the tavern. The others stumbled after him, hauling up their breeches and smoothing down their petticoats.

'Back to the boat, lads,' Tom told them, 'or get left behind.'

It was less than a hundred paces to the jetty where the longboat was tied up, but they had covered only half that distance when a stentorian bellow followed them.

'Thomas Courtney! Stand, in the name of the law.' Tom glanced over his shoulder and saw the two big men burst out through the tavern doorway and come pelting after them.

'I have a warrant signed by the Chief Justice of England! You are charged with the bloody murder of Lord Courtney.'

The challenge spurred Tom on. 'Run for it, lads!'

They reached the head of the stone steps well ahead of the bailiffs, but there they ran into a bottleneck on the narrow stairway, and the two big men gained on them rapidly. Each had drawn a sword from under his cloak, and their heavy boots pounded over the cobbles. 'Stop! In the name of the law!'

'I will hold them off!' Aboli rumbled, and turned to face them. 'Go into the boat!' Instead, Tom turned with him and they stood at the head of the stairs, shoulder to shoulder.

'Your wound. You cannot wield a sword yet. Will you never listen to me?' Aboli demanded.

'Only when you make sense!' Tom changed the Neptune sword into his left hand as the pain of his unhealed wound stabbed him in the side.

'I will kill you, if you force me to it,' he shouted at the approaching pair, in such a tone as to bring them up short.

They hesitated just out of sword-play. 'We are officers of the law. Touch one of us at your peril.' They were disconcerted by the odd pair who confronted them, the fresh-faced youth with the bent nose and the scarified black giant.

'And I am a murderer with bloody hands. One more death means little to me.' Tom laughed ghoulishly, 'This savage here eats men raw. He likes their heads best. He sucks the flesh off the bones.'

Aboli whipped the hat off his great bald head and scowled at them, contorting his tattooed face into a grotesque mask. The bailiffs stepped back involuntarily.

Behind his back Tom heard the last of his men tumble into the longboat, and the oars creaking in the rowlocks.

'Come on board, Captain,' Luke Jervis yelled.

'Shove off!' Tom yelled at Luke, and leaped forward to meet the two bailiffs. 'On guard! Defend yourselves!'

He thrust at the man in front of him, driving him back, flashing the blade inches from his eyes, snagging and splitting the fabric of his coat with the point, but always careful not to wound him.

The bailiffs had only to touch blades to realize that they were outclassed, and they retreated before the combined attack. Luke Jervis shouted again.

Tom glanced swiftly over his shoulder: the longboat hovered just off the wharf with the rowers resting on their oars. 'Time to go,' he said to Aboli in Arabic, and made two more rapid lunges at the bailiffs' faces that sent them stumbling backwards in panic. Then he and Aboli whirled and ran to the edge of the wharf. They leaped together far out and dropped into the water with their cloaks ballooning behind them.

As soon as they surfaced the longboat shot in to pick them up. Tom held the Neptune sword in his right hand and side-paddled with the other arm to meet the boat. The crew lifted him and Aboli out of the water and turned immediately, pulling mightily for where the *Swallow* lay. Once they were all safely aboard it took only minutes to recover the longboat and rope it down on the foredeck, while the other watch were on the windlass hoisting the anchor from the muddy bottom.

The bailiffs must have commandeered their skiff. They were halfway across from the wharf when the *Swallow* hoisted her mainsail and heeled to the night wind. As they bore away down the narrow inlet towards the open water of the Solent they passed the small boat close. One of the bailiffs stood up in the stern and pointed his drawn sword at Tom as he stood beside the *Swallow*'s helm. 'You can never escape,' he shouted across the gap between the two craft. 'You have blood on your hands, and we will smell you out, no matter where you go on the face of this earth.'

Tom made no reply, but looked dead ahead. They left the small boat bobbing in their wake.

The wind treated them like a lover. It came from the north, the harbinger of winter, cold and swift, but not so strong as to force them to put a reef in the main. Within a week they had cleared Ushant. Then the north wind whisked them across Biscay, that notorious breeder of gales and turbulent seas, and south past the Canaries and on into the doldrums.

Here they expected it to falter, become fluky and erratic, but it blew sweet and constant. One day, after the noon sun-shot, Tom marked their position on the line of the equator and a thousand nautical miles west of the massive bulge of the African continent.

'New course is south by east, Mr Tyler. Full and by.' He marked it on the traverse board.

Ned Tyler touched his forehead. 'Full and by it is, Captain.'

Tom looked up at the *Swallow*'s mainsail: it was swollen tight and white as an eight-month pregnant belly. Then he looked over the stern: the wake was slick and straight across the wind-ruffled Atlantic swells. 'With this wind we will raise the Cape in less than sixty days, and thirty days later we will drop our hook in Zanzibar Roads.' He had left all his doubts and misgivings far under the northern horizon, and now he felt strong and invulnerable.

Abd Muhammad al-Malik's dhow was in disarray. The fallen boom that had almost killed the Prince had left the ship drifting helplessly, bows to the wind, her decks smothered under the heavy woven matting sail, and her rigging in a shambles. Blocks were swinging and banging against the mast and hull in the strong gusts of the monsoon, and her rigging was whipping and snapping, threatening to flog itself and the ship into further ruin.

The first thing that had to be done to bring order out of this destruction was to capture the end of the main halyard. This heavy rope was flying from the top of the mast. Rove through the eye of the main block at the masthead, it could not be pulled back from the deck. This would merely compound the problem of hoisting the great lateen sail and getting the ship sailing again. Someone would have to climb the mast.

Unlike a square-rigged ship, no shrouds secured it and there was no other easy form of access to the masthead. With her mainsail down, the dhow was rolling wildly in the heavy swells. The captain was trying to keep her bows into the sea with the tiller as she made sternway, but every now and then a heavier sea would catch her broadside, and roll her almost clean over. The mast was like a gigantic pendulum as it whipped from side to side, aggravating these violent movements. The ship was in dire danger.

The captain could not leave the tiller, but he screeched orders at his men as they huddled as far from him as the deck would allow, all trying to avoid his eye. They knew full well what needed to be done but not one was willing to attempt the climb to the masthead.

Dorian watched all this pandemonium with excited fascination. There had never been anything so entertaining on the deck of the *Seraph*, not all this screaming and gesticulation.

'Ahmed, son of the great sow!' Fouad, the captain, singled out another victim and pointed with a shaking finger to the top of the mast. 'I will wrap your corpse in a pig skin before I throw you overboard if you do not obey me.' The man turned away his head and stared out to sea, as if he had been smitten deaf.

Dorian measured the climb with an experienced eye, and wondered what they were all so afraid of. He had danced a hornpipe with Tom on the main yard of the *Seraph*, one hand on his hip, the other touching the top of his head, while the ship ran with the Cape rollers under her stern and the south-easter blew half a gale. This mast was only a third the height of the *Seraph*'s main.

He could almost hear Tom's voice mocking him: 'Come on, Dorry. Show them what you can do. I'll give you guts!'

No one was looking at him – they had all forgotten him in the desperate exigency of the moment. Even the Prince had forsaken his customary aplomb and was clinging to one of the stays on the foredeck, staring up at the swaying masthead.

Dorian slipped off the long robe and threw it down on the deck. The skirts would tangle his legs. Naked as a new-born he ran to the foot of the mast and shot up it like a monkey pursued by a leopard. The Prince recovered his poise and shouted, 'Stop that child! He will kill himself.'

Dorian was well out of reach of the frantic hands trying to carry out the royal command. His agility and head for heights had been developed and refined in the rigging of the *Seraph* and, by those standards, it was an easy climb. He used the roll of the hull and the swing of the mast to propel himself upwards, gripping alternately with knees and hands. He reached the top of the mast and glanced down. He saw their terrified faces turned up

581

towards him, and could not resist the temptation to show off a little more. He wrapped both legs around the main stay and let go with one hand. He placed his thumb on the tip of his nose and wiggled his fingers down at the deck in a derisive gesture. Even though the crew had never seen this gesture before, the meaning was unmistakable. Dorian's naked body gleamed white as an oyster-shell in the sunlight and his bare bottom was round and pink. He waggled it at them to emphasize the insult.

A moan of dread and horror went up from the watchers below as he climbed higher. They knew that the Prince's wrath would be dreadful if any harm came to the boy, and that it would fall squarely upon their heads. They moaned again as Dorian reached out and gripped the flapping halyard.

'Belay the end!' he shouted down at the deck, using maritime English, but his order was clear to the captain who, having divined his meaning, then translated it into Arabic. Three men ran to grab the standing end of the heavy line.

As soon as they had it ready to break his fall, Dorian took two turns of the unravelled, worn tail end around his waist and then ran it back between his legs.

'Break my fall!' he yelled again. He waited for the right moment in the swing of the mast, then released his grip and kicked himself clear. The halyard squealed through the block as he dropped.

The men on the standing end of the line let it run through their leathery palms, braking his fall as Dorian came down. He was swooping far out over the water at each travel of the dhow's roll, and he whooped with the exhilaration of each swing through the air.

The men on the other end of the halyard judged his descent with sailors' skill, and allowed him to drop down the last few fathoms of the rope so lightly that his bare feet made no sound as they touched the deck. There was a rush to ensure he was safe and to secure the tail end of the halyard, which was wrapped around his waist.

As soon as a fresh rope was rove through the block at the masthead and the boom was hoisted once more, the dhow came on the wind, transformed by the press of the lateen sail from a helpless rolling hulk into a thing of the sea, agile and swift.

The Prince placed one hand on Dorian's shoulder and looked around the faces of his retinue. 'By his quickness of thought and action, this child has saved my life, and that of the ship,' he announced. 'Is there one of you who still doubts that this is the red-crowned orphan of the prophecy?' He laid his hand on Dorian's shining curls and looked each of his courtiers in the eyes. Not one could hold his gaze.

It was the mullah who spoke out first. 'It is the miracle of St Taimtaim,' he cried. 'I declare the Holy Word. This is the child of the prophecy!'

'It is the prophesy!' they chorused. 'Praise God's name!'

With his hand still on Dorian's head, the Prince said clearly, 'Let all men know that I take this child as my adopted son. Henceforth he shall be known as al-Ahmara ibn al-Malik, the Red One, son of al-Malik.'

The mullah smiled slyly at his master's cunning. By making the child his own son, he had neatly validated the prophecy of the saint. But other conditions had to be fulfilled, before the Prince could reap the rewards the old saint had promised. No doubt, in due season, these also could be met. 'It is the will of God!' cried the mullah.

The others intoned in chorus, 'God is great!'

Even without the Prince's commendation, over the weeks they spent at sea Dorian had earned himself a place in the affections of every member of the crew. It was clear to all of them that the boy was a bird of good omen, and each one secretly hoped that some of the promise of the prophecy might rub off on him. As Dorian moved about the deck even the most hardened, villainous sailors smiled and bantered with him, or touched his red head for luck.

The ship's cook made special sweetmeats and sugared delights for him, while the rest of the crew vied with each other for his attention, and pressed small gifts on him. One even took the charm he wore on a thong around his neck and placed it over Dorian's head. 'May this shield you,' he said, and made the sign against the evil eye.

'Little monkey with the heart of a lion,' Fouad, the captain, named him fondly and after evening prayers called Dorian to sit with him at the helm. He pointed out the navigational stars as they rose out of the sea, recited the names of the constellations and told Dorian the legends behind each one.

These Arabs were men of the deserts and the ocean. They lived their entire lives under the panoply of heaven, and the stars were always overhead. They had studied them over the centuries, and now the captain was sharing some of this knowledge with Dorian. It was a rare gift he was offering the child.

Dorian listened in fascination, his upturned face shining in the light of the heavens. Then in his turn he gave the captain the English names of the heavenly bodies, which he had learned from Aboli and Big Daniel.

The other crewmen gathered round them and listened

to the fables of the Seven Sisters, of Orion the hunter and of the scorpion, as Dorian related them in his sweet high voice. They loved the stars and they loved a good story.

Now that he had a free run of the ship there was so much to occupy him that Dorian had little time to feel lonely or sorry for himself. He would spend half the morning hanging over the dhow's side, watching a pod of long-nosed dolphins frolicking in the bow-wave, their wide tails pumping and their knowing eyes looking up at him as they dodged back and forth under the bows. Suddenly one of the creatures would spring from the dazzling blue water as high as where Dorian stood and grin at him with its wide mouth. Dorian waved at it, and burst into delighted peals of laughter. The Arab seamen closest to him would pause in their labours and smile in sympathy.

Whenever he became too involved in conversation with them, though, Fouad would call to him possessively, 'Come here, little monkey with the lion heart, steer the ship for me.' Dorian would take the tiller and his eyes sparkled as he held the running dhow on the wind, felt her tremble under his hands like a thoroughbred horse gathering itself for a jump.

Sometimes the Prince, sitting cross-legged on the silk carpet under his sun tent, would break off a discussion with his courtiers and watch the boy with a little smile on his lips.

As Dorian was still a boy and had not yet felt the circumcision knife, Tahi could go unveiled in his presence. She was that lowliest creature, a divorced woman. Her husband was one of the Prince's grooms. Unable to give him a son, Tahi had been discarded. Only al-Malik's beneficence and compassion had saved her from begging in the streets and souks of Lamu.

Tahi was big and plump and round all over, her skin well greased and brown. She loved her food and had a jolly laugh, and an easy-going disposition. Her loyalty and devotion to the Prince were the centre of her existence. Now, suddenly, Dorian was the son of her master.

Like all the others on board, Tahi was smitten by his beautiful red hair, his strange pale green eyes and milky white skin. When he unleashed the full force of his sunny smile and winning charm upon her she could not resist him. Childless herself, he assuaged all her maternal instincts, and very soon she had lost her heart to him.

When the Prince appointed her Dorian's official nurse, she wept with gratification. It did not take long for Dorian to discover that her bland, almost bovine features concealed a shrewd intelligence and a sharp political sense. She understood all the currents of power and influence in the Prince's court and navigated these with rare skill. She explained to him who were the great and important men in the Prince's retinue, their strengths and their failings, their foibles and how to treat each of them. She coached him in the etiquette of the court, and in how to comport himself in the presence of the Prince and his followers.

For Dorian the nights were the only bad times. In the dark, memories of Tom and his father crept up on him and overwhelmed him. One night Tahi woke to hear stifled sobs coming from where Dorian lay on his thin mattress on the far side of the little cabin they shared. An outcast herself, she understood instinctively the homesickness and loneliness of a small boy torn from his family and all things familiar and dear, cast among strangers of a different race, religion and way of life.

She rose quietly and went to him, lying beside him on the mattress and taking him into her warm, soft, motherly embrace. At first Dorian tried to resist, and pushed her away, but then he let himself relax and lie still in her arms. She murmured little endearments against the top of his shining head, all the love words she had bottled up inside her for the son her barren womb had denied her. After a while the rigidity went out of Dorian's body and he moved closer to her, cuddling his head between her great round breasts, and at last he slept. The next night he went to her mattress quite naturally and she opened her fat arms and drew him to her. 'My baby,' she whispered, in wonder at the depth of her emotion. 'My own beautiful baby.'

Dorian could not remember the comfort of his own mother's arms, but there was a deep need in him. Tahi soon came to fill a great part of that void.

As the dhow drew closer to her home port, Prince Abd Muhammad al-Malik sat under his awning not too deeply involved in affairs of state and business to lack time to ponder the prophecy of the saint, and to watch the boy with a veiled but keen appraisal. 'Al-Allama,' he used the family name of his mullah, 'what revelations have you received regarding the child?'

The mullah hooded his eyes, shielding his thoughts from the penetrating perception of his master. 'He is winsome, and he draws people to him as honey draws bees.'

'That is evident.' The Prince's voice had an edge to it. 'But it is not what I asked of you.'

'It seems that he has those attributes described by the holy Taimtaim,' al-Allama went on cautiously, 'but it will be many years hence before we can be certain of that.'

'In the meantime we must guard him well, and nurture those traits that are necessary to fulfil the prophecy,' al-Malik suggested.

'We will do all in our power, great Prince.'

'It will be your duty to lead him in the paths of righteousness, and reveal to him the wisdom of the Prophet so that he will in time come gently to the faith and submit himself to Islam.'

'He is a child still. We cannot hope to place a man's head on such young shoulders.'

'Every journey begins with the first step,' the Prince contradicted him. 'Already he speaks the sacred language

587

of the Faith better than some of my other children, and he has displayed some knowledge of religious matters. He has been tutored. It will be your sacred duty to foster that knowledge and enlarge upon it until, in time, he submits to Islam. Only in that way can the prophecy be fulfilled in its entirety.'

'As my lord commands.' Al-Allama made a sign of acquiescence, touching his lips and his heart. 'I will take the first step of the long journey this very day,' he vowed to the Prince, who nodded his appreciation.

'If it please Allah!'

After the midday prayers, and when the Prince had retired to his cabin in the stern to be with his concubines, al-Allama sought out the child. He was engrossed in discussion with Fouad. The captain was instructing him in navigation of the islands, pointing out to him the seabirds and clumps of drifting weed that indicated the run of the currents. He called these the rivers of the sea, and was explaining to Dorian how the islands and the shape of the coast affected these mighty rivers, bending and twisting them and subtly altering their shading of blue and green.

Under Ned Tyler's instruction Dorian had come to enjoy every facet of the art of navigation. Some of his most pleasant memories were of working through a sun-shot with Tom, or taking a bearing on a land feature, then marking the chart and writing up the results in the ship's log, arguing and laughing with his elder brother as they did so.

Now Fouad was teaching him the lore of these regions of the ocean, the names and habits of the seabirds and creatures, and the drifting weed. There were small birds with snowy plumage that dived and fluttered over the ship's wake. 'You will not find them further than ten leagues from land. Watch the direction of their flight, and they will lead you to it,' Fouad told him.

At another time he beckoned him to the ship's rail

and pointed overside. 'Look, little monkey! One of the monsters of the sea but gentle as an unweaned lamb.' They were passing so close to it that Dorian jumped onto the gunwale and looked down on its dappled back. He could see that it was not one of the whales they had encountered by the hundred in the southern reaches of the Atlantic. It seemed to be a species of shark, but it was almost as long as the dhow. Unlike the tiger or the hammerhead, which he knew, this beast moved lazily and unafraid though the clear waters. Dorian could see the shoal of little pilot fish that swam just ahead of its cavernous mouth. 'Are they not afraid they will be eaten?' he cried.

'The monster eats only the tiniest creatures of all. Slime and crawling things that float in the sea, smaller than rice grains.' Fouad was enjoying the enthusiasm of his pupil. 'When you see one of these gentle monsters it means that the monsoon is ready to change from the *kaskazi* to the *kusi*, from the north-west to the south-east.'

Al-Allama interrupted the pair, and led Dorian away to where they could talk in private. Dorian looked disappointed and followed him only reluctantly.

'Once, you spoke thus in reply to my question,' al-Allama reminded him. '"I am but a man like yourselves, but the inspiration has come to me that your God is one God. Whoever expects to meet his Lord, let him work righteousness."'

'Yes, holy one.' Dorian was not particularly interested in this new topic. He would have much preferred to continue his animated discussion with Fouad.

However, Tahi had warned him of how powerful the mullah was, and how he could protect or punish a small boy in his power. 'He is the servant of God and a voice of the Prophet. Treat him with great respect. For all our sakes,' Tahi had said, so Dorian was attentive.

'Who taught you these things?' al-Allama demanded.

'I had a teacher,' Dorian looked suddenly as though he

was on the point of tears, 'when I was with my father. His name was Alf, and he taught me Arabic.'

'So it was he who made you learn the Koran, the Sacred Book of the Prophet?'

'Only some verses to write and discuss. That verse from Sura eighteen was one of them.'

'Do you believe in God, al-Amhara?' the mullah insisted.

'Yes, of course,' Dorian said quickly. 'I believe in God eternal, in his Son eternal and the Holy Ghost eternal.' The litany of the Order that he had listened to Tom reciting by heart came readily to his tongue.

Al-Allama tried not to let his alarm and repugnance show in the face of such blasphemy. 'There is but one God,' he said solemnly, 'and Muhammad is his last true prophet.'

Dorian had no interest in this assertion, but he enjoyed arguing, especially with anyone in authority. 'How do you know that?' he challenged. 'How do you know I am wrong, and you are right?' Al-Allama rose to the challenge, and Dorian leaned back, let the torrent of religious rhetoric wash over him, while he dreamed of other things.

D orian wished there was a place for him at the masthead, as there had been on the *Seraph*, a place high above the sea where he could be alone. However, the lateen-rigged dhow did not afford this possibility, and he had to watch from the deck with the rest of the crew as the African mainland came up over the horizon, a dark, mysterious landmass. He wrinkled his nose as he smelt its animal odour on the air. It was the smell of dust and spice and mangrove swamp. The alien aroma was a mild shock to the senses, but it was alluring and enticing after the salt-seared airs of the ocean, which had cleared his nose and heightened his sense of smell.

Standing beside Fouad at the helm as they closed the land, Dorian had his first view of the island of Lamu. Fouad pointed out its main features and gave him a brief history of this jewel in the territories of the Caliphate of the Omani. 'My people have traded here since the time of the Prophet, and before when we were also infidels and strangers to the Great Truth,' he explained proudly. 'This was an important port when Zanzibar was still a crocodile-infested swamp.'

Laboriously the dhow tacked up the channel between the island and the mainland, and Fouad pointed out the dark green hills above the white beaches. 'The Prince has a palace on the mainland where he lives in the dry season, but in the wet he moves to the island.' He pointed out the white buildings that, from this distance, looked like surf breaking on a coral reef.

'Lamu is richer than Zanzibar. Her buildings are more beautiful and magnificent. The Sultan of Zanzibar is a vassal of our Prince and pays tribute to him.'

There was a gathering of craft in the anchorage, and dozens of other vessels were coming in or setting out to sea. Some were fishing boats and others were large, heavily laden traders or lighter, faster slavers, proof of the prosperity and importance of this thriving port.

Those ships they passed recognized the Prince's dhow by the green pennants she flew at her masthead, and by the impressive figure of Abd Muhammad al-Malik sitting under the awning on the foredeck, surrounded by his court. They dipped their colours in respect, and shouted their loyal greetings and blessings across the water. 'May the love of Allah and the smile of his Prophet follow you all your days.'

The dhows at anchor in the bay fired their guns and

beat their war drums. The boom of cannon shot carried to the shore, and as the Prince and his retinue sailed into the harbour they saw a vast crowd gathering on the beach and wharf to greet him.

In their tiny cabin Tahi dressed Dorian in a fresh white robe and covered his shining hair with a headcloth. She placed leather sandals on his feet, then took his hand and led him up on deck.

Fouad took the dhow in to the beach. The tide was running out swiftly, for here the tidal range at full springs was twenty feet. The ship took the ground and heeled as the tide ran out from under her. A gang of slaves waded out to the stranded vessel to carry the Prince and other notables to the beach. A huge black man clad only in a loincloth took the Prince on his back, and the waiting crowds fell to their knees and shouted their greetings. A band of musicians played a high-pitched wailing tune, which offended Dorian's ear. The pipes and fifes sobbed and the drums banged and boomed without rhythm.

Tahi would have carried Dorian to the beach, but he avoided her embrace and splashed joyfully through the surf, wetting himself to the armpits. There was a brief ceremony of welcome for the Prince on the beach, then al-Malik mounted a black stallion. From horseback he looked about quickly and caught Tahi's eye. She stood in the crowd, holding Dorian's hand. She rushed forward with Dorian and the Prince spoke to her imperiously. 'Take al-Amhara to the zenana. Kush will provide quarters for both of you.' Dorian was too interested in the Prince's horse to take much notice of the words that decided his fate. He loved horses almost as much as he did boats and the sea. Tom had taught him to ride as soon as he could walk. Al-Malik's mount was a magnificent animal, much different from those he had known at High Weald. It was smaller and more graceful, with large, limpid eyes and flared nostrils, a long back and strong delicate legs. He reached up and stroked its muzzle. The stallion snuffled his fingers, and then tossed its head.

'He's beautiful.' Dorian laughed.

The Prince looked down on him with a faint smile that softened his fierce hawk-handsome features. A boy who was a seaman born and who also loved horses had all his approval. 'Take good care of him. See to it that he does not try to run away,' he ordered Tahi and the eunuch, Kush, who had come forward to answer the Prince's charge. Al-Malik lifted the stallion's head with a touch on the reins, and rode away down the street of the port, which was carpeted with palm fronds in his honour. The musicians and the crowds closed in behind him, and singing and clapping followed his procession up towards the towering walls of the fort.

Kush gathered up the women from the Prince's household as they came ashore from the dhow. There were two of the youngest concubines, heavily veiled, but slim and graceful under the layers of black robes. Their hands and feet were beautifully formed, dyed with henna, and decorated with precious rings of sapphire and emerald on fingers and toes. They giggled a great deal, which annoyed Dorian, and their maidservants were even worse, noisy as a flock of starlings. He was pleased when they were shepherded by Kush into the first bullock cart.

Tahi led Dorian into the second. The bullocks were pure white, with a huge spread of horns and massive humps on their shoulders, like the drawings of camels Dorian had seen in the books of travel in the library at High Weald. He wanted to run beside the cart, but Kush restrained him with a podgy hand on his shoulder. There were gold rings on each of the eunuch's fingers, and the jewels set in them caught the bright tropical sunlight and sparked the eye.

'Ride beside me, little one,' he said, in a high, feminine voice, and when Dorian would have demurred Tahi pinched his arm so hard it hurt. He interpreted this as a warning that Kush was a man – or, rather, a thing – of power and must be placated.

The procession of carts left the seashore, passed through the outskirts of the port and into the countryside. They trundled down the narrow, dusty road into the interior of the verdant island. They rolled through groves of swaying coconut palms, and forests of wild fig trees. Flocks of brightly coloured parrots and wild green pigeons swarmed in the branches, greedily devouring the ripening fruits. Dorian had never seen birds like these before. He followed their jewelled flight with exclamations of wonder.

Kush studied him carefully through bright black eyes almost buried in rolls of fat. 'Who taught you, a Frank, to speak the language of the Prophet?' he asked suddenly, and with a sigh Dorian gave him the response that had become worn and weary with repetition.

'Are you of Islam? Or is it true that you are an infidel.'

'I am a Christian,' Dorian said proudly.

Kush screwed up his fat face as though he had tasted a green persimmon. 'Then how is it that your hair is the same colour as that of the Prophet?' he demanded. 'Or is this a lie? What colour is your hair? Why do you hide it?'

Dorian adjusted the drape of his headcloth. He was irked by the constant harping on this one subject. There was so much else of interest all around him. He wished the fat one would leave him alone to enjoy it all.

'Show me your hair,' Kush insisted, and reached for the headcloth. Dorian started to pull away, but Tahi spoke sharply and he allowed Kush to lift the cloth from his head. Kush gazed in amazement as Dorian's thick, curling locks tumbled down to his shoulders and flared in the sunlight like a fire in tall grass. The other passengers riding in the back of the cart exclaimed and called on Allah to witness the wonder of it, and even the bullock drivers turned back and walked beside the high wheel to stare up at him. Hastily Dorian covered his head.

After a mile the track wound out of the forest and ahead rose the high, blank wall of the zenana. It was built of coral blocks and painted with burnt limewash to a dazzling white. There were no windows, and the only opening was a gate, carved from teak and decorated with complicated designs of vines and foliage, obeying the Islamic stricture that forbids depictions of human forms or those of other living creatures.

The gates swung open as the little caravan of carts approached, and they proceeded through into the closed, forbidden world of the zenana. This was the home of women, and their offspring, and of the eunuchs who guarded them. Other than the Prince, no grown man might enter here at the peril of his very life.

The women and children had gathered just inside the gates to greet the procession of bullock carts. Many had not left these cloistered precincts since childhood. Any distraction delighted them. They chattered and shrieked with excitement and came close around the carts to inspect the occupants and to find any strange face among them.

'There he is!'

'It is true. He is a Frank!'

'Is his hair really red? Surely it cannot be.'

Here, in the seclusion of the harem, the females could go unveiled. The Prince had the choice of any girl in his realm, and most were young and comely. Their skin colours ranged from purple black through all shades of brown, gold and amber to soft buttery yellow. Their children danced around them, caught up in the excitement. The babes in the nurses' arms wailed in the uproar.

The women crowded forward to have a closer look at Dorian as he jumped down from the cart, then followed as Kush led them through a maze of courtyards and enclosed gardens. These were richly decorated with mosaic floors and elaborate archways. Sea shells had been inlaid in the plaster to form intricate designs. There were pools, filled with reeds and lotus plants. Gemlike fish glided beneath the water and dragonflies and bright kingfishers hovered over the surface.

Some of the elder children danced around Dorian, chanting and teasing him.

'Little white infidel!'

'Green devil-eyes.'

Kush pretended to swipe at them with the long staff he carried but he was grinning, and made no real attempt to drive them away. Swiftly they passed from the splendid and beautiful area of the zenana into the more dilapidated part, in the back regions of the main complex of buildings. It was clear that this was the least desirable section. The gardens were unkempt and the walls stained and unpainted. They passed several abandoned ruins, overgrown with tropical growth, and reached a dilapidated block. Kush took them to a small but sturdy door and ordered them to enter. They found themselves in a large living room, dark and not too clean. The walls were soot-stained, the floors dusty and covered with the droppings of gecko lizards and rats.

Kush closed the doors firmly behind them, and turned a massive key in the lock. Tahi shouted at him through the tiny grille in the door. 'Why are you locking us away? We are not prisoners. We are not criminals.'

'The mighty Prince Abd Muhammad al-Malik has ordered that the child be prevented from escaping.'

'He cannot escape. There is no place for him to run to.'

Kush ignored her protests and strode away, taking most of the others with him. For a while some of the royal children mocked them through the grille, but they soon tired of this and drifted away.

When all was quiet Dorian and Tahi began to explore their quarters. Apart from the living room, there were sleeping chambers, and a little kitchen with an open hearth. Next to it was the washroom with a tiled floor sloped to an open drain. Beyond was the latrine with covered buckets.

The furnishings were sparse: sleeping mats of plaited reeds and sitting rugs of woven wool. There were cooking-pots and water-jars in the kitchen, and naturally they would eat with their fingers in the Arabic fashion. There was a large ceramic rainwater cistern, which supplied fresh water.

Dorian looked up at the opening in the kitchen roof that allowed smoke to escape. 'I could easily climb out of there,' he boasted.

'If you do, Kush will thrash you with his staff,' Tahi told him, 'so do not even think of it. Come and help me clean out this sty.'

As they worked together, sweeping out the bare rooms with brooms of reeds then polishing the clay floors with half coconut shells, Tahi explained to him the rules of the zenana.

As a royal nursemaid since her husband had divorced her, Tahi had lived in the confines of the zenana, and she was an expert on the affairs of its restricted society. Over the days that followed she shared this knowledge with Dorian.

Prince Abd Muhammad al-Malik was in his early thirties. His elder brother, the Caliph, for reasons of his own succession, had prevented him from marrying until he was almost twenty. Thus it was that his eldest son was only little older than Dorian. His name was Zayn al-Din and, like Dorian, he had not yet reached puberty; he still lived with his mother in the zenana.

'Remember his name,' Tahi instructed. 'As the eldest son, he is very important.' Then she went on to list the names of the other male children by the other wives and concubines, but there were so many that Dorian made no effort to memorize them. Tahi did not even bother to mention the girls, because they were of no importance.

In the weeks that followed it seemed that the Prince had forgotten about his red-headed slave-boy. They heard nothing more from outside the walls of the zenana. Every day, under Kush's beady eye, slave-women came to bring them their rations of rice, meat and fresh fish, and to carry away the rubbish from the kitchen and the buckets from the latrine. Apart from that, Dorian and Tahi were left to themselves.

There were grille windows in the main room of their quarters, which overlooked a section of the gardens. To relieve the boredom of their confinement, they spent much of their time watching the comings and goings of the other members of the zenana from this vantage-point.

Tahi was able to point out Zayn al-Din to Dorian. He was a large, plump child, taller than any of his siblings. He had a sallow caramel complexion, his mouth was pouting and petulant. The skin around his eyes was discoloured, as though it was bruised. 'Zayn has a taste for sweet things,' Tahi explained. There were livid patches of prickly heat on the inside of his elbows and knees. He walked splay-legged to prevent his thighs rubbing together and the skin between them chafing.

Whenever Dorian saw him, Zayn was surrounded by a dozen or so of his siblings. One morning he watched as this pack pursued a smaller boy across the lawns, and trapped him against the outer wall of the zenana. They dragged him to Zayn, who had not exerted himself in the chase, but came waddling up when it was over. Tahi was watching also and she told Dorian that the victim was the son of a lesser concubine of the Prince, and therefore fair game for the eldest son of the first wife.

Dorian, who knew all about the rights of the first-born

from his dealings with brother William, felt his sympathy go out to the little boy as he watched Zayn twisting his ears until he sank to his knees, weeping with fear. 'As punishment for what you have done, I make you my horse,' Zayn told him loudly, and forced him down on to all fours. Then he bestrode him and lowered his full weight on to the other child's back. He had a cane in his hand, made from a palm frond from which the leaves had been stripped.

'Gallop, horse!' he ordered, and lashed him across the bottom. The palm frond was lithe and whippy. It snapped loudly, and the little boy wailed with shock and pain. He started forward on hands and knees with Zayn bouncing on his back.

The other children fell in behind them, prancing, jeering and urging them on. When the boy faltered, they joined in the beating, some running to break sticks from the nearest shrubs. One flipped up the child's robe and exposed his brown bottom, laced with angry stripes. They drove him twice around the lawns.

Tears were flooding down the victim's face when at last he collapsed under Zayn's weight and lay sobbing on the coarse grass. His knees were rubbed raw and bleeding. Zayn gave him a casual kick, then led the others away, leaving him to drag himself up and limp away.

'He is a bully,' Dorian said furiously. He could not think of the word in Arabic, so he spoke in English. Tahi shrugged.

'The Koran says that the strong should protect the weak.' Dorian lapsed back into Arabic.

Tahi advised him, 'Do not tell Zayn al-Din that. He will not like it.'

'I would like to take him for a ride,' Dorian said furiously, 'and see how much he likes it.'

Tahi made the sign to avert bad luck. 'Do not even think the thought. Walk wide of Zayn al-Din,' she warned. 'He is a vindictive boy. Surely he will hate you for the favour the Prince has shown you. He can do us much harm. Even Kush is afraid of him, for one day he will be the Prince.'

Over the following days she went on explaining to Dorian the hierarchy of the harem. The Prince was allowed four wives, by the decree of the Prophet. However, he could divorce and remarry as he wished, and there was no limit to the number of concubines with whom he might indulge himself. Those wives he had divorced but who had borne him children still lived in the zenana.

Thus almost fifty women were congregated within these walls. Fifty beautiful, bored, frustrated women, with nothing to fill the long days but intrigue, feud and jealous scheming. It was a complex society, filled with innumerable currents and subtle nuances.

Kush reigned over them all, so his favour or disfavour was important to the happiness and well-being of the inmates. Then the four current wives, in order of seniority, were next in importance. After that, the Prince's favourite of the moment, but she was usually some pretty child only just entered into womanhood and her star would soon wane. Then all the former wives and the concubines squabbled, fought and manoeuvred for position in the order of things. 'It is important for you to understand these things, al-Amhara. Important for both of us. I have no standing at all, I am only a poor old nursemaid. I can do little to protect you, and nobody will miss me.'

'Are you going somewhere?' Dorian demanded, with alarm. He had grown so fond of her in the short time they had been together and the prospect of being abandoned yet again frightened him. 'I will miss you.'

'I'm not going anywhere, my little one,' she assured him quickly, 'but people die here in the zenana, especially little people of no consequence who give offence to those above them.'

'Don't worry. I will protect you,' Dorian told her stoutly, and hugged her.

'I feel safer in your care,' she did not let him see her smile, 'but we do not yet know your position. It seems that the Prince looks upon you with some favour, but we cannot yet be sure. Why does he allow Kush to imprison us and treat us like animals in a cage? Why does he not send for you? Has he forgotten you?' She sighed and returned his embrace.

'Perhaps he does not know how Kush treats us,' Dorian suggested.

'Perhaps,' she agreed. 'So we must wait. In the meantime we must be careful, al-Amhara, very careful.'

Time passed, and the excitement of their arrival was forgotten. No one peered at them through the grille any more, and the children led by Zayn al-Din became bored with chanting insults under the windows, and found other occupations more rewarding. Each day Dorian chafed more cruelly at this confinement.

When he heard the shrill cries and happy laughter of other children at play in the gardens, and heard their running footsteps along the cloisters and across the courtyard outside his meagre quarters, he would rush to the window for a glimpse of them. This only aggravated his loneliness and sense of isolation. He felt as imprisoned as he had been in his cell on the island where al-Auf had chained him.

One morning as the pearly light of a new day filtered through the high window in his room, he lay naked on his sleeping mat, stripping the hard outer lining off a stick of sugar-cane with his teeth. He paused as someone began singing in the garden outside. It was a sweet, girlish voice, even though the words were repetitive and nonsensical, some nursery rhyme about palm dates and a hungry monkey. He lay and listened to it idly, chewing the sweet juice out of the cane and spitting out the pith.

Suddenly there came the shrill but unmistakable chatter of a monkey. The singer broke off the refrain and burst into peals of silvery laughter. Both sounds intrigued Dorian, who jumped up and went to the window. He peered out into the garden and saw a small girl sitting alone on the coping of the lotus pool below him. She had her back to him, but her hair hung down it, dark, almost iridescent black with a silver streak gleaming through the thick tresses. Dorian had never seen anything like it, and he was fascinated.

She wore an embroidered green shift, which left her brown arms bare, and a pair of baggy white cotton trousers. Her legs were doubled up under her and he could see that the soles of her small feet were dyed with henna to a bright ginger colour. She was holding up a sugared date, and a vervet monkey stood on its back legs and danced on the grass in front of her. Each time she gave a hand signal, the monkey chattered louder and spun in a circle. The girl laughed with delight. Finally she offered the sweetmeat, and called, 'Come to me, Jinni!' The monkey bounded up onto her shoulder and took the date from her fingers. It stuffed it into its pouch and began searching in the girl's hair with skinny black fingers, as though for fleas. The girl stroked its fluffy white belly and began singing again.

Suddenly, the ape looked up and saw Dorian's head in the window. It let out a squeak, shot off the girl's shoulder and up the wall. Hanging on the sill it thrust its hand through the window grille, palm up like a beggar, trying to wheedle the stick of sugar-cane from him.

Dorian laughed at the creature, which bared its teeth, bobbed its head at him, and tried to snatch the sugar-cane from his hand, at the same time gibbering and pulling faces.

The girl swung around and looked up. 'Make him do a trick,' she called. 'Don't feed him until he does.' Dorian saw that she also had a funny little monkey face, and huge eyes the colour of Devon honey when the heather on the moors was in bloom. 'Do this with your hand.' She demonstrated, and at the signal the monkey threw itself into an agile back somersault. 'Make him do it three times.' The girl clapped her hands. 'Jinni must do it three times.'

On the third somersault Dorian offered him the sugarcane. The monkey snatched it, galloped across the lawn on all fours, tail held high, and shot to the top branches of one of the tamarind trees. He sat there chewing it with the sweet juices dripping from his lips.

'I know who you are,' the girl announced solemnly, looking up at Dorian with those huge eyes.

'Who am I?'

'You are al-Amhara, the infidel.'

Until now he had been indifferent to what they called him, but suddenly it displeased him. 'My real name is Dorian, but you can call me Dorry. That's what my brother calls me.'

'Dowie.' She tried it out, but had difficulty rolling the R. 'It's a strange name, but I shall call you Dowie.'

'What is your name?' he wanted to know.

'Yasmini,' she told him, 'which means the flower of the jasmine.' She jumped up and came closer, staring up at him with an awed and serious expression. 'Your hair really is red. I thought they were making it up.' She held her head on one side. 'It is very pretty. I wish I could touch it.'

'Well, you cannot,' he told her shortly, but she showed no offence at his tone.

'I feel very sorry for you,' she said.

'Why should you?' He was taken aback.

'Because Zayn says you are an infidel, you will never be circumcised, and you can never enter the gardens of Paradise.'

'We have our own heaven,' Dorian told her loftily. He found discussion of his nether regions vaguely disconcerting.

'Where is it?' Yasmini wanted to know, and they fell into a long, involved discussion of the various merits of the two paradises. 'Our paradise is called Jannat,' she said. 'Allah said, "I have prepared for my righteous servants what no eye has seen and no ear has heard, and what the mind of man has not conceived."'

Dorian considered that in silence, and could think of no suitable retort – Jannat was difficult to beat – so he changed the subject to something of which he felt more certain.

'In England my father has fifty horses. How many does your father have?'

After that Yasmini came every morning, bringing Jinni with her. She sat under Dorian's window with the monkey on her shoulder and listened, her eyes glowing, as he tried to explain to her what ice was and how snow fell from the sky, why Englishmen had only one wife, and how some had hair the colour of the gold bangles on her ankles as well as flaming red like his, how the girls curled their golden hair with hot irons and the men shaved theirs off and wore wigs, the colour and style of the women's dresses and the fact that they did not wear trousers like she did but went naked under their skirts.

'That is very uncouth,' she said primly. 'And is it true, as Zayn says, that you even eat the flesh of pigs?'

'The skin goes all crackly when it's roasted,' he said, to shock her. 'It crunches in your teeth.'

She made her eyes wider still, and pretended to vomit. 'That is truly disgusting. No wonder you cannot go to Paradise with us.'

'We do not wash five times a day like your people do. Sometimes we don't wash at all during the entire winter. It's much too cold,' he told her with relish.

'Then you must smell as bad as the pigs you eat.'

She knew nothing of the world outside, but she was an expert on the affairs of the zenana. She told him that her mother was one of the divorced wives of the Prince, but that she had two brothers, so they were still in his favour. 'If it were only me, it would be different, because I am only a girl and my father does not like daughters.' She said it in a matter-of-fact tone, devoid of self-pity. 'But my mother is of royal blood. She is the niece of the Great Mogul, so the emperor is my great-uncle,' she told him proudly.

'So you are a princess?'

'Yes, but only a little one, and not very grand.' Her candour was disarming. 'Do you see the silver streak in my hair?' She pirouetted to display it. 'My mother has the same streak and my grandfather also. It is a mark of royalty.'

When she explained the relationship of the other children, Dorian listened with more attention than he had to Tahi.

'Zayn al-Din is my half-brother, but I do not like him. He is fat and cruel.' She considered Dorian thoughtfully. 'Is it true that my father has adopted you?'

'Yes, it is true.'

'Then you are also my brother. I think I like you better than Zayn, even though you eat pig meat. Do you like me, al-Amhara? Zayn says I look like Jinni.' She stroked the monkey on her shoulder. 'Do you think I look like a monkey?'

'I think you are very pretty,' Dorian told her gallantly, and when she smiled it was true.

'My mother says that my father, the Prince, has gone away to see my uncle, who is the Caliph in Muscat.'

'When will he return?' Dorian asked quickly. This must be the reason that he and Tahi had been neglected: the Prince was not here to protect them. 'Will he come back soon?'

'My mother says he may be gone a long time, perhaps a year or more.' Yasmini put her head on one side to study his face. 'If you are verily my brother, perhaps our father

605

will take you riding and hawking with him when he comes back. I wish I were a boy so I could go with you,' she said, and jumped up from where she sat on the edge of the lotus pond. 'I must go now. Kush must not catch me here. He has forbidden any of us to talk to you. He will beat me if he finds me.'

'Come again tomorrow,' he said, trying not to make it sound like a plea.

'Perhaps,' she flung over her shoulder, as she raced away across the lawn with Jinni prancing around her flying bare feet.

When she was gone Dorian looked up at the sky, watched the gulls wheeling overhead, listened to the distant sound of the surf beating on the shore, and thought desperately about trying to escape. He imagined climbing out through the open roof of the kitchen, of clambering over the outer wall of the zenana and finding a small boat on the beach. But where would I go in it? he wondered, and the fantasy shrivelled and died. I will have to wait for Tom to come. He resigned himself once more to the inevitable.

One morning, Kush came rattling his keys and shouted, in his shrill squeaky voice, 'Tahi, you are to prepare the boy to visit the holy mullah.' He threw down an armful of clean clothing. 'I will come back to fetch him after the midday prayers. Make certain that he is ready, or I will have you beaten until you bleed.'

The bullock cart was waiting at the gates and Dorian clambered on board, almost beside himself with excitement and the joy of being allowed out of his bleak prison. Tahi was not coming with him but she had been allowed to sun herself in the gardens during his absence.

Kush rode beside Dorian on the front seat of the cart, smiling and caressing him. 'These robes suit you well. They are of the finest quality. See the embroidery on the collar. It is of silk! Prince Abd Muhammad al-Malik has a robe just like this. I chose it specially for you. See how I spoil you.'

The closer they came to the palace, the more agitated and conciliatory Kush became. 'Have some of these sugared cinnamon cakes. They are my favourites. You will like them also. I want you to be happy, al-Amhara.'

When they came in sight of the white walls of the fort, Kush became more direct in his instruction. 'If al-Allama, blessed be his sainted name, should ask how I have treated you, you must tell him that I have been like a father to you. That you have been given the first choice of the finest foods, the freshest fish and the choicest fruits for your kitchen.'

'And that you have locked me in stinking hot rooms like a criminal?' Dorian asked innocently.

'That is not true. Perhaps I have been a little too concerned for your safety, that is all.' Though he was smiling, his eyes were as cold as those of a cobra. 'Do not try to make trouble for me, little infidel. I can be a better friend than an enemy – ask that fat old sow Tahi. She will tell you.'

They climbed down from the cart in the outer court-yard of the fort. Kush took his hand and led him into the labyrinth of the building. They climbed several staircases and at last came out on to a terrace, high above the harbour, which looked out across the waters of the channel to the mass of the African mainland.

Dorian looked about eagerly. It was a delight to see the sea again, and to have the salt-laden breeze of the monsoon in his face, cleaning his head of the stale smells of the zenana. He saw the mullah at once and made a bow

607

of respect, touching his heart and his lips. Al-Allama greeted him and said, 'May Allah keep you smiling, little one.'

There was another man sitting beside the mullah, cross-legged under the sun awning of split bamboo. He was sipping a small cup of thick black coffee, and a tall glass hookah stood close at hand.

'*Salaam aliekum*, old father,' Dorian said respectfully, and the man turned to look at him. Dorian's heart leaped and his face lit with joy as he recognized him. He rushed forward to embrace him.

'Ben Abram!' He clung to the old doctor. 'I thought I would never see you again. I thought you would still be with al-Auf on the island.'

Gently the old man fended off his embrace, and rearranged his ruffled beard. It was not seemly to allow the others to see the strength of the relationship he and the boy shared. 'Let me look at you.' He held Dorian away at arm's length and studied his face. His expression changed. 'You look pale. What has happened to you, my child?' He swivelled round and looked up at Kush, who was hovering anxiously at the rear of the terrace. 'You have been in charge of the boy. What have you done to him, eunuch?' Outside the zenana Kush was only a house-slave – a castrated slave at that. Ben Abram made no effort to disguise his contempt.

'I call on Allah and his saints to witness.' Kush's jowls quivered and a light sweat broke out on his chin. 'I have cherished him. He has been well fed and cosseted as though he was the true son of my master.'

Ben Abram looked to Dorian for confirmation, knowing he would receive a direct answer. 'He has locked me in a dingy little room since the day I arrived. He has fed us on pig swill, and I have not been allowed to speak to anyone but my nurse in all that time.'

Ben Abram stared at Kush coldly, and the eunuch fell

608

to his knees. 'It was on the orders of the Prince, your honour. He commanded me to keep the child from escaping.'

'The Prince paid a lakh of rupees in gold for this child. He has formally declared him his adopted son,' Ben Abram replied, in a soft voice filled with menace. 'When His Royal Highness returns from Muscat I shall inform him in person how you have cared for his son.'

'I only did my duty, merciful lord,' Kush blubbered.

'I know full well how you discharge that duty towards some of the children and women in your care, eunuch.' Ben Abram paused significantly.

'Sometimes it is my duty to punish those who disobey the Prince's commands.'

'I recall the girl Fatima,' Ben Abram mused.

'She was a whore and a harlot,' Kush justified himself.

'She was sixteen years of age and in love,' Ben Abram contradicted him.

'She had a lascivious animal come in to her over the wall of the zenana.'

'He was a young warrior, an officer of the royal guard,' Ben Abram corrected him.

'It was my duty, lord. I did not intend her to die. It was meant only to be a lesson to the others.'

Ben Abram raised his hand to quieten any further protestations of innocence. 'Hear me, eunuch, and believe what I tell you. If any further harm befalls this boy – Nay! If in the future you treat him with less than the greatest consideration, I will see to it that you scream even louder than did little Fatima.'

Al-Allama had been listening intently to all this. Now he spoke. 'All that Ben Abram has ordered, I endorse. The child and his nurse must be given decent quarters and well fed. You must not confine him nor place unnecessary restriction on him. He must be able to come and go like any other of the Prince's sons. He will come to me for instruction every other day and I shall question him strictly on how he has been treated. Now get out of my sight.' He waved Kush away. 'Wait below to take the boy back when he is ready.'

As Kush crept away he shot a glance, rank with venom, at Dorian.

Ben Abram turned back to Dorian. 'There is much I have to tell you. Did you hear of the fighting on the island after you had left?'

'No. No! I have heard none of this. Tell me, old father. Tell me everything.'

'Not all of it is good news,' Ben Abram warned him, and he began to talk quietly. Dorian listened intently. He exclaimed with pride and excitement when he heard of the attack on the fortress of Flor de la Mar, and how Tom had killed al-Auf with his own hands.

'Al-Auf was a beast. I am so proud of Tom. I wish I had been there to watch it.' But he wept when he heard of his father's wounding and how he had lost both of his legs.

'Is he dead, old father? Please tell me he is still alive.'

'In all truth, little one, I do not know. He was alive when your brother allowed me to leave the island. I think your brother planned to take him back to England.'

'To England?' Dorian was distraught. 'That is so far away. He may never come back. Has Tom deserted me?' The tears welled up and broke over his eyelids. He let them run unheeded down his cheeks.

Ben Abram took his hands, and found that the boy was trembling as though in the throes of a high fever. 'Your brother is a good man, a man of honour. He showed me great kindness.'

'But if he has gone back to England—' Dorian broke off and swallowed painfully. 'He will forget about me. I will never see him again.'

'Then that will be the will of God. In the meantime, you are the son of the Prince, and you must be attentive

610

to his wishes.' Ben Abram rose to his feet. 'Now you must obey the holy al-Allama, for he has returned from Muscat ahead of the Prince, and it is His Royal Highness's command that you should submit yourself to the mullah's instruction.'

Sipping numerous cups of coffee and sucking on the waterpipe, Ben Abram waited while the religious instruction went on through the hottest hours of the day. Once or twice he made a comment or asked a question, but mostly he listened in silence. Dorian was comforted by his quiet presence.

The sun was casting the long shadows of the palms over the beach below them when Ben Abram asked for the mullah's blessing and took Dorian to where Kush waited in the bullock cart to take him back to the zenana.

Ben Abram stopped out of earshot of the eunuch and spoke quietly, 'I will see you as often as I am able to,' he promised, 'whenever you come for lessons with the mullah.' He lowered his voice to a whisper. 'Your brother showed me great kindness. If it were not for him I, too, would have been sold into slavery. Because of this I promised him to bring you a message. I could not repeat it with the mullah listening. It is for you only to hear.'

'What was the message? Please tell me, old father.'

'Your brother asked me to tell you that he would always hold true to the oath he swore to you. Do you remember that oath?'

'He said he would come back for me,' Dorian whispered. 'He swore a dreadful oath.'

'Yes, little one. To me he affirmed his promise. He will return for you. I should not tell you this. It is against the interests of my master, but I could not deprive you of the comfort of your brother's words.'

'I knew he would never forget that oath.' Dorian touched the old man's sleeve. 'Thank you for telling me this.'

Ben Abram's and al-Allama's threats had a profound effect on Kush. The next day Dorian and Tahi were moved to more spacious quarters in a better part of the zenana. Now they had their own small courtyard with a freshwater fountain. Kush sent a slave-woman to help Tahi with the cooking and the heavy housework, such as changing the latrine buckets. He also sent Dorian a fresh wardrobe of clothing, and Tahi was allowed to meet the carts when they came up from the town each day laden with fresh produce and supplies. She was able to take her pick of the fresh meat and fish. Most importantly, during the day Dorian was allowed the run of the zenana. However, even though he complained bitterly, Kush would not allow him to leave the walled enclosure except to visit the mullah at the fort.

Even this changed when Dorian complained to Ben Abram. After that Dorian was allowed to roam the port and the entire island, although one of Kush's guards followed him closely and never let him out of sight. So great was his freedom that Dorian started to think once again of escaping from the island.

His plans were more a game of make-believe than of serious intent. When he started frequenting the beach where the fishing-boats came in to land their catches and tried to make friends among the fisher-folk, he discovered that Kush had forestalled him. He must have warned all the islanders not to speak to the infidel. With his guard always hovering close at hand there was not the slightest chance of stealing a boat, or of receiving any assistance from the local fishermen and sailors. Finally Dorian resigned himself to the futility of his plans to escape. He started to devote more time and effort to making friends among the soldiers at the fort, the grooms of the royal stables and the Prince's falconers.

Yasmini greeted his release from confinement with patent delight, and as soon as she divined that there was no obvious objection from Kush, she became Dorian's shadow. Of course, she was never allowed to place a foot outside the gates to the zenana, but she followed Dorian around the gardens and was a constant visitor to the quarters he shared with Tahi.

Her voice and laughter mingled with the chattering of Jinni to make the gloomy rooms seem brighter. Tahi started to teach her to cook over the smoky wood fire. This was something that Yasmini had never tried before and she took huge delight in the novelty, and she pressed her creations on Dorian. 'I made it just for you, Dowie,' she piped. 'You do like it, don't you?' Anxiously she watched each mouthful disappear. 'Is it good? Do you like it?'

When Dorian left the zenana for his visits to the beach, the harbour and the fort, she pined. She hung around Tahi's skirts waiting for his return and her monkey face lit up as he walked through the door and she ran to him.

At times her devotion became so cloying that Dorian made an excuse to leave the walls of the zenana simply to be away from her. He would go down to the royal stables and spend hours feeding, watering and grooming the magnificent animals of the Prince's string, for the privilege of being allowed to ride one. All his instruction by his father and elder brothers at High Weald came back to him. In the cool of the evening the grooms played the game of *pulu*, the Persian name for a ball, which was a passion among the royal Moguls, and had been adopted by the Omanis. The ball was carved from a bamboo root, and was struck by a mallet of the same material. When the head groom came to know Dorian better, he allowed him to join the younger boys on the practice field. Dorian loved the feel of the horse's sweating back between his legs and the thundering, shouting charge down the field, elbowing and jostling the others in the mêlée around the ball. Soon his aggression and skill made the old syces nod with approval. 'If Allah allows, he will be a worthy horseman.'

One of his other favourite retreats was the royal mews where the Prince's falcons were kept. Around the fierce yet lovely birds he was quiet and attentive, and soon the falconers accepted his interest, and began to impart their lore and wisdom to him. He learned their colourful language and terminology, and sometimes, at their invitation, rode out with them when they flew the birds along the edge of the mangrove swamps at the north end of the island.

At other times he would give his guard the slip, and sneak away alone to explore the shores of the island, finding coves and deserted beaches where he could throw off his clothes, plunge into the ocean and swim out over the reef, driving himself to the point of exhaustion. Then he would swim back and lie in the white sand, staring out into the south and imagining the topsails of Tom's ship coming up over the horizon.

When he went back to the zenana, where he knew Yasmini would be waiting for him, he always took a small gift with him to assuage his guilt. Sometimes it was a falcon feather from one of the moulting birds, or a bangle he had plaited from horse-tail hair, or sea shells that he had brought up from the reef. He strung these into necklaces for her.

'I wish I could come with you,' she told him wistfully. 'I would love to swim with you, or watch you ride the horses.'

'Well, you know that you cannot,' Dorian told her brusquely. He had realized what her life would be like in the years ahead. She would never be able to leave the zenana, except veiled and chaperoned. He was probably the only friend of the opposite sex who was not a blood relative she would ever know. Even that would end soon, for both of them were on the threshold of puberty. As soon as she became a woman she was to be married. Tahi told him that it had been arranged when Yasmini was only four years old. 'She is to be given to one of her cousins in the land of the Great Mogul across the ocean, to cement the ties between the two royal houses.' She watched the emotions that crossed Dorian's face at the thought of his little companion being sent away to a man she did not know in a land she had never seen.

'She is my sister. I don't want her to go,' Dorian blurted out impulsively. He was surprised by the strength of the responsibility he felt for her.

'It will make no difference to you,' Tahi told him roughly, hiding her compassion in her tone. 'Within the year the change of manhood will come upon you. Kush will be watching for it. He never misses it. At the very first sign you will be banished from the zenana for ever. Even if she were to stay here, you would never see Yasmini's face again after that day. Perhaps it is best that your friendship ends as cleanly as the stroke of the knife that will celebrate your own manhood.'

The reference to the knife perturbed him. He had heard the other boys discussing the rite of circumcision, and making crude jokes about it, but he had never thought that he himself would have to undergo it. Now Tahi had rudely brought it home to him. 'I am not a Mussulman,' he protested. 'They cannot do that to me.'

'You will never find a wife if you keep that bit of skin,' she warned him.

'I don't want a wife, and I don't want anyone to cut pieces off me.'

His fear of the blade was exacerbated by the incipient guilt he felt towards Yasmini at their enforced separation from each other. 'What will she do without me to look after her?' he worried. 'She is only a baby.'

He came home from his wanderings about the island one afternoon just after the afternoon prayers. His hair was still damp and stiff with sea-water. Tahi was squatting in front of the cooking-fire and she looked up as he stood in the doorway. With a long-suffering expression he answered her questions as to where he had been and what he had been doing, giving her only those details that he felt she need know. Then he looked around casually. 'Where is Yasmini?' he enquired, as though the answer was of no real concern.

'She was here until prayers, then she went to see Battuta who has a new pet. I think it is a grey parrot.' Dorian leaned over her shoulder and snatched one of the hot rounds of unleavened bread from the coals in front of her. She slapped his hand. 'That is dinner. Put it back at once.'

'May the Prophet open the doors of mercy to you, Tahi.' Laughing, he headed out into the gardens, breaking off pieces of bread and stuffing them into his mouth. He had a gift for Yasmini, a large spiral shell with an opalescent pink interior. He knew where to find her. There was a ruined tomb at the east side of the gardens that had been built in honour of one of the Islamic saints centuries before. There was a stone tablet on the wall of the tomb, whose text Dorian had deciphered laboriously: 'Abd Allah Muhammad Ali, died in the year of the Prophet 120.'

There was a high dome surmounted by a bronze symbol of the crescent moon, thick with verdigris. Below it was an open prayer terrace that faced in the direction of the Kabaa in Mecca. At one end there was large open rainwater cistern where once the faithful had performed *wudu*, the ritual ablutions, before prayers. Now it was disused and attracted flocks of wild birds in the afternoons.

Yasmini and her special friends among her half-sisters

liked to play on the terrace. Here they gossiped and bickered and played fantastic games, dressed up their pets in infants' clothing and nursed them, pretended to run a household and cook for their imaginary families.

Dorian had reached the foot of the staircase that led up to the terrace, when a scream from above froze him with one foot on the bottom step. Instantly he recognized Yasmini's voice, but what slashed his heart was the high-pitched agony that filled it. He sprang forward and flew up the ancient staircase driven by a series of those terrible cries, each shriller and more chilling than the one before.

Jinni, the vervet monkey, sat on the top of the dome of the old tomb. When he grew tired of being nursed and dressed like a human baby, he would escape to this favourite perch where Yasmini could not reach him. Now he scratched under his arm sleepily, his blue eyelids drooping over his big brown eyes. Every few minutes he would sway and almost fall from his perch, then jerk awake and blink down at the gardens spread below him.

Suddenly he smelt something that brought him fully awake: cinnamon cakes. There was nothing in all the world that Jinni loved more. He stood to his full height, using his long tail to balance on the rounded plaster dome, and looked around him eagerly.

Two boys came down one of the paths through the shrubbery. Even from this distance Jinni could see that their jaws were working and that the biggest of the pair carried a covered silver dish. Jinni did not need his eyes to tell him what was under the cover. He made a small, greedy, chittering sound, and skipped down off the dome and swung into the top of the peepul tree, which spread its wide branches below the terrace.

Hidden by the thick foliage, he watched the two boys

settle down in a hidden corner of the gardens and place the silver dish between them. Zayn al-Din lifted the cover, and Jinni stiffened his tail and rolled his eyes as he saw the mound of yellow cakes. He was torn between greed and fear. He knew Zayn al-Din only too well. He had a healed scar over one eye where a stone had struck him. Zayn was an expert with a slingshot. On the other hand, the cakes were still warm from the clay oven and their aroma was tantalizing, irresistible.

Jinni shot down the trunk of the peepul, keeping it between him and the boys. When he reached the ground he peered out from behind the tree. When he was sure he was still unobserved he left his hiding-place and darted across the lawn. From the depths of one of the shrubs he stole another look. He puffed out his cheeks and wiggled his nose. The scent of cinnamon was much stronger here. He watched Zayn lift one of the cakes to his mouth and bite into its fluffy yellow delights.

Ibn al-Malik Abubaker was the other boy, one of Zayn al-Din's numerous half-brothers. He stood up and went to one of the casuarina trees near the outer wall, and pointed up into the branches. 'There is a hawk nesting there,' he called to Zayn, who stood up and waddled across to join him. They had their backs turned to the silver dish and their heads were thrown back as they discussed the shaggy nest in the branches high above them.

'Perhaps it's a peregrine,' Zayn said hopefully. 'We can take the chicks when they are fledged.'

Jinni gathered his courage. He shot out from under the shrub, and covered the open ground in a grey streak. He reached the dish and filled both fists with the sticky cakes. He stuffed them into his mouth until his pouches bulged to the point of bursting. Half the cakes remained in the dish and he tried to fill his paws, but he couldn't manage them all, so he dropped those he already held and started again.

'The monkey!' Zayn's dreaded voice screeched behind him and Jinni knew he had been discovered. In his haste to escape he sent the dish flying, and raced away back to the safety of the peepul tree. He scattered a trail of broken cinnamon cakes across the lawn behind him.

As he sped up the trunk and reached the safety of the first high branch he ducked his head and looked back. The boys were in close pursuit, shouting their protests and outrage. '*Shaitan!* Devil monkey! Pig animal!'

Jinni reached the top branches and crouched in a fork. He felt safe here, and started to munch the remnants of the cakes that had survived the flight and the climb up the tree.

Below him Zayn opened the pouch on his belt and brought out his slingshot. He unwound the leather thongs and stretched them between spread arms, then he selected a perfectly rounded pebble, and fitted it into the pocket at the end of the double thongs. He moved around the base of the tree until he had a clear shot at Jinni. The monkey bobbed his head and opened his eyes wide, making a terrifying face to frighten him away.

'I will teach you such a lesson that you will never steal my cakes again,' Zayn promised him, and began to wind up for the throw. Round and round his head he swung the sling, building up speed until the thongs thrummed through the air, and then, at that exact moment, he released it. The pebble was a hissing white blur, too swift for Jinni to dodge. It struck the monkey's left arm below the elbow, and the bone snapped.

Jinni screeched and sprang high in the air, his broken arm flapping. As he came down he tried to grab at a branch but the arm would not respond and he tumbled halfway down the tree before he could catch hold with his right paw.

The two boys were shouting and dancing with excitement. 'You hit him, Zayn!' Abubaker exulted.

'I will kill you, you thieving *shaitan*!' Zayn was fitting another stone into the pocket of the sling. Jinni clawed his way single-armed back up the tree. He was whining and gibbering with pain as he reached the long branch that extended out over the terrace.

Zayn launched the next stone, which sang through the air and hit the branch just under Jinni's chest. He sprang in the air and raced towards the end of the branch with his broken arm dangling and swinging. He knew where he could find protection. Yasmini had heard his screams and, though she did not know what had caused them, she was calling him urgently. 'Jinni! What is it, my baby? Come to your mama.'

From the end of the branch Jinni launched himself, and dropped into Yasmini's arms, sobbing and chittering with pain and terror.

'Come!' Zayn shouted at Abubaker. 'Find a stick! We will finish him off!'

At the foot of the staircase the gardeners had left a pile of bamboo stakes. Each of the boys grabbed one and ran up the staircase. Puffing and laughing, Zayn was the first to reach the terrace. He stopped short when Yasmini confronted him with Jinni in her arms. 'Don't come near me!' she yelled at him. 'Leave us alone, Zayn al-Din.'

For a moment Zayn was disconcerted by the fury of the small girl, but then Abubaker came up behind him and pushed him forward. 'It's only Yasmini. She is a baby. I will hold her. You grab the monkey.'

Yasmini retreated before them, clutching the terrified animal to her chest, but they followed her threateningly, brandishing the bamboo stakes, egging each other on. 'The *shaitan* stole my cakes. I am going to kill him.'

'I will kill you first,' Yasmini shouted back at him, but her show of bravery was starting to crumble and tears welled in her eyes. She came up against the low wall of the rainwater cistern, and stood there, trapped and desperate. Her half-sisters had deserted her and run off at the first sign of trouble from their elder brother. Yasmini was alone. Her lips quivered, but she tried to keep her voice strong. 'Leave us alone. I will tell al-Amhara. He will punish you for what you have done to Jinni.'

Zayn jeered, 'You will tell al-Amhara? You frighten me! Al-Amhara is a pig-eating infidel.' They crowded her up against the cistern. Suddenly Abubaker jumped forward and grabbed her around the neck.

'Get the monkey!' he shouted, and Zayn seized Jinni by the leg. The three struggled and staggered around the terrace fighting over the screeching animal. Yasmini was clinging to Jinni with all her strength, screaming through her tears. Abubaker prised her fingers free one at a time, until she lost her grip and Zayn snatched the monkey from her.

'Give him back,' she pleaded. 'Please don't hurt him any more.'

Zayn held Jinni up by the scruff of the neck. 'Come and get him then, before I kill the filthy thing.'

Suddenly Jinni twisted in his grip and sank his teeth into Zayn's wrist. Zayn let out a howl of pain and surprise, lifted Jinni over his head and hurled him into the rainwater cistern. The monkey disappeared beneath the water, then splashed to the surface and swam to the edge. Zayn held up his bleeding wrist and stared at it. Then his sallow face darkened with fury. 'He bit me! Look at the blood!' He ran to the edge of the cistern, reached out with the bamboo stake and pushed Jinni's head under the water. As soon as it bobbed up again he thrust it under once more, now hooting with sadistic joy. 'Let us see how well it can swim!'

Yasmini tore herself out of Abubaker's grip and jumped on to Zayn's back. She screamed as she pummelled his head and shoulders. Zayn kept on hooting and jeering, taking no notice of her screams and her attack. He went on drowning Jinni, ducking his head every time it reappeared.

Jinni was weakening swiftly and sneezing water, his fur sodden and clinging to his skull. He no longer had the strength or the air in his lungs to scream, but Yasmini's voice rang louder and shriller. 'Leave him! I hate you. Leave my baby!'

Dorian raced up the last few steps and stopped at the top of the staircase. It took him a moment to grasp the meaning of the confused scene before him. He had been overtaken by a wild panic at the prospect of finding Yasmini badly injured and dying, but his fear gave way to cold anger as he saw what the two big boys were doing to her and Jinni. He launched himself at them.

Abubaker saw him coming and spun round to face him. He lifted the bamboo to hit at his head but Dorian ducked under the swing and crashed his shoulder into the centre of the other boy's chest, sending him reeling away. Abubaker struck the side wall of the terrace, and dropped the bamboo. Then he turned and fled to the head of the staircase and disappeared down it.

Dorian's only concern now was to get at Zayn and rescue Yasmini. He flew at him, and Zayn turned to meet him, but he was hampered by the small girl straddling his back and his swing with the bamboo was clumsy. Dorian blocked it and seized the stake with both hands. They stumbled in a circle, both tugging and heaving at the stake.

'Get Jinni!' Dorian gasped at Yasmini, and obediently she jumped down off Zayn's back and ran to the cistern. She reached in and grabbed the monkey as he floundered weakly. She dragged him out, sopping wet, coughing and sneezing water from his mouth and nose. She held him to her chest and crouched below the parapet of the cistern, trying to avoid the two boys who were struggling and pushing each other around the terrace.

Zayn was heavier than Dorian, and taller by two inches. He was starting to dominate this straight trial of strength. 'I am going to drown you just like the monkey, you devil-eyed infidel,' he threatened, and heaved with all his weight on the bamboo stave.

In his fury Dorian had forgotten everything that Tom had ever taught him, but now the insult steadied him and he let Zayn pull him in close. Then he released his grip on the stave and bunched his right fist. He shifted his feet, anchoring himself. 'Use the turn of the body, and the swing of the shoulders,' Tom had coached him. 'Go for the nose.'

Dorian launched the punch, his hands hardened by riding and his shoulders conditioned by swimming. He caught Zayn flush on the nose, which squashed like an overripe plum in a flood of scarlet juice. Zayn dropped the bamboo and clutched with both hands at his injured face. His eyes flooded with tears of pain, and blood ran from between his fingers and dripped on to his white *kanzu*.

Dorian set himself up for the next punch. Tom had shown him how to find the point of the jaw, making him clench his teeth and feel for it under his own ear. Dorian let the next punch go with all his weight coming in behind it.

Zayn had never heard of this kind of fighting. Making a hammer out of the hand and using it to beat in an opponent's face was something alien to his idea of combat. He had been taught to wrestle, but enjoyed it only when matched against a lighter, weaker boy.

The blow to his nose had flabbergasted him, the surprise even more crippling than the pain. He was unprepared for the next blow. It felt like a cannonball into the side of his face, and his senses tottered. Dorian did not yet have the weight or power to drop him senseless. But the punch struck exactly where he had aimed, and with enough force to send Zayn reeling backwards, unable to see through his streaming eyes, unable to defend himself, his legs turning boneless under him.

Then, to Zayn's bewilderment, there came another blow, slamming into his fat lips. He felt one of his front teeth break off, and the warm metallic taste of his own blood filled his mouth. With both arms covering his face he stumbled blindly to the head of the stairs.

Behind him Dorian picked up the bamboo, and belaboured his back and shoulders. Even through the pain of his mouth and nose, the sting of the bamboo made Zayn leap forward onto the top step.

Dorian swung the cane again, and Zayn yelled as though he had been stung by a scorpion and lost his footing. He went rolling in a tangle of arms and legs to the bottom, and crawled away sobbing wildly. Then he heard Dorian rushing down the stairs behind him, and looked back over his shoulder through swimming eyes.

The infidel's face was contorted into a crimson mask of fury, those pale green eyes were blazing and he had the bamboo held high in both hands. Zayn hauled himself to his feet and spat out the broken tooth in a spray of blood. He tried to run, but something was broken in his right foot, and he hopped, limped and lumbered away across the lawn, in pursuit of the fleeing Abubaker.

Dorian dropped the bamboo and let them go. He took a few deep breaths to bring his rage under control, then thought of the little girl. He ran back up the steps.

Yasmini was still crouched under the parapet. She was shaking and sobbing, and holding the sodden body of the monkey to her chest.

'Are you hurt, Yasmini? Did he hurt you?'

She shook her head and wordlessly held Jinni out towards him. The monkey's fur was soaked and flattened against his body, so that he appeared to be half his normal size, as though the skin had been flayed off him.

'His arm!' Yasmini whispered. 'It's broken.'

Dorian took the dangling limb gently between his fingers, and Jinni whimpered but did not resist. He watched Dorian with huge, trusting eyes. Dorian tried to remember all he had learned from watching Dr Reynolds working with the injuries of a sailor who had fallen from the rigging of the *Seraph*, and another who had caught his arm in the spinning bars of the capstan. He straightened Jinni's arm gently, using a short length of bamboo to secure it in that position, then bound it up with a strip of cotton torn from his *keffiya* headcloth. 'I must take him to Ben Abram,' he told Yasmini, and lifted the small body out of her arms.

'I wish I could come with you,' she whispered, but she knew that was not possible, and Dorian did not bother to reply. He made a cradle for Jinni out of a fold of his robe. Yasmini came with him as far as the gates of the zenana, and stood staring after him as he trotted off down the road through the palm groves heading for the town.

Within half a mile he caught up with one of the grooms from the stables leading a string of the Prince's horses.

'Mustapha!' he shouted. 'Give me a ride as far as the harbour.'

Mustapha took him up on the back of his mount and they galloped through the narrow streets of the town, down to the seafront.

Ben Abram was at work in his infirmary near the harbour. He came through from the small back room, scrubbing blood from his hands, and greeted Dorian and Jinni with astonishment.

'I have brought you a patient, old father, one who is in sore need of your great skills,' Dorian told him.

'Will the beast bite me?' Ben Abram peered at Jinni suspiciously.

'Have no fear. Jinni knows he can trust you.'

'The setting of bones is a skill that goes back into antiquity,' Ben Abram remarked, as he peered closely at the limb, 'but I doubt any of my forebears had such a patient as this.'

When he had finished, and the limb was splinted and bandaged, Ben Abram gave Jinni a draught of laudanum, and the monkey slept in Dorian's arms for all the long walk back to the zenana.

Yasmini was waiting for them just inside the gate. She took the drugged monkey out of Dorian's arms, and carried him tenderly to the living quarters where they found Tahi in a tearful turmoil of worry. 'What have you done, you stupid boy?' She attacked Dorian the instant he put his head through the doorway. 'The whole zenana is in an uproar. Kush has been here. He is in such a terrible rage that he can hardly speak. Is it true that Jinni has bitten Zayn al-Din and that you have broken his tooth and smashed his nose, and that the bone in his foot is broken? Kush says that Zayn may never be able to walk again – at the least he will be crippled for life.'

'He broke his foot with his own clumsiness.' Dorian was defiant and unrepentant, and Tahi seized him and hugged him to her ample bosom. She broke down and wept loudly. 'You do not know what danger you have brought on your own head!' she sobbed. 'From now onwards we must always be on the watch. You must never eat or drink anything that I have not tasted first. You must keep the bar on the door to your sleeping chamber.' She reeled off the list of precautions that they would take against the vengeance of Kush and Zayn al-Din. 'Allah only knows what the Prince will think of this when he returns from Muscat.' She ended her tirade with morbid relish.

Yasmini and Dorian left her wailing and dreaming of horrors over her kitchen pots, and carried Jinni through to Dorian's bedchamber. They laid him on the sleeping mat and sat over him side by side.

Neither spoke, but after a while Yasmini drooped like

a fading blossom and fell asleep against Dorian's shoulder. He put his arm around her, and much later Tahi found them asleep in each other's arms. She knelt beside the pair and studied their faces. 'They are so beautiful together, so young and so innocent. What a great pity that it can never be. They might have had red-haired children,' she whispered, and lifted Yasmini out of Dorian's protective arms to carry her back to her own mother's splendid quarters near the main gate, where she handed her over to one of the nurses.

Kush came again, early the following morning, full of bluster and threats. Despite these it was apparent that he was not prepared to flout the strictures of al-Allama and Ben Abram, and to bring any real harm to Dorian, but his malevolence shimmered around him like an aura of evil. At the door he looked back at Dorian, his swollen features filled with hatred. 'The day will soon come, if Allah is kind, when you will no longer be here in the zenana to trouble me.'

The atmosphere crackled like summer lightning with hostility towards Dorian. The other children, all except Yasmini, kept well away from him. As soon as they saw him they broke off their rowdy games and scuttled away tittering. The women covered their faces and drew the skirts of their robes aside as though contact with him would contaminate them.

Three days later he met Zayn as he came back through the gates from his lessons with al-Allama. Zayn was sitting with Abubaker and three other toadies. They were feasting on a dish of sweetmeats, but they fell silent as Dorian walked down the cloisters towards them, and watched him uneasily.

Zayn's nose was still swollen and there was a black

scab on his upper lip. Both his eye sockets were bruised even darker than their natural colour. His right foot was wrapped in bandages – perhaps it was true that he might be crippled for life, Dorian thought, but he never faltered, and he stared directly at Zayn. The bigger boy could not hold that cold green stare and turned away. He said something to Abubaker and both boys giggled nervously. Dorian strode past them and Zayn grew bolder as he walked away. 'Skin white as pus,' he said, and his breath whistled through the gap in his front teeth.

'Eyes green as pigs' pee,' Abubaker agreed.

'Only one who drinks it would know the colour so well,' Dorian said as loudly, and walked on without looking back.

Over the following weeks the feeling of dangerous hostility subsided. Though Dorian had become the outcast of the zenana, now the others simply ignored him. Even Zayn and Abubaker no longer reacted to his presence, but behaved with exaggerated nonchalance whenever they met. Zayn was still limping and over time it became clear that the damage to his right foot might indeed be permanent.

However, Tahi was not placated by the hostile truce between the two boys, and she missed no opportunity to lecture Dorian on the dangers of exposing himself to poison, or other macabre methods of dealing death at a distance. 'Always shake out your *kanzu* before donning it. Turn over your sandals. There is a small green scorpion that kills so swiftly that the victim does not have time to cry out after its sting. Kush knows well the ways of the scorpion, and all the other evil things.'

But none of this could dampen Dorian's naturally ebullient spirits for long. He spent less and less time within the walls of the zenana. When he was there, Yasmini was his constant companion.

As a credit to Ben Abram's skills, Jinni recovered

rapidly, and though he favoured the undamaged limb he was soon scampering along the top of the outer wall or scaling the highest branches of the peepul trees.

The long month of Ramadan came and then the new moon ended the fast. Within days Zayn al-Din was gone from the zenana. He had reached puberty and manhood, and, still limping from the injury Dorian had inflicted on him, had entered the outside world. Dorian and Yasmini rejoiced at his departure. They heard that he had been sent to Muscat to join the court of his uncle, the Caliph.

Tahi sniffed when they told her. 'He has been sent as a hostage to the Caliph to ensure the obedience of the Prince.'

This was not the first that Dorian had heard of the intrigues within the Omani royal family. However, Tahi repeated what he knew already. 'The Caliph has executed six of his brothers for treason, and he does not trust those he has spared.' She dropped her voice to a whisper. 'The Caliph is a cruel, evil man. Allah forbid that you should ever come to his notice as the child of the prophecy.' She shivered at the thought.

A few weeks after Zayn al-Din's abrupt departure, Yasmini came to Dorian's quarters before he was awake and shook his arm urgently. 'Jinni did not come for his food last night and he was not in my bed this morning.' She was drawn and shaky from grief and worry.

Dorian jumped up and flung on his *kanzu* while Yasmini lamented, 'I think something terrible has happened to my Jinni.'

'We will find him,' Dorian promised her. 'Come on!'

They started with all the most likely places, Jinni's favourite haunts. The chief of these was the tomb of the saint, Abd Allah Muhammad Ali. They searched every inch of the ancient structure, calling Jinni's name and offering cinnamon cakes. They knew that, if anything would, the aroma would bring him out of any hiding-place. When they failed there, they went systematically through the gardens, but with the same lack of success. By this time Yasmini was beside herself with grief. 'You saved him once, Dowie. Now Shaitan has come back for him again. He may have taken him away as a punishment.'

'Don't be a baby, Yassie.' Unconsciously he used the same words with which Tom had chided him. 'Shaitan does not concern himself with monkeys and small females.'

'What are we going to do?' Yasmini turned those haunted honey-coloured eyes on him with absolute trust.

'We will start again at the tomb. Jinni must be somewhere.'

The entrance to the tomb had been bricked and plastered closed centuries before, and though Dorian examined it minutely there was no hole through which even a monkey could pass. They went up onto the terrace and searched that again. Though they called until they were hoarse, there was still no sign of Jinni.

At last they sat in despair on the edge of the cistern and avoided each other's eyes, tired and dispirited. If they had not been absolutely silent they would never have heard the faint chittering. They heard it at the same time and Yasmini seized Dorian's arm, sinking her sharp little nails into his skin.

'Jinni!' she whispered.

They jumped down from the cistern and stared about eagerly, their tiredness forgotten. The sound seemed to emanate in the air around them, without any focal point.

'Where is it coming from, Dowie?' Yasmini asked, but he shushed her imperiously. Holding up a hand for silence, he tracked the faint sound across the terrace. When it stopped he whistled, and immediately Jinni called again, leading him to the far end.

There they seemed to reach a dead end, until Dorian went down on his knees and crawled along the juncture of the dome wall and the skirting of the terrace where Jinni's cries were perceptibly louder. Weeds and creepers blanketed the area, but he picked out a track through them that looked as though somebody or something had recently passed that way. He moved in, bending the weeds aside and lifting the dangling creepers to inspect the base of the dome wall.

He saw at once that the coral rag had disintegrated at one point and that there was an aperture large enough for Jinni to have squeezed through. When he put his ear to this opening his last doubts were dispelled. Jinni's cries were magnified as though by a speaking tube. 'He's down there!' he told Yasmini.

She clapped her hands joyfully. 'Can you get him out, Dowie?' Then she placed her mouth to the hole and shouted down it, 'Jinni, my baby! Can you hear me?' She was answered by faint but excited squeaks from the depths of the hole.

'Get out of the way.' Dorian pushed her aside, and began to work at enlarging the hole with his bare hands. The ragging was unmortared, and chunks of it came away in his hands. He sent Yasmini to bring him one of the bamboo staves from the pile at the bottom of the steps, and used this to prise out the more stubborn chunks of brick.

Within half an hour he had enlarged the opening enough so that he could squeeze through. However, when he peered down into the depths all he could see was the swirling dust of his labours, and darkness. 'Wait here, Yassie,' he ordered, and lowered his legs into the opening. Although he kicked around he was unable to touch the bottom or find a foothold. He clung to the lip with both hands and let himself down an inch at a time. Abruptly the section of the wall he was holding broke away, and with a shout of alarm he fell into the dark. He expected to plunge down hundreds of feet to his death, but he dropped only inches before he hit the ground. The impact was so unexpected that his legs gave way under him and he fell in a heap. He scrambled up.

Yasmini was calling down urgently, 'Are you all right, Dowie?'

'Yes.'

'Can I come down?'

'No! You stay there. Take your head out of the way to let the light in.'

When the dust had settled and his eyes became accustomed to the gloom he surveyed his surroundings. A faint ray of sunlight came from the opening above him and by its light he found himself in a narrow passage, which seemed to have been built into the centre of the massive outer wall of the tomb. It was just wider than his shoulders and high enough for him to stand upright.

Jinni's cries came from close at hand and he moved towards them, sneezing. Dorian found a wooden door, which shut off the passage. It was crumbling with age and damp mould, and it had fallen off its rotten leather hinges. Jinni must have swung on it, and even his small bulk had been enough to bring it down. Now he was trapped under it.

He had torn his fingernails on the wood trying to free himself, and his fur was thick with dust and wood chips. Dorian tugged and heaved at the heavy door, lifting it enough for the monkey to wriggle out from under it. Jinni was not injured and he shot up Dorian's body and onto his shoulder where he clung to his neck with both arms, chattering with relief.

'You stupid animal,' Dorian scolded in English, as he stroked Jinni's head to quieten him. 'This will teach you not to go wandering off to where you should not go, you idiot monkey.'

He carried him back and handed him up to Yasmini, who was hanging head and shoulders through the hole. Then he went back, lifted one end of the door and dragged it back. He leaned it against the wall of the passage and used it as a ladder to climb back through the opening into the sunlight.

He was covered with dust and dirt, so while Yasmini smothered Jinni in a loving embrace, he washed away the worst of the filth in the waters of the cistern.

Yasmini carried Jinni down the steps, but before he followed them Dorian went back on an impulse and arranged the weeds and the flowering creeper to conceal the hole in the base of the dome.

It was some days later that Dorian went back to explore the further reaches of the secret passage. He should never have told Yasmini what he planned, for she insisted on coming with him and bringing Jinni. Without letting Tahi know, Dorian took one of the lamps, and a steel and flint to light it.

They went through elaborate precautions to make certain that they were not followed by any of Kush's spies or henchmen, taking separate routes to the old tomb and meeting beside the cistern.

'Nobody followed you?' Dorian demanded, as Yasmini scuttled up the stairs with Jinni riding on her shoulder.

'Nobody!' she confirmed, almost dancing with excitement. 'What do you think we will find, Dowie? A great treasure of gold and jewels?'

'A secret room full of skulls and old bones,' he said, teasing.

She looked apprehensive. 'Will you go first?' she asked, and took his hand.

They crept into the weeds and pulled them closed

633

behind them, then Dorian lifted the creepers from the entrance to the passage and peered into the darkness. 'It's safe. Nobody has found it.' He squatted and worked with the flint and steel. When the lamp flame was burning evenly, he said, 'Pass it down to me when I tell you.' He lowered himself into the opening, and looked up. 'Give me the lamp.' He took it from her hands and set it out of the way. 'Now come down.'

He guided her dangling feet, placing them on the old door. 'You're nearly there. Jump!'

She hopped down and looked about her. Jinni came darting after her and shot up her leg. There was not enough headroom for him to ride on her shoulder so she took him on her hip. 'This is so exciting. I have never done anything like this before.'

'Don't make so much noise.' Dorian picked up the lamp. 'Now stay close behind me, but don't get in my way.'

He moved cautiously to where the old door had stood, but felt a slide of disappointment when he saw that the passage had been bricked shut only a few yards further on. It was a dead end.

'What is beyond the bricks?' Yasmini asked, in a whisper.

'It looks as if it once led into the tomb itself, but somebody closed it off. I wonder why they built it anyway.'

'So that the Angel Gibrael could come into the tomb to take the soul of the saint to Paradise,' Yasmini told him, with authority. 'Gibrael always comes down to fetch the souls of righteous men.'

Dorian was on the point of ridiculing her, when he saw how large and liquid her eyes looked in the light of the lamp. 'Perhaps you are right,' he agreed. 'But I wonder where the other end of the passage leads to.'

They turned, passing under the opening through which they had entered and went on slowly into the dusty darkness, which smelt of fungus and mould. In the feeble yellow lamplight the floor beneath their feet began to slope downwards and every few paces there were stone steps descending. The roof was only inches above Dorian's head.

'I'm frightened,' Yasmini whispered breathlessly. 'Perhaps the Angel will be angry with us for using his road.' She hugged Jinni close to her chest. With her other hand she reached out and took a firm grip on the back of Dorian's *kanzu*.

They moved on quietly. The passage continued to angle downwards until Dorian guessed that they were well below ground level, then it levelled out and ran straight. He counted the paces.

'What happens if the roof falls in?' Yasmini asked.

'It's been here for hundreds of years,' Dorian said confidently. 'Why would it suddenly fall in now?' He went on, counting the paces aloud.

'Three hundred and twenty-two,' he announced, then said, almost immediately, 'Look, there are steps going up again.'

They climbed them slowly. Dorian paused on each tread and held the lamp high to survey the way ahead. Suddenly he stopped again. 'It's blocked,' he said, with heavy disappointment. In the lamplight they saw that the roof and one of the side walls had fallen in. They stood uncertainly, staring at the tumbled masonry.

Suddenly Jinni jumped down from Yasmini's hip and darted forward. Before Dorian could grab his tail he disappeared into a small opening between the intact part of the roof and the pile of rubble.

'Jinni!' Yasmini pushed past Dorian and thrust her arm into the opening. 'He will get stuck again. Save him, Dowie.'

'Stupid monkey!' Dorian started clearing the masonry and trying to reach inside. Every few minutes they heard Jinni calling, but he would not come back to Yasmini though she pleaded with him. Dorian worked on doggedly, clearing the rubbish from the tunnel ahead. Then he stopped and climbed onto the heap. 'I can see light ahead.' He was jubilant. He jumped down and redoubled his efforts to clear away the rubble that still blocked the tunnel.

An hour later he wiped his face on the hem of his *kanzu*. His sweat had mingled with the dust into a paste of mud.

'I think I can crawl through now.' He worked his way, belly down, into the enlarged opening, and apprehensively Yasmini watched his body, then his legs and finally his feet disappear from view. Moments later he called, 'Yassie! It's all right. Come on.'

She was so much smaller than him that she could crawl on hands and knees. Within a short distance the light strengthened and she found Dorian squatting at the exit to the tunnel. A veil of vegetation hung down in front of them, but beyond that was brilliant sunlight.

'Where are we?' she asked, crowding in beside him.

'I don't know.'

Cautiously he parted the green foliage. They were in a saucer of ground, surrounded by fallen walls of coral bricks disintegrated by time and weather. The whole area was heavily overgrown. 'Stay there,' Dorian told her, and crept out into the sunlight. Gingerly he climbed to the top of the ruin and looked out. He saw palm trees and green mangrove forest and beyond that a glimpse of white beach and the vivid blue ocean. He recognized the area from his explorations outside the walls. 'We are outside the zenana,' he said, with astonishment. 'The tunnel goes under the wall.'

'I have never been outside in my whole life.' Yasmini climbed up beside him. 'Look, is that the beach? Can't we go down there, Dowie?'

They heard voices, and ducked down. A party of women passed below their hiding-place without looking up. They were Swahili slave-girls, black and unveiled, with

636

huge bundles of firewood balanced on their heads. They passed and their voices faded.

'Can we go down to the beach, Dowie?' Yasmini pleaded. 'For only a short time. Just this once.'

'No! You're a silly girl,' Dorian said sternly. 'The fishermen will see us and they'll tell Kush. Then there will be another grave in the cemetery. You know what happens to little girls who defy him.' He scrambled back into the mouth of the tunnel. 'Come on.'

'Perhaps it is the will of God that I should never swim in the ocean with you,' she said wistfully, still gazing down through the trees.

'Come down, Yassie. We must go back.'

Her words troubled him. Every time he went down to the beach by himself and swam out over the reef he felt guilty, and though she did not mention it again her appeal preyed upon his mind.

Over the weeks that followed he quietly scouted the area outside the east wall of the zenana, and found that there were many overgrown ruins among the trees. They were mostly covered with undergrowth, or by the sand dunes blown up from the beach by the monsoon. It took him some days to find the exact clump of bushes and old coral rag that hid the mouth of the tunnel. When he was certain that he was not being watched he climbed over the heap and down to the opening in its saucer.

He spent several hours working to clear the entrance so that access was easier and safer, then covered it again with fallen palm fronds and dried branches to hide it from casual discovery by the Swahili wood gatherers.

From his friend Mustapha, the groom at the stables, he begged a grubby, tattered *kanzu*, more patches than original material, and an equally filthy *keffiya*, which even the groom would no longer wear. He rolled these into a bundle and hid it in the exit of the tunnel. He waited until the moon was full, and then, when all was ready, he asked Yasmini, 'Would you really like to swim in the ocean?'

She stared at him in astonishment, and then her small face crumpled. 'Don't tease me, Dowie,' she pleaded.

'This evening you will come to eat dinner with Tahi and me. After the Maghrib prayers, you will thank Tahi and tell her that you are going back to your mother. Instead you will come here and hide behind the cistern.' Slowly her face lit up and her eyes sparkled. 'Your mother will think you are with Tahi, and Tahi will think you are with your mother. I will follow you shortly and find you here.'

'Yes, Dowie.' She nodded vigorously.

'You will not be frightened to come here in the dark, on your own?'

'No, Dowie.' She shook her head so vehemently that it seemed she might loosen it from her shoulders.

'You cannot bring Jinni. He must stay in his cage. Do you promise me?'

'I promise you with all my heart, Dowie.'

At dinner Yasmini was so restless and talkative that Tahi studied her shrewdly. 'What ails you, child? You're jabbering like a flock of parakeets and bouncing around as though you have a hot coal in your trousers. Have you been out in the sun again without a covering for your head?'

Yasmini gobbled down the last of the meal, scooping it from the bowl with the fingers of her right hand. Then she jumped up. 'I must go, Tahi. My mother charged me to return early.'

'You have not finished your food. I have your favourite, grated coconut cakes with saffron.'

'I'm not hungry tonight. I must go. I will come again tomorrow.'

'Your prayers first.' Tahi restrained her.

'All praise and thanks to the Almighty Allah for having given us to eat and drink, and having made of us Muslims,' Yasmini gabbled, and sprang to her feet. She was out of the room before Tahi could stop her again.

Dorian waited a short time, then stood up and stretched nonchalantly. 'I'm going for a walk in the gardens.'

Immediately Tahi was all concern. 'Remember to be very careful, al-Amhara. Do not think that Kush has forgiven you.'

Dorian retreated swiftly to avoid any further advice.

'Yassie?' he called softly, as he crept up the staircase to the terrace. His voice quavered and cracked: it had been playing tricks on him for a while now, in moments of nervousness or emotion, jumping up and down the scale. 'Yassie?' This time it came out gruffly.

'Dowie! I am here.' She crawled out from behind the cistern, and ran to meet him. The moon was just rising above the outer wall of the zenana, and by its light Dorian led her to the opening to the Angel's Road, as they had named their secret passage. He lowered himself into it and found the lamp, the flint and steel where he had left them. When the wick was burning evenly he called Yasmini down and caught her small body as she came sliding down the old door. She pressed close behind him, hanging on to the back of his robe as he led her along the tunnel.

When they reached the collapsed section that he had

cleared Dorian snuffed out the wick of the lamp. 'We must not show any light,' he warned her. They groped their way along the wall for the last few yards, and at last they could see the luminescence of the moon through the trailing creepers that masked the exit of the tunnel. Dorian searched for the bundle of old clothes he had hidden in a niche in the tunnel wall.

'Here! Put these on,' he ordered.

'They are smelly!' she protested.

'Do you want to come with me or not?'

She did not argue again, but there was the rustle of cloth as she stripped off her own clothes, and pulled the *kanzu* over her head.

'I am ready,' she said eagerly.

He led her out into the moonlight. The robe was too big for her. She tripped over the skirts. He knelt in front of her and ripped away the hem at the level of her ankles, then helped her arrange the *keffiya* over her head to hide her long hair. 'That will do,' he said as he looked her over. She looked like any one of the ragged urchins that ran wild through the streets of the town or along the beaches. The son of a fisherman, perhaps, or one of the gatherers of firewood or mangrove bark. 'Come on!'

They scrambled out of the ruins and then, with exaggerated caution, crept down through the palm groves to the head of the beach. Dorian knew this stretch of the coast intimately. He had chosen a spot where low sandstone cliffs screened a tidal pool.

In the face of the cliff there was a shallow cave, which was filled with shadows that hid them as they sat side by side on the hard-packed damp sand. They looked out on the silvery moon-bathed cove. The tide was out, and the coral sand was exposed. It was purest white and the moon shadows of the sculpted sandstone pillars were cast stark and blue on its flat, unmarked sands. The low surf on the outer reef glowed with phosphorescence, which lit up their faces intermittently.

'It's beautiful,' Yasmini whispered. 'I would never have believed how beautiful.'

'I am going to swim,' Dorian said, and stood up. He pulled off his *kanzu* and kicked away his sandals. 'Are you coming?'

Without waiting for an answer he walked out on the beach. At the edge of the pool he turned and looked back.

Yasmini emerged from the cave, moving like a fawn from the covert on legs that seemed too long for her child-like body. She had shed the tattered robe and was as naked as he. Dorian had seen slave-girls on the blocks in the market, but none had possessed this fairy grace. Her hair hung down her back to her small rounded buttocks, the streak through the sable hair was silver in the moonlight.

When she reached him she put out her hand in an innocent gesture and took his. Her creamy breast buds were barely defined, delicate swellings, but the little nipples stood proud, teased by the cool airs of the monsoon. He stared at them, and they made him feel strange, an unaccustomed tightness in the pit of his stomach.

Hand in hand they stepped into the pool. The water was warmer than the night air, warm as their own blood. Yasmini sank down into it, until her long hair floated out around her like the leaves of the water lotus, and she laughed with joy.

The moon was halfway to its zenith when at last he told her, 'We must not stay here longer. It grows late, we must go back.'

'I have never been so happy,' she said. 'Never in my life. I wish we could stay like this for ever.' But she stood up obediently and the silvery water gilded her long slim limbs. They walked back up the beach and left their footprints like a double string of beads on the pale sand.

At the mouth of the cave she turned to him, 'Thank you, Dowie.' Then suddenly she threw both her arms around him, and hugged him. 'I love you so much, my brother.' Dorian stood awkwardly in her embrace. The feeling of her small body against him, the warmth of her skin through the cool drops of sea-water, gave him that strange feeling again in the pit of his stomach.

She stepped back and giggled. 'I am all wet.' She took a hank of her thick dark hair and twisted it. The water dripped from it on to the sand.

Dorian picked up his *kanzu* from where he had dropped it. 'Turn around!' he said, and obediently she offered him the slim curve of her back. He dried it roughly, scrubbing it with the folds of his robe.

'The other side now.'

She turned to face him and he wiped the cloth over those small warm swellings on her chest, then down over her belly. 'That tickles!'

Her stomach was smooth and concave, the only blemish upon it the puckering of her navel, and at its base, the little vertical cleft of hairless skin between her thighs.

'Now put on your *kanzu*,' he ordered, and she turned and picked up the garment off the sand. He saw that her buttocks were small and perfectly rounded. He felt his chest constrict, and he drew the next breath with difficulty.

She straightened up, and dropped the dirty *kanzu* over her head, and as she pushed her head out through the opening he was still standing staring at her. She gave him a pixie smile. Then, while she wound her hair into a thick rope and pushed it under the *keffiya*, she studied his body openly, and without any sense of guilt or sin. 'You are so white, where the sun has not touched you – and look! You have hair down there also.' She pointed with surprise. 'It's the same colour as on your head. It sparkles like silk in the moonlight. It's pretty,' she marvelled.

He had forgotten the soft fuzz that had sprouted over the past months. For the first time he felt shy, almost guilty, in front of her, and swiftly he covered himself with his own damp robe. 'We must go!' he said, and she had to run to catch up with him as he headed back towards the zenana. In the safety of the tunnel she shed the grubby *kanzu* and changed back into her own clothing.

'Are you ready?' Dorian asked.

'Yes, Dowie.' But before he could start down the tunnel she grabbed his hand. 'Thank you, my brother,' she whispered. 'I will never forget what we did tonight, never, never!'

He tried to untangle her grip on his hand. His emotions confused him, and he felt almost angry with her for causing him to feel this way.

'Can we come again, Dowie?' she pleaded.

'I don't know.' He pulled his hand free. 'Perhaps.'

'Please, Dowie. It was so much fun.'

'Well, then, we will have to see.'

'I will be so good. I will do anything you say. I won't tease you or cheek you ever again. Just say yes. Please, Dowie.'

'All right, Yassie. We will come again.'

A few days after their foray down the Angel's Road, and before Dorian could make good his promise to take her again, Kush came to his living quarters. He appeared in the early morning, before the sun had risen, and with him were two of his eunuch slaves. Tahi met them at the door and tried to prevent them entering. 'What do you want with al-Amhara?' she demanded.

'Stand aside, you old cow,' Kush ordered. 'The boy is no longer your charge.'

'You have come to take him from me.' Her voice

quivered, and she snatched at his embroidered waistcoat as he tried to push past her.

'Stand back, I warned you!' He drove the butt of his staff into her belly, and she doubled over with pain.

'Bring out the infidel,' Kush ordered his two slaves and they rushed into Dorian's small chamber. He was sitting up on his mat, rudely wakened by Kush's penetratingly high tones from the room next door, rubbing the sleep out of his eyes. The eunuchs grabbed his arms and dragged him through to where Kush waited.

'Take that off.' Kush pointed with his staff at the *kikoi* cloth knotted around Dorian's hips. They pulled it off, and Kush grinned lasciviously. 'I thought so! A nice little garden you're growing there.' With the tip of his staff, he prodded the nest of fluffy red-gold curls that now covered Dorian's *mons pubis*. Dorian tried to cover himself, but they forced him upright.

'It is time for this to come off.' He prodded Dorian with one fat beringed finger. 'We will rid you of this smelly piece of skin.'

'Don't touch me!' Dorian shouted furiously, his voice cracking, his cheeks flushing bright scarlet with anger and humiliation. 'Take your fat white hands off me, you thing with no balls.'

The smirk dropped from Kush's lips and he jerked his hand away. 'Say your *salaams* to this old cow.' He glared at Tahi. 'You will see her no more. My fellows will wait with you while you pack your possessions. You are leaving the zenana. The knife awaits you, and a new life thereafter.'

At the door Tahi clung to him. 'You are the son I could never have,' she whispered. 'I will love you all my life.'

'And I will love you also, Tahi. I cannot remember my own mother, but she must have been like you.'

'Be a man and a warrior, al-Amhara. Make me proud.'

'Tell Yasmini—' He broke off. What message could he

send the little one? While he pondered it, the slaves pulled him out through the door. Desperately he called back to Tahi, 'Tell Yasmini I will never forget her. Tell her she will always be my little sister.'

The slaves took him out to where the bullock cart waited in the front courtyard of the zenana. A small crowd of children and women servants had gathered to watch him go, but Yasmini was not among them, although he looked for her as they rolled out through the gates.

'It is always more difficult and dangerous when the boy is older,' Ben Abram observed. 'This should have been done much earlier, not at thirteen, when he is on the threshold of manhood.'

'The boy comes from the world of the infidel and he is in a state of abomination until the ritual is performed. It must be done before the return of the Prince from Muscat,' al-Allama replied. 'If he is verily of the prophecy then Allah will protect the boy.'

Dorian stood naked before them. They were on the terrace of the palace, overlooking the harbour. Apart from the doctor and the holy mullah, there was a young black slave-girl with them, a pagan who could not be defiled by assisting Ben Abram.

Ben Abram laid out his instruments on the low table, then looked straight into Dorian's eyes. 'Pain is nothing to a man. Honour is everything. Remember that all your life, my son.'

'I will not fail, old father,' Dorian replied. They had discussed this many times before.

'Bismilla-hi Allahu akbar!' Ben Abram said quietly. 'I begin in the name of Almighty God. Allah is great!'

At the same time the mullah began to recite a sura from the Koran in a slow sonorous tone. '"We begin with the name of Allah, who is most kind and merciful. O Allah, grant him full faith, everlasting security, abundance of provisions, maturity of mind, beneficial knowledge, guidance to perform righteous deeds, noble character, honour and sound health."'

Ben Abram nodded to the slave-girl, who knelt in front of Dorian and took hold of his penis. She began to manipulate it with a milking motion. Swiftly it swelled and stiffened, and the girl modestly averted her eyes but she continued to fondle him until he was fully erect. Then Ben Abram selected a small, razor-sharp knife from the tray, and came to them. He said softly to the girl, 'Enough!' and she moved away.

'In the Name of Allah,' Ben Abram said, and made the first swift practised stroke of the blade.

Dorian stiffened at the sting, but he bit down and stopped the cry of pain before it reached his lips. Then came the next cut and the next, but still he fought back any outcry, and felt the blood run warm down his thighs.

At last Ben Abram laid aside the knife. 'In the Name of God, it is done!' And he bandaged the wound.

Dorian felt his legs quaking under him, but he kept all expression from his face, and his eyes open. Even al-Allama gave voice to his approval. 'Now you are a man.' He touched Dorian's forehead in blessing. 'And you have conducted yourself as a man indeed.'

Ben Abram took his arm and led him to a back room in the palace where a sleeping mat was laid ready for him. 'I will come in the morning to bandage the wound again,' he promised.

In the morning Dorian was flushed and hot, and the wound was ugly and inflamed. Ben Abram changed the dressing and laid on it a soothing ointment. Then he administered a bitter-tasting potion. Within days the fever had abated and the healing had begun. Before long, the scabs had come away and Ben Abram allowed Dorian to go alone to the ocean side of the island to swim in the warm clear waters, and to go down to the royal stables and help the grooms exercise the Prince's horses, galloping along the white fluffy sand of the beaches and joining in the wild rowdy games of *pulu*.

Soon after, a sail was sighted coming up the channel, and the lookouts on the palace walls picked out the royal pennant at the masthead. The entire population of the island flocked down to the beaches to welcome the return of Prince Abd Muhammad al-Malik from the Omani capital of Muscat.

The Prince stepped ashore to the boom of cannon from the battlements of the fort, the ululations of the women and shouts of adoration from the men. They fired their long-barrelled jezails into the air, while the drums beat and the fifes wailed.

Dorian was with the grooms, who were holding the horses at the head of the beach. He had helped to burnish the tack, and polish the turquoise gemstones that adorned the Prince's saddle and the cheekpieces of the bridle. As an adopted royal son, the head groom had accorded to Dorian the honour of leading al-Malik's stallion forward and holding him for the Prince to mount.

Dorian watched the Prince coming up the beach, the crowds opening before him and his subjects prostrating themselves, trying to kiss the hem of his robes as he passed by. It was over a year since he had last seen him, and Dorian had forgotten how tall and regal he was in his snowy robes with the great jewelled dagger at his waist, its hilt of polished rhinoceros horn glowing with the soft lustre of amber. The headband that held his *keffiya* in place was of twisted gold wire. He strode towards where Dorian waited for him, smiling and returning the greetings of his subjects with the elegant gesture of blessing, touching his heart and his lips.

'*Salaam aliekum*, great lord!' Dorian bowed. Even

though his voice was lost in the tumult of the crowd, the Prince looked into his face and Dorian saw, from the pleased expression in his dark eyes, that he recognized him. The Prince inclined his head slightly, then swung up into the saddle with the grace of an expert horseman and rode away towards the fort.

The Prince sat with his closest courtiers on the terrace of the palace, sipping coffee and listening to the reports of the men who had administered the islands and colonies in his absence. 'There have been many Frankish ships calling at Zanzibar,' his vizier told him. 'More each month now that the *kusi* wind brings them in from the south. They all seek to trade for ivory and slaves.'

The sultanate of Zanzibar was part of the Prince's domains, and a share of the profits from its markets found its way into his treasury. He could be sure that his subservient sultan would mulch the infidel for every rupee that the trade could stand.

'Ali Muhammad must warn the infidel captains that I will not tolerate their presence north of Zanzibar. I most strictly forbid it.' The gold and goods that the infidels brought with them were welcome, but al-Malik knew full well the avarice and ruthlessness of the Franks. They had already established factories and bases in the empire of the Great Mogul. Once they had a foothold they were impossible to budge. They must not be allowed to come as far north as Lamu.

'Ali Muhammad is fully aware of your commands. If any infidel ship ventures into these waters he will send report to Your Excellency by swift dhow.'

The Prince nodded. 'If the call for ivory is so great, how plentiful are our sources on the mainland?'

'Ivory is every year more scarce, and the call of the infidel for more always greater.'

In a great part, the markets on Zanzibar and Lamu relied on the pagan black tribes of the interior to supply their needs. The tribes did not have muskets with which to hunt the giant pachyderms. Their method was to set primitive pitfalls, lined with sharpened stakes, into which they tried to stampede the herds. There were a few intrepid hunters among them who were capable of bringing down the elephant with bow and arrow, but their harvest was meagre.

'Perhaps we should sell muskets to the chiefs to help them to gather greater quantities?' a courtier suggested cautiously, but the Prince shook his head vehemently.

'That is too dangerous,' he said. 'It may encourage them to revolt against our authority. We would be opening the door of the lion's cage.'

They discussed the question at length, and then the Prince turned his attention to the slave trade. 'As we harvest the slaves from coastal areas, they are driven further into the interior. Like the elephants, they become wilder and more wary. Each season the numbers we are able to obtain fall off.'

As with the ivory, the Arabs relied on the more warlike chiefs of the interior to fall upon their neighbours and to capture slaves from their traditional tribal enemies, then to bring them to the gathering points on the shores of the great lakes.

'We might consider sending our own warriors into the forests to capture slaves,' someone proposed.

The Prince stroked his beard thoughtfully. 'We would have to send good men and bold. We cannot know what they will encounter out there in the wilderness. We can only be sure that it will be dangerous and hard.' He paused to consider the suggestion further. 'I will give you my decision on this later, but in the meantime draw up a list of the names of fifty men who might be relied upon to lead such an expedition.'

He dealt with each of these matters concerning trade, but before he went on to other more serious topics, he dismissed the least important members of his council, and kept only five of his most senior and trusted men with him to hear the outcome of his visit to Muscat. This was perilous ground, which reeked of conspiracy and treachery. The Caliph, al-Uzar ibn Yaqub, was older than the Prince by forty years, born of one of their father's wives when he was a young man. Al-Malik was the child of his father's dotage and his father's last favourite, but as every horseman knew, 'An old stallion and a young mare breed the finest foals.'

The tiny Omani empire was under grave threat from the conquering Ottomans, that mighty empire that had its capitals in Istanbul and Baghdad, and which sprawled across most of the Arab world. The only states that had so far resisted them were a few small principalities beneath the notice of the Turkish caliphs in the north, or those who had succeeded in defending themselves from the depredations of the Ottomans.

Oman was protected by its strong fleet against attack from the sea. Any aggressor who tried to come at it overland from the north would be confronted by the ferocious sands of the Rub Al Khali, the Empty Quarter, and by the desert warriors who made up the small Omani army, and for whom the desert was home.

Oman had defied the Ottoman conquerors for a hundred years, and could do so for another hundred, if only it were led by a strong and resourceful man. Ibn Yaqub was not that man. He was past seventy years of age, and given to convoluted political intrigue and conspiracy, rather than the rigours and hardships of war. His chief concern was always to safeguard his own position of power, rather than hold together and protect his small nation. In the process he had lost the respect of his tribes, for the Omani were made up of many, each under its own sheikh. Without firm direction these hard desert men were losing their sense of purpose and resolve, they were beginning to squabble among themselves, resuscitating ancient tribal blood feuds, and spurning the rule of the vacillating, cruel and scheming old man in Muscat.

Ibn Yaqub's authority still held only close to his stronghold, but as it reached out into those burning deserts and across the endless waters of the Ocean of the Indies it grew ever more dilute and insubstantial. The desert sheikhs and the dhow commanders would follow only a man they respected.

Already some had sent secret emissaries to al-Malik, for he had proved himself a mighty man and a warrior without peer. They all knew that the Caliph had banished him to the outpost of the empire at Lamu because he was fearful of his half-brother's influence and popularity. The messengers promised that if he returned to Arabia, to the Omani, and headed a revolt against his brother then they would rise behind him. With him at the helm of the state they would once more unite against the Ottoman. 'It is your duty and your God-given right. If you come to us then the mullahs will declare *jihad*, righteous war, and we will ride behind you to overthrow the tyrant,' they promised.

These were dire matters, and fraught with terrible perils. If they should fail, none of the six men seated on the terrace could doubt what the consequences would be for them personally. They sat long, debating the chances of success, and the justice of their cause.

When the council began, the dhows on the beach below them had been stranded by the ebb, high and dry and heeled over. Long lines of slaves had wound out across the exposed sand to unload their cargoes. While the council talked, the tide began to flood, and gradually the ships righted themselves and floated free. They spread their matting sails and tacked out into the channel. Fresh arrivals from the mainland, heavily laden with cargo, came in to moor above the beach. Still the six men on the terrace talked and debated, and the tide reached high slack, then began its ebb.

All this time al-Malik listened, and spoke little, while he allowed each of the others to say what was in their hearts without check or restraint. Carefully he sifted the gems of wisdom from the dross.

They reviewed the order of battle of those forces on which they could rely, and made lists of those sheikhs who were uncommitted or doubtful. They compared these to the powers that ibn Yaqub commanded. Only when he had heard all they had to say did al-Malik make his decision. 'It will depend upon the tribes of the deep desert, the Saar, the Dahm and the Karab. They are the greatest warriors of all the Omani. Without them our cause cannot prosper. Yet we have not heard from them. We do not know in which direction they will point the war lance.'

His councillors murmured agreement, and al-Malik said softly, 'I must go to them.'

They were silent for a while, considering this bold course of action, and then al-Allama said, 'Your brother the Caliph will not allow it. If you insist, he will smell danger on the wind.'

'I will make the *haj*, the pilgrimage to Mecca, taking the ancient desert route to the Holy Places, the road that passes through the territory of the tribes. The Caliph cannot forbid a pilgrim, under penalty of eternal damnation.'

'There is great risk,' al-Allama said.

'There is never great gain without great risk,' al-Malik replied, 'and God is great.'

'*Allah akbar!*' they replied. 'Surely, God is great.'

Al-Malik made a graceful gesture of dismissal, and one by one they came to embrace him, kiss his hand and take their leave. Al-Allama was the last, and al-Malik said, 'Stay with me. It is the hour of Maghrib, the prayers at the setting of the sun. We will pray together.'

Two slave-girls brought pitchers of pure sweet well water and the two men performed the ritual purification, washing their hands in the water that the girls poured for them from the silver pitchers, rinsing their mouths three times, snuffing water cupped in the right palm three times and blowing it out of the nostril with the fingers of the left hand, then going on to bathe their faces, arms and feet.

The slave-girls left and al-Allama stood and faced the Kabaa in Mecca, thousands of miles to the north. Cupping his hands behind his ears, he began the call to prayer in a loud voice. 'God is great. I bear witness that Muhammad is the messenger of God. Come to prayer! Come to your own good!'

Below them in the courtyard and under the palm trees along the head of the beach, hundreds of robed figures assembled quietly and took up the posture of reverence, all facing in the same direction.

'The prayer has begun!' chanted al-Allama.

When it was ended, al-Malik gestured for the mullah to take a seat on the cushion close to his right hand. 'I saw the boy, al-Amhara, on the beach when I arrived. Tell me how he has fared in my absence.'

'He grows like a tamarind tree, strong and tall. Already he is a fine horseman. He has a quick mind and a ready tongue, sometimes too ready. He is often prone to lack respect for his elders and betters. He does not take readily to criticism or restraint. And when he is angry or thwarted, his choice of invective would make a sea captain pale,' al-Allama said primly.

Al-Malik hid his smile behind the rim of his coffee-cup. What he heard only made him like his infidel son the more. He would make a leader of men.

Al-Allama went on, 'He has come to manhood, and been properly circumcised by Ben Abram. When the time comes for him to accept Islam, he will be ready.'

'That is good,' the Prince said. 'And tell me, holy father, have your teachings borne fruit in that direction?'

'He now speaks our language as though born to it, and he can recite long sections of the Holy Koran from memory.' Al-Allama looked uneasy and evasive.

'Has he made any progress towards submitting himself to God?' al-Malik insisted. 'Without that the prophecy can have no effect.'

'The Prophet Himself has said that no man can be forced to convert to Islam. He must come to it in his own way and in his own time.'

'So your answer is no?'

'He glories in argument. Sometimes I think the only reason he memorizes the Koran is the better to argue with me. He glories in the religion of his own people and boasts that one day he will be inducted into some Christian religious order, which he calls the Knights of the Order of St George and the Holy Grail, like his grandfather and his father before him.'

'It is not for us to question the ways of Allah,' al-Malik said.

'God is great!' Al-Allama endorsed his assertion. 'But there is more to tell concerning the boy. We have had an enquiry from the English consul in Zanzibar concerning him.'

Al-Malik leaned forward earnestly. 'I thought that the consul in Zanzibar had been murdered over a year ago?'

'That was the man named Grey. Since his death the English have sent another to take his place.'

'I see. What form did this enquiry from the new man take?'

'He describes the boy accurately, his age and colouring. He knows that al-Amhara was captured by al-Auf, and that he was sold into slavery. He knows that he was bought by Your Excellency. He knows the name that we have given him – al-Amhara.'

'How has he learned all this?' Worry lines creased al-Malik's brow.

'I do not know, except that Ben Abram has told me much about the boy's lineage. He met and spoke to al-Amhara's elder brother when the Franks captured him at al-Auf's base.'

The Prince nodded. 'What does the doctor know concerning the boy?'

'His family is noble, close to the English King. Despite his youth, al-Amhara's brother is a formidable fighting mariner, and he has sworn a mighty oath to find and rescue his younger brother. Perhaps it is this family who is behind these enquiries from Zanzibar. We do not know this for certain, but it would be wise not to ignore these questions.'

Al-Malik pondered this, then asked, 'The English are buyers and owners of slaves. How can they object to the same practice in others? What can they do to force us to their will? Their land is far away, at the end of the earth. They cannot send an army against us.'

'Ben Abram says that the Franks have perfidious ways of making war. They issue *firman* to the captains of their armed merchant ships against their enemies. These men are like sharks, or barracudas. They come for plunder.'

'Would the English King declare war on us over one child?'

'Ben Abram fears that he might. Not only for the sake of the child but also for the excuse to send their ships into our waters, to seize the territory and the riches of the Omani.'

'I will think on all that you have told me.' Al-Malik dismissed him. 'Bring Ben Abram and the boy to me here tomorrow after the Zuhr prayers.'

Dorian came to his audience with the Prince consumed by both trepidation and excitement at the prospect. When he had first met the Prince, Dorian had been possessed of no such qualms: al-Malik had been only another Mussulman, an enemy and a pagan chief. However, he had learned much since he had been under the instruction of al-Allama and Ben Abram. He now knew that the Prince's claim to royalty stretched back as far as that of the English King, he knew of his exploits as a sailor and a warrior, of the reverence his subjects felt towards him. In addition to this, the spiritual umbilical cord that bound Dorian to England and Christianity was unravelling and eroding with time and great distance.

These days he never had opportunity to speak his own language, he thought in Arabic, and had difficulty recalling the English words for even the simplest ideas. Even his memories of his family were fading. He thought of his brother Tom only on occasion, and all ideas of escape from Lamu had been abandoned. He no longer thought of his state here on the island as one of captivity. Slowly he was being absorbed into the Arab world and the Arab way of thought. Now, confronted with the Prince again, he was overcome with awe and reverence.

When he knelt before al-Malik on the coral stones of the terrace and asked for his blessing, his heart ran faster with surprise and pleasure at the form in which the Prince returned his greeting. 'Come and sit beside me, my son. We have much to discuss.' This regal and impressive man had reaffirmed him as his son in front of these witnesses. Dorian felt proud, then experienced a sharp pang of guilt. He had a fleeting image of his true father, but the picture in his mind of Hal's face was blurring.

I will always be true to my real father, he promised himself staunchly, but he obeyed al-Malik's invitation promptly and gladly.

'In my absence you have become a man.' Al-Malik studied him keenly.

'Yes, my lord,' Dorian replied, and had to stop himself adding automatically, 'By the grace of Allah.'

'I can see that this is so.' Al-Malik picked out the outline of firm young muscle and breadth of shoulders beneath the *kanzu* that Dorian wore so naturally. 'And it is therefore fitting that you should relinquish the name of the child and take in its stead the name of the man. From henceforth you shall be called al-Salil.'

'It is the will of Allah,' al-Allama and Ben Abram said together. They both looked proud and pleased with this honour that the Prince had accorded their protégé. It redounded to their credit, for the name the Prince had chosen was a propitious one: it meant the Drawn Sword.

'Your beneficence is like the rising of the sun after the dark night,' Dorian replied, and al-Allama nodded his approval at the choice of words and their inflection.

'It is also fitting that you should have your own lance-bearer.' Al-Malik clapped his hands and a young man stepped out onto the terrace with a long, raking stride, like that of a racing camel. He was probably fifteen years older than Dorian, in his late twenties, and a warrior by his dress and mien. He wore a curved scimitar at his waist and carried a round bronze shield on his shoulder.

'This is Batula,' the Prince told him. 'He will make his oath to you.'

Batula came to Dorian and knelt in front of him. 'From this day forward you are my liege lord,' he said in a strong, clear voice. 'Your enemies are my enemies. Wherever you may ride, I shall carry your lance and your shield at your right hand.'

Dorian put his hand upon Batula's shoulder in acceptance of the pledge, and Batula rose to his feet. The two young men looked each other in the face, and instinctively Dorian liked what he saw there. Batula was not handsome of features, but his face was broad and honest, his nose large and hawkish. When he smiled his teeth were even and white. He wore his thick dark hair oiled with ghee and twisted into a braid over one wide shoulder.

'Batula is an exponent of the lance,' al-Malik said, 'and a warrior tried in battle. There is much he has to teach you, al-Salil.' The lance was the weapon of the true Arab horseman. Dorian had watched the novices at practice on the field of arms, and had thrilled to the charge of pounding hoofs, the steely flash of the lance-points as they picked a suspended brass finger ring out of the air at full charge.

'I shall be a willing pupil,' Dorian promised.

Al-Malik dismissed Batula. When he had left the terrace the Prince resumed, 'Very soon I shall undertake another long journey to the north, the pilgrimage to Mecca through the sands and the wilderness of the deserts. You will accompany me, my son.'

'My heart rejoices that you choose me, great lord.'

Al-Malik made the gesture of dismissal, and when Dorian had gone he turned back to al-Allama and Ben Abram. 'You will send a message to the Sultan in Zanzibar for him to pass on to the English consul there.' He paused to collect the words, then went on, 'Tell him that Prince al-Malik indeed purchased al-Amhara from al-Auf. He did this to take the boy under his protection and to shield him from harm. Tell him that, despite all al-Malik could do to protect him, al-Amhara fell sick of a pestilence and that he died a year ago. He is buried here on the island of Lamu. Tell him that al-Malik has spoken thus.'

Al-Allama bowed. 'It shall be as you command, Your Excellency.' He was impressed by this ingenious solution.

'Al-Amhara is dead,' al-Malik went on. 'You will erect a headstone in the cemetery with that name on it. Al-Amhara is dead. Al-Salil lives on.'

'By God's grace.' Al-Allama acknowledged the order.

'I shall take the boy with me into the desert and leave him with the Saar to hide him. There in the sands he will learn the warrior's way. In time the Franks will forget that he once existed.'

'This is a wise decision.'

'Al-Salil is more than a son to me, he is my living talisman. I shall never yield him to the demands of the Franks,' he said, softly but firmly.

The *Swallow* came up the channel, then tacked into the roads of Zanzibar. Ahead there were ten sail of square-rigged ships lying in the anchorage, besides a mass of Arab dhows. Tom Courtney looked them over carefully. They flew the flags of some of the great trading nations of the northern hemisphere, with a preponderance of Portuguese and Spaniards.

'Not a Frenchie in sight, Mr Tyler,' Tom announced, with relief. He did not relish the complications of sharing a neutral port with ships of the enemy.

'No,' agreed Ned. 'But there is at least one East India-man.' He pointed out the tall ship, a princess of the ocean, displaying the majesty of the Company. 'They will offer us an even frostier welcome than the Frenchies would have done.'

Tom grinned recklessly. 'I give not a fig for them,' he said. 'They can do nothing to us outside the courts of England, and we will not be back there for a while.' And added, under his breath, 'Not until they drag me there in chains.' He glanced up at his own masthead, devoid of any flag. He had not wanted to announce his nationality. 'As soon as we anchor, I will go ashore to pay a visit to the new consul,' he told Ned.

He had spoken to the captain of another English ship in Table Bay when they broke their long voyage at Good Hope. The captain had told him that Grey had a successor in the consular office in Zanzibar. 'He is some young fellow sent from Bombay, after Grey was murdered, to take over the consular duties for the Fever Coast, and, of course, more importantly, to see to the interest of John Company in those seas.'

'What is his name?' Tom had wanted to know.

'I don't recall. I've never met him, but by all accounts he is surly and difficult, enchanted by his own importance.'

Tom watched as Ned took the *Swallow* into the bay, and they dropped the anchor in water so clear they could see the multicoloured fish swarming over the coral heads four fathoms under the keel.

'I will take Aboli ashore with me,' Tom said, as soon as the longboat was launched.

The two landed on the stone jetty beneath the walls of the old Portuguese fort and made their way into the narrow streets.

The heat and the stinking bustle were all so familiar that Tom could hardly credit that it was almost two years since last he had come ashore here. They asked for directions from the Arab harbour master. 'No, no,' he told them. 'The new consulate is no longer in *effendi* Grey's old house in the town. I will send a boy to show you the way.' And he picked out one of the ragged urchins from the swarm who were pestering the *ferenghi* for alms. 'This son of Shaitan will guide you. Do not give him baksheesh of more than one anna.'

The boy danced ahead, leading them out of the jumble of narrow alleys and ramshackle buildings into the palm groves. Along a sandy road, a mile or more beyond the last hovel, they came to a large villa behind high walls. Although the house seemed old, the outer wall had been repaired recently and painted with burnt limewash. The roof of the main house that showed above the top of the wall was freshly thatched with palm fronds. There were two brass plaques on the gate. One was engraved: 'His Majesty's Consulate.' Below that was the Company's emblem of rampant lions and the legend: 'Office of the United Company of Merchants of England Trading to the East Indies.'

A servant answered Tom's ring at the outer gates in the wall, and Tom sent him with a note to his master. After a few minutes the man returned. Tom left Aboli to wait for him in the courtyard and followed him.

The main house was laid out around gardens and fountains in the Oriental style of architecture. The ceilings were high but the rooms sparsely furnished. There were, however, vases of tropical flowers in the rooms through which the servant led Tom, and these floral decorations and the arrangement of cushions on the austere hardwood furniture suggested a feminine hand. At last the servant led Tom into a large room with stone floors and bookcases lining the walls.

'Please to wait here, *effendi*. The master will come soon.'

Left to himself, Tom looked up at the slowly revolving fan and the arrangement of lines and pulleys that led through a hole in the wall to where a slave pulled rhythmically on a line to keep the fan turning.

Tom walked to the writing-desk in the centre of the floor, and glanced at the quill stand and ink-pot, set out precisely, and at the piles of documents bound with red ribbon and stacked with military precision. Then he turned from the desk and wandered along the bookshelves, trying to divine from their contents the character of the man he had come to meet. The shelves were filled with heavy ledgers and bound reports with the Company emblem embossed on the spine. There was nothing of a personal nature on display and the room had a soulless feel to it.

He was alerted by a footstep on the flags on the terrace outside the entrance to the inner courtyard, and he turned just as a tall, lean figure appeared in the doorway. The bright tropical sun was behind him, so Tom did not recognize him at once. The consul stopped and let his eyes adjust to the gloom of the room after the brilliant sunshine outside. He was dressed in a sober black serge costume with a white lace collar.

Then he stepped into the room and removed the wide-brimmed black hat from his head. Tom saw his face clearly for the first time. For a long moment his astonishment was so intense that he could neither move nor speak. Then he laughed and started forward. 'Guy! Is it really you?' Impulsively he opened his arms to embrace his twin brother.

It was obvious that Guy Courtney's surprise was as great as Tom's. A host of differing emotions showed briefly on his face, then were gone. His features became cold and stiff, and he stepped back from Tom's embrace.

'Thomas,' he said. 'I had no idea that it was you. You signed a false name on your note.'

'Neither had I any idea that it was you,' Tom said, and let his welcoming arms fall to his sides. He avoided the accusation of using a false name. He had deemed it wise not to use his real name here, in case by some strange chance a warrant for the murder of William had reached Zanzibar ahead of him. He watched Guy's expression for some sign that this had happened, and judged that he could not rely on his twin to shelter him from justice.

They stared at each other in silence for a minute, which seemed to Tom like all eternity. Then Guy held out his right hand. With relief Tom took it.

Guy's grip was limp and his flesh as cool as his expression. He dropped Tom's hand after only a brief contact, then turned away to his desk. 'Please be seated, Thomas.' He indicated the high-backed chair across the room, without looking directly at his brother. 'I trust that you have not returned to these waters to indulge in any form of trade. The fact that you use an assumed name makes me think that that may be the case.' When Tom did not reply at once, he went on, 'I must warn you that my first loyalty is to the Company,' he made it sound as though he was invoking the name of God, 'and I will immediately send a report to London.'

Tom stared at him, feeling his anger boil up swiftly. 'Merciful heavens, Guy, is that your first concern? Are we not brothers? Do you not want to know about Father and Dorian?'

'I am already aware of Father's death. The Company ship that lies in the harbour this day brought me a letter from Lord Childs and from our brother William in England,' Guy replied. Tom felt a surge of relief at this confirmation that he had not yet heard of William's death.

Guy replaced the quill in its holder, and went on, 'I have mourned Father's passing in my own way so there is nothing more to say on that score.' His mouth hardened. 'Besides, you were always his favourite. I meant little to him.'

'That is not true, Guy. Father loved us all equally,' Tom burst out.

'So you say.' Guy shrugged. 'As for Dorian, I heard that he was lost at sea, drowned and dead.'

'No, he was not.' Tom made no effort to keep his voice down. 'He was captured by the Mussulmen and sold into slavery.'

Guy laughed without humour. 'You were always one for a wild tale. I assure you as His Majesty's consul in these territories I have access to the most reliable sources of information.'

Despite his denial, Tom thought he detected a shiftiness in his expression. 'I was there, damn you, Guy. I saw it with my own eyes.'

663

Guy seated himself behind the desk and fiddled with the quill, stroking his own cheek with the plume. 'Ah, you actually saw him sold into slavery? How surprising that you did nothing to prevent it.'

'No, you puffed-up jackanapes!' Tom bellowed. 'I know that he was in the power of the Mussulman pirates, captured and not dead or drowned. I also know for certain that he was sold into slavery.'

'What proof do you—' Guy started, but Tom strode to the desk and slammed his hands on the top so that ink spurted up and splattered the piles of documents.

'The testimony of the Arabs we captured at Flor de la Mar, and proof of my own eyes and senses. Dorian is alive, I tell you, and it is your duty as a brother and an Englishman to help me find him.'

Guy leaped to his feet. His face was icy pale, his eyes blazing. 'How dare you come here into my house, into my territory, in your old overweening, blustering style and dictate to me what I must do?' he screamed at Tom, drops of spittle flying from his lips.

'Sweet Christ, Guy, don't tempt me further. I'll whip the hide off your craven back if you don't do your duty by our little brother.'

'Those days are long past, Thomas Courtney. I am the master here, the chosen representative of His Majesty and of the Company. You will find yourself thrown into prison, your fine ship seized and confiscated if you raise a hand to me.' He was shaking with rage. 'Don't you dare preach to me, not after what you did to Caroline!' His voice rose to a shriek at her name, and Tom recoiled as though struck in the chest by a musket-ball.

At the same time Guy stepped back, clearly appalled by what he had allowed to slip past his tongue in anger. Tom was cast into confusion by the accusation, which had struck home. They stared at each other speechlessly, and in the silence a small sound made them both turn to the door that led in from the garden.

A woman stood there. She was dressed in a pale green dress of Chinese silk, with slashed sleeves and high neck. Her full skirts covered her ankles and only the toes of her slippers showed. She was staring at Tom as though at her own ghost. One hand clutched her throat, the other held the hand of the child who toddled beside her.

'What are you doing here, Caroline?' Guy roared. 'You know well that you may not come here when I have visitors.'

'I heard voices.' Caroline faltered. Her hair was piled high in curls upon her head and ringlets hung down on her cheeks, but Tom saw that she was sallow of countenance, as though she had recently risen from a sick-bed. 'I heard my name called out.' She was still staring at Tom.

The child was in a smock and ribbons. His head was covered with blond curls and Tom had the impression of an angelic little face and perfect pink lips.

'Who's that man?' said the infant, and pointed at Tom with a chuckle.

'Take Christopher out of here,' Guy shouted at Caroline. 'Immediately!'

Caroline seemed not to have heard him. 'Tom?' she said, in a wondering, bemused tone. 'I never thought to see you again.' Christopher hung on her hand and tried to take an unsteady step towards him, but she pulled him back gently. 'How are you, Tom?'

'In good health,' Tom replied awkwardly, 'as I trust you are.'

'I have been ill,' Caroline whispered, staring at him. She moistened her lips. 'Since the birth of our—' She paused, blushing and thrown into confusion. 'The birth of Christopher.'

'I am sorry.' A shadow of regret passed over Tom's

face. 'Your family. How are your parents and your sisters?' He had to think of their names. 'Agnes and Sarah?'

'My father was appointed Governor of Bombay. He arranged the post of consul here in Zanzibar for Guy.' She glanced nervously at her husband, who was still glaring at her. 'My mother died of the cholera a year ago.'

'I am so sorry,' Tom interjected. 'She was a delightful lady.'

'Thank you.' Caroline inclined her head sadly. 'My sister Agnes married in Bombay.'

'But she was so young!' Tom protested, remembering those two tomboy sisters from the *Seraph*.

'She is no longer a child. She is seventeen,' Caroline corrected him. They were silent again, and Guy sank down into his chair, no longer trying to assert his authority over his wife.

Involuntarily, Tom looked down at the child who clung to Caroline's skirts. 'He is a beautiful child.' He raised his eyes back to her face.

She nodded, as though to a question that had not been uttered. 'Yes,' she said. 'He is like his father.'

Tom had an almost irresistible urge to go to the laughing infant and pick him up. Instead he stepped back a pace to prevent himself doing so.

'Caroline!' Guy intervened again, even more forcibly. 'I have business to conduct. Please take Christopher away.'

Caroline seemed to droop, and a desperate look came into her eyes as she studied Tom's face. 'It was good to see you again, Tom. Perhaps you will be able to visit us while you are in Zanzibar. Could you come to dine with us here at the consulate one evening?' There was a wistful note in the question.

'I do not think Thomas will be here long enough to make social calls.' Guy came to his feet again, and frowned at her, as if to silence her.

'That is a great pity,' Caroline said. 'Then I will say

666

farewell now.' She picked up the little boy. 'Goodbye, Tom.'

'Goodbye, Caroline.'

Carrying Christopher, she went through the door with a swish of silken skirts. The child looked back solemnly over his mother's shoulder at Tom.

For long after they had gone, both brothers were silent. Then Guy said, in a controlled, cold voice, 'You are to keep away from my family. I will not tolerate you speaking to my wife again. I challenged you to a duel once before. I will again, if you provoke me.'

'It would give me little pleasure to have to kill you. You were never a swordsman, Guy,' Tom said, and he thought of William. The guilt was still a sick feeling in the pit of his stomach. 'I have no wish to intrude on your private life. From now on, we will touch only on matters of business. Can we agree on that?'

'Distasteful as I find any contact with you, I agree,' Guy replied. 'And the first matter of business is for me to repeat my question. Do you intend to indulge in any form of trade in these waters? I have reports from the harbour that your ship is heavily laden. Do you have a trading licence from the Company? Do you carry trade goods?'

'We are eight thousand miles from London. We are beyond the line, sir, and I do not recognize your authority in English law to interfere with me or question my intentions.' Tom kept his temper under control with an effort. 'My first concern is only with Dorian. Have you made enquiry with the Sultan of Zanzibar concerning him?'

Guy became agitated. 'I have had no reason to approach the Sultan on the subject, and I forbid you to do so. I have managed to establish cordial relations with him. He is now favourably inclined towards England and the Company. I do not wish to have that state of affairs disturbed by anyone making accusations against his sovereign lord, Prince al-Malik.'

Tom's expression changed abruptly. 'How did you know that al-Malik was the one who bought Dorian as a slave? I never mentioned that name.'

Guy looked confused, and was silent for many seconds as he searched for a reply. 'Al-Malik is the sovereign overlord of this coast. It was natural for me to assume—'

'By God, Guy! It was not natural for you to assume anything! You know something about what has happened to Dorian. If you don't tell me, I will go to the Sultan myself.'

'You will not!' Guy sprang to his feet. 'I will not have you destroying all my work here.'

'You cannot stop me.'

'Listen to me.' Guy changed his tone. 'Very well, I will tell you the truth. I also heard these rumours about a white boy with red hair in the hands of the Arabs. Naturally I thought of Dorian, so I made enquiries of the Sultan. He promised to send a messenger to Prince al-Malik to find out the truth. I am waiting to hear from the Prince.'

'Why did you lie to me? Why did you not tell me this at once?' Tom demanded. 'Why did I have to force it out of you?'

'Because I know you well. I did not want you rushing in and antagonizing the Sultan. My dealings with him are very sensitive.'

'How long ago did you make these enquiries?' Tom demanded.

'I want you to keep out of this.' Guy sidestepped the question in spite of Tom's insistence. 'I have the whole business in my own hands.'

'How long ago?'

'Some time ago.' Guy looked down at his desk. 'Dealings with the Arabs take time.'

'When?' Tom came to him and thrust his face to Guy's.

'When I first arrived here on the island,' Guy admitted. 'A year ago.'

'A year ago?' Tom shouted. 'A year ago! Well, believe me, I will not wait that long. I will go to the Sultan this very day, and demand an answer.'

'I forbid it!' Guy cried. 'I am the consul!'

'Forbid all you will, Guy,' Tom told him grimly. 'I am on my way now to the fort.'

'I will send a full report of your behaviour to Lord Childs in London,' Guy threatened desperately. 'The Company ship in the harbour now will sail within days for England. Lord Childs will bring the full wrath of the Company down upon you.'

'There is no threat you can make that will stop me searching for Dorian. Send all the reports you wish, Guy, but it will be a year and more before you receive a reply. By then I will be a thousand miles away, with Dorian in my care.'

'Leave this house at once, sir!' Guy shouted. 'And don't dare set foot on my threshold again.'

'That is an invitation very much to my taste, sir.' Tom crammed his hat back onto his head. 'I wish you good morrow.'

He strode to the door without looking back, and smiled as Guy yelled after him, 'I forbid you to go near the Sultan's palace. I shall send word to him at once that you are an interloper and do not have the protection of His Majesty, the Company, or this office.'

Tom strode back along the sandy path towards the harbour, and Aboli had to step out to keep up with him. Aboli had had no reply to his initial questions so he was silent as he followed Tom.

Tom was in a black rage. He wanted to storm into the Sultan's fort above the harbour, take the heathen swine by the throat and choke the answers out of him. But he was at least able to recognize that his emotions were out of control, that once again he was on the verge of committing some violent act that could bring disaster on his enterprise. *I must get back on board the Swallow where I can do no more harm to myself, and talk to Aboli and Ned before I act,* he told himself, but his hand strayed to the hilt of the blue Neptune sword, and his anger flew off on another tack. *By God! If, to save Dorian, I have to take the little Swallow in against the whole Mussulman fleet, I will not flinch.*

There was a shout behind him, so faint that at first it did not penetrate his rage. Then there was the sound of galloping hoofs and the shout came again. 'Tom! Wait! Wait for me! I must talk to you.'

Tom swung round and glared back down the track. The horse came racing towards him, the rider leaning low on its neck, white sand spurting from under the hoofs.

'Tom!' This time he realized that it was a woman's voice. As the horse came closer he saw skirts billowing out behind and long hair blowing on the wind. His rage was forgotten in an instant, and he stared at her in astonishment.

She was riding astride and bareback, and he saw the flash of pale legs gripping the horse's flanks, naked to well above the knees where her skirts had rucked up. She lifted one slim arm and waved at him. 'Tom!' Despite her use of his Christian name, he did not recognize her. She brought the bay mare to a plunging halt beside where he stood, and in a rustle of skirts swung down to the ground. She tossed the reins to Aboli. 'Hold her, please, Aboli,' she said. The big man roused himself from his shock, and grabbed the reins.

'Tom! Oh, Tom!' The strange girl ran to him, and threw her arms around his neck. 'I thought I would never see you again.' She hugged him tightly, then stepped back and seized both his hands. 'Let me look at you.' She stared into his face, and he stared back.

Her long hair was a soft brown, but her face was not beautiful – the jaw too strong, her mouth too wide, especially when she smiled, as she was now. Her eyes were bright English blue, sparkling at him through long lashes. He saw at once that her skin was her main ornament. It was without blemish, but lightly touched by the tropical sun to an unfashionable golden brown. She was almost as tall as he was, her eyes looking straight into his, and she held herself easily and confidently with a boyish thrust of the hips and set of the shoulders.

'You don't recognize me, do you, Tom?' She laughed at him.

He shook his head dumbly. He found her face riveting, her eyes full of fun and alive with intelligence. 'Forgive me, madam,' he faltered. 'You have me at a disadvantage.'

'Madam indeed!' she chided him. 'I am Sarah.' She shook his hands. 'Sarah Beatty, Caroline's little sister. You used to call me the gadfly. "Why are you always buzzing around my head like a gadfly, Sarah?"' she mimicked. 'Now do you remember?'

'Sweet heavens, how you have changed!' he exclaimed in astonishment and, despite himself, looked down at the shapely swell of full breasts under her bodice.

'As you have, Tom. What happened to your nose?'

He touched the end in embarrassment. 'It was broken.'

'Poor Tom.' She made a face of mock sympathy. 'But it suits you well enough. Oh, Tom, it's so good to see you.' She linked her arm through his and led him down the track towards the town. Aboli fell in behind them at a respectful distance.

'I heard your voice when you were shouting at Guy. I could not believe it was yours, although I recognized it immediately.' She gave him a roguish sideways glance. 'So I listened outside the door. Guy would have beaten me if he had caught me at it.'

'Does he beat you?' Tom bristled protectively. 'We will see to that.'

'Oh, shush, don't be a booby. I can look after myself. But let's not waste time talking of Guy. I can only stay a moment. They will miss me, and send the servants to look for me.'

'Sarah, there is so much we have to discuss.' Tom felt strangely bereft at the thought of parting from her so soon. Her arm through his was strong and warm. There was a light fragrance around her, like an aura, that stirred something deep inside him.

'I know. I heard you talking to Guy about little Dorian. We all loved Dorian. I want to help you.' She thought quickly. 'There is an old ruined Jesuit monastery near the south point of the island. I will meet you there tomorrow, at two bells in the afternoon watch.' She laughed at him. 'You see? I remember all the sailor's things you taught me. Will you be there?'

'Of course.' She released his arm, turned back to Aboli and embraced him. 'Do you remember how we used to play horsey, Aboli? You carried me on your back.'

A smile lit Aboli's face, transforming it. 'Miss Sarah, you have grown beautiful!'

She took the reins from him. 'Hand me up!'

He cupped a huge palm and when she stepped into it he boosted her easily onto the mare's back. She flashed a

672

last smile at Tom. 'Don't forget!' she warned him. She wheeled and slapped her heels into the mare's flanks.

Tom watched her gallop away. 'No,' he said softly. 'I won't forget.'

'*E*ffendi, my master the Sultan is indisposed. He is not able to receive any visitors, not even those as important as your exalted self.' The vizier sneered at Tom. The harbour was filled with the ships of the Franks, all of their captains clamouring for an audience with his master, all seeking favours, licences to trade, permission to visit the forbidden territories further to the north.

'When will he see me?' Tom demanded. The vizier pursed his mouth with disapproval at such a crass, unsubtle question. He knew that this young infidel commanded a tiny vessel that could carry little in the way of goods for trade, and he did not have the smell of gold about him. He was hardly worthy of serious attention. Yet he was unusual: he spoke good intelligible Arabic, and understood the etiquette of business – he had offered suitable gifts to smooth the path to the Sultan.

'That is in the hands of Allah.' The vizier shrugged gracefully. 'Perhaps a week, perhaps a month, I do not know.'

'I will be back here tomorrow morning, and every day thereafter until the Sultan agrees to see me,' Tom assured him.

'And I will wait for your return each day, as the drought-struck earth awaits the rains,' said the vizier blandly.

Aboli was waiting for him at the gates of the fort, and Tom raised an eyebrow in reply to his unspoken question. He was too angry and frustrated to speak. They retraced their steps through the spice market, where the air was filled with the aroma of cloves and pepper, past the whipping-block in the slave market where some incorrigible woman was chained with the flesh of her back hanging in bloody festoons, down the street of the gold merchants, to the stone quay of the harbour where the longboat waited.

As he took his seat in the stern sheets Tom glanced up at the sky to judge the angle of the sun, then pulled the silver Tompion watch from his pocket and flipped open the cover. 'Row me around to the south point of the island,' he ordered. He had checked his chart the previous night, and found that the ruins of the old Jesuit monastery were marked upon it. A small cove close by should provide a landing.

As the rowers pulled down the channel, close in to the coral reef that showed its teeth through the snoring surf, Tom felt his ill-humour evaporate in the gay sunshine at the prospect of his rendezvous with Sarah.

Ahead of the longboat he saw the swells of the open sea beating with more force on the unprotected south point of the island. When he stood up and studied the shore ahead, he could pick out the course of the fresh-water stream marked by lush green vegetation as it ran down into the lagoon. There was always a pass through the reef where the sweet water inhibited the growth of the coral. As they came level with the stream he made out the deeper water of the pass and steered through it. The beach was deserted and there was no mark of a keel upon it. Tom jumped from the bows onto the hard white sand without wetting his boots. 'I will be back in an hour or so,' he told Aboli. 'Wait for me.'

He found an overgrown path that ran beside the stream, and forced his way along it, moving inland until it came out into the open groves of the palm trees. He saw the ruins of the monastery ahead. He increased his pace, and as he came under the tumbled walls he called out sharply, 'Sarah? Are you there?' There was a shriek as a flock of parakeets exploded out of the upper branches of a bo tree, whose roots were embedded in the tumbled stone blocks, but no other sound.

He continued on around the base of the walls, then heard a horse whinny just ahead of him. He ran forward, unable to restrain himself from showing his eagerness, and found the mare tied in the fallen gateway. Her saddle was stacked at the base of the wall, but there was no sign of her rider.

He was about to call again but thought better of it, and went on cautiously through the gateway. The building was roofless, overgrown with weed and newly germinated palm shoots from fallen coconuts. Blue-headed lizards scurried away among the stones, and butterflies with brilliant wings floated above the tops of the flowers.

He stood in the centre of the ancient courtyard, and placed his hands on his hips. He remembered her mischievous ways from long ago. It was clear that she had not improved, that she was hiding from him.

'I am going to count to ten,' he shouted, as he had when she was just a shrimp, 'and then I am coming to get you.' Once that threat had been enough to send her and her sister squealing for cover. 'One!' he counted, and her voice came from high above him. 'Guy says that you ravish young virgins.'

He spun round and saw her perched high on the arch of the gateway, her long legs dangling over the edge, her calves exposed beneath the hem of her skirts and her feet bare. He had walked right underneath her.

'He says that no decent Christian girl is safe when you are on the prowl.' She put her head on one side. 'Is that true?'

'Guy is a fool.' Tom grinned up at her.

'Guy does not like you very much. No brotherly

warmth in his heart.' Sarah started to swing her legs, and he stared at them. They were smooth and shapely. 'Is Christopher truly yours?'

Tom almost reeled at the directness of her question. 'Who told you that?' He tried to recover his composure.

'Caroline did,' she replied. 'She hasn't stopped crying since she saw you yesterday.'

Tom stared up at her, and all she had told him in those few sentences left him in confusion. He could think of nothing to say.

'If I come down, will you promise not to pounce on me and give me a baby also?' she asked sweetly, and stood up.

He felt a tremor of concern as she balanced easily on top of the rickety wall, and found his voice. 'Have a care. You will fall.'

As if she had not heard, she ran along the narrow top of the wall, jumping down from tier to tier until she could hop down the last few feet to the ground. She was as nimble as an acrobat. 'I brought a picnic basket for us to share.' She walked past him further into the ruins, and he followed her to one of the ancient monks' cells, which although roofless and open to the sky was shaded from the slanting sun. She pulled out the basket from where she had hidden it under a pile of palm fronds. She seated herself, twisting up her legs beneath her in that double-jointed feminine attitude that he found so appealing. She arranged her skirts artlessly, giving him another heart-stopping glimpse of those lovely calves.

She opened the basket and, as she set out the contents, she asked, 'Did you go to see the Sultan?'

'He refused me.' Tom sat down facing her, leaning his back against one of the blocks and crossing his legs.

'Of course! Guy sent word to him to warn him you were coming.' She changed the subject with bewildering rapidity. 'I helped myself to a bottle of wine from his cellar.' She held it up like a trophy. 'It's French, and came on the last ship from home.' She read the label. 'Corton Charlemagne. Is that good?'

'I don't know,' Tom admitted, 'but it sounds impressive.'

'Guy says it's superb. My brother-in-law fancies himself a great connoisseur. He is terribly proud of it. He would be furious if he knew we were drinking it. I am allowed only half a glass at supper. Will you open it?' She passed it to Tom, and set out platters of pies and cold meat. 'I was truly sorry to hear about the death of your father,' she said, and her face was sad suddenly. 'He was so kind to me and my family on the voyage out to Good Hope.'

'Thank you,' Tom replied, as he popped the cork out of the bottle, turning away to hide the shadow that passed across his face.

She sensed his sorrow and smiled to cheer him again. 'If my own father hadn't arranged the post of consul for Guy, he would still be a clerk in Bombay. He isn't such a Lord High and Mighty as he imagines he is.' She put on a solemn expression that was so faithful an imitation of his brother that Tom's mood changed and he grinned, as she mimicked Guy's pompous tone and inflection. '"I am the youngest consul in the service of His Majesty. I shall have a knighthood before I am thirty."' Tom guffawed. She was a delight to be with.

Then swiftly she changed again and became serious. 'Oh, Tom, what are we going to do about poor little Dorian? Guy doesn't really care. All he worries about is the Company's trade with the Arabs, and Lord Childs in London. He won't do anything to offend the Sultan and the Prince.'

Tom's expression again became grim. 'I will not let Guy or the Omani divert me. I have a fine, fast ship, and if they force me to it, I shall use it.'

'I know exactly how you are suffering, Tom. I feel as

though Dorian is my own brother. I will do everything I can to help you. But you must be careful. Guy says that the Prince has forbidden any Christian ships to go further north than Zanzibar, under penalty of seizure. He says that the Arabs will sell the crews into slavery if they transgress this decree.' She leaned across and placed her hand on his forearm. Her fingers were long and tapered. They felt cool against his skin. 'It will be terribly dangerous. I couldn't bear it if anything happened to you, dear Tom.'

'I can look after my ship and my crew,' he assured her, but her touch was distracting.

'I know you can.' She withdrew her hand, and sparkled at him. 'Pour Guy's wine.' She set out two pewter cups. 'Let's see if it is as good as he boasts.'

She took a sip. 'Mmm!' she murmured. 'You had best keep the bottle beside you. Caroline says that ravishers ply their innocent victims with strong drink before having their way with them.' She widened her eyes. 'And I *don't* want a child like Caroline. Not today, at least.'

She had a way of keeping him off-balance. The blouse she wore had slipped down to expose one shoulder, but she did not seem to have noticed. 'Agnes has a baby now too. She married a Captain Hicks in the Company army at Bombay. It seems both my sisters are brood mares. It may run in the family, so I have to be very careful. You aren't married, are you, Tom?'

'No.' His voice was husky. The skin on her shoulder and arm was smooth and sun-gilded and there were colourless hairs on her forearms, fine as silk, that caught the sun.

'That's good. So what are we going to do about Dorian? Do you want me to spy on Guy and find out everything I can? I don't think he will tell you much himself.'

'I would be most grateful for your help.'

'I can go through all his correspondence and eavesdrop on his visitors. There is a hole in the wall where the ropes

678

for the fan go through. It makes a fine confessional.' She looked mightily pleased with herself. 'But, of course, we will have to meet here regularly so that I can report to you.'

Tom found that prospect far from distasteful. 'Do you remember the concerts we used to have in the evenings on board the *Seraph*?' she asked, and burst spontaneously into the chorus of 'Spanish Ladies'. Her voice was true and unaffected, and Tom, tone-deaf as he was, was stirred by it. The hair on the back of his neck prickled and he was sorry when she stopped.

'What happened to Master Walsh, our teacher?' she asked. 'He was such a funny little man.'

'He is with me on the *Swallow*.' And he went on to tell her about all the crew she remembered from the *Seraph*.

She wept when he told her how Big Daniel Fisher had died, and he wanted to take her in his arms to comfort her. Instead he changed the subject, and told her about how they had captured the *Swallow*, and about the long voyage out.

She listened raptly, wiped away the tears, and applauded his courage and ingenuity. Soon she was chatting easily again, flitting from subject to subject, as though she had stored up a hundred questions for him in the years they had been apart.

Tom was intrigued. The longer he studied her face the more he decided that his first appraisal had been in error. Perhaps her features were not pretty, her nose and mouth *were* too large, her jaw too square, but put together with the animation and spirit that lit them he decided she was almost beautiful. Her eyes crinkled when she laughed, and she had a little trick of lifting her chin when she asked a question, which he liked.

The shadows moved out across the courtyard as they talked. Suddenly she broke off in the middle of a hilarious description of her family's arrival in Bombay, and their reaction to the unfamiliar, exotic new world. 'Oh, Tom, it's late. The time went so quickly. I have stayed too long.' Hastily she gathered up the plates and empty wine cups. 'I must go. Guy will be furious if he even suspects where I have been.'

'Guy is not your master.' Tom frowned.

'He is the master of our household. My father placed me in his care when Mother died. For Caroline's sake, I have to humour him. He takes out his ill-temper on her.'

'Are you happy living with Guy and Caroline, Sarah?' He felt that even in the short time they had spent together he knew her well enough to ask such a delicate question.

'I can think of other circumstances which would please me better,' she said, almost inaudibly, without looking up from the picnic basket. Then she pulled on her discarded shoes and jumped to her feet. Tom picked up the basket and she placed one slim hand on his arm as if she needed to steady herself over the uneven ground. It was only a short time ago, though, that he had seen her dancing along the top of the high wall.

'When will you come again to give me report of what Guy is doing?' Tom asked, as he lifted the pannier basket onto the mare's back.

'Not tomorrow, I have promised to help Caroline with Christopher, but the next day, at the same time.'

He placed his hands on her waist and lifted her up into the saddle. He hoped she realized the strength that that simple act had required for she was no delicate lily of a girl. Today she was riding side-saddle.

She hooked one leg around the horn, and he helped her arrange her long skirts. Then she looked down at him as he stood by her stirrup. 'Oh, Tom,' she said impulsively, 'it's been such fun. Life on the island is so restricted and boring. Guy won't even let me go into the town on my own. I cannot last remember when I enjoyed myself so

680

much.' Then she seemed overcome by embarrassment at her lack of restraint. Without waiting for his response she urged the mare away, and raced off down the sandy path through the palm groves. She sat tall and regal in the saddle.

As Tom came up the causeway from the harbour and passed below the portcullis of the fort, he saw two men coming towards him, deep in conversation. He caught a snatch of their words as they passed him, enough to be sure that they were speaking English, and he turned back after them. 'God love you, gentlemen,' he called, 'it's good to hear the Christian tongue spoken in this heathen land. May I introduce myself? Robert Davenport.' He used the pseudonym he had chosen to protect himself from the murder warrant that he knew must follow him. The two Englishmen turned to face him, their expressions guarded. Only then Tom recognized them as the captain and one of the officers from the East Indiaman in the harbour. He had seen them rowed ashore from the ship earlier in the day. 'I hope you have enjoyed a good voyage thus far?' Tom asked, when they had reluctantly introduced themselves and shaken hands, still stiff and reserved. 'I presume that you are coming from an audience of the Sultan?'

'Yes.' The captain nodded curtly. He did not volunteer further information, and Tom had to fish again.

'What is the fellow like? This will be my first meeting with him. Does he speak any English?'

'He speaks only his own God-forsaken lingo,' the man replied. 'I wish you luck in your dealings with him. He is a crafty devil, and you will need all the luck you can muster.' He bowed. 'And now if you will excuse me, sir . . .'

Tom strode into the fort, his anger bubbling over. He

now had proof of what Sarah had told him. At the instigation of Guy, his own brother, the vizier was fobbing him off.

A servant of the vizier tried to delay him in the antechamber, but Tom brushed past him: he knew his way to the inner cabinet. He jerked aside the thick silk curtains that covered the doorway and barged through.

The vizier was seated on the low platform at the far side of the room. The room stank of incense and hashish. There was a writing-tablet in front of him and a secretary beside him, offering documents one at a time for his signature. The vizier looked up, startled by Tom's precipitate entrance.

'A minute ago I spoke to the English captain who was coming from an audience of His Excellency,' Tom announced. 'I was pleased to hear that the Sultan has recovered so swiftly from his indisposition,' he went on, in Arabic, 'for this means that he is now able to meet me, and respond to my petition.'

The vizier scrambled to his feet, but Tom brushed past him, making for the doorway beyond. 'You cannot go in there!' he cried fearfully, but Tom ignored him.

'Guard!' the vizier shouted. 'Stop that man.'

A big man in a long robe and half-armour appeared in the doorway and blocked Tom's way. He had his hand on the pommel of the sheathed scimitar on his belt. Tom stepped up to him, and seized his sword arm at the wrist. The guard tried to draw his weapon but Tom held his arm, and crushed his wrist in a vicious grip that made him wince, looking over his shoulder into the room beyond.

'Greetings, mighty lord,' he called to the man who reclined on a mound of cushions. 'I call down all the blessings of Allah upon you, and offer you my humble and dutiful respects. I beg to address you on a matter of mercy. As the Prophet Himself has said, the small child and the widow are deserving of our compassion.'

The Sultan blinked at him, and sat upright. He wore a stiff jacket of heavily brocaded silk over scarlet pantaloons, gathered at the waist with a girdle of gold filigree. His turban was scarlet to match his trousers, and his beard was bushy and thick. He tugged at it nervously. He had not expected to be confronted by this barbaric Frank, quoting the sacred words of the Koran at him.

The vizier had run after Tom. Now he thrust himself between them. 'Forgive me, lord, I tried to stop him. This is the mean and worthless unbeliever of whom I told you. I will call the guard to have him removed.'

'Let him be,' the Sultan said. 'I will listen to what he has to say.'

Tom released the guard's wrist and pushed him aside. 'This mean and worthless unbeliever thanks the mighty Sultan Ali Muhammad, and presents his humble respects.'

His words were so much at odds with his behaviour that the Sultan smiled. 'Speak to me, then, on this compassionate matter,' he invited.

'I seek a child, my own brother. He was lost two years ago. I have good reason to suspect that he is being held captive in the territories of the Omani.'

The Sultan's expression became guarded.

'My brother is a subject of His Majesty King William the Third. There is a treaty between your Caliph and our King which forbids the enslavement of their subjects.'

'I know who you are.' The Sultan held up his hand to silence Tom. 'I have heard from the English consul concerning you. I have also received enquiries from the consul about this child. These matters are being investigated. There is nothing more I can tell you until I receive a reply from the court of the Caliph in Muscat.'

'It is a year and more since—' Tom began angrily, but the Sultan stopped him.

'I am sure that you must realize the folly of arousing

the displeasure of the Caliph by importuning him on such a trivial matter as this.'

'It is no trivial matter,' Tom protested. 'My family is noble, and wields much influence.'

'To the Caliph, it is a trivial matter. However, His Majesty is a man of great compassion. We can rest assured that we will hear from him if he can tell us anything about the boy. He will reply to these queries when he has something to tell us. In the meantime we must wait upon his grace.'

'How long?' Tom demanded. 'How long must we wait?'

'As long as is necessary.' The Sultan made the gesture of dismissal. 'Next time you burst in upon me like an enemy I will treat you as one, Englishman,' he warned coldly.

When Tom had been led away, the Sultan summoned his vizier and the man prostrated himself before him. 'Forgive me, mighty lord. I am dust before you. I tried to prevent that mad Frank—'

The Sultan silenced him with a wave of his hand. 'Send word to the English consul that I wish to speak to him immediately.'

'Guy went down to the fort yesterday. The Sultan sent for him,' Sarah told Tom. 'When he came back he had a black dog on his back. He beat one of the grooms senseless, and shouted at Caroline and me.'

'He didn't beat you?' Tom asked. 'I swear I will thrash him into a pulp if he raises a hand to you.'

'He tried that only once.' Sarah laughed, and shook out her hair so that it danced in the monsoon wind. 'I doubt he will do so again. I broke one of his precious

684

Chinese vases over his head. It didn't bleed much, but he behaved as if he was dying. But enough of that! I was giving you my report.'

'Stand by about!' Tom interrupted her, and she jumped to the mizen halyard of the little felucca. She was learning the ropes quickly and was already a handy crew. Tom had hired the craft in Zanzibar harbour for a few rupees a day, and they laid her on a tack to round the south point of the island. Then Sarah came back to sit beside him.

'So, after throwing the entire household into pandemonium, Guy spent the rest of the afternoon in his room. At supper he spoke hardly a word, but drank two bottles of port, and another of Madeira. It took two servants to help Caroline and me carry him up to bed.'

'So my twin has become a sot?' Tom asked.

'No, it was most unusual – the first time I have seen him drink himself into a stupor. You seem to have a strange effect on people.' She made the double-edged remark with such insouciance that Tom was not certain how to interpret it. She went on lightly, 'After we had tucked him up, and Caroline was beside him in the bed, I went down to his office, and found he had written a sheaf of letters. I made copies of those that concern us.'

She pulled out the folded pages from the pocket of her skirt. 'This one is to Lord Childs, and this to your brother William.' She handed them to him and the sheets fluttered in her hand.

'Take the tiller.' He handed it to her, and Sarah perched up on the transom, her skirts pulled up to her knees to let the sun and wind play on her skin. With an effort Tom averted his eyes from those long, strong limbs and focused his attention on the papers. He frowned as he read the first letter, and as he continued the frown turned into a dark scowl. 'The treacherous bastard!' he exclaimed, then was immediately contrite. 'Forgive me. I did not mean to use rough language.'

She laughed, crinkling her eyes. 'If Guy is a bastard that makes you one also. We had better choose another description. How about toad or bunghole?'

Tom felt himself blush, he had not expected to be outdone in the use of invective. Hurriedly he switched his attention back to the letter to William. It was an eerie feeling to read words directed to the man he had killed.

When he finished reading he tore both letters to shreds and threw them up into the air. They watched them fly away like white gulls on the wind.

'So tell me about your audience with the Sultan. Every last detail,' Sarah demanded.

Before replying Tom stood up and went to the foot of the mast. He lowered the lateen sail, and immediately the motion of the felucca changed: she no longer plunged and wrestled with the wind, but gave herself to it like a lover, with a gentle swoop and climb. He went back and sat close to Sarah, but not quite touching her. 'I had to force my way into his inner cabinet,' he said, 'but I had armed myself with a quotation from the Koran.' He described the meeting to her, repeating the exchanges word for word, and she listened solemnly, not interrupting once, which he realized even from their short acquaintance was unusual.

Once or twice during the recital Tom lost the thread and repeated himself. Her eyes were wide-set, and the whites were clear and so white that they seemed to be tinged with a faint bluish radiance, like those of a healthy infant. Their faces were so close together that he could trace that elusive fragrance to her breath. When he had finished speaking they were both silent, but neither made any move to pull apart.

Sarah broke the silence. 'Are you planning to kiss me, Tom?' She stroked the long tendrils of hair back from her face with one hand. 'Because if you are this is a good time for it. There is no one to spy on us.'

He moved his face towards hers, then stopped with only an inch between their lips, overcome by an almost religious sense of awe and sacrilege. 'I don't want to do anything that will give you offence,' he croaked.

'Don't be a booby, Tom Courtney.' Despite the insult her voice was husky, and her eyes closed slowly, the thick dark lashes interlacing. She ran the pink tip of her tongue over her lips, then pursed them expectantly.

Tom felt an almost irresistible urge to seize her and crush her body against his own. Instead he touched his lips to hers as lightly as a butterfly settling on a petal. The moisture on them tasted faintly sweet, and he felt that he might suffocate with the pressure in his chest. After a moment he drew back.

Her eyes flew open. They were startlingly green. 'Damn you, Tom Courtney,' she said. 'I have waited so long, and that was the best you could do.'

'You are so soft and beautiful,' he stammered. 'I don't want to hurt you or make you despise me.'

'If you don't want me to despise you, then you must do better than that.' She closed her eyes again and leaned towards him. He hesitated only a heartbeat longer then seized her, wrapped her in his arms, and crushed her mouth with his.

She made a small mewing sound of surprise and stiffened with shock at the unexpected power of his embrace, then flung herself forward, meeting his kiss with such abandon that their lips were forced open, their teeth clashed together, the softness and wetness of their mouths melded and their tongues entwined.

A larger wave hit the side of the drifting felucca and tumbled them from their perch on the transom. It did not break their embrace and they fell to the deck, oblivious of the smell of the bilges and of the dried fish scales that covered the hard planks beneath them.

'Tom! Tom!' She was trying to speak without lifting her mouth from his. 'Yes! So long! I never thought – oh, yes, you are so strong. Don't stop now.'

He wanted to devour her, to engulf her completely. The lining of her mouth was slippery, and her tongue was a maddening goad. His senses swam, the universe closed in upon him until this warm fragrant body in his arms was all of existence.

At last they had to free their mouths to breathe. It was only for a moment, just long enough for her to gasp, 'Tom. Oh, Tom. I have loved you from the first moment I saw you. All these years I thought I had lost you.'

Then they flew at each other again, moaning and clawing at each other, her arms locked about his neck, bruising their lips against each other's mouth and teeth. Blindly he groped for her breasts, and when he found them their shape and elastic weight made him cry out aloud as if in pain. He fumbled at the fastening of her bodice, but he was clumsy and inexpert. Impatiently she pushed away his hands and undid the ribbon. She reached in and scooped out one of her breasts and pushed it into his hand, closing his fingers over it.

'There,' she said, into his mouth, 'it's yours. Everything is yours.' He kneaded her flesh, and though she whimpered she exulted in the pain.

'Oh, I have hurt you.' He pulled away. 'I'm sorry. Truly, I'm sorry.'

'No, no!' She reached for his hands and replaced them on her bosom. 'Do it. Do whatever you want.'

He stared at the breast in his hand. It was as white as though it had been freshly carved from ivory, but with the pink marks of his rough fingers on it. It filled his cupped hand. The nipple was engorged and hard, dark with blood. 'So beautiful. I have never seen anything so beautiful.'

He bowed his head and placed his lips on the nipple. She arched her back, thrusting her chest up to meet him. She reached up with both hands, twisted and entwined her fingers in the thick, springing curls at the back of his head, guiding his mouth. When at last he lifted it to look at her face, she locked her mouth on his once more.

He was on top of her now, and suddenly she realized what that hardness was that he was pushing against her thighs and belly. She had never felt it before, but often she and Caroline had discussed it, and she had wheedled every detail out of her elder sister. As the realization struck her, she stopped breathing and stiffened with shock. Immediately Tom tried to break away again. 'I didn't mean to frighten you. We should stop now.'

The threat terrified her. She was desperate at the thought of being deprived of him and the hardness of his body. She pulled him back. 'Please, Tom, don't go away!'

Almost timidly he embraced her again, but he arched his lower body away from her. She wanted to feel him again, that wondrous man-thing hard against her. She reached around behind him and locked her hands over his buttocks, pulling him in and hunting for him with straining hips. 'Yes!' She had found him. 'Oh, yes.' She was in a transport, her emotions tumbling and twisting like a twig caught in a whirlpool. She felt him tugging at her clothing, reaching down between them, and she realized what he was trying to do.

She raised herself on her shoulders and heels, arching her bottom off the deck, and reached down to help him, pulling her skirts over her thighs, then as high as her navel. The monsoon wind was cool on her naked belly, and Tom was kneeling over her, plucking frantically at the fastenings of his breeches. She raised herself on her elbows, wanting to see him. Caroline's descriptions had been graphic, but she wanted to see for herself. Tom was taking so long, she felt she could not wait longer. She wanted to help him and stretched out her hand.

Then, with one movement, he wrenched his breeches down to his knees, and she gasped aloud. Nothing her sister had told her had prepared her for this. Staring at him, she fell back on the hard deck and her legs fell apart weakly as if she had no control of them.

A long time later he lay heavy and inert on top of her. He was gasping like a man rescued from drowning. Droplets of his sweat had fallen upon her like rain, and wet the front of her bodice, her face and her bare breast. She had locked her legs around him, and she held him still. The felucca under them rocked them like infants in the cradle.

Tom stirred and tried to rise, but she tightened the grip of her arms and legs to prevent him leaving her. He sighed raggedly and slumped back on top of her. She felt a strange sense of triumph and possession, as though she had achieved something of almost mystical importance, something beyond mere flesh. She could not find the words to describe it to herself, but she stroked his head and murmured gentle but incoherent endearments to him.

With infinite regret, and a sense of aching loss, she felt him shrivel inside her, and though she ached where he had forced his way into her, she tightened her muscles and tried to hold him in, but he slipped away, and she had to let him sit up. He looked about him with a bewildered expression. 'We have drifted a league out to sea.'

She sat up beside him, smoothing down her skirts, and saw that the island was a blue line on the horizon. Tom came up on his knees, pulling up his breeches, and she watched him. She felt maternal and protective, as though she had miraculously become a full woman, as though she had put her girlhood behind her, that she was now the strong one and he the child who must be fostered and cherished.

Tom staggered to the halyard, unsteady on his feet,

raised the sail and put the felucca on the wind. Sarah straightened her clothing and retied the ribbon of her bodice, then rose from the deck and went to sit with him at the tiller. He put his arm around her shoulders and she snuggled close to him. They were halfway back to the island before either of them spoke.

'I love you, Sarah Beatty,' he said.

She rejoiced to hear him say it and tightened her embrace. 'As I said before, I have loved you since the first day I laid eyes upon you, Tom Courtney. Even though I was only a child, I prayed that one day I would be your woman.'

'That day has come,' he said, and kissed her again.

They met as often as Sarah could escape the vigilance of Caroline and Guy. Sometimes the intervals between their meetings were two or three days, but then their passion was inflamed by the delay.

These trysts were always in the afternoons, for in the mornings Sarah helped her sister run the household, or looked after little Christopher. Neither could Tom leave the *Swallow* and his crew: the ship had suffered extensive storm damage to her hull and rigging after leaving Good Hope, and this had to be repaired, the ship made fully seaworthy again.

Most mornings Tom was up at the fort, for he was desperate to have news of Dorian from Muscat, and he was still waiting for his licence to trade. Although he lavished flattery and baksheesh on the vizier, he was still in bad grace and the vizier punished him with flowery excuses and apologies for the delay. Without the Sultan's *firman* in his hands Tom could not deal in the island markets.

Those precious hours when Tom and Sarah could be together sped by too swiftly for both of them. Some

691

afternoons they lay in each other's arms, not bothering to touch the delicacies that Sarah had brought with her, making love as though it were for the last time. In the intervals between they talked, breathless in their need to say everything they felt for each other, making fantastic plans for the future, for the time when they could escape the island together and, with Dorian, sail away in the *Swallow*.

On other days they took the felucca and sailed to the outer reefs, anchoring over the coral and fishing with hand lines, laughing and shouting with excitement as they dragged up the lovely creatures from the depths, kicking on the lines, sparkling like great gemstones in the sunlight as they were swung inboard.

One afternoon Sarah brought the box of duelling pistols her father had given her when they parted in Bombay, for her protection in this land of wild animals and wilder men. 'Papa promised to teach me to shoot, but he never found time,' she told him. 'Will you teach me now, Tom?'

They were magnificent weapons. The grips were carved from lustrous walnut, and the locks and long-rifled barrels were chased with gold and silver. There were ramrods of horn, and powder flasks of silver. Fitted into the case was a screw-topped pot containing fifty lead balls that had been selected to ensure that they were perfectly round and symmetrical. The patches were of oiled leather.

Tom loaded with half-measures of powder to reduce the recoil. Then he showed her how to place her feet, and address the target, turned half away, presenting her right shoulder. Then with her left fist on her hip, to bring up the weapon with a straight right arm, pick up the foresight bead in the notch of the back sight and fire as she swung through the target, rather than trying to hold her aim until her arm ached and shook.

He set up a coconut on top of one of the low walls of

the monastery, fifteen paces away. 'Knock it off!' he said, and called her misses. 'Low! Still low! Right!' He reloaded swiftly, and she changed pistols. With the fourth shot she sent the nut spinning and spraying milk. She squealed gleefully, and soon she was hitting more often than she missed.

'I should be given a prize for each hit,' she demanded.

'What sort of prize did you have in mind?'

'A kiss might be appropriate.'

With this incentive, she hit five nuts in succession, and Tom told her, 'Clever girl, you have won the grand prize.' He picked her up in his arms and carried her, protesting weakly and insincerely, through the gateway, into their secret place in the ruins.

A few days later he brought one of London's best muskets with him in the felucca, and showed her how to load and fire it. Tom had purchased four of these extraordinary weapons before they sailed from England. He could not afford to buy more, for they were staggeringly expensive.

The cheap military muskets were smooth-bored, and the ball did not fit snugly in the barrel, so spin was not imparted to it as it was driven through the lands. Because they were not stabilized, the balls flew erratically.

However, with this rifled weapon the accuracy was startling. Tom could be sure of hitting a coconut with every shot at a hundred and fifty paces. Sarah was tall and strong enough to be able to level the heavy musket from her shoulder without difficulty, and once again she proved she had the quickness of hand and eye to make her a natural marksman. Within an hour of practice she was able to claim her reward from him after almost every shot.

'I suppose the next thing I shall have to teach you is sword-play,' Tom remarked, as they lay together on the plaited sleeping mat with which they had now furnished their secret roofless cell in the monastery.

'You have done a fine job of that already.' She grinned wickedly, and reached down his body. 'Here is my trusty sword and, sir, I know already full well how to play with it.'

In serious mood, they discussed their plans for when Tom had succeeded in rescuing Dorian. 'I will come back for you,' he said, 'and take you with me, away from Zanzibar and Guy.'

'Yes.' She nodded as though she had never doubted that. 'And then we will sail back to England together, won't we, Tom?' She saw his expression change. 'What is it, my darling?' she asked anxiously.

'I can never return to England,' he said softly.

She scrambled to her knees and stared at him in dismay. 'What do you mean, never return home?'

'Listen to me, Sarah.' He sat up and took both her hands in his. 'Something terrible happened before I left England, something I never intended.'

'Tell me,' she pleaded. 'Anything that touches you, touches me.'

And so he told her about William. He started at the beginning, describing their childhood, and the growing tyranny the elder brother had exerted over the younger ones. He recounted many small incidents of heartless cruelty that William had inflicted. 'I think the only time that Dorian, Guy and I were happy was when we were free of him, those times when he was away at university,' he said.

Her expression was filled with sympathy. 'I did not like him when I met him at High Weald,' she agreed. 'He reminded me of a serpent, cold and poisonous.'

Tom nodded. 'I had almost forgotten how vindictive he could be when I was away from home, on the voyage of the *Seraph*. But when we took Father home after Flor de la Mar it was all brought back to me with a vengeance.'

He told her how William had treated their father

when he was dying, and how he had repudiated his oath to help find Dorian after Hal's death. 'We fought,' he said. 'We had fought before, often, but never like this.' He paused and the pain of the memory was so plain to see that she tried to embrace him to make him stop the recital. 'No, Sarah, I have to tell you everything. You have to listen, so that you can understand how it happened.' Sometimes halting, at other times in a fierce rush of words, he told her about that fight on his last night at High Weald. 'You asked how I broke my nose, and I could not tell you then.' He touched the lump. 'Billy did that.'

He described the battle in simple words that were so vivid and affecting that Sarah paled and clutched his arm, sinking her nails into his flesh. 'In the end I could not kill him, though he deserved it a hundred times. I was moved by Alice, as she stood there with the baby in her arms, pleading for his life, and I could not kill him. I put up my sword and rode away, thinking that that was the end of it. But I should have known my brother better than that.'

'There is more?' she asked in a small, frightened voice. 'I don't think I can bear to hear more.'

'I have to tell you all of it, and you must listen so that you can understand.'

He came at last to the fatal meeting on the river landing below the Tower of London. He described the fight with the band of hired cut-throats. His voice sank lower and lower, and there were long pauses as he searched for the words to describe the terrible climax. 'I still did not know it was Billy. It was dark. He wore a wide hat and his face was covered. I thought he was the boatman, and I ran to him, asking him to ferry us away. I was thunderstruck when he drew out the pistol. He fired and the ball struck me here.' He lifted his shirt and displayed the long pink scar across his ribs beneath his arm.

She stared at it, then reached out to trace the raised, twisted cicatrices with her fingertips. She had noticed the scar before, but when she had questioned him, he had been evasive and dismissive. Now she knew why. 'He might have killed you,' she breathed in awe.

'Yes, I thought he had. But, luckily, the ball struck my ribs and glanced away. It knocked me off my feet, and Billy stood over me and aimed the second barrel. That shot would have finished the business. The sword was in my hand. I was afraid, terrified. I threw with all my strength, and it hit him full in the chest and went through his heart.'

'Oh, merciful God.' Sarah stared at him. 'You killed your own brother.'

'I did not know it was Billy, not even then. Not until I lifted the hat from his head and saw his face.'

They were silent a while.

Sarah looked horrified. Then she rallied. 'He was trying to kill you,' she said firmly. 'You had to do it, Tom, to save yourself.' She saw the desolation in his eyes, reached out, took his head and pulled it to her bosom, holding him there, stroking his hair. 'There is no blame. You had to do it.'

'I have told myself that a thousand times.' Tom's voice was muffled. 'But he was my brother.'

'God is just. I know that He forgives you, my darling. You must put it behind you.'

He lifted his face, and she knew that there was nothing she could say to ease the pain. It would haunt him if he lived a hundred years. She kissed him. 'None of it makes any difference to us, Tom. I am your woman for ever. If we can never go back to England, then let it be so. I will follow you to the ends of the earth. Nothing matters but you and me, and our love.'

She drew him down onto the sleeping mat, and offered him the comfort of her body.

S till the *Swallow* waited in the harbour. They had completed the repairs long since, and she was once more sleek and lovely. Her hull glistened with new paint, but her canvas stayed furled and she snubbed restlessly on her anchor cables, like a falcon at bate.

Her crew were growing restless. There had been a number of ugly fights among them, their nerves rubbed raw by inactivity, and Tom knew he could not hold them much longer in idleness, like prisoners on their own ship. More and more Tom was tempted to defy the Sultan's decree and sail north into those forbidden seas where he knew Dorian was held captive, or to take the *Swallow* across to the mainland and search for those hidden places in the mysterious interior where the ivory, gold and gum arabic were harvested.

Aboli and Ned Tyler advised patience, but Tom rounded on them angrily. 'Patience is for old men. Fortune never smiled on patience.'

The monsoon fell away, into the breathless period of the doldrums, then swung right round the compass and whispered almost inaudibly out of the north-east, those first gentle breaths that herald the change of season, harbinger of the big rains of the *kaskazi*.

The *kaskazi* gathered strength, and the heavily laden trading ships in the harbour hoisted their anchors, spread their canvas to the fresh new wind and bore away southwards to round Good Hope.

The *Swallow* waited in the almost empty harbour. Then, on one of Tom's regular visits to the fort, the vizier greeted him as though he were newly arrived in the port, and offered him a seat on a brocaded cushion and a thimble cup of thick, sweet black coffee. 'All my efforts on your behalf have borne fruit. His Excellency, the Sultan, has looked favourably on your petition for a licence to trade.' He smiled disarmingly, and produced the document from the sleeve of his robe. 'Here is his *firman*.'

Tom reached for it eagerly, but the vizier slipped it back into his sleeve. 'The *firman* is restricted to the island of Zanzibar alone. It does not entitle you to sail further north, or to call at any port on the mainland. If you do so, your ship will be seized and the crew with it.'

Tom tried to hide his irritation. 'I understand, and I am grateful for the generosity of the Sultan.'

'A tax will be levied on any goods you acquire in the markets, which must be paid for in gold before the goods are loaded aboard your ship. The tax is one fifth part of the value of all goods.'

Tom swallowed hard, but kept on smiling politely. 'His Excellency is generous.'

The vizier held out the document, but as Tom reached for it, he again withdrew it, and exclaimed at his own forgetfulness. 'Ah! Forgive me, *effendi*. I have overlooked the small matter of the licence fee. A thousand rupees in gold and, of course, another five hundred rupees for my own intercession with His Excellency.'

With the royal *firman* at last in his grasp, Tom could visit the markets. Each day he came ashore at dawn, bringing Master Walsh and Aboli with him, and he returned to the ship only at the hour of Zuhr, the early-afternoon prayer, when the merchants closed their stalls to answer the call of the muezzin to their devotions.

For the first few weeks he made no purchases, but each day sat for hours with one or other of the merchants, drinking coffee and exchanging pleasantries, examining their wares without any show of enthusiasm, striking no deals, but comparing price and quality. Tom had believed at first that his bargaining power would be strengthened by most of the other European traders having sailed already with the *kaskazi*, and that there would be little competition for the goods on offer.

He soon found that this was far from the case. The other traders had picked over the goods, and selected the best. The ivory tusks remaining in the market were mostly immature, few any longer than his arm, many deformed and discoloured. There was nothing even approaching that mighty pair his father had purchased from Consul Grey on their first visit to the island. Despite the poor quality, the merchants were already fat with profits and they maintained their prices, shrugging indifferently when he protested.

'*Effendi*, there are few men who hunt the beasts. It is dangerous work, and each season they have to travel further to find the herds. Now it is very late in the season. The supply of ivory has been taken up by the other Frankish traders,' one of the merchants explained smoothly. 'However, I have a few fine slaves for your consideration.'

With all the grace he could muster, Tom refused the offer to examine these human chattels. Aboli had been captured as a slave in childhood, but every detail of the horrors inflicted upon him had remained starkly clear in his memory. Before he had ever sailed from the shores of England Tom had grown up with his descriptions of the heinous trade. During his many voyages Tom's father had accumulated first-hand knowledge of the trade, and he had helped instil in the young Tom an abhorrence of its inhuman practices.

Since he had first rounded Good Hope, Tom had come in regular contact with the slavers and their victims. During their long wait in Zanzibar Roads there had always been slave-ships anchored close to them, near enough for the stink and heartbreaking sounds to carry clearly to where the *Swallow* was lying.

Each day now he walked with Aboli through the slave

compounds, and it was more difficult to ignore the misery all around them: the wailing of children torn from their parents' arms, the weeping of bereaved mothers, and the dumb suffering in the dark eyes of young men and women deprived of their free, wild existence, chained like animals, abused in a language they did not understand, spreadeagled on the whipping-block, flogged with the vicious hippohide *kiboko* until their ribs showed white in the wounds. The very thought of making a profit out of the torment of these lost souls made the bile rise in the back of Tom's throat.

Back on the *Swallow* he discussed their predicament with his ship's officers. Although the foremost object of the voyage was to find Dorian, and Tom never wavered from that goal, he had a duty to his crew and he had inveigled many of them aboard with the promise of reward. So far there had been no rewards and there was little prospect of any profit to share with them.

'There are few bargains to be had hereabouts,' Master Walsh confirmed lugubriously. He opened his notebook, adjusted his gold-rimmed spectacles on his nose, and quoted the list of the ivory and gum arabic prices he had compiled before they left England. 'The price of spices is more favourable, but still leaves little profit when we take into account the hardships and expenses of the voyage. The cloves and pepper, now, there is always a ready market for them, and to a lesser extent for cinnamon and, of course, the cinchona bark is in demand in America and in the Mediterranean countries afflicted by malaria.'

'We must have a few hundredweight of cinchona for our own use,' Tom cut in. 'Now that the big rains are beginning there will be much fever among the men.' The boiled extract from the bark was bitter as gall but, a century ago, the Jesuit monks had discovered that it was a sovereign remedy for the malarial fever. It had been the fathers who had first introduced the cinchona trees to this island. Now it grew here profusely.

'Yes,' agreed Aboli softly. 'You will need the cinchona. Especially if you're going inland to search for your own ivory.'

Tom looked at him sharply. 'What made you think I would be so foolhardy as to flout the decrees of the Sultan and John Company, Aboli? Even you have counselled me strongly against such a course.'

'I have watched you sitting in the bows each evening and staring across the channel at the African mainland. Your thoughts were so loud that they almost deafened me.'

'It would be dangerous.' Tom stopped short of denying the accusation, but his head turned instinctively towards the west, and a dreamy look came into his eyes as he stared across at the hazy outline of the land fading into the dusk shadows.

'That has never stopped you before,' Aboli pointed out.

'I would not know where to begin. It is a land unknown, *terra incognita*.' He used the caption from the charts in his cabin that he studied so avidly. 'Not even you have travelled out there, Aboli. It would be folly to go without a guide to lead us.'

'No, I do not know this northern land,' Aboli agreed. 'I was born much further south, near the great River Zambezi, and it is many years since I was last there.' He paused. 'But I know where we can find somebody who could lead us into the interior.'

'Who?' Tom asked, unable to hide his excitement. 'Where will we find this man? What is his name?'

'I do not yet know his name or his face, but I will recognize him when I see him.'

Whe they went ashore the next morning, the first chained files of slaves were being led to the market from the barracoons where they had been incarcerated overnight.

Like all the other commodities at this late season, their ranks were thinned, and fewer than two hundred specimens were on offer. When the *Swallow* had first arrived, there had been several thousand for sale. Most of those remaining were old or frail, thin with sickness or scarred from the *kiboko*. Buyers were always chary of a whip-marked slave, for it usually meant that he or she was incorrigible, not amenable to training.

Previously, when passing through the market, Tom had averted his gaze, had tried to avoid studying them, his repugnance and pity too troubling. But now he and Aboli took up a position at the main gate of the slave-market from which they could watch the sorry columns being herded past. They scrutinized every individual as he came level with them.

There were two or three black men in the ranks who seemed to Tom to be of the type they were seeking, tall and strong and heroic despite their chains. But when he touched Aboli's arm and glanced at him in enquiry, Aboli shook his head impatiently.

'Nothing?' Tom asked quietly, despondent. The last of the slaves were filing past, and Aboli had shown no interest in any of them.

'Our man is there,' Aboli contradicted him, 'but the slave-masters were watching us. I could not point him out.'

The slaves were led to their stalls around the square and each was chained to his post. The masters took their seats in the shade, wealthy men, complacent, richly dressed, attended by their personal slaves who brewed

702

coffee for them and lit the hookahs. Eyes hooded and sly, they watched Tom and Aboli as they made a slow circuit of the market.

Aboli stopped at the first stall and examined one of the slaves, a big man and a warrior by his looks. The slave-master pulled open his mouth to show his teeth, as though he were a horse, and palpated his muscles. 'Not more than twenty years of age, *effendi*,' the Arab said. 'Look at these arms – strong as a bullock. There is another thirty years' hard work in him.'

Aboli spoke to the slave in one of the dialects of the forests, but the man stared back at him like a dumb animal. Aboli shook his head, and they passed on to the next stall, to repeat the routine.

Tom realized he was slowly working his way towards the man he had already selected. He looked ahead, trying to guess which he was, and then, with sudden certainty, he recognized him.

He was naked except for a brief loincloth, a small man, with a thin wiry body. There was no fat or soft flesh on him. His hair was a thick, unkempt bush, like that of a wild animal, but his eyes were bright and piercing.

Gradually Tom and Aboli approached the group in which he was tethered, and Tom was careful to feign disinterest in the one they had chosen. They inspected another man and a young girl, then, much to the slave-master's chagrin, made as if to move on. As if in after-thought, Aboli turned back to the little man. 'Show me his hands,' he demanded of the slave-master, who nodded to his assistant. Between them, they grabbed the slave's wrists, and the chains clanked as they forced him to extend his hands for Aboli's scrutiny. 'Turn them over,' Aboli ordered, and they turned them palm uppermost. Aboli concealed his satisfaction. The first two fingers of both the man's hands were calloused to the extent of being almost deformed. 'This is our man,' he said to Tom in English, but his inflection made it sound like a rejection. Tom shook his head as if confirming his rejection. They turned away, leaving the disappointed slave-master staring after them.

'What is it about his hands?' Tom asked, without looking back. 'What is it that has marked them that way?'

'The bowstring,' Aboli said curtly.

'Both hands?' Tom stopped with surprise.

'He is an elephant hunter,' Aboli explained, 'but keep walking and I will explain it to you. The elephant bow is so stiff that no man can draw it from the shoulder. The hunter creeps close – that close.' He pointed out a wall ten paces away. 'Then he lies on his back, both feet on the stock of the bow. He lays the tip of the arrow between his big toes and he draws with both hands on the string. Over the years of hunting the bowstring marks his fingers like that.'

Tom had difficulty visualizing a bow of that power. 'It must be a formidable weapon, this bow.'

'It can shoot an arrow clean through the body of an ox, from shoulder to shoulder, and go on to kill a man standing on the other side,' Aboli said. 'That man is one of the small intrepid brotherhood who live by hunting the great beasts.'

They completed their leisurely round of the market, then casually returned to where the little man stood. 'He is double chained, at ankles and wrists,' Aboli pointed out in English. 'And look at his back.' Tom saw the half-healed scars that criss-crossed the dark skin. 'They have beaten him savagely, trying to break him to their will, but you can see by his eyes that they have not succeeded.'

Aboli circled the little man slowly, peering at his muscular frame, and said something to him in a language Tom did not understand. There was no reaction from the slave. Tom watched his eyes and saw that they were sullen and uncomprehending. Aboli spoke two words in another of the forest dialects. There was still no sign from the little man that he understood.

Tom knew that, besides his mother tongue, the language Aboli had taught him when he was a child, Aboli spoke at least a dozen other lesser dialects of the far interior. Now, he switched again. This time the little man started and turned his head to stare at Aboli in confusion and amazement. He replied with a single word. 'Fundi!'

'That is his name,' Aboli explained to Tom, still in English. 'He is of the Lozi. A fierce warrior tribe. His name means the Adept.' Aboli smiled. 'He probably merits it.'

Tom accepted the slave-master's invitation to drink a cup of coffee, the essential accompaniment to any civilized session of bargaining. Within a very short time, Tom sensed that the slave-master was eager to rid himself of his small but truculent merchandise, and he was able to press the advantage. After an hour of haggling, the slave-master threw up his hands in despair. 'My children will starve. You have ruined me with your intransigence. You leave me a pauper, but take him! Take him and my very blood and bones with him.'

When they had Fundi, the Adept, on board the *Swallow*, Tom called for the blacksmith and had the chains knocked off his ankles and wrists. The little man rubbed the galled flesh and stared at them in astonishment. Then his eyes turned westward to the shadowy outline of the land from which he had been torn so cruelly.

'Yes.' Aboli read his thoughts. 'You can try to escape and flee back to your home. But can you swim that far?' He pointed across the forbidding blue expanse of water. 'Out there are sharks to greet you, larger than the greatest crocodiles you have ever seen, with teeth longer and sharper than the point of your arrows. If they do not eat you, then I will catch you and beat you so that you will think the blows of the Arabs were but the timid touch of a young virgin. Then I will chain you again like an animal.'

Fundi glared at him defiantly, but Aboli went on, 'Or, if you are wise, you will tell us about the land from which you have come, then lead us back there without chains, walking ahead of us like a warrior once more, a slayer of great elephants, free and proud.'

Fundi went on staring at him, but despite himself his expression changed, and his dark eyes widened. 'How do you know that I am a slayer of elephants? How do you speak the language of the Lozi? Why do you offer me my freedom again? Why do you wish to journey to the land of my fathers?'

'All these things I will explain to you,' Aboli promised. 'But for now think only that we are not your enemies. Here, there is food for you.'

Fundi was half starved, and he gorged himself on the bowl of rice and goat stew that Aboli placed before him. Gradually the food in his belly and Aboli's gentle questions lulled him, and he answered through a mouthful of half-chewed meat.

Aboli translated for Tom. 'He does not know how far it is, for he does not count distance as we do. But his land is distant, many months of travel. He says he lives beside a great river.'

It took time for Fundi to tell them all his story, but over the days that followed he filled in the details, and intrigued them with his description of lakes and mighty plains, of mountains crowned with shining white, like the heads of old men.

'Snow-capped mountains?' Tom was perplexed. 'Surely it is not possible in these tropical climes.'

He told them of immense herds of strange beasts, some of them larger than the hump-backed Zebu cattle of the Arabs, black and monstrous with sickle-shaped horns that could rip the guts out of a black-maned lion with a single thrust.

'Elephant?' Tom asked. 'Ivory?'

Fundi's eyes shone when he spoke of the mighty beasts. 'They are my goats,' he boasted to Aboli, and showed him the callouses on his fingers. 'My name is Fundi, the great slayer of elephants.' He held up both his hands with his fingers spread, and ten times closed them into double fists then flashed them again. 'This is how many elephants have fallen to my bow, shot through the heart by my arrows, every one of them a mighty bull with teeth longer than this.' He stood on tiptoe and stretched his arm up as high as he could reach.

'Are there still many elephant in his land?' Tom asked. 'Or has the mighty hunter, Fundi, killed them all?'

When Aboli put the question to him Fundi laughed, and his face became impish. 'Can you count the blades of grass on the great plains? How many fish are there in the lakes? What is the number of duck in the flocks that shade the sky in the season of the big rains? That is how many elephant there are in the land of the Lozi.'

Tom's excitement fed upon these intriguing tales, and he lay awake at night in his hard, narrow bunk, dreaming of the wild land the little man described to them. It was not only the promise of wealth and profit; he wanted to see these wonders with his own eyes, and pursue the mighty beasts, see the white-capped mountains and voyage on the wide, sweet waters of the lakes.

Then the wild flights of his imagination were checked by thoughts of Dorian and Sarah, and his commitment to them: Sarah has already promised that she will come with me wherever I travel. She is not like other girls. She is like me. She has adventure in her blood. But what of Dorian?

He thought of Dorian as he had not in all the years since they had parted. In his mind's eye he saw him as he had been on that fateful night when he had climbed to the window of his cell on Flor de la Mar, a little helpless child.

It took an effort to break his mind out of the rut in which it had travelled so long. What will he be like now?

Has he been changed by the hardships he has been forced to suffer? Is he still my little brother, or a different man from the boy I once knew? he wondered, alarmed at the thought of a stranger having taken Dorian's place. One thing I am sure of: he will never have changed as Guy has. There will still be the fire in him. He will want to come with me on this new adventure. The bond between us must still be strong. I am certain of it.

It seemed as though he had thrown down his gauntlet at the feet of the gods of chance, for the answer he sought came sooner than he expected. In the dawn light of the following morning a dirty little bum-boat rowed across from the stone quay of the harbour to where the *Swallow* lay at her moorings. When the boatman was still half a pistol shot from the ship's side, he stood on the thwart and hailed them. '*Effendi*, I have a paper for you from the English consul!' He held the document aloft and brandished it.

'Come alongside!' Ned Tyler gave him permission.

In his cabin Tom heard the shouts and had a strange premonition that something portentous was about to overtake him. In his shirtsleeves he hurried up on deck, just in time to snatch the letter out of the boatman's hands.

He saw that the address on the folded sheet was in Guy's handwriting. It had changed little since they had practised together under Master Walsh. The missive was addressed to Captain Thomas Courtney, aboard the *Swallow*, Zanzibar Roads.

When Tom tore it open hurriedly, the message it contained was terse: 'The Sultan has commanded both of us to an audience at noon this day. I shall meet you at the gate to the fort ten minutes before the hour. G.C.'

Predictably, Guy was precisely punctual. When he rode up with his syce in attendance his greeting was cool. He merely nodded, dismounted and tossed the reins to his servant. Then he glanced in Tom's direction. 'I would not

708

have troubled you, sir,' he said, distantly, not meeting Tom's eyes, 'but His Excellency insisted that you be present at this audience.' He drew his watch from the pocket of his waistcoat, glanced at it, then strode in through the gates without looking back.

The vizier greeted them with expressions of the greatest respect, bowing and smiling ingratiatingly, and backing away before them into the presence of the Sultan where he prostrated himself.

Guy bowed but not too low, conscious of his dignity as representative of His Majesty, and offered polite greetings. Tom followed his example. Then his gaze went to the man who sat at the Sultan's right hand: he looked well fed and his robe was of the finest quality. The hilt of his dagger was of gold and rhino horn. He was a high-ranking and dignified personage, of obvious importance, for even the Sultan deferred to him. He was studying Tom with more than ordinary interest, as though he knew who he was and had heard reports of him.

'I call down the blessings of Allah on you,' the Sultan said, and gestured to the cushions placed ready to receive them. Guy sat awkwardly, finding it difficult to manage his sword while he did so. Tom had spent many hours with the merchants in the markets and was accustomed to this position. He placed the scabbard of the Neptune sword across his lap.

'I am honoured to welcome to my court the holy mullah of the mosque of Prince Abd Muhammad al-Malik, the brother of the Caliph of Oman.' The Sultan inclined his head towards the man who sat beside him. Tom stiffened and felt his breathing come faster at the name of the Prince, the man who had bought Dorian from the corsair. He stared at the mullah, as the Sultan went on, 'This is the holy al-Allama. He has come from the Prince.'

Both Tom and Guy stared at him. Al-Allama made a

graceful gesture. His hands were small and smooth, like a girl's. 'May you find favour in the sight of God and His Prophet,' he said, and they bowed in acknowledgement.

'I trust that you have had a pleasant voyage, and when you left your home all was well in your household,' Tom said.

The mullah replied, 'I thank you for your concern. The *kaskazi* bore us kindly, and Allah smiled upon our enterprise.' Al-Allama smiled. 'I must congratulate you on the excellence of your Arabic. You speak the sacred language as if born to it.'

The compliments passed back and forth, but Tom found the long, complicated ritual of greetings and well-wishes hard to endure. This man came with news of Dorian: there could be no other reason for this audience. He studied al-Allama's face, trying to divine the nature of his tidings by the little signs, the twist of his lips, the inflection of his voice, and the expression in his eyes, but the mullah's face was bland, his manner urbane.

'Your trading in the markets of Zanzibar has been profitable?' the mullah asked. 'The Prophet approved of the honest merchant.'

'My main reason for visiting the domains of your Caliph was not to indulge in trade,' Tom told him, relieved to have an opening to address his real concerns. 'I come on a mission of compassion. I seek a dear one who is lost to me and my family.'

'My lord, the Prince al-Malik, has heard of your quest, and has received the petition you have addressed to him,' al-Allama replied. His tone was still expressionless, his face inscrutable.

'I have heard that your lord is a mighty man, but filled with compassion for the weak and that he is strong for justice and the law.'

'Prince Abd Muhammad al-Malik is all these things. That is the reason why he has sent me in person to deal

710

with your concerns, rather than sending a message that could not express the depth of his feelings for your loss.'

Tom felt a chill on his skin, even in the closed room and the hot incense-laden air. The mullah's choice of words was ominous. He felt Guy stir beside him, but he did not look at him. He waited for the mullah to speak again, dreading what he had to say. But al-Allama sipped delicately at his coffee, and looked down at his lap.

At last Tom was forced to press him, 'I have waited three years to have word of my brother. I beg you not to prolong my suffering.'

The mullah set down his cup and wiped his lips on the folded cloth that a slave handed him. 'My lord prince bids me speak thus.' He paused again as if gathering his thoughts. 'It is true that, some years ago, I purchased a young Frankish boy. He was named al-Amhara for his hair, which was a marvellous shade of red.'

Tom released a long, hissing sigh of relief. They had admitted it. There was to be no denial and subterfuge to battle against. Dorian was in the hands of the Mussulman Prince. 'Your words have lifted a great stone from my soul, a stone that threatened to crush the life out of me,' he said, and his voice was choked. He thought he might lose control and break down. Such weakness would be a terrible loss of prestige, and invite the scorn of all those present. He took a deep breath and lifted his chin to meet the mullah's eyes. 'What terms has your Prince set for the return of my brother to the bosom of his family?'

The mullah did not answer at once, but stroked and smoothed his beard, rearranging the perfumed braids on his chest.

'My lord ordered me to speak thus. "I, Abd Muhammad al-Malik, took the boy al-Amhara under my protection, paying a princely ransom for him, in order to protect him from the men who had captured him, and to ensure that no further hardship was inflicted upon him."'

'Your Prince is a mighty man and merciful,' Tom said, but he wanted to shout, 'Where is he? Where is my brother? What price do you want for his release?'

'My lord the Prince found the boy to be comely and well favoured. He took him to his heart, and to show his favour and shield him from all evil he declared al-Amhara his adopted son.'

Tom started to rise from the cushion, his face clearly displaying his alarm. 'His son?' he demanded, and foresaw the terrible obstacle that this had placed in his path.

'Yes, his own son. He treated him like a prince. I was given the task of educating the boy, and I also found him worthy of love.' Al-Allama dropped his eyes and for the first time showed emotion.

'I rejoice that my brother has found such favour in high places,' Tom said. 'But he is my brother. I have the right of blood. The Prophet of God has said that the tie of blood is as steel and cannot be sundered.'

'Your knowledge of the Holy Words of Islam does you credit,' the mullah said. 'My lord the Prince acknowledges your right of blood and offers you the payment of blood money for your loss.' Al-Allama summoned a servant who came forward carrying a small ebony chest inlaid with ivory and mother-of-pearl. He knelt in front of the two white men, placed the box on the tiles and opened the lid.

Tom had not moved, and now he did not even look down at the contents of the chest. However, Guy leaned forward and stared at the golden coins that filled the box to overflowing.

'Fifty thousand rupees,' said al-Allama. 'A thousand of your English pounds. A sum that takes into account that al-Amhara was a prince of the royal house of Oman.'

At last Tom found his voice again and the power of movement. He started up, his hand on the hilt of the Neptune sword. 'There is not enough gold in Arabia to buy me off,' he roared. 'I came here to find my brother, and I shall not leave until he is delivered to me.'

'That is not possible,' said al-Allama, and his voice was low and heavy with regret. 'Your brother is dead. He died almost two years ago of the malarial fever. There was nothing any man could do to save him though, Allah knows, we who loved him tried. Al-Amhara is dead.'

Tom dropped back on the cushion, his face blanched with shock. His eyes were haunted as he stared at al-Allama. He did not speak for a long time, and the only sound was the buzzing of a fat blue fly that bumped against the ceiling. 'I do not believe what you tell me,' he whispered, but his voice was hopeless, his expression desolate.

'I swear to you, as I love God and pray for his salvation, that I have seen al-Amhara's name on his tomb in the royal cemetery in Lamu,' al-Allama said, with infinite sorrow in his voice, so that Tom could no longer doubt him.

'Dorian,' he whispered. 'He was so young, so full of life.'

'Allah is kind. We can be sure that there is a place for him hereafter. My lord the Prince offers you consolation. He shares your sense of loss keenly,' the mullah offered.

Tom rose to his feet. It seemed to require a great effort to make such a simple movement. 'I thank your master,' he replied. 'I beg your forbearance but I must leave you now, to be alone to mourn my brother.' He turned to the door.

Guy stood and bowed to the two Arabs. 'We thank your lord the Prince for his compassion. We accept his offer of blood money.' He stooped, closed the lid of the chest and picked it up. 'All debts between Prince Abd Muhammad al-Malik and our family are discharged in full.'

He followed Tom to the door, hampered by the weight of the chest.

Sarah was on her usual perch high on the walls of the old monastery, from where she could spot Tom as soon as he appeared on the path that led up from the beach. 'Tom!' she called, and waved gaily, coming to her feet and running down the crumbled walls with her arms spread wide to balance herself. 'You are late! I have been waiting for hours. I had almost given you up.' She jumped down to the ground and raced, barefoot, down the sandy path. Ten feet from where he stood she came up short and stared into his face. 'Tom, what is it?' she whispered. She had never seen him like this before. His features were haggard, and his eyes filled with a terrible sorrow. 'Tom, what has happened to you?'

He took an uncertain step towards her, and held out his arms like a drowning man. She flew to him.

'Tom! Oh, Tom! What is it?' She held him with all her strength. 'Tell me, my darling. I want to help.'

He began to shake, and she thought he was sick, overcome by some terrible fever. He made a choking sound, and tears streamed down his face. 'You must tell me!' she pleaded. She had never imagined that he could succumb like this. She had always thought him strong and indomitable, but here he was in her arms, broken, devastated. 'Please, Tom, speak to me.'

'Dorian is dead.'

She went cold and still. 'It can't be,' she breathed, 'it just can't be. Are you certain. Is there no doubt?'

'The man who brought the news is a mullah, a holy man. He swore on his faith,' Tom said. 'There can be no doubt.'

Still holding each other, they sank together to their knees, and she was weeping with him. 'He was like my own brother,' she said, pressing her cheek against his so

714

that their tears mingled, bathing their faces. After a while she sniffed, and wiped her face on the sleeve of her blouse. 'How did it happen?' He was still unable to speak. 'Tell me, Tom,' she insisted. She knew instinctively that she must make him talk about it: like a surgeon, she had to lance the boil, let the pus and poison out. At last he began the story, the words coming hard, seeming to tear his throat as he forced them out. It took a long time, but at last he had told her everything, and she knew it must be true.

'What are we going to do now?' she asked, and stood up. She kept tight hold of his hands, and forced him to his feet. She had to stop him giving in to the dark waves of sorrow into which he was sinking.

'I don't know,' he said. 'I know only that Dorian is dead, that I could not save him. It was my fault. If only I had come to him sooner!'

'It is not your fault,' she said angrily. 'I will not even let you think that. You did all you could. No man could have done more.'

'I don't care any more,' Tom said.

'Yes, you do. You owe it to yourself and to me and the memory of Dorian. He always looked up to you. He knew how strong you were. He would not want this from you.'

'Please don't berate me, Sarah. I am exhausted with grief. Nothing else matters.'

'I will not let you give up. We must plan together.' She demanded, 'What are we going to do now?'

'I don't know,' he repeated, but he straightened his shoulders and dashed away the tears.

'Where are we going?' she asked. 'We cannot stay here, and we can't return to England. Where, Tom?'

'Africa,' he said. 'Aboli has found a man to guide us into the interior.'

'When do we leave?' she asked simply, not questioning the decision.

'Soon. A few days from now.' He had steadied himself, for the moment thrown off the debilitating sorrow. 'It will take that long to refill the water-barrels, to buy fresh provisions and to make the final arrangements.'

'I will be ready,' she said.

'It will be hard. A dangerous journey without end. Are you sure that is what you want? You must tell me now if you have any doubts.'

'Don't be a big booby, Tom Courtney,' she said. 'Of course I am going with you.'

When she left the monastery, Sarah took a circuitous route back to the consulate, riding first along the track she had discovered that led to one of the small villages on the seaward side of the island. She had gone only half a mile when she was seized by a certainty that someone was following her. She thought she heard hoofbeats on the track behind her so she reined in and swivelled in the saddle to look back.

The path was hemmed in on both sides by thick vegetation, the twisted stems and glossy leaves of the veloutia and clumps of lantana. She could not see further than the last turning in the path only a few paces behind her.

'Tom?' she called. 'Is that you?'

There was no reply, and in the silence she decided that she was starting at ghosts and shadows. 'You are being foolish,' she told herself firmly, and rode on.

When she reached the village she bought a basket of vegetables from one of the old women there, her excuse for her long absence, then rode almost to the port so that she could return to the consulate along the main road.

She had much to occupy her thoughts. Her mood swung from excited elation, at the prospect of the adventure ahead of her, to deep sadness when she faced the necessity of leaving Caroline and little Christopher. She loved them both dearly. Caroline had come to rely on her strength and fortitude in the dark unhappiness of her marriage to Guy, and Sarah looked upon baby Christopher as though he were her own. She worried how they would fare without her. 'Could they not come with us?' she wondered, and almost immediately knew that she was silly even to think it.

'I have to leave them.' She steeled herself. 'I love them both, but Tom is my man, and I love him more than life itself. I must go with him.'

She was so preoccupied with these thoughts that she rode into the stableyard without noticing Guy until he called to her sternly from the shade of the long veranda. 'Where have you been, Sarah?'

She looked up in confusion. 'You startled me, Guy.'

'Guilty conscience?' he accused.

'I've been buying vegetables.' She touched the basket tied to the back of her saddle. 'I am about to elope with a cabbage!' She laughed merrily, but Guy did not smile.

'Come to my office!' he ordered, and she noticed his syce hovering in the doorway of the stable. The boy was Guy's creature, a sly, pock-marked little fellow. His name was Assam. She had never liked or trusted him, and even less so now that she saw his grin was knowing and gloating. With a sinking feeling, Sarah wished she had taken more care to cover her tracks when she went to her assignation with Tom, and that she had given more weight to her feeling that she had been followed that afternoon.

'I wish to bathe and change for dinner,' she told Guy, trying to brazen it out, but he scowled and slapped his riding-crop against his boot.

'This will not take long,' he said. 'As your guardian, I must insist that you obey me. Assam will take your mare.'

With resignation she followed him down the veranda

and into the cool gloom of his office. He closed the doors behind them and left her standing in the centre of the floor as he took his seat behind his desk.

'You have been meeting him at the old monastery,' he said flatly.

'Who? What are you talking about?'

'Do not bother to deny it,' he said. 'On my instructions, Assam followed you.'

'You have been spying on me,' she flared at him. 'How dare you?' She tried to whip up her indignation, but it was not convincing.

'I am pleased that you do not insult my intelligence by denying it.'

'Why should I deny the man I love?' She drew herself up, tall and truly angry now.

'You have made yourself into a sailor's whore,' he said. 'Once he has had all he wants from between your legs, he will laugh and sail away, the way he did with your sister.'

'When he sails away, I will go with him.'

'I am your guardian, and you are only eighteen. You will go nowhere without my consent.'

'I am going with Tom,' she said, 'and nothing you can say or do will stop me.'

'We will see about that.' He stood up. 'You are confined to your rooms, and you will not leave them again until after the *Swallow* has sailed from Zanzibar.'

'You cannot treat me like a prisoner.'

'Yes, I can. There will be a guard at the door of your quarters, and others at the gates. I have given them their orders. Now go to your room. I will have your dinner sent up to you.'

Tom was so occupied with readying the *Swallow* for sea that he paid scant attention to the square-rigged ship that limped into the harbour after sunset. Even in the poor light he saw that she had been damaged by storms. It was the season when the cyclones swept down the Indian Ocean, and she must have encountered one of these devil winds. The name on her transom was the *Apostle*. She flew the tattered flag of the East India Company at her masthead, and once she had anchored Tom sent Luke Jervis across in the longboat to ask for the news.

Luke returned within the hour, and came to Tom's cabin, where he was writing up the ship's log. 'She is outward-bound from Bombay with a mixed cargo of cloth and tea,' Luke reported. 'She ran into a storm north of the Mascarenes. She intends to make her repairs here before resuming her voyage.'

'What news?'

'Most of it is stale, for the *Apostle* sailed from the Company dock months ago but the war against the French is going well. William is whipping their backsides. He is a good fighter, our Willy.'

'Great news!' Tom jumped up. 'Tell the crew and issue a good tot to every man to drink King Willy's health.'

What Tom could not know was that, apart from the news of the war, the *Apostle* carried a packet of letters and documents, sealed in a tarred canvas bag, from the Governor of Bombay and addressed to His Majesty's Consul at Zanzibar. The captain sent the packet ashore the following morning, and Guy Courtney opened it at the luncheon table on the long veranda of the consulate. Caroline sat opposite him, but Sarah was still locked in her own quarters.

'There is a personal letter from your father,' Guy told Caroline, as he picked it out of the assortment of gazettes and sealed papers.

'It is addressed to me,' Caroline protested, as he broke the wax seal and began to read it.

'I am your husband,' he said complacently.

Suddenly his expression changed and the sheet shook in his hands. 'By God! This passes all belief!'

'What is it?' Caroline laid down the silver spoon in her hand. It must be momentous news indeed to have that effect on her husband: Guy prided himself on his cool composure in even the most trying circumstances.

He was staring at the letter, and slowly his expression changed from consternation to jubilation. 'I have him now!'

'Who? What has happened?'

'Tom! He is a murderer. By God! Now he will pay the price on the gallows. He has murdered our dear brother, William, and there is a warrant out for his arrest. I intend to do my duty, and it will give me the greatest pleasure to cut him down to size.' Guy leaped to his feet, knocking the teapot off its stand. It shattered on the tiles, but he scarcely glanced at it.

'Where are you going, Guy?' Caroline stood up, her face white with shock, swaying on her feet.

'To the Sultan,' he said, and shouted to the servants, 'Tell Assam to saddle the grey, and to hurry.' He turned back to Caroline, and punched his fist into the palm of his other hand. 'At last! I have waited for this for so long. I will ask the Sultan for men from his guard. After the trouble Tom has caused him, he won't quibble. We will arrest Master Thomas and seize the *Swallow*. When we sell

720

the ship, she should bring in two thousand pounds at the very least. I deserve a reward for bringing a dangerous criminal to justice.' He laughed triumphantly. 'Master Tom will have a free berth on the *Apostle* back to London, in chains.'

'Guy, he is your brother! You cannot do this to him!' Caroline was distraught.

'Billy was Tom's brother also, yet the swine ran him through in cold blood. Now he will pay a high price for all his arrogance.'

She ran to him and clutched at his sleeve. 'No, Guy, you cannot do this!'

'So!' He rounded on her, his face darkening and seeming to swell with rage. 'You plead for him. You still love him, don't you? In a minute, you would pull up your skirts and open your legs for him like the dirty little slut you are.'

'That's not true.'

'You would love him to plant another bastard in your belly.' He struck her across the face, sending her reeling back against the low wall of the veranda. 'Well, your lover is going to make no more bastards.' He strode away down the terrace, bellowing for his horse.

Caroline leaned heavily against the wall, clutching the angry red weal on her cheek, until she heard his horse gallop away through the gates and down the track towards the harbour and the fort. Then she dragged herself to her feet.

When Guy had first told her of the liaison between Tom and her young sister, she had been horrified and torn with jealousy. Then last night she had gone to Sarah's room and spent nearly two hours with her. Slowly she had come to realize how deeply her sister was in love. She had long been aware that her own feelings for Tom were hopeless, so she had thrust them aside, and though the pain of the sacrifice was intense, she had kissed Sarah and promised to help her and Tom to elope. 'I have to warn them,' she whispered aloud, 'but there is so little time.'

She picked up a tray from the sideboard, loaded it with a plate of food for Sarah, and carried it down the veranda, past the nursery where Christopher was sleeping, to the last door. One of Guy's watchmen was squatting there, half asleep in the drowsy afternoon heat, with his musket across his lap. He started awake as she came towards him, then scrambled to his feet.

'*Salaam aliekum*, Donna.' He bowed. 'The master has given strict orders that no one should pass this door, coming or going.'

'I have food for the lady, my sister,' she said imperiously. 'Stand aside.'

He hesitated; his orders had not covered this eventuality. Then he bowed again. 'I am as dust under your feet,' he said, drew the big iron key from the folds of his robe and turned it in the lock. Caroline swept past him, but as the door closed she dropped the tray on the first table and ran through to Sarah's bedchamber.

'Sarah, where are you?'

Her sister lay on the bed under the tent-like mosquito net. A light sheet covered her, and she seemed to be sleeping, but as soon as she heard Caroline's voice she threw it back and sprang from the bed, fully clothed and wearing riding boots under her long skirts. 'Caroline! I am so glad you have come. I did not want to leave without saying goodbye to you.'

Caroline stared at her, and Sarah ran to her and embraced her. 'I am leaving with Tom. He is waiting for me on the beach below the old monastery, but I am late already.'

'How will you escape past Guy's guards?' Caroline asked.

Sarah reached under her skirts and drew out the duelling pistols. 'I will shoot anyone who tries to stop me.'

'Listen to me, Sarah. A letter has come from Father in Bombay. Tom is accused of the murder of his elder brother, and there is a warrant issued for his arrest.'

'I know that. Tom told me.' She pulled away. 'You cannot stop me, Caroline. It makes no difference, I know he is innocent and I am going away with him.'

'You don't understand.' Caroline seized her arm again. 'I have already promised that I will help you and Tom. I am not going back on my word. I came to tell you that Guy has ridden to the fort to inform the Sultan. They are going to arrest Tom, and send him back to England in chains, to his trial and execution.'

'No!' Sarah stared at her sister.

'You have to warn him, but you will not escape unless I help you.' She thought quickly. 'This is what we will do.' She spoke rapidly, filling out the plan as she went along. 'Do you understand?' she asked, when she had finished.

Sarah nodded. 'I am ready. I have made all my preparations, but hurry, Caroline. Tom will believe I am not coming. He will tire of waiting, and leave.'

Caroline went to the door, and called to the guard to open up. When she left, he locked the door behind her. Caroline went directly to the stables and shouted for Assam. 'Saddle my mare.'

When the groom hesitated, she stamped her foot. 'At once! Or I will have you beaten,' she snapped. 'I am in haste. I have promised to meet the master at the fort.'

Within minutes Assam brought out the horse and Caroline took the reins from him. 'Go to the gates and tell the guards to open up. I am coming out.' Thoroughly intimidated by now, Assam ran to obey.

Trying not to hurry, or show her agitation, Caroline led the saddled mare across the lawns to the end of the veranda. The guard at Sarah's door stood to greet her, and she proffered the letter from her father.

'Give this to my sister immediately,' she ordered. He slung the musket over his shoulder and took the letter from her. He went to the door and knocked upon it.

After a moment Sarah called from within, 'What is it?'

'A letter, Donna.'

'Give it to me.'

He unlocked the door, and swung it open. Sarah stepped out, and thrust the pair of pistols into his startled face. The hammers were cocked and her fingers were curled around the triggers. 'Lie down on your face,' she ordered, but instead of obeying the guard snatched the musket from his shoulder and tried to cock the hammer. Calmly Sarah lowered the aim of the pistol in her right hand and, at point-blank range, shot him in the knee. He squealed and collapsed on the tiles of the veranda, the shattered leg twisted under him. Sarah kicked away the fallen musket.

'Fool, you should have done as I ordered,' she told him harshly. 'The next ball will be in your head.' She touched the muzzle of the other pistol to his forehead.

He covered his face and cowered at her feet, and Sarah thrust the fired pistol into her belt, then stepped back into the doorway. She picked up the leather bag into which she had packed her most treasured possessions and dragged it out onto the veranda.

In the meantime Caroline had run forward to help her hoist the bag onto the saddle. Then the two sisters embraced swiftly but passionately.

'Go with God, my darling Sarah. I wish you and Tom all joy of each other.'

'I know that you love him also, Caroline.'

'Yes, but he is yours now. Treat him kindly.'

'Kiss Christopher for me.'

'We will both miss you, but go now! Hurry!' Caroline

made a step for her with her linked hands and boosted Sarah up into the saddle. 'Goodbye, my sister,' she called as Sarah urged the mare into a gallop and sped away across the lawns.

Assam saw her coming, and shouted to the other guards to close the gates, but Sarah rode straight at him and he had to throw himself aside to avoid being knocked down by the driving hoofs. The mare flew through the open gates and out into the forest. Sarah turned her onto the path that led southwards, through the palm groves to the ruined monastery.

'Please wait, Tom,' she whispered, and the wind flung away the words, and sent her long hair streaming out behind her like a flag. 'Please wait for me, my darling, I am coming.' She pushed the mare to the top of her speed and the boles of the palm trees streamed past her in a blur.

At the gates of the monastery she pulled the mare down from full gallop to a plunging halt. The animal fidgeted and threw her head, sweating nervously, unaccustomed to such rough treatment.

'Tom!' Sarah screamed, and the echoes from the ancient walls mocked her. 'Tom!'

He has gone, she thought. While the mare backed and circled under her, she leaned out of the saddle and searched the soft ground. She picked out Tom's fresh footprints coming up from the beach, and the trampled area in front of the gateway where he had paced back and forth, waiting for her. Then, his patience clearly exhausted, the string of his footprints headed back towards the beach.

'Tom!' she shouted in despair, and put the mare at the narrow track through the undergrowth. The branches whipped against her legs as they raced down beside the stream and at last burst out onto the white coral sands, with the limpid water of the lagoon in front of her.

She saw the mark that the keel of the felucca had left at the water's edge, and then she looked up and saw the tiny craft. It was moving slowly towards the gap in the reef, half a mile away. Tom was in the stern with the long bamboo pole in his hands, punting her over the shallow flats.

'Tom!' she screamed and waved. 'Tom!'

But the wind fretted in the palms and the surf boomed and boiled on the outer reef, smothering her cries. The tiny felucca moved away doggedly, and Tom did not look back.

She urged the mare into the water, and though at first she baulked, she was a game little horse and she plunged forward, leaping and lunging through the deeper holes, until the water reached halfway up her shoulders, and Sarah's boots and skirts were soaked. But the felucca was moving faster, drawing away from them.

'Tom!' Sarah called in agony. Then she pulled the second pistol from her belt, pointed it at the sky and fired. The report was an insignificant pop in the immensity of sea and wind. 'He has not heard!'

It took a long second for the sound to carry, then she saw Tom's distant figure start, and he looked back at her.

'Oh, praise God!' She almost wept with relief.

With an expert thrust of the pole Tom spun the felucca about, and sent it gliding back across the lagoon. 'Where were you? What has happened?' he shouted across as he came within hail.

'Guy has found out about you and William,' she called back. 'He has gone to the fort to raise the guard. They are going to seize you and your ship.'

She saw his expression harden, but he said nothing as he brought the boat alongside the mare. Then he threw down the punt pole, reached across to seize her around the waist and lift her from the saddle. He set her down on the deck.

'My bag!' she panted. He pulled the dirk from the

sheath on his belt and cut the thong that tied it to the pommel. He dragged it on board, slapped the mare, and she turned and floundered back towards the beach. Tom grabbed the bamboo pole and aimed the bows of the felucca at the pass once more.

'How long ago did Guy go to the fort?' he asked. 'How much time do we have?'

'Not much. He left the consulate well over two hours ago.'

'Stand by the halyard,' he ordered grimly. 'We will have to hoist the sail, and take a chance on the coral.'

The lateen sail flapped and snapped, then filled with the monsoon wind. The felucca heeled sharply, and raced towards the gap in the reef. She skimmed through and as soon as the water turned blue under her keel Tom stood at the tiller and brought her round on a heading for the harbour where the *Swallow* lay at anchor.

'Tell me everything,' he ordered. She came to him and put her arms around his waist. 'How did Guy find out?'

'A ship came in last night.'

'The *Apostle*,' he exclaimed. 'I should have expected this.' He listened intently as she related all the details. When she had finished, he murmured, 'God grant we are in time,' and looked ahead as the harbour of Zanzibar opened before them, and he saw the little *Swallow* lying tranquilly at her anchor.

'Thank God! They have not seized her yet,' he said fervently, but at that moment they both saw the flotilla of a dozen small boats that had left the stone quay below the fort and were streaming across the bay towards the ship. Tom shaded his eyes, and stared across the mile of water that separated them from the leading boat. He recognized the tall lean figure in the plumed hat in the bows. 'Guy is keen as a hound with the smell of the fox hot in his nostrils.'

The barge was riding low in the water under the weight of the armed men crowded into it. All the other craft in the flotilla were similarly laden.

'He has a hundred of the Sultan's rascals with him, at least,' Tom calculated. 'He is taking no chances.'

He glanced up at the masthead, and judged the strength and direction of the wind on his cheek. He had sailed the craft enough by now to know all her foibles well, and how to squeeze every foot of speed out of her. 'Harden her up a little,' he called to Sarah, who ran forward to the boom sheet. The felucca liked her touch and surged forward under their feet.

'It will be a near-run thing.' Tom eyed the leading boat, and calculated the difference in speed and course. They had the advantage of the wind, on a broad reach. Guy was close-hauled, making heavy weather of it with his overloaded hull deep in the water. Tom doubted that the other boat could reach the anchored *Swallow* on a single tack. On the other hand, the felucca must cut right across the bows of Guy's dhow. Tom narrowed his eyes as he judged the converging course.

'We are going to pass within easy musket shot of the leading boat,' he told Sarah. 'Pile those nets and fish boxes along the starboard rail and lie flat behind them.'

'What about you?' she asked anxiously.

'Didn't I tell you? I am immune to musket-balls.' He grinned. 'And, besides, all Arabs are poor shots.'

If she had not loved him so much, she might have been more impressed by his disregard of danger. 'My place is at your side,' she said stubbornly, trying to match his show of courage.

'Your place is where I say it is.' His expression became bleak and cold. 'Get down, woman.'

She had never seen him like this before, and it took her off-balance. She found herself obeying meekly, and only when she was lying flat on the smelly deck, protected by the nets and heavy wooden boxes, did she begin to recover her sense of independence.

I must not let him get the upper hand so soon, she warned herself, but her thoughts were interrupted by a faint shout. The Arabs in the leading dhow had spotted the little felucca racing across their quarter. The vessel heeled dangerously as they crowded to the rail to stare across the gap, jabbering and gesticulating, cocking and brandishing their long-barrelled jezails.

'Stop!' Guy's voice was faint on the wind, but they were close enough now for Tom to see clearly his dark, furious expression. 'Heave to, at once, Tom Courtney, or I will order my men to fire upon you.'

Tom laughed and waved cheerily. 'Piss into the wind, dear brother, and get it all back into your face.'

They were less than a hundred yards apart, a pistol shot, and Guy called to the Arab musketeers who crammed the open deck of the dhow and, with his drawn sword, pointed across at the felucca. In response they levelled their muskets and, despite his braggadocio, Tom felt a qualm of fear as he looked into the line of weapons aimed across the gap at him.

'Fire!' Guy yelled, with a sweep of his sword. There was a blast, and a bank of thick white powder smoke briefly obscured the dhow.

The air around Tom's head was filled with the whir and buzz of passing shot, the heavy lead balls kicked spurts of spray from the surface of the water all around the hull of the felucca and thudded into her side, knocking white splinters from her timbers.

Tom felt something pluck at the sleeve of his shirt, and when he glanced down there was a tear in the cloth, and a thin trickle of blood from the shallow wound across his biceps.

'Are you all right, Tom?' Sarah asked anxiously, from where she lay at his feet. He laughed again and turned half away so she could not see the blood on his sleeve.

'I told you they're poor shots.' He lifted his hat and with it gave Guy a mocking salute. But at the movement a few drops of scarlet splattered the dirty deck at his feet. Sarah saw the blood, and her face blanched. Then, without hesitation, she sprang to her feet and rushed back to the stern.

'Get back!' Tom snapped. 'Those are real musket-balls. You could be killed.'

Sarah ignored him, and placed herself four square in front of him, shielding him with her own body. She threw back the shawl from her shoulders and shook out her hair so that it flew out like a banner on the wind.

'Shoot!' she screamed across at the barge. 'Shoot me, if you dare, Guy Courtney!' They were close enough to see the frustration and fury on Guy's face.

'Get down, Sarah,' he yelled at her. 'If you are hit it will be your own doing.'

Tom tried to push her down on the deck but she flung both arms around his neck and clung to him. Her face was bright with fury as she glared across at the barge. 'If you want your brother, you will have to kill me first,' she shrieked at Guy.

Guy's expression changed from triumph to uncertainty. He looked back at his men. The musketeers were reloading frantically. Tom saw the tips of their ramrods pumping up and down as they drove fresh balls down the long barrels. It took even a good man fully two minutes to reload, and by the time the next volley was ready the two craft were as close as they would ever be as the felucca crossed the bows of the barge.

The quicker and more expert of the musketeers finished loading and priming. Four of them cocked and raised their jezails in unison, sighting over the long barrels at the pair in the stern of the felucca. Still Guy hesitated, but then his grim expression crumbled, and with a sweep of his sword blade he knocked up the weapon of the man beside him, and shouted in Arabic, 'Stop! Do not fire! You will hit the woman.'

One man ignored the order and fired. There was a spurt of blue smoke from the muzzle of his jezail and the ball thudded into the tiller bar in Tom's hand.

'Stop!' Guy yelled in fury, and slashed the sword down on the man's wrist. There was a flash of bright blood and the man clutched his injured arm and staggered away across the deck.

'Stop!' Guy turned on the other men and, reluctantly, one at a time, they lowered their muskets. The felucca head-reached on the barge, then drew away from her.

'You haven't won yet, Tom Courtney!' Guy shouted after them. 'From now on, every man's hand is against you. One of these days you will pay what you owe in full, I will see to that. I swear it!'

Tom ignored his brother's fading shouts of anger, and looked forward. The *Swallow* was now lying only a cable's length ahead, but the musket fire from the barge had alerted her crew. They were swarming over her deck and climbing into her rigging. Ned Tyler was not waiting for orders to get the ship under weigh.

Sarah hugged Tom around the waist, and looked back at the swarm of small boats that ploughed along behind them. 'That was exciting,' she said, and her eyes were sparkling.

'Don't you dare look so pleased with yourself, you little hussy.' Tom hugged her. 'You disobeyed my direct orders.'

'You had best accustom yourself to that.' She grinned up at him. 'For it may happen again, some day.' Then she became businesslike and with his dagger she cut the torn sleeve from his shirt. She used the cloth to bind up the flesh wound in his arm and staunch the bleeding. In the meantime they were coming up fast on the *Swallow*, and Tom told her, 'Belay that, and get ready to jump sharply.'

The capstan was clanking on the foredeck of the sloop as Ned Tyler hauled his anchor, and as the flukes pulled free of the bottom, the sloop paid off and began making stern way. Sarah pulled up her skirts and tucked them into her belt so that her legs were bare and free, and crouched by the rail.

Tom saw Aboli's head at the rail above him. As the hulls touched and Tom dropped the sail, Aboli jumped down like a great black panther ambushing a gazelle from the branch of a tree. His bare feet thudded on the deck as he landed beside Sarah. He swept her up in his arms. She shrieked in protest but in the same movement he sprang back, caught hold of the boarding ladder that dangled down the sloop's side and carried her up onto the *Swallow*'s deck.

Tom snatched up Sarah's leather bag from where it lay on the deck of the felucca and jumped across the narrow gap of water that separated the hulls, allowing the felucca to drift free, and he followed Aboli up. As he swung one leg over the rail, Ned Tyler saluted him solemnly from the helm. 'Welcome aboard, Captain,' he said.

'Thank you, Mr Tyler. I can think of no reason why we should linger here any longer. Get the ship on the wind, if you please.'

He dropped Sarah's bag on the deck and strode to the stern. As the *Swallow* came round, the dhow with Guy in her bows was two hundred yards dead astern, but the sloop drew away from it so swiftly that it seemed to be at anchor.

Guy's bare sword hung at his side, his shoulders were slumped dejectedly, and his face was contorted with frustration and hatred. When they saw Tom the men around him could no longer restrain themselves, and they opened a furious fusillade, banging away with their muskets, but

Guy seemed oblivious to them. All his attention was concentrated on his twin brother.

They stared at each other as the two vessels drew swiftly apart. Sarah came to stand beside Tom. Hand in hand they watched the shape of the barge dwindle until they could no longer make out Guy's tall figure. Then the *Swallow* rounded the point and the harbour of Zanzibar closed behind them and the dhow was lost to sight.

Dorian Courtney stood up. He had been on his knees praying to the God of his fathers. He wandered along the edge of the cliff, then stooped to pick up a pebble that had caught his eye. He wet it with his tongue then held it to the sunlight. It was pink agate striated with soft blue layers, and crowned with crystals of diamond clarity. It was beautiful.

He leaned out and let it drop from his fingers, then watched it fall five hundred sheer feet down the cliffs. It dwindled in size and disappeared before it hit the surface of the sea far below. It left neither splash nor ripple upon the surface, no sign of anything so lovely ever having existed. Suddenly, for the first time in almost seven years, he thought of little Yasmini, who had vanished from his life in the same way.

The wind tugged and his robe streamed out behind him, but his feet were planted wide and he felt no fear of the drop that opened at his feet. At his right hand the gaunt red rock cliff that stood so tall above the sea was riven by a narrow valley. In its depths, clinging precariously to the shore, were the palm groves, roofs and white domes of the village of Shihr. Dorian's men were encamped among the low acacia thorn trees and palms further up the valley. The blue smoke of their camp-fires rose in oily tendrils, straight into the air until it caught the eddy of the wind over the summit of the cliffs and streamed away towards the forbidding hills and dunes of the desert.

Dorian shaded his eyes and looked out to sea. The ships were closer now. Four stately dhows with high poops and matting sails, the flotilla of Prince al-Malik. They had been in sight since dawn, but the wind was against them, forcing them to tack and tack again. Dorian narrowed his eyes, judging their progress, and he saw that it would be many hours still before they could enter the bay and anchor off the beach.

He was impatient and restless. It was so long since last he had seen the Prince, his adoptive father. He turned away from the edge of the cliff, and started back along the path that led to the ancient tomb. It stood on the crest of this rocky promontory, its dome bleached by the desert suns of a hundred years.

Al-Allama and the sheikhs of the Saar were still at prayer, their rugs spread in the shadow of the tomb, turned in the direction of the holy city that lay hundreds of miles to the north across this burning land. Dorian slowed his pace, not wishing to arrive while they were still at their devotions.

The Saar did not know that he was not of Islam. On the instruction of the Prince, he had concealed that from them during all the time he had lived among them. He knew that they would never have taken him so readily into the tribe if they had guessed the truth, that he was an infidel. They believed that he was under a vow of penance not to pray in the community of believers, but to make his devotions to Allah in solitude. At the hour of prayer he would always leave them and wander away into the desert.

Alone he prayed to the God of his fathers, kneeling in the wilderness, but the words were becoming more difficult as time passed and his devotions more perfunctory. Gradually this strange sense of having been deserted by his own

God was overcoming him. He was losing his childhood faith, and he felt bewildered and bereft.

He stopped on the crest of the hill and watched the men kneeling and prostrating themselves in the shade of the mosque. Not for the first time he envied them their immutable faith. He waited at a distance until they had finished and begun to disperse. Most mounted up and trotted down the cliff path to the village below. Soon there were only two men left near the tomb.

Batula, his lance-bearer, was with the two camels, squatting with infinite patience in the patch of shade the animals threw. The bronze war shield was tied to the saddle of Dorian's riding camel, and in the leather boot were his jezail and long lance, its point bright in the sun and the green pennant fluttering. These were all the accoutrements of the desert warrior.

Al-Allama was also waiting for him, seated out of the wind, on an outcrop of red rock. Dorian turned towards him and strode up the path. The first streaks of grey now showed in the mullah's beard but his skin was still unlined, and despite the months of hard riding and lean rations, his girth had not shrunk. He inclined his head to one side as he watched al-Salil, the Drawn Sword, come towards him.

Al-Salil was tall now, and under the long, swirling robes he was lean and hard, his flesh pared down and tempered by the desert. He came on with a swinging gait, like the pace of a racing camel, and there was an air of authority and command in the set of his shoulders and the carriage of his veiled head.

'His name was well chosen,' al-Allama murmured to himself. When Dorian reached him, he made a sign of invitation and the young man dropped down beside him on the rock. His legs curled under him, he sat like one of the Saar, gracefully at ease, the curved sword in its silver and leather scabbard across his knees. Only Dorian's eyes were visible: the rest of his face was covered by the tail of his headdress, which was wound loosely over his nose, mouth and chin. The eyes were piercing, green and bright, and despite the desert sand and glare they were not shot with blood. Slowly Dorian unwound the cloth that covered his face and smiled at the mullah. 'It is good to have you back. I have missed you, holy father,' he said. 'Nobody to argue with, my life has been dull indeed.'

'Dull?' Al-Allama hid a smile. 'It is not what the sheikhs have told me of your stay with them. Sixteen of the enemy to your own lance.'

Dorian stroked his beard, which sprang into curls under his fingers, crackling in the dry desert air, bright as newly forged copper. 'The Ottoman are easy to kill,' he said deprecatingly, but the smile remained on his lips.

He is still as winsome as the child I first met on the island of Daar Al Shaitan. Al-Allama studied his face: the high, thoughtful forehead of the scholar offset by the hard line of mouth and jaw that bespoke the warrior and the leader of men.

'Why have you brought me here, old father?' Dorian asked, leaning forward to look into his face. 'You always have a reason for what you do.'

Al-Allama smiled and softly asked a question in reply. 'Do you know whose tomb this is?'

Dorian glanced up at the weathered dome and crumbling walls. 'That of a holy man,' he said. There were many such ancient tombs, some guarding the scattered oases of the interior, others on the cliffs and rugged hills along the Omani coast of southern Arabia.

'Yes,' al-Allama agreed. 'A holy man.'

'I cannot read the name,' Dorian said, for most of the inscriptions on the wall had been abraded by the sand-laden winds. There were many, some quotations from the Koran but others Dorian did not recognize. Perhaps they were the words of the dead man himself.

Al-Allama rose to his feet and circled the tomb, pausing to read any of the inscriptions that were still legible. After a moment Dorian stood up and followed him. 'There is a quotation from the saint who lies within. Perhaps it is of interest to you.' Al-Allama pointed high up the wall.

Dorian deciphered some of it with difficulty. '"The orphan who comes from the sea,"' he read aloud, and al-Allama nodded encouragement. '"With the tongue and the crown of the Prophet..."' Dorian stopped. 'I cannot read the next line. It is too faded.'

'"With the tongue and the crown of the Prophet, but with darkness in a pagan heart,"' al-Allama helped him. Dorian went closer to the wall, peering up at it.

'"When the light fills the pagan heart, he will bring together the sands of the desert that are divided, and his just and pious father shall ride upon the back of the elephant."'

Dorian came back to al-Allama's side. 'What is it? I do not recognize it from the Koran. As a poem, it rhymes neatly, but it makes no sense,' he said. 'What are the tongue and crown of the Prophet? How can an orphan have a father? Why the back of an elephant?'

'The Prophet was crowned with red hair and, of course, his tongue was Arabic, the sacred language,' al-Allama pointed out, and stood up. 'In the palace of Muscat stands the Elephant Throne of Oman, carved from mighty tusks of ivory. I will leave you to consider the rest of the prophecy. If he applies himself to it, even such a dull student as al-Salil should be able to find a solution to the riddle of the holy Taimtaim.'

'Taimtaim!' Dorian exclaimed. 'This is the tomb of the saint?' He stared at the eroded inscription, and now the saint's name appeared, like a figure seen through a dark mist. 'This is the prophecy! These are the words that have shaped my life.' He felt a sense of awe, but it was mingled with anger and resentment, that he had been deprived of so much, and been made to suffer for these few mystic words, written so long ago and now only barely legible. He wanted to challenge them, to protest and to refute them, but al-Allama was halfway down the path into the valley, leaving him in this desolate place to confront his destiny.

Dorian remained there for many hours. Sometimes he paced angrily along the walls of the tomb, searching the other inscriptions for any further fragments of knowledge. He read them aloud, testing the sound of the words rather than the sense, trying to divine the hidden meanings that lay behind them. Sometimes he squatted and studied a single word or phrase, then he sprang to his feet again and returned to the inscription that al-Allama had pointed out to him. 'If I am indeed the orphan you speak of, then you are wrong, old man. It can never come to pass. I am a Christian. I will never accept Islam.' He defied the ancient saint. 'I shall never bring together the sands of the desert, whatever your meaning there.'

'Lord!' Batula's voice broke into his meditation, and Dorian stood up. 'The ships.' Batula gestured down the cliffs. 'They are entering the bay.'

Batula had the camels up and moving towards the head of the path. Dorian broke into a run, catching them easily before they started down. He called to his own beast as he came loping up alongside her. 'Ibrisam! Silk Wind!' At the sound of his voice, she turned her head and looked down at him with those great dark eyes with their heavy double fringe of lashes, and roared softly, lovingly, to welcome him. She was a noble full-pointed Sherari. He swung up into the high saddle seven feet above the ground with a single effortless movement. He touched her neck with the tip of the long riding wand, and shifted his weight forward in the saddle, which was cushioned with the finest Nejd leather and hung with luxurious trappings, tassels and straps dyed with shades of red, yellow and blue, woven carrying-nets embroidered with silver stars and metal tissue.

Ibrisam responded to his touch and movement, stretching into that elegant, comfortable gait that once had carried her beloved master at ten miles every hour for eighteen hours without check, from the tongue of Wadi Taub across the grisly plain of Mudhail, strewn with the white bones of lost caravans, to the brackish waters of the oasis of Ma Shadid.

She loved Dorian like a faithful dog. After a full day's journey through the terrible places of the sands, she would not sleep in the desert night unless he lay down beside her. No matter how fierce her thirst or hunger, she would break off from drinking or grazing to come to him and nuzzle him, begging for his caress and the comfort of his voice.

They flew down the path, overtaking Batula before he reached the floor of the valley. The entire encampment was in turmoil, camels roaring, men shouting and ululating, firing joy shots into the air as they poured down through the groves towards the beach. Ibrisam carried Dorian to the head of this wild procession, and across the golden sands to the water's edge.

When Prince al-Malik stepped ashore, Dorian was the first to run forward to greet him. His face was unveiled and he fell to his knees and kissed the hem of the Prince's robe. 'May all your days be golden with glory, lord. Too long my eyes have hungered for sight of your face.'

The Prince lifted him to his feet and gazed into his face. 'Al-Salil! I would not have known you, but for the colour of your hair, my son.' He embraced Dorian, holding him to his breast. 'I can see that all the reports I have had of you are true. You have become a man indeed.'

Then the Prince turned to greet the sheikhs of the Saar, as they also pressed forward and surrounded him. When he had embraced them, the Prince moved slowly up the valley in a triumphal procession. The desert warriors strewed palm fronds at his feet, called blessings upon him, kissed the hem of his robe and fired their jezails in the air.

A leather tent, large enough to cover a hundred men, had been set up beside the well in the shade of the grove. The sides were open to allow the evening breeze off the sea to waft through, and rugs and cushions covered the sandy earth. The Prince took his seat in the centre of the floor and the sheikhs gathered around him. Slaves brought pitchers of well water for them to wash their hands. Then they presented huge bronze platters of food, piled high with yellow rice swimming in melted camel-milk butter, and fragrant stews of mutton and spices.

Al-Malik took a morsel from each dish delicately in his right hand. Some he tasted himself, other titbits he fed to the men around him. This was an honour he was bestowing, a mark of his favour, and these hard-bitten, hawkish warriors who could not count the war wounds that scarred their faces and bodies treated him with the respect and affection of loving children for their father.

When they had eaten, the Prince gestured for the still brimming platters to be taken out to the ranks of common warriors who squatted in the open, that they might share the banquet.

The red sun wheeled down behind the hills, and the stars pricked through the darkening desert sky. They washed their hands again, and the slaves lit the hookahs. The sides of the leather tent were lowered, the sheikhs clustered closer around the Prince and passed the ivory mouthpieces from hand to hand. The thick, curling clouds of Turkish tobacco smoke billowed around their heads. In the yellow light of the lamps they began to talk.

The first to speak said, 'The Porte has sent an army of fifteen thousand men to take Muscat. Yaqub has opened the gates of the city to them.' The Sublime Porte was the might and authority of the Turkish Ottoman empire, its seat in distant Istanbul. Al-Malik's elder brother, al-Uzar Ibn Yaqub, the weak and dissolute Caliph of Oman in Muscat, had at last capitulated to the Ottomans without offering battle. Allah alone knew what bribes and assurances he had received, but he had welcomed the occupying army of the Porte into his city, and now the freedom and independence of all the desert tribes was in the most terrible jeopardy.

'He is a traitor. Allah is my witness! He has sold us into slavery,' one of the other sheikhs said. They growled like a pride of lions, and looked to al-Malik.

'He is my brother, and my Caliph,' said the Prince. 'I am oath-bound to him.'

'By God, he is no longer a ruler of Oman,' a sheikh protested. 'He has become the plaything of the Porte.'

'He who has sodomized a thousand boys has become the bum whore of the Turks,' agreed another. 'By his treachery you, and all of us, are released from our vows of fealty.'

'Lead us, mighty lord,' urged another. 'We are your men. Lead us to the gates of Muscat and we will help you drive out the Ottoman, place you on the Elephant Throne of Oman.'

One after another they spoke, and all said the same thing. 'We have pleaded to you to come to us. Now we plead for you to lead us.'

'We, the Saar, are your oath-men. We can raise three thousand lances to ride at your back.'

'What of the other tribes?' the Prince asked, not rushing into such a dire decision. 'What of the Awamir and the Bait Imani? What of the Bait Kathir and the Harasis?'

'We of the Saar cannot speak for them,' they answered, 'for there are blood feuds between us and many of them.

But their sheikhs wait for you in the sands. Go to them and, God willing, they will raise the war lance and ride with us to Muscat.'

'Give us your decision,' they begged. 'Give us your decision, and we will give you our oath.'

'I will lead you,' said the Prince softly and simply, and their weathered brown faces lit with joy. One by one they knelt before him and kissed his feet. When he held out his curved dagger, they touched the steel with their lips. Then they took his hands, lifted the Prince to his feet and led him out of the tent to where the warriors waited in the moonlight.

'We give you the new Caliph of Oman,' they told their men, who shouted their allegiance and fired their muskets into the air. The war drums began to beat, and the eerie blast of the rams' horns echoed from the dark cliffs above the grove.

In the joyous commotion, Dorian came to his father and embraced him. 'I and my men are ready to take you to meet the sheikhs of the Awamir at the wells of Muhaid.'

'Then let us ride, my son,' the Prince agreed. Dorian left him and strode away through the grove, calling to his men, 'Saddle up! We ride at once!'

They ran to their camels, calling them by name, and soon the entire valley was in uproar as they broke camp. The camels bellowed and roared as they were loaded with the leather waterskins, and the tents were collapsed and packed.

Before the rise of the new moon, in the cool of the night, they were ready to ride, a long column of robed, veiled men on their tall beasts. The Prince's camel was a creamy yellow female. When he had seated himself in the saddle, Dorian commanded her to rise. With a groan she lurched to her feet. Al-Malik sat her easily: born in the desert and a warrior from boyhood, he made a noble picture in the first rays of the rising moon.

Dorian sent a vanguard of twenty men ahead, and a rearguard to come up behind. He rode close beside the Prince as the column started up the valley, and headed out into the desert.

They went swiftly, all racing camels and, but for the waterskins, lightly burdened. They climbed up and out of the valley and the desert stretched ahead, infinite and still, purple and dark hills of rock and shining dunes of silver sand stretching away to the north. Above the winding serpent of men and beasts, the stars were a dazzling field, like banks of wild white daisies after rain. The sand muted the fall of the camels' broad pads, and the only sound was the creak of leather and the occasional soft murmur of a voice warning, 'Beware! Hole.'

Dorian rode at ease, lulled by Ibrisam's rhythmic gait, and the harsh desert miles unwound beneath him. The dark hills formed strange, wondrous shapes around them, filled with shadows and mystery, and the stars and the crescent moon of Islam lit their way through the night. He gazed up at the sky, not merely to navigate through the darkness and the broken wilderness, but caught up in the mesmeric thrall of the ancient patterns of light and their inexorable march through the heavens.

Strangely, this was the time when he felt closer to his past, when he seemed to feel the presence of Tom still near to him. They had spent so many nights together under the starry firmament when they were lads aboard the old *Seraph*, perched up in the rigging. It had been Aboli, Big Daniel and Ned Tyler who had taught him the names of all the navigational stars, and he whispered them aloud now. So many had Arabic names: Al Nilam, Al Nitak, Mintaka, Saif . . .

Riding in the company of the man who had become his father, and these wild falcon-fierce warriors whom he commanded, Dorian pondered the ancient prophecy of St Taimtaim, as he had seen it written on the crumbling walls of the old sage's tomb. Slowly he was overcome with an almost religious sense of some immutable destiny awaiting him here under these desert skies.

They stopped after midnight, when the great Scorpion lay low on the stony hills. One of the sheikhs of the Saar came to the Prince to make his farewells and to reiterate his vows. 'I go to raise my levy,' he told al-Malik. 'Before the full of this moon I will meet you at the wells of Ma Shadid with five hundred lances at my back,' he promised.

They watched his camel pace away swiftly into the east until it was lost in the purple shadows, then they went on. Twice more in the night other sheikhs detached themselves from the main column and, after they had sought the Prince's blessing, slipped away into the sands, leaving with the promise to meet again at the wells of Ma Shadid in the full of the moon.

They went on until they discovered a field of lush *zahra*, which had sprung up where, months before, a thunderstorm had drenched a tiny part of the desert. They stopped and let the camels graze, while they cut bundles of 'the flower', for this was the finest of all camel foods and highly prized. When they had loaded it onto their mounts they rode on until the dawn turned the eastern horizon orange and pink.

They stopped again, this time to camp, couched the camels and fed them on the garnered *zahra*. Then they made coffee and cakes of meal over smoky fires of dried camel dung. When they had eaten, they lay down, wrapped in their robes. They slept through the hours of quivering heat when the rocks danced in the mirage. Dorian lay close beside Ibrisam, in her shadow, and the sound of her belches and the grinding of her jaws as she chewed the cud was familiar and lulling. He slept well and woke in the evening, when the air cooled.

While the column roused itself and prepared for the long night march, Dorian sent a small patrol under Batula to scout ahead along their intended line of march. Then he mounted Ibrisam, and rode back to sweep their back trail, making certain that they were not being followed.

This was the way of this hard, hostile land, where the tribes lived in a perpetual state of blood feud and war, where raids for camels and women were part of desert life, and vigilance was the centre of every man's existence.

Dorian found that the back trail was clear. He turned back, urged Ibrisam into a swinging trot and soon caught up with the main column. After midnight they reached the bitter wells at Ghail ya Yamin. A small encampment of the Saar was already there, and they came out of their tents and surrounded the Prince's camel, ululating and firing joy shots in the air.

They camped for two days under the straggly date palms at Ghail ya Yamin, where the water in the wells was so brackish that it could only be drunk when mixed with camel's milk. The men had to climb down deep into the earth to reach it, and they carried it up to the surface in leather bags to water the camels. After the long, waterless journey the camels drank with relish. Ibrisam drank repeatedly and sucked up twenty-five gallons during the next few hours.

The last of the sheikhs of the Saar left the column here and scattered out into the wilderness to find their people, leaving Prince al-Malik with only Dorian's small force to guide and protect him on the last leg of the journey to meet the Awamir at the wells of Muhaid.

It took them three nights of travel to cross the salt flats before the hills of Shiya. Even in the moonlight the flats were white as a snowfield, and the pads of the camels left a dark path over the shiny surface. On the third morning they saw the hills rise far ahead of them, a pale blue line, serrated like the fangs of a tiger shark against the dawn. They camped for the day in a shallow wadi where a growth of thorny ghaf trees gave them some shelter from the sun. Before he lay down to sleep, Dorian climbed to the lip of the wadi to study the line of hills that lay ahead. The red, rugged rock was highlighted by the rising sun.

The hills of Shiya marked the boundary between the territories of the Saar and the Awamir. Dorian picked out a peak shaped like a castle turret. The Saar called it the Witch's Tower. It marked the pass through the range that would take them into the domain of the Awamir. Dorian smiled with satisfaction that he had led the column across the trackless plains directly to the pass, then stood up and went down into the wadi to find shade and rest for the day.

That evening when the column was ready to continue the march Dorian rode back as usual to sweep the back trail. Half a mile from the camp he cut the spoor of a strange camel. By now he had grown so adept in the ways of the desert that he could recognize the tracks of every beast in their column. These tracks showed that the unknown rider had come out of the west and crossed their trail. Dorian read how the man had dismounted to examine their trail, then remounted and followed it for almost two miles, before sheering off and riding to a low shale bank that rose like the spine of an elephant out of the salt-white plain. Behind this cover he had left his camel and crawled to the top of the ridge. His snake-like drag marks were clear for Dorian to read.

When Dorian followed these to the crest of the ridge he found that he overlooked the camp among the ghaf trees where the column had spent the day. Dorian saw that the stranger had lain on the ridge for a while, then drawn back and run down to where he had tethered his camel. He had ridden off, making a wide circle around the encampment, then headed directly towards the hills of Shiya and the Witch's Tower above the pass. The spy had at least eight hours' lead on the column and would have reached the pass by now.

The implications were sinister. The news of the arrival of al-Malik and his journey through the desert to meet the leaders of the tribes would almost certainly have reached the Caliph in Muscat and his Ottoman allies. They might have sent a force to intercept him, and the logical place to set up an ambush would be at the pass of the Witch's Tower.

Dorian took only minutes to decide his next action. He swung up onto Ibrisam's saddle and urged her into a run. They sped away across the white flats and within a short time he saw the column ahead, dark shadows on the shining earth. The rearguard challenged him as he came up, then recognized Ibrisam. 'It is al-Salil, by God!'

'Where is Batula?' Dorian shouted, as he came within hail.

His lance-bearer galloped back to him. As he reached Dorian's side he threw back his veil and uncovered his face. 'You come in haste, master, there is danger?'

'A stranger rides in our shadow,' Dorian told him. 'He has watched us from afar while we camped, then he rode off towards the pass, perhaps to warn the men who are waiting there.' Quickly he explained to Batula what he had found, then sent him out with two companions to follow up the tracks of the stranger. He watched them ride away and urged Ibrisam on to catch up with the Prince.

Al-Malik listened intently while Dorian made his report. 'There are many enemies. Almost certainly these are the servants of the Ottoman or of my brother the Caliph. Allah knows, there are many who would prevent me reaching the tribes of the interior. What do you plan, my son?'

Dorian pointed ahead. The dark hills of Shiya were an unbroken barrier, rising five hundred feet above the salt flats. 'Lord, we do not know how many of the enemy there are. I have thirty men, and can laugh at twice or thrice that number of enemy. However, if the Ottoman have got wind of your journey they may have sent an army to find you.'

'That is likely.'

'The pass at the Witch's Tower is the main and swiftest route through the hills to reach the Awamir, but there is another lesser pass further to the west.' Dorian pointed across the silver plain. 'It is known as the Pass of the Bright Gazelle, and to reach it will take us many leagues out of our way, but I cannot risk riding into the Witch's Tower and being trapped in its gut by a large force of the Ottoman.'

Al-Malik nodded. 'How far to this other pass? Can we reach it before daybreak?'

'No,' Dorian replied. 'Even if we drive the camels hard we will not be there before the middle of the morning.'

'Then let us ride,' said al-Malik.

Dorian called to his men of the vanguard and ordered them to change direction towards the west. They closed up and, with the Prince in the centre of the line, every man alert for an ambush, they pushed the camels harder. The beasts were still fresh and strong and the salt crystals crunched under their pads. A soft white dustcloud rose up and sparkled behind them in the still night air as they sped forward.

They halted for a short while after midnight, to let the camels blow and to drink a cup of water mixed with camel's milk, then went on.

In that darkest hour of the night, four hours before dawn, there was a shout of alarm from the riders in the rearguard of the column. Dorian turned his camel and raced back.

'What is it?' he began, then broke off as he spotted the dark clump of camels coming towards them out of the night. There were few, but they might be the outriders of an army.

'Close up the ranks!' he ordered, and loosened the

748

butt of his lance in its leather boot. Swiftly the column evolved into a defensive formation, with the Prince in the centre where they could protect him. Then Dorian urged Ibrisam forward and challenged the approaching men with a shouted question.

'Al-Salil!' The response was immediate, and he recognized Batula's voice.

'Batula!' He rode to meet his lance-bearer. They came together at a gallop then Dorian turned Ibrisam to run alongside Batula's mount so they could talk.

'What news?'

'A war party, many men,' Batula replied. 'They were waiting at the Witch's Tower.'

'How many?'

'Five hundred, perhaps more.'

'Who?'

'Turks and Masakara.' The Masakara were the tribe from the coastal lands around Muscat and Sur. Dorian had no doubt that they were the Caliph's men, especially if Turks were with them.

'Encamped?'

'No, they are riding hard in pursuit of us.'

'How do they know we have changed direction?'

'I can only guess that they must have many scouts watching us, and we saw your dustcloud from many miles. It shines like a beacon fire in the moonlight.'

Dorian looked up and saw it obscuring half the sky above them. 'How far are they behind you?'

Batula threw back the cloth from his face and grinned in the starlight. 'If it were daylight you would be able to see their dustcloud clearly. Loosen your lance, al-Salil. There will be good fighting before the sun sets tomorrow.'

They raced onwards all that night, until the dawn flushed the eastern sky and the light grew stronger.

'Ride on!' Dorian called to the Prince, turned Ibrisam aside and headed for a pimple of dark lava that rose abruptly fifty feet out of the flat white plain to their left. When he reached it he jumped down from the saddle and scrambled to the top of it.

The dawn flared before his eyes, and the light came swiftly, that miraculous birth of the desert day. The wild hills of Shiya stood tall and serried ahead of him; their colours were as gorgeous as those of some tropical bird, bright gold and red with bars of purple and buttresses of crimson. He could clearly see the Pass of the Bright Gazelle, a dark blue cleft that split the sheer, rugged cliffs from top to bottom. The white sands were piled up at the base of the hills in a sloping ramp, and the wind had carved the soft dunes below the gaudy rockface into weird, fantastic shapes.

Then Dorian looked back the way they had come and saw the dustcloud of the Turks, billowing up from the glistening plain close behind him. At that moment the rising sun shot its first arrow of light through a gap in the crest of the hills. Although Dorian was still in shadow, the plain behind him was lit, and he saw the sunlight sparkle on the lance heads of the approaching riders.

'Batula was wrong,' he whispered, as he saw their multitudes. 'There are many more than he counted. A thousand, perhaps.'

They were spread out over a wide front, many squadrons, some obscured by the dust of those ahead.

'There must have been a traitor,' Dorian mused. 'They would not have sent this vast array had they not known for certain that the Prince was coming this way.'

The closest squadron of the enemy was near the centre of the line, a small band that had outstripped the main body, leaving them floundering along behind. They were so close that he could see the shapes of the camels and the riders on their backs through the gossamer sheets of rolling dust. He could not count them but he guessed there were two hundred in this group and, judging from the way in which they rode, they were hard-fighting men.

He narrowed his eyes as he tried to estimate their speed and compare it to the pace of the fleeing column of his own men. Those camels out there were fresh and fleet, while his own beast had run all night. The enemy were outrunning them, and it would be a close race to reach the Pass of the Bright Gazelle.

He ran down to where Ibrisam stood and leaped up onto her back. She sprang away at the touch of his riding wand and fled in pursuit of the column. As he emerged from behind the cover of the rocks, the pursuers spotted him and he heard their faint but warlike cries carrying in the cool morning air. Dorian swivelled in the saddle and looked back just in time to see the puffs of gunsmoke as the riders in the leading ranks fired at him.

The range was too long, and he did not even hear the flight of the musket-balls. Ibrisam, the Silk Wind, ran on untouched and caught up with their own band at the start of the sand ramp that led up to the foot of the cliffs. This was a slithering slope of loose, crystalline particles that gave under the weight of the camels and ran back like water beneath their pads.

The column struggled upwards, sliding back half a pace for every one they gained, and the camels moaned with fear at the treacherous footing. One of the leading animals went down on its haunches, lunging wildly to regain its feet, then rolled backwards, crushing its rider under the saddle. Dorian was close enough to hear the screams and the crackle of the bones as both the man's legs snapped. Then the heavy beast slid back in a tangle to the foot of the ramp, leaving the slope behind it littered with waterskins and broken equipment, dragging its rider down with it, caught in the traces.

Dorian jumped down and, with his sword, cut the

injured man free. Batula saw what he was doing and turned back to help him. His mount slid down the slope in sheets of flying sand, and at the bottom he jumped down beside Dorian. Between them they lifted the injured man, his shattered legs dangling, up onto Ibrisam's back.

The tail of the column was already halfway up the slope. The Prince and the vanguard had reached the foot of the rocks and were disappearing into the dark cleft of the pass through the hills.

Dorian seized Ibrisam's halter, dragged her head round and started her up the dune. He glanced back over the plain and saw the pursuit bearing down upon them. Their mounts were stretched out at full run, the dust boiling out behind them, the riders on their backs brandishing their weapons, howling war cries into the wind, robes streaming out behind them, racing in to cut them down while they struggled up the treacherous slope.

Abruptly, from high above, came the blast of musket fire. The Prince had rallied the men as they reached the mouth of the pass, and the crash of the volley echoed and boomed along the cliff face. Dorian saw at least three of the onrushing riders knocked from the saddle by the heavy lead balls, and one of the camels must have been struck in the brain, for it dropped so suddenly that it cartwheeled, haunches over head, flinging its rider high as it sprawled on the hard-baked earth. The charge lost speed and impetus, and as Dorian and Batula toiled up the soft slope another volley of musket fire swept over their heads.

It was answered by a rattle of rolling fire from the foot of the dunes where the enemy were dismounting and turning their jezails on the struggling pair exposed on the ramp above them. Lead balls kicked up spurts of sand around Dorian's feet, but there seemed a charm of protection over him, for despite the rain of shots he and Batula battled on.

Running with sweat and gasping for breath, they

dragged the camels over the top of the sand ramp and onto the stony ledge at the mouth of the pass. Dorian looked around him swiftly as he heaved and panted for breath.

The other camels had been led into shelter behind the first turn of the high stone walls, and his men had couched them there then run back to take up positions among the rocks from where they could fire down on the enemy.

Dorian looked out across the plain below and saw the Ottoman squadrons strung out over miles of the pale earth, but all headed in his direction. He made a swift count of their numbers.

'Certainly close to a thousand!' he decided, and wiped the stinging sweat from his eyes with his headcloth. Then he examined Ibrisam quickly, running his hands over her flanks and haunches, dreading to find blood from a bullet wound, but she was unharmed. He tossed the halter rope to Batula. 'Take the camels to safety,' he ordered, 'and have the injured man cared for.'

While Batula led the beasts deeper into the gut of the pass, Dorian went to find the Prince. Al-Malik squatted, musket in hand, unharmed and composed, quietly directing the musketeers among the rocks. Dorian crouched beside him. 'Lord, this is not your business. It is mine.'

The Prince smiled at him. 'You have done well thus far. You should have left that clumsy fellow to fend for himself. Your life is worth a hundred of his.'

Dorian ignored both the rebuke and the compliment. He said quietly, 'With half the men I can hold the enemy here for many days, until our water is spent. I will send Batula and the other half to escort you through the pass and on to the oasis of Muhaid.'

The Prince looked into his face, his expression grave. The odds would be twenty against a thousand, and though the position was strong, they could expect the enemy to be determined and resourceful. He knew the sacrifice Dorian was offering. 'Leave Batula here,' he said, 'and come with

753

me to Muhaid.' The tone of his voice was a question, not an order.

'No, my lord.' Dorian rejected it. 'I cannot do that. My place is here with my men.'

'You are right.' The Prince rose to his feet. 'I cannot force you to neglect your duty, but I can command you not to fight here to the death.'

Dorian shrugged. 'Death makes his own choices. He brooks no argument from us.'

'Hold them here for the rest of the day and the night,' al-Malik said. 'That will give me time to reach Muhaid and rally the Awamir. I will come back for you with an army.'

'As my lord commands,' said Dorian, but the Prince saw the battle lust in his green eyes, and it made him uneasy.

'Al-Salil,' he said firmly, and gripped Dorian's shoulder to reinforce the words, 'I cannot tell how long it will take for me to return with the men of the Awamir. Hold them here until dawn tomorrow, no longer than that. Then run to join me as fast as Ibrisam will carry you. You are my talisman, and I cannot afford to lose you.'

'Lord, you must leave at once. Every moment is precious.'

They went back together to the camels and Dorian gave swift orders, dividing the men into two groups: those who would stay to hold the pass and those who would ride with the Prince. They shared out what remained of the water and food, a fourth part for the Prince and the remainder for Dorian's party.

'We will leave all of our muskets with you, the five barrels of black powder and the bags of lead shot,' the Prince told Dorian.

'We will put it to good employment,' Dorian promised.

Within minutes it was done and the Prince and Batula mounted at the head of the departing party. The Prince looked down from the saddle at Dorian. 'Allah be your shield, my son,' he said.

'Go with God, my father,' Dorian replied.

'That is the first time you have called me that.'

'It is the first time I have felt it to be true.'

'You do me honour,' said al-Malik gravely, and touched his camel's neck with the riding wand. Dorian watched them wind away down the narrow passage between the high rock walls and disappear around the first turn. Then he put all else from his mind except the coming battle. He strode back to the entrance to survey the plain and the cliffs with a soldier's eye. He considered the height of the sun. It was only a little past noon. It was going to be a long day and an even longer night.

He picked out the weak spots in his defence which the enemy would exploit, and made his plans as to how he would counter each move they made. First they will try a direct assault, straight up the slope, he decided, as he looked at them massing below him on the edge of the plain. He went among his men, laughing and bantering with them, moving them into the best defensive positions among the rocks, making certain that each had full powder flasks and shot bags.

He had not finished setting out the last of his pickets before he heard a distant blast of a horn from the bottom of the slope, followed immediately by the beat of war drums and a swelling shout from the first wave of attackers, who rushed forward and started up the slope.

'Steady!' Dorian called to his men. 'Hold your fire, brothers of the warrior blood.' He slapped the shoulder of a man with long dark locks of tangled hair spilling over his shoulders and they grinned into each other's face. 'The first shot will be the sweetest, Ahmed. Make it tell.'

He went on down the line. 'Wait until they are staring down your barrel, Hassan.'

'I want a clean kill from you with your first bullet, Mustapha.'

'Let them get so close that even you cannot miss, Salim.'

Though he laughed and joked he was watching the attackers come up the slope. These were Turks, heavier men than the birdlike Arabs of the desert, with long moustaches and round bronze helmets with nosepieces, and gilets of chain armour over their robes of striped wool. Heavy gear for the desert, Dorian thought as they toiled up the ramp of loose sand, the first wild rush slowly becoming a laboured climb. Dorian walked out onto the lip of the slope as if to welcome them, and stood with his hands on his hips grinning down at them. Not only did he want to inspire his men by his example, he also wanted to make certain that none could disobey his order and open fire while he was standing in front of them.

One of the Turks below paused and threw up his musket. His face was shiny with sweat and his hands shook with the effort of the climb. Dorian steeled himself, and the Turk fired. The ball hissed past Dorian's head and the wind flipped a lock of his red-gold hair across his cheek and lips. 'Is that the best you goat-lovers can do?' He laughed down at them. 'Come up here. Come and taste the hospitality of the Saar.'

His taunts gave the leaders fresh wind, and they broke into a clumsy, lurching run up the last few yards of the ramp. Dorian stepped back into the ranks of his own men. 'Ready now, brethren,' he said quietly, and cocked the hammer of his jezail.

A line of Turks came shoulder to shoulder over the lip. Their faces were flushed darkly, bathed in sweat, as they staggered on to the levelled jezails of the Saar. Most had discarded their own muskets during the climb. Now they brandished their scimitars and, with a hoarse yell, threw themselves on the defenders.

'Now!' shouted Dorian, and the Saar fired together, twenty muskets in a single prolonged blast of gunsmoke and ball. It swept through the line of Turks. Dorian saw his own shot punch a gap in the yellow teeth of a burly, moustached Turk in front of him. The man's head snapped back. Blood and brain tissue burst out of the back of his skull and the sword flew from his hand. He fell back into the man who teetered on the crest of the slope behind him, throwing him off-balance so that they fell together and rolled down the sand ramp, knocking down another three men who were climbing up it, sending them all to the bottom.

'Take the blade to them now,' Dorian called, and they sprang out from behind the rocks and charged into the milling throng of Turks on the ledge. That murderous charge drove the Ottomans back, stumbling over their own dead, and over the edge of the ramp. The ledge was cleared, and the Saar met the men who were still struggling up towards them. They had the advantage of height, and the Turks were almost exhausted by the time they came within sword-play.

The struggle was swiftly over, and the attackers broken, dead and wounded. Those who had not been hurt slipped and slithered back down, ignoring the angry shouts of their captains, running over them and carrying them away in the rout.

The Saar danced on the ledge, beards and robes swirling, hurling taunts and obscene insults after the enemy. Dorian saw at a glance that he had not lost a single man, either killed or wounded, while at least a dozen Turkish corpses were half buried in the fine sand of the dune below. 'That was only the first course of the banquet.' He controlled his own jubilation. No more than a hundred Turks had come at them in that rash charge. 'They won't try that again.'

He strode among his men, shouting to them to reload

the muskets, but it took him some time to get them under control again. 'I want ten men up in the cliffs.' He picked them out by name, and sent them climbing up the rock walls to where they could observe the whole front of the hills and any move the enemy made. He guessed that they would now send men to climb the sand dunes on each side of the mouth of the pass, out of musket range of Dorian's men, then they would regroup on the ledge and close in from both sides. Combined with another frontal attack, this would be more difficult to resist.

Dorian knew that his men must eventually be driven back into the gut of the pass, and it was there in the narrow passage that they would be forced to make their final stand. Relying on the men he had posted high in the cliffs to give warning of the next attack, he took six men into the pass to select the best defensive position.

It was almost three years since he had last travelled this way, but he remembered that there was a narrow place where the rock pinched in. When he found it again the gap was barely wide enough for a loaded camel to pass through. Beyond it was a rockfall, and at his orders the six Saar laid aside their weapons and used the loose rock from the fall to fortify the gap, building a *sangar* across it, behind which they could shelter.

The camels were couched deeper in the pass beyond the next twist of the passage and Dorian went to check that they were saddled and ready for a quick escape when the enemy broke through the *sangar*. Ibrisam groaned with love when she saw him, and he caressed her head before he left her to go back to the mouth of the pass.

The men he had sent to climb the rock walls were in position above him, and the others were spread out along the ledge. They were loading the extra muskets that the Prince had left with them, and setting these close at hand. That would give them an extra shot when the fighting was heavy.

Dorian squatted on the ledge and looked down upon the enemy. Even though the sun was high now and the heat becoming fierce, the white salt flats swarmed with activity. Troops of mounted men were still coming up to swell the ranks of the enemy, and Turkish officers were riding back and forth along the foot of the sand dunes, studying the lie of the land. Their helmets and weapons sparkled, and the white dust hung in a shimmering curtain over them.

Suddenly there was an even more agitated movement among the troops directly below where Dorian sat, and a horn sounded a fanfare. A small party was approaching, the outriders carrying banners of green and scarlet, the colours of the Sublime Porte. There could be little doubt that this was the command party of the enemy force. As they drew closer, Dorian studied them with interest. He picked out two figures in the centre of the group who, judging by their splendid dress and the rich caparisons of their camels, were high-ranking officers. One was a Turk, for he carried the round bronze shield and wore the helmet with steel nosepiece. The Ottoman general, Dorian decided, and turned his attention to the second man, an Arab. Even at this distance there was something vaguely familiar about him, and Dorian stirred uneasily. He was swaddled in fine woollen robes, but Dorian could see he was a big man. The band of his headdress was of gold filigree and the scabbard of the curved dagger on his waist shone with the same lustrous metal. There were even gold sandals on his feet. The man was a dandy. Damn me, but I know him. Dorian's sense of recognition grew stronger, and he racked his memory to try to put a name to him.

The command party drew up at the foot of the dunes, well out of musket shot of Dorian's men on the ledge, and the Turkish commander lifted a telescope to his eye and peered up at the mouth of the pass. He completed a leisurely survey of the cliff face, then lowered the glass and spoke to his officers, who were grouped obsequiously behind him. Immediately they wheeled away, and began to give orders to the squadrons of waiting troops.

There was another burst of activity. They were doing exactly what Dorian had anticipated: within a short while hundreds of heavily armed men were climbing the slope on both sides of the mouth of the pass. They were keeping well out of musket shot of the little group of defenders, but Dorian knew that when they reached the ledge they would creep in, then try to rush the entrance to the pass.

'Al-Salil! The dung-eating Turks are coming up to us again.' Dorian's lookouts on the cliffs above called their observations down to him. From their vantage-points they could see more than he, and they warned him when the first of the enemy reached the ledge and began to move along it towards the centre.

'Shoot any who come within range,' Dorian shouted back, and immediately a fusillade of musket shots echoed along the cliffs. The Saar were firing down upon the ledge, and the Turks were returning their fire. Occasionally there came a scream as a man was hit, but the shouts from the lookouts warned that the enemy were gradually working into a position from which they could launch their first assault on the mouth of the pass.

Even though he was distracted by action all around him, Dorian kept watching the gold-bedecked Arab who rode beside the Turkish general. At last a train of baggage camels came up from the rear, and from these were offloaded a painted leather tent. Twenty men unrolled it, set it up on the white plain and spread rugs and cushions in its shade. The Turkish general dismounted and went to take his place on the rugs. The Arab dandy couched his camel also, and clambered down awkwardly from the saddle. He followed the Turk to the tent, and now Dorian could see the breadth of his shoulders and the swell of his belly under the woollen robe. He had not taken more than a few paces when Dorian noticed the limp: he was favouring his right foot. It was enough to jolt his memory. He remembered their fight on the steps of the old tomb in the garden of the zenana at Lamu, and the fall that had broken that foot.

'Zayn!' he whispered. 'Zayn al-Din!' It was his old enemy from childhood days, now costumed like a prince of Oman and riding at the head of an army.

Dorian felt all the old hatred and antagonism return in full flood. Zayn was the enemy once again. But what is he doing here, hunting his own father? Dorian puzzled. Does he know that I am here also?

He tried to make sense out of this strange, unlooked-for circumstance. Zayn had been at the court of Muscat for so long that he would have been caught up in the convoluted maelstrom of royal intrigue, probably trained and encouraged by his uncle the Caliph. Unless Zayn had changed greatly from the boy Dorian had known, he would have taken readily to the conspiracies of the court. It was clear that he had become another pawn of the Sublime Porte. Perhaps he was at the centre of the capitulation of Oman to the Ottoman.

'You traitorous swine,' Dorian muttered, staring down at him with loathing. 'You would sell your country and your people, even your own father. What was the price? What reward have the Porte offered you, Zayn? The throne itself, as their puppet in Muscat?'

Zayn al-Din took his seat beside the Turkish general in the shade of the tent fly, and a slave placed a cup in his hand. He sipped from it, and Dorian saw that he had grown a thin, straggling beard but that his cheeks were smooth and plump. He stared up directly at Dorian, who pulled off the headdress and shook out his shining gold curls. The cup slipped from Zayn's fingers as he recognized him.

Dorian waved gaily at him. Zayn made no reply, but

seemed to crouch a little lower, hunching down like a bloated toad. At that moment there was a sudden heavy burst of firing along the cliffs on the right, and Dorian turned away to bolster the defence on that side of the pass.

'Beware, al-Salil,' one of the lookouts called. 'They are coming!'

'How many?' Dorian shouted back, and dropped behind the rock with Ahmed.

'Many!' came the reply. 'Too many.'

On this side, the cliffs formed a jagged buttress that turned back upon itself so that they could not see more than twenty paces along the open ledge, but they could hear the voices of the men beyond the corner of the cliff and their footsteps as they pressed forward, the clatter of a bronze shield on rock, the creak of leather thongs on breastplate and scabbard belt.

'Steady!' Dorian called softly to his men. 'Wait for them. Let them come close.'

Suddenly, a rank of Turks charged around the corner of the cliff, straight at them. The ledge was only wide enough for three at a time, but others pressed close behind them, right on their heels.

'*Allah akbar!*' they howled. 'God is great!'

There was a tall pock-marked man in the front rank, with a steel Saracen helmet on his head, chain-mail covering his torso and a double-bladed battleaxe in his hands. He jumped out ahead of his comrades and singled out Dorian, locking eyes with him and charging straight at him with the axe held in both hands above his head.

He was an arm's length away. The muzzle of the long jezail almost touched his face as Dorian fired. The ball hit the Turk in the throat, and he dropped to his knees clutching the wound. A severed artery pumped out blood between his fingers in thick glutinous jets, and he fell forward on his face.

Dorian dropped the empty musket and snatched up

the loaded one that lay at hand and cocked the hammer. Another man jumped over the dying Turk and Dorian shot him in the chest. He went down kicking and twitching on the rock ledge.

Dorian threw down the empty musket and drew his sword. He stepped forward to block the ledge. Ahmed was on his right and Salim on the left, their shoulders touching. The enemy came at them in a mob, three at a time but with others close behind, ready to step into the gaps left by the men who fell. Dorian loved the feel of a good blade in his hand. This weapon he held now had been a parting gift from the Prince when he had sailed from Lamu. It was of Damascus steel, limber as a willow wand and sharp as the tooth of a serpent.

He killed the first man who came at him cleanly, lunging under the rim of his helmet into his dark eye, skewering the eyeball like a sheep's kidney on a kebab, and sending the steel on into his brain. Recovering swiftly, Dorian disengaged the blade and let his victim drop. Then the others rushed forward behind their bronze shields, and there was no longer space nor pause for fine sword-play. Shoulder to shoulder in the pack and surge, they hacked and stabbed and shouted, swaying back and forth and side to side, across the narrow ledge.

The warning cry from the Saar lookouts in the cliff face was almost drowned by the shouting, the clatter of steel on steel, the trampling and shoving.

'On the left side and the front!'

Dorian heard it, and cut down another man before he jumped back from the fight, letting Mustapha, who was behind him, move up into his place in the line.

He looked about him and saw that, while he had been fighting on the right, the Turks had launched a series of attacks at every other point. Five of his men were fighting desperately to hold the far side of the entrance, where the enemy were pressing forward along the ledge. At the same time two hundred Turks were coming directly up the sand slope to their front. In the few moments that it took him to make this appraisal, two of his men were killed. Salim had half his head cut away by the swing of an axe blade and Mustapha took a sword thrust through the lungs and dropped to his knees belching bright gouts of blood.

Dorian knew he could not afford these losses, and the Turks coming up the slope had almost reached the ledge. The men he had placed in the cliffs had not waited for his order but were scrambling down to join the fighting. He was grateful when they jumped the last ten feet onto the rock beside him. By now both his flanks were buckling under the pressure, and at any moment a wave of the enemy would come roaring over the front of the ledge.

'Back to back!' Dorian yelled. 'Cover each other! Back into the pass.'

They formed a tight, defensive ring, and the Turks bayed around them as they fell back quickly into the mouth of the pass, but they lost more men to the flashing blades and musket-balls fired at close range.

'Now!' Dorian gave the order. 'Run!'

They spun round and pounded back deeper into the pass, dragging their wounded with them, while the enemy jammed in the entrance, obstructing each other by their numbers as they tried to pursue.

Dorian was in the lead as they raced round the bend in the rock passage and he shouted to the six men behind the walls of the *sangar*, 'Hold your fire! It is us!'

The rock wall of the *sangar* was chest high and they had to scramble over it. The men waiting behind the wall helped to drag the wounded over the top.

As the last of the Saar fell over the wall the enemy came roaring down the rock passage close behind him. The six men who had not taken any part in the fighting so far were desperate to join in: they had loaded all the remaining muskets and stacked them along the side of the cliff, and they had planted the long lances in the earth, close at hand for when the Turks breached the *sangar*.

The first volley into the front rank of the Turks brought them up short, and there was confusion and dismay as those in front tried to retreat and their comrades coming up behind pushed them forward. Another close-quarter volley with the second battery of reloaded muskets tipped the balance, and the remaining Turks fled back down the passage to disappear around the bend in the rock. Although they were hidden by the curved rock wall, the voices of the Turks were magnified by the surrounding walls, and Dorian could hear every word as they cursed the Saar and urged each other to attack again. He knew that there would be only a brief respite before the next assault.

'Water!' he ordered. 'Bring a waterskin.' The heat in the pass was like a bread oven, and the fighting had been heavy and hot. They gulped down the foul, brackish liquid from the bitter wells at Ghail ya Yamin as though it were sweet sherbet.

'Where is Hassan?' Dorian asked, as he counted heads.

'I saw him fall,' one of his men replied, 'but I was carrying Zayid and I could not go back for him.'

Dorian felt the loss, for Hassan had been one of his favourites. Now he had only twelve men still able to fight. They had dragged back five of their wounded with them but others had had to be left to the mercy of the Turks. Now they carried the five wounded back to where the camels were couched, then Dorian divided the survivors into four equal groups.

The wall of the *sangar* was wide enough for only three of them to man it at a time. Dorian positioned the three other groups behind the leading rank, after each volley they would fall back to reload and the other ranks would step up to take their turn. In this fashion he hoped to maintain a steady fire into the Turks as they came forward to the attack. He might be able to hold them off until dark, but he doubted that they could survive the night.

So few of the Saar were still on their feet, and the Turks had a reputation as terrible and doughty fighters. He knew they would be resourceful enough to find some strategy to thwart their best efforts of defence. All he could hope for was to buy time for al-Malik, and in the end they would have to try to fight their way out with lance and sword.

They settled down behind the *sangar* in the hushed, heated air of the pass, husbanding their strength.

'I would trade my place in Paradise for a pipe of *kheef* now.' Misqha grinned as he wrapped a strip of filthy sweat-soaked cloth around the sword-cut in his upper arm. The heady smoke of the herb made the smoker fearless and oblivious to the pain of his wounds.

'I will make one for you and light it with my own hands when we sit in the halls of Muscat,' Dorian promised, then broke off as somebody called his name.

'Al-Salil, my brother!' the voice echoed and resonated from the rock. 'My heart rejoices to see you again.' It was high-pitched, almost girlish.

Although the timbre had changed, Dorian recognized it. 'How is your foot, Zayn al-Din?' he called back. 'Come, let me break the other for you, to balance your duck waddle.'

Out of sight behind the bend of the passage, Zayn giggled. 'We will come, my brother, believe me, we will come, and when we do I shall laugh while my Turkish allies lift the skirts of your robe and bend you over the saddle of your camel.'

'I think you would enjoy that more than I would, Zayn.' Dorian used the feminine form of address, as though he were speaking to a woman, and Zayn was silent for a while.

'Listen, al-Salil,' he shouted again. 'This is your blood brother Hassan. You left him behind when you ran like a cowardly jackal. He still lives.'

Dorian felt a chill of dread blow down his spine. 'He is a brave man, Zayn al-Din. Let him die with dignity,' he called back. Hassan had been his friend since the first day he had come to live among the Saar. He had two young wives and four little sons, the oldest only five years of age.

A terrible scream came down the passage, a scream of mortal agony and outrage, which descended into a sobbing moan.

'Here is a gift for you from your friend.' Something small, soft and bloody was lobbed around the corner of the passage. It rolled in the sandy earth and came to rest in front of the *sangar* wall. 'You are in need of another pair of balls, al-Salil, my brother,' Zayn al-Din called. 'There they are. Hassan will not need them where he is going.'

The Saar growled and cursed, and Dorian felt tears sting his eyelids. His voice choked as he shouted back, 'I swear, in the name of God, that I will do the same for you one day.'

'Oh, my brother,' Zayn called back, 'if this dog of a Saar is so dear to you, I will send him back to you. But before I do I wish to look at his liver.'

There was another terrible scream, then Hassan was thrust out into the open and sent staggering down the passage towards the *sangar*. He was naked, and between his legs was a dark hole, mushy with blood. They had ripped open his belly and his entrails dangled around his knees, slippery and purple. He reeled towards Dorian, his mouth open. He made a cawing animal sound, and his mouth was a blood-drenched cave. Zayn al-Din had cut out his tongue.

Before he reached the *sangar* wall he collapsed and lay wriggling weakly in the dust. Dorian leaped over the wall with the musket in his hand. He placed the muzzle at the back of Hassan's head and fired. His skull collapsed like a rotten melon. At the sound of the shot the Turks came pouring down the passage, like a wave of storm water. Dorian jumped back over the wall.

'Fire!' he shouted to his men, and the first volley of musket-balls slapped like thrown gravel into the front rank of the attackers.

The fighting raged back and forth for the few hours of daylight that remained. Gradually the passage clogged with the enemy dead, they were piled almost as high as the rock wall, and a thick fog of gunsmoke filled the depths of the pass, so that the air was hard to breathe and they panted and gasped as they fired and reloaded. The smoke mingled with the metallic smell of blood and the gas from the torn intestines, and in the heat the sweat poured down their bodies and burned their eyes with its salt.

Using their own dead as an assault ladder, the Turks managed to climb over the top of the wall three times, and three times Dorian and his Saar hurled them back. As darkness fell there were only seven Arabs still able to stand beside him and all were wounded. In the lull between each attack, they dragged their dead and wounded back to where the camels were couched. There was no one to tend the injured men, so Dorian placed a waterskin beside those who still had the strength to drink from it.

Jaub, who was nicknamed the Cat, had had his right shoulder shattered by the blow of a battleaxe, and Dorian could not staunch the pumping arterial bleeding. 'It is time for me to leave you, al-Salil,' Jaub whispered, as he struggled to his knees. 'Hold my sword for me.'

Dorian could not refuse this last request: he could not leave this comrade of a dozen battles to the Turks. With ice in his heart, he set the hilt of the sword firmly in the sand and placed the point of the curved blade in the notch below the sternum, aimed up towards the heart.

'The blessing of Allah and his Prophet on you, my friend,' Jaub thanked him and fell forward. The blade slid in full length and the point, smeared with blood, came out between his shoulder-blades. Dorian stood up and ran back to the wall just as another rush of Turks came howling down the gut of the pass. They hurled them back at last, but two more of the Saar had gone down. I had hoped to hold them longer, Dorian thought, as he leaned heavily on the blood-soaked wall. I had hoped to give my father more time to raise the Awamir, but there are too few of us left and it is almost over now.

It was becoming very dark in the passage. Soon the Turks would be able to creep up to the foot of the wall unseen.

'Bin-Shibam,' he croaked to the man beside him, for his throat was swollen with thirst and strained with shouting, 'bring the last waterskin and the bundles of firewood from the camel loads. We will drink and light the night with our last fire.'

The leaping flames lit the rock walls of the pass with a ruddy flickering light, and at intervals one of the Saar threw a burning brand over the wall to dispel the shadows in which the Turks might crawl forward.

There was a lull now. They could hear the Turks talking beyond the bend, and the groans of the wounded and dying were hideous, but still the next attack did not come. They sat in a small lonely huddle against the wall, drinking the last of the water and helping each other bind up their wounds. All of them were hurt, but although Dorian had been in the thick of the fighting all that day his injuries were the least grave. There was a deep cut on the back of his left arm, and a sword-thrust through the same shoulder. 'But I still have my right arm to wield a sword,' he told the man who was fashioning an arm sling for him from a length of rope from the camel tack. 'I think we have done all we can here. If any of you wishes to leave, take a camel and ride with my thanks and blessings.'

'This is a good place to die,' said the man beside him.

'The houris of Paradise will be sad that we disregard their call,' another refused Dorian's offer.

Then they all looked up in mild alarm as a pebble clattered down from high above, bouncing from wall to wall, striking tiny sparks from the rock.

'They have climbed the cliffs and are over our heads.' Dorian jumped to his feet. 'Douse the fire.' The flames would light them for the men high above to see their position. His warning came too late.

Suddenly the air around them was filled with a thunderous roar, like that of a great waterfall, and a bombardment of rocks came hurtling down upon them. Some of the boulders were the size of powder-kegs, others only as large as a man's head, but there was no shelter from this lethal rain in the gut of the pass.

Three more men were crushed in the first few moments and the others struck down as they ran back along the passage to the camels. Dorian was the only one to get through. He reached Ibrisam's side and threw himself into the saddle. 'Hut! Hut!' he urged her to her feet, but as she rose the bombardment of boulders ceased abruptly and the Turks swarmed over the wall behind him. They stabbed the wounded Arabs then, with barely a pause, rushed forward to surround Ibrisam.

Dorian hit one of them in the chest with the lance, driving the steel head in deeply against the clinging resistance of living flesh, but the shaft snapped off in his hand and he hurled the stump into the face of another Turk and drew his sword. He slashed at the heads of the men who were trying to pull him down from the saddle, and drove Ibrisam back down the passage. She kicked out at the men who stood in her way, clashing her huge yellow teeth, biting all the fingers off one man's hand and crushing another's ribs with a single blow from her forefoot. Then she bounded forward and broke through their ranks.

Dorian clung to the pommel of the saddle with his good hand as Ibrisam ran free, following the bends and convulsions of the pass. The bloodthirsty yells of the Turks dwindled behind them.

The pass ran a mile or more through the hills, a dry water-course formed when a softer stratum of rock had been washed out by storm-water over the millennia. Once they were clear of their pursuers Ibrisam shifted into that smooth-pacing trot that covered the ground swiftly and had given her the name Silk Wind.

Dorian fell into a trance from thirst, exhaustion and the stiffening pain of his wounds. The walls of the pass streamed past him endlessly, mesmerizing him further. Once he almost toppled from the saddle, but Ibrisam felt him slump and came to an abrupt halt. This roused Dorian and he sat more firmly in the saddle when she went on.

Only then did he become aware that her gait was hampered, but he was confused and dazed, barely able to keep his seat. The effort required to dismount and check her condition was too much for him.

Once again he dozed and when he started awake he found that they had emerged from the far end of the pass and were out into the open country of the Awamir. He could tell from the height of the moon and the position of the stars that it was after midnight.

The night was icy cold, a cruel contrast to the burning heat of the day. The blood and sweat that soaked his robe chilled him further and he was shivering and light-headed. Ibrisam was moving strangely under him, her pace short and her back hunched. At last he summoned the strength and resolve to order her to halt and couch.

He tested the waterskin that hung over her withers,

771

and found that it contained less than a gallon of the stinking water from Ghail ya Yamin. He took his thick woollen shawl out of the carrying-net and spread it over his shoulders. Still shivering, he examined Ibrisam to find the cause of her distress.

He saw at once that her rump was wet and shining in the moonlight, and discovered that she was scouring heavily. The liquid dung she was passing was dark red with blood. Dorian felt a plunge of dismay. His own injuries and misery forgotten, he palpated her sleek, smooth flanks but when he touched her belly, just forward of her back legs, she moaned softly and his hand came away wet and shining with blood.

A thrust from a Turkish lance had cut deep into her belly and ruptured her bowels. She was mortally wounded, and it was a miracle of love and determination that she had carried him this far. Dorian was so weak and sad that his tears welled. He untied the leather bucket from the load and filled it with the last of the water from the skin. He drank half a pint of the filthy liquid, then went to kneel at Ibrisam's head.

'My brave darling,' he said, and gave her to drink of what remained in the bucket. She sucked up the water eagerly, and when it was finished she snuffled the bottom. 'There is nothing more I can do for you,' he told her, as he stroked her ears. She loved him to do that. 'You will be dead by morning,' he said, 'and I with you, unless you can carry me a little further, for the Turks will follow closely. Will you carry me for the last time?' He stood up and called to her softly, 'Hut! Hut!'

She swung her head and looked at him with those great dark eyes swimming with agony.

'Hut! Hut!' he said, and she groaned, roared and heaved herself upright. Dorian dragged himself up into the saddle.

She went on at that cramped painful gait, following

the tracks that the Prince and Batula had left through the broken hills and deep wadis. Dorian almost toppled again, but he rallied and used the empty carrying-net to tie himself into the saddle. He dozed, jerked awake and dozed again, slowly sinking into a coma. He lost all track of time, speed, direction, and they wandered on, the dying beast and the man.

An hour after dawn, just as the cruel flail of the sun scourged them once again, Ibrisam went down for the last time. She died on her feet still trying to struggle forward. With a last low moan, she fell heavily, throwing him from the saddle to sprawl on the rock-strewn earth.

Dorian crawled to his knees then dragged himself into the shade of Ibrisam's carcass. He forced himself not to think about the death of his beloved beast, or the loss of so many of his men. He had to concentrate all his strength and wits on staying alive until Batula could lead the Awamir back to rescue him.

He saw the heavy tracks of many camels in the loose earth ahead of him, and realized that even in her death throes Ibrisam had still faithfully followed the route that Batula and the Prince had taken towards the oasis at Muhaid. That might yet save his life, for when they returned they would come back along their own tracks.

It was the rule of survival in the desert not to leave a place of safety and wander off into the wilderness, but Dorian knew that the Turks were following him. Zayn al-Din would not let him go so easily. The enemy must be close, and if they found him before Batula returned he could expect the same treatment that Zayn had given to the wounded he had captured at the Pass of the Bright Gazelle.

He must go on to meet Batula and he must try to keep ahead of the following Turks for as long as he had the strength to remain on his feet. He stood up shakily and looked down at the load that Ibrisam had carried. Was there anything that might be of use to him? He unhooked the waterskin, shook it, then held it high with both hands, the spout to his lips. A few bitter drops slid reluctantly into his mouth and he swallowed painfully, his throat already swelling. Then he dropped the empty skin.

Weapons. He looked to what he had with him. There was his jezail in the leather scabbard, and the powder flask and shot bag. The butt stock of the musket was inlaid with ivory and mother-of-pearl, the lock chased with silver. It weighed almost seven pounds, too heavy to carry. Leave it.

His broken lance had been left at the pass, and the sword would weigh him down – its weight would seem to double with every mile he walked. Sadly, he unbuckled the belt and let it drop. He kept the dagger, he would need that at the end. The edge was keen. He had honed it until he could shave the red-gold hairs from his own forearm with it. When the Turks closed in, he would fall on it, choosing a clean death, rather than emasculation and disembowelment.

He looked down at Ibrisam and said, 'There is one last thing I ask you for, my darling.' He knelt beside her and slit open her belly with the dagger. From her stomach he took handfuls of the contents and squeezed out the liquid between his fingers and drank it. It was bitter with gall, and he had to control the urge to vomit it out again, but he knew it would give him the strength to survive a few more hours under the cruel sun.

He rebound his wounds, found that the bleeding had stopped, and that black scabs had formed. Then he tightened the straps of his sandals, and spread the shawl over his head to fend off the brutal sunlight. Without looking back at Ibrisam he struck out along the tracks of the Prince's party, towards a horizon that was already wavering with the blue heat mirage.

An hour or so later he fell for the first time. His legs seemed to turn to water under him and he went down face first. His open mouth was filled with dry chalky earth, and he almost choked as he tried to spit it out. There was no saliva left in his mouth, and the dust was sucked into his lungs as he panted for air. He struggled into a sitting position, coughed and gasped. The effort saved him from sinking into coma. He wiped his face with the tail of his headdress and there was no spittle on his lips or sweat on his face. He forced himself back on to his feet. Though he lurched and staggered, almost fell again, he kept himself upright and some little strength returned to his legs.

He walked on and the sunlight burned deep into his eyes, seeming to cook the contents of his skull. He felt his dry lips tear like parchment as he tried to swallow, and there was the slow metallic weep of salty blood into his mouth.

The pain and thirst slowly receded, and he entered that dreamlike state where there was no feeling. He heard music, sweet and melodious. He stopped and looked about him blearily, saw Tom and Yasmini standing together on the crest of the slope he was climbing. They were both waving and laughing.

'Don't be a baby, Dorry!' Tom shouted.

'Come on, Dowie.' Yasmini danced like a dainty elf beside him, swirling her skirts. He had forgotten how pretty she was. 'Come with me, Dowie, I will take you down the Angel's Road again.'

Dorian broke into a shambling, unsteady run, and the pair on the hill turned and waved at him before they disappeared over the crest. He felt as though each pace he took was through deep loose sand, and he stumbled over a rock, had to windmill his arms to prevent himself falling, but he reached the crest and looked down into the valley beyond.

He stared in amazement, for the valley was filled with green trees laden with ripe, red fruit, and there were fields of lush English grass leading down to a lake of sparkling water. Tom had gone, but Yasmini stood naked at the edge of the lake. Her body was sleek and slim, her skin a lovely golden shade and her hair, with its silver blaze, rippled down to her waist. Her little apple-shaped breasts peered shyly through the shimmering curtain of her hair. 'Dowie!' she called, and her voice was as sweet as the dawn call of a desert thrush. 'Dowie, I have waited for you so long.'

He tried to run down to her, but his legs gave way again and he fell. He was too weary to lift his head. 'Just let me sleep a little, Yassie,' he pleaded, but no sound came from his swollen throat, and his tongue seemed to fill his mouth and cleave to the roof.

With another huge effort he opened his eyes, and with a terrible sense of loss he realized that Yasmini and the lake were gone. There was only the harsh, burning wilderness below him, rock, thorn and sand. He rolled over to look back down the hill and saw the patrol of Ottoman cavalry. They were coursing along his back track, fifty men on racing camels, still two sea miles behind him, but coming on apace. He knew that they, at least, were not phantoms.

He crawled a short way on hands and knees, then launched himself to his feet. His knees buckled but he fought off the weakness, and staggered over the crest of the hill. The gradient helped him to run on.

He heard the music again, but now it filled the heavens: hundreds of voices were singing. He lifted his eyes and saw the heavenly choir, a throng of angels clustered around the sun, so glorious that they starred his vision like the reflections from the facets of a great diamond.

'Come to God!' they sang. 'Surrender yourself to the Will of God!'

'Yes!' he mumbled, and the sound of his own voice was strange in his ears, coming from a great distance. 'Yes, I am ready.'

As he said it, a miracle occurred. God appeared to

him. God was tall, he wore a robe of blinding white and the rays of the sun behind his head formed a golden nimbus. His countenance was beautiful, noble, handsome and filled with great compassion. God lifted his right hand in a gesture of blessing, and his eyes were filled with love as he looked down at Dorian. Dorian felt as though God's strength was flowing into his body, charging his soul with an infinite sense of holiness and reverence. He fell to his knees and used this new strength to shout aloud, 'I bear witness that there is no God but God, and Muhammad is His Prophet!'

God's beautiful face shone with benevolence. He strode forward, lifted Dorian to his feet and embraced him, kissed his blackened, bleeding lips.

'My son!' God said, but he spoke with the voice of Prince Abd Muhammad al-Malik. 'Your acceptance of the one true faith fills my heart with joy. Now the prophecy fulfils itself, and I give thanks to God that we have found you in time.'

Dorian sagged in the Prince's arms and al-Malik shouted to the men who followed him closely, 'Water! Batula, bring water.'

Batula squeezed cool, sweet water from a sponge between Dorian's lips and lifted him onto the litter they had prepared for this moment. A dozen men of the Awamir raised it onto the back of one of the baggage camels.

High on the swaying litter, Dorian rolled his head and, through bloodshot eyes, between swollen lids, saw the hordes of the Awamir coming across the plain.

Then, on the skyline above, the Turkish patrol appeared and reined in their camels in their own dustcloud. They gazed down in astonishment, and sudden trepidation, on the army of the Awamir.

A great shout of 'Allah akbar!' went up from the ranks of the Awamir, they couched their long lances, and swept forward to battle. The Turks turned and fled before them.

Dorian sagged back on the litter, closed his eyes and let the darkness overwhelm him.

There were almost six thousand fighting men in the column of Awamir that streamed back through the Pass of the Bright Gazelle. The salt flats beyond the pass were clear of the enemy. Their scouts had reported the approach of the Prince's army and they had fled back into the north towards Muscat.

Al-Malik paused at the pass to give decent burial to the broken bodies of the Saar who had died there. Dorian was still too weak and sick to rise from his litter, but he had Batula and four others carry him to the graveside, and for the first time he prayed as a Muslim in the community of other believers as they recited the prayer for the dead.

Then the army went on across the salt flats to the bitter wells at Ghail ya Yamin, where the warriors of the Saar had already assembled, adding another three thousand lances to the Prince's array.

The sheikhs of the Saar came to the tent where Dorian lay that night, crowded around his litter and demanded that he tell them every detail of the fight at the Pass of the Bright Gazelle. They interrupted the recitation with exclamations of wonder as he told them how each of the Saar had died, the fathers and brothers of the dead men weeping with pride.

'By Allah, a fight in which Hassan would have been happy to die!'

'In God's Name, Salim was a man.'

'Allah will prepare a place in Paradise for my son, Mustapha.'

They were fierce for war and revenge, for the blood feud could be settled only in blood, and they spat in the sand and swore their oaths of retribution against Zayn al-

Din and the Turks. In his heart Dorian swore the same oaths with them.

Then each noon and evening that the army camped at Ghail ya Yamin they came again to his tent to hear the story repeated, and they corrected Dorian if he left out a single detail, pleading with him to remember every blow and shot, and exactly what each of the Saar had done and said before he died.

From Ghail ya Yamin, the army set out north on the next leg of the long journey to Muscat. At each well and pass through the mountains the other tribes came to join them, the Balhaf and the Afar, the Bait Kathir and the Harasis, so that by the time they reached Muqaibara they were fifteen thousand lances together, a mighty host that spread back ten miles across the desert.

Batula whispered the story of Dorian's conversion to one of his companions. No Arab could keep a secret, certainly not one as poignant as this, and the tale was told around every camp-fire, and the warriors repeated the prophecy of the ancient St Taimtaim, for many had read the text of it on the walls of his tomb. They debated it endlessly and swore in God's Name that al-Salil was verily the orphan of the prophecy, and that with him in their company the victory was assured. Before Ramadan came again, they would install Prince Abd Muhammad al-Malik on the Elephant Throne in the halls of Muscat.

In the weeks that it took the army to travel from Ghail ya Yamin to Muqaibara, Dorian's injuries healed cleanly, for in the desert there are no evil humours to make wounds corrupt and mortify. When he was ready to take his place in the ranks once more, the Prince sent for him. As he strode through the encampment every tribe cheered him and followed him to the tent of the Prince. They massed around the open doorway as Dorian knelt before al-Malik and asked of him, 'Give me your blessing, Father.'

'You have my gratitude and my blessing, son, and much more besides.' Al-Malik clapped his hands, and Batula led forward four beautiful thoroughbred racing camels. Each was richly caparisoned and carried lance, sword and jezail in the scabbards on their backs. 'This is my gift to you, to repay in a small coin what you lost at the Pass of the Bright Gazelle.'

'I thank you for your generosity, Father, though I look for no reward for what was only my duty.'

Al-Malik clapped his hands again, and two heavily veiled old women of the Saar came to Dorian and laid a bundle of folded silk at his feet. 'These are the mothers of Hassan and Salim, who died at the pass,' the Prince explained. 'They have begged me for the honour of sewing and embroidering your battle pennant.'

The women spread out the banner upon the floor of the tent. It was six feet long, of azure blue silk, and embroidered upon it, in silver metal thread, was the prophecy of St Taimtaim. The elegant script flowed and swirled upon the silken ground, like the currents and whirlpools in the surface of a swift blue river.

'Father, this is the pennant of a sheikh,' Dorian protested.

'And that is what you are now.' Al-Malik smiled fondly at him. 'I have raised you to that rank. I know that you will bear it with honour.'

Dorian stood up and held the banner high above his head, then ran with it out into the sunlight. The crowds opened before him, shouted their acclamation and fired their muskets in the air. The banner streamed out behind Dorian, like a blue serpent on the wind. He came back to the Prince's tent and prostrated himself before him. 'You do me too much honour, lord.'

'In the coming battle, you shall command the left flank, Sheikh al-Salil,' the Prince told him. 'I shall place four thousand lances under your pennant.'

Dorian sat up and looked gravely into the Prince's eyes. 'Father, may I speak to you in secrecy?'

Al-Malik gestured for the leather sides of the tent to be lowered, for al-Allama and his retinue to retire and leave the two of them together. 'What more do you ask of me, my son?' Al-Malik leaned closer to him. 'Speak, and you shall have it.'

In reply Dorian spread the azure banner and traced with his finger the words of the prophecy. '"He shall bring together the sands of the desert which are divided,"' he read aloud.

'Continue,' the Prince ordered, frowning. 'I do not know your meaning.'

'It seems that the holy saint placed a further duty upon me. It comes to me that when he speaks of the sands of the desert, the saint was speaking of the tribes who are divided and at war with each other.'

Now the Prince nodded. 'This may well be true,' he admitted. 'Although most of the tribes have come to us, the Masakara, the Harth and the Bani Bu Hasan still beat the war drum for Yaqub and the Sublime Porte.'

'Let me go to them under this banner,' Dorian pleaded. 'Let them see the colour of my hair, and I shall debate the prophecy with them. Then, if Allah is kind, I shall bring over another ten thousand lances to your side.'

'No!' Al-Malik started up in alarm. 'The Masakara are treacherous. They will disembowel you and peg you out in the sun. I cannot allow you to run such a risk.'

'I have fought against them,' Dorian said softly. 'They must accord me the respect of an honourable foe. If I came to them alone and placed myself in their power as a traveller, then they dare not go against the teachings of the Prophet. They must listen to what I have to say to them.'

The Prince looked unhappy, and stroked his beard in agitation, but what Dorian had said was true. The Prophet had placed a duty of host on his believers. They were obliged to protect the traveller in their midst. 'Still, I cannot allow you to place yourself in such jeopardy,' he said at last.

Dorian argued, 'One life at risk, but ten thousand lances as the stake. Father, you cannot deny me this chance to fulfil my destiny as it is written.'

At last the Prince sighed. 'How can the Masakara prevail against your eloquence? I cannot. You may go to them, al-Salil, as my emissary. But I swear on the red beard of the Prophet that if they harm you in any way there will be such a lopping of heads as will gorge every vulture in Araby until they cannot fly.'

At sunset the following evening the Prince sat alone on a rock on the crest of a low hill beyond the oasis. Four camels slipped out of the encampment of the army and rode past his hilltop, heading northwards into the purple shadows. Dorian rode the first, leading the second on a long rein. Batula followed him, also leading a second camel. Both men were veiled. When he looked up at the Prince, Dorian dipped his lance in salute and the Prince lifted his right hand in blessing.

Then Abd Muhammad al-Malik watched them ride away into the wilderness, his expression sad and bereft. It was dark and the stars were a blaze of glory overhead when at last he rose from the rock on which he was sitting and went down towards the glow of the camp-fires that filled the wide valley of Muqaibara.

I n the cool season, when the winds came off the sea, in the month before the feast of Ramadan, the army of al-Malik lay before Muscat and watched the Ottoman and the host of tribes loyal to the Caliph come out in battle array to meet them.

Al-Malik sat with his staff under a leather awning on a promontory that jutted out into the plain, his own army drawn up beneath him. He raised the long brass telescope to his eye and studied the formations of the enemy as they evolved before him. The Turks were in the centre, their cavalry squadrons in the van, and their camel men behind.

'How many?' he asked the men around him, who argued as though they were counting goats at a market.

'Twelve thousand Turks,' they decided at last. The centre glittered with bronze and steel, the green banners of the Sublime Porte waved and flapped in the sea breeze, the cavalry squadrons cantered forward then settled into a solid phalanx ready to advance to the attack.

'And the Masakara?' the Prince asked. 'How many?' They were on the right flank, a milling throng of camel men, restless as a flock of starlings.

'Six, seven thousand,' said a sheikh of the Harasis.

'At least that many,' said another. 'Perhaps more.'

Al-Malik looked to the other flank of the enemy where the black veils and headdresses marked them as the Bani Bu Hasan and the Harth. They were the wolves of the desert and there were as many of them as there were of the Masakara.

Al-Malik tasted once again the bitter gall of disappointment in the back of his throat. They were outnumbered almost two to one. Al-Salil had failed in his attempt to bring over the northern tribes: al-Malik had heard nothing of him since he had vanished into the desert almost two moons ago. He knew in his heart that they had miscalculated, that he should never have sent al-Salil to them. Every day he had dreaded receiving a gift from the Masakara, the severed head of his red-haired son in a leather bag. Although the grisly trophy had not arrived, the proof of his failure was out on the plain: almost fifteen thousand rebel lances drawn up against him.

Suddenly there was a disturbance along the centre of the Turkish line. Despatch riders galloped forward with orders from the Ottoman staff, and the horns sounded the advance. The Turkish cavalry moved forward, rank upon rank, rippling with sunlight off their accoutrements, but the Arab formations on the flanks held their positions, and allowed gaps to open in the front. This was unusual, and through his telescope the Prince watched with a sudden, keener interest.

There was another commotion among the enemy, and this time the staff gallopers sped out from the Turkish command in the centre, waving their arms, clearly urging their Arab allies to join in the general advance and close the dangerous gaps in the front.

Then at last the Arab formations began to move, but they wheeled right and left, towards the centre, where the Turks stood uncertainly, confused by this unexpected evolution.

'In the sweet Name of God,' whispered al-Malik, and he felt his heart swell so that his breath came short.

In the centre of the front rank of the Masakara he saw a strange new banner unfurl, carried by a tall rider on a honey-coloured thoroughbred camel. He turned his glass upon this warrior and saw that the banner was azure blue, shot through with gleaming silver script, and as he stared in wonder the rider threw off his headdress and couched his lance. His hair was red-gold and his lance was aimed at the Turkish flank.

'Allah! All praise to Allah! Al-Salil has done it. He has turned the rebel tribes to our cause.'

As he stared in wonder, the Arab formations on either flank of the Turks started forward, catching the Ottoman in enfilade, closing upon them like a fist of steel.

The Prince roused himself, gave the order, 'Advance! Charge at them,' the war drums boomed and the horns sounded an urgent, strident note.

With the Saar and the Awamir in the centre, the army of the south rolled forward, raising a towering cloud of dust to sully the high blue sky.

Dorian rode in the centre of the line, and his heart was singing. Right up to this last moment, he had not been certain that the sheikhs of the Masakara would hold true to their undertaking to turn upon the Ottoman. The fleet beast under him pulled ahead of the riders on each side of him, and only Batula could match him, riding hard a lance-length behind.

Ahead the Turks were in confusion, most still looking down the valley to where Prince al-Malik's army was rolling forward; only those closest to the right flank had seen the danger and were turning to meet the charge.

With a clash and shock, of body to body and shield to shield, they struck the Ottoman flank, and ripped through it. Dorian selected a man from the ranks, bulky in his chain-mail and bronze helmet, dark face contorted with rage and dismay as he struggled to control his plunging steed. Dorian dropped the tip of his lance and leaned low in the saddle. Under Batula's training he had learned to pick a thrown desert melon out of the air at full gallop. Now he aimed for the opening in the Turk's chain-mail shirt, into his left armpit.

The lance jolted in his hand as the tip found the opening unerringly and slipped through the man's chest until it struck the chain-mail on the far side, then the impact lifted the Turk clean out of the saddle and he hung on the supple lance, kicking.

Dorian dropped the tip and let him slide off the steel and roll in the dust, then he raised the lance again and picked out his next victim. This time the lance shattered in his hand at the force of the blow, but the steel head was firmly lodged in the throat of the man he had hit. The Turk gripped the stump with both hands and tried to pluck it out of his flesh, but he died before he could do so, then slipped down from the saddle to be dragged away by his fear-crazed horse.

Batula tossed the spare lance to Dorian, who caught it neatly and in the same movement couched the long shaft and dropped its bright head to the level of the next man's belly.

In the first few minutes of the charge the ranks of the Ottoman were ripped wide open, charged from both flanks, and while they still reeled the main army of the south crashed into their disordered front.

The locked armies revolved like a mass of debris caught up in the vortex of a whirlpool, and the uproar was deafening as men hacked and shoved, shouted and died. It could not last long, for the conflict was one-sided and the fury of the attackers too fierce. Caught in flank and front, outnumbered at every point, the Ottoman line bulged and began to give. The Arabs sensed the victory and pressed forward, like wolves around a dying camel, tearing, howling, ripping into them, until at last they broke, and the battle turned into a bloody, broken shambles.

Dorian's first charge had carried him deep into the mass of the enemy and, for a desperate while, he and Batula were cut off and surrounded. The second lance broke in his hands, so he drew out his sword and fought until his right arm was daubed with Turkish blood to the shoulder.

Then abruptly the fury of the enemy around him abated and they broke away, turning the heads of their mounts towards the rear. Dorian saw men throw down their weapons as the Arabs came racing through the gaps in their front. The Turks whipped their mounts into a gallop and fled. 'Full chase!' Dorian yelled. 'Chase them! Cut them down.'

Mingled like oil and water, the two armies streamed back across the plain together, the Arabs were ululating and swinging their bloody swords, shouting their war-cries as the battle turned into a rout and the fleeing Turks made little effort to defend themselves. Some threw themselves from their horses and knelt in the path of the attackers, begging for mercy, but the Arabs lanced them casually as they rode by, then wheeled back to strip the corpses of gold and booty.

Dorian fought his way through to the rear. Ahead he saw that the Ottoman staff had long ago abandoned the battle, and were also in desperate flight across the plain. The general and every one of his officers had grabbed a horse or a camel and were fleeing back towards the city. In all this multitude there was only one man Dorian wanted.

'Where is Zayn al-Din?' he shouted to Batula. Dorian had seen him earlier that morning as the army had debouched through the gates of Muscat. Zayn al-Din had been with the Turkish staff, riding behind the Ottoman general, wearing half-armour and carrying a lance as though he were eager for the fight. With him had been Abubaker, his old crony and henchman from the zenana at Lamu. Abubaker had grown tall and lean, with long moustaches, and he also was dressed in the accoutrements of a warrior. Although his two old enemies had ridden within two lance-lengths of Dorian, neither had recognized him among the ranks of the Masakara, for Dorian had been mounted on a strange camel and his face and red hair had been swathed in the folds of a black turban.

'Where is he?' he shouted to Batula. 'Can you see him?' He jumped up and stood tall on the wooden saddle frame of the running camel, a careless feat of skill, and from the height he scoured the open plain ahead, which was covered not only with the fleeing enemy but also with bolting loose horses and unmounted camels whose riders had been hacked down.

'There he is!' Dorian shouted, dropped back easily into the saddle and urged his mount forward. Zayn al-Din was half a mile ahead, mounted on the same bay stallion that Dorian had seen that morning. His plump body was unmistakable, as was the golden head-rope around his blue headdress. Dorian pushed his camel to the top of its speed. He overhauled and passed many other Turks, some high-ranking officers, but he ignored them and, like a cheetah coursing the gazelle of his choice, bore down swiftly on Zayn al-Din.

'Brother!' he called to him, as he ran close behind the bay stallion. 'Stay a while! I have something for you.'

Zayn looked back over his shoulder. The wind plucked off his headdress and his long dark hair and his beard fluttered. Terror turned his face the colour of rancid camel butter as he saw Dorian close behind him, saw the long curved sword in his hand, his face all speckled with other men's blood, his grin savage and merciless.

Zayn al-Din seemed paralysed with fear, clinging to the pommel of his saddle, his eyes fixed on Dorian as he came alongside and raised the scimitar on high. Then, with a shriek, Zayn released his grip and fell out of the saddle. He struck the hard ground and rolled like a boulder down a steep hillside, until he lay still at last in a dusty heap, like a pile of old clothing.

Dorian wheeled his camel and stood over him as Zayn crawled up on to his knees. His face was white with dust, and there was a raw graze down one cheek. He looked up at Dorian and began to blubber. 'Spare me, al-Salil. I will give you anything.'

'Throw me your lance,' Dorian called to Batula, without taking his eyes of Zayn's abject face. Batula tossed it across to him. Dorian lowered the point and placed it on Zayn's chest. Zayn began to weep, and the tears cut runnels through the dust that powdered his face. 'I have a lakh of gold rupees, my brother. It is all yours, if you spare me, I swear it.' His mouth was slack and his lips quivered and drooled with fear.

'Do you remember Hassan at the Pass of the Bright Gazelle?' Dorian asked grimly, leaning out from the saddle to stare into his face.

'God forgive me,' Zayn cried. 'It was in the heat of the fighting. I was not myself. Forgive me, my brother.'

'I wish only that I could bring myself to touch you, then surely I would cut out your testicles as you did to my friend, but rather would I touch a poisonous snake,' Dorian spat with disgust. 'You do not deserve the warrior's death by the steel of the lance, but because I am a compassionate man I shall give it to you.' He pressed forward with the long shaft and the bright point pricked Zayn al-Din's fat chest.

Then Zayn saved his own life. He found the only words that could avert Dorian's implacable wrath.

'In the name of the man who is our father. In the love of al-Malik, grant me mercy.'

Dorian's expression changed, his gaze wavered, and he withdrew the lance tip an inch. 'You ask for the judgement of the father you have betrayed. We both know it must be the garotte of the executioner. If that is the death you choose, over the clean death I offer you, so be it, then. I grant it to you.'

Dorian put up the lance, and rammed the butt down into the leather bucket behind his heel.

'Batula!' he called, and when his lance-bearer came up he ordered him, 'Bind the arms of this eater of swine flesh behind his back and place a noose around his neck.' Batula slipped down from the saddle and swiftly trussed Zayn's arms, then dropped a running noose over his head. He passed the end of the rope up to Dorian, who made it fast to one of the loops on his saddle.

'On your feet!' Dorian barked, and gave the rope a yank. 'I am taking you to the Prince.' Zayn lurched upright, then staggered after Dorian's camel. Once he lost his balance and rolled on the ground, but Dorian did not slacken the pace or even look back, and Zayn struggled up again, his robe ripped and his knees bloody. Before they had covered a mile of that sanguinary plain, on which the corpses of the Turks lay like seaweed on a storm-lashed beach, the golden sandals had been torn from Zayn's feet and his soles were raw. His face was swollen and black as the rope half choked him and he was so weak he could no longer call for mercy.

As Prince Abd Muhammad al-Malik rode up to the gates of Muscat at the head of his retinue, the citizens of the city and the courtiers of the Caliph al-Uzar ibn Yaqub threw open the gates and came out to greet him. They had torn their garments and poured ash and dust over their heads as a sign of repentance, and they knelt in front of his horse, pleading for their lives, swearing allegiance to him and hailing him as the new Caliph of Oman.

The Prince sat impassively on his horse, a noble, magisterial figure, but when the vizier of his brother Yaqub came forward bearing a stained sack over his shoulder, al-Malik's expression turned to sorrow for he knew what it contained.

The vizier emptied the sack into the dust of the roadway and Yaqub's severed head rolled to the feet of the Prince's mount, and stared up at him with dull, glazed eyes. His grey beard was matted and filthy, like that of a street beggar, and the flies settled in a humming cloud on his open eyes and bloody lips.

Al-Malik gazed down on him sadly, then looked up at the vizier and spoke softly. 'You seek to win my approval by murdering my brother and bringing me this sad broken thing?' he asked.

'Great lord, I did only what I thought would please you.' The vizier blanched and trembled.

The Prince gestured to the sheikh of the Awamir at his side. 'Kill him!' The sheikh leaned from the saddle and, with his sword, split the vizier's skull down to the chin. 'Treat my brother's remains with all respect and prepare him for burial before the setting of the sun. I shall lead the prayers for his soul,' said al-Malik. Then he looked at the cringing citizens of Muscat. 'Your city is now my city. Its people are now my people,' he told them. 'By my royal decree Muscat is exempt from plunder. Its women are protected by my word of honour from rape and its treasures from pillage.' He lifted his right hand in blessing and said, 'After you have sworn the oath of fealty, all your trespasses and crimes against me shall be forgiven and forgotten.'

Then he rode on into the city, to the halls of Muscat, and took his place upon the Elephant Throne of Oman, carved from great ivory tusks.

A hundred noblemen clamoured for the new Caliph's ear, and a hundred pressing affairs of state awaited his attention, but one of the first men for whom he sent was Sheikh al-Salil. When Dorian prostrated himself before the throne, al-Malik stepped down, lifted him to his feet and embraced him.

'I had thought you dead, my son. Then when I saw your banner flying in the ranks of the Masakara my heart

791

shouted aloud with joy. I owe you much, I shall never know just how much, for if you had not brought in the northern tribes under my flag the battle might have gone hard for us. Perhaps I might not be sitting on the Elephant Throne this day.'

'Father, during the battle I took a prisoner from the army of the Ottoman,' Dorian told him, and made a sign to Batula, who waited among the noblemen at the back of the throne room. He came forward, leading Zayn al-Din on the rope.

Zayn's attire was ragged and filthy with dust and dried blood, his hair and beard white with dust and his bare feet raw and bloodied like those of a pilgrim. At first al-Malik did not recognize him. Then Zayn stumbled forward and threw himself at his father's feet, and wept and wriggled his whole body like a whipped dog. 'Father, forgive me. Forgive my stupidity. I am guilty of treason and disrespect. I am guilty of greed. I was led astray by evil men.'

'How is this so?' the Caliph asked coldly.

'The Sublime Porte offered me the Elephant Throne if I would turn against you, and I was weak and stupid. I regret this with all my heart and if you should order me killed, I will shout my love for you to the heavens as the life flies from my body.'

'You richly deserve such a death,' the Caliph said. 'You have had nothing but love and kindness from me all your life, and you have repaid me with treachery and dishonour.'

'Allow me another chance to prove my love to you.' Zayn slobbered on his father's sandals and mucus streamed from his nose as the tears poured from his eyes.

'This glad day has already been marred by the death of my brother, Yaqub. There has been enough blood spilled,' said al-Malik thoughtfully. 'Stand up, Zayn al-Din. I grant you pardon, but in penance you must make the pilgrimage to the holy places at Mecca and ask forgiveness there also.

Do not show me your face again until you return with your soul cleansed.'

Zayn lumbered to his feet. 'All Allah's blessings upon you, Majesty, for your benevolence and your compassion. You shall find my love to be like a mighty river that flows on eternally.' Still grovelling, bowing and mouthing protestations of loyalty and duty, Zayn backed away down the length of the throne room, then turned and pushed his way through the crowds and out of the tall carved-ivory doors.

Ten days after the triumphal entry into Muscat, and a week before the commencement of Ramadan, the coronation of the new Caliph was celebrated in the halls of Muscat and the streets of the city. Most of the tribal warriors had drifted back into the wilderness to their villages around the tiny oases scattered down the length of Oman, for they were desert dwellers and unhappy behind the walls of a city. They swore their oaths of fealty to al-Malik, then rode away on their camels, laden with the spoils of the Ottoman army that they had destroyed.

Those who remained joined the celebrations in the streets of the city where whole carcasses of camels and sheep were roasted on the bonfires in every souk and square. The rams' horns sounded, the drums beat and men danced in the streets while veiled women watched from the upper floors of the huddled buildings.

The new Caliph walked in procession through the crowded streets, stopping every few paces to embrace one of the warriors who had fought in his army. The crowds ululated, fired joy shots in the air and fell at his feet.

It was well after midnight when the Caliph returned to the palace of Muscat, and Sheikh al-Salil was still at his side where he had been all that day.

'Stay with me yet a while,' the Caliph ordered, when they reached the door of his bedchamber. He took Dorian's arm and led him through and out onto the high balcony, which overlooked the sea and the streets of the city. The music and the shouts of the revellers carried faintly up to them, and the flames of the bonfires reflected off the walls and lit the dancers. 'I owe you an explanation for pardoning Zayn al-Din,' said the Caliph at last.

'You owe me nothing, Majesty,' Dorian protested. 'It is I who owe you everything.'

'Zayn deserved harsher punishment. He was a traitor, and I know how he treated your comrades at the Pass of the Bright Gazelle.'

'My concerns are nothing,' Dorian replied. 'It is what he did to you, and what he will one day do to you again, that angers me.'

'You think that his repentance was a sham?'

'He lusts for the Elephant Throne,' said Dorian. 'I would have been happier if you had taken a scorpion into your bosom and a cobra into your bed.'

The Caliph sighed sadly. 'He is my eldest son. I could not begin my reign with his murder. But I have placed you in great jeopardy, for his hatred of you is implacable.'

'I am able to defend myself, Father.'

'That you have proved.' The Caliph laughed softly. 'But now to other matters. I have another task for you, a dangerous and difficult one.'

'You have only to command me, Majesty.'

'Our trade with the African interior is most important to the prosperity of our people. We, who once were only poor desert nomads, are becoming a nation of seafarers and traders.'

'I understand that, Father.'

'Today I received a messenger from the Sultan of Zanzibar. Our African trade is under a new and grave threat, the very existence of our bases at Zanzibar and Lamu is at stake.'

'How is this possible?'

'A band of marauders is savaging our caravan routes between the Fever Coast and the Great Lakes. Our African trade is in jeopardy.'

'Are the black tribes rising in rebellion?' Dorian asked.

'Perhaps this is the case. We know that there are black tribesmen among the marauders, but there are also rumours that they are led by infidel Franks.'

'From which country?' Dorian asked.

The Caliph shrugged. 'This is not known. All that is certain is that they are ruthless in their attacks upon our slave caravans. We have lost almost the entire year's revenue from the sale of slaves, together with immense quantities of ivory and gold out of the interior.'

'What do you want me to do?' Dorian asked.

'I will give you a *firman* of authority, a commission as a general in my armies and as many fighting men as you need – a thousand, two thousand? I want you to sail south to Lamu then cross the channel and march inland to put an end to these depredations.'

'When do you wish me to leave?'

'You must sail with the new moon that ends the fast of Ramadan.'

The flotilla of Sheikh al-Salil, the Drawn Sword, anchored off the beach of the island of Lamu in the full of the moon. It comprised seven large sea-going dhows, carrying twelve hundred troops of the caliphate.

Dorian went ashore in the dawn to call upon the governor, to present his *firman* and to make arrangements for the reception and resupply of his army. He needed quarters for his men ashore to recuperate from the long voyage down the coast, and supplies of fresh food, horses and baggage animals.

The camels of the desert would not survive long on the humid, pestilent coast, and neither would Arabian horses from the north. Dorian needed animals that had been reared on the coast and had developed an immunity to the African diseases.

It took three days to get all his men and his baggage train ashore, and Dorian spent much of this time at the landing or in the newly built camp above the beach. On the evening of the third day he was walking back through the streets of the town, accompanied by Batula and three of his captains. They were almost at the gates of the fort when he heard his childhood name called. 'Al-Amhara!'

He spun round, for he recognized the voice, though he had not heard it in many years, and stared at the heavily veiled woman who crouched in the doorway of the old mosque across the narrow lane. 'Tahi? Is that you, old mother?'

'Praise be to God, my child, I thought you might not remember me.'

Dorian wanted to rush to her and embrace her, but it would be a grave breach of decorum and etiquette to do so in a public place. 'Stay there, and I will send someone to bring you to my quarters,' he told her, and walked on. He sent Batula back to bring her through the gates of the fort to the wing that the governor had placed at his disposal.

As soon as Tahi stepped through the door, she threw back her veil and rushed to him. She was weeping, almost incoherently. 'My little boy, my baby, how tall you have grown! The beard and the fierce eyes like a falcon – but I would have known you anywhere. What a great man you have become, and a sheikh also!'

Dorian laughed, held her and stroked her hair. 'What is this silver I see here, old mother? But you are still beautiful.'

'I am an old woman, but your embrace makes me young again.'

'Sit down.' He led her to the pile of rugs on the terrace, then sent a slave for sherbet and a platter of honeyed dates.

'There is so much I want to hear from you.' She reached across to stroke his beard and his cheek. 'My beautiful baby, who has become a beautiful man! Tell me everything you have done since you left Lamu.'

'That would take a day and a night,' he protested, smiling fondly at the old woman.

'I have the rest of my life to listen,' she said, so he answered all her questions, in the meantime holding back his own, although it took all his restraint.

At last he came to the end of the recital. 'And thus the Caliph has sent me back to Lamu and the Fever Coast, and I praise God that he has for now I am able to look on your beloved face again.' Her face was deeply lined with care and hardship, and her hair steely grey, but he loved her as much as he ever had. 'Tell me how you have fared since I went away.'

She told him how she had stayed on in the zenana, given menial duties by the head eunuch, Kush. 'At least I have had shelter and food in my mouth, for that I praise God's Name.'

'You shall come to live with me now,' he promised her, 'and I shall be able to repay all the love and kindness that you lavished upon me.' She wept again with happiness. Then, trying to make it sound casual, he asked the question, and waited for the answer he dreaded. 'What news of little Yasmini? She must be a woman by now, and long ago have been sent to India to marry her Mogul princeling.'

'He died of the cholera before she could go to him,' Tahi said, and watched his face shrewdly.

He tried to disguise his feelings from her, and sipped at the cup of sherbet. 'So they found another noble and important husband for her?' he asked softly.

'Yes,' Tahi agreed. 'The Emir of the al-Bil Khail in Abu Dhabi, a rich old man with fifty concubines, but only three wives, the eldest having died two years ago.' She saw the hurt and resignation in his green eyes.

'When was she married?' he asked.

She had to take pity on him. 'She is betrothed but not yet married. She will sail to meet her bridegroom when the winds change and the *kusi* blows again. In the meantime she waits sadly in the zenana here on Lamu.'

'Yasmini is still here on Lamu?' He stared at her. 'I did not know.'

'I was with her in the garden by the fountain this morning. She knows you are here. Everyone in the zenana knows it. You should have seen Yasmini's eyes when she spoke your name. They glowed like the stars of the great cross. She said, "I love al-Amhara, as a brother and more. I must see him one last time before I become an old man's bride and disappear from the world for ever."'

Dorian jumped up from the rug and strode to the end of the terrace. He stood there, gazing over the bay where his dhows rode at anchor. He felt a strange sense of elation, as though the wheel of his destiny had made another turn. During the hard years in the desert his memories of Yasmini had grown dim, but he had refused the offers of the sheikhs of the Saar to find him a wife from among their own daughters. He had not known until now that he had been waiting for something or someone else, for the memory of the little monkey-faced girl with the mischievous smile.

Then he felt a touch of dismay. There was so much that stood in their way. She was imprisoned in the zenana and betrothed to another man. In the eyes of Allah she was his sister, and he knew that the penalty for incest was a hideous death. If he violated a royal virgin and defiled the sanctity of the zenana, even the Caliph could not save him from death by stoning or decapitation. And what would they do to Yasmini? He shuddered as he remembered the tales, repeated in whispers, of Kush's treatment of any of his charges who strayed. They said that one girl had taken four days to die and that her screams had prevented anyone in the zenana from sleeping during all that harrowing time. 'I cannot let her take the risk,' he said aloud, and hugged shoulders, torn by emotions that swung him first one way then the other. 'And yet I cannot resist my heart's urging.' He turned and smashed his bunched fist into the wall of rough coral ragging and revelled in the pain. 'What shall I do?'

He strode back to where Tahi squatted patiently on the rug. 'Will you take a message back to her?'

'You know I will. What shall I tell her, my son?'

'Tell her that at moonrise tonight I will be waiting at the end of the Angel's Road.'

He would not let Batula accompany him, but at nightfall he took a horse and, heavily robed and veiled, rode out of the town towards the north. He remembered every track, stream, clump of forest and stretch of mangrove swamp.

He circled back through the palm groves and saw the walls of the zenana ahead, tall, massive and dark before the moonrise. He found the old ruin and tethered his mare in a patch of bush near by, where she would be hidden from anyone using the woodcutter's track. He did not expect any islander to be abroad at this hour, for they were superstitious and terrified of the forest djinns.

He climbed over the piles of fallen masonry and pushed his way through the thicket of bush and scrub until he stepped down into the hidden saucer in the centre. The entrance to the tunnel was overgrown and he could see that no one had used it in all the years that had passed.

He found a seat on a block of coral where he could watch both the entrance to the tunnel and keep an eye open for intruders. He did not have long to wait for soon the moonglow filled the eastern sky, and then, as it rose above the tops of the palms, it struck down into the saucer with a silver light.

He heard a soft sound, light footstep and a whisper from the entrance of the tunnel. 'Dowie? Are you there?' Her voice was more husky than he remembered, and goose pimples rose along his forearms, stirred the fine hairs at the back of his neck.

'I am here, Yassie.'

The branches that screened the entrance parted and she stepped out into the moonlight. She wore a simple white robe and a cloth over her head. He saw at once that she had grown inches taller, but her body was still slim and supple as a vine, her step quick and alert as a frightened gazelle. She saw him and stopped dead, then slowly reached up and drew aside the veil that covered her face.

He gasped. In the moonlight she was beautiful. Although no longer a child, her face was delicate and still elfin in quality, with high cheekbones and huge dark eyes. When she smiled her lips were full, her teeth white and even.

He stood up, and pulled back his own veil. She started. 'You have grown so tall, and the beard—' She broke off and stood, uncertain.

'And you have grown into a lovely woman.'

'Oh, I have missed you so,' she whispered. 'Every single day—'

Suddenly she ran to him, and he held out his arms.

She was trembling and sobbing softly against his chest. 'Don't cry, Yassie. Please don't cry.'

'I am so happy,' she sobbed. 'I have never been so happy in all my life.'

He drew her down on the coral block and she stopped weeping, pulled back at arm's length to gaze into his face. 'I have heard news of you even in the zenana, how you have become a mighty warrior, how you won a great fight in the desert and rode with our father to Muscat and won another fierce battle there.'

'Not single-handed.' He smiled and traced the line of her mouth with his fingertip. They talked quickly and eagerly, breaking in upon each other and leaving much only half said, before flitting on to another idea.

'What happened to your pet monkey, Jinni?' he asked.

Tears welled up into her eyes, sparkling in the moonlight. 'Jinni is dead,' she whispered. 'Kush found him in his precious garden and beat him to death with a spade. He sent his little body to me as a gift.'

Dorian changed the subject then, distracting her with other more pleasant childhood memories and soon she was laughing again. Then they both fell silent, and she lowered her eyes shyly. Without looking at him she whispered, 'Do you remember how you took me to swim in the sea when we were children? That was the first time I ever remember leaving the zenana.'

'I remember.' His voice was gruff.

'Will you take me again tonight?' She looked up at him. 'Please, Dowie.'

They went down through the trees hand and hand, and found the beach deserted and glistening in the moonlight. The shadows of the palms were purple-black on the sands and the water shone with the oily luminescence of a black pearl.

Since last they had been here, the cave in the sandstone had been excavated deeper by the wave action of the high tides. They paused at the entrance and turned to each other. 'Is what we are doing a sin?' she asked him.

'If it is I do not care,' he replied. 'I know only that I love you and that being with you does not feel to me like a sin.'

'I love you also,' she said. 'I could not love anyone or anything more, though I live a hundred years.' She untied the ribbon at her neck and let her shift drop onto the sand. She wore only pantaloons of silk.

Dorian could not breathe as he gazed at her. Her breasts had swelled, and the tips were dark and pointed. Her skin was smooth and gleamed like the lining of an oyster shell. 'You used to tease me that I looked like a monkey,' she said, half defiant and half timid, fearing his rejection.

'Not any more.' He had caught his breath. 'I have never seen anything more beautiful.'

'I was so afraid I would not please you. I want you to like me, Dowie. Tell me that you like me, please.'

'I love you,' he said. 'I want you to be my woman and my wife.'

She laughed with joy, took his hands and placed them on her breasts. They were warm and pliant, and the nipples hardened as he rolled them gently between his fingers. 'I am your woman. I think I have always been your woman. I do not know how it is done but I want to be your wife here tonight.'

'Are you sure, my darling? If others learned of this, it could mean disgrace and a terrible death.'

'To be without you would be a death far worse than anything that even Kush could contrive. I know that it cannot be for ever, but give me this one night to be your wife. Show me how, Dowie, please, show me how.'

So he spread his robes on the sand and laid her down upon them, and slowly, with infinite gentleness, small sounds of love and wonder, gasps of surprise and, in the end, a single long shuddering spasm of pain that was soon lost in the transport of joy that followed, they became lovers.

Over the days that followed, Dorian was embroiled in the planning of his coming campaign on the mainland across the channel. He purchased most of the draught animals and horses that were available on Lamu, and sent one of his captains with three dhows south to Zanzibar to do the same thing there. He also bought up much of the available grain stocks and trade goods in the markets.

Then he spent hours each day talking to the caravan masters, and the Arab traders who had been in the caravans the marauders had attacked and looted. He tried to find out the identity of the bandits, their numbers, how they were armed and the methods they used to carry out the attacks. He tallied the losses these men had suffered and the totals shocked him. Over three lakhs of gold dust had been stolen, twenty-seven tons of new ivory and almost fifteen thousand freshly captured slaves. The Caliph had every reason to be worried.

As to the marauders themselves, the reports were vague and contradictory. Some said there were white men, Franks, with black archers and spearmen. Another said they were but savages who fought with spear and arrow. One said that they carried out their raids only during the night when the caravans were encamped. Another told how they ambushed his long files of slaves and porters during the day, and murdered all the Arab escorts, and that he alone escaped. Another merchant told how they had spared him and all his men and set them free after stripping them of all their possessions. Dorian realized that there was no agreement as to who they were, and no clear pattern to their methods. Only one thing was clear: the marauders appeared like forest djinns out of the southern wilderness and disappeared back the same way. 'What do they do with the slaves they capture?' he asked, and the Arabs shrugged. 'They must sell them somewhere?' he insisted. 'They would need a fleet of large ships to transport such numbers.'

'There has been no sighting of such a fleet along the Fever Coast,' they told him, and Dorian's puzzlement increased.

He had so little certain information on which he could base his plans. All he could concentrate on was protecting the caravans and getting them moving again, for the trade had almost dried up. Faced with such heavy losses, few of the Arab merchants on Lamu and Zanzibar would take the risk of financing further expeditions.

His other planning revolved around taking the war to the bandits, following them into their fastnesses, tracking them down like the wild animals they were and destroying them. For this purpose he recruited all the scouts and caravan guides who had been left idle by the cessation of trade.

He could not begin the campaign until the weather on the mainland changed, for this was the season of the Big Wet, when the coastal lowlands were inundated with the rains and the Fever Coast lived up to its fearsome reputation. However, he must be ready to sail as soon as the rains ceased and the *kusi* wind started to blow again.

Thinking of the start of the *kusi* always brought his mind back to Yasmini. That same wind would carry her ship north to the Gulf and her marriage. The thought made his guts sour with anger and frustration. He thought of writing to the Caliph in Muscat and asking him to cancel the marriage plans. He even considered confessing his love to his adoptive father and asking him for dispensation to marry Yasmini.

They met each evening after dark, but when he broached this idea to her, Yasmini was terrified and trembled with fear. 'I think not about myself, Dowie, but if our father even suspects that there is the love of a man and a woman between us, no matter how much he loves you, he will be honour-bound to place your case before the mullahs to be judged by the Shari'ah laws. There could be only one verdict for both of us. No, Dowie, there is no escape that way. Our destiny is with God, and He is not always merciful.'

'I will take you away,' Dorian declared. 'We will take one of the dhows and a few of my best men and sail away, find some place where we can live out our love.'

'There is no such place,' Yasmini told him sadly. 'We are both of Islam, and there would be no place in Islam for us. We would be outcasts and wanderers for ever. Here, you are a great man, soon to be greater. You have the love and respect of our father and of all men. I will not let you throw all that away for me.'

They spent much of their precious time together discussing their terrible predicament. They lay in each other's arms in the moonlight and whispered endlessly. When they saw that there was no escape or release for them, they made love with an almost savage passion, as though to divert the fate that loomed before them.

Before dawn each morning, Dorian led her back to the entrance tunnel, where she kissed him as if for the last time, and took the Angel's Road back into the zenana. During the days the girl who had once been playful and happy, loved by all in the zenana, was now pale, silent and lethargic. Her friends and all the servants gradually became alarmed. And there was nothing that happened in that little enclosed world that did not come at last to the ears of Kush.

Their flawed idyll of love and desperation lasted through the months leading up to the change of the monsoon winds. The expeditionary force to the mainland was almost ready to sail, and the final preparations for Yasmini's wedding were complete. Her dowry had been sent from Muscat to her bridegroom in Abu Dhabi, her trousseau was packed and ready to go aboard the dhow that would carry her away to her new home thousands of miles to the north, and the confines of another royal zenana, in which she would pass the rest of her life.

'I cannot let this happen,' Dorian told her. 'I will rescue you from that, even if I have to forsake everything in this life.'

'No, Dowie, I will not let you do it. You will have many other wives in the years ahead, and you will win glory and happiness without me.'

'No,' he said. 'I do not care about the rest. I care only for you.'

'Then I can never come out to you again along the Angel's Road. Unless you promise me to put this madness out of your mind, this will be the last time we will meet, Dowie. You must swear to me.'

'I cannot do that.'

'Then I will never see you again.'

He saw that she was determined. 'Please, Yassie, you cannot be so cruel to both of us.'

'Then make love to me for the last time.'

'Yassie, I cannot go on without you.'

'You are strong. You will go on. Make love to me. Give me something to hold on to, to remember through the years ahead.'

So they parted at the entrance to the tunnel, and Yasmini ran back through the narrow passage, blinded with her tears. As she clambered out of the opening above the tomb of the saint, a huge hand closed on her arm and lifted her off her feet.

As she struggled and kicked, Kush giggled into her face, holding her easily. 'I have waited many years for this, my little harlot. I knew that one day you would place yourself in my power. You were always too bold and headstrong.'

'Leave me!' she screamed. 'Put me down.'

'No,' Kush replied. 'Now you are mine. Never again will you flout my rules. The other women will listen to your screams and they will quail in their beds, and think about the price of sin.'

'My father,' she cried. 'My future husband. They will make you pay dearly if you harm me.'

'Your father barely knows your name. He has many other daughters, and none of them is a whore. Your future husband would never accept rotten half-chewed fruit into his zenana. No, my little one, from now on you belong to Kush alone.'

Kush carried her to the little cell beside the cemetery, in the rear of the gardens, screened from the rest of the zenana by a hedge of flowering thorns. Two of his assistants were waiting there, eunuchs also, big men, gone to fat, but powerful. They had performed this punishment many times before, and they had made all the preparations.

Kush laid Yasmini on the hard wooden frame and carefully took off her clothing. All three were grinning with anticipation, stripped to loincloths but already sweating in the small hot cell. They touched her body as it was revealed, stroking her smooth limbs, sniffing her hair, pinching her small glossy breasts. Then, when she was naked, they strapped her wrists and ankles with leather thongs until she lay spreadeagled and pinioned. Then Kush stood between her legs and smiled down at her, in an almost avuncular fashion.

'You have been taken in harlotry. We know the man,

but it spites me that he is grown too powerful to bring to justice. His punishment will be to hear of your fate. The rest of the world beyond these walls will hear that you died of a fever. Many do, at this season of the year. However, I will make certain that your lover has the truth whispered in his ear. For the rest of his life he will live with the knowledge that he was responsible for your strange, particular death.'

Still smiling he leaned forward and placed his fat hand on her private parts, gently stroking the soft nest of fine dark hair between her thighs. 'I am sure you have heard what happens to all the bad girls who have come to this room. But, in case you are uncertain, I will explain it to you as we go along.'

He nodded to one of the other eunuchs, who came to stand beside Kush holding a wooden tray. On it lay two small packets. They were wrapped in fine rice-paper, fish-shaped, as long as a finger and tapered at both ends. They gleamed in the lamplight, for they had been heavily greased with sheep fat.

'These each contain five ounces of chilli powder. I grow the pods myself in my little garden. They are of the fiercest variety. The juice from my fruit will burn the skin and flesh from the mouth of a Mogul, fed all his life on the strongest curries. I have to wear gloves of dogskin to protect my hands when I grind the powder.'

Suddenly he thrust his fat forefinger deep into her. 'One for this pretty perfumed little hole in front.' He grinned down at her as she screamed with shock, pain and humiliation. Then he pulled out his finger, and thrust it in again further back. 'And the second packet for this other, darker cavern at the rear.' He withdrew his finger, sniffed it, wrinkled his nose and pulled a face at the other two eunuchs. They tittered with delight.

He picked up one of the packets from the tray. Yasmini stared at it in horror and struggled against her bonds. 'Hold her legs,' he grunted at the other two. One of them forced her knees as far apart as they would go. Kush spread the silky fur and the soft lips beyond. Then, with the expertise bred of practice, he slipped the greased packet into her body.

'See how al-Amhara has opened the way for me and made my task easier,' he said, then stood back and wiped his fingers on his loincloth. 'The front end done. Now for the rear,' he said, and picked up the other packet. His assistant reached under Yasmini's body and took one of her small round buttocks in each hand and drew them rudely apart.

She was gnawing her lips and her teeth were stained pink with her own blood. She whipped her lithe golden body back and forth as far as her bonds would allow, and tears ran back into her hair.

With his free hand Kush groped between her buttocks. 'Open it wider!' he told the other man. 'Yes, that's better. So sweet and tight.'

Yasmini's sobs ended with a sharp high squeal. 'Ah, yes,' Kush gloated. 'That's it. All the way. As far as I can reach.'

He stepped back. 'Shabash! It is done. Bind her ankles and her knees together so that she cannot expel the sweetmeats.' They worked swiftly, then stood back and surveyed their handiwork with satisfaction.

'Now go out and finish digging the whore's grave.' They went out into the cemetery, and soon there came the sound of their spades biting into the sandy earth, their jovial banter as they worked.

Kush came to Yasmini's side. 'Your bier is ready, and the sheet to cover you when we lower you into the earth.' He pointed them out to her against the far wall. 'And see, I have even carved your headboard with my own loving hands.' He held it up for her to read. 'It has the date of your death, and tells the world that you died of fever.'

Yasmini was silent now, her body rigid. Her eyes, wide and glittering with tears, were fastened on his face as he bent over her.

'You see, the chilli powder is so virulent that it will eat its way through the rice-paper, while from the outside the juices of your own body will moisten and weaken it further. Soon the packet will dissolve and the powder will be released into your secret places.'

He stroked her hair back from her forehead, then with his thumb wiped the tears from her eyelids with feminine gentleness. 'At first you will feel a tiny stinging, which will grow into a fire, a raging fire that will make you long for the lesser heat of hell. I have watched many whores die upon this wooden bed, but I do not think there are words to describe their suffering. It will eat out your womb and your bowels like a hundred rats burrowing into your soft-ness, and your screams will carry to every woman in the zenana. They will remember you when next they are tempted to sin.'

He was breathing heavily now, and his expression was rapt, deeply aroused by the picture of suffering he was painting. 'When will it begin?' he asked rhetorically. 'We cannot be sure. In an hour, or two, or even longer, there is no way of telling. How long will it last? I cannot tell you. I have seen the weak ones die in a day, and the strong ones last four days, screaming to the end. I think you are one of the strong ones, but we will see.'

He went to the doorway and called to the men who were digging the grave, 'Are you not finished yet? You cannot come and watch the fun until you are finished.'

'Soon.' One paused and leaned on his spade. Only the top of his shaved head was visible above the rim of the excavation. 'We will be finished before the first packet bursts open.'

Kush went back into the hut, and settled his bulk comfortably on the bench against the far wall. 'The waiting is the interesting part,' he told Yasmini. 'Some beg for mercy, but I know you are too proud for that. Sometimes the brave ones try to conceal from me the moment when the paper breaks open. They try to deny me my enjoyment, but not for long.' He giggled. 'Not for very long.'

He folded his arms across his soft, womanly breasts, and leaned back against the wall. 'I will be beside you to the end, Yasmini, to share each exquisite moment with you. And I shall probably shed a tear at your graveside, for I am a man of sentiment, and soft-hearted.'

The word that Kush had taken another girl to the little hut beside the graveyard spread swiftly through the zenana, and the instant that Tahi heard the rumour she knew with dreadful certainty who the girl was. She also knew exactly what she must do. She did not hesitate but threw on a shawl and veil, and picked up the basket in which she always brought back her purchases from the town when she was sent on errands by one of the royal wives or concubines. As an ancient free woman, she could pass without check between the zenana and the open world beyond the walls, and among her duties was the daily trip into the markets. She left her dingy room at the rear of the kitchen block, and hurried along the cloisters. She was terrified that one of the eunuchs would stop her before she reached the gates.

A deep, unnatural silence hung like a pall over the zenana and the gardens, and the cloisters were deserted. No child laughed, no woman sang, and the fires in the kitchen were dead and cold. Every inhabitant of the women's world had locked herself and her offspring in her own quarters. It was so quiet that, when Tahi stopped to listen, all she could hear was her own blood pulsing in her ears.

Only one of the eunuch guards was on the gate, but he knew her well. He was so distracted by the hushed air of drama that he hardly glanced at her face as she drew back her veil to identify herself. He waved her through with one pudgy, beringed hand.

The moment she was out of sight of the gate, she flung away the basket and broke into a heavy run. Within a mile her heart felt so swollen with fatigue that she could hardly breathe. She fell on the verge of the track and could not force her legs to carry her another step.

A slave-boy came out of the fields, driving two donkeys ahead of him, laden with bundles of mangrove bark, for tanning leather. Tahi staggered to her feet and hunted under her robes for her purse. 'My daughter is dying,' she called to the boy. 'I must fetch the doctor to her.' She held up a silver rupee. 'Take me to him and there will be another coin for you when we arrive at the fort.'

The lad ogled the coin then nodded vigorously. He untied one of the bundles of bark and let it fall on the verge. He boosted Tahi onto the donkey's back then whipped the little animal into a trot and ran behind it, laughing and calling to Tahi, 'Hold on tight, old mother. Rabat is swift as an arrow. We will have you at the port before you have time to blink twice.'

Dorian sat on the terrace with Ben Abram at his side. They were drinking cups of black tarry coffee and were engrossed in compiling a list of the medical supplies that would be needed by the expedition to the mainland. The pair had joyously renewed their friendship at almost the same minute that Dorian had stepped ashore on the beach at Lamu. Every day Ben Abram had come to join him in the morning prayers, and afterwards they sat long together in the pleasant, easy conversation of old friends.

'I am too old to leave the island,' Ben Abram was protesting at Dorian's insistence that he join the expedition to care for the health of the soldiers.

'We both know that you are as strong and as spry as the first day we met,' Dorian told him. 'Would you let me die of some horrible disease in the interior? I need you, Ben Abram.'

Dorian broke off as he heard a commotion at the end of the terrace. He stood up and shouted irritably at the guards, 'What is this uproar? You have my strict orders that I am not to be disturbed.'

'I am as dust under your feet, great sheikh. But there is an old crone here who kicks and scratches like a rabid wildcat.'

Dorian exclaimed with annoyance, and was about to order them to send the woman off with a swat across her buttocks, when she screeched, 'Al-Amhara! It is me, Tahi! In the name of Allah, let me speak to you of someone we both love.'

Dorian went cold with dread. Tahi would never have been so indiscreet unless some terrible disaster had over-taken Yasmini. 'Let her pass,' he shouted to the guards, and hurried to meet the old woman as she tottered down the terrace, far gone with fatigue and worry.

She collapsed at his feet and clung to his knees. 'Kush knows about you and the girl. He was waiting for Yasmini as she came back to the zenana and he has taken her to the little room beside the graveyard,' she blurted out.

From his own sojourn behind the zenana walls, Dorian knew about the little room. Although it was strictly forbid-den, the small boys of the zenana had dared each other to creep beyond the thorn hedge and go into it to touch the dreadful wooden frame. They terrified each other with horror stories of what Kush did to the women he took there. One of the most chilling memories of all Dorian's days within the zenana were the shrieks of a girl named Salima who had been taken there, after Kush had discovered her love for a young officer of the governor's guard. Those cries had lasted four days and three nights, growing slowly weaker all that time, and the silence at the end was more harrowing than the shrillest scream had been.

For long moments he was unmanned by Tahi's warning. He felt the strength go out of his legs so that he could not move them, and his mind went blank, as though trying to hide from the horror of it. Then, with a shudder, he threw off the weakness and turned to Ben Abram. The old doctor had come to his feet. His expression was filled with alarm tempered with compassion. 'I should not have heard those words, my son. You must have been foolish, mad, beyond any reason. But my heart breaks for you.'

'Help me, old friend,' Dorian pleaded. 'Yes, I have been foolish and I have committed a terrible sin, but it was the sin of love. You know what Kush will do to her.'

Ben Abram nodded. 'I have seen the fruits of his monstrous cruelty.'

'Ben Abram, I need your help.' By the sheer intensity of his gaze, Dorian tried to will him to it.

'I cannot enter the zenana,' the old man said.

'If I bring her out to you, will you help us?'

'Yes, my son. If you can bring her out to me, I will help you, if it is not too late.' Ben Abram turned to Tahi. 'When did he take her to the little room?'

'I know not. Perhaps two hours ago.' Tahi sobbed.

'Then we have very little time,' said Ben Abram briskly. 'I have the instruments I need with me. We can go at once.'

'You will never be able to keep pace with me, old father.' Dorian strapped on his sword-belt. 'Come after me as fast as you can ride. There is a secret way under the walls on the east side.' Swiftly he described how to find the entrance to the tunnel.

'I have ridden past there, and remember the old ruins,' Ben Abram murmured.

'Wait for me there,' Dorian said, then raced down the staircase, three steps at a time, and into the courtyard. As he ran to the stables, he saw that one of the grooms was leading out his black stallion to curry it in the yard. The horse had a halter on its lean Arabian head, and was one of the fleetest in Dorian's string of fine animals that the Caliph had pressed on him as a parting gift when he left Muscat.

He snatched the single rein out of the startled groom's hand and vaulted onto the stallion's bare back. As he hammered his heels into the horse's flanks the stallion jumped away, and before they reached the gates of the fort he was at full gallop.

They raced through the narrow streets, scattering chickens, dogs and terrified people from their path. As they burst out of the narrow lanes into the open country, Dorian lay flat along the stallion's neck and pushed him to the top of his speed. 'Go!' he whispered in his ear, and the stallion flicked back his ears to listen. 'Run for the very life of my love.'

There was a short-cut through the mangroves. Dorian turned the horse off the main road and they splashed through the mud for a hundred yards until they hit firm ground again then sped through the palm grove on the far side, saving almost half a mile.

The high walls of the zenana were white through the boles of the palms, and he sheered off towards the beach to keep out of sight of the gate. Once he was clear, he swung back again and galloped along the base of the wall. He saw the mound of ruins just ahead and leaped down with one arm around the stallion's neck, his feet skimming the earth. He let go before the horse had stopped and used the momentum to hurl himself up the side of the tumbled ruins and down into the saucer beyond.

He dragged aside the trailing branches and ran into the dark opening. The interior was narrower and lower than he remembered it, and it was pitch dark. When the uneven floor started to rise under his feet he almost fell. At last he saw ahead the dim light from the exit hole and could go on even faster. He jumped up, caught the rim of the opening and with a single movement heaved himself through and out onto the sunlit terrace where, long ago, Yasmini and her little friends had played with their dolls. It was deserted. He crossed it with long strides and dropped down the staircase on which Zayn al-Din had injured his ankle into the garden below.

At the bottom he paused to take his bearings. A pall of silence hung over the zenana and the gardens. None of the female slaves tended the flower-beds and fountains, no person moved, and there was no birdsong. In the hush the very breeze had dropped, as though all nature held its breath. The palm fronds drooped silently and not a leaf stirred on the high tops of the casuarina trees.

He drew his sword, knowing that he would kill without hesitation any of the eunuchs who tried to stop him, and went towards the north end of the enclosure, towards the mosque and the cemetery.

He ran down the narrow lane between the outer wall and behind the mosque. Ahead was the thorn hedge that surrounded the cemetery. He ducked through the well-remembered gap and looked across the burial ground. Each grave mound had a headboard set above it and some of the newer graves were still decorated with faded ribbons and flags.

The hut was on the far side, and the thorn hedge had almost overgrown and smothered it in the years since he had last seen it. The door was open and Dorian held his breath as he listened for any sound of suffering coming from the interior. The quiet was suffocating and ominous, seemingly charged with evil.

Then he heard voices, the high feminine chatter of a castrated man. He hid the sword under a fold of his robe and slipped forward silently. There was a gust of giggles and he saw one of the eunuchs sitting on the edge of a newly dug grave, his feet swinging into the hole, the rolls of his belly fat hanging into his lap. Dorian stepped up behind him. He could see the knuckles of his spine through the fat, as the man leaned forward to speak to somebody in the pit beneath him. Dorian drove the needle point of the long curved blade of his scimitar through the joint between two vertebrae, separating the spinal cord with a surgeon's stroke. The eunuch died without a murmur, collapsed and slid into the hole, his weight pulling him off the blade. He fell like a sack of lard on the man beneath him.

Trapped under his weight, the other man squealed with outrage and struggled to free himself. 'What are you doing, Sharif? Have you gone mad? Get off me.' He pushed off the corpse and rose to his feet. The top of his head was just below ground level, and he was still peering down at the dead man lying at his feet. 'Get up, Sharif. What game are you playing?'

The top of his shaven head looked like an ostrich egg. Dorian raised the sword, then slashed down, splitting his skull neatly in half down to the level of his teeth. With a twist of his wrist he levered the blade from the crisp bone of the skull and turned to the door of the hut.

He ran to it, and as he reached it Kush appeared before him, blocking the door with his huge bulk. They stared at each other for only a fleeting moment, but Kush recognized him. He had been among the crowd on the beach when Dorian had stepped ashore on his arrival with the flotilla from Muscat.

With astonishing speed and agility for such a gross

creature, he leaped back into the room, and snatched up a spade that stood against the wall. With another leap he put the heavy wooden frame on which Yasmini was stretched out between himself and Dorian, and raised the spade high over the girl.

'Stay back!' he screamed. 'With a single blow I can burst the bags inside her and release the poison.'

Yasmini lay naked under his threat, her long slim legs trussed tightly together at ankle and knee, and her arms stretched out over her head, pulling her tender golden breasts out of shape. She looked up at Dorian, but even her huge eyes were not large or deep enough to contain all her terror.

Dorian launched himself across the room, just as Kush started to bring down the spade with all his strength behind it. Dorian came in under the blow before it struck Yasmini in her tender midriff, spreading his body over hers, shielding her. The spade struck his back and he felt his ribs crack. Pain flared through his chest.

He rolled over the frame, forcing himself to ignore the pain, careful not to place his weight on her body and break the fragile sacks. Kush lifted the spade again and this time aimed at Dorian's head. His fat face was a mask of fury, and his great belly bulged forward over his loincloth. Dorian's whole left side was numb from the blow, and he was down on one knee, unable to rise in time to meet the next.

He still had the sword in his right hand. He reached out with the blade and drew the edge across Kush's belly from side to side at the level of his navel, opening him up the way a fishwife splits the stomach of a grouper. Kush dropped the spade, which clattered on the stone floor. He reeled back against the far wall and, with both hands, tried to hold the lips of the long wound closed. He stared down at it with an air of astonishment, and watched his own entrails bulge out between his fingers in slippery ropes. The hot, fetid stink of his ruptured gut filled the little room.

Dorian dragged himself to his feet. His left arm dangled at his side, numb and useless, and he leaned over Yasmini.

'I prayed that you would come,' she whispered. 'I did not think it was possible, and now it's too late. Kush has put terrible things inside me.'

'I know what he has done,' Dorian told her. 'Don't talk. Lie still.'

Kush gave a high, keening cry, but Dorian barely glanced at him as he slumped forward on his face then kicked and struggled weakly in the mess of his own guts.

Dorian slipped the blade of his scimitar between Yasmini's ankles and cut the leather thongs. Then he did the same for those at her knees. 'Don't try to sit up. Any contraction might burst the bags.'

With a touch of the razor edge he cut the bonds that held her wrists, then dropped the sword and massaged his paralysed left arm. With a surge of relief he felt it begin to tingle and the strength flowing down it to his fingertips. He slipped his arm under Yasmini's shoulders, lifted her carefully off the wooden frame and set her on her feet.

'Squat,' he ordered, 'slowly. Make no sudden movement.' He helped her down. 'Now spread your knees apart and push gently as though you were at stool.' He knelt down beside her and placed his arm around her shoulders. 'Gently to begin with, then harder.'

She took a deep breath and bore down, her face contorted and darkened with blood. There was a sudden spluttering sound and one of the packets was driven out of her body with such force that it hit the floor between her feet and burst open, spilling the red powder across the flagstones. The acrid chemical smell of chilli mingled with the stink of Kush's faeces, and stung their nostrils. 'Good!

Well done, Yassie.' He held her tighter. 'Can you do the same with the other sack?'

'I will try.' She took another breath and strained again. But after a minute she gave a sharp sigh and shook her head. 'No, it will not move. I can't do it.'

'Ben Abram is waiting at the end of the Angel's Road,' he said. 'I am taking you to him. He will know what to do.'

Gently he lifted her to her feet. 'You must not try to walk. The least movement might burst the bag. Slowly now, put one arm around my neck. Hold on.'

He slipped his good arm under her knees and lifted her easily. As he strode to the door, Kush was moaning and blubbering, 'Help me. Don't leave me. I am dying.' Dorian did not look back.

He skirted the open grave in the bottom of which lay the two dead eunuchs. He went quickly, dreading meeting another for he had left his scimitar on the floor of the hut, and he did not yet have full use of his injured arm. Much more, he dreaded jolting or squeezing Yasmini. He had to try to balance speed against caution, and he whispered soft reassurance to her as he went, trying to calm and comfort her. 'It will be all right, my little one. Ben Abram will be able to rid you of it. It will soon be over.'

He crossed the lawns with a smooth stride that cushioned his precious burden, and he climbed the staircase to the terrace of the saint's tomb one step at a time, treading lightly. He lowered her through the opening into the tunnel, and when he scrambled down beside her he peered anxiously into her face for any sign that the movement had triggered something unspeakable within her tender womanhood. 'Are you all right?' he asked. She nodded, and tried to smile. 'We are nearly there now. Ben Abram is waiting.' He lifted her again, and had to bend almost double to clear the low roof as he started down the tunnel.

He saw the light ahead and almost involuntarily took

a longer step. A fragment of loose coral rolled under his foot, and he stumbled and almost fell, bumping her into the wall.

'Ah!' Yasmini gasped as she was jolted, and Dorian felt his heart constrict.

'What is it, my darling?'

'It stings inside me,' she whispered. 'Oh, Allah, it burns!'

He ran the last few paces and carried her out into the sunlit saucer among the ruins.

'Ben Abram!' Dorian shouted. 'In God's Name, where are you?'

'Here, my son.' Ben Abram stood up from where he had been waiting in the shade and hurried to them, lugging his bag.

'It has begun, old father. Make haste.'

They laid her on the ground, and Dorian gasped out an almost incoherent explanation of how Yasmini had rid herself of one packet. 'But the other is still inside her, and it has begun to leak.'

'Hold her knees up like this,' Ben Abram said, and then, to Yasmini, 'I am going to hurt you. These are the instruments I use in childbirth.' They glittered in his hands.

She closed her eyes. 'I submit myself to the Will of God,' she murmured, and dug her fingernails into Dorian's forearm as Ben Abram went to work.

The evidence of her pain rippled across her lovely face, and tightened and twisted her lips. Once she made a small mewing sound, and Dorian whispered helplessly, 'I love you, flower of my heart.'

'I love you, Dowie,' she gasped, 'but there is a burning fire inside me.'

'I am going to cut you now,' Ben Abram said.

A moment later Yasmini cried out and her whole body stiffened. Dorian looked down and saw blood on Ben

Abram's hands as he took up a silver instrument, shaped like a double spoon. A minute later he sat back on his heels, with the blood-smeared, sodden, half-disintegrated packet captured between the spoons. 'I have it!' he said. 'But it has leaked the spice into her. We must get her down to the water quickly.'

Dorian snatched her up, his injured arm and the pain of his cracked ribs forgotten. He ran with Yasmini's naked body clutched to his chest. Ben Abram hobbled along behind them, losing distance as Dorian tore away between the palm trees. He ran down the beach and into the ocean, plunging Yasmini into the cool green water. Ben Abram came in after them with a brass enema syringe in his hand. Dorian held Yasmini's lower body beneath the surface while Ben Abram repeatedly filled the tube of the syringe with sea-water and forced it into her. It was almost half an hour before he was satisfied and allowed Dorian to carry her out of the water and up the beach.

She was trembling with shock and pain. Dorian wrapped her in his woollen shawl and they laid her in a shaded place under the trees. Ben Abram took a large bottle of salve from his bag, and anointed her injuries. After a while her shivering abated, and she told them, 'The pain is passing now. It still burns, but not as badly.'

'I was able to remove most of the poison in the spoons. I think I managed to flush out the rest before it did much damage. I had to cut you to reach the sack, but it is a clean cut and I will stitch it up now. The salve will heal the wound swiftly.' He smiled at her encouragingly as he prepared a needle and catgut. 'You have been lucky, and you have Tahi and al-Salil to thank for that.'

'What will we do now, Dowie?' She held out one hand to Dorian. He took it and squeezed it. 'I can never go back into the zenana.' She looked like the little monkey-faced girl again, pale and huddled in the shawl, bedraggled wet hair hanging limply over her shoulders, eyes underlined with purple shadows of pain.

'You are never going back into the zenana again, I give you my oath on it.' Dorian leaned across and kissed her bruised, swollen lips. Then he stood up and his expression turned grim. 'I must leave you here with Ben Abram while he finishes his work,' he said. 'I also have work to do, but I will return very soon, before Ben Abram is done. Be brave, my love.'

He strode back through the trees, jumped down into the saucer and went along the tunnel under the walls of the zenana. He climbed out cautiously onto the terrace of the saint's tomb, and took a minute to listen and watch. All was still deathly quiet, so he dropped down the stairs and crossed the lawns. He paused behind the thorn hedge of the graveyard and satisfied himself that the corpses of the eunuchs had not been discovered or the alarm raised. Then he went forward cautiously.

At the door of the hut he paused to allow his eyes to adjust to the gloom after the strong sunlight. Kush was curled up on the floor in the position of an unborn child in the womb. His bloody hands were still clutching his open stomach, and his eyes were closed. Dorian thought he was dead, but as he stepped up to the eunuch he opened his eyes. His expression changed. 'Please help old Kush,' he muttered. 'You were always a good boy, al-Amhara. You would not let me die.'

Dorian stooped and picked up his sword from the floor. Kush became more animated. 'No, don't kill me. In the name of Allah, I beg you for mercy.'

Dorian slid the blade into the scabbard on his belt, and Kush whimpered with relief, 'I said you were a good boy. Help me onto the litter.' He tried to crawl towards the bier that he would have used to take Yasmini to her grave, but the movement opened the great wound in his belly. Fresh blood trickled out, and he subsided again, clutching himself. 'Help me, al-Amhara. Call others to help carry me to a surgeon.'

Dorian's expression was merciless as he stooped and seized Kush's ankles, then leaned back and dragged him across the floor towards the door. 'No! Don't do that! You will open the wound further,' Kush squealed, but Dorian ignored his protests. There was a long slippery mark of blood and gastric juices on the flags behind Kush. Dorian hauled him feet first through the doorway into the sunlight. Kush moaned and grabbed the jamb of the door, hanging on to it with the strength of a drowning man. Dorian dropped his legs and in one movement almost too swift for the eye to follow he drew and swung his scimitar, lopping off the three fingers of Kush's right hand that were clawed around the doorpost. Kush howled and held his mutilated hand to his chest. He stared down at it in horrified astonishment. 'You have maimed me,' he stuttered.

Dorian sheathed the sword, seized the eunuch's ankles again, and dragged him through the dirt of the cemetery towards the open grave. They had covered half the short distance before Kush realized what he intended. Now his screams were high and girlish, and he rolled and struggled so that his dangling entrails flapped and twisted in the sand.

'The women listening to your caterwauling will think your foul packets have burst in Yasmini's belly,' Dorian grunted. 'Sing on, you great bag of pig fat. There is no one to help you now, this side of the devil in hell.'

With one last heave he tipped Kush into the grave, on top of the other two bodies, and looked down at him, standing with both hands on his hips while he recovered his breath, and waited for the pain in his broken ribs to subside a little. Kush read his own death in those green eyes.

'Mercy!' He tried to rise, but the agony in his guts was

too great and he drew up his knees to his chest, and huddled against the side wall of new-cut earth.

Dorian went back and fetched the spade. When he returned and took up the first spadeful of earth, Kush screamed, 'No, no! How can you do this thing to me?'

'As easily as you performed your unspeakable cruelties upon the defenceless women in your charge,' Dorian replied. Kush screamed and pleaded until the earth smothered his cries. Dorian worked on doggedly, until the grave was filled in over the three bodies. Then he stamped it down and shaped the mound neatly.

From the hut, he fetched the headboard with Yasmini's name carved on it, and planted it on the mound. He tied a burial ribbon around it with the prayer for the dead embroidered on it. Then he replaced the spade in the hut, gathered up the pieces of severed leather thongs and took down Kush's robes from where the eunuch had hung them on a peg in the wall. He rolled them into a bundle and tied it with a length of leather thong.

Before he left the room, he glanced around to make certain that all was in order, and smiled grimly. 'For the next hundred years the poets will sing of the disappearance of the three eunuchs after they had murdered and buried the lovely Princess Yasmini. Perhaps the devil himself came to escort them down to hell. Nobody will ever know. But what a fine legend it will make for posterity.'

Then he left the zenana for the last time along the Angel's Road.

When Dorian returned to where he had left them, Ben Abram had finished stitching Yasmini's injuries, and was binding them up with a wad of cotton.

'It is well done, al-Salil,' he assured Dorian. 'Seven days from now I will remove the stitches and within a month she will be completely healed, as though it never happened.'

Dorian wrapped Yasmini in Kush's soft robes of finest wool, then helped her gently onto the stallion's back, holding her across his lap, so that there was no pressure on her wounds. They started back at a sedate pace towards the fort. She was so completely swathed in the voluminous robes that no inquisitive person they passed on the road would be able to tell if she were man or woman.

'No one outside the zenana has ever seen your face before. They will never recognize you as the Princess Yasmini, for she lies under her headboard in the graveyard of the zenana.'

'Am I really free, Dowie?' she whispered with difficulty, for despite his care the stitches were pulling painfully.

'No, you silly little baggage. You are now the slave-boy who belongs to the great Sheikh al-Salil. You will never be free.'

'Never?' she asked. 'Promise me that I will be your slave for ever. That you will never let me go.'

'I swear it to you.'

'Then I am well content.' She laid her head on his shoulder.

For many weeks thereafter strange rumours were whispered in the souks of Lamu about the disappearance of Kush, the eunuch. He had been well known in the islands, feared and hated even outside the walls of the zenana. Some said that while walking on the road by night he had been taken by the forest djinns. In another version of the same story the abductor was Shaitan himself. The more pragmatic believed he had stolen from his master, Caliph al-Malik, and that, fearful of discovery and retribution, the eunuch had hired a dhow to take him across the channel and had fled into the interior of Africa. To give substance to this theory, the Sheikh al-Salil issued a warrant for the arrest of Kush and offered a reward of ten thousand rupees for his capture. After a month or so when nothing further was heard of the eunuch, the idlers in the souks lost interest in the case.

The new topic of discussion on the island became the cessation of the *kaskazi* winds, the beginning of the *kusi*, and the opening of a new trading season. Also, the imminent departure of the expeditionary army of Sheikh al-Salil for the mainland diverted interest from three missing eunuchs.

Among the sheikh's large retinue few took much notice of the new slave-boy, Yassie. Though the lad was remarkably pretty and graceful of body, even in his ankle-length robes, at first he seemed in ill health, shy and uncertain of himself. However, the servant-woman Tahi, the childhood nurse of the sheikh and herself a newcomer to the household, took the boy under her protection. Yassie shared her quarters, and soon his beauty and pleasant ways won over all the other servants and slaves.

Yassie had a trilling unbroken voice and played the sistrum with rare skill. When Sheikh al-Salil sent for him every evening to sing to him in his private chambers, soothing away the worries and cares of the day, none of the household thought it strange. Within weeks Yassie had obviously found special favour with his master, and was made one of the sheikh's body-servants. Then the sheikh ordered Yassie to spread his sleeping mat in the tiny curtained alcove off his sleeping chamber, within easy call of al-Salil's own bed, so that he could minister to his needs during the night.

On the first night of this new arrangement, al-Salil returned late from the war council with his dhow captains on the terrace. Yassie had been dozing while he waited for him, and sprang to his feet as al-Salil entered the chamber, attended by Batula. Yassie had pitchers of hot water ready on the brazier, and after Batula helped the sheikh strip down to his loincloth, Yassie poured the water over al-Salil's head and body so that he could bathe. In the meantime Batula hung his master's weapons on the pegs beside his bed, sword and dagger honed, shield burnished, then came to kneel for his master's pleasure.

'You may leave me now, Batula, but wake me in the hour before dawn, for there remains much still to be done before we sail.' As he spoke, al-Salil dried himself on the cloth Yassie handed him. 'Sleep well, Batula, and may the eyes of God watch over your slumbers.'

The moment the curtains fell over the doorway behind Batula, Dorian and Yasmini grinned at each other, and he reached out for her. 'I have waited too long,' he said, but she danced back out of reach.

'I have my duties to complete, noble master. I must dress your hair and oil your body.'

She knelt behind him while he sat on a silk rug and, with a cloth, she rubbed his hair until it was almost dry, then combed it out and plaited it into a single thick braid down his naked back. While she worked she gave small murmurs of admiration and awe. 'So thick and beautiful, the colour of gold and saffron.'

Then she massaged his shoulders with perfumed coconut oil, and touched the scars on his body. 'Where did this happen?'

'At a place called the Pass of the Bright Gazelle.' His eyes were closed and he submitted to the skilful touch of her fingers, for in the zenana she had been taught the arts of pleasing a future husband. When he was lulled and almost asleep, she leaned forward. 'Are you still so ticklish here, Dowie?' And she thrust her tongue deep into his ear.

It galvanized him, and he gasped in protest. Goose-pimples rose on his muscled forearms, and he reached back and grabbed her around the waist. 'You must be taught more respect, slave.' He carried her to the bed, dropped her on it and knelt astride her, pinning her arms above her head. For a while they laughed into each other's face, then the laughter stopped. He bent his head and laid his mouth on hers.

Her lips opened warm and wet to receive him, and she whispered, into his mouth, 'I did not know that my heart could hold so much love!'

'Thou hast too many clothes,' he murmered, and swiftly she wriggled out of them, arching her back to let him draw them out from under her and throw them onto the floor.

'Thou art beautiful beyond the telling of it,' he said, considering the silky golden length of her, 'but is thy body healed?'

'It is, completely. But do not take my word for it, master, prove it to thine own satisfaction, and to mine.'

Whenthe *kusi* wind blew steady and strong down the channel, and the skies were burning blue, devoid of thunderheads, the flotilla of Sheikh al-Salil sailed from Lamu, and three days later made its landfall on the African mainland.

Under the waving silk of the blue banner they disembarked, and the long lines of armed men and draught animals wound away from the Fever Coast, marching inland along the slave road into the interior.

The sheikh rode in the van, and close behind him followed the slave-boy, Yassie. Some of the men remarked on the adoration and hero-worship with which the lad looked at his master, and smiled indulgently.

For the long months after their escape from Zanzibar Tom Courtney explored the coast of the mainland. He kept well south of the Arab trade routes, avoiding any encounter with the Omani, either on land or sea. They were looking for the river mouth that Fundi, the elephant hunter, called the Lunga.

Without the little man's help they might never have found the entrance, for the channel doubled back upon itself, forming an optical illusion, so that from the sea the land seemed unbroken, and a ship might sail past without suspecting the existence of the river mouth.

Once the little vessel was safely into the channel, Tom launched the two longboats. In them he sent Luke Jervis and Alf Wilson to follow the main channel, and guide the *Swallow* through. There were many false channels and dead ends among the papyrus beds, but they threaded their way along them. Many a time they were forced to turn back when the channel they were following pinched out. It took them days of searching and gruelling labour to warp the *Swallow* through, and Tom gave thanks for her shallow draught. Without it they would never have been able to cross the numerous sandbars and shallows. Eventually they came out into the main flow of the river.

The papyrus beds were infested by villainous-looking crocodiles and grunting, bellowing river-horses. Over them hung a canopy of swarming insects. Vast flocks of shrieking, bleating wildfowl rose from the reeds as they passed.

Abruptly the reed beds fell away, and they sailed through stretches of meadowlike flood plains, and stands of open forest on either bank. Here, herds of strange animals lifted their heads from grazing and watched the little vessels pass, then snorted with alarm and stampeded away into the forest. Their numbers and variety were bewildering, and the sailors crowded the ship's rail to stare and marvel at them.

There were graceful antelope, some the size of English red deer, others much larger, with strange, fantastic horns, scimitar-shaped or lunate or corkscrewed, not antlered like the deer they knew from home. Each day they went ashore to hunt these animals. The game was confiding, obviously never having seen white men with firearms, so that the hunters were able to approach within easy musket shot and bring them down with a well-placed lead ball. They never lacked for meat, and they pickled and dried what they could not eat immediately.

Once they had butchered the kill, gutting and quartering the carcasses, even stranger creatures came to scavenge the bones and offal they left on the riverbank. The first to arrive were carrion birds, undertaker storks and vultures of half a dozen species, which filled the sky above with a dark, revolving cloud then swooped in to settle. Graceful and majestic in flight, they were grotesque and gruesome in repose.

After the birds came spotted dog-like creatures that whooped and wailed like banshees, and little red foxes with black backs and silver flanks. Then they saw the first lions. Tom did not need Aboli to tell him what these great maned cats were: he recognized them from the coats-of-arms of kings and noblemen in England, and from the illustrations in a hundred books in the library at High Weald. The roaring and monstrous grunting of these beasts in the night thrilled the men as they swung in their hammocks, and Sarah crept closer into Tom's arms in the narrow bunk in their little cabin.

In the forests and glades they searched for sign of elephant, their intended quarry, whose tusks would repay them for all this effort and endeavour. Fundi and Aboli pointed out great pad marks moulded rock hard in the sun-baked clay. 'These were made last season in the Big Wet,' they told Tom. Then they came across trees in the forest that had been cast down as though by a mighty wind, stripped of their topmost branches and bark. But the trees were dried out, and their injuries long ago withered.

'A year ago,' said Fundi. 'The herds have gone on and might not return for many seasons.'

The land became hilly and the Lunga river twisted through the valleys, becoming swifter, flawed with rapids. Soon they could force their way through only with difficulty, for boulders and sharp black rocks guarded the channel, and each mile they went put the little *Swallow* in deeper peril.

In the end there was a place where the river formed an oxbow around a low, forested hill. Tom and Sarah went ashore and climbed to the top. They sat together on the brow and Tom surveyed the land below them through his telescope. 'It's a natural fortress,' he said at last. 'We are surrounded on three sides by the river. We need only build a palisade across the narrow neck, and we will be secure from man and animal.' Then he turned and pointed out a small bay with smooth rock sides. 'There is a perfect mooring for the *Swallow*.'

'What will we do here?' Sarah asked. 'For there are still no elephants.'

'This will be our base camp,' he explained. 'From here we can press on into the interior by longboat or on foot, until we find the herds that Fundi has promised us.'

They built a palisade of heavy logs across the neck of the oxbow. They took ashore the cannon from the *Swallow* and mounted them in earthen emplacements to cover the glacis in front of the palisade. Then they constructed wooden huts and plastered the walls with mud, and thatched them with reeds from the riverbank.

Dr Reynolds set up his clinic in one of the huts and laid out his surgical instruments and medicines. Each day he forced every member of the party to swallow a spoonful of the bitter grey quinine powder he had purchased in the markets of Zanzibar, and though the drug made their ears sing, and they protested and cursed him for it, there was no fever in the camp. Sarah became his willing apprentice, and soon she could stitch up the gash in a foot caused by a carelessly swung axe or administer a purge or bleed a sick man with as much aplomb as her teacher.

Sarah chose the site for their living hut at a discreet distance from the others. It had a fine view over the river valley to blue mountains in the distance. She used cotton cloth from the bolts of trade goods to sew curtains and bedclothes. Then she designed the furniture and had the ship's carpenters build it for her.

Ned Tyler had a farmer's instincts, and to augment the diet of venison and biscuit, he started a vegetable garden with seeds he had brought from England. He watered them through irrigation ditches he dug on the riverbank. Then he fought a never-ending war with the monkeys and apes that came to raid the green sprouts as they pushed out through the soil.

Within a few months the camp was complete, and Sarah named it Fort Providence. A week later, Tom loaded the longboats with trade goods, powder, muskets and shot. With Fundi to guide them, he set out on a hunting and exploring expedition further upstream in search of the elusive elephant herds, and of the native tribes with whom they could open trade.

Ned Tyler was left, with five men, in charge of Fort Providence. Sarah remained with Ned also, for Tom would not allow her to make the journey upstream until he knew what dangers lay ahead. She would take over Dr Reynolds's duties from him in his absence, and she had plans to continue her home-building work. She stood on the landing and waved to Tom until the longboats disappeared around the next bend in the river.

Three days' travel beyond the fort, the longboats moored for the night at a confluence with a smaller stream. While they gathered firewood and built shelters of thorn branches to keep out nocturnal predators, Fundi and Aboli scouted the banks of the stream. They had been gone for only a short while before Fundi came scurrying back through the trees. His eyes were dancing with excitement as he poured out a flood of gabbled explanation. When he came to the end, Tom had understood only a few words. He had to wait for Aboli to come into camp to hear the full report.

'Fresh sign,' Aboli told him. 'A day old. A big herd, maybe a hundred, and a few big bulls with them.'

'We must follow them at once.'

Tom was more excited than the little hunter, but Aboli pointed to the sun, which stood only a finger's width above the treetops. 'It will be dark before we have gone a mile. We will start at first light in the morning. Such a herd will be easy to follow. They are moving slowly, feeding as they go, and they will leave a road through the forest.'

Before darkness fell, Tom had planned the expedition.

There would be four musketeers to attack the great beasts, himself and Aboli, Alf Wilson and Luke Jervis. Each hunter would have two men to carry the spare guns, to reload and to hand him a freshly charged musket after each discharge. Tom checked the weapons himself. They were the rifled muskets that he had purchased in London. He made certain there were spare flints for the locks, that the powder flasks were filled and the bullet bags bulged with antimony-hardened lead balls for the ten-bore firearms. Ten-bore signified that ten of the lead balls it threw weighed one pound. While he worked on the weapons, Aboli filled the waterskins and made certain they had biscuit and dried meat for a three-day journey.

Even after the long day of rowing and dragging the boats through the shallows, everyone in the party was too excited to sleep. They sat late around the fires, listening to the strange sounds of the African night, the whistle and hoot of the night birds, the idiotic giggling of the hyena and the rumbling roars of a pride of lions hunting the far hills.

Often in the short time he had been with them, Tom had listened to the stories of Fundi as he told of the hunt for the mighty grey beasts, but he asked the little man to repeat them now. Aboli translated when Tom could not follow, but his own knowledge of the Lozi language was burgeoning, and he could understand much of what Fundi said.

Fundi explained again how the elephant had very poor eyesight, but possessed a sense of smell that could warn him of a hunter a mile or more upwind. 'He can suck up your scent out of the air and hold it in the bone cavities of his head, run with it for a great distance and blow it through his trunk into the mouths of his companions.'

'Into the mouths?' Tom questioned him avidly. 'Not the nostrils?'

'The smell of the Nzou is in the top lip,' Fundi

explained. His name for the elephant denoted a wise old man, not an animal, and he used it with respect and affection, expressing the feeling of the true hunter for his quarry. 'There are pink buds in his mouth, like the flowers of the kigilia tree. With these he tastes the air.'

With a stick Fundi drew the outline of the beast in the dust and they craned forward in the firelight to watch as he explained where a man must place his arrow to bring down one of the giants.

'Here!' He touched a spot behind the shoulder of his drawing. 'With great care not to strike the bones of the leg, which are like tree trunks. Deep! Drive the iron in deep, for the heart and the lungs are hidden behind skin this thick.' He showed the span of his thumb. 'And muscle and ribs.' He held out his arms. 'You must go in this deep to kill the Nzou, the wise old grey man of the forest.'

When Fundi stopped talking at last, Tom implored him to continue, but he stood up with dignity. 'It will be a long, weary way tomorrow, and it is time to rest now. I will teach you more when we are on the spoor.'

Tom lay awake until the moon had almost completed its circuit of the heavens, excitement boiling in his blood. When he closed his eyes the image of the quarry appeared in his imagination. He had never laid eyes on the living beast, but he had seen hundreds of their tusks piled in the markets of the Spice Islands, and he remembered again the mighty pair that his father had bought from Consul Grey in Zanzibar, which now stood in the library at High Weald. 'I will kill another beast like that one,' he promised himself, and in the hour before the dawn he fell into a sleep so deep and dark that Aboli had to shake him awake.

Tom left two men to guard the longboats, and in the first chilly glimmer of dawn they struck out along the trail that the elephant herd had left down the riverbank.

As Aboli had told him, the sign was clear to read and they moved forward steadily. As the light strengthened they went faster, and the trees they passed were smashed and stripped of bark and branches. Huge piles of yellow dung littered the forest floor, and troops of monkeys and flocks of brown partridge-like wild birds were scratching in it for undigested seeds and fruits. 'Here!' Aboli pointed to one of these piles. 'This is the dropping of a very old bull, one that might carry heavy tusks. The ivory never stops growing until the beast dies.'

'How do you tell his dung from that of a young animal?' Tom wanted to know.

'The old man cannot digest his food properly.' Aboli dug his toe into the pile. 'See, the twigs are still whole, and the leaves entire. Here, the nuts of the ivory palm, with half the flesh still on the pip.' Tom considered the first scrap he had been thrown of the lore of the hunt.

In the late morning they reached the point where the herd had left the stream and turned west towards the hills. Here they crossed an area where the surface was of fine talc dust. In this medium the imprint of the elephant pads was so detailed that each crack and wrinkle was faithfully preserved.

'Here!' Aboli pointed out a string of pad marks. 'This is the spoor of the great bull. See the size of each footprint, the front foot round and the back foot more oval in shape.' Aboli placed his own arm beside one of the tracks, using its length from the tip of his finger to the elbow as a yardstick. 'So long means that he is a mighty bull, and see how his pads are worn smooth? He is of great age. Unless his tusks are worn or broken, this will truly be an animal worthy of the chase.'

They crossed the first line of hills, and in the lush valley beyond Fundi and Aboli divined from the sign that the herd had fed and rested the previous night. 'We have gained many hours on them,' Fundi exulted. 'They are not far ahead.' But Tom was to learn that day that Fundi's idea of distance did not coincide with his own. By nightfall they were still on the herd's tracks, and Fundi was still assuring them that they were not far ahead.

All the white men in the party were nearing exhaustion, for sailors are not accustomed to covering such distances on foot. They had hardly the will left to eat a biscuit and a stick of dried meat, to swallow a few mouthfuls of water from the skins, before they fell asleep on the hard earth.

The next morning while it was still dark they were away again after the herd. Before long it was clear from the sign that they had lost much of their gain of the previous day, for the herd had kept moving westward in the moonlight while they had slept. For most of the white men the march became an endless torment of thirst, aching muscles and blistered feet. Tom was still young and tough and eager enough to make light of the hardship, forging along behind the trackers, with the heavy musket over his shoulders.

'Close! We are very close now.' Fundi grinned with malicious glee, and the gruelling miles dropped behind them. By now the waterskins were almost empty, and Tom had to warn the men with dire threats not to drink without permission. Tiny black flies swarmed around their heads and crawled into their ears, eyes and nostrils. The sun beat down like a hammer on an anvil and reflected up from the stony ground. The hooked thorns clawed at their legs as they passed, ripping their clothing and leaving bloody lines on their skin.

At last they found where the herd had stopped in a patch of dense forest, had spent many hours resting, dusting themselves, and breaking down branches, before it drifted on again, and the hunters finally made a real gain upon it.

Aboli pointed out to Tom how the dung that the herd was now dropping had not had time to dry, and when he thrust his finger into one pile he could feel the residual body heat. Clouds of brightly coloured butterflies hovered over the warm turds to drink up the moisture. With renewed strength in their legs they increased the pace, and climbed another line of hills.

On the rocky slopes grew strange trees with swollen trunks and crowns of leafless branches on their tops, fifty feet above the ground. At the base of one tree huge furry seed-pods were heaped. Aboli cracked one open: the black seeds inside were coated with a yellow pithy layer. 'Suck the seeds,' he said. The pleasant sour taste made their saliva flow again, and relieved the burning thirst of the march.

The line of hunters, burdened by their weapons and waterskins, toiled on up the hill. Just below the crest their heads went up. An awful sound came to them on the heated air, distant but stirring as the blast on a war trumpet. Though Tom had never heard the like before, he knew instinctively what it was.

Quickly he ordered the column to halt below the crest of the hill. Most of the men collapsed thankfully in the shade. He, Aboli and Fundi crept up to the skyline. They used a tree trunk to break their silhouette as they peered over into the valley beyond, and Tom's heart leaped against his ribs like a caged beast.

Down the length of the valley below them was strung out a line of sparkling green pools, each surrounded by lush reed beds and spreading shade trees. The elephant herd was gathered around the pools, some of the huge animals standing in the shade, fanning themselves with their ears, which seemed to Tom as wide as the mainsail of the *Swallow*. Others were standing on the yellow sandbanks that surrounded the pools, dipping their trunks into the green water and sucking up gargantuan draughts, then curling their trunks into their mouths and sending it hissing down their throats with the force of a ship's bilge pump. Younger animals crowded into the pools. Like rowdy children they frolicked and splashed, beating the water white with their trunks, shaking their huge heads and flapping their ears. Their wet bodies were black and shining. Some lay flat then rolled on to their sides, disappearing entirely below the surface, leaving only their trunks writhing above the surface like a sea serpent.

Tom went down on one knee and raised his telescope to his eye. This first sighting of the legendary beasts was so far beyond anything he had imagined that he was lost in wonder. He delighted in every detail. One of the youngest calves, not much bigger than a large pig but mischievous and bumptious, charged out of the water and, with swinging trunk and murderous trumpeting, chased the white egrets that were perched on the edge of the pool. The birds rose in a gratifying white cloud, and the small elephant swaggered back into the water, slipped almost immediately in the mud and trapped itself under a submerged log.

Its now terrified squeals brought every protective female within earshot rushing to the rescue, convinced that the calf had been taken by a crocodile. It was dragged out of the water, its dignity destroyed, and it fled, chastened, to hide between the legs of its mother, and suckle for comfort at the milk-swollen udders between her front legs. Tom laughed aloud, then Aboli touched his shoulder and pointed out a group of three huge animals that stood aloof from the raucous behaviour of the cows and calves.

They were in a patch of dense bush on the far side of the water, standing shoulder to shoulder, ears flapping lazily. Occasionally one picked up a load of dust in his trunk and dashed it over his head and back. Apart from that they seemed to be sleeping on their feet.

Through the lens, Tom studied this towering trio, which dwarfed every other animal in the herd. He examined the long ivory shafts they carried, and saw at once that, though they were all massive, the bull in the centre carried tusks that protruded beyond his lip almost the length of a boat's oar, and were the girth of Sarah's slim waist. He felt the pulse of his hunter's blood pound in his ears at each pump of his heart. This was the bull he had dreamed of, and his instinct was to seize the musket he had propped against the tree beside him and rush down to do battle with the giant. But Aboli sensed his mood and laid a restraining hand on his shoulder. 'These are sage and wary creatures,' he warned Tom. 'It will not be easy to come up to that bull down there. His females will guard and protect him. It will call for all our cunning and caution to outwit them.'

'Explain to me what we must do,' said Tom, and Aboli and Fundi lay on each side of him and planned the hunt.

'The wind is the key,' Aboli told him. 'We must always keep below the wind.'

'There is no wind,' Tom said, and pointed to the leaves that hung lifelessly from the top branches of the trees in the heated noonday.

'There is always wind,' Aboli contradicted him, and let a handful of dust trickle through his fingers. The fine golden motes floated in the sunlight, then drifted slowly away. Aboli made a delicate gesture describing the movement down the valley.

'When they are alarmed they will always run with the wind in their faces, then they will circle to come above the wind and take the scent.' He made another gesture to illustrate this manoeuvre. 'We will place Alf and Luke there and there.' He pointed out the positions. 'When they are in place, you and I will come down there.' He pointed out the path of their stalk. 'We will creep in close. When we fire, the bulls will be driven on to the others.'

Tom gestured for Alf and Luke to come up beside him on the ridge. Once they had recovered from their initial amazement at the first sight of the quarry, he gave them their orders, sending them to circle out behind the ridge, and cross it a mile further down the valley where they would be out of sight and below the wind of the herd.

It was almost an hour later that, through the telescope, he made out the two parties of hunters moving up the valley into the positions he had assigned them. It was good to have men under him who knew his mind and could carry out his orders so faithfully.

Aboli leading, they slipped quietly over the skyline, using the trees and scrub to screen their crossing. The great beasts were not so dim-sighted that they could not pick up alien movement. They crept down towards the pools with painstaking stealth, taking care not to run into one of the females scattered among the trees. Tom could barely credit how such a huge animal could become virtually invisible when it stood still among the thick bush, grey on grey, even its legs resembling the tree trunks. Slowly they closed in on the trio of bulls. Although they were still invisible, the hunters were guided by their deep rumblings.

Tom whispered to Aboli, 'Is that the sound of their bellies?'

Aboli shook his head. 'The old men are speaking to each other.'

Occasionally they saw a cloud of dust rise above the tops of the bush as one of the bulls dusted himself. It guided them through the thick undergrowth. Step by cautious step they went forward, once having to pull back and circle around a young cow and her nursing calf in the scrub between them and their quarry.

At last Fundi stopped them with a gesture of his pink palm, then pointed ahead. Tom went down on one knee and, looking below the hanging vines and branches, made out the massive grey forelegs of the nearest bull. The sweat of excitement was trickling into his eyes and stinging like sea-water. He wiped it away with the bandanna knotted around his throat, and checked the lock and flint of his musket. Aboli nodded at him and he drew back the hammer to half cock. They began to crawl forward.

Slowly, more of the nearest beast came into view, the

droop of his belly, the baggy grey skin hanging in folds around his knees, then the lower curve of one thick, yellow tusk.

They crawled in closer still, and Tom saw that the tusk was stained with the juices of bark that the bull had stripped from the forest trees. Closer still and he could see every crease and wrinkle in the skin, each wiry hair in the stubby tail. Tom looked at Aboli and made the gesture of firing, but Aboli shook his head vehemently, and signed to him to move in closer still.

The bull was rocking gently on his feet, and then to Tom's amazement something extraordinary began to issue from between its back legs. It was thicker than a man's thigh and seemed to extend endlessly, until it was dangling almost to the ground. Tom had to make an effort to prevent himself laughing. Drowsy and contented, the old man was letting his member dangle out and engorge.

Again Tom glanced at Aboli for instruction, and again Aboli scowled and urged him forward, but at that moment the bull stepped back and reached up with his trunk to pluck a bunch of leaves from the branches above him. The movement revealed the other bull, which he had been screening with his bulk.

Tom drew breath with a soft hiss as he saw how much larger was the old patriarch than his attendant. His enormous head was drooping, and his ears flapped gently. They were tattered and worn like the sails of a storm-battered ship. His small eyes were closed, the thick pale lashes meshing, and the ooze from the gland behind his eye ran down his cheek in a long damp smear.

The bull's head was propped on his tusks. Tom marvelled at the length and girth of those ivory curves, which reached down to the earth. They were so thick and heavy that there was hardly any taper from the lip to the blunt tip. He could see the bulge under the grey skin where a quarter of the length was buried in the skull. They must be an onerous burden for even such a mighty animal to carry through all the days of its life, he mused.

Tom was so close now that he could clearly see a metallic blue fly settle on the bull's eyelashes. The elephant blinked to drive it away. At that moment Tom felt a light touch on his arm, and turned his head slowly to see Aboli nod at him. He turned back and focused his gaze on the outline of the bones of the bull's shoulder under the wrinkled, eroded skin. He picked out the exact spot Fundi had described to him, just behind the shoulder and two-thirds of the way down the mighty barrel of the chest.

He raised the musket and slowly drew back the hammer to full cock, muffling the click of the mechanism with his hand. Looking down the long barrel, he saw that the muzzle was almost touching the bull's flank. There was no need to use the pip of the foresight. Gently he took up the pressure of the trigger and the hammer dropped in a burst of blue-white sparks over the pan. There was that moment of delay that seemed as long as infinity, but was the smallest part of a second, then the heavy weapon bellowed and pounded into his shoulder, knocking him back on his haunches, and blinding him with a cloud of white powder smoke, which obscured the body of the elephant.

A moment after his shot he heard Aboli fire. All around him the tranquil forest erupted in a rush of mighty bodies. Trumpeting and squealing, the herd plunged through the undergrowth, and trees swayed and crashed down under the onslaught.

Tom dropped the empty gun, reached back, seized the second musket from the man behind him and sprang to his feet. He ran into the thick cloud of smoke. As he emerged on the far side he saw the plunging hindquarters of the bull disappear as the scrub closed behind him.

'Chase him!' Aboli shouted at his shoulder, and they raced after the fleeing bull. All around they heard the cows and squealing calves crashing through the undergrowth.

Thorns and branches tore at Tom, but he ignored the ripping of his clothing and the scratching at his skin and ran on along the pathway that the bull had riven through the scrub.

He burst out on to the open bank of one of the pools, and the beast was fifty feet ahead of him, his ears spread and the curves of his tusks showing yellow on each side of his baggy hindquarters as he bore directly away from Tom at full run. His stubby tail tuft was held high, and Tom could see the knuckles of his spine running down the curve of his back to join the tail.

He swung up the musket and fired at the spine, the bull dropped into a sitting position on his haunches, and skidded down the bank. But the ball must have grazed the spine rather than smashed it: he was paralysed for but a second. As he reached the bottom of the bank he came up on all four legs again and splashed through the head of the pool and up the far bank.

Aboli ran alongside Tom and fired across the pool. They both saw the ball raise a puff of dried mud from the back of the bull's skull, but he shook his head, clapping his ears against his flanks, and disappeared into the dense bush on the far side. Tom grabbed his third musket from the panting sailor who handed it to him, and plunged down the bank in pursuit of the bull.

Aboli ran beside him, and they could see the course the bull was breaking through the forest – the treetops were shaking and there was a rustling, crackling wake through the bush, like that of a breaching whale beneath the surface of the sea.

Suddenly there was a thudding outburst of musket fire out on the right flank where the other hunters were hidden, and Aboli grunted, 'The other bulls have run into Alf and Luke.'

Running together, they skirted the edge of the pool and plunged into the bush on the far side. The path the

845

bull had torn through was closing behind him, and they struggled on with difficulty, losing cloth and skin to the thorns.

'We will never catch him now,' Tom gasped. 'He will run clear away from us.'

But when they burst out into a clearing at last, they both shouted with triumph as they saw the great bull only a pistol shot ahead. He was hard hit. His run had been reduced to an unsteady walk, and his head was hanging, his tusks ploughing long furrows in the soft earth, and pale frothy blood was bubbling from the tip of his trunk.

'Your first shot was a lung hit!' Aboli shouted, and they ran forward with renewed vigour, swiftly overhauling the wounded beast. Ten paces behind him, Tom dropped on one knee. He was gasping for air, his heart pounding and his hands shaking, as he tried to take a bead on the swaying hindquarters, aiming once again for the spine.

He fired and this time the ball flew true from the rifled barrel. In the instant before the smoke obscured his vision, he saw it plough into the wide grey back, shattering the vertebrae above the tail. The bull dropped on to his haunches once again. Tom scrambled to his feet and ran out to one side so that he could see around the smoke bank.

The elephant was sitting facing him, shaking its head with fury and agony, the great tusks held high, blowing a carmine cloud of blood from the tip of its trunk. Its death squeals seemed loud enough to split Tom's skull and burst his eardrums.

Aboli fired at the head and though they both saw the ball strike on the domed forehead, it could not penetrate the fortress of bone in which the brain was buried. The maimed beast tried to drag its crippled back legs behind it and reach its tormentors.

Both men ran back, well out of reach of the swinging trunk and, with unsteady hands, poured powder into the muzzles of their muskets, rodded down the wadding and the balls, then crept forward, circling to find an opening, to get in close before firing into the barrel of the chest.

Again and again they ran back to reload, then came forward to fire. Gradually the strength of the beast leaked out of him from the mouths of twenty running wounds, and with a last groan he fell over on his side, stretched out those fabulous tusks and was still.

Tom went forward cautiously. He reached out and with the muzzle of the musket touched the tiny eye, fringed with pale lashes and brimming with almost human tears. It did not blink. The bull was dead at last. He wanted to shout his triumph, but instead he found himself overwhelmed by a strange, almost religious melancholy. Aboli came to stand beside him, and when their eyes met, Aboli nodded in understanding. 'Yes,' he said softly. 'You have learned what it means to be a true hunter, for you have understood the beauty and the tragedy of what we do.'

Between them, Alf and Luke had brought down one of the other bulls, but the third had escaped the ambush, and had run off unscathed with the rest of the herd into the forest. Tom wanted to follow him up but both Fundi and Aboli laughed at him. 'You will never see him again. He will run for twenty miles without stopping, and then he will walk another fifty miles faster than you could run.'

That evening they dined like princes on tough, rank elephant cheek meat, roasted on green-stick skewers over the coals, and drank the muddy pool water, tainted with elephant urine, as though it were the finest claret. They slept like dead men beside the fire.

Over the next two days they drew the tusks from the two bulls, chopping them out of the skull, taking infinite pains not to mark or mar the ivory. Fundi showed them how to free the long conical nerve from the cavity in the butt of each tusk and stuff the hole with green grass. Then they used bark rope to secure the four huge tusks to carrying poles. When they set out on the long march back to where they had left the boats, it took four men to carry each tusk.

When they reached the river again, they cached the tusks on the bank, burying them so deep that even the hyena could not dig them out and chew them to splinters. Then they went on upstream in the longboats. Each day they found fresh elephant sign more plentiful, and they followed on foot, sometimes killing within a few miles. At other times they were forced to march for days to catch up with the herds.

Within a month they had harvested enough ivory to make a full load for both longboats. All the white men were ragged and exhausted. The fat had been burned off them, their bearded faces were gaunt and their bodies skeletal. Only Aboli and Fundi seemed unaffected by the hardships of the hunt. There was general rejoicing when Tom announced his decision to turn back to Fort Providence.

That night at the camp-fire, Aboli and Fundi came to where Tom sat staring into the dying flames, thinking of Sarah, anticipating their reunion. They squatted on each side of him and he considered their dark faces thoughtfully before he spoke. 'This is grave business,' he said, with certainty. 'I can see that you mean to spoil my content-ment and my pleasure at the return to Fort Providence.' He sighed with resignation. 'Very well, what is it?'

'Fundi says that we are very close to the lands of his people, the Lozi.'

'How close?' Tom asked suspiciously. By now he spoke the Lozi language with confidence and he had learned what Fundi considered very close.

'Ten days' travel,' Fundi said confidently, but when Tom stared at him accusingly, he dropped his eyes. 'Or perhaps a very little further,' he admitted.

'So Fundi wishes to return to his own people?' Tom asked.

'And I will go with him,' said Aboli quietly.

Tom felt a stab of alarm. He stood up and led Aboli out of the firelight, then turned on him almost angrily. 'What is this?' Tom asked. 'Do you wish to leave me, and go back to Africa?'

Aboli smiled. 'I leave you only for a while. You and I have become branch and vine of the same tree. We can never be put asunder.'

'Then why do you go without me?'

'For many years the Lozi have been hounded by the slavers. If they caught a glimpse of your white face . . .' He shrugged expressively. 'No, I will go with Fundi. We will take trade goods with us, as much as we can carry. Fundi says that his tribe has a store of ivory, from the elephant they have taken in their pitfalls and from the carcasses of those old animals they have found dead in the forest. With Fundi to calm their fears and with samples of our goods to show them, perhaps I can open up a road of trade with the Lozi.'

'How will I find you again?'

'I will come to you at Fort Providence. Fundi says that I can buy a canoe from his tribe. Perhaps my canoe will be loaded with riches when we meet again.' Aboli placed an avuncular hand on Tom's shoulder. 'You have shown that you are a mighty hunter in these last days, but now it is time for you to rest. Go back to the woman who waits for you and make her happy. I shall return before the season changes and the Big Wet begins.'

The next morning Aboli and Fundi lifted the heavy bundles of trade beads, copper wire and cloth onto their heads, balancing them easily so their hands were free to hold their weapons, and set off westward along the river-bank. Tom walked a little way beside Aboli, then stopped and watched his old comrade disappear among the tall riverine forest trees before he turned away sadly and went down to where the longboats were loaded and moored against the bank.

'Shove off,' he ordered, as he took his seat at the tiller of the leading boat. 'Take us back to Fort Providence.' And they cheered him as they bent to the oars and ran down with the current towards the east.

T**he lookouts on the hill above Fort Providence spotted the longboats as soon as they rounded the last bend upstream, and Sarah was dancing with excitement on the beach when Tom stepped ashore. She rushed into his arms, but after the first embrace drew back and stared into his face, appalled by what she saw. 'You are starved!' she said. 'And dressed like a scarecrow, in rags!' Then she wrinkled her nose. 'When last did you bathe?'

She led him up the hill, but would not let him into the little cottage. 'You will stink out all my hard work.'

First she filled the galvanized hip bath, which stood under the wild fig tree in the backyard, with steaming water. Then she undressed him, set aside his rags for later washing and mending, and sat him in the bath as though he were a little boy. She sponged away the accumulated dust and filth of the weeks of hard hunting, combed out his thick black hair, and braided it into a sailor's pig-tail. With her scissors, she trimmed the shaggy bush of his beard into the neat, pointed style that King William had made fashionable. She anointed all the scratches and cuts that covered his legs and arms with a salve she fetched from Dr Reynolds's surgery. Tom revelled in the attention.

At last, she helped him into fresh, lovingly ironed shirt and breeches. Only then did she take his hand and lead him into the cottage. Proudly she displayed everything she had done in his absence, from the easy chair that the carpenters had made especially for him to the broad double bed in the back room and the mattress she had sewn and filled with dried kapok from the silk-cotton trees that grew along the riverbank.

Tom eyed the bed with a wicked grin. 'It looks to be a fine piece of work, but I'd best test it before I give a firm opinion,' he said, and chased her giggling twice around it before she allowed herself to be captured and lifted onto the embroidered covers.

Afterwards they lay and talked while the sun set, and then long into the night. He told her of all he had done and seen. He described the hunting to her, and the new strange lands they had found, the forests and the far blue mountains, and the marvellous animals and birds they had discovered. 'It is so big, and endless and beautiful and wild,' he told her, and held her close. 'We never saw another man, nor any sign of one in all our journey. It's all ours, Sarah. Ours for the taking.'

'Will you take me with you next time?' she asked, jealous of his attention, wanting to share the wonders of it all with him. Somehow she never doubted that there would be a next time. She saw that he had fallen in love with this land, as much as he was in love with her. She knew that from now on they were both a part of it.

'Yes,' he agreed. 'Next time you shall be with me to see it.'

There was so much to tell and to discuss that it took more than one long night. Over the lazy weeks that followed, while the men rested and recuperated from the hunting, Tom and Sarah spent hours alone each day. He read to her from the journal he had kept during the expedition so that he overlooked no detail, and when he had told it all to her, they discussed and planned the future.

'We have been lucky to discover this Lunga river or, rather, to have Fundi show it to us,' Tom told her. 'The old Portuguese explorers must have overlooked it, and the Arabs also. Fundi tells me that the Arab trading routes, the slave road, is a long way further to the north.' He smiled ruefully. 'If Fundi says it is a long way, you can believe it is a hundred miles or more. With luck, neither the Omani nor John Company will ever find us here. Fort Providence is a perfect entrepôt to the interior. The elephant herds hereabouts have never been hunted, and if Aboli and Fundi can make contact with the tribes, we can open up trade with them and have it all to ourselves.'

'But where will you sell the ivory?' she asked. 'Not in Zanzibar or any other Arab port, nor any place where the Company has a factory. Brother Guy will never let you rest if he finds where you are. We can never go back to England.' She tried not to sound wistful, and hurried on, 'Where can we sell our goods, and buy the necessities, powder and shot, medicines and flour, candles and oil, rope and canvas and pitch?'

'There is such a place close at hand,' Tom assured her. 'As soon as the long rains begin, the Big Wet, we will pull out of here and sail down to Good Hope. The Dutch at the Cape will be hot for our ivory, and even hotter to sell us all the goods we can pay for. Best of all, they won't give a brass guilder or a morsel of their old cheese for the warrant of arrest placed on me by the Lord Chancellor of England.'

There was much to keep every man in the fort busy during the weeks when they waited for Aboli to return. All the ivory had to be cleaned, weighed and packed with dry grass to prevent it being damaged during the voyage. Then the little *Swallow* had to be careened on the beach below the fort, her bottom scraped clean of weed. The ship-worm that had taken hold in her planking had to be burned out with boiling pitch. Once she was afloat again, they repainted her, stitched the rents in her canvas and made small changes to her rigging so that she would not be recognized as the ship in which they had escaped from England. It was a sailor's superstition that it was bad luck to change a ship's name, but there was no help for it. They scraped the old name from her transom, and painted the new one over it.

When they relaunched her, Sarah broke a bottle of brandy from the ship's stores over her bows. 'I rename this ship *Centaurus*,' she intoned. 'May God bless her and all who sail in her.'

Then the ivory was taken aboard the *Centaurus* and carefully loaded into her holds. They refilled her water casks and made all ready for the voyage southwards.

Now each afternoon the thunderheads began to build up along the northern horizon, mountains that reached up into the heavens. The sunset turned the cloud ranges purple and sullen scarlet, the lightning flickered in their bellies and the far thunder muttered the threat of the coming wet season.

The first rains burst upon them, sweeping across the hills in trailing robes of grey. For three days and nights, thunder bombarded them and the air was filled with water, as though they lay beneath a mighty waterfall. Then the stormclouds opened, and in that lull a dozen long dugout canoes came fast down the swollen waters of the Lunga river. In the lead canoe stood Aboli, tall and scar-faced. Tom shouted with joy and ran down to the beach to welcome him ashore.

Fundi was in the last canoe, but the oarsmen were all strangers. The bottom of each craft was stacked with elephant tusks, none as large as those that Tom's expedition had taken but valuable none the less.

The oarsmen were all of the Lozi tribe, kinsmen of Fundi. Despite his assurances, they were terrified of the strange white men of Fort Providence. They expected to be taken as slaves, chained together and marched away as had happened to so many of their tribe. Gone, never to be seen or heard of again.

They were mostly old men, grey and bent, or uninitiated striplings. They huddled together on the beach, not to be reconciled or comforted by any of Tom's reassurances in Lozi. 'They have come with us only because Bongola, their chief, ordered them to do so,' Aboli explained. 'When he saw the trade goods we brought with us, his greed surpassed his fear of the slavers. Still, he would not come himself to trade, but sent the least important members of the tribe in his stead.'

They brought the ivory ashore from the canoes and weighed it, then discussed a fair price for it with Fundi. 'I do not want to spoil the trade by overpaying them,' Tom explained to Sarah, 'but neither do I want to bilk them, and kill the trade before it begins.'

In the end the bags of Venetian trade beads, bolts of cloth, crates of hand-mirrors and axe-heads, and bales of copper wire were loaded into the canoes, and the rowers were sent home. Their little flotilla shot upstream against the current, propelled by men so thankful to have escaped with their lives that they rowed with the strength of demons, hysterically chanting their gratitude for their escape to their tribal gods and ancestors as they disappeared around the first bend.

'They will be back next season,' Aboli prophesied. 'Bongola will see to that.'

Fundi and three of the bolder Lozi, who had remained with him, agreed to stay on at Fort Providence during the Big Wet and protect the buildings and gardens against the ravages of the weather and wild animals. The rest of the party loaded the last of the ivory and went aboard the *Centaurus*. As the full onslaught of the rains washed over them, they let the swollen river and the monsoon wind drive the little *Centaurus* downstream and out into the Ocean of the Indies.

'The course to clear Madagascar and make for Good Hope is south-east by south. Mark it on the traverse board, if you please, Mr Tyler,' Tom ordered.

'South-east by south, it is, Captain.'

'Full and by, Mr Tyler,' said Tom, who took Sarah's hand and led her to the bows. They stood together and watched the flying fish explode from the surface of the Mozambique Channel and spin away in silvery blurs, like new-minted coins tossed across the blue current.

'If I can find a priest at Good Hope, will you marry me, Sarah Beatty?' he asked.

'That I will, Thomas Courtney.' She laughed and hugged him closer. 'That I will.'

The little *Centaurus* anchored in Table Bay on a sunny morning in which the south-easter chopped bursts of white off the tops of the wavelets. They went ashore under the towering mountain whose flat top was covered by the famous tablecloth, a stationary bank of roiling white cloud.

The settlement had grown in size since last they had visited the Cape. The strictures of the Dutch East India Company against foreigners owning land or taking up residence in its territory were every bit as draconian as those of its English counterpart. However, Tom soon discovered that, for a few golden guilders placed in the hands of the right official, these laws could be waived. Once they had paid their dues, the welcome they received from the burghers was convivial, especially as the *Centaurus* was well burdened, and the Dutch merchants smelt profits in their visit.

They planned to stay in the Cape until the rains on the Fever Coast had passed. As their quarters aboard the *Centaurus* were cramped, and the motion of the ship at anchor was uncomfortable, Tom found lodgings for himself and Sarah in one of the little guest-houses below the Company gardens run by a manumitted Malay woman, who was a wonderful cook and hostess.

In the first week Tom visited all the merchants whose warehouses lined the waterfront, and was delighted to find that the demand for ivory was strong. He struck several good bargains for the sale of their cargo. The crew were given their first pay and share of the profits since they had sailed from England. Over the next few months most of them spent everything they had earned in the ale shops and bawdy-houses of the town, but Ned Tyler and Dr Reynolds used theirs to purchase smallholdings of land in the Constantia valley on the far side of the mountain.

Tom and Aboli used nearly all of their share to buy the necessary stores for another season at Fort Providence, and a goodly stock of the trade goods on offer in the warehouses of the colony.

Tom gave Sarah fifty pounds from the prize, which she used to assemble her trousseau. It included a small harpsichord and a baby cradle on wooden rockers, which she painted with floral wreaths and choirs of cherubs.

The entire crew were in the congregation of the little church in the gardens when Tom and Sarah were married, and after the ceremony they carried the newly-weds on their shoulders down the street to their lodgings, singing all the way and pelting them with handfuls of rose petals.

In one of the waterside taverns Aboli found a sun-wizened little Dutchman named Andries van Houten, who had been brought out from Amsterdam as a gold-finder for the Dutch East India Company. 'I have scoured the mountains as far as Stellenbosch,' van Houten told Aboli after the third tankard of ale had slid effortlessly down his gullet, his Adam's apple bobbing in his red wrinkled throat. 'There is no gold in this devil-damned colony, but I can smell it in the north.' He sniffed the air. 'If only I could find a ship to take me up the coast.' And he looked at Aboli hopefully. 'But I don't have a guilder in my purse to pay my passage.'

Aboli brought him to see Tom, and they talked every evening for a week. In the end, Tom agreed to purchase all the prospecting equipment that van Houten needed and take him to Fort Providence when they sailed.

Those pleasant days at Good Hope passed too swiftly, and they were soon reloading the *Centaurus*, taking great care with Sarah's harpsichord and the cradle. As the season changed, and the oak trees that lined the streets dropped their leaves, they hoisted the anchor and sailed northwards around Cape Point and into the Mozambique Channel again.

When they entered the mouth of the Lunga river and forged their way upstream, they saw the high-water mark on the banks, and the debris hanging in the branches of the trees that showed just how strong had been the flood during the months of the Big Wet. When they reached the hilly country, the forest was green and burgeoning with new growth.

Faithful to the trust they had placed in him, Fundi met them at the landing below Fort Providence, and proudly showed Tom how well he had cared for everything in their absence. They set to rethatching the roofs of the huts, and repairing the weak spots in the palisade. Sarah had her new harpsichord installed in the front room of their cottage, and played and sang for Tom every evening after dinner.

She placed the painted baby cradle beside their bed in

the back room. The first night Tom eyed it as he sat on the bed and pulled off his boots. 'I take that as a challenge, Mistress Courtney,' he told her. 'Shall we see what we can do about filling it?'

They did not have much time to devote to the task, for within weeks Tom was ready to take the first hunting party upriver.

Van Houten was in the leading boat, sitting on his wooden box of chemicals with his gold pans stacked at hand. He prospected every gravel-bed and sandbank they passed. When they went ashore to hunt the elephant herds, van Houten did not join them but wandered away with his two Lozi helpers to search the hills and streams for traces of the precious metal.

The hunting was good this season. Within a month they had filled the boats with ivory, and set out to retrace their steps to Fort Providence.

Sarah accompanied Tom on the second expedition, bringing with her the paintbox she had bought in Good Hope. She filled the pages of her sketchbooks with images of the journey.

They followed the river further than ever before, and at last reached the country of the Lozi. At the first village the entire population fled into the forest, and it took several days before they came creeping out timidly from among the trees. After Fundi and Aboli had overcome their initial fear and suspicion, they began a friendly relationship with the tribe.

They found that the Lozi were generally a pleasant and cheerful people. Though small in stature, they were well formed and handsome. Some of the women were beautiful, with fine Nilotic features. They went bare-breasted and their carriage was graceful and proud.

Aboli had a long, serious discussion with the village elders, and the outcome was that, for a few rolls of copper wire and a small bag of glass beads, he acquired two of the prettiest, plumpest virgins as wives. The girls were named Falla and Zete. It was difficult to tell who was better pleased with the bargain, the bridegroom or the little brides, preening in the new finery Aboli had given them as part of the bride price and gazing at their husband with awe and reverence.

Dr Reynolds, with Sarah to assist him, successfully treated many of the sick Lozi, which sealed the good relations with the tribe. When the expedition went on upriver to the capital *kraal* of the Lozi, the drums carried ahead of them the news of their coming. Their paramount chief Bongola, came down to the landing to welcome them and lead them to new huts that had been built especially in their honour.

Bongola's village was a cluster of several hundred thatched huts built along the riverbank and on the slopes of the hills. Each hut was set around with a *shamba* of mango and plantain trees and manioc plants. *Kraals* of logs housed the scrubby cattle and goats of the tribe, and kept them safe from the nocturnal forays of leopard and hyena.

By this time Tom and Aboli were both fluent in the language, and they held long *indabas* with Bongola each day of their stay. Bongola was a naturally garrulous little man and he related the recent history of the tribe to Tom. The Lozi had once held rich lands on the banks of the great freshwater lake to the north, but then the slavers had arrived and fallen upon them, like the cheetah on the gazelle herds of the plains. The survivors had fled southwards, and for almost two decades now had evaded further depredations. But each day they lived in terror of the slavers whom they knew were slowly driving their raiding columns deeper into the interior. 'We know that one day we will have to fly again,' Bongola told Tom. 'That was why we were filled with such alarm when we heard of your arrival.'

Tom remembered Aboli's stories of how he had been

captured by the slavers when he was a child. He remembered also those unfortunates he had seen in the slave-markets of Zanzibar, and felt once again that deep abhorrence of the trade, and anger at his own inability to ease the plight of these people.

The trading was profitable with Bongola, who brought out many fine ivory tusks from his hoard to sell. Then van Houten came in from one of his forays into the wilderness and proudly showed Tom five porcupine quills, each stoppered at one end. When he removed the stopper from one and poured the contents into the bowl of his gold scale, Tom stared at the tiny pile of metallic flakes and granules, which gleamed yellow in the sunlight.

'Gold dust?' he asked. 'I have heard tell of the fool's gold. Are you certain this is not it?'

Van Houten bridled at the slur on his professional integrity, and showed Tom how to test the flakes with acid from his box of chemicals. 'The acid will eat any of the base metals but not the noble one,' he explained. They watched it bubble and fizz as he dipped the flake into it but when he brought it out the metal was bright and unscarred.

He took Tom to the place where he had panned the dust, and showed him the string of gravel-beds and sand-bars along the course of a stream down one of the valleys. At Tom's request Bongola sent them fifty women of the tribe: traditionally the men would not engage in such menial labour as working in the field or digging holes in the stream bed.

Van Houten gave each of the women a pan and showed her how to use it, dip and swing, swirling the gravel in the pan and letting the dross flow away over the lip, until only the gleaming tail remained. Swiftly the women learned the art and Tom promised them a measure of glass beads for each quill of the noble dust that they brought to him.

Van Houten's alluvial goldfield proved so rich that

a hard-working woman could fill a quill in less than a day, and soon gold panning was the preferred activity of the tribe. When some of the men wanted to join in such a profitable pastime, the women drove them away indignantly.

The rains threatened, and it was time to head downriver again. The longboats were low in the water under their cargoes of ivory, and Tom had almost a hundred ounces of gold dust locked in the ship's strong-box.

When Aboli told Falla and Zete that he was leaving them with their families until he returned next season, they burst into distraught wails and fountains of tears. Sarah remonstrated with him at such treatment. 'How can you be so cruel, Aboli? You have made them love you, and now you are breaking their little hearts.'

'They would die of terror and seasickness on the voyage down to Good Hope, and even if they survived they would pine for their mothers every day they were away. They would make my life as miserable as their own. No, they must stay here, and wait for me, as good wives should.'

The desolation of the two girls was miraculously relieved by the parting gifts of beads, cloth and handmirrors that Aboli bestowed on them, enough to make them the richest wives in the village. Both girls were bubbling over with giggles and smiles as they waved farewell to his tall figure at the tiller of the leading longboat.

When they returned to Lozi Land at the beginning of the following dry season, both Falla and Zete were huge with child, their glossy black bellies bulging out over their loincloths and their breasts big as ripe melons. They gave birth within days of each other. Sarah acted as midwife and delivered two baby boys.

'By God!' said Tom as he examined the infants. 'There is no doubt they are yours, Aboli. The poor little devils only lack a tattoo to be as ugly as their father.'

Aboli was a changed man. Gone was his dignified reserve and regal bearing when he held a chubby drooling son on each knee. The scarified visage that had struck terror into a thousand enemies became benign and close to beautiful. 'This one is Zama,' he told Tom and Sarah, 'for he will be a mighty warrior. And this one is Tula, for he will be a poet and a wise man.'

That night, in the darkness of their hut, Sarah laid her cheek on Tom's and whispered into his ear, 'I want a son also. Please, Tom. Please, my darling, give me a baby to hold and love.'

'I will try,' he promised. 'With all my heart, I will try.' But as the years passed, part of each spent at Fort Providence or travelling in the wilderness of Lozi Land, the other part spent in the Cape of Good Hope, Sarah remained slim and tall and flat-bellied, with nothing to swell her womb or puff out her shapely bosom.

Both Zama and Tula grew swiftly into strong little boys, taking after their father, tall for their age and natural leaders of the other boys of their age group. They spent their days in the forest and on the grassy plains along the river, tending the communal cattle herds of the tribe, and learning to handle bow and spear, coming to know the ways of the wild creatures of the forests. In the evenings they sat at Aboli's feet at the fireside, and listened wide-eyed to his stories of the sea, of battles and adventures in faraway places.

'Take us with you, Father,' Zama pleaded. As Aboli had predicted he was the taller and stronger of the brothers.

'Please, honoured father,' Tula piped. 'Take us and show us these wonders.'

'You must stay with your mothers, and tend your duties

here until you have been circumcised and initiated into manhood,' Aboli promised them. 'Then Lord Klebe and I will take you with us into the world beyond Lozi Land.'

The elephant hunting was good in Lozi Land, and van Houten discovered a new alluvial goldfield three days' march to the north of the original one, which brought in a steady trickle of gold dust to Fort Providence. Both the tribe and Tom prospered, and each season of the big rains the *Centaurus* took a full cargo down to the Cape.

An Amsterdam bank of good repute had an office on the Heerengracht above the waterfront. Tom already had two thousand pounds deposited with them, and after this season the amount was doubled. At last he was a wealthy man.

He had to face one bitter disappointment. When the time came to sail north again, Ned Tyler declared himself too old to undertake another voyage. By now his hair was as fine and white as new-picked cotton, his back was bowed and his once clear eyes were clouded and rheumy. 'Leave me on my little farm here in the Constantia valley,' he begged. 'Let me tend my chickens and vegetables.'

'I am going to stay with Ned,' Dr Reynolds decided, 'I have had enough adventure to last my lifetime.' Only when he looked carefully at the surgeon's red, bluff face did Tom realize how he had aged along with Ned. 'I have had all I want of bandaging and stitching up your rascals. I want to plant a few vines, perhaps make a good wine before I die.'

'But who will look after us?' Tom protested. 'You cannot send us out to die of malaria in the wilderness.'

'You have a fine little surgeon with you,' the old doctor replied. 'I have taught Mistress Sarah all I know about setting a broken leg or mixing a potion. I place you in her good hands and, like as not, you will be better off. Lord knows, she is prettier than I am, and has a kinder heart.'

Alf Wilson took over as first officer of the *Centaurus*, and he had the helm as they pushed into the mouth of the Lunga river at the beginning of the next hunting season. Every man and woman aboard was consumed with excitement on these annual returns to Fort Providence. They were all eager to see how Fundi had taken care of the settlement during the rains, to learn if the elephant were still plentiful upon the hills of Lozi Land, and to find out how much gold dust the women had collected in their absence.

Aboli tried unsuccessfully to conceal his eagerness to be reunited with his wives and children again: by this time Falla and Zete had added generously to their brood. There were two small daughters and another two sons.

As always, Fundi met them on the landing below the fort, and welcomed Tom and Sarah ashore. All was well in the fort, and there was little rain damage to be repaired. Sarah unwrapped the canvas cover from her harpsichord, played a chord, then smiled when the notes were true. She launched into the chorus of 'Spanish Ladies'.

Aboli demanded from Fundi the news of the tribe and his family, but there was none for the rains had been heavy that season and the river not navigable. No canoe from Bongola's village had reached the fort. Aboli fretted through the time that it took to unload the cargo from the *Centaurus*, to repair the fort and to make the final preparations for the expedition upstream to Lozi Land. He was at the tiller of the leading longboat when they were ready at last to leave Fort Providence.

The first intimation of something seriously amiss came when they reached the outlying villages of the Lozi, and found them all deserted. Though they searched the area around each cluster of huts they found no living soul, nor any clue as to what had happened to the inhabitants.

Dreading what they would find there, they went on towards Bongola's village as fast as they could row, dragging the boats through the shallows and keeping going as long as there was light enough to make out the banks on either side and steer around the rocks in the channel.

They came to it in the early afternoon. A dreadful hush hung over the hills, no sound of drum or horn or shouted welcome. They saw at once that the outlying gardens were overrun with weed. Then they passed the first hut on the bank. The roof thatch had been burned and the walls stood gaunt and bare, the mud plaster washed away by the rains.

Nobody in the boats spoke, but as he pulled with all his strength on the long oar, Aboli's face was a terrible mask of despair. They stared at the ruins of the village as they passed, the burned huts, neglected gardens and empty cattle pens. The top branches of the trees were lined with rows of roosting vultures, grim silhouettes, hunch-backed and hook-billed. The sickly sweet stench of death and putrefaction was on the air.

A single canoe lay on the beach of the landing, but its bottom had been staved in. The fish racks on which the men dried the catch had fallen down, and the nets were abandoned in untidy heaps. Aboli jumped overside when the water was waist-deep, waded ashore and ran up the beach to the overgrown path that led to the huts of Falla and Zete.

Tom followed him but did not catch up with Aboli until he came to the small cluster of huts surrounded by a *boma* of thorn branches. Aboli stood in the open gateway, staring at the burned-out huts of his wives and children. Tom stopped beside him, but neither man spoke. Then Aboli walked forward and knelt. From the soft blue ash, he picked up a tiny human skull and held it cupped in both hands as though it were a sacred chalice. The cranium had been crushed by a heavy blow. He stared into the empty eye sockets, and the tears washed down his scarred face. Yet his voice was steady as he looked up at Tom and said,

'The slavers always kill the babies for they are too young to survive the march to the coast. Their weight only weakens the mothers who are forced to carry them.'

He touched the deep dent in the dome of the tiny skull. 'See how they held my little daughter by the ankles and dashed her head on the doorpost of the hut? This was my beautiful baby, Kassa,' he said, lifted the skull to his mouth and kissed the ghastly wound.

Tom could not watch his sorrow. He looked away, and saw that somebody had written on the wall of the roofless hut with a stick of charcoal in Arabic script, 'God is great. There is no God but God.' That made certain the identity of the perpetrators of this atrocity. He stared at the legend while he tried to compose himself. When at last he spoke, his voice was stifled with horror. 'When did this happen?' he asked.

'Perhaps a month ago.' Aboli stood up. 'Maybe a little longer than that.'

'The slave columns must move slowly?' Tom asked. 'With the chains and the women and children?'

'Yes,' Aboli agreed. 'They move very slowly, and it is a long weary road to the coast.'

'We can catch them,' Tom's voice grew surer and stronger, 'if we start at once and march hard.'

'Yes,' said Aboli, 'we will catch them. But first I must bury my dead. Make the preparations for the march, Klebe, and I will be ready to leave before noon.'

Aboli found two more tiny skeletons among the ruins and weeds. The bones were scattered and chewed by the carrion eaters, but he identified his babies by the bead bracelets he had given them, which were still entwined with the small bones. They were of his two youngest sons, not yet two years old. He gathered up their remains and placed them in a tanned leather cloak.

He dug their grave in the floor of the hut in which

they had been conceived, and buried them together. Then he opened a vein in his own wrist, dribbled his blood on to the grave and prayed to his ancestors to receive the souls of his children kindly.

When he came down to the landing he found that Tom had almost completed the order of march. From years of experience in hunting the elephant herds, each man knew his duty. There were three bands of five men each. They were commanded by Tom, Alf Wilson and Luke Jervis. Three sailors would be left to guard the boats.

Each man of the expedition carried his weapons, powder and shot, his waterskin and blanket, and enough food for a week. That was a full load of sixty pounds in weight, and once it was expended they would live off the land.

'You must stay here with the boats,' Tom told Sarah, as he unwrapped the blue sword from the canvas roll in which he kept it. He did not carry the long weapon on the elephant hunts for it hampered his gait, but he would need it now. 'There will be fighting and danger,' he explained, as he belted the scabbard around his waist.

'That is why I must go with you. There will be many wounded and hurt, and none to minister to them. I cannot stay here,' she replied, and he saw the determination in her set expression, the cold light in her eyes. She had already packed her medicine chest and blanket. He knew from long experience it would serve no purpose to argue with her. He gave in.

'Keep close to me. If we run into danger, do as I tell you, woman, and for once do not stop to argue.'

Led by Aboli and Fundi, they went in single file through the remains of the village. They passed many more skeletons along the path, all that remained of the old men and women and small children judged too weak by the slavers to survive the march to the coast. It was a relief to leave behind this scene of death and desolation, and to follow the trail left by the shuffling lines of Lozi prisoners as they were driven northwards into the hills.

Aboli and Fundi set a killing pace. Fundi carried his great elephant bow over one shoulder and a quiver of poisoned arrows over the other. He, too, had lost his family in the slaughter and the pillage.

By Tom's reckoning they covered ten miles in that first march, and he declared a halt only after the moonless night became too dark to allow them to make out the ground under their feet. He slept only fitfully with Sarah beside him under their blankets. Soon after midnight he sprang to his feet as a ghostly cry echoed from the summit of the hill above them. It was a human voice, calling down to them in the language of the Lozi. 'What manner of men are you?'

'I am Klebe, your friend,' Tom shouted back.

'I am Aboli, husband of Falla and Zete.' Aboli threw more wood on the fire, which flared up brightly.

'I am Fundi, the hunter of elephants. Come down to us, men of the Lozi.'

They appeared among the dark trees, moving shadows in the firelight that materialized into human shapes. There were less than a hundred survivors of the raid, many of them women, but over fifty warriors who still carried their weapons, throwing spears and the heavy elephant bows with quivers of poisoned arrows.

They squatted in a dense mass around the fire and one at a time the elders described the attack that had caught the village by surprise, the massacre and the slave-taking that had followed.

'Some of us were able to run into the forest, and others were out hunting or gathering roots and wild honey, so we escaped,' they explained.

'What of my family,' Aboli asked.

'They have taken Falla and Zete, and your sons Zama

868

and Tula,' they told him. 'We saw them in chains when we spied upon the slavers' caravan from afar.'

They sat all the rest of that night, reciting the long roll of those who had perished and those who had been captured. In the dawn, when it was time to resume the pursuit, Tom ordered the old men and the women back to the ruined village to bury the dead and plant crops to ward off the famine that must inevitably follow this disaster. 'Some of my men are there. They will hunt game to feed you until the crops are ripe.' They went back obediently, and Tom assembled the remaining Lozi warriors. He knew most of them by name, and had hunted with some. 'We are going after the caravan. We will fight to free those who have been captured,' he told them. 'Will you join us?'

'We wanted to follow them, but the Arabs have fire sticks, and we were afraid,' they said. 'But you also have the terrible fire sticks, so we will come with you.'

Fundi picked out the most intrepid, skilful hunters among them, and sent them to scout ahead, to discover any ambush or snare the slavers might have set. When they started out again, he kept the rest of the Lozi with them, following the well-worn slave road into the north.

They marched hard from first light of day until dark, and though the signs of the slave caravan were too old and eroded for even Fundi and Aboli to read accurately, they knew that they had covered in a day the same ground that it had taken the long files of chained slaves six days to make good. During the day they had passed the rudely thatched shelters and dead camp-fires of that number of overnight camps.

The next day they were away again at first light, and before noon they came upon the remains of the first casualties among the slaves. There were only a few bone chips and blood-caked scraps of loincloth lying beside the path, for the Arabs had removed the chains from the corpses and the forest scavengers had devoured the rest.

'These were the weak ones,' Fundi said. 'They died of weariness and broken hearts. We will find many more before we catch up with the caravan.'

On each day's march now the sign became fresher and clearer to read. Always the road was marked by the old camps where the caravan had passed the nights, and by the remains of those who had not survived the rigours of the journey.

Ten days out, and they came upon the junction of the roads, where the slave column from Lozi Land in the south joined up with another more numerous column coming in from the country of the great freshwater lakes in the west. Fundi and Aboli examined the abandoned site where the two caravans had camped the first night after they had met. 'There are now over two thousand slaves in the column. I have counted their sleeping places.' Aboli showed Tom where the slaves had flattened the grass when they lay down for the night. 'Most are carrying heavy loads, some made up of food supplies, grain and dried game meat.'

'How do you know that?' Tom demanded.

'Their deep heelprints in the dust show that they are burdened. Then they have discarded a few of the empty food baskets beside the cooking-fires, and left a few kernels of grain and scraps of meat in them,' Aboli explained. 'But they are also being forced by the Arabs to carry many ivory tusks as well.'

'Ivory?' Tom's interest was piqued. 'Where would they find ivory?'

'The Arabs have plundered it from the villages they have raided, and the Omani are also hunters, as you are.' Fundi had joined in the discussion.

'How can you tell this, about the ivory?'

Aboli took him to the far side of the camp-site, and pointed to marks in the earth. 'This is where they stacked the tusks while they rested for the night.' The long curved imprints in the earth were clear for even Tom to read.

'There are about a hundred and sixty Arab guards and merchants with the caravan.' Aboli led him to the thatched *bomas* of thorn branches that had housed the guards for the night, and pointed out the mattresses of cut grass on which they had slept. 'One for each man, and I have also counted the footprints.'

'How can you tell the footprints of Arab from those of slave?' Tom wanted to know.

'The Arabs wear sandals. Many have big dogs on leashes – here you can see the pad marks. They use them to frighten the slaves, and to catch the runaways.'

'We have wasted almost an hour here,' Tom cut in. 'We know how many enemy there are to deal with. Let us go after them.'

This huge agglomeration of heavily burdened men and women moved even slower than before, and the much smaller file of pursuers, hardened by years of hunting the elephant herds, gained on them rapidly.

In the middle of the morning of the seventeenth day since leaving Bongola's village, two of the scouts came running back to the head of the pursuit column, where Sarah marched beside Tom, matching him stride for stride on her long legs. 'We have seen the smoke from their camp-fires ahead,' they shouted, before they reached the head of the column.

'Stay with Luke and Alf,' Tom ordered Sarah, and he beckoned to Aboli. The two moved forward, falling into the steady trot they used to close in on the elephant herds in the final stage of the hunt. The Lozi scouts guided them to the top of a small granite hill from which they had a good view over miles of the country ahead.

The smoke from hundreds of small cooking-fires was scribbled against the cloudless blue of the sky not more than a few miles ahead. 'We have them now,' Tom exulted, and led the others down the hill at the same ground-eating trot. Within the hour they reached the deserted encampment and the fires were still smoking. The wide pathway beaten by thousands of bare feet wound away among the trees, and they ran along it.

They stopped involuntarily to a distant sound: a mournful dirge sung by a thousand voices, soft in the harsh midday sun but heartbreakingly beautiful. The slaves were singing a lament to a lost land, to the home and loved ones they would never see again.

Tom surveyed the land ahead. 'We will circle out to the right.' He pointed. 'We must get ahead of the column and watch as it passes so that we know the exact numbers and the formation they are keeping.'

They came out of the edge of the trees and before them lay an open plain that reached to the horizon, the pale yellow grassland shimmering with mirage in the sunlight. Isolated *kopjes* lay like small islands on the wide expanse, and here and there stood a flat-topped acacia tree. Herds of game were scattered across the open plain, zebra, wildebeest and gazelle. Giraffe stretched up their stately necks to feed on the top leaves of the acacia, and here and there a rhinoceros stood, massive, horned and dark, against the pale grass.

Two or three miles out on their left flank a fine mist of dust marked the position of the slave caravan, and Tom and Aboli agreed quickly on their next move. One of the conical granite hills stood fairly in the path of the distant column. Its summit would afford an ideal vantage-point, but they had to move swiftly. They left the Lozi scouts hidden in the trees, and the two broke into a full run across the plain.

They were almost blown by the time they reached the foot of the little hill on the opposite side from the approaching caravan, and they threw themselves on the ground and struggled for breath. As soon as they had recovered sufficiently to sit up, they drank a few mouthfuls from the waterskin. Then they pulled themselves to their feet and climbed the rocky side of the hill.

Just below the summit they threw themselves flat once more, and peeped cautiously over the top. The head of the slave caravan was a mile distant across the grassland, and would pass close to the foot of their hill.

Thousands of tiny figures were strung out in a straggling file, reaching back almost three miles to the edge of the forest. It was exactly as Tom had pictured it from Aboli's reading of the sign. At the head of the column rode an impressive figure on an Arab stallion. He was dressed in long green robes, and his head and face were covered in a flowing turban of the same colour. Only his eyes were left uncovered. Two stark naked black female slaves trotted beside the horse, holding a large tasselled sunshade over the rider.

The other Arabs were marching on the flanks of the column. Through the telescope Tom counted a hundred and fifty-four of them all told. A hundred and thirty-six were foot soldiers, and the others were mounted. They were all robed and heavily armed. The mounted men rode back and forth along the column, urging it on.

The slaves were too numerous to count accurately, but Tom saw that Aboli's initial estimate of two thousand must be close to the mark. Most, both men and women, were naked. A few wore scraps of leather or ragged trade cloth around their waists. They were all fettered. The children were tied together in groups of five or six, with ropes of plaited bark or rawhide around their necks. The slavers had not used up on them their supply of chains.

The heads and bodies of all the slaves were coated grey with dust, through which sweat had streaked giving them an unearthly appearance. They were all carrying something; even the children had gourds or grain baskets balanced on their heads. The women held the bedrolls and possessions of the slave masters, or baskets and waterskins. The men brought the ivory. Through the lens of his telescope Tom saw they had hundreds of tusks between them. A few were so large that it took four men to carry one.

Closer and closer the column crept to the foot of the hill on which they lay and they could make out more details and hear the mournful singing. One of the women near the head of the line dropped the basket from her head and slumped to the ground, pulling down the three others who were chained to her. Those around her tried to lift her to her feet again, but she was too weak to stay upright.

The disturbance brought four of the slave-masters running. They gathered around the fallen girl, and Tom could hear their angry shouts as they tried to get her up again. Then one of them laid into her with a *kiboko*. He swung from on high, aiming first at the back of her legs and, when that had no effect, raining cutting blows across her back and buttocks. The sharp clap of the lash on bare skin carried clearly in the heated air.

At last the guards resigned themselves to the loss of another piece of trade goods. One knelt and unlocked the shackles from the girl's wrist, then he seized her ankles and dragged her body off the path. His comrades urged the halted column forward, and they left the girl's naked, dusty body where it lay.

Now the column was passing so close to the *kopje* that they could make out the faces of the slaves with the naked eye. Suddenly Aboli stiffened and grasped Tom's arm. He pointed to the centre of the line and it took Tom a moment to see what had excited him. There, another file of children marched, boys and girls mixed indiscriminately, linked together with a long light rope around their waists. Each child carried a bundle or basket balanced on his or her head, the size and weight of each load graduated to the age and strength of the one who carried it. The boy at the head of the file was the tallest. He walked proudly and lithely where the others slumped with weariness and despair.

'Zama,' said Aboli. 'My eldest son. And that is Tula behind him.' His voice was level but his eyes held a great, burning anger. 'There are Zete and Falla also, in the rank behind them.' The two women were naked, chained at the necks, their breasts heavy and full of the unsucked milk left by their massacred infants.

Tom had nothing to say for his old friend's comfort, so they lay quietly and watched the sorry procession wind past them. So slow was the pace that it took almost two hours, but the slave-masters drove them on with shouts and flicking whips.

In the wake of the column a pack of hyena and jackals followed. They gobbled up the excrement left on the veld by the dysentery-racked slaves and any other discarded waste and offal. Tom thought that the abandoned slave-girl must have died but he was wrong. When the hyena gathered around her in a circle, giggling and hooting with greedy excitement, she struggled up on one elbow and tried to rise to her feet, but the effort was too much. She collapsed and drew up her knees to her chest, covering her dusty head with bare arms.

The hyena pack drew back a little, but then edged forward again, circling her. One stretched out its neck and tried to sniff her foot. The girl picked up a stone, threw it, and the beast backed away. Then another of the huge dog-like animals rushed at her from behind and sank its fangs into her shoulder. While she rolled and kicked in the dust, it worried her, shaking its massive head, until it had bitten out a lump of her flesh, which it swallowed, while the girl collapsed sobbing on the dusty earth. The smell of fresh blood was too much for the others to resist. Another hyena darted in and seized her foot. It ran off with her, dragging her like a sledge on her back. Tom jumped to his feet, ready to rush down the hillside to save her, but Aboli pulled him down again. 'The Arabs are still too close.' He pointed at the tail of the column half a mile away. 'They will see you. There is nothing we can do for her.'

Aboli was right, of course. Tom slumped down again and watched another hyena rush in and bite into the girl's stomach, leaning back against the drag of the first animal. They had her stretched out between them, and her wild screams carried to the men on the hilltop. Then a dozen other beasts joined in, ripping her apart, crunching her bones with their great jaws, wolfing down her flesh while her struggles weakened, then ended. Within minutes there was nothing left of her but the wet and bloody patch of earth. The pack loped on after the disappearing slave caravan.

Tom and Aboli climbed down from their vantage-point and followed after them, shadowing the caravan while the day dwindled away and the sun crept down towards the horizon. When the slave-masters ordered the night halt and the column went into bivouac, they crept even closer. Using the cover of a grove of acacia trees, they assessed the layout of the camp, carefully noting the horse lines and the *bomas* of the Arabs.

When the sun set and darkness fell they left the camp and hurried back. Within the hour they met up with the rest of their party coming up behind them. They built a screened fire to cook the evening meal, and while they ate hurriedly Tom held his war council and gave each of his lieutenants their orders for the night attack on the Arab camp. As soon as they had finished eating, they moved forward again.

They could see the glow of the camp-fires from two miles away across the plain, and moved in. Tom and Aboli placed each of the Lozi archers in his allotted position, and repeated their orders so that there could be no misunderstanding. Then they moved into their own positions and began the long wait. Tom wanted to attack in that darkest time between midnight and dawn, when the spirits and vigour of the Arabs would be at their lowest ebb.

Slowly the camp-fires of the caravan flickered lower, then burned down to puddles of red ash. The great Scorpion of stars, tail held high, crept down across the sky above them then sank towards the horizon. The voices and the singing of the slaves died away, and a profound silence settled over the encampment.

'It is time,' Tom said at last, and stood up. They moved in closer and made one last inspection of the encampment, making certain that nothing had altered. The only fire still burning brightly was the one at the horse lines among a grove of acacia trees on the near side of the camp.

Against the flames they saw three of the Arab guards sitting together, drinking coffee and talking quietly. They were staring into the fire. That will blind them, Tom thought grimly, and then whispered to Aboli, 'Take the one nearest you.'

They moved in until they were at the edge of the circle of firelight. Both had kept their swords covered so there would be no reflection of firelight to alert a sentry.

'Have at them!' Tom slipped his blade from the scabbard and ran lightly up behind the seated Arabs. He killed the first cleanly, with a thrust in the back of the neck. Across the fire Aboli killed another. The dead man fell face forward into the fire and his turban and long bushy hair burst into flames and flared like a torch.

The third Arab let out a startled shout and started to his feet, but Tom stabbed him in the throat. The blue sword slid in sweetly and the next shout drowned, gurgling, in the man's own blood.

Tom and Aboli crouched over their victims' bodies, listening for the alarm, but the horse lines were set apart from the main camp and the dying Arab had made no more noise than a sleeping man in a nightmare. All was still. They moved to where the horses were tethered. Another dark shadow came to meet them from among the trees. Tom challenged with a low two-toned whistle, the call of a night-jar. The recognition signal came at once and Luke Jervis stepped forward.

'All secure!' he murmured, letting Tom know that the other Arabs in the horse lines had been taken care of. Tom ran to one of the horses. He had picked out the bay stallion the Arab leader had ridden that day, and marked its position in the lines. Now he untied its halter and spoke to it softly, stroking its forehead, gentling it with hand and voice. Then he swung up onto its bare back. Aboli had chosen another horse, and when he was mounted Tom whistled softly to Luke.

Luke ran back to where his men had surrounded one of the sleeping *bomas* of the Arab guards. Almost immediately there came thudding volleys of musket fire all around the periphery of the camp and spurts of muzzle flame pricked the darkness as the sailors fired into the sleeping Arabs at close range. A low buzz ran through the camp as it came awake, and quickly built up into a screaming, shouting uproar. The Arab slave-masters came stumbling out of the *bomas*, half asleep and fumbling with their weapons to be met by volley after volley of musket fire and flights of whistling Lozi arrows.

The slaves were unable to move, for they had been chained down to the iron stakes that the slave-masters had driven into the hard earth. They lay where they were fettered and wailed and howled with terror, adding to the confusion.

Some of the Arabs were firing back, and a determined resistance was mounting. Tom galloped down the line towards the *boma* of thorn branches where, at sundown, he had watched the caravan leader take shelter. He carried a burning brand from the guards' camp-fire in one hand, and now he hurled it on to the thatched roof of the hut. It caught quickly and the flames soared up, showering sparks and lighting the night for a hundred yards around. Driven out by the heat, the Arab leader came running from the hut with a jezail in one hand. He was without a turban and his oiled grey hair fell to his shoulders. His beard was in tangled disarray. Tom wheeled the horse and charged straight at him. The Arab stood to meet him, and threw up the jezail. Tom lay along the stallion's neck and drove it on straight into the muzzle of the musket.

The Arab fired and in the bloom of powder smoke Tom heard the ball whir close past his head. He expected the old man to turn and run once his weapon was fired. Instead he stood proudly, helpless and unarmed, but with head up and fierce eye to meet his death. Tom felt a pang of admiration and respect as he leaned out and drove the glittering blue blade through the man's heart with such force that the Arab was lifted clean off his feet and died before he struck the ground again. Tom rode back and looked down at him. Moved by the night breeze, his silver beard feathered across his chest. Tom might have felt remorse, but then he remembered Aboli's massacred children, the girl who had been eaten alive by the hyena pack, and his guilt withered stillborn.

He wheeled away and, from the back of the stallion, looked down the line. At two places the slave-masters had taken cover and grouped together in small pockets of resistance. Tom called urgently to Aboli, 'We must break them up. Ride with me.' They stormed down upon them, swords bared, and, yelling with the furious ecstasy of battle, they cut them down. The Arabs who survived broke up under this onslaught. They threw down their empty muskets and ran out into the darkness.

'Let them go!' Tom stopped his men from pursuing

them and consoled himself. 'They will not get far and I will send Fundi and his archers after them as soon as it is light.'

In the fighting he had become separated from Aboli. He rode down the slave lines, searching for him. The fighting was over, but the encampment was a shambles. Many of the slaves had pulled up their stakes and were stumbling about in the firelight shouting and howling. The din was deafening, and Tom could not make his orders heard. When he tried to beat sense into some of the slaves with his scabbard, it only made them more witless with terror. He gave up any effort to quieten them and rode on looking for Aboli. He saw his horse, but with no rider. He felt a painful stab of concern that Aboli had been shot off its back. He urged his own horse forward, but then in the crowd he saw Aboli on foot, carrying two small boys in his arms, hugging their naked dusty bodies against his chest.

'They are unharmed, Klebe, both of them,' Aboli shouted to him, and Tom waved and wheeled back to find Sarah. He knew she would be somewhere in this sea of black bodies trying to minister to those who needed her help, and he felt real concern for her in this dangerous, volatile atmosphere: she could easily be trampled by the surging mob or run into an escaping Arab who carried a curved dagger on his belt.

He saw her golden hair like a beacon in the firelight, and pushed the stallion through the throng to reach her. He bent down, slipped an arm around her waist, lifted her up onto the horse's withers in front of him and kissed her.

She threw both arms around his neck and hugged him so hard that it hurt. 'You did it, my darling. They are free.'

'And there is a fine load of Arab ivory to pick up.' He grinned.

'You base creature.' She smiled back at him. 'Is that all you can think of in this glorious moment?'

'My father taught me, "Do good to all men, but at the end remember to collect your fee."'

It took the rest of the night to restore order among the hordes of slaves. Most were still in chains, but as soon as it was light they began the work of freeing them. Tom found an enormous bunch of keys on the belt around the waist of the old Arab headman he had killed. The keys fitted the locks, and as they were released, Tom ordered the slaves to be placed in separate groups, divided by tribes and villages. Then he made them the responsibility of their own chieftains and headmen.

Sarah tended first to Aboli's family. The two boys were unhurt and still healthy. Zete and Falla were beside themselves with terror but Aboli spoke to them sternly, and they quietened. When Sarah was certain they no longer needed her help, she went among the others. First she picked out the children who needed medical attention. Many were smitten with dysentery and she dosed them with a binding potion, then treated their chain and rope galls with healing ointment. Though she worked tirelessly through the night and into the following day, she could not do enough with her small medicine chest for the hundreds who called to her for help.

While this was going on Tom sent Fundi and his band of archers after the fleeing Arabs who had escaped during the night. They had not gone far, and most were unarmed. Fundi's men hunted them down quickly, and finished them off with the wickedly barbed arrows. The poison turned the flesh around the entry wounds purple, then ran through the blood like liquid fire. It was not a kind death, but when the hunters brought back the severed heads of their victims as proof of the kill, Tom looked upon them dispassionately. The deeds of the dead men were fresh in his mind, and his anger was not yet appeased.

Under their officers the sailors ransacked the camp, and piled the spoils in a heap for Tom to count and enter in his log book. Apart from the mountain of ivory, they found a small iron chest in the ashes of the caravan master's hut. It had withstood the heat of the flames, and when they broke it open they found it contained gold dinar coins worth almost three hundred pounds. 'That adds up to fair profit for a day's work of good deeds,' Tom said to Sarah, with satisfaction.

They gathered up the food baskets and the muskets, the kegs of powder and the bars of lead for casting shot, bales of trade cloth, sacks of beads and mounds of other valuable equipment.

'How are you going to carry all this back to Fort Providence?' Sarah wanted to know. 'You may be forced to leave it here.'

'We will see to that,' Tom promised grimly, and had Fundi and Aboli bring all the headmen of the released slaves to him. He explained to them that he would divide up the food stores between the people from the different tribes, and that the women and children were free to return to their villages. However, in exchange for their freedom every one of the men must act as porter to carry the spoils down to Lozi Land. After that, they would be free to follow the women back to their homes. He explained to them that they would be paid in trade goods for their labour. The chieftains were delighted with this arrangement, for naturally all the wages of their subjects would come directly to them. Until that moment they had not realized that they were free again, and had believed that they had merely exchanged one set of slave-masters for another.

It took several days to share out the food and make up the splinter caravans before Tom was able to send the women on their way home. They went singing their thanks and praises to the white men who had saved them. Then the heavily burdened caravan of men started into the south, with Tom and Sarah, mounted on captured Arab horses, at the head of the column.

Tom left Fundi and twenty of his most intrepid hunters to patrol the slave road during the rest of the dry season. As soon as they spotted the approach of another Arab caravan Fundi had his orders to send runners to Fort Providence to alert Tom.

When they reached Fort Providence, Tom realized that he had more than a full cargo of ivory for the little *Centaurus*.

'We will not be forced to hunt again, for this season at least,' he told Sarah. 'I will be able to concentrate all my efforts on freeing more of these miserable slaves from the clutches of the wicked Mussulmen.'

His expression was pious and virtuous, but she saw the twinkle in his eyes and was not taken in. 'I wish those were honest sentiments, Thomas Courtney, but I know you too well. You are in this for the ivory and the fun of a good fight.'

'You are too harsh a judge, my pretty darling,' he protested, with a grin, 'but why should you quibble? It's those brats you care about, and I am giving them into your care. This way we both have our heart's desire.'

'It won't be as easy next time,' she warned him. 'The Arab merchants will be expecting you.'

'Ah! But I also have a few ideas on that score.'

They had captured almost two hundred Arab muskets, and a goodly store of powder and lead. Instead of elephant hunting, Tom and his crew trained fifty Lozi warriors as musketeers. They had picked the most promising men, but even these had difficulty in mastering a weapon so alien to their culture. They never truly overcame their fear and awe of the firearm, or the instinct to close their eyes tightly in anticipation of the discharge. Tom soon realized that they would never be marksmen. He accepted this, and instead drilled them to fire massed volleys at close range, loading the jezails with a handful of specially cast buckshot that would spread, rather than a single ball.

Within weeks, one of Fundi's runners had come into Fort Providence from the north with news of another slave caravan coming down from the lake country. 'Time to see if my new strategy works,' Tom said to Sarah. 'I don't suppose I can prevail upon you to remain here at Fort Providence out of harm's way?' For answer she smiled and went to pack her medical stores.

When at last they came up with the caravan, they found that it was even larger and richer than the first, but more heavily escorted with Arab infantry and mounted men. Tom's men were outnumbered by almost two to one. He and Aboli shadowed the Arabs for days while they worked out a plan to attack them.

Very soon it became clear that the Arab slave-masters had learned of the fate of the first caravan. They were very much on the alert. On the march they threw out a screen of scouts, and at the first sign of trouble pulled back into defensive formations in businesslike style. They went into carefully constructed defensive *bomas* when they halted at night, and kept a vigilant cordon of sentries around their encampments to guard against a night attack.

Tom and Aboli scouted ahead of the column and found the ford of a wide river where the slave caravan would be forced to cross. They moved their own force up and concentrated all their men in the dense riverine forest on the far bank.

When the slave caravan reached the river, the long unwieldy column began the crossing. Tom allowed the head of it to cross unmolested. Then, when half of the slaves and their escorts were across, he cut them off and fell on the head of the column.

From their carefully concealed positions, the Lozi musketeers fired massed volleys at point-blank range into the Arab guards. Using the spread of small shot, even they could not miss and the effect was murderous. For a while the fighting was fierce but the Arab advance guard was outnumbered and shot to pieces by those first volleys. When their comrades on the far bank tried to cross the river to reinforce them, they were forced to wade almost chest-deep through the current, and were driven back in confusion by the accurate fire of Tom's sailors.

By nightfall the fighting on this bank was over. Tom's men had captured the head of the caravan and wiped out all the Arab guards. They had also captured the entire Arab stores of black powder. Tom now had the advantage of numbers, and the remaining Arabs on the far bank were desperately short of ammunition.

Tom moved his men across the river, and launched a series of lightning raids on the Arab positions, forcing the slave-masters to defend themselves and use up the last of their powder. Once their muskets were empty he attacked in earnest and shattered the Arab line. With the last of their powder gone, the defenders were wiped out in desperate hand-to-hand fighting in which the Lozi used their short stabbing spears to savage effect. The last of the Arabs was driven into the river where, drawn by the scent of blood in the water, the crocodiles had gathered.

In the aftermath of the fighting, Tom freed over three thousand slaves, and marched south to Fort Providence with a long file of porters carrying vast booty.

Although Fundi's scouts maintained the watch on the slave roads, that was the last caravan to try to win through to the Fever Coast during that dry season. 'We must pray for better business next time,' Tom said to Sarah, as they stood together on the quarterdeck of the little *Centaurus* as she ran downriver to the ocean at the beginning of the Big Wet.

'If business grows any better, you will sink the ship under us,' she told him. 'I cannot even use my cabin because it's stuffed so full of elephant tusks.'

'It's all these children of yours that weigh us down,' Tom said accusingly.

Sarah had not been able to resist taking into her care four of the most appealing orphans from the released slave caravans. She lavished her maternal instincts upon them, and now they clustered around her, dressed in the clothes she had sewn for them, sucking their thumbs and clinging to her skirts. 'Thomas Courtney, I do declare you are jealous of a few little babies.'

'When we reach Good Hope I will buy you a pretty bonnet to win back your love,' he promised.

She opened her mouth to tell him she would prefer a baby son, but that was a painful subject for both of them. Instead she smiled. 'And a pretty dress to go with it. I have lived in rags these past months.' She hugged his arm. 'Oh, Tom, it will be so good to reach civilization again. Even for so short a time.'

The Caliph of Oman, Abd Muhammad al-Malik, was dying in his Muscat palace, and not even the wisest of his physicians could fathom the cause of the mysterious disease that had assailed him. They had purged him until blood dribbled out of his anus. They had lanced the veins in his arms and bled him until his gaunt face was *écru* and sallow, with plum-coloured eye-sockets. They had blistered his chest and back with hot irons to burn out the sickness, all to no avail.

The disease had begun to manifest itself shortly after

Prince Zayn al-Din had returned from the long pilgrimage to Mecca and the holy places of Islam that his father had ordered him to undertake as a penance for his treachery. On his return to Muscat, Zayn al-Din had once again made the most abject petitions to his father. He tore his fine raiment and slashed his cheeks and chest with a sharp knife. He poured ash and dust on his head and crawled on his hands and knees into his father's presence, wailing for forgiveness.

Al-Malik had stepped down from the ivory throne, lifted him to his feet and, with the hem of his own robe, had wiped away the blood and dirt from his son's fat face. Then he kissed him on the lips. 'You are my son, and although once I had lost you, now you are restored to me,' he said. 'Go and bathe yourself, change your apparel. Put on the blue robes of a royal Omani and take your seat on the cushion at my right hand.'

Soon after this the terrible headaches began, which left the Caliph confused and drowsy. Then he was attacked by fits of convulsions and vomiting. His stomach ached and his stools were black and tarry, his urine dark red with blood.

While the physicians treated him and looked for improvement, the disease worsened. His fingernails turned blue. His hair and his beard fell out in tufts. He drifted in and out of coma and his flesh melted away, so that his bald and hairless head resembled that of a cadaver.

Knowing that the end was near, thirty of his sons gathered around his bed in the dark, shuttered, airless bedchamber. The eldest, Zayn al-Din, sat closest to his bed and led the chanted prayers for the intervention of Allah in their father's suffering.

Once, in the pause between prayers, Zayn al-Din lifted his tear-filled eyes and looked sorrowfully across the chamber at his half-brother. Ibn al-Malik Abubaker was the son of one of the lesser concubines. He had always been Zayn al-Din's trusted companion from their child-hood days in the zenana on Lamu island. Because of his lowly status in the royal household Abubaker might have dropped into obscurity. However, there is a saying in the desert that every man needs a camel to carry him over the sands. Zayn al-Din was Abubaker's camel. On the back of his elder half-brother, Abubaker was determined to ride one day to power. He knew also that Zayn al-Din needed him, for Abubaker was the faithful servant, shrewd and resourceful, committed to his brother. He had been at Zayn al-Din's side at the battle of Muscat, and had tried to protect him when the Ottoman Turks had been routed, but in the mêlée he had been lanced in the chest and thrown from his horse.

After the battle he had recovered from his wound, and received a pardon from the new Caliph; al-Malik was always benevolent and generous to his sons. Instead of being grateful for this mercy, though, Abubaker was fiercely resentful. Like Zayn al-Din, he was ambitious and devious, a born conspirator, and greedy for power. He knew that, despite his father's expression of forgiveness, his treachery would be remembered for the rest of the Caliph's life. May that be short, he thought, as he looked across the crowded bedchamber, fogged with incense smoke, and caught the eye of Zayn al-Din. His brother gave him a barely percep-tible nod, and Abubaker lowered his eyes then smoothed his moustache as a sign that he had understood.

It was Abubaker who had provided the bitter white powder that was doing the business for them. One of the physicians tending the sinking Caliph was Abubaker's man. Administered in tiny doses, the poison accumulated in the body of the victim so that the symptoms became gradually more acute. Silently Abubaker agreed with his brother that it was time to give the Caliph the lethal dose that would end it.

Abubaker covered his face with the black headcloth,

as if to hide his sorrow, and smiled. By this time tomorrow his elder brother Zayn al-Din would be seated on the Elephant Throne. He, ibn al-Malik Abubaker, would be commander of the armies and fleets of Oman. Zayn al-Din had promised him that, and the rank of *imam* and two lakhs of rupees from the royal treasury. Abubaker had always seen himself as a mighty warrior, and he knew that at last his star was rising and beginning to burn brightly. 'All thanks to my sainted brother, Zayn al-Din. May Allah shower ten thousand blessings upon his head,' he whispered.

At dusk the physicians gave the Caliph a potion to help him sleep and to strengthen him against the assaults of the night demons. Although al-Malik coughed, dribbled the medicine down his chin and rolled his head away, the doctors held him gently and spooned every last drop down his throat.

He lay so still and pale on the cushions that twice during the long, hot night the doctors opened his eyelids, held a lamp in front of his face and watched for the shrinking of the pupils. 'In the love and kindness of Allah, the Caliph yet lives,' they intoned each time.

Then, as the first coppery rays of dawn light pricked through the fretwork of the shutters of the east window, the Caliph started up suddenly and gave a strong, clear cry. 'God is great!' Then he fell back on the sweat-soaked cushions of his bed, and a slow trickle of blood ran from his nostrils and down his cheeks into the bed-linen.

The doctors rushed forward, forming a circle around the body, and though all his sons craned for a glimpse of their father, he was hidden from them. The chief surgeon whispered to the vizier of the court in lugubrious tones. Then the vizier faced the rows of seated princes and intoned, in a voice of heavy portent, 'Abd Muhammad al-Malik, Caliph of Oman, is dead. Allah receive his spirit!'

'In God's Name,' they replied in solemn chorus, many faces raddled with grief.

'In accordance with his father's wishes, Zayn al-Din is the successor to the Elephant Throne of Oman. May Allah bless him and grant him a long, glorious reign.'

'In God's Name!' they repeated, but none showed any joy at the announcement. They knew that dark days were ahead.

Outside the city walls, jutting out into the sea, was a rocky headland. The cliffs on the point fell sheer into deep water, so clear that every detail of the coral below was etched like a marble mosaic. The new Caliph had ordered a pavilion of polished pink granite blocks built upon the lip of the precipice. He named it the Palace of Retribution. From his seat in the shaded colonnade he could look down to the surface of the sea and watch the long, dark shadows of the sharks gliding over the reef far below. There had been no sharks when first the palace was built, but now there were many, and they were well fed.

Zayn al-Din was eating a ripe pomegranate when they brought another of his father's officers barefoot before him. They had shaved his head and beard, and placed a chain around his neck as a symbol of condemnation. 'You were unkind to me, bin-Nabula,' the Caliph said, 'when I was in disgrace and out of my father's favour, may Allah bless his sainted soul!' He spat one of the pomegranate pips, which hit the proud old man in the face. He did not even blink but stared back coldly at his tormentor. Bin-Nabula had commanded the former Caliph's army and fleet: he was a soldier proud.

'You called me the fat puppy.' Zayn al-Din wagged his head sorrowfully. 'That was very cruel of you.'

'It was a name that fitted you well,' the condemned man replied. 'And since then you have grown wider in girth and more repulsive in mien. I give thanks to Allah that your noble father cannot know what a plague he has visited upon his people.'

'Old man, you were always garrulous, but I have a certain cure for that vice.' Zayn al-Din nodded to the new general of his army. 'My little friends down there are hungry. Do not keep them waiting.'

Abubaker bowed. He was dressed in burnished half-armour with a spiked helmet and embroidered silk neck flap. When he straightened he was smiling. The smile on that narrow face, with the snaggle teeth of a barracuda, was dreadful to look upon but bin-Nabula did not flinch. 'Many good men have gone along this road ahead of me,' bin-Nabula said. 'I prefer their company to yours.'

The executions had been conducted daily over the last months since the accession of the new Caliph. Hundreds of once powerful and important men had gone over the cliff to the waiting shark pack. Zayn al-Din had a long memory for a slight or an insult and neither he nor General Abubaker tired of the sport.

'Remove the chain,' Abubaker ordered his men. He did not want bin-Nabula to sink too swiftly. They lifted the heavy links from his neck, and led him to the block.

'Both feet,' Abubaker commanded, and they placed his legs across the block. Abubaker had refined the punishment: with his feet gone, the condemned man could splash on the surface but not swim to the shore, and the blood in the water would rouse the shark pack and drive it into a feeding frenzy.

He drew his sword and slashed the blade through the air above bin-Nabula's legs, smiling at him with those uneven teeth. The old general looked back at him steadily, without any sign of fear. Abubaker could have delegated this duty to any of his men, but he took pleasure in doing his brother's work himself. He laid the edge of the curved blade against the old man's ankle, judging his stroke with narrowed eyes.

'A single clean stroke,' Zayn al-Din encouraged him, 'or I shall claim a penalty from you, my brother.'

Abubaker lifted the blade, paused at the top, then swung down. The steel hissed in the air, then sliced through flesh and bone and thudded into the wooden block. The white foot with its blue veins dropped on to the polished granite floor, and Zayn al-Din clapped his hands. 'A fair stroke indeed. But can you do the same again?'

Abubaker wiped the blade on a square of silk that a slave handed him, then lined up on the other ankle. Hiss and clunk, the steel sank deep into the wood of the block. Zayn al-Din hooted with laughter.

The soldiers carried bin-Nabula to the edge of the cliff, leaving a wet red trail across the pink polished granite flags. Zayn al-Din jumped up from his cushions and limped to the low parapet that protected him from the drop. He leaned over the wall and looked down. 'My little fishes are waiting for you, bin-Nabula. Go with God.'

The soldiers threw him over the edge and his robes ballooned around him as he fell, but he made no sound. Some of them screamed all the way down, and Zayn al-Din enjoyed that. Bin-Nabula struck the surface and was driven deep by the impetus of his fall. Then the disturbed water cleared and they saw him float up to the surface. He floundered there, trying to keep his head above the water but the water clouded red around him.

'There!' Zayn al-Din pointed down with a trembling finger and shrieked with excitement. 'Look at my lovely fish.'

The dark shapes moved with agitation, speeding up as they rose towards the surface, circling the struggling old man.

'Yes, my little ones, come! Come!'

Then the first shot in and bin-Nabula was plucked below the surface. But the water was so clear that Zayn al-Din could follow every detail of the banquet he had set.

When the sport was ended and there was nothing further to watch, he returned to the pile of cushions under the silk canopy and called for cold sherbet to drink. Then he beckoned his brother to come to him. 'That was well done, Abubaker, but it is more satisfying when they scream. I believe the old *shaitan* remained silent merely to diminish my enjoyment.'

'Bin-Nabula was always an obstinate old goat,' Abubaker agreed. 'There were six hundred and twelve names on the list you gave me. It is sad, Majesty, but bin-Nabula was number six hundred. We are almost at the end of the list.'

'No. No, my dearest brother, we are not nearly at an end. One of the chiefs of all our enemies has not been dealt with yet.'

'Give me the rascal's name.' Abubaker showed his uneven teeth in a grimace that was too savage to be a smile. 'Tell me where to find him, and I will seek him out for you.'

'But, my brother, you know him well. You also have a reckoning with him.' Zayn al-Din leaned forward, his belly sagging into his lap, and drew up the hem of his robe. Tenderly he massaged the deformed joint of his ankle. 'Even after all the years my foot still aches when there is thunder in the air.' Understanding dawned in Abubaker's dark eyes, and Zayn al-Din went on softly, 'I did not enjoy being dragged on a rope's end to the gates of Muscat.'

'Al-Salil.' Abubaker nodded. 'The red-headed green-eyed devil. I know where to find him. Our sainted father, Allah bless his memory, sent him to Africa to reopen the trade routes for our caravans.'

'Take as many ships and men as you need, Abubaker. Go to Africa. Find him and bring him back to me, broken, if you wish, but not dead. Do you understand me?'

'Broken, but not dead. I understand you perfectly, Majesty.'

Yasmini waded out from the shore. She sucked in her already flat belly at the cold, and raised her hands above her head. Dorian lay on the crisp white sand and watched her. Although they had made love only minutes before, he never tired of looking at that cream and ivory body. She had bloomed since leaving the stultifying bounds of the zenana walls. Now she bubbled with interest and excitement for all the wonders around her, and when they were alone her sense of fun and mischief enchanted him.

Waist-deep in the lake, Yasmini scooped a double handful of the sweet water and raised it to her lips. As she swallowed, a few droplets spilled from between her fingers and dribbled on to her chest. They caught the sunlight and sparkled like a diamond necklace on her smooth skin. Her nipples puckered at the chill and stood out crisply.

She turned and waved at him. Then, with a shudder of protest at the cold water, she lowered herself until only her head showed. Her hair, shot through with the silver blaze, floated in a dark cloud around her lotus face.

'Have courage, master! Come in!' she invited, but he waved a lazy hand in refusal. This respite was so delightful after the months of hard marching up from the coast.

'Is the great sheikh, the mighty warrior and victor of Muscat, afraid of a little cold water?' she mocked.

He smiled at her and shook his head. 'I do not fear the water, but you have exhausted all my strength, O brazen one.'

'That was my purpose!' She tinkled with laughter, and suddenly rose up and splashed a sheet of the cold water over him.

'Wicked woman!' He sprang up. 'You have exhausted my forbearance also.' He charged into the lake in a storm of spray and, though she tried to escape, he seized her and plunged both of them below the surface. They came up clinging together and spluttering with laughter. After a while, her expression became solemn.

'I fear that you have not been truthful with me, lord,' she said. 'I am holding in my right hand that which proves your strength is far from exhausted.'

'Is it enough that I ask your forgiveness for deceiving you?'

'No, it is not nearly enough.' She placed both slim arms around his neck. 'This is how the fish and crocodiles punish their mates when they err.' She hopped up and beneath the surface gripped his hips in the scissors of her legs.

A while later they waded back to the beach, still clinging together, and laughing breathlessly. They flopped down at the edge of the water, and Dorian looked up at the height of the sun. He murmured regretfully, 'The morning is almost spent. We must go back now, Yassie.'

'Just a little longer,' she pleaded. 'Sometimes I grow weary of playing the slave-boy.'

'Come!' he ordered, and pulled her to her feet. They went to where their clothing lay in an untidy heap, and dressed quickly. The little sailing dhow was drawn up on the sand, but before she stepped on board Yasmini paused and looked about her slowly, taking leave of this wondrous place where for an hour they had been happy and free.

On the top of the tallest tree of the island perched a

pair of snowy-headed fish eagles, their sleek bodies black washed with cinnamon. One of the birds threw back its head and uttered a yelping chant. 'I will never forget that cry,' Yasmini said. 'It is the very voice of this wild land.'

The hills on the far side of the lake were just an outline, paler blue than the water. A long line of pink flamingo flew low along the far shore. The head of the flight rose on a thermal of warm air then dropped again. Every following bird rose as it reached the same point in the air and then dropped exactly as the bird before it had. The effect was extraordinary, as though a long, pink serpent undulated above the azure waters.

'Nor will I ever forget such beauty,' Yasmini whispered. 'I would like to stay here for ever with you.'

'This is the country of God, where man counts for nothing,' Dorian said. 'But come. We cannot afford such a dream. Duty has me in its iron grasp. Tomorrow we must leave this place and begin the march back to the Fever Coast.'

'Just a moment longer, lord,' she begged, and pointed to a strange dark cloud, a mile out from where they stood, that rose from the surface of the lake, five hundred feet straight into the unsullied blue of the African sky.

'What is that? It is as though the water is on fire and sends smoke into the air.'

'Tiny insects,' Dorian told her. 'They breed on the bottom of the lake in their multitudes then rise to the surface and spin tiny sails of gossamer. On these sails they float into the air and are carried away.'

'The ways of Allah are wonderful,' she murmured, eyes shining.

'Come,' he urged again, 'and remember that you are once more Yassie, the slave-boy, and that you must show me duty and respect.'

'Yes, master.' She bowed low with her palms together touching her lips, and her entire demeanour changed. She was a consummate actress, and when she straightened up she held herself like a servant, not a princess, and moved like a boy as she pushed the dhow out into the lake and scrambled in over the bows.

They sat apart as the tiny craft rounded the end of the island and came in full view of the village on the mainland a league away across the water. Even at that distance many eyes would be watching them.

Although these waters were so expansive as to seem like the ocean itself, they were months of travel from the Fever Coast, and the climate was drier and healthier up here on the high plateau of the continent. The village of Ghandu was spread along several miles of the lakeshore, for this was the centre of all Omani trade with the interior. From here the long slave road wound down to the coast. In sight now were a dozen or more canoes and sailing dhows, plying in towards the port of Ghandu. They had voyaged down hundreds of miles of lakeshore, and they carried cargoes of dried fish, ivory, slaves, hides and gum arabic they had gathered from the vast wilderness.

As Dorian and Yasmini sailed in towards the village, she wrinkled her nose with distaste. The sweet air was tainted with the stench of the fish racks and the slave barracoons. When Dorian stepped ashore Bashir al-Sind, his chief lieutenant, was there to meet him with the rest of the army staff. Yassie hung back self-effacingly while Dorian was plunged immediately into the duty and responsibility of his command, a duty he had escaped for those few precious moments on the island with Yasmini.

'The women have arrived, lord,' Bashir told him, 'and the merchants have gathered to listen to your orders for the march.'

Dorian strode through the village, between the seething barracoons where the slaves were penned, through the squalor and misery that was in such bitter contrast to the beauty and serenity he and Yasmini had experienced a short while before. In the main souk, seated on their cushioned stools under their gaudy silk sunshades, each surrounded by his own entourage of robed guards and house-slaves, the five merchants awaited him. These men controlled all trade coming through Ghandu. They were all pious, learned men; their speech was cultured and the compliments they paid him were florid. Their deportment was dignified and noble, and they were exceedingly rich. Yet Dorian had come to despise them in the short time he had been at Ghandu and exposed to the savagery of the trade that supported them.

Dorian had been a slave once, but al-Malik had never treated him as one. Slavery had been a constant fact of his adult life, but for this reason he had given it little thought. Most of the slaves he had ever known were tamed or born into captivity, resigned to it and, in almost every case, treated kindly as valuable chattels. But since arriving here at Ghandu he had been confronted by the raw, brutal reality. He had been forced to witness the bringing in of the freshly captured people, and it had not been a comfortable lesson.

He found himself torn by his own humanity, and his love and duty to his adoptive father, the Caliph. He understood how the prosperity and well-being of the nation depended on this trade. He would not shirk the duty of protecting it, but he took no pleasure in what he had to do.

It was the hour of the midday prayers, so they made their ablutions. Yassie poured water for Dorian to wash, and he prayed with the merchants as they knelt in a row on the silk rugs, facing the holy places in the north. When they resumed their seats under the sunshades Dorian felt a strong desire to forgo the elaborate opening speeches of the merchants, the further exchange of compliments, and to come to the business that had to be discussed. However, he was now so Arabic in his ways that he could not bring himself to such gaucherie. The sun was well past its zenith before one of the merchants mentioned, almost in passing, that they had two hundred female slaves ready for him as he had requested.

'Bring them to me,' he ordered, and when the merchants gave the orders the women were paraded before him. Dorian saw at once that they had fobbed him off with the oldest and most sickly. Many would never survive the gruelling march to the coast. He felt his anger stir. He had come here to save these men from ruin. He had a *firman* from the Caliph commanding their obedience, and now they were niggardly and obstructive. He controlled his anger. The condition of the women was not vital to the success of his plans. He intended to place them in the caravan merely to lull the marauders into attacking. A slave column composed entirely of men must excite suspicion.

Out of hand Dorian rejected fifty of the women, the weak old crones and the women far gone in pregnancy. The rigours of the march would kill the old and bring those pregnant into labour long before their time, and Dorian could not take on his conscience the inevitable deaths of their infants. For the same reason he had refused the offer of children the merchants made. 'When we leave Ghandu, I want your lightest marching chains on these wretches,' he warned the merchants. He rose to his feet as a signal that the meeting was ended.

It was a relief to leave the odious village and to go up into the hills above the lake where the air was sweeter and cooler, the view glorious. Dorian had sited his camp upon the slopes. He had learned from his own experience that his men remained healthier if they were kept away from crowded villages, if the latrine pits were built away from the water supply and if the halal laws of food preparation were strictly observed. He had often wondered if the ritual washing before prayers also contributed to healthier troops.

Certainly there were fewer diseases in his camps than his father had experienced on the crowded little English ships on which Dorian had sailed as a child.

Although it was late afternoon by this time, his work was not yet finished for the day. There would be an early start tomorrow on the first leg of the march, and he had to review the order of his caravan.

Five hundred of his own men, together with the female slaves, were to make up his decoy. The coloration of the captured slaves was almost purple-black. Not even the darkest-complexioned of his Arabs were that colour, so Dorian had used the infusion of tanning bark, in which the lake fishermen soaked their nets, to dye their bodies to a more natural African shade. It was still not perfect, but he depended on the dust and grime of the march to make the deception more effective.

He had encountered further difficulties: none of his men would strip naked in public – religious modesty forbade that – so he was forced to allow them to wear loincloths, although he made certain these were filthy and ragged. They had also baulked at shaving their heads, but no African slave had flowing locks and Dorian had insisted sternly. They would wear light chains, but these would not be locked and could be cast off in an instant. With very poor grace the five merchants of Ghandu had contributed a hundred elephant tusks to sweeten the bait. These were small and light, so that the men could carry their weapons in bundles on their heads along with the ivory.

Dorian would lead the column, mounted, robed and veiled, just as the marauders would expect. He would keep Yassie close at hand. She had learned to ride astride on the march up from the coast. He would have a small detachment of Arab guards flanking the column, not so weak as to excite suspicion, but not so strong as to deter an attack.

Bashir al-Sind would bring up the rearguard with another thousand fighting men, keeping two or three leagues back so that his dust would not be visible to the enemy scouts. The signal that the vanguard was under attack would be a red Chinese rocket. At the signal Bashir would rush up and surround the attackers, while Dorian and his men would pin them down until Bashir could get his forces into position.

'It's a simple plan,' Dorian decided, after he and Bashir had gone over it together for the tenth time. 'There will be many things we cannot foresee, but those are the chances of war, and we will counter each as it arises. Perhaps the *fisi* will not come at all.' *Fisi* was the Swahili word for hyena, and that was what they had called the marauders.

'They will come, al-Salil,' Bashir predicted. 'They have the taste for Omani blood now, and they are addicted to it.'

'Pray to Allah that you are right,' said Dorian, and went to his own tent where the slave-boy, Yassie, had his evening meal prepared for him.

'There is something about this that troubles me,' said Aboli, as he studied the distant caravan through the lens.

'Share your anxiety with me,' Tom invited, with scarely veiled sarcasm.

Aboli shrugged. 'Those men are small-boned, delicately built. They walk with a strange grace, light-footed as cats. I have never seen slaves march like that.'

Three miles from where they lay in wait, the Arab caravan was descending the escarpment of the hills, winding down it like a serpent. 'They have been marching only a few weeks since leaving the lake country,' Tom explained, for himself rather than for Aboli. 'They are still fresh and strong.' He did not want to accept any evidence that might counsel against carrying out the attack. This was the first caravan of the dry season that they had been able to intercept and he had feared that the source and wellspring of their fortunes had dried up. He was determined that this prize would not slip through his net.

'Yes, the men are young and strong, but look at the women.' Tom took back the telescope, and studied them. He felt a little stir of unease in his guts. The women were different in skin tone, age and body structure from their men. 'They are of a different tribe,' Tom said, with more confidence in his tone than he felt.

'There are no children,' said Aboli. 'Where are the children?'

'God love you, Aboli!' Tom was exasperated. 'Sometimes you could make a fresh-plucked rose smell like a wet fart.'

They were both silent for a while. Tom swung the glass to the head of the caravan. The Arab headman rode on a grey dappled mare with rich trappings. At a glance Tom saw that he was a fine horseman, probably young. He rode tall and at ease in the saddle. He carried his long jezail slung over his back, and his shield on his shoulder. A lance-bearer rode at his right hand, ready to pass across the weapon, and a young boy rode at his other hand. A hand-slave or a favourite bum-boy, Tom guessed. The Arab wore the blue turban of the royal house of Oman, and the tail of the cloth was wound over the lower part of his face so that only his eyes were exposed.

'I would like to test his steel.' Tom forced himself to ignore his own misgivings. 'By God, he looks as though he could give good account.'

'The ivory is small and, by the ease with which they carry it, light,' Aboli said softly.

Tom rounded on him. 'I have come a hundred miles to gather in that ivory, light or heavy, and I mean to have it. I will not slink home again because you have had a bad dream, Aboli.'

I should never have told him about the dream, Aboli chided himself, then said aloud, 'I have followed you into every wild and reckless venture you have ever conceived, Klebe. Perhaps it is an old man's folly, but I intend to die at your side. So then, if you insist, let us go down and take these rich and easy pickings.'

Tom snapped the telescope shut and grinned at him. 'Let's not talk of dying on such a glorious day as this, old friend.' He stood up. 'First we will cast their back trail, then go ahead of the column to find a good place to transact the main business.' They went down to where Fundi held the horses at the base of the hill.

Batula rode up to the head of the long column as it wound through the open forest, and made his salute to al-Salil. 'The *fisi* are sniffing along our back trail,' he reported.

Dorian swung his horse out of the file. It skittered and threw its head. 'When?'

'After we had gone into bivouac yesterday evening. Two horsemen came up from the south, followed by two others on foot.'

'What else did you make of them?'

'When they dismounted to study our spoor, both riders were shod with leather. Though they have savages with them, I think that these are Franks. They walked back and forth, then remounted and followed us. From a hill they overlooked our camp, then turned back into the south.'

'Did it seem that they had become aware that Bashir al-Sind is following behind us?'

'No, lord, it seems to me that they are unaware.'

'In Allah's name, it begins,' Dorian said, with satisfaction. 'Make the signal to warn Bashir al-Sind that the *fisi* are near, and that he can close up.' Three innocent-looking cairns of stones, placed in a certain pattern in the road behind them, would mean nothing to anyone except al-Sind. Batula rode back to the tail of the caravan. When he returned he told Dorian, 'It is done as you ordered, lord.'

'Now, take three men with you and ride ahead to find the place where they will most likely come at us,' Dorian ordered. 'Ride openly, and make no suspicious move.'

It was afternoon when Dorian saw the patrol returning. Batula rode up calmly. 'Lord, ahead of us there is such a place as favours the design of our enemies.' Dorian waited for him to continue. Batula went on, 'Our head will reach the place in an hour. The road goes down another escarpment, winding through a narrow place between broken ground. Bowmen can lie concealed close on each hand. Halfway down there is an even steeper place. Here the path descends, like a ladder, down natural stone steps. This is a place where they can cut our column in half.'

'Yes.' Dorian nodded. 'I remember this place from when we marched up from the coast. There is a river in the valley below, with a pool where we rested for four days.'

'It is the same place,' Batula confirmed.

'That is where they will make their attack,' Dorian said, with certainty, 'for beyond the river is a wide plain of many days' march that does not suit their purpose so well.'

Above the natural stone ladder hung a crenellated buttress of red lichen-painted rock, a hundred feet high and rotten. It was split by deep, vertical cracks and overhung the narrow pass below. Tom sat on the edge, swinging his feet over the drop, and looked into the narrow passage. He had discovered and made a note of this place two years earlier, after their first success against the slavers.

No more than five horses can pass abreast, he estimated, and it's too rugged to ride them up or down it. They will have to dismount and lead them. That was good, because the Lozi archers had proved unreliable in the face of a cavalry charge. However, they were formidable fighters in confined hand-to-hand encounters. There was not another place along all the hundreds of miles of the entire slave road that lent itself so perfectly to an ambush and the kind of fighting in which his men excelled.

Under the supervision of Luke Jervis, ten men were toiling over the broken ground behind where Tom sat. Each carried a fifty-pound keg of black powder on his back. Tom stood up and went to direct them to the mouth of the crack in the rocky buttress. They stacked the kegs, then threw themselves down to rest.

Quickly Aboli fashioned a crude boatswain's chair from a plank and a coil of rope. With three of the men belaying the rope's end, he lowered himself into the crack. When he reached the bottom they sent the powder-kegs swaying down to him. Tom knew that Aboli could do this kind of work better than any, so he left him to it and made another circuit of the cliff's edge to check his dispositions, and assure himself of their escape route if the attack failed. Sarah would wait with the horses in a bush-choked gully well back from the fighting, but close enough if all turned against them and they were forced to make a run for it.

When he returned to the mouth of the crack, he found that Aboli had finished placing the explosive and was being hauled up again. 'I have laid three separate fuses,' he told Tom, and pointed to the long white snakes dangling down the rock face, 'in case one might fail.'

'Two hundred and fifty pounds.' Tom grinned. 'That will open their eyelids and loosen their teeth for them.'

They went back across the high broken ground to a vantage-point from which they could overlook the approaching slave caravan. They saw the dustcloud long before the column came into view among the trees of the open miombo forest. Tom studied the head of it through the lens, but could detect no change in the speed or composition of the column. The slaves still marched three and four abreast, their chains dangling and clanking. The Arab guards flanked them, and the blue-turbaned headman still rode at the point.

'There is no singing,' Aboli remarked.

It was true, Tom realized. Always before there had been slave-singing. 'They must be a gloomy lot.'

'The slave-masters never use the whip on them,' Aboli went on. 'Think of another clever reason for that, Klebe.'

Tom rubbed the lump of his broken nose. 'We have come across the only kind-hearted Mussulmen in Araby. You waste your breath, Aboli, and test my patience. These are mine, and I will have them.'

Aboli shrugged. 'It is not your fault, Klebe. Your father was a stubborn man, and your grandfather before him. It runs in the blood.'

Tom changed the subject. 'Do you think they will camp tonight at the mouth of the pass or come straight in?'

Aboli considered the height of the sun. 'If they

attempt to make the passage this day, it will be dark before they are through.'

'Darkness will suit our plans well enough.'

'Put away your spyglass now, Klebe. They are close. The angle of the sun could send a flash of light down to them, and startle the game.'

Dorian reined in his horse, and stood in the saddle to survey the mouth of the pass. It opened gradually, the sides growing deeper and steeper as the ground fell away. He remembered the terrain clearly: he had memorized its perils when first he passed through it. It was the perfect place for an ambush. He felt the skin prickle at the nape of his neck, the premonition of danger, which he trusted from long experience. 'Batula, take two men with you and go down the pass to scout it.' That was what any prudent caravan master must do. 'Make a show of searching for sign, but if you discover any do not call the alarm. Come back to me. Before you reach me shout loudly that the road is clear and all is safe.'

Batula dipped his lance-tip, rode into the pass and disappeared beyond the first turn. Dorian dismounted stiffly, and behind him the long column shuffled to a halt, the slaves sank to the earth and set aside their loads. The slave-boy, Yassie, set up a sunshade for the sheikh then blew on the coals in the copper brazier that he carried on the back of his saddle. When they burst into bright flame he placed the coffee pot over them. The coffee bubbled, and Yassie drew a thimble of it then knelt to offer it to his master.

'Stay close to me when the fighting begins,' Dorian whispered to Yassie. 'Under no circumstances pick up a weapon or make any warlike gesture. If you are menaced by an enemy, throw yourself down and scream for mercy. If you are captured do not let them know you are a woman, lest they use you as one.'

'As you command, master. But with you at my side I am not afraid of anything.'

'Know that I love you, little one, and that I shall always love you.'

'As I love you, master.'

A shout from the mouth of the pass interrupted them. 'The road is clear, and all is safe.' Dorian looked up to see Batula waving his lance back and forth, the blue pennant fluttering at its tip.

Dorian mounted and stood in the stirrups to give the forward command. That was all that was needed, for every one of his men knew his duty. Ponderously the caravan rolled down into the maw of red rock.

The walls of stone closed in upon them. This was one of the old elephant roads, and over the ages the pads of the great pachyderms had worn the rock floor smooth. Dorian wound the blue headcloth tighter over his mouth and nose and, without leaning forward to make it obvious, he examined the ground for recent sign of the marauders. The stone was clean, but that meant nothing: these were dangerous men and they would not have been so careless as to mark the path.

As the pass narrowed, the ranks of slaves and guards were compressed until they marched with shoulders touching. There was no talking in the column, no singing, for none of the Arabs could imitate the cadence and rhythm of wild Africa.

High on the wall of the pass, Dorian saw a flicker of movement, a tiny flash of grey. His heart skipped and beat faster. Then he saw that it was only a tiny klipspringer, one of the hare-sized gazelle that lived among the rocks. It stood poised on the crest of a boulder, all four minute hoofs held together, its straight horns and ears pricked, watching the men below with large, startled eyes.

Halfway down the escarpment the steep pitch began as the pass squeezed between high portals of weathered, eroded rock, then dropped down a flight of natural stone stairs. Dorian swung off the saddle of the grey, and led it down the treacherous footing. From the bottom he looked back up the pitch. His soldier's instincts crawled to see his men in such a cramped, perilous situation: they were confined in the narrow stone gut, so cramped that they would only be able to swing an edged weapon or aim a musket with difficulty.

He drew the horse off the path and they squeezed against the wall to let the files of slaves and guards pass. Now he searched the walls on either side, looking for the flash of gunmetal, the movement of a human head against the sky. There was nothing, and half the column was down the stone ladder. The second half of the caravan was squeezing through the red rock portals. It must come now. He judged the moment: they were fairly in the trap. He glanced back at Yassie. She had stopped close behind him, and pulled her own horse off the track. She had wedged herself against a large boulder to let the files of men pass her.

Dorian looked back at the sky. A single vulture was sailing in the tall blue on widespread pinions. It was a funereal black with a bald red head and hooked beak. It turned its head and looked down on the mass of men as it circled.

Patience, foul bird, Dorian thought grimly. This day we will lay such a feast that will satiate even your lust for flesh.

Before he could complete the thought, the air was driven in upon his eardrums with such force that he reeled backwards. It seemed as though a mighty vice had closed upon his chest, and the solid rock jumped and shivered beneath his feet.

He saw a tower of smoke, dust and red rock fragments shoot into the sky as high as the circling vulture. Then the earth was riven open, the buttress of rock split apart. The cliff shuddered, then swung outwards. It moved so slowly that he had time to think as he watched it. Black powder! I should have guessed it. They have blown out the buttress.

The collapsing cliff fell more swiftly, rumbled, ground and roared. The screams of the men beneath it were puny and thin. It fell upon them and snuffed out their fruitless calls to God. The pass was blocked, and the long caravan cut in half like the body of a python divided by a single sword-cut.

While Dorian still clung to his horse's neck, his ears ringing and senses whirling, he saw the first flights of arrows dropping on to his men like clouds of locusts, and volleys of musket fire crashed down from the walls of the pass. Spurting powder smoke fogged the hot, still air, and he heard the lead shot splattering like hail on stone and living flesh alike.

A hundred or more of his men had been crushed under the avalanche. Less than fifty of his warriors had escaped below the still dust-smoking ruins. The rest of his force was cut off in the top end of the pass. In an instant, he saw that the attackers had wrested the advantage, and he knew that in the next instant they would charge in to finish the bloody work they had begun so well. He swung up into the saddle and drew his scimitar.

He and Batula were separated, but that was of little consequence for the press was too close for lance-work. It would be the sword and dagger when the *fisi* came down. The slaves had thrown themselves flat, as he had ordered. As they crouched against the stone floor in simulated terror, they were slipping off their chains and drawing out their weapons from the bundles they had carried on their heads.

From the saddle he saw the *fisi* leap up from the ambush, and storm down the steep sides – black men in war feathers, brandishing light shields of raw hide, bounding from rock to rock, howling some savage war-cry. They carried short spears and heavy clubs. Then, with astonishment, Dorian saw a white man in the van, then another and a third.

'God is great!' Dorian roared.

The crouching half-naked Arabs sprang up to meet the charge, scimitars in hand, and answered his cry. 'God is great! *Allah akbar!*'

Dorian spurred forward to reach a position from which he could command the battle, but a heavy lead musketball took his horse in the shoulder with a thump and it went down in a tangle of kicking limbs and equipment. Dorian jumped clear, and landed lightly on his feet. All around him was uproar, but through it he heard a single voice sing out: 'Have at them, lads! Chop out their pagan bungholes!' It was an English voice, rich with the earthy burr of Devon, and it shocked Dorian more than the explosion of gunpowder.

'Englishmen!' He had not heard the language spoken in many a long year. Suddenly all those years were brushed away. These were his countrymen. He found himself caught up in a whirlpool of divided emotions. He looked about him for a way in which to halt the battle, to save the lives of his own troops and his countrymen, who were pitted against each other.

But the war-lance was sped and it was too late to change its flight. He looked for Yassie – she was still cowering under the shelter of her boulder. But she shouted a high warning and pointed beyond him. 'At your back, lord!' Dorian whirled to meet the man who rushed at him.

He was a big, square-shouldered rogue, with a twisted nose and a curling bush of black beard. His face was deeply tanned by sun and wind, but there was something about his eyes, that green sparkle, that touched a deep chord in Dorian's memory. There was not a moment for him to dwell on it, for the man came at him with a speed and poise that belied his size.

Dorian caught the first thrust, but it was so powerful that it thrilled his right arm to the shoulder. He went into riposte, fluid and graceful, and the Englishman met him, caught his blade high in the natural line and swept it into the classic prolonged engagement, rolling their two blades together so that the steel shrieked and sang.

In that instant Dorian realized three things: that the Englishman was the finest swordsman he had ever faced, that if he tried to break he was a dead man, and that he recognized the sword that had trapped his own blade. He had last seen it hanging at his father's side as he stood on the quarterdeck of the old *Seraph*. The blue steel and the gold inlay shimmered and dazzled the eye. It was unmistakable.

Then his opponent spoke for the first time, his voice hardly blunted by the effort he was extending to keep Dorian's blade in check. 'Come, Abdulla, let me slice another inch off your bald prickhead for you.'

He spoke in Arabic, but Dorian knew that voice.

'*Tom!*' he wanted to shout, but the shock was so intense that his voice choked in his throat and no sound reached his lips. The muscles in his right arm went soft, and he dropped the point.

No man living could afford to drop the point when Tom Courtney had him locked in prolonged engagement, and the killing stroke came like a flash of lightning out of a sunny blue summer sky. At the last moment Dorian twisted aside, disturbing his brother's aim by a bare thumb's width but then he felt the hit, high right in the chest, and the long slide of steel into his flesh. The scimitar spun from his nerveless fingers and he went down on his knees with the blade still in him.

'Tom!' He tried to call his name again, but no sound came. Tom reared back, plucking the steel out of his chest with a soft, sucking sound, like an infant releasing the teat. Dorian toppled forward on to his face. Tom stepped over him and sighted down the blade to finish it. Before he could make the killing stroke, a small body hurled itself between them, covering Dorian's body protectively.

'Damn you,' Tom shouted, but held the stroke. 'Get out of this!' The boy, who was using his own body as a shield, was a mere child, and the act of sacrifice touched Tom even in his battle rage. He could have killed them both with a single thrust, through and through. But he could not bring himself to do it. He stepped back and tried to kick the youth off the Arab headman's supine body, but the little fellow clung to his master like an oyster to a rock.

He was screaming pitifully in Arabic. 'Mercy! In the name of Allah, mercy!'

At that moment Aboli shouted a warning: 'At your back, Klebe!' Tom spun round, his point high, to meet the rush of two half-naked men. For an instant he thought they were slaves who had been released miraculously from their chains and were now attacking him with scimitars they had conjured up from who knew where. Then he saw that their features were not negroid, but Arabic. By God, they were not slaves at all but fighting Mussulmen. He countered right and left, bringing them up short, then killed one and sent the other staggering away with a slash across his bare shoulder.

'Klebe, it is a trap!' Aboli roared again, and Tom had a moment to look around. Every one of the erstwhile slaves was free of his chains, and armed. They were swift and purposeful in their counter-attack. Already the Lozi spearmen were breaking up before their onslaught and most were in flight, scrambling back up the sides of the gorge in wild disarray.

From the front of the column Tom saw a red Chinese rocket whoosh into the sky on a long tail of white smoke, and knew that it must be a signal to bring Arab reinforcements swarming down on them.

Over the tumbled wall of raw red rock that blocked the back section of the pass came a wave of more Mussulmen, some in robes, the others in loincloths, rushing down to join the fight. Aboli and the little band of English seamen were already far outnumbered. Within minutes they would be cut off and overwhelmed by this fresh tide of warriors.

'Get out, Klebe! It is lost. Get out!'

'On me!' Tom bellowed. 'On me the *Centaurus*.' He called the others to him. Alf Wilson and Luke Jervis broke through the enemy ranks and ran to his side. With Aboli and all the remaining seamen they formed a circle of steel, and retreated in the formation they had practised so often. With their headman down and out of the fighting, the Arabs seemed suddenly indecisive and reluctant to press themselves on to the hedge of swords. Tom reached the point at the foot of the cliff from where they could begin the climb back, and snapped, 'Away with you, lads. Every man for himself, and the devil take the hindmost.'

They climbed hand over hand, sweating and cursing and panting. Before they reached the top the Arabs below had rallied and sent the first volleys of musket fire thudding into the rocks around them, loose chips showering on their heads, and the ricochets humming away. One of the English seamen was struck: the ball caught him in the back. He arched out and loosened his grip, then went sliding and rolling down the face. Tom glanced back and the moment his man reached the bottom he saw the Arabs swarm over his body and cut him to pieces. 'Nothing we can do for poor Davie. Keep climbing,' he grunted.

Tom and Aboli scrambled over the crest together and were shielded from the fire below. They paused to draw breath and rally the others around them.

The sweat was streaming down Aboli's scarified face, and when he looked at Tom he shook his great bald head, needing no words to express his feelings eloquently.

'Do not say it, Aboli. You have proved once again that you are as wise as God, but somewhat older and not so beautiful.' Tom laughed raggedly, still out of breath. 'Come on, lads. Let's get back to the horses.'

Sarah was holding them in the dense bush of the gully. She took one look at their faces as they came scrambling back, dragging two wounded men with them, and asked no questions. Most of them were cut and bleeding, and all were drenched with sweat. There were not enough mounts for all, so Tom took Sarah up behind his saddle. Luke had one of the wounded with him, Alf Wilson the other, while the rest of the seamen grabbed a stirrup leather each and were dragged along as they headed back into the south. The Lozi warriors had scattered long before into the bush.

'We have brought the whirlwind down upon ourselves. They will send an army after us,' said Aboli.

'Our days at Fort Providence have come to an end,' Tom agreed, riding hard beside him. 'Thank God, the *Centaurus* has no cargo to carry. The river is low but she will ride light, and we can be away downriver, before the Mussulmen can catch up with us.'

Dorian lay where he had fallen in the gut of the pass. Ben Abram, the old surgeon, would not allow them to move him until he had placed a compress on the wound, and bound it up tightly to staunch the bleeding. 'It has missed the heart and the lung,' he said grimly, 'but he is still in mortal danger.'

They made a litter out of lance-shafts and a leather tent-fly, and eight men carried him gently through the shambles of the battlefield, where the other wounded groaned and called for water. Yasmini walked beside the litter. She had wound her headcloth tightly over her face to stifle her sobs and hide her tears.

When they reached the grove of tall shade trees beside the river pool at the foot of the escarpment, the camp servants had already recovered the sheikh's tent from among the scattered baggage and set it up. They laid al-Salil on his sleeping mat and propped him on the silk cushions. Ben Abram gave him a draught of the poppy, and he sank into an uneasy doze.

'He will not die?' Yasmini pleaded with Ben Abram. 'Please tell me he will not die, old father.'

'He is young and strong. With God's grace, he will live, but it will take time for him to recover, and to regain the use of his right arm.'

'I will stay by his side and will not rest until he does.'

'I know you will, child.'

Within the hour, there were loud voices outside the tent. Yassie flew out to protect her lord and drive them away. But even in his drugged state Dorian recognized the voices of Bashir al-Sind and Batula. 'Let them enter!' he called weakly, and Yassie had to stand aside.

Bashir bowed at the entrance. 'Lord Sheikh, I call down Allah's protection upon you.'

'What of the enemy?'

'We came up as soon as we saw the rocket but we were too late. They had escaped.'

'How many of the enemy were killed?'

'Many black *kaffirs*, and three Franks.'

'Was one of the Franks a big man with a black beard?'

Bashir shook his head. 'None of them. Two were small and thin, one bigger infidel had a grey beard.'

Dorian felt a surge of relief. Tom had escaped. Then Batula spoke unbidden, his voice sharp and eager. 'Lord, I have followed the sign of those *fisi* who fled the battlefield. They had horses hidden close by, and are running south, moving fast. But give the order and we will follow them.'

Bashir cut in as eagerly, 'Al-Salil, I have a thousand men ready and mounted, eager to hunt them down. I wait only for your order and then, by Allah, none will survive.'

'No!' The exclamation was torn from Dorian in pain, and Bashir blinked at the strength of his refusal.

'Forgive my impertinence, great lord, but I do not understand. It was the centrepiece of our plans that we hunt down the infidel bandits.'

'You are not to follow them. I forbid it.' Dorian mustered all the force he had left to emphasize the order.

'If we do not follow at once they will get clear away!' Bashir saw the chance for glory snatched from him, and glanced across at Ben Abram. 'Perhaps the severity of your wound has clouded your judgement, mighty lord.'

Dorian struggled up on one elbow. 'In the name of Allah, I swear this! If you flout my orders, I will carry your head on the point of my lance, and bury your body in a pigskin.'

There was a long silence, then at last Bashir spoke softly. 'Will the great lord, al-Salil, repeat these orders in front of the senior officers of the staff, that they may bear witness that it is not cowardice on my part that kept me in bate while the beaten enemy escaped?'

The four senior officers came to the tent and Dorian repeated his command in front of them, then sent them away. When Bashir made to follow them Dorian stopped him. 'There are matters here so deep that I cannot explain to you, Bashir. Forgive me that I seem to disparage you. Know only that you are still high in my favour.' Bashir bowed, touched his heart and his lips, but his expression was cold and aloof as he backed out of the tent. Outside they heard him shouting angry orders to his troops to stand down.

Dorian seemed to sink into a deep sleep. The silence in the tent was heavy, and Yasmini wiped the sweat from his brow with a damp cloth. After a long while, Dorian stirred and opened his eyes. He looked first at her and then at Ben Abram.

'Are we alone?' he asked, and they both nodded.

'Come closer, old father. There is aught I must tell you.' When Yasmini made as if to rise and leave the tent, he laid a hand on her arm to restrain her. As they both hovered over him, Dorian said quietly, 'The man who struck me down was my brother. That was why I could not send Bashir after him.'

'Is this possible, Dowie?' Yasmini stared into his eyes.

'Yes.' Ben Abram spoke for him. 'I know this brother and it is possible.'

'Tell her, please, old father. I find it tiring to speak. Explain it to her.'

Ben Abram took a minute to gather his words, then began to speak softly so that no one outside the tent could hear him. He told Yasmini how Dorian had been captured as a child and sold into slavery; how al-Malik had bought him from the pirates and adopted him. 'I met him face to face, this brother of al-Salil. I came to know him well on the island after he had destroyed the lair of the pirates. His name is Tom. I was his captive, but he set me free and sent me with a message to al-Salil. He promised that he would never give up searching for him, and that one day he would find him and rescue him.'

Yasmini looked to Dorian for confirmation, and he nodded. 'Then why did he not hold to his oath to free you, this loyal brother of yours?' she asked.

Dorian looked abashed. 'I cannot answer that,' he admitted. 'Brother Tom was never one to take his oath

918

lightly. I suppose, in the end, after all the years, he simply forgot me.'

'No,' said Ben Abram. 'There was something you never knew and that I could not tell you. Your brother came back to Zanzibar, searching for you. The Prince al-Malik would not surrender you. He sent the mullah al-Allama with a message to your brother. He told him that al-Amhara was dead of the fever, and they had placed a marker in the cemetery with your name upon it.'

'That was when my father changed my name to al-Salil.' Dorian's voice became stronger and sharper as he understood. 'It was to hide the truth from Tom. No wonder my brother gave up the search for me.'

He closed his eyes and was silent. Yasmini thought he had fallen into coma, but then she saw a single tear squeeze out between his closed lids. Her heart contracted with pity for him. 'What will you do, my love?' She stroked his fiery red head.

'I know not,' he said. 'It is all too cruel. I feel a sword dividing my soul.'

'You are of Islam now,' Ben Abram said. 'Can you ever go back to your origins?'

'Would your brother believe that you are alive, after you have been dead to him all these years?' Yasmini asked.

'And can you embrace him now, when he is the sworn enemy of your father, the Caliph al-Malik, and of your God and your people?' Ben Abram twisted the knife in his heart.

Dorian had no answer for either of them. He turned his face to the leather wall of the tent and took refuge in his weakness from the wound. Yasmini never left his side while he drifted in and out of consciousness, tormented by physical pain and by the emotional forces that tore at his heart and threatened to rend it apart.

The army stagnated for days in the camp below the escarpment while their sheikh lay sequestered in his tent.

Under Bashir's direction, they gathered in the wounded and built thatched shelters for them beneath the shade trees. Ben Abram tended them. They buried their dead, but left undisturbed those who were already interred beneath the red rock of the avalanche. They repaired the smashed equipment and resharpened their weapons. Then they waited for further orders. None came. Bashir al-Sind strode angrily through the camp, lashing out at any man who crossed his path, and the men shared his frustration. They burned for a chance to avenge their comrades who had died in the narrows of the pass, but they could not move without the orders of al-Salil.

Ugly rumours spread through the camp, that Bashir would rebel and take over command from the ailing sheikh. That the sheikh had died, that he had recovered, that he had sneaked away in the night and left them to their fate.

Then another, stranger rumour flared through the ranks, that a second grand expeditionary force under the command of a prince of the royal house of Oman was marching up from the coast to join them. With this combined force, they would be allowed at last to pursue the infidel into his lair. This rumour was only hours old when they heard the low thump of distant war drums, at first so soft that it seemed to be the beating of their own hearts. The Arab soldiers crowded the high ground to look out across the plain, and thrilled to the blast of a ram's-horn trumpet. They saw a splendid host approaching, with a staff of high-ranking officers riding at the head.

They gathered in awe as these strangers rode into the

camp. The officer who led the cohorts wore half-armour in the Turkish style with a pot-shaped helmet, spiked on top and with a padded neck flap. From the back of his horse this splendid figure addressed them in ringing tones.

'I am Prince ibn al-Malik Abubaker. Men of Oman, loyal soldiers and true, I bring you sad tidings. Abd Muhammad al-Malik, my father and your Caliph, is dead in the Muscat palace, struck down in his prime by the sword of the black angel.'

A groan went up from the ranks, for most of them had fought at Muscat to place al-Malik on the Elephant Throne and they had loved their Caliph. They threw themselves down on their knees, and cried out, 'May God have mercy on his soul.'

Abubaker let them give expression to their sorrow, then he held up a gloved hand for their silence. 'Soldiers of the Caliph, I bring you salutations from your new ruler. Zayn al-Din, beloved elder son of al-Malik, who is now the Caliph. He bids me call you to swear allegiance and loyalty to him.'

They knelt in rows with Bashir al-Sind at the head of the army and swore the oath of fealty, calling on God to witness it. By the time the ceremony was over, the sun was setting. Then Abubaker dismissed them, and called Bashir to him.

'Where is that coward and traitor, al-Salil?' he demanded. 'On behalf of the Caliph, I have urgent business with him.'

Dorian heard the pronouncement of his adoptive father's death while he lay on the sleeping mat in his tent, for Abubaker's voice carried clearly through the leather side wall. It seemed that all the foundations of his life were being torn out one at a time. He felt too weak and sick to surmount these shocks and hardships.

Then he heard Zayn al-Din's name, and the news of his accession to the Elephant Throne, and realized that his predicament was even worse than he had fancied. With a vast effort he put aside his sorrow for his father and his own debilitating physical suffering, took Yasmini's hand and drew her closer to his bed. She was shaken by the news of al-Malik's death, but not as deeply as Dorian, for she had hardly known her father as a man. She recovered from her sorrow swiftly when he shook her. 'We are in great danger, Yassie. Now we are both completely in Zayn's power. I do not have to tell you what that means, for Kush was a saint in comparison to our brother.'

'How can we escape him, for you cannot move, Dowie? What can we do?'

He told her what she must do for them, speaking softly and urgently, making her repeat every detail. 'I would give you a written letter, but I cannot write with this arm. You must carry my message by word of mouth alone, but learn it well for otherwise it will not be believed.'

She was quick-witted and, even in her confused state, she memorized it all perfectly at the first attempt, although she had difficulty in enunciating some of the words he taught her. There was no time for her to perfect them.

'That will do. He will understand. Now, go!' he ordered her.

'I cannot leave you, lord,' she pleaded.

'Abubaker will recognize you if you stay by me. In his clutches, you will be no help to either of us.'

She kissed him once, tenderly and lovingly, then rose to leave him, but there came a heavy tramp outside the tent and she shrank back into a corner, covered her head and shoulders with her shawl. At that moment the tent flap was thrown open and Bashir al-Sind stepped in. Ben Abram tried to intervene, and prevent him approaching the bed on which Dorian lay.

'Al-Salil is sorely wounded and must not be disturbed.'

Bashir pushed him aside contemptuously. 'General Abubaker, the emissary of the Caliph, approaches!' he warned Dorian, and his expression was cold and malicious. Dorian knew that he had changed allegiance and was no longer his loyal friend and ally.

Behind him, Abubaker stepped into the tent, and stood with his hands on his hips. 'So, the traitor yet lives. That is good. Al-Salil, who was once al-Amhara in the zenana at Lamu where we were playmates.' He sniggered sarcastically. 'I have come to take you to the Caliph to answer capital charges of treason. We will march for the coast tomorrow at dawn.'

Ben Abram intervened again. 'Noble Prince, he cannot be moved. His wound is grievous. It will endanger his very life.'

Abubaker stepped close to the bed, and looked down at Dorian. 'A wound, you say. How can I be certain he is not shirking?'

Suddenly he reached down and grasped the padded dressing that covered Dorian's chest. With one brutal gesture he ripped it away. The fresh-formed scab was stuck to the bandage, and as it came away Dorian stiffened and hissed with agony. Fresh blood started from the wound and trickled down his chest. In the corner of the tent Yasmini whimpered with sympathy, but none of them took notice of her. 'It is but a mere scratch.' Abubaker gave his opinion as he pretended to examine the open wound. 'Not enough to keep a traitor from justice.' He grabbed a handful of Dorian's thick red hair and dragged him from the bed. 'Get on your feet, traitor pig.'

He pulled Dorian upright. 'See, Doctor, how strong is your patient. He has been duping you. There is little wrong with him.'

'Noble Prince, he will not survive such treatment, or the long march to the coast.'

'Ben Abram, you doddering old goat, if he dies before we reach the coast I will have your head. Let it be a contest between you and me.' He smiled, and showed all his uneven teeth. 'You must do your best to keep al-Salil alive. For my part, I will do my best to kill him by degrees. We shall see who wins.' He threw Dorian back onto his sleeping mat, and turned to stride out of the tent. Bashir followed him.

Yasmini sprang up and rushed to Dorian. Although his face was contorted with agony, he whispered to her fiercely, 'Go, woman. Waste not another moment. Find Batula and ride.'

Tom and his band reached Fort Providence in three days of hard riding, and immediately started to make preparations to abandon the settlement. Aboli sent Fundi and three of his men upriver to fetch his family. 'I cannot sail without them,' he told Tom simply.

'I would not expect that,' Tom replied. 'But they must make haste. We can be sure the Mussulmen are hard on our tracks.'

Tom sent out pickets to cover all the approaches to the fort, so that they would have warning when the Arab forces appeared. Then, in haste, they began to load the *Centaurus* for her departure down the Lunga river. They fetched the light nine-pounder cannon from the emplacements on the stockade wall and placed them in their carriages on the upper deck. There was no ivory to take with them but they reloaded all the trade goods they had brought up from Good Hope at the beginning of the season. Sarah gathered all her treasures and brought them aboard, the linen and cutlery, pots and pans, medical stores and books almost filling their tiny cabin. Tom argued about the harpsichord.

'I will buy you another,' he promised, but when he saw that peculiar expression of hers he knew he was wasting his breath. With poor grace he allowed two seamen to carry it up the gangplank and sway it down into the hold.

It was strange, but still there was no sign of pursuit from the north, and Tom sent out Aboli to make certain that the pickets covering the northern trails were alert and at their posts. This calm was unnatural. Surely retribution must come soon.

The days passed. Then, at last, Fundi returned downriver from Lozi Land with two dugout canoes carrying Zete and Falla, the two boys Zama and Tula, and the new babies. Sarah took them all under her wing. Tom sent an urgent messenger after Aboli, bidding him bring in the pickets for all was at last in readiness for the departure.

Two days later there was a shout from the sentry on the watch-tower above the fort. 'Riders coming from the north!'

Tom climbed up the ladder, telescope in hand. 'Where away?' he demanded, and when the sentry pointed, he focused the telescope.

Sarah climbed up to the top of the tower beside him. 'Who is it?' she asked anxiously.

'It's Aboli, bringing in the pickets.' He whistled softly with relief and satisfaction. 'And no sign of pursuit. It looks as though we might get clear away without a fight. I had not thought that possible. I cannot understand why the Mussulmen have let us off so lightly. Get all your little brats on board. We will shove off downriver as soon as Aboli steps on deck.'

She started down the ladder, but he stopped her with another whistle. 'Aboli is bringing in two strangers. Arabs, by God. Prisoners, by the look of it, for Aboli has them well trussed up. He has bagged himself a couple of enemy scouts. Like as not they will be able to tell us where their main force is.'

Tom and Sarah were waiting for them when Aboli marched his captives aboard the *Centaurus*.

'What fine fish are these you have netted, Aboli?' Tom asked, as he eyed them. By their apparel they were Arabs, one a warrior, and a dangerous one by the look of him. The other was a slip of a boy, a pretty lad with big dark eyes, who was timid and fearful. 'An unlikely pair,' Tom said.

The boy seemed encouraged by his easy tone. '*Effendi*, you speak my language?' he asked softly, and his voice was sweet and unbroken.

'Yes, boy. I speak Arabic.'

'Your name is Tom?'

'Damn you, you little scamp.' Tom frowned and stepped towards him threateningly. 'How did you know that?'

'Tom, wait!' Sarah stopped him. 'She is a girl.'

Tom stared hard into Yasmini's face, then laughed. He snatched off her headcloth and her long dark hair tumbled around her shoulders. 'So she is, and a mighty pretty one too. Who are you?'

'I am the Princess Yasmini, and I bring you a message from Dowie.'

'From who?'

'From Dowie.' She looked desperate. 'Dowie! Dowie!'

She repeated it with different inflections, but Tom shook his head, puzzled.

'I think she is trying to say Dorry,' Sarah intervened, and relief rushed across Yasmini's face.

'Yes! Yes! Dowie! Dowie! Your brother.'

Tom's face turned ugly, swelling with dark blood. 'You come here to mock me. My brother Dorry has been dead these many years. What are you playing at, you little bitch? Is this a trap?' he shouted into her face.

Her eyes welled with tears, but she drew herself up and began to sing. Her voice was hesitant at first, but then it steadied, became sweet and true, but she sang in the semi-quavers of the Orient, alien to the European ear. The tune was twisted and the words were a parody of the English language. They all stared at her, in total incomprehension.

Then Sarah gasped, 'Tom, it's "Spanish Ladies". She is trying to sing "Spanish Ladies"!' She rushed forward and embraced Yasmini. 'It must be true. Dorian is alive, and the song is his sign that this girl comes from him.'

'Dorian! Is it possible? Where is he?' Tom grabbed one of Yasmini's arms and shook it violently. 'Where is my brother?'

It came out in a garbled rush of words. Yasmini started another sentence before she had finished the one that preceded it, tripping over her tongue in her haste to tell it all, and leaving much out, so that she had to go back and start again.

'Dorry needs help.' Tom picked out the essentials, and turned to Aboli. 'Dorry is alive, and in dire straits, and has sent them to fetch us.'

'The horses are still saddled,' Aboli said calmly. 'We can ride at once.'

Tom turned back to Yasmini, who was still gabbling out her story to Sarah. 'Enough, girl!' he stopped her.

'There will be time later to tell the rest of it. Can you take us to Dorry?'

'Yes!' she said vehemently. 'Batula and I can lead you to him.'

Tom leaned down from the saddle to give Sarah a final hasty kiss. For once she had not insisted on accompanying this expedition. Tom should have realized by this unusual behaviour and by her recent reticence that something was afoot, but he was so distracted that he gave it not a thought.

'Make sure Alf Wilson keeps everyone aboard, and all secure. When we return we will be in great haste, like as not with half of Araby hard on our heels.' He gathered the reins, lifted his horse's head and looked around for the others.

Yasmini and Batula had already started, and were halfway up the first hill above the Lunga river. Luke and Aboli were hanging back, waiting for Tom to catch up with them. Everyone was dressed in Arab robes and led a spare horse on a rein. Tom clapped his heels into his horse's flanks, and waved back at Sarah as it bounded forward under him.

'Come back soon and safe!' Sarah called after him, with one hand pressed lightly to her stomach.

It had taken them four days, riding hard, changing horses every hour, using every glimmer of light from dawn to the brief African dusk, to catch up with the Arab column.

Tom had ridden beside Yasmini all the way, and they had talked until their throats were dry with the dust and the heat. She had told him everything that had happened to Dorian since she had first met him in the zenana until his arrest by Abubaker only days before. This time her story was coherent and lucid, touched with humour and pathos, so at times Tom laughed with delight and at others was moved to the brink of tears. She showed him what type of man Dorian had become and made Tom proud. She told him of her and Dorian's love for each other, and in the process won Tom's affection and liking. He was enchanted by her pretty sparkle and her sunny nature. 'So now you will be my little sister.' He smiled at her fondly.

'I like that, *effendi*.' She smiled back. 'It makes me very happy.'

'If I am to be your brother, you must call me Tom.'

When she reminded him of the fight in the pass, and explained how he had cut down his own brother, nearly run her through too, he was smitten with remorse. 'He never showed his face! How could I know?'

'He understands, Tom. He loves you still.'

'I might have killed both of you. It was as though something outside me held my hand.'

'God's ways are marvellous, and not for us to question.'

She led him through the complicated maze of royal Omani politics, explained how they had been caught up in them, and the consequences to Dorian of Zayn al-Din's accession to the caliphate. 'So now Abubaker takes him back to Muscat to face the spite and vengeance of Zayn,' she said, and the tears ran down her dusty face.

He leaned across and patted her arm like a brother. 'We will see to that, Yasmini. Please do not weep.'

They cut the wide deep spoor of the marching Arab army and closed in on it until they could make out the dustcloud above the forest. Then Batula went ahead while the rest hung back and waited until night fell. He would be able to infiltrate the loose mass of veiled riders without drawing attention or suspicion.

Just as the sun was setting he returned along the back trail. 'Praise God, al-Salil is still alive,' were his first words. To Tom, the use of Dorian's Arab name still sounded strange. 'I have seen him from afar, but did not try to reach him. They bear him on a drag litter behind a horse.'

'How strong did he seem?' Tom demanded.

'He can walk a little,' Batula replied. 'I saw Ben Abram help him from the litter and lead him to the tent where they have him now. His right arm is still in a sling. He moves slowly, stiffly, like an old man, but he carries his head high. He is stronger than when we left him.'

'Praise God's Name,' whispered Yasmini.

'Can you lead us to his tent, Batula?' Tom asked.

Batula nodded. 'Yes, but they guard him well.'

'Have they put chains on him?'

'No, *effendi*. They must consider his wound enough restraint.'

'We will bring him out this very night,' Tom decided. 'This is how we will do it.'

They approached the camp from upwind so that their horses would not smell those of the Arabs and whinny to them. They left Yasmini to hold them, and went forward to the edge of the forest. The camp was as murmurous as a beehive and the air was blue and thick with the smoke of hundreds of cooking-fires. There was constant movement, grooms and slaves coming and going from the horse lines, men drifting into the surrounding bush on personal business and returning to their sleeping mats, the cooks bearing steaming rice pots through the camp and doling out the evening meal. Few sentries were set, and little order enforced.

'Abubaker is no real soldier,' Batula said contemptuously. 'Al-Salil would never allow such lack of discipline.'

Tom sent Batula into the camp first, and the rest followed him singly at intervals, moving casually, veiled and robed with their weapons concealed. Batula went towards a hollow in the centre of the encampment where a leather tent had been set up in isolation from the others. In the firelight Tom saw that the scrub around it had not been cleared, but that at least three guards were posted around it. They squatted with their weapons across their laps.

Batula settled down under a twisting-branched marula tree, a hundred yards from the prison tent. The others came up casually and joined him, squatting in a circle and spreading their robes around them until, in the semi-darkness, they seemed like any of the other small groups of Omani soldiers scattered about, talking softly, drinking coffee and sharing a pipe.

Suddenly there was a stir as a group of three splendidly apparelled Arabs came striding towards them, followed closely by their bodyguards. Tom felt a flutter of panic, certain that somehow their presence had been discovered, but the men passed close by them and went on towards the tent.

'He with the blue headcloth and gold rope is Prince Abubaker, the one I told you of,' whispered Batula. 'The other two are al-Sind and bin Tati, both fierce soldiers and liegemen of Abubaker.'

Tom watched the three enter the tent in which Dorian lay prisoner. They were close enough to hear the murmur of voices from behind the leather walls. Then there came the sound of a blow and a cry of pain. Tom half rose to his feet, but Aboli reached out a hand and drew him down. There was more talking within the tent, then Abubaker stooped out through the fly and paused to look back. 'Keep him alive, Ben Abram, that he may die with more passion.' Abubaker laughed and came back, passing so close that Tom could have touched the hem of his robe.

'*Salaam aliekum*, mighty lord,' Tom murmured, but Abubaker never glanced in his direction, and went on to where his own tent stood in the centre of the encampment.

Slowly a hush settled. Voices died away, and men curled up in their shawls around the fires and the flames burned down to ash. Tom and his men lay down around the small fire Batula had built, and covered their heads but did not sleep. As the fires died, the darkness deepened. Tom watched the stars to judge the passage of time. It went infinitely slowly. At last he reached across and touched Aboli's back.

'It is time.' He stood up slowly and moved towards Dorian's tent. He had been watching the sentry who sat at the rear. He had seen his head droop, then come up with a jerk, only to droop again.

Tom walked up softly behind him, leaned over him and struck him across the temple with the barrel of his pistol. He felt the thin bone break and the man sagged forward without a sound. Tom squatted in his place, assuming the same position with the man's musket across his lap. He waited for a long minute to make certain that there was no alarm. Then he eased himself forward on his haunches until he was close to the rear wall of the tent.

He had no way of knowing if they had posted a guard inside the tent at Dorian's bedside. He wet his lips, drew breath, then softly whistled the opening bar of 'Spanish Ladies'.

Someone stirred behind the leather wall, and then came a voice he did not remember. It was not the voice of the child Dorian had been when they had parted. It was the voice of a man.

'Tom?'

'Aye, lad. Is it safe within?'

'Only Ben Abram and me.'

Tom slipped out his jack-knife and the leather wall of the tent fell apart beneath the blade. A hand reached out to him through the gap, pale in the starlight. Tom seized it, squeezed hard, and Dorian drew him through the gap into the tent where they embraced, kneeling chest to chest.

Tom started to speak, but his voice was choked. He hugged Dorian with all his strength, and drew another breath. 'God love you, Dorian Courtney. I know not what to say.'

'Tom!' Dorian reached up with his good hand and seized a handful of the thick dust-stiff curls at the back of his brother's head. 'It's so good to see you.' The English words were alien on his tongue, and he was weeping, overwhelmed by the weakness of his wound and by a towering joy.

'Don't do that, Dorry, or you'll set me off,' Tom protested, and pulled away to wipe his eyes on the back of his arm. 'Let's get you out of here, lad. How badly are you hurt? Can you walk if Aboli and I help you?'

'Aboli? Is he here with you?' Dorian's voice trembled.

'I am here, Bomvu,' Aboli rumbled beside his ear, 'but there will be time for all this later.' He had dragged in the fallen sentry through the cut in the tent wall. Now Tom and he rolled the Arab onto the sleeping mat, and covered his body with Dorian's woollen blanket. In the meantime Ben Abram was helping Dorian into his robe, covering those shining red curls with a turban.

'Go with God, al-Salil,' he whispered, and turned to Tom. 'I am Ben Abram. Do you remember me?'

'I shall never forget you and your kindness to my brother, old friend.' Tom gripped his arm. 'All God's blessing be upon you.'

'You have kept your oath,' Ben Abram said softly. 'Now you must gag and bind me, else Abubaker will treat me cruelly when he finds al-Salil gone.'

They left Ben Abram trussed up and took Dorian through the back wall. Outside the tent they lifted him to his feet and supported him between them. Then they started slowly through the sleeping camp. Batula and Luke Jervis went ahead, moving like dark ghosts, and they skirted one of the camp-fires. A sleeping Arab stirred, sat up and stared at them as they passed close to where he lay, but let them go unchallenged, sank down to the earth again and covered his head again.

'Bear up, Dorry,' Tom whispered in his ear. 'Nearly out of it.' They went on towards the edge of the forest and, as the trees closed around them, Tom almost exclaimed aloud with relief, but at that moment a harsh voice challenged them in Arabic from close at hand.

'What manner of men are you? Stand, in God's Name, and deliver yourselves.'

Tom reached for the sword under his robe, but Dorian caught his hand and replied in the same language, 'The peace of Allah on you, friend. I am Mustapha of Muhaid, and I am devoured by the dysentery. My friends take me to a private place in the bush.'

'You are not alone in your suffering, Mustapha. There is much of this sickness in the camp,' the sentry sympathized. 'Peace upon you, and on your bowels also.'

They moved on slowly. Suddenly Batula appeared again out of the night. 'This way, *effendi*!' he whispered. 'The horses are close.'

They heard the stamp of a hoof, and suddenly Yasmini's small figure detached itself from the darkness and raced to Dorian. They clung to each other, exchanging embraces and soft, loving whispers until Tom drew them gently apart and led Dorian to the strongest horse. Between them Aboli and Tom boosted him into the saddle, where he swayed unsteadily. Tom tied his ankles together with a leather thong stretched under the horse's belly, and they swung Yasmini up behind him.

'Hold him steady, little sister,' Tom told her. 'Do not let him slide off.'

He mounted his own horse, and took the lead rein of Dorian's mount. 'Take us home, Aboli,' he said, and looked back through the trees towards the sleeping camp. 'We will not have more than a few hours' start at best. Then they will be after us like a swarm of hornets.'

They used the horses cruelly. The animals had been driven hard on the ride up from Fort Providence, given almost no rest and time to graze, except during the brief night halts. Now the treatment was the same on the ride back. It was baking hot at noon, and the stretches between water were long. The hard ground and flinty stones ripped into the animals' hoofs.

They lost the first horse before they had gone twenty miles. It was the mount carrying Dorian and Yasmini. It went stone lame in all four hoofs, and could barely hobble. Tom turned it loose, knowing in his heart that lions and hyena would have the brave beast that same night. They put Dorian up on one of the spares and went on at the same pace. By the third day they had burned up all the spare horses and had only those they rode. As they were about to mount again after the brief noon stop at a muddy waterhole, Aboli said quietly, 'The muskets will be no use to us against an army, and the weight is killing the horses.'

They abandoned their firearms and powder flasks, shot bags and every stick of baggage, keeping only their edged weapons and the waterskins. Tom turned his back so that none would see what he did, and slipped one of the loaded pistols into his belt below his shirt.

It was a double-barrelled weapon. He knew from what Yasmini had told him of the fate that awaited her and Dorian if the Arabs caught up with them. The pistol was for them, one barrel each. 'God give me the strength to do it when the time comes,' he prayed silently.

Though they had drastically lightened the load, they lost another two horses that day. Luke, Aboli and Tom

935

took turns trotting beside the mounted men, hanging on to the stirrup leathers to keep up with the driving pace of the march.

That evening, for the first time, they spotted the pursuing column of Arabs. They were crossing another line of those hills that ran with the grain of this wild country. When they looked back they saw the dustcloud rising three leagues behind them.

That night they stopped only for an hour, then went on by starlight, following the high beacon of the great cross in the constellation of Centaurus. Despite this long night march, and that the Arabs must be burning up their mounts even as they were, they discovered when the dawn broke that they had gained no ground on the pursuit. In the early sunlight the dustcloud rose, red as blood, on the horizon still three leagues behind them.

During the night marches, even Aboli had lost all sense of distance covered and their exact position in this wilderness of forest and broken, hilly country. That evening they crossed another line of hills, hoping to see the shining waters of the Lunga below them, but their hopes were dashed as ahead rose yet another line of green hills. They struggled across the intervening valley, the horses almost finished, and all of them nearing the limit of their endurance. Even Aboli was suffering, trying to conceal the limp caused by a strained ligament in his knee. His face was dry and dusty grey with all the moisture sweated out of him. Dorian was gaunt, his body skeletal beneath his robe, his wound weeping fresh blood from under the filthy dressing. Yasmini had almost exhausted the last of her strength trying to hold him in the saddle. The last horse staggered under their combined weight.

It fell just below the crest of the hills, going down as though it had taken a musket-ball through the brain. Tom cut the thong that held Dorian's ankles together and dragged him out from under it.

'It's shanks's pony from here, lad. Can you go on?' he asked him.

Dorian tried to smile. 'I can go on as long as you can, Tom.' But when Tom tried to lift him, his knees gave way under him and he sagged to the stony ground.

Close behind them the red dustcloud rose in the valley they had just crossed. They cut a short pole and Aboli and Tom took the ends. They sat Dorian in the middle of it, placed his arms around their shoulders and staggered down the side of the hill into the valley, carrying him between them.

They stopped during the night for a few minutes at a time, then picked up Dorian on his pole and carried him forward until they could not take another pace and sagged to the ground for another rest. It took them all that night to cross the wide valley. They could only hope that the pursuit had halted in the dark behind them, unable to follow their spoor.

Dawn caught them toiling up the slope on the far side of the valley. When they looked back the Arabs were so close that their lance-tips caught the early light and twinkled merrily.

'They have halved the distance,' Tom gasped, as they lowered Dorian to the ground for another rest. 'At the speed we are making they will be up to us in an hour.'

'Leave me here, Tom,' Dorian whispered. 'Save yourselves.'

'You are mad!' Tom cried. 'The last time I turned my back on you, you were gone for years. I'll not take that risk again.'

They hoisted him, and set off again. Yasmini was walking a few paces ahead. Her leather sandals were ripped and torn almost off her feet, and her heels were bleeding where the blisters had burst open. She fell before they reached the crest, and though she crawled to the nearest tree and tried to use the trunk to pull herself upright, she was too weak to regain her feet.

'Luke, take my place here! You, Batula, help him.' Tom handed over the end of the carrying pole to them and went to where Yasmini crouched against the tree, sobbing softly.

'I am a stupid, weak woman,' she wept as he stooped over her.

'Yes,' he agreed, 'but much too pretty to leave behind.' He lifted her, and though she was fragile and bird-like, the effort strained every sinew and muscle in his aching back and shoulders. He held her to his chest, and braced himself to take another step upwards.

There was a faint shout far behind them, and he looked back over his shoulder. The outriders of the Arab pursuit column had reached the foot of the hill below them. One raised his jezail and powder smoke spurted from the long barrel. Seconds later they heard the thud of the shot. But the range was still too long, and the ball came nowhere near them.

'Almost at the top,' Tom sang out, trying to sound cheerful and gay. 'One more tilt at it, lads.' He stepped out on the top of the hill, blinded by sweat. He knew he could go no further. He lowered Yasmini to the ground and wiped his eyes, but his vision was still blurred and starred with bright lights. He reeled on his feet, looked back at the others, and saw that they, too, were finished. Even Aboli had used up the last of his giant strength. He could hardly take the last few steps onto the crest.

This is where we will die, Tom thought. I still have the blue sword to make a decent fight of it, and in the end I will have the pistol for Yasmini and Dorian. He fumbled under his shirt and touched the butt.

Then, suddenly, Aboli was beside him, shaking his arm, unable to speak, pointing down into the valley ahead. For a moment Tom thought it must be a mirage, but then he realized that the dazzle that hurt his squinting eyes was the sunlight off the wide surface of the Lunga river, and that the little *Centaurus* was moored against the bank. They were so close that they could see tiny human figures on the open deck.

Tom felt new strength flow into his legs. He drew the pistol from under his shirt and fired both barrels in the air. There was a sudden stir on the ship, and Tom saw the flash of a telescope lens as it was aimed up at them. He waved wildly, and the tall figure of Alf Wilson waved back.

Tom turned and looked behind him. The Arab outriders were coming on at a gallop, already halfway up the hill. Without another word, Tom picked up Yasmini and launched himself down the slope towards the river. Gravity took hold of his legs, and he could hardly keep up with them. Each pounding step jarred his spine, as the ground flew past under his feet. He heard Aboli and the others coming down after them, but he could not look back. It took all his wits and strength to stay on his feet. Yasmini closed her eyes in fear, and clung to him with both arms around his neck.

Suddenly there was a shout from behind them and a volley of musket fire. The Arabs had reached the top of the hill. A musket-ball knocked a slab of bark and a burst of wet white splinters from the bole of the tree close beside Tom. He could not keep up the pace and, with Yasmini's weight, he could not stop. He felt one of his legs give way under him and he fell. He and the girl rolled in a tangle together, until they slid into a boulder and lay stunned.

Aboli came past them, with Dorian on his back, bouncing and staggering, Batula and Luke Jervis trying to keep up with him. Aboli's legs were beyond his control. He could not stop to help Tom, but Luke grabbed Tom's arm and dragged him up, while Batula lifted Yasmini in his arms and took a few more unsteady paces down the hill.

There was the rumble of hoofs as the Arabs charged

their mounts down upon them. They had already couched their lances and Tom could see the expressions of triumph on their dark faces. Then he heard Sarah shout his name. 'Tom! We're coming!'

He spun round and saw that she was astride a bay, dragging two spare horses on lead reins behind her, coming straight up the hill at full pelt. Alf Wilson was a length behind her, on a black mare from their herd. He also had two spares. Sarah reined in beside him and Tom snatched Yasmini out of Batula's arms and almost threw her light body over the withers of Sarah's mount. Sarah grabbed her and prevented her from slipping over the other side of the horse.

'Go!' Tom gasped. 'Get her out of here!'

Sarah said not a word, but tossed him the reins of the spare horses and wheeled away down the hill with Yasmini bumping like a wet sack before her.

Tom left one horse for Luke and Batula, and threw himself onto the back of the other. He caught up with Aboli swiftly and plucked Dorian's bleeding, battered body off his back. 'Take a mount from Alf!' he shouted at Aboli as he swept past, and tore down the hill after Sarah. He heard Arabic howls and driving hoofs close behind him, and expected a lance thrust into his back at any instant. But he could not spare a backward glance – he was too busy clutching Dorian. In despair he felt him slip from his grasp and could not hold him. Then, suddenly, Aboli was riding beside him. He leaned across and pushed Dorian upright so that Tom could get a fresh grip around his shoulders.

When they hit the level ground of the riverbank, Tom and Aboli were riding knee to knee, hard behind Sarah, who still held Yasmini. Next came Alf, Batula and Luke in a group. Close behind charged the Arab cavalry. They were gaining, reaching forward eagerly with the long lances.

Sarah did not hesitate when she reached the river. She pushed her mount straight on. It leaped out from the high bank then hit the water in a burst of spray and went clean under. Tom and Aboli followed her over the edge without checking their gallop, then the others jumped almost on top of them. They came up swimming beside their straining mounts, heading out into the stream towards where the *Centaurus* lay.

Behind them, the Arabs reined up on the bank in a swirl, trying to draw their jezails out of the boots as their horses reared and plunged. The first blast of grapeshot from one of the *Centaurus*'s nine-pounders caught them, and half went down in a bloody, broken tangle of men and animals. The rest wheeled away in panic and tore back up the hill as another broadside from the *Centaurus* shattered the trees around them.

The swimming horses reached the ship's side, and the seamen dragged the riders on board. As soon as he reached the deck, Tom ran straight to Sarah and the two embraced, with water streaming from hair and sodden clothing. 'In a fix, you are worth ten men to me, my beauty.' Then he pulled back from her. 'Dorian is sore hurt. He will need all your care. Yasmini is done in also. Look to them while I get the ship away.'

He strode to the helm, and glanced up at the rigging. Alf Wilson had everything shipshape and ready.

'If you please, Mr Wilson, will you get us under way downriver?' Tom ordered, then sought out Aboli. 'We are going to need the horses to drag the ship through the shallows. Take them down to the south bank, on the far side of the river from the Mussulmen. You should be able to keep pace with the ship.'

Aboli called to his sons, Zama and Tula, 'Now I have man's work for you. Come with me.' They followed him over the ship's side to help round up the herd.

Tom felt the ship come alive under his feet, and swing

out into the current. The banks started to stream past on either hand. He looked to the south bank and saw that Aboli and his boys had the horses gathered into a compact herd and were bringing them along the bank at a canter.

He swung round and looked to the north, just in time to see the vanguard of the main Arab army come over the crest, and start down towards the river in a solid stream of glittering armour, lances and musket barrels. Tom snatched the telescope from Alf Wilson's hand and focused it on the head of the advancing column. He picked out Abubaker's Turkish helmet and al-Sind's yellow turban riding beside him. 'I think we will have an honour guard all the way downriver,' he told Alf grimly. 'They won't be able to trouble us much until we reach the shallows.'

Before they reached the sea, they would have to negotiate the shallows, where the river spread out and slowed its plunge towards the ocean. Here the sand bars were always changing depth and position. With the present height of the water there would be barely enough to float the *Centaurus* through. He could expect Abubaker and al-Sind to follow them down and harass them all the way.

Tom had only hours before they reached this treacherous stretch, and he set all hands to making the preparations for warping the ship over the bars and for defending her from enemy attack while she was most vulnerable.

He seized a moment to visit the cabin where Sarah had taken Dorian and Yasmini. With relief he found his brother resting easily in the little bunk. Sarah had changed the dressing on his wound, and she nodded at Tom to let him know all was well. Yasmini had recovered enough to help her, and she was feeding Dorian from a pewter bowl of soup. Tom spent only a minute with them before he hurried on deck again.

The first thing he saw as he stepped over the coaming was the long column of Omani cavalry streaming down the north bank after them.

'Five hundred or more,' he estimated, and Alf Wilson agreed.

'Enough to do us some mischief in a straight fight, Captain.'

'We best not let it come to that.' Tom smiled with more confidence than he felt. 'How long before we reach the shallows?'

'Two hours at this speed.'

'Right, then. We're going to lighten the ship. Throw everything overboard that is not essential to our voyage,' he ordered. Then he lowered his voice so that it would not carry to Sarah in the cabin below: 'You can start with that harpsichord.'

With splash after high splash they jettisoned the cargo. After the harpsichord they sent over the bales of trade goods, left them bobbing in the wake as they bore down swiftly on the sand bars. Most of the powder-kegs went over the side and all the iron roundshot – Tom kept just enough powder and grape to fight during an hour of heavy engagement.

'Drain half the water from the barrels. Leave just enough to allow us to reach Good Hope on short rations,' Tom cried. That would be a terrible hardship for the women and children – but capture by the Omani would be a lot worse, he consoled himself.

While the crew worked, Tom kept an eye on the following cavalry. Where the current sped through the narrows the *Centaurus* pulled ahead of the Omani column, but when it slowed up and the wind became fluky in the middle of the day, the sails flapped lazily, and the Arabs regained all the ground they had lost.

Tom loaded one of the stern cannon with a double charge of powder and a hatful of grapeshot. When the head of the column came within extreme range he fired at it. He did little damage but the horses bucked and danced, and the Arabs fell back respectfully.

Aboli and the two boys leading the horses on the south bank were keeping up well. Their herd was rested and strong, while the Arab mounts had been worn down by the long pursuit, and could not match them.

They came down a last chute of racing water, steering the wooden hull between outcrops of ugly black rock, then all the speed and power went out of the current and they idled down to where the sandbanks almost choked off the river with their yellow humps of gravel.

'Get the women and children into the longboats,' Tom ordered. 'Every pound of weight will make a difference to our draught.'

Dorian was too weak to be sent ashore, and Yasmini stayed to take care of him. Sarah took the helm to free a man for the heavy work of warping. All the other passengers were taken across to the south bank and placed in Aboli's care. Then the longboat came back and stood by ready to take the ship in tow if she went aground.

Tom stood by the helm, and an anxious silence fell over the little *Centaurus* as she ran down on the first meandering bend where they could see the shape of the bottom through the clear green water. The Arab cavalry column seemed to sense their opportunity, and closed up eagerly. Tom cast a glance at them, but although they were now within easy shot, he was too busy to serve the little cannon and he had to let them come on.

The *Centaurus* swept easily into the bend, and Tom let out his breath with relief. But it was premature. Suddenly she jarred and lurched under their feet as she touched the bottom, then shook herself free and slid on down the green river.

'Close call,' Tom breathed, and then to Sarah at the helm, 'Hold her fair in the green channel.'

The next turn came up and the ship was moving slowly now. The Arabs were half a musket shot back, cantering in formation down the flat, sandy north bank, lances glittering and headcloths blowing in the wind of their ride.

The *Centaurus* hit the sand with her keel and slid to a halt so suddenly that they were almost thrown to the deck. Tom grabbed at the binnacle to steady himself. The *Centaurus* was grounded solidly.

'Boats away!' Tom yelled, and every man aboard scrambled down into the longboats. Tom shouted to Sarah, 'Keep the helm centred!' Then he left her to it, and dropped down into the longboat.

The coxswains in the stern of each longboat picked up the ends of the tow lines, which were lying ready, and made them fast. Then, the rowers hauling with all their strength, the two boats raced out ahead of the *Centaurus* until the lines came up hard. They strained at the long sweeps and tried to drag her off the clinging sand.

From the south bank, Aboli charged his horse into the water and picked up the end of the long line Sarah tossed to him. He swam his horse back with it and as his mount lunged out of the river onto the bank, he hitched the end of the line to the team of waiting horses.

'Ya! Ya! Haul away!' He cracked his whip over their backs and they took up the strain, then threw their full weight against the traces.

The *Centaurus* grated forward over the gravel, then stuck fast again. On the bank the Arab horsemen broke into a gallop and swept forward, deploying as they came on. As they drew level with the stranded ship, the first rank wheeled and couched their lances. They struck the river in a wall of white spray and came straight at the men in the longboats.

The water reached the bellies of the horses then rose up to their shoulders. Now the leading horses were swimming, but their riders had the lances poised as they reached the leading longboat, and swarmed around it like a pack of sharks around a dead whale.

The seamen fired their pistols into the Arabs at close range then stood up to beat them off with the long sweeps. But the boat was rocking wildly, and must soon capsize under the sheer weight of the enemy.

On the north bank the next rank of cavalry wheeled into position for the charge, lining the edge of the sand bar in a solid mass. Abubaker was in the centre of the line, his cuirass and spiked helmet shining. He brandished his scimitar, and led his horsemen forward, at a trot that broke into a canter then into a wild gallop.

Sarah could not leave the wheel. Over the bows she saw the longboats surrounded by struggling masses of horses and men. Tom was standing in the stern with the blue sword in his hand, hacking at the heads of the Arabs in the water. Some of the Arabs were trying to cut the tow rope at the stern, sawing at it with their scimitars. Other were throwing their full weight and that of their steeds on to the gunwale. The boat was canting over until the water poured in over the side. It would soon swamp.

Abubaker's squadron charged into the river, and even Sarah could see that it would soon be over. She was helpless to intervene. Until now she had not seen Dorian come up from the cabin, Yasmini's shoulder under his armpit to support him. Using her as a crutch, he hobbled painfully to the nearest cannon. He seized the marlin spike to traverse the stubby black barrel. Then he grabbed the smoking slow-match out of the sand tub and pressed the end to the touchhole.

The weapon crashed back on its tackle, and a storm of grapeshot hit the front rank of the charging Arab horsemen just as they reached the water's edge. Clinging to the wooden ship's rail, Yasmini stared across the channel. She saw a two-ounce ball of lead strike Abubaker full in the mouth. His teeth exploded out from between his lips in sparkling chips, then the ball burst through his jawbone and out through the back of his skull. His spiked helmet was lifted from his head and spun high in the air.

The men around him were torn from the saddle, and the ranks buckled and turned back from the water's edge. Dorian stumbled to the next cannon and laid the aim. The horsemen saw the muzzle of the cannon turning towards them and spurred away in panic. The buzzing cloud of grapeshot caught them in enfilade and a dozen horses went down. In seconds the ranks were reduced to chaos. They had all seen General Abubaker's head shot away, and now Bashir al-Sind was down too, his horse killed under him. The fight went out of them. They broke and galloped away to avoid the next devastating blast of grapeshot.

Yasmini grabbed Dorian's arm as he tottered and almost fell, then led him to the next cannon. As it fired the *Centaurus* heeled slightly to the recoil and slid reluctantly over the sand. The Arabs around the longboats saw their comrades on the bank riding away, leaving them unsupported. They turned their horses back towards the shore.

'Pull! Pull to burst your guts!' Tom shouted at his crew, and they fell to the oars again. The *Centaurus* crept forward and touched again. Dorian fired another cannon shot, and as the ship rocked Aboli lashed the horse team in the traces. Slowly and reluctantly, the *Centaurus* slid over the sand and floated free in the deep channel beyond.

'Back on board!' Tom roared triumphantly. 'Get the women and children back on board.'

Aboli piled his wives and all their offspring into the longboat as its keel touched the beach. Then he cut the traces of the horses and slapped their rumps to send them galloping into the forest. He ran back and jumped over the gunwale of the boat as the rowers pulled after the *Centaurus*. The ship was floating away swiftly downstream, and they had to pull hard to catch her.

'It's a clear run down to the mouth from here,' Aboli told Tom, as he came to where he stood beside the helm. They both looked back at the shattered Arab force on the north bank. They were making no effort to regroup and continue the pursuit.

'Stand the men down, Mr Wilson,' said Tom. 'And give them all a double tot of rum for their trouble.'

Alf Wilson touched his cap. 'Begging your pardon, Captain, but you threw the rum barrel overboard. Do you want to put the ship about and go back to fetch it?' His tone was serious but his lips twitched.

'I think the men will have to wait for it until we reach Good Hope,' Tom replied, as solemnly.

Tom stood at the stern rail as the *Centaurus* made her offing and the dark mass of the African mainland slowly merged with the gathering night far behind. There was a light step on the deck beside him, and he reached out to pull Sarah in front of him so that her back was pressed against his chest. He hugged her hard to him, and reached over her shoulder to kiss her ear. She shuddered deliciously as his beard tickled the back of her neck. 'Dorry is asking for you,' she said.

'I will go to him presently,' he answered, but made no move to leave her.

After a long silence she asked, 'What happens now, Tom?'

'I know not, lass. Good Hope first, and after that, let come as will.'

'Well, one thing only is certain. I shall have a little surprise for you once we reach Good Hope.'

'Ah!' He sounded interested. 'What is it?'

'If I tell you it will be no surprise.' She reached behind her, took both his hands and placed them firmly on her stomach. It took him a moment to understand. Then he let out a roar of delighted laughter. 'Jesus love you, Sarah Courtney. I know not what to say.'

She knew that that was his most extravagant expression of joy. 'Then hold your peace, you great booby, and give me a kiss instead.'